Robin Cook

THREE COMPLETE NOVELS

Robin Cook

THREE COMPLETE NOVELS

TERMINAL

FATAL CURE

ACCEPTABLE RISK

G.P. Putnam's Sons•New York

These are works of fiction. The characters
and events described in these books are imaginary,
and any resemblance to actual persons,
living or dead, is purely coincidental.

G. P. Putnam's Sons
Publishers Since 1838
a member of
Penguin Putnam Inc.
200 Madison Avenue
New York, NY 10016

Library of Congress Cataloging-in-Publication Data

Cook, Robin, date.
[Selections.   1997]
Robin Cook: three complete novels / Robin Cook.
p.   cm.
Contents: Terminal—Fatal cure—Acceptable risk.
ISBN 0-399-14319-X
1. Detective and mystery stories, American.   2. Medicine—Fiction.
I. Title.
PS3553.O5545A6   1997   97-6480 CIP
813'.54—dc21

Printed in the United States of America
1   3   5   7   9   10   8   6   4   2

This book is printed on acid-free paper. ∞

Book design by Amanda Dewey

CONTENTS

TERMINAL

To Jean with love and appreciation

ACKNOWLEDGMENTS

I would like to thank Matthew Bankowski, Ph.D., for his patience and generosity in tolerating my questions about his arena of expertise, and for his willingness to read and comment upon the original manuscript of *Terminal*.

I would also like to thank Phyllis Grann, my friend and editor, for her valuable input. I would also like to apologize for any deleterious effects the lateness of the manuscript of *Terminal* may have had on her longevity.

Finally I would like to thank the basic science departments of the College of Physicians and Surgeons at Columbia University for providing me with the background that makes it possible for me to understand and appreciate the fast-paced developments in molecular biology.

Science without conscience is
but the ruin of the soul.

—*François Rabelais*

PROLOGUE

JANUARY 4 • MONDAY, 7:05 A.M.

Helen Cabot gradually awoke as dawn emerged from the winter darkness blanketing Boston, Massachusetts. Fingers of pale, anemic light pierced the darkness of the third-floor bedroom in her parents' Louisburg Square home. At first she didn't open her eyes, luxuriating under the down comforter of her canopied bed. Totally content, she was mercifully unaware of the terrible molecular events occurring deep inside her brain.

The holiday season had not been one of Helen's most enjoyable. In order to avoid missing any classes at Princeton where she was enrolled as a junior, she'd scheduled an elective D&C between Christmas and New Year's. The doctors had promised that removing the abnormally heavy endometrial tissue lining the uterus would eliminate the violently painful cramps that left her incapacitated each time she got her period. They'd also promised it would be routine. But it hadn't been.

Turning her head, Helen gazed at the soft morning light diffusing through the lace curtains. She had no sensation of impending doom. In fact, she felt better than she had in days. Although the operation had gone smoothly with only mild post-operative discomfort, the third day after surgery she had developed an unbearable headache, followed by fever, dizziness, and most disturbing of all, slurred speech. Thankfully, the symptoms had cleared as quickly as they had appeared, but her parents still insisted she keep her scheduled appointment with the neurologist at the Massachusetts General Hospital.

Drifting back to sleep Helen heard the barely perceptible click of her father's computer keyboard. His study was next to Helen's bedroom. Opening her eyes just long enough to see the clock, she realized it was just past seven. It was amazing how hard her father worked. As the founder and chairman of the board of one of the most powerful software companies in the world, he could afford to rest on his laurels. But he didn't. He was driven, and the family had become astoundingly wealthy and influential as a result.

Unfortunately the security that Helen enjoyed from her family circumstances did not take into account that nature does not respect temporal wealth and power. Nature works according to its own agenda. The events occurring in Helen's brain, unknown to her, were being dictated by the DNA molecules that comprised her genes. And on that day in early January, four genes in several of her brain's neurons were gearing up to produce certain encoded proteins. These neurons had not divided since Helen was an infant, which was normal. Yet now because of these four genes and their resultant proteins, the neurons would be forced to divide again, and to keep on dividing. A particularly malignant cancer was about to shatter Helen's life. At age twenty-one, Helen Cabot was potentially "terminal," and she had no idea.

JANUARY 4 • 10:45 A.M.

Accompanied by a slight whirring noise, Howard Pace was slid out of the maw of the new MRI machine at the University Hospital in St. Louis. He'd never been more terrified in his life. He'd always been vaguely anxious about hospitals and doctors, but now that he was ill, his fears were full-fledged and overwhelming.

At age forty-seven Howard had been in perfect health until that fateful day in mid-October when he'd charged the net in the semifinals of the Belvedere Country Club's annual tennis tournament. There'd been a slight popping noise, and he'd sprawled ignominiously as the unreturned ball sailed over his head. Howard's anterior cruciate ligament had snapped inside his right knee.

That had been the beginning of it. Fixing the knee had been easy. Despite some mild problems his doctors ascribed to the aftereffects of general anesthesia, Howard had returned to work in just a few days. It had been important for him to get back quickly; running one of the nation's largest airplane manufacturing firms was not easy in an era of sharply curtailed defense budgets.

With his head still stabilized in the vise-like apparatus for the MRI, Howard was unaware of the technician's presence until the man spoke.

"You okay?" he asked as he began to release Howard's head.

"Okay," Howard managed to reply. He was lying. His heart was thumping in terror. He was afraid of what the test would reveal. Behind a glass divider he could discern a group of white-coated individuals studying a CRT screen. One of them was his doctor, Tom Folger. They were all pointing, gesturing, and, most disturbing of all, shaking their heads.

The trouble had begun the day before. Howard had awakened with a headache, a rare occurrence unless he'd "tied one on," which he hadn't. In fact, he'd not had anything to drink since New Year's Eve. After taking a dose of aspirin and eating a bit of breakfast, the pain had abated. But later that morning in the middle of a board meeting, with no warning whatsoever, he'd vomited. It had been so violent and so unexpected, with no preceding nausea, that he'd not even been able to lean aside. To his utter mortification, his undigested breakfast had spewed over the boardroom table.

With his head now freed, Howard tried to sit up, but the movement caused his headache to return in full force. He sank back to the MRI table and closed his eyes until his doctor gently touched his shoulder. Tom had been the family internist for over twenty years. He and Tom had become good friends over the years, and they knew each other well. Howard did not like what he saw in Tom's face.

"It's bad, isn't it?" Howard asked.

"I've always been straight with you, Howard . . ."

"So don't change now," Howard whispered. He didn't want to hear the rest, but he had to.

"It doesn't look good," Tom admitted. He kept his hand on Howard's shoulder. "There are multiple tumors. Three to be exact. At least that's how many we can see."

"Oh, God!" Howard moaned. "It's terminal, isn't it?"

"That's not the way we should talk at this point," Tom said.

"Christ it isn't," Howard snapped. "You just told me you've always been straight with me. I asked a simple question. I have a right to know."

"If you force me to answer, I'd have to say yes; it could be terminal. But we don't know for sure. For the present we've got a lot of work to do. First thing we have to do is find out where it's come from. Being multifocal suggests it's spread from someplace else."

"Then let's get on with it," Howard said. "If there's a chance, I want to beat this thing."

January 4 • 1:25 p.m.

When Louis Martin first awoke in the recovery room, he felt as if his throat had been scorched with an acetylene torch. He'd had sore throats before, but nothing had even come close to the pain he'd felt as he tried to swallow after his surgery. To make matters worse, his mouth had been as dry as the central Sahara.

The nurse who had materialized at his bedside seemingly out of nowhere had explained that his discomfort was due to the endotracheal tube the anesthesiologist had inserted prior to his operation. She gave him a damp washcloth to suck on and the pain had abated.

By the time he was wheeled back to his room, a different pain had started, located somewhere between his legs and radiating into the small of his back. Louis knew the cause of that discomfort. It was the site of his surgery to reduce an enlarged prostate gland. The damn thing had been forcing him to get up to urinate four or five times each night. He'd scheduled the surgery for the day after New Year's. Traditionally that was a slow time for the computer giant he ran north of Boston.

Just as the pain was getting the best of him, another nurse gave him a bolus of Demerol through the IV which was still attached to his left hand. A bottle of fluid hung on a T-shaped pole protruding from the head of his bed.

The Demerol put him back into a drugged sleep. He wasn't sure how much time had passed when he became aware of a presence next to his head. It took all his strength to open his eyes; his eyelids felt like lead. At the head of his bed was a nurse fumbling with plastic tubing coming from the IV bottle. In her right hand was a syringe.

"What's that?" Louis mumbled. He sounded inebriated.

The nurse smiled at him.

"Sounds as if you'd had one too many," she said.

Louis blinked as he tried to focus on the woman's swarthy face. In his drugged state, the nurse was a blur. Yet she was correct about how he sounded.

"I don't need any more pain medicine," Louis managed to say. He struggled to a half-sitting position, leaning on an elbow.

"It's not pain medicine," the nurse said.

"Oh," Louis said. While the nurse completed the injection, Louis slowly realized he still didn't know what he was being given. "What kind of medicine is it?" Louis asked.

"A wonder drug," the nurse said, quickly capping the syringe.

Louis laughed in spite of himself. He was about to ask another question, but the nurse satisfied his curiosity.

"It's an antibiotic," she said. She gave Louis's shoulder a reassuring squeeze. "Now you close your eyes and rest."

Louis flopped back onto his bed. He chuckled. He liked people with a sense of humor. In his mind he repeated what the nurse had said: *a wonder drug.* Well, antibiotics were wonder drugs, there was no doubt. He recalled that Dr. Handlin had told him he might be put on antibiotics as a precaution after his operation. Louis vaguely wondered what it had been like to be in a hospital before antibiotics had been discovered. He felt thankful that he was living when he was.

Closing his eyes, Louis followed the nurse's suggestion and let his body relax. The pain was still present, but because of the narcotic, it didn't bother him. Narcotics were wonder drugs as well, and so were the anesthetic agents. Louis was the first to admit he was a coward when it came to pain. He could never have tolerated surgery back when none of the "wonder drugs" were available.

As Louis drifted off to sleep, he wondered what kind of drugs the future would bring. He decided he'd have to ask Dr. Handlin's opinion.

JANUARY 4 • 2:53 P.M.

Norma Kaylor watched the drops fall into the millipore chamber hanging below her IV bottle. The IV ran through a large-bore catheter into her left arm. She had such mixed feelings about the medicine she was getting. She hoped the powerful chemotherapeutic agents would cure her breast cancer which, she'd been told, had spread into her liver and lungs. At the same time she knew the medicines were cellular poisons, capable of wreaking havoc on her body as well as on her tumor. Dr. Clarence had warned her about so many dreadful side effects that she'd made a conscious effort to screen out his voice. She'd heard enough. She'd signed the consent form with a feeling of numbed detachment.

Turning, Norma looked out the window at the intensely blue Miami sky, filled with massive bubbles of white cumulus clouds. Since her cancer had been diagnosed, she tried hard not to ask *why me?* When she'd first felt the lump she had hoped it would go away of its own accord, like so many lumps had done in the past. It wasn't until several months had passed and the skin over the lump had suddenly dimpled that she'd forced herself to see a doctor, only to learn that her fears had been justified: the lump was malignant. So just before her thirty-third birthday she'd undergone a radical mastectomy. She hadn't fully recovered from the surgery before the doctors began the chemotherapy.

Determined to end her self-pity, she was reaching for a novel when the door to her private room opened. She didn't even look up. Staff at the Forbes Cancer Center was constantly in and out adjusting her IV, injecting her medicine. She had gotten so used to the constant comings and goings, they barely interrupted her reading anymore.

It was only after the door had closed again that she became aware she had been given some new drug. The effect was unique, causing the strength suddenly to drain from her body. Even the book she was holding fell from her hands. But what was more frightening was the effect on her breathing; it was as if she were being smothered. In agony she tried to get air, but she had progressive difficulty, and soon she was totally paralyzed except for her eyes. The image of her door being quietly opened was the last thing she knew.

"Oh, God, here she comes!" Sean Murphy said. Frantically he grabbed the charts stacked in front of him and ducked into the room behind the nurses' station on the seventh floor of the Weber Building of the Boston Memorial Hospital.

Confused at this sudden interruption, Peter Colbert, a fellow third-year Harvard medical student, surveyed the scene. Nothing was out of the ordinary. It appeared like any busy internal medicine hospital ward. The nurses' station was a beehive of activity with the floor clerk and four RN's busy at work. There were also several orderlies pushing patients on gurneys. Organ music from the soundtrack of a daytime soap could be heard drifting out of the floor lounge. The only person approaching the nurses' station who didn't belong was an attractive female nurse who Peter felt was an eight or nine out of a possible ten. Her name was Janet Reardon. Peter knew about her. She was the daughter of one of the old Boston Brahmin families, aloof and untouchable.

Peter pushed back from the counter where he had been sitting next to the chart rack and shoved open the door to the back room. It was an all-purpose office with desk-high countertops, a computer terminal, and a small refrigerator. The nurses held their reports in there at the end of each shift, and those who brown-bagged it used it as a lunchroom. In the back was a lavatory.

"What the hell's going on?" Peter demanded. He was curious to say the least. Sean was against the wall with his charts pressed to his chest.

"Shut the door!" Sean commanded.

Peter stepped into the room. "You've been making it with Reardon?" It was part question, part stunned realization. It had been almost two months ago at the outset of Peter's and Sean's rotation on third-year medicine that Sean had spotted Janet and had asked Peter about her.

"Who the hell is that?" Sean had demanded. His mouth had gone slack. In front of him was one of the most beautiful women he'd ever seen. She was climbing down from the counter after retrieving something from the inaccessible top shelf of a wall cabinet. He could tell she had a figure that could have graced any magazine.

"She's not your type," Peter had said. "So close your mouth. Compared to you she's royalty. I know some guys who have tried to date her. It's impossible."

"Nothing is impossible," Sean had said, watching Janet with stunned appreciation.

"A townie like you could never get to first base," Peter had said. "Much less hit a home run."

"Want to bet?" Sean had challenged. "Five bucks says you are wrong. I'll have her thirsting for my body by the time we finish medicine."

At the time, Peter had just laughed. Now he appraised his partner with renewed respect. He thought he'd gotten to know Sean over the last two months of grueling work, and yet here he was on the last day of medicine surprising him.

"Open the door a crack and see if she's gone," Sean said.

"This is ridiculous," Peter said, but he opened the door several inches nonetheless. Janet was at the counter talking to Carla Valentine, the head nurse. Peter let the door shut.

"She's right outside," he said.

"Damn!" Sean exclaimed. "I don't want to talk to her right now. I've got too much to do, and I don't want a scene. She doesn't know I'm leaving for Miami for that elective at the Forbes Cancer Center. I don't want to tell her until Saturday night. I know she's going to be pissed."

"So you *have* been dating her?"

"Yeah, we've gotten pretty hot and heavy," Sean said. "Which reminds me: you owe me five bucks. And let me tell you, it wasn't easy. At first she'd barely talk to me. But eventually, utter charm and persistence paid off. My guess is that it was mostly the persistence."

"Did you bag her?" Peter asked.

"Don't be crude," Sean said.

Peter laughed. "Me crude? That's the best example of the pot calling the kettle black that I've ever heard."

"The problem is she's getting serious," Sean said. "She thinks because we slept together a couple of times, it's leading to something permanent."

"Am I hearing marriage here?" Peter asked.

"Not from me," Sean said. "But I think that's what she has in mind. It's insane, especially since her parents hate my guts. And hell, I'm only twenty-six."

Peter opened the door again. "She's still there talking with one of the other nurses. She must be on break or something."

"Great!" Sean said sarcastically. "I guess I can work in here. I've got to get these off-service notes written before I get another admission."

"I'll keep you company," Peter said. He went out and returned with several of his own charts.

They worked in silence, using the three-by-five index cards they carried in

their pockets bearing the latest laboratory work on each of their assigned patients. The idea was to summarize each case for the medical students rotating on
service come March 1.

"This one has been my most interesting case," Sean said after about half an
hour. He held the massive chart aloft. "If it hadn't been for her I wouldn't even
have heard about the Forbes Cancer Center."

"You talking about Helen Cabot?" Peter asked.

"None other," Sean said.

"You got all the interesting cases, you dog. And Helen's a looker, too. Hell,
on her case consults were pleading to be called."

"Yeah, but this looker turned out to have multiple brain tumors," Sean said.
He opened the chart and glanced through some of its two hundred pages. "It's
sad. She's only twenty-one and she's obviously terminal. Her only hope is that
she gets accepted by the Forbes. They have been having phenomenal luck with
the kind of tumor she has."

"Did her final pathology report come back?"

"Yesterday," Sean said. "She's got medulloblastoma. It's fairly rare; only about
two percent of all brain tumors are this type. I did some reading on it so I could
shine on rounds this afternoon. It's usually seen in young children."

"So she's an unfortunate exception," Peter commented.

"Not really an exception," Sean said. "Twenty percent of medulloblastomas
are seen in patients over the age of twenty. What surprised everyone and why no
one even came close to guessing the cell type was because she had multiple
growths. Originally her attending thought she had metastatic cancer, probably
from an ovary. But he was wrong. Now he's planning an article for the *New England Journal of Medicine*."

"Someone said she was not only beautiful but wealthy," Peter said, lamenting anew he'd not gotten her as a patient.

"Her father is CEO of Software, Inc.," Sean said. "Obviously the Cabots
aren't hurting. With all their money, they can certainly afford a place like the
Forbes. I hope the people in Miami can do something for her. Besides being
pretty, she's a nice kid. I've spent quite a bit of time with her."

"Remember, doctors are not supposed to fall in love with their patients,"
Peter said.

"Helen Cabot could tempt a saint."

Janet Reardon took the stairs back to pediatrics on the fifth floor. She'd used her
fifteen-minute coffee break trying to find Sean. The nurses on seven said they'd
just seen him, working on his off-service notes, but had no idea where he'd gone.

Janet was troubled. She hadn't been sleeping well for several weeks, waking
at four or five in the morning, way before her alarm. The problem was Sean and
their relationship. When she'd first met him, she'd been turned off by his coarse,

cocky attitude, even though she had been attracted by his appealing Mediterranean features, black hair, and strikingly blue eyes. Before she'd met Sean she hadn't known what the term "Black Irish" meant.

When Sean had initially pursued her, Janet had resisted. She felt they had nothing in common, but he refused to take no for an answer. And his keen intelligence pricked her curiosity.

She finally went out with him thinking that one date would end the attraction. But it hadn't. She soon discovered that his rebel's attitude was a powerful aphrodisiac. In a surprising about-face, Janet decided that all her previous boyfriends had been too predictable, too much the Myopia Hunt Club crowd. All at once she realized that her sense of self had been tied to an expectation of a marriage similar to her parents' with someone conventionally acceptable. It was then that Sean's Charlestown rough appeal had taken a firm hold on her heart, and Janet had fallen in love.

Reaching the nurses' station on the pediatric floor, Janet noticed she still had a few minutes left on her break. Pushing through the door to the back room, she headed for the communal coffee machine. She needed a jolt to get her through the rest of the day.

"You look like you just lost a patient," a voice called.

Janet turned to see Dorothy MacPherson, a floor nurse with whom she'd become close, sitting with her stockinged feet propped upon the countertop.

"Maybe just as bad," Janet said as she got her coffee. She only allowed herself half a cup. She went over and joined Dorothy. She sat heavily in one of the metal desk chairs. "Men!" she added with a sigh of frustration.

"A familiar lament," Dorothy said.

"My relationship with Sean Murphy is not going anywhere," Janet said at length. "It's really bothering me, and I have to do something about it. Besides," she added with a laugh, "the last thing I want to do is to be forced to admit to my mother that she'd been right about him all along."

Dorothy smiled. "I can relate to that."

"It's gotten to the point that I think he's avoiding me," Janet said.

"Have you two talked?" Dorothy asked.

"I've been trying," Janet said. "But talking about feelings is not one of his strong points."

"Regardless," Dorothy said. "Maybe you should take him out tonight and say what you've just said to me."

"Ha!" Janet laughed scornfully. "It's Friday night. We can't."

"Is he on call?" Dorothy asked.

"No," Janet said. "Every Friday night he and his Charlestown buddies get together at a local bar. Girlfriends and wives are not invited. It's the proverbial boys' night out. And in his case, it's some kind of Irish tradition, complete with brawls."

"Sounds disgusting," Dorothy said.

"After four years at Harvard, a year of molecular biology at MIT, and now three years of medical school, you'd think he'd have outgrown it. Instead, these Friday nights seem to be more important to him than ever."

"I wouldn't stand for it," Dorothy said. "I used to think my husband's golf fetish was bad, but it's nothing compared to what you're talking about. Are there women involved in these Friday night escapades?"

"Sometimes they go up to Revere. There's a strip joint there. But mostly it's just Sean and the boys, drinking beer, telling jokes, and watching sports on a big-screen TV. At least that's how he's described it. Obviously I've never been there."

"Maybe you should ask yourself why you're involved with this man," Dorothy said.

"I have," Janet said. "Particularly lately, and especially since we've had so little communication. It's hard even to find time to talk with him. Not only does he have all the work associated with med school, but he has his research too. He's in an M.D.-Ph.D. program at Harvard."

"He must be intelligent," Dorothy offered.

"It's his only saving grace," Janet said. "That and his body."

Dorothy laughed. "At least there's a couple of things to justify your anguish. But I wouldn't let my husband get away with that juvenile Friday night stuff. Hell, I'd march right in and embarrass the heck out of him. Men will be boys, but there have to be some limits."

"I don't know if I could do that," Janet said. But as she took a sip from her coffee, she gave the idea some thought. The problem was that she'd always been so passive in her life, letting things happen, then reacting after the fact. Maybe that's how she got herself into this kind of trouble. Maybe she needed to encourage herself to be more assertive.

"Damn it, Marcie!" Louis Martin shouted. "Where the hell are those projections? I told you I wanted them on my desk." To emphasize his displeasure, Louis slapped his hand on his leather-bound blotter, sending a flurry of papers wafting off into the air. He had been feeling irritable ever since he'd awakened at four-thirty that morning with a dull headache. While in the bathroom searching for aspirin, he'd vomited into the sink. The episode had shocked him. His retching had come with no warning and no accompanying nausea.

Marcie Delgado scurried into her boss's office. He'd been yelling at her and criticizing her all day. Meekly she reached across the desk and pushed a stack of papers bound with a metal clip directly in front of the man. In block letters on the front cover was: PROJECTIONS FOR BOARD MEETING FEBRUARY 26.

Without even an acknowledgment, much less an apology, Louis snatched up the documents and stormed out of the office. But he didn't get far. After half a dozen steps, he couldn't recall where he was going. When he finally remembered he was headed for the boardroom, he wasn't sure which door it was.

"Good afternoon, Louis," one of the directors said, coming up behind him and opening the door on the right.

Louis stepped into the room feeling disoriented. He hazarded a furtive glance at the people sitting around the long conference table. To his consternation, he was unable to recognize a single face. Lowering his eyes to stare at the packet of papers he'd carried in with him, he let them slip from his grasp. His hands were shaking.

Louis Martin stood for another moment while the babble of voices in the room quieted. All eyes were drawn to his face, which had turned ghostly pale. Then Louis's eyes rolled up inside his head, and his back arched. He fell backward, his head striking the carpeted floor with a dull thump. Simultaneous with the impact on the floor, Louis's body began to tremble before being overwhelmed by wild tonic and clonic muscular contractions.

None of Louis's board of directors had ever seen a grand mal seizure, and for a moment they were all stunned. Finally, one man overcame his shock and rushed to the side of his stricken chairman. Only then did others respond by racing off to nearby telephones to call for help.

By the time the ambulance crew arrived, the seizure had passed. Except for a residual headache and lethargy, Louis felt relatively normal. He was no longer disoriented. In fact, he was dismayed to be told he'd had a seizure. As far as he was concerned, he'd only fainted.

The first person to see Louis in the emergency room at the Boston Memorial Hospital was a medical resident who introduced himself as George Carver. George seemed harried but thorough. After conducting a preliminary examination he told Louis that he would have to be admitted even though Louis's private internist, Clarence Handlin, had not yet been consulted.

"Is a seizure serious?" Louis asked. After his prostate operation two months earlier, Louis was not happy about the prospect of being hospitalized.

"We'll get a neurology consult," George said.

"But what's *your* opinion?" Louis asked.

"Seizures with sudden onset in an adult suggests structural brain disease," George said.

"How about talking English," Louis said. He hated medical jargon.

The resident fidgeted. "Structural means exactly that," he said evasively. "Something abnormal with the brain itself, not just its function."

"You mean like a brain tumor?" Louis asked.

"It could be a tumor," George said reluctantly.

"Good Lord!" Louis said. He felt himself break out in a cold sweat.

After calming the patient the best he could, George went into the "pit," as the center of the emergency room was called by those that worked there. First he checked to see if Louis's private physician had called in yet. He hadn't. Then he paged a neurology resident stat. He also told the ER clerk to call the medical student who was up for the next admission.

"By the way," George said to the clerk as he was returning to the cubicle where Louis Martin was waiting. "What's the name of the medical student?"

"Sean Murphy," the clerk said.

"Crap!" Sean said as his beeper went off. He was certain that Janet had long since disappeared, but just to be sure, he opened the door carefully and scanned the area. He didn't see her, so he pushed through. He had to use the phone out in the nurses' station since Peter was hogging the one in the back room, trying to get last-minute lab reports.

Before Sean called anybody, he approached Carla Valentine, the head nurse. "You guys looking for me?" he asked expectantly. He was hoping they were because then the page would involve some easily performed scut work. What Sean feared was that the page was coming from either admitting or the ER.

"You're all clear for the moment," Carla said.

Sean then dialed the operator and got the bad news. It was the ER with an admission.

Knowing the sooner he got the history and physical done, the better off he'd be, Sean bid farewell to Peter, who was still on the phone, and went downstairs.

Under normal circumstances Sean liked the ER and its constant sense of excitement and urgency. But on the afternoon of his last day on his medicine rotation, he didn't want another case. The typical Harvard medical student's workup took hours and filled between four and ten pages of tightly written notes.

"It's an interesting case," George said when Sean arrived. George was on hold on the phone with radiology.

"That's what you always say," Sean said.

"Truly," George said. "Have you ever seen papilledema?"

Sean shook his head.

"Grab an ophthalmoscope and look at the guy's nerve heads in both eyes. They'll look like miniature mountains. It means the intracranial pressure is elevated." George slid the ER clipboard along the countertop toward Sean.

"What's he got?" Sean asked.

"My guess is a brain tumor," George said. "He had a seizure at work."

At that moment someone came on the phone line from radiology, and George's attention was directed at scheduling an emergency CAT scan.

Sean took the ophthalmoscope and went in to see Mr. Martin. Sean was far from adept at using the instrument, but after persistence on his part and patience on Louis's part, he was able to catch fleeting glimpses of the mounded nerve heads.

Doing a medical student history and physical was a laborious task under the best of circumstances, and doing it in the emergency room and then up in X-ray while waiting for a CAT scan made it ten times more difficult. Sean persisted, asking as many questions as he could think of, especially about the current illness. What Sean learned that no one else had was that Louis Martin had had some transient headache, fever, and nausea and vomiting about a week after his prostate surgery in early January. Sean had stumbled onto this information just before Louis began his enhanced CAT scan. The technician had to order Sean out of the CAT scanner room and into the control room moments before the study commenced.

Besides the technician running the CAT scanner, there were a number of other people in the control room including Dr. Clarence Handlin, Louis Martin's internist, George Carver, the medical resident, and Harry O'Brian, the on-call neurology resident. They were all grouped around the CRT screen, waiting for the first "cuts" to appear.

Sean pulled George aside and told him about the earlier headache, fever, and nausea.

"A good pickup," George said while he pulled pensively at the skin at the edge of his jaw. He was obviously trying to relate these earlier symptoms to the current problem. "The fever is the curious part," he said. "Did he say it was a high fever?"

"Moderate," Sean said. "102 to 103. He said it was like having a cold or mild flu. Whatever it was, it went away completely."

"It might be related," George said. "At any rate this guy is a 'sickie.' The preliminary CAT scan showed two tumors. Remember Helen Cabot upstairs?"

"How can I forget?" Sean said. "She's still my patient."

"This guy's tumors look very similar to hers," George said.

The group of doctors around the CRT screen began talking excitedly. The first cuts were coming out. Sean and George stepped behind them and peered over their shoulders.

"Here they are again," Harry said, pointing with the tip of his percussion hammer. "They're definitely tumors. No doubt at all. And here's another small one."

Sean strained to see.

"Most likely metastases," Harry said. "Multiple tumors like this have to come from someplace else. Was his prostate benign?"

"Completely," Dr. Handlin said. "He's been in good health all his life."

"Smoke?" Harry asked.

"No," Sean said. The people in front moved to give Sean a better view of the CRT screen.

"We'll have to do a full metastatic workup," Harry said.

Sean bent over close to the CRT screen. The areas of reduced uptake were apparent even to his inexperienced eye. But what really caught his attention was how much they resembled Helen Cabot's tumors, as George had said. And like hers, they were all in the cerebrum. That had been a point of particular interest with Helen Cabot, since medulloblastomas generally occurred in the cerebellum, not the cerebrum.

"I know statistically you have to think of a metastasis from lung, colon, or prostate," George said. "But what are the chances we're seeing a tumor similar to Helen Cabot's? In other words, multifocal primary brain cancer like medulloblastoma."

Harry shook his head. "Remember, when you hear hoofbeats you should think of horses, not zebras. Helen Cabot's case is unique even though there have been a couple of similar cases recently reported around the country. Nonetheless, I'll be willing to wager anyone that we're looking at metastatic tumors here."

"What service do you think he should be on?" George asked.

"Six of one, half dozen of another," Harry said. "If he's on neurology, we'll need an internal medicine consult for the metastatic workup. If he's on internal medicine, he'll need the neuro consult."

"Since we took Cabot," George suggested, "why don't you guys take him. You interact better with neurosurgery anyway."

"Fine by me," Harry said.

Sean groaned inwardly. All his work doing the history and physical was for naught. Since the patient would be admitted to neurology, the medical student on neurology would get credit for it. But at least that meant Sean was free.

Sean motioned to George that he'd see him later on rounds, then slipped out of the CAT scan room. Although he was behind on his off-service notes, Sean took the time for a visit. Having been thinking and talking about Helen Cabot, he wanted to see her. Getting off the elevator on the seventh floor, he walked directly down to room 708 and knocked on the half-open door.

Despite her shaved head and a series of blue marker stains on her scalp, Helen Cabot still managed to look attractive. Her features were delicate, emphasizing her large, bright green eyes. Her skin had the translucent perfection of a model. Yet she was pale, and there was little doubt she was ill. Still, her face lit up when she saw Sean.

"My favorite doctor," she said.

"Doctor-to-be," Sean corrected her. He didn't enjoy the charade of playing doctor like many medical students. Ever since he graduated from high school he'd felt like an imposter, playacting first at the role of a Harvard undergraduate, then an MIT fellow, and now a Harvard medical student.

"Have you heard the good news?" Helen asked. She sat up despite her weakness from the many seizures she'd been having.

"Tell me," Sean said.

"I've been accepted into the Forbes Cancer Center protocol," Helen said.

"Fantastic!" Sean said. "Now I can tell you I'm heading there myself. I've been afraid to mention it until I heard you were going too."

"What a marvelous coincidence!" Helen said. "Now I'll have a friend there. I suppose you know that with my particular type of tumor they've had a one hundred percent remission."

"I know," Sean said. "Their results are unbelievable. But it's no coincidence we'll be down there together. It was your case that made me aware of the Forbes. As I've mentioned to you, my research involves the molecular basis of cancer. So discovering a clinic where they are having hundred-percent success treating a specific cancer is extraordinarily exciting for me. I'm amazed I hadn't read about it in the medical literature. Anyway, I want to go down there and find out exactly what they're doing."

"Their treatment is still experimental," Helen said. "My father emphasized that to me. We think the reason they've avoided publishing their results is that they first want to be absolutely sure of their claims. But whether they've published or not, I can't wait to get there and start treatment. It's the first ray of hope since this nightmare started."

"When are you going?" Sean asked.

"Sometime next week," Helen said. "And you?"

"I'll be on the road the crack of dawn on Sunday. I should be there early Tuesday morning. I'll be waiting for you." Sean reached out and gripped Helen's shoulder.

Helen smiled, placing her hand over Sean's.

After completing report, Janet returned to the seventh floor to look for Sean. Once again the nurses said he'd been there only moments earlier but apparently had disappeared. They suggested paging him, but Janet wanted to catch him off guard. Since it was now after four she thought the best place to find him would be Dr. Clifford Walsh's lab. Dr. Walsh was Sean's Ph.D. advisor.

To get there, Janet had to leave the hospital, brace herself against the winter wind, walk partway down Longfellow Avenue, cross the medical school quadrangle, and climb to the third floor. Even before she opened the door to the lab, she knew she'd guessed correctly. She recognized Sean's figure through the frosted glass. It was mostly the way he moved that was so familiar. He had surprising grace for such a stocky, muscular frame. There was no wasted motion. He went about his tasks quickly and efficiently.

Entering the room, Janet closed the door behind her and hesitated. For a moment she enjoyed watching Sean. Besides Sean there were three other people busily working. A radio played classical music. There was no conversation.

It was a rather dated and cluttered lab with soapstone-topped benches. The newest equipment were the computers and a series of desk-sized analyzers. Sean had described the subject of his Ph.D. thesis on several occasions, but Janet still wasn't a hundred percent certain she understood it all. He was searching for specialized genes called oncogenes that had the capability of encouraging a cell to become cancerous. Sean had explained that the origins of oncogenes seemed to be from normal "cellular control" genes that certain types of viruses called retroviruses had a tendency to capture in order to stimulate viral production in future host cells.

Janet had nodded at appropriate times during these explanations but had always found herself more interested by Sean's enthusiasm than the subject matter. She also realized that she needed to do some more basic reading in the area of molecular genetics if she was to understand Sean's particular area of research.

Sean had a tendency to assume that she had more knowledge than she had, in a field where advances came at a dizzying pace.

As Janet watched Sean from just inside the door, appreciating the V that his broad shoulders and narrow waist formed, she became curious about what he was currently doing. In sharp contrast to many other visits she'd made over the last two months, he wasn't preparing one of the analyzers to run. Instead he seemed to be putting objects away and cleaning up.

After watching for several minutes, expecting him to notice her, Janet stepped forward and stood right next to him. At five-six Janet was relatively tall, and since Sean was only five-nine, they could just about look each other in the eye, especially when Janet wore heels.

"What may I ask are you doing?" Janet said suddenly.

Sean jumped. His level of concentration had been so great he'd not sensed her presence.

"Just cleaning up," he said guiltily.

Janet leaned forward and looked into his startlingly blue eyes. He returned her stare for a moment, then looked away.

"Cleaning up?" Janet asked. Her eyes swept around the now pristine lab bench. "That's a surprise." Janet redirected her eyes at his face. "What's going on here? This is the most immaculate your work area has ever been. Is there something you haven't told me?"

"No," Sean said. Then he paused before adding, "Well, yes, there is. I'm taking a two-month research elective."

"Where?"

"Miami, Florida."

"You weren't going to tell me?"

"Of course I was. I planned on telling you tomorrow night."

"When are you leaving?"

"Sunday."

Janet's eyes angrily roamed the room. Absently, her fingers drummed on the countertop. She questioned to herself what she'd done to deserve this kind of treatment. Looking back at Sean, she said: "You were going to wait until the night before to tell me this?"

"It just came up this week. It wasn't certain until two days ago. I wanted to wait until the right moment."

"Considering our relationship, the right moment would have been when it came up. Miami? Why now?"

"Remember that patient I told you about? The woman with medulloblastoma."

"Helen Cabot? The attractive coed?"

"That's the one," Sean said. "When I read about her tumor, I discovered . . ." He paused.

"Discovered what?" Janet demanded.

"It wasn't from my reading," Sean corrected himself. "One of her attendings said that her father had heard about a treatment that is apparently achieving one hundred percent remission. The protocol is only administered at the Forbes Cancer Center in Miami."

"So you decided to go. Just like that."

"Not exactly," Sean said. "I spoke to Dr. Walsh, who happens to know the director, a man named Randolph Mason. A number of years ago they worked together at the NIH. Dr. Walsh told him about me, and got me invited."

"This is the wrong time for this," Janet said. "You know I've been disturbed about us."

Sean shrugged. "I'm sorry. But I have the time now, and this is potentially consequential. My research involves the molecular basis of cancer. If they are experiencing a hundred-percent remission rate for a specific tumor, it has to have implications for all cancers."

Janet felt weak. Her emotions were raw. Sean's leaving for two months at this time seemed the worst possible situation as far as her psyche was concerned. Yet his reasons were noble. He wasn't going to the Club Med or something. How could she get angry or try to deny him. She felt totally confused.

"There is the telephone," Sean said. "I'm not going to the moon. It's only a couple of months. And you understand that this could be very important."

"More important than our relationship?" Janet blurted out. "More important than the rest of our lives?" Almost immediately Janet felt foolish. Such comments sounded so juvenile.

"Now let's not get into an argument comparing apples and oranges," Sean said.

Janet sighed deeply, fighting back tears. "Let's talk about it later," she managed. "This is hardly the place for an emotional confrontation."

"I can't tonight," Sean said. "It's Friday and . . ."

"And you have to go to that stupid bar," Janet snapped. She saw some of the other people in the room turn to stare at them.

"Janet, keep your voice down!" Sean said. "We'll get together Saturday night as planned. We can talk then."

"Knowing how upset this leaving would make me, I cannot understand why you can't give up drinking with your trashy buddies for one night."

"Careful, Janet," Sean warned. "My friends are important to me. They're my roots."

For a moment their eyes met with palpable hostility. Then Janet turned and strode from the lab.

Self-consciously, Sean glanced at his colleagues. Most avoided his gaze. Dr. Clifford Walsh did not. He was a big man with a full beard. He wore a long white coat with the sleeves rolled up to the elbows.

"Turmoil does not help creativity," he said. "I hope your leaving on this sour note does not influence your behavior down in Miami."

"Not a chance," Sean said.

"Remember, I've gone out on a limb for you," Dr. Walsh said. "I assured Dr. Mason you'd be an asset to his organization. He liked the idea that you've had a lot of experience with monoclonal antibodies."

"That's what you told him?" Sean questioned with dismay.

"I could tell from our conversation that he'd be interested in that," Dr. Walsh explained. "Don't get your dander up."

"But that was what I did three years ago at MIT," Sean said. "Protein chemistry and I have parted ways."

"I know you're interested in oncogenes now," Dr. Walsh said, "but you wanted the job and I did what I thought was best to get you invited. When you are there, you can explain you'd rather work in molecular genetics. Knowing you as I do, I'm not worried about you making your feelings known. Just try to be tactful."

"I've read some of the work of the chief investigator," Sean said. "It's perfect for me. Her background is in retroviruses and oncogenes."

"That's Dr. Deborah Levy," Dr. Walsh said. "Maybe you can get to work with her. But whether you do or not, just be grateful you've been invited at this late date."

"I just don't want to get all the way down there and get stuck with busy-work."

"Promise me you won't cause trouble," Dr. Walsh said.

"Me?" Sean asked with eyebrows arched. "You know me better than that."

"I know you too well," Dr. Walsh said. "That's the problem. Your brashness can be disturbing, to put it mildly, but at least thank the Lord for your intelligence."

FEBRUARY 26 • FRIDAY, 4:45 P.M.

"Just a second, Corissa," Kathleen Sharenburg said as she stopped and leaned against one of the cosmetic counters of Neiman Marcus. They'd come to the mall just west of Houston to shop for dresses for a school dance. Now that they had made their purchases, Corissa was eager to get home.

Kathleen had had a sudden sensation of dizziness giving her the sickening sensation that the room was spinning. Luckily, as soon as she touched the countertop, the spinning stopped. She then shuddered through a wave of nausea. But it too passed.

"You all right?" Corissa asked. They were both juniors in high school.

"I don't know," Kathleen said. The headache she'd had off and on for the last few days was back. It had been awakening her from sleep, but she hadn't said anything to her parents, afraid that it might be related to the pot she'd smoked the weekend before.

"You look white as a ghost," Corissa said. "Maybe we shouldn't have eaten that fudge."

"Oh my God!" Kathleen whispered. "That man over there is listening to us. He's planning on kidnapping us in the parking garage."

Corissa spun about, half expecting some fearful man to be towering over them. But all she saw was a handful of peaceful, women shoppers, mostly at the cosmetic counters. She didn't see any man.

"What man are you talking about?" she asked.

Kathleen's eyes stared ahead, unblinking. "That man over there near the coats." She pointed with her left hand.

Corissa followed the direction of Kathleen's finger and finally saw a man almost fifty yards away. He was standing behind a woman who was shuffling through a rack of merchandise. He wasn't even facing toward them.

Confused, Corissa turned back to her best friend.

"He's saying we cannot leave the store," Kathleen said.

"What are you talking about?" Corissa questioned. "I mean, you're starting to scare me."

"We have to get out of here," Kathleen warned. Abruptly she turned and headed in the opposite direction. Corissa had to run to catch up with her. She grabbed Kathleen's arm and yanked her around.

"What is wrong with you?" Corissa demanded.

Kathleen's face was a mask of terror. "There are more men now," she said urgently. "They are coming down the escalator. They're talking about getting us as well."

Corissa turned. Several men were indeed coming down the escalator. But at such a distance Corissa couldn't even see their faces much less hear what they said.

Kathleen's scream jolted Corissa like an electric charge. Corissa spun around and saw Kathleen begin to collapse. Reaching out, Corissa tried to keep Kathleen from falling. But they were off balance, and they both fell to the floor in a tangle of arms and legs.

Before Corissa could extract herself, Kathleen began to convulse. Her body heaved wildly against the marble floor.

Helping hands got Corissa to her feet. Two women who'd been at a neighboring cosmetic counter attended to Kathleen. They restrained her from hitting her head on the floor and managed to get something between her teeth. A trickle of blood oozed from Kathleen's lips. She had bitten her tongue.

"Oh my God, oh my God!" Corissa kept repeating.

"What's her name?" one of the women attending Kathleen asked.

"Kathleen Sharenburg," Corissa said. "Her father is Ted Sharenburg, head of Shell Oil," she added, as if that fact would somehow help her friend now.

"Somebody better call an ambulance," the woman said. "This girl's seizure has to be stopped."

It was already dark as Janet tried to see out the window of the Ritz Café. People were scurrying past in both directions on Newbury Street, their hands clasped to either coat lapels or hat.

"I don't know what you see in him anyway," Evelyn Reardon was saying. "I told you the day you brought him home he was inappropriate."

"He's earning both his Ph.D. and an M.D. from Harvard," Janet reminded her mother.

"That doesn't excuse his manners, or lack thereof," Evelyn said.

Janet eyed her mother. She was a tall, slender woman with straight, even features. Few people had trouble recognizing that Evelyn and Janet were mother and daughter.

"Sean is proud of his heritage," Janet said. "He likes the fact that he's from working stock."

"There's nothing wrong in that," Evelyn said. "The problem is being mired in it. The boy has no manners. And that long hair of his . . ."

"He feels convention is stifling," Janet said. As usual she found herself in the unenviable position of defending Sean. It was particularly galling at the moment since she was cross with him. What she'd hoped for from her mother was advice, not the same old criticism.

"How trite," Evelyn said. "If he was planning on practicing like a regular doctor, there might be hope. But this molecular biology, or whatever it is, I don't understand. What is he studying again?"

"Oncogenes," Janet said. She should have known better than to turn to her mother.

"Explain what they are once more," Evelyn said.

Janet poured herself more tea. Her mother could be trying, and attempting to describe Sean's research to her was like the blind leading the blind. But she tried nonetheless.

"Oncogenes are genes that are capable of changing normal cells into cancer cells," Janet said. "They come from normal cellular genes present in every living cell called proto-oncogenes. Sean feels that a true understanding of cancer will come only when all the proto-oncogenes and oncogenes are discovered and defined. And that's what he's doing: searching for oncogenes in specialized viruses."

"It may be very worthwhile," Evelyn said. "But it's all very arcane and hardly the type of career to support a family on."

"Don't be so sure," Janet said. "Sean and a couple of his fellow students at MIT started a company to make monoclonal antibodies while he was getting his master's degree. They called it Immunotherapy, Inc. Over a year ago it was bought out by Genentech."

"That's encouraging," Evelyn said. "Did Sean make a good profit?"

"They all did," Janet said. "But they agreed to reinvest it in a new company. That's all I can say at the moment. He's sworn me to secrecy."

"A secret from your mother?" Evelyn questioned. "Sounds a bit melodramatic. But you know your father wouldn't approve. He's always said that people should avoid using their own capital in starting new enterprises."

Janet sighed in frustration. "All this is beside the point," she said. "What I wanted to hear is what you think about my going to Florida. Sean's going to be there for two months. All he'll be doing is research. Here in Boston he's doing research plus schoolwork. I thought maybe we'd have a better chance to talk and work things out."

"What about your job at Memorial?" Evelyn asked.

"I can take a leave," Janet said. "And I can certainly work down there. One of the benefits of being a nurse is that I can find employment just about anywhere."

"Well, I don't think it is a good idea," Evelyn said.

"Why?"

"It's not right to go running after this boy," Evelyn said. "Particularly since you know how your father and I feel about him. He's never going to fit into our family. And after what he said to Uncle Albert I wouldn't even know where to seat him at a dinner party."

"Uncle Albert was teasing him about his hair," Janet said. "He wouldn't stop."

"That's no excuse for saying what he did to one's elder."

"We all know that Uncle Albert wears a toupee," Janet said.

"We may know but we don't mention it," Evelyn said. "And calling it a rug in front of everyone was inexcusable."

Janet took a sip of her tea and stared out the window. It was true the whole family knew Uncle Albert wore a toupee. It was also true that no one ever commented on it. Janet had grown up in a family where there were many unspoken rules. Individual expression, especially in children, was not encouraged. Manners were considered of paramount importance.

"Why don't you date that lovely young man who brought you to the Myopia Hunt Club polo match last year," Evelyn suggested.

"He was a jerk," Janet said.

"Janet!" her mother warned.

They drank their tea in silence for a few moments. "If you want to talk to him so much," Evelyn finally said, "why not do it before he leaves? Go see him tonight?"

"I can't," Janet said. "Friday night is his night with the boys. They all hang out at some bar near where he went to high school."

"As your father would say, I rest my case," Evelyn said with uncamouflaged satisfaction.

———

A hooded sweatshirt under a wool jacket insulated Sean from the freezing mist. The cinch for the hood had been drawn tight and tied beneath his chin. As he jogged along High Street toward Monument Square in Charlestown, he passed a basketball from one hand to the other. He'd just finished playing a pickup game at the Charlestown Boys Club with a group called "The Alumni." This was a motley assortment of friends and acquaintances from age eighteen to sixty. It had been a good workout, and he was still sweating.

Skirting Monument Square with its enormous phallic monument commemorating the Battle of Bunker Hill, Sean approached his boyhood home. As a plumber his father, Brian Murphy, Sr., had had a decent income, and back before it became fashionable to live in the city, he had purchased a large Victorian town house. At first the Murphys had lived in the ground-floor duplex, but after his father had died at age forty-six from liver cancer the rental from the duplex had been sorely needed. When Sean's older brother, Brian, Jr., had gone away to school, Sean, his younger brother Charles, and his mother Anne had moved into one of the single-floor apartments. Now she lived there alone.

As he reached the door, Sean noticed a familiar Mercedes parked just behind his Isuzu 4×4, indicating older brother Brian had made one of his surprise visits. Intuitively, Sean knew he was in for grief about his planned trip to Miami.

Taking the stairs two at a time, Sean unlocked his mother's door and stepped inside. Brian's black leather briefcase rested on a ladder-back chair. A rich smell of pot roast filled the air.

"Is that you, Sean?" Anne called from the kitchen. She appeared in the doorway just as Sean was hanging up his coat. Dressed in a simple housedress covered by a worn apron, Anne looked considerably older than her fifty-four years. After her long, repressing marriage to the hard-drinking Brian Murphy, her face had become permanently drawn, her eyes generally tired and forlorn. Her hair, which she wore in an old-fashioned bun, was naturally curly and although it had been an attractive dark brown, it was now streaked with gray.

"Brian's here," Anne said.

"I guessed as much."

Sean went into the kitchen to say hello to his brother. Brian was at the kitchen table, nursing a drink. He'd removed his jacket and draped it over a chair; paisley suspenders looped over his shoulders. Like Sean, he had darkly handsome features, black hair, and brilliant blue eyes. But the similarities ended there. Where Sean was brash and casual, Brian was circumspect and precise. Unlike Sean's shaggy locks, Brian's hair was neatly trimmed and precisely parted. He sported a carefully trimmed mustache. His clothing was decidedly lawyer-like and leaned toward dark blue pinstripes.

"Am I responsible for this honor?" Sean asked. Brian did not visit often even though he lived nearby in Back Bay.

"Mother called me," Brian admitted.

It didn't take Sean long to shower, shave, and dress in jeans and a rugby shirt. He was back in the kitchen before Brian finished carving the pot roast. Sean helped set the table. While he did so, he eyed his older brother. There had been a time when Sean resented him. For years his mother had introduced her boys as my wonderful Brian, my good Charles, and Sean. Charles was currently off in a seminary in New Jersey studying to become a priest.

Like Sean, Brian had always been an athlete, although not as successful. He'd been a studious child and usually at home. He'd gone to the University of Massachusetts, then on to law school at B.U. Everybody had always liked Brian. Everyone had always known that he would be successful and that he would surely escape the Irish curse of alcohol, guilt, depression, and tragedy. Sean, on the other hand, had always been the wild one, preferring the company of the neighborhood ne'er-do-wells and frequently in trouble with the authorities involving brawls, minor burglary, and stolen-car joyrides. If it hadn't been for Sean's extraordinary intelligence and his facility with a hockey stick, he might have ended up in Bridgewater Prison instead of Harvard. Within the ghettos of the city the dividing line between success and failure was a narrow band of chance that the kids teetered on all through their turbulent adolescent years.

There was little conversation during the final dinner preparations. But once they sat down, Brian cleared his throat after taking a sip of his milk. They'd always drunk milk with dinner throughout their boyhoods.

"Mother is upset about this Miami idea," Brian said.

Anne looked down at her plate. She'd always been self-effacing, especially when Brian Sr. was alive. He'd had a terrible temper made worse by alcohol, and alcohol had been a daily indulgence. Every afternoon after unplugging drains, fixing aged boilers, and installing toilets, Brian Sr. would stop at the Blue Tower bar beneath the Tobin Bridge. Nearly every night he'd come home drunk, sour, and vicious. Anne was the usual target, although Sean had come in for his share of blows when he tried to protect her. By morning Brian Sr. would be sober, and consumed by guilt; he'd swear he would change. But he never did. Even when he'd lost seventy-five pounds and was dying from liver cancer, his behavior was the same.

"I'm going down there to do research," Sean said. "It's no big deal."

"There's drugs in Miami," Anne said. She didn't look up.

Sean rolled his eyes. He reached over and grasped his mother's arm. "Mom, my problem with drugs was in high school. I'm in medical school now."

"What about that incident your first year of college?" Brian added.

"That was only a little coke at a party," Sean said. "It was just unlucky the police decided to raid the place."

"The lucky thing was my getting your juvenile record sealed. Otherwise you would have been in a hell of a fix."

"Miami is a violent city," Anne said. "I read about it in the newspapers all the time."

"Jesus Christ!" Sean exclaimed.

"Don't use the Lord's name in vain," Anne said.

"Mom, you've been watching too much television. Miami is like any city, with both good and bad elements. But it doesn't matter. I'll be doing research. I won't have time to get into trouble even if I wanted to."

"You'll meet the wrong kind of people," Anne said.

"Mom, I'm an adult," Sean said in frustration.

"You are still hanging out with the wrong people here in Charlestown," Brian said. "Mom's fears are not unreasonable. The whole neighborhood knows Jimmy O'Connor and Brady Flanagan are still breaking and entering."

"And sending the money to the IRA," Sean said.

"They are not political activists," Brian said. "They are hoodlums. And you choose to remain friends."

"I have a few beers with them on Friday nights," Sean said.

"Precisely," Brian said. "Like our father, the pub is your home away from home. And apart from Mom's concerns, this isn't a good time for you to be away. The Franklin Bank will be coming up with the rest of the financing for Oncogen. I've got the papers almost ready. Things could move quickly."

"In case you've forgotten, there are fax machines and overnight delivery," Sean said, scraping his chair back from the table. He stood up and carried his plate over to the sink. "I'm going to Miami no matter what anybody says. I believe the Forbes Cancer Center has hit on something extraordinarily important. And now if you two co-conspirators will allow me, I'm going out to drink with my delinquent friends."

Feeling irritable, Sean struggled into the old pea coat that his father had gotten back when the Charlestown Navy Yard was still functioning. Pulling a wool watch cap over his ears, he ran downstairs to the street and set out into the freezing rain. The wind had shifted to the east and he could smell the salt sea air. As he neared Old Scully's Bar on Bunker Hill Street, the warm incandescent glow from the misted windows emanated a familiar sense of comfort and security.

Pushing open the door he allowed himself to be enveloped by the dimly lit, noisy environment. It was not a classy place. The pine wood paneling was almost black with cigarette smoke. The furniture was scraped and scarred. The only bright spot was the brass footrail kept polished by innumerable shoes rubbing across its surface. In the far corner a TV was bolted to the ceiling and tuned to a Bruins hockey game.

The only woman in the crowded room was Molly, who shared bartending duties with Pete. Before Sean could even say anything a brimming mug of ale slid along the bar toward him. A hand grasped his shoulder as a cheer spread through the crowd. The Bruins had scored a goal.

Sean sighed contentedly. It was as if he were at home. He had the same comfortable feeling he'd get whenever he was particularly exhausted and settled into a soft bed.

As usual, Jimmy and Brady drifted over and began to brag about a little job they'd done in Marblehead the previous weekend. That led to humorous recollections of when Sean had been "one of the guys."

"We always knew you were smart the way you could figure out alarms,"

Brady said. "But we never guessed you'd go to Harvard. How could you stand all those jerks."

It was a statement, not a question, and Sean let it pass, but the comment made him realize how much he'd changed. He still enjoyed Old Scully's Bar, but more as an observer. It was an uncomfortable acknowledgment because he didn't truly feel part of the Harvard medical world either. He felt rather like a social orphan.

A few hours later when Sean had had a few drafts, and he was feeling more mellow and less an outcast, he joined in the raucous decisionmaking involving a trip up to Revere to one of the strip joints near the waterfront. Just at the moment the debate was reaching a frenzied climax, the entire bar went dead silent. One by one heads turned toward the front door. Something extraordinary had happened, and everyone was shocked. A woman had breached their all-male bastion. And it wasn't an ordinary woman, like some overweight, gum-chewing girl in the laundromat. It was a slim, gorgeous woman who obviously wasn't from Charlestown.

Her long blond hair glistened with diamonds of moisture, and it contrasted dramatically with the rich deep mahogany of her mink jacket. Her eyes were almond shaped and pert as they audaciously scanned the room, leaping from one stunned face to another. Her mouth was set in determination. Her high cheekbones glowed with color. She appeared like a collective hallucination of some fantasy female.

A few of the guys shifted nervously, guessing that she was someone's girlfriend. She was too beautiful to be anyone's wife.

Sean was one of the last faces to turn. And when he did, his mouth dropped open. It was Janet!

Janet spotted him about the same time he saw her. She walked directly up to him and pushed in beside him at the bar. Brady moved away, making an exaggerated gesture of terror as if Janet were a fearful creature.

"I'd like a beer, please," she said.

Without answering, Molly filled a chilled mug and placed it in front of Janet.

The room remained silent except for the television.

Janet took a sip and turned to look at Sean. Since she was wearing pumps she was just about eye level. "I want to talk with you," she said.

Sean hadn't felt this embarrassed since he'd been caught with his pants off at age sixteen with Kelly Parnell in the back of her family's car.

Putting his beer down, Sean grasped Janet by her upper arm, just above the elbow, and marched her out the door. When they got out on the sidewalk Sean had recovered enough to be angry. He was also a little tipsy.

"What are you doing here?" he demanded.

Sean allowed his eyes to sweep around the neighborhood. "I don't believe this. You know you weren't supposed to come here."

"I knew nothing of the kind," Janet said. "I knew I wasn't invited, if that's what you mean. But I didn't think my coming constituted a capital offense. It's important I talk with you, and with you leaving on Sunday, I think it's more important than drinking with these so-called friends of yours."

"And who is making that value judgment?" Sean demanded. "I'm the one who decides what is important to me, not you, and I resent this intrusion."

"I need to talk to you about Miami," Janet said. "It's your fault you've waited until the last minute to tell me."

"There's nothing to talk about," Sean said. "I'm going and that's final. Not you, not my mother, and not my brother are going to stop me. Now if you'll excuse me, I have to go back in and see what I can salvage of my self-respect."

"But this can impact the rest of our lives," Janet said. Tears began to mix with the rain running down her cheeks. She'd taken an emotional risk coming to Charlestown, and the idea of rejection was devastating.

"I'll talk with you tomorrow," Sean said. "Good night, Janet."

Ted Sharenburg was nervous, waiting for the doctors to tell him what was wrong with his daughter. His wife had gotten in touch with him in New Orleans where he'd been on business, and he had gotten the company Gulfstream jet to fly him directly back to Houston. As the CEO of an oil company that had made major contributions to the Houston hospitals, Ted Sharenburg was afforded special treatment. At that moment his daughter was inside the huge, multimillion-dollar MRI machine having an emergency brain scan.

"We don't know much yet," Dr. Judy Buckley said. "These initial images are very superficial cuts." Judy Buckley was the chief of neuroradiology and had been happy to come into the hospital at the director's request. Also in attendance were Dr. Vance Martinez, the Sharenburgs' internist, and Dr. Stanton Rainey, chief of neurology. It was a prominent group of experts to be assembled at any hour, much less at one o'clock in the morning.

Ted paced the tiny control room. He couldn't sit still. The story he'd been told about his daughter had been devastating.

"She experienced an acute paranoid psychosis," Dr. Martinez had explained. "Symptoms like that can occur, especially with some sort of involvement of the temporal lobe."

Ted reached the end of the room for the fiftieth time and turned. He looked through the glass at the giant MRI machine. He could just barely see his daughter. It was as if she were being swallowed by a technological whale. He hated being so helpless. All he could do was watch, and hope. He'd felt almost as vulnerable when she'd had her tonsils out a few months earlier.

"We've got something," Dr. Buckley said.

Ted hurried over to the CRT screen.

"There's a hyperintense circumscribed area in the right temporal lobe," she said.

"What does it mean?" Ted demanded.

The doctors exchanged glances. It was not customary for the relative of a patient to be in the room during such a study.

"It's probably a mass lesion," Dr. Buckley said.

"Can you put that in lay terms?" Ted asked, trying to keep his voice even.

"She means a brain tumor," Dr. Martinez said. "But we know very little at this point, and we should not jump to conclusions. The lesion might have been there for years."

Ted swayed. His worst fears were materializing. Why couldn't he be in that machine and not his daughter?

"Uh-oh!" Dr. Buckley said, forgetting the effect such an exclamation would have on Ted. "Here's another lesion."

The doctors clustered around the screen, transfixed by the vertically unfolding images. For a few moments they forgot about Ted.

"You know, it reminds me of the case I told you about in Boston," said Dr. Rainey. "A young woman in her twenties with multiple intracranial tumors and negative metastatic workup. She was proved to have medulloblastoma."

"I thought medulloblastoma occurs in the posterior fossa," Dr. Martinez said.

"It usually does," Dr. Rainey said. "It also usually occurs in younger kids. But twenty percent or so of the incidents are in patients over twenty, and it's occasionally found in regions of the brain besides the cerebellum. Actually, it would be wonderful if it turns out to be medulloblastoma in this case."

"Why?" Dr. Buckley asked. She was aware of the high mortality of the cancer.

"Because a group down in Miami has had remarkable success in getting remissions with that particular tumor."

"What's their name?" Ted demanded, clutching onto the first hopeful news he'd heard.

"The Forbes Cancer Center," Dr. Rainey said. "They haven't published yet but word of that kind of a result gets around."

MARCH 2 • TUESDAY, 6:15 A.M.

When Tom Widdicomb awoke at 6:15 to begin his workday, Sean Murphy had already been on the road for several hours, planning on reaching the Forbes Cancer Center by mid-morning. Tom did not know Sean, and had no idea he was expected. Had he known that their lives would soon intersect, his anxiety would have been even greater. Tom was always anxious when he decided to help a patient, and the night before he'd decided to help not one but two women. Sandra Blankenship on the second floor would be the first. She was in great pain and already receiving her chemotherapy by IV. The other patient, Gloria D'Amataglio, was on the fourth floor. That was a bit more worrisome since the last patient he'd helped, Norma Taylor, had also been on the fourth floor. Tom didn't want any pattern to emerge.

His biggest problem was that he constantly worried about someone suspecting what he was doing, and on a day that he was going to act, his anxiety could be overwhelming. Still, sensitive to gossip on the wards, he'd heard nothing that suggested that anyone was suspicious. After all, he was dealing with women who were terminally ill. They were expected to die. Tom was merely saving everyone from additional suffering, especially the patient.

Tom showered, shaved, and dressed in his green uniform, then went into his mother's kitchen. She always got up before he did, insistent every morning as far back as he could remember that he should eat a good breakfast since he wasn't as strong as other boys. Tom and his mother, Alice, had lived together in their close, secret world from the time Tom's dad died when Tom was four. That was when he and his mother had started sleeping together, and his mother had started calling him "her little man."

"I'm going to help another woman today, Mom," Tom said as he sat down to eat his eggs and bacon. He knew how proud his mother was of him. She had always praised him even when he'd been a lonely child with eye problems. His schoolmates had teased him mercilessly about his crossed eyes, chasing him home nearly every day.

"Don't worry, my little man," Alice would say when he'd arrive at the house in tears. "We'll always have each other. We don't need other people."

And that was how things worked out. Tom had never felt any desire to leave home. For a while, he worked at a local veterinarian's. Then at his mother's suggestion, since she'd always been interested in medicine, he'd taken a course to be an EMT. After his training, he got a job with an ambulance company but had trouble getting along with the other workers. He decided he would be better off as an orderly. That way he wouldn't have to relate to so many people. First he'd worked at Miami General Hospital but got into a fight with his shift supervisor. Then he worked at a funeral home before joining the Forbes housekeeping staff.

"The woman's name is Sandra," Tom told his mother as he ran his dish under the faucet at the sink. "She's older than you. She's in a lot of pain. The 'problem' has spread to her spine."

When Tom spoke to his mother, he never used the word "cancer." Early in her illness, they'd decided not to say the word. They preferred less emotionally charged words like "problem" or "difficulty."

Tom had read about succinylcholine in a newspaper story about some doctor in New Jersey. His rudimentary medical training afforded an understanding of the physiologic principles. His freedom as a housekeeper allowed him contact with anesthesia carts. He'd never had any problem getting the drug. The problem had been where to hide it until it was needed. Then one day he found a convenient space above the wall cabinets in the housekeeping closet on the fourth floor. When he climbed up and looked into the area and saw the amount of accumulated dust, he knew his drug would never be disturbed.

"Don't worry about anything, Mom," Tom said as he prepared to leave. "I'll be home just as soon as I can. I'll miss you and I love you." Tom had been saying that ever since he had gone to school, and just because he'd had to put his mother to sleep three years ago, he didn't feel any need to change.

It was almost ten-thirty in the morning when Sean pulled his 4×4 into the parking area of the Forbes Cancer Center. It was a bright, clear, summer-like day. The temperature was somewhere around seventy, and after the freezing Boston rain Sean felt he was in heaven. He'd enjoyed the two-day drive, too. He could have made it faster, but the clinic wasn't expecting him until late that day so there'd been no need. He spent his first night in a motel just off I95 in Rocky Mount, North Carolina.

The next day had taken him deep into Florida where the depth of spring seemed to increase with every passing mile. The second night had been spent in perfumed delight near Vero Beach, Florida. When he asked the motel clerk about the wonderful aroma in the air he was told it came from the nearby citrus groves.

The last lap of the journey turned out to be the most difficult. From West Palm Beach south, particularly near Fort Lauderdale and into Miami, he fought rush-hour traffic. To his surprise even eight-laned I95 coagulated into a stop-and-go mess.

Sean locked his car, stretched, and gazed up at the imposing twin bronzed, mirrored towers of the Forbes Cancer Center. A covered pedestrian bridge constructed of the same material connected the buildings. He noted from the signs that the research and administration center was on the left while the hospital was on the right.

As Sean started for the entrance, he thought about his first impressions of Miami. They were mixed. As he'd come south on I95 and neared his turnoff, he'd been able to see the gleaming new downtown skyscrapers. But the areas adjacent to the highway had been a mélange of strip malls and low-income housing. The area around the Forbes Center, which was situated along the Miami River, was also rather seedy although a few modern buildings were interspersed among the flat-roofed cinder block structures.

As Sean pushed through the mirrored door, he thought wryly about the difficulty everyone had given him about this two-month elective. He wondered if his mother would ever get over the traumas he'd caused her as an adolescent. "You're too much like your father," she'd say, and it was meant as a reproach. Except for enjoying the pub, Sean felt little similarity with his father. But then he had been presented with far different choices and opportunities than his father ever had.

A black felt sign stood on an easel just inside the door. Spelled out in white plastic letters was his name and a message: Welcome. Sean thought it was a nice touch.

There was a small lounge directly behind the front door. Entrance into the building itself was blocked by a turnstile. Next to the turnstile was a Corian-covered desk. Behind the desk sat a swarthy, handsome Hispanic man dressed in a brown uniform complete with epaulets and peaked military-style hat. The outfit reminded Sean of a cross between those seen in Marine recruitment posters and those seen in Hollywood Gestapo movies. An elaborate emblem on the guard's left arm said "Security" and the name tag above his left pocket proclaimed that his name was Martinez.

"Can I help you?" Martinez asked in heavily accented English.

"I'm Sean Murphy," Sean said, pointing to the welcome sign.

The guard's expression did not change. He studied Sean for a beat then picked up one of several telephones. He spoke in rapid, staccato Spanish. After he hung up he pointed to a nearby leather couch. "A few moments, please."

Sean sat down. He picked up a copy of *Science* from a low coffee table and idly flipped the pages. But his attention was on Forbes' elaborate security system. Thick glass partitions separated the waiting area from the rest of the building. Apparently the guarded turnstile provided the only entrance.

Since security was all too frequently neglected in health care institutions, Sean was favorably impressed and said as much to the guard.

"There are some bad areas nearby," the guard replied but didn't elaborate.

Presently a second security officer appeared, dressed identically to the first. The turnstile opened to allow him into the lounge.

"My name is Ramirez," the second guard said. "Would you follow me, please."

Sean got to his feet. As he passed through the turnstile he didn't see Martinez press any button. He guessed the turnstile was controlled by a foot pedal.

Sean followed Ramirez for a short distance, turning into the first office on the left. "Security" was printed in block letters on the open door. Inside was a control room with banks of TV monitors covering one wall. In front of the monitors was a third guard with a clipboard. Even a cursory glance at the monitors told Sean that he was looking at a multitude of locations around the complex.

Sean continued to follow Ramirez into a small windowless office. Behind the desk sat a fourth guard who had two gold stars attached to his uniform and gold trim on the peak of his hat. His name tag said: Harris.

"That will be all, Ramirez," Harris said, giving Sean the feeling he was being inducted into the army.

Harris studied Sean, who stared back. There was an almost immediate feeling of antipathy between the men.

With his tanned, meaty face, Harris looked like a lot of people Sean had known in Charlestown when he was young. They usually had jobs of minor authority that they practiced with great officiousness. They were also nasty drunks.

Two beers and they'd want to fight about a call a referee had made on a televised sporting event if you suggested you disagreed with their perception. It was crazy. Sean had learned long ago to avoid such people. Now he was standing across the desk from one.

"We don't want any trouble here," Harris was saying. He had a faint southern accent.

Sean thought that was a strange way to begin a conversation. He wondered what this man thought he was getting from Harvard, a parolee? Harris was in obvious good physical shape, his bulging biceps straining the sleeves of his short-sleeved shirt, yet he didn't look all that healthy. Sean toyed with the idea of giving the man a short lecture on the benefits of proper nutrition, but thought better of the idea. He could still hear Dr. Walsh's admonitions.

"You're supposed to be a doctor," Harris said. "Why the hell are you wearing your hair so long? And I'd hazard to say that you didn't shave this morning."

"But I did put on a shirt and tie for the occasion," Sean said. "I thought I was looking quite natty."

"Don't mess with me, boy," Harris said. There was no sign of humor in his voice.

Sean shifted his weight wearily. He was already tired of the conversation and of Harris.

"Is there some particular reason you need me here?"

"You'll need a photo ID card," Harris said. He stood up and came around from behind the desk to open a door to a neighboring room. He was several inches taller than Sean and at least twenty pounds heavier. In hockey Sean used to like to block such guys low, coming up fast under their chins.

"I'd suggest you get a haircut," Harris said, as he motioned for Sean to pass into the next room. "And get your pants ironed. Maybe then you'll fit in better. This isn't college."

Stepping through the door Sean saw Ramirez look up from adjusting a Polaroid camera mounted on a tripod. Ramirez pointed toward a stool in front of a blue curtain, and Sean sat down.

Harris closed the door to the camera room, went back to his desk, and sat down. Sean had been worse than he'd feared. The idea of some wiseass kid coming down from Harvard had not appealed to him in the first place, but he hadn't expected anyone looking like a hippie from the sixties.

Lighting a cigarette, Harris cursed the likes of Sean. He hated such liberal Ivy League types who thought they knew everything. Harris had gone through the Citadel, then into the army where he'd trained hard for the commandos. He'd done well, making captain after Desert Storm. But with the breakup of the Soviet Union, the peacetime army had begun cutting back. Harris had been one of its victims.

Harris stubbed out his cigarette. Intuition told him Sean would be trouble. He decided he'd have to keep his eye on him.

With a new photo ID clipped to his shirt pocket, Sean left security. The experience didn't mesh with the welcome sign, but one fact did impress him. When he'd asked the reticent Ramirez why security was so tight, Ramirez had told him that several researchers had disappeared the previous year.

"Disappeared?" Sean asked with amazement. He'd heard of equipment disappearing, but people!

"Were they found?" Sean had asked.

"I don't know," Ramirez had said. "I only came this year."

"Where are you from?"

"Medellín, Colombia," Ramirez had said.

Sean had not asked any more questions, but Ramirez's reply added to Sean's unease. It seemed overkill to head security with a man who acted like a frustrated Green Beret and staff it with a group of guys who could have been from some Colombian drug lord's private army. As Sean followed Ramirez into the elevator to the seventh floor his initial positive impression of Forbes security faded.

"Come in, come in!" Dr. Randolph Mason repeated, holding open his office door. Almost immediately Sean's unease was replaced by a feeling of genuine welcome. "We're pleased to have you with us," Dr. Mason said. "I was so happy when Clifford called and suggested it. Would you like some coffee?"

Sean acquiesced and was soon balancing a cup while sitting on a couch across from the Forbes director. Dr. Mason looked like everyone's romantic image of a physician. He was tall with an aristocratic face, classically graying hair, and an expressive mouth. His eyes were sympathetic and his nose slightly aquiline. He seemed the type of man you could tell a problem to and know he'd not only care but he'd solve it.

"The first thing we must do," Dr. Mason said, "is have you meet our head of research, Dr. Levy." He picked up the phone and asked his secretary to have Deborah come up. "I'm certain you will be impressed by her. I wouldn't be surprised if she were soon in contention for the big Scandinavian prize."

"I've already been impressed with her earlier work on retroviruses," Sean said.

"Like everyone else," Dr. Mason said. "More coffee?"

Sean shook his head. "I have to be careful with this stuff," he said. "It makes me hyper. Too much and I don't come down for days."

"I'm the same way," Dr. Mason said. "Now about your accommodations. Has anyone discussed them with you?"

"Dr. Walsh just said that you would be able to provide housing."

"Indeed," Dr. Mason said. "I'm pleased to say that we had the foresight to purchase a sizable apartment complex several years ago. It's not in Coconut Grove, but it's not far either. We use it for visiting personnel and patients' families. We're delighted to offer you one of the apartments for your stay. I'm certain you will find it suitable, and you should enjoy the neighborhood as it's so close to the Grove."

"I'm pleased I didn't have to make my own arrangements," Sean said. "And as far as entertainment is concerned, I'm more interested in working than playing tourist."

"Everyone should have a balance in life," Dr. Mason said. "But rest assured, we have plenty of work for you to do. We want your experience here to be a good one. When you go into practice we hope you will be referring us patients."

"My plan is to remain in research," Sean said.

"I see," Dr. Mason said, his enthusiasm dimming slightly.

"In fact, the reason I wanted to come here . . ." Sean began, but before he could complete the statement, Dr. Deborah Levy walked into the room.

Deborah Levy was a strikingly attractive woman with dark olive skin, large almond-shaped eyes, and hair even blacker than Sean's. She was stylishly thin and wore a dark blue silk dress beneath her lab coat. She walked with the confidence and grace of the truly successful.

Sean struggled to get to his feet.

"Don't bother to get up," Dr. Levy said in a husky yet feminine voice. She thrust a hand at Sean.

Sean shook Dr. Levy's hand while balancing his coffee in the other. She gripped his fingers with unexpected strength and gave Sean's arm a shake that rattled his cup in its saucer. Her gaze bore into him with intensity.

"I've been instructed to say welcome," she said, sitting across from him. "But I think we should be honest about this. I'm not entirely convinced your visit is a good idea. I run a tight ship here in the lab. You'll either pitch in and work or you'll be out of here and on the next plane back to Boston. I don't want you to think . . ."

"I drove down," Sean interrupted. He knew he was already being provocative, but he couldn't help himself. He didn't expect such a brusque greeting from the head of research.

Dr. Levy stared at him for a moment before continuing. "The Forbes Cancer Center is no place for a holiday in the sun," she added. "Do I make myself clear?"

Sean cast a quick glance at Dr. Mason, who was still smiling warmly.

"I didn't come here for a holiday. If Forbes had been in Bismarck, North Dakota, I would have wanted to come. You see, I've heard about the results you've been getting with medulloblastoma."

Dr. Mason coughed and moved forward in his seat, placing his coffee on the table. "I hope you didn't expect to work on the medulloblastoma protocol," he said.

Sean's gaze shifted between the two doctors. "Actually, I did," he said with some alarm.

"When I spoke with Dr. Walsh," Mason said, "he emphasized that you have had extensive and successful experience with the development of murine monoclonal antibodies."

"That was during my year at MIT," Sean explained. "But that's not my interest now. In fact, I feel it is already yesterday's technology."

"That's not our belief," Dr. Mason said. "We think it's still commercially viable and will be for some time. In fact, we've had a bit of luck isolating and producing a glycoprotein from patients with colonic cancer. What we need now is a monoclonal antibody in hopes it might be an aid to early diagnosis. But, as you know, glycoproteins can be tricky. We've been unable to get mice to respond antigenically, and we've failed to crystallize the substance. Dr. Walsh assured me you were an artist when it comes to this kind of protein chemistry."

"I was," Sean said. "I haven't been doing it for some time. My interest has changed to molecular biology, specifically oncogenes and oncoproteins."

"This is just what I feared," Dr. Levy said, turning to Dr. Mason. "I told you this was not a good idea. We are not set up for students. I'm much too busy to baby-sit a medical student extern. Now if you'll excuse me, I must get back to my work."

Dr. Levy got to her feet and looked down at Sean. "My rudeness is not meant to be personal. I'm very busy, and I'm under a lot of stress."

"I'm sorry," Sean said. "But it is difficult not to take it personally since your medulloblastoma results are the reason I took this elective and drove all the way the hell down here."

"Frankly, that's not my concern," she said, striding toward the door.

"Dr. Levy," Sean called out. "Why haven't you published any articles on the medulloblastoma results? With no publications, if you'd stayed in academia, you'd probably be out looking for a job."

Dr. Levy paused and cast a disapproving look at Sean. "Impertinence is not a wise policy for a student," she said, closing the door behind her.

Sean looked over at Dr. Mason and shrugged his shoulders. "She was the one who said we should be honest about all this. She hasn't published for years."

"Clifford warned me that you might not be the most diplomatic extern," Dr. Mason said.

"Did he now?" Sean questioned superciliously. He was already beginning to question his decision to come to Florida. Maybe everybody else had been right after all.

"But he also said you were extremely bright. And I think Dr. Levy came on a bit stronger than she meant. At any rate she has been under great strain. In fact we all have."

"But the results you've been getting with the medulloblastoma patients are fantastic," Sean said, hoping to plead his case. "There has to be something to be learned about cancer in general here. I want desperately to be involved in your protocol. Maybe by looking at it with fresh, objective eyes I'll see something that you people have missed."

"You certainly don't lack self-confidence," said Dr. Mason. "And perhaps someday we could use a fresh eye. But not now. Let me be honest and open with you and give you some confidential information. There are several reasons you won't be able to participate in our medulloblastoma study. First, it is already a clinical protocol and you are here for basic science research. That was made clear to your mentor. And second of all we cannot permit outsiders access to our current work because we have yet to apply for the appropriate patents on some of our unique biological processes. This policy is dictated by our source of funding. Like a lot of research institutions, we've had to seek alternate sources for operating capital since the government started squeezing research grants to everything but AIDS. We have turned to the Japanese."

"Like the Mass General in Boston?" Sean questioned.

"Something like that," Dr. Mason said. "We struck a forty-million-dollar deal with Sushita Industries, which has been expanding into biotechnology. The agreement was that Sushita would advance us the money over a period of years in return for which they would control any patents that result. That's one of the reasons we need the monoclonal antibody to the colonic antigen. We have to produce some commercially viable products if we hope to continue to receive Sushita's yearly payments. So far we haven't been doing too well in that regard. And if we don't maintain our funding we'll have to shut our doors which, of course, would hurt the public which looks to us for care."

"A sorry state of affairs," Sean said.

"Indeed," Dr. Mason agreed. "But it's the reality of the new research environment."

"But your short-term fix will lead to future Japanese dominance."

"The same can be said about most industries," Dr. Mason said. "It's not limited to health-related biotechnology."

"Why not use the return from patents to fund additional research?"

"There's no place to get the initial capital," Dr. Mason said. "Well, that's not entirely true in our case. Over the last two years we've had considerable success with old-fashioned philanthropy. A number of businessmen have given us hefty donations. In fact, we are hosting a black-tie charity dinner tonight. I would very much like to extend an invitation to you. It's at my home on Star Island."

"I don't have the proper clothes," Sean said, surprised at being invited after the scene with Dr. Levy.

"We thought of that," Dr. Mason said. "We've made arrangements with a tux rental service. All you have to do is call in your sizes, and they will deliver to your apartment."

"That's very thoughtful," Sean said. He was finding it difficult to deal with this on-again, off-again hospitality.

Suddenly the door to Dr. Mason's office burst open and a formidable woman in a white nurse's uniform rushed in, planting herself in front of Dr. Mason. She was visibly distressed.

"There's been another one, Randolph," she blurted out. "This is the fifth breast cancer patient to die of respiratory failure. I told you that . . ."

Dr. Mason leapt to his feet. "Margaret, we have company."

Recoiling as if slapped, the nurse turned to Sean, seeing him for the first time. She was a woman of forty, with a round face, gray hair worn in a tight bun, and solid legs. "Excuse me!" she said, the color draining from her cheeks. "I'm terribly sorry." Turning back to Dr. Mason, she added, "I knew Dr. Levy had just come in here, but when I saw her return to her office, I thought you were alone."

"No matter," said Dr. Mason. He introduced Sean to Margaret Richmond, director of nursing, adding, "Mr. Murphy will be with us for two months."

Ms. Richmond shook hands perfunctorily with Sean, mumbling it was a pleasure to meet him. Then she took Dr. Mason by the elbow and steered him outside. The door closed, but the latch didn't catch, and it drifted open again.

Sean could not help but overhear, especially with Ms. Richmond's sharply penetrating voice. Apparently, another patient on standard chemotherapy for breast cancer had unexpectedly died. She'd been found in her bed totally cyanotic, just as blue as the others.

"This cannot go on!" Margaret snapped. "Someone must be doing this deliberately. There's no other explanation. It's always the same shift, and it's ruining our stats. We have to do something before the medical examiner gets suspicious. And if the media gets ahold of this, it will be a disaster."

"We'll meet with Harris," Dr. Mason said soothingly. "We'll tell him he has to let everything else slide. We'll tell him he has to stop it."

"It can't go on," Ms. Richmond repeated. "Harris has to do more than run background checks on the professional staff."

"I agree," Dr. Mason said. "We'll talk to Harris straightaway. Just give me a moment to arrange for Mr. Murphy to tour the facility."

The voices drifted away. Sean moved forward on the couch hoping to hear more, but the outer office remained silent until once again the door burst open. Guiltily he sat back as someone else dashed into the room. This time it was an attractive woman in her twenties dressed in a checkered skirt and white blouse. She was tanned, bubbly, and had a great smile. Hospitality had refreshingly returned.

"Hi, my name's Claire Barington."

Sean quickly learned that Claire helped run the center's public relations department. She dangled keys in front of his face, saying: "These are to your palatial apartment at the Cow's Palace." She explained that the center's residence had gotten its nickname in commemoration of the size of some of its earlier residents.

"I'll take you over there," Claire said. "Just to make certain it's all in order and you're comfortable. But first Dr. Mason told me to give you a tour of our facility. What do you say?"

"Seems like a good idea to me," Sean said, pulling himself up from the couch. He'd only been at the Forbes Center for about an hour, and if that hour were any indication of what the two months would be like, it promised to be a curiously interesting sojourn. Provided, of course, he stayed. As he followed the shapely Claire Barington out of Dr. Mason's office, he began seriously considering calling Dr. Walsh and heading back to Boston. He'd certainly be able to accomplish more there than here if he was to be relegated to busywork involving monoclonal antibodies.

"This, of course, is our administrative area," Claire said as she launched into a practiced tour. "Henry Falworth's office is next to Dr. Mason's. Mr. Falworth is the personnel manager for all non-professional staff. Beyond his office is Dr. Levy's. Of course, she has another research office downstairs in the maximum containment lab."

Sean's ears perked up. "You have a maximum containment lab?" he asked with surprise.

"Absolutely," Claire said. "Dr. Levy demanded it when she came on board. Besides, the Forbes Cancer Center has all the most up-to-date equipment."

Sean shrugged. A maximum containment lab designed to safely handle infectious microorganisms seemed a bit excessive.

Pointing in the opposite direction, Claire indicated the clinical office shared by Dr. Stan Wilson, chief of the hospital's clinical staff, Margaret Richmond, director of nursing, and Dan Selenburg, hospital administrator. "Of course, these people all have private offices on the top floor of the hospital building."

"This doesn't interest me," Sean said. "Let's see the research areas."

"Hey, you get the twenty-five-dollar tour or none at all," she said sternly. Then she laughed. "Humor me! I need the practice."

Sean smiled. Claire was the most genuine person he'd met so far at the Center. "Fair enough. Lead on!"

Claire took him over to an adjacent room with eight desks manned by busy people. A huge collating copy machine stood off to the side busily functioning. A large computer with multiple modems was behind a glass enclosure like some kind of trophy. A small glass-fronted elevator that was more like a dumbwaiter occupied another wall. It was filled with what appeared to be hospital charts.

"This is the important room!" Claire said with a smile. "It's where all the bills are sent for hospital and outpatient services. These are the people who deal with the insurance companies. It's also where my paychecks come from."

After seeing more of administration than Sean would have liked, Claire finally took him downstairs to see the laboratory facilities which occupied the middle five stories of the structure.

"The first floor of the building has auditoriums, library, and security," Claire droned as they entered the sixth floor. Sean followed Claire down a long central corridor with labs off either side. "This is the main research floor. Most of the major equipment is housed here."

Sean poked his head into various labs. He was soon disappointed. He'd been expecting a futuristic lab, superbly designed and filled with state-of-the-art technology. Instead he saw basic rooms with the usual equipment. Claire introduced him to the four people they came upon in one of the labs: David Lowenstein, Arnold Harper, Nancy Sprague, and Hiroshi Gyuhama. Of these people only Hiroshi expressed any more than a passing interest in Sean. Hiroshi bowed deeply when introduced. He seemed genuinely impressed when Claire mentioned that Sean was from Harvard.

"Harvard is a very good school," Hiroshi said in heavily accented English.

As they continued down the corridor, Sean began to notice that most of the rooms were empty.

"Where is everybody?" he asked.

"You've met pretty much the whole research staff," Claire said. "We have a tech named Mark Halpern, but I don't see him at the moment. We don't have many personnel presently, although word has it that we are about to start expanding. Like all businesses, we've been through some lean times."

Sean nodded, but the explanation did little to allay his disappointment. With the impressive results of the medulloblastoma work, he'd envisioned a large group of researchers working at a dynamic pace. Instead, the place seemed relatively deserted, which reminded Sean of Ramirez's unsettling remark.

"Down in security they told me some of the researchers had disappeared. Do you know anything about that?"

"Not a lot," Claire admitted. "It was last year and it caused a flap."

"What happened?"

"They disappeared all right," Claire said. "They left everything: their apartments, their cars, even their girlfriends."

"And they were never found?" Sean asked.

"They turned up," Claire said. "The administration doesn't like to talk about it, but apparently they are working for some company in Japan."

"Sushita Industries?" Sean asked.

"That I don't know," Claire said.

Sean had heard about companies luring away personnel, but never so secretly. And never to Japan. He realized it was probably just another indication that times were changing in the arena of biotechnology.

Claire brought them to a thick opaque glass door barring further progress down the corridor. In block letters were the words: No Entry. Sean glanced at Claire for an explanation.

"The maximum containment facility is in there," she said.

"Can we see it?" Sean asked. He cupped his hands and peered through the door. All he could see were doors leading off the main corridor.

Claire shook her head. "Off limits," she said. "Dr. Levy does most of her work in there. At least when she's in Miami. She splits her time between here and our Basic Diagnostic lab in Key West."

"What's that?" Sean asked.

Claire winked and covered her mouth as if she were telling a secret. "It's a minor entrepreneurial spin-off for Forbes," she said. "It does basic diagnostic work for our hospital as well as for several hospitals in the Keys. It's a way of generating some additional income. The trouble is the Florida legislature is giving us some trouble about self-referral."

"How come we can't go in there?" Sean asked, pointing through the glass door.

"Dr. Levy says there is some kind of risk, but I don't know what it is. Frankly, I'm happy to stay out. But ask her. She'll probably take you in."

Sean wasn't sure Dr. Levy would do him any favors after their initial meeting. He reached out and pulled the door open a crack. There was a slight hiss as the seal was broken.

Claire grabbed his arm. "What are you doing?" She was aghast.

"Just curious to see if it was locked," Sean said. He let the door swing shut.

"You are a trip," she said.

They retraced their route and descended another floor. The fifth floor was dominated by a large lab on one side of the corridor and small offices on the other. Claire took Sean into the large lab.

"I was told that you would have this lab for your use," Claire said. She switched on the overhead lights. It was an enormous room by the standards of the labs Sean was accustomed to work in at both Harvard and MIT where fights for space among researchers were legendary for their acrimony. In the center was a glass-enclosed office with a desk, a telephone, and a computer terminal.

Sean walked around, fingering the equipment. It was basic but serviceable. The most impressive items were a luminescence-spectrophotometer and a binocular microscope to detect fluorescence. Sean thought he could have some fun with those instruments under the right circumstances, but he didn't know if the Forbes provided the right environment. For one thing, Sean realized that he'd probably be working in this large room alone.

"Where are all the reagents and things?" he asked.

Claire motioned for Sean to follow, and they descended another floor where Claire showed him the supply room. As far as Sean was concerned, this was the most impressive area he'd seen so far. The supply room was filled with everything a molecular biological lab would need. There was even a generous selection of various cell lines from the NIH.

After cursorily touring through the rest of the lab space, Claire led Sean down to the basement. Scrunching up her nose, she took him into the animal room. Dogs barked, monkeys glared, and mice and rats skittered about their cages. The air was moist and pungent. Claire introduced Sean to Roger Calvet, the animal keeper. He was a small man with a severe hunchback.

They only stayed a minute and as the doors closed behind them, Claire made a gesture of relief. "My least favorite part of the whole tour," she confided. "I'm not sure where I stand on the animal-rights issue."

"It's tough," Sean admitted. "But we definitely need them. For some reason mice and rats don't bother me as much as dogs or monkeys."

"I'm supposed to show you the hospital too," Claire said. "Are you game?"

"Why not?" Sean said. He was enjoying Claire.

They took the elevator back to the second floor and crossed to the clinic by way of the pedestrian bridge. The towers were some fifty feet apart.

The second floor of the hospital housed the diagnostic and treatment areas as well as the ICU and the surgical suites. The chemistry lab and radiology were also there along with medical records. Claire took Sean in to meet her mother, who was one of the medical librarians.

"If I can be of any assistance," Mrs. Barington said, "just give me a call."

Sean thanked her and moved to leave, but Mrs. Barington insisted she show him around the department. Sean tried to be interested as he was shown the Center's computer capabilities, the laser printers, the hoist they used to bring charts up from the basement storage vault, and the view they had over the sleepy Miami River.

When Claire and Sean got back to the corridor, she apologized.

"She's never done that," she added. "She must have liked you."

"That's just my luck," Sean said. "The older set and the prepubescent are taken by me. It's the women in between I have trouble with."

"I'm sure you expect me to believe that," Claire said sarcastically.

Sean was next treated to a rapid walk through the modern eighty-bed hospital. It was clean, well designed, and apparently well staffed. With its tropical colors and fresh flowers, it was even cheerful despite the gravity of many of the patients' illnesses. On this leg of the tour, Sean learned that the Forbes Cancer Center had teamed up with the NIH to treat advanced melanoma. With the powerful sunshine, there was a lot of melanoma in Florida.

With the tour completed, Claire told Sean it was time for her to lead him over to the Cow Palace and see that he got settled. He tried to suggest he'd be fine, but she wouldn't hear of it. With strict orders to stay close, he followed her car out of the Forbes Cancer Center and headed south on Twelfth Avenue. He drove carefully, having heard that most people in Miami carry pistols in their glove compartments. Miami has one of the world's highest mortality rates from fender-bender accidents.

At Calle Ocho they turned left, and Sean glimpsed the rich Cuban culture that has placed such an indelible mark on modern Miami. At Brickell they turned right and the city changed again. Now he drove past gleaming bank buildings, each an open testament to the financial power of the illicit drug trade.

The Cow Palace was not imposing to say the least. Like so many buildings in the area, it was two stories of concrete block with aluminum sliding doors and windows. It stretched for almost a block with asphalt parking in both the front and the back. The only attractive thing about the place was the tropical plantings, many of which were in bloom.

Sean pulled up next to Claire's Honda.

After checking the apartment number on the keys, Claire led the way upstairs. Sean's unit was halfway down the hall at the back. As Claire struggled to get the key into the lock, the door directly opposite opened.

"Just moving in?" a blond man of about thirty asked. He was stripped to the waist.

"Seems that way," Sean said.

"Name's Gary," the man said. "Gary Engels from Philadelphia. I'm an X-ray tech. Working nights, looking for an apartment by day. How about you?"

"Med student," Sean said as Claire finally opened the door.

The apartment was a furnished one-bedroom with a full kitchen. Sliding glass doors led from both the living room and the bedroom to a balcony that ran the length of the building.

"What do you think?" Claire asked as she opened the living-room slider.

"Much more than I expected," Sean said.

"It's hard for the hospital to recruit certain personnel," Claire said. "Especially high-caliber nurses. They have to have a good temporary residence to compete with other local hospitals."

"Thank you for everything," Sean said.

"One last thing," Claire said. She handed him a piece of paper. "This is the number of the tux rental place that Dr. Mason mentioned. I assume you'll be coming tonight."

"I'd forgotten about that," Sean said.

"You really should come," Claire said. "These affairs are one of the perks for working at the Center."

"Are they frequent?" Sean asked.

"Relatively," Claire said. "They really are fun."

"So you'll be there?" Sean asked.

"Most definitely."

"Well then, maybe I'll come," he said. "I haven't worn a tux too many times. It should be entertaining."

"Wonderful," Claire said. "And since you might have trouble finding Dr. Mason's home, I don't mind picking you up. I live in Coconut Grove just down the way. How about seven-thirty?"

"I'll be ready," Sean said.

Hiroshi Gyuhama had been born in Yokosuka, south of Tokyo. His mother had worked in the U.S. Naval base, and from an early age Hiroshi had been interested in America and Western ways. His mother felt differently, refusing to let him take English in school. An obedient child, Hiroshi acquiesced to his mother's wishes without question. It wasn't until after her death when he was at the university studying biology that he was able to take English, but once he began he displayed an unusual proficiency.

After graduation Hiroshi was hired by Sushita Industries, a huge electronics corporation that had just begun expanding into biotechnology. When Hiroshi's supervisors discovered how fluent he was in English, they sent him to Florida to supervise their investment in Forbes.

Except for an initial difficulty involving two Forbes researchers who refused to cooperate, a dilemma which had been handled expeditiously by bringing them to Tokyo and then offering them enormous salaries, Hiroshi had faced no serious problems during his tenure at Forbes.

Sean Murphy's unexpected arrival was a different story. For Hiroshi and the Japanese in general any surprise was disturbing. Also, for them, Harvard was more of a metaphor than a specific institution. It stood for American excellence and American ingenuity. Accordingly Hiroshi worried that Sean could take some of Forbes's developments back to Harvard where the American university might beat them to possible patents. Since Hiroshi's future advancement at Sushita rested on his ability to protect the Forbes investment, he saw Sean as a potential threat.

His first response had been to send a fax via his private telephone line to his Japanese supervisor. From the outset the Japanese had insisted they be able to communicate with Hiroshi without going through the Center switchboard. That had been only one of their conditions.

Hiroshi had then called Dr. Mason's secretary to ask if it would be possible for him to see the director. He'd been given a two o'clock appointment. Now, as he ascended the stairs to the seventh floor, it was three minutes before the hour. Hiroshi was a punctilious man who left little to chance.

As he entered Mason's office, the doctor leapt to his feet. Hiroshi bowed deeply in apparent respect though in reality he did not think highly of the American physician, believing Dr. Mason lacked the iron will necessary in a good manager. In Hiroshi's estimation, Dr. Mason would be unpredictable under pressure.

"Dr. Gyuhama, nice of you to come up," Dr. Mason said, motioning toward the couch. "Can we get you anything? Coffee, tea, or juice?"

"Juice, please," Hiroshi replied with a polite smile. He did not want any refreshment but did not care to refuse and appear ungrateful.

Dr. Mason sat down across from Hiroshi. But he didn't sit normally. Hiroshi noticed that he sat on the very edge of his seat and rubbed his hands together. Hiroshi could tell he was nervous, which only served to lower further Hiroshi's estimation of the man as a manager. One should not communicate one's feelings so openly.

"What can I do for you?" Dr. Mason asked.

Hiroshi smiled again, noting that no Japanese would be so direct.

"I was introduced to a young university student today," Hiroshi said.

"Sean Murphy," Dr. Mason said. "He's a medical student at Harvard."

"Harvard is a very good school," Hiroshi said.

"One of the best," Dr. Mason said. "Particularly in medical research." Dr. Mason eyed Hiroshi cautiously. He knew Hiroshi avoided direct questions. Mason always had to try to figure out what the Japanese man was getting at. It was frustrating, but Mason knew that Hiroshi was Sushita's front man, so it was important to treat him with respect. Right now it was apparent that he had found Sean's presence disturbing.

Just then, the juice arrived and Hiroshi bowed and said thank you several times. He took a sip, then placed the glass on the coffee table.

"Perhaps it might be helpful if I explain why Mr. Murphy is here," Dr. Mason said.

"That would be very interesting," Hiroshi said.

"Mr. Murphy is a third-year medical student," Dr. Mason said. "During the course of the year third-year students have blocks of time which they can use to choose an elective and study something that particularly interests them. Mr. Murphy is interested in research. He'll be here for two months."

"That's very good for Mr. Murphy," Hiroshi said. "He comes to Florida during the winter."

"It is a good system," Dr. Mason agreed. "He'll get the experience of seeing a working lab in operation, and we'll get a worker."

"Perhaps he'll be interested in our medulloblastoma project," Hiroshi said.

"He is interested," Dr. Mason said. "But he will not be allowed to participate. Instead he will be working with our colonic cancer glycoprotein, trying to crystallize the protein. I don't have to tell you how good it would be for both Forbes and Sushita if he were able to accomplish what we've so far failed to do."

"I was not informed of Mr. Murphy's arrival by my superiors," Hiroshi said. "It is strange for them to have forgotten."

All at once, Dr. Mason realized what this circuitous conversation was about. One of Sushita's conditions was that they review all prospective employees before they were hired. Usually it was a formality, and where a student was concerned, Dr. Mason had not given it a thought, particularly since Murphy's stay was so temporary.

"The decision to invite Mr. Murphy for his elective happened rather quickly. Perhaps I should have informed Sushita, but he is not an employee. He does not get paid. Besides, he's a student with limited experience."

"Yet he will be entrusted with samples of glycoprotein," Hiroshi said. "He will have access to the recombinant yeast that produces the protein."

"Obviously he will be given the protein," Dr. Mason said. "But there is no reason for him to be shown our recombinant technology for producing it."

"How much do you know about this man?" Hiroshi asked.

"He comes with a recommendation from a trusted colleague," Dr. Mason said.

"Perhaps my company would be interested in his resumé," Hiroshi said.

"We have no resumé," Dr. Mason said. "He's only a student. If there had been anything important to know about him, I'm confident my friend Dr. Walsh would have informed me. He did say that Mr. Murphy was an artist when it came to protein crystallization and making murine monoclonal antibodies. We need an artist if we are going to come up with a patentable product. Besides, the Harvard cachet is valuable to the clinic. The idea we have been training a Harvard graduate student will not do us any harm."

Hiroshi got to his feet and, with his continued smile, bowed, but not as deeply nor for as long a period as when he'd first come into the office. "Thank you for your time," he said. Then he left the room.

After the door clicked behind Hiroshi, Dr. Mason closed his eyes and rubbed them with his fingertips. His hands were shaking. He was much too anxious, and if he wasn't careful, he'd aggravate his peptic ulcer. With the possibility of some psychopath killing metastatic breast cancer patients, the last thing he needed was trouble with Sushita. He now regretted doing Clifford Walsh the favor of inviting his graduate student. It was a complication he didn't need.

On the other hand, Dr. Mason knew he needed something to offer the Japanese or they might not renew their grant, irrespective of other concerns. If Sean could help solve the problem associated with developing an antibody to their glycoprotein, then his arrival could turn into a godsend.

Dr. Mason ran a nervous hand through his hair. The problem was, as Hiroshi made him realize, he knew very little about Sean Murphy. Yet Sean would have access to their labs. He could talk to other workers; he could access the computers. And Sean struck Dr. Mason as definitely the curious type.

Snatching up the phone, Dr. Mason asked his secretary to get Clifford Walsh from Boston on the line. While he waited, he ambled over to his desk. He wondered why he hadn't thought of calling Clifford earlier.

Within a few minutes, Dr. Walsh was available on the phone. Dr. Mason sat while he talked. Since they'd spoken just the previous week, their small talk was minimal.

"Did Sean get down there okay?" Dr. Walsh asked.

"He arrived this morning."

"I hope he hasn't gotten into trouble already," Dr. Walsh said.

Dr. Mason felt his ulcer begin to burn. "That's a strange statement," he said. "Especially after your excellent recommendations."

"Everything I said about him is true," Dr. Walsh said. "The kid is just short of a genius when it comes to molecular biology. But he's a city kid and his social skills are nowhere near his intellectual abilities. He can be headstrong. And he's physically stronger than an ox. He could have played professional hockey. He's the type of guy you want on your side if there's going to be a brawl."

"We don't brawl down here much," Dr. Mason said with a short laugh. "So we won't be taking advantage of his skills in that regard. But tell me something else. Has Sean ever been associated with the biotechnology industry in any way, like worked summers at a company? Anything like that?"

"He sure has," Dr. Walsh said. "He not only worked at one, he owned one. He and a group of friends started a company called Immunotherapy to develop murine monoclonal antibodies. The company did well as far as I know. But then I don't keep up with the industrial side of our field."

The pain in Mason's gut intensified. This was not what he wanted to hear.

Mason thanked Dr. Walsh, hung up the phone, and immediately swallowed two antacid tablets. Now he had to worry about Sushita learning of Sean's association with this Immunotherapy company. If they did, it might be enough to cause them to break the agreement.

Dr. Mason paced his office. Intuition told him he had to act. Perhaps he should send Sean back to Boston as Dr. Levy had suggested. But that would mean losing Sean's potential contribution to the glycoprotein project.

Suddenly Dr. Mason had an idea. He could at least find out all there was to know about Sean's company. He picked up the phone again. This number he didn't have his secretary dial. He dialed it himself. He called Sterling Rombauer.

True to her word, Claire showed up at Sean's apartment at seven-thirty on the dot. She was wearing a black dress with spaghetti straps and long dangly earrings. Her brunette hair was pulled back at the sides with rhinestone-studded barrettes. Sean thought she looked terrific.

He wasn't at all sure of his own outfit. The rented tux definitely needed the suspenders; the pants showed up two sizes too large and there hadn't been time to change them. The shoes were also a half size too large. But the shirt and the jacket fit reasonably well, and he tamed his hair back on the sides with some hair gel he borrowed from his friendly neighbor, Gary Engels. He even shaved.

They took Sean's 4×4 since it was roomier than Claire's tiny Honda. With Claire giving directions, they skirted the downtown high rises and drove up Biscayne Boulevard. People of all races and nationalities crowded the street. They passed a Rolls Royce dealership, and Claire said that she'd heard most of the sales were for cash; people walked in with briefcases full of twenty-dollar bills.

"If the drug traffic stopped tomorrow, it would probably affect this city," Sean suggested.

"The city would collapse," Claire said.

They turned right on the MacArthur Causeway and headed toward the southern tip of Miami Beach. On their right they passed several large cruise ships moored at the Dodge Island seaport. Just before they got to Miami Beach, they turned left and crossed a small bridge where they were stopped by an armed guard at a gatehouse.

"This must be a ritzy place," Sean commented as they were waved through.

"Very," Claire answered.

"Mason does okay for himself," Sean said. The palatial homes they were passing seemed inappropriate for a director of a research center.

"I think she's the one with the money," Claire said. "Her maiden name was Forbes, Sarah Forbes."

"No kidding." Sean cast a glance at Claire to be sure she wasn't teasing him.

"It was her father who started the Forbes Cancer Center."

"How convenient," Sean said. "Nice of the old man to give his son-in-law a job."

"It's not what you think," Claire said. "It's quite a soap opera. The old man started the clinic, but when he passed away he made Sarah's older brother, Harold, executor of the estate. Then Harold went and lost most of the foundation's money in some central Florida land development scheme. Dr. Mason was a latecomer to the Center and only arrived when it was about to go under. He and Dr. Levy have turned the place around."

They pulled into a sweeping drive in front of a huge white house with a portico supported by fluted Corinthian columns. A parking attendant quickly took charge of the car.

The inside of the house was equally impressive. Everything was white: white marble floors, white furniture, white carpet, and white walls.

"I hope they didn't pay a decorator a lot of money for picking the colors," Sean said.

They were motioned through the house to a terrace overlooking Biscayne Bay. The bay was dotted with lights from other islands as well as hundreds of boats. Beyond the bay was the city of Miami shimmering in the moonlight.

Nestled in the center of the terrace was a large kidney-shaped pool illuminated from beneath the water. To its left was a pink and white striped tent where long tables were laden with food and drink. A calypso steel band played next to the house and filled the velvety night air with melodious percussion. At the water's edge beyond the terrace was a gigantic white cruiser moored to a pier. Hanging from davits off the yacht's stern was yet another boat.

"Here come the host and hostess," Claire warned Sean, who'd been momentarily mesmerized by the scene.

Sean turned in time to see Dr. Mason guide a buxom bleached blonde toward them. He was elegant in a tuxedo that obviously was not rented and patent leather slippers complete with black bows. She was squeezed into a strapless peach gown so tight that Sean feared the slightest movement might bare her impressive breasts. Her hair was slightly disheveled and her makeup more suitable to a girl half her age. She was also clearly drunk.

"Welcome, Sean," Dr. Mason said. "I hope Claire has been taking good care of you."

"The best," Sean said.

Dr. Mason introduced Sean to his wife, who fluttered heavily mascaraed lashes. Sean dutifully squeezed her hand, drawing the line at her expected kiss on the cheek.

Dr. Mason turned and motioned for another couple to join them. He introduced Sean as a Harvard medical student who would be studying at the Center. Sean had the uncomfortable feeling he was on display.

The man's name was Howard Pace, and from Dr. Mason's introduction, Sean learned that he was the CEO of an aircraft manufacturing company in St. Louis, and it was he who was about to make the donation to the Center.

"You know, son," Mr. Pace said, putting his arm around Sean's shoulder. "My gift is to help train young men and women like yourself. They are doing wonderful things at Forbes. You will learn a lot. Study hard!" He gave Sean a final man-to-man thump on the shoulder.

Mason began introducing Pace to some other couples and Sean suddenly found himself standing alone. He was about to snag a drink when a wavering voice stopped him. "Hello, handsome."

Sean turned to face the bleary eyes of Sarah Mason.

"I want to show you something," she said, grabbing Sean's sleeve.

Sean cast a desperate glance around for Claire, but she was nowhere in sight. With resignation rare for him, he allowed himself to be led down the patio steps and out onto the dock. Every few steps he had to steady Sarah as her heels slipped through the cracks between the planking. At the base of the gangplank leading to the yacht, Sean was confronted by a sizable Doberman with a studded collar and white teeth.

"This is my boat," Sarah said. "It's called Lady Luck. Would you like a tour?"

"I don't think that beast on deck wants company," Sean said.

"Batman?" Sarah questioned. "Don't worry about him. As long as you're with me he'll be a lamb."

"Maybe we could come back later," Sean said. "To tell the truth, I'm starved."

"There's food in the fridge," Sarah persisted.

"Yeah, but I had my heart set on those oysters I saw under the tent."

"Oysters, huh?" Sarah said. "Sounds good to me. We can see the boat later."

As soon as he got Sarah back on land, Sean ducked away, leaving her with an unsuspecting couple who'd ventured toward the yacht. Searching through the crowd for Claire, a strong hand gripped his arm. Sean turned and found himself gazing into the puffy face of Robert Harris, head of security. Even a tux didn't dramatically change his appearance, with his Marine-style crew cut. His collar must have been too tight since his eyes were bulging.

"I want to give you some advice, Murphy," Harris said with obvious disdain.

"Really?" Sean questioned. "This should be interesting, since we have so much in common."

"You're a wiseass," Harris hissed.

"Is that the advice?" Sean asked.

"Stay away from Sarah Forbes," Harris said. "I'm only telling you once."

"Damn," Sean said. "I'll have to cancel our picnic tomorrow."

"Don't push me!" Harris warned. With a final glare, he stalked off.

Sean finally found Claire at the table featuring oysters, shrimp, and stone crab. Filling his plate, he scolded her for allowing him to fall into the clutches of Sarah Mason.

"I suppose I should have warned you," Claire said. "When she drinks she's notorious for chasing anything in pants."

"And here I thought I was irresistible."

They were still busy with the seafood when Dr. Mason stepped to the podium and tapped the microphone. As soon as the crowd was silent, he introduced Howard Pace, thanking him profusely for his generous gift. After a resounding round of applause, Dr. Mason turned the microphone over to the guest of honor.

"This is a bit syrupy for my taste," Sean whispered.

"Be nice," Claire chided him.

Howard Pace began his talk with the usual platitudes, but then his voice cracked with emotion. "Even this check for ten million dollars cannot adequately express my feelings. The Forbes Cancer Center has given me a second chance at life. Before I came here all my doctors believed my brain tumor was terminal. I almost gave up. Thank God I didn't. And thank God for the dedicated doctors at the Forbes Cancer Center."

Unable to speak further, Pace waved his check in the air as tears streamed down his face. Dr. Mason immediately appeared at his side and rescued the check lest it waft out into the wine-dark Biscayne Bay.

After another round of applause, the formal events of the evening were over. The guests surged forward, all overcome with the emotion Howard Pace had expressed. They had not expected such intimacy from such a powerful person.

Sean turned to Claire. "I hate to be a drag," he said. "But I've been up since five. I'm fading fast."

Claire put down her drink.

"I've had enough as well. Besides, I've got to be at work early."

They found Dr. Mason and thanked him, but he was distracted and barely realized they were leaving. Sean was thankful Mrs. Mason had conveniently disappeared.

As they drove back over the causeway Sean was the first to speak. "That speech was actually quite touching," he said.

"It's what makes it all worthwhile," Claire agreed.

Sean pulled up and parked next to Claire's Honda. There was a moment of awkwardness. "I did get some beer this afternoon," he said after a pause. "Would you like to come up for a few minutes?"

"Fine," Claire said enthusiastically.

As Sean climbed the stairs behind her he wondered if he'd overestimated his endurance. He was almost asleep on his feet.

At the door to his apartment, he awkwardly fumbled with the keys, trying to get the right one in the lock. When he finally turned the bolt, he opened the door and groped for the light. Just as his fingers touched the switch, there was a violent cry. When he saw who was waiting for him, his blood ran cold.

"Easy now!" Dr. Mason said to the two ambulance attendants. They were using a special stretcher to lift Helen Cabot from the Learjet that had brought her to Miami. "Watch the steps!"

Dr. Mason was still dressed in his tuxedo. Margaret Richmond had called just as the party was ending to say that Helen Cabot was about to land. Without a second's hesitation, Dr. Mason had jumped into his Jaguar.

As gently as possible the paramedics eased Helen into the ambulance. Dr. Mason climbed in after the gravely ill woman.

"Are you comfortable?" he asked.

Helen nodded. The trip had been a strain. The heavy medication had not completely controlled her seizures. On top of that they'd hit bad turbulence over Washington, D.C.

"I'm glad to be here," she said, smiling weakly. Dr. Mason gripped her arm reassuringly, then got out of the ambulance and faced her parents, who had followed the stretcher from the jet. Together they decided that Mrs. Cabot would ride in the ambulance while John Cabot would ride with Dr. Mason.

Dr. Mason followed the ambulance from the airport.

"I'm touched that you came to meet us," Cabot said. "From the look of your clothes I'm afraid we have interrupted your evening."

"It was actually very good timing," Mason said. "Do you know Howard Pace?"

"The aircraft magnate?" John Cabot asked.

"None other," Dr. Mason said. "Mr. Pace has made a generous donation to the Forbes Center, and we were having a small celebration. But the affair was winding down when you called."

"Still, your concern is reassuring," John Cabot said. "So many doctors are distracted by their own agendas. They are more interested in themselves than the patients. My daughter's illness has been an eye-opening experience."

"Unfortunately your complaints are all too common," Dr. Mason said. "But at Forbes it's the patient who counts. We would do even more if we weren't so strapped for funds. Since government began limiting grants, we've had to struggle."

"If you can help my daughter I'll be happy to contribute to your capital needs."

"We will do everything in our power to help her."

"Tell me," Cabot said. "What do you think her chances are? I'd like to know the truth."

"The possibility of a full recovery is excellent," Dr. Mason said. "We've had remarkable luck with Helen's type of tumor, but we must start treatment immediately. I tried to expedite her transfer, but your doctors in Boston seemed reluctant to release her."

"You know the doctors in Boston. If there's another test available, they want to do it. Then, of course, they want to repeat it."

"We tried to talk them out of biopsying the tumor," Dr. Mason said. "We can now make the diagnosis of medulloblastoma with an enhanced MRI. But they wouldn't listen. You see, we have to biopsy it regardless of whether they did or not. We have to grow some of her tumor cells in tissue culture. It's an integral part of the treatment."

"When can it be done?" John Cabot asked.

"The sooner the better," Dr. Mason said.

"But you didn't have to scream," Sean said. He was still shaking from the fright he'd experienced when he'd flipped on the light switch.

"I didn't scream," Janet said. "I yelled 'surprise.' Needless to say, I'm not sure who was more surprised, me, you, or that woman."

"That woman works for the Forbes Cancer Center," Sean said. "I've told you a dozen times. She's in their public relations department. She was assigned to deal with me."

"And dealing with you means coming back to your apartment after ten at night?" Janet asked with scorn. "Don't patronize me. I can't believe this. You haven't even been here twenty-four hours and you have a woman coming to your apartment."

"I didn't want to invite her in," Sean said. "But it was awkward. She'd brought me here this afternoon, then took me to a Forbes function tonight. When we pulled up outside for her to get her car, I thought I'd try to be hospitable. I offered her a beer. I'd already told her I was exhausted. Hell, you're usually complaining about my lack of social graces."

"It seems strangely convenient for you to gain some manners just in time to bestow them on a young, attractive female," Janet fumed. "I don't think my being skeptical is unreasonable."

"Well, you're making more of this than it deserves," Sean said. "How did you get in here, anyway?"

"They gave me the apartment two doors down," Janet said. "And you left your sliding door open."

"Why are they letting you stay here?"

"Because I've been hired by the Forbes Cancer Center," Janet said. "That's part of the surprise. I'm going to work here."

For the second time that evening, Janet had Sean stunned. "Work here?" he repeated as if he hadn't heard correctly. "What are you talking about?"

"I called the Forbes hospital," Janet said. "They have an active nurses' recruitment program. They hired me on the spot. They, in turn, called the Florida Board of Nursing and arranged for a temporary 120-day endorsement so I can practice while the paperwork is being completed for my Florida nursing license."

"What about your job at Boston Memorial?" Sean asked.

"No problem," Janet said. "They gave me an immediate leave of absence. One of the benefits of being in nursing these days is that we are in demand. We get to call the shots about our terms of employment more than most employees."

"Well, this is all very interesting," Sean said. For the moment that was all he could think of to say.

"So we'll still be working at the same institution."

"Did you ever think that maybe you should have discussed this idea with me?" Sean asked.

"I couldn't," Janet said. "You were on the road."

"What about before I left?" Sean asked. "Or you could have waited until I'd arrived. I think we should have talked about this."

"Well, that's the whole point," Janet said.

"What do you mean?"

"I came here so we can talk," Janet said. "I think this is a perfect opportunity for us to talk about us. In Boston you're so involved with school and your research. Here your schedule will undoubtedly be lighter. We'll have the time we never had in Boston."

Sean pushed off the couch and walked over to the open slider. He was at a loss for words. This whole episode of coming to Florida was working out terribly. "How'd you get here?" he asked.

"I flew down and rented a car," Janet said.

"So nothing's irreversible?" Sean said.

"If you think you can just send me home, think again," Janet said, an edge returning to her voice. "This is probably the first time in my life I've gone out on a limb for something I think is important." She still sounded angry, but Sean sensed she could also be on the verge of tears. "Maybe we're not important in your scheme of things . . ."

Sean interrupted her. "It isn't that at all. The problem is, I don't know whether I'm staying."

Janet's mouth dropped open. "What are you talking about?" she asked.

Sean came back to the couch and sat down. He looked into Janet's hazel eyes as he told her about his disturbing reception at the Center with half the people being hospitable, the other half rude. Most importantly, he told her that Dr. Mason and Dr. Levy were balking at allowing him to work on the medulloblastoma protocol.

"What do they want you to do?" she asked.

"Busywork as far as I'm concerned," Sean said. "They want me to try to make a monoclonal antibody to a specific protein. Failing that, I'm to crystallize it so that its three-dimensional molecular shape can be determined. It will be a waste of my time. I'm not going to be learning anything. I'd be better off going back to Boston and working on my oncogene project for my dissertation."

"Maybe you could do both," Janet suggested. "Help them with their protein and in return get to work on the medulloblastoma project."

Sean shook his head. "They were very emphatic. They are not about to change their minds. They said the medulloblastoma study had moved into clinical trials, and I'm here for basic research. Between you and me, I think their reluctance has something to do with the Japanese."

"The Japanese?" Janet questioned.

Sean told Janet about the huge grant Forbes had accepted in return for any patentable biotechnology products. "Somehow I think the medulloblastoma protocol is tied up in their deal. It's the only way I can explain why the Japanese would offer Forbes so much money. Obviously they expect and intend to get a return on their investment someday—and probably sooner rather than later."

"This is awful," Janet said, but her response was personal. It had nothing to do with Sean's research career. She'd been so consumed by the effort of coming to Florida that she'd not prepared herself for this kind of reversal.

"And there's another problem," Sean said. "The person who gave me the chilliest reception happens to be the director of research. She's the person I directly report to."

Janet sighed. She was already trying to figure how to undo everything she had done to get her down to the Forbes Center in the first place. She'd probably have to go back on nights at Boston Memorial, at least for a while. Janet pushed herself out of the deep armchair where she'd been sitting and wandered over to the sliding door. Coming to Florida had seemed like such a good idea to her when she'd been in Boston. Now it seemed like the dumbest thing she'd ever thought of.

Suddenly Janet spun around. "Wait a minute!" she said. "Maybe I have an idea."

"Well?" Sean questioned when Janet remained silent.

"I'm thinking," she said, motioning for him to be quiet for a moment.

Sean studied her face. A few moments ago she'd looked depressed. Now her eyes sparkled.

"Okay, here's what I think," she said. "Let's stay here and look into this medulloblastoma business together. We'll work as a team."

"What do you mean?" Sean sounded skeptical.

"It's simple," Janet said. "You mentioned that the project had moved into clinical trials. Well, no problem. I'll be on the wards. I'll be able to determine the treatment regiments: the timing, the dosages, the works. You'll be in the lab and you can do your thing there. That monoclonal stuff shouldn't take all your time."

Sean bit his lower lip as he gave Janet's suggestion some thought. He had actually considered looking into the medulloblastoma issue on the sly. His biggest obstacle had been exactly what Janet would be in a position to provide, namely clinical information.

"You'd have to get me charts," Sean said. He couldn't help but be dubious.

Janet had always been a stickler for hospital procedures and rules, in fact for any rules.

"As long as I can find a copy machine, that should be no problem," she said.

"I'd need samples of any medication," Sean said.

"I'll probably be dispensing the medicine myself," she said.

He sighed. "I don't know. It all sounds pretty tenuous."

"Oh, come on," Janet said. "What is this, role reversal? You're the one who's always telling me I've lived too sheltered a life, that I never take chances. Suddenly I'm the one taking the chances and you turn cautious. Where's that rebel spirit you've always been so proud of?"

Sean found himself smiling. "Who is this woman I'm talking to?" he said rhetorically. He laughed. "Okay, you're right. I'm acting defeated before trying. Let's give it a go."

Janet threw her arms around Sean. He hugged her back. After a long moment, they looked into each other's eyes, then kissed.

"Now that our conspiracy has been forged, let's go to bed," Sean said.

"Hold on," Janet said. "We're not sleeping together if that's what you mean. That's not going to happen until we have some serious talk about our relationship."

"Oh, come on, Janet," Sean whined.

"You have your apartment and I have mine," Janet said as she tweaked his nose. "I'm serious about this talk business."

"I'm too tired to argue," Sean said.

"Good," Janet said. "Arguing is not what it's going to take."

At eleven-thirty that night, Hiroshi Gyuhama was the only person in the Forbes research building except for the security man who Hiroshi suspected was sleeping at his post at the front entrance. Hiroshi had been alone in the building since nine when David Lowenstein had departed. Hiroshi wasn't staying late because of his research; he was waiting for a message. At that moment he knew it was one-thirty in the afternoon the following day in Tokyo. It was usually after lunch that his supervisor would get the word from the directors regarding anything Hiroshi had passed on.

As if on cue, the receiving light on the fax machine blinked on, and the LCD flashed the message: *receiving.* Eagerly Hiroshi's fingers grasped the sheet as soon as it slid through. With some trepidation he sat back and read the directive.

The first part was as he'd expected. The management at Sushita was disturbed by the unexpected arrival of the student from Harvard. They felt that it violated the spirit of the agreement with the Forbes. The directive went on to emphasize the company's belief that the diagnosis and treatment of cancer would be the biggest biotechnology/pharmaceutical prize of the twenty-first century. They felt that it would surpass in economic importance the antibiotic bonanza of the twentieth century.

It was the second part of the message that dismayed Hiroshi. It mentioned that the management did not want to take any risks, and that Hiroshi was to call Tanaka Yamaguchi. He was to tell Tanaka to investigate Sean Murphy and act accordingly. If Murphy was considered a threat, he was to be brought to Tokyo immediately.

Folding the fax paper several times lengthwise, Hiroshi held it over the sink and burned it. He washed the ashes down the drain. As he did, he noticed his hands were trembling.

Hiroshi had hoped the directive from Tokyo would have given him peace of mind. But it only left him even more agitated. The fact that Hiroshi's superiors felt that Hiroshi could not handle the situation was not a good sign. They hadn't said it directly, but the instruction to call Tanaka said as much. What that suggested to Hiroshi was he was not trusted in matters of crucial importance, and if he wasn't trusted, then his upward mobility in the Sushita hierarchy automatically was in question. From Hiroshi's perspective he'd lost face.

Unswervingly obedient despite his growing anxiety, Hiroshi got out the list of emergency numbers he'd been given before coming to Forbes over a year ago. He found the number for Tanaka and dialed. As the phone rang, Hiroshi felt his anger and resentment for the Harvard medical student rise. If the young doctor-to-be had never come to Forbes, Hiroshi's stature vis-à-vis his superiors would never have been tested this way.

A mechanical beep followed a message in rapid Japanese urging the caller to leave his name and number. Hiroshi did as he was told, but added he would wait for the call back. Hanging up the phone, Hiroshi thought about Tanaka. He didn't know much about the man, but what he did know was disquieting. Tanaka was a man frequently used by various Japanese companies for industrial espionage of any sort. What bothered Hiroshi was the rumor that Tanaka was connected to the Yakusa, the ruthless Japanese mafia.

When the phone rang a few minutes later, its raucous jangle sounded unnaturally loud in the silence of the deserted lab. Startled by it, Hiroshi had the receiver off the hook before the first ring had completed.

"Moshimoshi," Hiroshi said much too quickly, betraying his nervousness.

The voice that answered was sharp and piercing like a stiletto. It was Tanaka.

4

MARCH 3 • WEDNESDAY, 8:30 A.M.

When Sean's eyes blinked open at eight-thirty, he was instantly awake. He snatched up his watch to check the time, and immediately became annoyed with himself. He'd intended to get to the lab early that day. If he was going to give this plan of Janet's a shot, he'd have to put in more of an effort.

After making himself reasonably decent by pulling on his boxer shorts, he padded down the balcony and gently knocked on Janet's slider. Her curtains were still closed. After he knocked again harder, her sleepy face appeared behind the glass.

"Miss me?" Sean teased when Janet slid the door open.

"What time is it?" Janet asked. She blinked in the bright light.

"Going to nine," Sean said. "I'll be leaving in fifteen or twenty minutes. Want to go together or what?"

"I'd better drive myself," Janet said. "I've got to find an apartment. I only get to stay here a few nights."

"See you this afternoon," Sean said. He started to leave.

"Sean!" Janet called.

Sean turned.

"Good luck!" Janet said.

"You too," Sean said.

As soon as he was dressed, Sean drove over to the Forbes Center and parked in front of the research building. It was just after nine-thirty when he walked in the door. As he did, Robert Harris straightened up from the desk. He'd been explaining something to the guard on desk duty. His expression was somewhere between angry and morose. Apparently the man was never in a good mood.

"Banker's hours?" Harris asked provocatively.

"My favorite Marine," Sean said. "Were you able to keep Mrs. Mason out of trouble, or was she desperate enough to take you on a tour of Lady Luck?"

Robert Harris glared at Sean as Sean leaned against the bar of the turnstile to show his ID to the guard at the desk. But Harris couldn't think of an appropriate retort fast enough. The guard at the desk released the bar and Sean pushed through.

Unsure how to approach the day, Sean first took the elevator to the seventh floor and went to Claire's office. He was not looking forward to meeting her since they'd parted on such uncomfortable terms. But he wanted to clear the air.

Claire and her superior shared an office with their desks facing each other. But when Sean found her, Claire was alone.

"Morning!" Sean said cheerfully.

Claire looked up from her work. "I trust you slept well," she said sarcastically.

"I'm sorry about last night," Sean offered. "I know it was unpleasant and awkward for everyone. I apologize that the evening had to end that way, but I assure you Janet's arrival was totally unexpected."

"I'll take your word for it," Claire said coolly.

"Please," Sean asked. "Don't you turn unfriendly. You're one of the few people here who has been nice to me. I'm apologizing. What more can I do?"

"You're right," Claire said, finally softening. "Consider it history. What can I do for you today?"

"I suppose I have to talk with Dr. Levy," Sean said. "How do you suggest I find her?"

"Page her," Claire said. "All of the professional staff carry beepers. You should get one yourself." She picked up the phone, checked with the operator that Dr. Levy was in, then had her paged.

Claire only had time to tell Sean where to go to get a beeper when her phone rang. It was one of the administrative secretaries calling to say that Dr. Levy was in her office only a few doors down from Claire's.

Two minutes later Sean was knocking on Dr. Levy's door, wondering what kind of reception he'd get. When he heard Dr. Levy call out to come in, he tried to talk himself into being civil even if Dr. Levy wasn't.

Dr. Levy's office was the first place that appeared like the academic scientific environment Sean was accustomed to. There was the usual clutter of journals and books, a binocular microscope, and odd assortments of microscopic slides, photomicrographs, scattered color slides, Erlenmeyer flasks, culture dishes, tissue culture tubes, and lab notebooks.

"Beautiful morning," Sean said, hoping to start off on a better note than the day before.

"I asked Mark Halpern to come up when I heard you were on the floor," Dr. Levy said, ignoring Sean's pleasantry. "He is our chief and currently our only lab tech. He will get you started. He can also order any supplies and reagents you might need and we don't have, although we have a good stock. But I have to approve any orders." She pushed a small vial across her desk toward Sean. "Here is the glycoprotein. I'm sure you'll understand when I tell you that it does not leave this building. I meant what I said yesterday: stick to your assignment at hand. You should have more than enough to keep you busy. Good luck, and I hope you are as good as Dr. Mason seems to believe you are."

"Wouldn't it be more comfortable if we were a bit more friendly about all this?" Sean asked. He reached over and picked up the vial.

Dr. Levy pushed a few wayward strands of her glistening black hair away from her forehead. "I appreciate your forthrightness," she said after a brief pause. "Our relationship will depend on your performance. If you work hard, we'll get along just fine."

Just then, Mark Halpern entered Dr. Levy's office. As they were introduced, Sean studied the man and guessed he was around thirty. He was a few inches taller than Sean and was meticulously dressed. Sporting a spotless white apron over his suit, he looked more like men Sean had seen around cosmetic counters in department stores than a tech in a scientific lab.

Over the next half hour, Mark set Sean up for work in the large empty fifth floor that Claire had shown him the day before. By the time Mark left, Sean was satisfied with the physical aspects of his work situation; he only wished he was working on something he was truly interested in.

Picking up the vial Dr. Levy had given him, Sean unscrewed the cap and looked in at the fine white powder. He sniffed it; it had no smell. Pulling his stool closer to the counter, he set to work. First he dissolved the powder in a variety of solvents to get an idea of its solubility. He also set up a gel electrophoresis to get some approximation of its molecular weight.

After about an hour of concentration, Sean was suddenly distracted by movement that he thought he'd seen out of the corner of his eye. When he looked in that direction, all he saw was empty lab space extending over to the door to the stairwell. Sean paused from what he was doing. The only detectable sound came from the hum of a refrigerator compressor and the whirring of a shaking platform Sean was using to help super-saturate a solution. He wondered if the unaccustomed solitude was making him hallucinate.

Sean was seated near the middle of the room. Putting down the utensils in his hands, he walked the length of the lab, glancing down each aisle. The more he looked the more uncertain he became that he'd seen something. Reaching the door to the stairwell, he yanked it open and took a step forward, intending to look up and down the stairs. He hadn't really expected to find anything, and he involuntarily caught his breath when his sudden move put him face-to-face with someone who'd been lurking just beyond the door.

Recognition dawned swiftly as Sean realized that it was Hiroshi Gyuhama who stood before him, equally startled. Sean remembered meeting the man the day before when Claire had introduced them.

"Very sorry," Hiroshi said with a nervous smile. He bowed deeply.

"Quite all right," Sean said, feeling an irresistible urge to bow back. "It was my fault. I should have looked through the window before opening the door."

"No, no, my fault," Hiroshi insisted.

"It truly was my fault," Sean said. "But I suppose it is a silly argument."

"My fault," Hiroshi persisted.

"Were you coming in here?" Sean asked, pointing back into his lab.

"No, no," Hiroshi said. His smile broadened. "I'm going back to work." But he didn't move.

"What are you working on?" Sean asked, just to make conversation.

"Lung cancer," Hiroshi said. "Thank you very much."

"And thank you," Sean said by reflex. Then he wondered why he was thanking the man.

Hiroshi bowed several times before turning and climbing the stairs.

Sean shrugged and walked back to his lab bench. He wondered if the movement he'd seen originally had been Hiroshi, perhaps through the small window in the stairwell door. But that would mean Hiroshi had been there all along, which didn't make sense to Sean.

As long as his concentration had been broken, Sean took the time to descend to the basement to seek out Roger Calvet. Once he found him, Sean felt uncomfortable talking to the man whose back deformity prevented him from looking at Sean when he spoke. Nonetheless, Mr. Calvet managed to isolate a group of appropriate mice so that Sean could begin injecting them with the glycoprotein in hopes of eliciting an antibody response. Sean didn't expect success from this effort since others at the Forbes Center had undoubtedly tried it already, yet he knew he had to start from the beginning before he resorted to any of his "tricks."

Back in the elevator Sean was about to press the button for the fifth floor when he changed his mind and pressed six. He wouldn't have guessed it of himself, but he felt isolated and even a bit lonely. Working at Forbes was a distinctly uncomfortable experience, and not simply because of the bevy of unfriendly people. There weren't *enough* people. The place was too empty, too clean, too ordered. Sean had always taken the academic collegiality of his previous work environments for granted. Now he found himself needing some human interaction. So he headed for the sixth floor.

The first person Sean encountered was David Lowenstein. He was an intense, thin fellow bent over his lab bench examining tissue culture tubes. Sean came up to his left side and said hello.

"I beg your pardon?" David said, glancing up from his work.

"How's it going?" Sean asked. He reintroduced himself in case David had forgotten him from the day before.

"Things are going as well as can be expected," David said.

"What are you working on?" Sean asked.

"Melanoma," David answered.

"Oh," Sean said.

The conversation went downhill from that point, so Sean drifted on. He caught Hiroshi looking at him, but after the stairwell incident Sean avoided him. Instead he moved on to Arnold Harper, who was busily working under a hood. Sean could tell he was doing some kind of recombinant work with yeast.

Attempts at conversation with Arnold were about as successful as those with David Lowenstein had been. The only thing Sean learned from Arnold was that he was working on colon cancer. Although he'd been the source of the glycoprotein Sean was working with, he didn't seem the least interested in discussing it.

Sean wandered on and came to the glass door to the maximum containment lab with its No Entry sign. Cupping his hands as he'd done the day before, he again tried to peer through. Just like the previous day, all he could see was a corridor with doors leading off it. After glancing over his shoulder to make sure no one was in sight, Sean pulled open the door and stepped inside. The door shut behind him and sealed. This portion of the lab had a negative pressure so that no air would move out when the door was opened.

For a moment Sean stood just inside the door and felt his pulse quicken with excitement. It was the same feeling he used to get as a teenager when he, Jimmy, and Brady would go north to one of the rich bedroom communities like Swampscott or Marblehead and hit a few houses. They never stole anything of real value, just TVs and stuff like that. They never had trouble fencing the goods in

Boston. The money went to a guy who was supposed to send it over to the IRA, but Sean never knew how much of it ever got to Ireland.

When no one appeared to protest Sean's presence in the No Entry area, Sean pushed on. The place didn't have the look or feel of a maximum containment lab. In fact, the first room he looked into was empty except for bare lab benches. There was no equipment at all. Entering the room, Sean examined the surface of the counters. At one time they had been used, but not extensively. He could see some marks where the rubber feet of a countertop machine had sat, but that was the only telltale sign of use.

Bending down, Sean pulled open a cabinet and gazed inside. There were a few half-empty reagent bottles as well as assorted glassware, some of which was broken.

"Hold it right there!" a voice shouted, causing Sean to whirl around and rise to a standing position.

It was Robert Harris poised in the doorway, hands on his hips, feet spread apart. His meaty face was red. Dots of perspiration lined his forehead. "Can't you read, Mr. Harvard Boy?" Harris snarled.

"I don't think it's worth getting upset over an empty lab," Sean said.

"This area is off limits," Harris said.

"We're not in the army," Sean said.

Harris advanced menacingly. Between his height and weight advantage, he expected to intimidate Sean. But Sean didn't move. He merely tensed. With all his street experience as a teenager, he instinctively knew what he'd hit and hit hard if Harris threatened to touch him. But Sean was reasonably confident Harris wouldn't try.

"You are certainly one wiseass," Harris said. "I knew you'd be trouble the moment I laid eyes on you."

"Funny! I felt the same way about you," Sean said.

"I warned you not to mess with me, boy," Harris said. He moved within inches of Sean's face.

"You have a couple of blackheads on your nose," Sean said. "In case you didn't know."

Harris glared down at Sean and for a moment he didn't speak. His face got redder.

"I think you are getting entirely too worked up," Sean said.

"What the hell are you doing in here?" Harris demanded.

"Pure curiosity," Sean said. "I was told it was a maximum containment lab. I wanted to see it."

"I want you out of here in two seconds," Harris said. He stepped back and pointed toward the door.

Sean walked out into the hall. "There are a few more rooms I'd like to see," he said. "How about we take a tour together?"

"Out!" Harris shouted, pointing toward the glass door.

Janet had a late morning meeting with the director of nursing, Margaret Richmond. She used the time from Sean's wakeup call until the moment she had to leave to take a long shower, shave her legs, blow-dry her hair, and press her dress. Although she knew her job at the Forbes hospital was assured, meetings such as the one she was anticipating still made her nervous. And on top of that, she was still anxious about Sean's potential for heading back to Boston. All in all she had plenty of reason to be upset; she had no idea what the next few days would bring.

Margaret Richmond was not what Janet anticipated. Her voice on the telephone had conjured up an image of a delicate, slight woman. Instead, she was powerful and rather severe. Yet she was still cordial and businesslike, and conveyed to Janet a sincere appreciation for Janet's coming to the Forbes hospital. She even gave Janet her choice of shifts. Janet was pleased to opt for days. She had assumed she'd have to start on nights, a shift she disliked.

"You indicated a preference for floor duty," Ms. Richmond said as she consulted her notes.

"Correct," Janet said. "Floor duty gives me the type of patient contact that I find the most rewarding."

"We have an opening for days on the fourth floor," Ms. Richmond said.

"Sounds good," Janet said cheerfully.

"When would you like to start?" Ms. Richmond asked.

"Tomorrow," Janet said. She would have preferred a few days' delay to give herself a chance to find an apartment and get settled, but she felt an urgency about delving into the medulloblastoma protocol.

"I'd like to use today to try to find a nearby apartment," Janet added.

"I don't think you should stay around here," Ms. Richmond said. "If I were you I'd go out to the beach. They've done a nice job restoring the area. Either that or Coconut Grove."

"I'll take your advice," Janet said. Assuming the meeting was over, she stood.

"How about a quick tour of the hospital?" Ms. Richmond asked.

"I'd like that," Janet said.

Ms. Richmond first took Janet across the hall to meet Dan Selenburg, the hospital administrator. But he wasn't available. Instead, they went to the first floor to see the outpatient facilities, the hospital auditorium, and the cafeteria.

On the second floor Janet peered into the ICU, the surgical area, the chemistry lab, the radiology department, and medical records. Then they went up to the fourth floor.

Janet was impressed with the hospital. It was cheerful, modern, and appeared to be adequately staffed, which was particularly important from a nursing point of view. She'd had her misgivings about oncology and the fact that all the patients would be cancer patients, but given the otherwise pleasant environment and the variety in the patients she saw—some old, some gravely ill, others seemingly normal—she decided the Forbes hospital was definitely a place she could work. In many ways, it wasn't dissimilar to the Boston Memorial, just newer and more pleasantly decorated.

The fourth floor was arranged in the same configuration as other patient floors. It was a simple rectangle with private rooms on either side of a central corridor. The nurses' station was situated in the middle of the floor near the elevators and formed a large U-shaped counter. Behind it was a utility room and a small closet-like pharmacy with a dutch door. Across from the nurses' station was a patients' lounge. A housekeeping closet with a slop sink was across from the elevators. At either end of the long central hall were stairways.

Once their tour was completed, Ms. Richmond turned Janet over to Marjorie Singleton, the head nurse on days. Janet liked Marjorie immediately. She was a petite redhead with a smattering of freckles across the bridge of her nose. She seemed in a constant flurry of activity and never without a smile. Janet met other staffers as well, but the profusion of names overwhelmed her. Aside from Ms. Richmond and Marjorie, she didn't think she'd remember a single person to whom she'd been introduced except for Tim Katzenburg, the ward secretary. He was a blond-haired Adonis who looked more like a beach boy than a hospital ward secretary. He told Janet he was taking pre-med courses at night school since discovering the limited utility of a philosophy degree.

"We're really glad to have you," Marjorie said when she rejoined Janet after taking care of a minor emergency. "Boston's loss is our gain."

"I'm happy to be here," Janet said.

"We've been shorthanded since the tragedy with Sheila Arnold," Marjorie said.

"What happened?"

"The poor woman was raped and shot in her apartment," Marjorie said. "And not too far from the hospital. Welcome to big-city life."

"How terrible," Janet said. She wondered if that was the reason Ms. Richmond had warned her against the immediate neighborhood.

"Currently we happen to have a small contingent of patients from Boston," Marjorie said. "Would you like to meet them?"

"Sure," Janet said.

Marjorie bounded off. Janet practically had to run to keep up with her. Together they entered a room on the west side of the hospital.

"Helen," Marjorie called softly once she stood beside the bed. "You have a visitor from Boston."

Bright green eyes opened. Their intense color contrasted dramatically with the patient's pale skin.

"We have a new nurse joining our staff," Marjorie said. She then introduced the two women.

The name Helen Cabot immediately registered in Janet's mind. Despite the mildly jealous feelings she'd had back in Boston, she was pleased to find Helen at the Forbes. Her presence would undoubtedly help keep Sean in Florida.

After Janet had spoken briefly with Helen, the two nurses left the room.

"Sad case," Marjorie said. "Such a sweet girl. She's scheduled for a biopsy today. I hope she responds to the treatment."

"But I've heard that you people have had a hundred percent remission with her particular type of tumor," Janet said. "Why wouldn't she respond?"

Marjorie stopped and stared at Janet. "I'm impressed," she said. "Not only are you aware of our medulloblastoma results, you made an instantaneous and correct diagnosis. Are you endowed with powers we should know about?"

"Hardly," Janet said with a laugh. "Helen Cabot was a patient at my hospital in Boston. I'd heard about her case."

"That makes me feel more comfortable," Marjorie said. "For a second there I thought I was witnessing the supernatural." She began walking again. "I'm concerned about Helen Cabot because her tumors are far advanced. Why did you people keep her for so long? She should have been started on treatment weeks ago."

"That's something I know nothing about," Janet admitted.

The next patient was Louis Martin. In contrast to Helen, Louis did not appear ill. In fact, he was sitting in a chair fully dressed. He'd arrived only that morning and was still in the process of being admitted. Although he didn't look sick, he did appear anxious.

Marjorie went through introductions again, adding that Louis had the same problem as Helen, but that thankfully he'd been sent to them much more swiftly.

Janet shook hands with the man, noting his palm was damp. She looked into the man's terrified eyes, wishing there was something she could say that would comfort him. She also felt a little guilty realizing that she was somewhat pleased to learn of Louis's plight. Having two patients on her floor under the medulloblastoma protocol would give her that much more opportunity to investigate the treatment. Sean would undoubtedly be pleased.

As Marjorie and Janet returned to the nurses' station, Janet asked if the medulloblastoma cases were all on the fourth floor.

"Heavens no," Marjorie said. "We don't group patients according to tumor type. Their assignment is purely random. It just so happens we'll currently have three. As we speak we're admitting another case: a young woman from Houston named Kathleen Sharenburg."

Janet hid her elation.

"There's one last patient from Boston," Marjorie said as she stopped outside of room 409. "And she's a doll with an incredibly upbeat attitude that's been a source of strength and support for all the other patients. I believe she said she's from a section of town called the North End."

Marjorie knocked on the closed door. A muffled "Come in" could be heard. Marjorie pushed open the door and stepped inside. Janet followed.

"Gloria," Marjorie called. "How's the chemo going?"

"Lovely," Gloria joked. "I've just started the IV portion today."

"I brought you somebody to meet," Marjorie said. "A new nurse. She's from Boston."

Janet looked at the woman in the bed. She appeared to be about Janet's own age. A few years earlier, Janet would have been shocked. Prior to working in a hospital she'd been under the delusion that cancer was an affliction of the elderly. Painfully, Janet had learned that just about anyone was fair game for the disease.

Gloria was olive-complected with dark eyes and what had been dark hair. Presently her scalp was covered with a dark fuzz. Although she'd been a buxom woman, one side of her chest was now flat beneath her lingerie.

"Mr. Widdicomb!" Marjorie said with surprised irritation. "What are you doing in here?"

Her attention focused on the patient, Janet had not realized there was another person in the room. She turned to see a man in a green uniform with a mildly distorted nose.

"Don't go giving Tom a bad time," Gloria said. "He's only trying to help."

"I told you I wanted room 417 cleaned," Marjorie said, ignoring Gloria. "Why are you in here?"

"I was about to do the bathroom," Tom said meekly. He avoided eye contact while fidgeting with the mop handle sticking out of his bucket.

Janet watched. She was fascinated. Tiny Marjorie had been transformed from an amiable pixie to a commanding powerhouse.

"What are we to do with the new patient if the room is not ready?" Marjorie demanded. "Get down there at once and get it done." She pointed out the door.

After the man had left, Marjorie shook her head. "Tom Widdicomb is the bane of my existence here at Forbes."

"He means well," Gloria said. "He's been an angel to me. He checks on me every day."

"He's not employed as part of the professional staff," Marjorie said. "He's got to do his own job first."

Janet smiled. She liked working on wards that were well run by someone capable of taking charge. Judging by what she'd just seen, Janet was confident she'd get along fine with Marjorie Singleton.

Some of the soapy water sloshed out of his bucket as Tom raced down the corridor and into room 417. He released the doorstop and let the door close. He leaned against it. His breaths came in hissing gasps, a legacy of the terror that had flashed through him when the knock had first sounded on Gloria's door. He'd been seconds away from giving her the succinylcholine. If Marjorie and that new nurse had happened by a few minutes later, he would have been caught.

"Everything is fine, Alice," Tom reassured his mother. "There's no problem whatsoever. You needn't be worried."

Having reined in his fear, Tom was now angry. He'd never liked Marjorie, not from the first day that he'd met her. That bubbly good nature was just a sham. She was a meddlesome bitch. Alice had warned him about her, but he hadn't listened. He should have done something about her like he'd done to that other busybody nurse, Sheila Arnold, who'd started asking questions about why he was hanging around an anesthesia cart. All he'd have to do was get Marjorie's address sometime when he was cleaning up in administration. Then he'd show her who was in charge, once and for all.

Having calmed himself with thoughts of taking care of Marjorie, Tom pushed off from the door and eyed the room. He didn't care for the actual cleaning part of his job, just the freedom it provided. He'd preferred the job with the ambulance except for having to deal with fellow EMTs. With housekeeping, he didn't have to deal with anyone except for rare run-ins with the likes of Marjorie. Also, with housekeeping he could go anyplace in the hospital almost anytime he wanted. The only catch was he occasionally had to clean. But most of the time he was able to get by just pushing things around, since nobody was watching him.

If Tom was honest with himself, he had to admit that the job he'd liked the best had been one he'd held way back when he'd first left high school. He'd gotten a job with a vet. Tom liked the animals. After he'd worked there for a while the vet had designated Tom as the person in charge of putting the animals to sleep. They were usually old, sick animals that were suffering, and the work gave Tom a lot of satisfaction. He could remember being disappointed when Alice didn't share his enthusiasm.

Opening the door, Tom peered up the corridor. He had to return to the housekeeping closet to retrieve his housekeeping cart, but he didn't want to run into Marjorie for fear she'd start in on him again. Tom was afraid he might not be able to control himself. On many occasions he'd felt like striking her because that's what she needed. Yet he knew he couldn't afford to do that, no way.

Tom knew he would have trouble helping Gloria now that he'd been seen in her room. He would have to be more careful than usual. He'd also have to wait a day or so. He'd just have to hope she'd still be on IVs by then. He didn't want to inject the succinylcholine intramuscularly because that might make it detectable if it occurred to the medical examiner to look for it.

Slipping out of the room, Tom headed up the hall. As he passed 409, he glanced inside. He didn't see Marjorie, which was good, but he did see that other nurse, the new one.

Tom slowed his steps as a new fear gripped him. What if the new nurse who'd been hired to replace Sheila was actually hired to find him? Maybe she was a spy. That would explain why she had suddenly appeared in Gloria's room with Marjorie!

The more Tom thought about it, the more sure he became, especially since the new nurse was still in Gloria's room. She was out to trap him and stop his crusade against breast cancer.

"Don't worry, Alice," he assured his mother. "I'll listen this time."

Anne Murphy felt better than she had in weeks. She'd been depressed for several days after she'd learned of Sean's plans to go to Miami. To her, the city was synonymous with drugs and sin. Somehow, the news hadn't surprised her. Sean had been a bad child from an early age and, like men in general, he certainly wasn't likely to change, despite his surprising academic performances late in high school and then in college. At first when he talked about going to medical school, she'd felt a ray of hope. But the hope had been shattered when he told her he did not plan to practice medicine. Like so many other junctures in her life, Anne recognized she just had to endure and stop praying for miracles.

Still the question of why Sean couldn't be more like Brian or Charles plagued her. What had she done wrong? It had to have been her fault. Maybe it was because she hadn't been able to breast-feed Sean as a baby. Or maybe it was because she'd been unable to stop her husband from beating the child during some of his drunken rages.

Leave it to her youngest son, Charles, to provide a bright spot in the days subsequent to Sean's departure. Charles had called from his seminary in New Jersey with the glorious news that he would be home for a visit the following evening. Wonderful Charles! His prayers would save them all.

In anticipation of Charles's arrival, Anne had gone out shopping that morning. She planned to spend the day baking and preparing dinner. Brian said he'd try to make it although he had an important meeting that night that might run late.

Opening the refrigerator, Anne began putting away the cold items while her mind reveled in anticipation of the pleasures she'd enjoy that evening. But then she caught herself. She knew such thoughts were dangerous. Life was such a weak thread. Happiness and pleasure were invitations for tragedy. For a moment she tortured herself about how she'd feel if Charles were killed on the way to Boston.

The doorbell interrupted Anne's worries. She pressed the intercom and asked who was calling.

"Tanaka Yamaguchi," a voice said.

"What do you want?" Anne asked. The doorbell did not ring often.

"I want to talk to you about your son Sean," Tanaka said.

The color drained from Anne's face. Instantly she scolded herself for having entertained pleasurable thoughts. Sean was in trouble again. Had she expected anything less?

Pressing the door-release button, Anne went to the door to her apartment and pulled it open in anticipation of her unexpected guest. Anne Murphy was surprised enough that someone was paying a house call; when she saw that he was an Oriental, she was shocked. The fact that the man's name was Oriental hadn't registered.

The stranger was about Anne's height but stocky and muscular with coal-black short hair and tanned skin. He was dressed in a dark, slightly shiny business suit with a white shirt and dark tie. Over his arm he carried a belted Burberry coat.

"I beg your pardon," Tanaka said. He had only a slight accent. He bowed and extended his business card. The card simply read: Tanaka Yamaguchi, Industrial Consultant.

With one hand pressed against her throat and the other clutching the business card, Anne was at a loss for words.

"I must speak to you about your son Sean," Tanaka said.

As if recovering from a blow, Anne found her voice: "What's happened? Is he in trouble again?"

"No," Tanaka said. "Has he been in trouble before?"

"As a teenager," Anne said. "He was a very headstrong boy. Very active."

"American children can be troublesome," Tanaka said. "In Japan the children are taught to respect their elders."

"But Sean's father could be difficult," Anne said, surprised at her admission. She felt flustered and wasn't sure if she should invite the man in or not.

"I'm interested in your son's business dealings," Tanaka said. "I know he is a fine student at Harvard, but is he involved with any companies that produce biological products?"

"He and a group of his friends started a company called Immunotherapy," Anne said, relieved that the conversation was turning to the more positive moments of her son's checkered past.

"Is he still involved with this Immunotherapy?" Tanaka asked.

"He doesn't talk to me about it too much," Anne said.

"Thank you very much," Tanaka said with another bow. "Have a nice day."

Anne watched as the man turned and disappeared down the stairs. She was almost as surprised at the sudden end to the conversation as she'd been at the man's visit. She stepped out into the hall just in time to hear the front door close two floors down. Returning to her apartment, she closed the door and bolted it behind her.

It took her a moment to pull herself together. It had been a strange episode. After glancing at Tanaka's card, she slipped it into her apron pocket. Then she went back to putting food into the refrigerator. She thought about calling Brian but decided she could tell him about the Japanese man's visit that evening. Provided, of course, that Brian came. She decided that if he didn't come, then she'd call.

An hour later Anne was absorbed in making a cake when the door buzzer startled her again. At first she worried that the Japanese man had returned with more questions. Maybe she should have called Brian. With some trepidation she pressed the intercom button and asked who was there.

"Sterling Rombauer," a deep masculine voice replied. "Is this Anne Murphy?"

"Yes . . ."

"I would very much like to speak to you about your son Sean Murphy," Sterling said.

Anne caught her breath. She couldn't believe yet another stranger was there to ask questions about her second born.

"What about him?" she asked.

"I'd rather talk to you in person," Sterling said.

"I'll come down," Anne said.

Rinsing her hands of flour, Anne started down the stairs. The man was standing in the foyer, a camel-hair coat thrown over his arm. Like the Japanese man, he was wearing a business suit and white shirt. His tie was a bright red foulard.

"I'm sorry to bother you," Sterling said through the glass.

"Why are you asking about my son?" Anne demanded.

"I've been sent by the Forbes Cancer Center in Miami," Sterling explained.

Recognizing the name of the institution where Sean was working, Anne opened the door and gazed up at the stranger. He was an attractive man with a broad face and straight nose. His hair was light brown and mildly curly. Anne thought he could have been Irish except for his name. He was over six feet tall with eyes as blue as those of her own sons.

"Has Sean done something I should know about?" she asked.

"Not that I'm aware of," Sterling said. "The management of the clinic routinely looks into the background of the people who work there. Security is an important issue with them. I merely wanted to ask you a few questions."

"Like what?" Anne asked.

"Has your son been involved with any biotechnology companies to your knowledge?"

"You are the second person to ask that question in the last hour," Anne said.

"Oh?" Sterling said. "Who may I ask made similar inquiries?"

Anne reached into her apron pocket and drew out Tanaka's business card. She handed it to Sterling. Anne could see the man's eyes narrow. He handed her the card back.

"And what did you tell Mr. Yamaguchi?" Sterling asked.

"I told him my son and a few friends had started their own biotechnology company," Anne said. "They called it Immunotherapy."

"Thank you, Mrs. Murphy," Sterling said. "I appreciate your talking with me."

Anne watched the elegant stranger descend the steps in front of her house and climb into the back seat of a dark sedan. His driver was in uniform.

More baffled than ever, Anne went back upstairs. After some indecision she picked up the phone and called Brian. After apologizing for interrupting his busy day, she told him about her two curious visitors.

"That's odd," Brian said when she was finished.

"Should we be worried about Sean?" Anne asked. "You know your brother."

"I'll call him," Brian said. "Meanwhile, if anyone else comes asking questions, don't tell them anything. Just refer them to me."

"I hope I didn't say anything wrong," Anne said.

"I'm sure you didn't," Brian assured her.

"Will we be seeing you later?"

"I'm still working on it," Brian said. "But if I'm not there by eight eat without me."

With the Miami street map open on the seat next to her, Janet managed to find her way back to the Forbes residence. She was pleased when she saw Sean's Isuzu in the parking lot. She was hoping to find him home since she had what she thought was good news. She'd found an airy, pleasant furnished apartment on the southern tip of Miami Beach that even had a limited view of the ocean from the bathroom. When she'd first started looking for apartments she'd been discouraged since it was "in season." The place she found had been reserved a year in advance, but the people had unexpectedly canceled. Their cancellation had come in five minutes before Janet stepped into the real estate office.

Grabbing her purse and her copy of the rental agreement, Janet went up to her apartment. She took a few minutes to wash her face and change into shorts and a tank top. Then with lease in hand she walked down the balcony to Sean's slider. She found him glumly slouched on the couch.

"Good news!" Janet said cheerfully. She plopped down in the armchair across from him.

"I could use some of that," Sean said.

"I found an apartment," she announced. She brandished the lease. "It's not fabulous, but it's a block from the beach, and best of all it's a straight shot out the expressway to the Forbes."

"Janet, I don't know whether I can stay here," Sean said. He sounded depressed.

"What happened?" Janet asked, feeling a shiver of anxiety.

"The Forbes is nuts," Sean said. "The atmosphere sucks. For one thing, there's a Japanese weirdo who I swear is watching me. Every time I turn around, there he is."

"What else?" Janet asked. She wanted to hear all Sean's objections so she could figure a way to deal with them. Having just signed a lease for two months made her commitment to remaining in Miami that much more binding.

"There's something basically wrong with the place," Sean said. "People are either friendly or unfriendly. It's so black and white. It's not natural. Besides, I'm working by myself in this huge empty room. It's crazy."

"You've always complained about the lack of space," Janet said.

"Remind me never to complain again," Sean said. "I never realized it, but I need people around me. And another thing: they have this secret maximum containment lab which is supposed to be off limits. I ignored the sign and went in anyway. You know what I found? Nothing. The place was empty. Well, I didn't get to go in every room. In fact, I hadn't gotten far when this frustrated Marine who heads up the security department stormed in and threatened me."

"With what?" Janet asked with alarm.

"With his gut," Sean said. "He came up real close and gave me this nasty look. I was this far from giving him a shot in the nuts." Sean held up his thumb and index finger about a half inch apart.

"So what happened?" Janet asked.

"Nothing," Sean said. "He backed off and just told me to get out. But he was all worked up, ordering me out of an empty room as if I'd done something really wrong. It was insane."

"But you didn't see the other rooms," Janet said. "Maybe they're redoing the room you were in."

"It's possible," Sean admitted. "There's a lot of potential explanations. But it's still weird, and when you add all the weird stuff together, it makes the whole joint seem plain crazy."

"What about the work they want you to do?"

"That's okay," Sean said. "In fact, I don't know why they've had so much trouble. Dr. Mason, the director, came in during the afternoon, and I showed him what I was doing. I'd already gotten some minuscule crystals. I told him that I could probably get some decent crystals in a week or so. He seemed pleased, but after he left, I thought about it, and I'm not wild about helping to make money for some Japanese holding company, which is essentially what I'd be doing if I get crystals that they can defract."

"But that's not all you'll be doing," Janet said.

"How's that?"

"You'll also be investigating the medulloblastoma protocol," Janet said. "Tomorrow I'm starting on the fourth floor and guess who's there?"

"Helen Cabot?" Sean guessed. He pulled in his feet and sat up.

"You got it," Janet said. "Plus another patient from Boston. A Louis Martin."

"Does he have the same diagnosis?" Sean asked.

"Yup," Janet said. "Medulloblastoma."

"That's amazing!" Sean remarked. "And they certainly got him down here quickly!"

Janet nodded. "Forbes is a bit perturbed that Helen had been kept in Boston so long," Janet said. "The head nurse is worried about her."

"There'd been a lot of argument about whether or not to biopsy her and which of her tumors to go after," Sean explained.

"And there was another young woman being admitted while I was there," Janet said.

"Medulloblastoma too?" Sean asked.

"Yup," Janet said. "So there are three patients on my floor who are just beginning their treatments. I'd say that was pretty convenient."

"I'll need copies of their charts," Sean said. "I'll need drug samples as soon as they start actual treatment, unless of course the drugs are named. But that's not going to be the case. They won't be using chemo on these people; at least not chemo exclusively. The drugs will probably be coded. And I'll need each patient's regimen."

"I'll do what I can," Janet said. "It shouldn't be difficult with the patients on my floor. Maybe I'll even be able to arrange to care for at least one of them personally. I've also located a convenient copy machine. It's in medical records."

"Be careful there," Sean warned. "The mother of the woman in public relations is one of the medical librarians."

"I'll be careful," Janet said. She eyed Sean warily before going on. She was learning what a mistake it was to push him to any conclusions before he was ready to make them. But she just had to know. "So this means you're still game?" she asked. "You'll stay? Even if it means doing that bit of work with the protein, even if it is for the Japanese?"

Sean leaned forward with his head down, elbows on his knees, and rubbed the back of his head. "I don't know," he said. "This whole situation is absurd. What a way to do science!" He looked up at Janet. "I wonder if anybody in Washington had any idea what limiting research funding would do to our research establishments. It's all happening just when the country needs research more than ever."

"All the more reason for us to try to do something," Janet said.

"You're serious about this?" Sean asked.

"Absolutely," Janet said.

"You know we'll have to be resourceful," Sean said.

"I know."

"We'll have to break a few rules," he added. "Are you sure you can handle that?"

"I think so," Janet said.

"And once we start, there's no turning back," Sean said.

Janet started to answer but the ringing of the phone on the desk startled them both.

"Who the hell could that be?" Sean wondered. He let it ring.

"Aren't you going to answer it?" Janet asked.

"I'm thinking," Sean said. What he didn't say was that he was afraid it might be Sarah Mason. She'd called him that afternoon, and despite a temptation to aggravate Harris, Sean did not want any association with the woman whatsoever.

"I think you should answer it," Janet said.

"You answer it," Sean suggested.

Janet jumped to her feet and snatched up the receiver. Sean watched her expression as she asked who was calling. She showed no strong reaction as she extended the phone to him.

"It's your brother," she said.

"What the hell?" Sean mumbled as he pulled himself out of the couch. It wasn't like his brother to call. They didn't have that type of relationship, and they had just seen each other Friday night.

Sean took the phone. "What's wrong?" he asked.

"I was about to ask you the same question," Brian said.

"You want an honest answer or platitudes?" Sean asked.

"I think you'd better tell me straight," Brian said.

"This place is bizarre," Sean said. "I'm not so sure I want to stay. It might be a complete waste of time." Sean glanced over at Janet, who rolled her eyes in exasperation.

"Something weird's going on up here too," Brian said. He told Sean about the two men who'd visited their mother, asking about Immunotherapy.

"Immunotherapy is history," Sean said. "What did Mom say?"

"Not much," Brian said. "At least according to her. But she got a bit flustered. All she said was that you and some friends started it."

"She didn't say we sold out?"

"Evidently not."

"What about Oncogen?"

"She said she didn't mention it because we'd told her not to discuss it with anyone."

"Good for her," Sean said.

"Why would these people be up here talking to Mom?" Brian asked. "The Rombauer guy told her he represented the Forbes Cancer Center. He said that they routinely look into their employees for security reasons. Have you done anything to suggest you're a security risk?"

"Hell, I've only been here for a little over twenty-four hours," Sean said.

"You and I know of your penchant to provoke discord. Your blarney would try the patience of Job."

"My blarney is nothing compared to your blather, brother," Sean teased. "Hell, you've made an institution of it by becoming a lawyer."

"Since I'm in a good mood, I'll let that slam slide," Brian said. "But seriously, what do you think is going on?"

"I haven't the slightest idea," Sean said. "Maybe it's like the man said: routine."

"But neither guy seemed to know about the other," Brian said. "That doesn't sound routine to me. And the first man left his card. I have it right here. It says: Tanaka Yamaguchi, Industrial Consultant."

"Industrial consultant could mean anything," Sean said. "I wonder if his involvement is somehow related to the fact that a Japanese electronics giant called Sushita Industries has invested heavily in Forbes. They're obviously looking for some lucrative patents."

"Why can't they stick to cameras, electronics, and cars?" Brian said. "They're already screwing up the world's economy."

"They're too smart for that," Sean said. "They are looking toward the long term. But why they would be interested in my association with piss-ant Immunotherapy, I haven't the foggiest."

"Well, I thought you should know," Brian said. "It's still a little hard for me to believe you're not stirring things up down there, knowing you."

"You'll hurt my feelings talking like that," Sean said.

"I'll be in touch as soon as the Franklin Bank comes through for Oncogen," Brian said. "Try to stay out of trouble."

"Who, me?" Sean asked innocently.

Sean dropped the receiver into the cradle as soon as Brian said goodbye.

"Have you changed your mind again?" Janet asked with obvious frustration.

"What are you talking about?" Sean questioned.

"You told your brother that you weren't sure you wanted to stay," Janet said. "I thought we'd decided to go for it."

"We had," Sean said. "But I didn't want to tell Brian about the plan. He'd worry himself sick. Besides, he'd probably tell my mother and who knows what would happen then."

"That was very nice indeed," Sterling told the masseuse. She was a handsome, healthy Scandinavian from Finland, dressed in what could have passed for a tennis outfit. He gave her an extra five-dollar tip; when he'd made the arrangements for the massage through the Ritz's concierge, he'd already included an adequate tip in the charge added to his account, but he'd noticed she'd gone over the allotted time.

While the masseuse folded her table and gathered her oils, Sterling pulled on a thick white terry-cloth robe and slipped off the towel cinched around his waist. Dropping into the club chair near the window he lifted his feet onto the ottoman and poured a glass of the complimentary champagne. Sterling was a regular visitor at Boston's Ritz Carlton.

The masseuse called a goodbye from the door, and Sterling thanked her again. He decided he'd ask for her by name the next time. A regular massage was one of the expenses Sterling's clients had learned to expect. They'd complain on occasion, but Sterling would merely say that they could accept his terms or hire someone else. Invariably they'd agree because Sterling was extremely effective at the service he performed: industrial espionage.

There were other, more sanitized, descriptions for Sterling's work such as trade counsel or business consultant, but Sterling preferred the honesty of industrial espionage, although for propriety's sake, he left it off his business card. His card merely read: consultant. It didn't read "industrial consultant" as did the card he'd seen earlier that day. He felt the word "industrial" suggested a limitation to manufacturing. Sterling was interested in all business.

Sterling sipped his drink and gazed out the window at the superb view. As usual, his room was on a high floor overlooking the magical Boston Garden. As the sunlight waned, the park's lamps lining the serpentine walkways had blinked on, illuminating the swan boat pond with its miniature suspension bridge. Although it was early March, the recent cold snap had frozen the pond solid. Skaters dotted its mirrored surface, weaving in effortless, intersecting arcs.

Raising his eyes, Sterling could see the fading dazzle of the gold-domed Massachusetts State House. Ruefully he bemoaned the sad fact that the legislature had systematically destroyed its own tax base by enacting shortsighted, anti-business legislation. Unfortunately Sterling had lost a number of good clients who'd either been forced to flee to a more business-oriented state or forced to leave business altogether. Nevertheless, Sterling enjoyed his trips to Boston. It was such a civilized city.

Pulling the phone over to the edge of the table, Sterling wanted to finish work for the day before he indulged in dinner. Not that he found work a burden. Quite the contrary. Sterling loved his current employ, especially considering that he didn't have to work at all. He'd trained at Stanford in computer engineering, worked for Big Blue for several years, then founded his own successful computer chip company, all before he was thirty. By his middle thirties he was tired of an unfulfilling life, a bad marriage, and the stultifying routine of running a business. First he divorced, then he took his company public and made a fortune. Then he engineered a buyout and made another fortune. By age forty he could have bought a sizable portion of the State of California if he'd so desired.

For almost one year he indulged himself in the adolescence he felt he'd somehow missed. Eventually, he got extremely bored with such places as Aspen. That was when a business friend asked him if he would look into a private matter for him. From that moment on, Sterling had been launched on a new career which was stimulating, never routine, rarely dull, and which utilized his engineering background, his business acumen, his imagination, and his intuitive sense for human behavior.

Sterling called Randolph Mason at home. Dr. Mason took the call from his private line in his study.

"I'm not sure you will be happy about what I've learned," Sterling said.

"It's better I learn it sooner rather than later," Dr. Mason responded.

"This young Sean Murphy is an impressive young fellow," Sterling said. "He founded his own biotechnology company called Immunotherapy while a graduate student at MIT. The company turned a profit almost from day one marketing diagnostic kits."

"How's it doing now?"

"Wonderfully," Sterling said. "It's a winner. It's done so well that Genentech bought them out over a year ago."

"Indeed!" Dr. Mason said. A ray of sunshine entered the picture. "Where does that leave Sean Murphy?"

"He and his young friends realized a considerable profit," Sterling said. "Considering their initial investment, it was extremely lucrative indeed."

"So Sean's no longer involved?" Dr. Mason asked.

"He's completely out," Sterling said. "Is that helpful?"

"I'd say so," Dr. Mason said. "I could use the kid's experience with monoclonals, but not if he's got a production facility behind him. It would be too risky."

"He could still sell the information to someone else," Sterling said. "Or he could be in someone else's employ."

"Can you find that out?"

"Most likely," Sterling said. "Do you want me to continue on this?"

"Absolutely," Dr. Mason said. "I want to use the kid but not if he's some kind of industrial spy."

"I've learned something else," Sterling said as he poured himself more champagne. "Someone besides myself has been investigating Sean Murphy. His name is Tanaka Yamaguchi."

Dr. Mason felt the tortellini in his stomach turn upside down.

"Have you ever heard of this man?" Sterling asked.

"No," Dr. Mason said. He'd not heard of him, but with a name like that, the implications were obvious.

"My assumption would be he's working for Sushita," Sterling said. "And I know that he is aware of Sean Murphy's involvement with Immunotherapy. I know because Sean's mother told him."

"He'd been to see Sean's mother?" Dr. Mason asked with alarm.

"As have I," Sterling said.

"But then Sean will know he's being investigated," Dr. Mason sputtered.

"Nothing wrong in that," Sterling said. "If Sean is an industrial spy, it will give him pause. If he's not, it will only be a matter of curiosity or at worst a minor irritation. Sean's reaction should not be your concern. You should be worried about Tanaka Yamaguchi."

"What do you mean?"

"I've never met Tanaka," Sterling said. "But I have heard a lot about him since we're competitors of sorts. He came to the United States many years ago for college. He's the eldest son of a wealthy industrial family, heavy machinery I believe. The problem was he adapted to 'degenerate' American ways a bit too easily for the family's honor. He was swiftly Americanized and became too individualistic for Japanese tastes. The family decided they didn't want him home so they funded a lavish lifestyle. It's been a kind of exile, but he's been clever to augment his allowance by doing what I do, only for Japanese companies operating in the U.S. But he's like a double agent of sorts, frequently representing the Yakusa at the same time he's representing a legitimate firm. He's clever, he's ruthless, and he's effective. The fact that he's involved means your Sushita friends are serious."

"You think he was involved with our two researchers who disappeared and whom you found happily working for Sushita in Japan?"

"I wouldn't be surprised," Sterling said.

"I can't afford to have this Harvard student disappear," Dr. Mason said. "That would be the kind of media event that could destroy the Forbes."

"I don't think there is a worry for the moment," Sterling said. "My sources tell me Tanaka is still here in Boston. Since he has access to a lot of the same information as I, he must think Sean Murphy is involved in something else."

"Like what?" Dr. Mason asked.

"I'm not sure," Sterling said. "I haven't been able to locate all that money those kids made when they sold Immunotherapy. Neither Sean nor his friends have any personal money to speak of, and none of them indulged themselves with expensive cars or other high-ticket items. I think they are up to something, and I believe Tanaka thinks so too."

"Good God!" Dr. Mason said. "I don't know what to do. Maybe I should send the kid home."

"If you think Sean can help you with that protein work you told me about," Sterling said, "then hold tight. I believe I have everything under control. I have made inquiries with numerous contacts, and because of the computer industry here, I'm well connected. All you have to do is tell me to remain on the case and continue paying the bills."

"Keep on it," Dr. Mason said. "And keep me informed."

MARCH 4 • THURSDAY, 6:30 A.M.

Janet was up, dressed in her white uniform, and out of the apartment early since her shift ran from seven to three. At that time of the morning there was very little traffic on I95, especially northbound. She and Sean had discussed driving together but in the end decided it would be better if each had their own wheels.

Janet felt a little queasy entering the Forbes Hospital that morning. Her anxiety went beyond the usual nervousness associated with starting a new job. The prospect of breaking rules was what had her on edge and tense. She already felt guilty to a degree; it was guilt by intent.

Janet made it to the fourth floor with time to spare. She poured herself a cup of coffee and proceeded to familiarize herself with the locations of the charts, the pharmacy locker, and the supply closet: areas she would need to be familiar with to carry out her job as a floor nurse. By the time she sat down for report with the night shift going off duty and the day shift coming on, she was significantly calmer than she had been when she first arrived. Marjorie's cheerful presence no doubt helped put her at ease.

Report was routine except for Helen Cabot's deteriorating condition. The poor woman had had several seizures during the night, and the doctors said that her intracranial pressure was rising.

"Do they think the problem is related to the CAT scan–driven biopsy yesterday?" Marjorie asked.

"No," Juanita Montgomery, the night shift supervisor, said. "Dr. Mason was in at three A.M. when she seized again, and he said the problem was probably related to the treatment."

"She's started treatment already?" Janet asked.

"Absolutely," Juanita said. "Her treatment started Tuesday, the night she got here."

"But she just had her biopsy yesterday," Janet said.

"That's for the cellular aspect of her treatment," Marjorie chimed in. "She'll be pheresed today to harvest T lymphocytes which will be grown and sensitized to her tumor. But the humoral aspect of her treatment was started immediately."

"They used mannitol to bring down her intracranial pressure," Juanita added. "It seemed to work. She hasn't seized again. They want to avoid steroids and a shunt if possible. At any rate, she's got to be monitored carefully, especially with the pheresis."

As soon as report was over and the bleary-eyed night shift had departed, the day's work began in earnest. Janet found herself extremely busy. There were a lot of sick patients on the floor, representing a wide range of cancers, and each was on an individual treatment protocol. The most heartrending for Janet was an angelic boy of nine who was on reverse precautions while they waited for a bone marrow transplant to repopulate his marrow with blood-forming cells. He'd been given a strong dose of chemotherapy and radiation to wipe out completely his own leukemic marrow. At the moment he was completely vulnerable to any microorganisms, even those normally not pathogenic for humans.

By mid-morning, Janet finally had a chance to catch her breath. Most of the nurses took their coffee breaks in the utility room off the nurses' station where they could put up their tired feet. Janet decided to take advantage of the time to have Tim Katzenburg show her how to access the Forbes computer. Every patient had a traditional chart and a computer file. Janet wasn't intimidated by computers, having minored in computer science in college. But it still helped to have someone familiar with the Forbes system get her started.

When Tim was distracted for a moment by a phone call from the lab, Janet called up Helen Cabot's file. Since Helen had been there less than forty-eight hours, the file was not extensive. There was a computer graphic showing which of her three tumors they had biopsied and the location of the trephination of the skull just above the right ear. The biopsy specimen was grossly described as firm, white, and of an adequate amount. It said that the specimen had been immediately packed in ice and sent to Basic Diagnostics. In the treatment section it said that she'd begun on MB-300C and MB-303C at a dosage of 100mg/Kg/day of body weight administered at 0.05 ml/Kg/minute.

Janet glanced over at Tim, who was still busy on the phone. On a scrap of paper, she wrote down the treatment information. She also wrote down the alpha numeric designator, T-9872, that was listed as the diagnosis along with the descriptive term: medulloblastoma, multiple.

Using the diagnostic designator, Janet next called up the names of the patients with medulloblastoma who were currently in the hospital. There were a total of five including the three on the fourth floor. The other two were Margaret Demars on the third floor, and Luke Kinsman, an eight-year-old, in the pediatric wings of the fifth floor. Janet wrote down the names.

"Having trouble?" Tim asked over Janet's shoulder.

"Not at all," Janet said. She quickly cleared the screen so that Tim wouldn't see what she'd been up to. She couldn't afford to arouse suspicion on her very first day.

"I've got to enter these lab values," Tim told her. "It will only take a sec."

While Tim was absorbed with the computer terminal, Janet scanned the chart rack for Cabot, Martin, or Sharenburg. To her chagrin, none of those charts was there.

Marjorie breezed into the station to get some narcotics from the pharmacy locker. "You're supposed to be on your coffee break," she called to Janet.

"I am," Janet said, holding up her Styrofoam cup. She mentally made a note to bring a mug into work. Everyone else had his or her own.

"I'm already impressed with you," Marjorie teased from inside the pharmacy. "You needn't work through your break. Kick back, girl, and take a load off your feet."

Janet smiled and said that she'd be taking that kind of break after she was fully acclimated to the ward's routine. When Tim was finished with the computer terminal, Janet asked him about the missing charts.

"They're all down on the second floor," Tim said. "Cabot's getting pheresed while Martin and Scharenburg are being biopsied. Naturally the charts are with them."

"Naturally," Janet repeated. It seemed tough luck that not one of those charts could have been there when she had the chance to look at them. She began to suspect that the clinical espionage she'd committed herself to might not be quite as easy as she'd thought when she suggested her plan to Sean.

Giving up on the charts for the moment, Janet waited for one of the other shift nurses, Dolores Hodges, to finish up in the pharmacy closet. Once Dolores had headed down the hall, Janet made sure no one was watching before slipping into the tiny room. Each patient had an assigned cubbyhole containing his or her prescribed medications. The drugs had come up from the central pharmacy on the first floor.

Finding Helen's cubbyhole, Janet quickly scanned the plethora of vials, bottles, and tubes that contained anti-seizure medication, general tranquilizers, anti-nausea pills, and non-narcotic pain pills. There were no containers designated MB300C or MB303C. On the chance that these medications were secured with the narcotics, Janet checked the narcotics locker, but she found only narcotics there.

Next Janet located Louis Martin's cubbyhole. His was a low one, close to the floor. Janet had to squat down to search through it, but first she had to close the lower half of the Dutch door to make room. As with Helen's cubby, Janet could find no drug containers with special MB code designations on the label.

"My goodness, you startled me," Dolores exclaimed. She had returned in haste and had practically tripped headlong over Janet crouched before Louis Martin's cubbyhole. "I'm so sorry," Dolores said. "I didn't think anyone was in here."

"My fault," Janet said, feeling herself blush. She was instantly afraid she was giving herself away and that Dolores would wonder what she'd been up to. Yet Dolores showed no signs of being suspicious. Instead, once Janet stepped back and out of the way, she came in to get what she needed. In a moment she was gone.

Janet left the pharmacy closet visibly trembling. This was only her first day and though nothing terrible had happened, she wasn't sure she had the nerves for the furtive behavior espionage demanded.

When Janet reached Helen Cabot's room, she paused. The door was propped open by a rubber stopper. Stepping inside, Janet gazed around. She didn't expect to find any drugs there, but she wanted to check just the same. As she'd expected, there weren't any.

Having recovered her composure, Janet headed back toward the nurses' station, passing Gloria D'Amataglio's room on the way. Taking a moment, Janet stuck her head through the open door. Gloria was sitting up in her armchair with a stainless steel kidney dish clutched in her hand. Her IV was still running.

When they'd chatted the day before Janet had learned that Gloria had gone to Wellesley College just as she herself had. Janet had been in the class a year ahead. After thinking about it overnight, Janet had decided to ask Gloria if she'd known a friend of hers who'd been in Gloria's class. Getting Gloria's attention, she posed her question.

"You knew Laura Lowell!" Gloria said with forced enthusiasm. "Amazing! I was great friends with her. I loved her parents." It was painfully obvious to Janet that Gloria was making an effort to be sociable. Her chemotherapy was no doubt leaving her nauseous.

"I thought you might," Janet said. "Everybody knew Laura."

Janet was about to excuse herself and allow Gloria to rest when she heard a rattle behind her. She turned in time to see the housekeeping man appear at the door, then immediately disappear. Fearing her presence had interrupted his schedule, Janet told Gloria she'd stop by later and went out into the hall to tell the housekeeper the room was all his. But the man had disappeared. She looked up and down the corridor. She even checked a couple of the neighboring rooms. It was as if he'd simply vanished into thin air.

Janet headed back to the nurses' station. Noticing she still had a bit of break time left, she took the elevator down to the second floor in hopes of getting a glimpse at one or more of the missing charts. Helen Cabot was still undergoing pheresis and would be for some time. Her chart was unavailable. Kathleen Sharenburg was undergoing a biopsy at that moment, and her chart was in the radiology office. With Louis Martin, Janet lucked out. His biopsy was scheduled to follow Kathleen Sharenburg's. Janet discovered him on a gurney in the hallway. He was heavily tranquilized and soundly sleeping. His chart was tucked under the gurney pad.

After checking with a technician and learning that Louis would not be biopsied for at least an hour, Janet took a chance and pulled out his chart. Walking quickly as if leaving the scene of a crime with the evidence in hand, she carried the chart into medical records. It was all she could do not to break into a full sprint. Janet admitted to herself that she was probably the worst person in the world to be involved in this kind of thing. The anxiety she'd felt in the pharmacy locker came back in a flash.

"Of course you can use the copy machine," one of the medical record librarians told her when she asked. "That's what it's here for. Just indicate nursing on the log."

Janet wondered if this librarian was the mother of the woman in public relations who'd been in Sean's apartment on the night of her arrival. She'd have to be careful. As she walked over to the copy machine, she glanced over her shoulder. The woman had gone back to the task she'd been doing when Janet had entered, paying no attention to Janet whatsoever.

Janet quickly copied Louis's entire chart. There were more pages than she would have expected, particularly since he had only been hospitalized for one day. Glancing at some of them, Janet could tell that most of the chart consisted of referral material that had come from Boston Memorial.

Finished at last, Janet hurried the chart back to the gurney. She was relieved to see that Louis had not been moved. Janet slipped the chart under the pad, positioning it exactly as she'd found it. Louis didn't stir.

Returning to the fourth floor, Janet panicked. She hadn't given any thought to what she would do with the copy of the chart. It was too big to fit into her purse, and she couldn't leave it lying about. She had to find a temporary hiding place, somewhere the other nurses and nursing assistants would not be likely to go.

With no break time left, Janet had to think fast. The last thing she wanted to do on her first day of work was take more time off than she was due. Frantically, Janet tried to think. She considered the patient lounge, but it was currently occupied. She thought of one of the lower cabinets in the pharmacy closet, but dismissed that idea as too risky. Finally she thought of the housekeeping closet.

Janet looked up and down the corridor. There were plenty of people around, but they all seemed absorbed by what they were doing. She saw the housekeeper's cart parked outside a nearby patient room, suggesting the man was busy cleaning within. Taking a breath, Janet slipped into the closet. The door with its automatic closer shut behind her instantly, plunging her into darkness. She groped for the light switch and turned it on.

The tiny room was dominated by a generous slop sink. On the wall opposite was a countertop with undercounter cabinets, a bank of shallow overcounter wall cabinets, and a broom closet. She opened the broom closet. There were a few shelves above the compartment that held the brooms and mops, but they were too exposed. Then she looked at the overcounter cabinets and her eyes kept rising.

Placing a foot on the edge of the slop sink, she climbed up atop the counter. Reaching up, she groped the area above the wall cabinets. As she'd guessed, there was a narrow depressed space between the top of the cabinets and the ceiling. Confident she'd found what she'd been looking for, she slipped the chart copy over the front lip and let it drop down. A bit of dust rose up in a cloud.

Satisfied, Janet climbed down, rinsed her hands in the sink, then emerged into the hall. If anybody had wondered what she'd been up to, they didn't give any indication. One of the other nurses passed her and smiled cheerfully.

Returning to the nurses' station, Janet threw herself into her work. After five minutes she began to calm down. After ten minutes even her pulse had returned to normal. When Marjorie appeared a few minutes later, Janet was calm enough to inquire about Helen Cabot's coded medication.

"I've been going over each of the patients' treatments," Janet said. "I want to familiarize myself with their medications so I'll be prepared for whomever I'm assigned to for the day. I saw reference to MB300C and MB303C. What are they, and where would I find them?"

Marjorie straightened up from bending over the desk. She grasped a key strung around her neck on a silver-colored chain and pulled it out in front of her. "MB medicine you get from me," she said. "We keep it in a refrigerated lockup right here in the nursing station." She pulled open a cabinet to expose a small refrigerator. "It's up to the head nurse on each shift to dispense it. We control the MBs somewhat like narcotics, only a bit stricter."

"Well, that explains why I couldn't find it in the pharmacy," Janet said, forcing a smile. All at once she realized that getting samples of the medicine was going to be a hundred times more difficult than she'd envisioned. In fact, she wondered if it was possible at all.

Tom Widdicomb was trying to calm down. He'd never felt so wired in his life. Usually his mother was able to calm him down, but now she wouldn't even talk to him.

He'd made it a point to arrive extra early that morning. He'd kept an eye on that new nurse, Janet Reardon, from the moment she'd arrived. He'd trailed her carefully, watching her every move. After tracking her for an hour, he'd decided his concerns had been unjustified. She'd acted like any other nurse, so Tom had felt relieved.

But then she'd ended up in Gloria's room again! Tom could not believe it. Just when he'd let his guard down, she'd reappeared. That the same woman would thwart his attempt to relieve Gloria's suffering not once but twice went past coincidence. "Two days in a row!" Tom had hissed in the solitude of his housekeeping closet. "She's gotta be a spy!"

His only consolation was that this time he'd walked in on her rather than vice versa. Actually, it was even better than that. He'd almost walked in on her. He didn't know whether she'd seen him or not, although she probably had.

From then on he'd followed her again. With her every step he became more and more convinced she was there to get him. She was not acting like a regular nurse, no way. Not with the sneaking around she was doing. The worst was when she'd sneaked into his housekeeping closet and started opening cabinets. He could hear her from the hall. He knew what she had been looking for, and he'd been sick with worry that she'd find his stuff. As soon as she'd left, he'd stepped inside. Climbing up on the counter, he'd blindly reached up on top of the wall cabinet at the very far end in the corner to feel for his succinylcholine and syringes. Thankfully they were there and hadn't been disturbed.

After climbing down from the cabinet, Tom struggled to calm himself. He kept telling himself he was safe since the succinylcholine was still there. At least he was safe for the moment. But there was no doubt that he would have to deal with Janet Reardon, just as he'd had to deal with Sheila Arnold. He couldn't let her stop his crusade. If he did, he might risk losing Alice.

"Don't worry, Mother," Tom said aloud. "Everything will be all right."

But Alice wouldn't listen. She was scared.

After fifteen minutes, Tom felt calm enough to face the world. Taking a fortifying breath, he pulled open the door and stepped into the hall. His housekeeping cart was to his right pushed against the wall. He grabbed it and started pushing.

He kept his eyes directed at the floor as he headed toward the elevators. As he passed the nurses' station he heard Marjorie yell to him about cleaning a room.

"I've been called to administration," Tom said without looking up. Every so often if there'd been an accident, like spilled coffee, he'd be called up there to clean it up. Regular cleaning of the administration floor was handled by the night crew.

"Well, get back here on the double," Marjorie yelled.

Tom swore under his breath.

When he got to the administration floor, Tom pushed his cleaning cart directly into the main secretarial area. It was always busy there, no one ever looking at him twice. He parked his cart directly in front of the wall chart of the floor plan of the Forbes residence in southeast Miami.

There were ten apartments on each floor, and each had a little slot for a name. Tom quickly found Janet Reardon's name in the slot marked 207. Even more handy was a key box attached to the wall just below the chart. Inside were multiple sets of keys, all carefully labeled. The box was supposed to be locked, but the key to open it was always in the lock. Since the box was obscured by his cart, Tom calmly helped himself to a set for apartment 207.

To justify his presence Tom emptied a few wastebaskets before pushing his cart back to the elevators.

As he waited for an elevator to arrive he felt a wave of relief. Even Alice was willing to talk to him now. She told him how proud of him she was now that he would be able to take care of things. She told him that she'd been worried about this new nurse, Janet Reardon.

"I told you that you didn't have to worry," Tom said. "Nobody will ever bother us."

Sterling Rombauer had always liked the adage that his schoolteacher mother had espoused: *Chance favors the prepared mind.* Figuring there were only a limited number of hotels in Boston that Tanaka Yamaguchi would find acceptable, Sterling had decided to try calling some of the hotel employee contacts he'd cultivated over the years. His efforts had been rewarded with immediate success. Sterling smiled when he learned that not only did he and Tanaka share the same profession, they shared the same taste in hotels.

This was a felicitous turn of events. Thanks to his frequent stays at Boston's Ritz Carlton, Sterling's contacts in the hotel were simply sterling. A few discreet inquiries revealed some helpful information. First, Tanaka had hired the same livery company Sterling himself used, which wasn't surprising since it was by far the best. Second, he was scheduled to remain in the hotel at least another night. Finally, he'd made a lunch reservation in the Ritz Café for two people.

Sterling went right to work. A call to the maître d' in the café, a rather crowded, intimate environment, produced a promise that Mr. Yamaguchi's party would be seated at the far banquette. The neighboring corner table, literally inches away, would be reserved for Mr. Sterling Rombauer. A call to the owner of the livery company resulted in a promise of the name of Mr. Yamaguchi's driver as well as a transcript of his stops.

"This Jap is well connected," the owner of the livery company said when Sterling phoned him. "We picked him up from general aviation. He came in on a private jet, and it wasn't one of those dinky ones either."

A call to the airport confirmed the presence of the Sushita Gulfstream III and gave Sterling its call number. Phoning his contact at the FAA in Washington and providing the call numbers, Sterling obtained a promise to keep him informed of the jet's movements.

With so much accomplished without even leaving his hotel room and a bit of time to spare before the luncheon rendezvous, Sterling walked across Newbury Street to Burberry's to treat himself to several new shirts.

With his legs crossed and stretched out in front of him, Sean sat in one of the molded plastic chairs in the hospital cafeteria. His left elbow was resting on the table, cradling his chin; his right arm dangled over the back of the chair. Mood-wise, he was in approximately the same state of mind as he'd been the night before when Janet had come through his living-room slider. The morning had been an aggravating rerun of the previous day, confirming his belief that the Forbes was a bizarre and largely unfriendly place to work. Hiroshi was still trailing him like a bad detective. Practically every time Sean turned around when he was up on the sixth floor using some equipment not available on the fifth, he'd see the Japanese fellow. And the moment Sean looked at him, Hiroshi would quickly look away as if Sean were a moron and wouldn't know that Hiroshi had been watching him.

Sean checked his watch. The agreement had been that he'd meet Janet at twelve-thirty. It was already twelve-thirty-five, and although a steady stream of hospital personnel continued to pour by, Janet had yet to appear. Sean began to fantasize about going down to the parking lot, getting into his Isuzu, and hitting the road. But then Janet came through the door, and just seeing her lightened his mood.

Although Janet was still pale by Florida standards, her few days in Miami had already given a distinctively rosy cast to her skin. Sean thought she'd never looked better. As he admiringly watched her sensuous movements as she weaved through the tables, he hoped that he'd be able to talk her out of whatever it was that was keeping her in her own apartment and out of his.

She took the seat across from him, barely saying hello. Under her arm she clutched an unfolded Miami newspaper. He could tell she was nervous, the way she continually scanned the room like some wary, vulnerable bird.

"Janet, we're not in some spy movie," Sean said. "Calm down!"

"But I feel like I am," Janet said. "I've been sneaking around, going behind people's backs, trying not to arouse suspicion. But I feel like everyone knows what I'm doing."

Sean rolled his eyes. "What an amateur I have for an accomplice," he joked. Then, more seriously, he added, "I don't know whether this is going to work if you're stressed out now, Janet. This is only the beginning. You haven't even done anything yet compared to what's coming. But, to tell you the truth, I'm jealous. At least you're doing something. I, on the other hand, have spent a good part of the morning in the bowels of the earth injecting mice with the Forbes protein plus Freund's adjuvant. There's been no intrigue and certainly no excitement. This place is still driving me nuts."

"What about your crystals?" Janet asked.

"I'm deliberately slowing down on that," Sean said. "I was doing too well. I won't let them know how far I've gotten. That way, when I need some time for some investigative work, I'll take it and still be able to have results to show as a cover. So how'd you do?"

"Not great," Janet admitted. "But I made a start. I copied one chart."

"Just one?" Sean questioned with obvious disappointment. "You're this nervous about one chart?"

"Don't give me a hard time," Janet warned. "This isn't easy for me."

"And I'd never say I told you so," Sean quipped. "Never. Not me. That's not my style."

"Oh, shut up," Janet said as she handed the newspaper to Sean under the table. "I'm doing the best I can."

Sean lifted the newspaper and placed it on top of the table. He spread it out and opened it, exposing the copied pages which he immediately removed. He pushed the newspaper aside.

"Sean!" Janet gasped, as she furtively scanned the crowded room. "Can't you be a little more subtle?"

"I'm tired of being subtle," he said. He started going through the chart.

"Even for my benefit?" Janet asked. "There might be some people from my floor here. They might have seen me give these copies to you."

"You give people too much credit," Sean said distractedly. "People aren't as observant as you might think." Then, referring to the copies Janet had brought, he said, "Louis Martin's chart is nothing but referral material from the Memorial. This history and physical is mine. That lazy ass on neurology just copied my workup."

"How can you tell?" Janet asked.

"The wording," Sean said. "Listen to this: the patient 'suffered through' a prostatectomy three months ago. I use expressions like 'suffered through' just to see who reads my workups and who doesn't. It's a little game I play with myself. No one else uses that kind of phraseology in a medical workup. You're supposed to just give facts, not judgments."

"Imitation is the highest form of flattery, so I guess you should be flattered," Janet said.

"The only thing of interest here is in the orders," Sean said. "He's being given two coded drugs: MB300M and MB305M."

"That code is comparable to the one I saw in Helen Cabot's computer file," Janet said. She handed him the paper on which she'd written the treatment information she'd gotten from the computer.

Sean glanced at the dosage and the administration rate.

"What do you think it is?" Janet asked.

"No idea," Sean said. "Did you get any of it?"

"Not yet," Janet admitted. "But I finally located the supply. It's kept in a special locker, and the shift supervisor has the only key."

"This is interesting," Sean said, still studying the chart. "From the date and time of the order they started treatment as soon as he got here."

"Same with Helen Cabot," Janet said. She told him what Marjorie had explained to her, namely that they started the humoral aspect of the treatment immediately whereas the cellular aspect didn't begin until after the biopsy and T-cell harvesting.

"Starting treatment so soon seems odd," Sean said. "Unless these drugs are merely lymphokines or some other general immunologic stimulant. It can't be some new drug, like a new type of chemo agent."

"Why not?" Janet asked.

"Because the FDA would have had to approve it," Sean said. "It has to be a drug that's already been approved. How come you only got Louis Martin's chart? What about Helen Cabot's?"

"I was lucky to get Martin's," Janet said. "Cabot is getting pheresed as we speak, and the other young woman, Kathleen Sharenburg, is being biopsied. Martin was a 'to follow' for his biopsy so his chart was available."

"So these people are on the second floor right now?" Sean asked. "Right above us?"

"I believe so," Janet said.

"Maybe I'll skip lunch and take a walk up there," Sean said. "With all the usual commotion in most diagnostic and treatment areas, the charts are usually just kicking around. I could probably get a look at them."

"Better you than me," Janet said. "I'm sure you're better at this than I."

"I'm not taking over your job," Sean said. "I'll still want copies of the other two charts as well as daily updates. Plus I want a list of all the patients they've treated to date who have had medulloblastoma. I'm particularly interested in their outcomes. Plus I want samples of the coded medicine. That should be your priority. I have to have that medicine; the sooner the better."

"I'll do my best," Janet said. Knowing how much trouble it had been merely to copy Martin's chart, she had misgivings about getting everything Sean wanted with the kind of speed he was implying. Not that she was about to voice those concerns to Sean. She was afraid he'd give up and leave for Boston.

Sean stood up. He gripped Janet's shoulder. "I know this isn't easy for you," he said. "But remember, it was your idea."

Janet put a hand on Sean's. "We can do it," she said.

"I'll see you at the Cow Palace," he said. "I suppose you'll be there around four. I'll try to get back about the same time."

"See you then," Janet said.

Sean left the cafeteria and used the stairs to get to the second floor. He emerged at the south end of the building. The second floor was a center of activity and as bustling as he'd expected. All the radiation therapy as well as diagnostic radiology was done there; so was all the surgery and any treatment that could not be done at the bedside.

With all the confusion Sean had to squeeze between gurneys carrying people to and from their procedures. A number of the gurneys with their human passengers were parked along the walls. Other patients sat on benches dressed in hospital robes.

Sean excused himself and pushed through the tumult, bumping into hospital personnel as well as ambulatory patients. With a modicum of difficulty he proceeded down the central corridor, checking each door as he went. Radiology and chemistry were on the left, treatment rooms, ICU, and the surgical suites were on the right. Knowing that the pheresis was a long procedure and not labor-intensive, Sean decided to try to find Helen Cabot. Besides looking at her chart, he wanted to say hello.

Spotting a hematology technician sporting rubber tourniquets attached to her belt loops, Sean asked her where pheresis was done. The woman guided Sean through a side corridor and pointed toward two rooms. Sean thanked her and checked the first. A male patient was on the gurney. Sean closed the door and opened the other. Even from the threshold he recognized the patient: it was Helen Cabot.

She was the only one there. Outflow and inflow lines were attached to her left arm as her blood was being passed through a machine that separated the elements, isolating the lymphocytes and returning the rest of the blood to her body.

Helen turned her bandaged head in Sean's direction. She recognized him immediately and tried to smile. Instead, tears formed in her large green eyes.

From her color and general appearance Sean could see that her condition had dramatically worsened. The seizures she'd been suffering had been taking a heavy toll.

"It's good to see you," Sean said as he bent down to bring his face close to hers. He resisted an urge to hold and comfort her. "How are you doing?"

"It's been difficult," Helen managed to say. "I had another biopsy yesterday. It wasn't fun. They also warned me I might get worse when they started the treatment, and I have. They told me I was not to lose faith. But it's been hard. My headaches have been unbearable. It even hurts to talk."

"You have to hold on," Sean said. "Keep remembering that they have put every medulloblastoma patient into remission."

"That's what I keep reminding myself," Helen said.

"I'll try to come to see you every day," Sean said. "Meanwhile, where's your chart?"

"I think it's out in the waiting room," Helen said, pointing with her free hand toward a second door.

Sean gave her a warm smile. He squeezed her shoulder, then stepped into the small waiting room that connected to the corridor. On a counter was what he was searching for: Helen's chart.

Sean picked it up and flipped to the order sheets. Drugs similar to those he'd seen in Martin's chart were duly noted: MB300C and MB303C. He then turned to the beginning of the chart and saw a copy of his own workup which had been sent as part of the referral package.

Flipping the pages quickly, Sean came to the progress note section, and he read the entry for the biopsy that had been taken the day before, indicating they had gone in over the right ear. The note went on to say that the patient had tolerated the procedure well.

Sean had just begun to scan for the laboratory section to see if a frozen section had been done when he was interrupted. The door to the hallway crashed open and slammed against the wall with such force that the doorknob dented the plaster.

The sudden crash startled Sean. He dropped the chart onto the plastic laminate countertop. In front of him and filling the entire doorway was the formidable figure of Margaret Richmond. Sean recognized her immediately as the nursing director who'd burst into Dr. Mason's office. Apparently the woman made a habit of such dramatic entries.

"What are you doing in here?" she demanded. "And what are you doing with that chart?" Her broad, round face was distorted with outrage.

Sean toyed with the idea of giving her a flip answer, but he thought better of it.

"I'm looking in on a friend," Sean said. "Miss Cabot was a patient of mine in Boston."

"You have no right to her chart," Ms. Richmond blustered. "Patients' charts are confidential documents, available only to the patient and his doctors. We view our responsibility in this regard very seriously."

"I'm confident the patient would be willing to give me access," Sean said. "Perhaps we should step into the next room and ask her."

"You are not here as a clinical fellow," Ms. Richmond shouted, ignoring Sean's suggestion. "You are here in a research capacity only. Your arrogance in thinking that you have a right to invade this hospital is inexcusable."

Sean saw a familiar face appear over Ms. Richmond's intimidating shoulder. It was the puffy, smug countenance of the frustrated Marine, Robert Harris. Sean suddenly guessed what had happened. Undoubtedly he'd been picked up by one of the surveillance cameras, probably one in the second-floor corridor. Harris had called Richmond and then had come over to watch the slaughter.

Knowing that Robert Harris was involved, Sean could no longer resist the urge to lash back, particularly since Ms. Richmond wasn't responding to his attempts to be reasonable.

"Since you people aren't in the mood to discuss this like adults," Sean said, "I think I'll wander back to the research building."

"Your impertinence only makes matters worse," Ms. Richmond sputtered. "You're trespassing, invading privacy, and showing no remorse. I'm surprised the governors of Harvard University would let someone like you into their institution."

"I'll let you in on a secret," Sean said. "They weren't all that impressed with my manners. They liked my facility with a puck. Now, I'd really like to stay and chat with you people, but I've got to get back to my murine friends who, by the way, have more pleasant personalities than most of the staff here at Forbes."

Sean watched as Ms. Richmond's face empurpled. This was just one more of a series of ridiculous episodes that had him fed up. Consequently he derived perverse pleasure out of goading and angering this woman who could easily have played linebacker for the Miami Dolphins.

"Get out of here before I call the police," Ms. Richmond yelled.

Sean thought that calling the police would be interesting. He could just imagine some poor uniformed rookie trying to figure out how to categorize Sean's offense. Sean could see it in the paper: Harvard extern actually looks into his patient's chart!

Sean stepped forward, literally eye to eye with Ms. Richmond. He smiled, pouring on his old charm. "I know you'll miss me," he said, "but I really must go."

Both Ms. Richmond and Harris followed him all the way to the pedestrian bridge that spanned the gulf between the hospital and the research building. The whole time they maintained a loud dialogue about the degeneracy of current-day youth. Sean had the feeling he was being run out of town.

As Sean walked across the bridge he recognized how much he would have to depend on Janet for clinical material pertaining to the medulloblastoma study, provided, of course, he stayed.

Returning to his fifth-floor lab, Sean tried to lose himself in his work to repress the anger and frustration he felt toward the ridiculous situation he found himself in. Like the empty room upstairs, Helen's chart didn't have anything in it to get upset about. But as he cooled down, Sean was able to acknowledge that Ms. Richmond did have a point. As much as he hated to admit it, the Forbes was a private hospital. It wasn't a teaching hospital like the Boston Memorial, where teaching and patient care went hand in hand. Here, Helen's chart was confidential. Yet even if it was, Ms. Richmond's fury was hardly appropriate for his infraction.

In spite of himself, within an hour Sean became engrossed in his crystal-growing attempts. Then, as he held a flask up against the overhead light, he caught a bit of movement out of the corner of his eye. It was a rerun of the incident on his first day. Once again the movement had come from the direction of the stairwell.

Without so much as looking in the direction of the stairwell, Sean calmly got off his stool and walked into the storeroom as if he needed some supplies. Since the storeroom was connected to the central corridor, Sean was able to dash the length of the building to the stairwell opposite the one where he'd seen the movement.

Racing down a flight, he ran the length of the fourth floor to enter the opposite stairwell. Moving as silently as possible, he climbed the stairs until the fifth-floor landing came into view. As he'd suspected, Hiroshi was there furtively looking through the glass of the door, obviously baffled as to why Sean had not returned from the storeroom.

Sean tiptoed up the remaining stairs until he was standing directly behind Hiroshi. Then he screamed as loud as he was able. Within the confines of the stairwell, Sean was impressed with the amount of noise he was capable of generating.

Having seen a few Chuck Norris martial arts movies, Sean had been a little concerned that Hiroshi might turn into a karate demon by reflex. But instead Hiroshi practically collapsed. Conveniently he'd had one hand on the door handle. It was that support which kept him standing.

When Hiroshi recovered enough to comprehend what had happened, he stepped away from the door and started to mumble an explanation. But he was backing up at the same time, and when his foot hit the riser of the first stair, he turned and fled up, disappearing from view.

Disgusted, Sean followed, not to pursue Hiroshi, but rather to seek out Deborah Levy. Sean had had enough of Hiroshi's spying. He thought Dr. Levy would be the best person to discuss the matter with since she ran the lab.

Going directly to the seventh floor, Sean walked down to Dr. Levy's office. The door was ajar. He looked in. The office was empty.

The pool secretaries did not have any idea of her whereabouts but suggested Sean have her paged. Instead, Sean went down to the sixth floor and sought out Mark Halpern, who was dressed as nattily as ever in his spotless white apron. Sean guessed he washed and ironed the apron every day.

"I'm looking for Dr. Levy," Sean said irritably.

"She's not here today," Mark said. "Is there something I can help you with?"

"Will she be here later?" Sean asked.

"Not today," Mark said. "She had to go to Atlanta. She travels a lot for work."

"When will she be back?"

"I'm not sure," Mark said. "Probably tomorrow late. She said something about going to our Key West facility on her way back."

"Does she spend much time there?" Sean asked.

"Fair amount," Mark said. "Several Ph.D.s who'd originally been here at Forbes were supposed to go to Key West, but they left instead. Their absence left Dr. Levy with a burden. She's had to pick up the slack. I think Forbes is having trouble replacing them."

"Tell her I'd like to talk to her when she comes back," Sean said. He wasn't interested in the Forbes's recruiting problems.

"Are you sure there's nothing I can do?" Mark said.

For a second Sean toyed with the idea of talking with Mark about Hiroshi's behavior, but decided against it. He had to speak to someone in authority. There wasn't anything Mark would be able to do.

Frustrated that he could get no satisfaction for his anger, Sean started back toward his lab. He was almost to the stairwell door when he thought of another question for Mark.

Returning to his tiny office, Sean asked the tech if the pathologists over in the hospital cooperated with the research staff.

"On occasion," Mark said. "Dr. Barton Friedburg has coauthored a number of research papers that require a pathologic interpretation."

"What kind of guy is he?" Sean asked. "Friendly or unfriendly? Seems to me that people fall into one camp or the other around here."

"Definitely friendly," Mark said. "Besides, I think you might be confusing unfriendly with being serious and preoccupied."

"You think I could call him up and ask him a few questions?" Sean asked. "Is he that friendly?"

"Absolutely," Mark said.

Sean went down to his lab, and using the phone in the glass-enclosed office so he could sit at a desk, he phoned Dr. Friedburg. He took it as an auspicious sign when the pathologist came on the line directly.

Sean explained who he was and that he was interested in the findings of a biopsy done the day before on Helen Cabot.

"Hold the line," Dr. Friedburg said. Sean could hear him talking with someone else in the lab. "We didn't get any biopsy from a Helen Cabot," he said, coming back.

"But I know she had it done yesterday," Sean said.

"It went south to Basic Diagnostics," Dr. Friedburg said. "You'll have to call there if you want any information on it. That sort of thing doesn't come through this lab at all."

"Who should I ask for?" Sean asked.

"Dr. Levy," Dr. Friedburg said. "Ever since Paul and Roger left, she's been running the show down there. I don't know who she has reading the specimens now, but it's not us."

Sean hung up the phone. Nothing about Forbes seemed to be easy. He certainly wasn't about to ask Dr. Levy about Helen Cabot. She'd know what he was up to in a flash, especially after she heard from Ms. Richmond about his looking at Helen's chart.

Sean sighed as he looked down at the work he was doing trying to grow crystals with the Forbes protein. He felt like throwing it all into the sink.

For Janet, the afternoon seemed to pass quickly. With patients coming and going for therapy and diagnostic tests, there was the constant tactical problem of organizing it all. In addition, there were complicated treatment protocols that required precise timing and dosage. But during this feverish activity Janet was able to observe the way patients were divided among the staff. Without much finagling she was able to arrange to be the nurse assigned to take care of Helen Cabot, Louis Martin, and Kathleen Sharenburg the following day.

Although she didn't handle them herself, she did get to see the containers the coded drugs came in when the nurses in charge of the medulloblastoma patients for the day got the vials from Marjorie. Once they'd received them, the nurses took them into the pharmacy closet to load the respective syringes. The MB300 drug was in a 10cc injectable bottle while the MB303 was in a smaller 5cc bottle. There was nothing special about these containers. They were the same containers many other injectable drugs were packaged in.

It was customary for everyone to have a mid-afternoon as well as a mid-morning break. Janet used hers to go back down to medical records. Once there she used the same ploy she'd used with Tim. She told one of the librarians, a young woman by the name of Melanie Brock, that she was new on the staff and that she was interested in learning the Forbes system. She said she was familiar with computers, but she could use some help. The librarian was impressed with Janet's interest and was more than happy to show her their filing format, using the medical records' access code.

Left on her own after Melanie's introduction, Janet called up all patients with the T-9872 designator which she'd used to pull up current medulloblastoma cases on the ward's workstation. This time, Janet got a different list. Here there were thirty-eight cases on record over the last ten years. This list did not include the five cases currently in the hospital.

Sensing a recent increase, Janet asked the computer to graph the number of cases against the years. In a graph form, the results were rather striking.

Looking at the graph, Janet noted that over the first eight years there had been five medulloblastoma cases, whereas during the last two years there had been

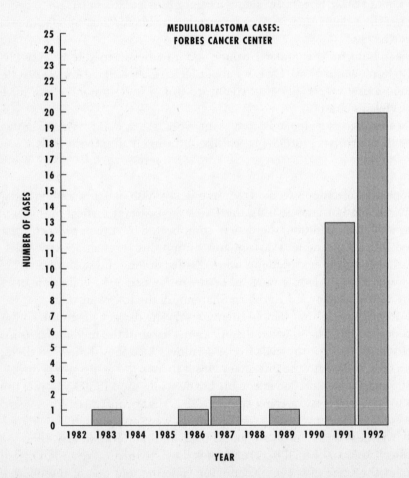

MEDULLOBLASTOMA CASES:
FORBES CANCER CENTER

thirty-three. She found the increase curious until she remembered that it had been in the last two years that the Forbes had had such success with its treatment. Success sparked referrals. Surely that accounted for the influx.

Curious about the demographics, Janet called up a breakdown by age and sex. Sex showed a preponderance of males in the last thirty-three cases: twenty-six males and seven females. In the earlier five cases there had been three females and two males.

When she looked at ages, Janet noted that in the first five cases there was one twenty-year-old. The other four were below the age of ten. Among the recent thirty-three cases Janet saw that seven cases were below the age of ten, two between the ages of ten and twenty, and the remaining twenty-four were over twenty years of age.

Concerning outcome, Janet noted that all of the original five had died within two years of diagnosis. Three had died within months. In the most recent thirty-three, the impact of the new therapy was dramatically apparent. All thirty-three patients were currently alive, although only three of them were nearing two years after diagnosis.

Hastily, Janet wrote all this information down to give to Sean.

Next Janet randomly picked out a name from the list. The name was Donald Maxwell. She called up his file. As she went through the information, she saw that it was rather abbreviated. She even found a notation that said: *Consult physical chart if further information is needed.*

Janet had become so absorbed in her investigative work, she was shocked when she glanced at her watch. She'd used up her coffee break and then some, just as she had that morning.

Quickly she had the computer print out a list of the thirty-eight cases with their ages, sexes, and hospital numbers. Nervously, she went over to the laser printer as the sheet emerged. Turning from the printer, she half expected to find someone standing behind her, demanding an explanation. But no one seemed to have taken notice of her activities.

Before heading back to her floor, Janet sought out Melanie for one quick and final question. She found her at the copy machine.

"How do I go about getting the hospital chart of a discharged patient?" Janet asked.

"You ask one of us," Melanie said. "All you have to do is provide us with a copy of your authorization, which in your case would come from the nursing department. Then it takes about ten minutes. We keep the charts in the basement in a storage vault that runs beneath both buildings. It's an efficient system. We need access to them for patient care purposes, like when the patients come for outpatient care. Over in administration they need access to them for billing and actuarial purposes. The charts come up on dumbwaiters." Melanie pointed to the small glass-fronted elevator set into the wall.

Janet thanked Melanie, then hurried out to the elevator. She was disappointed about the authorization issue. She couldn't imagine how she would arrange that without completely giving herself away. She hoped Sean would have an idea.

As she pressed the elevator button impatiently, Janet wondered if she would have to apologize for again extending her break. She knew she couldn't keep doing it. It wasn't fair, and Marjorie was bound to complain.

Sterling was extremely pleased with the way the day was proceeding. He had to smile to himself as he rose up in the paneled elevator of the Franklin Bank's home office on Federal Street in Boston. It had been a sublime day with minimal effort and maximum gain. And the fact that he was being handsomely compensated for enjoying himself made it all that much more rewarding.

The luncheon at the Ritz had been heavenly, especially since the maître d' had been accommodating enough to bring a white Meursault down from the main dining room wine cellar. Sitting as close as he had to Tanaka and his guest, Sterling had been able to hear most of their conversation from behind his *Wall Street Journal.*

Tanaka's guest was a personnel executive from Immunotherapy. Since the buyout, Genentech had left the company largely intact. Sterling did not know how much money was in the plain white envelope that Tanaka had placed on the table, but he did notice that the personnel executive had slipped it into his jacket in the blink of an eye.

The information Sterling overheard was interesting. Sean and the other founding partners had sold Immunotherapy in order to raise capital for a totally new venture. Tanaka's informer wasn't one hundred percent certain, but it was his understanding that the new company would also be a biotechnology firm. He couldn't tell Tanaka its name or its proposed product line.

The gentleman knew there had been a holdup in forming the new company when Sean and his partners realized they would be undercapitalized. The reason he knew this was that he'd been approached to move to the new company and he'd agreed, only to be informed that there would be a delay until sufficient funds could be raised. From the sound of the gentleman's voice at this juncture, Sterling understood that the delay had engendered significant ill will between him and the new management.

The final bit of information that the gentleman had delivered was the name of the bank executive at the Franklin who was in charge of the negotiation of the loan for additional start-up capital. Sterling was acquainted with a number of people at the Franklin, but Herbert Devonshire was not one of them. But that was soon to change since it was Herbert whom Sterling was presently on his way to see.

The luncheon had also afforded Sterling an opportunity to observe Tanaka up close. Knowing a considerable amount about the Japanese character and culture, particularly in relation to business, Sterling was fascinated by Tanaka's performance. Flawlessly deferential and respectful, it would have been impossible for an uninitiated American to pick up the clues that suggested Tanaka clearly despised his lunch companion. But Sterling immediately discerned the subtle signs.

There'd been no way for Sterling to eavesdrop on Tanaka's meeting with Herbert Devonshire. Sterling had not even considered it. But he wanted to know its location so that he would be able to suggest he did know the content when he spoke to Mr. Devonshire. Accordingly, Sterling had the limousine company's president order Tanaka's driver to call it in to him. The president had then relayed the information to Sterling's driver.

After being tipped off, Sterling had entered City Side, a popular bar in the south building of Faneuil Hall Market. There'd been a chance Tanaka might recognize him from lunch, but Sterling had decided to risk it. He wouldn't be getting too close. He'd observed Tanaka and Devonshire from afar, noting their location in the bar and what they ordered. He also noted the time Tanaka had excused himself to make a call.

Armed with this information, Sterling had felt confident confronting Devonshire. He'd been able to get an appointment for that afternoon.

After a brief wait that he judged was designed to impress him with Mr. Devonshire's busy schedule, Sterling was shown into the banker's imposing office. The view was to the north and east, commanding a spectacular vista over the Boston Harbor as well as Logan International Airport in East Boston and the Mystic River Bridge arching over to Chelsea.

Mr. Devonshire was a small man with a shiny bald pate, wire-rimmed glasses, and conservative dress. He stood up behind his antique partner's desk to shake hands with Sterling. He couldn't have been over five feet five by Sterling's estimation.

Sterling handed the man one of his business cards. They both sat down. Mr. Devonshire positioned the card in the center of his blotter and aligned it perfectly parallel with the blotter's borders. Then he folded his hands.

"It's a pleasure to meet you, Mr. Rombauer," Herbert said, leveling his beady eyes at Sterling. "What can the Franklin do for you today?"

"It's not the Franklin I'm interested in," Sterling said. "It's you, Mr. Devonshire. I'd like to establish a business relationship with you."

"Our motto has always been personal service," Herbert said.

"I shall come directly to the point," Sterling said. "I'm willing to form a confidential partnership with you for our mutual benefit. There is information I need and information your superiors should not know."

Herbert Devonshire swallowed. Otherwise, he didn't move.

Sterling leaned forward to bring his eyes to bear on Herbert. "The facts are simple. You met with a Mr. Tanaka Yamaguchi this afternoon at the City Side Bar, not the usual business location, I'd venture to say. You ordered a vodka gimlet and then gave Mr. Yamaguchi some information, a service that, while not illegal, is of questionable ethics. A short time later a sizable portion of the monies

Sushita Industries keeps on deposit at the Bank of Boston was wire-transferred to the Franklin with you designated as the private banker involved."

Herbert's face blanched at Sterling's words.

"I have an extensive network of contacts throughout the business world," Sterling said. He settled back in his chair. "I'd very much like to add you to this intimate, very anonymous, but stellar network. I'm certain we can provide each other with useful information as time goes by. So the question is, would you care to join? The only obligation is that you never, ever, disclose the source of any information I pass on to you."

"And if I choose not to join?" Herbert asked, his voice raspy.

"I will pass on the information about you and Mr. Yamaguchi to people here at the Franklin who have some minor say in your future."

"This is blackmail," Herbert said.

"I call it free trade," Sterling said. "And as for your initiation fee, I would like to hear exactly what you told Mr. Yamaguchi about a mutual acquaintance, Sean Murphy."

"This is outrageous," Herbert said.

"Please," Sterling warned. "Let's not allow this conversation to dissolve into mere posturing. The fact is, your behavior was outrageous, Mr. Devonshire. What I am asking is a small price to pay for the benefits you will accrue from landing such a customer as Sushita Industries. And I can guarantee I will be useful to you in the future."

"I gave very little information," Herbert said. "Entirely inconsequential."

"If it makes you more comfortable to believe that, that's fine," Sterling said.

There was a pause. The two men stared at each other across the expanse of antique mahogany. Sterling was happy to wait.

"All I said was that Mr. Murphy and a few associates were borrowing money to start a new company," Herbert said. "I gave no figures whatsoever."

"The name of the new company?" Sterling asked.

"Oncogen," Herbert said.

"And the proposed product line?" Sterling asked.

"Cancer-related health products," Herbert said. "Both diagnostic and therapeutic."

"Time frame?"

"Imminent," Herbert said. "Within the next few months."

"Anything else?" Sterling asked. "I should add that I have ways of checking this information."

"No," Herbert said. His voice had developed an edge.

"If I learn you've deliberately prevaricated," Sterling warned, "the result will be as if you refused to cooperate."

"I have more appointments," Herbert said tersely.

Sterling stood up. "I know it is irritating to have your hand forced," he said. "But remember, I feel indebted and I always repay. Call me."

Sterling took the elevator down to the ground floor and hurried over to his sedan. The driver had locked the doors and had fallen asleep. Sterling had to thump on the window to get him to release the rear locks. Once inside, Sterling called his contact at the FAA. "I'm on a portable phone," he warned his friend.

"The bird's scheduled to leave in the morning," the man said.

"What destination?"

"Miami," the man said. Then he added: "I sure wish I was going."

"Well, what do you think?" Janet asked as Sean poked his head into the bedroom. Janet had brought Sean out to Miami Beach to see the apartment she'd rented.

"I think it's perfect," he said, looking back into the living room. "I'm not sure I could take these colors for long, but it does look like Florida." The walls were bright yellow, the rug was Kelly green. The furniture was white wicker with tropical floral print cushions.

"It's only for a couple of months," Janet said. "Come in the bathroom and look at the ocean."

"There it is!" Sean said as he peered through the slats of the jalousie window. "At least I can say I've seen it." A narrow wedge of ocean was visible between two buildings. Since it was after seven and the sun had already set, the water looked more gray than blue in the gathering darkness.

"The kitchen's not bad either," Janet said.

Sean followed her, then watched as she opened cabinets and showed him the dishes and glassware. She'd changed out of her nurse's uniform and had on her tank top and shorts. Sean found Janet incredibly sexy, particularly when she was so scantily clad. Sean felt himself at a distinct disadvantage with the way she was dressed, especially as she bent over showing him the pots and pans. It was difficult to think.

"I'll be able to cook," she said, straightening up.

"Wonderful," Sean said, but his mind was concerned with other basic appetites.

They moved back into the living room.

"Hey, I'm ready to move in tonight," Sean said. "I love it."

"Hold on," Janet said. "I hope I haven't given you the impression we're moving in together just like that. We've got some serious talking to do. That's the whole reason I came down here."

"Well, first we have to get going on this medulloblastoma thing," Sean said.

"I didn't think the two issues would be mutually exclusive," Janet said.

"I didn't mean to imply that they were," Sean said. "It's just that it's hard for me at the moment to think about much beyond my role here at Forbes and whether I should stay. The situation is kind of dominating my mind. I think it's pretty understandable."

Janet rolled her eyes.

"Besides, I'm starved," Sean said. He smiled. "You know I can never talk when I'm hungry."

"I'll be patient to a point," Janet conceded. "But I don't want you to forget I need some serious communicating. Now, as far as dinner is concerned, the real estate person told me there's a popular Cuban restaurant just up Collins Avenue."

"Cuban?" Sean questioned.

"I know you rarely venture from your meat and potatoes," Janet said. "But while we're in Miami we can be a bit more adventuresome."

"Groan," Sean murmured.

The restaurant was close enough to walk, so they left Sean's 4×4 where they'd found a parking spot across from the apartment. Walking hand in hand, they wandered north up Collins Avenue beneath huge silver- and gold-tipped clouds that reflected the reddened sky over the distant Everglades. They couldn't see the ocean, but they could hear the waves hit against the beach on the other side of a block of recently renovated and refurbished Miami art deco buildings.

The entire beach neighborhood was alive with people strolling up and down the streets, sitting on steps or porches, Rollerblading, or cruising in their cars. Some of the car stereos had the bass pumped up to a point that Sean and Janet could feel the vibration in their chests as the cars thumped past.

"Those guys aren't going to have functional middle ears by the time they're thirty," Sean commented.

The restaurant gave the impression of frenzied disorganization with tables and people crammed everywhere. The waiters and waitresses were dressed in black pants or skirts and white shirts or blouses. Each had on a soiled apron. They ranged in age from twenty to sixty. Shouting back and forth, they communicated among themselves and to the steam table in expressive bursts of Spanish while they ran and weaved among the tables. Over the entire tumult hung a succulent aroma of roast pork, garlic, and dark roasted coffee.

Carried along by a current of people, Sean and Janet found themselves squeezed among other diners at a large table. Frosted bottles of Corona with lime wedges stuck in their mouths appeared as if by magic.

"There's nothing on here for me to eat," Sean complained after studying the menu for a few minutes. Janet was right; he rarely varied his diet.

"Nonsense," Janet said. She did the ordering.

Sean was pleasantly surprised when their food came. The marinated and heavily garlic-flavored roast pork was delicious, as was the yellow rice and the black beans covered with chopped onions. The only thing he didn't care for was the yucca.

"This stuff tastes like potato covered with mucoid exudate," Sean yelled.

"Gross!" Janet exclaimed. "Stop sounding so much like a medical student."

Conversation was almost impossible in the raucous restaurant, so after dinner they wandered over to Ocean Drive and ventured into Lummus Park where they could talk. They sat under a broad banyan tree and gazed out at the dark ocean dotted with the lights of merchant ships and pleasure boats.

"Hard to believe it's still winter in Boston," Sean said.

"It makes me wonder why we put up with slush and freezing rain," Janet said. "But enough small talk. If, as you said, you can't talk about us for the moment, then let's talk about the Forbes situation. Was your afternoon any better than your morning?"

Sean gave a short, mirthless laugh. "It was worse," he said. "I wasn't on the second floor for five minutes before the director of nursing burst into the room like a raging bull, yelling and screaming because I was looking at Helen's chart."

"Margaret Richmond was mad?" Janet asked.

Sean nodded. "All two hundred and fifty snarling pounds of her. She was out of control."

"She's always been civil with me," Janet said.

"I've only seen her twice," Sean said. "Neither time would I describe her as civil."

"How did she know you were there?" Janet asked.

"The Marine commando was with her," Sean said. "They must have picked me up on a surveillance camera."

"Oh, great!" Janet said. "Something else I have to worry about. I never thought of surveillance cameras."

"You don't have to worry," Sean said. "I'm the one who the head of security can't abide. Besides, the cameras are most likely only in the common areas, not patient floors."

"Did you get to talk with Helen Cabot?" Janet asked.

"For a moment," Sean said. "She doesn't look good at all."

"Her condition's been deteriorating," Janet said. "There's talk of doing a shunt. Did you learn anything from her chart?"

"No," Sean said. "I didn't have time. They literally chased me back over the bridge to the research building. Then, as if to cap off the afternoon, that Japanese guy appeared again, sneaking around, watching me in the lab from the stairwell. I don't know what his story is, but this time I got him. I scared the living willies out of him by sneaking up behind him and letting out this bloodcurdling yell. He nearly dropped his pants."

"The poor fellow," Janet said.

"Poor fellow nothing!" Sean said. "This guy's been watching me since I arrived."

"Well, I've had some luck," Janet said.

Sean brightened. "Really! Great! Did you get some of the miracle medicine?"

"No, no medicine," Janet said. She reached into her pocket and pulled out the computer printout and the sheet with her hastily scribbled notes. "But here's the list of all the medulloblastoma patients for the last ten years: thirty-eight in all; thirty-three in the past two years. I've summarized the data on the sheet."

Sean eagerly took the papers. But to read them he had to hold it over his head to catch the light coming from the streetlights along Ocean Drive. As he

looked it over, Janet explained what she'd learned about the sex and age distribution. She also told him that the computer files were abridged and that there
had been a notation to consult the charts themselves for more information. Finally, she told him what Melanie had said about obtaining those charts in as little as ten minutes providing, of course, you had the proper authorization.

"I'll need the charts," Sean said. "Are they right there in medical records?"

"No." Janet explained what Melanie had said about the chart storage vaults
extending beneath both buildings.

"No kidding," Sean said. "That might be rather handy."

"What do you mean?" Janet asked.

"It means that I might be able to get to them from the research building,"
Sean said. "After the episode today, it's pretty clear I'm persona non grata in the
hospital. This way I can attempt to get at those charts without running afoul of
Ms. Richmond and company."

"You're thinking of breaking into the storage vault?" Janet asked with alarm.

"I kinda doubt they'd leave the door open for me," Sean said.

"But that's going too far," Janet said. "If you did that, you'd be breaking the
law, not just a hospital rule."

"I warned you about this," Sean said.

"You said we'd have to break rules, not the law," Janet reminded him.

"Let's not get into semantics," Sean said with exasperation.

"But there's a big difference," Janet said.

"Laws are codified rules," Sean said. "I knew we'd get around to breaking the
law in some form or fashion, and I thought you did too. But, be that as it may,
don't you think we're justified? These Forbes people have obviously developed
a very effective treatment for medulloblastoma. Unfortunately, they have chosen to be secretive about it, obviously so they can patent their treatment before
anyone else catches on. You know, this is what bugs me about the private funding of medical research. The goal becomes a return on investment instead of the
public interest. The public weal is in second place if it is considered at all. This
treatment for medulloblastoma undoubtedly has implications for all cancers,
but the public is being denied that information. Never mind that most of the
basic science these private labs base their work on was obtained through public
funds at academic institutions. These private places just take. They don't give.
The public gets cheated in the process."

"Ends never justify means," Janet said.

"Go ahead and be self-righteous," Sean said. "Meanwhile, you're forgetting
this whole thing was your idea. Well, maybe we should give up, and maybe I
should go back to Boston and get something done on my dissertation."

"All right!" Janet said with frustration. "All right, we'll do what we have
to do."

"We need the charts and we need the miracle medicine," Sean said. He stood
up and stretched. "So let's go."

"Now?" Janet questioned with alarm. "It's nearly nine at night."

"First rule of breaking and entering," Sean said. "You do it when no one is at home. This is a perfect time. Besides, I have a legitimate cover: I should inject more of my mice with the primary dose of the glycoprotein."

"Heaven help me," Janet said as she allowed Sean to pull her up from the bench.

Tom Widdicomb guided his car into the slot at the extreme end of the parking area for the Forbes residence. He inched forward until the wheels touched the curb restraint. He had pulled up under the protective branches of a large gumbo-limbo tree. Alice had told him to park there just in case someone noticed the car. It was Alice's car, a lime green 1969 Cadillac convertible.

Tom opened the car door and stepped out after making certain no one was in sight. He pulled on a pair of latex surgical gloves. Then he reached under the front seat and grasped the chef's knife he'd brought from home. Light glinted off its polished surface. At first he'd planned on bringing the gun. But then thinking about noise and the thinness of the residence walls, he'd settled on the knife instead. Its only drawback was that it could be messy.

Being careful of the knife's cutting edge, Tom slipped the blade up inside the right sleeve of his shirt, cupping the handle in the palm of his hand. In his other hand he carried the keys to 207.

He made his way along the rear of the building, counting the sliders until he was below 207. There were no lights on in the apartment. Either that nurse was already in bed or she was out. Tom didn't care. Either way had its benefits and disadvantages.

Walking around to the front of the building, Tom had to pause while one of the tenants came out and headed for his car. After the man had driven away, Tom used one of the keys to enter the building. Once inside, he moved quickly. He preferred not to be seen. Arriving outside of 207, he inserted the key, opened the door, stepped inside, and closed the door behind him in one swift, fluid motion.

For several minutes he stood by the door without moving, listening for the slightest sound. He could hear several distant TVs, but they were from other apartments. Pocketing the keys, he allowed the long-bladed chef's knife to slide out from his sleeve. He clutched its handle as if it were a dagger.

Slowly he inched forward. By the light coming from the parking area he could see the outline of the furniture and the doorway into the bedroom. The bedroom door was open.

Looking into the gloom of the bedroom, which was darker than the living room due to the closed drapes, Tom could not tell if the bed was occupied or empty. Again he listened. Aside from the muffled sound of the distant TVs plus the hum of the refrigerator which had just kicked on, he heard nothing. There was no steady breathing of someone asleep.

Advancing into the room a half step at a time, Tom bumped gently against the edge of the bed. Reaching out with his free hand, he groped for a body. Only then did he know for sure: the bed was empty.

Not realizing he'd been holding his breath, Tom straightened up and breathed out. He felt relief of tension on the one hand, yet profound disappointment on the other. The anticipation of violence had aroused him and satisfaction would be delayed.

Moving more by feel than by sight, he managed to find his way to the bathroom. Reaching in, he ran his free hand up and down the wall until he found the light switch. Turning it on, he had to squint in the brightness, but he liked what he saw. Hanging over the tub were a pair of lacy pastel panties and a bra.

Tom placed the chef's knife down on the edge of the sink and picked up the panties. They were nothing like the ones Alice wore. He had no idea why such objects fascinated him, but they did. Sitting on the edge of the tub, he fingered the silky material. For the moment he was content, knowing that he'd be entertained while he waited, keeping the light switch and the knife close at hand.

"What if we get caught?" Janet asked nervously as they headed toward the Forbes Center. They'd just come from the Home Depot hardware store where Sean had bought tools that he said should work almost as well as a locksmith's tension bar and double ball pick.

"We're not going to get caught," Sean said. "That's why we're going there now when no one will be there. Well, we don't know that for sure, but we'll check."

"There will be plenty of people on the hospital side," Janet warned.

"And that's the reason why we stay away from the hospital," Sean said.

"What about security?" Janet asked. "Have you thought about that?"

"Piece of cake," Sean said. "Except for the frustrated Marine, I haven't been impressed. They're certainly lax at the front door."

"I'm not good at this," Janet admitted.

"Tell me something I didn't know!" Sean said.

"And how are you so acquainted with locks and picks and alarms?" Janet asked.

"When I grew up in Charlestown, it was a pure-blooded working-class neighborhood," Sean said. "The gentrification hadn't started. Each of our fathers was in a different trade. My father was a plumber. Timothy O'Brien's father was a locksmith. Old man O'Brien taught his son some of the tricks of the trade, and Timmy showed us. At first it was a game; kind of a competition. We liked to believe there weren't any locks in the neighborhood we couldn't open. And Charlie Sullivan's father was a master electrician. He put in fancy alarm systems in Boston, mostly on Beacon Hill. He often made Charlie come along. So Charlie started telling us about alarms."

"That's dangerous information for kids to have," Janet said. Her own childhood couldn't have been further from Sean's among the private schools, music lessons, and summers on the Cape.

"You bet," Sean agreed. "But we never stole anything from our own neighborhood. We'd just open up locks and then leave them open as a practical joke. But then it changed. We started going out to the 'burbs like Swampscott or Marblehead with one of the older kids who could drive. We'd watch a house for a while, then break in and help ourselves to the liquor and some of the electronics. You know, stereos, TVs."

"You stole?" Janet questioned with shock.

Sean glanced at her for a second before looking back at the road. "Of course we stole," he said. "It was thrilling at the time and we used to think all the people who lived on the North Shore were millionaires." Sean went on to tell how he and his buddies would sell the goods in Boston, pay off the driver, buy beer, and give the rest to a fellow raising money for the Irish Republican Army. "We even deluded ourselves into thinking we were youthful political activists even though we didn't have the faintest idea of what was going on in Northern Ireland."

"My God! I had no idea," Janet said. She'd known about Sean's adolescent fights and even about the joyrides, but this burglary was something else entirely.

"Let's not get carried away with value judgments," Sean said. "My youth and yours were completely different."

"I'm just a little concerned you learned to justify any type of behavior," Janet said. "I would imagine it could become a habit."

"The last time I did any of that stuff was when I was fifteen," Sean said. "There's been a lot of water over the dam since then."

They pulled into the Forbes parking lot and drove to the research building. Sean cut the engine and turned out the lights. For a moment neither moved.

"You want to go ahead with this or not?" Sean asked, finally breaking the silence. "I don't mean to pressure you, but I can't waste two months down here screwing around with busywork. Either I get to look into the medulloblastoma protocol or I go back to Boston. Unfortunately, I can't do it by myself; that was made apparent by the run-in with hefty Margaret Richmond. Either you help, or we cancel. But let me say this: we're going in here to get information, not to steal TV sets. And it's for a damn good cause."

Janet stared ahead for a moment. She didn't have the luxury of indecision, yet her mind was a jumble of confusing thoughts. She looked at Sean. She thought she loved him.

"Okay!" Janet said finally. "Let's do it."

They got out of the car and walked to the entrance. Sean carried the tools he'd gotten at the Home Depot in a paper bag.

"Evening," Sean said to the security guard, who blinked repeatedly as he stared at Sean's ID card. He was a swarthy Hispanic with a pencil-line mustache. He seemed to appreciate Janet's shorts.

"Got to inject my rats," Sean said.

The security guard motioned for them to enter. He didn't speak, nor did he take his eyes off Janet's lower half. As Sean and Janet passed through the turnstile they could see he had a miniature portable TV wedged on top of the bank of security monitors. It was tuned to a soccer match.

"See what I mean about the guards?" Sean said as they used the stairs to descend to the basement. "He was more interested in your legs than my ID card. I could have had Charlie Manson's photo on it and he wouldn't have noticed."

"How come you said rats instead of mice?" Janet asked.

"People hate rats," Sean said. "I didn't want him deciding to come down and watch."

"You do think of everything," Janet said.

The basement was a warren of corridors and locked doors, but at least it was adequately lighted. Sean had made many trips to the animal room and was generally familiar with that area, but he hadn't gone beyond it. As they walked, the sound of their heels echoed off the bare concrete.

"Do you have any idea where we're going?" Janet asked.

"Vaguely," Sean said.

They walked down the central corridor taking several twists and turns before coming to a T intersection.

"This must be the way to the hospital," Sean said.

"How can you tell?"

Sean pointed to the tangle of pipes lining the ceiling. "The power plant is in the hospital," he said. "These lines are coming over to feed the research building. Now we have to figure out which side has the chart vault."

They proceeded down the corridor toward the hospital. Fifty feet down there was a door on either side of the narrow hall. Sean tried each. Both were locked.

"Let's give these a try," he said. He set down his bag and removed some tools, including a slender jeweler-like allen wrench and several short pieces of heavy wire. Holding the allen wrench in one hand and one of the pieces of heavy wire in the other, he inserted both into the lock.

"This is the tricky part," he said. "It's called raking the pins."

Sean closed his eyes and proceeded by feel.

"What do you think?" Janet asked as she looked up and down the corridor, expecting someone to appear at any moment.

"Piece of cake," Sean said. There was a click and the door opened. Finding a light, Sean turned it on. They had broken into an electrical room with huge wall-sized electrical buses facing each other.

Sean turned out the light and closed the door. Next he went to work on the door across the corridor. He had it open in less time than the first.

"These tools make a decent tension bar and pick," he said. "Nothing like the real thing, but not bad."

Switching on a light, he and Janet found themselves in a long, narrow room filled with metal shelving. Arranged on the shelves were hospital charts. There was a lot of empty space.

"This is it," Sean said.

"A lot of room to expand," Janet commented.

"Don't move for a couple of minutes," Sean said. "Let me make sure there are no alarms."

"Good grief!" Janet said. "Why don't you tell me these things in advance."

Sean took a quick turn around the room looking for infrared sensors or motion detectors. He found nothing. Rejoining Janet and taking out the computer printout sheet he said: "Let's divide these charts up between us. I only want the ones from the last two years. They'll reflect the successful treatment."

Janet took the top half of the list and Sean took the lower. In ten minutes they had a stack of thirty-three charts.

"It's easy to tell this isn't a teaching hospital," Sean said. "In a teaching hospital you'd be lucky to find one chart, much less all thirty-three."

"What do you want to do with them?" Janet asked.

"Copy them," Sean said. "There's a copy machine in the library. The question is, is the library open? I don't want the guard seeing me pick that lock. There's probably a camera there."

"Let's check," Janet said. She wanted to get this over with.

"Wait," Sean said. "I think I have a better idea." He started toward the research building end of the chart vault. Janet struggled to keep up. Rounding the last bank of metal shelves, they came to the end wall. In the center of the wall was a glass door. To the right of the door was a panel with two buttons. When Sean pushed the lower of the two, a deep whirring noise broke the silence.

"Maybe we're in luck," he said.

Within several minutes the dumbwaiter appeared. Sean opened the door and began removing the shelves.

"What are you doing?" she asked.

"A little experiment," Sean said. When he had enough of the racks removed, he climbed inside. He had to double up with his knees near his chin.

"Close the door and push the button," he said.

"Are you sure?" Janet asked.

"Come on!" Sean said. "But after the motor stops, wait for a couple of beats, then be sure to push the 'down' button to get me back."

Janet did as she was told. Sean ascended with a wave and disappeared from view.

With Sean gone, Janet's anxiety grew. The gravity of their actions hadn't sunk in when Sean had been with her. But in the eerie silence the reality of where she was and what she was doing hit her: she was burglarizing the Forbes Cancer Center.

When the whirring stopped, Janet counted to ten, then pressed the down button. Thankfully, Sean quickly reappeared. She opened the door.

"Works like a charm," Sean said. "It goes right up to finance in administration. Best of all, they've got one of the world's best copy machines."

It took them only a few minutes to carry the charts over to the electric dumbwaiter.

"You first," Sean said.

"I don't know whether I want to do this," Janet said.

"Fine," Sean said. "Then you wait here while I copy the charts. It'll probably take about a half hour." He started to climb back in the dumbwaiter.

Janet grabbed his arm. "I changed my mind. I don't want to wait here by myself, either."

Sean rolled his eyes and got out of the dumbwaiter. Janet climbed into the hoist. Sean handed her most of the charts, closed the door, and pushed the button. When the motor stopped, he pressed again and the dumbwaiter reappeared. With the remaining charts in hand, he piled into the dumbwaiter a second time and waited a few uncomfortable minutes until Janet pushed the button upstairs in administration.

When Janet opened the door for him, he could tell she was becoming frantic.

"What's the matter now?" he asked as he struggled out of the dumbwaiter.

"All the lights are on up here," she said nervously. "Did you turn them on?"

"Nope," Sean said, gathering up an armload of the charts. "They were on when I came up. Probably the cleaning service."

"I never thought of that," Janet said. "How can you be so calm through all this?" She sounded almost angry.

Sean shrugged. "Must have been all that practice I had as a kid."

They quickly fell into a system at the copy machine. By taking each chart apart, they could load it into the automatic feed. Using a stapler they found on a nearby desk, they kept the copies organized and reassembled the originals as soon as they'd been copied.

"Did you notice that computer in the glass enclosure?" Janet asked.

"I saw it on my tour on day one," Sean said.

"It's running some kind of program," Janet said. "When I was waiting for you to come up, I glanced in. It's connected to several modems and automatic dialers. It must be doing some kind of survey."

Sean looked at Janet with surprise. "I didn't know you knew so much about computers. That's rather odd for an English lit major."

"At Wellesley I majored in English literature but computers fascinated me," she explained. "I took a lot of computer courses. At one point I almost changed majors."

After loading more sets of charts into the copy machine, Sean and Janet walked over to the glass enclosure and looked in. The monitor screen was flashing digits. Sean tried the door. It was open. They went inside.

"Wonder why this is in a glass room?" he asked.

"To protect it," Janet said. "Big machines like this can be affected by cigarette smoke. There's probably a handful of smokers in the office."

They looked at the figures flashing on the screen. They were nine-digit numbers.

"What do you think it's doing?" Sean asked.

"No idea," Janet said. "They're not phone numbers. If they were, there'd be seven or ten digits, not nine. Besides, there's no way it can be calling phone numbers that rapidly."

The screen suddenly went blank, then a ten-digit number appeared. Instantly an automatic dialer went into motion, its tones audible above the hum of the air-conditioning fans.

"Now that's a phone number," Janet said. "I even recognize the area code. It's Connecticut."

The screen went blank again, then resumed flashing more nine-digit numbers. After a minute the list of numbers froze at a specific number and the computer printout device activated. Both Sean and Janet glanced over to the printer in time to see the nine-digit number print out followed by: *Peter Ziegler, age 55, Valley Hospital, Charlotte, North Carolina, Achilles tendon repair, March 11.*

Suddenly, an alarm sounded. As the computer reverted to flashing its nine-digit numbers, Sean and Janet looked at each other, Sean with confusion, Janet with panic.

"What's happening?" she demanded. The alarm kept ringing.

"I don't know," Sean admitted. "But it isn't a burglar alarm." He turned to look out into the office just in time to see the door to the hallway opening.

"Down!" he said to Janet, forcing her to her hands and knees. Sean figured that whoever was coming into the room was coming to check the computer. He frantically motioned to Janet to crawl behind the console. In utter terror, Janet did as she was told, fumbling over coiled computer cables. Sean was right behind her. Hardly had they gotten out of sight when the door to the glass enclosure was opened.

From where they were huddled, they could see a pair of legs enter the room. Whoever it was, it was a woman. The alarm that initiated the episode was turned off. The woman picked up a phone and dialed.

"We have another potential donor," she said. "North Carolina."

At that moment, the laser printer began printing yet again, and again the alarm sounded for a brief moment.

"Did you hear that?" the woman asked. "What a coincidence. We're getting another, as we speak." She paused, waiting for the printer. "Patricia Southerland, age forty-seven, San Jose General, San Jose, California, breast biopsy, March 14. Also sounds good. What do you think?"

There was a pause before she spoke again: "I know the team's out. But there's time. Trust me. This is my department."

The woman hung up. Sean and Janet heard her tear off the sheet that had just printed. Then the woman turned and left.

For a few minutes neither Sean nor Janet spoke.

"What the hell did she mean, a potential donor?" Sean whispered at last.

"I don't know and I don't care," Janet whispered back. "I want out of here."

"Donor?" Sean murmured. "That sounds creepy to me. What do we have here? A clearinghouse for body parts? Reminds me of a movie I saw once. I tell you, this place is nuts."

"Is she gone?" Janet asked.

"I'll check," Sean said. Slowly he backed out from their hiding place, then peeked over the countertop. The room was empty. "She seems to be gone," Sean said. "I wonder why she ignored the copy machine."

Janet backed out and gingerly raised her head. She scanned the room as well.

"Coming in, the computer alarm must have shielded the sound," Sean said. "But going out, she had to have heard it."

"Maybe she was too preoccupied," Janet offered.

Sean nodded. "I think you're probably right."

The computer screen that had been flashing the innumerable nine-digit numbers suddenly went blank.

"The program seems to be over," Sean said.

"Let's get away from here," Janet said, her voice quavering.

They ventured out into the room. The copy machine had finished the latest stack of charts and was silent.

"Now we know why she didn't hear it," Sean said, going up to the machine and checking it. He loaded the last of the charts.

"I want out of here!" Janet said.

"Not until I have my charts," Sean said. He pushed the copy button and the copier roared to life. Then he began removing the originals and the copies already done, stapling the copies and reassembling the charts.

At first, Janet watched, terrified that any moment the same woman would reappear. But after she recognized the faster they were finished, the sooner they would leave, she pitched in. With no further interruptions they had all the charts copied and stapled in short order.

Returning to the small elevator, Sean discovered that it was possible to push the button with the door ajar. Then, when the door was closed, the dumbwaiter operated. "Now I don't have to worry about you forgetting to bring me down," he said teasingly.

"I'm in no mood for humor," Janet remarked as she climbed into the hoist. She held out her arms to take as many charts and copies as possible.

Repeating the procedure that had brought them up to the seventh floor, they returned the charts to the vault. To Janet's chagrin, Sean insisted they take the time to return the charts to their original locations. With that accomplished, they carried the chart copies to the animal room where Sean hid them beneath the cages of his mice.

"I should inject these guys," Sean said, "but to tell you the truth, I don't much feel like it."

Janet was pleased to leave but didn't start to relax until they were driving out of the parking lot.

"That has to have been one of the worst experiences of my life," she said as they traversed Little Havana. "I can't believe that you stayed so calm."

"My heart rate was up," Sean admitted. "But it went smoothly except for that little episode in the computer room. And now that it's over, wasn't it exciting? Just a little?"

"No!" Janet said emphatically.

They drove in silence until Sean spoke again: "I still can't figure out what that computer was doing. And I can't figure out what it has to do with organ donation. They certainly don't use organs from deceased cancer patients. It's too risky in relation to transplanting the cancer as well as the organ. Any ideas?"

"I can't think about anything at this point," Janet said.

They pulled into the Forbes residence.

"Geez, look at that old Caddy convertible," Sean said. "What a boat. Barry Dunhegan had one just like it when I was a kid, except his was pink. He was a bookmaker and all us kids thought he was cool."

Janet cast a cursory glance at the finned monster parked within the shadow of an exotic tree. She marveled how Sean could go through such a wrenching experience, then think about cars.

Sean pulled to a stop and yanked on the emergency brake. They got out of the car and entered the building in silence. Sean was thinking about how nice it would be to spend the night with Janet. He couldn't blame the security guard for ogling her. As Sean climbed the stairs behind Janet, he was reminded how fabulous her legs were.

As they came abreast of his door he reached out and drew her to him, enveloping her in his arms. For a moment they merely hugged.

"What about staying together tonight?" Sean forced himself to ask. His voice was hesitant; he feared rejection. Janet didn't answer immediately, and the longer she delayed, the more optimistic he became. Finally he used his left hand to take out his keys.

"I don't think it's a good idea," she said.

"Come on," Sean urged. He could smell her fragrance from having held her close.

"No!" Janet said with finality after another pause. Although she'd been wavering, she'd made a decision. "I know it would be nice, and I could use the sense of security after this evening, but we have to talk first."

Sean rolled his eyes in frustration. She could be so impossibly stubborn. "Okay," he said petulantly, trying another tack. "Have it your way." He let go of her, opened his door, and stepped inside. Before shutting the door, he glanced at her face. What he wanted to see was sudden concern that he was miffed. Instead he saw irritation. Janet turned and walked away.

After closing his door, Sean felt guilty. He went to his slider, opened it, and stepped out on the balcony. A few doors down he saw Janet's light in her living room go on. Sean hesitated, not sure what to do.

"Men," Janet said aloud with ire and exasperation. She hesitated inside her door, going over the conversation outside Sean's door. There was no reason for him to get angry with her. Hadn't she gone along with his risky plan? Didn't she generally defer to his wishes? Why couldn't he ever even try to understand hers?

Knowing that nothing would be solved that evening, Janet walked into the bedroom and turned on the light. Although she would later remember it, it didn't completely register that her bathroom door was closed. When Janet was by herself she never closed doors. It had been a habit developed as a child.

Pulling off her tank top and unhooking her bra, Janet tossed them on the armchair by the bed. She undid the clip on the top of her head and shook her hair free. She felt exhausted, irritable, and as one of her roommates at college used to say, fried. Picking up the hair dryer she'd tossed on her bed in haste that morning, Janet opened the bathroom and entered. The moment she turned on the light, she became aware of a hulking presence to her left. Reacting instinctively, Janet's hand shot out as if to fend off the intruder.

A scream started in Janet's throat but was stalled before it could get out by the hideousness of the image that confronted her. A man was in her bathroom dressed in baggy dark clothes. A knotted segment of nylon stocking had been drawn over his head so that his features were grotesquely compressed. At shoulder height he clutched a butcher's knife menacingly.

For an instant, neither of them moved. Janet quiveringly aimed the ineffectual hair dryer at the ghoulish face as if it were a Magnum revolver. The intruder stared down the barrel in shocked surprise until he realized he was looking at heating coils, not the innards of a handgun.

He was the first to react, reaching out and snatching the hair dryer from Janet's hand. In a burst of rage he threw the apparatus aside; it smashed the mirror of the medicine cabinet. The shattering of the glass jolted Janet from her paralysis, and she bolted from the bathroom.

Tom reacted swiftly and managed to grab Janet's arm, but Janet's momentum pulled them stumbling into the bedroom. His original intent had been to stab her in the bathroom. The hair dryer had thrown him off guard. He hadn't planned on her getting out of the bathroom. And he didn't want her to scream, but she did.

Janet's first scream had been stifled by shock, but she more than made up for it with a second scream that reverberated in the confines of her small apartment and penetrated the cheaply built walls. It was probably heard in every apartment in the building, and it sent a shiver of fear down Tom's spine. As angry as he was, he knew that he was in trouble.

Still holding on to Janet's arm, Tom whipped her around so that she careened off the wall before falling crossways on the bed. Tom could have killed her there and then, but he didn't dare take the time. Instead he rushed to the slider. Fumbling with the curtains and then the lock, he yanked the door open and disappeared into the night.

Sean had been loitering on the balcony outside Janet's open living room slider, trying to build up the courage to go in and apologize for trying to make Janet feel guilty. He was embarrassed at his behavior, but since apologies weren't his strong suit, he was having difficulty motivating himself.

Sean's hesitation dissolved in an instant at the sound of the shattering mirror. For a moment he struggled with the screen, trying to slide it open. When he heard Janet's bloodcurdling scream followed by a loud thud, he gave up opening the screen properly and threw himself through it. He ended up on the shag carpet, his legs still bound in the mesh. Struggling to his feet he launched himself through the doorway into the bedroom. He found Janet on the bed, wide-eyed with terror.

"What's the matter?" Sean demanded.

Janet sat up. Choking back tears, she said, "There was a man with a knife in my bathroom." Then she pointed to the open bedroom slider. "He went that way."

Sean flew to the sliding glass door and whipped back the curtain. Instead of one man, there were two. They came through the door in tandem, roughly shoving Sean back into the room prior to everyone recognizing each other. The newcomers were Gary Engels and another resident who'd responded to Janet's scream just as Sean had.

Frantically explaining that an intruder had just left, Sean led the two men back out onto the balcony. As they reached the handrail they heard the screech of tires coming from the parking lot behind the building. While Gary and his companion ran for the stairs, Sean returned to Janet.

Janet had recovered to a degree. She'd slipped on a sweatshirt. When Sean entered she was sitting on the edge of the bed finishing an emergency call to the police. Replacing the receiver, she looked up at Sean, who was standing above her.

"You okay?" he asked gently.

"I think so," she said. She was visibly shaking. "God, what a day!"

"I told you you should have stayed with me." Sean sat next to her and put his arms around her.

In spite of herself, Janet gave a short laugh. Leave it to Sean to try to smooth over any situation with humor. It did feel wonderful to be in his arms.

"I'd heard Miami was a lively city," she said, taking his lead, "but this is too much."

"Any idea how the guy got in here?" Sean asked.

"I left the slider in the living room open," Janet admitted.

"This is learning the hard way," Sean said.

"In Boston the worst thing that ever happened to me was an obscene phone call," Janet said.

"Yeah, and I apologized," Sean said.

Janet smiled and threw her pillow at him.

It took the police twenty minutes to arrive. They pulled up in a squad car with lights flashing but no siren. Two uniformed officers from the Miami police department came up to the apartment. One was a huge bearded black man, the other was a slim Hispanic with a mustache. Their names were Peter Jefferson and Juan Torres. They were solicitous, respectful, and professional as they spent an unhurried half hour going over Janet's story. When she mentioned that the man was wearing latex rubber gloves, they canceled a crime scene technician who was scheduled to come over after finishing a homicide case.

"The fact that nobody got hurt puts this incident into a different category," Juan said. "Obviously homicides get more attention."

"But this could have been a homicide," Sean protested.

"Hey, we do the best we can with the manpower we got," Peter said.

While the policemen were still there gathering facts, someone else showed up: Robert Harris.

Robert Harris had carefully cultivated and nurtured a relationship with the Miami police department. Although he decried their lack of discipline and their poor physical shape, characteristics that set in approximately a year subsequent to their graduation from the police academy, Harris was enough of a pragmatist to understand that he needed to be on their good side. And this attack on a nurse at the Forbes residence was a case in point. Had he not developed the connections he had, he probably wouldn't have heard about the incident until the following morning. As far as Robert was concerned, such a situation would be unacceptable for the head of security.

The call had come from the duty commander while Harris was using his Soloflex machine in front of his TV at home. Unfortunately, there'd been a delay of nearly half an hour following the dispatch of the patrol car, but Harris was not in a position to complain. Arriving late was better than not arriving at all. Harris just didn't want the case to be cold by the time he got involved.

As Harris had driven to the residence, he thought back to the rape and murder of Sheila Arnold. He couldn't shake the suspicion—improbable though it might seem—that Arnold's death was somehow related to the deaths of the breast cancer patients. Harris wasn't a doctor so he had to go on what Dr. Mason had told him a few months ago, namely that it was his belief that the breast cancer patients were being murdered. The tip-off was the fact that these patients' faces were blue, a sign they were being somehow smothered.

Dr. Mason had made it clear that getting to the bottom of this situation should be Harris's primary task. If word leaked to the press, the damage to the

Forbes might be irreparable. In fact, Dr. Mason had made it sound like Harris's tenure depended on a quick and unobtrusive resolution of this potentially embarrassing problem. The quicker that resolution came about, the better for everyone.

But Harris had not made any progress over the last few months. Dr. Mason's suggestion that the perpetrator was probably a doctor or a nurse had not panned out. Extensive background checks on the professional staff had failed to uncover any suspicious discrepancies or irregularities. Harris's attempts at keeping an unobtrusive eye on the Forbes breast cancer patients hadn't turned anything up. Not that he'd been able to keep watch over all of them.

Harris's suspicion that Miss Arnold's death was related to the breast cancer patient deaths had hit him the day after her murder while he'd been driving to work. It was then he'd remembered that the day before she was killed a breast cancer patient on her floor had died and turned blue.

What if Sheila Arnold had seen something, Harris wondered. What if she'd witnessed or overheard something whose significance she hadn't appreciated—something that made the perpetrator feel threatened nonetheless. The idea had seemed reasonable to Harris, although he did wonder if it were the product of a desperate mind.

In any case, Harris's suspicion hadn't left him with much to go on. He had learned from the police that a witness had seen a man leaving Miss Arnold's apartment the night of the murder, but the description had been hopelessly vague: a male of medium height and medium build with brown hair. The witness had not seen the man's face. In an institution the size of the Forbes Cancer Center, such a description had been of limited use.

So when Harris was told of yet another attack on a Forbes nurse, he again considered a possible connection to the breast cancer deaths. There had been another suspicious blue death on Tuesday.

Harris entered Janet's apartment eager to talk with her. He was extremely chagrined to find her in the company of the wiseass medical student, Sean Murphy.

Since the police were still questioning the nurse, Harris took a quick look around. He saw the shattered mirror in the bathroom along with the broken hair dryer. He also noticed the panties amid the debris on the floor. Wandering into the living room, he noted the large hole in the screen. It was obvious the screen had been a point of entry, not escape.

"Your witness," Peter Jefferson joked, coming into the living room. His partner followed in his shadow. Harris had met Peter on several occasions in the past.

"Anything you can tell me?" Harris asked.

"Not a whole lot," Peter said. "Perp was wearing a nylon stocking over his face. Medium build, medium height. Apparently didn't say a word. Girl's lucky. The guy had a knife."

"What are you going to do?" Harris asked.

Peter shrugged. "The usual," he said. "We'll file a report. We'll see what the sarge says. One way or another it'll get turned over to an investigative unit. Who knows what they'll do." Peter lowered his voice. "No injury, no robbery. It's not likely this will become a number-one priority. If she'd gotten whacked it'd be a different story."

Harris nodded. He thanked the officers and they left. Harris stepped into the bedroom. Janet was packing a bag; Sean was in the bathroom collecting her toiletries.

"On behalf of Forbes, I want to tell you I'm terribly sorry about this," he said.

"Thank you," Janet said.

"We've never felt the need for security here," Harris added.

"I understand," Janet said. "It could have happened anyplace. I did leave the door open."

"The police told me you had difficulty describing the guy," Harris said.

"He had a stocking over his head," Janet said. "And it all happened so fast."

"Is it possible that you might have seen him before?" Harris asked.

"I don't think so," Janet said. "But it really is impossible to say for sure."

"I want to ask you a question," Harris said. "But I want you to think for a minute before answering. Has anything unusual happened to you recently at Forbes?"

Janet's mouth went instantly dry.

Overhearing this exchange, Sean immediately guessed what was going through Janet's mind: she was thinking about their break-in into the chart room.

"Janet has had a rather difficult experience," Sean said, stepping into the room.

Harris turned. "I'm not talking to you, boy," he said menacingly.

"Listen, jughead," Sean said. "We didn't call the Marines. Janet has spoken to the police. You can get your information from them. She doesn't have to talk to you, and I think she's been through enough tonight. She doesn't need you pestering her."

The two men faced off, glaring at each other.

"Please!" Janet shouted. Fresh tears welled in her eyes. "I can't stand any tension just now," she told them.

Sean sat down on the bed, put his arm around her, and leaned his forehead against hers.

"I'm sorry, Miss Reardon," Harris said. "I understand. But it is important for me to ask you if you've seen anything unusual while you worked today. I know it was your first day."

Janet shook her head. Sean glanced up at Harris and with his eyes motioned for him to leave.

Harris fought hard to keep himself from slapping the kid around. He even fantasized about sitting on him and shaving his head. But instead he turned and left.

———

As the night advanced toward dawn Tom Widdicomb's anxiety gradually increased. He was in the storeroom off the garage huddled in the corner beside the freezer. He had his arms around himself and his knees drawn up as if he were cold. He even intermittently shivered as his mind constantly tortured him by replaying over and over the disastrous events at the Forbes residence.

Now he was a total failure. Not only had he failed to put Gloria D'Amataglio to sleep, he'd failed to get rid of the nurse who'd prevented him from doing so. And despite the nylon stocking he'd worn, she'd seen him up close. Maybe she could recognize him. More than anything, Tom was mortified to have mistaken that stupid hair dryer for a gun.

Because of his idiocy, Alice wasn't speaking to him. He'd tried to talk with her, but she wouldn't even listen. He'd disappointed her. He wasn't "her little man" anymore. He deserved to be laughed at by the other children. Tom had tried to reason with her, promising that he would help Gloria that morning, and that as soon as he could he'd rid them of the meddlesome nurse. He promised and cried, but to no avail. Alice could be stubborn.

Getting stiffly to his feet, Tom stretched his cramped muscles. He'd been crouched in the corner without moving for hours, thinking his mother would eventually feel sorry for him. But it hadn't worked. She'd ignored him. So he thought he'd try talking to her directly.

Moving in front of the chest freezer he snapped open the lock and raised the lid. The frozen mist inside the freezer swirled as it mixed with a draft of moist, warm Miami air. Gradually the mist dissipated, and out of the fog emerged the desiccated face of Alice Widdicomb. Her dyed red hair was frozen into icy tangles. The skin of her face was sunken, blotchy, and blue. Crystals had formed along the edges of her open eyelids. Her eyeballs had contracted slightly, dimpling the surface of her corneas which were opaque with winter-like frost. Her yellow teeth were exposed by the retraction of her lips, forming a horrid grimace.

Since Tom and his mother had lived such isolated lives, Tom had little difficulty after he'd put her to sleep. His only mistake had been that he'd not thought of the freezer soon enough, and after a couple of days she'd started to smell. One of the few neighbors with whom they occasionally spoke had even mentioned it, throwing Tom into a panic. That was when he'd thought of the freezer.

Since then nothing had changed. Even Alice's social security checks continued to arrive on schedule. The only close call had been when the freezer compressor conked out one hot Friday night. Tom hadn't been able to get someone to come to fix it until Monday. He had been terrified the guy would need to open the freezer, but he didn't. The man did tell Tom that he thought he might have some bad meat in there.

Supporting the lid, Tom gazed at his mother. But she still refused to say a word. She was understandably scared.

"I'll do it today," Tom said pleadingly. "Gloria will still be on IVs. If not, I'll think of something. And the nurse. I'll get rid of her. There's not going to be any problem. No one is going to come to take you away. You're safe with me. Please!"

Alice Widdicomb said nothing.

Slowly Tom lowered the lid. He waited for a moment in case she changed her mind, but she didn't. Reluctantly he left her and went through to the kitchen into the bedroom they'd shared for so many years. Opening the bedside table he took out Alice's gun. It had been his father's originally, but after he'd died, Alice had taken it over, frequently showing it to Tom, saying that if anyone ever tried to come between them, she'd use it. Tom had learned to love the sight of the mother-of-pearl handle.

"Nobody's ever coming between us, Alice," Tom said. So far he'd only used the gun once, and that was when the Arnold girl tried to interfere by taking him aside to say she'd seen him take some medicine off the anesthesia cart. Now he'd have to use it again for this Janet Reardon before she caused more trouble than she already had.

"I'll prove to you that I'm your little man," Tom said. He slipped the cold gun into his pocket and went into the bathroom to shave.

MARCH 5 • FRIDAY, 6:30 A.M.

As she drove along the General Douglas MacArthur Causeway heading for work, Janet tried to distract herself by admiring the impressive view over Biscayne Bay. She even tried to fantasize about taking a cruise with Sean on one of the dazzling white cruise ships lined up at the Dodge Island seaport. But nothing worked. Her mind kept returning to the previous night's events.

After confronting that man in her bathroom, Janet wasn't about to spend the night in 207. Not even Sean's apartment seemed a safe haven to her. Instead, she insisted on moving to the Miami Beach unit she'd rented. Not wanting to be alone, she'd invited Sean to come with her and was relieved when he accepted and even offered to sleep on the couch. But once they got there, even Janet's best resolutions fell to the wayside. They slept together in what Sean described as the "Platonic fashion." They didn't make love, but Janet had to admit, it felt good to be close to him.

Almost as much as the intruder's break-in, Janet was troubled by her escapade with Sean. The episode in the administration office the previous night troubled her deeply. She couldn't stop thinking about what would have happened had they been caught. On top of that, she'd begun to wonder what kind of man Sean was. He was smart and witty, of that there was no doubt. But given this new revelation of his past experience of thievery, she questioned what his true morals were.

All in all Janet felt profoundly distraught, and to make matters worse she was facing a day in which she was expected to obtain deceitfully a sample of medicine that was highly controlled. If she failed, she faced the possibility of Sean packing his things and leaving Miami. As she neared the hospital Janet found herself thinking longingly about Sunday, the first day she was scheduled to have off. The fact that she was already thinking about vacation time at the start of her second day on the job gave an indication of her level of stress.

The bustling atmosphere of the floor turned out to be a godsend for Janet's troubled mind. Within minutes of her arrival, she was swept up in the tumult of the hospital. Nursing report gave the oncoming day shift a hint of the work ahead of them. Between diagnostic tests, treatments, and complicated medication protocols, all the nurses knew they would have little free time. The most disturbing news was that Helen Cabot had not improved overnight as the doctors had hoped. In fact, the night nurse taking care of her felt she'd actually lost ground, having had a small seizure around four A.M. Janet listened carefully to this part of the briefing since she'd arranged to be assigned to Helen Cabot for the day.

Regarding the controlled medicines, Janet had concocted a plan. Having seen the type of vials they came in, she'd made it a point to obtain similar vials that were empty. Now all she needed was some time alone with the medicine.

After report had concluded, Janet launched into work. The first order of business was to start an IV line for Gloria D'Amataglio. It was Gloria's last day of IV medication on her current chemotherapy cycle. Having shown an early facility with venipuncture, Janet was in demand for the procedure. During report she'd offered to start Gloria's IV since there had been some problems doing so in the past. The nurse scheduled to care for Gloria for the day had readily agreed.

Armed with all the necessary paraphernalia, Janet went into Gloria's room. Gloria was sitting on the bed, leaning against a bank of pillows, obviously feeling better than she had the day before. While they chatted nostalgically about the beauty of the pond on the Wellesley campus and how romantic it had been on party weekends, Janet got the IV going.

"I hardly felt that," Gloria said in admiration.

"Glad to help," Janet said.

Leaving Gloria's room, Janet felt her stomach tighten as she prepared herself for her next task: getting to the controlled medication. She had to dodge several gurneys, then did a kind of sidestep dance to get around the housekeeper and his bucket.

Reaching the nurses' station, Janet got out Helen Cabot's chart and turned to the order sheet. It indicated that Helen was to get her MB300C and MB303C starting at eight A.M. First Janet got the IV bottle and syringes; she then got the empty containers which she'd put aside. Finally she went to Marjorie and asked for Helen's medication.

"Just a sec," Marjorie said. She ran down the corridor to the elevators to give a completed X-ray form to an orderly taking a patient down to X-ray.

"That guy never remembers the requisition," Tim commented with a shake of his head.

Marjorie returned to the nurses' station at a jog. As she rounded the counter, she was already removing the key from around her neck for the special medication locker.

"What a day!" she said to Janet. "And to think it's just starting!" She was obviously preoccupied with the welter of activity hospital wards faced at the beginning of each workday. Opening the small but stoutly built refrigerator, she reached in and brought out the two vials of Helen Cabot's medicine. Consulting a ledger that was also stored in the refrigerator, she told Janet she should take 2 ccs of the larger vial and a half cc of the smaller. She showed Janet where to initial after she administered the medication and where Marjorie would initial when Janet was finished.

"Marjorie, I have Dr. Larsen on the line," Tim said, interrupting them.

With the vials of clear fluid safely in hand, Janet retreated to the pharmacy closet. First she turned on the hot water in the small sink. After making sure no one was watching, she held the two MB vials under the hot water. When the gummed labels came loose, Janet pulled them off and placed them on the empty vials. She tucked the now unlabeled vials into the utility drawer back behind an assortment of plastic dosage cups, pencils, pads, and rubber bands.

After another precautionary glance into the busy nurses' station, Janet held the two empty vials over her head and let them fall to the tile floor. Both smashed into tiny shards. After pouring a small amount of water onto the glass pieces, Janet turned and left the pharmacy closet.

Marjorie was still on the phone, and Janet had to wait for her to disconnect. As soon as she did, Janet put a hand on her arm.

"There's been an accident," Janet said. She tried to sound upset, which wasn't difficult considering her nervousness.

"What happened?" Marjorie asked. Her eyes widened.

"I dropped the two vials," Janet said. "They slipped out of my hand and broke on the floor."

"Okay, okay!" Marjorie said, reassuring herself as well as Janet. "Let's not get too excited. Accidents happen, especially when we're busy and rushing about. Just show me."

Janet led her back to the pharmacy closet and pointed at the remains of the two vials. Marjorie squatted down and, using her thumb and forefinger, gingerly pulled out the shards attached to the labels.

"I'm terribly sorry," Janet said.

"It's okay," Marjorie said. She stood up and shrugged. "As I said, accidents happen. Let's call Ms. Richmond."

Janet followed Marjorie back to the nurses' station, where Marjorie placed a call to the director of nursing. After she explained what had happened, she had to get out the ledger from the medicine refrigerator. Janet could see the vials for the other two patients as she did so.

"There was 6cc in the larger and 4cc in the smaller," Marjorie said into the phone. She listened, agreed several times, then hung up.

"No problem," Marjorie said. She made an entry into the ledger, then handed the pen to Janet. "Just initial where I indicated what was lost," she said.

Janet wrote her initials.

"Now head over to Ms. Richmond's office in the research building, seventh floor," Marjorie said. "Bring these labels with you." She put the broken glass fragments with their attached labels in an envelope and handed them to Janet. "She'll give you several new vials, okay?"

Janet nodded and apologized again.

"It's all right," Marjorie assured her. "It could have happened to anyone." Then she asked Tim to page Tom Widdicomb to get him to mop up the pharmacy closet.

With her heart pounding and knowing her face was flushed, Janet walked toward the elevators as calmly as she could. Her ruse had worked, but she didn't feel good about it. She felt like she was taking advantage of Marjorie's trust and good nature. She was also concerned that someone might stumble across the unlabeled vials in the utility drawer. Janet would have liked to have removed them, but she felt she couldn't risk it until later when she could give them directly to Sean.

Despite her preoccupation with Helen's drugs, as Janet came abreast of Gloria's door she noticed it was closed. Having just started her IV, this disturbed her. Except for the one incident when Marjorie had introduced Janet to Gloria, Gloria's door was always ajar. Gloria had even commented that she liked to have it open so she could stay in touch with life on the ward.

Perplexed, Janet stopped and stared at the door, debating with herself what she should do. She was already behind with her work, so she should get over to Ms. Richmond's office. Yet Gloria's door bothered her. Fearing Gloria might be feeling poorly, Janet stepped over to the door and knocked. When there was no response, she knocked again louder. When there was still no answer, Janet pushed the door open and peered inside. Gloria was flat on the bed. One of her legs was dangling over the side of the mattress. It seemed an unnatural position for a nap.

"Gloria?" Janet called.

Gloria didn't respond.

Propping the door open with its rubber foot, Janet approached the bed. Off to the side was a slop bucket with a mop, but Janet didn't see it because as she got closer she noted with alarm that Gloria's face was a deep cyanotic blue!

"Code, room 409!" Janet shouted at the operator after snatching the phone from its cradle. She tossed the envelope with the glass shards on the bedside table.

Pulling Gloria's head back and after making certain her mouth was clear, Janet started mouth-to-mouth resuscitation. With her right hand pinching Gloria's nostrils, Janet forcibly inflated Gloria's lungs several times. Noting the ease with which she was able to do this, she became confident there was no blockage. With her left hand she felt for a pulse. She found one, but it was weak.

Janet blew several more times as people began to arrive. Marjorie was there first, but soon others followed. By the time Janet was relieved from her resuscitative efforts by one of the other nurses, there were at least ten people in the room trying to help. Janet was impressed by the quick response: even the housekeeper was there.

Gloria's color responded quickly, to everyone's relief. Within three minutes several doctors including an anesthesiologist arrived from the second floor. By then a monitor had been set up showing a slow but otherwise normal heartbeat. The anesthesiologist deftly inserted an endotracheal tube and used an Ambu bag to inflate Gloria's lungs. This was more efficient than mouth-to-mouth, and Gloria's color improved even more.

But there were bad signs as well. When the anesthesiologist shone a penlight into Gloria's eyes her widely dilated pupils did not react. When another doctor tried to elicit reflexes, she was unable to do so.

After twenty minutes Gloria started to make efforts to breathe. Minutes later, she was breathing on her own. Reflexes also returned but in a fashion that did not bode well. Her arms and legs extended while her hands and feet flexed.

"Uh-oh," the anesthesiologist said. "Looks like some signs of decerebrate rigidity. That's bad."

Janet did not want to hear this.

The anesthesiologist shook his head. "Too long without oxygen to the brain."

"I'm surprised," one of the other doctors said. She tilted the IV bottle to see what was running in. "I didn't think respiratory failure was a complication of this regimen."

"Chemo can do unexpected things," the anesthesiologist said. "It could have started with a cerebral vascular incident. I think Randolph better hear about this."

After rescuing her envelope, Janet stumbled out of the room. She knew scenes like this came with the territory, but knowing that hard fact didn't make them any easier to bear.

Marjorie came out of Gloria's room, saw Janet, and came over. She shook her head. "We're not having much luck with these advanced breast cancer patients," she said. "I think the powers that be better start questioning the treatment protocol."

Janet nodded but didn't speak.

"Being the first one on the scene is always tough," she said. "You did all you could."

Janet nodded again. "Thanks," she said.

"Now get that medicine for Helen Cabot before we have more trouble," Marjorie said. She gave Janet a sisterly pat on the shoulder.

Janet nodded. She took the stairs to get to the second floor, then crossed to the research building. She took an elevator to the seventh floor and, after asking for Ms. Richmond, was directed to her office.

The nursing director was expecting her and reached for the envelope. Opening it she poured the contents onto her desk blotter. With her index finger she pushed the shards around until she could read the labels.

Janet remained standing. Ms. Richmond's silence made her fear that somehow the woman knew exactly what Janet had done. Janet began to perspire.

"Did this cause a problem?" Ms. Richmond asked finally in her surprisingly soft voice.

"What do you mean?" Janet asked.

"When you broke these vials," Ms. Richmond said. "Did the glass cut you?"

"No," Janet said with relief. "I dropped them on the floor. I wasn't injured."

"Well, it's not the first time or the last," Ms. Richmond said. "I'm glad you didn't hurt yourself."

With surprising agility for her size, Ms. Richmond sprang up from behind her desk and went to a floor-to-ceiling cabinet that concealed a large, locked refrigerator. Unlocking and opening the refrigerator door, she took out two vials similar to the ones Janet had broken. The refrigerator was almost filled with such vials.

Ms. Richmond returned to her desk. Searching in a box in a side drawer, she took out printed labels identical to those on the shards on her desk. Licking the backs, she began applying the appropriate label to each vial. Before she was finished her phone rang.

Ms. Richmond answered and continued to work, holding the phone against her ear with a raised shoulder. But almost immediately the call took her full attention.

"What?" she cried. Her soft voice turned querulous. Her face reddened.

"Where?" Ms. Richmond demanded. "Fourth floor!" she said after a pause. "That's almost worse! Damnation!"

Ms. Richmond slammed the phone down and for a moment stared ahead without blinking. Then, noting Janet's presence with a start, she got up and handed over the vials. "I've got to go," she said urgently. "Be careful with that medicine."

Janet nodded and started to respond, but Ms. Richmond was already on her way out the door.

Janet paused at the threshold of Ms. Richmond's office and watched her walk rapidly away. Looking over her shoulder, she gazed at the cabinet which concealed the locked refrigerator. Something wasn't right about all this, but she wasn't sure what it was. Too much was happening.

————

Randolph Mason marveled at Sterling Rombauer. He had some idea of Sterling's personal wealth as well as of his legendary business acumen, but he had no idea what motivated the man. Chasing around the country at other people's bidding would not be the life Mason would lead if he had command of the assets Sterling did. Nonetheless, Mason was grateful for Sterling's chosen occupation. Every time he hired the man, he got results.

"I don't think you have anything to worry about until the Sushita plane shows up here in Miami," Sterling was saying. "It had been waiting for Tanaka in Boston and was scheduled to go to Miami, but then it went to New York and on to Washington without him. Tanaka had to fly down here on a commercial flight."

"And you will know if and when the plane comes?" Dr. Mason asked.

Sterling nodded.

Dr. Mason's intercom crackled on. "Sorry to disturb you, Dr. Mason," Patty, his secretary, said. "But you told me to warn you about Ms. Richmond. She's on her way in and she seems upset."

Dr. Mason swallowed hard. There was only one thing that could set Margaret off. He excused himself from Sterling and left his office to intercept his director of nursing. He caught her near Patty's desk and drew her aside.

"It's happened again," Ms. Richmond snapped. "Another breast cancer patient with a cyanotic respiratory arrest. Randolph, you have to do something!"

"Another death?" Dr. Mason asked.

"Not a death yet," Ms. Richmond said. "But almost worse, especially if the media gets involved. The patient is in a vegetative state with obvious brain damage."

"Good Lord," Dr. Mason exclaimed. "You're right; it could be worse if the family starts asking questions."

"Of course they will ask questions," Ms. Richmond said. "Once again, I must remind you that this could ruin everything we've worked for."

"You don't have to tell me," Dr. Mason said.

"Well, what are you going to do?"

"I don't know what else to do," Dr. Mason admitted. "Let's get Harris up here."

Dr. Mason had Patty call Robert Harris and told her to buzz him the moment Harris arrived. "I have Sterling Rombauer in my office," he told Ms. Richmond. "Maybe you should hear what he has to say about our medical student extern."

"That brat!" Ms. Richmond said. "When I caught him over in the hospital sneaking a look at Helen Cabot's chart I felt like throttling him."

"Calm down and come in and listen," Dr. Mason said.

Ms. Richmond reluctantly allowed Dr. Mason to lead her into his office. Sterling got to his feet. Ms. Richmond told him he didn't have to stand on her account.

Dr. Mason had everybody sit, then asked Sterling to bring Ms. Richmond up to date.

"Sean Murphy is an interesting and complicated individual," Sterling said as he casually crossed his legs. "He's lived a rather double life, changing drastically when he got into Harvard undergraduate school, yet still clinging to his blue-collar Irish roots. And he's been successful. Currently he and a group of friends are about to start a company they intend to call Oncogen. Its goal will be to market diagnostic and therapeutic agents based on oncogene technology."

"Then it's clear what we should do," Ms. Richmond said. "Especially considering his being insufferably brash."

"Let Sterling finish," Dr. Mason said.

"He's extremely bright when it comes to biotechnology," Sterling said. "In fact I'd have to say he's gifted. His only real liability, as you've already guessed, is in the social realm. He has little respect for authority and manages to irritate a lot of people. That said, he's already been involved with the founding of a successful company that was bought out by Genentech. And he's had no significant difficulty finding funding for his second venture."

"He's sounding more and more like trouble," Ms. Richmond said.

"Not in the way you think," Sterling said. "The problem is that Sushita knows approximately as much as I do. It's my professional opinion that they will deem Sean Murphy a threat to their investment here at Forbes. Once they do, they'll be inspired to act. I'm not convinced a move to Tokyo and, essentially, a buyout, will work with Mr. Murphy. Yet if he stays here, I think they'll consider reneging on renewing your grant."

"I still don't understand why we don't send him back to Boston," Ms. Richmond said. "Then it's over. Why take the risk of jeopardizing our relationship with Sushita?"

Sterling looked at Dr. Mason.

Dr. Mason cleared his throat. "From my perspective," he said, "I don't want to be rash. The kid is good at what he does. This morning I went down to where he's working. He's got a whole generation of mice accepting the glycoprotein. On top of that, he showed me some promising crystals that he's been able to grow. He insists he'll have better in a week. No one else has been able to get this far. My problem is I'm caught between a rock and a hard place. A more dire threat to our Sushita funding is the fact that we have yet to provide them with a single patentable product. They expected something by now."

"In other words, you think we need this brat even with the risks," Ms. Richmond said.

"That's not the way I would phrase it," Dr. Mason said.

"Then why don't you call Sushita and explain it to them," Ms. Richmond said.

"That would not be advisable," Sterling said. "The Japanese prefer indirect communication so that confrontation can be avoided. They would not understand such a direct approach. Such a ploy would cause more anxiety than it would alleviate."

"Besides, I already alluded to all this with Hiroshi," Dr. Mason said. "And they still went ahead to investigate Mr. Murphy on their own."

"The Japanese businessman has a great problem with uncertainty," Sterling added.

"So what is your take on this kid?" Ms. Richmond asked. "Is he a spy? Is that why he's here?"

"No," Sterling said. "Not in any traditional sense. He's obviously interested in your success with medulloblastoma, but it's from an academic point of view, not a commercial one."

"He was very open about his interests in the medulloblastoma work," Dr. Mason said. "The first time I met him he was clearly disappointed when I informed him he would not be permitted to work on the project. If he'd been some kind of spy, I think he'd keep a lower profile. Rocking the boat only draws further scrutiny."

"I agree," Sterling said. "As a young man he's still motivated by idealism and altruism. He has not yet been poisoned by the new commercialism of science in general and medical research in particular."

"Yet he's already started his own company," Ms. Richmond pointed out. "That sounds pretty commercial to me."

"But he and his partners were essentially selling their products at cost," Sterling said. "The profit motive did not play a role until the company was bought out."

"So what's the solution?" Ms. Richmond asked.

"Sterling will monitor the situation," Dr. Mason said. "He'll keep us informed on a daily basis. He'll protect Mr. Murphy from the Japanese as long as he is a help to us. If Sterling decides he is acting as a spy, he'll let us know. Then we'll send him back to Boston."

"An expensive baby-sitter," Ms. Richmond said.

Sterling smiled and nodded in agreement. "Miami in March is very agreeable," he said. "Particularly at the Grand Bay Hotel."

A short burst of static from Dr. Mason's intercom preceded Patty's voice: "Mr. Harris is here."

Dr. Mason thanked Sterling, indicating the meeting was over. As he accompanied Sterling out of the office, Dr. Mason couldn't help but agree with Ms. Richmond's assessment: Sterling was an expensive baby-sitter. But Dr. Mason was convinced the money was well spent and, thanks to Howard Pace, readily available.

Harris was standing next to Patty's desk, and for the sake of propriety, Dr. Mason introduced him to Sterling. As he did, he couldn't help but feel each man was the other's antithesis.

After sending Harris into his office, Dr. Mason thanked Sterling for all he'd done and implored him to keep them informed. Sterling assured him he would, and left. Dr. Mason then went back into his office to deal with the current crisis.

Dr. Mason closed the door behind him. He noticed Harris was standing stiffly in the center of the room; his patent leather visored hat with its gold trim was wedged under his left arm.

"Relax," Dr. Mason said as he went around behind his desk and sat down.

"Yes, sir," Harris said smartly. He didn't move.

"For crissake, sit down!" Dr. Mason said when he noticed Harris was still standing.

Harris took a seat, his hat remaining beneath his arm.

"I suppose you've heard another breast cancer patient has died," Dr. Mason said. "At least for all practical purposes."

"Yes, sir," Harris said crisply.

Dr. Mason eyed his head of security with mild irritation. On the one hand he appreciated the professionalism of Robert Harris; on the other hand the militaristic playacting bothered him. It wasn't appropriate for a medical institution. But he'd never complained because until these breast cancer deaths, security had never been a problem.

"As we told you in the past," Dr. Mason said, "we believe some misguided demented individual is doing this. It's becoming intolerable. It has to be stopped.

"I've asked you to make this your number-one priority. Have you been able to turn anything up?"

"I assure you, this problem has my undivided attention," Harris said. "Following your advice I've done extensive background checks on most all of the professional staff. I've checked references by calling hundreds of institutions. No discrepancies have turned up so far. I'll now be expanding the checks to other personnel who have access to patients. We tried to monitor some of the breast cancer patients, but there are too many to keep tabs on all the time. Perhaps we should consider putting security cameras in all the rooms." Harris did not mention his suspicion of the possible connection between these cases and the death of a nurse and the attempted assault of another. After all, it was only a hunch.

"Maybe cameras in every breast cancer patient's room is what we have to do," Ms. Richmond said.

"It would be expensive," Harris warned. "Not only the cost of the cameras and the installation, but also the additional personnel to watch the monitors."

"Expense might be an academic concern," Ms. Richmond said. "If this problem continues and the press gets hold of it, we might not have an institution."

"I'll look into it," Harris promised.

"If you need additional manpower, let us know," Dr. Mason said. "This has to be stopped."

"I understand, sir," Harris said. But he didn't want help. He wanted to do this on his own. At this point it had become a matter of honor. No screwball psychotic was going to get the best of him.

"And what about this attack last night at the residence?" Ms. Richmond asked. "I have a hard enough time recruiting nursing personnel. We can't have them attacked in the temporary housing we offer them."

"It is the first time security has been a problem at the residence," Harris said.

"Maybe we need security people there during the evening hours," Ms. Richmond suggested.

"I'd be happy to put together a cost analysis," Harris said.

"I think the patient issue is more important," Dr. Mason said. "Don't dilute your efforts at the present time."

"Yes, sir," Harris said.

Dr. Mason looked at Ms. Richmond. "Anything else?"

Ms. Richmond shook her head.

Dr. Mason glanced back at Harris. "We're counting on you," he said.

"Yes, sir," Harris said as he got to his feet. By reflex he started to salute, but he caught himself in time.

"Very impressive!" Sean said aloud. He was sitting by himself in the glass-enclosed office in the middle of his expansive lab. He was at an empty metal desk, and he had the copies of the thirty-three charts spread out in front of him. He'd chosen the office in case someone suddenly appeared. If they did he'd have enough time to sweep the charts into one of the empty file drawers. Then he'd pull over the ledger featuring the protocol he'd developed to immunize the mice with the Forbes glycoprotein.

What Sean found so impressive were the statistics concerning the medulloblastoma cases. The Forbes Cancer Center had indeed achieved a one hundred percent remission rate over the last two years, which contrasted sharply with the one hundred percent fatality rate over the eight years prior to that. Through follow-up MRI studies, even large tumors were shown to have completely disappeared after successful treatment. As far as Sean was concerned, such consistent results were unheard of in the treatment of cancer except for the situation of cancer *in situ*, meaning extremely small, localized neoplasia that could be completely excised or otherwise eliminated.

For the first time since he'd arrived, Sean had had a reasonable morning. No one had bothered him; he hadn't seen Hiroshi or any of the other researchers. He'd started the day by injecting more of the mice which had given him a chance to get the copies of the charts up to his office. Then he'd toyed with the crystallization problem, growing a few crystals that he thought would keep Dr. Mason content for a week or so. He'd even had the director come down to see some of the crystals. Sean knew he'd been impressed. At that point, reasonably confident he wouldn't be disturbed, Sean had retired into the glass office to review the charts.

First he'd read through all the charts to gain an overall impression. Then he'd gone back, checking on epidemiological aspects. He'd noted that the patients represented a wide range of ages and races. They were also of varying sex. But the predominant group consisted of middle-aged white males, not the typical group seen with medulloblastoma. Sean guessed that the statistics were skewed due to economic considerations. The Forbes was not a cheap hospital. People needed adequate medical insurance or sizable savings accounts to be patients there. He also noted that the cases came from various major cities around the country in a truly national distribution.

But then, as if to show how dangerous generalizations were, he discovered a case from a small southwestern Florida town: Naples, Florida. Sean had seen the town on a map. It was the southernmost town on the west coast of Florida, just north of the Everglades. The patient's name was Malcolm Betencourt, and he was nearing two years since the commencement of his treatment. Sean noted the man's address and phone number. He thought he might want to talk with him.

As for the tumors themselves, Sean noted that most were multifocal rather than being a single lesion, which was more common. Since they were multifocal, the attending physicians in most cases had initially believed they were dealing with a metastatic tumor, one that had spread to the brain from some other organ like lung, kidney, or colon. In all these cases, the referring physicians had expressed surprise when the lesions turned out to be primary brain tumors arising from primitive neural elements. Sean also noted that the tumors were particularly aggressive and fast-growing. They would have undoubtedly led to rapid death had not therapy been instituted.

Concerning therapy, Sean noted that it did not vary. The dosage and rate of administration of the coded medication was the same for all patients although it was adjusted for weight. All patients had experienced about a week of hospitalization and after discharge were followed in the outpatient clinic at intervals of two weeks, four weeks, two months, six months, then annually. Thirteen of the thirty-three patients had reached the annual-visit stage. Sequelae from the illness were minimal and were associated with mild neurological deficits secondary to the expanding tumor masses prior to treatment rather than to the treatment itself.

Sean was also impressed with the charts themselves. He knew he was looking at a wealth of material that would probably take him a week to digest.

Concentrating as deeply as he was, Sean was startled when the phone on his desk began to ring. It was the first time it had ever rung. He picked it up, expecting a wrong number. To his surprise, it was Janet.

"I have the medicine," she said tersely.

"Great!" Sean said.

"Can you meet me in the cafeteria?" she asked.

"Absolutely," Sean said. He could tell something was wrong. Her voice sounded strained. "What's the matter?"

"Everything," Janet said. "I'll tell you when I see you. Can you leave now?"

"I'll be there in five minutes," Sean said.

After hiding all the charts, Sean descended in the elevator and crossed over the pedestrian bridge to the hospital. He guessed he was being observed by camera and felt like waving to indicate as much, but resisted the temptation.

When he arrived in the cafeteria Janet was already there, sitting at a table with a cup of coffee in front of her. She didn't look happy.

Sean slid into a chair across from her.

"What's wrong?" he asked.

"One of my patients is in a coma," Janet said. "I'd just started an IV on her. One minute she was fine, the next minute not breathing."

"I'm sorry to hear that," Sean said. He'd had some exposure to the emotional traumas of hospital life, so he could empathize to an extent.

"At least I got the medicine," she said.

"Was it difficult?" Sean asked.

"Emotionally more than anything else," Janet said.

"So where is it?"

"In my purse," she said. She glanced around to make sure no one was watching them. "I'll give the vials to you under the table."

"You don't have to make this so melodramatic," Sean said. "Sneaking around draws more attention than just acting normal and handing them over."

"Humor me," Janet said. She fumbled with her purse.

Sean felt her hand hit his knee. He reached under the table and two vials dropped into his hand. Respecting Janet's sensitivity he slipped them into his pockets, one on each side. Then he scraped back his chair and stood up.

"Sean!" Janet complained.

"What?" he asked.

"Do you have to be so obvious? Can't you wait five minutes like we're having a conversation?"

He sat down. "People aren't watching us," he said. "When are you going to learn?"

"How can you be so sure?" she asked.

Sean started to say something, then thought better of it.

"Can we talk about something fun for a change?" Janet asked. "I'm completely stressed out."

"What do you want to talk about?"

"What we can do come Sunday," Janet said. "I need to get away from the hospital and all this tension. I want to do something relaxing and fun."

"Okay, it's a date," Sean promised. "Meanwhile, I'm eager to get back to the lab with this medicine. Would it be so obvious if I were to leave now?"

"Go!" Janet commanded. "You're impossible."

"See you back at the beach apartment," Sean said. He moved away quickly lest Janet say something about his not being invited. He looked back and waved as he left the cafeteria.

Hurrying over the bridge between the two buildings, he thrust his hands into his pockets and palmed the two vials. He couldn't wait to get started. Thanks to Janet, he felt some of the investigative excitement he'd expected when he'd made the decision to come to the Forbes Cancer Center.

Robert Harris carried the cardboard box of employee files into his small windowless office and set them on the floor next to his desk. Sitting down, he opened the top of the box and pulled out the first file.

After the conversation with Dr. Mason and Ms. Richmond, Harris had gone directly to personnel. With the help of Henry Falworth, the personnel manager, he'd compiled a list of non-professionals who had access to patients. The list included food service personnel who distributed menus and took orders and those who delivered meals and picked up the trays. The list also included the janitorial and maintenance staffs who were occasionally called to patient rooms for odd jobs. Finally, the list ran to housekeeping: those who cleaned the rooms, the halls, and the lounges of the hospital.

All in all, the number of people on the list was formidable. Unfortunately he had no other ideas to pursue save for the camera surveillance, and he knew such an operation would prove too costly. He would investigate prices and put together a proposal, but he knew Dr. Mason would find the price unacceptable.

Harris's plan was to go through the fifty or so files rather quickly to see if anything caught his attention, anything that might seem unlikely or strange. If he found something that was questionable, he'd put the file in a group to investigate first. Harris wasn't a psychologist any more than he was a doctor, but he thought that whoever was crazy enough to be killing patients would have to have something weird on his record.

The first file belonged to Ramon Concepcion, a food service employee. Concepcion was a thirty-five-year-old man of Cuban extraction who'd worked a number of food service jobs in hotels and restaurants since he was sixteen. Harris read through his employment application and looked at the references. He even glanced at his health care utilization. Nothing jumped out at him. He tossed the file on the floor.

One by one, Harris worked through the box of files. Nothing caught his eye until he came to Gary Wanamaker, another food service employee. Under the heading experience Gary had listed five years' work in the kitchen at Rikers Island Prison in New York. In the employment photo the man had brown hair. Harris put that file on the corner of his desk.

It was only five files later that Harris came across another file that caught his eye. Tom Widdicomb worked in housekeeping. What got Harris's attention was the fact that the man had trained as an emergency medical technician. Even though he'd had a series of housekeeping jobs subsequent to his EMT training, including a stint at Miami General Hospital, the thought of a guy with emergency medical training working housekeeping seemed odd. Harris looked at the employment photo. The man had brown hair. Harris put Widdicomb's file on top of Wanamaker's.

A few files later, Harris came across another file that tweaked his curiosity. Ralph Seaver worked for the maintenance department. This man had served time for rape in Indiana. There it was right in the file! Included was even a phone number of the man's former probation officer in Indiana. Harris shook his head. He'd not expected to find such fertile material. The professional staff files had been boring in comparison. Except for a few substance abuse problems and one child molestation allegation, he'd not found anything. But with this group, he'd only gone through a quarter of the files and had already yanked three that he thought deserved a closer look.

Instead of sitting down and having coffee on her afternoon coffee break, Janet took the elevator to the second floor and visited the intensive care unit. She had a lot of respect for the nurses who worked there. She never understood how they could take the constant strain. Janet had tried the ICU after graduation. She found the work intellectually stimulating, but after a few weeks decided it wasn't for her. There was too much tension, and too little patient interaction. Most of the patients were in no position to relate on any level; many of them were unconscious.

Janet went over to Gloria's bed and looked down at her. She was still in a coma and had not improved, although she was still breathing without mechanical assistance. Her widely dilated pupils had not constricted, nor did they react to light. Most disturbing of all, an EEG showed very little brain activity.

A visitor was gently stroking Gloria's forehead. She was about thirty years old with coloring and features similar to Gloria's. As Janet raised her head, their eyes met.

"Are you one of Gloria's nurses?" the visitor asked.

Janet nodded. She could tell the woman had been crying.

"I'm Marie," she said. "Gloria's older sister."

"I'm very sorry this happened," Janet said.

"Well," Marie said with a sigh, "maybe it's for the best. This way she won't have to suffer."

Janet agreed for Marie's benefit, although in her own heart she felt differently. Gloria had still had a shot at beating breast cancer, especially with her positive, upbeat attitude. Janet had seen people with even more advanced disease go into remission.

Fighting tears of her own, Janet returned to the fourth floor. Again, she threw herself into her work. It was the easiest way to avoid thoughts that would only leave her cursing the unfairness of it all. Unfortunately the ruse was only partly successful, and she kept seeing the image of Gloria's face as she thanked Janet for starting her IV. But then suddenly the ruse was no longer needed. A new tragedy intervened that matched Gloria's and overwhelmed Janet.

A little after two, Janet gave an intramuscular injection to a patient whose room was at the far end of the corridor. On her way back to the nurses' station, she decided to check in on Helen Cabot.

Earlier that morning and about an hour after Janet had added the coded medication to Helen's IV and adjusted the rate, Helen complained of a headache. Concerned about her condition, Janet had called Dr. Mason and informed him of this development. He'd recommended treating the headache minimally and asked to be called back if it got worse.

Although the headache had not gone away after the administration of an oral analgesic, it had not grown worse. Nevertheless, Janet had checked on Helen frequently at first, then every hour or so throughout the day. With the headache unchanged and her vital signs and level of consciousness remaining normal, Janet's concern had lessened.

Now, almost 2:15, as Janet came through the door, she was alarmed to discover that Helen's head had lolled to the side and off the pillow. Approaching the bed, she noticed something even more disturbing: the woman's breathing was irregular. It was waxing and waning in a pattern that suggested a serious neurological dysfunction. Janet phoned the nurses' station and told Tim she had to speak with Marjorie immediately.

"Helen Cabot is Cheyne-Stoking," Janet said when Marjorie came on the line, referring to Helen's breathing.

"Oh no!" Marjorie exclaimed. "I'll call the neurologist and Dr. Mason."

Janet took the pillow away and straightened Helen's head. Then she took a small flashlight she always carried and shined it in each of Helen's pupils. They weren't equal. One was dilated and unresponsive to the light. Janet shuddered. This was something she'd read about. She guessed that the pressure had built up inside Helen's head to the point that part of her brain was herniating from the upper compartment into the lower, a life-threatening development.

Reaching up, Janet slowed Helen's IV to a "keep open" rate. For the moment that was all she could do.

Soon other people started to arrive. First it was Marjorie and other nurses. Then the neurologist, Dr. Burt Atherton, and an anesthesiologist, Dr. Carl Seibert, rushed in. The doctors began barking orders in an attempt to lower the pressure inside Helen's head. Then Dr. Mason arrived, winded by his run from the research building.

Janet had never met Dr. Mason, although she'd spoken with him on the phone. He was titularly in charge of Helen's case, but in this neurological crisis he deferred to Dr. Atherton.

Unfortunately, none of the emergency measures worked, and Helen's condition deteriorated further. It was decided that emergency brain surgery was needed. To Janet's dismay, arrangements were made to transfer Helen to Miami General Hospital.

"Why is she being transferred?" Janet asked Marjorie when she had a moment.

"We're a specialty hospital," Marjorie explained. "We don't have a neuro-surgical service."

Janet was shocked. The kind of emergency surgery Helen needed required speed. It did not require an entire neurosurgical service, just an operating room and someone who knew how to make a hole in the skull. Obviously with the biopsies they'd been doing, that expertise was available at the Forbes.

With frantic preparations, Helen was readied to leave. She was moved from her bed onto a gurney. Janet aided in the transfer, moving Helen's feet, then running alongside holding the IV bottle aloft as the gurney was rushed to the elevator.

In the elevator Helen took a turn for the worse. Her breathing, which had been irregular when Janet had entered her room, now stopped altogether. Helen's pale face quickly began to turn blue.

For the second time that day, Janet started mouth-to-mouth resuscitation while the anesthesiologist yelled for someone to get an endotracheal tube and an Ambu bag as soon as they got to the first floor.

When the elevator stopped and the doors opened, one of the fourth-floor nurses rushed out. Another kept the doors from closing. Janet continued her efforts until Dr. Seibert nudged her aside and deftly slipped in an endotracheal tube. After connecting the Ambu bag, he began to inflate Helen's lungs to near capacity. The blue cast to Helen's face transformed into a translucent alabaster.

"Okay, let's go," Dr. Seibert yelled.

The tightly packed group rushed Helen out to the ambulance receiving dock, collapsed the gurney, and pushed it inside the waiting vehicle. Dr. Seibert boarded with Helen, maintaining her respiration. The doors were slammed shut and secured.

With flashing light and piercing siren, the ambulance roared out of the parking bay and disappeared around the building.

Janet turned to look at Marjorie, who was standing next to Dr. Mason. She was consoling him with her hand on his shoulder.

"I can't believe it," Dr. Mason was saying with a halting voice. "I suppose I should have prepared myself. It was bound to happen. But we've been so lucky with our medulloblastoma treatments. With every success, I thought just maybe we could avoid this kind of tragedy."

"It's the people in Boston's fault," Ms. Richmond said. She'd appeared on the scene just before the ambulance had left. "They wouldn't listen to us. They kept her too long."

"We should have put her in the ICU," Dr. Mason said. "But she'd been so stable."

"Maybe they'll save her at Miami General," Marjorie said, trying to be optimistic.

"It would be a miracle," Dr. Atherton said. "It was pretty clear her uncus had herniated below the calyx and was compressing her medulla oblongata."

Janet repressed an urge to tell the man to keep his thoughts to himself. She hated the way some doctors hid behind their jargon.

All at once, as if on some unseen cue, the entire group turned and disappeared through the swinging doors of the Forbes ambulance dock. Janet was left outside. She was just as glad to be alone. It was suddenly so peaceful by the lawn. A huge banyan tree graced the grounds. Behind the banyan was a flowering tree Janet had never seen before. A warm, moist tropical breeze caressed her face. But the pleasant scene was still marred by the undulating siren of the receding ambulance. To Janet, it sounded like a death knell for Helen Cabot.

Tom Widdicomb wandered from room to room in his mother's ranch house, alternately crying and cursing. He was so anxious he couldn't sit still. One minute he was hot, the next freezing. He felt sick.

In fact, he'd felt so sick he'd gone to his supervisor and told him as much. The supervisor had sent him home, commenting that he was pale. He'd even noticed that Tom was shaking.

"You've got the whole weekend," the supervisor had said. "Go to bed, sleep it off. It's probably a touch of the 'snowbird flu.' "

So Tom had gone home, but he'd been unable to rest. The problem was Janet Reardon. He'd almost had a heart attack when she'd come knocking on Gloria's door minutes after he'd put Gloria to sleep. In an absolute panic he'd fled into the bathroom, sure that he'd been cornered. He'd gotten desperate enough to take his gun out.

But then the pandemonium in the room gave him the diversion he needed to get away. When he'd emerged from the bathroom, no one had even noticed. He'd been able to slip into the hall with his bucket.

The problem was that Gloria was still alive. Janet Reardon had saved her, and Gloria was still suffering, although now she was out of reach. She was in the ICU where Tom was not allowed to go.

Consequently, Alice still wouldn't talk to him. Tom had continued to plead, but without success. Alice knew Tom couldn't get to Gloria until she was transferred out of the ICU and put back into a private room.

That left Janet Reardon. To Tom, she seemed like a devil sent to destroy the life that he and his mother had created. He knew he had to get rid of her. Only now he didn't know where she lived. Her name had been removed from the residence chart in administration. She'd moved out.

Tom checked his watch. He knew her shift ended when his would have ended: three P.M. But he also knew nurses stayed longer because of their report. He'd have to be in the parking lot when she came out. Then he could follow her home and shoot her. If he was able to do that he was reasonably confident Alice would break this petulant silence and talk with him.

"Helen Cabot died!" Janet repeated through sudden tears. As a professional it wasn't like her to cry over the death of a patient, but she was extra sensitive since there'd been two tragedies in the same day. Besides, Sean's response frustrated her. He was more interested in where Helen's body was than the fact that the woman was dead.

"I understand she died," Sean said soothingly. "I don't mean to sound callous. Part of the way I respond is to cover the pain I feel. She was a wonderful person. It's such a shame. And to think that her father runs one of the largest computer software companies in the world."

"What difference does that make?" Janet snapped. She wiped under her eyes with the knuckle of her index finger.

"Not much," Sean admitted. "It's just that death is such a leveler. Having all the money in the world makes no difference."

"So now you're a philosopher," Janet said wryly.

"All of us Irish are philosophers," Sean said. "It's how we deal with the tragedy of our lives."

They were sitting in the cafeteria where Sean had agreed to come when Janet called him. She'd called him after report, before she left for the apartment. She'd said she needed to talk.

"I don't mean to upset you," Sean continued. "But I'm truly interested in the location of Helen's body. Is it here?"

Janet rolled her eyes. "No, it's not here," she said. "I don't know where it is truthfully. But I suppose it's over at the Miami General."

"Why would it be there?" Sean asked. He leaned across the table.

Janet explained the whole episode, indicating her indignation that they couldn't do an emergency craniotomy at the Forbes.

"She was in extremities," Janet said. "They never should have transferred her. She never even made it to the OR. We heard she died in the Miami General emergency room."

"How about you and me driving over there?" Sean suggested. "I'd like to find her."

For a moment, Janet thought Sean was kidding. She rolled her eyes again, thinking Sean was about to make some sick joke.

"I'm serious," Sean said. "There's a chance they'll do an autopsy. I'd love to have a tumor sample. For that matter, I'd like to have some blood and even some cerebrospinal fluid."

Janet shuddered in revulsion.

"Come on," Sean said. "Remember, we're in this thing together. I'm really sorry she died—you know I am. But now that she's dead, we should concentrate on the science. With you in a nursing uniform and me in a white coat, we'll have the run of the place. In fact, let's bring some of our own syringes just in case."

"In case of what?" Janet asked.

"In case we need them," Sean said. He winked conspiratorially. "It's best to be prepared," he added.

Either Sean was the world's best salesman or she was so stressed out, she was incapable of resisting. Fifteen minutes later she found herself climbing into the passenger side of Sean's 4×4 to head over to a hospital she'd never visited, in hopes of obtaining the brain tissue of one of her patients who'd just expired.

"That's him." Sterling pointed at Sean Murphy through the car's windshield for Wayne Edwards's benefit. Wayne was a formidable Afro-American whose services Sterling enlisted when he did business in south Florida. Wayne was an ex–Army sergeant, ex-policeman, and ex–small businessman who'd gone into the security business. He was an ex from as many things as Sterling was, and like Sterling, he now used his varied experience for a similar career. Wayne was a private investigator, and although he specialized in domestic squabbles, he was talented and effective in other areas as well. Sterling had met him a few years previously when both were representing a powerful Miami businessman.

"He looks like a tough kid," Wayne said. He prided himself on instantaneous assessments.

"I believe he is," Sterling said. "He was an all-star hockey player from Harvard who could have played professionally if he'd been inclined."

"Who's the chick?" Wayne asked.

"Obviously one of the nurses," Sterling said. "I don't know anything about his female liaisons."

"She's a looker," Wayne said. "What about Tanaka Yamaguchi? Have you seen him lately?"

"No, I haven't," Sterling said. "But I think I will. My contact at the FAA told me the Sushita jet has just refiled a flight plan to Miami."

"Sounds like action," Wayne said.

"In a way, I hope so," Sterling said. "It will give us a chance to resolve this problem."

Wayne started his dark green Mercedes 420SEL. The windows were heavily tinted. From the outside it was difficult to see within, especially in bright sunlight. He eased the car away from the curb and headed for the exit. Since a hospital shift had changed half an hour earlier, there was still considerable traffic leaving the parking area. Wayne allowed several cars to come between his car and Sean's. Once on Twelfth, they headed north over the Miami River.

"I got sandwiches and drinks in the cooler in the back seat," Wayne said while motioning over his shoulder.

"Good thinking," Sterling said. That was one of the things he liked about Wayne. He thought ahead.

"Well, well," Wayne said. "Short trip. They're turning already."

"Isn't this another hospital?" Sterling asked. He leaned forward to survey the building Sean was approaching.

"This area is hospital city, man," Wayne said. "You can't drive a mile without running into one. But they're heading to the mama hospital. That's Miami General."

"That's curious," Sterling said. "Maybe the nurse works there."

"Uh-oh," Wayne said. "I do believe we have company."

"What do you mean?" Sterling asked.

"See that lime green Caddy behind us?" Wayne asked.

"It would be hard to miss it," Sterling said.

"I've been watching it since we crossed the Miami River," Wayne said. "I have the distinct impression it's following our Mr. Murphy. I wouldn't have noticed it except I used to have wheels just like it in my younger days. Mine was burgundy. Good car, but a devil to parallel park."

Sterling and Wayne watched as Sean and his companion entered the hospital through the emergency entrance. Not far behind was the man who'd arrived in the lime green Cadillac.

"I think my initial impression was correct," Wayne said. "Looks to me like that dude is tighter on their tail than we are."

"I don't like this," Sterling said. He opened the passenger door, got out, and glanced back at the dumpy Cadillac. Then he bent down to talk to Wayne. "This is not Tanaka's style, but I can't risk it. I'm going in. If Murphy comes out, follow him. If the man in the Cadillac comes out first, follow him. I'll be in touch over the cellular phone."

Grabbing his portable phone, Sterling hurried after Tom Widdicomb, who was climbing the steps on the side of the ambulance dock outside the Miami General emergency room.

With the assistance of a harried resident in the emergency room who'd given them directions, it did not take Sean and Janet long to find the pathology department. Once there, Sean sought out another resident. He told Janet that between the residents and the nurses you could find out anything you wanted to know about a hospital.

"I'm not doing autopsies this month," the resident said, trying to rush away.

Sean blocked his path. "How can I find out if a patient will be posted?" he asked.

"You have the chart number?" the resident asked.

"Just the name," Sean said. "She died in the ER."

"Then we probably won't be autopsying the case," the resident said. "ER deaths are usually assigned to the medical examiner."

"How can I be sure?" Sean persisted.

"What's the name?"

"Helen Cabot," Sean said.

The resident graciously went over to a nearby wall phone and made a call. It took him less than two minutes to ascertain that Helen Cabot was not scheduled.

"Where do bodies go?" Sean asked.

"To the morgue," the resident said. "It's in the basement. Take the main elevators to B1 and follow the red signs with the big letter M on them."

After the resident hurried on, Sean looked at Janet. "You game?" he asked. "If we find her then we'll know her disposition for sure. We might even be able to get a little body fluid."

"I've come this far," Janet said with resignation.

Tom Widdicomb felt calmer than he had all day. At first he'd been dismayed when Janet had appeared with a young guy in a white coat, but then things took a turn for the better when the two went directly to the Miami General. Having worked there, Tom knew the place from top to bottom. He also knew that Miami General would be crowded with people at that time of day since formal visiting hours had just started. And crowds meant chaos. Maybe he would get his chance at Janet and wouldn't even have to follow her home. If he had to shoot the fellow in the white coat, too bad!

Following the couple within the hospital had not been easy, especially once they went to pathology. Tom had thought he'd lost them and was about to return to the parking lot to keep an eye on the 4×4 when they suddenly reappeared. Janet came so close, he was sure she'd recognize him. He'd panicked, but luckily hadn't moved. Fearing Janet would scream as she had in the Forbes residence, he'd gripped the pistol in his pocket. If she had screamed he would have had to shoot her on the spot.

But Janet glanced away without reacting. Obviously she'd failed to identify him. Feeling more secure, Tom followed the pair more closely. He even rode down in the same elevator with them, something he'd not been willing to do when they'd gone up to pathology.

Janet's friend pushed the button for B1, and Tom was ecstatic. Of all the locations in Miami General, Tom liked the basement the best. When he'd worked at this hospital, he snuck down there many times to visit the morgue or to read the newspaper. He knew the labyrinthine tunnels like the back of his hand.

Tom's anxiety about Janet recognizing him returned when everyone else but a doctor and a uniformed maintenance man got off on the first floor. But even with so slim a crowd to lose himself in, Janet failed to remember him.

As soon as the elevator reached the basement, the doctor and the maintenance man turned right and walked quickly away. Janet and Sean paused briefly, looking in both directions. Then they turned left.

Tom waited behind in the elevator until the doors began to shut. Bumping them open, he stepped out and followed the couple, keeping at a distance of about fifty feet. He slipped his hand in his pocket and gripped the gun. He even put his finger between the trigger and its guard.

The farther from the elevators the couple walked, the better Tom liked it. This was a perfect location for what he had to do. He couldn't believe his luck.

They were entering an area of the basement few people visited. The only sounds were their footfalls and the slight hissing of steam pipes.

"This place feels appropriately like Hades," Sean said. "I wonder if we're lost."

"There haven't been any turnoffs since the last M sign," Janet said. "I think we're okay."

"Why do they always put morgues in such isolated places?" Sean said. "Even the lighting is getting lousy."

"It's probably near a loading dock," Janet said. Then she pointed ahead. "There's another sign. We're on the right track."

"I think they want their mistakes as far away as possible," Sean quipped. "It wouldn't be good advertising to have the morgue near the front entrance."

"I forgot to ask how you made out with the medicine I got for you."

"I haven't gotten very far," Sean admitted. "What I did was start a gel electrophoresis."

"That tells me a lot," Janet said sarcastically.

"It's actually simple," Sean said. "I suspect the medicine is made up of proteins because they have to be using some sort of immunotherapy. Since proteins all have electric charges, they move in an electrical field. When you put them in a specific gel, which coats them with a uniform charge, they move only in relation to their size. I want to find out how many proteins I'm dealing with and what their approximate molecular weight is. It's a first step."

"Just make sure you learn enough to justify the effort for getting it," Janet said.

"I hope you don't think you're off the hook with this one sample," Sean said. "Next time I want you to get some of Louis Martin's."

"I don't think I can do it again," Janet said. "I can't break any more vials. If I do, they'll be suspicious for sure."

"Try a different method," Sean suggested. "Besides, I don't need so much."

"I thought by bringing the whole vial you'd have plenty," Janet said.

"I want to compare the medicines from different patients," Sean said. "I want to find out how they differ."

"I'm not sure they differ," Janet said. "When I went up to Ms. Richmond's office to get another vial, she took it from a large stock. I got the feeling they are all being treated by the same two drugs."

"I can't buy that," Sean said. "Every tumor is distinct antigenically, even the same kind of tumor. Oat cell cancer from one person will be different antigenically from the same type of cancer from another. In fact, if it arises as a new tumor even in the same person it will be antigenically distinct. And antigenically distinct tumors require different antibodies."

"Maybe they use the same drug until they biopsy the tumor," Janet suggested.

Sean looked at her with renewed respect. "That's an idea," he said.

Finally they rounded a corner and found themselves in front of a large insulated door. A metal sign at chest level read: *Morgue. Unauthorized Entry Forbidden.* Next to the door were several light switches.

"Uh-oh," Sean said. "I guess they were expecting us. That's a rather formidable bolt action lock. And I didn't bring my tools."

Janet reached out and yanked on the door. It opened.

"I take that back," Sean said. "Guess they didn't expect us. At least not today."

A cool breeze issued from the room and swirled about their legs. Sean flipped on the lights. For a split second there was no response. Then raw fluorescent light blinked on.

"After you," Sean said gallantly.

"This was your idea," Janet said. "You first."

Sean stepped in with Janet immediately following. Several wide, concrete supporting piers blocked a view of the entire space, but it was obviously a large room. Old gurneys littered the room haphazardly. Each bore a shrouded body. The temperature, according to a gauge on the door, was forty-eight degrees.

Janet shivered. "I don't like this."

"This place is huge," Sean said. "Either the architects had a low opinion of the competence of the medical staff, or they planned for a national disaster."

"Let's get this over with," Janet said, hugging herself. The cold air was damp and penetrating. The smell was like a musty wet basement that had been closed for years.

Sean yanked back a sheet. "Oh, hello," he said. The bloodied face of a partially crushed construction worker stared up at him. He was still in his work clothes. Sean covered the man and went to the next.

Despite her revulsion, Janet did the same, going in the opposite direction.

"Too bad they're not in alphabetical order," Sean said. "There must be fifty bodies in here. This is one scene the Miami Chamber of Commerce wouldn't want to get up north."

"Sean!" Janet called, since they'd moved apart. "I think your humor is tasteless."

They worked around opposite ends of one of the concrete piers.

"Come on, Helen," Sean called in a childlike singsong. "Come out, come out wherever you are."

"That's especially crude," Janet said.

Tom Widdicomb was filled with excited anticipation. Even his mother had decided to break her long silence to tell him how clever he'd been to follow Janet and her friend into Miami General. Tom was well acquainted with the morgue. For what he intended to do, he couldn't have found a better place.

Approaching the insulated door, Tom pulled his gun from his pocket. Holding the pistol in his right hand, he pulled the thick door open and looked inside.

Not seeing Janet or her friend, he stepped into the morgue and let the door ease closed. He couldn't see the couple but he could hear them. He distinctly heard Janet tell the man in the white coat to shut up.

Tom grasped the brass knob of the heavy lock on the door and slowly turned it. Silently the bolt slid into the striker plate. When Tom had worked at Miami General, the lock had never been used. He doubted if a key existed. Locking it ensured that he would not be disturbed.

"You're a smart man," Alice whispered.

"Thank you, Mom," Tom whispered back.

Holding the gun in both hands as he'd seen them do on TV, Tom moved forward, heading toward the nearest of the concrete piers. He could tell from Janet and her friend's voices that they were just on the opposite side of it.

"Some of these people have been in here for a while," Sean said. "It's like they've been forgotten."

"I was thinking the same thing," Janet said. "I don't think Helen Cabot's body is here. It would have been near the door. After all, she just died a few hours ago."

Sean was about to agree when the lights went out. With no windows and the door heavily girdled with insulating weather stripping, it wasn't just dark, it was absolutely black, like the vortex of a black hole.

The instant the lights went out there was an ear-piercing scream followed by hysterical sobbing. At first Sean thought it was Janet, but having known where she was before the darkness enveloped him, he could tell that the crying was coming from behind the wall near the door to the hall.

So if it wasn't Janet, Sean thought, who was it?

The agony was infectious. Even the sudden darkness wouldn't have disturbed Sean ordinarily, but combined with the terrorized wailing, he found himself on the border of panic. What kept him from losing control was concern about Janet.

"I hate the dark," the voice cried out suddenly amid weeping. "Someone help me!"

Sean didn't know what to do. From the direction of the wailing came the sounds of frenzied commotion. Gurneys were bumping into each other, spilling their bodies onto the concrete floor.

"Help me!" the voice screamed.

Sean thought about calling out to try to calm the anguished individual, but he couldn't decide if that was a good idea or not. Unable to decide, he stayed quiet.

After the sound of more gurneys clanking against each other, there was a low-pitched thump as if someone had hit up against the insulated door. That was followed by a mechanical click.

For a moment a small amount of light fingered its way around the concrete pier. Sean caught sight of Janet with her hands pressed against her mouth. She was only about twenty feet from him. Then the darkness descended again like a heavy blanket. This time it was accompanied by silence.

"Janet?" Sean called softly. "You okay?"

"Yes," she answered. "What in God's name was that?"

"Move toward me," Sean said. "I'm coming toward you."

"All right," Janet said.

"This place is nuts," Sean said, wanting to keep talking as they groped toward each other. "I thought Forbes was weird, but this place takes the prize hands down. Remind me not to match here for my internship."

At last their groping hands met. Holding on to each other, they weaved their way through the gurneys in the direction of the door. Sean's foot nudged a body on the floor. He warned Janet she'd have to step over it.

"I'll have nightmares about this the rest of my life," Janet said.

"This is worse than Stephen King," Sean said.

Sean collided with the wall. Then, moving laterally, he felt the door. He pushed it open, and they both stumbled into the deserted corridor, blinking in the light.

Sean cupped Janet's face in his hands. "I'm sorry," he said.

"Life is never boring with you," Janet said. "But it wasn't your fault. Besides, we made it. Let's get out of here."

Sean kissed the end of her nose. "My feelings exactly."

Mild concern they would have trouble finding their way to the elevators proved unwarranted. In minutes the two were climbing into Sean's 4×4 and heading out of the parking lot.

"What a relief," Janet said. "Do you have any idea what happened in there?"

"I don't," Sean said. "It was so weird. It was like it was staged to scare us to death. Maybe there's some troll living in the basement who does that to everyone."

As they were about to exit the parking area, Sean put on the brake suddenly, enough to make Janet reach out to support herself against the dash.

"What now?" she asked.

Sean pointed. "Look what we have here. How convenient," he said. "That brick building is the medical examiner's office. I had no idea it was so close. It must be fate telling us that Helen's body is over there. What do you say?"

"I'm not wild about the idea," Janet admitted. "But as long as we're here . . ."

"That's the ticket," Sean said.

Sean parked in visitor parking, and they entered the modern building. Inside they approached an information desk. A cordial black woman asked if she could be of assistance.

Sean told her that he was a medical student and Janet was a nurse. He asked to speak with one of the medical examiners.

"Which one?" the receptionist asked.

"How about the director?" Sean suggested.

"The chief is out of town," the receptionist said. "How about the deputy chief?"

"Perfect," Sean said.

After a short wait they were buzzed through an inner glass door and directed to a corner office. The deputy chief was Dr. John Stasin. He was about Sean's height but of slight build. He seemed genuinely pleased that Sean and Janet had stopped by.

"Teaching is one of our major functions," he said proudly. "We encourage the professional community to take an active interest in our work."

"We're interested in a specific patient," Sean said. "Her name is Helen Cabot. She died this afternoon in the Miami General emergency room."

"Name doesn't ring a bell," Dr. Stasin said. "Just a minute. Let me call downstairs." He picked up the phone, mentioned Helen's name, nodded, and said "yeah" a few times, then hung up. It all happened extremely rapidly. It was apparent that grass did not grow under Dr. Stasin's feet.

"She arrived a few hours ago," Dr. Stasin said. "But we won't be posting her."

"Why not?" Sean asked.

"Two reasons," Dr. Stasin said. "First, she had documented brain cancer which her attending physician is willing to aver as the cause of death. Second, her family has expressed strong feelings against our posting her. In this kind of circumstance we feel it is better not to do it. Contrary to popular opinion, we're receptive to the family's wishes unless, of course, there is evidence of foul play or a strong suggestion that the public weal would be served by an autopsy."

"Is there a chance of getting any tissue samples?" Sean asked.

"Not if we don't do the autopsy," Dr. Stasin said. "If we did, the tissues removed would be available at our discretion. But since we're not posting the patient, property rights rest with the family. Besides, the body has already been picked up by the Emerson Funeral Home. It's on its way to Boston sometime tomorrow."

Sean thanked Dr. Stasin for his time.

"Not at all," he said. "We're here every day. Give a call if we can help."

Sean and Janet retraced the route to the car. The sun was setting; rush hour was in full swing.

"Surprisingly helpful individual," Janet said.

Sean only shrugged. He leaned his forehead against the steering wheel.

"This is depressing," he said. "Nothing seems to be going our way."

"If anyone should be melancholy it should be me," Janet reminded him, noting how glum he'd suddenly become.

"It's an Irish trait to be melancholy," Sean said. "So don't deny me. Maybe these difficulties we're having are trying to tell me something, like I should be heading back to Boston to do some real work. I never should have come down here."

"Let's go get something to eat," Janet said. She wanted to change the subject. "We could go back to that Cuban restaurant on the beach."

"I don't think I'm hungry," Sean said.

"A little *arroz con pollo* will make all the difference in the world," Janet said. "Trust me."

Tom Widdicomb had every light on in the house despite the fact that it wasn't even dark outside. But he knew it would be dark soon, and the idea terrified him. He did not like the dark. Even though it was hours after the terrible episode in the Miami General morgue he was still shaking. His mother had done something similar to him once when he was about six. He'd gotten irritated at her when she said he couldn't have any more ice cream, and he'd threatened to tell the teacher at school that they slept together unless she gave him more. Her response had been to shut him in a closet overnight. It had been Tom's worst experience. He'd been afraid of both the dark and closets ever since.

Tom had no idea how the lights had gone off in the morgue except that when he had finally found the door and pushed it open, he'd practically collided with a man dressed in a suit and tie. Since Tom had still had the gun in his hand, the man had backed away, giving Tom the opportunity to bolt down the corridor. The man had given chase, but Tom had lost him easily in the network of tunnels, corridors, and connecting rooms he knew so well. By the time Tom exited from an isolated basement door with outside steps leading to the parking area, the man was nowhere in sight.

Still panicked, Tom had run to his car, started it, and had headed toward the parking area exit. Fearing that whoever had chased him in the basement might have somehow gotten out faster than he, Tom had been watchful as he drove, and since the parking lot was not busy at that time, he'd seen the green Mercedes almost immediately.

Passing his intended exit, Tom had gone to another one that was seldom used. When the green Mercedes had followed suit, Tom was convinced he was being followed. Consequently, he concentrated on losing the car in the afternoon rush hour. Thanks to a traffic light and a few cars that had come between them, Tom had been able to speed away. He had driven aimlessly for half an hour just to make sure he was no longer being followed. Only then did he return home.

"You never should have gone into Miami General," Tom said, lambasting himself for his mother's benefit. "You should have stayed outside, waited, and followed her home."

Tom still had no idea where Janet lived.

"Alice, talk to me!" he shouted. But Alice wasn't saying a word.

All Tom could think to do was wait until Janet got off work on Saturday. Then he'd follow her. He'd be more careful. Then he'd shoot her.

"You'll see, Mom," Tom said to the freezer. "You'll see."

Janet had been right, although Sean wasn't about to admit it. What had especially perked him up were the tiny cups of Cuban coffee. He'd even tried what the people at the neighboring table had done. He'd drunk them like shots of alcohol, letting the mouthful of strong, thick, sweet fluid fall into his stomach in a bolus. The taste had been intense and the mild euphoria almost immediate.

The other thing that had helped Sean out of his dejected mood was Janet's positive attitude. Despite her difficult day and the episode at Miami General, she'd found the stamina to remain upbeat. She reminded Sean that they were doing rather well for only two days' effort. They had the thirty-three charts of the previous medulloblastoma patients and she'd managed to get two vials of the secret medicine. "I think that's pretty good progress," Janet said. "At this rate we're sure to get to the bottom of the Forbes success in treating these people. Come on, cheer up! We can do it!"

Janet's enthusiasm and the caffeine finally combined to win Sean over.

"Let's find out where this Emerson Funeral Home is located," he said.

"Why?" Janet asked, leery of such a suggestion.

"We can do a drive-by," Sean said. "Maybe they're working late. Maybe they give out samples."

The funeral home was on North Miami Avenue near the city cemetery and Biscayne Park. It was a well-cared-for two-story Victorian clapboard structure with dormers. It was painted white with a gray slate roof and was surrounded on three sides by a wide porch. It gave the impression that it had been a private home.

The rest of the neighborhood was not inviting. The immediately adjacent buildings were constructed of concrete block. There was a liquor store on one side and a plumbing supply store on the other. Sean parked directly in front in a loading zone.

"I don't think they're open," Janet said, gazing up at the building.

"Lots of lights," Sean said. All the ground-floor lights were on except for the porch lights. The second floor was completely dark. "I think I'll give it a try."

Sean got out of the car, climbed the steps, and rang the bell. When no one answered, he looked into the windows. He even looked into some of the side windows before he came back to the car and got in. He started the engine.

"Where are we going now?" she asked.

"Back to the Home Depot," Sean said. "I need some more tools."

"I don't like the sound of this," Janet said.

"I can drop you off at the apartment," Sean suggested.

Janet was silent. Sean drove first to the apartment out on Miami Beach. He pulled over to the curb and stopped. They hadn't spoken en route.

"What exactly are you planning to do?" she asked at last.

"Continue my quest for Helen Cabot," Sean said. "I won't be long."

"Are you planning on breaking into that funeral home?" Janet asked.

"I'm going to 'ease in,'" Sean said. "That sounds better. I just want a few samples. If worse comes to worst, how bad is it? She's already dead."

Janet hesitated. At that point she had the door open and one foot out. As crazy as Sean's plan was, she felt responsible to a degree. As Sean had already pointed out several times, this whole venture had been her idea. Besides, she thought she'd go crazy sitting in the apartment waiting for him to return. Pulling her foot back into the car, Janet told Sean that she'd changed her mind and that she'd go along.

"I'm coming as a voice of rationality," she said.

"Okay by me," Sean said equably.

At Home Depot Sean bought a glass cutter, a suction device for lifting large pieces of glass, a Sheetrock knife, a small handheld jigsaw, and a cooler. After that he stopped at a 7-Eleven, where he bought ice for the cooler and a few cold drinks. Then he drove back to the Emerson Funeral Home and parked again in the loading zone.

"I think I'll wait here," Janet said. "By the way, I think you're crazy."

"You're entitled to your opinion," Sean said. "I'd rather think of myself as determined."

"A cooler and cold drinks," Janet commented. "It's as if you think you're going on a picnic."

"I just like to be prepared," Sean said.

Sean hefted his pack of tools and the cooler and went up onto the funeral home porch.

Janet watched him check the windows. Several cars drove by in both directions. She was amazed at his sangfroid. It was as if he believed himself to be invisible. She watched as he went to a side window toward the back and put down his sack. Bending over, he took out some of the tools.

"Damn it all!" Janet said. With irritation she opened the door, climbed the funeral home's front steps, and walked around to where Sean was busily working. He'd attached the suction device to the window.

"A change of heart?" Sean asked without looking at Janet. He ran the glass cutter deftly around the perimeter of the window.

"Your lunacy floors me," Janet said. "I can't believe you're doing this."

"Brings back fond memories," Sean said. With a decisive tug, he pulled a large segment of the window glass out and laid it on the porch planking. After leaning inside, he told Janet that the alarm was a simple sash alarm, which was what he'd guessed.

Sean reached in with his tools and the cooler and set them on the floor. After stepping through the window himself, he leaned back out.

"If you're not coming in, it would be better if you waited in the car," he said. "A beautiful woman hanging around on a funeral home porch at this hour might attract some attention. This might take me a few minutes if I find Helen's body."

"Give me a hand!" Janet said impulsively as she tried to follow Sean's easy step through the window.

"Watch the edges!" Sean warned. "They're like razors."

Once Janet was inside, Sean hefted the tools and handed the cooler to Janet. "Nice of them to leave the lights on for us," he said.

The two big rooms in the front were viewing rooms. The room they'd entered was a casket display room with eight caskets exhibited. Their lids were propped open. Across a narrow hall was an office. In the rear of the house, extending from one side to the other was the embalming room. The windows were covered with heavy drapes.

There were four stainless steel embalming tables. Two were occupied by shrouded corpses. The first was a heavyset woman who looked lifelike enough to be asleep except for the large Y-shaped, crudely sutured incision on the front of her torso. She'd been autopsied.

Moving to the second body, Sean lifted the sheet.

"Finally," Sean said. "Here she is."

Janet came over and mentally prepared herself before looking. The sight was less disturbing than she'd imagined. Like the other woman, Helen Cabot appeared in sleeplike repose. Her color was better than it had been in life. Over the last few days she'd become so pale.

"Too bad," Sean commented. "She's already been embalmed. I'll have to forgo the blood sample."

"She appears so natural," Janet said.

"These embalmers must be good," Sean said. Then he pointed to a large glass-fronted metal cabinet. "See if you can find me some needles and a scalpel."

"What size?"

"I'm not choosy," Sean said. "The longer the needle the better."

Sean plugged in the jigsaw. When he tried it, it made a fearful noise.

Janet found a collection of syringes, needles, even suture material, and latex rubber gloves. But no scalpels. She brought what she'd found over to the table.

"Let's get the cerebrospinal fluid first," Sean said. He pulled on a pair of the gloves.

He had Janet help roll Helen onto her side so that he could insert a needle in the lumbar area between two vertebrae.

"This will only hurt for a second," Sean said as he patted Helen's upturned hip.

"Please," Janet said. "Don't joke around. You'll only upset me more than I already am."

To Sean's surprise he got cerebrospinal fluid on the first try. He'd only performed the maneuver on living patients a couple of times. He filled the syringe, capped it, and put it on the ice in the cooler. Janet let Helen roll back supine.

"Now for the hard part," he said, coming back to the embalming table. "I'm assuming you've seen an autopsy."

Janet nodded. She'd seen one but it had not been a pleasant experience. She braced herself as Sean prepared.

"No scalpels?" he asked.

She shook her head.

"Good thing I got this Sheetrock knife," Sean said. He picked up the knife and extended the blade. Then he ran it around the back of Helen's head from one ear to the other. Grasping the top edge of the incision, Sean yanked. With the kind of ripping sound of a weed being uprooted, Helen's scalp pulled away from her skull. Sean pulled it all the way down over Helen's face.

He palpated the craniotomy hole on the left side of Helen's skull that had been done at the Boston Memorial, then looked for the one on the right, the one done at Forbes two days previously.

"That's weird," he said. "Where the hell is the second craniotomy hole?"

"Let's not waste time," Janet said. Although she'd been nervous when they had entered, her anxiety was steadily increasing with each passing minute.

Sean continued to look for the second craniotomy hole, but finally gave up. Picking up the jigsaw, he looked at Janet. "Stand back. Maybe you don't want to watch. This isn't going to be pretty."

"Just do it," Janet said.

Sean pushed the jigsaw blade into the craniotomy hole he'd found and turned the saw on. It bit into the bone and almost yanked itself out of his hands. The job would not be as easy as Sean had envisioned.

"You have to steady the head," Sean told Janet.

Grasping either side of Helen's face, Janet vainly tried to keep the head from jerking from side to side as Sean struggled to hold the bucking jigsaw. With great difficulty he managed to saw off a skull cap of bone. He had intended to keep the blade depth equal to the thickness of the skull, but it had been impossible. The saw blade had dug into the brain in several places, shredding the surface.

"This is disgusting," Janet said. She straightened up and brushed herself off.

"It's not a bone saw," Sean admitted. "We had to improvise."

The next part was almost as difficult. The Sheetrock knife was much larger than a scalpel, and Sean had difficulty inserting it below the brain to cut through the spinal cord and cranial nerves. He did the best he could. Then, inserting his hands on either side within the skull, he grasped the mutilated brain and yanked it out.

After taking the cold drinks out of the cooler, Sean dropped the brain onto the ice. Then he popped the top on one of the drinks and offered it to Janet. Sweat was beading his forehead.

Janet declined. She watched as he took a long drink, shaking her head in amazement. "Sometimes I don't believe you," she said.

Suddenly they both heard a siren. Janet panicked and started back for the display room, but Sean restrained her.

"We have to get out of here," Janet whispered urgently.

"No," Sean said. "They wouldn't come with a siren. It has to be something else."

The sound of the siren built. Janet felt her heart racing faster and faster. Just when the siren sounded as if it were coming into the house, its pitch abruptly changed.

"Doppler effect," Sean said. "A perfect demonstration."

"Please!" Janet pleaded. "Let's go. We got what you wanted."

"We have to clean up," Sean said, putting his drink down. "This is supposed to be a clandestine operation. See if you can find a broom or a mop. I'll put Helen back together so no one will know the difference."

Despite her agitation, Janet did as Sean asked. She worked feverishly. When she was done, Sean was still suturing the scalp back in place using subcutaneous stitches. When he was finished, he pulled her hair over the incision. Janet was impressed. Helen Cabot's body appeared undisturbed.

They carried the tools and the cooler back to the casket display room.

"I'll go out first and you hand me the stuff," Sean said. He ducked and stepped through the window.

Janet handed out the things.

"You need help?" Sean asked. His arms were full.

"I don't think so," Janet said. Coming in had not been that difficult.

Sean started toward the car with his bundles.

Janet mistakenly grasped the edge of the glass before stepping through. In her haste she'd forgotten Sean's earlier warning. Feeling the razor-sharp edge cut into four of her fingers, she recoiled in pain. Glancing at her hand she saw an oozing line of blood. She clutched her hand and silently cursed.

Since she was on the inside now, she decided it would be far easier and less dangerous to get out by opening the window. There was no need to risk getting cut by the glass again. Without thinking, she undid the lock and pushed up the sash. Immediately the alarm sounded.

Struggling out the window, Janet ran after Sean. She got to the car just after he'd stashed the cooler on the floor of the back seat. In unison, they jumped into the front and Sean started the car.

"What happened?" he demanded as he pulled the car into the street.

"I forgot about the alarm," Janet admitted. "I opened the window. I'm sorry. I told you I wasn't good at this."

"Well, no problem," Sean said as he turned right at the first intersection and headed east. "We'll be long gone before anybody responds."

What Sean didn't see was the man who'd come out of the liquor store. He'd responded to the alarm immediately, and he'd seen Janet and Sean getting into the 4×4. He also got a good look at the license plate. Returning inside his store he wrote down the numbers before he forgot them. Then he called the Miami police.

Sean drove back to Forbes so that Janet could get her car. By the time they pulled into the parking area, Janet had calmed down to some degree. Sean stopped next to her rental car. She opened the door and started to get out.

"Are you coming right back to the apartment?" she asked.

"I'm going to head up to my lab," Sean said. "You want to come?"

"I have to work tomorrow," Janet reminded him. "And it's been a tough day. I'm exhausted. But I'm afraid to let you out of my sight."

"I'm not going to be long," Sean said. "Come on! There are only a couple of things I want to do. Besides, tomorrow is Saturday and we'll go on that little vacation I promised you. We'll leave after you get off work."

"Sounds like you've already decided where we'll go," Janet said.

"I have," Sean said. "We'll drive across the Everglades to Naples. I hear it is quite a place."

"All right, it's a deal," Janet said, closing her door. "But tonight you have to get me home before midnight at the latest."

"No problem," Sean said as he drove around to the research building side of the parking lot.

"At least the Sushita jet hasn't left Washington," Sterling said. He was sitting in Dr. Mason's office. Wayne Edwards was there too, as were Dr. Mason and Margaret Richmond. "I don't believe Tanaka will make a move until the jet is here and available," he added.

"But you said Sean had been followed," Dr. Mason said. "Who was following him?"

"I was hoping you could enlighten us," Sterling said. "Do you have any idea why someone would be following Mr. Murphy? Wayne noticed him when we crossed the Miami River."

Dr. Mason glanced at Ms. Richmond, who shrugged. Dr. Mason looked back at Sterling. "Could this mystery individual be in the employ of Tanaka?"

"I doubt it," Sterling said. "It's not Tanaka's style. If Tanaka makes a move, Sean will just disappear. There won't be any warning. It will be smooth and professional. The individual who was following Sean was disheveled. He was wearing a soiled open-necked brown shirt and trousers. And he certainly wasn't acting like the sort of professional Tanaka would enlist."

"Tell me exactly what happened," Dr. Mason demanded.

"We followed Sean and a young nurse out of the Forbes parking area around four," Sterling said.

"The nurse would be Janet Reardon," Ms. Richmond interjected. "The two are friends from Boston."

Sterling nodded. He motioned for Wayne to write the name down. "We'll need to investigate her as well. It's important to eliminate the possibility of them working as a team."

Sterling described following Sean to Miami General and his instructions to Wayne to follow the unknown man in brown if he came out first.

Dr. Mason was surprised to learn that Sean and his nurse friend had headed to the morgue. "What on earth were they doing there?"

"That was something else I was hoping you could tell us," Sterling said.

"I can't imagine," Dr. Mason said, shaking his head. He again looked at Ms. Richmond. She shook her head as well.

"When the mysterious man entered the morgue behind Sean Murphy and Miss Reardon," Sterling continued, "I only got a quick glimpse. But it was my impression he was holding a gun. That later proved to be correct. At any rate I was concerned for Mr. Murphy's safety, so I rushed to the morgue door only to find it locked."

"How dreadful," Ms. Richmond said.

"There was only one thing I could do," Sterling said. "I turned off the lights."

"That's a nice touch," Dr. Mason said. "Good thinking."

"I'd hoped the people within wouldn't hurt each other until I could conceive of a way to get the door open," Sterling said. "But there was no need. The man in brown apparently has a strong phobia of the dark. Within a short time he burst from the room significantly distraught. It was then that I saw the gun clearly. I gave chase, but unfortunately I was attired in leather-soled shoes, which put me at a distinct disadvantage to his running shoes. Besides, he seemed entirely familiar with the terrain. When it was clear that I'd lost him, I returned to the morgue. By then Sean and Miss Reardon had already departed as well."

"And Wayne followed the man in brown?" Dr. Mason asked.

"He tried," Sterling said.

"I lost him," Wayne admitted. "It was rush hour, and I was unlucky."

"So now we have no idea where Mr. Murphy is," Dr. Mason moaned. "And we have a new worry about an unknown assailant."

"We have a colleague of Mr. Edwards watching the Forbes residence for Sean's return," Sterling said. "It is important we find him."

The phone on Dr. Mason's desk rang. Dr. Mason answered it.

"Dr. Mason, this is Juan Suarez in security," the voice at the other end told him. "You asked me to call if Mr. Sean Murphy appeared. Well, he and a nurse just came in and went up to the fifth floor."

"Thank you, Juan," Dr. Mason said with relief. He hung up the phone. "Sean Murphy is safe," he reported. "He just came into the building, probably to inject more mice. What dedication! I tell you, I think the kid is a winner and worth all this trouble."

It was after ten o'clock at night when Robert Harris left Ralph Seaver's apartment. The man had not been particularly cooperative. He'd resented Harris's bringing up his rape conviction in Indiana which he'd dubbed "ancient history." Harris didn't think much of Seaver's self-serving assessment, but he mentally took the man off his list of suspects the minute he laid eyes on him. The attacker had been described as being of medium height and medium build. Seaver was at least six-eight and probably weighed two hundred and fifty pounds.

Climbing into his dark blue Ford sedan, Harris picked up the last file in his priority category. Tom Widdicomb lived in Hialeah, not too far from where Harris was. Despite the hour, Harris decided to drive by the man's home. If the lights were on, he'd ring the bell. Otherwise he'd let it go until morning.

Harris had already made several background calls regarding Tom Widdicomb. He'd found out that the man had taken an EMT course and had passed the exam for his license. A call to an ambulance firm where Tom had worked didn't yield much information. The owner of the company refused to comment, explaining that the last time he talked about a former employee the tires of two of his ambulances were slashed.

A call to Miami General had been a bit more helpful but not by much. A personnel officer said that Mr. Widdicomb and the hospital had parted ways by mutual agreement. The officer admitted he'd not met Mr. Widdicomb; he was merely reading from the employment file.

Harris had also checked with Glen, the housekeeping supervisor at the Forbes Hospital. Glen said that Tom was dependable from his point of view, but that he frequently clashed with his colleagues. He said that Tom worked better on his own.

The last call Harris had made was to a veterinarian by the name of Maurice Springborn. That number, however, was no longer in service and information did not have another number. So all in all, Harris hadn't turned up anything incriminating concerning Tom Widdicomb. As he drove into Hialeah and searched for 18 Palmetto Lane, he was not optimistic.

"Well, at least the lights are on," Harris said as he pulled over to the curb in front of an ill-kept ranch-style house. In sharp contrast to the other modest homes in the neighborhood, Tom Widdicomb's was lit up like Times Square on New Year's Eve. Every light inside and outside the house was blazing brightly.

Getting out of the car, Harris stared at the house. It was amazing how much light emanated from it. Shrubbery three houses away cast sharp shadows. As he walked up the driveway, he noticed the name on the mailbox was Alice Widdicomb. He wondered how she and Tom were related.

Mounting the front steps, Harris rang the bell. As he waited he eyed the house. It was decorated in a plain style with faded pastel colors. The trim was badly in need of paint.

When no one responded to the bell, Harris rang again and put his ear to the door to make sure the bell was functioning. He heard it clearly. It was hard to believe no one was home with all the lights on.

After a third ring, Harris gave up and returned to his car. Rather than leave immediately, he sat staring at the house, wondering what could motivate people to illuminate their house so brightly. He was just about to start his engine when he thought he saw some movement by the living room window. Then he saw it again. Someone in the house had definitely moved a drape. Whoever it was seemed to be trying to catch a peek at Harris.

Without a moment's hesitation, Harris climbed out of his car and went back to the stoop. He leaned on the doorbell, giving it one long blast. But still no one came.

Disgustedly, Harris returned to his car. He used his car phone to call Glen to see if Tom Widdicomb was scheduled to work the next day.

"No, sir," Glen said with his southern accent. "He's not scheduled to work until Monday. Good thing, too. He was under the weather today. He looked terrible. I sent him home early."

Harris thanked Glen before hanging up. If Widdicomb wasn't feeling well and was home in bed, why all the lights? Was he feeling so bad he couldn't even come to the door? And where was Alice, whoever she was?

As Harris drove away from Hialeah he pondered what he should do. There was something weird going on at the Widdicombs'. He could always go back and stake out the house, but that seemed extreme. He could wait until Monday when Tom showed up for work, but what about in the meantime? Instead, he decided he'd go back the following morning to see if he could catch a glimpse of Tom Widdicomb. Glen had said he was of medium height and medium build with brown hair.

Harris sighed. Sitting in front of Tom Widdicomb's house was not his idea of a great Saturday, but he was desperate. He felt he'd better make some headway on the breast cancer deaths if he was interested in remaining employed at Forbes.

Sean was whistling softly while he worked, the picture of contented concentration. Janet watched from a high stool similar to Sean's that she'd dragged over to the lab bench. In front of him was an array of glassware.

It was at quiet times like this that Janet found Sean so appealingly attractive. His dark hair had fallen forward to frame his downturned face with soft ringlets, which had an almost feminine look in stark contrast to his hard, masculine features. His nose was narrow at the top where it joined the confluence of his heavy eyebrows. It was a straight nose except for the very tip where it slanted inward before joining the curve of his lips. His dark blue eyes were fixated unblinkingly on a clear plastic tray in his strong but nimble fingers.

He glanced up to look directly at Janet. His eyes were bright and shining. She could tell he was excited. At that moment she felt inordinately in love, and even the recent episode at the funeral home receded into her mind for the moment. She wanted him to take her in his arms and tell her that he loved her and wanted to spend the rest of his life with her.

"These initial silver stain electrophoresis gels are fascinating," Sean said, shattering Janet's fantasy. "Come and look!"

Janet pushed off her stool. At the moment she wasn't interested in electrophoresis gels, but she felt she had little choice. She didn't dare risk lessening his enthusiasm. Still, she was disappointed he didn't sense her affectionate feelings.

"This is the sample from the larger vial," Sean explained. "It's a non-reducing gel so you can tell by the control that it has only one component, and its molecular weight is about 150,000 daltons."

Janet nodded.

Sean picked up the other gel and showed it to her. "Now, the medicine in the small vial is different. Here there are three separate bands, meaning there are three separate components. All three have much smaller molecular weights. My guess is that the large vial contains an immunoglobulin antibody while the small vial most likely contains cytokines."

"What's a cytokine?" Janet asked.

"It's a generic term," Sean said. He got off his own stool. "Follow me," he said. "I've got to get some reagents."

They used the stairs. As they walked, Sean continued to explain. "Cytokines are protein molecules produced by cells of the immune system. They're involved in cell-to-cell communication, signaling cues like when to grow, when to start doing their thing, when to get ready for an invasion of virus, bacteria, or even tumor cells. The NIH has been busy growing the lymphocytes of cancer patients in vitro with a cytokine called interleukin-2, then injecting the cells back into the patient. In some cases they've had some good results."

"But not as good as the Forbes with their medulloblastoma cases," Janet said.

"Definitely not as good," Sean said.

Sean loaded himself and Janet with reagents from the storeroom; then they started back to his lab.

"This is an exciting time in biological science," Sean said. "The nineteenth century was the century for chemistry; the twentieth century was the century for physics. But the twenty-first century will belong to molecular biology; it's when all three—chemistry, physics, and biology—are going to merge. The results will be astounding, like science fiction come true. In fact, we're already seeing it happen."

By the time they got back in the lab Janet found herself becoming genuinely interested despite the day's emotional traumas and her fatigue. Sean's enthusiasm was infectious.

"What's the next step with these medicines?" she asked.

"I'm not sure," Sean admitted. "I suppose we should see what kind of reaction we get between the unknown antibody in the large vial and Helen Cabot's tumor."

Sean asked Janet to get out some scissors and a scalpel from a drawer near where she was standing. Sean took the cooler over to the sink, and after putting on a pair of latex rubber gloves, he lifted out the brain and rinsed it off. From beneath the sink he pulled out a cutting board. He put the brain on the board.

"I hope I don't have trouble finding the tumor," he said. "I've never tried to do anything like this before. Judging by the MRI we did in Boston, her largest tumor is in the left temporal lobe. That was the one they biopsied up there. I suppose that's the one I should go after." Sean oriented the brain so that he could determine the front from the back. Then he made several slices into the temporal lobe.

"I have an almost irresistible urge to joke about what I'm doing here," he said.

"Please don't," Janet said. It was hard for her to deal with the fact that this was the brain of a person with whom she'd so recently related.

"Now this looks promising," Sean said. He spread the edges of his most recent incision. At the base was a comparatively dense and more yellow-appearing tissue bearing tiny but visible cavities. "I think those spots might be areas where the tumor outgrew its own blood supply."

Sean asked Janet to give him a hand, so she pulled on a pair of the rubber gloves and held the cut edges of the brain apart while Sean took a sample of the tumor with the scissors.

"Now we have to separate the cells," he said, putting the sample in tissue culture medium, then adding enzymes. He put the flask in the incubator to give the enzymes a chance to work.

"Next we have to characterize this immunoglobulin," he said, holding up the larger of the two vials of unknowns. "And to do this we have a test called ELISA where we use commercially made antibodies to identify specific types of immunoglobulins." He placed the large vial on the countertop and picked up a plastic plate that had ninety-six tiny circular wells. In each of the wells he put a different capture antibody and allowed it to bind. Then he blocked any remaining binding sites in the wells with bovine serum albumin. Next he put a small aliquot of the unknown in each of the wells.

"Now I have to figure out which antibody has reacted to the unknown," he said, washing each of the wells to rid them of any of the unknown immunoglobulin that hadn't reacted. "We do this by adding to each well the same antibody that was originally in the well, only this time tagged with a compound that's enzymatically capable of yielding a colored reaction." This last substance had the characteristic of turning a pale lavender.

The whole time Sean was doing this test, he kept up a running explanation for Janet. She'd heard of the test but had never seen it performed.

"Bingo!" Sean said when one of the many wells turned the appropriate color to match controls he'd set up in sixteen of the end wells. "The unknown is no longer an unknown. It's a human immunoglobulin called IgG1."

"How did Forbes make it?" Janet asked.

"That's a good question," Sean said. "I'd guess by monoclonal antibody technique. Although it is not out of the question to make it by recombinant DNA technology. The problem there is that it's a big molecule."

Janet had a vague idea of what Sean was talking about and had definitely become interested in the process of figuring out what these unknown medicines were, but suddenly her physical exhaustion could no longer be ignored. Glancing at her watch she could understand why. It was almost midnight.

Feeling ambivalent about interrupting Sean's enthusiasm which she'd been trying hard to bolster, she reached out and grasped his arm. He was holding a Pasteur pipette. He'd started ELISA plates for the second unknown.

"Do you have any idea of the time?" she asked.

Sean glanced at his watch. "My word, time does fly when you're having a good time."

"I've got to work tomorrow," she said. "I've got to get some sleep. I suppose I could go back to the apartment by myself."

"Not at this hour," Sean said. "Just let me finish what I'm doing here, then I want to run a quick immuno-fluorescence test to see the level of reaction between the IgGl and Helen's tumor cells. I'll use an automatic diluter. It will only take a few minutes."

Janet reluctantly agreed. But she couldn't sit on a stool any longer. Instead she dragged out an armchair from the glass-enclosed office. Less than half an hour later, Sean's enthusiasm went up another notch. The ELISA test on the second unknown had identified three cytokines: interleukin-2, which as he explained to Janet was a T lymphocyte growth factor; tissue necrosis factor alpha, which was a stimulant for certain cells to kill foreign cells like cancer cells; and interferon gamma, which was a substance that seemed to help activate the entire immune system.

"Aren't the T cells the ones that disappear in AIDS?" Janet asked. She was having progressive difficulty staying awake.

"Right on," Sean said. He was now holding a number of slides on which he'd run fluorescence antibody tests at different dilutions of the unknown immunoglobulin. Slipping one of the very high dilution slides under the objective of the fluorescein scope, Sean put his eyes to the eyepiece.

"Wow!" he exclaimed. "The intensity of this reaction is unbelievable. Even at a one to ten thousand dilution this IgGl antibody reacts with the tumor four plus. Janet, come and take a look at this!"

When Janet didn't respond, Sean looked up from the eyepieces of the binocular scope. Janet was slouched in the chair. She'd fallen fast asleep.

Seeing Janet sleeping, Sean immediately felt guilty. He hadn't considered how exhausted she must be. Standing up and stretching his tired arms, he stepped over to Janet and looked down at her. She seemed particularly angelic in her repose. Her face was framed by her fine blond hair. Sean felt an urge to kiss her. Instead, he gently shook her shoulder.

"Come on," he whispered. "Let's get you to bed."

Janet was already buckled in Sean's car when her sleepy mind reminded her she'd brought her own car that morning. She mentioned it to Sean.

"Are you in any condition to drive?" Sean asked.

She nodded. "I want my car," she said, leaving no room for discussion.

Sean pulled around to the hospital and let her out. Once she had her car started, he let her lead the way. And as they pulled out into the street, Sean was too intent on Janet to notice the dark green Mercedes which slowly began to follow them both without the benefit of its headlights.

MARCH 6 • SATURDAY, 4:45 A.M.

As soon as Sean's eyes fluttered open, he was instantly awake. He couldn't wait to get to the lab to unravel more of the medulloblastoma mystery cure. The little work that he'd been able to do the night before had merely whetted his appetite. Despite the early hour, he slipped out of bed, showered, and dressed.

When Sean was ready to leave for the lab he tiptoed back into the dark bedroom and gently nudged Janet. He knew she'd want to sleep until the last possible moment but there was something he wanted to tell her.

Janet rolled over and groaned: "Is it time to get up already?"

"No," Sean whispered. "I'm off to the lab. You can go back to sleep for a few minutes. But I wanted to remind you to pack some things for our overnight trip to Naples. I want to leave this afternoon when you get off work."

"Why do I have the feeling you have some ulterior motive in this?" Janet asked, rubbing her eyes. "What's with Naples?"

"I'll tell you on our way there," Sean said. "If we leave from the Forbes we'll beat the traffic out of Miami. Don't pack a lot of stuff. All you'll need is something for dinner tonight, a bathing suit, and jeans. One other thing," Sean added, leaning over her.

Janet looked into his eyes.

"I want you to get some of Louis Martin's medicine this morning," he said.

Janet sat up. "Great!" she exclaimed sarcastically. "How do you expect me to do that? I told you how hard it was to get Helen's samples."

"Calm down," Sean said. "Just give it a try. It could be important. You said that you thought the medicine all came from a single batch. I want to prove it's impossible. I don't need a lot, and just some from the larger vial. Even a few cc's will do."

"They control the medicine more carefully than a narcotic," Janet complained.

"What about diluting it with saline?" Sean suggested. "You know, the old trick of putting water in your parents' liquor bottles. They're not going to know the concentration changed."

Janet thought about the suggestion. "You think it could hurt the patient?"

"I can't see how," Sean said. "More than likely it's designed with a wide safety margin."

"All right, I'll try," Janet said with reluctance. She hated being deceptive and devious with Marjorie.

"That's all I can ask," Sean said. He kissed her on the forehead.

"Now I can't get back to sleep," she complained as Sean headed for the door.

"We'll be sure to get lots of sleep over the weekend," he promised.

As Sean made his way out to his 4×4 there was only a slight hint of dawn in the eastern sky. To the west the stars twinkled as if it were still the middle of the night.

Pulling away from the curb, he was already preoccupied with the work ahead in the lab and oblivious to his surroundings. Once again he failed to notice the dark green Mercedes as it too pulled out into the light traffic several cars behind.

Inside the Mercedes Wayne Edwards was dialing his car phone, calling Sterling Rombauer at the Grand Bay Hotel in Coconut Grove.

A sleepy Sterling picked up on the third ring.

"He's left the lair and is heading west," Wayne said. "Presumably to Forbes."

"Okay," Sterling said. "Stay with him. I'll join you. I was just informed a half an hour ago that the Sushita jet is winging south at this very moment."

"Sounds like game time," Wayne said.

"That's my assumption," Sterling said.

Anne Murphy was depressed again. Charles had come home, but he'd only stayed one night. And now that he was gone, the apartment seemed so lonely. He was such a pleasure to be with, so calm and so close to God. She was still in bed, wondering if she should get up, when the front door buzzer sounded.

Anne reached for her plaid robe and headed for the kitchen. She wasn't expecting anyone, but then she hadn't been expecting the two callers inquiring about Sean, either. She remembered her promise not to talk to any strangers about Sean or Oncogen.

"Who is it?" Anne asked, pressing the talk button of her intercom.

"Boston police," a voice replied.

A shiver went down Anne's spine as she buzzed the door open. She was sure this visit meant Sean had reverted to his old ways. After quickly brushing out her hair, she went to the door. A man and a woman were standing there, dressed in Boston police uniforms. Anne had never seen either of them before.

"Sorry to bother you, ma'am," the female officer said. She held up her identification. "I'm Officer Hallihan and this is Officer Mercer."

Anne was clutching the lapels of her robe, holding it closed. The police had come to the door a number of times when Sean had been a teenager. This visit brought back bad memories.

"What's the problem?" Anne asked.

"Are you Anne Murphy, mother of Sean Murphy?" Officer Hallihan asked. Anne nodded.

"We're here at the request of the Miami police," Officer Mercer said. "Do you know where your son Sean Murphy is currently?"

"He's at the Forbes Cancer Center in Miami," Anne said. "What's happened?"

"We don't know that," Officer Hallihan said.

"Is he in trouble?" Anne asked, afraid to hear the answer.

"We really have no information," Officer Hallihan said. "Do you have an address for him there?"

Anne went to the telephone table in the hall, copied down the address of the Forbes residence, and gave it to the police.

"Thank you, ma'am," Hallihan said. "We appreciate your cooperation."

Anne closed the door and leaned against it. In her heart, she knew that what she'd feared had happened: Miami had been the bad influence she'd suspected; Sean was in trouble again.

As soon as she thought she was composed enough, Anne called Brian at home.

"Sean's in trouble again," she blurted when Brian answered. Tears came as soon as she got the words out.

"Mom, try to control yourself," Brian said.

"You have to do something," Anne said between sobs.

Brian got his mother to calm down enough to tell him what had happened and what the police had said.

"It's probably some traffic violation," Brian said. "He probably drove over someone's lawn, something like that."

"I think it's worse," Anne sniffled. "I know it is. I can feel it. That boy will be the death of me."

"How about if I come over?" Brian said. "I'll make some calls in the meantime and check it out. I bet it's something minor."

"I hope so," Anne said as she blew her nose.

While Anne waited for Brian to drive over from Marlborough Street, she dressed and began putting her hair up. Brian lived across the Charles River in Back Bay, and since it was Saturday with no traffic, he was there in half an hour. When he buzzed to let her know he was on his way up, Anne was putting in the last of her hairpins.

"Before I left my apartment I put in a call to a lawyer colleague in Miami by the name of Kevin Porter," Brian told his mother. "He works for a firm we do business with in the Miami area. I told him what had happened, and he said he had an in with the police and could find out what's going on."

"I know it's bad," Anne said.

"You don't know it's bad!" Brian said. "Now don't get yourself all worked up. Remember last time you ended up in the hospital."

The call from Kevin Porter came within minutes of Brian's arrival.

"I'm afraid I don't have great news for you," Kevin said. "A liquor store owner got your brother's tag leaving the scene of a burglary."

Brian sighed and looked at his mother. She was sitting on the very edge of a straight-backed chair with her hands clasped together in her lap. Brian was furious with Sean. Didn't he ever consider the effects of his escapades on their poor mother?

"It's a weird story," Kevin continued. "It seems that a dead body was mutilated and, you ready for this . . . ?"

"Let me have the whole story," Brian said.

"Somebody stole the brain out of the body," Kevin said. "And this body wasn't some derelict. The deceased was a young woman whose father is some business bigwig up there in Beantown."

"Here in Boston?"

"Yup, and there's a big ruckus down here because of his connections," Kevin said. "Pressure is being put on the police to do something. The state's attorney has drawn up a list of charges a mile long. The medical examiner who looked at the body guessed the skull had been opened with a jigsaw."

"And Sean's 4×4 was seen leaving the scene?" Brian asked. He was already trying to think of a defense.

"Afraid so," Kevin said. "Plus one of the medical examiners says your brother and a nurse were at the medical examiner's office only a few hours before asking about the same body. Seems they wanted samples. Looks like they got them. Obviously the police are looking for your brother and the nurse for questioning and probably arrest."

"Thanks, Kevin," Brian said. "Let me know where you'll be today. I might need you, especially if Sean is arrested."

"You can reach me all weekend," Kevin said. "I'll leave word at the station to call me if your brother is picked up."

Brian slowly replaced the receiver and looked at his mother. He knew she wasn't ready for this, especially since she thought Sean was alone in Sodom and Gomorrah.

"Do you have Sean's phone numbers handy?" he asked. He tried to keep the concern out of his voice.

Anne got them for him without speaking.

Brian called the residence first. He let it ring a dozen times before giving up. Then he tried calling the Forbes Cancer Center research building. Unfortunately all he got was a recording saying that the switchboard was open Monday through Friday, eight until five.

Picking the phone back up decisively, he called Delta Airlines and made a reservation on the noon flight to Miami. Something strange was going on, and he thought he'd better be there in the thick of things.

"I was right, wasn't I?" Anne said. "It's bad."

"I'm sure it's all some misunderstanding," Brian said. "That's why I think I should go down there and clear things up."

"I don't know what I did wrong," Anne said.

"Mother," Brian said. "It's not your fault."

Hiroshi Gyuhama's stomach was bothering him. His nerves were on edge. Ever since Sean had frightened him in the stairwell, he'd been reluctant to spy on the man. But this morning he'd had no choice. He checked on Sean as soon as he saw the 4×4 in the parking lot so early in the day. When he saw that Sean was feverishly working in his lab, Hiroshi returned to his office.

Hiroshi was doubly upset now that Tanaka Yamaguchi was in town. Hiroshi had met him at the airport two days earlier and had driven him to the Doral Country Club where he planned to stay and play golf until the final word came from Sushita.

The final word had come late Friday night. After reviewing Tanaka's memorandum, the Sushita board had decided that Sean Murphy was a risk to the Forbes investment. Sushita wanted him in Tokyo forthwith where they would "reason" with him.

Hiroshi was not at all comfortable around Tanaka. Knowing of the man's associations with the Yakusa made Hiroshi extremely wary. And Tanaka gave subtle hints that he did not respect Hiroshi. He'd bowed when they met, but he hadn't bowed very low, and not for very long. Their conversation on the way to the hotel had been inconsequential. Tanaka did not mention Sean Murphy. And once they arrived at the hotel, Tanaka had ignored Hiroshi. Worst of all he did not invite Hiroshi to play golf.

All these slights were painfully obvious to Hiroshi; the implications were clear.

Hiroshi dialed the Doral Country Club Hotel and asked to speak with Mr. Yamaguchi. He was transferred to the clubhouse since Mr. Yamaguchi had scheduled a tee time in twenty minutes.

Tanaka came on the line. He was particularly curt when he heard Hiroshi's voice. Speaking in rapid Japanese, Hiroshi got directly to the point.

"Mr. Sean Murphy is here at the research center," Hiroshi said.

"Thank you," Tanaka said. "The plane is on its way. All is in order. We will be at Forbes this afternoon."

Sean had started the morning off in high spirits. After the initial ease of identifying the immunoglobulin and the three cytokines, Sean had expected just as rapid progress in determining exactly what kind of antigen the immunoglobulin reacted to. Since it reacted so strongly with the tumor cell suspension, he reasoned that the antigen had to be membrane-based. In other words, the antigen had to be on the surface of the cancer cells.

To assure himself of this assumption as well as confirm that the antigen was at least partially a peptide, Sean had treated intact cells from Helen's tumor with trypsin. When he tried to see if these digested cells reacted with the immunoglobulin, he quickly learned they did not.

But from that moment on, Sean had run into trouble. He could not characterize this membrane-based antigen. His idea was to try innumerable known antigens and see if they reacted with the antigen binding portion of the unknown immunoglobulin. None reacted. Using literally hundreds of cell lines grown in tissue culture, he spent hours filling the little wells, but he got no reaction. He was particularly interested in cell lines whose origins were from neural tissues. He tried normal cells and transformed or neoplastic cells. He tried digesting all the cells with detergents in increasing concentration, first to open the cell membranes and expose cytoplasmic antigens, then to open nuclear membranes to expose nuclear antigens. Still nothing reacted. There wasn't a single episode of immunofluorescence in any of hundreds of tiny wells.

Sean couldn't believe how difficult it was turning out to be to find an antigen to react with the mysterious immunoglobulin. So far he hadn't even gotten a partial reaction. Just when he was losing patience, the phone rang. He walked to a wall extension to answer it. It was Janet.

"How's it going, Einstein?" she asked brightly.

"Terrible," Sean said. "I'm not getting anywhere."

"I'm sorry to hear that," Janet said. "But I've got something that might brighten your day."

"What?" Sean asked. At the moment he couldn't imagine anything except the antigen he was seeking. But Janet certainly wouldn't be able to supply that.

"I got a sample of Louis Martin's large vial medicine," Janet said. "I used your idea."

"Great," Sean said without much enthusiasm.

"What's the matter?" Janet questioned. "I thought you'd be pleased."

"I am pleased," he said. "But I'm also frustrated with the stuff I have; I'm at a loss."

"Let's meet so I can give you this syringe," Janet said. "Maybe you need a break."

They met as usual in the cafeteria. Sean took advantage of the time to get something to eat. As before, Janet passed Sean the syringe under the table. He slipped it into his pocket.

"I brought my overnight bag, as requested," she said, hoping to lighten Sean's mood.

Sean merely nodded as he ate his sandwich.

"You seem a lot less excited about our trip than you did this morning," Janet commented.

"I'm just preoccupied," Sean said. "I never would have guessed I'd not find some antigen that would react with the mysterious immunoglobulin."

"My day hasn't been so great either," Janet said. "Gloria is no better. If anything, she's a little worse. Seeing her makes me depressed. I don't know about you, but I'm really looking forward to getting away. I think it will do us both some good. Maybe a little time away from the lab will give you some ideas."

"That would be nice," Sean said dully.

"I'll be off sometime around three-thirty," Janet said. "Where shall we meet?"

"Come over to the research building," Sean said. "I'll meet you downstairs in the foyer. If we leave from that side, we'll miss the shift-change crowd in the hospital."

"I'll be there with bells on," Janet said brightly.

Sterling reached over the seat and nudged Wayne. Wayne, who'd been sleeping in the back, sat up quickly.

"This looks promising," Sterling said. He pointed through the windshield at a black stretch Lincoln Town Car that was parking at the curb midway between the hospital building and the research building. Once the car stopped, a Japanese man got out of the rear and gazed up at the two buildings.

"That's Tanaka Yamaguchi," Sterling said. "Can you tell how many people are in the limousine with your glasses?"

"It's difficult to see through the tinted windows," Wayne said, using a small pair of binoculars. "There's a second man sitting in the back seat. Wait a sec. The front door is opening as well. I can see two more. That's four people total."

"That's what I'd expect," Sterling said. "I trust that they're all Japanese."

"You got it, man," Wayne said.

"I'm surprised they're here at Forbes," Sterling said. "Tanaka's preferred technique is to abduct people in an isolated location so there will be no witnesses."

"They'll probably follow him," Wayne suggested. "Then just wait for the right spot."

"I imagine you are right," Sterling said. He saw a second man get out of the limousine. He was tall compared to Tanaka. "Let me have a look with those binoculars," Sterling said. Wayne passed them over the seat. Sterling adjusted the focus of the glasses and studied the two Orientals. He didn't recognize the second one.

"Why don't we go over there and introduce ourselves?" Wayne suggested. "Let them know this is a risky operation. Maybe they'd give up the whole plan."

"That would only serve to alert them," Sterling said. "It's better this way. If we announce ourselves too soon they'll merely operate more clandestinely. We have to catch them in the act so we have something we can use to bargain with them."

"It seems like such a cat-and-mouse game," Wayne said.

"You are absolutely correct," Sterling said.

Robert Harris had been sitting in his car a few doors down from Tom Widdicomb's home on Palmetto Lane in Hialeah since early that morning. Although he'd been there for over four hours, Harris had seen no sign of life except that the lights had all gone out. Once he thought he saw the curtains move the way they had the night before, but he couldn't be certain. He thought maybe in his boredom his eyes were playing tricks on him.

Several times Harris had been on the verge of giving up. He was wasting too much valuable time on one individual who was suspicious only because of a career switch, the fact that he kept all his lights on, and because he wouldn't answer his doorbell. Yet the idea that the attack on the two nurses could be related to the cancer patient episodes gnawed at Harris. With no other current ideas or leads, he stayed where he was.

It was just after two P.M., and just when Harris was about to leave to deal with hunger and other bodily needs, that he first saw Tom Widdicomb. The garage door went up, and there he was, blinking in the bright sunlight.

Physically, Tom fit the bill. He was of medium height and medium build with brown hair. His clothes were mildly disheveled. His shirt and pants were unpressed. One sleeve of his shirt was rolled up to mid-forearm, the other was down but unbuttoned. On his feet were old, lightweight running shoes.

There were two cars in the garage: a huge, vintage lime green Cadillac convertible and a gray Ford Escort. Tom started the Ford with some difficulty. Once the engine caught, black smoke billowed out of the exhaust as if the car had not been started for some time. Tom backed it out of the garage, closed the garage door manually, then got back into the Escort. When he pulled out of the driveway, Harris let him build up a lead before following.

Harris did not have any preconceived plan. When he first saw Tom the moment the garage door opened, he considered getting out of the car and having a conversation with the man. But he'd held back, and now he was following him for no specific reason. But soon it became apparent where Tom was headed, and Harris got progressively interested. Tom was heading for the Forbes Cancer Center.

When Tom entered the parking lot, Harris followed but purposefully turned in the opposite direction to avoid Tom's noticing him. Harris stopped quickly, opened the door, and stood on the running board as he watched Tom cruise around the parking lot and finally stop near the entrance to the hospital.

Harris got back into his car and worked his way closer, finding a vacant spot about fifty feet from the Escort. What was going through his mind was the possibility that Tom Widdicomb might be stalking the second nurse to be attacked, Janet Reardon. If that were true, perhaps he'd been the one who had attacked her, and if he had, maybe he was the breast cancer patients' killer.

Harris shook his head. It was all so conjectural, with so many "ifs" and so contrary to the way he liked to think and act. He liked facts, not vague suppositions. Yet this was all he had for the moment, and Tom Widdicomb was acting strange: staying in a house with every light on; hiding out most of the day; now loitering in the hospital parking area on his day off, especially when he was supposed to be home sick. As ridiculous as it all might have sounded from a rational point of view it was enough to keep Harris sitting in his car wishing he'd had the foresight to bring sandwiches and Gatorade.

When Sean returned from his meeting with Janet, he changed the direction of his investigations. Instead of attempting to characterize the antigenic specificity of Helen Cabot's medicine, he decided to determine exactly how Louis Martin's medicine differed from hers. A rapid electrophoresis of the two showed them to be of approximately the same molecular weight, which he'd expected. An equally rapid ELISA test with the anti-human immunoglobulin IgGl confirmed it was the same class of immunoglobulins as Helen's. He'd also expected that.

But then he discovered the unexpected. He ran a fluorescence antibody test with Louis Martin's medicine with Helen's tumor and got just as strong a positive reaction as he'd gotten with Helen's medicine! Even though Janet believed that the medicines came from the same source, Sean did not believe they could be the same. From what he knew about the antigenic specificity of cancers and their antibodies, it was extremely improbable. Yet now he was faced with the fact that Louis's medicine reacted with Helen's tumor. He almost wished he could get his hands on Louis's biopsy just so he could run it against Helen's medicine to confirm this baffling finding.

Sitting at the lab bench, Sean tried to think what to do next. He could subject Louis Martin's medicine to the same battery of antigens he'd tried with Helen's medicine, but that would probably be futile. Instead, he decided to characterize the antigenic binding areas of the two immunoglobulins. Then he could compare their amino acid sequences directly.

The first step of this procedure was to digest each of the immunoglobulins with an enzyme called papain to split off the fragments that were associated with antigen binding. After the splitting, Sean separated these segments, then "unfolded" the molecules. Finally, he introduced these compounds into an automated peptide analyzer that would do the complicated work of sequencing the amino acids. The machine was on the sixth floor.

Sean went to the sixth floor and primed the automated instruments. There were a few other researchers working that Saturday morning, but Sean was too engrossed in his work to start any conversations.

Once the analyzer was prepared and set to run, Sean returned to his lab. Since he had more of Helen's medicine than he did of Louis's, he used hers to continue trying to find something that would react with its antigen binding area. He tried to think what kind of surface antigen could be on her tumor cells and reasoned that it was probably some kind of glycoprotein that formed a cellular binding site.

That was when he thought of the Forbes glycoprotein that he had been trying to crystallize.

As he had been doing with numerous other antigen candidates, he tested the reactivity of the Forbes glycoprotein with Helen's medicine using an immunofluorescence test. Just as he was scanning the plate for signs of reactivity, which he didn't see, he was startled by a husky female voice.

"Exactly what are you doing?"

Sean turned to see Dr. Deborah Levy standing directly behind him. Her eyes sparkled with a fierce intensity.

Sean was taken completely by surprise. He'd not even taken the precaution of coming up with a convincing cover story for all his immunological testing. He hadn't expected anyone to interrupt him on Saturday morning, particularly not Dr. Levy; he didn't even think she was in town.

"I asked a simple question," Dr. Levy said. "I expect an answer."

Sean looked away from Dr. Levy, his eyes sweeping over the mess of reagents on the lab bench, the profusion of cell culture tubes, and the general disarray. He stammered, trying to think up some reasonable explanation. Nothing came to mind except the crystal work he was supposed to be doing. Unfortunately that had nothing to do with immunology.

"I'm trying to grow crystals," Sean said.

"Where are they?" Dr. Levy asked evenly. Her tone indicated she would take some convincing.

Sean didn't answer right away.

"I'm waiting for an answer," Dr. Levy said.

"I don't know exactly," Sean said. He felt like a fool.

"I told you I run a tight ship here," Dr. Levy said. "I have a feeling you didn't take my word."

"I did," Sean hastened to say. "I mean, I do."

"Roger Calvet said you haven't been by to inject any more of your mice," Dr. Levy said.

"Yes, well . . ." Sean began.

"And Mr. Harris said he caught you in our maximum containment area," Dr. Levy interrupted. "Claire Barington said she told you specifically that area was closed."

"I just thought . . ." Sean started to say.

"I let you know from the start that I did not approve of your coming here," Dr. Levy said. "Your behavior thus far has only confirmed my reservations. I want to know what you are doing with all this equipment and expensive reagents. One doesn't use immunologic materials to grow protein crystals."

"I'm just fooling around," Sean said lamely. The last thing he wanted to admit was that he was working on medulloblastoma, particularly after he'd been forbidden access.

"Fooling around!" Dr. Levy repeated contemptuously. "What do you think this place is, your personal playground?" Despite her dark complexion, color rose in her cheeks. "No one does any work around here without submitting a formal proposal to me. I'm in charge of research. You are to work on the colonic glycoprotein project and on that alone. Do I make myself clear? I want to see defractable crystals by next week."

"Okay," Sean said. He avoided looking at the woman.

Dr. Levy stayed for another minute, as if to make sure her words had sunk in. Sean felt like a child caught red-handed in a naughty act. He didn't have a thing to say for himself. His usual talent for witty retort had momentarily abandoned him.

At long last, Dr. Levy stalked out of the lab. Silence returned.

For a few minutes Sean merely stared at the mess in front of him without moving. He still had no idea where the crystal work was. It had to be there someplace, but he didn't make any move to find it. He simply shook his head. What a ridiculous situation. His sense of frustration came back in a rush. He'd really had it with this place. He never should have come—and never would have had he known the Forbes Center's terms. He should have left in protest as soon as he'd been informed. It was all he could do to restrain himself from using his hand to sweep the countertop of all the glassware, pipettes, and immunologic reagents and allow them to smash to the floor.

Sean looked at his watch. It was just after two in the afternoon. "The hell with it all," he thought. Gathering up the immunoglobulin unknowns, he stashed them in the back of the refrigerator along with Helen Cabot's brain and the sample of her cerebrospinal fluid.

Sean grabbed his jean jacket and headed for the elevators, leaving behind the mess he'd created.

Emerging into the bright, warm Miami sunshine, Sean felt a bit of relief. Tossing his jacket into the back seat of his 4×4, he climbed in behind the wheel. The engine roared to life. He made it a point to burn a little rubber as he exited the parking area and sped south toward the Forbes residence. He was so wrapped up in his thoughts, he didn't notice the stretch limo pull out after him, bumping its undercarriage on the dip as it struggled to keep Sean in sight, nor did he spot the dark green Mercedes tailing the limo.

Sean sped back to his apartment, slammed the car door with extra force, and kicked the front door of the residence shut. He was in a foul mood.

Going into his apartment, he heard the door across the hall open. It was Gary Engels dressed in his usual jeans without a shirt.

"Hey, man," Gary said casually, leaning against the doorjamb. "You had some company earlier."

"What kind of company?" Sean asked.

"The Miami police," Gary said. "Two big burly cops came in here nosing around, asking all sorts of questions about you and your car."

"When?" Sean asked.

"Just minutes ago," Gary said. "You could have passed them in the parking lot."

"Thanks," Sean said. He went into his apartment and closed the door, irritated anew with another problem. There was only one explanation for the police's visit: someone had noted his license plate after the funeral home alarm went off.

The last thing Sean wanted now was a hassle with the police. He grabbed a small suitcase and filled it with a dop kit, underwear, a bathing suit, and shoes. In his garment bag he packed a shirt, tie, slacks, and a jacket. In less than three minutes he was headed back down the stairs.

Before stepping out of the building he looked to see if there were any police cars, marked or otherwise. The only vehicle that looked out of place was a limousine. Confident the cops wouldn't be coming after him in a limo, Sean made a dash for his 4×4, then headed back to the Forbes Cancer Center. En route he stopped to use a pay phone.

The idea the police were looking for him bothered Sean immensely. It brought back bad memories of his unruly youth. Parts of his brief life of petty crime had been exhilarating, but his brushes with the judicial system had only been tedious and disheartening. He never wanted to get bogged down in that bureaucratic quagmire again.

The first person Sean thought to call after hearing about the police was his brother Brian. Before Sean spoke to any police, he wanted to speak to the best lawyer he knew. He hoped his brother would be home. He usually was on Saturday afternoon. But instead of Brian he got Brian's answering machine with its inane message complete with background elevator music. Sometimes Sean wondered how they could have grown up in the same house.

Sean left a message saying that it was important that they talk, but that he couldn't leave a number. He said he'd call later. Sean would try again once he got to Naples.

Returning to his car, Sean sped back toward the Forbes. He wanted to be sure to be at their appointed meeting place when Janet got off work.

MARCH 6 • SATURDAY, 3:20 P.M.

By three-twenty when the last details of report were being given, Janet fell asleep. She'd been exhausted when Sean had awakened her that morning, but after a shower and coffee, she'd felt reasonably good. She'd needed more coffee midway through the morning and then again in the middle of the afternoon. She'd done well until she'd sat down for report. As soon as she was stationary, her fatigue became overpowering, and she embarrassed herself by nodding off. Marjorie had to give her a nudge in the ribs.

"You look like you're burning the candle at both ends," Marjorie said.

Janet merely smiled. Even if she could tell Marjorie all she'd been up to the previous afternoon and evening, she doubted Marjorie would have believed her. In fact, she wasn't sure she believed it herself.

As soon as report was over, Janet got her things together and crossed over to the Forbes research building. Sean was sitting in the foyer reading a magazine. He smiled as soon as he saw her. She was glad to see his mood had improved since they'd met in the cafeteria.

"You ready for our little trip?" Sean asked, getting to his feet.

"Couldn't be more ready," Janet said. "Although I would like to get this uniform off and take a shower."

"The uniform we can handle," Sean said. "There's a ladies' room right here in the foyer where you can change. The shower will have to wait, but beating the traffic is worth the sacrifice. Our route will take us right by the airport, and I'm sure there's traffic there every afternoon."

"I was only kidding about the shower," Janet said. "But I will change."

"Be my guest," Sean said. He pointed to the ladies' room door.

Tom Widdicomb had his hand in his pants pocket clutching his pearl-handled "Saturday night special" revolver. He'd been standing off to the side of the hospital entrance watching for Janet Reardon to emerge. He thought that there might be a chance he could shoot her as she got into her car. In his mind's eye he saw himself walk up just as she got in behind the wheel. He'd shoot her in the back of the head and keep walking. With all the clutter and confusion of people and cars and the noise of car engines starting, the sound of the gun would be lost.

But there was one problem. Janet had not appeared. Tom had seen other familiar faces, including nurses from the fourth floor, so it was not as if report had held her up.

Tom looked at his watch. It was three-thirty-seven, and the mass exodus of the day shift had slowed to a trickle. Most people had now left, and Tom was confused and frantic; he had to find her. He'd made the effort to be sure she was working, but where was she?

Pushing off from where he'd been leaning against the building, Tom walked around the edge of the hospital and headed in the direction of the research building. He could see the walkway spanning the two structures. He wondered if she could have crossed and exited on the research side.

He was midway between the two buildings when the sight of a long black limousine gave him pause. Tom figured that some celebrity was being treated in the outpatient department. It had happened before.

Scanning the parking lot in a wide arc, Tom nervously tried to think what he should do. He wished he knew what kind of car Janet drove because then he'd know if she'd slipped away or not. If she had, there was a big problem. He knew she was scheduled to be off the next day, and unless he found out where she lived, she'd be inaccessible for the rest of the weekend. And that was trouble. Without some kind of definitive information, Tom hated the thought of going home to a silent house. Alice hadn't spoken to him all night.

Tom was still trying to figure out what to do when he saw the black 4×4 he'd followed the day before. He started moving toward it for a closer look when suddenly, there she was! She'd just exited the research building.

Tom was relieved to see her at last but chagrined that she was not alone. Accompanying her was the same man she'd been with the previous afternoon. Tom watched as they walked toward the 4×4. She was carrying an overnight bag. Tom was about to sprint back to his car when he saw that they weren't climbing into the Isuzu. Instead they merely got out an additional suitcase and a garment bag.

Tom knew that shooting Janet in the parking lot was out of the question now that the day shift had left. Besides, being with someone meant he'd have to shoot both if he didn't want to leave a witness.

Tom started back for his car, keeping an eye on the couple as he did. By the time he got to his Escort, Janet and Sean had arrived at a red Pontiac rent-a-car. Tom got into his car and started it while he watched Janet and Sean put their bags in the Pontiac's trunk.

Robert Harris had been watching every move Tom Widdicomb made. He'd seen Sean and Janet before Tom had, and when Tom initially didn't react, Harris had been disappointed, thinking that his whole "house of cards" theory was in error. But then Tom had spotted them and had scurried back to his Escort. In response Harris started his own car and drove out of the parking lot, thinking and hoping that Tom intended to follow Janet. At the corner of Twelfth Street he pulled over to the side of the road. If he were correct, Tom would soon be exiting, and Harris's suspicion would be significantly reinforced.

Presently Sean and Janet drove by and turned north to cross the Miami River. Then, just as Harris expected, Tom came and turned in the same direction. Only a black limo separated Tom from his apparent quarry.

"This is looking more and more interesting," Harris said to himself as he started to pull out. Behind him a horn blasted and Harris jammed on his brakes. A big green Mercedes missed him by inches.

"Damn!" Harris growled. He didn't want to lose Tom Widdicomb and had to tromp on the gas pedal to catch up. He was determined to follow the man to see if he made any overt threatening gestures toward Janet Reardon. If he did, then Harris would nail him.

Harris was content until Tom turned west instead of east on the 836 East-West Expressway. As he passed Miami International Airport, then merged with Florida's Turnpike heading south, Harris realized this was going to be a far longer trip than he'd anticipated.

"I don't like this," Sterling said as they exited Florida's Turnpike at Route 41. "Where are these people going? I wanted them to go home or stay in crowds."

"If they turn west up here at the next intersection, they're on their way into the Everglades," Wayne said. He was doing the driving. "Either that or they're heading across Florida. Route 41 cuts through the Everglades from Miami to the Gulf Coast."

"What's on the Gulf Coast?" Sterling asked.

"Not much, in my book," Wayne said. "Nice beaches and good weather, but it's subdued. Naples is the first real town. There are also a couple of islands like Marco and Sanibel. Mostly it's condo heaven with a lot of retirees. Pretty low-key, but high end. You can spend millions for a condo in Naples."

"Looks like they're turning west," Sterling said, his eyes on the limousine ahead of them. They were following Tanaka, not Sean, assuming Tanaka would keep Sean in sight.

"What's between here and Naples?" Sterling asked.

"Not a lot," Wayne said. "Just alligators, saw grass, and Cypress swamp."

"This is making me very nervous," Sterling said. "They're playing directly into Tanaka's hands. Let's hope they don't stop in some isolated pull-out."

Sterling glanced to the right and did a double take. In the blue sedan along-side them was a familiar face. It was Robert Harris, head of security at Forbes. Sterling had just been introduced to the man the previous day.

Sterling pointed Harris out to Wayne and explained who he was. "This is a disturbing complication," he said. "Why would Mr. Harris be following Sean Murphy? Chances are he'll only serve to make this situation significantly more difficult than it need be."

"Would he know about Tanaka?" Wayne asked.

"I cannot imagine he would," Sterling said. "Dr. Mason would not be so fool-ish."

"Maybe he's got a crush on the chick," Wayne offered. "Maybe he's follow-ing Reardon, not Murphy."

Sterling sighed. "It's disconcerting how quickly an operation can go awry. A minute ago I was confident we would be able to control the course of events since we had the informational edge. Unfortunately, I no longer believe that. I'm beginning to have that uncomfortable feeling that chance will become a major factor. Suddenly there are too many variables."

Brian hadn't checked any luggage. He'd simply brought a carry-on and his brief-case. After getting off the plane he went directly to the Hertz counter. After a short ride on the Hertz shuttle bus he found his rental car in the lot: a cream-colored Lincoln Town Car.

Armed with a detailed street map of Miami, Brian first drove south to the Forbes residence. He'd tried calling Sean's number several times from the airport in Boston, but there hadn't been any answer. Concerned, he'd called Kevin from the plane, but Kevin had assured him that the police had not yet picked Sean up.

At the Forbes residence, Brian knocked on Sean's door, but there was no response. Hoping Sean would soon return, Brian left him a note saying that he was in town and would be staying at the Colonnade Hotel. Brian jotted down the hotel's phone number. Just as he was slipping the note under Sean's door, the door opposite opened.

"You looking for Sean Murphy?" a shirtless young man in jeans asked.

"Yes," Brian said. He then introduced himself as Sean's brother.

Gary Engels introduced himself. "Sean was here this afternoon around two-thirty," he said. "I told him the police had been here looking for him so he didn't stay long."

"Did he say where he was going?" Brian asked.

"Nope," Gary said. "But he took a suitcase and a garment bag with him when he left."

Brian thanked Gary, then returned to his rental car. The idea of Sean leaving with luggage did not sound promising. Brian only hoped his brother wasn't dumb enough to be trying to make a run for it. Unfortunately, with Sean, anything was possible.

Brian headed for the Forbes Cancer Center. Although the switchboard was closed, Brian thought that the building itself would be open, and it was. He went into the foyer.

"I'm looking for Sean Murphy," he told the guard. "My name is Brian Murphy. I'm Sean's brother from Boston."

"He's not here," the guard said with a heavy Spanish accent. He consulted a log in front of him. "He left at two-twenty. He came back at three-oh-five, but left again at three-fifty."

"Do you have any way to get in touch with him?" Brian asked.

The guard consulted another book. "He's staying at the Forbes residence. Would you like that address?"

Brian told the guard he already had that information and thanked him. He walked outside and got back into his car, wondering what he should do. He questioned the wisdom of his coming to Miami without having spoken to Sean first and wondered where his brother could be.

Deciding to check into his hotel, Brian started his car and made a U-turn to head out of the parking lot. In the process he spotted a black Isuzu that looked suspiciously like Sean's. Steering closer to it, he noticed that the plates were from Massachusetts. Putting his Lincoln in park, Brian hopped out to peer into the 4×4. It was Sean's, all right. The interior was filled with his fast-food wrappers and empty Styrofoam cups.

It seemed odd that Sean would leave it parked in the hospital lot. Going back into the building, Brian mentioned the car's presence to the guard and asked if he could account for it. The guard simply shrugged his shoulders.

"Is there any way to get in touch with the director of the Center before Monday?" Brian asked.

The guard shook his head.

"If I were to leave my name and hotel number," Brian said, "would you call your supervisor and ask if he could pass it on to the director of the Center?"

The guard nodded agreeably and even got out a pen and paper for Brian to write on. Brian wrote the note quickly, then handed it to the guard along with a five-dollar bill. The guard's face lit up with a big smile.

Brian returned to his car, drove to his hotel, and checked in. Once in his room, the first thing he did was call Kevin to give him the number. Kevin again assured him there'd been no arrest.

Brian then called Anne to reassure her that he'd gotten to Miami safely. He admitted he'd not yet spoken with Sean but expected to do so soon. He gave her his number at the hotel before hanging up.

After speaking with his mother, Brian kicked off his shoes and opened his briefcase. If he was stuck in a hotel room, at least he could get some work done.

"This is more like the scenery I expected to see in South Florida," Sean said. They had finally left civilization behind. The four-lane highway lined with strip malls and condominiums had given way to a two-lane road slicing straight across the Everglades.

"It's breathtakingly beautiful," Janet said. "It looks almost prehistoric. I half expect to see a brontosaurus rise up from one of these ponds," she added with a laugh.

They were cruising past oceans of saw grass interspersed with hummocks of pine, palm, and cypress. Exotic birds were everywhere. Some were ghostly white, others iridescent blue. Huge cumulus clouds billowed in the distance, looking whiter than usual against the intense blue sky.

The drive had done much to help calm Janet. She was glad to be leaving Miami and her patients behind. With Sean driving, she had her shoes off and her bare feet planted on the dash. She was dressed in her most comfortable pair of jeans with a simple white cotton shirt. For work she'd had her hair tied back, but she'd taken it down as soon as they'd pulled out of the Forbes lot. With all the car windows rolled down, it was blowing free.

The only problem was the sun. Since they were heading due west, bright sunlight was streaming through the windshield with a vengeance. Both Sean and Janet were wearing their sunglasses, and they had tilted the sun visors in an attempt to keep their faces shaded from the harsh rays.

"I think I'm beginning to understand Florida's attraction," Janet said, the sun notwithstanding.

"It makes winter in Boston seem extra cruel," Sean said.

"How come you didn't want to take your Isuzu?" Janet asked.

"There's a little problem with my car," Sean said.

"What kind of problem?" Janet asked.

"The police are interested in talking to its owner."

Janet took her feet down from the dash. "I don't think I like what I'm hearing," she said. "What's with the police?"

"The police came to the Forbes residence," Sean said. "Gary Engels talked with them. I think someone got the tag number from my license plate after the alarm went off at the funeral home."

"Oh, no!" Janet exclaimed. "Then the police are looking for us."

"Correction," Sean said. "They're looking for me."

"Oh, God!" Janet said. "If someone saw the license plate then they saw both of us." She closed her eyes. This was the kind of nightmare she'd feared.

"All they have is a tag number," Sean said. "That's hardly evidence."

"But they can get our fingerprints," Janet said.

Sean shot her a look of mild disdain. "Be serious," he said. "They're not about to send a team of crime scene investigators out to dust the site over a broken window and a cadaver's missing brain."

"How do you know?" Janet shot back. "You're no law enforcement expert. I think we should turn ourselves in to the police and explain everything."

Sean gave a scornful laugh. "Please! We're not giving ourselves up. Don't be ridiculous. Remember, they're looking for me. They want to talk with me. If worse comes to worst, I'll take the rap. But it's not going to come to that. I put in a call to Brian. He knows people in Miami. He'll fix it."

"Did you speak to Brian?" Janet asked.

"No, not yet," Sean admitted. "But I left a message on his answering machine. When we get to the hotel, I'll try again and leave the hotel number if he's still not in. By the way, did you bring your credit card?"

"Of course I brought my credit card," Janet said.

"Thank heaven for your trust fund," Sean said. He reached over and gave Janet's knee a playful slap. "I made a reservation at the Ritz Carlton. The Quality Inn was full."

Janet stared out the passenger-side window, wondering what she was doing with her life. It had nothing to do with the credit card issue. She didn't mind picking up the tab every now and again. Sean was generous with his money when he had it, and she had more than enough. What bothered her was the fact that they were wanted by the police. It was gallant of Sean to offer to take the rap alone, but Janet knew she couldn't let him do it even if it did fly, which it probably wouldn't. Whoever had seen that license plate had seen her too. Falling in love with Sean seemed to be bringing her nothing but grief, first emotionally and now potentially professionally. She wasn't sure how the Forbes Center would react to having a nurse on staff who was charged with God knows what in connection with a funeral home break-in. She couldn't think of too many employers who would view that kind of record as a plus.

Janet was on the verge of panic, yet there was Sean, as calm and cocky as ever. He really seemed to be enjoying himself. How he could be so cool and collected knowing the Miami police were searching for him was beyond her. She wondered if she would ever truly understand him.

"What's the story with Naples, Florida?" Janet asked, deciding to change the subject. "You said you'd explain once we were on our way."

"Very simple," Sean said. "One of the patients from that group of thirty-three lives in Naples. His name is Malcolm Betencourt."

"One of the medulloblastoma patients in remission?" Janet asked.

"Yup," Sean said. "One of the first to be treated. He's been in remission for almost two years."

"What do you plan to do?"

"Call him up."

"And say what?"

"I don't know exactly," Sean said. "I'll have to improvise. I think it would be interesting to hear about the Forbes treatment from the patient's point of view. I'm especially curious as to what they told him. They had to have told him something just to get the informed consent forms signed."

"What makes you think he'll talk to you?" Janet asked.

"How could he resist my Irish charm?" Sean said.

"Seriously," Janet said. "People don't like to talk about their infirmities."

"Infirmities, perhaps," Sean admitted. "But recovery from an otherwise terminal illness is something else. You'd be surprised. People love to talk about that kind of thing and the world-famous doctor who made it happen. Have you ever noticed how people like to think their doctor is world famous, even if he practices someplace like Malden or Revere?"

"I think you have a lot of chutzpah," Janet said. She wasn't convinced that Malcolm Betencourt would be receptive to Sean's call, but she also knew she wouldn't be able to do anything to prevent Sean from trying. Besides, except for this new worry about the Miami police, the idea of a weekend away was still delicious, even if Sean had an ulterior aim in mind. She even thought that she and Sean might finally have a moment to talk about their future. After all, aside from Malcolm Betencourt, she'd have Sean to herself without interruption.

"How did you make out with the sample of Louis Martin's medicine?" Janet asked. She thought she'd keep the conversation light until they got to dinner. She could imagine a candlelight dinner on a terrace overlooking the sea. Then she'd talk about commitment and love.

Sean flashed Janet a look of frustration. "I was interrupted by the charming head of research," he said. "She read me the riot act and told me I had to go back to the Forbes glycoprotein baloney. She really caught me off guard; for once words failed me. I couldn't think of anything clever to say."

"I'm sorry," Janet said.

"Well, it was bound to happen sooner or later," Sean said. "But even before the harpy showed up I wasn't doing that great. I haven't been able to get Helen's medicine to react with any antigen, cellular, viral, or bacterial. But you must be right about the medicine all coming from a single batch. I ran a sample of Louis's medicine against Helen's tumor and it reacted just as strongly at the same dilutions as Helen's."

"So they use the same medicine," Janet said. "What's the big deal? When people are treated with an antibiotic, they all get the same drug. Labeling the drug for each patient is probably more a matter of control than anything else."

"But cancer immunotherapy is not comparable to antibiotics," Sean said. "Like I said before, cancers are antigenically distinct, even the same type of cancer."

"I thought one of the tenets of scientific reasoning involved the issue of an exception," Janet said. "If an exception is found to a hypothesis then one is forced to reconsider the original hypothesis."

"Yeah, but . . ." Sean said, but he hesitated. Janet was making good sense. The fact was that Forbes was getting one hundred percent remission, apparently with medication that was not individualized. Sean had seen that success documented in the thirty-three cases. Therefore, there had to be an error in his insistence on the immunological specificity of cancer cells.

"You have to admit I have a point," Janet persisted.

"Okay," Sean said, "but I still think there's something strange with all this. Something I'm missing."

"Obviously," Janet said. "You don't know what antigen the immunoglobulin reacts with. That's what's missing. Once you figure that out maybe everything else will fall into place. Let's see what a relaxing weekend will do for your creativity. Maybe by Monday you'll have an idea that will get you around this apparent roadblock."

After passing through the heart of the Everglades, Sean and Janet began to see signs of civilization. First there was an isolated resort or two, then the road expanded to four lanes. Quickly the saw grass gave way to strip malls, convenience gas station/food stores, and miniature golf courses equally ugly as on the Miami side.

"I'd heard Naples was upscale," Janet said. "This hardly looks upscale."

"Let's hold our verdict until we get to the Gulf," Sean said.

The road suddenly turned north, and the unattractive profusion of unrestricted signs and commercial development continued.

"How can so many strip malls survive?" Janet asked.

"It's one of the mysteries of American culture," Sean said.

With map in hand, Janet did the navigating. She gave Sean plenty of warning before they had to turn left toward the water.

"It's starting to look a bit more promising," Sean said.

After a mile or so of more scenic vistas, the Mediterranean-style Ritz Carlton loomed out of the mangroves to the left of the road. The profusion of lush tropical plants and exotic flowers was staggering.

"Ah, home!" Sean said as they pulled beneath the porte cochere.

A man in a blue morning coat and a black top hat opened their car doors. "Welcome to the Ritz Carlton," the liveried gentleman said.

They entered through oversized glass doors into a haze of polished pink marble, expansive Oriental carpets, and crystal chandeliers. High tea was being served on the dais beneath the huge arched windows. Off to the side was a grand piano complete with tuxedoed pianist.

Sean put his arm around Janet as they meandered over to the registration desk. "I think I'm going to like this place," he told her.

Tom Widdicomb had gone through a range of emotions during his two-hour pursuit. Initially when Janet and Sean had headed out of town toward the Everglades, he'd been disturbed. Then he'd decided it was a good thing. If they were on some mini-vacation, they'd be lax and unsuspecting. In the city, people were naturally more suspicious and careful. But as one hour turned into two, and Tom began to eye his gas gauge, he'd become angry. This woman had caused him so much trouble, he began to wish they'd just pull over to the side of the road. Then he could stop and shoot them both and put an end to it all.

As he pulled into the Ritz Carlton, he wondered if he had any gas at all. The gauge had registered empty for the last five miles.

Avoiding the front entrance, Tom drove around and parked in a large lot next to the tennis courts. Getting out of his car he ran up the drive, slowing when he saw the red rental car parked directly in front of the entrance. Clutching the handle of the pistol in his pocket, Tom walked around the car and fell in with a group of guests and entered the hotel. He was afraid someone might try to stop him, but no one did. Nervously, he scanned the lavish foyer. He spotted Janet and Sean standing at the registration desk.

With his anger giving him courage, Tom boldly walked to the registration desk and stood next to Sean. Janet was just on the other side of him. Being so close sent a shiver down Tom's spine.

"We're out of nonsmoking rooms with an ocean view," the desk person said to Sean. She was a petite woman with large eyes, golden hair, and the type of tan that made dermatologists cringe.

Sean looked at Janet and raised his eyebrows. "What do you think?" he asked.

"We can see how bad the smoking room is," she suggested.

Sean turned back to the receptionist. "What floor is your room with the ocean view?" he asked.

"Fifth floor," the receptionist said. "Room 501. It's a beautiful room."

"Okay," Sean said. "Let's give it a try."

Tom moved away from the registration desk, silently mouthing "Room 501" as he headed for the elevators. He saw a heavyset man in a business suit with a small earphone in his ear. Tom avoided him. The whole time he kept his hand in his pocket, clutching his pistol.

Robert Harris stood by the piano racked by indecision. Like Tom, he'd been exhilarated early in the chase. Tom's obvious pursuit of Janet seemed to confirm his fledgling theory. But as the procession left Miami, he'd become irritated, especially when he too thought he might run out of gas. On top of that, he was starved; his last meal had been early that morning. Now that they had made it all the way through the Everglades to the Ritz Carlton in Naples, he was having doubts as to what exactly the journey proved. It certainly was no crime to drive to Naples, and Tom could contend he hadn't been following anybody. Sadly, Harris had to admit that as of yet, he hadn't come up with anything conclusive. The link between Tom and the attack on Janet or the breast cancer patient deaths was tenuous at best, still made up only of hypothesis and conjecture.

Harris knew he'd have to wait for Tom to make an overtly aggressive move toward Janet, and he hoped he would. After all, Tom's apparent interest in the nurse could be chalked up to some crazy obsession. The woman wasn't bad. In fact she was reasonably attractive and sexy; Harris himself had appreciated that.

Feeling distinctly out of place dressed as he was in shorts and T-shirt, Harris skirted the piano as Tom Widdicomb disappeared from view down the hallway past reception. Walking quickly, Harris passed Janet and Sean, who were still busy checking in.

Up ahead, Harris could see Tom round a corner and disappear from sight. Harris was about to pick up his pace when he felt a hand grab his arm. Turning, he looked into the face of a heavyset man with an earphone stuck in his right ear. He was dressed in a dark suit, presumably to blend in with the guests. He wasn't a guest. He was hotel security.

"Excuse me," the security man said. "May I help you?"

Harris cast a quick glance in the direction Tom had gone, then looked back at the security man who still had hold of his arm. He knew he had to think of something quickly. . . .

"What are we going to do?" Wayne asked. He was hunched over the steering wheel. The green Mercedes was parked at the curb near the main entrance to the Ritz Carlton. Ahead of them was the limousine parked on one side of the porte cochere. No one had gotten out of the limousine although the liveried doorman had spoken with the driver, and the driver had handed him a bill, presumably a large denomination.

"I truly don't know what to do," Sterling said. "My intuition tells me to stay with Tanaka, but I'm concerned about Mr. Harris's entering the hotel. I have no idea what he plans to do."

"Uh-oh!" Wayne uttered. "More complications." Ahead they saw the front passenger-side door of the limousine open. An immaculately dressed, youthful Japanese man climbed out. He placed a portable phone on top of the car, adjusted his dark tie, and buttoned his jacket. Then he picked up the phone and went into the hotel.

"Do you think they might be considering killing Sean Murphy?" Wayne asked. "That dude looks like a professional to me."

"I would be terribly surprised," Sterling said. "It's not the Japanese way. On the other hand, Tanaka is not your typical Japanese, especially with his connections to the Yakusa. And biotechnology has become an extremely big prize. I'm afraid I'm losing confidence in my ability to predict his intentions. Perhaps you'd better follow the Japanese man inside. Whatever you do, make sure he does not harm Mr. Murphy."

Relieved to get out of the car, Wayne lost no time going into the hotel.

After Wayne slipped inside the hotel, Sterling's eyes drifted back to the limousine. He tried to imagine what Tanaka was thinking, what he was planning next. Absorbed by these thoughts, he suddenly remembered the Sushita jet.

Reaching for the car phone, Sterling called his contact at the FAA. The contact asked him to hold while he punched the query into his computer. After a brief pause, he came back on the line.

"Your bird has flown the coop," he said.

"When?" Sterling asked. This he didn't want to hear. If the plane was gone, Wayne might be correct. Tanaka certainly wasn't planning on bringing Sean to Japan if he no longer had the Sushita jet at his command.

"It left just a short time ago," the contact said.

"Is it going back up the East Coast?" Sterling asked.

"Nope," the contact said. "It's going to Naples, Florida. Does that mean anything to you?"

"Indeed it does," Sterling said with relief.

"From there it's going to Mexico," the contact said. "That will take it out of our jurisdiction."

"You've been most helpful," Sterling said.

Sterling hung up the phone. He was glad he'd called. Now he was certain Sean Murphy was not about to be killed. Instead he was about to be offered a free trip across the Pacific.

"I can't smell any cigarette smoke in here," Janet said as she sniffed around the spacious room. Then she opened the French doors and stepped out onto the terrace. "Sean, come out here!" she called. "This is gorgeous."

Sean was sitting on the edge of the bed reading the directions for making a long-distance call. He got up and joined Janet on the terrace.

The view was spectacular. A beach shaped like a scimitar swept to the north in a gigantic arc, ending in the distance at Sanibel Island. Directly below their terrace was the lush greenery of a mangrove swamp. To the south the beach ran a straight line, eventually disappearing behind a line of high-rise condominiums. To the west, the sun was slanting through a sheath of red clouds. The Gulf was calm and deep green. A few wind surfers dotted the surface, their sails offering bright splashes of color.

"Let's go to the beach for a swim," Janet suggested. Her eyes sparkled with enthusiasm.

"You're on," Sean said. "But first I want to call Brian and Mr. Betencourt."

"Good luck," Janet said over her shoulder. She was already on her way inside to change.

With Janet in the bathroom putting on her suit, Sean dialed Brian's number. It was after six, and Sean fully expected him to be home. It was disappointing to hear the damn answering machine kick on and have to sit through Brian's message yet again. After the beep Sean left the number of the Ritz and his room number and asked his brother to please call. As an afterthought he added that it was important.

Next, Sean dialed Malcolm Betencourt's number. Mr. Betencourt himself answered on the second ring.

Sean winged it. He explained that he was a medical student at Harvard who was taking an elective at the Forbes Cancer Center. He said he'd been reviewing charts of patients who'd been on the medulloblastoma protocol and who had been doing well. Having had an opportunity to review Mr. Betencourt's chart, he'd appreciate the chance to talk to Mr. Betencourt in person about his treatment, if that would be at all possible.

"Please call me Malcolm," Mr. Betencourt said. "Where are you calling from, Miami?"

"I'm in Naples," Sean said. "My girlfriend and I just drove over."

"Splendid. So you're already in the neighborhood. And you're a Harvard man. Just the med school or undergrad too?"

Sean explained that he was on leave from the M.D./Ph.D. program but that he'd been an undergrad at Harvard too.

"I went to Harvard myself," Malcolm said. "Class of '50. I'll bet that sounds like a century ago. You play any sports while you were there?"

Sean was somewhat surprised by the direction the conversation was taking, but he decided to go with it. He told Malcolm that he'd been on the ice hockey team.

"I was on the crew team, myself," Malcolm said. "But it's my time at the Forbes you're interested in, not my glory days of youth. How long will you be in Naples?"

"Just the weekend."

"Hang on a second, young fella," Malcolm said. In a minute, he came back on the line. "How about coming over for dinner?" he asked.

"That's awfully kind," Sean said. "Are you sure it's not an imposition?"

"Hell, I already checked with the boss," Malcolm said cheerfully. "And Harriet will be tickled to have some youthful company. How's eight-thirty sound? Dress is casual."

"Perfect," Sean said. "How about some directions."

Malcolm told Sean that he lived on a street called Galleon Drive in Port Royal, an area just south of Naples's old town. He then gave specific directions which Sean wrote down.

No sooner had Sean hung up the phone than there was a knock on the door. Sean read over the directions as he walked to the door. Absentmindedly, he opened the door without asking who it was or looking through the security peephole. What he didn't realize was that Janet had hooked the security chain. When he pulled the door open, it abruptly stopped, leaving only a two-inch crack.

Through the crack Sean saw a momentary glint of metal in the hand of whoever was at the door. The significance of that glint failed to register. Sean was too embarrassed to have bungled opening the door to focus on it. As soon as he reopened the door properly, he apologized to the man standing there.

The man, dressed in a hotel uniform, smiled and said there was no need for an apology. He said he should apologize for disturbing them, but the management was sending up fruit and a complimentary bottle of champagne because of the inconvenience of not having a nonsmoking ocean-view room.

Sean thanked the man and tipped him before seeing him out, then he called to Janet. He poured two glasses.

Janet appeared at the bathroom doorway in a black one-piece bathing suit cut high on her thighs and low in the back. Sean had to swallow hard.

"You look stunning," he said.

"You like it?" Janet asked as she pirouetted into the room. "I got it just before I left Boston."

"I love it," Sean said. Once again he appreciated Janet's figure, remembering it had been her figure that had first attracted him to her when he'd seen her climbing down from that countertop.

Sean handed her a glass of champagne, explaining the management's gift.

"To our weekend escape," Janet said, extending her glass toward Sean.

"Hear, hear!" Sean said, touching her glass with his.

"And to our discussions this weekend," Janet added, thrusting her glass at him again.

Sean touched her glass for a second time, but his face assumed a quizzical expression. "What discussions?" he asked.

"Sometime in the next twenty-four hours I want to talk about our relationship," Janet said.

"You do?" Sean winced.

"Don't look so mournful," Janet said. "Drink up and get your suit on. The sun's going to set before we get out there."

Sean's nylon gym shorts had to double as a bathing suit. He'd not been able to find his real bathing suit when he'd packed in Boston. But it hadn't worried him. He hadn't planned on going to the beach much, and if he did, it would have been just to walk and look at the girls. He hadn't planned on going into the water.

After they'd each had a glass of champagne, they donned terry-cloth robes provided by the hotel. As they rode down in the elevator, Sean told Janet about Malcolm Betencourt's invitation. Janet was surprised by this development, and a little disappointed. She'd been envisioning a romantic dinner for just the two of them.

On the way to the beach they walked by the hotel's pool, which was a free-form variation of a clover leaf. There were half a dozen people in the water, mostly children. After crossing a boardwalk spanning a narrow tongue of mangrove swamp, they arrived at the Gulf of Mexico.

Even at this hour, the beach was dazzling. The sand was white and mixed with the crushed, sun-bleached remains of billions of shellfish. Redwood beach furniture and blue canvas umbrellas dotted the beach directly in front of the hotel. Groups of dawdling sunbathers were scattered to the north, but to the south, the sand was empty.

Opting for privacy, they turned to the south, angling across the sand to reach the apogee of the small waves as they washed up on the beach. Expecting the water to feel like Cape Cod in the summer, Sean was pleasantly surprised. It was still cool, but certainly not cold.

Holding hands, they walked on the damp, firm sand at the water's edge. The sun was dipping toward the horizon, casting a glistening path of golden light along the surface of the water. A flock of pelicans silently glided by overhead. From the depths of a vast mangrove swamp came the cry of a tropical bird.

As they walked past the beachfront condominiums just south of the Ritz Carlton, real estate development gave way to a line of Australian pine trees mixed with sea grapes and a few palms. The Gulf changed from green to silver as the sun sank below the horizon.

"Do you honestly care for me?" Janet asked suddenly. Since she wouldn't get a chance to talk seriously with Sean at dinner, she decided there was no time better than the present to at least get a discussion started. After all, what could be more romantic than a sunset walk on the beach?

"Of course I care for you," Sean said.

"Why don't you ever tell me?"

"I don't?" Sean asked, surprised.

"No, you don't."

"Well, I think it all the time," Sean said.

"Would you say you care for me a lot?"

"Yeah, I would," Sean said.

"Do you love me, Sean?" Janet asked.

They walked for a way in silence watching their feet press into the sand.

"Yeah, I do," Sean said.

"Do what?" Janet asked.

"What you said," Sean replied. He glanced off at the spot on the horizon where the sun had set. It was still marked by a fiery glow.

"Look at me, Sean," Janet said.

Reluctantly, Sean looked into her eyes.

"Why can't you tell me you love me?" she asked.

"I'm telling you," Sean said.

"You can't say the words," Janet said. "Why not?"

"I'm Irish," Sean said, trying to lighten the mood. "The Irish aren't good at talking about their feelings."

"Well, at least you admit it," Janet said. "But whether you truly care for me or not is an important issue. It's futile to have the kind of talk I want if the basic feelings aren't there."

"The feelings are there," Sean insisted.

"Okay, I'll let you off the hook for the moment," Janet said, pulling Sean to a halt. "But I have to say it's a mystery to me how you can be so expressive about everything else in life and so uncommunicative when it comes to us. But we can talk about that later. How about a swim?"

"You really want to go in the water?" he asked reluctantly. The water was so dark.

"What do you think going for a swim means?" Janet asked.

"I get the point," Sean said. "But this really isn't a bathing suit." He was afraid that once his shorts got wet it would be akin to wearing nothing.

Janet couldn't believe that after they'd come this far he was balking at going into the water because of his shorts.

"If there's a problem," she said, "why don't you just take them off?"

"Listen to this!" Sean said mockingly. "Miss Proper is suggesting I skinny-dip. Well, I'd be happy to as long as you'll do the same."

Sean glared at Janet in the half-light. Part of him relished making her feel uncomfortable. After all, hadn't she just made him squirm on this issue of expressing feelings? He wasn't quite sure she'd rise to his challenge, but then Janet had been surprising him a lot lately, starting with her following him to Florida.

"Who first?" she asked.

"We'll do it together," he said.

After a moment's hesitation they both peeled off their terry-cloth robes, then their suits, and pranced naked into the light surf. As evening deepened toward night, they frolicked in the shallow water, letting the miniature waves cascade over their nude bodies. After the controlling grip of Boston winter it seemed like the epitome of abandon, especially for Janet. To her surprise, she was enjoying the sensation immensely.

Fifteen minutes later they drew themselves out of the water and rushed up the beach to gather their clothes, giggling like giddy adolescents. Janet immediately began to step into her suit, but Sean had different ideas. Grabbing her hand, he pulled her up into the shadows of the Australian pines. After spreading their robes on the sandy bed of pine needles at the edge of the beach, they lay down in tight, joyous embrace.

But it didn't last long.

Janet was the first to sense something was wrong. Lifting her head, she looked out at the luminous line of white sand beach.

"Did you hear that?" she asked.

"I don't think so," Sean replied without even listening.

"Seriously," Janet said. She sat up. "I heard something."

Before either could move a figure stepped out of the shadows enveloping the copse of pine trees. The stranger's face was lost in shadow. All they could see clearly was the pearl-handled gun pointed at Janet.

"If this is your property we'll just go," Sean said. He sat up.

"Shut up!" Tom hissed. He couldn't take his eyes off Janet's nakedness. He'd planned on stepping out of the darkness and immediately shooting them both, but now he found himself hesitating. Although he couldn't see much in the half-light, what he could see was mesmerizing. He was finding it difficult to think.

Sensing Tom's penetrating eyes, Janet snatched up her bathing suit and pressed it against her chest. But Tom was not to be denied. With his free hand he wrenched the suit away and let it drop to the sand.

"You never should have interfered," Tom snapped.

"What are you talking about?" Janet asked, unable to take her eyes off the gun.

"Alice told me girls like you would try to tempt me," Tom said.

"Who's Alice?" Sean asked. He got to his feet. He hoped to keep Tom talking.

"Shut up!" Tom barked, swinging the gun in Sean's direction. He decided it was time to get rid of this guy. He extended his arm, tightening his grip on the trigger until the gun fired.

But the bullet went wide. At the exact moment Tom pulled the trigger a second shadowy figure hurled out of the darkness, tackling Tom, knocking him sideways a number of yards.

The gun sprang from Tom's grip with the stranger's impact. It fell to the ground inches from Sean's foot. With the sound of the shot still ringing in his ears, Sean looked down at the weapon with shock. He couldn't believe it; someone had fired a gun at him!

"Get the gun!" Harris managed to grunt as he wrestled with Tom. They rolled against the trunk of one of the pine trees. Tom momentarily broke free. He started out onto the beach, but he only got fifty feet away before Harris tackled him again.

Both Sean and Janet got over their initial shock and began to react at the same moment. Janet snatched up their robes and suits. Sean picked up the gun. They could see Harris and Tom rolling around in the sand close to the water.

"Let's get out of here!" Sean said urgently.

"But who saved us?" Janet asked. "Shouldn't we help him?"

"No," Sean said. "I recognize him. He doesn't need any help. We're out of here."

Sean grabbed Janet's reluctant hand, and together they ran out from beneath the canopy of pine onto the beach and then north toward the hotel. Several times Janet tried to look over her shoulder, but each time Sean urged her on. As they neared the hotel they stopped long enough to slip into their robes.

"Who was that man who saved us?" Janet demanded between gasping breaths.

"Head of security at Forbes," Sean said, equally winded. "His name is Robert Harris. He'll be okay. We should worry about that other fruitcake."

"Who was he?" Janet asked.

"I haven't the slightest idea," Sean said.

"What are we going to tell the police?" Janet asked.

"Nothing," Sean said. "We're not going to the police. I can't. They're looking for me. I can't go until I talk to Brian."

They ran past the pool and into the hotel.

"The man with the gun had to be associated with Forbes too," Janet said. "Otherwise, the head of security wouldn't have been here."

"You're probably right," Sean said. "Unless Robert Harris is after me just like the police are. He could be playing bounty hunter. I'm sure he'd like nothing better than to get rid of me."

"I don't like any of this," Janet admitted as they rode up in the elevator.

"Me neither," Sean said. "Something weird's happening, and we don't have a clue."

"What are we going to do?" Janet asked. "I still think we should go to the police."

"First thing we're going to do is change hotels," Sean said. "I don't like Harris knowing where we're staying. It's bad enough he knows we're in Naples."

Once in the room they quickly got their things together. Janet again tried to talk Sean into going to the police, but he adamantly refused.

"Now here's the plan," Sean said. "I'll take the bags and go down to the pool, then slip out by the tennis courts. You go down to the front door, get the car, then come and pick me up."

"What are you talking about?" Janet demanded. "Why all this sneaking around?"

"We were followed here at least by Harris," Sean said. "I want everybody to think we're still staying here."

Janet decided it was easier just to go along with Sean. She could tell he was in no mood to argue. Besides, he might be right to be this paranoid.

Sean left first with the bags.

Wayne Edwards walked back to the Mercedes at a fast clip and climbed into the passenger seat. Sterling had moved behind the wheel.

Up ahead Sterling could see the youthful Japanese man climbing back into the limousine.

"What's happening?" Sterling asked.

"I'm not sure," Wayne said. "The Jap just sat in the foyer and read magazines. Then the girl appeared alone. She's under the porte cochere waiting for the car. No sign of Sean Murphy. I bet those guys in the limo are as confused as we are."

A parking valet drove by in the red Pontiac. He parked under the porte cochere.

The limousine started up, spewing a puff of black smoke from its tailpipe.

Sterling started the Mercedes. He told Wayne that the Sushita jet was on its way to Naples.

"Not much doubt something's going to happen," Wayne said.

"I'm sure it will be tonight," Sterling said. "We've got to be prepared."

Presently the red Pontiac went by with Janet Reardon at the wheel. Behind her came the limo. Sterling made a U-turn.

At the base of the drive the Pontiac turned right. The limo followed.

"I smell a fish," Wayne said. "Something's not right with this picture. To get to the road you have to turn left. This right is a dead end."

Sterling turned right to follow the others. Wayne was correct; the road dead-ended. But just before the dead end they came to an entrance to a large parking lot that was partially obscured by foliage. Sterling pulled in.

"There's the limo," Wayne said, pointing off to the right.

"And there's the Pontiac," Sterling said, motioning toward the tennis courts. "And there is Mr. Murphy loading luggage in the trunk. This is a rather unorthodox departure."

"I suppose they think they're being clever," Wayne said, shaking his head.

"Maybe this move has something to do with Mr. Robert Harris," Sterling suggested.

They watched the red Pontiac drive by and out the exit. The limo followed. After waiting a bit, Sterling did the same.

"Watch for Harris's blue sedan," Sterling advised.

Wayne nodded. "I've been watching," he assured him.

They drove south for four or five miles, then cut west toward the Gulf. Eventually they ended up on Gulf Shore Boulevard.

"This area is a lot more built up," Wayne said. Either side of the road had condominium buildings with manicured lawns and pampered flower beds.

They drove for a short time before they saw the red Pontiac pull up a ramp to the first-floor entrance of the Edgewater Beach Hotel. The limo pulled off the road but remained on the ground level, turning in under the building. Sterling pulled off the road and parked in a diagonal spot to the right of the ramp. He turned off the ignition. At the top of the ramp they could see Sean directing the removal of their luggage from the Pontiac's trunk.

"A nice little hotel," Wayne said. "Less ostentatious."

"I believe you'll find the facade misleading," Sterling said. "Through some of my banking connections I've heard this place had been purchased by a charming Swiss fellow who added significant European elegance."

"You think Tanaka will try to make his move from here?" Wayne asked.

"I believe he's hoping Sean and his companion will go out so that he can corner them in some isolated location."

"If I were with that chick I think I'd bolt the door and order room service."

Sterling picked up the car phone. "Speaking of Mr. Murphy's companion, let's see what my contacts in Boston have learned about her."

MARCH 6 • SATURDAY, 7:50 P.M.

"This is a fabulous room," Janet said as she opened the large wooden tropical shutters.

Sean joined her. "It looks almost as if we're cantilevered out over the beach," he said. They were on the third floor. The beach was illuminated all the way down to the water's edge. A line of Hobie Cats was directly below them.

They were both making an attempt to put the disturbing beach experience behind them. At first Janet wanted to go back to Miami, but Sean talked her into staying. He'd said whatever the explanation for the episode was, at least it was now behind them. He'd said that since they'd driven all the way over to Naples, they should at least enjoy themselves.

"Let's get a move on," Sean said. "Malcolm Betencourt is expecting us in forty minutes."

While Janet showered, Sean sat down and tried Brian one more time. He was frustrated when he got the answering machine yet again. He left a third message instructing his brother to disregard the previous phone number. He gave the Edgewater Beach number and the room number, adding that he'd be out for dinner, but to call later, no matter the time. He said it was vitally important for them to talk.

Sean then called the Betencourt residence to say they might be a few minutes late. Mr. Betencourt assured him it wasn't a problem and thanked him for calling.

Sitting on the edge of the bed with Janet still in the shower, Sean took out the pistol he'd picked up on the beach. Snapping open the cylinder, he shook out some sand. It was an ancient .38 Smith and Wesson detective special. There were four remaining cartridges. Sean shook his head when he thought how close he'd come to being shot. He also thought about the irony of being saved by someone he'd disliked from the moment he'd first met him.

Snapping the cylinder of the revolver closed, Sean put the gun under his shirt. There had been a few too many inexplicable brushes with disaster in the last twenty-four hours for him to pass up this chance to arm himself. Sean sensed that something bizarre was happening, and like any good medical diagnostician, he was trying to relate all the symptoms to a single illness. Intuitively, he felt he should keep the gun just in case. Inwardly he was still shaking from the feeling of helplessness he'd had just before the gun had gone off.

After Janet got out of the shower, Sean got in. Janet was still complaining about not having reported the man with the gun, and said as much as she was applying her makeup. But Sean remained unwavering, adding that he believed Robert Harris was fully capable of handling the situation.

"Won't it look suspicious if we have to explain after the fact why we didn't go to the police?" Janet persisted.

"Probably," Sean agreed, "but it is just something else Brian will have to handle. Let's stop talking about it for a while and try to enjoy ourselves a little."

"One more question," Janet said. "The man said something about my interfering. What do you think he meant?"

Sean threw up his hands in exasperation. "The guy was obviously crazy. He was probably in the middle of some acute paranoid psychotic episode. How am I supposed to know what he was talking about?"

"All right," Janet said. "Take it easy. Did you try Brian again?"

Sean nodded. "The bum is still not home," he said. "But I left this number. He'll probably call while we're at dinner."

When they were ready to leave, Sean phoned the parking valet to have the car brought up to the entrance. As they exited the room, Sean pocketed the Smith and Wesson, unbeknownst to Janet.

As they drove south on Gulf Shore Boulevard, Janet finally began to calm down. She even began to notice the surroundings again and to appreciate all the flowering trees. She noticed there was no debris or graffiti or any signs of homeless people. The problems of urban America seemed a long way from Naples, Florida.

While she was trying to get Sean to look at a particularly beautiful flowering tree, she noticed that he was spending an inordinate amount of time looking in the rearview mirror.

"What are you looking for?" she questioned.

"Robert Harris," Sean said.

Janet glanced behind them, then at Sean.

"Have you seen him?" she asked with alarm.

Sean shook his head. "No," he said. "I haven't seen Harris, but I think a car is following us."

"Oh great!" Janet said. The weekend was not turning out as she'd envisioned at all.

All of a sudden, Sean made a U-turn in the middle of the road. Janet had to grab the dash to steady herself. In the blink of an eye they were traveling north, returning in the direction from which they'd come.

"It's the second car," Sean said. "See if you can tell what kind of car it is and if you can see the driver."

There were two cars bearing down on them from the opposite direction, their headlights cutting a swath in the darkness. The first car went by. Sean slowed, and then the second car passed them.

"It's a limousine," Janet said with surprise.

"Well, that shows how paranoid I'm getting," Sean said with a touch of chagrin. "That's certainly not the kind of car Robert Harris would be driving."

Sean made another sudden U-turn, and they were again heading south.

"Would you give me a little warning when you are about to do one of your maneuvers?" Janet complained. She resettled herself in her seat.

"Sorry," Sean said.

As they traveled south beyond the old section of town they noticed the homes got progressively larger and more impressive. Within Port Royal they were even more lavish, and when they pulled into Malcolm Betencourt's driveway lined with blazing torches, they were awed. They parked in an area designated "visitor parking" at least a hundred feet from the door.

"This looks more like a transplanted French château," Janet said. "It's huge. What does this man do?"

"He runs some enormous for-profit hospital corporation," Sean said. He got out of the car and came around to open the door for Janet.

"I didn't know there was so much money in for-profit medicine," Janet said.

The Betencourts were gracious hosts. They welcomed Sean and Janet as if they were old friends. They even teased them for parking in an area reserved for the "trades."

Armed with glasses of the finest champagne flavored with a mere drop of cassis, Sean and Janet were treated to a grand tour of the twenty-thousand-square-foot home. They also had a walk around the grounds, which included two pools, one cascading into the other, and a hundred-and-twenty-foot teak sailboat moored to a sizable pier.

"Some people might say that this house is a bit too big," Malcolm said when they were seated in the dining room. "But Harriet and I are accustomed to a lot of room. Our home up in Connecticut is actually a little larger."

"Plus we entertain regularly," Harriet said. She rang a little bell and a servant appeared with the first course. Another poured crisp white wine.

"So you are studying at Forbes?" Malcolm said to Sean. "You're a lucky man, Sean. It's a great place. You've met Dr. Mason, I presume?"

"Dr. Mason and Dr. Levy," Sean said.

"They're doing great things," Malcolm said. "Of course, I don't have to tell you that. As you know, I'm living proof."

"I'm certain you are grateful," Sean said. "But . . ."

"That's an understatement," Malcolm interrupted. "They've given me a second chance at life, so we're more than grateful."

"We've donated five million from our foundation," Harriet said. "We in the United States have to put our resources in those institutions that are successful instead of following those pork barrel policies of Congress."

"Harriet's sensitive about the research issue," Malcolm explained.

"She's got a good point," Sean admitted. "But, Mr. Betencourt, as a medical student I'm interested in your experience as a patient, and I'd like to hear it in your own words. How did you understand the treatment you were given? Especially considering the business you are in, I'm sure you were interested."

"You mean the quality of the treatment or the treatment per se?"

"The treatment per se," Sean said.

"I'm a businessman, not a doctor," Malcolm said. "But I consider myself an informed layperson. When I got to Forbes they immediately started me on immunotherapy with an antibody. On the first day they took a biopsy of the tumor, and they took white blood cells from my body. They incubated the white blood cells with the tumor to sensitize them to become 'killer cells.' Finally, they injected my own sensitized cells back into my bloodstream. As I understand it, the antibody coated the cancer cells and then the killer cells came along and ate 'em up."

Malcolm shrugged and looked at Harriet to see if she wanted to add anything.

"That's what happened," she agreed. "Those little cells went in there and gave those tumors hell!"

"At first my symptoms got a little worse," Malcolm said. "But then they got progressively better. We followed the progression on MRI. The tumors just melted away. And today I feel great." To emphasize his point he gave his chest a thump with his fist.

"And now you are treated in the outpatient?" Sean asked.

"That's right," Malcolm said. "I'm scheduled at present to go back every six months. But Dr. Mason is convinced I'm cured, so I expect to extend it out to once a year. Each time I go I get a dose of antibody just to be sure."

"And no more symptoms?" Sean asked.

"Nothing," Malcolm said. "I'm fit as a fiddle."

The first-course dishes were removed. The main course arrived along with a mellow red wine. Sean felt relaxed despite the episode on the beach. He glanced at Janet, who was having a separate conversation with Harriet; it turned out they had family friends in common. Janet smiled back at Sean when he caught her eye. Clearly she, too, was enjoying herself.

Malcolm took an appreciative taste of his wine. "Not bad for an '86 Napa," he said. He put his glass down on the table and looked over at Sean. "Not only have I no symptoms from the brain tumor, but I feel great. Better than I have in years. Of course, I'm probably comparing it to the year before I got the immunotherapy, which was pure hell. Not much else could have gone wrong. First I had knee surgery, which wasn't fun, then encephalitis, and then the brain tumor. This year I've been great. Haven't even had a cold."

"You had encephalitis?" Sean asked, his fork poised halfway to his mouth.

"Yes," Malcolm said. "I was a medical oddity. Somebody could have gone through medical school just studying me. I had a bout of headache, fever, and was generally feeling crappy, and . . ." Malcolm leaned over and spoke behind his hand. "There was some burning in my pecker when I peed." He glanced over to be sure the women hadn't overheard.

"How did you know it was encephalitis?" Sean asked. He put his full fork down on his plate.

"Well, the headache was the worst part," Malcolm said. "I went to my local internist who sent me down to Columbia Presbyterian. They're used to seeing strange stuff down there, all kinds of exotic, tropical diseases. They had these high-powered infectious-disease people see me. They were the ones who first suspected encephalitis and then proved it with some new method called polymerase something or other."

"Polymerase Chain Reaction," Sean said as if he were in a trance. "What kind of encephalitis was it?"

"They called it SLE," Malcolm said. "It stands for St. Louis encephalitis. They were all surprised, saying it was kinda out of season. But I had been on a couple of trips. Anyway, the encephalitis was mild, and after some bed rest I felt fine. Then of course, two months later, bam! I got a brain tumor. I thought I was done for. So did my doctors up north. First they thought it had spread from someplace else like my colon or my prostate. But when they all proved clean, they decided to biopsy. The rest, of course, is history."

Malcolm took another bite of his food, chewed and swallowed it. He took a taste of his wine, then glanced back at Sean. Sean hadn't moved. He appeared stunned. Malcolm leaned across the table to look him in the eye. "You okay, young fella?"

Sean blinked as if he were emerging from hypnosis. "I'm fine," he stammered. He quickly apologized for seeming distracted, saying that he was just astounded by Malcolm's story. He thanked Malcolm profusely for being willing to share it with him.

"My pleasure," Malcolm said. "If I can help train a few of you medical students, I'll feel like I'm repaying a little of the interest I owe on my debt to the medical profession. If it weren't for your mentor Dr. Mason and his colleague Dr. Levy, I wouldn't be here today."

Malcolm then turned his attention to the women, and while everyone but Sean ate his dinner, the conversation switched to Naples and why the Betencourts had decided to build their house there.

"How about we take our dessert out on the terrace above the pool," Harriet suggested after the dishes had been cleared.

"I'm sorry but we'll have to skip dessert," Sean said, speaking up after a long silence. "Janet and I have been working tremendously hard. I'm afraid we'll have to get back to our hotel before we fall asleep on our feet. Right, Janet?"

Janet nodded and smiled self-consciously, but it was not a smile motivated by cheerful assent. It was an attempt to hide her mortification.

Five minutes later they were saying goodbye in the Betencourts' grand foyer with Malcolm insisting that if Sean had any more questions he should call him directly. He gave Sean his private direct-dial number.

When the door closed behind them, and they started out the massive drive-way, Janet was incensed. "That was a rude way to end the evening," she said. "After they'd been so gracious with us, you practically walk out in the middle of the meal."

"That was the end of the meal," Sean reminded her. "Harriet was talking about dessert. Besides, I couldn't sit there another minute. Malcolm made me re-alize several extraordinary things. I don't know if you were listening when he de-scribed his illnesses."

"I was talking with Harriet," Janet said irritably.

"He told me he had an operation, encephalitis, and then his brain tumor all within a period of a few months."

"What did that tell you?" Janet asked.

"It made me realize that both Helen Cabot and Louis Martin had the same history," Sean said. "I know because I did their history and physicals."

"You think these illnesses are related somehow?" she asked. Some of the anger was gone from her voice.

"It seems to me I saw a similar sequence and timing in a number of the charts we copied," Sean said. "I'm not positive because I wasn't looking for it, but even with three, the possibility of it happening by chance is pretty small."

"What are you saying?" Janet asked.

"I don't know for sure," Sean said. "But it convinced me I want to go to Key West. Forbes has a spin-off diagnostic lab down there where they sent the biop-sies. It's a favorite trick of hospitals to have quasi-independent labs to maximize the profits they can make out of diagnostic lab work, self-referral limitations be damned."

"I have next weekend off," Janet said. "Both Saturday and Sunday. I wouldn't mind visiting Key West."

"I don't want to wait," Sean said. "I want to go right away. I think we're onto something here." He was also thinking that between the police looking for him and not being able to reach Brian, he might not have the luxury of waiting a week.

Janet stopped dead in her tracks and glanced at her watch. It was after ten. "Are you talking about going there tonight?" she asked with disbelief.

"Let's find out how far it is," Sean said. "Then we can decide."

Janet started walking again, passing Sean, who'd paused when she had. "Sean, you are getting more incomprehensible and crazier all the time," she said. "You call people up at the last minute, get them to graciously invite you to din-ner, then you walk out in the middle because you suddenly have the idea of going to Key West. I give up. But I'll tell you something: this lady is not going to Key West tonight. This lady is . . ."

Janet didn't finish her angry monologue. Rounding the Pontiac, which was partially hidden by a large banyan tree, she'd practically collided with a figure in a dark suit, white shirt, and dark tie. His face and hair were obscured by shad-ows.

Janet gasped. She was still on edge from the episode on the beach, and confronting yet another man coming out of the dark frightened her terribly. Sean started toward her but was stopped by a similarly shadowy figure on his side of the car.

Despite the darkness, Sean could tell the man before him was Asian. Before Sean knew it, a third man had stepped behind him. For a moment no one spoke. Sean glanced back at the house and estimated how long it would take him to cover the distance to the front door. He also thought about what he'd do once he got there. Unfortunately, a lot depended on how quickly Malcolm Betencourt responded.

"If you please," the man in front of Sean said in flawless English. "Mr. Yamaguchi would be most grateful if you and your companion would come and have a word with him."

Sean looked at each man in turn. All of them exuded an aura of total confidence and tranquillity that Sean found unnerving. Sean could feel the weight of Tom's pistol in his jacket pocket, but he dared not pull it out. He had no experience with guns, and there was no way he could shoot these people. And he hesitated to think how these men might retaliate.

"It would be regretful if there is trouble," the same man said. "Please, Mr. Yamaguchi is waiting in a car parked on the street."

"Sean," Janet called over the top of the car in a wavering voice, "who are these people?"

"I don't know," Sean answered her. Then, to the man in front of him, he said: "Can you give me an idea who Mr. Yamaguchi is, and why he particularly wants to talk with us?"

"Please," the man repeated. "Mr. Yamaguchi will tell you himself. Please, the car is just a few steps away."

"Well, since you are being so nice about it," Sean said. "Sure, let's say hello to Mr. Yamaguchi."

Sean turned and started around the car. The man who was standing behind him stepped aside. Sean put an arm around Janet's shoulder and together they started toward the street. The taller Japanese man, the one who had been in front of Sean, led the way. The other two silently followed.

The limousine was parked beneath a line of trees and was so dark it was difficult to see it until they were only a few feet away. The taller man opened the rear door and motioned for Sean and Janet to climb inside.

"Can't Mr. Yamaguchi come out?" Sean asked. He wondered if this was the same limo that he thought had been following them on their way to the Betencourts'. He guessed it was.

"Please," the taller Japanese man said. "It will be far more comfortable inside."

Sean motioned for Janet to get in, and he climbed in after her. Almost immediately the other rear door opened, and one of the silent Japanese men crowded in next to Janet. Another man followed immediately behind Sean. The taller man got in the front behind the wheel and started the car.

"What's going on here, Sean?" Janet asked. Her initial shock was changing to alarm.

"Mr. Yamaguchi?" Sean asked. In front of him he could just make out the figure of a man sitting in one of the seats to the side of a console with a small built-in TV set.

"Thank you very much for joining me," Tanaka said with a slight bow. His accent was barely perceptible. "I apologize for the inconvenient seating, but we shall have only a short ride."

The car lurched forward. Janet grabbed Sean's hand.

"You people are very polite," Sean said. "And we appreciate that. But we would also appreciate some idea what this is all about and where we're going."

"You have been invited on a vacation," Tanaka said. His white teeth flashed in the dark. When they passed a streetlamp, Sean got his first glimpse of the man's face. It was calm but determined. There was no sign of emotion.

"Your trip is compliments of Sushita Industries," Tanaka continued. "I can assure you that you will be treated extremely well. Sushita would not go through this effort unless they had great respect for you. I am sorry it has to be done in this furtive, barbaric fashion, but I have my orders. I'm also sorry that your companion has been caught up in this affair, but your hosts will treat her with equal respect. Her presence at this point is helpful since I'm certain you would not want to see any harm befall her. So please, Mr. Murphy, do not attempt any heroics. My colleagues are professionals."

Janet began to complain, but Sean squeezed her hand to silence her.

"And where are we going?" Sean asked.

"To Tokyo," Tanaka said as if there had been no question.

They drove in strained silence as they worked their way in a northeasterly direction. Sean considered his options. There weren't many. The threat of violence toward Janet was sobering, and the pistol in his pocket was not reassuring.

Tanaka had been correct about the ride. In less than twenty minutes they pulled into the general aviation area of the Naples airport. As late as it was on a Saturday night, there were minimal signs of life, only a few lights in the main building. Sean tried to think of ways of alerting whomever he could, but the specter of harm to Janet kept him in check. Although he certainly did not want to be taken forcibly to Japan, he couldn't think of a plausible way to forestall it.

The limo drove through a gate in a chain-link fence and out onto the tarmac. Skirting the rear of the general aviation building, they headed for a large private jet that was clearly prepared to take off at any moment. Its engines were running, its anti-collision and navigational lights were flashing, its door was open, and its retractable steps were extended.

The limousine stopped about fifty feet from the plane. Sean and Janet were politely asked to climb out of the car and walk the short distance to the steps. Cupping their hands over their ears to shield them from the whine of the jet engine, Sean and Janet reluctantly headed for the plane as commanded. Once again, Sean considered his options. Nothing seemed promising. He caught Janet's eye. She looked distraught. They paused at the base of the plane's steps.

"Please," Tanaka yelled over the sound of the engines as he motioned for Sean and Janet to move up the stairs.

Sean and Janet again exchanged glances. Sean nodded for her to board, then followed her up. They had to duck to enter, but once inside they could stand up. To their left was the cockpit with its door closed.

The interior of the plane was simple yet elegant, featuring darkly stained mahogany and tan leather. The carpeting was dark green. The seating included a banquette and a series of reclinable club chairs that could rotate to face any direction. Toward the rear of the plane was a galley and a door to a lavatory. On a counter in the galley was an open bottle of vodka and a sliced lime.

Sean and Janet paused near the door, unsure of where they were to go. One of the near club chairs was occupied by a Caucasian man dressed in a business suit. Like the Japanese, he exuded an aura of calm confidence. His features were angular and handsome; his hair was mildly curly. In his right hand he held a drink. Sean and Janet could hear the ice tinkle against the glass as he brought it to his lips.

Tanaka, who had boarded directly behind Sean and Janet, saw the Caucasian man seconds after Sean and Janet had. He seemed startled.

The taller of the Japanese men bumped into Tanaka since Tanaka had stopped so abruptly. The collision prompted a rapid outpouring of angry-sounding Japanese from Tanaka.

The taller Japanese began to respond, but he was interrupted by the Caucasian.

"I should warn you," he said in English. "I speak fluent Japanese. My name is Sterling Rombauer." He put his drink down in a depression in the arm of his chair made for that purpose, stood up, pulled out a business card, and handed it to Tanaka with a deferential bow.

Tanaka bowed in unison with Sterling as he accepted the card, and despite the surprise he obviously felt concerning Sterling's presence, he examined the card with care and bowed again. Then he spoke in rapid Japanese to his companion behind him.

"I believe I can best answer that," Sterling said casually as he reclaimed his seat and lifted his drink. "The pilot, copilot, and cabin crew are not in the cockpit. They are resting in the lavatory." Sterling gestured over his shoulder.

Tanaka spoke more angry Japanese to his cohort.

"Please excuse me for interrupting again," Sterling said. "But what you are asking your associate to do is unreasonable. I'm certain that if you carefully consider the situation, you'll agree that it would not serve my purposes to be here alone. And indeed, if you look out the starboard side you will see a vehicle occupied by an accomplice who is currently holding a portable phone programmed to speed-dial the police. In this country, abduction is a crime, a felony, to be more specific."

Tanaka looked again at Sterling's business card as if there was something he could have missed on his first examination. "What is it you want?" he asked in English.

"I believe we need to talk, Mr. Tanaka Yamaguchi," Sterling said. He rattled the ice cubes in his drink and took a last sip. "I am currently representing the interests of the Forbes Cancer Center," he continued. "Its director does not want to jeopardize the Center's relationship with Sushita Industries, but there are limits. He does not want to see Mr. Murphy spirited away to Japan."

Tanaka was silent.

"Mr. Murphy," Sterling called, ignoring Tanaka for the moment. "Would you mind allowing Mr. Yamaguchi and myself a few moments alone? I suggest you and your companion deplane and join my associate in the car. You can wait for me there; I will not be long."

Tanaka made no effort to countermand Sterling's suggestion. Not needing a second invitation, Sean grabbed Janet's hand, and together they pushed past Tanaka and his cohort, descended the short flight of stairs, and ran toward the darkened car parked perpendicular to the plane.

Reaching the Mercedes, Sean went to the passenger-side rear door and opened it. He allowed Janet to climb in. He followed. Before he closed the door Wayne Edwards greeted them with a warm "Hi, folks." Although he'd briefly glanced at them as they got in, he quickly turned his attention back to the plane, which could be seen clearly through his windshield. "I don't mean to sound inhospitable," he continued, "but maybe it would be better for you to wait in the terminal building."

"Mr. Rombauer told us to join you," Sean said.

"Hey, I know," Wayne said. " 'Cause that was the plan. But I've been thinking ahead. If something goes awry, and that plane starts to move, I'm driving straight into its nose gear. There aren't any air bags in the back seat."

"I get the picture," Sean said. He got out and gave Janet a hand. Together they headed toward the general aviation building.

"This keeps getting more and more confusing," Janet complained. "Spending time with you is living on the edge, Sean Murphy. What is going on?"

"I wish I knew," Sean said. "Maybe they think I know more than I do."

"And what is that supposed to mean?"

Sean shrugged his shoulders. "One thing I do know is that we've just missed an unwanted trip to Japan," Sean said.

"But why Japan?" Janet asked.

"I don't know for sure," Sean said. "But that Hiroshi character at Forbes has been watching me ever since I showed up, and some Japanese man recently visited my mother asking about me. The only explanation I can think of is that they somehow see me as a risk to their investment in Forbes."

"This whole situation is insane," Janet said. "Who was that man in the plane who got us out of there?"

"I've never seen him before," Sean said. "It's just another part to the mystery. He did say he was working for Forbes."

They arrived at the general aviation building only to find the door locked.

"Now what?" Janet asked.

"Come on!" Sean said. "We're not staying here." He grabbed her hand, and together they skirted the two-story cement structure, exiting the airfield through the same gate the limo had entered through. In front of the building was a sizable parking lot. Sean began going from car to car, trying doors.

"Don't tell me, let me guess," Janet said. "Now you're going to steal a car just to round out the evening!"

"Borrow is a better term," Sean said. He found a Chevrolet Celebrity with its doors unlocked. After leaning in so he could feel under the dash, he got in behind the wheel. "Get in," he called to her. "This will be easy."

Janet hesitated, feeling more and more that she was being drawn into something she didn't want any part of. The idea of riding in a stolen car was not appealing, particularly given the trouble they were already in.

"Get in!" Sean called again.

Janet opened the door and did as she was told.

Sean got the car started instantly, much to Janet's dismay. "Still a pro," she commented scornfully.

"Practice makes perfect," Sean said.

Where the airport entrance met the county road, Sean took a right. They drove for a time in silence.

"Am I allowed to ask where we're going?" Janet asked.

"I'm not sure where," Sean said. "I'd like to find someplace where I can ask directions to Key West. Trouble is that this town is pretty quiet even though it's only eleven on a Saturday night."

"Why don't you take me back to the Betencourts'," Janet said. "I'll get my rental car and go back to the hotel. Then you can go to Key West if you're so inclined."

"I don't think that's a good idea," Sean said. "Those Japanese guys didn't show up at the Betencourts' by accident. They were in that limo that I thought was following us earlier. Obviously they followed us from the Edgewater Beach Hotel, which means they must have been following us from the Ritz Carlton. More likely, they've been following us all the way from Forbes."

"But the others had followed us, too," Janet said.

"We must have been a regular caravan coming across the Everglades," Sean agreed. "But the point is we can't go back to the car or the hotel. Not unless we want to risk further pursuit."

"And I suppose we can't go to the police," Janet said.

"Of course not," Sean snapped.

"What about our belongings?" Janet asked.

"We'll call from Miami and have them sent," Sean said. "We'll call the Betencourts about the car. Hertz will have to get it. It's not that important. It's more important that we're no longer followed."

Janet sighed. She felt indecisive. She wanted to go to bed, yet Sean was making some sense in a situation that didn't make any sense whatsoever. The episode with the Japanese had frightened her, in some ways just as badly as the episode on the beach.

"Here are some people," Sean said. "I can ask them." Ahead, they could see a line of cars pulled up near a big sign heralding the Oasis, some sort of nightclub/disco. Sean pulled over to the side of the road. The line for valet parking snaked through a parking lot that was half-filled with trailered boats. The Oasis shared a parking lot with a land-locked marina.

Sean got out of the Celebrity and weaved his way among the parked cars toward the disco's entrance. Spine-jangling bass emanated from the open door. After waiting at the parking valet's podium, Sean cornered one of the men and asked directions to the city dock. The harried man quickly described the route to Sean with flamboyant hand gestures. A few minutes later Sean was back in the car. He repeated the directions to Janet so she could help.

"Why are we going to the city dock?" Janet asked. "Or is that a stupid question?"

"Hey, don't be mad at me," Sean complained.

"Who else can I be mad at?" Janet said. "This weekend so far is hardly what I had anticipated."

"Reserve your anger for that kook on the beach or those paranoid Japanese," Sean said.

"What about the city dock?" Janet asked again.

"Key West is due south of Naples," Sean said. "That much I remember from seeing it on a map. The Keys curve to the west. Going by boat could be easier and probably faster. We could even get some sleep. Plus, we wouldn't be using a 'borrowed' car."

Janet didn't even comment. The idea of a night-long boat ride would be a fitting end to such an insane day.

They found the city dock with ease at the base of a short cul-de-sac with a large flagpole at its entrance. But the docks were a disappointment as far as Sean was concerned. He'd expected it to be much busier, having heard that sportfishing was popular on the west coast of Florida. The only marina was shut tight. There were a few offers for fishing boat charters on a bulletin board, but not much else. After parking the car, they walked out on the pier. The larger, commercial boats were all dark.

Returning to the car, Janet leaned on the hood. "Any more bright ideas, Einstein?"

Sean was thinking. The idea of getting to Key West by boat still appealed to him. It was certainly too late to rent another car. Besides, they'd be exhausted when they arrived. Next to the city dock was a restaurant/bar appropriately called The Dock. Sean pointed.

"Let's go in there," he said. "I could use a beer, and we can see if the bartender knows any charter boat people."

The Dock was a rustic, casual affair constructed of planked, pressure-treated wood and furnished with epoxy-filled hatch-cover tables. There were no windows, just screened openings that could be closed with shutters. In lieu of drapes was a collection of fishnets, buoys, and other nautical gear. Ceiling fans turned slowly overhead. A darkly burnished wood bar in the shape of a J stretched around one wall.

A small crowd was grouped around the bar watching a basketball game on a TV positioned high on the wall in a corner by the entrance. It wasn't like Old Scully's back in Charlestown, but Sean thought the place had a comfortable feel. In fact, it made him a little homesick.

Sean and Janet found room at the bar, their backs to the TV. There were two bartenders, one tall, serious, and mustached, the other stocky with a constant smirk on his face. Both were casually dressed in printed short-sleeved shirts and dark shorts. Short aprons were tied around their waists.

The taller bartender came over immediately and tossed circular cardboard coasters in front of Sean and Janet with a practiced flick of his wrist.

"What'll it be?" he asked.

"I see you have conch fritters," Sean said, eyeing a large menu attached to the wall.

"Sure do," the bartender said.

"We'll have an order," Sean said. "And I'll have a light draft." Sean looked at Janet.

"I'll have the same," she said.

Frosted mugs of beer were soon before them, and Sean and Janet had only a moment to comment on the relaxed character of the place before the conch fritters arrived.

"Wow!" Sean commented. "That was fast."

"Good food takes time," the bartender said.

In spite of all that had happened that evening, both Sean and Janet found themselves laughing. The bartender, like any good comedian, never cracked a smile.

Sean used the opportunity to ask about boats.

"What kind of boat you interested in?" the bartender asked.

Sean shrugged. "I don't know enough about boats to say," he admitted. "We want to go to Key West tonight. How long would it take?"

"Depends," the bartender said. "It's ninety miles as the crow flies. With a good-sized boat you can be down there in three or four hours."

"Any idea how we could find someone to take us?" Sean said.

"It'll cost you," the bartender said.

"How much?"

"Five, six hundred," the bartender said with a shrug.

"They take credit cards?" Sean asked.

Janet started to complain, but Sean gripped her leg under the edge of the bar. "I'll pay you back," he whispered.

The bartender stepped around the corner where he used a telephone.

Sterling dialed Randolph Mason's home number with malicious pleasure. Well paid though he was, Sterling wasn't pleased to be working at two o'clock in the morning. He thought that Dr. Mason should be equally inconvenienced.

Even though Dr. Mason's voice was groggy and full of sleep, he sounded pleased to hear from Sterling.

"I have resolved the Tanaka-Sushita conundrum," Sterling announced. "We even received fax confirmation from Tokyo. They will not abduct Mr. Murphy. He can stay at the Forbes Cancer Center provided you personally guarantee that he will not be exposed to patentable secrets."

"I cannot make that guarantee," Dr. Mason said. "It's too late."

Sterling was too surprised to speak.

"There's been a new development," Dr. Mason explained. "Sean Murphy's brother, Brian Murphy, has shown up here in Miami concerned about Sean. Unable to locate him, he got in touch with me. He has informed me that the Miami police are looking for Sean in connection with a break-in at a funeral home and the unauthorized theft of a cadaver's brain."

"Does this cadaver's brain involve the Forbes Cancer Center?" Sterling asked.

"Most definitely," Dr. Mason said. "The deceased was a patient at Forbes. She'd been one of our medulloblastoma patients, the only one to die in the last several years, I might add. The problem is, our treatment protocol has no patent protection yet."

"You mean to say that Sean Murphy could be in possession of patentable secrets by having this brain at his disposal?"

"Exactly," Dr. Mason said. "As usual, you are right on target. I've already instructed security at Forbes to deny Mr. Murphy access to our labs. What I want you to do is see that he is turned over to the police."

"That might be difficult," Sterling said. "Mr. Murphy and Miss Reardon have vanished. I'm calling from their hotel. They have left their belongings, but I do not think they are planning on returning. It's now after two in the morning. I'm afraid I underestimated their fortitude. I thought that after being rescued from the prospect of abduction, their relief would have rendered them passive. Quite the contrary. My guess is that they commandeered an automobile and drove away."

"I want you to find them," Dr. Mason said.

"I appreciate your confidence in my abilities," Sterling said. "But the character of this assignment is changing. I think you would do better to hire a regular private investigator whose fees are considerably less than mine."

"I want you to stay on the job," Dr. Mason said. There was a hint of desperation in his voice. "I want Sean Murphy turned over to the police as soon as possible. In fact, knowing what I now know, I wish you'd let the Japanese take him. I'll pay you time and a half. Just do it."

"That is very generous," Sterling said, "but, Randolph . . ."

"Double time," Dr. Mason said. "There'd be too much lag time attempting to get someone else involved at this point. I want Sean Murphy in police custody now!"

"All right," Sterling said reluctantly. "I will stay with the assignment. But I have to warn you that unless Miss Reardon uses her Visa card, I'll have no way of tracking him until he turns up in Miami again."

"Why her card?" Dr. Mason asked.

"That's how they paid for their hotel bills," Sterling said.

"You've never let me down," Dr. Mason said.

"I will do my best," Sterling promised.

After Sterling had disconnected, he indicated to Wayne that he had to make another call. They were in the lobby of the Edgewater Beach Hotel. Wayne was comfortably ensconced on a couch with a magazine in his lap.

Sterling dialed one of his many bank contacts in Boston. Once he was sure the man was awake enough to be coherent, Sterling gave him the details he'd learned about Janet Reardon, including the fact that she had used her Visa card at two hotels that evening. Sterling asked for him to call back on Sterling's portable line if the card was used again.

Rejoining Wayne, Sterling informed him that they were to remain on the assignment, but the goal had changed. He told him what Dr. Mason had said and that they were to see that Mr. Murphy was turned over to the police. Sterling also asked if Wayne had any suggestions.

"Just one," Wayne said. "Let's get a couple of rooms and get some shut-eye."

Janet felt her stomach lurch. It was as if the steak with green peppercorn sauce she'd had for dinner at the Betencourts' had reversed its progress in her digestive tract. She was lying on a bunk in the bow of the forty-two-foot boat that was taking them to Key West. In the bunk across the narrow room, Sean was fast asleep. In the half-light he looked so peaceful. The fact that he could be so relaxed under the circumstances left Janet exasperated. It made her discomfort that much more trenchant.

Despite the Gulf's apparent calm during their sunset walk, it now felt as violent as a rough ocean. They were traveling due south and hitting oncoming swells at forty-five degrees. The boat alternately bounced dizzily up to the right only to crash down with a shudder to the left. Through it all was the constant, deep-throated roar of the diesel engines.

They had not been able to get under way until two-forty-five in the morning. At first they'd motored on calm waters with hundreds of dark mangrove-covered islands visible in the moonlight. As exhausted as she was, Janet had gone down to sleep only to be awakened by the sudden pounding of the boat against the waves and the sound of suddenly strong wind. She hadn't heard Sean come down, yet when she awoke, there he was, sleeping peacefully.

Throwing her feet over the side of the bunk, Janet braced herself as the boat thumped into the trough of another wave. Holding on with both hands, she made her way aft and up into the main salon. She knew she would be sick if she didn't get air. Below deck the slight smell of diesel only compounded her nascent nausea.

Holding on for dear life, Janet managed to get to the stern of the careening boat where there were two swivel deep-sea fishing chairs mounted to the deck. Fearing these chairs were too exposed, Janet collapsed onto a series of cushions covering a seat along a port side. The starboard side was getting drenched with spray.

The wind and fresh air did wonders for Janet's stomach, but there was no opportunity for rest. She literally had to hold on. With the roar of the engines and the pounding magnified where she was in the stern, Janet could not fathom what people saw in powerboating. Up ahead under a canopy sat Doug Gardner, the man who'd been willing to forgo a night's sleep to ferry them to Key West—for a price. He was silhouetted against an illuminated cluster of dials and gauges. He didn't have much to do since he'd put the boat on automatic pilot.

Janet looked up at the canopy of stars and recalled how she used to do the same thing on summer evenings when she was a teen. She'd lie there dreaming about her future. Now she was living it and one thing was for sure: it wasn't quite what she used to imagine.

Maybe her mother had been right, Janet thought reluctantly. Maybe it had been foolish for her to come to Florida to try to talk to Sean. She smiled a wry smile. The only talk they'd managed thus far was the little they'd done on the beach that evening, when Sean had merely echoed her own expression of love. It had been less than satisfying.

Janet had come to Florida in hopes of taking command of her life, but the longer she was with Sean, the less in command she felt.

Sterling got even more satisfaction out of calling Dr. Mason at three-thirty A.M. than he had at two. It took four rings for the doctor to answer. Sterling himself had just been awakened by a call from his banking contact in Boston.

"I now know the destination of the infamous couple," Sterling said. "Fortunately, the young lady used her credit card again for a rather sizable sum. She paid five hundred and fifty dollars to be ferried from Naples to Key West."

"That's not good news," Dr. Mason said.

"I thought you'd be pleased to know we've learned where they're going," Sterling said. "I consider it a bit of good luck."

"The Forbes has a facility in Key West," Dr. Mason said. "It's called Basic Diagnostics. I imagine that's where Mr. Murphy is headed."

"Why do you believe he would go to Basic Diagnostics?" Sterling asked.

"We send a lot of our lab work there," Dr. Mason said. "With current third-party payment schemes, it's cost effective."

"Why do you care if Mr. Murphy visits the facility?"

"The medulloblastoma biopsies are sent there," Dr. Mason said. "I don't want Mr. Murphy exposed to our techniques of sensitizing patient T lymphocytes."

"And Mr. Murphy might be able to deduce these techniques by a mere visit?" Sterling asked.

"He's very savvy as far as biotechnology is concerned," Dr. Mason said. "I can't take the risk. Get yourself down there immediately and keep him out of that lab. See that he is turned over to the police."

"Dr. Mason, it is three-thirty in the morning," Sterling reminded him.

"Charter a plane," Dr. Mason said. "We're paying the expenses. The manager's name is Kurt Wanamaker. I'll give him a call right after I hang up and tell him to expect you."

After Sterling got Mr. Wanamaker's phone number, he hung up. Despite the money that he was being paid, he was not happy with the idea of rushing off to Key West in the middle of the night. He felt that Dr. Mason was overreacting. After all, it was Sunday and the lab very likely wasn't even open.

Yet Sterling got out of bed and walked into the bathroom.

MARCH 7 • SUNDAY, 5:30 A.M.

Sean's first glimpse of Key West in the pre-dawn light was of a line of low-rise clapboard buildings nestled in tropical greenery. A few taller brick structures poked out of the skyline here and there, but even they were no taller than five stories. The water's edge from the northwest was dotted with marinas and hotels all cheek to jowl.

"Where's the best place to drop us off?" Sean asked Doug.

"Probably the Pier House pier," Doug said as he cut back the engines. "It's right at the base of Duval Street, which is Key West's main drag."

"You familiar with the area?" Sean asked.

"I've been here a dozen or so times," Doug said.

"Ever hear of an organization called Basic Diagnostics?"

"Can't say that I have," Doug said.

"What about hospitals?" Sean asked.

"There are two," Doug replied. "There's one right here in Key West, but it's small. There's a larger one on the next key called Stock Island. That's the main facility."

Sean went below and woke Janet up. She wasn't pleased about having to get up. She told Sean she'd only come down below fifteen or twenty minutes earlier.

"When I came down here hours ago you were sleeping like a baby," Sean said.

"Yeah, but as soon as we hit rough seas, I had to go back out on deck. I didn't get to sleep the whole trip like you did. Some restful weekend this has turned out to be."

The docking was uneventful since there was no other boating activity so early on a Sunday morning. Doug waved goodbye and motored away as soon as Sean and Janet jumped to the pier.

While Sean and Janet strolled off the pier and began to look around, they had the strange feeling they were the only living beings on the island. There was plenty of evidence of the previous night's partying; empty beer bottles and other debris were haphazardly strewn about in the gutters. But there were no people. There weren't even any animals. It was like the calm after the storm.

They walked up Duval Street with its complement of T-shirt stores, jewelers, and souvenir shops all shuttered as if they expected a riot. The famous Conch Tour Train appeared abandoned by its bright yellow ticket kiosk. The place was as much of a honky-tonk as Sean expected, yet the net effect was surprisingly charming.

As they passed Sloppy Joe's Bar the sun peeked tentatively over the Atlantic Ocean and filled the deserted street with misty morning light. Half a block farther on they were enveloped by a delicious aroma.

"That smells suspiciously like . . ." Sean began.

"Croissants," Janet finished.

Following their noses they turned into a French bakery *cum* café. The delectable smell was coming from open windows off a terrace dotted with tables and umbrellas. The front door was locked so Sean had to yell through the open window. A woman with red frizzy hair came out wiping her hands on an apron.

"We're not open yet," she said with the hint of a French accent.

"How about a couple of those croissants?" Sean suggested.

The woman cocked her head while she gave the idea some thought. "I suppose," she said. "I could offer you some café au lait that I've made for myself. The espresso machine hasn't been turned on yet."

Sitting under one of the umbrellas on the deserted terrace, Sean and Janet savored the oven-fresh pastries. The coffee revived them.

"Now that we're here," Janet said, "what's the plan?"

Sean stroked his heavily whiskered chin. "I'll see if they have a phone book," he said. "That will give me the address of the lab."

"While you do that, I think I'll use the ladies' room," Janet said. "I feel like something the cat dragged in."

"A cat would be afraid to go near you," Sean said. He ducked when Janet threw her crumpled napkin at him.

By the time Janet returned, looking much fresher, Sean had not only gotten the address, he'd gotten directions from the red-haired woman.

"It's kinda far," he said. "We'll need a ride."

"And of course that will be easy," Janet said. "We can either hitchhike or just take one of the many cabs streaming by." They hadn't seen a single car since they'd arrived.

"I was thinking about something else," Sean said as he left a generous tip for their hostess. He stood up.

Janet looked at him questioningly for a moment before realizing what he had in mind. "Oh, no!" she said. "We're not stealing another car."

"Borrow," Sean corrected her. "I'd forgotten how easy it is."

Janet refused to have anything to do with "borrowing" a car, but Sean proceeded undeterred.

"I don't want to break anything," he said, going from car to car on a side street, trying all the doors. Every one was locked. "Must be a lot of suspicious people around here." Then he stopped, staring across the street. "I just changed my mind. I don't want a car."

Crossing over to a large motorcycle teetering on its kickstand, Sean got the engine going almost as quickly as he would have if he'd had the ignition key. Straddling the bike and kicking back the kickstand, he motioned for Janet to join him.

Janet studied Sean with his unshaven face and rumpled clothes as he revved the motorcycle's engine. How could she have fallen in love with a guy like this? she asked herself. Reluctantly, she threw a leg over the machine and threw her arms around Sean's waist. Sean hit the gas and they sped off, shattering the early morning silence.

They traveled back down Duval Street in the direction from which they'd come, then turned north at the Conch Train kiosk and followed the shoreline. Eventually they came to an old wharf. Basic Diagnostics occupied a two-story brick warehouse that had been nicely refurbished. Sean drove around to the back of the building and parked the bike behind a shed. Once the motorcycle engine was off the only sound they could hear was the cry of distant seagulls. Not a soul was around.

"I think we're out of luck," Janet said. "It doesn't look open."

"Let's check it out," Sean said.

They mounted some back stairs and peered in the rear door. There were no lights on inside. A platform ran along the north side of the building. They tried the doors along the platform, including a large overhead door, but everything was locked tight. In the front of the building there was a sign on the double-door entry that announced that the lab was open from twelve noon to five P.M. on Sundays and holidays. There was a small metal drop door for leaving samples during off hours.

"Guess we'll have to come back," Janet said.

Sean didn't respond. He cupped his hands and peered through the front windows. Rounding the corner, he did the same at another window. Janet followed him as he went from window to window working his way back the way they'd come.

"I hope you're not getting any ideas," Janet said. "Let's find someplace where we can sleep for a few hours. Then we can return after noon."

Sean didn't answer. Instead he stepped away from the last window he'd been peering through. Without warning he gave the glass a sudden karate-like chop with the side of his hand. The window imploded, shattering on the floor within. Janet leapt back, then quickly looked over her shoulder to see if there were any witnesses. Then, looking back at Sean, she said: "Let's not do this. The police are already looking for us from the episode in Miami."

Sean was busy removing a few of the larger shards. "No shatter alarm," he said.

He quickly climbed through the window, then turned around to inspect it carefully. "No alarm at all," he said. Unlocking the sash, he pulled it up. Then he extended a hand toward Janet.

Janet held back. "I don't want to be part of this," she said.

"Come on," he insisted. "I wouldn't be breaking in here unless I thought it was mighty important. Something bizarre is going on, and there might be some answers here. Trust me."

"What if someone comes?" Janet asked. She gave another nervous glance over her shoulder.

"No one is going to come," Sean said. "It's seven-thirty Sunday morning. Besides, I'm only going to look around. We'll be out of here in fifteen minutes, I promise. And if it makes you feel any better, we'll leave a ten-dollar bill for the window."

After everything they'd been through, Janet figured there wasn't much point in resisting now. She let Sean help her through the window.

They were standing in a men's lavatory. There was the scented smell of disinfectant coming from an oval pink cake in the base of the urinal attached to the wall.

"Fifteen minutes!" Janet said as they cautiously opened the door.

Outside the men's room was a hall running the length of the building. A cursory check of the floor revealed a large laboratory across from the men's room that also ran the length of the building. On the same side as the men's room were a ladies' room, a storeroom, an office, and a stairwell.

Sean opened each door and peered inside. Janet looked over his shoulder. Entering the laboratory proper he walked down the central aisle, glancing from side to side. The floor was a gray vinyl, the cabinets a lighter gray plastic laminate, and the countertops stark white.

"Looks like a normal, garden-variety clinical lab," he said. "All the usual equipment." He paused in the microbiological section and looked into an incubator filled with petri dishes.

"Are you surprised?" Janet asked.

"No, but I expected more," Sean said. "I don't see a pathology section where they'd process biopsies. I was told the biopsies are sent here."

Returning down the main hall, Sean went to the stairwell. He mounted the steps. At the top was a stout metal door. It was locked.

"Uh-oh," Sean said. "This might take more than fifteen minutes."

"You promised," Janet said.

"So I lied," Sean said as he inspected the lock. "If I can find some appropriate tools it might be sixteen minutes."

"It's been fourteen already," Janet said.

"Come on," Sean said. "Let's see if we can find something to act as a tension bar and some heavy wire to use as picks." He retreated down the stairs. Janet followed.

Sterling's chartered Sea King touched down with a squeal of rubber at seven-forty-five in the morning at the Key West airport and taxied over to general aviation. At the commercial terminal right next door an American Eagle commuter plane was in the final boarding process.

By the time Sterling had gotten a call back from the charter company it had been close to five A.M. After some persuasion which included a promise of extra money, the plane was supposed to have departed around six, but because of refueling problems it wasn't ready to leave until six-forty-five.

Both Sterling and Wayne took advantage of the delay to catch some sleep, first at the Edgewater Beach Hotel, then in the waiting area at the airport. Then they had slept most of the flight.

Arriving at the general aviation building in Key West, Sterling saw a short balding man in a floral print short-sleeved shirt gazing out the front window. He was holding a steaming Styrofoam cup.

As Sterling and Wayne deplaned, the balding man came out and introduced himself. He was Kurt Wanamaker. He was of stocky build with a broad, suntanned face. What hair he had was bleached by the sun.

"I went by the lab about seven-fifteen," Kurt said on the way to his Chrysler Cherokee. "Everything was quiet. So I think you've beaten them if they are planning on coming at all."

"Let's go directly to the lab," Sterling said. "I'd like to be there if and when Mr. Murphy breaks in. Then we could do more than merely deliver him to the police."

"This should work," Sean said. He had his eyes tightly closed while he fiddled with the two ballpoint pen refills. He'd bent the end of one to a right angle to serve as a tension bar.

"What exactly are you doing in there?" Janet asked.

"I told you back at Forbes," Sean said. "When we were trying to get in the chart vault. It's called raking the pins. There are five of the little guys in there keeping the cylinder from turning. Ah, there we go." The lock opened with a click. The door swung in.

Sean entered first. Since there were no windows, the interior was as dark as a moonless night, save for the light that spread up through the stairwell. Groping on the wall to the left of the door, Sean's hand hit against a panel of switches. He flipped them all on at once and the entire ceiling lit up in a wink.

"Well, look at this!" Sean said in utter amazement. Here was the lab he'd expected to see at the Forbes Cancer Center research building. It was enormous, encompassing the entire floor. It was also very white, with its white floor tiles, white cabinets, and white walls.

Slowly Sean walked down the center aisle, appreciating the equipment. "Everything is brand new," he said admiringly. He put his hand on a desktop machine. "And strictly top notch. This is an automated southern blotting instrument. It runs at least twelve thousand dollars. And here is the latest chemiluminescence spectrophotometer. It's a cool twenty-three. And over there is a high phase liquid chromatography unit. That's around twenty grand. And here's an automatic cell sorter. That's at least one hundred and fifty thousand. And my God!"

Sean stopped in awe in front of a peculiar egg-shaped apparatus. "Don't let your credit card get near to this big guy," he said. "It's a nuclear magnetic resonator. You have any idea what this baby costs?"

Janet shook her head.

"Try half a million dollars," Sean said. "And if they have that, it means they have an X-ray defractor as well."

Walking on, Sean came to a glass-enclosed area. Inside he could see a Type III maximum containment hood as well as banks and banks of tissue culture incubators. Sean tried the glass door. It opened out, so he had to work against the suction holding it closed. In order to prevent the escape of any organisms, the pressure inside the viral lab was kept lower than the rest of the laboratory.

Stepping into the maximum containment area, Sean motioned for Janet to stay where she was. First he went to a floor freezer and opened its hood. The temperature on an internal gauge stood at minus seventy degrees Fahrenheit. Nestled inside the freezer were multiple racks containing small vials. Each vial contained a frozen viral culture.

Closing the freezer, Sean glanced in some of the tissue culture incubators.

They were being kept at ninety-eight point six degrees Fahrenheit, mimicking the normal internal temperature of a human being.

Moving on to the desk, Sean picked up some electron photomicrographs of isometric viruses as well as accompanying engineering-style drawings of the viral capsids. The drawings were done to study the icosahedral symmetry of the viral shells and included actual measurement of the capsomeres. Sean noted that the viral particle had an overall diameter of 43 nanometers.

Leaving the maximum containment area, Sean proceeded into an area in which he felt very much at home. A whole section of the lab seemed dedicated to oncogene study, just what Sean was doing back in Boston. The difference, however, was that in this lab the equipment was all brand new. Sean longingly looked at shelf upon shelf of appropriate reagents for the isolation of oncogenes and their products, the oncoproteins.

"This place is state of the art in every regard," he said. In the oncogene section there were additional tissue culture incubators the size of thousand-bottle wine coolers. He opened the door of one and glanced at the cell lines. "This is a place I could work," he said, closing the incubator.

"Is this what you expected?" Janet asked. She'd followed behind like a puppy except when he went into the maximum containment area.

"More than I expected," Sean said. "This must be where Levy works. I'd guess that most of this equipment has come from the off-limits area of the sixth floor of the Forbes research building."

"What is all this telling you?" Janet asked.

"It's telling me I need a few hours in the lab back at Forbes," Sean said. "I believe . . ."

Sean didn't get to finish. The sounds of voices and footsteps were heard coming up the stairway. Janet put a hand over her mouth in panic. Sean grabbed her, his eyes desperately sweeping that area of the lab for a place to hide. There was no escape.

MARCH 7 • SUNDAY, 8:05 A.M.

"Here they are!" Wayne Edwards announced. He'd just pulled open a stout metal door to a small storage closet near the glass-enclosed maximum containment lab.

Sean and Janet blinked with the sudden intrusion of light.

Sterling stepped toward Wayne's discovery. Kurt was at his side.

"They may not look like fugitives or agents provocateurs," Sterling said. "Though of course we know the truth."

"Out of the closet!" Wayne commanded.

A subdued and remorseful Janet and a defiant Sean stepped out into the bright light.

"You people should not have left the airport last night," Sterling scolded. "And to think of the effort we'd expended on your behalf to thwart your abduction. Some gratitude. I'm curious to know if you're aware of how much trouble you've caused."

"How much trouble I *am* causing," Sean corrected.

"Ah, Dr. Mason mentioned you were brash," Sterling said. "Well, we'll allow you to vent your impertinence on the Key West police. They can do battle with their Miami counterparts as to jurisdiction of your case now that you've committed a felony here as well."

Sterling picked up a phone in preparation to dial.

Sean pulled the long-dormant gun from his jacket pocket and pointed it at him. "Put the phone down," he commanded.

Janet sucked in her breath at the sight of the gun in Sean's hand.

"Sean!" she cried. "No!"

"Shut up," Sean snapped. The threesome surrounding him in a wide arc made him nervous. The last thing he wanted to do was let Janet give them an opportunity to overpower him.

As Sterling replaced the receiver, Sean motioned for the three men to group together.

"This is extremely foolish behavior," Sterling commented. "Breaking and entering in the possession of a deadly weapon is a far more serious crime than mere breaking and entering."

"Into the closet!" Sean commanded, motioning toward the space he and Janet had just vacated.

"Sean, this is going too far!" Janet said. She stepped up to Sean.

"Get out of my way!" Sean snarled. He shoved her roughly to the side.

Already dismayed at the appearance of the gun, Janet was doubly shocked at the sudden change in Sean's personality. The cruel and vicious sound of his voice and the expression on his face cowed her.

Sean succeeded in herding the three men into the narrow closet. He quickly closed and locked the door behind them. Pocketing the gun, he moved some sizable furniture against the door, including a heavy five-drawer file cabinet.

Satisfied, he grabbed Janet's hand and started toward the exit. Janet tried to hold back. They got halfway to the stairway when she managed to pull free.

"I'm not going with you," she said.

"What are you talking about?" Sean whispered forcibly.

"The way you talked to me back there," she said. "I don't know you."

"Please!" Sean voiced through clenched teeth. "That was theatrics for the benefit of the others. If things don't go the way I imagine they will, you'll be able to contend that you were coerced into this whole affair. With the work I have to do back at the lab in Miami, there's a chance things might get worse before they get better."

"Be straight with me," Janet said. "Stop talking in riddles. What's going through your mind?"

"It's a bit much to explain at the moment," Sean said. "Right now we have to get out of here. I can't tell how long that storage closet will hold those three. Once they're out, the cat's out of the bag."

More confused than ever, Janet followed Sean down the stairs, through the first-floor lab, and out the front of the building. Kurt Wanamaker's Cherokee was angled in from the street. Sean motioned for Janet to get in.

"Convenient and thoughtful of them to have left the keys," Sean said.

"As if that would have made any difference to you," Janet said.

Sean started the car, but then immediately killed the engine.

"What now?" Janet asked.

"In the excitement I forgot that I need some of those reagents from upstairs," Sean said. He got out of the car and leaned in the window. "This won't take but a minute. I'll be right back."

Janet tried to protest, but Sean was gone. Not that he'd cared much about her feelings about any of this mess so far. She got out of the car and began to pace the length of it nervously.

Thankfully, Sean returned in a few minutes carrying a large cardboard box, which he shoved into the back seat. He got in behind the wheel and started the car. Janet got in next to him. They pulled out into the road and headed north.

"See if there's a map in the glove compartment," he said.

Janet searched and found one. She opened it up to the Florida Keys. Sean took the map and studied it while driving. "We can't count on getting all the way to Miami with this car," he said. "As soon as those three get out of the closet, they'll realize it's missing. The police will start looking for it and since there's only one road north, it won't be hard to find."

"I'm a fugitive," Janet marveled. "Just like the man said when they found us in the closet. I don't believe it. I don't know whether to laugh or cry."

"There's an airport at Marathon," Sean said, ignoring Janet's comment. "We'll leave the car there and either rent a car or fly depending on the flight schedule."

"I presume we're going back to Miami," Janet said.

"Absolutely," Sean said. "We'll go directly to Forbes."

"What's in the cardboard box?" Janet asked.

"A lot of reagents they don't have in Miami," Sean said.

"Like what?" Janet asked.

"Mostly DNA primer pairs and DNA probes for oncogenes," Sean said. "I also found some primers and probes for virus nucleic acid, particularly those used for St. Louis encephalitis."

"And you're not about to tell me what all this is all about?" Janet said.

"It will sound too preposterous," Sean admitted. "I want some proof first. I've got to prove it to myself before I tell anyone, even you."

"At least give me a general idea of what you use these primers and probes for," Janet said.

"DNA primers are used to find particular strands of DNA," Sean said. "They seek out a single strand from millions of others, then react with it. Then, by a process called the Polymerase Chain Reaction, the original DNA strand can be amplified billions of times. That way it can be easily detected by a labeled DNA probe."

"So using these primers and probes is like looking for the proverbial needle in the haystack with a powerful magnet," Janet said.

"Exactly," Sean said, impressed with how quickly she grasped the science. "A very, very powerful magnet. I mean, it can find one particular DNA strand out of a solution of millions of others. In that sense it's almost a magical magnet. I think the guy who developed the process should get the Nobel Prize."

"Molecular biology is making big strides," Janet said sleepily.

"It's unbelievable," Sean agreed. "Even those in the field have trouble keeping up."

Janet struggled against ponderously heavy eyelids made worse by the muffled drone of the engine and the gentle jostling. She wanted to press Sean for more of an explanation of what was going through his mind, and she thought the best way to do that was to get him to talk about molecular biology and what he was planning to do when he got back to the lab at Forbes. But she was too exhausted to go on.

Janet had always found driving calming. Between the little amount of sleep she'd gotten aboard the boat and all the running around they'd been doing, it wasn't long before she nodded off. She fell into a deep, much needed sleep and rested undisturbed until Sean pulled off Route 1 onto the grounds of the Marathon Airport.

"So far so good," Sean said when he noticed Janet was stirring. "No roadblocks and no police."

Janet sat up. For a moment she had no idea where she was, but then reality came back in a numbing flash. Now she felt worse than she had when she'd fallen asleep. Running her fingers through her hair made her think of a bird's nest. It was hard for her to imagine what she looked like. She decided not to try.

Sean parked the car in the most crowded part of the parking lot. He thought its presence would be less likely to be noticed that way and thereby give them more time. Hefting the cardboard box from the back seat, he carried it into the terminal. He sent Janet to check on commuter flights to Miami while he went to inquire about the availability of rental cars. He was still searching for a rental agent when Janet returned to tell him that a flight to Miami left in twenty minutes.

The airline agent helpfully taped Sean's box closed after plastering the outside with "fragile" stickers. The agent guaranteed the parcel would be treated with the utmost care. Later, as Sean was boarding the small turboprop commuter plane, he saw someone casually tossing his box onto a luggage cart. But Sean wasn't worried. He'd found bubble wrap back at Basic Diagnostics when he packed the reagents. He was reasonably confident his primers and probes would survive the trip.

Once at the Miami airport, he and Janet rented a car. They used Avis, avoiding Hertz in case the Hertz computer indicated that Janet Reardon was already in possession of a red Pontiac.

With the primers and probes in the back seat, they drove directly to Forbes. Sean parked next to his 4×4 near the entrance to the research building. He got out his Forbes ID card.

"You want to come in or what?" Sean asked. Exhaustion was catching up with him at this point too. "You can take this car back to the apartment if you want."

"I've come this far," Janet said. "I want you to explain what you're doing as you do it."

"Fair enough," Sean said.

They got out of the car and walked into the building. Sean did not expect any trouble, so he was surprised when the guard stood up. None of the guards had ever done that. This one's name was Alvarez. Sean had seen him before on several occasions.

"Mr. Murphy?" Alvarez questioned with a definite Spanish accent.

"That's me," Sean said. He'd bumped into the turnstile arm, which Alvarez had failed to release. Sean had his ID in his hand visible for Alvarez to see. The cardboard box was under his other arm. Janet was behind him.

"You are not permitted in the building," Alvarez said.

Sean put down his cardboard box.

"I work here," Sean said. He leaned over to hold his ID closer to Alvarez's face in case the guard had missed it.

"Orders from Dr. Mason," Alvarez said. He leaned back from Sean's ID as if it were somehow repulsive. He picked up one of his telephones with one hand and flipped through a Rolodex with the other.

"Put the phone down," Sean said, struggling to control his voice. Between everything he'd been through and his general fatigue, he was at the end of his patience.

The guard ignored Sean. He found Dr. Mason's phone number and started punching in the numbers.

"I asked you nicely," Sean said. "Put the phone down!" He spoke now with considerably more force.

The guard finished dialing, then calmly eyed Sean as he waited for the connection to go through.

With lightning speed, Sean reached across the Corian desk and grabbed the phone line where it disappeared into the woodwork. A sharp yank tore the cable free. Sean held the end of the cable up to the surprised guard's face. It was a tangled mass of tiny red, green, and yellow wires.

"Your phone is out of order," Sean said.

Alvarez's face turned red. Dropping the receiver, he snatched up a truncheon and started around the desk.

Instead of retreating, which the guard expected, Sean lunged ahead to meet Alvarez as if throwing a body check in a hockey game. Sean came up from below. The base of his forearm connected with the guard's lower jaw. Alvarez was lifted off his feet and smashed back against the wall before he could try anything with the truncheon. On impact Sean could hear a definite crack like a piece of dried kindling being snapped. Sean also heard the man grunt when he hit the wall as the breath was forced from his lungs. When Sean pulled away, Alvarez fell to the floor, his body limp.

"Oh, God!" Janet cried. "You've hurt him."

"Geez, what a jaw," Sean said as he rubbed the base of his forearm.

Janet stepped around Sean to get to Alvarez, who was bleeding from his mouth. Janet half feared that he was dead, but she quickly determined he was merely unconscious.

"When is this going to end?" she moaned. "Sean, I think you've broken this man's jaw, and he's bitten his tongue. You knocked him out."

"Let's walk him over to the hospital side," Sean suggested.

"They don't have trauma capability here," Janet said. "We'll have to take him over to Miami General."

Sean rolled his eyes and sighed. He eyed his cardboard box of primers and probes. He needed a few hours, maybe even as much as four, up in the lab. He looked at his watch. It was just after one in the afternoon.

"Sean!" Janet commanded. "Now! It's only three minutes away. We can come back once we've dropped him off. We can't just leave him this way."

Reluctantly, Sean pushed his cardboard box behind the guard's desk, then helped Janet carry Alvarez outside. Between the two of them, they got him out to the rental car and into the back seat.

Sean could see the wisdom in taking Alvarez to the emergency room at Miami General. It wasn't smart to leave a bleeding, unconscious man unattended. If Alvarez took a turn for the worse, Sean would be in serious trouble, the kind even his clever brother would have a hard time getting him out of. But Sean wasn't about to get caught now just because he'd agreed to this mission of mercy.

Even though it was midday Sunday, Sean counted on a busy ER. He wasn't disappointed. "This is a quick dropoff," he warned Janet. "A speedy in and out. Once we get him in the ER, we're out of there. The staff there will know what to do."

Janet wasn't in complete agreement, but she knew better than to disagree.

Sean left the engine idling, the gear in park, while he and Janet struggled with Alvarez's still-limp body. "At least he's breathing," Sean said.

Just inside the door to the ER, Sean spotted an empty gurney. "Put him on this," he ordered Janet.

With Alvarez safely laid atop it, Sean gave the gurney a gentle shove. "Possible code," Sean shouted as the gurney rolled down the hall. Then he grabbed Janet by the arm. "Come on, let's go," he said.

As they raced back to the car, Janet said, "He wasn't a code."

"I know," Sean admitted. "But it was all I could think of to get some action. You know how emergency rooms are. Alvarez could have lain around for hours before anyone did something for him."

Janet only shrugged. Sean did have a point. And before they'd left she'd been relieved to see a male nurse already intercepting the gurney.

On the way back to Forbes, neither Sean nor Janet said another word. Both were exhausted. On top of that, Janet was unnerved by Sean's explosive violence; it was yet more behavior she had not anticipated from him.

Meanwhile, Sean was trying to figure out how he could ensure himself four hours of uninterrupted lab time. Between the unfortunate episode with Alvarez and the fact the Miami police were already looking for him, Sean knew he would have to come up with something creative to hold off the hordes. Suddenly he had an idea. It was radical, but it would definitely work. His plan brought a smile to his face despite his exhaustion. There was a kind of poetic justice involved that appealed to him.

Sean felt justified in using extreme measures at this point. The more he thought about his current theory of what was going on at the Forbes Cancer Center, the more convinced he was that he was correct. But he needed proof, and to get proof, he needed lab time. And to get the lab time, he needed something drastic. In fact the more drastic it was, the better it would work.

When they made the final turn into the parking lot at Forbes, Sean broke the silence: "The night you arrived in Florida I'd gone to an affair at Dr. Mason's," he said. "A medulloblastoma patient donated money to Forbes, big money. He headed up an airplane manufacturing firm in St. Louis."

Janet was silent.

"Louis Martin is the CEO of a computer hardware manufacturing firm north of Boston," Sean said. He glanced at Janet as he parked. She looked puzzled.

"Malcolm Betencourt runs a huge for-profit chain of hospitals," Sean continued.

"And Helen Cabot was a college student," Janet said at last.

Sean opened his door, but he didn't get out. "True, Helen was a college student. But it's also true that her father is founder and CEO of one of the world's top software companies."

"What are you trying to say?" Janet asked.

"I just want you to think about all this," Sean said as he finally got out of the car. "And when we get upstairs, I want you to look at the thirty-three charts we copied and think about the economic demographics. Just let me know what they say to you."

Sean was pleased that no new guard had come on duty. He retrieved his cardboard box from behind the front desk. Then both he and Janet ducked under the turnstile and took the elevator to the fifth floor.

Sean first checked the refrigerator to make certain that Helen's brain and sample of cerebrospinal fluid had not been disturbed. Next he got the charts out from their hiding place and gave them to Janet. He eyed the mess at his lab bench but didn't touch it.

"While you're perusing the charts," Sean said casually, "I'll be heading out. But I'll be back shortly, maybe in an hour."

"Where are you going?" Janet asked. As usual, Sean was full of surprises. "I thought you needed lab time. That's why we rushed here."

"I do," Sean assured her. "But I'm afraid I'm going to be interrupted because of Alvarez and also because of that group I locked in the closet in Key West. They must be out and fit to be tied by now. I have to make some arrangements to keep the barbarians at bay."

"What do you mean by arrangements?" Janet asked warily.

"Maybe it's better if you don't know," Sean said. "I came up with a great idea that's guaranteed to work, but it's a bit drastic. I don't think you should be involved."

"I don't like the sound of this at all," Janet said.

"If anybody comes in here while I'm gone and asks for me," Sean said, ignoring Janet's concerns, "tell them that you have no idea where I am, which will be the truth."

"Who might come?" Janet asked.

"I hope no one," Sean said. "But if someone does come, it will probably be Robert Harris, the guy who saved the day on the beach. If Alvarez calls anyone, he'll call him."

"What if he asks what I'm doing here?"

"Tell him the truth," Sean said. "Tell him you're going over these charts to try to understand my behavior."

"Oh, please!" Janet said superciliously. "I'm not going to understand your behavior from these charts. That's ridiculous."

"Just read them and keep in mind what I just told you."

"You mean about the economic demographics?" Janet asked.

"Exactly," Sean said. "Now I've got to get out of here. But I need to borrow something. Can I have that container of Mace you always carry in your purse?"

"I don't like this at all," Janet repeated, but she got the container of Mace and handed it to Sean. "This is making me very nervous."

"Don't worry," Sean said. "I need the Mace in case I run into Batman."

"Give me a break," Janet said with exasperation.

Sean knew his time was limited. Alvarez would be regaining consciousness soon if he hadn't already. Sean was quite confident the guard would eventually get the message to someone that he was no longer guarding the Forbes research building and that Sean Murphy was back in town.

Using the rental car, Sean drove to the City Yacht Basin near the municipal auditorium. He parked the car and went into one of the marinas where he rented a sixteen-foot Boston Whaler. Leaving the yacht basin, he drove the boat across Biscayne Bay and around the Dodge Island seaport. Since it was Sunday afternoon, a number of cruise ships were lined up at the dock with people boarding for Caribbean adventures. There was also a horde of pleasure craft, from jet skis to large oceangoing yachts.

Crossing the sea lane was treacherous because of the chop created by a combination of wind and other waterborne traffic, but Sean made it safely to the bridge connecting the MacArthur Causeway to Miami Beach. Passing under the bridge he saw his objective off to the left: Star Island.

It was easy to find the Masons' home since their huge white yacht, *Lady Luck*, was moored to the pier in front. Sean angled his Boston Whaler in behind the yacht where a floating dock was connected to the pier by a ship's ladder. As Sean expected, by the time he secured his boat, Batman, the Masons' Doberman, was at the top of the ladder growling and baring his formidable teeth.

Sean climbed the ladder saying "good dog" over and over. Batman leaned out from the pier as far as he dared and responded to Sean's cajoling by curling his upper lip into a menacing snarl. The volume of his growling rose as he showed more teeth.

Coming within twelve inches of the canine's canines, Sean gave Batman a blast from Janet's Mace canister that sent the dog howling toward its lair on the side of the garage.

Confident that there was only one dog, Sean clambered up onto the pier and surveyed the grounds. What he had to do, he had to do quickly, before any phone calls could be made. The sliders opening out from the living room to the pool were cast open. The sound of opera issued forth.

From where he was standing, Sean couldn't see anyone. As nice a day as it was, he'd expected to see Sarah Mason sunning herself on one of the chaises by the pool. Sean did see a towel, some suntan lotion, and a portion of the Sunday paper, but no Sarah.

Moving quickly, Sean rounded the pool and approached the open sliders. Screen doors obscured his view inside. The closer he got to the house, the louder the music became.

Reaching the door, Sean tried the screen. It was unlocked. Silently he slid it open. Stepping into the room he tried to listen for sounds of people over the opera's sudden crescendo.

Advancing to the stereo, Sean searched among its dazzling array of dials and gauges. Finding the power button, he turned the system off, plunging the room into relative silence. He was hoping that cutting off the *Aida* aria in the middle would have a summoning effect. It did.

Almost immediately, Dr. Mason appeared at the door to his study, gazing at the stereo with a quizzical expression on his face. He took a few steps into the room before he saw Sean. He stopped, obviously flabbergasted.

"Good afternoon, Dr. Mason," Sean said with a voice that was more chipper than he felt. "Is Mrs. Mason around?"

"What in heaven's name is the meaning of this . . . ?" Dr. Mason blustered. He couldn't seem to find the right words.

"Intrusion?" Sean suggested.

Sarah Mason appeared, apparently equally baffled by the sudden silence. She was dressed, if that was the word, in a shiny black bikini. The skimpy suit barely covered her ample flesh. Over the bikini she wore a diaphanous jacket with rhinestone buttons, but the jacket was so transparent, it hardly made for a more modest appearance. Completing the outfit were black, backless high-heeled slippers decorated with a tuft of feathers over each instep.

"I've come to invite you two to the lab," Sean said matter-of-factly. "I suggest you bring some reading material. It may be a long afternoon."

Dr. and Mrs. Mason exchanged glances.

"Trouble is, I don't have a lot of time," Sean added. "Let's get a move on. We'll use your car, since I came in a boat."

"I'm going to call the police," Dr. Mason announced. He started to turn back into his study.

"I don't think that is part of the game plan," Sean said. He pulled out Tom's gun and held it up in the air to be sure both of the Masons could see it clearly.

Mrs. Mason gasped. Dr. Mason stiffened.

"I was hoping a mere invitation would be sufficient," Sean said. "But I do have this gun if need be."

"I think you are making a big mistake, young man," Dr. Mason said.

"With all due respect," Sean said, "if my suspicions are correct, then you're the one who's made big mistakes."

"You won't get away with this," Dr. Mason warned.

"I don't intend to," Sean said.

"Do something!" Mrs. Mason commanded her husband. Tears had formed in the corners of her eyes, threatening her eyeliner.

"I want everybody to stay cool," Sean said. "No one will get hurt. Now if we can all just go to the car." Sean motioned with the gun.

"I'll have you know we're expecting company," Dr. Mason said. "In fact, we're expecting your—"

"That just means we have to get out of here faster," Sean interrupted. Then he yelled: "Move!" With gun in hand, he motioned to the hall.

Reluctantly, Dr. Mason put a protective arm around his wife and walked her to the front door. Sean opened it for them. Mrs. Mason was sobbing, saying that she couldn't go dressed as she was.

"Out!" Sean yelled, his impatience obvious.

They got halfway to Dr. Mason's parked car when another car pulled up to the curb.

Dismayed at this intrusion, Sean slipped the gun into his jacket pocket. He was thinking that he'd have to add this visitor to his pair of hostages. When he saw who it was, he had to blink several times: it was his own brother Brian.

"Sean!" Brian called the moment he recognized his brother. He ran up the lawn, his face reflecting both surprise and pleasure. "I've been looking for you for twenty-four hours! Where have you been?"

"I've been calling you," Sean said. "What in God's name are you doing in Miami?"

"It's a good thing you've arrived, Brian," Dr. Mason interjected. "Your brother was in the process of kidnapping us."

"He has a gun!" Mrs. Mason warned between sniffles.

Brian looked at his brother incredulously. "Gun?" he echoed in disbelief. "What gun?"

"It's in his pocket," Mrs. Mason snapped.

Brian stared at Sean. "Is this true?"

Sean shrugged. "It's been a crazy weekend."

"Let me have the gun," Brian said, extending his hand.

"No," Sean said.

"Let me have the gun," Brian repeated, this time more firmly.

"Brian, there's more involved here than meets the eye," Sean said. "Please don't interfere right now. Obviously I'm going to need your legal talents later, so don't go away. Just cool out for a few hours."

Brian took another step closer to Sean, bringing him within arm's reach. "Give me the gun," he repeated. "I'm not letting you commit this kind of crime. Abduction with a deadly weapon is a serious felony. It carries a compulsory prison term."

"I understand you have good intentions," Sean said. "I know you're older, and you are a lawyer. But I can't explain everything right now. Trust me!"

Brian reached out and jammed his hand into Sean's jacket pocket, groping toward the conspicuous bulge. His fingers wrapped around the gun. Sean grabbed Brian's wrist in an iron grip.

"You're older," Sean said, "but I'm stronger. We've been through this before."

"I'm not letting you do this," Brian said.

"Let go of the gun," Sean ordered.

"I'm not about to let you throw your life away," Brian said.

"Don't make me do this," Sean warned.

Brian tried to wrench his arm from Sean's grip while maintaining a hold on the gun.

Sean reacted by throwing a left uppercut into the pit of Brian's stomach. With lightning speed, he followed his punch with a sharp jab to the nose. Brian went down like a sack of potatoes, curling into a tight ball as he struggled to catch his breath. A bit of blood trickled out of his nose.

"I'm sorry," Sean said.

Dr. and Mrs. Mason, who'd been watching this exchange, bolted for the garage. Sean leapt after them, catching Mrs. Mason first. Dr. Mason, who had hold of Mrs. Mason's other arm, was pulled up short as well.

Having just struck his brother, Sean was in no mood for further argument. "In the car," he growled. "Dr. Mason, you drive."

Sheepishly, the Masons complied. Sean got in the back seat. "The lab, please," he said.

As they pulled out of the driveway, Sean caught a glimpse of Brian, who'd managed to push himself into a sitting position. Brian's face reflected a mixture of confusion, hurt, and anger.

"It's about time," Kurt Wanamaker snapped as he, Sterling, and Wayne stumbled out of the storage closet. They were dripping with perspiration. Despite the air-conditioning in the main lab, the temperature in the unventilated closet had soared.

"I just heard you," the technician explained.

"We've been shouting since noon," Kurt complained.

"It's hard to hear from downstairs," the technician said. "Especially with all the equipment running. Plus, we never come up here."

"I don't understand how you couldn't have heard," Kurt said.

Sterling went directly to a phone and dialed Dr. Mason's private number. When Dr. Mason didn't answer, Sterling cursed as he pictured Dr. Mason spending a relaxing Sunday afternoon at a country club.

Replacing the receiver, Sterling considered what he should do next. With decisive speed, he rejoined Kurt and Wayne and said that he'd like to go back to the airport.

As they descended the stairs, Wayne broke the strained silence. "I never would have picked Sean Murphy for somebody carrying a piece."

"It was a definite surprise," Sterling agreed. "I believe it is further evidence that Sean Murphy is a far more complex individual than we have surmised."

When they got to the front of the building, Kurt Wanamaker was thrown into a panic. "My car's gone!" he moaned.

"Undoubtedly compliments of Mr. Murphy," Sterling said. "He seems to be thumbing his nose at us."

"I wonder how Murphy and his girl got out here from the center of town," Wayne said.

"There's a motorcycle in the back that doesn't belong to anyone who works here," the technician said.

"I guess that answers it," Sterling said. "Call the police and give them the details about your missing automobile. Since he took the car I think it's safe to presume he's left the island. Perhaps the police can pick him up."

"It's a new car," Kurt whined. "I've only had it three weeks. This is awful."

Sterling held his tongue. He felt nothing but contempt for this nervous, tiresome, balding man with whom he'd spent more than five uncomfortable hours crammed into a tiny closet. "Perhaps you could ask one of your technicians to give us a ride to the airport." He took solace in the hope that this would be the last thing he'd ever have to say to the man.

MARCH 7 • SUNDAY, 2:30 P.M.

As soon as Dr. Mason pulled into the Forbes parking lot, Sean tried to peer into the research building foyer to see if anything had changed since he'd left. With sunlight reflecting off the windows, it was impossible to see in. Sean couldn't tell if another guard had come on duty or not.

It was only after they'd parked, and Sean entered the building, keeping the Masons close ahead, that he saw another guard had indeed come on duty. The man's ID badge read "Sanchez."

"Tell him who you are and ask for his passkeys," Sean whispered as the trio neared the turnstile.

"He knows who I am," Dr. Mason snapped.

"Tell him you want no one else in the building until we come down," Sean said. He knew such a command would be ignored as the afternoon progressed, but he thought he might as well try.

Dr. Mason did as he was told. He passed the large key ring to Sean as soon as Sanchez had given it to him. The guard eyed them strangely as they went through the turnstile. Big-breasted blondes wearing black bikinis and feathered high heels weren't exactly regulars at the Forbes research building.

"Your brother was right," Dr. Mason said after Sean closed and locked the entrance doors beyond the turnstile. "This is a serious felony. You'll go to prison. You're not going to get away with this."

"I told you, I don't intend to get away with it," Sean said.

Sean locked the stairwell doors. On the second floor he closed and locked the fire doors leading to the bridge to the hospital. Once they got to the fifth floor he locked off the elevator, then summoned the second car. When it arrived, he locked that off as well.

Ushering the Masons into his lab, Sean waved to Janet. She was inside the glass-enclosed office reading the charts. She came out and looked quizzically at the Masons. Sean hastily introduced them, then sent the Masons into the glass-enclosed office, telling them to stay put. He closed the door behind them.

"What are they doing here?" Janet asked with concern. "And what's Mrs. Mason doing in a swimsuit? It looks like she's been crying."

"She's a bit hysterical," Sean explained. "There wasn't time for her to change.

I brought them here to keep others from disturbing me. Besides, as soon as I do what I'm planning on doing, Dr. Mason is the first person I want to tell."

"Did you force them to come here?" Janet asked. Even after everything else Sean had resorted to, this had to be past the limit.

"They would have preferred to listen to the rest of *Aida*," Sean admitted. He began clearing a work area on his bench, particularly under one of the exhaust hoods.

"Did you use that gun you're carrying?" Janet asked. She didn't want to hear the answer.

"I had to show it to them," Sean admitted.

"Heaven help us," Janet exclaimed, looking up toward the ceiling and shaking her head.

Sean got out some fresh glassware including a large Erlenmeyer flask. He pushed away some of the debris near the sink to make space.

Janet reached out and grasped Sean's arm. "This whole thing has gone too far," she said. "You've kidnapped the Masons! Do you understand that?"

"Of course," Sean said. "What do you think, I'm crazy?"

"Don't make me answer that," Janet said.

"Did anybody come by while I was gone?" Sean asked.

"Yes," Janet said. "Robert Harris came like you thought he might."

"And?" Sean asked, looking up from his work.

"I told him what you told me to say," Janet replied. "He wanted to know if you'd gone back to the residence. I said I didn't know. I think he went there to look for you."

"Perfect," Sean said. "He's the one I'm the most afraid of. He's too gung ho. Everything has to be in place by the time he returns." Sean went back to work.

Janet didn't know what to do. She watched Sean for a few minutes as he mixed reagents in the large Erlenmeyer flask, creating a colorless, oily liquid.

"What exactly are you doing?" she asked.

"I'm making a large batch of nitroglycerin," he said. "Plus an ice bath for it to sit in and cool."

"You're joking," Janet said with fresh concern. It was hard to keep up with Sean.

"You're right," Sean said, lowering his voice. "It's show time. This is really for the benefit of Dr. Mason and his beautiful bride. As a doctor, he knows just enough chemistry to make this believable."

"Sean, you're acting bizarre," Janet said.

"I am a bit manic," Sean agreed. "By the way, what did you think of those charts?"

"I guess you were right," Janet said. "Not all the charts had reference to economic status, but those that did indicated that the patients were CEOs or family members of CEOs."

"All part of the Fortune 500, I'd guess," Sean said. "What does that make you think?"

"I'm too exhausted to draw conclusions," Janet said. "But I suppose it's a strange coincidence."

Sean laughed. "What do you think the statistical probability would be of that happening by chance?"

"I don't know enough about statistics to answer that," Janet said.

Sean held up the flask and swirled the contained solution. "This looks good enough to pass," he said. "Let's hope old Doc Mason remembers enough of his inorganic chemistry to be impressed."

Janet watched Sean carry the flask into the glass enclosure. She wondered if he was losing touch with reality. Granted, he'd been driven to increasingly desperate acts, but abducting the Masons at gunpoint was a mind-numbing quantum leap. The legal consequences of such an act had to be severe. Janet didn't know much law, but she knew she was implicated to an extent. She doubted Sean's proposed coercion theory would spare her. She only wished she knew what to do.

Janet watched as Sean presented the fake nitroglycerin to the Masons as the real thing. Judging by the impression he made on Dr. Mason, she gathered that the Forbes director recalled enough of his inorganic chemistry to make the presentation plausible. Dr. Mason's eyes opened wide. Mrs. Mason brought a hand to her mouth. When Sean gave the flask a violent swirl both the Masons stepped back in fear. Then Sean jammed the flask into the ice bath he'd set up on the desk, collected the charts Janet had left in there, and came out into the lab. He dumped the charts on a nearby lab bench.

"What did the Masons say?" Janet asked.

"They were suitably impressed," Sean said. "Especially when I told them the freezing point is only fifty-five degrees Fahrenheit and that the stuff is extraordinarily unstable in a solid form. I told them to be careful in there because bumping the table would detonate it."

"I think we should call this whole thing off," Janet said. "You're going too far."

"I beg to differ," Sean said. "Besides, it's me that's doing this, not you."

"I'm involved," Janet said. "Just being here probably makes me an accessory."

"When all is said and done, Brian will work it out," Sean said. "Trust me."

Janet's attention was caught by the couple in the glass office. "You shouldn't have left the Masons alone," Janet said. "Dr. Mason is making a call."

"Good," Sean said. "I fully expected him to call someone. In fact, I hope he calls the police. You see, I want a circus around here."

Janet stared at Sean. For the first time, she thought he might be experiencing a psychotic break. "Sean," she said gently, "I have a feeling that you're decompensating. Maybe you've been under too much pressure."

"Seriously," Sean said. "I want a carnival atmosphere. It will be much safer. The last thing I want is some frustrated commando like Robert Harris crawling around through the air ducts with a knife in his mouth trying to be a hero. That's when people would get hurt. I want the police and the fire department out there scratching their heads but keeping the would-be paladins at bay. I want them to think I'm crazy for four hours or so."

"I don't understand you," Janet said.

"You will," Sean assured her. "Meanwhile, I got some work for you to do. You told me you know something about computers. Head up to administration on the seventh floor." He handed her the ring of pass keys. "Go into that glass room that we saw when we copied the charts, the one where the computer was running that program, flashing those nine-digit numbers. I think those numbers are social security numbers. And the phone numbers! I think those were numbers for insurance companies that write health insurance. See if you can corroborate that. Then see if you can hack your way into the Forbes mainframe. I want you to look for travel files for the clinic, especially for Deborah Levy and Margaret Richmond."

"Can't you tell me why I'm doing this?" Janet asked.

"No," Sean said. "It's like a double blind study. I want you to be objective."

Sean's mania was oddly compelling—and persuasive. Janet took the keys and walked to the stairwell. Sean gave her a thumbs-up in parting. Whatever the resolution of this madcap, reckless escapade would be, she'd know within four or five hours.

Before he got down to work, Sean picked up a telephone and called Brian's number in Boston and left a long message. First he apologized for hitting him. Then he said that in case something happened to go horribly wrong, he wanted to tell him what he believed was happening at the Forbes Cancer Center. It took him about five minutes.

Lieutenant Hector Salazar of the Miami Police Department normally used Sunday afternoons as an opportunity to finish the reams of paperwork generated by Miami's typically busy Saturday nights. Sundays were generally quiet. Auto accidents, which the uniformed patrol and their sergeants could handle, comprised the biggest portion of the day's workload. Later on Sundays, after the football games were over, domestic violence often flared. Sometimes that could involve the watch commander, so Hector wanted to get as much done as he could before the phone started to ring.

Knowing that the Miami Dolphins game was still in progress, Hector answered the phone at three-fifteen with little concern. The call was patched through the complaint room to a landline.

"Sergeant Anderson here," the voice said. "I'm at the Forbes Cancer Center hospital building. We got a problem."

"What is it?" Hector asked. His chair squeaked as he leaned back.

"We got a guy holed up in the research building next door with two, maybe three hostages," Anderson said. "He's armed. There's also a bomb of some kind involved."

"Christ!" Hector said as his chair tipped forward with a thump. From experience, he knew the paperwork this kind of scene could generate. "Anyone else in the building?"

"We don't think so," Anderson said. "At least not according to the guard. To make matters worse, the hostages are VIPs. It's the director of the center, Dr. Randolph Mason, and his wife, Sarah Mason."

"You have the area secured?" Hector asked. His mind was already jumping ahead. This operation would be a hot potato. Dr. Randolph Mason was well known in the Miami area.

"We're doing it now," Anderson said. "We're running yellow crime scene tape around the whole building."

"Any media yet?" Hector asked. Sometimes the media got to a scene faster than backup police personnel. The media often monitored the police radio bands.

"Not yet," Anderson said. "That's why I'm using this landline. But we expect a blizzard any minute. The hostage taker's name is Sean Murphy. He's a medical student working at the clinic. He's with a nurse named Janet Reardon. We don't know if she's an accomplice or a hostage."

"What do you mean by 'some kind of bomb'?" Hector asked.

"He mixed up a big flask of nitroglycerin," Anderson said. "It's standing in ice on a desk in the room with the hostages. Once it freezes, slamming the door can set it off. At least, that's what Dr. Mason said."

"You've talked with the hostages?" Hector asked.

"Oh, yeah," Anderson said. "Dr. Mason told me he and his wife are in a glass office along with the nitro. They're terrified, but so far they're unharmed and they have a phone. He says he can see the perp. But the girl is gone. He doesn't know where she went."

"What's Murphy doing?" Hector asked. "Has he made any demands yet?"

"No demands yet," Anderson said. "Apparently he's real busy doing some kind of experiment."

"What do you mean experiment?" Hector asked.

"No clue," Anderson said. "I'm just repeating what Dr. Mason said. Apparently Murphy had been disgruntled because he'd been denied permission to work on a particular project. Maybe he's working on that. At any rate, he's armed. Dr. Mason said he waved the gun in front of them when he broke into their home."

"What kind of gun?"

"Sounds like a .38 detective special, from Dr. Mason's description," Anderson said.

"Make sure the building is secure," Hector said. "I want no one going in or out. Got it?"

"Got it," Anderson said.

After telling Anderson that he'd be out on site in a few minutes, Hector made three calls. First he called the hostage negotiating team and spoke with the supervisor, Ronald Hunt. Next he called the shift SWAT team commander, George Loring. Finally he called Phil Darell, the bomb squad supervisor. Hector told all three to assemble their respective teams and to rendezvous at the Forbes Cancer Center ASAP.

Hector heaved his two-hundred-and-twenty-pound frame out of the desk chair. He was a stocky man who'd been all muscle during his twenties. During his early thirties, a lot of that muscle had turned to fat. Using his stubby, shovel-like hands, he attached to his belt the police paraphernalia he'd removed to sit at his desk. He was in the process of slipping into his Kevlar vest when the phone rang again. It was the chief, Mark Witman.

"I understand there's a hostage situation," Chief Witman said.

"Yes, sir," Hector stammered. "I was just called. We're mobilizing the necessary personnel."

"You feel comfortable handling this?" Chief Witman said.

"Yes, sir," Hector answered.

"You sure you don't want a captain running the show?" Chief Witman asked.

"I believe there'll be no problem, sir," Hector said.

"Okay," Chief Witman said. "But I must tell you I have already had a call from the mayor. This is a politically sensitive situation."

"I'll keep that in mind, sir," Hector said.

"I want this handled by the book," Chief Witman said.

"Yes, sir," Hector said.

Sean attacked his work with determination. Knowing that his time was limited, he tried to work efficiently, planning each step in advance. The first thing he did was slip up to the sixth floor to check on the automatic peptide analyzer that he'd set up on Saturday to sequence the amino acids. He thought there was a good chance his run had been disturbed since Deborah Levy had appeared to read him the riot act just after he'd started it. But the machine hadn't been touched, and his sample was still inside. He tore off the readout from the printer.

The next thing Sean did was carry two thermal cyclers down from the sixth floor to the fifth. They were going to be his workhorses for the afternoon. It was in the thermal cyclers that the polymerase chain reactions were carried out.

After a quick check on the Masons, who seemed to be spending most of their time arguing over whose fault it was that they'd been taken hostage, Sean got down to real work.

First he went over the readout from the peptide analyzer. The results were dramatic. The amino acid sequences of the antigen binding sites of Helen Cabot's medicine and Louis Martin's medicine were identical. The immunoglobulins were the same, meaning all the medulloblastoma patients were being treated, at least initially, with the same antibody. This information was consistent with Sean's theory, so it fanned his excitement.

Next, Sean got out Helen's brain and the syringe containing her cerebrospinal fluid from the refrigerator. He took another general sample of tumor from the brain, then returned the organ to the refrigerator. After cutting it into small pieces, Sean put the tumor sample in a flask with the appropriate enzymes to create a cell suspension of the cancer cells. He put the flask in the incubator.

While the enzymes worked on the tumor sample, Sean began loading some of the ninety-six wells of the first thermal cycler with aliquots of Helen's cerebrospinal fluid. To each well of cerebrospinal fluid he added an enzyme called a reverse transcriptase to change any viral RNA to DNA. Then he put the paired primers for St. Louis encephalitis virus into the same well. Finally, he added the reagents to sustain the polymerase chain reaction. These reagents included a heat stable enzyme called Taq.

Turning back to the cell suspension of Helen's cancer, Sean used a detergent designated NP-40 to open the cells and their nuclear membranes. Then, by painstaking separation techniques, he isolated the cellular nucleoproteins from the rest of the cellular debris. In a final step he separated the DNA from the RNA.

He loaded samples of the DNA into the remaining wells of the first thermal cycler. Into these same wells Sean carefully added the paired primers for oncogenes, a separate pair for each well. Finally he dosed each well with an appropriate amount of reagents for the polymerase chain reaction.

With the first thermal cycler fully loaded, Sean turned it on.

Turning to the second thermal cycler, Sean added samples of Helen's tumor cell RNA to each well. In the second run he was planning to look for messenger RNA made from oncogenes. To do this he had to add aliquots of reverse transcriptions to each well, the same enzyme that he'd added to the samples of cerebrospinal fluid. While he was in the tedious process of adding the oncogene primer pairs, a pair in each well, the phone rang.

At first Sean ignored the phone, assuming that Dr. Mason would answer it. When Mason failed to do so, the continuous ringing began to grate on Sean's nerves. Putting down the pipette he was using, Sean walked over to the glass-enclosed office. Mrs. Mason was sitting glumly in an office chair pushed into the corner. She'd apparently cried herself out and was just sniffling into a tissue. Dr. Mason was nervously watching the flask in the ice bath, concerned that the ringing phone might disturb it.

Sean pushed open the door. "Would you mind answering the phone?" Sean said irritably. "Whoever it is, be sure to tell them that the nitroglycerin is just on the verge of freezing."

Sean gave the door a shove. As it clunked into its jamb, Sean could see Dr. Mason wince, but the doctor obediently picked up the receiver. Sean turned back to his lab bench and his pipetting. He'd only loaded a single well when his concentration was again broken.

"It's a Lieutenant Hector Salazar from the Miami Police Department," Dr. Mason called. "He'd like to talk with you."

Sean looked over at the office. Dr. Mason had the door propped open with his foot. He was holding the phone in one hand, the receiver in the other. The cord snaked back into the office.

"Tell him that there will be no problems if they wait for a couple more hours," Sean said.

Dr. Mason spoke into the phone for a few moments, then called out: "He insists on talking with you."

Sean rolled his eyes. He put his pipette back down on the lab bench, stepped over to the wall extension, and pushed the blinking button.

"I'm very busy right now," he said without preamble.

"Take it easy," Hector said soothingly. "I know you're upset, but everything is going to work out fine. There's someone here who'd like to have a word with you. His name is Sergeant Hunt. We want to be reasonable about all this. I'm sure you do too."

Sean tried to protest that he didn't have time for conversation when Sergeant Hunt's gruff voice came over the line.

"Now I want you to stay calm," Sergeant Hunt said.

"That's a little difficult," Sean said. "I've got a lot to do in a short time."

"No one will get hurt," Sergeant Hunt said. "We'd like you to come down here so we can talk."

"Sorry," Sean said.

"I've heard that you've been angry about not being able to work on a particular project," Sergeant Hunt said. "Let's talk about it. I can understand how upsetting that might be. You may want to lash out at the people you think are responsible. But we should also talk about the fact that holding people against their will is a serious offense."

Sean smiled when he realized the police had surmised he'd taken the Masons hostage as a result of being kept off the medulloblastoma protocol. In a way, they weren't far off.

"I appreciate your concern and your presence," Sean said. "But I don't have a lot of time to talk. I've got to get back to work."

"Just tell us what you want," Sergeant Hunt said.

"Time," Sean said. "I only want a little time. Two or three, or perhaps four hours at most."

Sean hung up. Returning to his bench, he lifted his pipette and went back to work.

Ronald Hunt was a six-foot redheaded man. At thirty-seven, he'd been on the police force for fifteen years, ever since graduating from community college. His major had been law enforcement, but he'd minored in psychology. Attempting to combine psychology with police work, he'd jumped at the chance to join the Hostage Negotiating Team when a slot became available. Although he didn't get to use his skills as often as he would have liked, when he did he'd enjoyed the challenge. He'd even been inspired to take more psychology at night school at the University of Miami.

Sergeant Hunt had been successful in all his previous operations and had developed confidence in his abilities. After the successful resolution of the last episode, which involved a discontented employee at a soft-drink bottling plant who'd taken three female colleagues hostage, Ronald had received a citation from the force for meritorious service. So when Sean Murphy hung up on him, it was a blow to his ego.

"The twerp hung up on me!" Ron said indignantly.

"What did he say he wanted?" Hector asked.

"Time," Ron said.

"What do you mean, time?" Hector asked. "Like the magazine? Does he want to be in *Time*?"

"No," Ron said. "Time like hours. He told me he has to get back to work. He must be working on that project he'd been forbidden to work on."

"What kind of project?" Hector asked.

"I don't know," Ron said. He then pushed the redial on the portable phone. "I can't negotiate unless we talk."

Lieutenant Hector Salazar and Sergeant Ronald Hunt were standing behind three blue-and-white Miami police cars parked in the Forbes parking lot directly across from the entrance to the Forbes research building. The squad cars were parked in the form of a letter U facing away from the building. In the heart of this U they'd set up a mini–command center with a couple of phones and a radio on a folding card table.

The police presence at the site had swelled considerably. Initially there had only been four officers: the original two uniformed patrolmen who'd answered the call, plus their sergeant and his partner. Now there was a small crowd. Besides dozens of regular uniformed police, including Hector, there was the two-man negotiating team, a five-man bomb squad, and a ten-man SWAT team dressed in black assault uniforms. The SWAT team was off to the side warming up with some jumping jacks.

In addition to the police, Forbes was represented by Dr. Deborah Levy, Margaret Richmond, and Robert Harris. They had been allowed near the command post but had been asked to keep to the side. A small crowd, including local media, had gathered just beyond the yellow crime scene tape. Several TV vans were parked as close as possible with their antennae extended. Reporters with microphones in hand and camera crews at their heels were scouring the crowd to interview anyone who seemed to have any information about the drama transpiring within.

While the crowd of spectators swelled, the police tried to go about their business.

"Dr. Mason says that Murphy flat out refuses to get back on the phone," Ron said. He was clearly offended.

"You keep trying," Hector advised him. Turning to Sergeant Anderson, Hector said: "I trust that all entrances and exits are covered."

"All covered," Anderson assured him. "No one is going in or coming out without our knowing it. Plus we have sharpshooters on the roof of the hospital."

"What about that pedestrian bridge connecting the two buildings?" Hector asked.

"We got a man on the bridge on the hospital side," Anderson said. "There aren't going to be any surprises in this operation."

Hector motioned to Phil Darell to come over. "What's the story on the bomb?" Hector asked.

"It's a little unorthodox," Phil acknowledged. "I spoke with the doctor. It's a flask of nitroglycerin. He estimates about two or three hundred cc's. It's sitting in an ice bath. Apparently Murphy comes in every so often and dumps ice into the bath. Every time he does it, it terrifies the doctor."

"Is it a problem?" Hector asked.

"Yeah, it's a problem," Phil said. "Especially once it solidifies."

"Would slamming a door detonate it?" Hector asked.

"Probably not," Phil replied. "But a shake might. A fall to the floor certainly would."

"But can you handle it?"

"Absolutely," Phil said.

Next Hector waved Deborah Levy over.

"I understand you run the research here."

Dr. Levy nodded.

"What do you think this kid is doing?" Hector asked. "He told our negotiator he wanted time to work."

"Work!" Dr. Levy said disparagingly. "He's probably up there sabotaging our research. He's been angry that we haven't allowed him to work on one of our protocols. He has no respect for anyone or anything. Frankly, I thought he was disturbed from the first moment I met him."

"Can he be working on that protocol now?" Hector asked.

"Absolutely not," Dr. Levy said. "That protocol has moved into clinical trials."

"So you think he's up there causing trouble," Hector said.

"I know that he is causing trouble!" Dr. Levy said. "I think you should go up there and drag him out."

"We have the safety of the hostages to consider," Hector said.

Hector was about to confer with George Loring and his SWAT team when one of the uniformed patrolmen got his attention.

"This man insists on talking with you, Lieutenant," the patrolman said. "He claims to be the brother of the guy who's holed up inside."

Brian introduced himself. He explained that he was a lawyer from Boston.

"Any insight into what's going on here?" Hector asked.

"No, I'm sorry," Brian said. "But I know my brother. Although he's always been headstrong, he would not do anything like this unless there was a damn good reason. I want to be sure that you people don't do anything rash."

"Taking hostages at gunpoint and threatening them with a bomb is more than headstrong," Hector said. "That kind of behavior puts him in an unstable, unpredictable, and dangerous category. We have to proceed on that basis."

"I admit what he's done here appears foolhardy," Brian said. "But Sean's ultimately rational. Maybe you should let me talk to him."

"You think he might listen to you?" Hector asked.

"I think so," Brian said, despite still feeling the effects of the episode at the Masons'.

Hector got the phone away from Ronald Hunt and let Brian try calling. Unfortunately no one answered, not even Dr. Mason.

"The doctor has been answering until a few minutes ago," Ron said.

"Let me go in and talk with him," Brian said.

Hector shook his head. "There are enough hostages in there as it is," he said.

"Lieutenant Salazar," a voice called. Hector turned to see a tall, slender Caucasian approaching, along with a bearded, powerfully built Afro-American. Sterling introduced himself and Wayne Edwards. "I'm acquainted with your chief, Mark Witman, quite well," Sterling said after the introductions. Then he added: "We heard about this situation involving Sean Murphy so we came to offer our services."

"This is a police matter," Hector said. He eyed the newcomers with suspicion. He never liked anyone who tried to bully him by saying he was bosom buddies with the chief. He wondered how they'd managed to cross the crime scene barrier.

"My colleague and I have been following Mr. Murphy for several days," Sterling explained. "We are in the temporary employ of the Forbes Cancer Center."

"You have some explanation of what's going on here?" Hector asked.

"We know that this dude's been getting progressively crazy," Wayne said.

"He's not crazy!" Brian said, interrupting. "Sean is brash and imprudent, but he's not crazy."

"If someone does a string of crazy things," Wayne said, "it's fair to say he's crazy."

At that moment everyone ducked reflexively as a helicopter swept over the building, then hovered over the parking lot. The thunderous thump of the rotor blades rattled everyone's rib cage. Every bit of dust and dirt smaller than medium-sized gravel became airborne. A few papers on the card table were swept away.

George Loring, commander of the SWAT team, came forward. "That's our chopper," he yelled into Hector's ear. The noise of the aircraft was deafening. "I called it over so we can get to the roof the moment you give the green light."

Hector was having trouble keeping his hat on. "For crissake, George," he screamed back. "Tell the goddamn chopper to move off until we call it."

"Yes, sir!" George yelled back. He pulled a small microphone clipped to one of his epaulets. Shielding it with his hands he spoke briefly to the pilot. To everyone's relief the chopper dipped, then swept away to land on a helipad next to the hospital.

"What's your take on this situation?" Hector asked George now that they could talk.

"I looked at the floor plans supplied by the head of security, who's been very cooperative," George said, pointing out Robert Harris for Hector. "I think we'd only need a six-man team on the roof: three down each stairwell. The suspect's in the fifth-floor lab. We'd only need one, but we'd probably go ahead and use two concussion grenades. It would be over in seconds. A piece of cake."

"What about the nitroglycerin in the office?" Hector asked.

"I didn't hear about any nitro," George said.

"It's in a glass-enclosed office," Hector said.

"It would be a risk," Phil interrupted, having overheard the conversation. "The concussive waves could detonate the nitroglycerin if it's in a solid state."

"Hell, then," George said. "Forget the grenades. We can just come out of both stairwells simultaneously. The terrorist wouldn't know what hit him."

"Sean's no terrorist!" Brian said, horrified at this talk.

"I'd like to volunteer to be with the assault team," Harris said, speaking up for the first time. "I know the terrain."

"This is not amateur hour," Hector said.

"I'm no amateur," Harris said indignantly. "I trained as a commando in the service and carried out a number of commando missions in Desert Storm."

"I think something should be done sooner rather than later," Dr. Levy said. "The longer that crazy kid is left up there, the more damage he can do to our ongoing experiments."

Everyone ducked again as another helicopter made a low pass over the parking area. This one had "Channel 4 TV" on its side.

Hector yelled for Anderson to call the complaint room to have them call Channel 4 to get their goddamn helicopter away from the scene or he'd let the SWAT team have a go at it with their automatic weapons.

Despite the noise and general pandemonium, Brian picked up one of the telephones and pressed the redial button. He prayed it would be answered, and it was. But it wasn't Sean. It was Dr. Mason.

Sean had no idea how many cycles he should let the thermal cyclers run. All he was looking for was a positive reaction in any of the approximately one hundred and fifty wells he'd prepared. Impatient, he stopped the first machine after twenty-five cycles and removed the tray containing the wells.

First he added a biotinylated probe and the enzymatic reagents used to detect whether the probe had reacted in the series of wells containing Helen Cabot's cerebrospinal fluid. Then he introduced these samples into the chemiluminescence instrument and waited by the printout to see if there was any luminescence.

To Sean's surprise, the very first sample was positive. Although he fully expected it to be positive eventually, he hadn't expected a reaction so soon. What this established was that Helen Cabot—just like Malcolm Betencourt—had contracted St. Louis encephalitis in the middle of the winter, which was strange since the normal vector for the illness is a mosquito.

Sean then turned his attention to the other wells where he would be searching for the presence of oncogenes. But before he could start adding the appropriate probes, he was interrupted by Dr. Mason.

Although the phone had rung intermittently after he'd spoken with Sergeant Hunt, Sean had ignored it. Apparently Dr. Mason had ignored it too, because on several occasions it rang for extended periods. Sean had finally turned the ringer off on his extension. But apparently it had rung again and apparently this time Dr. Mason had answered it because he'd gingerly opened the door to tell Sean that his brother was on the line.

Although Sean hated to interrupt what he was doing, he felt guilty enough about Brian to take his call. The first thing he did was apologize for striking him.

"I'm willing to forgive and forget," Brian said. "But you have to end this nonsense right now and come down here and give yourself up."

"I can't," Sean said. "I need another hour or so, maybe two at the most."

"What in God's name are you doing?" Brian asked.

"It'll take too long to explain," Sean said. "But it's big stuff."

"I'm afraid you have no idea of the hullabaloo you're causing," Brian said. "They've got everyone here but the National Guard. You've gone too far this time. If you don't come out this minute and put a stop to this, I won't have anything to do with you."

"I only need a little more time," Sean said. "I'm not asking for the world."

"There's a bunch of gung-ho nuts out here," Brian said. "They're talking about storming the building."

"Make sure they know about the purported nitroglycerin," Sean said. "That's supposed to dissuade them from heroics."

"What do you mean, 'purported nitroglycerin'?" Brian asked.

"It's mostly ethanol with just a little acetone," Sean said. "It looks like nitroglycerin. At least, it's close enough to fool Dr. Mason. You didn't think I'd make up a batch of the real thing, did you?"

"At this point," Brian said, "I wouldn't put anything past you."

"Just talk them out of any commando action," Sean said. "Get me at least one more hour."

Sean could hear Brian continue to protest, but Sean didn't listen. Instead he hung up the phone and turned back to the first thermal cycler tray.

Sean hadn't gotten far with the oncogene probes when Janet came through the stairwell door trailing computer printout sheets.

"No problem finding the Forbes travel file," she said. She thrust the computer paper at Sean. "For whatever it's worth, Dr. Deborah Levy does a lot of traveling, but it's mostly back and forth to Key West."

Sean glanced at the printout. "She does keep on the move," he agreed. "But notice all these other cities. That's what I expected. What about Margaret Richmond?"

"No travel to Key West," Janet said. "But moderate travel around the country. About once a month she's off to another city."

"What about that automated program we saw?" Sean asked.

"You were right about that," Janet said. "It was running when I got up there, so I copied two of the numbers we thought might have been phone numbers. When I tried to call direct I could tell it was a computer link, so I used the mainframe and its modem to connect. Both of them were insurance companies: one was Medi-First; the other was Healthnet."

"Bingo," Sean said. "It's all falling into place."

"How about letting me in on the revelation," Janet said.

"What I'd be willing to bet is that the computer searches for medical insurance companies' precertification files for specific social security numbers. It probably does it on a nightly basis during the week and on Sunday afternoons."

"You mean precertification for surgery?" Janet asked.

"That's exactly what I mean," Sean said. "In an attempt to cut down on unnecessary surgery, most if not all health plans require the doctor or the hospital to notify the insurance company of proposed surgery in advance. Usually it's merely a rubber-stamp exercise so it's pretty casual. I doubt there's any concern about confidentiality. That computer upstairs is printing out proposed elective surgery on a specific list of social security numbers."

"Those are the numbers that are flashing on the screen," Janet said.

"That's what it has to be," Sean said.

"So why?" Janet asked.

"I'll let you figure that out," Sean said. "While I continue processing these thermal cycler samples, you look at the referring histories on these thirty-three charts we copied. I think you'll find most will mention that the patient had elective surgery within a relatively short period before their diagnosis of medulloblastoma. I want you to compare the dates of those surgeries with Dr. Levy's travel schedule."

Janet stared at Sean without blinking. Despite her exhaustion, she was beginning to assimilate the facts as Sean understood them and therefore starting to comprehend the direction Sean's thoughts were headed. Without saying another word, she sat down with the charts and the computer printout she'd brought down from the seventh floor.

Turning back to his own work, Sean loaded a few more wells with the appropriate oncogene probes. He hadn't gotten far when Dr. Mason interrupted him.

"My wife is getting hungry," Dr. Mason announced.

With his general fatigue Sean's nerves were raw. After all that had happened he could not abide the Masons, particularly Mrs. Mason. The fact that they thought it appropriate to bother him with her being hungry threw him into a momentary rage. Putting down the pipette, he raced back toward the glass office.

Dr. Mason saw Sean coming and quickly guessed his state of mind. He let go of the door and backed into the office.

Sean threw open the office door so that it banged against the doorstop. He flew into the office, snatched the Erlenmeyer flask from the ice bath, and gave it a shake. Some of its contents had solidified and cakes of ice clunked against the sides of the container.

Dr. Mason's face blanched as he cringed in anticipation of an explosion. Mrs. Mason buried her face in her hands.

"If I hear one more sound from you people I'm going to come in here and shatter this flask on the floor," Sean yelled.

When no explosion occurred Dr. Mason opened his eyes. Mrs. Mason peeked out between her fingers.

"Do you people understand?" Sean snapped.

Dr. Mason swallowed hard, then nodded.

Disgusted with the Masons and his own temper tantrum, Sean went back to his lab bench. Guiltily he glanced over at Janet, but she'd not paid any attention. She was too engrossed in the charts.

Picking up the pipette, Sean went back to work. It was not easy, and he had to concentrate. He had to put the right probe in the right well, and he had the primer pairs and probes for over forty oncogenes, a rather extensive list.

A number of the first samples were negative. Sean didn't know if he'd taken them from the thermal cycler after an insufficient number of cycles or if they were truly negative. By the fifth sample he was beginning to become discouraged. For the first time since he'd put this drama into motion, he seriously questioned the conclusions which by then he'd come to view as rock solid. But then the sixth sample proved positive. He'd detected the presence of an oncogene known by the designation ERB-2, which referred to avian erythroblastosis virus, a virus whose normal host was chickens.

By the time Janet finished with the charts, Sean had found another oncogene, called v-myc, which stood for myelocytoma virus, another virus that grew in chickens.

"Only about three-quarters of the charts have the surgery dates," Janet said. "But of those, most of them match the dates and destinations of Dr. Levy's travel."

"Hallelujah!" Sean exclaimed. "It's all fitting into place like a jigsaw puzzle."

"What I don't understand," Janet said, "is what she did in those cities."

"Nearly everyone who's post-surgery is on an IV," Sean said. "It keeps people hydrated, plus if there's a problem the medical staff has a route for medication. My guess is that Deborah Levy gave them an injection into their IV."

"Of what?" Janet asked.

"An injection of St. Louis encephalitis virus," Sean said. He told Janet about the positive test for the SLE virus in Helen Cabot's cerebrospinal fluid. He also told her that Louis Martin had had transient neurological symptoms similar to Helen's several days after his elective surgery.

"And if you look back at the charts," Sean continued, "I think you'll find most of these people had similar fleeting symptoms."

"Why didn't they get full-blown encephalitis?" Janet asked. "Especially if it was injected through their IVs?"

"That's the truly clever part about all this," Sean said. "I believe the encephalitis viruses were altered and attenuated with the inclusion of viral oncogenes. I've already detected two such oncogenes in Helen's tumor. My guess is that I'll find another. One of the current theories on cancer is that it takes at least three isolated events in a cell to make it cancerous."

"How did all this occur to you?" Janet asked. It sounded too complicated, too involved, too complex, and most of all too hideous, to be true.

"Gradually," Sean said. "Unfortunately it took me a long time. I suppose initially my index of suspicion was so low; it's the last thing I expected. But when you told me they started immunotherapy with a specific agent from day one, I thought something was out of whack. That flew in the face of everything I knew about the specificity of immunotherapy. It takes time to develop an antibody and everybody's tumor is antigenically unique."

"But it was at the Betencourts' that you started acting strangely," Janet said.

"Malcolm Betencourt was the one who emphasized the sequence," Sean said. "Elective surgery, followed by neurological symptoms, and then brain tumor. Helen Cabot and Louis Martin had the same progression. Until I heard Malcolm's story, I hadn't realized its significance. As one of my medicine professors said, if you are painstakingly careful in your history-taking, you should be able to make every diagnosis."

"So you believe the Forbes Cancer Center has been going around the country giving people cancer," Janet said, forcing herself to put into words her awful fear.

"A very special kind of cancer," Sean said. "One of the viral oncogenes I've detected makes a protein that sticks out through the cell membrane. Since it's homologous to the protein that forms the receptor for growth hormone, it acts like a switch in the 'on' position to encourage cell growth and cell division. But besides that, the portion that sticks through the cell is a peptide and probably antigenic. My guess is the immunoglobulin they give these people is an antibody for that extracellular part of the ERB-2 oncoprotein."

"You're losing me," Janet admitted.

"Let's give it a try," Sean said. "Maybe I can show you. It will only take a moment since I have some of the ERB-2 oncoprotein from the Key West lab. Let's see if Helen Cabot's medicine reacts with it. Remember that I wasn't able to get it to react with any natural cellular antigen. The only thing it would react with was her tumor."

As Sean quickly prepared the immunofluorescence test, Janet tried to absorb what Sean had said so far.

"In other words," Janet said after a pause, "what makes this medulloblastoma cancer so different is that not only is it man-made, it's curable."

Sean looked up from his work with obvious admiration. "Right on!" he said. "You got it. They created a cancer with a tumor-specific antigen for which they already had a monoclonal antibody. This antibody would react with the antigen and coat all the cancer cells. Then all they'd have to do was to stimulate the immune system both in vivo and in vitro to get as many 'killer' cells as possible. The only minor problem was that the treatment probably made the symptoms worse initially because of the inflammation it would undoubtedly cause."

"Which is why Helen Cabot died," Janet said.

"That's what I'd guess," Sean said. "Boston kept her too long during the diagnostic stage. They should have sent her right down to Miami. The trouble is that Boston can't believe someone else might be better for any medical problem."

"How could you be so sure of all this?" Janet asked. "By the time we got back here you hadn't any proof. Yet you were sure enough to force the Masons over here by gunpoint. Seems to me you were taking a huge risk."

"The clincher was some engineer-style drawings of viral capsids I saw in the lab in Key West," Sean explained. "As soon as I saw them, I knew it all had to be true. You see, Dr. Levy's particular area of expertise is virology. The drawings were of a spherical virus with icosahedral symmetry. That's the kind of capsule an SLE virus has. The scientifically elegant part of this vile plot is that Deborah Levy was able to package the oncogenes into the SLE viral capsule. There wouldn't be room for more than one oncogene in each virus because she'd have to leave much of the SLE virus genome intact so that it would still be infective. I don't know how she did it. She also must have included some retroviral genes as well as the oncogene in order to get the oncogene to insert into the infected cell's chromosomes. My guess is that she transformed a number of the viruses with the oncogenes and only those brain cells that were unlucky enough to get all the oncogenes simultaneously became cancerous."

"Why an encephalitis virus?" Janet asked.

"It has a natural predilection for neurons," Sean said. "If they wanted to cause a cancer they could treat, they needed a tumor which they could count on giving early symptoms. Brain cancer is one of them. Scientifically, it's all quite rational."

"Diabolical is a better term," Janet said.

Janet glanced over into the glass-enclosed office. Dr. Mason was pacing the room although carefully avoiding the desk and the flask in the ice bath. "Do you think he knows all this?" she asked.

"That I don't know," Sean said. "But if I had to guess, I'd say yes. It would be hard to run this elaborate operation without the director knowing. After all, it was a fund-raiser in the final analysis."

"That's why they targeted CEOs and their families," Janet said.

"That's my assumption," Sean said. "It's easy to find out which health in-surance company a large firm uses. It's also not difficult to find out someone's social security number, especially for quasi–public figures. Once they had the subscriber's social security number, it would be an easy step to get their depen-dents'."

"So that evening when we were here copying the charts and heard the word donor, they were referring to money, not organs."

Sean nodded. "At that moment our imaginations were too active," he said. "We forgot that specialty hospitals and associated research centers have become increasingly desperate as NIH grants are getting harder and harder to come by. Creating a group of wealthy, grateful patients is a good way to make it through to the twenty-first century."

Meanwhile, the immunofluorescence test involving the ERB-2 and Helen Cabot's medicine had registered strongly positive, even stronger than it had with the tumor cells. "There you go!" Sean said smugly. "There's the antigen-antibody reaction I've been searching for."

Next Sean turned back to his hundreds of samples in the two thermocyclers.

"Can I help?" Janet asked.

"Definitely," Sean said. He showed her how to handle a twelve-channel pipette, then gave her a series of oncogene probes to add to the thermocycler wells.

They worked together for almost three-quarters of an hour, concentrating on the meticulous work. They were both physically exhausted and emotionally overwrought from the magnitude of the conspiracy they suspected. After the final well was probed and analyzed for its luminescence, they'd uncovered two more oncogenes: Ha-ras, named after the Harvey sarcoma virus which normally infected rats, and SV40 Large T from a virus usually found in monkey kidneys. From the RNA studies in the second thermocycler, where Sean had run a quan-titative polymerase chain reaction, it was determined that all the oncogenes were "mega" expressed.

"What an oncogene cocktail!" Sean said with awe as he stood and stretched his weary muscles. "Any nerve cell that got those four would undoubtedly be-come cancerous. Dr. Levy was leaving as little to chance as possible."

Janet put down the pipette she was holding and cradled her head in her hands. In a tired voice she spoke without looking up: "What now?"

"We give up, I guess," Sean said. As he tried to contemplate the next step, he glanced into the office at the Masons, who were arguing again. Mercifully, the glass partition dampened the sound of their voices considerably.

"How are we going to manage the giving up?" Janet asked sleepily.

Sean sighed. "You know, I hadn't given it much thought. It could be tricky."

Janet looked up. "You must have had some idea when you came up with this plan."

"Nope," Sean admitted. "I didn't think that far ahead."

Janet pushed off her seat and went to the window. From there she could see down into the parking lot. "You got that circus you wanted," she said. "There are hundreds of people out there, including a group in black uniforms."

"They're the ones who make me nervous," Sean admitted. "I'd guess they're a SWAT team."

"Maybe the first thing we should do is send the Masons out to tell them that we're ready to come out."

"That's an idea," Sean said. "But you'll go with them."

"But then you'll be in here alone," Janet said. She came back and sat down. "I don't like that. Not with all those black-uniform guys itching to come charging in here."

"The biggest problem is Helen Cabot's brain," Sean said.

"Why?" Janet asked with a sigh of exasperation.

"It's our only evidence," Sean said. "We cannot allow the Forbes people to destroy the brain, which I'm certain they'd do if given the chance. My guess is that I'll not be very popular with anybody when we end this. During the confusion there's a good chance the brain could get into the wrong hands. I doubt anyone is going to take the time to stop and hear me out."

"I'd have to agree," Janet said.

"Wait a second!" Sean said with sudden enthusiasm. "I've got an idea."

MARCH 7 • SUNDAY, 4:38 P.M.

It took Sean twenty minutes to convince Janet that the best thing for her to do was join the Masons in the office. It was Sean's hope that the idea she'd been coerced would be easier to put forth if she was considered a hostage. Janet was skeptical, but in the end she relented.

With that issue decided, Sean packed Helen Cabot's brain in ice and put it in the cooler he'd used to transport it to the lab. Then with some cord that he'd found in the supply closet, he made a large parcel out of the thirty-three chart copies plus the computer printout of the Forbes Cancer Center travel file. When all was ready, Sean picked up the passkeys and with the cooler in one hand and the charts in the other, he climbed up to the administration floor.

Using the passkey, Sean went into the finance section. After taking out the shelving from the dumbwaiter, he squeezed himself in along with his two parcels. He rode the dumbwaiter down the seven floors to the basement, trying hard to keep his elbows in so they wouldn't rub on the walls.

The chart vault was a problem. The light switch was at the entrance, and Sean had to negotiate the entire length of the room in utter blackness. Remembering at least the general layout of the shelving, he was able to move with a modicum of confidence although several times he became disoriented. Eventually, he found the sister dumbwaiter. Within minutes he was riding up the two stories to medical records in the hospital building.

When he opened the dumbwaiter door he was thankful for the lights being on but disappointed to hear someone giving muffled dictation. Before stepping out of the cramped car, Sean determined that the voice was coming from a small cubicle that was out of sight. As quietly as possible he got himself out of the hoist; then he crept into the hall, clutching his two parcels, one under each arm.

Once in the hall, Sean could sense the electricity in the air. It was apparent that the clinical chemistry and radiology departments had been informed of the hostage situation in the neighboring building; the excitement provided an almost holiday atmosphere for the weekend skeleton staff. Most of them were in the hall at the floor-to-ceiling windows opposite the elevators that faced the research building. None of them paid any attention to Sean.

Shunning the elevators, Sean took the stairs down to the first floor. When he came out into the main lobby, he felt immediately at ease. Conveniently, it was visiting hours so there was quite a mob of people clustered around the lobby entrance. Despite his bulky parcels, two-day growth of whiskers, and rumpled clothes, Sean was able to blend in.

Sean walked out of the hospital unimpeded. Crossing the parking lot to the research side he began to appreciate the number of people who'd showed up for his hostage show. They were milling about the handful of cars parked there, including his own 4×4.

Passing near his Isuzu, Sean contemplated dropping the brain and the charts off. But he decided it would be better to give them directly to Brian. Sean was confident his brother was still there despite his threats to abandon him.

The police had stretched the yellow vinyl crime scene tape from vehicle to vehicle all the way around the front of the research building. Behind the building they used trees to seal off the area completely. All along the tape at regular intervals uniformed police officers stood guard.

Sean noticed that the police had set up a command central at a card table positioned behind a group of squad cars. A crowd of several dozen police officials were gathered in the vicinity in the central spot. Off to the left was the black-suited SWAT team, some of whom were doing calisthenics, others checking an assortment of impressive weaponry.

Sean paused at the tape and scanned the crowd. He was able to pick Brian out instantly. He was the only man dressed in a white shirt and paisley suspenders. Brian was off to the side locked in an animated conversation with a black-suited SWAT team member with black face paint smeared under each eye.

Stepping over to one of the uniformed police officers manning the crime scene tape, Sean waved to get his attention. He was busy clipping his nails.

"Sorry to be a bother," Sean said. "I'm related to the individual who took the hostages and that's my brother over there talking with a member of the SWAT team." Sean pointed toward Brian. "I think I can help resolve the dilemma."

The policeman raised the tape without saying a word. He merely gestured for Sean to enter. Then he went back to his nails.

Sean kept clear of Deborah Levy and Robert Harris, whom he spotted near one of the squad cars. Fortunately they weren't looking in his direction. He also steered away from one of the men he'd locked in the closet in Key West, the same man who'd been waiting on the Sushita jet in Naples, whom he saw near the card table.

Sean went directly to his brother, coming up behind him. He caught bits and pieces of the argument, which dealt with the issue of storming the building. It was obvious they held contrary views.

Sean tapped Brian on the shoulder, but Brian shrugged the intrusion off with a disinterested shrug. He was busy making a point by pounding a fist into an open palm. He continued his emotional monologue until Sean drifted around into the corner of his vision. Brian stopped in midsentence, his mouth agape.

George Loring followed the line of Brian's gaze, sized Sean up as a homeless person, then looked back at Brian. "You know this guy?" he asked.

"We're brothers," Sean said as he nudged the shocked Brian aside.

"What the hell . . . ?" Brian exclaimed.

"Don't make a scene!" Sean warned, pulling his brother farther away. "If you're still mad about me tagging you, I'm sorry. I didn't want to hit you, but you left me with little choice. It was an inconvenient moment for you to pop up."

Brian threw a quick but concerned glance toward the command post a mere forty feet away. Redirecting his attention to Sean, he said: "What are you doing here?"

"I want you to take this cooler," Sean said, handing it over. "Plus these chart copies. But it's the cooler that's most important."

Brian adjusted his posture to deal with the weight of the charts. "How on earth did you get out of there? They assured me the place had been sealed off, that no one could go in or out."

"I'll tell you in a few minutes," Sean said. "But first about this cooler: it's got a brain in it. Not a very pretty brain, but an important one."

"Is this the brain you stole?" Brian asked. "If it is, it's stolen property."

"Hold your legal blarney," Sean said.

"Whose brain is it?"

"A patient's," Sean said. "And we'll need it to indict a number of people here at Forbes Cancer Center."

"You mean it's evidence?" Brian asked.

"It's going to blow a lot of people's minds," Sean promised.

"But there's no appropriate chain of custody," Brian complained.

"The DNA will solve that," Sean said. "Just don't let anybody have it. And the chart copies are important too."

"But they're no good as evidence," Brian said. "They're not authenticated copies."

"For crissake, Brian!" Sean snapped. "I know it was thoughtless of me not to have had the foresight to have a notary with me when I copied them, but we can use them for the grand jury. Besides, the copies will show us what we need to subpoena, and we can use them to be sure they don't change any of the originals." Sean lowered his voice. "Now, what do we do to end this carnival with no loss of life, particularly mine? These idle SWAT team guys give me the willies."

Brian glanced around again. "I don't know," he said. "Let me think. You're always throwing me off balance. Being your brother is a full-time job for several lawyers. I wish I could trade you in for a nice sister."

"That's not how you felt when we sold the stock in Immunotherapy," Sean reminded him.

"I suppose we could just walk away from here," Brian said.

"Whatever is best," Sean said agreeably.

"But then they could charge me as an accessory after the fact," Brian mused.

"Whatever you say," Sean said. "But I should tell you that Janet is upstairs."

"Is she that rich girl you've been dating in Boston?" Brian asked.

"That's the one," Sean said. "She surprised me and showed up down here the same day I arrived."

"Maybe it's best if you just give yourself up right here," Brian reasoned. "It will probably sit well with the judge. The more I think about it, the more I like it. Come on, I'll introduce you to Lieutenant Hector Salazar. He's running the show, and he seems like a decent guy."

"Fine by me," Sean said. "Let's do it before one of these black-suited SWAT team members doing calisthenics pulls a groin muscle and I get sued for loss of consortium."

"You'd better have one hell of an explanation for all of this," Brian warned.

"It'll blow your socks off," Sean said. "Guaranteed."

"Let me do the talking," Brian said. They started toward the card table.

"I wouldn't think of interfering," Sean said. "It's the one thing you do well."

As they approached the card table Sean eyed Sterling Rombauer and Robert Harris, who were arguing off to the side. Sean tried to turn away from them and walk sideways lest they recognize him and cause some kind of panic. But he needn't have been concerned. They were too engrossed in their conversation to notice him.

Coming up behind Hector Salazar's bulk, Brian cleared his throat to get the policeman's attention, but to no avail. Hector had taken over where Brian had left off with George Loring. George was eager to get the nod for action. Hector was advocating patience.

"Lieutenant!" Brian called.

"Goddamn it," Hector bellowed. "Anderson, did you call complaints about that TV chopper? Here it comes again."

All conversation had to halt as the Channel 4 helicopter flew low overhead and banked around the parking area. Hector flipped the cameraman a finger, which he'd later regret when he had to watch it replay again and again on TV.

Once the helicopter disappeared, Brian got Hector's attention.

"Lieutenant," Brian said buoyantly. "I'd like you to meet my brother Sean Murphy."

"Another brother!" Hector said, not making the proper connection. "What is this, a family reunion?" Then to Sean he said: "Do you think you might have some influence on that nutty brother of yours up in the lab? We have to get him to start talking to our negotiating team."

"This is Sean!" Brian said. "He's the one who was up there. But he's out now, and he wants to apologize for all this trouble."

Hector looked back and forth between the two brothers as his mind tried to make sense of this sudden, mind-boggling turn of events.

Sean stuck his hand out. Hector took it automatically, still too stunned to speak. The two men shook hands as if they'd just been introduced at a cocktail party.

"Hi!" Sean said, giving Hector one of his best smiles. "I want to personally thank you for all your effort. It really saved the day."

MARCH 8 • MONDAY, 11:15 A.M.

Sean preceded Brian through the swinging doors of the Dade County Courthouse and let the sun and cool fresh air wash over him while he waited for Brian to emerge. Sean had been in the lockup overnight after having been arrested and booked the previous evening.

"That was worse than medical school," Sean said, referring to the night in jail, as he and Brian descended the broad, sun-drenched steps.

"You're eyeball to eyeball with a long prison sentence if this case doesn't go perfectly smoothly," Brian said.

Sean stopped. "You're not serious, are you?" he asked with alarm. "Not after what I've told you these Forbes people have been up to."

"It's now in the hands of the judicial system," Brian said with a shrug. "Once it goes to a jury, it's a crapshoot. And you heard that judge in there at your arraignment. He was none too happy with you despite your giving yourself up and despite the nitroglycerin's not being nitroglycerin. As long as your captives thought it was nitroglycerin, it makes no difference what it was. You'd better thank me that I took the time and trouble to get your juvenile record sealed. If I hadn't you probably wouldn't have gotten out on bail."

"You could have made sure Kevin Porter told the judge there were extenuating circumstances," Sean complained.

"An arraignment is not a trial," Brian explained. "I told you that already. It's only a time for you to hear the formal charges against you and for you to enter your plea. Besides, Kevin alluded to extenuating circumstances during the bail portion."

"That's another thing," Sean said. "Five hundred thousand dollars bail! My God! Couldn't he have done better than that? Now we've tied up part of our seed capital of Oncogen."

"You're lucky to be out on bail, period," Brian said. "Let's go over your charges again: conspiracy, grand larceny, burglary, burglary with a deadly weapon, assault, assault with a deadly weapon, false imprisonment, kidnapping, mayhem, and mutilation of a dead body. My God, Sean, why'd you leave out rape and murder!"

"What about the Dade County District Attorney?" Sean asked.

"They call him State's Attorney down here," Brian said. "I met with him and with the U.S. District Attorney last night. While you were comfortably sleeping in jail, I was working my butt off."

"What did they say?"

"They were both interested, obviously," Brian said. "But without any evidence to present to them other than some circumstantial travel records and copies of hospital charts, they wisely withheld comment."

"What about Helen Cabot's brain?" Sean asked. "That's the evidence."

"It's not evidence yet," Brian said. "The tests you say you ran haven't been reproduced."

"Where is the brain itself?" Sean asked.

"It's been impounded by the police," Brian said. "But it is in the physical custody of the Dade County Medical Examiner. Remember, it's stolen property. So that's an added problem about its status as evidence."

"I hate lawyers," Sean said.

"And I have a feeling you'll be liking them even less by the time this is over," Brian said. "I heard this morning that in light of your irresponsible and slanderous statements that Forbes has retained one of the country's most successful and flamboyant lawyers as well as the backup of Miami's largest firm. A number of powerful people from all over the country are incensed by your allegations and are flooding Forbes with money for legal representation. In addition to the criminal charges, you'll be facing a blizzard of civil suits."

"I'm not surprised that important businesspeople are standing behind Forbes," Sean said. "But these same people will have a change of heart when they learn that the fantastic cure Forbes provided them was for a brain cancer that Forbes caused."

"You'd better be right about that," Brian said.

"I'm right," Sean said. "The tumor I checked had four viral oncogenes. Even finding one in a natural tumor would have been astounding."

"But that's only one tumor out of thirty-eight cases," Brian said.

"Don't worry," Sean said. "I'm right about this."

"But the other evidence has already been thrown into question," Brian said. "Through its lawyers, Forbes is saying that the fact that Dr. Deborah Levy happened to be in relevant cities the same day subsequent Forbes patients underwent elective surgery was purely coincidental."

"Oh, sure," Sean said sarcastically.

"They do have a point," Brian said. "First of all, her travel did not match all the cases."

"So they sent someone else," Sean said. "Like Margaret Richmond. You'll have to subpoena all their travel records."

"There's more to it," Brian said. "Forbes contends that Dr. Levy is an on-site inspector for the College of American Pathology. I already checked it out. It's true. She often travels around the country making clinical lab inspections necessary for hospitals to maintain accreditation. I've also already checked some of the hospitals. It seems Dr. Levy did make inspections on those specific days."

"What about the program running at night with the social security numbers?" Sean asked. "That's pretty incriminating."

"Forbes has already categorically denied it," Brian said. "They say that they access insurance companies on a regular basis but purely to process claims. They say they never access precertification files for elective surgery. And what's more, the insurance companies claim that all their files are secure."

"Of course the companies would say that," Sean said. "I'm sure they're all quaking in their boots that they might be drawn in on the civil side of this. But in regard to the program at Forbes, Janet and I saw it running."

"It will be tough to prove," Brian said. "We'd need the program itself, and they certainly aren't going to give it to us."

"Well, damn!" Sean said.

"It's all going to come down to the science and whether we can get a jury to believe it or even understand it," Brian said. "I'm not sure I do. It's pretty esoteric stuff."

"Where's Janet?" Sean asked. They started walking again.

"She's in my car," Brian said. "Her arraignment was much earlier and a bit easier, but she wanted to get out of the courthouse. I can't blame her. This whole experience has unnerved her. She's not accustomed to being in trouble the way you are."

"Very funny," Sean said. "Is she being charged?"

"Of course she's being charged," Brian said. "What do you think, these people down here are morons? She was an accomplice for everything except assault with a deadly weapon and the kidnapping. Fortunately, the judge seemed to believe her biggest crime is associating with you. He didn't set bail. She was released on her own recognizance."

As they neared Brian's rental car, Sean could see Janet sitting in the front seat. She had her head leaning back on the headrest and she appeared to be asleep. But as Sean came alongside the car, her eyes popped open. Seeing Sean, she scrambled out of the car and hugged him.

Sean hugged her back, feeling self-conscious with his brother standing next to them.

"Are you all right?" Janet asked, pulling her head away but keeping her arms around Sean's neck.

"Fine, and you?"

"Being in jail was an eye-opener," she admitted. "I guess I got a little hysterical at first. But my parents flew down with a family attorney who speeded up my arraignment."

"Where are your parents now?" Sean asked.

"Back at a hotel," Janet said. "They're mad I wanted to wait for you."

"I can imagine," Sean said.

Brian consulted his watch. "Listen, you two," he said. "Dr. Mason has scheduled a news conference at noon at Forbes. I think we should go. I was worried we'd still be tied up here at the courthouse, but there's time. What do you say?"

"Why should we go?" Sean asked.

"I'm concerned about this case, as you can tell," Brian said. "I'm worried about getting a fair trial here in Miami. I'd prefer that this news conference not turn into the public relations bonanza I believe Forbes expects it to be. Your being there will tone down their rhetoric. It will also help establish you as a responsible individual who is serious about his allegations."

Sean shrugged. "Okay by me," he said. "Besides, I'm curious what Dr. Mason will say."

"Okay by me," Janet said.

Because of traffic, it took more time than Brian expected to drive from the Dade County Courthouse, but they were still on time for the news conference when they finally pulled into the Forbes parking area. The conference was scheduled to be held in the hospital auditorium, and all the parking spaces near the hospital were occupied. Several TV vans were parked in the fire lane near the hospital's front door. Brian had to drive around by the research building to find a space.

As they walked around to the hospital, Brian commented on how much media attention the affair was getting. "Let me warn you, this is hot. It's just the kind of case that gets played out in the media as much as it gets played out in the courts. What's more, it's being played on the Forbes's turf. Don't be surprised if your reception is less than cool."

A throng of people was milling about in front of the hospital. Many were reporters, and unfortunately several recognized Sean. They mobbed him, fighting with each other to thrust microphones into his face, everyone asking hostile questions at the same time. Flashbulbs flashed; TV camera lights flooded the scene. By the time Sean, Brian, and Janet reached the front door, Sean was angry. Brian had to restrain him from taking a swing at a few of the photographers.

Inside wasn't much better. News of Sean's arrival sent ripples through the surprisingly large crowd. As the three entered the auditorium, Sean heard a chorus of boos rise from the members of the Forbes medical staff who were attending.

"I see what you mean about chilly receptions," Sean said as they found seats. "Hardly neutral territory."

"It's a lynch mob mentality," Brian said. "But this gives you an idea of what you're up against."

The booing and hissing directed at Sean ceased abruptly and was replaced by respectful applause when Dr. Randolph Mason appeared from the wings of the small stage. He walked resolutely to the podium, placing a sizable manila envelope on it. Grasping either side of the podium, he looked out over the audience with his head slightly tilted back. His bearing and appearance were commendably professional, his classically graying hair perfectly coiffed. He was dressed in a dark blue suit, white shirt, and subdued tie. The only splash of color was a lavender silk foulard handkerchief in his breast pocket.

"He looks like everyone's romantic image of a physician," Janet whispered. "The kind you'd see on TV."

Brian nodded. "He's the kind of man juries tend to believe. This is going to be an uphill battle."

Dr. Mason cleared his throat, then began speaking. His resonant voice easily filled the small auditorium. He thanked everyone for coming and for supporting the Forbes Cancer Center in the face of the recent accusations.

"Will you be suing Sean Murphy for slander?" one of the reporters yelled out from the second row. But Dr. Mason didn't have to answer. The entire auditorium erupted in a sustained hiss in response to the reporter's rudeness. The reporter got the message and meekly apologized.

Dr. Mason adjusted the position of the manila envelope as he collected his thoughts.

"These are difficult times for hospitals and research facilities, particularly specialty hospitals, which have the dual objectives of patient care and research. Clinical reimbursement schemes based on diagnosis and standard therapy do not work in environments such as Forbes where treatment plans often follow experimental protocols. Treatment of this sort is intensive and therefore expensive.

"The question is, where is the money supposed to come from for this type of care? Some people suggest it should come from research grants since it is part of the research process. Yet our public funding for general research has gone down, forcing us to seek other sources for financial support, like industry, or even, in exceptional cases, foreign industry. But even this source has limits, especially when the global economy is floundering. Where else can we turn but to the oldest method: private philanthropy."

"I can't believe this guy," Sean whispered. "This is like a fund-raiser pep talk."

A few people turned to glare at Sean.

"I have devoted my life to the relief of suffering," Dr. Mason continued. "Medicine and the fight against cancer have been my life since the day I entered medical school. I have always kept the good of mankind as my motivating force and goal."

"Now he sounds like a politician," Sean whispered. "When is he going to address the issue?"

"Quiet!" a person behind Sean snapped.

"When I took the position as director of the Forbes Center," Dr. Mason continued, "I knew the institution was in financial difficulty. Restoring the institution to a solid financial basis was a goal consistent with my desire to work for the good of mankind. I've given this task my heart and my soul. If I've made some mistakes, it is not for lack of altruistic motives."

There was spotty applause when Dr. Mason paused and fumbled with his manila envelope, undoing the string that held it closed.

"This is a waste of time," Sean whispered.

"That was just his introduction," Brian whispered in return. "Pipe down. I'm sure he's about to get to the meat of the news conference now."

"At this time I would like to take leave of you," Dr. Mason said. "To those who have helped me in this difficult period, my heartfelt thanks."

"Is this whole rigmarole so he can resign?" Sean asked out loud. He was disgusted.

But no one answered Sean's question. Instead, gasps of horror rippled through the audience when Dr. Mason reached into the envelope and pulled out a nickel-plated .357 Magnum revolver.

Murmurs crescendoed as a few people nearest the podium rose to their feet, unsure whether to flee or approach Dr. Mason.

"I don't mean for people to become upset," Dr. Mason said. "But I felt . . ."

It was clear Dr. Mason had more to say, but two reporters in the front row made a move for him. Dr. Mason motioned them to keep away, but the two men edged closer. Dr. Mason took a step back from the podium. He looked panicked, like a cornered deer. All the color had drained from his face.

Then, to everyone's dismay, Dr. Mason put the barrel of the revolver in his mouth and pulled the trigger. The bullet went through his hard palate, liquefied part of his brain stem and cerebellum, and carried away a five-centimeter disk of skull before burying itself deeply into the wooden cornice molding. Dr. Mason fell backward while the gun was propelled forward. The revolver hit the floor and skidded beneath the first row of seats, sending the people still seated there scattering.

A few people screamed, a few cried, most felt momentarily ill. Sean, Janet, and Brian looked away at the moment the gun went off. When they looked again the room was in pandemonium. No one knew quite what to do. Even the doctors and nurses felt helpless; clearly Dr. Mason was beyond help.

All Sean, Janet, and Brian could see of Dr. Mason were his shoes pointing upward and a foreshortened body. The wall behind the podium was splattered as if someone had hurled a handful of ripe red berries against it.

Sean's mouth had gone dry. He found it difficult to swallow.

A few tears welled in Janet's eyes.

Brian murmured: "Holy Mary, mother of God!"

Everyone was stunned and emotionally drained. There was little conversation. A few hearty souls, including Sterling Rombauer, ventured up to view Dr. Mason's corpse. For the moment most people remained where they were—all except for one woman, who got up from her seat and struggled toward an exit. Sean saw her pushing dumbfounded people aside in her haste. He recognized her immediately.

"That's Dr. Levy," Sean said, getting to his feet. "Somebody should stop her. I'll bet she's planning on fleeing the country."

Brian grabbed Sean by the arm, preventing him from giving chase. "This is not the time or place for you to play a paladin. Let her go."

Sean watched as Dr. Levy got to an exit and disappeared from view. He looked down at Brian. "The charade is beginning to unravel."

"Perhaps," Brian said evasively. His legal mind was concerned about the sympathy this shocking event was likely to evoke in the community.

Gradually, the crowd began to disperse. "Come on," Brian said. "Let's go."

Brian, Janet, and Sean shuffled out in silence and pushed through the subdued crowd gathered at the hospital entrance. They headed toward Brian's car. Each struggled to absorb the horrible tragedy they'd just had the misfortune of witnessing. Sean was the first to speak.

"I'd say that was a rather dramatic mea culpa," he said. "I suppose we have to give him credit for at least being a good shot."

"Sean, don't be crude," Brian said. "Black humor is not my cup of tea."

"Thank you," Janet said to Brian. Then to Sean she said: "A man is dead. How can you joke about it?"

"Helen Cabot is dead, too," Sean said. "Her death bothers me a lot more."

"Both deaths should bother you," Brian said. "After all, Dr. Mason's suicide could be attributed to all the bad publicity Forbes has received thanks to you. The man had reason to be depressed. His suicide wasn't necessarily an admission of guilt."

"Wait a second," Sean said, bringing the party to a halt. "Do you still have any doubts about what I've told you concerning this medulloblastoma issue after what we just witnessed?"

"I'm a lawyer," Brian said. "I'm trained to think in a specific fashion. I try to anticipate the defense."

"Forget being a lawyer for two seconds," Sean said. "What do you feel as a human being?"

"Okay," Brian relented. "I'll have to admit, it was an extremely incriminating act."

EPILOGUE

The big Delta jet banked, then entered its final approach into Logan Airport. It was landing to the northwest, and Sean, sitting in a window seat, had a good view of Boston out the left side of the plane. Brian was sitting next to him but had his nose buried in a law journal. Below they passed over the Kennedy Library on Columbus Point and then the tip of South Boston with its shorefront of clapboard three-decker houses.

Next Sean was treated to a superb view of the downtown Boston skyline with the Boston inner harbor in the foreground. Just before they touched down, he caught a quick glimpse of Charlestown with the Bunker Hill obelisk jutting up into the afternoon sky.

Sean breathed a sigh of relief. He was home.

Neither of them had checked luggage, so after deplaning they went directly to a cab stand and got a taxi. First they went to Brian's office in Old City Hall on School Street. Sean told the cabbie to wait and got out with Brian. They hadn't spoken much since they'd left Miami that morning, mainly because they'd been under such tension and had spoken so much during the prior three days. They had gone to Miami so Sean could testify before a Florida grand jury concerning the case *The State of Florida v. The Forbes Cancer Center.*

Sean eyed his brother. Despite their differences and their frequent arguments, he felt a rush of love for Brian. He stuck out his hand. Brian grasped it firmly and they shook. But it wasn't enough. Sean let go of Brian's hand and embraced him in a strong, sustained hug. When they parted both felt a moment of awkwardness. Rarely did they convey their affection physically. Generally they didn't touch save for jabs to the shoulder and pats on the back.

"Thanks for all you've done," Sean said.

"It pales in comparison to what you've done for a lot of potential Forbes victims," Brian said.

"But without your legal follow-through," Sean said, "Forbes would still be in business today."

"It's not over yet," Brian cautioned. "This was merely the first step."

"Well, whatever," Sean said. "Let's get back to putting our efforts into Oncogen. The Forbes matter is in the hands of the Florida State's Attorney and the U.S. District Attorney. Who do you think will prosecute the case?"

"Maybe they'll cooperate," Brian said. "With all the media attention, both obviously see the case as having great political potential."

Sean nodded. "Well, I'll be in touch," he said as he climbed back into the cab.

Brian grabbed the door before Sean had a chance to pull it closed. "I hate to sound captious," Brian said, "but as your older brother, I feel I should offer some advice. You'd make things so much easier for yourself if you'd only tone down that brazen side of your personality. I'm not talking about a big change, either. If you could just shed some of that townie abrasiveness. You're holding on to your past way too much."

"Aw, come on," Sean said with a wry smile. "Lighten up, Brian."

"I'm serious," Brian said. "You make enemies of those people less intelligent than yourself, which unfortunately is most of us."

"That's the most backhanded compliment I've ever received," Sean said.

"Well, it's not meant as a compliment," Brian said. "You're like some idiot savant. As smart as you are in some areas, you're retarded in others, like social skills. Either you're unaware of what other people are feeling, or you don't care. But either way, the results are the same."

"You're out of control!" Sean said with a laugh.

"Give it some thought, brother," Brian said. He gave Sean's shoulder a friendly poke.

Sean told the cabdriver to take him to the Boston Memorial Hospital. It was getting on toward three, and Sean was eager to catch Janet before her shift was over. Sitting back, Sean thought about what Brian had said. He smiled. As likable as his brother was, he could be such a nerd at times.

At the hospital, Sean went straight to Janet's floor. At the nurses' station he learned she was down in 503 medicating Mrs. Mervin. Sean headed down the hall toward the patient's room. He couldn't wait to give Janet the good news. He found her injecting antibiotic into Mrs. Mervin's IV.

"Well, hello, stranger," Janet said when she caught sight of Sean. She was pleased to see him although she was obviously preoccupied. She introduced Sean to Mrs. Mervin, telling her that he was one of the Harvard medical students.

"I just love all you boys," Mrs. Mervin said. She was an elderly white-haired woman with pink cheeks and sparkling eyes. "You can come visit me anytime," she said with a titter.

Janet winked at Sean. "Mrs. Mervin is on the mend."

"I can see that," Sean agreed.

Janet made a notation on a 3×5 card and stuck it into her pocket. After picking up her medication tray, she said goodbye to Mrs. Mervin, advising her to ring if she wanted anything.

In the hall, Sean had to scurry to keep up with Janet's pace.

"I'm anxious to talk with you," Sean said, coming alongside. "In case you couldn't guess."

"I'd love to chat," Janet said, "but I'm really busy. Report's coming up and I've got to finish these medications."

"The indictment against Forbes was handed down by the grand jury," Sean said.

Janet stopped and gave him a big, warm smile.

"That's great!" she said. "I'm pleased. And I'm proud of you. You must feel vindicated."

"As Brian says, it's an important first step," Sean said. "The indictment includes Dr. Levy, although she hasn't been seen or heard from since Mason's mea culpa news conference. No one knows where the heck she is. The indictment also includes two clinical staff doctors and the director of nursing, Margaret Richmond."

"It's still all so hard to believe," Janet said.

"It is until you realize how thankful the Forbes medulloblastoma patients have been," Sean said. "Up until we put an end to it all, they'd given over sixty million dollars in essentially unrestricted donations."

"What's happened to the hospital?" Janet asked, eyeing her watch.

"The hospital is in receivership," Sean said. "But the research institute is closed. And in case you're interested, the Japanese were fooled by the scam as well. They had no part in it. Since the lid blew off, they cut their losses and ran."

"I'm sorry about the hospital," Janet said. "I personally think it's a good hospital. I hope they make it."

"One other piece of news," Sean said. "You know that crazy guy that caught us on the beach and scared us half to death? His name is Tom Widdicomb, and he's crazier than the mad hatter. He'd kept his dead mother in a freezer at his house. Seems he thought she was telling him to put all advanced breast cancer patients to sleep with succinylcholine. The mother had had the same disease."

"My God," Janet said. "Then that's what happened to Gloria D'Amataglio."

"Apparently so," Sean said. "And a number of others."

"I even remember Tom Widdicomb," Janet said. "He was the housekeeper who bugged Marjorie so much."

"Well, apparently you bugged him," Sean said. "Somehow in his distorted thinking, he decided that you had been sent to stop him. That's why he was after you. They think he was the guy in your bathroom at the Forbes residence, and he definitely was the person who followed us into the Miami General morgue."

"Good Lord!" Janet exclaimed. The idea that a psychotic had been stalking her was terribly unnerving. It reminded her again of how different her trip to Florida had been from what she'd anticipated when she'd decided to go.

"Widdicomb will be tried," Sean continued. "Of course he's pleading insanity, and if they bring the mother in the freezer in to testify, he won't have a problem." Sean laughed. "Needless to say, it's because of him that the hospital is in receivership. Every family that lost a breast cancer patient under suspicious circumstances is suing."

"None of the medulloblastoma cases are suing?" Janet asked.

"Not the hospital," Sean said. "There'd been two entities: the hospital and the research center. The medulloblastoma patients will have to sue the research center. After all, at the hospital, they got cured."

"All except for Helen Cabot," Janet said.

"That's true," Sean agreed.

Janet glanced at her watch again and shook her head. "Now I'm really behind," she said. "Sean, I've got to go. Can't we talk about all this tonight, maybe over dinner or something?"

"Not tonight," Sean said. "It's Friday."

"Oh, of course!" Janet said coolly. She thumped her head with the heel of her hand. "How stupid of me to forget. Well then, when you get a chance, give me a call." Janet started down the hall.

Sean took a few steps and grasped her arm, pulling her to a stop.

"Wait!" he said, surprised at her abrupt end to their conversation. "Aren't you going to ask me about the charges against you and me?"

"It's not that I'm not interested," Janet said. "But you've caught me at a bad time, and of course, you're busy tonight."

"It'll only take a second," he said with exasperation. "Brian and I spent most of last evening bargaining with the State's Attorney. We got his word that all charges against you will be dropped. As far as I'm concerned, in return for testifying, all I have to do is plead guilty to disturbing the peace and malicious mischief. What do you think?"

"I think that's great," Janet said. "Now if you'll excuse me." She tried to get her arm free, but Sean wouldn't let go.

"There's something else," Sean said. "I've been doing a lot of thinking now that this Forbes thing is out of the way." Sean averted his gaze and shifted his weight uneasily. "I don't know how to say this, but remember when you said you wanted to talk about our relationship when you came down to Florida, how you wanted to talk about commitment and all that? Well, I think I want to do that. That is, if you're still thinking about what I think you were."

Stunned, Janet looked Sean directly in his deep blue eyes. He tried to look away. Janet reached out and, grasping his chin, turned his head back to face her. "Is all this double-talk an attempt to talk about marriage?"

"Well, yeah, sorta," Sean equivocated. He pulled away from Janet's hold on his chin to gaze down the hall. It was difficult for him to look at her. He made some gestures with his hands as if he were about to say more, but no words came.

"I don't understand you," Janet said, color spreading across her cheeks. "To think of all the times I wanted to talk and you wouldn't, and now you bring this up here and now! Well, let me tell you something, Sean Murphy. I'm not sure I can deal with a relationship with you unless you're willing to make some big changes, and frankly I don't think you're capable. After that experience down in Florida, I'm not sure you are what I want. It doesn't mean I don't love you, because I do. It just means I don't think I could live with the kind of relationship you're capable of."

Sean was shocked. For a moment he was incapable of speech. Janet's response had been totally unexpected. "What do you mean by change?" he asked finally. "Change what?"

"If you don't know and if I have to tell you, then it's futile. Of course, we could talk about it more tonight, but you have to go out with the boys."

"Don't get on my case," Sean said. "I haven't seen the guys for weeks with all this legal malarkey going on."

"That's undeniably true," Janet said. "And you have fun." Again she started down the hall. After a few steps she turned to face him. "Something else unexpected came out of my Florida trip," she said. "I'm seriously thinking of going to medical school. Not that I don't love nursing, and God only knows what a challenge it is, but all that material you introduced me to concerning molecular biology and the medical revolution it's spawning has turned me on in a way no other academic subject has been able to do. I think I want to be a part of it."

"Well, don't be a stranger, Sean," Janet added as she continued down the hall. "And close your mouth."

Sean was too stunned to speak.

It was a little after eight when Sean pushed into Old Scully's Bar. Not having been able to go for many weeks, he was filled with pleasant anticipation. The bar was jammed with friends and acquaintances and was brimming with good cheer. A number of people had been there since five and were feeling no pain. A Red Sox game was on the tube and at the moment Sean looked at it, Roger Clemens was giving the camera the evil eye while waiting for the sign from the catcher. There were a few cheers of encouragement from a knot of die-hard fans grouped directly under the TV. The bases were loaded.

Standing just inside the door, Sean paused to take in the scene. He saw Jimmy O'Connor and Brady Flanagan at the dartboard laughing to the point of tears. Someone's dart had missed the board. In fact, it had missed the wall and was embedded in one of the muntin bars of the window. Obviously, the two were smashed.

At the bar, Sean could see Molly and Pete tirelessly going about their business filling mugs of ale and stout, occasionally holding four or five of the frosted, brimming glasses in a single hand. Shots of Irish whiskey dotted the bar. The day's problems melted into oblivion much faster with these nips between the drafts of beer.

Sean eyed the guys at the bar. He recognized Patrick FitzGerald, or Fitzie, as they called him. He'd been the most popular guy in high school. Sean could remember as if it were yesterday how Fitzie had stolen his girl when they were in ninth grade. Sean had fallen head over heels for Mary O'Higgins only to have her disappear at a party he'd brought her to in order to make out with Fitzie in the back of Frank Kildare's pickup.

But since his high school triumph, Fitzie had put on considerable weight around his middle and his face had assumed a puffy, pasty look. He worked on the maintenance crew down at the old Navy Yard when he worked, and he was married to Anne Shaughnessy, who'd blown up to two hundred pounds after giving birth to twins.

Sean took a step toward the bar. He wanted to be drawn into his old world. He wanted people to slap him on the back, tease him about his brother becoming a priest. He wanted to remember those days when he thought his future was a limitless road to be traveled along with the whole gang. Fun and meaning were to be had in shared experiences that could be enjoyed over and over through reminiscences. In fact, the experiences became more enjoyable with the inevitable embellishment that accompanied each retelling.

But something held Sean back. With a disturbing, almost tragic sense, he felt apart. The feeling that his life had taken a different track from his old friends' came back to him with crushing clarity. He felt more like an observer of his old life; he was no longer a participant. The events at the Forbes clinic were forcing him to look at broader issues beyond the confines of his old friends in Charlestown. He no longer had the insulation that innocence of the world provided. Seeing his former friends all half drunk or worse made him appreciate their limited opportunities. For a confusing combination of social and economic reasons, they were caught in a web of repeated mistakes. They were condemned to repeat the past.

Without having spoken a single word to anyone, Sean abruptly turned and stumbled out of Old Scully's Bar. He quickened his step when he felt a powerful voice coaxing him back to the warm familiarity of this haven of his youth. But Sean had made up his mind. He would not be like his father. He would look to the future, not to the past.

Responding to a knock on her apartment door, Janet heaved her feet off the ottoman and struggled out of her deep club chair. She'd been perusing a ponderous book she'd picked up in the medical school bookstore called *Molecular Biology of the Cell*. At the door she peered through the security port. She was shocked to see Sean making a stupid face at her.

Fumbling with the locks, Janet finally swung the door open wide.

"I hope I'm not disturbing you," Sean said.

"What happened?" Janet asked. "Did that favorite haunt of yours burn down?"

"Maybe figuratively," Sean said.

"None of your old friends show up?" Janet asked.

"They were all there," Sean said. "May I come in?"

"I'm sorry," Janet said. "Please." She stepped aside, then closed the door behind him. "I've forgotten my manners. I'm just so surprised to see you. Can I get you something? A beer? A glass of wine?"

Sean thanked her but said no. He sat awkwardly on the edge of the couch. "I went as usual to Old Scully's . . ." he began.

"Oh, now I know what happened," Janet interrupted. "They ran out of beer."

"I'm trying to tell you something," Sean said with exasperation.

"Okay, I'm sorry," Janet said. "I'm being sarcastic. What happened?"

"Everybody was there," Sean said. "Jimmy O'Connor, Brady Flanagan, even Patrick FitzGerald. But I didn't talk to anyone. I didn't get much past the door."

"Why not?"

"I realized by going there I was condemning myself to the past," Sean said. "All of a sudden I had an idea about what you and even Brian were talking about concerning change. And you know something? I want to change. I'm sure I'll have occasional relapses, but I certainly don't want to be a 'townie' all my life. And what I'd like to know is whether or not you'd be willing to help me a little."

Janet had to blink away a sudden rush of tears. She looked into Sean's blue eyes and said, "I'd love to help you."

*This book is dedicated to the spirit of health-care reform
and the sanctity of the doctor-patient relationship.
It is my fervent hope that they need not
be mutually exclusive.*

PROLOGUE

February seventeenth was a fateful day for Sam Flemming.

Sam considered himself an extremely lucky person. As a broker for one of the major Wall Street firms, he'd become wealthy by the age of forty-six. Then, like a gambler who knew when to quit, Sam had taken his earnings and fled north from the concrete canyons of New York to idyllic Bartlet, Vermont. There he'd begun to do what he'd always wanted to do: paint.

Part of Sam's good fortune had always been his health, yet at half past four on February seventeenth, something strange began to happen. Numerous water molecules within many of his cells began to split apart into two fragments: a relatively inoffensive hydrogen atom and a highly reactive, viciously destructive hydroxyl free radical.

As these molecular events transpired, Sam's cellular defenses were activated. But on this particular day those defenses against free radicals were quickly exhausted; even the antioxidant vitamins E, C, and beta-carotene which he diligently took each day could not stem the sudden, overwhelming tide.

The hydroxyl free radicals began to nibble away at the core of Sam Flemming's body. Before long, the cell membranes of the affected cells began to leak fluid and electrolytes. At the same time some of the cells' protein enzymes were cleaved and inactivated. Even many DNA molecules were assaulted, and specific genes were damaged.

In his bed at Bartlet Community Hospital, Sam remained unaware of the high-stakes molecular battle within his cells. What he did notice was some of its sequelae: an elevation of his temperature, some digestive rumblings, and the beginnings of chest congestion.

Later that afternoon when Sam's surgeon, Dr. Portland, came in to see him, the doctor noted Sam's fever with disappointment and alarm. After listening to Sam's chest, Dr. Portland tried to tell Sam that a complication had apparently set in. Dr. Portland said that a touch of pneumonia was interfering with Sam's otherwise smooth recovery from the operation to repair his broken hip. But by then Sam had become apathetic and mildly disoriented. He didn't understand Dr. Portland's report on his status. The doctor's prescription for antibiotics and his assurances of a rapid recovery failed to register with him.

Worse still, the doctor's prognosis proved wrong. The prescribed antibiotic failed to stop the developing infection. Sam never recovered enough to appreciate the irony that he'd survived two muggings in New York City, a commuter plane crash in Westchester County, and a bad four-vehicle accident on the New Jersey Turnpike, only to die from complications arising from a fall on a patch of ice in front of Staley's Hardware Store on Main Street, Bartlet, Vermont.

THURSDAY • MARCH 18

Standing before Bartlet Community Hospital's most important employees, Harold Traynor paused long enough to relish the moment. He'd just called the meeting to order. The group assembled—all heads of departments—had obediently fallen silent. All eyes were riveted on him. Traynor's dedication to his office as chairman of the hospital board was a point of pride. He savored moments such as this when it became clear his very presence inspired awe.

"Thank you all for coming out on this snowy evening. I've called this meeting to impress upon you how seriously the hospital board is taking the unfortunate assault on Nurse Prudence Huntington in the lower parking lot last week. The fact that the rape was thwarted by the serendipitous arrival of a member of the hospital security staff does not in any way lessen the seriousness of the offense."

Traynor paused, his eyes falling significantly on Patrick Swegler. The head of hospital security averted his gaze to avoid Traynor's accusatory glance. The attack on Miss Huntington had been the third such episode in the last year, and Swegler felt understandably responsible.

"These attacks must be stopped!" Traynor looked to Nancy Widner, the director of nursing. All three victims had been nurses under her supervision.

"The safety of our staff is a prime concern," Traynor said as his eyes jumped from Geraldine Polcari, head of dietary, to Gloria Suarez, head of housekeeping. "Consequently, the executive board has proposed the construction of a multistoried parking facility to be built in the area of the lower parking lot. It will be directly attached to the main hospital building and will contain appropriate lighting and surveillance cameras."

Traynor gave Helen Beaton, president of the hospital, a nod. On his cue, Beaton lifted a cloth from the conference table to reveal a detailed architectural model of the existing hospital complex as well as the proposed addition: a massive, three-story structure protruding from the rear of the main building.

Amid exclamations of approval, Traynor stepped around the table to position himself next to the model. The hospital conference table was often a repository for medical paraphernalia under consideration for purchase. Traynor reached over to remove a rack of funnel-shaped test tubes so that the model could be better seen. Then he scanned his audience. All eyes were glued to the model; everyone except Werner Van Slyke had gotten to his feet.

Parking had always been a problem at Bartlet Community Hospital, especially in inclement weather. So Traynor knew that his proposed addition would be popular even before the recent string of attacks in the lower lot. He was pleased to see that his unveiling was progressing as successfully as he'd anticipated. The room was aglow with enthusiasm. Only sullen Van Slyke, the head of engineering and maintenance, remained impassive.

"What's the matter?" Traynor asked. "Doesn't this proposal meet with your approval?"

Van Slyke looked at Traynor, his expression still vacant.

"Well?" Traynor felt himself tense. Van Slyke had a way of irritating him. Traynor had never liked the man's laconic, unemotional nature.

"It's okay," Van Slyke said dully.

Before Traynor could respond the door to the conference room burst open and slammed against its stop on the floor. Everyone jumped, especially Traynor.

Standing in the doorway was Dennis Hodges, a vigorous, stocky seventy-year-old with rough-hewn features and weathered skin. His nose was rosy and bulbous, his beady eyes rheumy. He was dressed in a dark green boiled wool coat over creaseless corduroy trousers. On top of his head was a red plaid hunter's cap dusted with snow. In his raised left hand he was clutching a sheaf of papers.

There was no doubt Hodges was angry. He also smelled strongly of alcohol. His dark, gun-barrel-like eyes strafed the gathering, then trained in on Traynor.

"I want to talk to you about a few of my former patients, Traynor. You too, Beaton," Hodges said, throwing her a quick, disgusted look. "I don't know what kind of hospital you think you've been running here, but I can tell you I don't like it one bit!"

"Oh, no," Traynor muttered as soon as he'd recovered from Hodges' unexpected arrival. Irritation quickly overtook his shock. A rapid glance around the room assured him that the others were about as happy to see Hodges as he was.

"Dr. Hodges," Traynor began, forcing himself to be civil. "I think it is quite apparent that we are having a meeting here. If you will excuse us . . ."

"I don't care what the hell you people are doing," Hodges snapped. "Whatever it is, it pales in respect to what you and the board have been up to with my patients." He stalked toward Traynor. Instinctively, Traynor leaned back. The smell of whiskey was intense.

"Dr. Hodges," Traynor said with obvious anger. "This is not the time for one of your interruptions. I'll be happy to meet with you tomorrow to talk about your grievances. Now if you will kindly leave and let us get on with our business . . ."

"I want to talk now!" Hodges shouted. "I don't like what you and your board are doing."

"Listen, you old fool," Traynor snapped. "Lower your voice! I have no earthly idea what is on your mind. But I'll tell you what I and the board have been doing: we've been breaking our necks in the struggle to keep the doors of this hospital open, and that's no easy task for any hospital in this day and age. So I resent any implication to the contrary. Now be reasonable and leave us to our work."

"I ain't waiting," Hodges insisted. "I'm talking to you and Beaton right now. Nursing, dietary, and housekeeping nonsense can wait. This is important."

"Ha!" Nancy Widner said. "It's just like you, Dr. Hodges, bursting in here and suggesting that nursing concerns aren't important. I'll have you know . . ."

"Hold on!" Traynor said, extending his hands in a conciliatory gesture. "Let's not get into a free-for-all. The fact of the matter is, Dr. Hodges, we are here talking about the rape attempt that occurred last week. I'm sure you are not suggesting that one rape and two attempted rapes by a man in a ski mask are not important."

"It's important," Hodges agreed, "but not as important as what's on my mind. Besides, the rape problem is obviously an in-house affair."

"Just one second!" Traynor demanded. "Are you implying that you know the identity of the rapist?"

"Let's put it this way," Hodges said. "I have my suspicions. But right now I'm not interested in discussing them. I'm interested in these patients." For emphasis he slammed the papers he'd been holding onto the table.

Helen Beaton winced and said: "How dare you come charging in here as if you own the place, telling us what is important and what isn't. As administrator emeritus that's hardly your role."

"Thank you for your uninvited advice," Hodges said.

"All right, all right," Traynor sighed with frustration. His meeting had dissolved into a verbal melee. He picked up Hodges' papers, thrust them into the man's hand, then escorted the doctor from the room. Hodges resisted initially, but ultimately let himself be ushered out.

"We've got to talk, Harold," Hodges said once they were in the hall. "This is serious stuff."

"I'm sure it is," Traynor said, trying to sound sincere. Traynor knew that at some point he'd have to hear Hodges' grievances. Hodges had been the hospital administrator back when Traynor was still in grammar school. Hodges had taken the position when most doctors hadn't been interested in the responsibility. In his thirty years at the helm, Hodges had built Bartlet Community Hospital from a small rural hospital to a true tertiary care center. It was this sprawling institution he'd passed on to Traynor when he'd stepped down from his position three years before.

"Look," Traynor said, "whatever is on your mind, it can surely wait until tomorrow. We'll talk at lunch. In fact, I'll arrange for Barton Sherwood and Dr. Delbert Cantor to join us. If what you want to discuss concerns policy, which I assume it does, then it would be best to have the vice chairman and the chief of the professional staff there as well. Don't you agree?"

"I suppose," Hodges admitted reluctantly.

"Then it's settled," Traynor said soothingly, eager to get back and salvage what he could of his meeting now that Hodges was placated for the time being. "I'll contact them tonight."

"I might not be administrator any longer," Hodges added, "but I still feel responsible for what goes on around here. After all, if it hadn't been for me you wouldn't have been named to the board, much less elected chairman."

"I understand that," Traynor said. Then he joked: "But I don't know whether to thank you or curse you for this dubious honor."

"I'm worried you've let the power go to your head," Hodges said.

"Oh, come on!" Traynor said. "What do you mean, 'power'? This job is nothing but one headache after another."

"You're essentially running a hundred-million-dollar entity," Hodges said. "And it's the largest employer in this whole part of the state. That means power."

Traynor laughed nervously. "It's still a pain in the neck. And we're lucky to be in business. I don't have to remind you that our two competitors no longer are. Valley Hospital closed, and the Mary Sackler has been turned into a nursing home."

"We might still be open, but I'm afraid you money men are forgetting the hospital's mission."

"Oh, bullcrap!" Traynor snapped, losing a bit of control. "You old docs have to wake up to a new reality. It's not easy running a hospital in the current environment of cost-cutting, managed care, and government intervention. It isn't cost-plus anymore like you had it. Times have changed, demanding new adaptations and new strategies for survival. Washington is mandating it."

Hodges laughed derisively: "Washington sure isn't mandating what you and your cohorts are doing."

"The hell they aren't," Traynor argued. "It's called competition, Dennis. Survival of the fittest and the leanest. No more sleight-of-hand cost-shifting like you used to get away with."

Traynor paused, realizing that he was losing his composure. He wiped away the perspiration that had broken out on his forehead. He took a deep breath. "Listen, Dennis, I've got to get back into the conference room. You go home, calm down, relax, get some sleep. We'll get together tomorrow and go over whatever is on your mind, okay?"

"I am a bit tuckered," Hodges admitted.

"Sure you are," Traynor agreed.

"Tomorrow for lunch? Promise? No excuses?"

"Absolutely," Traynor said as he gave Hodges a prodding pat on the back. "At the inn at twelve sharp."

With relief Traynor watched his old mentor trudge toward the hospital lobby with his distinctive lumbering gait, rocking on his hips as if they were stiff. Turning back toward the conference room, Traynor marveled at the man's uncanny flair for causing turmoil. Unfortunately, Hodges was going beyond being a nuisance. He was becoming a virtual albatross.

"Can we have some order here," Traynor called out over the bedlam to which he returned. "I apologize for the interruption. Unfortunately, old Doc Hodges has a particular knack for showing up at the most inopportune times."

"That's an understatement," Beaton said. "He's forever barging into my office to complain that one of his former patients isn't getting what he considers VIP treatment. He acts as if he's still running this place."

"The food is never to his liking," Geraldine Polcari complained.

"Nor is the room cleaning," added Gloria Suarez.

"He comes into my office about once a week," Nancy Widner said. "It's always the same complaint. The nurses aren't responding quickly enough to his former patients' requests."

"He's their self-elected ombudsman," Beaton said.

"They're the only people in the town that can stand him," Nancy said. "Just about everyone else thinks he's a crotchety old coot."

"Do you think he knows the identity of the rapist?" Patrick Swegler asked.

"Heavens, no," Nancy said. "The man's just a blowhard."

"What do you think, Mr. Traynor?" Patrick Swegler persisted.

Traynor shrugged. "I doubt he knows anything, but I'll certainly ask when I meet with him tomorrow."

"I don't envy you that lunch," Beaton said.

"I'm not looking forward to it," Traynor admitted. "I've always felt he deserved a certain amount of respect, but to be truthful my resolve is wearing a bit thin.

"Now, let's get back to the matter at hand." Traynor soon had the meeting back on track, but for him the joy of the evening had been lost.

Hodges trudged straight up Main Street in the middle of the road. For the moment there were no vehicles moving in either direction. The plows hadn't come through yet; two inches of powdery new snow blanketed the town as still more flakes fell.

Hodges cursed under his breath, giving partial vent to his unappeased anger. Now that he was on his way home he felt angry for having allowed Traynor to put him off.

Coming abreast of the town green with its deserted, snow-covered gazebo, Hodges could see north past the Methodist church. There, in the distance, directly up Front Street, he could just make out the hospital's main building. Hodges paused, gazing wistfully at the structure. A sense of foreboding descended over him with a shiver. He'd devoted his life to the hospital so that it would serve the people of the town. But now he feared that it was faltering in its mission.

Turning away, Hodges recommenced his trek up Main Street. He jammed the copy-machine papers he was holding into his coat pocket. His fingers had gone numb. Half a block farther he stopped again. This time he gazed at the mullioned windows of the Iron Horse Inn. A beckoning, incandescent glow spilled out onto the frigid, snow-covered lawn.

It only took a moment of rationalization for Hodges to decide he could use another drink. After all, now that his wife, Clara, spent more time with her family in Boston than she did with him in Bartlet, it wasn't as if she'd be waiting up for him. There were certainly some advantages to their virtual estrangement. Hodges knew he would be glad for the extra fortification for the twenty-five-minute walk he faced to get home.

In the outer room Hodges stomped the snow from his rubber-soled work-boots and hung up his coat on a wooden peg. His hat went into a cubbyhole above. Passing an empty coat-check booth used for parties, Hodges went down a short hallway and paused at the entryway of the bar.

The room was constructed of unfinished pine that had an almost charred look from two centuries of use. A huge fieldstone fireplace with a roaring fire dominated one wall.

Hodges scanned the chamber. From his point of view, the cast of characters assembled was unsavory, hardly reminiscent of NBC's "Cheers." He saw Barton Sherwood, the president of the Green Mountain National Bank, and now, thanks to Traynor, vice chairman of the hospital's board of directors. Sherwood was sitting in a booth with Ned Banks, the obnoxious owner of the New England Coat Hanger Company.

At another table, Dr. Delbert Cantor was sitting with Dr. Paul Darnell. The table was laden with beer bottles, baskets of potato chips, and platters of cheese. To Hodges they looked like a couple of pigs at the trough.

For a split second Hodges thought about pulling his papers from his coat and getting Sherwood and Cantor to sit down and talk with him. But he abandoned the idea immediately. He didn't have the energy and both Cantor and Darnell hated his guts. Cantor, a radiologist, and Darnell, a pathologist, had both suffered when Hodges had arranged for the hospital to take over those departments five years earlier. They weren't likely to be a receptive audience for his complaints.

At the bar stood John MacKenzie, another local Hodges would just as soon avoid. Hodges had had a long-standing disagreement with the man. John owned the Mobil station out near the interstate and had serviced Hodges' vehicles for many years. But the last time he'd worked on Hodges' car, the problem had not been fixed. Hodges had had to drive all the way to the dealership in Rutland to get it repaired. Consequently he'd never paid John.

A couple of stools beyond John MacKenzie, Hodges saw Pete Bergan, and he groaned inwardly. Pete had been a "blue baby" who'd never finished the sixth grade. At age eighteen he dropped out of school and supported himself by doing odd jobs. Hodges had arranged for his job helping the hospital grounds crew but had had to acquiesce to his firing when he proved too unreliable. Since then Pete had held a grudge.

Beyond Pete stretched a row of empty bar stools. Beyond the bar and down a step were two pool tables. Music thudded out of an old-fashioned fifties-style jukebox against the far wall. Grouped around the pool tables were a handful of students from Bartlet College, a small liberal arts institution that had recently gone coed.

For a moment Hodges teetered on the threshold, trying to decide if a drink was worth crossing paths with any of these people. In the end the memory of the cold and the anticipation of the taste of the scotch propelled him into the room.

Ignoring everyone Hodges went to the far end of the bar and climbed up on an empty stool. The radiant heat from the fire warmed his back. A tumbler appeared in front of him, and Carleton Harris, the overweight bartender, poured him a glass of Dewar's without ice. Carleton and Hodges had known each other for a long time.

"I think you'll want to find another seat," Carleton advised.

"Why's that?" Hodges asked. He'd been pleased that no one had noticed his entrance.

Carleton nodded at a half-empty highball glass on the bar two stools away. "I'm afraid our fearless chief of police, Mr. Wayne Robertson, has stopped in for a snort. He's in the men's room."

"Oh, damn!" Hodges said.

"Don't say I didn't warn you," Carleton added as he headed toward several students who'd approached the bar.

"Hell, it's six of one, half a dozen of the other," Hodges murmured to himself. If he moved to the other end, he'd have to face John MacKenzie. Hodges decided to stay where he was. He lifted his glass to his lips.

Before he could take a drink, Hodges felt a slap on his back. It was all he could do to keep his drink from clanking against his teeth and spilling.

"Well, if it isn't the Quack!"

Swinging around, Hodges glared into the inebriated face of Wayne Robertson. Robertson was forty-two and heavyset. At one time he'd been all muscle. Now he was half muscle and half fat. The most prominent aspect of his profile was his abdomen, which practically draped his official belt buckle. Robertson was still in uniform, gun and all.

"Wayne, you're drunk," Hodges said. "So why don't you just go home and sleep it off." Hodges turned back to the bar and tried once more to take a sip of his drink.

"There's nothing to go home to, thanks to you."

Hodges slowly turned around again and looked at Robertson. Robertson's eyes were red, almost as red as his fat cheeks. His blond hair was clipped short in a fifties-style butch.

"Wayne," Hodges began, "we're not going over this again. Your wife, rest her soul, was not my patient. You're drunk. Go home."

"You were running the freakin' hospital," Robertson said.

"That doesn't mean I was responsible for every case, you lunkhead," Hodges said. "Besides, it was ten years ago." He again tried to turn away.

"You bastard!" Robertson snarled. Reaching out, he grabbed Hodges' shirt at the collar and tried to lift Hodges off the barstool.

Carleton Harris came around the bar with a swiftness that belied his bulk and insinuated himself between the two men. He opened Robertson's grip on Hodges' shirt one finger at a time. "Okay, you two," he said. "Off to your own corners. We don't allow sparring here at the Iron Horse."

Hodges straightened his shirt indignantly, snatched up his drink, and walked to the other end of the bar. As he passed behind John MacKenzie he heard the man mutter: "Deadbeat." Hodges refused to be provoked.

"Carleton, you shouldn't have interfered," Dr. Cantor called out to the bartender. "If Robertson had blown old Hodges away half the town would have cheered."

Dr. Cantor and Dr. Darnell laughed uproariously at Cantor's comment. Each one encouraged the other until they were slapping their knees and choking on their beers. Carleton ignored them as he stepped around the bar to help Barton Sherwood, who'd approached for refills.

"Dr. Cantor's right," Sherwood said loud enough for everyone in the bar to hear. "Next time Hodges and Robertson face off, leave them be."

"Not you too," Carleton said as he deftly mixed Sherwood's drinks.

"Let me tell you about Dr. Hodges," Sherwood said, still loud enough for everyone to hear. "A good neighbor he isn't. By a historical accident he owns a little tongue of land that happens to separate my two lots. So what does he do? He builds this gigantic fence."

"Of course I fenced that land," Hodges called out, unable to hold his tongue. "It was the only way to keep your goddamn horses from dropping their shit all over my property."

"Then why not sell the strip of land?" Sherwood demanded, turning to face Hodges. "It's of no use to you."

"I can't sell it because it's in my wife's name," Hodges answered.

"Nonsense," Sherwood said. "The fact that your house and land are in your wife's name is merely a legacy of an old ruse to protect your assets from any malpractice judgment. You told me so yourself."

"Then perhaps you should know the truth," Hodges said. "I was trying to be diplomatic. I won't sell you the land because I despise you. Is that easier for your pea brain to comprehend?"

Sherwood turned to the room and addressed everyone present. "You're all witnesses. Dr. Hodges is admitting he's acting out of spite. No surprise, of course, and hardly a Christian attitude."

"Oh, shut up," Hodges retorted. "It's a bit hypocritical for a bank president to question someone else's Christian ethics with all the foreclosures on your conscience. You've put families out of their homes."

"That's different," Sherwood said. "That's business. I have my stockholders to consider."

"Oh, bull," Hodges said with a wave of dismissal.

A sudden commotion at the door caught Hodges' attention. He turned in time to see Traynor and the rest of the attendees of the hospital meeting troop into the bar. He could tell that Traynor was not at all pleased to see him. Hodges shrugged and turned back to his drink. But he couldn't dismiss the fortuitous fact that all three principals were there: Traynor, Sherwood, and Cantor.

Grabbing his whiskey, Hodges slipped off his stool and followed Traynor to Sherwood and Banks' table. Hodges tapped him on his shoulder.

"How about talking now?" Hodges suggested. "We're all here."

"Goddamn it, Hodges," Traynor blurted out. "How many times do I have to tell you? I don't want to talk tonight. We'll talk tomorrow!"

"What does he want to talk about?" Sherwood asked.

"Something about a few of his old patients," Traynor said. "I told him that we'd meet him for lunch tomorrow."

"What's going on?" Dr. Cantor asked, joining the fray. He'd sensed blood and had been drawn over to the table like a shark attracted to chum.

"Dr. Hodges isn't happy with the way we are running the hospital," Traynor said. "We're to hear about it tomorrow."

"No doubt the same old complaint," Sherwood interjected. "No VIP treatment for his old patients."

"Some gratitude!" Dr. Cantor said, interrupting Hodges, who'd tried to respond. "Here we are donating our time pro bono to keep the hospital afloat and what do we get in return: nothing but criticism."

"Pro bono my ass," Hodges sneered. "None of you fool me. Your involvement isn't charity. Traynor, you've come to use the place to support your newly discovered grandiosity. Sherwood, your interest isn't even that sophisticated. It's purely financial, since the hospital is the bank's largest customer. And Cantor, yours is just as simple. All you're interested in is the Imaging Center, that joint venture I allowed in a moment of insanity. Of all the decisions I made as hospital administrator, that's the one I regret the most."

"You thought it was a good deal when you made it," Dr. Cantor said.

"Only because I thought it was the only way to update the hospital's CAT scanner," Hodges said. "But that was before I realized the machine would pay for itself in less than a year which, of course, made me realize you and the other private radiologist were robbing the hospital of money it should have been earning."

"I'm not interested in opening this old battle," Dr. Cantor said.

"Nor am I," Hodges agreed. "But the point is there's little or no charity involved with you people. Your concern is financial gain, not the good of your patients or the community."

"You're no one to talk," Traynor snapped. "You ran the hospital like a personal fiefdom. Tell us who's been taking care of that house of yours all these years?"

"What do you mean?" Hodges stammered, his eyes darting back and forth among the men in front of him.

"It's not a complicated question," Traynor said, his anger driving him on. He'd stuck Hodges with a knife and now he wanted to push it in to the hilt.

"I don't know what my house has to do with this," Hodges managed.

Traynor went up on his toes to survey the room. "Where's Van Slyke?" he asked. "He's here somewhere."

"He's by the fire," Sherwood said, pointing. He had to struggle to suppress a contented smile. This issue about Hodges' house had nettled him for some time. The only reason he'd never brought it up was that Traynor had forbidden it.

Traynor called to Van Slyke, but the man didn't seem to hear. Traynor called again, this time loud enough for everyone in the bar to hear. Conversation stopped. Except for the music emanating from the jukebox, the room was momentarily silent.

Van Slyke moved slowly across the room, uncomfortable in the spotlight. He was aware most of the people were watching him. But they soon lost interest and conversations recommenced where they had left off.

"Good grief, man," Traynor said to Van Slyke. "You look like you're moving through molasses. Sometimes you act eighty years old instead of thirty."

"Sorry," Van Slyke said, maintaining his bland facial expression.

"I want to ask you a question," Traynor continued. "Who has been taking care of Dr. Hodges' house and property?"

Van Slyke looked from Traynor to Hodges, a wry smile curling on his lips. Hodges looked away.

"Well?" Traynor questioned.

"We have been," Van Slyke said.

"Be a little more specific," Traynor said. "Who is 'we'?"

"The hospital grounds crew," Van Slyke said. He didn't take his eyes off Hodges. Nor did his smile change.

"How long has this been going on?" Traynor asked.

"Since way before I arrived," Van Slyke said.

"It's going to stop as of today," Traynor said. "Understand?"

"Sure," Van Slyke said.

"Thank you, Werner," Traynor said. "Why don't you go over to the bar and have a beer while we finish chatting with Dr. Hodges." Van Slyke returned to his place by the fire.

"You know that old expression," Traynor said, " 'People in glass houses . . .' "

"Shut up!" Hodges snapped. He started to say something else but stopped himself. Instead he stalked from the room in a fit of frustrated anger, grabbed his coat and hat, and plunged out into the snowy night.

"You old fool," Hodges muttered as he headed south out of town. He was furious at himself for allowing a "perk" to derail momentarily his indignation about patient care. Yet it was true that hospital maintenance had been taking care of his grounds. It had started years ago. The crew had simply shown up one day. Hodges had never asked for the service, but he'd never done anything to stop it, either.

The long walk home in the frosty night helped dampen Hodges' guilt about the yard service. After all, it didn't have anything to do with patient care. As he turned into his unplowed driveway he resolved to offer to pay some reasonable figure for the services rendered. He wasn't about to allow this affair to stifle his protest about more serious matters.

When Hodges reached the midpoint of his long driveway he could see down into the lower meadow. Through the blowing snow he could just make out the fence that he'd erected to keep Sherwood's horses from crossing his property. He'd never sell that strip of land to that bastard. Sherwood had gotten the second piece of land on a foreclosure of a family whose breadwinner had been one of Hodges' patients. In fact, he was one of the patients whose hospital admission summary Hodges had in his pocket.

Leaving the driveway, Hodges took a shortcut that skirted the frog pond. He could tell some of the neighborhood kids had been skating because the snow had been pushed off the ice and a makeshift hockey goal had been erected. Beyond the pond Hodges' empty house loomed out of the snowy darkness.

Rounding the building, Hodges approached the side door of the clapboard addition that connected the house with the barn. He knocked the snow off his boots and entered. In the mudroom he removed his coat and hat and hung them up. Fumbling in his coat pocket he pulled out the papers he'd been carrying and took them into the kitchen.

After placing the papers on the kitchen table, Hodges headed for the library to pour himself a drink in lieu of the one he'd abandoned at the inn. Insistent knocking at his door stopped him midway across the dining room.

Hodges looked at his watch in puzzlement. Who could be calling at that hour and on such a night? Reversing his direction, he went back through the kitchen and into the mudroom. Using his shirtsleeve he wiped away the condensation on one of the door's panes of glass. He could just make out the figure outside.

"What now?" Hodges muttered as he reached down and unlatched the door. He pulled it wide open and said: "Considering everything it's a bit strange for you to come visiting, especially at this hour."

Hodges stared at his visitor, who said nothing. Snow swirled in around Hodges' legs.

"Oh, hell," Hodges said with a shrug. "Whatever you want, come in." He let go of the door and headed toward the kitchen. "Just don't expect me to play the role of the hospitable host. And close the door behind you!"

When Hodges reached the single step up to the kitchen level, he started to turn to make sure the door had been closed tight against the weather. Out of the corner of his eye he saw something speeding toward his head. By reflex, he ducked.

The sudden movement saved Hodges' life. A flat metal rod glanced off the side of his head, but not before cutting deeply into his scalp. The force of the blow carried the metal rod to the top of his shoulder, where it fractured his collarbone. Its power also sent the stunned Hodges hurtling into the kitchen.

Hodges collided with the kitchen table. His hands clutched the edges, keeping him on his feet. Blood spurted in tiny pulsating jets from the open scalp wound onto his papers. Hodges turned in time to see his attacker closing in on him with arm raised. In a gloved hand he clutched a rod that looked like a short, flat crowbar.

As the weapon started down for a second blow, Hodges reached up and grabbed the exposed forearm, impeding the impact. Still, the metal cut into Hodges' scalp at the hairline. Fresh blood squirted from severed arteries.

Hodges desperately dug his fingernails into the assailant's forearm. He knew intuitively he could not let go; he had to keep from being struck again.

For a few moments the two figures struggled against each other. In a dance of death they pirouetted around the kitchen, smashing into the walls, upsetting chairs, and breaking dishes. Blood spattered indiscriminately.

The attacker cried in pain as he pulled his arm free from Hodges' grip. Once again the steel rod rose up to a frightening apogee before smashing down onto Hodges' raised forearm. Bones snapped like twigs under the impact.

Again the metal bar was lifted above the now hapless Hodges and brought down hard. This time its arc was unhindered, and the weapon impacted directly onto the top of Hodges' unprotected head, crushing in a sharply defined fragment of his skull and driving it deeply into his brain.

Hodges fell heavily to the floor, mercifully insensitive.

"We're coming to a river up ahead," David Wilson said to his daughter, Nikki, who was sitting in the passenger seat next to him. "Do you know what its name is?"

Nikki turned her mahogany eyes toward her father and pushed a wisp of hair to the side. David hazarded a glance in her direction, and with the help of the sunlight coming through the windshield, he caught some of the subtle spokes of yellow that radiated from her pupils through her irises. They were matched with strands of honey in her hair.

"The only rivers I know," Nikki said, "are the Mississippi, the Nile, and the Amazon. Since none of them are here in New England, I'll have to say I don't know."

Neither David nor his wife, Angela, could suppress a giggle.

"What's so funny?" Nikki demanded indignantly.

David looked into the rearview mirror and exchanged knowing glances with Angela. Both were thinking the same thought, and they had spoken of it often: Nikki frequently sounded more mature than expected for her chronological age of eight. They considered the trait an endearing one, indicative of her intelligence. At the same time, they realized their daughter was growing up faster than she might otherwise have because of her health problems.

"Why did you laugh?" Nikki persisted.

"Ask your mother," David said.

"No, I think your father should explain."

"Come on, you guys," Nikki protested. "That's not fair. But I don't care if you laugh or not because I can find the name of the river myself." She took a map from the glove compartment.

"We're on Highway 89," David said.

"I know!" Nikki said with annoyance. "I don't want any help."

"Excuse me," David said with a smile.

"Here it is," Nikki said triumphantly. She twisted the map on its side so she could read the lettering. "It's the Connecticut River. Just like the state."

"Right you are," David said. "And it forms the boundary between what and what?"

Nikki looked back at the map for a moment. "It separates Vermont from New Hampshire."

"Right again," David said. And then, gesturing ahead, he added: "And here it is."

They were all quiet as their blue, eleven-year-old Volvo station wagon sped over the span. Below the water roiled southward.

"I guess the snow is still melting in the mountains," David said.

"Are we going to see mountains?" Nikki asked.

"We sure are," David said. "The Green Mountains."

They reached the other side of the bridge where the highway gradually swung back toward the northwest.

"Are we in Vermont now?" Angela asked.

"Yes, Mom!" Nikki said with impatience.

"How much further to Bartlet?" Angela asked.

"I'm not quite sure," David said. "Maybe an hour."

An hour and fifteen minutes later the Wilsons' Volvo passed the sign reading: "Welcome to Bartlet, Home of Bartlet College."

David let up on the accelerator and the car slowed. They were on a wide avenue aptly called Main Street. The street was lined with large oaks. Behind the trees were white clapboard homes. The architecture was a potpourri of colonial and Victorian.

"So far it looks storybookish," Angela said.

"Some of these New England towns look like they belong in Disney World," David said.

Angela laughed. "Sometimes I think you feel a replica is better than an original."

After a short drive the homes gave way to commercial and civic buildings which were constructed mostly of brick with Victorian decorations. In the downtown area stood rows of three- and four-story brick structures. Engraved stone plaques announced the year each was constructed. Most of the dates were either late nineteenth century or early twentieth.

"Look!" Nikki said. "There's a movie theater." She pointed at a shabby marquee announcing a current movie in large block letters. Next to the movie theater was a post office with a tattered American flag snapping in the breeze.

"We're really lucky with this weather," Angela remarked. The sky was pale blue and dotted with small, puffy white clouds. The temperature was in the high sixties.

"What's that?" Nikki questioned. "It looks like a trolley with no wheels."

David laughed. "That's called a diner," he said. "They were popular back in the fifties."

Nikki was straining against her seat belt, excitedly leaning forward to peer out the front windshield.

As they approached the heart of the town they discovered a number of gray granite buildings that were significantly more imposing than the brick structures, especially the Green Mountain National Bank with its corbeled and crenellated clock tower.

"That building really looks like something out of Disney World," Nikki said.

"Like father, like daughter," Angela said.

They came to the town green, whose grass had already achieved a luxurious, almost midsummer color. Crocuses, hyacinths, and daffodils dotted the park, especially around the gingerbread central gazebo. David pulled the car over to the side of the road and stopped.

"Compared with the section of Boston around Boston City Hospital," David said, "this looks like heaven."

At the north end of the park was a large white church whose exterior was rather plain except for its enormous steeple. The steeple was neo-Gothic, replete with elaborate tracery and spires. Its belfry was enclosed by columns supporting pointed arches.

"We've got several hours before our interviews. What do you think we should do?" David asked.

"Why don't we drive around a little more, then have lunch?" Angela said.

"Sounds good to me." David put the car in gear and continued along Main Street. On the west side of the town green they passed the library which, like the bank, was constructed of gray granite. But it looked more like an Italian villa than a castle.

Just beyond the library was the elementary school. David pulled over to the side of the road so Nikki could see it. It was an appealing turn-of-the-century three-story brick building connected to a nondescript wing of more recent vintage.

"What do you think?" David asked Nikki.

"Would that be where I'd go to school if we come here to live?" Nikki asked.

"Probably," David said. "I can't imagine they'd have more than one school in a town of this size."

"It's pretty," Nikki said noncommittally.

Driving on, they quickly passed through the commercial section. Then they found themselves in the middle of the Bartlet College campus. The buildings were mostly the same gray granite they'd seen in the town and had the same white trim. Many were covered with ivy.

"A lot different from Brown University," Angela said. "But charming."

"I often wonder what it would have been like if I'd gone to a small college like this," David said.

"You wouldn't have met Mommy," Nikki said. "And then I wouldn't be here."

David laughed. "You're so right and I'm so happy I went to Brown."

Looping through the college, they headed back toward the center of town. They crossed over the Roaring River and discovered two old mill buildings. David explained to Nikki how waterpower was used in the old days. One of the mills now housed a computer software company, but its waterwheel was slowly turning. A sign advertised that the other mill was now the New England Coat Hanger Company.

Back in town David parked at the town green. This time they got out and strolled up Main Street.

"It's amazing, isn't it: no litter, no graffiti, and no homeless people," Angela said. "It's like a different country."

"What do you think of the people?" David asked. They had been passing pedestrians since they'd gotten out of the car.

"I'd say they look reserved," Angela said. "But not unfriendly."

David stopped outside of Staley's Hardware Store. "I'm going to run in and ask where we should eat."

Angela nodded. She and Nikki were looking into the window of the neighboring shoe store.

David was back in a flash. "The word is that the diner is best for a quick lunch, but the Iron Horse Inn has the best food. I vote for the diner."

"Me too," Nikki said.

"Well, that settles that," Angela said.

All three had hamburgers the old-fashioned way: with toasted buns, raw onion, and lots of ketchup. When they were through, Angela excused herself.

"There's no way I'm going to an interview until I brush my teeth," she said.

David took a handful of mints after paying the check.

On the way back to the car they approached a woman coming in their direction with a golden retriever puppy on a leash.

"Oh, how cute!" Nikki exclaimed.

The woman graciously stopped so Nikki could pet the dog.

"How old is she?" Angela asked.

"Twelve weeks," the woman said.

"Could you direct us to the Bartlet Community Hospital?" David asked.

"Certainly," the woman said. "Go up to the town green. The road on the right is Front Street. Take that right up to the hospital's front door."

They thanked the woman and moved on. Nikki walked sideways to keep the puppy in sight. "He was darling," she said. "If we come to live here, may I have a dog?"

David and Angela exchanged glances. Both were touched. Nikki's modest request after all the medical problems she'd been through melted their hearts.

"Of course you may have a dog," Angela said.

"You can even pick it out," David said.

"Well, then I want to come here," Nikki said with conviction. "Can we?"

Angela looked at David in hopes he would answer, but he gestured for her to field the question. Angela wrestled with her answer. She didn't know what to say. "Whether we come here or not is a difficult decision," she said finally. "There are many things we have to consider."

"Like what?" Nikki asked.

"Like whether they want me and your father," Angela said, relieved to have come up with a simple explanation, as the three got back in their car.

Bartlet Community Hospital was larger and more imposing than David or Angela had expected, even though they knew it was a referral center for a significant portion of the state.

Despite a sign that clearly said "Parking in the Rear," David pulled to the curb in the turnout before the front entrance. He put the car in park but left the engine running.

"This is truly beautiful," he said. "I never thought I would say that about a hospital."

"What a view," Angela said.

The hospital was midway up a hill just north of the town. It faced south and its facade was bathed in bright sunlight. Just below them at the base of the hill they could see the whole town. The Methodist church's steeple was especially prominent. In the distance the Green Mountains provided a scalloped border to the horizon.

Angela tapped David's arm. "We'd better get inside," she said. "My interview is in ten minutes."

David put the car in gear and drove around to the back of the hospital. There were two parking lots rising up in terraced tiers separated by a stand of trees. They found visitor slots next to the hospital's rear entrance in the lower lot.

Appropriately placed signs made finding the administrative offices easy, and a helpful secretary directed them to Michael Caldwell's office. Michael Caldwell was Bartlet's medical director.

Angela knocked on the jamb of the open door. Inside, Michael Caldwell looked up from his desk, then rose to greet her. He immediately reminded Angela of David with his olive coloring and trim, athletic build. He was also close to David's age of thirty, as well as his height of six feet. Like David's, his hair tended to form a natural center part. But there the similarities ended. Caldwell's features were harder than David's; his nose was hawk-like and narrower.

"Come in!" Caldwell said with enthusiasm. "Please! All of you." He quickly got more chairs.

David looked at Angela for guidance. Angela shrugged. If Caldwell wanted to interview the whole family, it was fine with her.

After brief introductions, Caldwell was back behind his desk with Angela's folder in front of him. "I've been over your application, and I have to tell you I am indeed impressed," he said.

"Thank you," Angela said.

"Frankly, I didn't expect a woman pathologist," Caldwell said. "Subsequently I've learned it's a field that is appealing to more and more women."

"The hours tend to be more predictable," Angela said. "It makes the practice of medicine and having a family more compatible." She studied the man. His comment made her slightly uncomfortable, but she was willing to withhold judgment.

"From your letters of recommendation I have the feeling that the department of pathology at the Boston City Hospital thinks you have been one of their brightest residents."

Angela smiled. "I've tried to do my best."

"And your transcript from Columbia's medical school is equally impressive," Caldwell said. "Consequently, we would like to have you here at Bartlet Community Hospital. It's as simple as that. But perhaps you have some questions for me."

"David has also applied for a job in Bartlet," Angela said. "It's with one of the major health maintenance organizations in the area: Comprehensive Medical Vermont."

"We call it CMV," Caldwell said. "And it's the only HMO in the area."

"I indicated in my letter that my availability is contingent on his acceptance," Angela said. "And vice versa."

"I'm well aware of that," Caldwell said. "In fact I took the liberty of contacting CMV and talking about David's application with the regional manager, Charles Kelley. CMV's regional office is right here in our professional building. Of course I cannot speak for them officially, but it is my understanding there is no problem whatsoever."

"I'm to meet with Mr. Kelley as soon as we're through here," David said.

"Perfect," Caldwell said. "So, Dr. Wilson, the hospital would like to offer you a position as associate pathologist. You'll join two other full-time pathologists. Your first year's compensation will be eighty-two thousand dollars."

When Caldwell looked down at the folder on his desk, Angela looked David's way. Eighty-two thousand dollars sounded like a fortune after so many years of burdensome debt and meager income. David flashed her a conspiratorial smile in return, obviously sharing her thoughts.

"I also have some information in response to your query letter," Caldwell said. He hesitated, then added: "Perhaps this is something we should talk about privately."

"It's not necessary," Angela said. "I assume you are referring to Nikki's cystic fibrosis. She's an active participant in her care, so there are no secrets."

"Very well," Caldwell said. He smiled meekly at Nikki before continuing. "I found out that there is a patient with that condition here in Bartlet. Her name is Caroline Helmsford. She's nine years old. I've arranged for you to meet with her doctor, Dr. Bertrand Pilsner. He's one of CMV's pediatricians."

"Thank you for making such an effort," Angela said.

"No problem," Caldwell said. "Obviously we want you folks to come here to our delightful town. But I must confess that I didn't read up on the condition when I made the inquiries. Perhaps there is something I should know in order to be of more assistance."

Angela looked at Nikki. "Why don't you explain to Mr. Caldwell what cystic fibrosis is."

"Cystic fibrosis is an inherited problem," Nikki said in a serious and practiced tone. "When both parents are carriers there is a twenty-five percent chance a child will have the condition. About one in every two thousand babies is affected."

Caldwell nodded and tried to maintain his smile. There was something unnerving about getting a lecture from an eight-year-old.

"The main problem is with the respiratory system," Nikki continued. "The mucus in the lungs is thicker than in the lungs of normal people. The lungs have difficulty clearing the thicker mucus, which leads to congestion and infection. Chronic bronchitis and pneumonia are the big worries. The condition is quite variable: some people are severely affected; others, like me, just have to be careful not to catch colds and do our respiratory therapy."

"Very interesting," Caldwell said. "You certainly sound professional. Maybe you should be a doctor when you grow up."

"I intend to," Nikki said. "I'm going to study respiratory medicine."

Caldwell got up and gestured toward the door. "How about you doctors and doctor-to-be going over to the medical office building to meet Dr. Pilsner."

It was only a short walk from the hospital's administrative area in the old central building to the newer professional building. In just a few minutes they passed through a fire door, and the corridor covering changed from vinyl tile to posh carpet.

Dr. Pilsner was in the middle of his afternoon office hours but graciously took time to meet the Wilsons. His thick white beard made him look a bit like Kris Kringle. Nikki took to him immediately when he bent down and shook her hand, treating her more like an adult than a child.

"We've got a great respiratory therapist here at the hospital," Dr. Pilsner said to the Wilsons. "And the hospital is well equipped for respiratory care. On top of that I took a fellowship in respiratory medicine at Children's in Boston. So I think we can take care of Nikki just fine."

"Wow!" Angela said, obviously impressed, and relieved. "This is certainly comforting. Ever since Nikki's diagnosis we take her special needs into consideration in all our decision-making."

"And indeed you should," Dr. Pilsner said. "Bartlet would be a good choice with its low pollution and clean, crisp air. Provided she has no tree or grass allergies, I think it would be a healthy environment for your daughter."

Caldwell escorted the Wilsons to CMV's regional headquarters. Before he left he made them promise to return to his office after David's interview.

The CMV receptionist directed the Wilsons to a small waiting area. The three of them barely had time to pick up magazines before Charles Kelley emerged from his private office.

Kelley was a big man who towered eight inches over David as they shook hands. His face was tanned and his sandy-colored hair had pure blond streaks running through it. He was dressed in a meticulously tailored suit. His manner was outgoing and ebullient, more like a high-powered super-salesman than a health care administrator.

Like Caldwell, Kelley invited the whole Wilson family into his office. He was also equally complimentary.

"Frankly, we want you, David," Kelley said, tapping a closed fist on his desk. "We need you as part of our team. We're pleased that you've taken an internal medicine residency, especially at a place like the Boston City Hospital. As more of the city moves to the country, we're finding we need your kind of expertise. You'll be an enormous addition to our primary care/gatekeeper crew, no doubt about it."

"I'm pleased you're pleased," David said with an embarrassed shrug.

"CMV is expanding rapidly in this area of Vermont, especially in Bartlet itself," Kelley boasted. "We've signed up the coat-hanger mill, the college, and the computer software company, as well as all the state and municipal employees."

"Sounds like a monopoly," David joked.

"We'd rather think it has to do with our dedication to quality care and cost control," Kelley said.

"Of course," David agreed.

"Your compensation will be forty-one thousand the first year," Kelley said.

David nodded. He knew he'd be in for some teasing from Angela even though they'd known all along that her earnings would be significantly larger than his. On the other hand, they hadn't expected hers would be double his.

"Why don't I show you your prospective office," Kelley said eagerly. "It will give you a better feeling for our operation and what it will be like working here."

David looked at Angela. Kelley's approach was certainly a harder sell than was Caldwell's.

To David's mind the office was dream-like. The view south over the Green Mountains was so picture-perfect, it looked like a painting.

David noticed four patients sitting in the waiting area reading magazines. He looked to Kelley for an explanation.

"You'll be sharing this suite with Dr. Randall Portland," Kelley explained. "He's an orthopedic surgeon. A good guy, I might add. We've found that sharing receptionists and nurses is an efficient use of resources. Let me see if he's available to say hello."

Kelley walked over and tapped on what David thought was merely a mirror. It slid open. Behind it was a receptionist. Kelley spoke to her for a moment before the mirrored partition slid closed.

"He'll be out in a second," Kelley said, rejoining the Wilsons. He then explained the layout of the office. Opening a door on the west side of the waiting room, he gave them a tour of empty, newly redecorated examining rooms. He also took them into the room that would be David's private office. It had the same fabulous view to the south as the waiting room.

"Hello everybody," a voice called out. The Wilsons turned from gaping out the window to see a youthful but strained-appearing man stride into the room. It was Dr. Randall Portland. Kelley introduced them all, even Nikki, who shook hands as she'd done with Dr. Pilsner.

"Call me Randy," Dr. Portland said as he shook David's hand.

David sensed the man was sizing him up.

"You play basketball?" Randy asked.

"Occasionally," David said. "Lately I haven't had much time."

"I hope you come to Bartlet," Randy said. "We need some more players around here. At least someone to take my place."

David smiled.

"Well, it's nice to meet you folks. I'm afraid I have to get back to work."

"He's a busy man," Kelley explained after Dr. Portland left. "We currently only have two orthopedists. We need three."

David turned back to the mesmerizing view.

"Well, what do you say?" Kelley questioned.

"I'd say we're pretty impressed," David said. He looked at Angela.

"We'll have to give it all a lot of thought," Angela said.

After leaving Charles Kelley, the Wilsons returned to Caldwell's office. He insisted on taking David and Angela on a quick tour of the hospital. Nikki was left in the hospital day-care center, run by pink-frocked volunteers.

The first stop on the tour was the laboratory. Angela was not surprised to find that the lab was truly state-of-the-art. After he showed her the pathology section where she'd be doing most of her work, Caldwell took her in to meet the department chairman, Dr. Benjamin Wadley.

Dr. Wadley was a distinguished-looking, silver-haired gentleman in his fifties. Angela was immediately struck by how much he reminded her of her father.

After the introductions, Dr. Wadley said he understood that David and Angela had a little girl. Before they could respond, he raved about the local school system. "My kids really thrived. One is now at Wesleyan in Connecticut. The other is a senior in high school and has already gotten early acceptance into Smith College."

A few minutes later, after bidding Dr. Wadley goodbye, Angela pulled David aside as they followed Caldwell.

"Did you notice the similarity between Dr. Wadley and my father?" Angela whispered.

"Now that you say it, yes," David said. "He has that same kind of poise and confidence."

"I thought it was rather remarkable," Angela said.

"Let's not have any hysterical transference," David joked.

Next on the tour was the ER, followed by the Imaging Center. David was particularly impressed with the newly acquired MRI machine.

"This is a better machine than the one at Boston City Hospital," David remarked. "Where did the money come from for this?"

"The Imaging Center is a joint venture between the hospital and Dr. Cantor, one of the staff doctors," Caldwell explained. "They upgrade the equipment all the time."

After the Imaging Center, David and Angela toured the new radiotherapy building which boasted one of the newest linear accelerators. From there they returned to the main hospital and the new neonatal critical care unit.

"I don't know what to say," David admitted when the tour was over.

"We'd heard the hospital was well equipped," Angela said, "but this is far better than we'd imagined."

"We're understandably proud of it," Caldwell said as he led them back into his office. "We had to significantly upgrade in order to land the CMV contract. We had to compete with the Valley Hospital and the Mary Sackler Hospital for survival. Luckily, we won."

"But all this equipment and upgrading had to cost a fortune," David said.

"That's an understatement," Caldwell agreed. "It's not easy these days running a hospital, especially in this era of government-mandated competition. Revenues are down, costs are going up. It's hard just to stay in business." Caldwell handed David a manila envelope. "Here's a packet of information about the hospital. Maybe it will help convince you to come up here and accept our job offers."

"What about housing?" Angela asked as an afterthought.

"I'm glad you asked," Caldwell said. "I was supposed to ask you to go down to the Green Mountain National Bank to see Barton Sherwood. Mr. Sherwood is the vice chairman of the hospital board. He's also president of the bank. He'll give you an idea how much the town supports the hospital."

After rescuing a reluctant Nikki from the day-care center where she'd been enjoying herself, the Wilsons drove back to the town green and walked to the bank. Typical of their reception in Bartlet, Barton Sherwood saw them immediately.

"Your applications were favorably discussed at the last executive board meeting," Barton Sherwood told them as he leaned back in his chair and hooked his thumbs in his vest pockets. He was a slight man, nearing sixty, with thinning hair and a pencil-line mustache. "We sincerely hope you'll be joining the Bartlet family. To encourage you to come to Bartlet, I want you to know that Green Mountain National Bank is prepared to offer both first and second mortgages so that you'll be able to buy a house."

David and Angela were stunned and their jaws dropped in unison. Never in their wildest imaginations had they thought they would have been able to buy a house the first year out of their residencies. They had very little cash, and a mountain of tuition debt: over a hundred and fifty thousand dollars.

Sherwood went on to give them the specifics, but neither David nor Angela could focus on the details. It wasn't until they were back in their car that they dared to speak.

"I can't believe this," David said.

"It's almost too good to be true," Angela agreed.

"Does this mean we're coming to Bartlet?" Nikki asked.

"We'll see," Angela said.

Since David had driven up from Boston, Angela offered to drive home. As she drove, David perused the information packet Caldwell had given them.

"This is interesting," David said. "There's a clip from the local paper about the signing of the contract between Bartlet Community Hospital and CMV. It says that the deal was consummated when the hospital board, under the leadership of Harold Traynor, finally agreed to CMV's demand to provide hospitalization for an unspecified monthly capitation fee, a method of cost control encouraged by the government and favored by HMO organizations."

"That's a good example of how providers like hospitals and doctors are being forced to make concessions," Angela said.

"Right you are," David agreed. "By accepting capitation the hospital has been forced to act like an insurance organization. They are assuming some of the health risk of the CMV subscribers."

"What's capitation?" Nikki asked.

David swung around. "Capitation is when an organization is paid a certain amount of money per person," he explained. "With health plans it's usually by the month."

Nikki still looked puzzled.

David tried again. "Let's be specific. Say that CMV pays Bartlet Hospital a thousand dollars each month for each person in the plan. Then if anybody has to be hospitalized during the month for whatever reason, CMV doesn't have to pay any more. So if no one gets sick for the month, the hospital makes out like a bandit. But what if everybody gets sick and has to go to the hospital? What do you think will happen then?"

"I think you still might be over her head," Angela said.

"I understand," Nikki said. "If everybody got sick the hospital would go broke."

David smiled with satisfaction and gave Angela a playful poke in the ribs. "Hear that?" he said triumphantly. "That's my daughter."

A few hours later, they were back home near their Southend apartment. Angela was lucky enough to find a spot only half a block from their door. David gently woke Nikki, who'd drifted off to sleep. Together the three walked to their building and mounted the stairs to their fourth-floor walk-up.

"Uh-oh!" Angela said. She was the first to reach their apartment.

"What's the matter?" David asked. He looked over her shoulder.

Angela pointed at the door. The trim was split from the point where a crowbar had been inserted. David reached out and pushed the door. It opened with no resistance. All three locks had been broken.

David reached in and turned on the light. The apartment had been ransacked: furniture upended and the contents of cabinets and drawers scattered about the floor.

"Oh, no!" Angela cried as tears welled in her eyes.

"Easy!" David said. "What's been done is done. Let's not get hysterical."

"What do you mean, 'Let's not get hysterical'?" Angela demanded. "Our home's been ruined. The TV's gone."

"We can get another TV," David said calmly.

Nikki came back from her room and reported that it hadn't been touched.

"At least we can be thankful for that," David said.

Angela disappeared into their bedroom while David surveyed the kitchen. Except for a partially empty container of ice cream melted on the counter, the kitchen was fine.

David picked up the phone and dialed 911. While he was waiting for the call to go through, Angela appeared with tears streaming down her face, holding a small, empty jewelry box.

After David gave the details to the 911 operator, he turned to Angela. She was struggling to maintain control.

"Just don't say anything super-rational," Angela managed through her tears. "Don't say we can get more jewelry."

"Okay, okay," David said agreeably.

Angela dried her face on her sleeve. "Coming home to this rape of our apartment makes Bartlet seem that much more appealing," she said. "At this point I'm more than ready to leave urban ills behind."

"I don't have anything against him personally," Dr. Randall Portland told his wife, Arlene, as they got up from the dinner table. She motioned their two sons, Mark and Allen, to help clear the table. "I just don't want to share my office with an internist."

"Why not?" Arlene asked, taking the dishes from her sons and scraping food scraps into the disposal.

"Because I don't want my post-ops sharing a waiting room with a bunch of sick people," Randy snapped. He recorked the unfinished bottle of white wine and put it into the refrigerator.

"Okay," Arlene said. "That I can understand. I was afraid it was some juvenile surgeon-internist squabble."

"Don't be ridiculous," Randy said.

"Well, you remember all the jokes you used to have about internists when you were a resident," Arlene reminded him.

"That was healthy verbal sparring," Randy said. "But this is different. I don't want infectious people around my patients. Call it superstitious, I don't care. But I've been having more than my share of complications with my patients and it has me depressed."

"Can we watch TV?" Mark asked. Allen, with his angelically huge eyes, was standing behind him. They were seven and six years old respectively.

"We already agreed that . . ." Arlene began, but then she stopped. It was hard to resist her sons' pleading expressions. Besides, she wanted a moment alone with Randy. "Okay, a half hour."

"Yippie!" Mark exclaimed. Allen echoed him before they dashed off to the family room.

Arlene took Randy by the arm and led him into the living room. She had him sit on the couch, and she took the chair opposite. "I don't like the way you are sounding," she said. "Are you still upset about Sam Flemming?"

"Of course I'm still upset about Sam Flemming," Randy said irritably. "I didn't lose a patient all through my residency. Now I've lost three."

"There are some things you cannot control," Arlene said.

"None of them should have died," Randy said. "Especially under my care. I'm just a bone doctor screwing around with their extremities."

"I thought you were over your depression," Arlene said.

"I'm having trouble sleeping again," Randy admitted.

"Maybe you should call Dr. Fletcher," Arlene suggested.

Before Randy could respond the phone rang. Arlene jumped. She'd been learning to hate its sound, especially when Randy had post-ops in the hospital. She answered on the second ring, hoping that it was a social call. Unfortunately it wasn't. It was one of the floor nurses at Bartlet Community Hospital wanting to speak with Dr. Portland.

Arlene handed the phone to her husband. He took it reluctantly and put it to his ear. After he'd listened for a moment, his face blanched. He replaced the receiver slowly and raised his eyes to Arlene's.

"It's the knee I did this morning," Randy said. "William Shapiro. He's not doing well. I can't believe it. It sounds the same. He's spiked a fever and he's disoriented. Probably pneumonia."

Arlene stepped up to her husband and put her arms around him and gave him a squeeze. "I'm sorry," she said, not knowing what else to say.

Randy didn't respond. Nor did he try to move for a few minutes. When he did, he silently disengaged Arlene's arms, and went out the back door without speaking. Arlene watched from the kitchen window as his car descended the driveway and pulled out into the street. She straightened up and shook her head. She was worried about her husband, but she didn't know what to do.

Monday • May 3

Harold Traynor fingered the mahogany and inlaid gold gavel he'd bought for himself at Shreve Crump & Low in Boston. He was standing at the head of the library table in the Bartlet Community Hospital. In front of him was the lectern that he had had built for the hospital conference room. Scattered on its surface were his extensive notes which he'd had his secretary type up early that morning. Stretching out from the lectern and scattered down the center of the table was the usual collection of medical paraphernalia in various stages of evaluation by the hospital board. Dominating the confusion was the model of the proposed parking garage.

Traynor checked his watch. It was exactly six P.M. Taking the gavel in his right hand, he struck it sharply against its base. Attentiveness to detail and punctuality were two characteristics Traynor particularly prized.

"I would like herewith to call to order the Executive Committee of the Bartlet Community Hospital," Traynor called out with as much pompousness as he could muster. He was dressed in his best pin-striped suit. On his feet were freshly polished elevator shoes. He was only five foot seven and felt cheated as far as stature was concerned. His dark, receding hair was neatly trimmed and carefully combed over his apical bald spot.

Traynor spent a great deal of time and effort preparing for hospital board meetings, both in terms of content and his appearance. That day he'd gone directly home to shower and change clothes after a day trip to Montpelier. With no time to spare, he did not stop at his office. Harold Traynor was an attorney in Bartlet specializing in estate planning and tax work. He was also a businessman with interests in a number of commercial ventures in the town.

Seated before him were Barton Sherwood, vice chairman; Helen Beaton, president and CEO of the hospital; Michael Caldwell, vice president and medical director of the hospital; Richard Arnsworth, treasurer; Clyde Robeson, secretary; and Dr. Delbert Cantor, current chief of staff.

Strictly following parliamentary procedure as specified in *Robert's Rules of Order*, which he'd purchased after being elected to the chairmanship, Traynor called on Clyde Robeson to read the minutes of the last meeting.

As soon as the minutes had been read and approved, Traynor cleared his throat in preparation for his monthly chairman's report. He looked at each member of his executive committee in turn, making sure they were all attentive. They were, except for Dr. Cantor who was, typically, bored and busily cleaning under his fingernails.

"We face significant challenges here at the Bartlet Community Hospital," Traynor began. "As a referral center we have been spared some of the financial problems of smaller rural hospitals, but not all of them. We're going to have to work even harder than we have in the past if the hospital is to survive these difficult days.

"However, even in these dark times there is occasional light. As some of you have undoubtedly heard, an esteemed client of mine, William Shapiro, passed away last week of pneumonia coming on after knee surgery. While I very much regret Mr. Shapiro's untimely passing, I am pleased to announce officially that Mr. Shapiro had generously designated the hospital as the sole beneficiary of a three-million-dollar insurance policy."

A murmur of approval spread through the people present.

Traynor lifted his hand for silence. "This charitable gesture couldn't have come at a better time. It will pull us out of the red and push us into the black, although not for long. The bad news for the month is the recent discovery that our sinking fund for our major bond issues is considerably short of its projected goals."

Traynor looked directly at Sherwood, whose mustache twitched nervously.

"The fund will need to be bolstered," Traynor said. "A good portion of the three-million-dollar bequest will have to go to that end."

"It wasn't all my fault," Sherwood blurted out. "I was urged to maximize return on the fund. That necessitated risk."

"The chair does not recognize Barton Sherwood," Traynor snapped.

For a moment, Sherwood looked as if he might respond, but instead he remained silent.

Traynor studied his notes in an effort to compose himself after Sherwood's outburst. Traynor hated disorder.

"Thanks to Mr. Shapiro's bequest," Traynor went on, "the sinking fund debacle will not be lethal. The problem is to keep any outside examiners from getting wind of the shortfall. We can't afford to have our bond rating change. Consequently, we will be forced to put off floating a bond issue for the parking garage until the sinking fund is restored.

"As a temporary measure to forestall assaults on our nurses I have instructed our CEO, Helen Beaton, to have lighting installed in the parking lot."

Traynor glanced around the room. According to the *Rules of Order*, the matter should have been presented as a motion, debated, and voted on, but no one moved to be recognized.

"The last item concerns Dr. Dennis Hodges," Traynor said. "As you all know, Dr. Hodges disappeared last March. During this past week I met with our chief of police, Wayne Robertson, to discuss the case. No clues as to his whereabouts have surfaced. If Dr. Hodges did meet with foul play, there has been no evidence of it, although Chief Robertson allowed that the longer Dr. Hodges is missing, the more likely it is that he is no longer living."

"My guess is he's still around," Dr. Cantor said. "Knowing that bastard, he's probably sitting down in Florida, laughing himself silly every time he thinks of us wrestling with all this bureaucratic bullshit."

Traynor used his gavel. "Please!" he called out. "Let's maintain some order here."

Cantor's bored expression changed to disdain, but he remained silent.

Traynor glared at Dr. Cantor before resuming: "Whatever personal feelings we may have about Dr. Hodges, the fact remains that he played a crucial role in the history of this hospital. If it hadn't been for him this institution would be merely another tiny, rural hospital. His welfare merits our concern.

"I wanted the executive committee to know that Dr. Hodges' estranged wife, Mrs. Hodges, has decided to sell her home. She relocated to her native

Boston some years ago. She had held out some hope that her husband might resurface, but based on her conversations with Chief Robertson, she has decided to sever her connections with Bartlet. I only raise this matter now because I think that sometime in the near future the board might wish to erect a memorial befitting Dr. Hodges' considerable contributions to Bartlet Community Hospital."

Having finished, Traynor gathered up his notes and formally turned the meeting over to Helen Beaton so that she could give her monthly president's report. Beaton stood up in her place, pushing her chair back from the table. She was in her mid-thirties with reddish-brown hair cut short. Her face was wide, not unlike Traynor's. She wore a businesslike blue suit accented with a silk scarf.

"I've spoken to several civic groups this month," she said. "My topic on each occasion was the financial plight of the hospital. It was interesting for me to ascertain that most people were generally unaware of our problems even though health-care issues have been almost constantly in the news. What I emphasized in my talks was the economic importance of the hospital to the town and the immediate area. I made it very clear that if the hospital were to close, every business and every merchant would be hurt. After all, the hospital is the largest employer in this part of the state. I also reminded everyone that there is no tax base for the hospital and that fund-raising has been and will remain key to keeping the doors open."

Beaton paused as she turned over the first page of her notes. "Now for the bad news," she said, referring to several large graphs illustrating the information she was about to relay. She held the graphs at chest height as she spoke. "Admissions for April were twelve percent over forecast. Our daily census was up eight percent over March, and our average length of stay was up six percent. Obviously these are serious trends, as I'm sure our treasurer, Richard Arnsworth, will report."

Beaton held up the last graph. "And finally I have to report that there has been a drop in utilization of the emergency room, which, as you know, is not part of our capitation agreement with CMV. And to make matters worse, CMV has refused to pay a number of our ER claims, saying the subscribers violated CMV rules."

"Hell, that's not the hospital's fault," Dr. Cantor said.

"CMV doesn't care about such technicalities," Beaton said. "Consequently, we've been forced to bill the patients directly and they are understandably upset. Most have refused to pay, telling us to go to CMV."

"Health care is becoming a nightmare," Sherwood said.

"Tell that to your representative in Washington," Beaton said.

"Let's not digress," Traynor said.

Beaton looked back at her notes, then continued: "Quality indicators for April were within normal expectations. Incident reports were actually fewer than in March and no new malpractice actions have been initiated."

"Will wonders never cease," Dr. Cantor commented.

"Other disturbing news for April involved union agitation," Beaton continued. "It was reported to us that both dietary and housekeeping have been targeted. Needless to say, unionization would significantly add to our financial problems."

"It's one crisis after another," Sherwood said.

"Two areas of under-utilization," Beaton continued, "are the neonatal intensive care unit and the linear accelerator. During April, I discussed this situation with CMV since our fixed costs for maintaining these units are so high. I emphasized it had been they who demanded these services. CMV promised me that they would look into ferrying patients from areas without these facilities to Bartlet and reimbursing us accordingly."

"That reminds me," Traynor said. As chairman, he felt he had the right to interrupt. "What is the status of the old cobalt-60 machine that the linear accelerator replaced? Have there been any inquiries from the state licensing division or the nuclear regulatory commission?"

"Not a word," Beaton answered. "We informed them the machine is in the process of being sold to a government hospital in Paraguay and that we are waiting for the funds."

"I don't want to get involved in any bureaucratic snafu with that machine," Traynor warned.

Beaton nodded and turned to the last page of her notes. "And finally, I'm afraid I have some additional bad news. Last night just before midnight there was another attempted assault in the parking lot."

"What?" Traynor cried. "Why wasn't I informed about this?"

"I didn't hear about it until this morning," Beaton explained. "I tried to call you as soon as I heard, but you weren't in. I left a message for you to call back but you never did."

"I was in Montpelier all day," Traynor explained. He shook his head in dismay. "Damn, this has to stop. It's a PR nightmare. I hate to imagine what CMV thinks."

"We need that garage," Beaton said.

"The garage has to wait until we can float a bond issue," Traynor said. "I want that lighting done quickly, understand?"

"I've already talked to Werner Van Slyke," Beaton said. "And he's already gotten back to me that he's been in touch with the electrical contractor. I'll follow up on it so that it's done ASAP."

Traynor sat down heavily and blew through pursed lips. "It's almost mindboggling what running a hospital today entails. Why did I get myself into this?" He picked up the current meeting's agenda, glanced at it, then called Richard Arnsworth, the treasurer, to give his report.

Arnsworth got to his feet. He was a bespectacled, precise, accountant type whose voice was so soft everyone had to strain to hear him. He started by referring everyone to the balance sheet each had received in his information packet that morning.

"What's immediately obvious," Arnsworth said, "is that the monthly expenses still significantly outstrip the monthly capitation payments from CMV. In fact, the gap has expanded relative to the increase in admissions and lengths of stay. We're also losing money on all Medicare patients not enrolled in CMV as well as all indigents who are not enrolled in any plan. The percentage of paying patients or those with standard indemnity insurance is so tiny we cannot cost-shift enough to cover our losses.

"As a result of this continued loss, the hospital's cash position has deteriorated. Consequently, I recommend switching from one hundred and eighty days investing to thirty days."

"It's already been taken care of," Sherwood announced.

When Arnsworth took his seat, Traynor asked for a motion to approve the treasurer's report. It was immediately seconded and carried with no opposition. Traynor then turned to Dr. Cantor to give the medical staff report.

Dr. Cantor got to his feet slowly and leaned his knuckles on the table. He was a big, heavyset man with a pasty complexion. Unlike other presenters he didn't refer to notes.

"Just a couple of things this month," he said casually. Traynor glanced over at Beaton and caught her eye, then shook his head in disgust. He hated Cantor's jaded behavior at their meetings.

"The anesthesiologists are all up in arms," Dr. Cantor said. "But of course it's expected now that they have been officially informed that the hospital is taking over the department, and they're to be on straight salary. I know how they feel since I experienced the same situation during Hodges' tenure."

"Do you think they'll sue?" Beaton asked.

"Of course they'll sue," Dr. Cantor said.

"Let them," Traynor said. "The precedent's been well established with pathology and radiology. I cannot believe they'd think they could continue with private billing while we're under capitation. It doesn't make sense."

"A new utilization manager has been chosen," Dr. Cantor said, changing the subject. "His name is Dr. Peter Chou."

"Will Dr. Chou cause any problems for us?" Traynor asked.

"I doubt it," Dr. Cantor said. "He didn't even want the position."

"I'll meet with him," Beaton said.

Traynor nodded.

"And the last item concerning the medical staff," Dr. Cantor said, "involves M.D. 91. I've been told he's not been drunk all month."

"Leave him on probation just the same," Traynor said. "Let's not take any chances. He's relapsed before."

Dr. Cantor sat down.

Traynor asked if there was any new business. When no one moved, he asked for a motion to adjourn. Dr. Cantor eagerly "so moved." After a resounding chorus of "yeas," Traynor struck the gavel and ended the meeting.

Traynor and Beaton slowly gathered up their papers. Everyone else trooped out of the conference room, heading for the Iron Horse Inn. When the sound of the outer door closing behind the departing group drifted back to the room, Traynor's eyes met Beaton's. Leaving his briefcase, Traynor stepped around the table and passionately embraced her.

Hand in hand they hurriedly left the conference room and retreated across the hall to a couch in Beaton's office as they had so many times before. There in the semidarkness they made frenzied love just as they had after each executive committee meeting for almost a year. It was a familiar scenario and didn't take long. They didn't bother to remove their clothes.

"I thought it was a good meeting," Traynor said as they rearranged their apparel after they were through.

"I agree," Beaton said. She turned on a light and went over to a wall mirror. "I liked the way you handled the lighting issue for the parking lot. It avoided needless debate."

"Thank you," Traynor said, pleased with himself.

"But I'm worried about the financial situation," Beaton admitted as she reapplied her makeup. "The hospital has to break even at the very least."

"You're right," Traynor admitted with a sigh. "I'm worried too. I'd love to wring some of those CMV people's necks. It's ironic that this 'managed competition' nonsense could very well force us into bankruptcy. That whole year of negotiations with CMV was a lose-lose situation. If we hadn't agreed to capitate, we wouldn't have gotten the contract and we would have had to close like the Valley Hospital. Now that we did agree to capitate, we still might have to close."

"Every hospital is having trouble," Beaton said. "We should keep that in mind, although it's hardly consolation."

"Do you think there is any chance we could renegotiate the contract with CMV?" Traynor asked.

Beaton laughed scornfully. "Not a chance," she said.

"I don't know what else to do," Traynor said. "We're losing money despite our DUM plan that Dr. Cantor proposed."

Beaton laughed with true mirth. "We have to alter that acronym. It sounds ridiculous. How about changing from Drastic Utilization Measures to Drastic Utilization Control? DUC sounds a lot better than DUM."

"I kind of like DUM," Traynor said. "It reminds me that it was dumb to set our capitation rate so low."

"Caldwell and I have come up with an idea that might help significantly," she said. She pulled a chair over and sat down in front of Traynor.

"Shouldn't we be getting down to the Iron Horse?" Traynor said. "We don't want anybody getting suspicious. This is a small town."

"This will only take a moment," Beaton promised. "What Caldwell and I did was brainstorm about how the consultants we hired came up with a capitation rate that has proved to be too low. What we realized was that we'd provided

them with hospitalization statistics that CMV had given us. What no one remembered was that those statistics were based on experience CMV had with its
own hospital in Rutland."

"You think CMV gave us fraudulent numbers?" Traynor asked.

"No," Beaton said. "But like all HMOs when they are dealing with their own
hospitals, CMV has an economic incentive for their doctors to limit hospitalization, something the public has no idea about."

"You mean like actual payments to the doctors?" Traynor asked.

"Exactly," Beaton said. "It's a bonus bribe. The more each doctor cuts his hospitalization rates the bigger the bonus. It's very effective. Caldwell and I believe
we can fashion a similar economic incentive here at Bartlet Community Hospital. The only problem is that we will have to fund it with some start-up capital.
Once it's operational, it will pay for itself by reducing hospitalization."

"Sounds great," Traynor said with enthusiasm. "Let's pursue it. Maybe this
kind of program, combined with DUM, will eliminate the red ink."

"I'll arrange a meeting with Charles Kelley to discuss it," Beaton said as she
got her coat.

"While we're on the topic of utilization," Beaton said as they started down
the long hall toward the exit, "I hope to heaven that we're not going to get the
Certificate of Need for open-heart surgery. It's crucial we don't. We have to
keep CMV sending their bypass patients to Boston."

"I agree wholeheartedly," Traynor said as he held the door open for Beaton.
They passed out of the hospital into the lower parking area. "That was one of the
reasons I was in Montpelier today. I've started some behind-the-scenes negative
lobbying."

"If we get that CON we'll be looking at a lot more red ink," Beaton warned.

They arrived at their respective cars, which were parked side by side. Before
he climbed behind the wheel, Traynor glanced around the dark parking area, particularly up toward the copse of trees that separated the lower lot from the
upper.

"It's darker out here than I remembered," he called over to Beaton. "It's like
asking for trouble. We need those lights."

"I'll get right on it," she promised.

"What a pain!" Traynor said. "With everything else we have to worry about,
we've got to worry about a damn rapist. What are the details about last night's
episode?"

"It occurred about midnight," Beaton said. "And this time it wasn't a nurse.
It was one of the volunteers, Marjorie Kleber."

"The teacher?" Traynor asked.

"That's right," Beaton said. "Ever since she got sick herself she's been doing
a lot of volunteering on weekends."

"How about the rapist?" Traynor asked.

"Same description: about six feet, wearing a ski mask. Ms. Kleber said he had
handcuffs."

"That's a nice touch," Traynor said. "How'd she get away?"

"It was just lucky," Beaton said. "The night watchman just happened along while making his rounds."

"Maybe we should beef up security," Traynor suggested.

"That's money we don't have," Beaton reminded him.

"Maybe I should talk to Wayne Robertson and see if the police can do any more," Traynor said.

"I've already done that," Beaton said. "But Robertson doesn't have the manpower to have someone up here every night."

"I wonder if Hodges really did know the rapist's identity?"

"Do you think his disappearance could have had anything to do with his suspicions?" Beaton asked.

Traynor shrugged. "I hadn't thought of that. I suppose it's possible. He wasn't one to keep his opinion to himself."

"It's a scary thought," Beaton said.

"Indeed," Traynor said. "Regardless, I want to be informed about any such assaults immediately. They can have disastrous consequences for the hospital. I especially don't want any surprises at an executive board meeting. It makes me look bad."

"I apologize," Beaton said, "but I did try to call. From now on I'll make sure you are informed."

"See you down at the Iron Horse," Traynor said as he got into his car and started the engine.

THURSDAY • MAY 20

"I've got to leave to pick up my child from her after-school program," Angela said to one of her fellow residents, Mark Danforth.

"What are you going to do about all these slides?" Mark asked.

"What can I do?" Angela snapped. "I've got to get my daughter."

"Okay," Mark said. "Don't jump on me. I was only asking. I thought maybe I could help."

"I'm sorry," Angela said. "I'm just strung out. If you could just see these few I'd be forever in your debt." She picked five slides from the rack.

"No problem," Mark said. He added Angela's to his own stack.

Angela covered her microscope, grabbed her things, and ran out of the hospital. No sooner had she pulled out of the lot than she was bogged down in rush-hour Boston traffic.

When Angela finally pulled up to the school, Nikki was sitting forlornly on the front steps. It was not a pretty area. The school was awash with graffiti and surrounded by a sea of concrete. Except for a group of sixth- and seventh-graders shooting baskets beyond a high chain-link fence, there were no grammar-school-aged children in sight. A group of listless teenagers in ridiculously oversized clothing loitered alongside the building. Directly across the street was the cardboard shanty of a homeless person.

"I'm sorry I was late," Angela said as Nikki climbed into the car and plugged in her seat belt.

"It's all right," Nikki said, "but I was a little scared. There was a big problem in school today. The police were here and everything."

"What happened?"

"One of the sixth-grade boys had a gun in the playground," Nikki said calmly. "He shot it and got arrested."

"Was anybody hurt?"

"Nope," Nikki said with a shake of her head.

"Why did he have a gun?" Angela asked.

"He's been selling drugs," Nikki replied.

"I see," Angela said, trying to maintain her composure as well as her daughter could. "How did you hear about this? From the other kids?"

"No, I was there," Nikki said, suppressing a yawn.

Angela's grip on the steering wheel involuntarily tightened. Public school had been David's idea. The two of them had gone to considerable effort in choosing the one that Nikki attended. Up until this episode, Angela had been reasonably satisfied. But now she was appalled, partly because Nikki was able to talk about the incident so matter-of-factly. It was frightening to realize that Nikki viewed this as an ordinary event.

"We had a substitute again today," Nikki said. "And she wouldn't let me do my postural lung drainage after lunch."

"I'm sorry, dear," Angela said. "Do you feel congested?"

"Some," Nikki said. "I was wheezing a little after being outside, but it went away."

"We'll do it as soon as we get home," Angela said. "And I'll call the school office again, too. I don't know what their problem is."

Angela did know what the problem was: too many kids and not enough staff, and what staff they had was always changing. Every few months Angela had to call to tell them about Nikki's need for respiratory therapy.

While Nikki waited in the car, Angela double-parked and dashed into the local grocery store for something to make for dinner. When she came out there was a parking ticket under the windshield wiper.

"I told the lady you'd be right out," Nikki explained, "but she said 'Tough' and gave it to us anyway."

Angela cursed under her breath.

For the next half hour they cruised around their immediate neighborhood looking for a parking space. Just when Angela was about ready to give up they found a spot.

After putting cold groceries in the refrigerator, Angela and Nikki attended to Nikki's respiratory physiotherapy. Usually they only did it in the morning. But on certain days, usually those with heavy pollution, they had to do it more often.

The routine they had established started with Angela listening with her stethoscope to make sure Nikki didn't need a bronchodilating drug. Then, by using a large beanbag chair that they'd bought at a garage sale, Nikki would assume nine different positions that utilized gravity to help drain specific areas of her lungs. While Nikki held each position, Angela percussed over the lung area with a cupped hand. Each position took two or three minutes. In twenty minutes they were finished.

With the respiratory therapy done, Nikki turned to her homework while Angela went into the galley-like kitchen to start dinner. A half hour later David came home. He was exhausted, having been up the entire previous night attending a number of sick patients.

"What a night!" he said. He tried to give Nikki a kiss on the cheek, but she pulled away, concentrating on her book. She was sitting at the dining-room table. Her bedroom wasn't large enough for a desk.

David stepped into the kitchen and was similarly rebuffed by Angela, who was busy with the dinner preparations. Twice spurned, David turned to the refrigerator. After having some difficulty getting the door open with both him and Angela in the same small area, he pulled out a beer.

"We had two AIDS patients come in through the ER with just about every disease known to man," he said. "On top of that, there were two cardiac arrests. I never even got to see the inside of the on-call room, much less get any sleep."

"If you're looking for sympathy you're talking to the wrong person," Angela said as she put some pasta on to boil. "You are also in my way."

"You're in a great mood," David said. He moved out of the tiny kitchen and draped himself over one of the stools at the counter that separated the kitchen from the living and dining area.

"My day has been stressful too," she said. "I had to leave unfinished work in order to pick Nikki up from school. I don't think it's fair that I have to do it every day."

"So this is what you're hysterical about?" David said. "Picking Nikki up? I thought that had been discussed and decided. Hell, you're the one who offered, saying your schedule was so much more predictable than mine."

"Can't you two be more quiet?" Nikki said. "I'm trying to read."

"I'm not hysterical!" Angela snapped sotto voce. "I'm just stressed out. I don't like depending on others to do my work. And on top of that, Nikki had some disturbing news today."

"Like what?" David asked.

"Ask her," Angela said.

David slipped off the barstool and squeezed into one of the dining-room chairs. Nikki told him about her day. Angela came into the room and began setting the table around Nikki's books.

"Are you still as supportive of public school when you hear about guns and drugs in the sixth grade?" Angela asked.

"Public schools have to be supported," David said. "I went to public school."

"Times have changed," Angela said.

"If people like us run away," David said, "the schools don't have a chance."

"I'm not willing to be idealistic when it comes to my daughter's safety," Angela snapped.

Once dinner was ready, they ate their spaghetti marinara and salads in strained silence. Nikki continued to read, ignoring her parents. Angela sighed loudly several times and ran her fingers through her hair. She was on the verge of tears. David fumed. After working as hard as he had for the previous thirty-six hours he did not think he deserved this kind of treatment.

Angela suddenly scraped back her chair, picked up her dish, and dropped it into the sink. It broke and both David and Nikki jumped.

"Angela," David said, struggling to keep his voice under control. "You're being overly emotional. Let's talk about picking Nikki up. There has to be another solution."

Angela wiped a few wayward tears from the corners of her eyes. She resisted the temptation to lash back at David and tell him that his conception of himself as the rational, agreeable partner was hardly reality.

Angela turned around from facing the sink. "You know," she said, "the real problem is that we have been avoiding making a decision about what to do come July first."

"I hardly think this is the opportune time to discuss what we are going to do with the rest of our lives," David said. "We're exhausted."

"Oh, beans," Angela said. She returned to the table and took her seat. "You never think it's the right time. The problem is time is running out, and no decision is a decision of sorts. July first is less than a month and a half away."

"Okay," David said with resignation. "Let me get my lists." He started to get up. Angela restrained him.

"We hardly need your lists," Angela said. "We have three choices. We've been waiting for New York to respond and they did three days ago. Here are our choices in a nutshell: we can go to New York and I'll start a fellowship in forensics and you in respiratory medicine; we can stay here in Boston where I'll do forensics and you'll go to the Harvard School of Public Health; or we can go to Bartlet and start to work."

David ran his tongue around the inside of his mouth. He tried to think. He was numb from fatigue. He wanted his lists, but Angela still had a hold on his arm.

"It's a little scary leaving academia," David said finally.

"I couldn't agree more," Angela said. "We've been students for so long it's hard to think of any other life."

"It's true we've had little personal time over these last four years," he said.

"Quality of life has to become an issue at some point," Angela agreed. "The reality is that if we stay here in Boston we'll probably have to stay in this apartment. We have too much debt to do anything else."

"It would be about the same if we went to New York," David said.

"Unless we accepted help from my parents," Angela said.

"We've avoided that in the past," David reminded her. "There have always been too many strings attached to their help."

"I agree," Angela said. "Another thing that we have to consider is Nikki's condition."

"I want a dog," Nikki said.

"Nikki's been doing okay," David said.

"But there's a lot of pollution here and in New York," Angela said. "That's bound to take its toll. And I'm getting pretty tired of all the crime here in the city."

"Are you saying you want to go to Bartlet?" David asked.

"No," Angela said, "I'm just trying to think of all the issues. But I have to admit, when I hear about guns and drugs in the sixth grade, Bartlet starts to sound better and better."

"I wonder if it is as heavenly as we remember," David questioned. "Since we go so few places maybe we've idealized it too much."

"There's one way to find out," Angela said.

"Let's go back!" Nikki cried.

"All right," David said. "Today's Thursday. How about Saturday?"

"Sounds good to me," Angela said.

"Yippee!" Nikki said.

FRIDAY • MAY 21

Traynor signed all the letters he'd dictated that morning and piled them neatly on the corner of his desk. Eagerly he got up and pulled on his coat. He was on his way through the outer office en route to the Iron Horse for lunch when his secretary, Collette, called him back to take a call from Tom Baringer.

Muttering under his breath, Traynor returned to his desk. Tom was too important a client to miss his call.

"You'll never guess where I am," Tom said. "I'm in the emergency room waiting for Dr. Portland to come in to put me back together."

"My God, what happened?" Traynor asked.

"Something stupid," Tom admitted. "I was cleaning some leaves out of my gutters when the ladder I was on fell over. I broke my damn hip. At least that's what the doctor tells me here in the emergency room."

"I'm sorry," Traynor said.

"Oh, it could be worse," Tom said. "But obviously I won't be able to make the meeting we had scheduled for this afternoon."

"Of course," Traynor said. "Was there something important you wanted to discuss?"

"It can wait," Tom said. "But listen, as long as I have you on the phone, how about giving the powers that be here at the hospital a call. I figure I deserve some VIP attention."

"You got it," Traynor said. "I'll see to it personally. I'm just on my way out to have lunch with the hospital's CEO."

"Good timing," Tom said. "Put in the good word."

After hanging up, Traynor told his secretary to cancel Tom's appointment and leave the slot open. The break would give him a chance to catch up on dictation.

Traynor was first to arrive for his luncheon meeting. After ordering a dry martini, he scanned the beam-ceilinged room. As usual of late, he'd been given the best table in the house, one in a cozy bay with a particularly dramatic view of the Roaring River, which raced past the rear of the inn. Traynor's pleasure was enhanced when he saw Jeb Wiggins, his old rival and a scion of one of the few old moneyed families of Bartlet, sitting at a far less conspicuous table. Jeb had always treated Traynor with condescension. Traynor's father had worked in the coat-hanger factory, which at that time had been one of the Wigginses' holdings. Traynor relished the role reversal: now he was running the biggest business in town.

Helen Beaton and Barton Sherwood arrived together. "Sorry we're late," Sherwood said, holding back Beaton's chair.

Beaton and Sherwood were served their usual drinks and they all ordered their meals. As soon as the waiter left them, Beaton spoke: "I have some good news. I met with Charles Kelley this morning, and he has no problem with our idea of instituting a bonus program for the CMV doctors. His only concern is whether it would cost CMV anything, which it won't. He promised to run the idea past his bosses, but I don't anticipate any problem."

"Wonderful," Traynor said.

"We'll be meeting again on Monday," Beaton added. "I'd like you to attend if you have the time."

"By all means," Traynor said.

"Now all we need is the start-up capital," Beaton said. "So I met with Barton and I think we have it solved." Beaton gave Sherwood's arm a squeeze.

Sherwood leaned forward and spoke in hushed tones: "Remember that small slush fund we'd created with the kickbacks from the construction on the radiotherapy building? I'd deposited it in the Bahamas. What I'll do is bring it back in small increments as needed. Also we can use some of it for vacations in the Bahamas. That's the easiest. We can even pay for the air tickets in the Bahamas."

The food arrived and no one spoke until the waitress had departed.

"We thought a vacation in the Bahamas could function as a grand prize," Beaton explained. "It could be awarded to the doctor with the lowest hospitalization percentage for the year."

"That's perfect," Traynor said. "This whole idea is sounding better and better."

"We'd better get it up and running ASAP," Beaton said. "So far the May figures are worse than those for April. Admissions are higher and the money loss correspondingly greater."

"I have some good news," Sherwood said. "The hospital sinking fund is back to its projected level with the infusion of the cash from the insurance bequest. It was done in a way that none of the bond examiners will ever detect."

"It's just one crisis after another," Traynor complained. He wasn't about to give Sherwood credit for fixing a problem he'd created.

"Do you want me to go ahead with the bond issue for the parking garage?" Sherwood asked.

"No," Traynor answered. "Unfortunately, we can't. We have to go back to the Board of Selectmen for another vote. Their approval had been contingent on starting the project immediately." With a scornful expression Traynor gestured with his head toward a neighboring table. "The Selectmen's chairman, Jeb Wiggins, thinks the tourist season might get screwed up if we build during the summer."

"How unfortunate," Sherwood said.

"I've got a bit of good news myself," Traynor added. "I just heard this morning that our CON for open-heart surgery has been turned down for this year. Isn't that terrible?"

"Oh, what a tragedy," Beaton said with a laugh. "Thank God!"

After the coffee had been served, Traynor remembered the call from Tom Baringer. He relayed the information on to Beaton.

"I'm already aware of Mr. Baringer's admission," Beaton said. "Some time ago I programmed a tickler file into the computer to alert me when such a patient is hospitalized. I've already spoken to Caldwell and he'll be taking care to be sure Mr. Baringer gets proper VIP treatment. What's the value of the fund?"

"One million," Traynor said. "It's not huge, but nothing to scoff at."

After they had finished their lunch, they walked out into the bright late spring sunshine.

"What's the status on the lighting of the parking lots?" Traynor asked.

"It's all done," Beaton said. "It's been done for over a week. But we decided to restrict the lighting to the lower lot. The upper is used only during the day, and by doing only the lower, we saved a considerable amount of money."

"Sounds reasonable," Traynor said.

Close to the Green Mountain National Bank they ran into Wayne Robertson. His wide-brimmed, trooper style hat was low on his forehead to shield his eyes from the sun. As added protection he was wearing highly reflective sunglasses.

"Afternoon," Traynor said amicably.

Robertson touched the brim of his hat in a form of salute.

"Any startling developments in the Hodges case?" Traynor asked.

"Hardly," Robertson said. "In fact, we're thinking about dropping it."

"I wouldn't be too premature," Traynor warned. "Remember, that old geezer had a penchant for appearing when least expected."

"And unwanted," Beaton added.

"Dr. Cantor thinks he's in Florida," Robertson said. "I'm starting to believe it myself. I think that little scandal about the hospital taking care of his house embarrassed him enough to leave town."

"I would have thought he'd have thicker skin than that," Traynor said. "But who am I to guess."

After exchanging farewells and good wishes for the weekend, the four returned to their respective jobs.

As Beaton drove up the hill toward the hospital, she thought about Traynor and her relationship with him. She wasn't happy; she wanted more. Trysts once or twice a month were hardly what she'd expected.

Beaton had met Traynor several years previously when he'd come to Boston to take a refresher course in tax law. She'd been working in the city as an assistant administrator in one of the Harvard hospitals. The attraction was instantaneous and mutual. They spent a torrid week together, then rendezvoused intermittently until he'd recruited her to come to Bartlet to run the hospital. She'd been led to believe that they would eventually live together, but so far it hadn't happened. Traynor had not gotten the divorce he'd promised was imminent. Beaton felt she had to do something to rectify the situation; she just didn't know what.

Back at the hospital, Beaton went directly to room 204, where she expected to find Tom Baringer. She intended to make sure he was comfortable. He wasn't there. Instead Beaton was surprised to discover another patient: a woman by the name of Alice Nottingham. Beaton set her jaw, descended to the first floor, and marched into Caldwell's office.

"Where's Baringer?" she asked curtly.

"Room 204," Caldwell said.

"Unless Mr. Baringer has had a sex change operation and is going by the name of Alice, he's not in 204."

Caldwell quickly got to his feet. "Something's gone wrong." He pushed past

Beaton and hurried across the hall to admissions. There he sought out Janice Sperling and asked her what had happened to Tom Baringer.

"I put him in 209," Janice said.

"I told you to put him in 204," Caldwell said.

"I know," Janice admitted. "But since we talked, 209 came available. It's a larger room. You said Mr. Baringer was a special patient. I thought he'd like 209 better."

"204 has a better view, plus it has the new orthopedic bed," Caldwell said. "The man has a broken hip. Either change rooms or change beds."

"Okay," Janice said, rolling her eyes. Some people could never be pleased.

Caldwell went to Beaton's office and stuck his head through the door. "I'm sorry for not having followed up on that situation," he said. "But it will be rectified within the hour. I promise."

Beaton nodded and went back to her work.

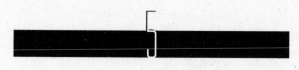

SATURDAY • MAY 22

David had set the alarm for five forty-five as if it were a normal workday. By six-fifteen he was on his way to the hospital. The temperature had already climbed into the low seventies and the skies were clear. Before nine he was finished with his rounds and on his way home.

"Okay, you guys," he called as he entered the apartment. "I don't want to spend this whole day waiting. Let's get this show on the road."

Nikki appeared in her doorway. "That's not fair, Daddy. We've been waiting for you."

"Just kidding," David said with a laugh as he gave Nikki a playful tickle.

Soon they were off. Before long, urban sprawl gave way to tree-dotted suburbia followed by long stretches of forest. The farther north they went, the prettier the surroundings became, especially now that leaves were on the trees.

When they reached Bartlet, David slowed to a crawl. Like eager tourists they drank in the sights.

"This is even more picturesque than I remembered," Angela said.

"There's that same puppy!" Nikki cried. She pointed across the street. "Can we stop?"

David pulled into an empty diagonal parking slot. "You're right," he said. "I recognize the lady."

"I recognize the dog," Nikki said. She opened the car door and got out.

"Just a second," Angela called. She jumped out of the car and took Nikki's hand to cross the street. David followed.

"Hello again," the woman said when Nikki approached. The puppy caught sight of Nikki and strained at its leash. As Nikki bent down, the dog licked her face. Nikki laughed with surprise.

"I don't know if you'd be interested, but Mr. Staley's retriever just had puppies a few weeks ago," the woman said. "They're right over in the hardware store across the street."

"Can we go see them?" Nikki pleaded.

"Why not," David said. He thanked the woman.

Recrossing the street the Wilsons entered the hardware store. Near the front in a makeshift playpen was Mr. Staley's dog, Molly, suckling five floppy puppies.

"They're adorable," Nikki cried. "Can I pet them?"

"I don't know," David said. He turned to look for a store attendant and practically bumped into Mr. Staley, who was standing directly behind them.

"Sure, she can pet them," Mr. Staley said after introducing himself. "In fact, they're for sale. No way I need six golden retrievers."

Nikki collapsed on her knees and, reaching into the pen, gently stroked one of the puppies. He responded by attaching himself to Nikki's finger as if it were a teat. Nikki squealed with delight.

"Pick him up if you like," Mr. Staley said. "He's the brute of the litter."

Nikki scooped the puppy up in her arms. The tiny dog snuggled against her cheek and licked her nose.

"I love him," Nikki said. "I wish we could get him. Can we? I'll take care of him."

David felt an unexpected surge of tears that he had to forcibly suppress. He took his eyes off Nikki and looked at Angela. Angela dabbed a tissue into the corners of her eyes and glanced up at her husband. Their eyes met in a moment of complete understanding. Nikki's modest request affected them even more than it had on their first visit to Bartlet. Considering all that she'd been through with her cystic fibrosis, it wasn't much to ask for.

"Are you thinking what I'm thinking?" David asked.

"I think so," Angela said. Her tears gave way to a smile. "It would mean we could buy a house."

"Goodbye, crime and pollution," he said. He looked down at Nikki. "Okay," he said. "You can have the dog. We're moving to Bartlet!"

Nikki's face lit up. She hugged the puppy to her chest as it licked her face.

David turned to Mr. Staley and settled on a price.

"I figure they will be ready to leave the mother in four weeks or so," Mr. Staley said.

"That will be perfect," David said. "We'll be coming up here at the end of the month."

With some difficulty, Nikki was separated from her puppy, and the Wilsons went back outside.

"What will we do now?" Angela asked with excitement.

"Let's celebrate," David said. "Let's have lunch at the inn."

A few minutes later they were sitting at a cloth-covered table with a view of the river. David and Angela each ordered a glass of white wine. Nikki had a cranberry juice. They touched their glasses.

"I'd like to toast our arrival in the Garden of Eden," David said.

"And I'd like to toast the beginning of paying back our debt," Angela said.

"Hear, hear!" David said, and they drank.

"Can you believe it?" Angela asked. "Our combined income will be over one hundred and twenty thousand dollars."

David sang a few bars of the song "We're in the Money."

"I think I'll call my dog Rusty," Nikki said.

"That's a wonderful name," David said.

"What do you think about me earning twice what you do?" Angela teased.

David had known the barb would come at some point, so he was prepared. "You'll be earning it in your dark, dreary lab," he teased back. "At least I'll be seeing real, live, appreciative people."

"Won't it challenge your delicate masculinity?" Angela continued.

"Not in the slightest," David said. "Also it's nice to know that if we ever get divorced I'll get alimony."

Angela lunged across the table to give David a poke in the ribs.

David parried Angela's playful gesture. "Besides," he said, "that kind of differential won't last much longer. It's a legacy of a past era. Pathologists, like surgeons and other overpaid specialists, will soon be brought down to earth."

"Says who?" Angela demanded.

"Says me," David said.

After lunch, they decided to go straight to the hospital to let Caldwell know their decision. Once they presented themselves to his secretary, they were ushered in right away.

"That's fantastic!" Caldwell said when they informed him of their decision. "Does CMV know yet?" he asked.

"Not yet," David said.

"Come on," Caldwell said. "Let's go give them the good news."

Charles Kelley was equally pleased with the news. After a congratulatory handshake he asked David when he thought he'd be ready to start seeing patients.

"Just about immediately," David said without hesitation. "July first."

"Your residency isn't over until the thirtieth," Kelley said. "Don't you want some time to get settled?"

"With our debt," David said, "the sooner we start working the better we'll feel."

"Same for you?" Caldwell asked Angela.

"Absolutely," Angela answered.

David asked if they could go back to the office he'd be assigned. Kelley was happy to oblige.

David paused outside the waiting room door, fantasizing how his name would look in the empty slot under Dr. Randall Portland's name. It had been a long, hard road, starting from the moment in the eighth grade when he'd decided to become a doctor, but he'd finally made it.

David opened the door and stepped over the threshold. His reverie was broken when a figure dressed in surgical scrubs leaped off the waiting room couch.

"What is the meaning of this?" the man angrily demanded.

It took David a moment to recognize Dr. Portland. It was partly due to the unexpectedness of the encounter, but it was also because Dr. Portland had changed in the month since David had last seen him. He'd lost considerable weight; his eyes seemed sunken, even haunted, and his cheeks were gaunt.

Kelley pushed his way to the front of the group, reintroduced David and Randall, and then explained to Randall why they were there. Dr. Portland's anger waned. Like a balloon losing its air, he collapsed back onto the couch. David noticed that not only had Randall lost weight but he was pale.

"Sorry to have bothered you," David said.

"I was just getting a bit of sleep," Dr. Portland explained. His voice was flat. He sounded as exhausted as he looked. "I did a case this morning, and I felt tired."

"Tom Baringer?" Caldwell asked.

Dr. Portland nodded.

"I hope it went okay," Caldwell said.

"The operation went fine," Dr. Portland said. "Now we have to keep our fingers crossed for the post-op course."

David apologized again, then herded everyone, including himself, out of the office.

"Sorry about that," Kelley said.

"What's wrong with him?" David asked.

"Nothing that I know of," Kelley said.

"He doesn't look well," David said.

"I thought he looked depressed," Angela said.

"He's busy," Kelley admitted. "I'm sure he's just overworked."

The group stopped outside Kelley's office. "Now that we know you are coming," Kelley said, "is there anything that we can do to help?"

"We'll have to go look at a few houses," Angela said. "Who do you suggest we call?"

"Dorothy Weymouth," Caldwell said.

"He's right," Kelley said.

"She's far and away the best realtor in town," Caldwell added. "Come back to my office and use my phone."

A half hour later, the whole family was in Dorothy Weymouth's office on the second floor of the building across the street from the diner. She was a huge, pleasant woman attired in a shapeless, tent-like dress.

"I have to tell you, I'm impressed," Dorothy said. Her voice was surprisingly high-pitched for such a large woman. "While you were on your way over here from the hospital, Barton Sherwood called to tell me the bank is eager to help you. Now it doesn't happen often that the president of the bank calls before I've even met the client.

"I'm not sure exactly what your tastes are," Dorothy said as she began putting photos of properties currently on the market out on her desk. "So you'll have to help me. Do you think you'd like a white clapboard house in town or an isolated stone farmhouse? What about size? Is that an important consideration? Are you planning any more children?"

Both David and Angela tensed at the question of whether they would have more children. Until Nikki's birth, neither had suspected they were carriers of the cystic fibrosis gene. It was a reality they could not ignore.

Unaware she'd hit a nerve, Dorothy continued laying out photos of homes, while she maintained a steady monologue.

"Here's a particularly charming property that's just come on the market. It's a beauty."

Angela caught her breath. She picked up the photo. Nikki tried to look over her shoulder.

"I do like this one," Angela said. She handed the picture to David. It was a brick, late Georgian or early Federal style home with double bow windows on either side of a central, paneled front door. Fluted white columns held up a pedimented portico over the door. Above the pediment was a large Palladian window.

"That's one of the oldest brick homes in the area," Dorothy said. "It was built around 1820."

"What's this in the back?" David asked, pointing to the photo.

Dorothy looked. "That's the old silo," she said. "Behind the house and connected to it is a barn. You can't see the barn in that photo because the picture was taken directly in front of the house, down the hill. The property used to be a dairy farm, quite a profitable one, I understand."

"It's gorgeous," Angela said wistfully. "But I'm sure we could never afford it."

"You could according to what Barton Sherwood told me," Dorothy said. "Besides, I know that the owner, Clara Hodges, is very eager to sell. I'm sure we could get you a good deal. Anyway, it's worth a look. Let's pick four or five others and go see them."

Cleverly orchestrating the order of the visits, Dorothy left the Hodges house for last. It was located about two and a half miles south of the town center on the crest of a small hill. The nearest house was an eighth of a mile down the road. When they pulled into the driveway, Nikki noticed the frog pond and was immediately sold.

"The pond is not only picturesque," Dorothy said, "it's also great for skating in the wintertime."

Dorothy pulled to a halt between the house and the frog pond and slightly to the side. From there they had a view of the structure with its connected barn. Neither Angela nor David said a word. They were both awed by the home's noble and imposing character. They now realized that the house was three stories instead of two. They could see four dormers on each side of the pitched slate roof.

"Are you sure Mr. Sherwood thinks we can afford this?" David asked.

"Absolutely," Dorothy said. "Come on, let's see the interior."

In a state of near hypnosis, David and Angela followed Dorothy around the inside of the house. Dorothy continued her steady stream of realtor chatter, saying things like "This room has so much promise" and "With just a little creativity and work, this room would be so cozy." Any problems such as peeling wallpaper or dry-rotted window sashes she minimized. The good points, like the sizes of the many fireplaces and the beautiful cornice work, she lauded with an uninterrupted flow of superlatives.

David insisted on seeing everything. They even descended the gray granite steps into the basement, which seemed exceptionally damp and musty.

"There seems to be a strange smell," he said. "Is there a water problem down here?"

"Not that I've heard of," Dorothy said. "But it is a nice big basement. There's room enough for a shop if you're the handy type."

Angela suppressed a giggle as well as a disparaging comment. She'd been about to say that David had trouble changing light bulbs, but she held her tongue.

"There's no floor," David said. He bent down and pried up a bit of dirt with his fingernail.

"It's a packed earth floor," Dorothy explained. "It's common in older homes like this. And this basement has other features typical of a nineteenth-century dwelling." She pulled open a heavy wooden door. "Here's the old root cellar."

There was shelving for preserves and bins for potatoes and apples. The room was poorly lit with one small bulb.

"It's scary," Nikki said. "It's like a dungeon."

"This will be handy if your parents ever come to visit," David said. "We can put them up down here."

Angela rolled her eyes.

After showing them the root cellar, Dorothy took them over to the other corner of the basement and proudly pointed out a large freezer chest. "This house has both the old and the new methods of food storage," she said.

Before they left the basement Dorothy opened a second door. Behind it was a second flight of granite steps which led up to a hatch-like door. "These stairs lead out to the back yard," Dorothy explained. "That's why the firewood is here." She pointed to several cords of firewood neatly stacked against the wall.

The last thing of note in the basement was the huge furnace. It looked almost like an old-fashioned steam locomotive. "This used to burn coal," Dorothy explained, "but it was converted to oil." She pointed out a large fuel tank perched on cinder blocks in the corner opposite the freezer chest.

David nodded, though he didn't know much about furnaces no matter what they burned.

On the way back up the steps to the kitchen, David smelled the musty smell again and asked about the septic system.

"The septic system is fine," Dorothy said. "We had it inspected. It's to the west of the house. I can point out the leach field if you like."

"As long as it's been inspected, I'm sure it's okay," David said. He had no idea what a leach field was or what it should look like.

David and Angela had Dorothy drop them off at the Green Mountain National Bank. They were nervous and excited at the same time. Barton Sherwood saw them almost immediately.

"We found a house that we like," David said.

"I'm not surprised," Sherwood said. "There are lots of wonderful houses in Bartlet."

"It's a house owned by Clara Hodges," David continued. He handed over the real estate summary sheet. "The asking price is two hundred and fifty thousand dollars. What does the bank think about the property and the price?"

"It's a great old house," Sherwood said. "I know it well." He scanned the summary sheet. "And the location is fabulous. In fact it borders my own property. As far as the price is concerned, I think it's a steal."

"So the bank would be willing to underwrite our purchase at that price?" Angela questioned. She wanted to be sure. It seemed too good to be true.

"Of course, you'll offer less," Sherwood said. "I'd suggest an initial offer of one hundred and ninety thousand. But the bank will be willing to back the purchase up to the asking price."

Fifteen minutes later David, Angela, and Nikki stepped back out into the warm Vermont sunshine. They had never bought a house before. It was a monumental decision. Yet having decided to come to Bartlet they were in a decisive frame of mind.

"Well?" David asked.

"I can't imagine finding something we'd like better," Angela said.

"I can even have a desk in my room," Nikki said.

David reached out and tousled Nikki's hair. "With as many rooms as that house has, you can have your own study."

"Let's do it," Angela said.

Back in Dorothy's office they told the pleased realtor their decision. A few minutes later Dorothy had Clara Hodges on the phone, and although it was a bit unconventional, a deal was concluded orally at a price of two hundred and ten thousand dollars.

As Dorothy drew up the formal documents, David and Angela exchanged glances. They were stunned to realize they were the new owners of a home more gracious than they could have ever hoped to have owned for years to come. Yet there was some anxiety as well. Their debt had more than doubled, to over three hundred and fifty thousand dollars.

By the end of the day, after a bit of shuttling back and forth between Dorothy's office and the bank, all the appropriate papers were filled out and a closing date was set.

"I have some names for you," Dorothy said when they were through with the paperwork. "Pete Bergan does odd jobs around the town. He's not the world's smartest fellow, but he does good work. And for painting, I use John Murray."

David wrote the names down with their phone numbers.

"And if you need a sitter for Nikki, my older sister, Alice Doherty, would be delighted to help out. She lost her husband a few years ago. Besides, she lives out your way."

"That's a wonderful tip," Angela said. "With both of us working we'll need someone just about every day."

Later that same afternoon David and Angela met the handyman and the painter out at their new home. They arranged to have a general cleaning as well as a minimum of painting and repairing to make the house weatherproof.

After one more visit to the hardware store so Nikki could pet Rusty one last time and say goodbye, the Wilsons got on the road for the drive back to Boston. Angela drove. Neither David nor Nikki dozed. They were all keyed up from what they'd accomplished and full of dreams about their new life that was imminently to begin.

"What did you think about Dr. Portland?" David asked after a period of silence.

"What do you mean?" said Angela.

"The man was hardly friendly," David said.

"I think we woke him up."

"Still, most people wouldn't act that irritable. Besides, he looked like death warmed over. He's changed so drastically in a month."

"I thought he sounded and looked depressed."

David shrugged. "He wasn't even that friendly the first time we met him, now that I think of it. All he wanted to know was whether I played basketball. Something about him makes me feel uncomfortable. I hope sharing an office with him doesn't become a sore spot."

It was dark by the time they returned to Boston; they'd stopped for dinner on the way. When they got back to their apartment, they looked around in wonderment, amazed that they'd been able to live for four years in such a tiny, claustrophobic space.

"This entire apartment would fit into the library of the new house," Angela commented.

David and Angela decided to call their parents to share the excitement.

David's were delighted. Having retired to Amherst, New Hampshire, they felt like Bartlet was next door. "We'll get to see a lot more of you guys," they said.

Angela's parents had a different response.

"It's easy to drop out of the academic big leagues," Dr. Walter Christopher said. "But it's hard getting back in. I think you could have asked my opinion before you made such a foolish move. Here's your mother."

Angela's mother came on the line and expressed her disappointment that Angela and David hadn't come to New York. "Your father spent a lot of time talking to all sorts of people to make sure you had good positions here," she said. "I think it was inconsiderate of you not to take advantage of his effort."

After Angela hung up she turned to David. "They've never been particularly supportive," she said. "So I suppose I shouldn't have expected them to change now."

MONDAY • MAY 24

Traynor arrived at the hospital with time to spare for his afternoon meeting. Instead of going directly to Helen Beaton's office, he went to the patient area on the second floor and walked down to room 209. After taking a breath to fortify himself, he pushed the door open. Being chairman of the board of directors of the hospital had not changed Traynor's aversion to medical situations, particularly bad medical situations.

Conscious of breathing shallowly in the presence of the seriously ill, Traynor moved across the darkened room and approached the large orthopedic bed. Bending over and scrupulously avoiding touching anything, he peered at his client, Tom Baringer. Tom didn't look good, and Traynor didn't want to get too close lest he catch some awful illness. Tom's face was gray and his breathing was labored. A plastic tube snaked from behind his head, feeding oxygen into his nose. His eyes were closed with tape, and ointment oozed out between his eyelids.

"Tom," Traynor called softly. When there was no response, he called louder. But Tom did not move.

"He's beyond responding."

Traynor jumped and the blood drained from his own face. Except for Tom, he'd thought he was alone.

"His pneumonia is not responding to treatment," the stranger said angrily. He'd been sitting in a corner of the room. He was cloaked in shadows; Traynor could not see his face.

"He's dying like the others," the man said.

"Who are you?" Traynor asked. He wiped his forehead where perspiration had instantly appeared.

The man got to his feet. Only then could Traynor see that he was dressed in surgical scrubs, covered with a white jacket.

"I'm Mr. Baringer's doctor, Randy Portland." He advanced to the opposite side of the bed and gazed down at his comatose patient. "The operation was a success but the patient is about to die. I suppose you've heard a variation of that quip before."

"I suppose I have," Traynor said nervously. Shock at Dr. Portland's presence was changing to anxious concern. There was something decidedly strange about the man's manner. Traynor wasn't sure what he would do next.

"The hip has been repaired," Dr. Portland said. He lifted the edge of the sheet so Traynor could see the tightly sutured wound. "No problem whatsoever. But unfortunately it's been a fatal cure. There's no way Mr. Baringer will walk out of here." Portland dropped the sheet and defiantly raised his eyes to Traynor's. "There's something wrong with this hospital," he said. "I'm not going to take all the blame."

"Dr. Portland," Traynor said hesitantly. "You don't look well to me. Maybe you should see a doctor yourself."

Dr. Portland threw back his head and laughed. But it was a hollow, mirthless laugh which ended as suddenly as it had begun. "Maybe you're right," he said. "Maybe I'll do that." He then turned and left the room.

Traynor felt stunned. He looked down at Tom as if he expected him to wake up and explain Dr. Portland's behavior. Traynor could understand how doctors might become emotionally involved in their patients' conditions, but Portland seemed unhinged.

Traynor tried one last time to communicate with Tom. Recognizing the futility, he backed away from the bed and slipped out of the room. Warily he looked for Dr. Portland. When he didn't see him, Traynor quickly walked to Beaton's office. Caldwell and Kelley were already there.

"Do you all know Dr. Portland?" Traynor asked as he took a chair.

Everyone nodded. Kelley spoke: "He's one of ours. He's an orthopedic surgeon."

"I just had a very peculiar and unnerving encounter with him," Traynor said. "On my way here I popped in to see my client, Tom Baringer, who's very sick. Dr. Portland was sitting in the corner of Tom's darkened room. I didn't even see him when I first went in. When he spoke, he acted strangely, even belligerently. I imagine he's distraught over Tom's condition, but he said something about not taking all the blame and that there was something wrong with the hospital."

"I think he's been under strain from overwork," Kelley said. "We're short at least one orthopedic surgeon. Unfortunately our recruiting efforts have been unsuccessful so far."

"He looked ill to me," Traynor said. "I advised him to see a doctor, but he only laughed."

"I'll have a talk with him," Kelley promised. "Maybe he needs a little time off. We can always get a locum tenens for a few weeks."

"Well, so much for that," Traynor said, trying to compose himself more in keeping with his role as chairman of the board. "Let's get our meeting under way."

"Before we do that," Kelley said, flashing one of his winning smiles, "there's something I have to say. My superiors are very upset about the negative ruling on the CON for open-heart surgery."

"We were disappointed about that as well," Traynor said nervously. He didn't like beginning on a negative note. "Unfortunately it's out of our hands. Montpelier turned us down even though we thought we'd made a good case."

"CMV had expected the open-heart program to be up and running by now," Kelley said. "It was part of the contract."

"It was part of the contract provided we got the CON," Traynor corrected. "But we didn't. So let's look at what has been done. We've updated the MRI, built the neonatal ICU, and replaced the old cobalt-60 machine with a new state-of-the-art linear accelerator. I think we have been showing remarkably good faith, and we've been doing all this while the hospital has been losing money."

"Whether the hospital loses money or not is not CMV's concern," Kelley said. "Especially since it's probably due to minor management inefficiencies."

"I think you are wrong," Traynor said, swallowing his anger at Kelley's insulting insinuation. He hated being put on the defensive, especially by this young, brazen bureaucrat. "I think CMV has to be concerned if we are losing money. If things get much worse we could be forced to close our doors. That would be bad for everyone. We have to work together. There's no other choice."

"If Bartlet Community Hospital goes under," Kelley said, "CMV would take its business elsewhere."

"That's not so easy anymore," Traynor said. "The two other hospitals in the area are no longer functioning as acute care facilities."

"No problem," Kelley said casually. "If need be, we would ferry our patients to the CMV hospital in Rutland."

Traynor's heart skipped a beat. The possibility of CMV ferrying its patients had never occurred to him. He'd hoped that the lack of nearby hospitals would give him some bargaining power. Apparently it didn't.

"I don't mean to imply that I'm not willing to work together with you people," Kelley said. "This should be a dynamic relationship. After all, we have the same goal: the health of the community." He smiled again as if to show off his perfectly straight white teeth.

"The problem is the current capitation rate is too low," Traynor said bluntly. "Hospitalization from CMV is running more than ten percent above projections. We can't support such an overrun for long. We need to renegotiate the capitation rate. It's that simple."

"The capitation rate doesn't get renegotiated until the contract term is over,"

Kelley said amicably. "What do you take us for? You offered the present rate in a competitive bidding process. And you signed the contract. So it stands. What I can do is start negotiations on a capitation rate for ER services, which was left out of the initial agreement."

"Capitating the ER is not something we can do at the moment," Traynor said, feeling perspiration run down the insides of his arms. "We have to stem our red ink first."

"Which is the reason for our meeting this afternoon," Beaton said, speaking up for the first time. She then presented the final version of the proposed bonus program for CMV physicians.

"Each gatekeeper CMV physician will be allocated a bonus payment provided his number of monthly hospital days per assigned subscriber stays at a given level. As the level goes down, the payment goes up and vice versa."

Kelley laughed. "Sounds like clever bribery to me. As sensitive as doctors are to economic incentives, it certainly should reduce hospitalization and surgery."

"It's essentially the same plan CMV has in effect at the CMV hospital in Rutland."

"If it works there then it should work here," Kelley said. "I have no trouble with it, provided it doesn't cost CMV anything."

"It will be totally funded by the hospital," Beaton said.

"I'll present it to my superiors," Kelley said. "Is that it for this meeting?"

"That's it," Beaton said.

Kelley got to his feet.

"We'd appreciate all the speed you can muster," Traynor said. "I'm afraid we're looking at a lot of red ink on our balance sheet."

"I'll do it today," Kelley promised. "I'll try to have a definitive answer by tomorrow." With that, he shook hands with everyone and left the room.

"I'd say that went as well as could be expected," Beaton said once he was gone.

"I'm encouraged," Caldwell said.

"I didn't appreciate his impudent suggestion of incompetent management," Traynor said. "I don't like his cocky attitude. It's unfortunate we have to deal with him."

"What I didn't like hearing was the threat to ferry patients to Rutland," Beaton said. "That worries me. It means our bargaining position is even weaker than I thought."

"Something just occurred to me," Traynor said. "Here we've had this high-level meeting that could possibly determine the fate of the hospital and there were no doctors present."

"It's a sign of the times," Beaton said. "The burden of dealing with the health-care crisis has fallen on us administrators."

"I think it's the medical world's equivalent of the expression, 'War is too important to leave up to the generals,' " Traynor said.

They all laughed. It was a good break from the tension of the meeting.

"What about Dr. Portland?" Caldwell asked. "Should I do anything?"

"I don't think there's anything to be done," Beaton said. "I haven't heard anything but good things about his surgical abilities. He certainly hasn't violated any rules or regulations. I think we'll have to wait and see what CMV does."

"He didn't look good to me," Traynor reiterated. "I'm no psychiatrist and I don't know what someone looks like when they're about to have a nervous breakdown, but if I had to guess, I'd guess they'd look the way he does."

The buzz of the intercom surprised them all, especially Beaton, who'd left explicit instructions there were to be no interruptions.

"Some bad news," she said once she hung up. "Tom Baringer has died."

The three fell silent. Traynor was the first to speak: "Nothing like a death to remind us that for all the red and black ink, a hospital really is a very different kind of business."

"It's true," Beaton said. "The burden of the work is that the whole town, even the whole region, becomes like an extended family. And as in any large family, someone is always dying."

"What is our death rate here at Bartlet Community Hospital?" Traynor asked. "It's never occurred to me to ask."

"We're just about in the middle of the road," Beaton said. "Plus or minus a percentage point. In fact, our rate is better than most of the inner-city teaching hospitals."

"That's a relief," Traynor said. "For a moment I was afraid there was something else I had to worry about."

"Enough of this morbid talk," Caldwell said. "I have some good news. The husband-and-wife team that we and CMV have been recruiting so actively has decided to come to Bartlet. So we'll be getting a superbly trained pathologist."

"I'm glad to hear it," Traynor said. "That brings pathology up to speed."

"They've even purchased the old Hodges house," Caldwell added.

"No kidding!" Traynor said. "I like that. There's something wonderfully ironic about it."

Charles Kelley slipped into his Ferrari coupe, started the engine, and gave it some gas. It responded like the engineering marvel it was, pressing him against the seat as he accelerated out of the hospital parking lot. He loved to drive the car, especially in the mountains. The way it hugged the road and cornered was a true delight.

After the meeting with the Bartlet Hospital people Kelley had phoned Duncan Mitchell directly, thinking it was a good opportunity to make his presence known to the man at the pinnacle of power. Duncan Mitchell was the CEO of CMV, as well as of several other HMOs and hospital management companies in the South. Conveniently the home office was in Vermont where Mr. Mitchell had a farm.

Kelley had not known what to expect and had been nervous when he called, but the CEO turned out to be gracious. Although Kelley had caught the man preparing to go to Washington, he had generously agreed to meet with Kelley outside the Burlington Airport general aviation building.

With CMV's Learjet in its final stages of fueling, Mitchell invited Kelley into the back of his limousine. He offered Kelley a drink from the limo's bar. Kelley politely refused.

Duncan Mitchell was an impressive man. He wasn't as tall as Kelley, yet he emanated a sense of power. He was meticulously dressed in a conservative business suit with a silk tie and gold cuff links. His Italian loafers were dark brown crocodile.

Kelley introduced himself and gave a brief history of his association with CMV, mentioning that he was the regional director for the area centered around Bartlet Community Hospital, just in case Mitchell didn't know. But Mitchell seemed acquainted with Kelley's position.

"We eventually want to buy that facility," he said.

"I assumed as much," Kelley said. "And that's why I wanted to come to talk with you directly."

Mr. Mitchell slipped a gold cigarette case from his vest pocket and took out a cigarette. He tapped it thoughtfully against the case's flat front surface. "There's a lot of profit to be squeezed out of these rural hospitals," Mitchell said. "But it takes careful management."

"I couldn't agree more," Kelley said.

"What is it you wanted to talk about?" Mr. Mitchell asked.

"Two issues," Kelley said. "The first involves a bonus program the hospital wants to initiate similar to our own with our hospitals. They want to cut down on hospitalization."

"And what's the other?" Mitchell asked. He blew smoke up toward the ceiling of the car.

"One of our CMV physicians has begun acting bizarrely in response to post-operative complications in his patients," Kelley said. "He's saying things like he's not to blame and there's something wrong with the hospital."

"Does he have a psychiatric history?" Mr. Mitchell asked.

"Not that we can determine," Kelley said.

"Regarding the first issue, let them have their bonus program. At this point it doesn't matter about their balance sheet."

"What about the doctor?" Kelley asked.

"Obviously you'll have to do something," Mitchell said. "We can't let that type of behavior go on."

"Any suggestions?" Kelley asked.

"Do what you need to do," Mitchell said. "I'll leave the details up to you. Part of the skill of running a large organization like ours is knowing when to delegate responsibility. This is one of those times."

"Thank you, Mr. Mitchell," Kelley said. He was pleased. It was obvious to him that he was being given a vote of confidence.

Elated, Kelley climbed out of the limousine and got back into his Ferrari. As he was pulling out of the airport he caught a glimpse of Mitchell walking from his car to the CMV jet.

"Someday," Kelley vowed, "it'll be me using that plane."

WEDNESDAY · JUNE 30

Both the internal medicine department and the pathology department had small, informal ceremonies for that year's group of graduates, marking the end of their residencies. After collecting their diplomas, David and Angela passed up the parties scheduled for that afternoon and hurried home. This was the day they would leave Boston for their new home and careers in Bartlet, Vermont.

"Are you excited?" David asked Nikki.

"I'm excited to see Rusty," Nikki announced.

They'd rented a U-Haul truck to help make the move. It took quite a few trips up and down the stairs to get their possessions in the two vehicles. Once they were finally packed, Angela got in their station wagon and David got in the U-Haul. For the first half of the trip, Nikki elected to ride with her dad.

David used the time to talk with Nikki about starting at a new school and ask her if she'd miss her friends.

"Some of them I'll miss," Nikki said, "but others I won't. Anyway, I think I'll cope."

David smiled, promising himself that he would remember to tell Angela about Nikki's precocious comment.

Just south of the New Hampshire border, they stopped for lunch. Eager to arrive at their new home, they ate quickly.

"I feel wonderful about leaving the frantic, crime-filled city behind," Angela said as they left the restaurant and approached their vehicles. "At this point I don't care if I ever go back."

"I don't know," David joked. "I'm going to miss hearing sirens, gunshots, breaking glass, and cries for help. Country life is going to be so boring."

Both Nikki and Angela pummeled him in mock anger.

For the rest of the trip Nikki joined Angela in the station wagon.

As they drove north the weather improved. In Boston it had been hot, muggy, and hazy. By the time they crossed into Vermont it was still warm but clear and much less humid.

Bartlet appeared serene in the early summer heat. Flower-filled window boxes adorned almost every sill. Slowing down, the Wilsons' two-vehicle caravan crept through the lazy town. Few people were on the streets. It was as if everyone were napping.

"Can we stop and get Rusty?" Nikki asked as they neared Staley's Hardware Store.

"Let's get a bit settled first," Angela said. "We'll have to build something to keep him in until he gets housebroken."

David and Angela pulled into their driveway and parked side by side. Now that the house was officially theirs they felt even more awed than they had on their initial visit.

David climbed out of the truck, his eyes glued to the house. "The place is lovely," he said. "But it looks like it needs more attention than I realized."

Angela walked over to David and followed his line of sight. Some of the decorative dentil work had fallen from the cornice. "I'm not worried," she said. "That's why I married someone who is handy around the house."

David laughed. "I can see it'll take some effort to make a believer out of you."

"I'll try to keep an open mind," she teased.

With a key they had been sent in the mail, they opened the front door and stepped inside. It looked very different without furniture. When they'd seen it before it had been filled with the Hodgeses' belongings.

"It has a dance hall feel," David said.

"There's even an echo," Nikki said. She yelled "Hello" and the word reverberated.

"That's when you know you've arrived at your proper station in life," David said, affecting an English accent. "When your house has an echo."

The Wilsons slowly passed through the foyer. Now that there were no rugs, their heels clicked on the wide wooden flooring. They had forgotten their new home's enormity, especially in contrast to their Boston apartment. Aside from a few pieces of furniture they'd agreed Clara would leave behind—a stool, a kitchen table—the place was bare.

In the center hall just before the grand staircase an imposing chandelier hung. There was a library and dining room to the left and a huge living room to the right. A central hall led to a spacious country kitchen which stretched across the back of the house. Beyond the kitchen was the two-story clapboard addition that connected the house to the barn. It had a mudroom, several storerooms, and a back staircase leading up to the second level.

Returning to the grand staircase, the Wilsons climbed up to the second story. There were two bedrooms with connecting baths on each side and a master suite over the kitchen area.

Opening a door off the central hallway next to the master suite, they climbed a narrow staircase up to the third level where there were four unheated rooms.

"Plenty of storage," David quipped.

"Which room will be my bedroom?" Nikki asked.

"Whatever room you want," Angela said.

"I want the room facing the frog pond," she said.

They went down to the second level and walked into the room Nikki wanted. They discussed where her furniture would go, including the desk she did not yet own.

"Okay, you guys," Angela commanded. "Enough procrastination. Time to unload."

David gave her a military salute.

Returning to the vehicles, they began to bring their belongings into the house and put them into the appropriate rooms. The couch, the bedding, and the heavy boxes of books made it quite a struggle. When they were finished David and Angela stood beneath the archway leading into the living room.

"It would be funny if it wasn't so pathetic," Angela said. The rug that had been almost wall to wall in their apartment seemed little better than a doormat in the middle of the expansive room. Their threadbare couch, two armchairs, and coffee table looked like they had been rescued from a garage sale.

"Understated elegance," David said. "Minimalist decor. If it were in *Architectural Digest*, everyone would be trying to imitate it."

"What about Rusty?" Nikki asked.

"Let's go get him," David said. "You've been a good sport and a big help. You want to come, Angela?"

"No, thanks," Angela said. "I'll stay and get more organized, especially in the kitchen."

"I assumed we'd eat down at the inn tonight," David said.

"No, I want to eat here in our new home," Angela answered.

While David and Nikki went to town, Angela unpacked a few of the boxes in the kitchen including their pots, pans, dishes, and flatware. She also figured out how to work the stove and got the refrigerator running.

Nikki returned carrying the adorable puppy with its wrinkled face and floppy ears. She had the dog pressed against her chest. He'd grown considerably since they'd seen him last. His feet were the size of Nikki's fists.

"He's going to be a big dog," David said.

While Nikki and David fashioned a pen for Rusty in the mudroom, Angela made dinner for Nikki. Nikki wasn't happy about eating before her parents, but she was too tired to complain. After she'd eaten and done some postural drainage, she and Rusty, both exhausted, were put to bed.

"Now I have a little surprise for you," Angela said as she and David descended from Nikki's room. She took him by the hand and led him into the kitchen. Opening the refrigerator, she pulled out a bottle of Chardonnay.

"Wow," David exclaimed, inspecting the label. "This isn't our usual cheap stuff."

"Hardly," Angela said. Reaching back into the refrigerator, she took out a dish covered with a paper towel. Lifting the towel she exposed two thick veal chops.

"I have the feeling we're in for a feast," David said.

"You'd better believe it," Angela said. "Salad, artichokes, wild rice, and veal chops. Plus the best Chardonnay I could buy."

David cooked the meat on an outdoor barbecue built into the side of the terrace off the library. By the time he came in Angela had the rest of the food on the table in the dining room.

Night had descended softly, filling the house with shadow. In the darkness the glow from the two candles that formed the centerpiece on the table only illuminated the immediate area. The disarray of the rest of the house was hidden.

They sat at opposite ends of the table. They didn't speak. Instead they merely gazed at each other as they ate. Both of them were moved by the romantic atmosphere, realizing that romance had been missing from their lives over the last years; the demands of their respective residencies and Nikki's ongoing health problems had taken precedence.

Long after they'd finished eating they continued to sit and stare at each other while a symphony of sounds of a Vermont summer night drifted in through the open windows. The candle flames flickered sensuously as the clean, cool air wafted across the room and caressed their faces. It was a magical moment they both wanted to savor.

Mutual desire drove them from the dining room into the dark living room. They fell onto the couch, their lips meeting as they enveloped each other in a warm embrace. They removed their clothing, each eagerly aiding the other. With a chorus of crickets in the background, they made love in their new home.

Morning brought mass confusion. With the dog barking to be fed and Nikki whining that she couldn't find her favorite jeans, Angela felt her patience was at an end. David was no help. He couldn't find the list he'd made of what was in each of the dozens of boxes left to be unpacked.

"All right, that's enough," Angela shouted. "I don't want to hear any more whining or barking."

For the moment, even Rusty quieted down.

"Calm down, dear," David said. "Getting upset isn't going to solve anything."

"And don't you tell me not to get upset," Angela cried.

"All right," David said calmly. "I'll go get the baby-sitter."

"I'm not a baby," Nikki whined.

"Oh, save me," Angela said with her face raised to the ceiling.

While David was off fetching Alice Doherty, Dorothy Weymouth's older sister, Angela was able to regain control of herself. She realized that it had been a mistake to tell their respective employers that they would be willing to start on July first. They should have given themselves a few days to get settled.

Alice turned out to be a godsend. She looked quite grandmotherly with her warm caring face, a twinkle in her eye, and snow-white hair. She had an engaging manner and surprising energy for a woman of seventy-nine. She also had the compassion and patience a chronically ill, willful child like Nikki required. Best of all, she loved Rusty, which immediately endeared her to Nikki.

The first thing Angela did was show her how to do Nikki's respiratory therapy. It was important for Alice to learn the procedure, and she proved to be a quick study.

"Don't you two worry about a thing," Alice called to David and Angela as they went out the back door. Nikki was holding Rusty, and she waved the dog's paw to say goodbye.

"I want to ride my bike," David announced once he and Angela got outside.

"Are you serious?" Angela asked.

"Absolutely," David said.

"Suit yourself," Angela said as she climbed into the Volvo and started the engine. She waved once to David as she descended the long drive and turned right toward town.

Although Angela was confident about her professional capabilities, she still felt nervous about starting her first real job.

Mustering her courage and reminding herself that first-day jitters were natural, she reported to Michael Caldwell's office. Caldwell immediately took her to meet Helen Beaton, the president of the hospital. Beaton happened to be in conference with Dr. Delbert Cantor, the chief of the professional staff, but she interrupted the meeting to welcome Angela. She invited Angela into her office and introduced her to Dr. Cantor as well.

While shaking her hand, Dr. Cantor unabashedly looked Angela up and down. She had chosen to wear one of her best silk dresses for her first day. "My, my," he said. "You certainly don't look like the few girls in my medical school class. They were all dogs." He laughed heartily.

Angela smiled. She felt like saying her class was just the opposite—the few men were all dogs—but she held her tongue. She found Dr. Cantor instantly offensive. He was clearly part of the old-school minority that still wasn't comfortable with women in the medical profession.

"We are so glad to have you join the Bartlet Community Hospital family," Beaton said as she escorted Angela to the door. "I'm confident you'll find the experience both challenging and rewarding."

Leaving the administration area, Caldwell took Angela to the clinical lab. As soon as Dr. Wadley saw her he leaped up from his desk and even gave her a hug as if they were old friends.

"Welcome to the team," Dr. Wadley said with a warm smile, his hands still gripping Angela's arms. "I've been anticipating this day for weeks."

"I'll be off," Caldwell said to Angela. "I can see you're in good hands here."

"Great job recruiting this talented pathologist," Wadley told Caldwell. "You're to be commended."

Caldwell beamed.

"A good man," Wadley said, watching him leave.

Angela nodded, but she was thinking about Wadley. Although she was again aware of how much the man reminded her of her father, now she was equally aware of their differences. Wadley's enthusiastic fervor was a welcome change from her father's aloof reserve. Angela was even charmed by Wadley's demonstrative welcome. It was reassuring to feel so wanted on her first day.

"First things first," Wadley said, rubbing his hands together. His green eyes shone with childlike excitement. "Let me show you your office."

He pushed open a connecting door from his own office into another that looked as though it had been recently decorated. The room was entirely white: the walls, the desk, everything.

"Like it?" Wadley asked.

"It's wonderful," Angela said.

Wadley pointed back toward the connecting door. "That will always be open," he said. "Literally and figuratively."

"Wonderful," Angela repeated.

"Now let's tour the lab again," Wadley said. "I know you saw it once, but I want to introduce you to the staff." He took a long, crisp, professional white coat from a hook and put it on.

For the next fifteen minutes Angela met more people than she could hope to remember. After circling the lab, they stopped at a windowless office next to the microbiology section. The office belonged to Dr. Paul Darnell, Angela's fellow pathologist.

In contrast to Wadley, Darnell was a short man whose clothing was rumpled and whose white coat was spotted haphazardly with stains used in preparing pathological slides. He seemed agreeable but plain and retiring, almost the antithesis of the affable and flamboyant Wadley.

After the tour was over, Wadley escorted Angela back to his office where he explained her duties and responsibilities. "I'm going to try to make you one of the best pathologists in the country," he said with a true mentor's enthusiasm.

David had enjoyed his three-and-a-half-mile bicycle ride immensely. The clean, crisp morning air had been delicious, and the bird life even more abundant than he'd imagined. He'd spotted several hummingbirds along the way. To top it off, he caught a fleeting glimpse of several deer across a dew-laden field just after crossing the Roaring River.

Arriving at the professional building, David discovered he was too early. Charles Kelley didn't show up until almost nine.

"My word, you are eager!" Kelley said when he spotted David perusing magazines in the CMV waiting area. "Come on in."

David followed Kelley into his office where Kelley had him fill out a few routine forms. "You're joining a crackerjack team," Kelley said while David worked. "You're going to love it here: great facilities, superbly trained colleagues. What else could you want?"

"I can't think of anything," David admitted.

When the paperwork was completed and after Kelley explained some of the ground rules, he accompanied David to his new office. As Kelley opened the office suite door and entered, David stopped to admire his nameplate that had already been installed in the slot on the outside of the door. He was surprised to see the name "Dr. Kevin Yansen" above his.

"Is this the same suite?" David asked in a lowered voice after catching up with Kelley. There were six patients in the waiting room.

"Same one," Kelley said. He knocked on the mirror, and after it had slid open, he introduced David to the receptionist he would be sharing with Dr. Yansen.

"Glad to meet you," Anne Withington said in a heavy South Boston accent. She cracked her gum, and David winced.

"Come in to see your private office," Kelley said. Over his shoulder he told Anne to send Dr. Yansen in to meet Dr. Wilson when he appeared between patients.

David was confused. He followed Kelley into what had been Dr. Portland's office. The walls had been repainted a light gray, and new gray-green carpet had been installed.

"What do you think?" Kelley asked, beaming.

"I think it's fine," David said. "Where did Dr. Portland go?"

Before Kelley could respond, Dr. Yansen appeared at the doorway and whisked into the room with his hand outstretched. Ignoring Kelley, he introduced himself to David, telling David to call him Kevin. He then slapped David on the back. "Welcome! Good to have you join the squad," he said. "You play basketball or tennis?"

"A little of both," David said, "but none recently."

"We'll have to get you back in the swing," Kevin said.

"Are you an orthopedist?" David asked as he looked at his new suitemate. He was a squarely built man with an aggressive-looking face. A mildly hooked nose supported thick glasses. He was four inches shorter than David, and standing next to Kelley, he appeared diminutive.

"Orthopedist?" Kevin laughed scornfully. "Hardly! I'm at the opposite end of the operative spectrum. I'm an ophthalmologist."

"Where's Dr. Portland?" David asked again.

Kevin looked at Kelley. "You haven't told him yet?"

"Haven't had a chance," Kelley said, spreading his hands, palms up. "He just got here."

"I'm afraid Dr. Portland is no longer with us," Kevin said.

"He's left the group?" David asked.

"In a manner of speaking," Kevin said with a wry smile.

"I'm afraid Dr. Portland committed suicide back in May," Kelley said.

"Right here in this room," Kevin said. "Sitting there at that desk." He pointed at the desk. Then Kevin formed his hand into a pistol with his index finger serving as the barrel, and pointed it at his forehead. "Bam!" he said. "Shot himself right through the forehead out the back. That's why the walls had to be painted and the carpet changed."

David's mouth went bone-dry. He gazed at the blank wall behind the desk and tried not to imagine what it had looked like after the incident. "How awful," David said. "Was he married?"

"Unfortunately," Dr. Yansen said with a nod. "Wife and two young boys. A real tragedy. I knew something was wrong. All of a sudden he stopped playing basketball on Saturday mornings."

"He didn't look good the last time I saw him," David said. "Was he ill? He'd looked as if he'd lost a lot of weight."

"Depressed," Kelley said.

David sighed. "Boy, you never know!"

"Let's move on to a happier subject," Kelley said after he'd cleared his throat. "I took you at your word, Dr. Wilson. We've scheduled patients for you this morning. Are you up to it?"

"Absolutely," David said.

Kevin wished David well and headed back to one of the examining rooms. Kelley introduced David to Susan Beardslee, the nurse he'd be working with. Susan was an attractive woman in her mid-twenties, with dark hair cut short to frame her face. What David immediately liked about her was her lively, enthusiastic personality.

"Your first patient is already in the examining room," Susan said cheerfully. She handed him the chart. "When you need me, just buzz. I'll be getting the next patient ready." She disappeared into the second examining room.

"I think this is where I leave," Kelley said. "Good luck, David. If there are any questions or problems, just holler."

David flipped open the cover of the chart and read the name: Marjorie Kleber, aged thirty-nine. The complaint was chest pain. He was about to knock on the examining room door when he read the diagnostic summary: breast cancer treated with surgery, chemotherapy, and radiation. The cancer had been diagnosed four years previously at age thirty-five. At the time of the discovery, the cancer had spread to the lymph nodes.

David quickly scanned the rest of the chart. He was mildly unnerved and needed a moment to prepare himself. A patient with breast cancer that had metastasized, or spread from the breast to other areas of the body, was a serious case with which to begin his medical career. Happily Marjorie had been doing well.

David knocked on the door and entered. Marjorie Kleber was sitting patiently on the examining table dressed in an examining gown. She looked up at David with large, sad, intelligent eyes. Her smile was the kind of smile that warmed his heart.

David introduced himself and was about to ask about her current complaint when she reached out and took one of his hands in hers. She squeezed it and held it to her chest at the base of her neck.

"Thank you for coming to Bartlet," she said. "You'll never know how much I have prayed for someone like you to come here. I'm truly overjoyed."

"I'm happy to be here," David stammered.

"Prior to your coming, I've had to wait up to four weeks to be seen," she said as she finally released David's hand. "That's the way it's been since the school's health-care coverage was switched to CMV. And every time it's been a different doctor. Now I've been told that you will be my doctor. It's so reassuring."

"I'm honored to be your doctor," David said.

"Waiting four weeks to be seen was so scary," Marjorie continued. "Last winter I had the flu so bad that I thought it was pneumonia. Luckily, by the time I was seen I was over the worst of it."

"Maybe you should have gone to the emergency room," David suggested.

"I wish I could have," Marjorie said. "But we're not allowed. I did go once the winter before last, but CMV refused to pay because it turned out to be the flu. Unless my problem is life-threatening, I have to come here to the office. I can't go to the emergency room without prior approval from a CMV physician. If I do, they won't pay."

"But that's absurd," David said. "How can you know in advance if your problem is life-threatening?"

Marjorie shrugged. "That's the same question I asked, but they didn't have an answer. They just reiterated the rule. Anyway, I'm glad you're here. If I have a problem I'll call you."

"Please do," David said. "Now let's start talking about your health. Who is following you in regard to your cancer?"

"You are," Marjorie said.

"You don't have an oncologist?" David asked.

"CMV doesn't have an oncologist," Marjorie said. "I'm to see you routinely and Dr. Mieslich, the oncologist, when you think it is necessary. Dr. Mieslich is not a CMV physician. I can't see him unless you order it."

David nodded, recognizing that there were realities about his new practice that would take time to learn. He also knew he'd have to spend considerable time going over Marjorie's chart in detail.

For the next fifteen minutes, David applied himself to the process of "working up" Marjorie's chest pain. While listening to her chest and in between her deep breathing, he asked her what she did at the school.

"I'm a teacher," Marjorie said.

"What grade?" he asked. He took his stethoscope from his ears and began preparations to run an EKG.

"Third grade," she said proudly. "I taught second grade for a number of years, but I much prefer third. The children are really blossoming then."

"My daughter is to start the third grade in the fall," David said.

"How wonderful," Marjorie said. "Then she'll be in my class."

"Do you have a family?" David asked.

"My word, yes!" Marjorie said. "My husband, Lloyd, works at the computer software company. He's a programmer. We have two children: a boy in high school and a girl in the sixth grade."

Half an hour later David felt confident enough to reassure Marjorie that her chest pain was not at all serious and that it had nothing to do with either her heart or her cancer, Marjorie's two chief concerns. She thanked him profusely once again for coming to Bartlet before he stepped out of the room.

David ducked into his private office with a sense of exuberance. If all his patients were as warm and appreciative as Marjorie, he could count on a rewarding career in Bartlet. He put her chart on his desk for further study.

Taking the file from its holder on the second examining room door, David perused his next patient's chart. The diagnostic summary read: leukemia treated with massive chemotherapy. David inwardly groaned; it was another difficult case that would require more "homework." The patient's name was John Tarlow. He was a forty-eight-year-old man who'd been under treatment for three and a half years.

Stepping into the room, David introduced himself. John Tarlow was a handsome, friendly man whose face reflected intelligence and warmth equal to Marjorie's. Despite his complicated history, John's complaint of insomnia was both easier and quicker to deal with than Marjorie's chest pain. After a short conversation it was clear to David that the problem was an understandable psychological reaction to a death in the family. David gave him a prescription for some sleeping medication that he was certain would help John get back to his usual routine.

After he was through with John, David added his chart to Marjorie's for further review. Then he searched for Susan. He found her in the tiny lab used for simple, routine tests.

"Are there a lot of oncology patients in the practice?" David asked hesitantly.

David very much admired the sort of people who chose to go into oncology. He knew himself well enough to know that he was not suited for the specialty. So it was with some trepidation that he discovered his first two CMV patients were both dealing with cancer.

Susan assured him that there were only a few such patients. David wanted to believe her. When he went back to get the chart out of the box on examining room one, he felt reassured. It wasn't an oncological problem; the case concerned diabetes.

David's morning passed quickly and happily. The patients had been a delight. They'd all been affable, attentive to what David had to say, and, in contrast to the non-compliant patients he'd dealt with during his residency, eager to follow his recommendations. All of them had also expressed appreciation for David's arrival, not as fervently as Marjorie, but enough to make David feel good about his reception.

For lunch, David met Angela at the coffee shop run by the volunteers. Over sandwiches, they discussed their morning.

"Dr. Wadley is terrific," Angela said. "He's very helpful and interested in teaching. The more I see him, the less he reminds me of my father. He's far more demonstrative than my father ever would be—far more enthusiastic and affectionate. He even gave me a hug when I arrived this morning. My father would die before he'd do that."

David told Angela about the patients he'd seen. She was particularly touched to hear about Marjorie Kleber's reaction to David's arrival.

"She's a teacher," David added. "In fact she teaches the third grade so she'll be Nikki's teacher."

"What a coincidence," Angela said. "What's she like?"

"She seems warm, giving, and intelligent," David said. "I'd guess she's a marvelous teacher. The problem is she's had metastatic breast cancer."

"Oh, dear," Angela said.

"But she's been doing fine," David said. "I don't think she's had any recurrence yet, but I haven't gone over her chart in detail."

"It's a bad disease," Angela said, thinking how many times she'd worried about it herself.

"The only complaint I have so far about the practice is that I've seen too many oncology patients," David said.

"I know that's not your cup of tea," Angela said.

"The nurse says it was just a coincidence that I started with two in a row," David said. "I'll have to keep my fingers crossed."

"Now don't get depressed," Angela said. "I'm sure your nurse was right." Angela remembered all too well David's response to the deaths of several oncology patients when he'd been a junior resident.

"Talk about depression," David said. He leaned closer and whispered. "Did you hear about Dr. Portland?"

Angela shook her head.

"He committed suicide," David said. "He shot himself in the office that I'm now using."

"That's terrible," Angela said. "Do you have to stay there? Maybe you can move to a different suite."

"Don't be ridiculous," David said. "What am I going to say to Kelley? I'm superstitious about death and suicide? I can't do that. Besides, they repainted the walls and recarpeted the floor." David shrugged. "It'll be okay."

"Why did he do it?" Angela asked.

"Depression," David said.

"I knew it," Angela said. "I knew he was depressed. I even said it. Remember?"

"I didn't say he wasn't depressed," David said. "I said he looked ill. Anyway, he must have killed himself soon after we met him, because Charles Kelley said he'd done it in May."

"The poor man," Angela said. "Did he have a family?"

"A wife and two young boys."

Angela shook her head. Suicide among doctors was an issue of which she was well aware. One of her resident colleagues had killed herself.

"On a lighter note," David said, "Charles Kelley told me that there's a bonus plan to reward me for keeping hospitalization at a minimum. The less I hospitalize the more I get paid. I can even win a trip to the Bahamas. Can you believe it?"

"I've heard of that kind of incentive plan," Angela said. "It's a ploy health maintenance organizations use to reduce costs."

David shook his head in disbelief. "Some of the realities of this 'managed care' and 'managed competition' stuff are really mind-boggling. I personally find it insulting."

"Well, on a lighter note of my own, Dr. Wadley's invited us to his home for dinner tonight. I told him I'd have to ask you. What do you think?"

"Do you want to go?" David asked.

"I know we have a lot to do at home, but I think we should go. He's being so thoughtful and generous. I don't want to appear ungrateful."

"What about Nikki?" David asked.

"That's another piece of good news," Angela said. "I found out from one of the lab technicians that Barton Sherwood has a daughter in high school who does a lot of sitting. They are our closest neighbors. I called and she's eager to come over."

"Think Nikki will mind?" David asked.

"I already asked her," Angela said. "She said she didn't care and that she's looking forward to meeting Karen Sherwood. She's one of the cheerleaders."

"Then let's go," David said.

Just before seven Karen Sherwood arrived. David let her in. He wouldn't have guessed she was a cheerleader. She was a thin, quiet young woman who unfortunately looked a lot like her father. Yet she was pleasant and intuitive. When she was introduced to Nikki she was smart enough to say she loved dogs, especially puppies.

While David drove Angela finished putting on her makeup. David could tell she was tense, and he tried to reassure her that everything would be fine and that she looked terrific. When they pulled up to the Wadley home, both were impressed. The house wasn't as grand as theirs, but it was in far better condition and the grounds were immaculate.

"Welcome," Wadley said as he threw open his front door to greet the Wilsons.

The inside of the house was even more impressive than the outside. Every detail had been attended to. Antique furniture stood on thick oriental carpets. Pastoral nineteenth-century paintings adorned the walls.

Gertrude Wadley and her courtly husband were significantly different people, lending credence to the saying "opposites attract." She was a retiring, mousy woman who had little to say. It was as if she'd been submerged by her husband's personality.

Their teenage daughter, Cassandra, seemed more like her mother initially, but as the evening progressed, she became more like her outgoing father.

But it was Wadley who dominated the evening. He pontificated on a number of subjects. And he clearly doted on Angela. At one point he looked skyward and thanked the fates that he had been rewarded with such a competent team now that Angela had arrived.

"One thing is for sure," David said as they drove home, "Dr. Wadley is thrilled with you. Of course, I can't blame him."

Angela snuggled up to her husband.

Arriving home, David accompanied Karen across the fields to her home, even though she insisted she'd be fine. When David got back, Angela met him at the door in lingerie she hadn't worn since their honeymoon.

"It looks better now when I'm not pregnant," Angela said. "Don't you agree?"

"It looked great then and it looks great now."

Stealing into the semidark living room, they lowered themselves onto the couch. Slowly and tenderly they made love again. Without the frenzy of the previous evening, it was even more satisfying and fulfilling.

Once they were through, they held each other and listened to the symphony of chirping crickets and croaking frogs.

"We've made love more here in the last two days than in the previous two months in Boston," Angela said with a sigh.

"We've been under a lot of stress."

"It makes me wonder about another child," Angela said.

David moved so that he could make out Angela's profile in the darkness. "Really?" he asked.

"With a house this size, we could have a litter," Angela said with a little laugh.

"We'd want to know if the child had cystic fibrosis. I suppose we could always rely on amniocentesis."

"I suppose," Angela said without enthusiasm. "But what would we do if it were positive?"

"I don't know," David said. "It's scary. It's hard to know what the right thing to do is."

"Well, like Scarlett O'Hara said, let's think about it tomorrow."

SUMMER IN VERMONT

Days melted into weeks and weeks into months as summer advanced. The sweet white corn grew chest-high across the road from the Wilsons' house and could be heard rustling in the evening breeze from the front porch. Plump tomatoes ripened to a deep red in the garden by the terrace. Crab apples the size of golf balls began to drop from the tree next to the barn. Cicadas buzzed incessantly in the midmorning August heat.

David and Angela's work continued to be stimulating and rewarding as they settled into their jobs. Each day brought some new experience that they enthusiastically shared with each other as they lingered over quiet suppers.

Rusty's appetite remained undiminished and a source of wonder as he grew quickly and with great exuberance, catching up to the size of his feet. Yet despite his growth he maintained the same adorable quality he'd had as a tiny puppy. Everyone found it impossible to pass him without offering a pat on the head or a scratch behind a golden ear.

Nikki flourished in the new environment. Her respiratory status remained normal and her lungs stayed clear. She also made new friends. She was closest to Caroline Helmsford by far; Caroline was a petite child a year older than Nikki who also suffered from cystic fibrosis. Having had so many unique experiences in common, the girls formed a particularly strong bond.

They had met quite by accident. Although the Wilsons had been told about Caroline on their first visit to Bartlet, they'd made no attempt to contact her. The two girls had bumped into each other in the local grocery store which Caroline's parents owned and ran.

Nikki also befriended the Yansen boy, Arni, who happened to be exactly Nikki's age. Their birthdays were only a week apart. Arni was like his father: short, squarely built, and aggressive. He and Nikki hit it off and spent hours in and out of the barn, never at a loss for things to do.

As much as they loved their work, the Wilsons delighted in their weekends. Saturday mornings David rose with the sun to make hospital rounds, then played three-on-three basketball in the high school gym with a group of physicians.

Saturday and Sunday afternoons David and Angela devoted to work on the house. While Angela worked on the interior, busying herself with curtains and stripping old furniture, David tackled outdoor projects like fixing the porch or replacing the drainpipes. David proved even less handy than Angela had feared. He was forever running off to Staley's Hardware Store for more advice. Fortunately, Mr. Staley took pity on David and gave him many lectures on fixing broken screens, leaky faucets, and burned-out electrical switches.

On Saturday, the twenty-first of August, David got up early as usual, made himself coffee, and left for the hospital. Rounds went quickly since he only had to see one patient, John Tarlow, the leukemia victim. Like David's other oncology patients, John had to be hospitalized frequently for a variety of problems. This latest hospitalization resulted from an abscess on his neck. Fortunately, he was doing fine. David anticipated discharging him in the next few days.

After completing his rounds, David biked over to the high school for basketball. Entering the gym he discovered that there were more people than usual waiting to play. When David finally got into the game he noticed that the competition was fiercer than usual. The reason was that no one wanted to lose because the losers had to sit out.

David responded to the heightened competition by playing more vigorously himself. Coming down from a rebound, his elbow collided solidly with Kevin Yansen's nose.

David stopped mid-stride, turning in time to see Kevin cradling his nose in both hands. Blood was dripping between his fingers.

"Kevin," David called in alarm. "Are you all right?"

"Chrissake," Kevin snarled through his cupped hands. "You ass!"

"I'm sorry," David said. He felt embarrassed at his own aggressiveness. "Let me see." David reached out and tried to ease Kevin's hands away from his face.

"Don't touch me," Kevin snapped.

"Come on, Mr. Aggressive," Trent Yarborough called from across the floor. Trent was a surgeon and one of the better ballplayers. He'd played at Yale. "Let's see the old schnozzola. Frankly, I'm glad to see you get a little of your own medicine."

"Screw you, Yarborough," Kevin said. He lowered his hands. His right nostril dripped blood. The bridge of his nose bent to the right.

Trent came over for a better look. "Looks like your beak's been broken."

"Shit!" Kevin said.

"Want me to straighten it?" Trent asked. "I won't charge much."

"Let's just hope your malpractice insurance is paid up," Kevin said. He tilted his head back and closed his eyes.

Trent grabbed Kevin's nose between his thumb and the knuckle of his index finger and snapped it back into position. The cracking sound that resulted made everyone—even the surgeon—wince.

Trent stepped back to admire his handiwork. "Looks better than the original," he said.

David asked if he could give Kevin a ride home, but Kevin told him he'd drive himself, still sounding angry.

A sub stepped into the game, taking Kevin's place. For a moment David stood and gazed at the door where Kevin had exited. Then he winced as someone slapped him on the back. David turned and looked into Trent's face.

"Don't let Kevin bother you," Trent said. "He's broken two other people's noses here that I know of. Kevin is not a particularly good sport, but otherwise he's okay."

Reluctantly, David resumed the game.

When David returned home, Nikki and Angela were ready for the day's outing. There were to be no projects that Saturday because they had been invited to a nearby lake for an overnight stay. An afternoon of swimming was to be followed by a cookout. The Yansens, the Yarboroughs, and the Youngs, the "three Y's" as they called themselves, had rented a lakeside cottage for the month. Steve Young was an obstetrician/gynecologist as well as one of the basketball regulars.

"Come on, Daddy," Nikki said impatiently. "We're already late."

David looked at the time. He'd played basketball longer than usual. Running upstairs, he jumped into the shower. A half hour later they were in the car and on their way.

The lake was an emerald green jewel nestled into a lushly wooded valley between two mountains. One of the mountains boasted a ski resort that David and Angela were told was one of the best in the area.

The cottage was charming. It was a rambling, multi-bedroomed structure built around a massive fieldstone fireplace. A spacious screened porch fronted the entire house and faced the lake. Extending out from the porch was a large deck. A flight of wooden steps connected the deck to a T-shaped dock that ran out fifty feet into the water.

Nikki immediately teamed up with Arni Yansen, and they ran off into the forest where Arni was eager to show her a treehouse. Angela went into the kitchen where Nancy Yansen, Claire Young, and Gayle Yarborough were happily involved in the food preparation. David joined the men who were nursing beers while casually watching a Red Sox game on a portable TV.

The afternoon passed languidly, interrupted only by the minor tragedies associated with eight active children who had the usual proclivities of tripping over rocks, skinning knees, and hurting each other's feelings. The Yansens had two children, the Youngs had one, and the Yarboroughs had three.

The only blip in the otherwise flawless day was Kevin's mood. He'd developed mildly black eyes from his broken nose. On more than one occasion he yelled at David for being clumsy and fouling him continuously. David finally took him aside, amazed that Kevin was making such an issue of the affair.

"I apologized," David said. "And I'll apologize again. I'm sorry. It was an accident. I certainly didn't mean it."

Kevin irritably eyed David, giving David the impression that Kevin was not going to forgive him. But then Kevin sighed. "All right," he said. "Let's have another beer."

After dinner the adults sat around the huge table while the children went out onto the dock to fish. The sky was still red in the west and the color reflected off the water. The tree frogs and crickets and other insects had long since started their incessant nightly chorus. Fireflies dotted the deep shadows under the trees.

At first the conversation dealt with the beauty of the surroundings and the inherent benefits of living in Vermont where most people only got to visit for short vacations. But then the conversation turned to medicine, to the chagrin of the other three wives.

"I'd almost rather hear sports trivia," Gayle Yarborough complained. Nancy Yansen and Claire Young heartily agreed.

"It's hard not to talk about medicine with all this so-called 'reform' going on," Trent said. Neither Trent nor Steve were CMV physicians. Although they had been trying to form a preferred provider organization with a large insurance company and Blue Shield, they were not having much luck. They were a little late. Most of the patient base had been snapped up by CMV because of the plan's aggressive, competitive marketing.

"The whole business has got me depressed," Steve said. "If I could think of some way of supporting myself and my family, I'd leave medicine in the blink of an eye."

"That would be a terrible waste of your skill," Angela said.

"I suppose," Steve said. "But it would be a hell of a lot better than blowing my brains out like you-know-who."

The reference to Dr. Portland intimidated everyone for a few moments. It was Angela who broke the silence. "We've never heard the story about Dr. Portland," she said. "I've been curious, I have to admit. I've seen his poor wife. She's obviously having enormous trouble dealing with his death."

"She blames herself," Gayle Yarborough said.

"All we heard was that he was depressed," David said. "Was it about something specific?"

"The last time he played basketball he was all uptight about one of his hip fracture patients dying," Trent said. "It was Sam Flemming, the artist. Then I think he lost a couple of others."

David felt a shiver pass down his spine. The memory of his own reaction as a junior resident to the deaths of several of his patients passed through him like an unwelcome chill.

"I'm not even sure he killed himself," Kevin said suddenly, shocking everyone. Other than complaining about David's clumsiness, Kevin had said very little that day. Even his wife Nancy looked at him as if he'd blasphemed.

"I think you'd better explain yourself," Trent said.

"Not much to explain except Randy didn't have a gun," Kevin said. "It's one of those nagging details that no one has been able to explain. Where'd he get it? No one has stepped forward to say that he'd borrowed it from him. He didn't go out of town. What did he do, find it along the road?" Kevin laughed hollowly. "Think about it."

"Come on," Steve said. "He must have had it, just no one knew."

"Arlene said she didn't know anything about it," Kevin persisted. "Plus he was shot directly through the front of the head and angled downward. That's why it was his cerebellum that was splattered against the wall. I've personally never heard of anyone shooting himself like that. People usually put the barrel in their mouths if they want to be sure not to mess it up. Other people shoot themselves in the side of the head. It's hard to shoot yourself from the front, especially with a long-barreled Magnum." Kevin made a pistol with his hand as he'd done on David's first day of work. This time when he tried to point the gun straight into his forehead, he made the gesture look particularly awkward.

Gayle shivered through fleeting nausea. Even though she was married to a doctor, talk of blood and guts made her ill.

"Are you trying to suggest he was murdered?" Steve said.

"All I'm saying is I'm personally not sure he killed himself," Kevin repeated. "Beyond that, everybody can make his own assessment."

The sounds of crickets and tree frogs dominated the night as everyone pondered Kevin's disturbing comments. "Well, I think it's all poppycock," Gayle Yarborough said finally. "I think it was cowardly suicide, and my heart goes out to Arlene and her two boys."

"I agree," Claire Young said.

Another uncomfortable silence followed until Steve broke it: "What about you two?" he asked, looking across the table at Angela and David. "How are you finding Bartlet? Are you enjoying yourselves?"

David and Angela exchanged glances. David spoke first: "I'm enjoying it immensely," he said. "I love the town, and since I'm already part of CMV I don't have to worry about medical politics. I walked into a big practice, maybe a little too big. I've got more oncology patients than I'd anticipated and more than I'd like."

"What's oncology?" Nancy Yansen asked.

Kevin gave his wife an irritated look of disbelief. "Cancer," he said disdainfully. "Jesus, Nance, you know that."

"Sorry," Nancy said with equal irritation.

"How many oncology patients do you have?" Steve asked.

David closed his eyes and thought for a moment. "Let's see," he said. "I've got John Tarlow with leukemia. He's in the hospital right now. I've got Mary Ann Schiller with ovarian cancer. I've got Jonathan Eakins with prostatic cancer. I've got Donald Anderson, who they thought had pancreatic cancer but who ended up with a benign adenoma."

"I recognize that name," Trent said. "That patient had a Whipple procedure."

"Thanks for telling us," Gayle said sarcastically.

"That's only four patients," Steve said.

"There's more," David said. "I've also got Sandra Hascher with melanoma and Marjorie Kleber with breast cancer."

"I'm impressed you've committed them all to memory," Claire Young said.

"It's easy," David said. "I remember them because I've befriended them all. I see them on a regular basis because they have a lot of medical problems, which is hardly surprising considering the amount of treatment they've undergone."

"Well, what's the problem?" Claire asked.

"The problem is that now that I've befriended them and accepted responsibility for their care, I'm worried they'll die of their illness and I'll feel responsible."

"I know exactly what he means," Steve said. "I don't understand how anybody can go into oncology. God bless them. Half the reason I went into OB was because it's generally a happy specialty."

"Ditto for ophthalmology," Kevin said.

"I disagree," Angela said. "I can understand very well why people go into oncology. It has to be rewarding because people with potentially terminal illnesses have great needs. With a lot of other specialties you never truly know if you have helped your patients or not. There's never a question with oncology."

"I know Marjorie Kleber quite well," Gayle Yarborough said. "Both TJ and my middle, Chandler, had her as their teacher. She's a marvelous woman. She had this creative way to get the kids interested in spelling with tiny plastic airplanes moving across a wall chart."

"I enjoy seeing her every time she comes in for an appointment," David admitted.

"How's your job?" Nancy Yansen asked Angela.

"Couldn't be better," Angela said. "Dr. Wadley, the chief of the department, has become a true mentor. The equipment is state-of-the-art. We're busy but not buried. We're doing between five hundred and a thousand biopsies a month, which is respectable. We see interesting pathology because Bartlet Hospital is acting as a tertiary care center. We even have a viral lab which I didn't expect. So all in all it's quite challenging."

"Have you had any run-ins with Charles Kelley yet?" Kevin asked David.

"Not at all," David said with surprise. "We've gotten along fine. In fact just this week I met with Kelley and the CMV quality management director from Burlington. They were both complimentary about the responses patients had given on forms asking them to evaluate care and satisfaction."

"Ha!" Kevin laughed scornfully. "Quality management is a piece of cake. Wait until you have your utilization review. It usually takes two or three months. Let me know what you think of Charles Kelley then."

"I'm not concerned," David said. "I'm practicing good, careful medicine. I don't give a hoot about the bonus program concerning hospitalization and I'm certainly not in the running for one of the grand prize trips to the Bahamas."

"I wouldn't mind," Kevin said. "I think it's a good program. Why not think twice before hospitalizing someone? Patients around here follow your orders. People are better off home than in the hospital. If the hospital wants to send Nance and me to the Bahamas, I'm not going to complain."

"It's a bit different for ophthalmology than for internal medicine," David said.

"Enough of this medical talk," Gayle Yarborough said. "I was just thinking we should have brought the movie *The Big Chill*. It's a great movie to watch with a group like this."

"Now that would stimulate some discussion," Nancy Yansen said. "And it would be a lot more stimulating than this medical drivel."

"I don't need the movie to think about whether I would be willing to let my husband make love to one of my friends so she could have a baby," Claire Young said. "No way, period!"

"Oh, come on," Steve said, sitting up from his slouch. "I wouldn't mind, especially if it were Gayle." He reached over and gave Gayle a hug. Gayle was sitting next to him. She giggled and pretended to squirm in his arms.

Trent poured a bit of beer over the top of Steve's head. Steve tried to catch it with his tongue.

"It would have to be a desperate situation," Nancy Yansen said. "Besides, there's always the turkey baster."

For the next several minutes everyone except David and Angela doubled up with laughter. Then followed a series of off-color jokes and sexual innuendoes. David and Angela maintained half smiles and nodded at punch lines, but they didn't participate.

"Wait a minute, everybody," Nancy Yansen said amid laughter after a particularly salacious doctor's joke. She struggled to contain herself. "I think we should get the kids off to bed so we can have ourselves a skinny dip. What do you say?"

"I say let's do it," Trent said as he clicked beer bottles with Steve.

David and Angela eyed each other, wondering if the suggestion was another joke. Everyone else stood up and started calling for their children, who were still down on the dock fishing in the darkness.

Later in their room as Angela washed her face at the wall sink she complained to David that she thought the group had suddenly regressed to some early, adolescent stage. As she spoke they both could hear the rest of the adults leaping from the dock amid giggles, shouts, and splashing.

"It does smack of college fraternity behavior," David agreed. "But I don't think there's any harm. We shouldn't be judgmental."

"I'm not so sure," Angela said. "What worries me is feeling that we're in a John Updike novel about suburbia. All that loose sexual talk and now this acting out makes me uncomfortable. I think it could be a reflection of boredom. Maybe Bartlet isn't the Eden we think it is."

"Oh, please!" David said with amazement. "I think you're being overly critical and cynical. I think they just have an exuberant, fun-loving, youthful attitude toward life. Maybe we're the ones with hang-ups."

Angela turned from the sink to face David. Her expression was one of surprise, as if David were a stranger. "You're entirely welcome to go out there naked and join the bacchanalia if you so desire," she said. "Don't let me stop you!"

"Don't get all bent out of shape," David said. "I don't want to participate. But at the same time I don't see it in such black-and-white terms as you apparently do. Maybe it's some of your Catholic baggage."

"I refuse to be provoked," Angela said, turning back to the sink. "And I specifically refuse to be baited into one of our pointless religious discussions."

"Fine by me," David said agreeably.

Later when they had gotten into bed and turned out the light the sounds of merriment from the dock had been replaced by the frogs and insects. It was so quiet they could hear the water lapping against the shore.

"Do you think they're still out there?" Angela whispered.

"I haven't the faintest idea," David said. "Moreover I don't care."

"What did you think of Kevin's comments about Dr. Portland?" Angela asked.

"I don't know what to think," David said. "To be truthful, Kevin has become somewhat of a mystery to me. He's a weird duck. I've never seen anyone carry on so much about getting bumped in the nose in a pickup basketball game."

"I found his comments unsettling to say the least," Angela said. "Thinking about murder in Bartlet even for a second leaves me strangely cold. I'm beginning to have this uncomfortable nagging feeling that something bad is going to happen, maybe because we're too happy."

"It's that hysterical personality of yours," David said, half in jest. "You're always looking for the dramatic. It makes you pessimistic. I think we're happy because we made the right decision."

"I hope you are right," Angela said as she snuggled into the crook of David's arm.

MONDAY · SEPTEMBER 6

Traynor pulled his Mercedes off the road and bumped across the field toward the line of cars parked near a split-rail fence. During the summer months, the fairgrounds beyond the fence were used most often for crafts fairs, but today Traynor and his wife, Jacqueline, were headed there for the eighth annual Bartlet Community Hospital Labor Day picnic. Festivities had begun at nine starting with field day races for the children.

"What a way to ruin a perfectly good holiday," Traynor said to his wife. "I hate these picnics."

"Fiddlesticks!" Jacqueline snorted. "You don't fool me for a second." She was a petite woman, mildly overweight, who dressed inordinately conservatively. She was wearing a white hat, white gloves, and heels even though the outing was a cookout with corn, steamed clams, and Maine lobster.

"What are you talking about?" Traynor asked as he pulled to a stop and turned off the ignition.

"I know how much you love these hospital affairs, so don't play martyr with me. You love basking in the limelight. You play your part of Mr. Chairman of the Board to the hilt."

Traynor eyed his wife indignantly. Their marriage was filled with antagonism, and it was his routine to lash back, but he held his tongue. Jacqueline was right about the picnic, and it irritated him that over their twenty-one years of marriage, she'd come to know him so well.

"What's the story?" Jacqueline asked. "Are we going to the affair or not?"

Traynor grunted and got out of the car.

As they trudged back along the line of parked cars, Traynor saw Beaton, who waved and started to come to meet them. She was with Wayne Robertson, the chief of police, and Traynor immediately suspected something was wrong.

"How convenient," Jacqueline said, seeing Beaton approach. "Here comes one of your biggest sycophants."

"Shut up, Jacqueline!" Traynor snarled under his breath.

"I've got some bad news," Beaton said without preamble.

"Why don't you head over to the tent and get some refreshments," Traynor told Jacqueline. He gave her a nudge. After she tossed Beaton a disparaging look, she left.

"She seems less than happy to be here this morning," Beaton commented.

Traynor gave a short laugh of dismissal. "What's the bad news?"

"I'm afraid there was another assault on a nurse last night," Beaton said. "Or rather, this morning. The woman was raped."

"Damn it all!" Traynor snarled. "Was it the same guy?"

"We believe so," Robertson said. "Same description. Also the same ski mask. This time the weapon was a gun rather than a knife, but he still had the handcuffs. He also forced her into the trees, which is what he's done in the past."

"I'd hoped the lighting would have prevented it," Traynor said.

"It might have," Beaton said hesitantly.

"What do you mean?" Traynor demanded.

"The assault occurred in the upper lot, where there are no lights. As you remember, we illuminated only the lower lot to save money."

"Who knows about this rape?" Traynor asked.

"Not very many people," Beaton said. "I took it upon myself to contact George O'Donald at the Bartlet Sun, and he's agreed to keep it out of the paper. So we might get a break. I know the victim's not about to tell many people."

"I'd like to keep it away from CMV if it's at all possible," Traynor said.

"I think this underlines how much we need that new garage," Beaton said.

"We need it, but we might not get it," Traynor said. "That's my bad news for tonight's executive meeting. My old nemesis, Jeb Wiggins, has changed his mind. Worse still, he's convinced the Board of Selectmen that the new garage is a bad idea. He's got them all convinced it would be an eyesore."

"Is that the end of the project?" Beaton asked.

"It's not the end, but it's a blow," Traynor admitted. "I'll be able to get it on the ballot again, but once something like this gets turned down, it's hard to resurrect it. Maybe this rape, as bad as it is, could be the catalyst we need to get it to pass."

Traynor turned to Robertson. Traynor could see two bloated images of himself in Robertson's mirrored sunglasses. "Can't the police do anything?" he asked.

"Short of putting a deputy up there on a nightly basis," Robertson said, "there's not much we can do. I already have my men sweep the lots with their lights whenever they're in the area."

"Where's the hospital security man, Patrick Swegler?" Traynor asked.

"I'll get him," Robertson said. He jogged off toward the pond.

"Are you ready for tonight?" Traynor asked once Robertson was out of earshot.

"You mean for the meeting?" Beaton asked.

"The meeting and after the meeting," Traynor said with a lascivious smile.

"I'm not sure about after," Beaton said. "We need to talk."

"Talk about what?" Traynor asked. This was not what he wanted to hear.

"Now isn't a good time," Beaton said. She could already see Patrick Swegler and Wayne Robertson on their way over.

Traynor leaned against the fence. He felt a little weak. The one thing he counted on was Beaton's affection. He wondered if she were cheating on him, seeing someone like that ass Charles Kelley. Traynor sighed; there was always something wrong.

Patrick Swegler approached Traynor and looked him squarely in the eye. Traynor thought of him as a tough kid. He'd played football for Bartlet High School during the brief era that Bartlet dominated their interscholastic league.

"There wasn't much we could have done," Swegler said, refusing to be intimidated about the incident. "The nurse had done a double shift and she did not call security before she left as we'd repeatedly instructed nurses to do whenever they leave late. To make matters worse, she'd parked in the upper lot when she'd come to work for the day shift. As you know, the upper lot is not illuminated."

"Jesus H. Christ!" Traynor muttered. "I'm supposed to be supervising the running of a multimillion-dollar operation, and I've got to worry about the most mundane details. Why didn't she call security?"

"I wasn't told, sir," Swegler said.

"If we get the new garage, the problem will be over," Beaton said.

"Where's Werner Van Slyke of engineering?" Traynor said. "Get him over here."

"You of all people know Mr. Van Slyke doesn't attend any of the hospital's social functions," Beaton said.

"Dammit, you're right!" Traynor said. "But I want you to tell him for me that

I want that upper parking lot lit just like the lower. In fact, tell him to light it up like a ballfield."

Traynor then turned back to Robertson. "And why haven't you been able to find out who this goddamn rapist is, anyway? Considering the size of the town and the number of rapes all presumably by the same person, I'd think you'd have at least one suspect."

"We're working on it," Robertson said.

"Would you like to head over to the tent?" Beaton asked.

"Why not?" Traynor fumed. "At least I'd like to get a few clams out of this." Traynor took Beaton by the arm and headed for the food.

Traynor was about to get back to the subject of their proposed rendezvous when Caldwell and Cantor spotted them and approached. Caldwell was in a particularly cheerful mood.

"I guess you've already heard how well the bonus program is working," he said to Traynor. "The August figures are encouraging."

"No, I haven't heard," Traynor said, turning to Beaton.

"It's true," Beaton said. "I'll be presenting the stats tonight. The balance sheet is okay. August CMV admissions are down four percent over last August. That's not a lot, but it's in the right direction."

"It's warming to hear some good news once in a while," Traynor said. "But we can't relax. I was talking with Arnsworth on Friday, and he warned me that the red ink will reappear with a vengeance when the tourists leave. In July and August a good portion of the hospital census has been paying patients, not CMV subscribers. Now that it's past Labor Day, the tourists will be going home. So we cannot afford to relax."

"I think we should reactivate our strict utilization control," Beaton said. "It's our only hope of holding out until the current capitation contract runs out."

"Of course we have to recommence," Traynor said. "We don't have any choice. By the way, for everyone's information, we have officially changed the name from DUM to DUC. It's now 'drastic utilization control.'"

Everyone chuckled.

"I have to say I'm disappointed," Cantor said, still chuckling. "As the architect for the plan I was partial to DUM." Despite the long, sunny summer his facial pallor had changed very little. The skin on his surprisingly slender legs was paler still. He was wearing bermuda shorts and black socks.

"I have a policy question," Caldwell said. "Under DUC, what's the status of a chronic disease like cystic fibrosis?"

"Don't ask me," Traynor said. "I'm no doctor. What the hell is cystic fibrosis? I mean, I've heard the term but that's about all."

"It's a chronic inherited illness," Cantor explained. "It causes a lot of respiratory and GI problems."

"GI stands for gastro-intestinal," Caldwell explained. "The digestive system."

"Thank you," Traynor said sarcastically. "I know what GI means. What about the illness; is it lethal?"

"Usually," Cantor said. "But with intensive respiratory care, some of the patients can live productive lives into their fifties."

"What's the actuarial cost per year?" Traynor asked.

"Once the chronic respiratory problems set in it can run twenty thousand plus per year," Cantor said.

"Good Lord!" Traynor said. "With that kind of cost, it has to be included in utilization considerations. Is it a common affliction?"

"One in every two thousand births," Cantor said.

"Oh, hell!" Traynor said with a wave. "Then it's too rare to get excited over."

After promises to be prompt for the executive board meeting that night, Caldwell and Cantor went their separate ways. Caldwell headed over to a volleyball game in the process of forming on the tiny beach at the edge of the pond. Cantor made a beeline for the tub of iced beer.

"Let's get to the food," Traynor said.

Once again they set out toward the tent that covered the rows of charcoal grills. Everyone Traynor passed either nodded or called out a greeting. Traynor's wife was right: he did love this kind of public occasion. It made him feel like a king. He'd dressed casually but with decorum: tailored slacks, his elevator loafers without socks, and an open-necked short-sleeved shirt. He'd never wear shorts to such an occasion and was amazed that Cantor cared so little about his appearance.

His happiness was dampened by the approach of his wife. "Enjoying yourself, dear?" she asked sarcastically. "It certainly appears that way."

"What am I supposed to do?" he asked rhetorically. "Walk around with a scowl?"

"I don't see why not," Jacqueline said. "That's the way you are most of the time at home."

"Maybe I should leave," Beaton said, starting to step away.

Traynor grabbed her arm, holding her back. "No, I want to hear more about August statistics for tonight's meeting."

"In that case, I'll leave," Jacqueline said. "In fact, I think I'll head home, Harold, dear. I've had a bite and spoken to the two people I care about. I'm sure one of your many colleagues will be more than happy to give you a lift."

Traynor and Beaton watched Jacqueline totter away through the deep grass in her pumps.

"Suddenly I'm not hungry," Traynor said after Jacqueline had disappeared from sight. "Let's circulate some more."

They walked down by the lake and watched the volleyball game for a while. Then they strolled toward the softball diamond.

"What is it you want to talk about?" Traynor asked, marshaling his courage.

"Us, our relationship, me," Beaton said. "My job is fine. I'm enjoying it. It's stimulating. But when you recruited me, you implied that our relationship would go somewhere. You told me you were about to get a divorce. It hasn't happened.

I don't want to spend the rest of my life sneaking around. These trysts aren't enough. I need more."

Traynor felt a cold sweat break out on his forehead. With everything else going on at the hospital, he couldn't handle this. He didn't want to stop his affair with Helen, but there was no way he could face Jacqueline.

"You think about it," Beaton said. "But until something changes, our little rendezvous in my office will have to stop."

Traynor nodded. For the moment it was the best he could hope for. They reached the softball field and absently watched. A game was in the process of being organized.

"There's Dr. Wadley," Beaton said. She waved and Wadley waved back. Next to him was a young, attractive woman with dark brown hair, dressed in shorts. She was wearing a baseball cap turned jauntily to the side.

"Who is that woman with him?" Traynor asked, eager to change the subject.

"She's our newest pathologist," Beaton said. "Angela Wilson. Want to meet her?"

"I think that would be appropriate," Traynor said.

They walked over and Wadley did the honors. During his lengthy introduction, he extolled Traynor as the best chairman of the board the hospital had ever had and Angela as the newest and brightest pathologist.

"I'm delighted to meet you," Angela said.

A yell from the other players took Wadley and Angela away. The game was ready to start.

Beaton watched as Wadley shepherded Angela to her position at second base. He was playing shortstop.

"There's been quite a change in old Doc Wadley," Beaton commented. "Angela Wilson has evoked the suppressed teacher in the man. She's given him a new lease on life. He's been on cloud nine ever since she got here."

Traynor watched Angela Wilson field practice ground balls and lithely throw them to first base. He could well understand Wadley's interest, only unlike Beaton, he didn't attribute it purely to a mentor's enthusiasm. Angela Wilson didn't look like a doctor, at least not any doctor Traynor had ever met.

FALL IN VERMONT

Even though David and Angela had spent four years in Boston during their residencies, they hadn't truly experienced the full glory of a New England fall. In

Bartlet it was breathtaking. Each day the splendiferous color of the leaves became more intense, as if trying to surpass the previous day's efforts.

Besides the visual treats, fall brought more subtle pleasures associated with a sense of well-being. The air turned crisp and crystal clear and more pure to breathe. There was a feeling of invigoration in the atmosphere that made waking up in the morning a pleasure. Each day was filled with energy and excitment; each evening offered cozy contentment, with the sound of a crackling fire to keep the nighttime chill at bay.

Nikki loved her school. Marjorie Kleber became her teacher and, as David had surmised, she was superb. Although Nikki had always been a good student, she now became an excellent one. She looked forward to Mondays when a new schoolweek would commence. At night she was full of stories about all she had learned that day in class.

Nikki's friendship with Caroline Helmsford blossomed and the two became inseparable during after-school activities. Nikki's friendship with Arni also grew. After much discussion of the pros and cons Nikki won the right to ride her bike to school provided she stayed off main roads. It was an entirely new type of freedom for Nikki, and one that she loved. The route took her past the Yansen house, and every morning Arni waited for her. The last mile they rode together.

Nikki's health continued to be good. The cool, dry, clean air seemed therapeutic for her respiratory system. Except for her daily morning therapy in her beanbag chair, it was almost as if she were not afflicted by a chronic disease. The fact that she was doing so well was a source of great comfort to David and Angela.

One of the big events of the fall was the arrival of Angela's parents in the latter part of September. Angela had felt a great amount of ambivalence about whether to invite them. David's support had tipped the balance.

Dr. Walter Christopher, Angela's father, was reservedly complimentary about the house and the town but condescending about what he called "rural medicine." He stubbornly refused to visit Angela's lab with the excuse that he spent too much of his life inside hospitals.

Bernice Christopher, Angela's mother, found nothing to be complimentary about. She thought the house was too large and much too drafty, especially for Nikki. It was also her opinion that the color of the leaves was just as good in Central Park as in Bartlet, and that no one needed to drive six hours to look at trees.

The only truly uncomfortable episode occurred at the dinner table Saturday night. Bernice insisted on drinking more than her share of wine, and, as usual, became tipsy. She then accused David and his family of being the source of Nikki's illness.

"There's never been cystic fibrosis on our side," she said.

"Bernice!" Dr. Christopher said sharply. "Displays of ignorance are unbecoming."

Strained silence ensued until Angela managed to contain her anger. She then changed the subject to her and David's quest for furniture in the neighboring antique and used furniture shops.

Everyone was relieved when the time of the Christophers' departure arrived midday on Sunday. David, Angela, and Nikki dutifully stood alongside the house and waved until the Christophers' car disappeared down the road. "Kick me next time I talk about them coming up here," Angela said. David laughed and assured her it hadn't been that bad.

The magnificent fall weather continued well into October. Although there had been some cool days in late September, Indian summer arrived and brought days as warm as those of summer itself. An auspicious combination of temperature and moisture preserved the peak foliage long after what the Bartlet natives said was usual.

In mid-October during a break in Saturday morning basketball, Steve, Kevin, and Trent cornered David.

"How about you and your family coming with us this weekend?" Trent said. "We're all going over to Waterville Valley in New Hampshire. We'd love to have you guys come along."

"Tell him the real reason we want them to come," Kevin said.

"Shut up!" Trent said, playfully rapping Kevin on the top of his head.

"The real reason is that we've rented a condo with four bedrooms," Kevin persisted, ducking away from Trent. "These tightwads will do anything to reduce the cost."

"Bull," Steve said. "The more people the more fun."

"Why are you going to New Hampshire?" David asked.

"It'll be the last weekend for foliage for sure," Trent said. "It's different over in New Hampshire. More rugged scenery. Some people think the foliage is even more spectacular there."

"I can't imagine it could be any prettier than it is right here in Bartlet," David said.

"Waterville's fun," Kevin said. "Most people know it only for winterskiing. But it's got tennis, golf, hiking, even a basketball court. The kids love it."

"Come on, David," Steve said. "Winter will be here soon enough. You've got to get out and take advantage of fall as long as possible. Trust us."

"It sounds okay to me," David said. "I'll run it by Angela tonight, and I'll give one of you guys a call."

With that decided, the group joined the others to finish their basketball game.

That night Angela was not enthused when David mentioned the invitation. After the experience of the weekend at the lake combined with being busy around the house, David and Angela had not socialized much. Angela did not want to participate in another weekend of off-color jokes and sexual innuendo. Despite David's feelings to the contrary, Angela continued to wonder if their friends were bored, especially the women, and the idea of being together in such close quarters sounded a little too claustrophobic for her.

"Come on," David said. "It will be fun. We should see more of New England. As Steve said, winter will be here all too soon, and for the most part we'll be imprisoned indoors."

"It'll be expensive," Angela said, trying to think up reasons not to go.

"Come on, Mom," Nikki said. "Arni told me Waterville was neat."

"How can it be expensive?" David questioned. "We'll be splitting the condo four ways. Besides, consider our income."

"Consider our debt," Angela countered. "We've got two mortgages on the house, one of which is a balloon, and we've started paying off our student loans. And I don't know if the car will make it through a Vermont winter."

"You're being silly," David said. "I'm keeping close tabs on our finances, and we are doing perfectly well. It's not as if this is some extravagant cruise. With four families in a condo it will be no more expensive than a camping trip."

"Come on, Mom!" Nikki cried.

"All right," Angela said at last. "I can tell when I'm outnumbered."

As the week progressed excitement about the trip grew. David got one of the other CMV doctors, Dudley Markham, to cover his practice. Thursday night they packed to leave the following afternoon.

The initial plan was to leave at three P.M., but the difficulties of getting five doctors away from the hospital in the middle of the afternoon proved impossible to overcome. It wasn't until after six that they actually departed.

They took three vehicles. The Yarboroughs took their own van with their three children; the Yansens and Youngs doubled up in the Yansens' van; David, Angela, and Nikki took the Volvo. They could have squeezed in with the Yarboroughs, but Angela liked the independence of having their own vehicle.

The condo was enormous. Besides the four bedrooms, there was an upper loft where the kids could sleep in sleeping bags. After the trip everyone was tired. They headed straight for bed.

The next morning, Gayle Yarborough took it upon herself to wake everyone early. She marched through the house drumming a wooden spoon on the bottom of a saucepan, calling out that they were to leave for breakfast in half an hour.

Half an hour turned out to be an optimistic estimate of the time of departure. Although there were four bedrooms and a sleeping loft, there were only three and a half baths. Showers, hair drying, and shaving were a traffic control nightmare. On top of that, Nikki had to do her postural drainage. It was almost an hour and a half before the group was ready to go.

Climbing into the vehicles in the same order as the night before, they motored out of the valley with its circle of mountains and headed up Interstate 93.

Driving through Franconia Notch both David and Angela were taken by the riotous beauty of the fall foliage silhouetted against stark, sheer walls of gray granite.

"I'm starved," Nikki said after a half hour of driving.

"Me too," Angela said. "Where are we going?"

"A place called Polly's Pancake Parlor," David said. "Trent told me it's an institution up here in northern New Hampshire."

Arriving at the restaurant, they were informed there would be a forty-minute wait for a table. Fortunately, as soon as they finally started eating, everybody said the wait had been worth it. The pancakes, smothered in pure New Hampshire maple syrup, were delicious, as were the smoked bacon and sausage.

After breakfast they toured around New Hampshire looking at the leaves and the mountain scenery. There were arguments about whether the fall foliage was better in Vermont or New Hampshire. No one won. As Angela said, it was like comparing superlatives.

As they drove back toward Waterville Valley on a particularly scenic stretch of road called the Kancamagus Highway, David noticed that high cirrus clouds had drifted over the vast dome of the sky. By the time they got back to Waterville the clouds were thicker, effectively blocking out the sun and causing the temperature to plummet into the mid-fifties.

Once they were back at the condo, Kevin was eager for a game of tennis. No one was interested, but he managed to talk David into playing. After driving most of the day, David thought that some exercise would do him good.

Kevin was an accomplished player, and he usually beat David with relative ease. But on this particular occasion, he wasn't up to his usual game. To Kevin's chagrin, David began winning.

With his keen competitive nature, Kevin tried harder, but his intensity only caused him to make more mistakes. He began getting angry at himself, then at David. When David called a shot out, Kevin dropped his racket in a show of disbelief.

"That was not out," Kevin yelled.

"It was," David answered. David circled the mark in the clay with his racket. Kevin walked all the way around the net to look.

"That wasn't the mark," Kevin said angrily.

David looked at his officemate. He could see the man was angry. "Okay," David said, hoping to defuse the tension. "Why don't we play the point over?"

When they replayed the point David won again, and in an attempt to lighten the atmosphere, he called out: "Cheating shows."

"Screw you," Kevin called back. "Serve the ball!"

Any enjoyment that David derived from the game was destroyed by Kevin's poor attitude. Kevin got more and more angry, contesting almost all of David's calls. David suggested they stop. Kevin insisted they play to the bitter end. They did and David won.

Walking back to the condo Kevin refused to talk, and David gave up trying to make conversation. A few sprinkles urged them on. When they arrived Kevin went into one of the bathrooms and slammed the door. Everyone looked at David. David shrugged. "I won," he said and felt strangely guilty.

Despite a cheerful fire, plenty of good food, and lots of beer and wine, the evening was overshadowed by Kevin's gloom. Even his wife, Nancy, told him he was acting childish. The comment sparked a nasty exchange between husband and wife that left everyone feeling uncomfortable.

Eventually Kevin's despondency spread. Trent and Steve began to lament that their practices had fallen to a point where they had to think seriously of leaving Bartlet. CMV had already hired people in their specialties.

"A lot of my former patients have told me they'd like to come back to me," Steve said, "but they can't. Their employers have negotiated with CMV for health coverage. If these patients see me they have to pay out of their pockets. It's a bad scene."

"Maybe you're better off getting the hell out while you can," Kevin said, speaking up for the first time without having been specifically spoken to.

"Now that's a sufficiently cryptic comment to beg an explanation," Trent said. "Does Dr. Doom and Gloom have some privileged information that we mortals are unaware of?"

"You wouldn't believe me if I told you," Kevin said while staring into the fire. The glow of the embers reflected off the surface of his thick glasses, giving him an eerie, eyeless appearance.

"Try us," Steve encouraged.

David glanced at Angela to see how she was faring amid this depressing evening. As far as David was concerned he found the experience much more disturbing than the one at the lake in August. He could handle sexual innuendo and crude jokes, but he had a lot of trouble with hostility and despondency, especially when it was openly expressed.

"I've learned a little more about Randy Portland," Kevin said without taking his eyes away from the fire. "But you people wouldn't believe any of it. Not after the way you responded to my suggestion that maybe his death wasn't suicide."

"Come on, Kevin," Trent said. "Stop making such a damn production out of this. Tell us what you heard."

"I had lunch with Michael Caldwell," Kevin said. "He wants me to serve on one of his innumerable committees. He told me that the chairman of the hospital board, Harold Traynor, had had a weird conversation with Portland the day he died. And Traynor related what was said to Charles Kelley."

"Yansen, get to the point," Trent said.

"Portland said there was something wrong with the hospital."

Trent's mouth dropped open in mock horror. "Something is wrong with the hospital? I'm shocked, just shocked." Trent shook his head. "Good gravy, man, there's plenty wrong with the hospital. If that's the payoff to this story, I'm not exactly impressed."

"There was more," Kevin said. "Portland told Traynor that he wouldn't take the blame."

Trent looked at Steve. "Am I missing something here?"

"Was Portland referring to a patient when he was making these claims?" Steve asked.

"Obviously," Kevin said. "But that's too subtle for a surgeon like Trent to pick up. What's clear to me is that Portland thought that something weird was going on with one of his patients. I think he should have kept his mouth shut. If he had, he'd probably still be around today."

"Sounds like Portland was just getting paranoid," Trent said. "He was already depressed. I don't buy it. You're trying to make a conspiracy out of nothing. What did Portland's patient die of, anyway?"

"Pneumonia and endotoxin shock," Steve said. "That's how it was presented in death conference."

"There you go," Trent said. "There's not a lot of mystery about a death when there's a bunch of gram-negative bacteria running around in the corpse's bloodstream. Sorry, Kev, you haven't convinced me."

Kevin stood up suddenly. "Why do I bother?" he said, throwing up his hands. "You're all blind as bats. But you know something? I don't give a rat's ass."

Stepping over Gayle, who'd sprawled on the floor in front of the fire, Kevin stomped up the half flight of stairs to the bedroom he and Nancy were occupying. He slammed the door behind him hard enough to rattle the bric-a-brac on the wooden mantel.

Everyone stared into the fire. No one spoke. Rain could be heard hitting the skylight like so many grains of rice. Finally Nancy stood up and said she'd be turning in.

"Sorry about Kevin," Trent said. "I didn't mean to provoke him."

"It's not your fault," Nancy said. "He's been a bear lately. There's something he didn't tell you. He recently lost a patient himself—which isn't exactly a common occurrence for an ophthalmologist."

The next day they woke to gusty wind, a heavy mist, and a cold, driving rain. When Angela looked out the window, she cried out for David. Fearing some catastrophe, David leaped from the bed. With heavily lidded eyes he looked out. He saw the car. He saw the rain.

"What am I supposed to be seeing?" he asked sleepily.

"The trees," Angela said. "They're bare. There are no leaves. All the foliage has vanished in one night!"

"It must have been the wind," David said. "It rattled the storm windows all night." He dropped onto the bed and burrowed back under the comforter.

Angela stayed at the window, captivated by the skeletal remains of the trees. "They all look dead," she said. "I can't believe what a difference it makes. It's hard not to see it as an omen. It adds to that feeling I've had that something bad is going to happen."

"It's melancholia left over from last night's conversational requiem," David said. "Don't get morbidly dramatic on me. It's too early. Come on back to bed for a few minutes."

The next shock was the temperature. Even by nine in the morning it was still in the thirties. Winter was on its way.

The gloomy weather did not improve the general moodiness of the adults, who'd awakened with the same sullenness they'd taken to bed. The children were initially happy, although even they started to be affected by their parents' ill humor. David and Angela were relieved to get away. As they drove down the mountain David asked Angela to remind him never to play tennis with Kevin again.

"You men can be such children with your sports," Angela said.

"Hey!" David snapped. "I wasn't the problem. He was the problem. He's so competitive. I didn't even want to play."

"Don't get so riled up," Angela said.

"I resent you implying I was at fault," David said.

"I wasn't implying anything of the kind," Angela said. "I was merely making a comment about men and their sports."

"All right, I'm sorry," David said. "I suppose I'm a bit out of sorts. It drives me crazy to be around morose people. This wasn't the most fun weekend."

"It's a strange group of people," Angela said. "They seem normal on the surface, yet underneath I'm not so sure. But at least they didn't get into any sexual discussions or start acting out like at the lake. On the other hand they did manage to dredge up the Portland tragedy again. It's like an obsession with Kevin."

"Kevin's weird," David said. "That's what I've been trying to tell you. I hate to be reminded of Portland's suicide. It makes going into my office an ordeal. Whenever he brings it up, I can't help but picture what the wall must have looked like behind my desk, splattered with blood and brains."

"David," Angela said sharply. "Please! If you don't have any concern for my sensibilities, think about Nikki's."

David glanced into the rearview mirror at Nikki. She was staring ahead without moving.

"You all right, Nikki?" David asked.

"My throat hurts," Nikki said. "I don't feel good."

"Oh, no!" Angela said. She turned around and looked at her daughter. She reached out and put the back of her hand to Nikki's forehead.

"And you insisted on going on this stupid trip," Angela muttered.

David started to defend himself, but changed his mind. He didn't want to get into an argument. He already felt irritable enough.

MONDAY • OCTOBER 18

Nikki did not have a good night, nor did her parents. Angela was particularly distressed. By the wee hours of morning it was clear that Nikki was becoming progressively more congested. Well before dawn Angela tried the usual postural drainage combined with percussion. When they were through, she listened to Nikki's chest with her stethoscope. She heard rales and rhonchi, sounds that meant Nikki's breathing tubes were becoming clogged with mucus.

Before 8:00 A.M., David and Angela called their respective offices to explain that they would be late. Bundling Nikki in multiple layers of clothing, they took her to see Dr. Pilsner. Initially their reception was not encouraging. The receptionist informed them that Dr. Pilsner had a full schedule. Nikki would have to return the following day.

Angela was not to be denied. She told the receptionist that she was Dr. Wilson from pathology and that she wanted to talk with Dr. Pilsner. The receptionist disappeared into the interior of the office. Dr. Pilsner himself appeared a moment later and apologized.

"My girl thought you folks were just the usual CMV subscriber," Dr. Pilsner explained. "What's the problem?"

Angela told the doctor how a sore throat had led to congestion overnight and that the congestion did not respond to the usual postural drainage. Dr. Pilsner took Nikki into one of the examining rooms and listened to her chest.

"Definitely clogged up," he said, removing the stethoscope from his ears. Then, giving Nikki's cheek a playful pinch, he asked her how she felt.

"I don't feel good," Nikki said. Her breathing was labored.

"She's been doing so well," Angela said.

"We'll have her back to normal in a wink," Dr. Pilsner said, stroking his white beard. "But I think we'd better admit her. I want to start intravenous antibiotics and some intensive respiratory therapy."

"Whatever it takes," David said. He stroked Nikki's hair. He felt guilty for having insisted on the New Hampshire weekend.

Janice Sperling in admissions recognized both David and Angela. She commiserated with them about their daughter.

"We've got a nice room for you," she said to Nikki. "It has a beautiful view of the mountains."

Nikki nodded and allowed Janice to slip on a plastic identification bracelet. David checked it. The room was 204, one that indeed had a particularly pleasant view.

Thanks to Janice, the admitting procedure went smoothly. In only a few minutes they were on their way upstairs. Janice led them to room 204 and opened the door.

"Excuse me," Janice said with confusion. Room 204 was already occupied; there was a patient in the bed.

"Mrs. Kleber," Nikki said with surprise.

"Marjorie?" David questioned. "What on earth are you doing in here?"

"Just my luck," Marjorie said. "The one weekend you go away, I have trouble. But Dr. Markham was very kind."

"I'm so sorry to bother you," Janice said to Marjorie. "I can't understand why the computer gave me room 204 when it was already occupied."

"No trouble," Marjorie said. "I like the company."

David told Marjorie he'd be back shortly. The Wilsons followed Janice to the nurses' station where she phoned admitting.

"I want to apologize for the mix-up," Janice said after the call. "We'll put Nikki in room 212."

Within minutes of their arrival in room 212, a team of nurses and technicians appeared and attended to Nikki. Antibiotics were started, and the respiratory therapist was paged.

When everything was under control, David told Nikki he'd be back to check on her periodically throughout the day. He also told her to do everything the nurses and the technicians asked her to do. He gave Angela a peck on the cheek, Nikki one on the forehead, and was on his way.

David returned directly to Marjorie's room and gazed down at his patient. She'd become one of his favorites over the months. She appeared tiny in the large orthopedic bed. David thought that Nikki would have been dwarfed.

"Okay," David said, feigning anger, "what's the story here?"

"It started on Friday afternoon," Marjorie said. "Problems always start on Friday when you are reluctant to call the doctor. I didn't feel well at all. By Saturday morning my right leg started to hurt. When I called your office they switched me to Dr. Markham. He saw me right away. He said I had phlebitis and that I had to go into the hospital to get antibiotics."

David examined Marjorie and confirmed the diagnosis.

"You think it was necessary for me to come into the hospital?" Marjorie asked.

"Absolutely," David assured her. "We don't like to take chances with phlebitis. Inflammation of veins goes hand in hand with blood clots. But it's looking good. I'd guess it's already improved."

"There's no doubt it's improved," Marjorie said. "It feels twenty times better than it did when I came in on Saturday."

Although he was already late getting to the office, David spent another ten minutes talking with Marjorie about her phlebitis to be sure she understood the problem. When he was finished he went to the nurses' station and read her chart. All was in order.

Next he called Dudley Markham to thank him for covering for him over the weekend and for seeing Marjorie.

"No problem," Dudley said. "I enjoyed Marjorie. We got to reminisce. She had my oldest in the second grade."

Before leaving the nurses' station David asked the head nurse, Janet Colburn, why Marjorie was in an orthopedic bed.

"No reason," Janet said. "It just happened to be in there. At the moment, it's not needed elsewhere. She's better off in that one, believe me. The electronic controls to raise and lower the head and feet never break down, something I can't say about our regular beds."

David wrote a short note in Marjorie's chart to make it official that he was assuming responsibility for her care; then he checked in on Nikki. She was already doing much better, even though the respiratory therapist had yet to arrive. Her improvement was probably due to hydration from her IV.

Finally, David headed over to the professional building to start seeing his patients. He was almost an hour late.

Susan was upset when David arrived. She had tried to juggle the patients' appointments and cancel those that she could, but there were still a number waiting. David calmed her as he slipped into his office to put on his white coat. She followed him like a hound, ticking off phone messages and consult requests.

With his white jacket half on, David abruptly stopped moving. Susan halted in mid-sentence, seeing David's face go pale.

"What's the matter?" Susan asked with alarm.

David didn't move or speak. He was staring at the wall behind his desk. To his tired, sleep-deprived eyes, the wall was covered with blood.

"Dr. Wilson!" Susan called. "What is it?"

David blinked and the disturbing image disappeared. Stepping over to the wall, he ran his hand over its smooth surface to reassure himself it had been a fleeting visual hallucination.

David sighed, marveling at how suggestible he'd become. He turned from the wall and apologized to Susan. "I think maybe I watched too many horror pictures when I was a kid," he said. "My imagination is working overtime."

"I think we better start seeing patients," Susan said.

"I agree."

Launching into work with gusto, David made up for lost time. By mid-morning he was caught up. He took a brief time-out from seeing patients in order to return some of the phone calls. The first person he tried was Charles Kelley.

"I was wondering when you would call," Kelley said. His voice was unusually businesslike. "I have a visitor in my office. His name is Neal Harper. He's from CMV utilization in Burlington. I'm afraid there's something we have to go over with you."

"In the middle of my office hours?"

"This won't take long," Kelley said. "I'm afraid I must insist. Could you please come over?"

David slowly put the receiver down. Although he didn't know why, he felt immediately anxious, as if he were a teenager being asked to come to the principal's office.

After telling Susan where he was going, David left. As he arrived at the CMV offices, the receptionist told him to go right in.

Kelley got up from behind his desk, appearing tall and tan as usual. But his manner was different. He was serious, almost dour, a far cry from his usual ebullient self. He introduced Neal Harper, a thin, precise man with pale skin and a small amount of acne. To David he appeared the apotheosis of the bureaucrat who'd been forever locked in his office, filling out his forms.

They all sat down. Kelley picked up a pencil and played with it with both hands.

"The statistics are in for your first quarter," Kelley said in a somber tone. "And they are not good."

David looked back and forth between the two men, feeling increasingly anxious.

"Your productivity is not satisfactory," Kelley continued. "You are in the lowest percentile in the whole CMV organization according to the number of patient visits per hour. Obviously you are spending entirely too much time with each patient. To make matters worse, you are in the highest percentile in ordering laboratory tests per patient from the CMV lab. As far as ordering consults from outside the CMV community, you're completely off the graph."

"I didn't know these statistics were gathered," David said lamely.

"And that's not all," Kelley said. "Too many of your patients have been seen in the Bartlet Community Hospital emergency room rather than in your office."

"That's understandable," David said. "I'm fully booked out for two weeks plus. When someone calls with an obviously acute problem needing immediate attention, I send them to the ER."

"Wrong!" Kelley snapped. "You don't send patients to the ER. You see them in your office provided they're not about to croak."

"But such disruptions throw my schedule into a turmoil," David said. "If I take time out to deal with emergencies, I can't see my scheduled patients."

"Then so be it," Kelley said. "Or make the so-called emergency patients wait until you've seen the people with appointments. It's your call, but whatever you decide, don't use the ER."

"Then what's the ER for?" David asked.

"Don't try to be a wiseass with me, Dr. Wilson," Kelley said. "You know damn well what the ER is for. It's for life-and-death emergencies. And that reminds me. Don't suggest that your patients call an ambulance. CMV will not pay for an ambulance unless there is pre-approval and pre-approval is only granted in cases that are truly life-threatening."

"Some of my patients live alone," David said. "If they're ill—"

"Let's not make this more difficult than it need be," Kelley interrupted. "CMV doesn't operate a bus service. All this is pretty simple. Let me spell it out for you. You must seriously increase your productivity, you must lower your use of laboratory tests drastically, you must reduce, or better yet stop, using consults outside the CMV family, and you must keep your patients out of the ER. That's all there is to it. Understand?"

David stumbled out of the CMV office. He was flabbergasted. He'd never considered himself extravagant in the use of medical resources. He'd prided himself on always keeping the patient's needs to the fore. Kelley's tirade was unnerving to say the least.

Reaching his office suite, David limped inside. He caught sight of Kevin disappearing behind a closed door with a patient and remembered his prophecy about the utilization evaluation. Kevin had been right on target; it had been devastating. What also bothered David was that Kelley had not made a single reference to quality or patient approval.

"You'd better get hopping," Susan said the instant she saw him. "You're getting behind again."

Midmorning Angela ducked out of the lab and went to check on Nikki. She was pleased to find her doing as well as she was. The fact that she wasn't running a fever was particularly encouraging. There was also a definite subjective decrease in Nikki's congestion following a prolonged visit by the respiratory therapist. Angela used a nurse's stethoscope to listen to Nikki's chest. There were still sounds of excessive mucus, but not nearly as much as there had been that morning.

"When can I go home?" Nikki asked.

"You just got here," Angela said, giving Nikki's hair a tousle. "But if you continue to improve the way you've been going, I'm sure Dr. Pilsner won't want to keep you long."

Returning to the lab, Angela went to the microbiology section to check on Nikki's sputum swab; she wanted to make certain it had been plated. It was crucial to determine the mix of bacteria in Nikki's respiratory tract. The technician assured her it had been done.

Returning to her office, Angela hung up her white coat in preparation to read a series of hematology slides. Just before she sat down she noticed the connecting door between her office and Wadley's was ajar.

Angela went over to the door and peeked in. Wadley was sitting at a double-headed teaching microscope. He caught sight of her and waved for her to come over.

"This is something I want you to see," Wadley said.

Angela stepped over to the 'scope and sat opposite her mentor. Their knees almost touched beneath the table. She put her eyes to the eyepiece and peered in. Immediately she recognized the specimen as a sample of breast tissue.

"This is a tricky case," Wadley said. "The patient is only twenty-two years old. We have to make a diagnosis, and we have to be right. So take your time." To make his point, he reached under the table and grasped Angela's thigh just above the knee. "Don't be too impulsive about your impression. Look carefully at all the ducts."

Angela's trained eye began to scan the slide in an orderly fashion, but her concentration faltered. Wadley's hand had remained on her thigh. He continued talking, explaining what he thought were the key points for making the diagnosis. Angela had trouble listening. The weight of his hand made her feel acutely uncomfortable.

Wadley had touched her often in the past, and she had had occasion to touch him as well. But it had always been within acceptable social bounds, such as contact on an arm, or a pat on the back, or an exuberant hug. They had even done several "high fives" during the softball game at the Labor Day picnic. There had never been any implication of intimacy until now, when his hand remained rooted to her leg with his thumb on the inside of her thigh.

Angela wanted to move away or remove his hand, but she did neither. She kept hoping that Wadley would suddenly realize how uncomfortable she felt and withdraw. But it didn't happen. His hand stayed on her thigh throughout a long explanation about why the biopsy had to be considered positive for cancer.

Finally Angela got up. She knew she was trembling. She bit her tongue and turned back toward her office.

"I'll be ready to review those hematology slides as soon as you are through with them," Wadley called after her.

Closing the connecting door between the offices, Angela went over to her desk and sank into her chair. Near tears, she cradled her face in her hands as a flood of thoughts cascaded through her mind. Going over the course of events of the previous months, she recalled all the episodes when Wadley offered to stay late to go over slides, and all the times he appeared when she had a few free moments. If she ever went to the coffee shop he appeared and always took the seat next to her. And as far as touching was concerned, now that she thought about it, he never passed up an opportunity.

All at once the mentor-like effort and demonstrative affection Wadley had been expending had a different, less generous, more unpleasant connotation. Even the recent talk of attending a pathology meeting in Miami during the next month made her feel uneasy.

Lowering her hands Angela stared ahead. She wondered if she was overreacting. Maybe she was blowing this episode way out of proportion, getting herself all worked up. After all, David was forever accusing her of being overly dramatic. Maybe Wadley hadn't been aware. Maybe he'd been so engrossed in his didactic role, he didn't realize what he was doing.

She angrily shook her head. Deep down she knew she wasn't overreacting. She was still grateful for Wadley's time and effort, but she could not forget how it felt to have his hand on her thigh. It was so inappropriate. He had to have known. It had to have been deliberate. The question was what she could do to put an end to his unwanted familiarity. After all, he was her boss.

At the end of his office hours, David walked over to the central hospital building to check on Marjorie Kleber and a few other patients. Once he determined that all were doing well, he stopped by to see Nikki.

His daughter was feeling fine thanks to a judicious combination of antibiotics, mucolytic agents, bronchodilators, hydration, and physical therapy. She was leaning back against a pile of pillows with a TV remote in her hand. She was watching a game show, a pastime frowned upon at home.

"Well, well," David said. "If it isn't a true woman of leisure."

"Come on, Dad," Nikki said. "I haven't watched much TV. Mrs. Kleber came to my room, and I even had to do some schoolwork."

"That's terrible," David said with improvised dismay. "How's the breathing?"

After so many sojourns in the hospital, Nikki was truly experienced at assessing her condition. Pediatricians had learned to listen to her evaluations.

"Good," Nikki said. "It's still a little tight, but it's definitely better."

Angela appeared at the doorway. "Looks like I'm just in time for a family reunion," she said. She came in and gave both Nikki and David a hug. With Angela sitting on one side of the bed and David on the other, they talked with Nikki for half an hour.

"I want to go home," Nikki whined when David and Angela got up to go.

"I'm sure you do," Angela said. "And we want you home, but we have to follow Dr. Pilsner's orders. We'll talk to him in the morning."

After waving goodbye and watching her parents disappear down the hall, Nikki wiped a tear from the corner of her eye and reached for the TV remote. She was accustomed to being in the hospital, but she still didn't like it. The only good thing about it was that she could watch as much TV as she wanted and any type of programming—something she definitely couldn't get away with at home.

David and Angela didn't talk until they were outside under the awning covering the hospital's rear entrance. Even then the conversation was minimal. David merely said that it was silly for both of them to get wet and then ran to get the car.

On the way home there was no conversation. The only noise was the repetitive and lugubrious sound of the windshield wipers. David and Angela both thought the other was responding to a combination of Nikki's hospitalization, the disappointing weekend, and the incessant rain.

As if to confirm David's suspicions Angela broke the silence as they pulled into their driveway by telling David that a preliminary look at Nikki's sputum culture suggested pseudomonas aeruginosa. "That's not a good sign," Angela continued. "When that type of bacteria gets established in someone with cystic fibrosis it usually stays."

"You don't have to tell me," David said.

Dinner was a stifled affair without Nikki's presence. They ate at the kitchen table as the rain pelted the windows. Finally, after they'd finished eating, Angela found the emotional strength and the words to describe what had happened between herself and Wadley.

David's mouth had slowly opened as the story unfolded. By the time Angela was finished his mouth was gaping in astonishment. "That bastard!" David said. He slammed his palm down onto the table and angrily shook his head. "There were a couple of times it passed through my mind he was acting a bit too enamored, like the day at the hospital picnic. But then I convinced myself I was being ridiculously jealous. But it sounds like my intuition was right."

"I don't know for sure," Angela said. "Which is partly why I hesitated to tell you. I don't want us to jump to conclusions. It's confusing as much as it is aggravating. It's so unfair that we women have to deal with this kind of problem."

"It's an old problem," David said. "Sexual harassment has been around forever, especially since women joined the workforce. It's been part of medicine for a long time, especially back when all doctors were men and all nurses were women."

"And it's still around despite the rapid increase in the number of women physicians," Angela said. "You remember some of the bullcrap I had to put up with from some of the medical school instructors."

David nodded. "I'm sorry this has happened," he said. "I know how pleased you'd been with Dr. Wadley. If you'd like I'll get in the car, drive over to his house, and punch him in the nose."

Angela smiled. "Thanks for the support."

"I thought you were being quiet tonight because you were worried about Nikki," David said. "Either that or angry about the weekend."

"The weekend is history," Angela said. "And Nikki is doing fine."

"I had a bad day too," David finally admitted. He got himself a beer from the refrigerator, took a long drink, and then told Angela about his utilization review with Kelley and the CMV man from Burlington.

"That's outrageous!" Angela said when David was finished. "What nerve to talk to you like that. Especially with the kind of positive response you've been getting from your patients."

"Apparently that's not a high priority," David said despondently.

"Are you serious? Everyone knows that doctor-patient relationships are the cornerstone of good medical care."

"Maybe that's passé," David said. "The current reality is determined by people like Charles Kelley. He's part of a new army of medical bureaucrats being created by government intervention. All of a sudden economics and politics have reached the ascendancy in the medical arena. I'm afraid the major concern is the bottom line on the balance sheet, not patient care."

Angela shook her head.

"The problem is Washington," David said. "Every time the government gets seriously involved in medical care they seem to screw things up. They try to please everybody and end up pleasing no one. Look at Medicare and Medicaid; they're both a mess and both have had a disastrous effect on medicine in general."

"What are you going to do?" Angela asked.

"I don't know," David said. "I'll try to compromise somehow. I guess I'll just take it a day at a time and see what happens. What about you?"

"I don't know either," Angela said. "I keep hoping that I was wrong, that I'm overreacting."

"It's possible, I suppose," David said gently. "After all, this is the first time you've felt this way. And all along Wadley's been a touchy-feely kind of guy. Since you never said anything up to this point, maybe he doesn't think you mind being touched."

"What exactly are you implying?" Angela demanded sharply.

"Nothing really," David said quickly. "I was just responding to what you said."

"Are you saying I brought this on myself?"

David reached across the table and grasped Angela's arm. "Hold on!" he said. "Calm down! I'm on your side. I don't think for a second that you are to blame."

Angela's sudden anger abated. She realized that she was overreacting, reflecting her own uncertainties. There was the possibility that she had been unknowingly encouraging Wadley. After all, she'd wanted to please the man as any student might, especially since she felt a debt to him for all the time and effort he'd expended on her behalf.

"I'm sorry," Angela said. "I'm just stressed out."

"Me too," David said. "Let's go to bed."

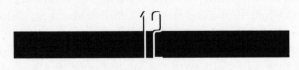

TUESDAY • OCTOBER 19

To David's and Angela's disappointment, it was still raining in the morning. In contrast to the gloomy weather, however, Nikki was in high spirits and doing marvelously. Even her color had returned. The sore throat, presaging an extended illness, had disappeared with the antibiotics, indicating that if it had been infectious, it had been bacterial rather than viral in origin. Thankfully there was still no fever.

"I want to go home," Nikki repeated.

"We haven't talked with Dr. Pilsner," David reminded her. "But we will, sometime this morning. Be patient."

After the visit with Nikki, Angela left for the lab while David went to the nurses' station to pick up Marjorie's chart. He'd been considering discharging her until he walked into her room. Her response to his greeting told him something was wrong.

"Marjorie, what's the matter?" David asked as he felt his own pulse quicken. She was lethargic. He touched the back of his hand to her forehead and her arms. Her skin was warm to the touch. He guessed she had a fever.

Marjorie responded to David's persistent questioning with barely intelligible mumbling. She acted drugged although not in any apparent pain.

Noticing Marjorie's breathing was mildly labored, David listened carefully to her chest. He heard faint sounds of congestion. Next he checked the area of phlebitis and found it was all but resolved. With mounting anxiety David examined the rest of his patient. Finding nothing he hurried back to the nurses' station and ordered a barrage of stat laboratory tests.

The first thing to come back from the lab was her blood count, but it only added to David's puzzlement. Her white cell level, which had been appropriately falling with the resolution of the phlebitis, had continued to fall and was now in the lower percentile of normal.

David scratched his head. The low white count seemed contradictory to her clinical state, which suggested developing pneumonia. Getting up from the desk, David went back to Marjorie's room and listened to her chest again. The incipient congestion was real.

Returning to the nurses' station, David debated what to do. More lab tests came back, but they were all normal, even the portable chest X ray, and hence no help. David thought about calling in some consults, but after his poor utilization review the day before, he was reluctant. The problem was that the consults who might have been helpful were not part of the CMV organization.

Instead of requesting any consults, David took the *Physicians' Desk Reference* off the bookshelf. Since his main concern was that a gram-negative bacteria might have appeared as a superinfection, he looked up an antibiotic that was specific for such an eventuality. When he found one he felt confident it would take care of the problem.

After the appropriate orders were written, including a request to be called immediately if there was any change in Marjorie's status, David headed over to his office.

It was Angela's turn to handle the day's surgical frozen sections. She always found the task nerve-racking since she knew that while she worked, the patient remained under anesthesia awaiting her verdict whether the biopsy was cancerous or benign.

The frozen sections were done in a small lab within the operating suite. The room was tucked off to the side and visited infrequently by the operating room staff. Angela worked with intense concentration, studying the patterns of cells in the specimen under the microscope.

She did not hear the door silently open behind her. She was unaware that anyone was in the room until he spoke.

"Well, honey, how's it going?"

Startled, Angela's head shot up as a bolus of adrenaline coursed through her body. With her pulse pounding in her temples, she found herself looking into Wadley's smiling face. She hated to be called "honey" by anyone, except maybe David. And she didn't appreciate being snuck up on.

"Any problems?" Wadley asked.

"No," Angela said sharply.

"Let me take a look," Wadley said, motioning toward the microscope. "What's the case?"

Angela gave Wadley her seat. Succinctly she gave the history. He glanced at the slide, then stood up.

For a moment they talked about the slide in pathological jargon. It was apparent they agreed the growth was benign, happy news for the anesthetized patient.

"I want to see you later in my office," Wadley said. He winked.

Angela nodded, ignoring the wink. She turned away and was about to sit down again when she felt Wadley's hand brush across her buttocks.

"Don't work too hard, honey!" he called out. And with that, he slipped out the door.

The episode had happened so fast that Angela had not been able to respond. But she knew it had not been inadvertent, and now she knew for certain that the thigh-touching the day before had not been an innocent oversight.

For a few minutes Angela sat in the tiny lab and trembled with indignation and confusion. She wondered what was encouraging this sudden boldness. She certainly had not changed her behavior over the last few days. And what should she do? She couldn't just idly sit by and allow it to go on. That would be an open invitation.

Angela decided she had two possibilities. She could confront Wadley directly or she could go to the medical director, Michael Caldwell. But then she thought about Dr. Cantor, the current chief of staff. Maybe she should go to him.

Angela sighed. Neither Caldwell nor Cantor struck her as ideal authorities to turn to in a case of sexual harassment. Both were macho types, and Angela remembered their responses when she'd first met them. Caldwell had seemed shocked that women were actually pathologists while Cantor had offered that ignorant remark about the few women in his medical school class being "dogs."

She thought again about confronting Wadley herself, but she didn't like that alternative any better.

The raucous buzz of static coming over the intercom shocked Angela back to reality. The static preceded the voice of the head nurse. "Dr. Wilson," she said. "They are waiting on the biopsy results down in OR three."

David found concentrating on his patients' problems harder that morning than the previous afternoon. Not only was he still upset about his review with Kelley, now he had Marjorie Kleber's worsening condition to worry about.

Midmorning, David saw another of his frequent visitors, John Tarlow, the leukemia patient. John didn't have an appointment; David had Susan squeeze him in as a semi-emergency after he'd called that morning. Only the day before David would have directed John to the ER, but feeling chastened by Kelley's lecture, he felt obliged to see the man himself.

John was feeling poorly. Following a meal of raw shellfish the night before, he'd developed severe GI problems with both vomiting and diarrhea. He was dehydrated and in acute discomfort with colicky abdominal pain.

Seeing how bad John was and remembering his leukemic history, David hospitalized him immediately. He ordered a number of tests to try to determine the cause of John's symptoms. He also started intravenous fluid to rehydrate him. For the moment he held off on antibiotics, preferring to wait until he had some idea of what he was dealing with. It could have been a bacterial infection or it could have been merely a response to toxins: food poisoning, in the vernacular.

Just before eleven in the morning Traynor was told the bad news by his secretary, Collette. She'd just been informed by phone that Jeb Wiggins had again carried the Board of Selectmen. The final vote on the hospital parking garage, which Traynor had managed once more to get on the agenda, had been thumbs down. Now there probably wasn't even a way to get it on the ballot again before spring.

"Goddamn it," Traynor raged. He pummeled the surface of his desk with both hands. Collette didn't flinch. She was accustomed to Traynor's outbursts. "I'd love to grab Wiggins around that fat neck of his and choke him until he turns blue."

Collette discreetly left the room. Traynor paced the area in front of his desk. The lack of support he had to deal with when it came to running the hospital galled him. He could not understand how the Board of Selectmen could be so shortsighted. It was obvious that the hospital was the most important enterprise in the entire town. It was equally obvious that the hospital needed the parking garage.

Unable to work, Traynor grabbed his raincoat, hat, and umbrella and stormed out of his office. Climbing into his car he drove up to the hospital. If there was to be no parking garage, he would at least personally inspect the lighting. He didn't want to risk any more rapes in the hospital parking lot.

Traynor found Werner Van Slyke in his windowless cubbyhole that served as the engineering/maintenance department's office. Traynor had never been particularly comfortable around Van Slyke. Van Slyke was too quiet, too much of a loner, and mildly unkempt. Traynor also found Van Slyke physically intimidating; he was several inches taller than Traynor and significantly huskier, with the kind of bulky muscles that suggested weight lifting was a hobby.

"I want to see the lights in the parking lots," Traynor said.

"Now?" Van Slyke asked, without the usual rise in the pitch of his voice that normal people use when asking questions. Every word he said was flat and it grated on Traynor's ears.

"I had a little free time," Traynor explained. "I want to make sure it's adequate."

Van Slyke pulled on a yellow slicker and walked out of the office. Outside the hospital he pointed to each of the lights in the lower lot, walking from one to the next without comment.

Traynor tagged along beneath his umbrella, nodding at each fixture. As he followed Van Slyke through the copse of evergreen trees and climbed the wooden steps that separated the two lots, Traynor wondered what Van Slyke did when he wasn't working. He realized he never saw Van Slyke walking around the town or shopping in the shops. And the man was notorious for not attending hospital functions.

Uncomfortable with the continued silence, Traynor cleared his throat: "Everything okay at home?" he asked.

"Fine," Van Slyke said.

"House okay, no problems?"

"Nope," Van Slyke said.

Traynor started feeling challenged to get Van Slyke to respond with more than monosyllables. "Do you like civilian life better than the navy?"

Van Slyke shrugged and began pointing out the lights in the upper lot. Traynor continued to nod at each one. There seemed to be plenty. Traynor made a mental note to swing up there with his car some evening to see how light it was after dark.

"Looks good," Traynor said.

They started back toward the hospital.

"You being careful with your money?" Traynor asked.

"Yeah," Van Slyke said.

"I think you are doing a great job here at the hospital," Traynor said. "I'm proud of you."

Van Slyke didn't respond. Traynor looked over at Van Slyke's wet profile with its heavy five o'clock shadow. He wondered how Van Slyke could be so unemotional, but then again he realized that he'd never understood the boy ever since he'd been little. Sometimes Traynor found it hard to believe they were related, yet they were. Van Slyke was Traynor's only nephew, the son of his deceased sister.

When they reached the stand of trees separating the two lots, Traynor stopped. He looked among the branches. "How come there are no lights on this path?"

"No one said anything about lights on the path," Van Slyke said. It was the first full sentence he had uttered. Traynor was almost pleased.

"I think one or two would be nice," Traynor said.

Van Slyke barely nodded.

"Thanks for the tour," Traynor said in parting. He was relieved to make his escape. He had always felt guilty for feeling so estranged from his own kin, but Van Slyke was such an enigma. Traynor had to admit that his sister hadn't exactly been a paragon of normality. Her name had been Sunny, but her disposition had been anything but. She'd always been quiet, retiring, and had suffered from depression for most of her life.

Traynor still had a hard time understanding why Sunny had married Dr. Werner Van Slyke, knowing the man was a drunk. Her suicide was the final blow. If she'd only come to him, he would have tried to help.

In any case, given Werner Van Slyke's parentage, it was hardly a surprise that he was as strange as he was. Yet with his naval machinist's training he'd been both helpful and reliable. Traynor was glad he'd suggested that the hospital hire him.

Traynor roused himself from this reflection and headed for Beaton's office.

"I've got some bad news," Traynor said as soon as Beaton's secretary admitted him. He told her about the Board of Selectmen's vote on the parking garage.

"I hope we don't have any more assaults," Beaton said. She was clearly disappointed.

"Me too," Traynor said. "Hopefully the lights will be a deterrent. I just walked around the parking lots and took a look at them. They seem adequate enough, except on the path between the two lots. I asked Van Slyke to add a couple there."

"I'm sorry I didn't do both lots from the start," Beaton said.

"How are the finances looking for this month?" Traynor questioned.

"I was afraid you'd ask," Beaton said. "Arnsworth gave me the mid-month figures just yesterday and they are not good. October will definitely be worse than September if the second half of the month is anything like the first. The bonus program is helping, but admissions for CMV are still over the projected level. To make matters worse, we seem to be getting sicker patients."

"I suppose that means we have to put more pressure on utilization," Traynor said. "DUC has to save the day. Other than the bonus program, we're on our own. I don't anticipate any more insurance bequests in the near future."

"There are a few other nuisances of which you should be aware," Beaton said. "M.D. 91 has relapsed. Robertson picked him up on a DUI. He was driving his car on the sidewalk."

"Pull his privileges," Traynor said without hesitation. "Alcoholic physicians have already caused enough heartache in my life." He recalled once again his sister's good-for-nothing husband.

"The other problem," Beaton said, "is that Sophie Stephangelos, the head nurse in the OR, has discovered significant theft of surgical instruments over the last year. She thinks one of the surgeons is taking them."

"What next?" Traynor said with a sigh. "Sometimes I think running a hospital is an impossible task."

"She has a plan to catch the culprit," Beaton said. "She wants an okay to go ahead with it."

"By all means," Traynor said. "And if she catches him let's make an example out of him."

Coming out of one of his examining rooms, David was surprised to find that the basket on the other room's door was empty.

"No charts?" he asked.

"You're ahead of yourself," Susan explained. "Take a break."

David took advantage of the opportunity to dash over to the hospital. The first stop was Nikki's room. When he walked in he was surprised to find both Caroline and Arni sitting on Nikki's bed. Somehow the two kids had managed to get into the hospital without being challenged. They were supposed to be accompanied by an adult.

"You won't get us into trouble, will you, Dr. Wilson?" Caroline asked. She looked much younger than nine. Her illness had stunted her growth much more than it had Nikki's. She looked more like a child of seven or eight.

"No, I won't get you in trouble," David assured them. "But how did you get out of school so early?"

"It was easy for me," Arni said proudly. "The substitute teacher doesn't know what's going on. She's a mess."

David turned his attention to his daughter. "I spoke with Dr. Pilsner, and he said it's okay for you to go home this afternoon."

"Cool," Nikki said excitedly. "Can I go to school tomorrow?"

"I don't know about that," David said. "We'll have to discuss it with your mother."

After leaving Nikki's room, David looked in on John Tarlow to make sure that he was settled, his IV was started, and the tests David had ordered were in progress. John said he didn't feel any better. David told him to be patient and assured him there'd be improvement after he'd been hydrated.

Finally David stopped in to see Marjorie. He hoped that the added antibiotic would have already improved her condition, but it hadn't. In fact, David was shocked to see how much she had deteriorated; she was practically comatose.

Panic-stricken, David listened to Marjorie's chest. There was more congestion than earlier but still not enough to explain her clinical state. Rushing back to the nurses' station, David demanded to know why he hadn't been called.

"Called on what?" Janet Colburn asked. She was the head nurse.

"Marjorie Kleber," David yelled while he wrote orders for more stat blood-work and another portable chest X ray.

Janet consulted with several of the other floor nurses, then told David that no one had noticed any change. She even said that one of the LPNs had just been in Marjorie's room less than half an hour previously and had reported no change.

"That's impossible," David snapped as he grabbed the phone and started making calls. Earlier, he'd been reluctant to call in consults. Now he was panicked to get them to come in as soon as possible. He called Marjorie's oncologist, Dr. Clark Mieslich, and an infectious disease specialist, Dr. Martin Hasselbaum. Neither of them were CMV doctors. David also called a neurologist named Alan Prichard, who was part of the CMV organization.

All three specialists were available for David's call. When they heard David's frantic appeal and his description of the case, they all agreed to come in immediately. David then called Susan to alert her to what was happening. He told her to advise the patients who came into the office that he would be delayed.

The oncologist was the first to arrive, followed in short order by the infectious disease specialist and the neurologist. They reviewed the chart and discussed the situation with David, before descending en masse on Marjorie. After examining her closely they withdrew to the nurses' station to confer. But hardly had they begun to discuss Marjorie's condition when disaster struck.

"She's stopped breathing," a nurse yelled from Marjorie's room. She'd stayed behind to clean up the debris left by the examining specialists.

While David and the consults raced back, Janet Colburn called the resuscitation team. They arrived in minutes and converged on room 204.

With so much manpower immediately available, Marjorie was quickly intubated and respired. It had been done with such dispatch that her heart rate did not change. Everyone was confident she'd experienced only a short period of decreased oxygen. The problem was they did not know why she'd stopped breathing.

As they began to discuss possible causes, her heart suddenly slowed and then stopped. The monitor displayed an eerie flat line. The resuscitation team shocked her in hopes of restarting her heart, but there was no response. They quickly shocked her again. When that didn't work, they began closed chest cardiac massage.

They worked frenetically for thirty minutes, trying every trick they could think of, but nothing worked. The heart would not even respond to external pacing. Gradually, discouragement set in, and finally, by general consensus, Marjorie Kleber was declared dead.

While the resuscitation team unhooked their wires and the nurses cleaned up, David walked back to the nurses' station with the consults. He was devastated. He could not imagine a worse scenario. Marjorie had come into the hospital with a relatively minor problem while he was off enjoying himself. Now she was dead.

"It's too bad," Dr. Mieslich said. "She was such a terrific person."

"I'd say she did pretty well considering the history in the chart," Dr. Prichard said. "But her disease was bound to catch up with her."

"Wait a second," David said. "Do you think she died of her cancer?"

"Obviously," Dr. Mieslich said. "She had disseminated cancer when I first saw her. Although she'd done better than I would have predicted, she was one sick lady."

"But there wasn't any clinical evidence of her tumor," David said. "Her problems leading up to this fatal episode seemed to suggest some sort of immune system malfunction. How can you relate that to her cancer?"

"The immune system doesn't control breathing or the heart," Dr. Prichard said.

"But her white count was falling," David said.

"Her tumor wasn't apparent, that's true," Dr. Mieslich said. "But if we were to open her up, my guess is that we would find cancer all over, including in her brain. Remember, she had extensive metastases when she was originally diagnosed."

David nodded. The others did the same. Dr. Prichard slapped David on the back. "Can't win them all," he said.

David thanked the consults for coming in. They all politely thanked him for the referral, then went their separate ways. David sat at the nurses' station desk. He felt weak and disconsolate. His sadness and sense of guilt at Marjorie's passing was even more acute than he'd feared. He'd come to know her too well. To make it even worse, she was Nikki's beloved teacher. How would he explain this to her?

"Excuse me," Janet Colburn said softly. "Lloyd Kleber, Marjorie's husband, is here. He'd like to talk to you."

David stood up. He felt numb. He didn't know how long he'd been sitting at the nurses' station. Janet directed him into the patients' lounge.

Lloyd Kleber was staring out the window at the rain. David guessed he was in his mid-forties. His eyes were red from crying. David's heart went out to the man. Not only had he lost a wife, but now he had the responsibility of two motherless children.

"I'm sorry," David said lamely.

"Thank you," Lloyd said, choking back tears. "And thank you for taking care of Marjorie. She really appreciated your concern for her."

David nodded. He tried to say things that reflected his compassion. He never felt adequate at moments like this, but he did the best he could.

Finally, David ventured to ask for permission to do an autopsy. He knew it was a lot to ask, but he was deeply troubled by Marjorie's swift deterioration. He wanted desperately to understand.

"If it could help others in some small way," Mr. Kleber said, "I'm sure Marjorie would want it done."

David stayed and talked with Lloyd Kleber until more members of the immediate family arrived. Then David, leaving them to their grief, walked over to the lab. He found Angela at the desk in her office. She was pleased to see him and told him so. Then she noticed his strained expression.

"What's wrong?" she asked anxiously. She stood up and took his hand.

David told her. He had to stop a few times to compose himself.

"I'm so sorry," Angela said. She put her arms around him and gave him a re-assuring hug.

"Some doctor!" he chided himself, fighting tears. "You'd think I'd have ad-justed better to this kind of thing by now."

"Your sensitivity is part of your charm," Angela assured him. "It's also what makes you a good doctor."

"Mr. Kleber agreed to an autopsy," David said. "I'm glad because I haven't the slightest idea why she died, especially so quickly. Her breathing stopped and then her heart. The consults all think it was her cancer. It probably was. But I'd like Bartlet to confirm it. Could you see that it gets done?"

"Sure," Angela said. "But please don't get too depressed over this. It wasn't your fault."

"Let's see what the autopsy shows," David said. "And what am I going to tell Nikki?"

"That's going to be hard," Angela admitted.

David returned to his office to try to see his patients in as short order as pos-sible. For their sake, he hated being so backed up, but there had been no way to avoid it. He'd only managed to see four when Susan waylaid him between ex-amining rooms.

"Sorry to bother you," she said, "but Charles Kelley is in your private office, and he demands to see you immediately."

Fearing Kelley's visit had something to do with Marjorie's death, David stepped across the hall into his office. Kelley was impatiently pacing. He stopped when David arrived. David closed the door behind himself.

Kelley's face was hard and angry. "I find your behavior particularly galling," he said, towering over David.

"What are you talking about?" David asked.

"Just yesterday I spoke with you about utilization," Kelley said. "I thought it was pretty clear and that you understood. Then today you irresponsibly ordered two non-CMV consults to see a hopelessly terminal patient. That kind of be-havior suggests that you have no comprehension of the major problem facing medicine today: unnecessary and wasteful expense."

With his emotions raw, David struggled to keep himself under control. "Just a minute. I'd like you to tell me how you know the consults were unnecessary."

"Oh, brother!" Kelley said with a supercilious wave of his head. "It's obvious. The patient's course wasn't altered. She was dying and she proceeded to die. Everyone must die at some time or another. Money and other resources should not be thrown away for the sake of hopeless heroics."

David stared into Kelley's blue eyes. He didn't know what to say. He was dumbfounded.

Hoping to avoid Wadley, Angela sought out Dr. Paul Darnell in his windowless cubicle on the other side of the lab. His desk was piled high with bacterial culture dishes. Microbiology was his particular area of interest.

"Can I speak to you for a moment," Angela called from Paul's doorway.

He waved her in and leaned back in his swivel chair.

"What's the autopsy protocol around here?" she asked. "I haven't seen any done since I got here."

"That's an issue you'll have to discuss with Wadley," Paul said. "It's a policy problem. Sorry."

Reluctantly, Angela went to Wadley's office.

"What can I do for you, honey?" Wadley said. He smiled a kind of smile Angela had previously seen as paternal but now saw as lewd.

Wincing at being addressed as "honey," Angela swallowed her pride and asked about the procedure for arranging an autopsy.

"We don't do autopsies," Wadley said. "If it's a medical examiner case, the body goes to Burlington. It costs too much to do autopsies, and the contract with CMV doesn't include them."

"What if the family requests it?" Angela asked, knowing this wasn't precisely true in the Kleber case.

"If they want to shell out eighteen hundred and ninety dollars, then we'll accommodate them," Wadley said. "Otherwise, we don't do it."

Angela nodded, then left. Instead of getting back to her own work, she walked over to the professional building and went into David's office. She was appalled by the number of patients waiting to be seen. Every chair in the waiting room was occupied; a few people were even standing in the hall. She caught David as he shuttled between examining rooms. He was clearly frazzled.

"I can't do an autopsy on Marjorie Kleber."

"Why not?" David asked.

Angela told him what Wadley had said.

David shook his head with frustration and blew out between pursed lips. "My opinion of this place is going downhill fast," he said. He then told Angela about Kelley's opinion of his handling of the Kleber case.

"That's ridiculous," Angela said. She was incensed. "You mean he suggested that the consults were unnecessary because the patient died. That's crazy."

"What can I tell you?" David said with a shake of his head.

Angela didn't know what to say. Kelley was beginning to sound dangerously uninformed. Angela would have liked to talk more, but she knew David didn't have the time. She motioned over her shoulder. "You've got an office full of patients out there," she said. "When do you think you'll be done?"

"I haven't the slightest idea."

"How about I take Nikki home and you give me a call when you're ready to leave. I'll come back and pick you up."

"Sounds good," David said.

"Hang in there, dear," Angela said. "We'll talk later."

Angela went back to the lab, finishing up for the day, collected Nikki, and drove home. Nikki was ecstatic to get out of the hospital. She and Rusty had an exuberant reunion.

David called at seven-fifteen. With Nikki comfortably ensconced in front of the TV, Angela returned to the hospital. She drove slowly. It was raining so hard the wipers had to struggle to keep the windshield clear.

"What a night," David said as he jumped into the car.

"What a day," Angela said as she started down the hill toward town. "Especially for you. How are you holding up?"

"I'm managing," David said. "It was a help to be so busy. I was grateful for the diversion. But now I have to face reality; what am I going to tell Nikki?"

"You'll just have to tell her the truth," Angela said.

"That's easier said than done," David said. "What if she asks me why she died? The trouble is I don't know, neither physiologically nor metaphysically."

"I've thought more about what Kelley said," Angela said. "It seems to me he has a fundamental misunderstanding about the basics of patient care."

"That's an understatement," David said with a short, sarcastic laugh. "The scary part is that he's in a supervisory position. Bureaucrats like Kelley are intruding into the practice of medicine under the guise of health-care reform. Unfortunately the public has no idea."

"I had another minor run-in with Wadley today," Angela said.

"That bastard!" David said. "What did he do now?"

"He called me 'honey' a few times," Angela said. "And he brushed his hand across my backside."

"God! What an insensitive jerk," David said.

"I really have to do something. I just wish I knew what."

"I think you should talk to Cantor," David said. "I've given it some thought. At least Cantor is a physician, not just a health-care bureaucrat."

"His comment about 'the girls,' as he called them, in his medical school class was not inspiring," Angela said.

They pulled into their driveway. Angela came to a stop as close as possible to the door to the mudroom. They both prepared to run for shelter.

"When is this rain going to stop?" David complained. "It's been raining for three days straight."

Once they were inside, David decided to make a fire to cheer up the house while Angela reheated the food she'd made earlier for herself and Nikki. Descending into the basement, David noticed that moisture was seeping through the grout between the granite foundation blocks. Along with the moisture was the damp, musty odor he'd occasionally smelled before. As he collected the wood, he comforted himself with the thought of the earthen floor. If a significant amount of water were to come into the basement, it would just soak in and eventually disappear.

After eating, David joined Nikki in front of the TV. Whenever she was ill they were lenient about how much time she was allowed to watch. David feigned interest in the show in progress, while he built up the courage to tell Nikki about Marjorie. Finally, during a commercial break, David put his arm around his daughter.

"I have to tell you something," he said gently.

"What?" Nikki asked. She was contentedly petting Rusty, who was curled up on the couch next to her.

"Your teacher, Marjorie Kleber, died today," David said gently.

Nikki didn't say anything for a few moments. She looked down at Rusty, pretending to be concerned about a knot behind his ear.

"It makes me very sad," David continued, "especially since I was her doctor. I'm sure it upsets you, too."

"No, it doesn't," Nikki said quickly with a shake of her head. She brushed a strand of hair away from her eyes. Then she looked at the television as if she were interested in the commercial.

"It's okay to be sad," David said. He started to talk about missing people you cared about when Nikki suddenly threw herself at him, enveloping him in a flood of tears. She hugged him tighter than he could ever remember her having hugged him.

David patted her on the back and continued to reassure her.

Angela appeared at the doorway. Seeing David holding their sobbing child, she came over. Gently pushing Rusty aside, she sat down and put her arms around both David and Nikki. Together the three held on to each other, rocking gently as the rain beat against the windows.

WEDNESDAY • OCTOBER 20

Despite Nikki's sustained protests, David and Angela insisted that she stay home from school another day. Considering the weather and the fact that she was still on antibiotics there was no reason to take a chance.

Although Nikki was not as cooperative as usual, they carried out her morning respiratory therapy with great diligence. Both David and Angela listened to her chest afterward and both were satisfied.

Alice Doherty arrived exactly at the time she promised. David and Angela were thankful to have someone so reliable and so conveniently available.

As Angela and David climbed into their blue Volvo, David complained that he'd not been able to ride his bike all week. It wasn't raining as hard as it had been, but the clouds were low and ponderous, and a heavy mist rose out of the saturated earth.

They got to the hospital at seven-thirty. While Angela headed off for the lab,

David went up to the patient floor. When he entered John Tarlow's room he was surprised to find drop cloths, stepladders, and an empty bed. Continuing on to the nurses' station he inquired after his patient.

"Mr. Tarlow has been moved to 206," Janet Colburn said.

"How come?" David asked.

"They wanted to paint the room," Janet said. "Maintenance came up and informed us. We let admitting know, and they told us to transfer the patient to 206."

"I think that's inconsiderate," David complained.

"Well, don't blame us," Janet said. "Talk to maintenance."

Feeling irritated for his patient's sake, David took Janet's suggestion and marched down to maintenance. He knocked on the jamb of the maintenance/engineering office. Inside and bent over a desk was a man close to David's age. He was dressed in rumpled, medium-green cotton twill work shirt and pants. His face was textured with a two-day growth of whiskers.

"What?" Van Slyke asked as he looked up from his scheduling book. His voice was flat and his expression was emotionless.

"One of my patients was moved from his room," David said. "I want to know why."

"If you are talking about room 216, it's being painted," Van Slyke said in a monotone.

"It's obvious it's being painted," David said. "What isn't obvious is why it's being painted."

"We have a schedule," Van Slyke said.

"Schedule or no schedule," David said, "I hardly think patients should be inconvenienced, especially patients who are ill, and patients in the hospital are invariably ill."

"Talk to Beaton if you have a problem," Van Slyke said. He went back to his book.

Taken aback by Van Slyke's insolence, David stood stunned in the doorway for a moment. Van Slyke ignored him with ease. David shook his head, then turned to go. On his way back to the patient floor, he was seriously considering taking Van Slyke's advice to discuss the situation with the hospital administrator until he walked into John Tarlow's new room. Suddenly David was presented with a more pressing problem: John Tarlow's condition was worse.

John's diarrhea and vomiting, which initially had been controlled, had returned with a vengeance. On top of that, John was obtunded, and when aroused, apathetic. David could not understand these symptoms since John had been on IVs since his admission and was clearly not dehydrated.

David examined his patient carefully but couldn't find an explanation for the marked change in his clinical state, particularly his depressed mental status. The only thing David could think of was the possibility John could have been overly sensitive to the sleeping medication that David had prescribed as a PRN order, meaning it was to be given if the patient requested it.

Hurrying back to the nurses' station, David pulled John's chart from the rack. He desperately pored over the data that had returned overnight from the lab in an attempt to understand what was going on and to try to decide what to do next. As a result of the run-in with Kelley the day before he was reluctant to request any consults since neither of the two he wanted—oncology and infectious disease—were CMV doctors.

David closed his eyes and rubbed his temples. He did not feel he was making much progress. Unfortunately, a key piece of information was lacking: the results of the stool cultures plated the day before were not yet available. Consequently David still didn't know if he was dealing with a bacteria or not, and if he was, what kind of bacteria it was. On the positive side was the fact that John was still afebrile.

Redirecting his attention to the chart, David ascertained that John had been given the PRN sleeping medication. Thinking that it might have contributed to John's lethargy, David canceled it. He also ordered another stool culture and another blood count. As a final request, he asked for John's temperature to be taken every hour along with the express order for David to be called if it rose above normal.

After completing the last scheduled biopsy, Angela tidied up the small pathology lab in the OR suite and headed for her office. Her morning had been productive and pleasant; she'd managed to avoid Wadley entirely. Unfortunately, she knew she'd eventually have to see him, and she worried about his behavior. Although she considered herself an optimistic person, she was fearful that the problem with Wadley would not spontaneously resolve.

Entering the office, Angela immediately noticed the connecting door from her office into Wadley's was ajar. As silently as possible she moved over to the door and began to close it.

"Angela!" Wadley called out, making Angela flinch. She hadn't realized how tense she was. "Come in here. I want to show you something fascinating."

Angela sighed and reluctantly opened the door. Wadley was sitting at his desk in front of his regular microscope, not the teaching microscope.

"Come on," Wadley called again. He waved Angela over and tapped the top of his microscope. "Take a gander at this slide."

Warily Angela advanced into the room. Several feet away she hesitated. As if sensing her reluctance, Wadley gave himself a little push, and his chair rolled back from the desk. Angela stepped up to the microscope and leaned over to adjust the eyepieces.

Before she could look in Wadley lunged forward and grabbed her around the waist. He pulled her onto his lap and locked his arms around her.

"Gotcha!" Wadley cried.

Angela shrieked and struggled to get away. The unexpected forcefulness of the contact shocked her. She'd been concerned about him touching her subtly, not manhandling her.

"Let me go!" Angela demanded angrily, trying to unlock his fingers and break his grip.

"Not until you let me tell you something," Wadley said. He was chuckling.

Angela stopped struggling. She had her eyes closed. She was as humiliated as she was furious.

"That's better," Wadley said. "I've got good news. The trip is all set. I even got the tickets already. We're going to the pathology meeting in Miami in November."

Angela opened her eyes. "Wonderful," she said with as much sarcasm as she could muster. "Now let me go!"

Wadley released her and Angela sprang from his lap. But as she pulled away he managed to grab her wrist. "It's going to be fantastic," Wadley said. "The weather will be perfect. It's the best time of year in Miami. We'll be staying on the beach. I got us rooms in the Fontainbleau."

"Let go!" Angela demanded through clenched teeth.

"Hey," Wadley said. He leaned forward and looked at her closely. "Are you mad or something? I'm sorry if I scared you. I just wanted it to be a surprise." He let go of her hand.

Angela was beside herself with anger. Biting her tongue to keep herself from exploding, she dashed into her office. Mortified and demeaned, she slammed the connecting door.

Forcibly she rubbed her face with both hands, trying to regain a modicum of control. She was shaking from the adrenaline coursing through her body. It took her a few minutes to settle down and for her breathing to return to normal. Once it had, she grabbed her coat and angrily stalked out of her office. At least Wadley's oafishly inappropriate advances had finally spurred her to action.

Avoiding the misty rain as much as possible, she dashed from the main hospital building to the Imaging Center. Once under the projecting eaves she slowed to a fast walk. Inside she went directly to Cantor's office.

Not having called beforehand, Angela had to wait almost a half hour before Dr. Delbert Cantor could see her. While she waited she calmed down considerably and even began once more to question if she were partly to blame for Wadley's behavior. She wondered if she should have anticipated it and not have been so naive.

"Come in, come in," Cantor said agreeably when he could finally see her. He'd gotten up from his disordered desk to escort Angela into the room. He had to move a stack of unopened radiology journals from a chair for her to sit down. He offered her some refreshment. She politely refused. He sat down, crossed his legs and arms, and asked what he could possibly do for her.

Now that she was face-to-face with the chief of the professional staff, Angela was not encouraged. All her misgivings about the man and his attitude toward women came back in a rush. His face had assumed a smirk as if he had already decided that whatever was on her female mind was of little consequence.

"This is not easy for me," Angela began. "So please bear with me. It was hard for me to come here, but I don't know what else to do."

Cantor encouraged her to continue.

"I'm here because I'm being sexually harassed by Dr. Wadley."

Cantor uncrossed his legs and leaned forward. Angela was encouraged that at least he was interested, but then she noticed that the smirk had remained.

"How long has this been going on?" Cantor asked.

"Probably the whole time I've been here," Angela said, intending to elaborate, but Cantor interrupted her.

"Probably?" he questioned with raised eyebrows. "You mean you're not sure?"

"It wasn't apparent initially," Angela explained. "At first I just thought he was acting like a particularly enthusiastic mentor, almost parental." She then went on to describe what had happened from the beginning; how it started as a problem of boundaries. "He always took advantage of opportunities to be close to me and touch me seemingly innocently," Angela explained. "He also insisted on confiding in me about personal family issues that I felt were inappropriate."

"This behavior you are describing can all be within the framework of friendship and the role of the mentor," Cantor said.

"I agree," Angela said. "That's why I allowed it to go on. The problem is that it has progressed."

"You mean it has changed?" Cantor asked.

"Most definitely," Angela said. "Quite recently." She then described the hand-on-the-thigh incident, feeling strangely embarrassed as she did so. She mentioned the hand brushing her backside and Wadley's sudden use of the appellation "honey."

"I personally don't see anything wrong with the word 'honey,' " Cantor said. "I use it all the time with my girls here in the Imaging Center."

Angela could only stare at the man while she wondered how the women in the Center felt about his behavior. Clearly she was in the wrong place. She couldn't begin to expect a fair hearing from a doctor whose views on women were probably more archaic than Wadley's. Nonetheless, she figured she should finish what she started, so she described the most recent incident: Wadley's pulling her onto his lap to announce their trip to Miami.

"I don't know what to say about all this," Cantor said once she finished. "Has Dr. Wadley ever implied that your job depends on sexual favors?"

Inwardly Angela groaned, fearing that Cantor's comprehension of sexual harassment was limited to the most overt circumstances. "No," she said. "Dr. Wadley has never intimated anything like that. But I find his unwanted familiarity extremely upsetting. It goes way beyond the bounds of friendship or a professional relationship, or even mutual respect. It makes working very difficult."

"Maybe you're overreacting. Wadley is just an expressive guy. You yourself said he's enthusiastic." When Cantor saw the look on Angela's face he added, "Well, it's a possibility."

Angela stood up. She forced herself to thank him for his time.

"Not at all," Cantor said as he pushed himself upright. "Keep me informed, young lady. Meanwhile, I promise I'll talk with Dr. Wadley as soon as I have an opportunity."

Angela nodded at this final offer and walked out. As she returned to her office, she couldn't help but feel that turning to Cantor wasn't going to help matters any. If anything, it was only going to make the situation worse.

Throughout the afternoon David had dashed over to check on John Tarlow every chance he had. Unfortunately, John hadn't improved. At the same time he hadn't deteriorated since David had made sure his IVs had kept up with his fluid loss from his vomiting and diarrhea. As David entered his room late in the afternoon for his final visit of the day, he hoped he would at least find John's mental status improved. But it wasn't. John was as listless as he'd been that morning, perhaps even a degree more so. When pressed, John could still say his name, and he knew he was in the hospital, but as to the month or the year, he had no clue.

Back at the nurses' station David went over the laboratory and diagnostic results that he had available, most of which were normal. The blood count done that day showed some decrease in John's white count, but in light of John's leukemic history, David had no idea how to interpret the drop. The preliminary stool culture which was now available was negative for pathological bacteria.

"Please call me if Mr. Tarlow's temperature goes up or his GI symptoms get worse," he told the nurses before he left their station.

David and Angela met in the hospital lobby. Together they ran for their car. The weather was getting worse. Not only was it still raining, it had gotten much colder.

On their way home, Angela told David about the latest incident with Wadley and Cantor's reaction to her complaint.

David shook his head. "Wadley I give up on. He's an ass. But I'd expected more from Cantor, especially in his position as chief of the professional staff. Even if he's insensitive you'd think he'd be aware of the law—and the hospital's liability. Do you think he's slept through the last decade's worth of legal decisions on sexual harassment?"

Angela shrugged. "I don't want to think about it anymore. How was your day? Has Marjorie's death been on your mind?"

"I haven't had time to dwell on it," David said. "I've got John Tarlow in the hospital and he's scaring me."

"What's wrong?"

"That's just it: I don't know," David said. "That's what scares me. He's become apathetic, much the way Marjorie was. He has a lot of functional GI complaints. That's what brought him into the hospital, and they have gotten worse. I don't know what's going on, but my sixth sense is setting off alarm bells. The trouble is I don't know what to do. At this point I'm just treating his symptoms."

"That's the kind of story that makes me glad I went into pathology," Angela said.

David then told Angela about his visit to Werner Van Slyke. "The man was more than rude," David complained. "He hardly gave me the time of day. It gives you an idea of the doctor's position in the new hospital environment. Now the doctor is just another employee, merely working in a different department."

"It makes it hard to be a patient advocate when even the maintenance department isn't responsive."

"My thoughts exactly," David said.

When David and Angela arrived home, Nikki was happy to see them. She'd been bored for most of the day until Arni stopped over to tell her about their new teacher.

"He's a man," Arni told David. "And real strict."

"I hope he's a good teacher," David said. He felt another stab of guilt about Marjorie's passing.

While Angela started dinner David drove Arni home. When David returned, Nikki met him at the door with a complaint. "It feels cold in the family room," she said.

David walked into the room and patted the radiator. It was blisteringly hot. He walked over to the French doors leading to the terrace and made sure they were closed. "Where did you feel cold?" David asked.

"Sitting on the couch," Nikki said. "Come over and try it."

David followed his daughter and sat down next to her. Immediately he could feel a cool draft on the back of his neck. "You're right," he said. He checked the windows behind the couch. "I think I've made the diagnosis," he said. "We need to put up the storm windows."

"What are storm windows?" Nikki asked.

David launched into an involved explanation of heat loss, convection currents, insulation, and Thermopane windows.

"You're confusing her," Angela called from the kitchen. She'd overheard a portion of the conversation. "All she asked was what a storm window was. Why don't you show her one?"

"Good idea," David said. "Come on. We'll get firewood at the same time."

"I don't like it down here," Nikki said as they descended the cellar stairs.

"Why not?" David asked.

"It's scary," Nikki protested.

"Now, don't be like your mother," David teased her. "One hysterical female in the house is enough."

Leaning against the back of the granite staircase was a stack of storm windows. David moved one away from the others so Nikki could see it.

"It looks like a regular window," Nikki said.

"But it doesn't open," David said. "It traps air between this glass and the glass of the existing window. That's what serves as insulation."

While Nikki inspected the window, David noticed something for the first time.

"What is it, Daddy?" Nikki asked, aware that her father had become distracted.

"Something I've never noticed before," David said. He reached over the stack of storm windows and ran his hand over the wall that formed the back of the stairs. "These are cinder blocks."

"What are cinder blocks?" Nikki asked.

Preoccupied with his discovery, David ignored Nikki's question.

"Let's move these storm windows," David said. He lifted the window he was holding and carried it over to the foundation wall. Nikki tipped the next one upright.

"This wall is different from the rest of the basement," David said after the last window had been moved away. "And it doesn't appear to be that old. I wonder why it's here."

"What are you talking about?" Nikki asked.

David showed her that the staircase was made of granite. Then he took her back beneath the stairs and showed her the cinder blocks. He explained that they must be covering some kind of triangular storage space.

"What's in it?" Nikki asked.

David shrugged. "I wonder." Then he said: "Why don't we take a peek. Maybe it's a treasure."

"Really?" Nikki asked.

David got the sledgehammer that was used along with a wedge to split the firewood and brought it over to the base of the stairs.

Just as David hefted the sledgehammer Angela called down the stairs to ask what mischief they were getting themselves into. David lowered the sledgehammer and put a finger to his lips. Then he shouted up to Angela that they'd be coming up with the firewood in a minute.

"I'll be upstairs taking a shower," Angela called down. "After that we'll eat."

"Okay," David called back. Then to Nikki he said: "She might take a dim view of our busting out part of the house."

Nikki giggled.

David waited long enough for Angela to get to the second floor before picking up the sledgehammer again. After telling Nikki to avert her eyes, David knocked out a portion of a cinder block near the top of the wall, creating a small hole.

"Run up and get a flashlight," David said. A musty odor wafted out of the walled-off space.

While Nikki was gone, David used the sledgehammer to enlarge the hole. With a final blow a whole cinder block came loose, and David lifted it out of the wall. By then Nikki was back with the flashlight. David took it and peered in.

David's heart jumped in his chest. He pulled his head out of the hole so quickly he skinned the back of his neck on the sharp edge of the cinder block.

"What did you see?" Nikki asked. She didn't like the look on her father's face.

"It's not a treasure," David said. "I think you'd better get your mother."

While Nikki was gone, David enlarged the hole even more. By the time Angela came down the stairs in her bathrobe David had a whole course of the cinder blocks dismantled.

"What's going on?" Angela demanded. "You've got Nikki upset."

"Take a look," David said. He handed Angela the flashlight and motioned for her to come see.

"This better not be a joke," Angela said.

"It's no joke," David assured her.

"My God!" Angela said. Her voice echoed in the small space.

"What is it?" Nikki asked. "I want to see too."

Angela pulled her head out and looked at David. "It's a body," she said. "And it's obviously been in there for some time."

"A person?" Nikki asked with disbelief. "Can I see?"

Angela and David both nearly shouted, "No."

Nikki started to protest, but her voice lacked conviction.

"Let's go upstairs and build that fire," David said. He took Nikki over to the woodpile and handed her a log. Then he picked up an armload himself.

While Angela phoned the town police David and Nikki worked on the fire. Nikki was full of questions that David couldn't answer.

Half an hour later a police cruiser turned into the Wilsons' driveway and pulled up to the house.

Two policemen had responded to Angela's call.

"My name's Wayne Robertson," the shorter of the pair said. He was dressed in mufti with a quilted cotton vest over a plaid flannel shirt. On his head was a Boston Red Sox baseball cap. "I'm chief of police and this is one of my deputies, Sherwin Morris."

Sherwin touched the brim of his hat. Tall and lanky, he was dressed in uniform. He was carrying a long flashlight: the kind that took four batteries.

"Officer Morris stopped by to pick me up after you called," Robertson explained. "I wasn't on duty, but this sounded important."

Angela nodded. "I appreciate your coming," she said.

Angela and David led the way. Only Nikki remained upstairs. Robertson took the flashlight from Morris and poked his head into the hole.

"I'll be damned!" he said. "It's the quack."

Robertson faced the Wilsons. "Sorry this has happened to you folks," he said. "But I recognize the victim despite the fact that he looks a little worse for wear. His name is Dr. Dennis Hodges. In fact, this was his house, as you probably are aware."

Angela's eyes met David's and she stifled a shiver. Gooseflesh had appeared on the back of her neck.

"What we have to do is knock the rest of this wall down so we can remove the body," Robertson continued. "Do you folks have any problem with that?"

David said that they didn't.

"What about calling the medical examiner?" Angela asked. Through her interest in forensics, she knew it was protocol to call the medical examiner on any suspicious death. This one certainly qualified.

Robertson regarded Angela for a few moments trying to think of something to say. He didn't like anyone telling him how to do his job, especially a woman. The only problem was that Angela was right. And now that he'd been reminded he couldn't ignore it.

"Where's the phone?" Robertson said.

"In the kitchen," Angela said.

Nikki had to be pried from the phone. She'd been back and forth between Caroline and Arni with the exciting news about finding a body in their basement.

Once the medical examiner had been called, Robertson and Morris set to work removing the cinder block wall.

David brought down an extension cord and a floor lamp to help them see what they were doing. The added light also gave them all a better look at the body. Although it was generally well preserved, there was some skeletonization of the lower half of the face. Some of the jawbones and most of the teeth were garishly exposed. The upper part of the face was surprisingly intact. The eyes were hideously open. In the center of the forehead at the hairline was a caved-in area covered with a green mold.

"That pile of stuff in the corner looks like empty cement bags," Robertson said. He was using the beam of the flashlight as a pointer. "And there's the trowel. Hell, he's got everything in there with him. Maybe it was a suicide."

David and Angela looked at each other with the same thought: Robertson was either the world's worst detective or a devotee of crude humor.

"I wonder what those papers are?" Robertson said, directing the light at a number of scattered sheets of paper in the depths of the makeshift tomb.

"Looks like copy machine paper," David said.

"Well, look at that," Robertson said as he directed the flashlight at a tool that was partially concealed under the body. It resembled a flat crowbar.

"What is it?" David asked.

"That's a pry bar," Robertson said. "It's an all-purpose tool, used mostly for demolition."

Nikki called down the stairs to say that the medical examiner had arrived. Angela went up to meet him.

Dr. Tracy Cornish was a thin man of medium height with wire-rimmed spectacles. He carried a large, old-fashioned black leather doctor's bag.

Angela introduced herself and explained that she was a pathologist at Bart-let Community Hospital. She asked Dr. Cornish if he'd had formal forensic training. He admitted he hadn't, and he explained that he filled in as a district medical examiner to supplement his practice. "But I've been doing it for quite a number of years," Dr. Cornish added.

"I was only asking because I have an interest in forensics myself," Angela said. She hadn't meant to embarrass the man.

Angela led Dr. Cornish down to the tomb. He stood and stared at the scene for a few minutes. "Interesting," he said finally. "The body is in a particularly good state of preservation. How long has he been missing?"

"About eight months," Robertson said.

"Shows what a cool, dry place will do," Dr. Cornish said. "This tomb has been like a root cellar. It's even dry after all this rain."

"Why is there some skeletonization around the jaws?" David asked.

"Rodents, probably," Dr. Cornish answered as he bent down and snapped open his bag.

David shuddered. His mouth had gone dry at the thought of rodents gnaw-ing on the body. Glancing at Angela, he could tell that she had taken this infor-mation in stride and was fascinated by the proceedings.

The first thing Dr. Cornish did was take a number of photos, including ex-treme close-ups. Then he donned rubber gloves and began removing the objects from the tomb, placing them in plastic evidence bags. When he got to the papers, everyone crowded around to look at them. Dr. Cornish made certain that no one touched them.

"They're part of medical records from Bartlet Community Hospital," David said.

"I'll bet these stains are all blood," Dr. Cornish said, pointing to large brown areas on the papers. He put all the papers into a plastic bag, which he then sealed and labeled.

When all the objects had been removed, Dr. Cornish turned his attention to the body. The first thing he did was search the pockets. He immediately found the wallet with bills still inside. There were also a number of credit cards in Den-nis Hodges' name.

"Well, it wasn't a robbery," Robertson said.

Dr. Cornish then removed Hodges' watch, which was still running. The time was correct.

"One of the battery manufacturers should use this for one of their zany commercials," Robertson suggested. Morris laughed until he realized no one else was.

Dr. Cornish then pulled a body bag out of his satchel and asked Morris to give him a hand getting Hodges into it.

"What about bagging the hands?" Angela suggested.

Dr. Cornish thought for a moment, then nodded. "Good idea," he said. He got paper bags from his kit and secured them over Hodges' hands. That done, he and Morris got the body into the bag and zipped it closed.

Fifteen minutes later the Wilsons watched as the police cruiser and the medical examiner's van turned around, descended their driveway, and disappeared into the night.

"Anyone hungry?" Angela asked.

Both Nikki and David groaned.

"I'm not either," Angela admitted. "What a night."

They adjourned to the family room where David stoked the fire and added wood. Nikki turned on the television. Angela sat down to read.

By eight o'clock all three decided they might eat something after all. Angela reheated the dinner she had made while David and Nikki set the table.

"Every family has a skeleton in the closet," David said when they were midway through the meal. "Ours just happened to be in the cellar."

"I don't think that's very funny," Angela said.

Nikki said she didn't get it, and Angela had to explain the figurative meaning. Once Nikki understood, she didn't think it was funny either.

David was not pleased about the gruesome discovery in their basement. He was particularly concerned about the potential effect on Nikki. He'd hoped bringing a little humor to the situation might defuse the tension. But even he had to admit his joke fell flat.

After Nikki's respiratory treatment, they all went to bed. Though not an antidote, sleep seemed to be the best alternative. Although Nikki and David were sleepy, Angela wasn't, and as she lay in bed she became acutely aware of all the sounds the house made. She had never realized how noisy it was, particularly on a windy, rainy night. From deep in the basement she heard the oil burner kick on. There was even an intermittent, very low-pitched whine from wind coming down the master bedroom flue.

A sudden series of thumps made Angela jump, and she sat upright.

"What's that?" Angela whispered nervously. She gave David a shove.

"What's what?" David asked, only half awake.

Angela told him to listen. The thumping occurred again. "There," Angela cried. "That banging."

"That's the shutters hitting against the house," David said. "Goodness sake, calm down!"

Angela lay back against the pillow, but her eyes were wide open. She was even less sleepy than she was when she'd gotten into bed.

"I don't like what has been happening around here," Angela said.

David audibly groaned.

"Really," Angela said. "I can't believe so much has changed in so few days. I was worried this was going to happen."

"Are you talking specifically about finding Hodges' body?" David asked.

"I'm talking about everything," Angela said. "The change in the weather,

Wadley's harassing me, Marjorie's death, Kelley's harassing you, and now a body in our basement."

"We're just being efficient," David said. "We're getting all the bad stuff out of the way at one time."

"I'm being serious, and . . ." Angela began to say, but she was interrupted by a scream from Nikki.

In a flash both David and Angela were out of bed and running down the central corridor. They dashed into Nikki's room. She was sitting in bed with a dazed look on her face. Rusty was next to her, equally confused.

It had been a nightmare about a ghoul in the basement. Angela sat on one side of Nikki's bed and David on the other. Together they comforted their daughter. Yet they didn't know quite what to say. The problem was that Nikki's nightmare had been a mixture of dream and reality.

David and Angela did their best to comfort Nikki. In the end they invited her to come sleep with them in their bed. Nikki agreed, and they all marched back to the master bedroom. Climbing into bed, they settled down. Unfortunately David ended up sleeping on the very edge because inviting Nikki also meant inviting Rusty.

THURSDAY • OCTOBER 21

The weather was not much better the next morning. The rain had stopped, but it was misting so heavily that it might as well have been raining. There was no break in the heavy cloud cover and it seemed even chillier than it had the day before.

While Nikki was doing her postural drainage the phone rang. David snatched it up. Considering the early morning hour, he was afraid the call was about John Tarlow. But it wasn't. It was the state's attorney's office requesting permission to send over an assistant to look at the crime scene.

"When would you like to come?" David asked.

"Would it be too inconvenient now?" the caller said. "We have someone in your immediate area."

"We'll be here for about an hour," David said.

"No problem," the caller replied.

True to their word, an assistant from the state's attorney's office arrived within fifteen minutes. She was a pleasant woman with fiery red hair. She was dressed conservatively in a dark blue suit.

"Sorry to bother you so early," the woman said. She introduced herself as Elaine Sullivan.

"No trouble at all," David said, holding the door open for her.

David led her down the cellar steps and turned on the floor lamp to illuminate the now empty tomb. She took out a camera and snapped a few pictures. Then she bent down and stuck a fingernail into the dirt of the tomb's floor. Angela came down the stairs and looked over David's shoulder.

"I understand that the town police were here last night," Elaine said.

"The town police and a district medical examiner," David said.

"I think I'll recommend that the state police crime-scene investigators be called," she said. "I hope it won't be a bother."

"I welcome the idea," Angela said. "I don't think the town police are all that accustomed to a homicide investigation."

Elaine nodded, diplomatically avoiding comment.

"Do we have to be here when the crime-scene people come?" David asked.

"That's up to you," Elaine said. "An investigator may want to talk with you at some point. But as far as the crime-scene people are concerned, they can just come in and do their thing."

"Will they come today?" Angela asked.

"They'll be here as soon as possible," Elaine said. "Probably this morning."

"I'll arrange for Alice to be here," Angela said. David nodded.

Shortly after the state's attorney's assistant had left, the Wilsons were off themselves. This was to be Nikki's first day back to school since she got out of the hospital. She was beside herself with excitement and had changed her clothes twice.

As they took her to school, Nikki couldn't talk about anything besides the body. When they dropped her off, Angela suggested that she refrain from talking about the incident, but Angela knew her request was futile: Nikki had already told Caroline and Arni, and they'd undoubtedly passed the story on.

David put the car in gear, and they started for the hospital.

"I'm concerned about how my patient will be this morning," he said. "Even though I haven't gotten any calls I'm still worried."

"And I'm worried about facing Wadley," Angela said. "I don't know if Cantor has spoken to him or not, but either way it won't be pleasant."

With a kiss for luck, David and Angela headed for their respective days.

David went directly to check on John Tarlow. Stepping into the room he immediately noticed that John's breathing was labored. That was not a good sign. David pulled out his stethoscope and gave John's shoulder a shake. David wanted him to sit up. John barely responded.

Panic gripped David. It was as if his worst fears were coming to pass. Rapidly David examined his patient and immediately discovered that John was developing extensive pneumonia.

Leaving the room, David raced down to the nurses' station, barking orders that John should be transferred to the ICU immediately. The nurses were in the middle of their report; the day shift was taking over from the night shift.

"Can it wait until we finish report?" Janet Colburn asked.

"Hell, no!" David snapped. "I want him switched immediately. And I'd like to know why I haven't been called. Mr. Tarlow has developed bilateral pneumonia."

"He was sleeping comfortably the last time we took his temperature," the night nurse said. "We were supposed to call if his temperature went up or if his GI symptoms got worse. Neither of those things happened."

David grabbed the chart and flipped it open to the temperature graph. The temperature had edged up a little, but not the way David would have expected having heard the man's chest.

"Let's just get him to the ICU," David said. "Plus I want some stat blood work and a chest film."

With commendable efficiency John Tarlow was transferred into the ICU. While it was being done, David called the oncologist, Dr. Clark Mieslich, and the infectious disease specialist, Dr. Martin Hasselbaum, to ask them to come in immediately.

The lab responded quickly to lab work requested for the ICU, and David was soon looking at John's results. His white count, which had been low, was even lower, indicating that John's system was overwhelmed by the developing pneumonia. It was the kind of lack of response one might expect from a patient undergoing chemotherapy, but David knew that John hadn't been on chemo for months. Most ominous of all was the chest X ray: it confirmed extensive, bilateral pneumonia.

The consults arrived in short order to examine the patient and go over the chart. When they were finished they moved away from the bed. Dr. Mieslich confirmed that John was not on any chemotherapy and hadn't been for a long time.

"What do you make of the low white count?" David asked.

"I can't say," Dr. Mieslich admitted. "I suppose it is related to his leukemia. We'd have to do a bone marrow sample to find out, but I don't recommend it now. Not with the infection he's developing. Besides, it's academic. I'm afraid he's moribund."

This was the last thing David wanted to hear although he had begun to expect it. He couldn't believe he was about to lose a second patient in his brief Bartlet career.

David turned to Dr. Hasselbaum.

Dr. Hasselbaum was equally blunt and pessimistic. He thought that John was developing massive pneumonia with a particularly deadly type of bacteria and that, secondarily, he was suffering from shock. He pointed to the fact that John's blood pressure was low and that his kidneys were failing. "It doesn't look good. Mr. Tarlow seems to have very poor physiological defenses, undoubtedly due to his leukemia. If we treat, we'll have to treat massively. I have access to some experimental agents created to help combat this type of endotoxin shock. What do you think?"

"Let's do it," David said.

"These drugs are expensive," Dr. Hasselbaum said.

"A man's life hangs in the balance," David said.

An hour and fifteen minutes later, when John's treatment had been instituted and there was nothing else to be done, David hurried to his office. Once again, every seat in the waiting room was occupied. Some patients were standing in the hall. Everyone was upset, even the receptionist.

David took a deep breath and plunged into his appointments. In between patients he called the ICU repeatedly to check on John's status. Each time he was told there had been no change.

In addition to his regularly scheduled patients, a number of semi-emergencies added to the confusion by having to be squeezed in. David would have sent these cases to the emergency room if it hadn't been for Kelley's lecture. Two of these patients seemed like old friends: Mary Ann Schiller and Jonathan Eakins.

Although he was somewhat spooked by the way Marjorie Kleber's and now John Tarlow's cases had progressed, David felt compelled to hospitalize both Mary Ann and Jonathan. David just didn't feel comfortable treating them as outpatients. Mary Ann had an extremely severe case of sinusitis and Jonathan had a disturbing cardiac arrhythmia. Providing them with admitting orders, David sent them both over to the hospital.

Two other semi-emergency patients were night-shift nurses from the second floor. David had met them on several occasions when he'd been called into the hospital for emergencies. Both had the same complaints: flu-like syndromes consisting of general malaise, low-grade fever, and low white counts, as well as GI troubles including crampy pain, nausea, vomiting, and diarrhea. After examining them, David sent them home for bed rest and symptomatic therapy.

When he had a minute he asked his nurse, Susan, if a flu was going around the hospital.

"Not that I've heard," Susan said.

Angela's day was going better than expected. She'd not had any run-ins with Wadley. In fact, she hadn't seen him at all.

Midmorning she phoned the chief medical examiner, Dr. Walter Dunsmore, having gotten his number from the Burlington directory. Angela explained that she was a pathologist at the Bartlet Community Hospital. She went on to explain her interest in the Hodges case. She added that she had once considered a career in forensic pathology.

Dr. Dunsmore promptly invited her to come to Burlington someday to see their facility. "In fact, why don't you come up and assist at Hodges' autopsy?" he said. "I'd love to have you, but I have to warn you, like most forensic pathologists, I'm a frustrated teacher."

"When do you plan to do it?" Angela asked. She thought that if it could be put off until Saturday, she might be able to go.

"It's scheduled for late this morning," Dr. Dunsmore said. "But there's some flexibility. I'd be happy to do it this afternoon."

"That's very generous," Angela said. "Unfortunately, I'm not sure what my chief would say about my taking the time."

"I've known Ben Wadley for years," Dr. Dunsmore said. "I'll give him a call and clear it with him."

"I'm not sure that would be a good idea," Angela said.

"Nonsense!" Dr. Dunsmore said. "Leave it to me. I look forward to meeting you."

Angela was about to protest further when she realized that Dr. Dunsmore had hung up. She replaced the receiver. She had no idea what Wadley's reaction to Dr. Dunsmore's call would be, but she imagined she'd learn soon enough.

Angela heard even sooner than she expected. Hardly had she hung up than it rang again.

"I'm caught up here in the OR," Wadley said agreeably. "I just got a call from the chief medical examiner. He tells me he wants you to come up to assist with an autopsy."

"I just spoke with him. I wasn't sure how you'd feel about it." It was obvious to Angela from Wadley's cheerfulness that Cantor had not yet spoken with Wadley.

"I think it's a great idea," Wadley said. "My feeling is that whenever the medical examiner asks for a favor, we do it. It never hurts to stay on his good side. You never know when we'll need a favor in return. I encourage you to go."

"Thank you," Angela said. "I will." Hanging up she called David to let him know her plans. When he came on the line, David's voice sounded tense and weary.

"You sound terrible," Angela said. "What's wrong?"

"Don't ask," David said. "I'll have to tell you later. Right now I'm behind again and the natives are restless."

Angela quickly told him about the medical examiner's invitation and that she'd been cleared to go. David told her to enjoy herself and rang off.

Grabbing her coat, Angela left the hospital. Before setting out for Burlington, she headed home to change clothes. As she approached the house she was surprised to see a state police van parked in front of her house. Evidently the crime scene investigators were still there.

Alice Doherty met her at the door, concerned that something was wrong. Angela immediately put her at ease. She then asked about the state police people.

"They are still downstairs," Alice said. "They've been there for hours."

Angela went down to the basement to meet the technicians. There were three. They had the entire area around the back of the stairs blocked off with crime scene tape and brightly illuminated with floodlights. One man was using advanced techniques in an attempt to lift fingerprints from the stone. Another man was carefully sifting through the dirt that formed the floor of the tomb. The third was using a handheld instrument called a luma-light, looking for fibers and latent prints.

The only man who introduced himself was the gentleman working on the fingerprints. His name was Quillan Reilly.

"Sorry we're taking so much time," Quillan said.

"It doesn't matter," Angela assured him.

Angela watched them work. They didn't talk much, each absorbed by his task. She was about to leave when Quillan asked her if the interior of the house had been repainted in the last eight months.

"I don't think so," Angela said. "We certainly haven't."

"Good," said Quillan. "Would you mind if we came back this evening to use some luminol on the walls upstairs?"

"What's luminol?" Angela asked.

"It's a chemical used to search for bloodstains," Quillan explained.

"The house has been cleaned," Angela said, taking mild offense that they thought any blood would still be detectable.

"It's still worth a shot," Quillan said.

"Well, if you think it might be helpful," Angela said. "We want to be cooperative."

"Thank you, ma'am," Quillan said.

"What happened to the evidence taken by the medical examiner?" Angela asked. "Do the local police have it?"

"No, ma'am," Quillan said. "We have it."

"Good," Angela said.

Ten minutes later, Angela was on her way. In Burlington, she found the medical examiner's office with ease.

"We're waiting for you," Dr. Dunsmore said as Angela was ushered into his modern and sparsely furnished office. He made her feel instantly at ease. He even asked her to call him Walt.

In minutes, Angela was dressed in a surgical scrub suit. As she donned a mask, a hood, and goggles, she felt a rush of excitement. The autopsy room had always been an arena of discovery for her.

"I think you'll find we are quite professional here," Walt said as they met outside the autopsy room. "It used to be that forensic pathology was somewhat of a joke outside of the major cities. That's not the case any longer."

Dennis Hodges was laid out on the autopsy table. X rays had been taken and were already on the X-ray view box. Walt introduced the diener to Angela, explaining that Peter would assist them in the procedure.

First they looked at the X rays. The penetrating fracture at the top of the forehead was certainly a mortal wound. There was also a linear fracture in the back of the head. In addition, there was a fracture of the left clavicle, the left ulna, and the left radius.

"There's no doubt it was a homicide," Walt said. "Looks like the poor old guy put up quite a fight."

"The local police chief suggested suicide," Angela said.

"He was joking, I hope," Walt said.

"I really don't know," Angela said. "He didn't impress me or my husband with his investigative skills. It's possible he's never handled a homicide."

"Probably not," Walt said. "Another problem is that some of the older local law enforcement people haven't had much formal training."

Angela described the pry bar that was found with the body. Using a ruler for determining the size of the penetrating fracture and then examining the wound itself they determined that the pry bar could have been the murder weapon.

Then they turned their attention to the bagged hands.

"I was delighted when I saw the paper bags," Walt said. "I've been trying to get my district MEs to use them on this kind of case for a long time."

Angela nodded, secretly pleased that she'd suggested it to Dr. Cornish the night before.

Walt carefully slipped the hands out of their covers and used a magnifying glass to examine under the nails.

"There is some foreign material under some of them," Walt said. He leaned back so Angela could take a look.

"Any idea what it is?" Angela asked.

"We'll have to wait for the microscopic," Walt said as he carefully removed the material and dropped it into specimen jars. Each was labeled according to which finger it came from.

The autopsy itself went quickly; it was as if Angela and Walt were an established team. There was plenty of pathology to make things interesting, and, as promised, Walt enjoyed his didactic role. Hodges had significant arteriosclerosis, a small cancer of the lung, and advanced cirrhosis of the liver.

"I'd guess he liked his bourbon," Walt said.

After the autopsy was completed, Angela thanked Walt for his hospitality and asked to be kept informed about the case. Walt encouraged her to call whenever she wanted.

On the way back to the hospital, Angela felt in a better mood than she had for days. Doing the autopsy had been a good diversion. She was glad that Wadley had let her go.

Pulling into the hospital parking lot, she couldn't find a space in the reserved area near the back entrance. She had to park way up in the upper lot instead. Without an umbrella, she was quite wet by the time she got inside.

Angela went directly to her office. No sooner had she hung up her coat than the connecting door to Wadley's office banged open. Angela jumped. Wadley loomed in the doorway. His square jaw was set, his eyes narrowed, and his customarily carefully combed silver hair was disheveled. He looked furious. Angela instinctively stepped back and eyed the door to the hall with the thought of fleeing.

Wadley stormed into the room, coming right up to Angela and crowding her against her desk.

"I'd like an explanation," he snarled. "Why did you go to Cantor of all people with this preposterous story, these wild, ridiculous, ungrounded accusations? Sexual harassment! My God, that's absurd."

Wadley paused and glared at Angela. She shrank back, not sure if she should say anything. She didn't want to provoke the man. She was afraid he might hit her.

"Why didn't you say something to me?" Wadley screamed.

Wadley paused in his tirade, suddenly aware that Angela's door to the hall was ajar. Outside, the secretaries' keyboards had gone silent. Wadley stomped to the door and slammed it shut.

"After all the time and effort I've lavished on you, this is the reward I get," he yelled. "I don't think I have to remind you that you are on probation around here. You'd better start walking a narrow path, otherwise you'll be looking for work with no recommendation from me."

Angela nodded, not knowing what else to do.

"Well, aren't you going to say anything?" Wadley's face was inches from Angela's. "Are you just going to stand there and nod your head?"

"I'm sorry that we've reached this point," she said.

"That's it?" Wadley yelled. "You've besmirched my reputation with baseless accusations and that's all you can say? This is slander, woman, and I'll tell you something: I might take you to court."

With that, Wadley spun on his heels, strode into his own office, and slammed the door.

Angela let out her breath unevenly as she fought back tears. She sank into her chair and shook her head. It was so unfair.

Susan poked her head into one of the examining rooms and told David that the ICU was on the line. Fearing the worst, David picked up the phone. The ICU nurse said that Mr. Tarlow had just gone into cardiac arrest and the resuscitation team was working on him at that very moment.

David slammed the phone down. He felt his heart leap in his chest, and he instantly broke out in a cold sweat. Leaving a distressed office nurse and receptionist, he dashed over to the ICU, but he was too late. By the time he arrived it was over. The ER physician in charge of the resuscitation team had already declared John Tarlow dead.

"Hey, there wasn't much point," the doctor said. "The man's lungs were full, his kidneys shot, and he had no blood pressure."

David nodded absently. He stared at his patient while the ICU nurses unhooked all the equipment and IV lines. As they continued to clean up, David went over to the main desk and sat down. He began to wonder if he were suited to be a doctor. He had trouble with this part of the job, and repetition seemed to make it more difficult, certainly not easier.

Tarlow's relatives came and, like the Kleber family, they were understanding and thankful. David accepted their kind words feeling like an impostor. He hadn't done anything for John. He didn't even know why he'd died. His history of leukemia wasn't a real explanation.

Even though he'd now been informed about the hospital autopsy policy, David asked the family if they would allow one. As far as David was concerned, there was no harm in trying. The family said they'd consider it.

Leaving the ICU area, David had enough presence of mind to check on Mary Ann Schiller and Jonathan Eakins. He wanted to be certain that they had been settled and their respective treatments started. He particularly wanted to be sure that the CMV cardiologist had visited Eakins.

Unfortunately, David discovered something that gave him pause. Mary Ann had been put in room 206: the room that John Tarlow had so recently vacated. David had half a mind to have Mary Ann moved, but he realized he was being irrationally superstitious. What would he have said to admitting: he never wanted one of his patients in room 206 again? That was clearly ridiculous.

David checked her IV. She was already getting her antibiotic. After promising he'd be back later, David went into Jonathan's room. He too was comfortable and relaxed. A cardiac monitor was in place. Jonathan said that the cardiologist was expected imminently.

When he returned to his office, Susan greeted David with word that Charles Kelley had called. "He wants to see you immediately," she said. "He stressed immediately."

"How many patients are we behind?" David asked.

"Plenty," Susan said. "So try not to be too long."

Feeling as if he were carrying the world on his shoulders, David dragged himself over to the CMV office. He wasn't exactly sure what Charles Kelley wanted to see him about, but he could guess.

"I don't know what to do, David," Charles Kelley said once David was sitting in his office. Kelley shook his head. David marveled at his role-playing ability. Now he was the wounded friend.

"I've tried to reason with you, but either you're stubborn or you just don't care about CMV. The very day after I talk to you about avoiding unnecessary consults outside of the CMV community, you do it again with another terminal patient. What am I going to do with you? Do you understand that the costs of medical care have to be considered? You know there's a crisis in this country?"

David nodded. That much was true.

"Then why is this so hard for you?" Kelley asked. He was sounding angrier. "And it's not only CMV that is upset this time. It's the hospital too. Helen Beaton called me moments ago complaining about the enormously expensive biotechnology drugs that you ordered for this sad, dying patient. Talk about heroics! The man was dying, even the consults said that. He'd had leukemia for years. Don't you understand? This is wasting money and resources."

Kelley had worked himself up to a fevered pitch. His face had become red. But then he paused and sighed. He shook his head again as if he didn't know what to do. "Helen Beaton also complained about your requesting an autopsy," he said in a tired voice. "Autopsies are not part of the contract with CMV, and you were informed of that fact just recently. David, you have to be reasonable. You have to help me or . . ." Kelley paused, letting the unfinished sentence hang in the air.

"Or what?" David said. He knew what Kelley meant, but he wanted him to say it.

"I like you, David," Kelley said. "But I need you to help me. I have people above me I have to answer to. I hope you can appreciate that."

David felt more depressed than ever as he stumbled back toward his office. Kelley's intrusion irritated him, yet in some ways Kelley had a point. Money and resources shouldn't be thrown away on terminal patients when they could be better spent elsewhere. But was that the issue here?

More confused and dejected than he could remember being, David opened the door to his office. He was confronted by a waiting room full of unhappy patients angrily glancing at their watches and noisily flipping through magazines.

Dinner at the Wilson home was a tense affair. No one spoke. Everyone was agitated. It was as if their Shangri-la had gone the way of the weather.

Even Nikki had had a bad day. She was upset about her new teacher, Mr. Hart. The kids had already nicknamed him Mr. Hate. When David and Angela arrived home that evening, she described him as a strict old fart. When Angela chided her about her language, Nikki admitted the description had been Arni's.

The biggest problem with the new teacher was that he had not allowed Nikki to judge her own level of appropriate exercise during gym and he'd not allowed Nikki to do any postural drainage. The lack of communication had led to a confrontation that had embarrassed Nikki.

After dinner David told everyone that it was time to cheer up. In an attempt to improve the atmosphere he offered to build a cozy fire. But when he descended to the basement, he suffered the shock of seeing yellow crime scene tape around his own basement stairs. It brought back the gruesome image of Hodges' body.

David gathered the wood quickly and dashed back upstairs. Normally he wasn't superstitious or easily spooked, but with the recent events he was becoming both.

After building the fire, David began to talk enthusiastically about the upcoming winter and the sports they would soon enjoy: skiing, skating, and sledding. Just when Angela and Nikki were getting in the spirit he'd hoped, headlight beams traversed the wall of the family room. David went to the window.

"It's a state police van," he said. "What on earth could they want?"

"I totally forgot," Angela said, getting to her feet. "When the crime scene people were here today they asked if they could come by when it was dark to look for bloodstains."

"Bloodstains? Hodges was killed eight months ago."

"They said it was worth a try," Angela explained.

The technicians were the same three men who had been there that morning. Angela was impressed with the length of their workday.

"We do a lot of traveling around the state," Quillan said.

Angela introduced Quillan to David. Quillan seemed to be in charge.

"How does this test work?" David asked.

"The luminol reacts with any residual iron from the blood," Quillan said. "When it does, it fluoresces."

"Interesting," David said, but he remained skeptical.

The technicians were eager to do their test and leave, so David and Angela stayed out of their way. They started in the mudroom, setting up a camera on a tripod. Then they turned out all the lights.

They sprayed luminol on the walls using a spray bottle similar to those used for window cleaner. The bottle made a slight hiss with each spray.

"Here's a little," Quillan said in the darkness. David and Angela leaned into the room. Along the wall was a faint, spotty, eerie fluorescence.

"Not enough for a picture," one of the other technicians said.

They circled the room but didn't find any more positive areas. Then they moved the camera into the kitchen. Quillan asked if the lights could be turned off in the dining room and the hallway. The Wilsons readily complied.

The technicians continued about their business. David, Angela, and Nikki hovered at the doorway.

Suddenly portions of the wall near the mudroom began to fluoresce.

"It's faint, but we got a lot here," Quillan said. "I'll keep spraying, you open the shutter on the camera."

"My God!" Angela whispered. "They're finding bloodstains all over my kitchen."

The Wilsons could see vague outlines of the men and hear them as they moved around the kitchen. They approached the table which had been left behind by Clara Hodges and which the Wilsons used when they ate in the kitchen. All at once the legs of the table began to glow in a ghostly fashion.

"My guess is this is the murder site," one of the technicians said. "Right here by the table."

The Wilsons heard the camera being moved, then the loud click of its shutter opening followed by sustained hissing from the spray bottle. Quillan explained that the bloodstains were so faint, the luminol had to be sprayed continuously.

After the crime-scene investigators had left, the Wilsons returned to the family room even more depressed than they had been earlier. There was no more talk of skiing or sledding on the hill behind the barn.

Angela sat on the hearth with her back to the fire and looked at David and Nikki, who had collectively collapsed on the couch. With her family arrayed in front of her, a powerful protective urge swept through Angela. She did not like what she had just learned: her kitchen had the remains of blood spatter from a brutal murder. This was the room that in many ways she regarded as the heart of their home and which she had thought she had cleaned. Now she knew that it had been desecrated by violence. In Angela's mind it was a direct threat to her family.

Suddenly Angela broke the gloomy silence. "Maybe we should move," she said.

"Wait one second," David said. "I know you're upset; we're all upset. But we're not going to allow ourselves to become hysterical."

"I'm hardly hysterical," Angela shot back.

"Suggesting that we have to move because of an unfortunate event which didn't involve us and which occurred almost a year ago is hardly rational," David said.

"It happened in this house," Angela said.

"This house happens to be mortgaged to the roof. We have both a first and second mortgage. We can't just walk away because of an emotional upset."

"Then I want the locks changed," Angela said. "A murderer has been in here."

"We haven't even been locking the doors," David said.

"We are from now on and I want the locks changed."

"Okay," David said. "We'll change the locks."

Traynor was in a rotten mood as he pulled up to the Iron Horse Inn. The weather seemed to fit his temperament: the rain had returned to tropical-like intensity. Even his umbrella proved uncooperative. When he couldn't get it open, he cursed and threw it into the back. He decided he'd simply have to make a run for the Inn's door.

Beaton, Caldwell, and Sherwood were already sitting in a booth when he arrived. Cantor got there just after him. As the two men sat down, Carleton Harris, the bartender, came by to take their drink orders.

"Thank you all for coming out in this inclement weather," Traynor said. "But I'm afraid that recent events mandated an emergency session."

"This isn't an official executive board meeting," Cantor complained. "Let's not be so formal."

Traynor frowned. Even in a crisis, Cantor persisted in irritating him.

"If I may continue," Traynor said, staring Cantor down.

"For chrissake, Harold," Cantor said, "get on with it."

"As you all know by now, Hodges' body turned up in rather unpleasant circumstances."

"The story has attracted media attention," Beaton said. "It made the front page of the Boston Globe."

"I'm concerned about this publicity's potentially negative effect on the hospital," Traynor said. "The macabre aspects of Hodges' death may attract still more media. The last thing we want is a bunch of out-of-town reporters poking around. Thanks largely to Helen Beaton, we've been able to keep word of our ski-masked rapist out of the headlines. But big-city reporters are bound to stumble across that brewing scandal if they're in town. Between that and Hodges' unseemly demise, we could be in for a slew of bad press."

"I've heard from Burlington that Hodges' death is definitely being ruled a homicide," Cantor said.

"Of course it will be ruled a homicide," Traynor snapped. "What else could it be ruled? The man's body was entombed behind a wall of cinder blocks. The issue before us is not whether or not his death was a homicide. The issue is what can we do to lessen the impact on the hospital's reputation. I'm particularly anxious about how these events impact our relationship with CMV."

"I don't see how Hodges' death is the hospital's problem," Sherwood said. "It's not like we killed him."

"Hodges ran the hospital for twenty-plus years," Traynor said. "His name is intimately associated with Bartlet. Lots of people know he wasn't happy with the way we were running things."

"I think the less the hospital says the better," Sherwood said.

"I disagree," Beaton said. "I think that the hospital should issue a statement regretting his death and underlining the great debt owed him. The statement should include condolences to his family."

"I agree," Cantor said. "Ignoring his death would seem peculiar."

"I agree," Caldwell said.

Sherwood shrugged. "If everyone else feels that way, I'll go along."

"Has anyone spoken to Robertson?" Traynor asked.

"I have," Beaton said. "He doesn't have any suspects. Braggart that he is, he surely would have let on if he had."

"Hell, the way he felt about Hodges he could be a suspect himself," Sherwood said with a laugh.

"So could you," Cantor said to Sherwood.

"And so could you, Cantor," Sherwood said.

"This isn't a contest," Traynor said.

"If it were a contest, you'd be a leading contestant," Cantor said to Traynor. "It's common knowledge how you felt about Hodges after your sister committed suicide."

"Hold on," Caldwell said. "The point is that no one cares who did it."

"That might not be entirely true," Traynor said. "CMV might care. After all, this sordid affair still reflects poorly on both the hospital and the town."

"And that's why I think we should issue a statement," Beaton said.

"Would anyone like to make a motion for a vote?" Traynor said.

"Jesus, Harold," Cantor said. "There are only five of us here. We don't have to follow parliamentary procedure. Hell, we all agree."

"All right," Traynor said. "Does everybody concur that we should make a formal statement along the lines Beaton discussed?"

Everyone nodded.

Traynor looked at Beaton. "I think it should come from your office," he said. "I'll be happy to do it," Beaton said.

FRIDAY • OCTOBER 22

It had been a turbulent night at the Wilson house. Just after two o'clock in the morning Nikki had begun screaming again and had to be awakened from yet another terrifying nightmare. The episode had upset everyone and had kept them all up for over an hour. David and Angela regretted having allowed Nikki to watch crime-scene technicians work, guessing they had contributed to her terror.

At least the day dawned bright and clear. After five days of continuous rain the sky was pale blue and cloudless. In place of the rain was a big chill. The temperature had plunged into the upper teens, leaving the ground blanketed with an exceptionally heavy hoarfrost.

There was little conversation as the Wilsons dressed and breakfasted. Everyone avoided making reference to the luminal test although Angela refused to sit at the kitchen table. She ate her cereal standing at the sink.

Before Angela and Nikki left, David asked Angela about lunch. Angela told him she'd meet him in the lobby at twelve-thirty.

On the way to school, Angela tried to encourage Nikki to give Mr. Hart more than one day's chance. "It's difficult for a teacher to take over someone else's class. Especially someone special like Marjorie."

"Why couldn't Daddy save her?" Nikki asked.

"He tried," Angela said. "But it just wasn't to be. Doctors can only do so much."

Pulling up to the front of the school, Nikki jumped out and was about to dash up the walk when Angela called her back.

"You forgot the letter," Angela said. She handed Nikki a letter Angela had written explaining Nikki's health problems and needs. "Remember, if Mr. Hart has any questions he should give either me or Dr. Pilsner a call."

Angela was relieved to find that Wadley wasn't around when she arrived at the lab. Quickly she immersed herself in her work, but no sooner had she started than one of the secretaries let her know that the chief medical examiner was on the phone.

"I have some interesting news," Walt said. "The material that we teased from beneath Dr. Hodges' fingernails was indeed skin."

"Congratulations," Angela said.

"I've already run a DNA screen," Walt said. "It is not Hodges' skin. I'd bet a thousand dollars it belongs to his assailant. It could prove to be critical evidence if a suspect is charged."

"Have you ever found evidence like this before?" Angela asked.

"Yes, I have," Walt said. "It's not rare in mortal struggles to find remnants of the attacker's skin under the victim's nails. But I have to admit that this case represents the longest interval from the time of the crime to the discovery of the body. If we can make an I.D. with a suspect it might be worth writing it up for one of the journals."

Angela thanked him for keeping her informed.

"I almost forgot," Walt added. "I found some black carbon particles embedded in the skin samples. It looks strange. It's as if the killer had scraped up against a hearth or a wood stove during the struggle. Anyway, I thought it was curious and that it might help the crime-scene investigators."

"I'm afraid it might only confuse them," Angela said. She explained about the luminol test the night before. "The blood spatter wasn't anywhere near a fireplace or the stove. Maybe the killer picked up the carbon earlier, someplace else?"

"I doubt it," Walt said. "There was no inflammation, just a few red blood cells. The carbon had to be picked up contemporaneous to the struggle."

"Maybe Hodges had carbon under his nails," Angela suggested.

"That's a good thought," Walt said. "The only trouble is the carbon is evenly distributed in the skin samples."

"It's a mystery," Angela said. "Especially since it doesn't jibe with what the crime-scene people found."

"It's the same with any mystery," Walt said. "To solve it you have to have all the facts. We're obviously missing some crucial piece of information."

After having been denied the opportunity to ride his bike for an entire week, David thoroughly enjoyed the trip from his home to the hospital. Taking a little extra time, he followed a route that was slightly longer than usual but much more scenic.

The exhilaration of the cold, crisp air and the views of the frost-filled meadows cleared David's mind. For a few minutes he was relieved of his anguish over his recent medical failures. Entering the hospital he felt better than he had for several days. The first patient he visited was Mary Ann Schiller.

Unfortunately Mary Ann was not bright and cheerful. David had to wake her up, and while he was examining her, she fell back asleep. Beginning to feel a little concerned, David woke her up again. He asked her how it felt when he tapped over her antral sinuses. With a sleep-slurred voice she said she thought there was less discomfort, but she wasn't sure.

David then listened to her chest with his stethoscope, and while he was con-centrating on her breath sounds, she fell asleep again. David allowed her to fall back onto the pillows. He looked at her peaceful face; it was in sharp contrast to his state of mind. Her drowsiness was alarming him.

David went to the nurses' station to go over Mary Ann's chart. At first he felt a little better, seeing that the low-grade fever she had developed the day be-fore had remained unchanged. But his apprehension grew when he read the nurses' notes and learned that GI symptoms had appeared during the night. She'd suffered from nausea, vomiting, and diarrhea.

David couldn't account for these symptoms. He wasn't sure how to proceed. Since her sinusitis seemed to be slightly better, he did not alter her antibiotics even though there was a slight chance the antibiotics were causing the GI prob-lems. But what about the drowsiness? As a precaution, he canceled her PRN sleep order as he'd done with John Tarlow.

Going on to Jonathan Eakins' room, David's relatively buoyant spirits re-turned. Jonathan was in an expansive mood. He was feeling chipper and re-ported that his cardiac monitor had been beeping as regularly as a metronome without the slightest suggestion of irregularity.

Taking out his stethoscope, David listened to Jonathan's chest. He was pleased to hear that Jonathan's lungs were perfectly clear. David wasn't sur-prised with Jonathan's rapidly improved status. He had spent several hours going over the case with the cardiologist the previous afternoon. The cardiologist had been certain there would be no problems with the heart.

The rest of David's hospital patients were all doing as well as Jonathan. He was able to move from one to the other swiftly, even discharging a few. With his rounds finished, David headed to his office, happy to be early. After the experi-ences of the last few days, he'd made a vow to make every effort not to get be-hind again.

As the morning progressed, David remained acutely aware of the amount of time he spent with each patient. Knowing that his productivity was being mon-itored, he tried to keep each visit short. Although he didn't feel good about it, he was afraid he didn't have much choice. Kelley's implied threat of firing him had left him shaken. With their debt, the family could not afford for him to be out of work.

Having gotten an early start, David was able to keep ahead all morning. When two second-floor nurses called and asked to be seen as semi-emergencies, David was able to take them the moment they came in the door.

Both had flu-like symptoms identical to the two previous nurses. David treated them the same way: recommending bed rest and symptomatic therapy for their GI complaints.

With ample time to attend to other matters, David even had an opportunity to slip over to Dr. Pilsner's office. He told the pediatrician that he'd been seeing some flu already, and he asked him about Nikki's flu shot.

"She's already had it," Dr. Pilsner said. "I haven't seen any flu in my practice yet, but I don't wait to see it before I give the shots, especially to my cystic fibrosis patients."

David also asked Dr. Pilsner about his opinion regarding the use of prophylactic antibiotics for Nikki. Dr. Pilsner said he was not in favor of it. He thought it best to wait until Nikki's condition suggested she needed them.

David finished his morning patients before noon and even had time to dictate some letters before meeting Angela in the hospital lobby.

"With the weather as nice as it is, what do you say we go into town and have lunch at the diner?" David suggested. He thought some fresh air would be good for both of them.

"I was about to suggest the same thing," Angela said. "But let's get take-out. I want to stop by the police station and find out how they intend to proceed with the Hodges investigation."

"I don't think that's a good idea," David said.

"Why not?" Angela questioned.

"I'm not entirely sure," David admitted. "Intuition, I guess. And it's not like the town police have inspired much confidence. To tell you the truth, I didn't get the impression they were all that interested in investigating the case."

"That's why I want to go," Angela said. "I want to be sure they know that we're interested. Come on, humor me."

"If you insist," David said with reluctance.

They got tuna sandwiches to go and ate them on the steps of the gazebo. Although it had been well below freezing that morning, the bright sun had warmed the air to a balmy seventy degrees.

After finishing their meal they walked over to the police station. It was a plain, two-story brick structure standing on the town green directly across from the library.

The officer at the front desk was gracious. After a quick call he directed David and Angela down a creaky wooden corridor to Wayne Robertson's office. Robertson invited them in and hastily took newspapers and Dunkin' Donuts bags off two metal chairs. When David and Angela were seated, he leaned his expansive backside against his matching metal desk. He crossed his arms and smiled. Despite the lack of direct sunlight in the room, he was wearing his reflective aviator-style sunglasses.

"I'm glad you folks stopped in," he said once David and Angela were seated. He had a slight accent that had a vague similarity to a southern drawl. "I'm sorry we had to intrude the other night. I'd like to apologize for upsetting your evening."

"We appreciated your coming," David said.

"What can I do for you folks?" Robertson asked.

"We're here to offer our cooperation," Angela said.

"Well now, we appreciate that," Robertson said. He smiled widely, revealing square teeth. "We depend on the community. Without its support, we couldn't do our job."

"We want to see the Hodges murder case solved," Angela said. "We want to see the killer behind bars."

"Well, you're certainly not alone," Robertson said with his smile plastered on his face. "We want to see it solved as well."

"Living in a house where there's been a murder is very distressing," Angela said. "Particularly if the murderer is still on the streets. I'm sure you understand."

"Absolutely," Robertson said.

"So we'd like to know what we can do to help," Angela said.

"Well, let's see," Robertson said, showing signs of unease. He stammered, "Actually, there's not a whole bunch anybody can do."

"What exactly are the police doing?" Angela asked.

The smile faded from Robertson's face. "We're working on it," Robertson said vaguely.

"Which means what?" Angela persisted.

David started to stand up, concerned about the direction and tone of the conversation, but Angela wouldn't budge.

"Well, the usual," Robertson said.

"What's the usual?" Angela asked.

Robertson was clearly uncomfortable. "Well, to be truthful we're not doing much right now. But back when Hodges disappeared, we were working day and night."

"I'm a little surprised that there hasn't been a resurgence of interest now that there is a corpse," Angela said testily. "And the medical examiner has unquestionably ruled the case a homicide. We've got a killer walking around this town, and I want something done."

"Well, we certainly don't want to disappoint you folks," Robertson said with a touch of sarcasm. "What exactly would you like done so that we'll know in advance you'll be pleased?"

David started to say something, but Angela shushed him. "We want you to do what you normally do with a homicide," she said. "You have the murder weapon so test it for fingerprints, find out where it was purchased, that sort of thing. We shouldn't have to tell you how to carry out an investigation."

"The spoor is a little cold after eight months," Robertson said, "and frankly I don't take kindly to your coming in here telling me how to do my job. I don't go up to the hospital and tell you how to do yours. Besides, Hodges wasn't the most popular man in town, and we have to set priorities with our limited manpower. For your information we have a few more pressing matters just now, including a series of rapes."

"It's my opinion that the basics ought to be done on this case," Angela said.

"They were," Robertson said. "Eight months ago."

"And what did you learn?" Angela demanded.

"Lots of things," Robertson snapped. "We learned there was no break-in or robbery, which has now been confirmed. We learned there was a bit of a struggle . . ."

" 'A bit of a struggle'?" Angela echoed. "Last night the state police crime-scene investigators proved that the killer chased the doctor through our house bashing him with a pry bar, spattering blood all over the walls. Dr. Hodges had multiple skull fractures, a fractured clavicle, and a broken arm." Angela turned to David, throwing her hands in the air. "I don't believe this!"

"Okay, okay," David said, trying to calm her. He had been afraid she'd make a scene like this. She had little tolerance for incompetence.

"The case needs a fresh look," Angela said, ignoring David. "I got a call today from the medical examiner confirming that the victim had skin from his attacker under his fingernails. That's the kind of struggle it was. Now all we need is a suspect. Forensics can do the rest."

"Thank you for this timely tip," Robertson said. "And thank you for being such a concerned citizen. Now if you'll excuse me, I have work to do."

Robertson stepped over to the door and held it open. David practically had to yank Angela from the office. It was all he could do to keep her from saying more on her way out.

"Did you catch any of that?" Robertson asked when one of his deputies appeared.

"Some of it," the deputy said.

"I hate these big-shot city people," Robertson said. "Just because they went to Harvard or someplace like that they think they know how to do everything."

Robertson stepped back inside his office and closed the door. Picking up the phone, he pressed one of the automatic dial buttons.

"Sorry to bother you," Robertson said deferentially, "but I think we might have a problem."

"Don't you dare paint me as an hysterical female," Angela said as she got into the car.

"Baiting the local chief of police like that certainly isn't rational," David said. "Remember, this is a small town. We shouldn't be making enemies."

"A person was brutally murdered, the body dumped in our basement, and the police don't seem too interested in finding out who did it. You're willing to let it rest at that?"

"As deplorable as Hodges' death was," David said, "it doesn't involve us. It's a problem that should be left up to the authorities."

"What?" Angela cried. "The man was beaten to death in our house, in our kitchen. We're involved whether you want to admit it or not, and I want to find out who did it. I don't like the idea of the murderer walking around this town, and I'm going to do something about it. The first thing is we should learn more about Dennis Hodges."

"I think you're being overly dramatic and unreasonable," David said.

"You've already made that clear," Angela said. "I just don't agree with you."

Angela seethed with anger, mostly at Robertson but partly at David. She wanted to tell him that he wasn't the paragon of rationality and agreeableness that he thought he was. But she held her tongue.

They reached the hospital parking lot. The only space available was far from the entrance. They got out and started walking.

"We already have plenty to worry about," David said. "It's not as if we don't have enough problems at the moment."

"Then maybe we should hire somebody to do the investigating for us," Angela said.

"You can't be serious," David said, coming to a halt. "We don't have the money to throw away on such nonsense."

"In case you haven't been listening to me," Angela said, "I don't think it's nonsense. I repeat: there's a murderer loose in this town. Someone who has been in our house. Maybe we've already met him. It gives me the creeps."

"Please, Angela," David said as he started walking again. "We're not dealing with a serial killer. I don't think it's so strange that the killer hasn't been found. Haven't you read stories about murders in small towns where no one would come forward even though it was common knowledge who the killer was? It's a kind of down-home justice where the people think the victim got what he deserved. Apparently Hodges wasn't uniformly admired."

They reached the hospital and entered. Just inside the door they paused.

"I'm not willing to chalk this up to down-home justice," Angela said. "I think the issue here is one of basic social responsibility. We're a society of laws."

"You're too much," David said. Despite his aggravation, he smiled. "Now you're ready to give me a lecture on social responsibility. You can be such an idealist sometimes, it blows my mind. But I do love you." He leaned over and gave her a peck on the cheek. "We'll talk more later. For now, calm down! You've got enough problems with Wadley to keep you occupied without adding this."

With a final wave David strode off toward the professional building. Angela watched him until he rounded the corner and disappeared from sight. She was touched by his sudden display of affection. Its unexpectedness mollified her for the moment.

But a few minutes later as she was sitting at her desk trying to concentrate, she replayed the conversation with Robertson in her mind and got furious all over again. She left her office to look for Paul Darnell. She found him where he always was: hunched over stacks of petri dishes filled with bacteria.

"Have you lived in Bartlet all your life?" Angela asked.

"All except four years of college, four of medical school, four of residency, and two in the navy."

"I'd say that makes you a local," Angela said.

"What makes me a local is the fact that Darnells have been living here for four generations."

Angela stepped into Paul's office and leaned against the desk. "I suppose you heard the gossip about the body found in my home," she said.

Paul nodded.

"It's really bothering me," Angela said. "Would you mind if I asked you a few questions?"

"Not at all," Paul said.

"Did you know Dennis Hodges?"

"Of course."

"What was he like?"

"He was a feisty old codger few people miss. He had a penchant for making enemies."

"How did he get to be hospital administrator?" Angela asked.

"By default," Paul said. "He took over the hospital at a time when no other doctors wanted the responsibility. Everybody thought that running the hospital was below their physician status. So Hodges had a free hand, and he built the place like a feudal estate, associating with a medical school for prestige and billing the place as a regional medical center. He even sank some of his own money into it in a crisis. But Hodges was the world's worst diplomat, and he didn't care one iota about other people's interests when they collided with the hospital's."

"Like when the hospital took over pathology and radiology?" Angela asked.

"Exactly," Paul said. "It was a good move for the hospital, but it created a lot of ill will. I had to take an enormous cut in my income. But my family wanted to stay in Bartlet so I adjusted. Other people fought it and eventually had to move away. Obviously Hodges made a lot of enemies."

"Dr. Cantor stayed as well," Angela remarked.

"Yes, but that was because he talked Hodges into a joint venture between himself and the hospital to create a world-class imaging center. Cantor wound up doing well financially, but he was the exception."

"I just had a conversation with Wayne Robertson," Angela said. "I got the distinct impression that he's dragging his feet about investigating who killed Hodges."

"I'm not surprised," Paul said. "There's not a lot of pressure to solve the case. Hodges' wife has moved back to Boston, and she and Hodges weren't getting along at the time of his death. They'd essentially lived apart these last few years. On top of that, Robertson could have done it himself. Robertson always had it in for Hodges. He even had an altercation with him the night Hodges disappeared."

"Why was there animosity between those two?" Angela asked.

"Robertson blamed his wife's death on Hodges," Douglas said.

"Was Hodges Robertson's wife's physician?" Angela asked.

"No, Hodges' practice was minuscule by then. He was running the hospital full time. But as director he allowed Dr. Werner Van Slyke to practice even though most everybody knew Van Slyke had a drinking problem. Actually Hodges left the issue of Van Slyke's privileges up to the medical staff. Van Slyke bungled Robertson's wife's appendicitis case while under the influence. Afterward, Robertson blamed Hodges. It wasn't rational, but hate usually isn't."

"I'm getting the feeling that finding out who killed Hodges won't be easy," Angela said.

"You don't know how right you are," Paul said. "There's a second chapter to the Hodges–Van Slyke affair. Hodges was friends with Traynor, who is the present chairman of the hospital board. Traynor's sister was married to Van Slyke, and when Hodges finally denied Van Slyke privileges . . ."

"All right," Angela said, holding up her hand, "I'm getting the idea. You're overwhelming me. I had no idea the town was quite this byzantine."

"It's a small town," Paul said. "A lot of families have lived here a long time. It's practically incestuous. But the fact of the matter is there were a lot of people who didn't care for Hodges. So when he disappeared, not too many people were broken up about it."

"But that means Hodges' murderer is walking around," Angela said. "Presumably a man who is capable of extreme violence."

"You're probably right about that."

Angela shivered. "I don't like it," she said. "This man was in my home, maybe many times. He probably knows my house well."

Paul shrugged. "I understand how you feel," he said. "I'd probably feel the same way. But I don't know what you can do about it. If you want to learn more about Hodges, go talk to Barton Sherwood. As president of the bank he knows everyone. He knew Hodges particularly well since he's been on the hospital board forever and his father had been before that."

Angela went back to her office and again attempted to work, but she still couldn't concentrate. It was impossible to get Hodges out of her mind. Reaching for the phone, she called Barton Sherwood. She remembered how friendly he'd been when they bought the house.

"Dr. Wilson," Sherwood said when he came on the line. "How nice to hear from you. How are you folks making out in that beautiful house of yours?"

"Generally well," Angela said, "but that's what I'd like to chat with you about. If I were to run over to the bank, would you have a few moments to speak with me?"

"Absolutely," Sherwood said. "Anytime."

"I'll be right over," Angela said.

After telling the secretaries that she'd be back shortly, Angela grabbed her coat and ran out to the car. Ten minutes later she was sitting in Sherwood's office. It seemed like just yesterday that she, David, and Nikki were there, arranging to buy their first house.

Angela came right to the point. She described how uncomfortable she felt about Hodges having been murdered in her house and about the murderer being on the loose. She told Sherwood she hoped he would be willing to help.

"Help?" Sherwood questioned. He was leaning back in his leather desk chair with both thumbs tucked into his vest pockets.

"The local police don't seem to care about solving the case," Angela said. "With your stature in the town a word from you would go a long way in getting them to do something."

Sherwood thumped forward in his chair. He was clearly flattered. "Thank you for your vote of confidence," he said, "but I truly don't think you have anything to worry about. Hodges was not the victim of senseless, random violence or of a serial killer."

"How do you know?" Angela asked. "Do you know who killed him?"

"Heavens no," Sherwood said nervously. "I didn't mean to imply that. I meant . . . well, I thought . . . there's no reason for you and your family to feel at risk."

"Do a lot of people know who killed Hodges?" Angela asked, recalling David's theory of down-home justice.

"Oh, no. At least, I don't think so," Sherwood said. "It's just that Dr. Hodges was an unpopular man who'd hurt a number of people. Even I had trouble getting along with him." Sherwood laughed nervously, then went on to tell Angela about the spit of land that Hodges had owned, fenced, and refused to sell out of spite, keeping Sherwood from using his own two parcels.

"What you're trying to tell me is the reason no one cares who killed Hodges is because he was disliked."

"Essentially, yes," Sherwood admitted.

"In other words, what we have here is a conspiracy of silence."

"I wouldn't put it that way," Sherwood said. "It's a situation where people feel that justice has been served, so no one cares much whether someone is arrested or not."

"I care," Angela said. "The murder took place in my house. Besides, there's no place for vigilante justice in this day and age."

"Normally I would be the first to agree with you," Sherwood said. "I'm not trying to justify this affair on moral or legal grounds. But Hodges was different. What I think you should do is go talk with Dr. Cantor. He'll be able to give you an idea of the kind of animosity and turmoil that Hodges was capable of causing. Maybe then you'll understand and be less judgmental."

Angela drove back up the hill toward the hospital feeling confused about what she should do. She did not agree with Sherwood for one second, and the more she learned about the Hodges affair, the more she wanted to know. Yet she did not want to speak with Cantor, not after the conversation she'd had with him the day before.

Entering the hospital, Angela went directly to the section of the pathology lab where slides were stained and prepared. Her timing was perfect: slides that she'd been anticipating that morning had just been completed. Taking the tray, she hurried back to her office to get to work.

The moment she entered her office Wadley appeared at the connecting door. Like the day before, he was visibly distressed. "I just paged you," he said irritably. "Where the hell were you?"

"I had to make a quick trip to the bank," Angela said nervously. Her legs suddenly felt weak. She feared Wadley was about to lose control the way he had the day before.

"Restrict your visits to the bank to your lunch hour," he said. He hesitated for a moment, then stepped back into his office and slammed the door.

Angela breathed a sigh of relief.

Sherwood had not moved from his desk following Angela's departure. He was trying to decide what to do. He couldn't believe this woman was making such a issue about Hodges. He hoped he hadn't said something that he would regret.

After some deliberation, Sherwood picked up the phone. He'd come to the conclusion that it was best for him to do nothing other than pass on the information.

"Something has just happened that I thought you should know about," Sherwood said when the connection went through. "I just had a visit from the newest member of the hospital's professional staff and she's concerned about Dr. Hodges . . ."

David finished with his last office patient for the day, dictated a few letters, then hurried over to the hospital to make his late afternoon rounds. Fearing what he'd find, he left Mary Ann Schiller for last. As he'd intuitively suspected, she'd taken a turn for the worse.

Her low-grade fever had gradually climbed during the afternoon. Now it hovered a little over one hundred and one. The fever bothered David, especially since it had risen while she was on antibiotics, but there was something that bothered him more: her mental state.

That morning Mary Ann had been drowsy, but now as David tried to talk to her, he found her both drowsy and apathetic. It had been a distinct change. Not only was it hard to wake her and keep her awake, but when she was awake she didn't care about anything and paid little attention to his questions. She was also disoriented with respect to time and place although she still knew her name.

David rolled her on her side and listened to her chest. When he did so he panicked. He heard a chorus of rhonchi and rales. She was developing massive pneumonia. It was like John Tarlow all over again.

David raced back to the nurses' station, where he ordered a stat blood count as well as a portable chest film. Going over Mary Ann's chart he found nothing abnormal. The nurses' notes for the day suggested that she had been doing fine.

The stat blood count came back showing very little cellular response to the developing pneumonia, a situation reminiscent of both Tarlow and Kleber. The portable chest film confirmed his fear: extensive pneumonia developing in both lungs.

At a loss, David called Dr. Mieslich, the oncologist, to confer by phone. After all the trouble with Kelley he was reluctant to ask for a formal consult even though that would have been far better.

Without having seen the patient, Dr. Mieslich could offer little help. He did confirm that the last time he had seen Mary Ann in his office there had been no evidence of her ovarian cancer. At the same time he told David that her cancer had been extensive prior to treatment and that he fully expected a recurrence.

While David was on the phone with the oncologist, a nurse appeared in front of the nurses' station and yelled that Mary Ann was convulsing.

David slammed down the phone and raced to the bedside. Mary Ann was indeed in the throes of a grand mal seizure. Her back was arched and her legs and arms were rhythmically thrashing against the bed. Fortunately, her IV had not become dislodged, and David was able to control the seizure quickly with intravenous medication. Nevertheless, in the wake of the seizure, Mary Ann remained comatose.

Returning to the nurses' station, David put in a stat call to the CMV neurologist, Dr. Alan Prichard. Since he was in the hospital making his own rounds, he called immediately. After David told him about the seizure along with a capsule history, Dr. Prichard told David to order either a CAT scan or an MRI, whichever machine was available. He said he'd be over to see the patient as soon as he could.

David sent Mary Ann to the Imaging Center for her MRI accompanied by a nurse in case she seized again. Then he called the oncologist back, explained what had happened, and asked for a formal consult. As he'd done with Kleber and Tarlow, he also called Dr. Hasselbaum, the infectious disease specialist.

David couldn't help but worry about Kelley's reaction to these non-CMV consults, but David felt he had little choice. He could not allow concern about Kelley to influence his decision making in light of the grand mal seizure. The gravity of Mary Ann's condition was apparent.

As soon as David was alerted that the MRI study was available, he dashed over to the Imaging Center. He met the neurologist in the viewing room as the first images were being processed. Along with Dr. Cantor they silently watched the cuts appear. When the study was complete David was shocked that there was no sign of a metastatic tumor. He would have sworn such a tumor was responsible for the seizure.

"At this point I cannot say why she had a seizure," Dr. Prichard said. "It could have been some micro emboli, but I'm only speculating."

The oncologist was equally surprised about the MRI result. "Maybe the lesion is too small for the MRI to pick up," he suggested.

"This machine has fantastic resolution," Dr. Cantor said. "If the tumor was too small for this baby to pick up, then the chances it could have caused a grand mal seizure are even smaller."

The infectious disease consult was the only one with anything specific to add, but his news wasn't good. He confirmed David's diagnosis of extensive pneumonia. He also demonstrated that the bacteria involved was a gram-negative type organism similar but not identical to the bacteria that had caused Kleber's and Tarlow's pneumonia. Worse still, he suggested that Mary Ann was already in septic shock.

From the Imaging Center David sent Mary Ann to the ICU where he insisted on the most aggressive therapy available. He allowed the infectious disease consult to handle the antibiotic regimen. The respiratory care he turned over to an anesthesiologist. By then Mary Ann's breathing was so labored she needed a respirator.

When everything that could be done for Mary Ann had been done and after all the consults had departed, David felt dazed. His group of oncology patients had become far more emotionally draining than he'd originally feared. Finally he left the ICU, and just to be reassured, he stopped in again to see Jonathan. Thankfully Jonathan was doing marvelously.

"I only have one complaint," Jonathan said. "This bed has a mind of its own. Sometimes when I press the button nothing happens. Neither the head nor the foot rises."

"I'll take care of it," David assured him.

Thankful for a problem that had an easy solution, David went back to the nurses' station and mentioned the problem to the evening head nurse, Dora Maxfield.

"Not his too," Dora said. "Some of these old beds break down a little too often. But thanks for telling us. I'll have maintenance take care of it right away."

David left the hospital and got on his bike. The temperature had dropped as soon as the sun had dipped below the horizon, but he felt the cold was somehow therapeutic.

Arriving home David found a bedlam of activity. Nikki had both Caroline and Arni over, and they were racing around the downstairs with Rusty in hot pursuit. David joined the melee, enjoying being pummeled and trampled by three active children. The laughter alone was worth the punishment. For a few minutes he forgot about the hospital.

When it was almost seven Angela asked David if he would take Caroline and Arni home. David was happy to do it, and Nikki came along. After the two children had been dropped off, David was glad for the moments alone with his daughter. First they talked about school and her new teacher. Then he asked her if she thought much about the body discovered in the basement.

"Some," Nikki said.

"How does it make you feel?" David asked.

"Like I don't want to ever go in the basement again."

"I can understand that," David said. "Last night when I was getting firewood I felt a little scared."

"You did?"

"Yup," David said. "But I have a little plan that might be fun and it might help. Are you interested?"

"Yeah!" Nikki said with enthusiasm. "What?"

"You can't tell anybody," David said.

"Okay," Nikki promised.

David outlined his plan as they continued home. "What do you say?" he asked once he had finished.

"I think it's cool," Nikki said.

"Remember, it's a secret," David said.

"Cross my heart."

As soon as David got into the house, he called the ICU to check on Mary Ann. He had been distressed that the floor nurses had missed the worsening condition of his two patients who had died. At the same time he recognized that his patients' vital signs had shown little change as their clinical states markedly deteriorated.

"There has been no alteration in Mrs. Schiller's status," the ICU nurse told him over the phone. She then gave him a lengthy review of Mrs. Schiller's vital signs, lab values, and even the settings on her respirator. The nurse's professionalism bolstered David's confidence that Mary Ann was receiving the best care possible.

Intentionally avoiding the kitchen table after the previous night's revelation, Angela served dinner in the dining room. It seemed huge with just three people and their skimpy dining-room furniture. But Angela tried to make it cozy with a fire in the fireplace and candles on the table. Nikki complained it was so dark she could hardly see her food.

After they had finished eating, Nikki excused herself to watch her half-hour allotment of television. David and Angela lingered at the table.

"Don't you want to ask me how my afternoon went?" Angela asked.

"Of course," David said. "How was it?"

"Interesting," Angela said. She told him about her conversations with Paul Darnell and Barton Sherwood concerning Dennis Hodges. She conceded that David might have been right when he suggested that some people in town knew who did it.

"Thanks for giving me credit," David said, "but I'm not happy about your asking questions about Hodges."

"Why not?" Angela asked.

"For a number of reasons," David said. "Mainly because we both have other things to worry about. But beyond that, did it occur to you that you might wind up questioning the killer himself?"

Angela admitted she hadn't thought of that, but David wasn't listening. He was staring into the fire.

"You seem distracted," she said. "What's wrong?"

"Another one of my patients is in the ICU fighting for her life."

"I'm sorry," Angela said.

"It's another disaster," David said. His voice faltered as he struggled with his emotions. "I'm trying to deal with it, but it's hard. She's doing very poorly. Frankly, I'm worried she'll die just like Kleber and Tarlow. Maybe I don't know what I'm doing. Maybe I shouldn't even be a doctor."

Angela came around the table to put an arm around David. "You are a wonderful doctor," she whispered. "You have a real gift. Patients love you."

"They don't love me when they die," David said. "When I sit in my office in the same spot where Dr. Portland killed himself, I start thinking that now I know why he did it."

Angela shook David's shoulders. "I don't want to hear any talk like that," she said. "Have you been speaking with Kevin Yansen again?"

"Not about Portland," David said. "He seems to have lost interest in the subject."

"Are you depressed?"

"Some," David admitted. "But it's not out of hand."

"Promise me you'll tell me if it gets out of hand?" Angela said.

"I promise," David said.

"What's this new patient's problem?" Angela asked. She sat down in the seat next to his.

"That's part of what's so upsetting," David said. "I don't really know. She came in with sinusitis which was improving with antibiotics. But then she began to develop pneumonia for some unknown reason. Actually, first she became drowsy. Then she became apathetic, and finally she had a seizure. I've had neurology, oncology, and infectious disease look at her. No one has any bright ideas."

"Then you shouldn't be so hard on yourself," Angela said.

"Except I'm responsible," David said. "I'm her doctor."

"I wish I could help," Angela said.

"Thank you," David said. He reached out and gave Angela's shoulder a squeeze. "I appreciate your concern because I know you mean it. Unfortunately, there's nothing you can do directly except understand why I can't get so worked up about Hodges' death."

"I can't just let it go," Angela said.

"But it could be dangerous," David said. "You don't know who you're up against. Whoever killed Hodges isn't likely to be thrilled by your poking around. Who knows what such a person might do? Look what he did to Hodges."

Angela looked into the fire, mesmerized for the moment by the white-hot coals that shimmered ominously in the intense heat. Potential danger to her family was her motivation for wanting Hodges' murder solved. She hadn't considered that her investigation itself could put them in greater jeopardy. Yet all she had to do was close her eyes and see the luminol glow in her kitchen or remember the horrid fractures on the X rays in the autopsy room to know that

David had a point: a person capable of that kind of violence was not someone who should be provoked.

Worried about Mary Ann, David was up before the sun. He stole out of the house without waking Angela and Nikki and got on his bike. Just as the sun was inching above the eastern horizon, he crossed the Roaring River. It was as cold as it had been the previous morning. Another heavy frost blanketed the fields and covered the naked branches of the leafless trees with a vitreous sheen.

David's early-morning arrival surprised the ICU nurses. Mary Ann's condition had not changed dramatically although she had developed moderately severe diarrhea. David was amazed and grateful for how the nurses took such a development in stride. It was a tribute to their compassion and dedication.

Reviewing Mary Ann's case again from the beginning, David did not have any new ideas. He even called one of his past professors in Boston whom he knew to be a chronic early riser. After hearing about the case, the professor volunteered to come immediately. David was overwhelmed by the man's commitment and generosity.

While he waited for his professor to arrive, David made the rounds to see his other hospitalized patients. Everyone was doing fine. He thought about sending Jonathan Eakins home but decided to keep him another day just to be sure his cardiac status was truly stable.

Once his professor arrived some hours later, David presented Mary Ann as if he were back in his training program. The professor listened intently, examined Mary Ann with great care, then went over the chart in detail. But even he had no new insights. David saw him out to his car, thanking him profusely for having made the trip.

With nothing else to do at the hospital, David headed home. He avoided Saturday morning basketball since he was still smarting from the unpleasant confrontation with Kevin Yansen over their tennis match. In his precarious emotional state, David felt that he'd do well to avoid Kevin's unpleasant competitiveness for another week.

When he got home, Angela and Nikki were just finishing breakfast. David teased them that they'd missed half the day. While Angela tended to Nikki's respiratory treatment, David went down into the basement and removed the crime scene tape. Then he took some of the storm windows out to the yard via the steps leading outdoors.

He'd put the first-floor windows up by the time Nikki joined him.

"When are we going to . . ." Nikki began to ask.

David put his finger to his lips to shush Nikki while he pointed to the nearby kitchen window where Angela could be seen. "As soon as we clean up," he said.

David let Nikki help him carry each of the screens down into the basement. He could have done it more easily himself, but she liked to think she was helping. They leaned them up against the base of the stairs where the storm windows had originally been.

With that accomplished, David and Nikki announced to Angela that they were heading into town on a shopping mission. Then they rode off on their bikes. Angela enjoyed seeing them having so much fun, though she did feel excluded.

Left alone, Angela began to feel a little edgy. She noticed every creak the empty house made. She tried to immerse herself in the book she was reading, but before long she was up locking the doors and even the windows. Ending up in the kitchen, Angela could not suppress her imagination from coating the walls with blood.

"I can't live like this," Angela said aloud, realizing how paranoid she was becoming. "But what am I going to do?"

She stepped over to the kitchen table, the legs of which she had scrubbed with the strongest disinfectant Mr. Staley had in his hardware store. Her fingers brushed its surface. She wondered if luminol would still fluoresce now that she had cleaned it so thoroughly. She still didn't like the idea that Hodges' killer was free. Yet she took to heart David's warning that it was dangerous for her to be snooping around about the murder.

Walking over to the phone directory, she looked up "private investigators" but didn't find any entries. Then she looked up "detectives" and found a list. Most were security businesses, but there were several individuals listed as well. One— a Phil Calhoun—was in Rutland, which was only a short drive away.

Before she had time to reconsider, Angela dialed the number. A man with a husky, slow, and deliberate voice answered.

Angela hadn't given much thought to what she would say. She finally stammered that she wanted to investigate a murder.

"Sounds interesting," Calhoun said.

Angela tried to picture the man on the other end of the wire. Judging from the voice she imagined a powerfully built man with broad shoulders, dark hair, maybe even a mustache.

"Perhaps we could meet," Angela suggested.

"You want me to come there or do you want to come here?" Calhoun asked.

Angela thought for a moment. She didn't want David finding out what she was up to—not just yet.

"I'll come to you," she said.

"I'll be waiting," Calhoun said after he gave her directions.

Angela ran upstairs, changed clothes, then left a note saying "Gone shopping" for David and Nikki.

Calhoun's office was also his home. She had no trouble finding it. In the driveway she noticed his Ford pickup truck had a rifle rack in the back of the cab and a sticker on the back bumper that read: "This Vehicle Climbed Mount Washington."

Phil Calhoun invited her into his living room and offered her a seat on a threadbare sofa. He was far from her romantic image of a private investigator. Although he was a big man, he was overweight and considerably older than she'd guessed from his voice. She figured he was in his early sixties. His face was a little doughy, but his gray eyes were bright. He was wearing a wool black and white checkered hunting shirt. His cotton work pants were held up by black suspenders. On his head was a cap with the words "Roscoe Electric" emblazoned above the visor.

"Mind if I smoke?" Calhoun asked, holding up a box of Antonio y Cleopatra cigars.

"It's your house," Angela said.

"What's the story about this murder?" Calhoun asked as he leaned back in his chair.

Angela gave a capsule summary of the whole affair.

"Sounds interesting to me," Calhoun said. "I'll be delighted to take the case on an hourly basis. Now about me: I'm a retired state police officer and a widower. That's about it. Any questions?"

Angela studied Calhoun as he casually smoked. He was laconic like most New Englanders. He seemed forthright, a trait she appreciated. Beyond that, she had no way of judging the man's competence, although having been a state policeman seemed auspicious.

"Why did you leave the force?" Angela asked.

"Compulsory retirement," Calhoun said.

"Have you ever been involved in a murder case?" Angela asked.

"Not as a civilian," Calhoun said.

"What type of cases do you usually handle?" Angela asked.

"Marital problems, shoplifting, bartender embezzlement, that sort of thing."

"Do you think you could handle this case?" Angela asked.

"No question," Calhoun said. "I grew up in a small Vermont town similar to Bartlet. I'm familiar with the environment; hell, I even know some of the people who live there. I know the kinds of feuds that simmer for years and the mindset of the people involved. I'm the right man for the job because I can ask questions without sticking out like a sore thumb."

Angela drove back to Bartlet wondering if she'd done the right thing in hiring Phil Calhoun. She also wondered how and when she'd tell David.

Arriving at home Angela was distressed to find that Nikki was by herself.

David had gone to the hospital to check on his patient. Angela asked Nikki if David had tried to get Alice to come over while he was away.

"Nope," Nikki said, unconcerned. "Daddy said he'd be back soon and that you'd probably show up before he did."

Angela decided she'd talk with David. Under the circumstances, she did not like Nikki being in the house by herself. She could hardly believe that David would leave Nikki alone, and the fact that he did eliminated any reservations Angela had about hiring Phil Calhoun.

Angela told Nikki that she wanted to keep the doors locked, and they went around to check them all. The only one that was open was the back door. As she prepared a quick snack for Nikki, she casually asked what she and her father had been doing that morning, but Nikki refused to say.

When David returned, Angela took him aside to discuss his leaving Nikki by herself. David was defensive at first but then agreed to avoid it in the future.

Soon David and Nikki were thick as thieves again, but Angela ignored them. Saturday afternoons were one of her favorite times. With little opportunity to cook during the week, she liked to spend a good portion of the day hovering over her recipe books and putting together a gourmet meal. It was a therapeutic experience for her.

By midafternoon she had the menu planned. Leaving the kitchen, she opened the cellar door and started down. She was on her way to the freezer to get some veal bones to make a golden stock when she realized she'd not been back to the basement since the technicians had been there. Angela's steps slowed. She was a little nervous going down in the cellar by herself and toyed with the idea of asking David to accompany her. But she realized she was being silly. Besides, she didn't want to spook Nikki any more than she already was.

Angela continued the rest of the way down the stairs and headed toward the freezer against the far wall. As she walked she glanced in the direction of Hodges' former tomb and was relieved to see that David had stacked the window screens over the hole.

Angela was just reaching into the freezer when she heard a scraping sound behind her. She froze. She could have sworn the noise had come from behind the stairs. Angela allowed the freezer to close before she slowly turned around to face the dimly lit cellar.

With utter horror, Angela saw the screens begin to move. She blinked, then looked again, hoping that it had been her imagination. But then the screens fell over with a loud, echoing crash.

Angela tried to scream, but no sound came out of her mouth. She tried to move, but she couldn't. With great effort, she at last took a step, then another. But she was only halfway to the stairs when Hodges' partially skeletonized face emerged from the tomb. Then the man himself staggered out. He seemed disoriented until he saw Angela. Then he started toward her, his arms extended.

Angela's terror translated to motion. She ran for the stairs in earnest, but she was too late. Hodges cut her off and grabbed her arm.

Feeling the creature's hand on her wrist unlocked Angela's voice. She screamed, struggling to free herself. Then she saw another ghoul emerge from the tomb, a smaller but equally hideous fiend with the exact same face. Suddenly Angela realized that Hodges was laughing.

Angela could only stare, dumbfounded, as David pulled off a rubber mask. Nikki, the smaller ghoul, pulled an identical mask from her face. Both of them were laughing hysterically.

At first Angela was embarrassed, but her humiliation quickly turned to fury. There was nothing funny about this gag. She pushed David aside and stomped upstairs.

David and Nikki continued to laugh, but their laughter soon faltered as they began to understand how much they had frightened Angela.

"Do you think she's really mad?" Nikki asked.

"I'm afraid so," David said. "I think we'd better go up and talk with her."

Angela refused to even look at them as she busied herself in the kitchen.

"But we're sorry," David repeated for the third time.

"We both are, Mom," Nikki insisted. But then both Nikki and David had to suppress giggles.

"We never imagined you'd be fooled for a minute," David said, trying to control himself. "Honest! We thought you'd guess immediately; it was so corny."

"Yeah, Mom," Nikki said. "We thought you'd guess because next Sunday's Halloween. These are going to be our Halloween costumes. We even bought the same mask for you."

"Well, you can just throw it away," Angela said.

Nikki's face fell. Her eyes welled with tears.

Angela looked at her and her anger melted. "Now don't you get upset," she said. She drew Nikki to her. "I know I'm overreacting," she added, "but I was really scared. And I don't think it was funny."

Eager to get started on what was easily the most intriguing case he'd landed since he started his little side business to supplement his pension and social security, Phil Calhoun drove into Bartlet in the middle of the afternoon. He parked his pickup truck within the shade of the Bartlet library and walked across the green to the police station.

"Wayne around?" he asked the duty officer.

The duty officer merely pointed down the hall. He was reading a copy of the *Bartlet Sun*.

Calhoun walked down and knocked on Robertson's open door. Robertson looked up, smiled, and invited Phil to take a load off his feet.

Robertson tipped back in his chair and accepted an Antonio y Cleopatra from Calhoun.

"Working late on a Saturday," Calhoun said. "Must be a lot going on here in Bartlet."

"Goddamned paperwork," Robertson said. "It sucks. And it gets worse every year."

Calhoun nodded. "I read in the paper that old Doc Hodges turned up," he said.

"Yeah," Robertson said. "Caused a little stir, but it's already died down. Good riddance. The man was a pain in the ass."

"How so?" Calhoun asked.

Robertson's face became red as he aired yet again his litany against Dr. Dennis Hodges. He admitted that there had been numerous times he'd almost decked the man.

"I gather Hodges wasn't the most popular man in town," Calhoun said.

Robertson gave a short, caustic laugh.

"Much action on the case?" Calhoun asked casually, blowing smoke up toward the ceiling.

"Nah," Robertson said. "We spun our wheels a bit back when Hodges disappeared, but it was mostly going through the motions. Nobody cared much, not even his wife. Practically ex-wife. She'd just about moved back to Boston even before Hodges disappeared."

"What about now?" Calhoun asked. "The *Boston Globe* said the state police were investigating."

"They were just going through the motions, too," Robertson said. "The medical examiner called the state's attorney. State's attorney sent some junior assistant to check it out. This assistant called in the state police, who then sent some crime-scene investigators to the site. But after that a state police lieutenant called me. I told him it wasn't worth his time and that we'd handle it. And as you know better than most people, the state police take their cue from us local guys on a case of this sort unless there's pressure from someplace like the state attorney's office or from some politician. Hell, the state police have more pressing cases to attend to. Same with us. Besides, it's been eight months. The trail's stone cold."

"What are you guys working on these days?" Calhoun asked.

"We've had a series of rapes and attacks up in the hospital parking lot," Robertson said.

"Any luck snagging the perpetrator?" Calhoun asked.

"Not yet," Robertson said.

After leaving the police station, Calhoun wandered down Main Street and stopped in the local bookstore. The proprietor, Jane Weincoop, had been a friend of Calhoun's wife. Calhoun's wife had been a big reader, especially the last year of her life when she'd been confined to bed.

Jane took Calhoun into her office, which was only a tiny desk stuck in the corner of the stock room. Calhoun said he was just passing through and after a bit of chitchat and catching up, he managed to steer the conversation to Dennis Hodges.

"The discovery of his body was certainly news in Bartlet," Jane admitted.

"I understand he wasn't a popular man," Calhoun said. "Who all had it in for him?"

Jane gave Calhoun a look. "Is this a professional or personal visit?" she asked with a wry smile.

"Just curiosity," Calhoun said with a wink. "But I'd still appreciate it if you'd keep my question to yourself."

Half an hour later Calhoun wandered back out into the fading afternoon sunlight clutching a list of over twenty people who had disliked Hodges. The list included the president of the bank, the owner of the Mobil station near the interstate, the town's retarded handyman, the chief of police whom Calhoun already knew about, a handful of merchants and store owners, and a half dozen doctors.

Calhoun was surprised by the length of the list but not unhappy. After all, the longer the list, the more billable hours he'd be logging in.

Continuing his trek up Main Street, Calhoun stopped into Harrison's Pharmacy. The pharmacist, Harley Strombell, was the brother of one of Calhoun's fellow troopers, Wendell Strombell.

Harley wasn't fooled any more than Jane had been about the nature of Calhoun's inquiries, but he promised to be discreet. He even added to Calhoun's list by offering his own name as well as those of Ned Banks, the owner of the New England Coat Hanger Company, Harold Traynor, and Helen Beaton, the new hospital administrator.

"Why did you dislike the man?" Calhoun asked.

"It was a personal thing," Harley said. "Hodges lacked even the rudimentary social graces." Harley explained that he'd had a small branch pharmacy up at the hospital until one day without explanation or warning, Hodges just kicked him out.

"I mean it was natural for the expanding hospital to have its own outpatient pharmacy," Harley said. "I understood that. But it was handled very badly, thanks to Dennis Hodges."

Calhoun left the pharmacy wondering how long his list would get before he could start whittling it down to serious suspects. He had close to twenty-five names and there were still a few more contacts in Bartlet he could check out before he considered the list complete.

Since most of the shops were closing for the night, Calhoun crossed the street and headed for the Iron Horse Inn. It was an establishment that held many pleasant memories for him. It had been his wife's favorite restaurant for special-occasion dinners, like celebrating anniversaries and birthdays.

Carleton Harris, the bartender, recognized Calhoun from across the room.

By the time Calhoun got to the bar a glass of Wild Turkey neat was waiting for him. Carleton even drew half a mug's worth of draft beer for himself so they could clink glasses in a toast.

"Working on anything interesting these days?" Carleton asked after downing his spot of beer.

"I think so," Calhoun said. He leaned in toward the bar and Carleton instinctively did the same.

Angela didn't say a word to David and avoided eye contact as they got ready for bed. David guessed that Angela was still irritated about the basement prank with the Halloween masks. He disliked moodiness and wanted to clear the air.

"I'm getting the message you're still upset about Nikki and me scaring you," he said. "Can't we talk about it?"

"What makes you say I'm angry?" Angela asked innocently.

"Come on, Angela," David said. "You've been giving me the silent treatment ever since Nikki went to bed."

"I suppose I'm disappointed you'd do such a thing when you know how upset I am about that body. I would have thought you'd have been more sensitive."

"I said I was sorry," David said. "I still can't believe you just didn't laugh the second you saw us. It never occurred to me you'd get as frightened as you did. Besides, it wasn't just an idle prank. I did it for Nikki's benefit."

"What do you mean?" Angela asked skeptically.

"With the nightmares she's been having, I thought it would help to treat the subject with humor. It was a ruse to get her in the basement without being afraid. And it worked: she was so focused on surprising you, she didn't think about her fears."

"You could have at least warned me."

"I didn't think I had to. Like I said, I never thought you'd be fooled. And the conspiratorial nature of the activity is what got Nikki so involved."

Angela eyed her husband. She could tell he was remorseful as well as sincere. Suddenly she felt more embarrassed she'd fallen for the trick than angry. She put down her toothbrush and went over to David and gave him a hug. "I'm sorry I got so mad," she said. "I guess I'm stressed out. I love you."

"I love you, too," David echoed. "I should have told you what we were doing. You could have pretended not to know. I just didn't think. I've been so distracted lately. I feel so stressed out, too. Mary Ann Schiller is no better. She's going to die. I just know it."

"Come on now," Angela said. "You can never be sure."

"I don't know about that," David said. "Come on, let's get to bed." As they finished washing he told Angela about his professor's having driven all the way from Boston and that even he had nothing to add.

"Are you any more depressed?" Angela asked.

"About the same," David said. "I woke up at four-fifteen this morning and couldn't go back to sleep. I keep thinking there's something I'm missing with these patients; maybe they've picked up some unknown viral disease. But I feel as though my hands are tied. It's so frustrating to have to think about Kelley and CMV every time I order a test or a consult. It's gotten so bad that I even feel like I have to rush through my daily office schedule."

"You mean to see more patients?" Angela asked. They moved from the bathroom into the bedroom.

David nodded. "More pressure from CMV via Kelley," he said. "I hate to admit it, but what it means is that I have to avoid talking with patients and answering their questions. It's not hard because it's easy to bully patients, but I don't like it. I wonder if the patients realize they are being shortchanged. A lot of critical clues for making the right diagnosis come from the kind of spontaneous comments patients make when you spend a little time with them."

"I have a confession to make," Angela said suddenly.

"What are you talking about?" David asked as he got into bed.

"I also did something today I should have spoken to you about before I did it," Angela said.

"What?" he asked.

As Angela slipped under the covers, she told David about going to Rutland and hiring Phil Calhoun to investigate Hodges' murder.

David looked at her, then looked away. He didn't say anything. Angela knew he was angry.

"At least I took your suggestion that it was dangerous for me to investigate it," Angela said. "Now we have a professional doing it."

"What makes this man a professional?" David asked, looking back at Angela.

"He's a retired state policeman."

"I was hoping you were going to be reasonable about this Hodges affair," David said. "Hiring a private investigator is going a little overboard. It's throwing money away."

"It's not throwing money away if it is important to me," Angela said. "And it should be important to you if you expect me to continue living in this house."

David sighed, turned out his bedside light, and rolled away from Angela.

She knew she should have warned him about hiring the investigator. She too sighed as she reached for her light. Maybe she didn't go about it the right way, but she was still confident that hiring Calhoun had been a good idea.

Hardly had the lights been turned out than they heard several loud thumps followed by the sound of Rusty's barking.

Angela turned her light back on and got out of bed. David did the same. They grabbed their robes and stepped into the hall. David turned on the hall light. Rusty was at the top of the stairs, looking down toward the darkened first floor. He was growling ferociously.

"Did you check to see if the front door was locked?" Angela whispered.

"Yes," David said. He walked down the hall and patted Rusty's head. "What is it, big fellow?"

Rusty went down the stairs and began barking at the front door. David followed him. Angela stood at the top of the stairs.

David unlocked the front door.

"Be careful," Angela warned.

"Why don't you slip on one of those Halloween masks," David called up to Angela. "We'll give whoever it is a good scare."

"Stop joking," Angela said. "This isn't funny."

David stepped out onto the porch holding on to Rusty's collar. The dark sky was strewn with stars. A quarter moon provided enough light to see all the way down to the road, but there wasn't anything unusual to be seen.

"Come on, Rusty," David urged as he turned around. As he approached the door he saw a typed note nailed to the muntin. He pulled it off. It read: "Mind your own business. Forget Hodges."

Closing the door and locking it, David climbed the stairs and handed the note to Angela. She followed David into the bedroom.

"I'll take this to the police," Angela said.

"Hell, it could have come from the police," David replied. He climbed back into bed and turned out the light. Angela did the same. Rusty padded back down the hall to rejoin Nikki, who'd evidently not stirred.

"Now I'm wide awake," David complained.

"So am I," Angela said.

The jangle of the telephone made them both jump. David answered it on the first ring. Angela turned on the light and watched her husband. His face fell as he listened. Then he hung up the phone.

"Mary Ann Schiller had another seizure and died," he said. "I told you it would happen." He raised a hand to his face and covered his eyes. Angela moved over and put her arms around him. She could tell he was crying silently.

"I wonder if this ever gets easier," he said. He wiped his eyes, then began to get dressed.

Angela accompanied him as far as the back door. After she saw him off, she locked the door behind him, then watched as the Volvo's taillights descended the driveway and disappeared.

Stepping from the mudroom into the kitchen, Angela could still see the eerie glow of the luminol in her mind's eye. She shivered. She did not like being in the huge old house at night without David.

At the hospital, David met Mary Ann's husband, Donald, for the first time. Donald, his teenage son Matt, and Mary Ann's parents were in the patients' lounge across from the ICU quietly talking and consoling each other. As with the Kleber family and the Tarlow family, they were appreciative of David's efforts. None of them had a bad word for him or a complaint.

"We had her for longer than Dr. Mieslich estimated," Donald said. His eyes were red and his hair was tousled as if he had been sleeping. "She even got to go back to her job at the library."

David commiserated with the family, telling them what they wanted to hear: she hadn't suffered. But David had to confess his confusion as to the cause of her seizures.

"You didn't expect seizures?" Donald asked.

"Not at all," David said. "Especially since her MRI was normal."

Everyone nodded as if they understood. Then, on the spur of the moment, David went against Kelley's orders and asked the family if they would permit an autopsy. He explained that it might answer a lot of questions.

"I don't know," Donald said. He looked over at his in-laws. They were equally indecisive.

"Why don't you think about it overnight?" David suggested. "We'll keep the body here."

Leaving the ICU, David felt despondent. He didn't go directly home. Instead, he wandered over to the dimly lit second-floor nurses' station. It was a quiet time of the night. Trying to keep his mind on other things, he glanced at Jonathan Eakins' chart. As he was perusing it, one of the night nurses told David that Mr. Eakins was awake, watching TV. David walked down and poked his head in.

"Everything okay?" David asked.

"What a committed doctor," Jonathan said with a smile. "You must live here."

"Is that ticker of yours staying nice and regular?" David asked.

"Like clockwork," Jonathan said. "When do I get to go home?"

"Probably today," David said. "I see they changed your bed."

"Sure did," Jonathan said. "They couldn't seem to fix the old one. Thanks for giving them a nudge. My complaints fell on deaf ears."

"No problem," David said. "See you tomorrow."

David left the hospital and got into his car. He started the engine but didn't put the car in gear. He'd had three unexpected deaths in one week: patients other doctors had been keeping alive and healthy. He couldn't help but question his competence. He wondered if he were meant to be a doctor. Maybe those three patients would still be alive if they'd had another physician.

He knew he couldn't sit in the hospital parking lot all night, so David finally put the car in gear and drove home. He was surprised to see a light on in the family room. By the time he'd parked and gotten out of the car, Angela was at the door. She was holding a medical journal.

"Are you all right?" she asked as she closed and locked the door behind David.

"I've been better," David said. "Why are you still up?" He removed his coat and motioned for Angela to precede him into the kitchen.

"There was no way I would sleep without you here," Angela said over her shoulder as she passed through the kitchen into the hall. "Not after that note was nailed to our door. And I've been thinking. If you have to go out in the middle of the night like this, I want to have a gun here."

David reached out and pulled Angela to a stop. "We'll have no guns in our house," he said. "You know the statistics as well as I do about guns in houses where there are children."

"Such statistics are not for physicians' families with a single, intelligent child," Angela countered. "Besides, I'll take responsibility for making sure Nikki is well acquainted with the gun and its potential."

David let go of his wife and headed for the stairs. "I don't have the energy or the emotional strength to argue with you."

"Good," Angela said as she caught up with him.

Upstairs, David decided to take another shower. When he came into the bedroom Angela was reading her pathology journal. She was as wide awake as he.

"Last night after dinner you said that you wished you could help me," David said. "Do you remember?"

"Of course I remember," Angela said.

"You might get your wish," David said. "An hour ago I asked the Schiller family if they would permit an autopsy. They said they'd think about it overnight and talk to me tomorrow."

"Unfortunately, it's not up to the family," Angela said. "The hospital doesn't do autopsies on CMV patients."

"But I have another idea," David said. "You could do it on your own."

Angela considered the suggestion. "Maybe I could," she said. "Tomorrow is Sunday and the lab is closed except for emergency chemistries."

"That was exactly my thought," David said.

"I could go to the hospital with you tomorrow and talk to the family," Angela said, warming to the idea.

"I'd appreciate it," David said. "If you could find some specific reason why she died, it would make me feel a whole lot better."

SUNDAY • OCTOBER 24

David and Angela were exhausted in the morning, but Nikki was well rested. She'd slept through the night without a nightmare and was eager to begin the day.

On Sundays the Wilsons got up early for church, followed by brunch at the Iron Horse Inn.

Attending church had been Angela's idea. Her motivation wasn't religious, it was social. She thought it would be a good way to join the Bartlet community. She'd settled on the Methodist church on the town green. It was far and away the most popular in town.

"Do we have to go?" David whined that morning. He was sitting on the side of the bed. He was trying to dress with clumsy fingers. He'd again awakened before dawn despite having gone to sleep so late. He'd lain awake for several hours. He'd just fallen back asleep when Nikki and Rusty had come bounding into the room.

"Nikki will be disappointed if we don't go," Angela called from the bathroom.

David finished dressing with resignation. A half hour later, the family climbed into the Volvo and drove into town. From past experience they knew to park in the Inn's parking lot and walk to the green. Parking near the church itself was always a disaster. The traffic on a Sunday was so bad it had to be supervised by one of the town's policemen.

That morning Wayne Robertson was on duty as traffic controller. A stainless-steel whistle protruded from his mouth.

"Isn't this handy," Angela said as soon as she spotted him. "You guys wait here."

Darting away before David could stop her, Angela went directly to the chief of police with the anonymous note in hand.

"Excuse me," Angela said. "I have something I'd like you to see. This was nailed to our door last night while we were in bed." She handed him the note, then rested her knuckles on her hips, her arms akimbo, waiting for his response.

Robertson allowed the whistle to drop from his mouth. It was attached by a cord around his neck. He glanced at the note, then handed it back. "I'd say it's a good suggestion. I recommend that you take the advice."

Angela chuckled. "I'm not asking your opinion as to the note's suggestion," she said. "I want you to find out who left it on our door."

"Well, now," he said slowly, scratching the back of his head, "it's not a lot to go on except for the fact that it was obviously typed on a nineteen fifty-two Smith Corona with a defective lowercase 'o.' "

For an instant, Angela began to reevaluate her estimation of Robertson's abilities. But then she realized he was making fun of her.

"I'm sure you'll do your best," Angela said with commensurate sarcasm, "but considering your attitude toward the Hodges murder case, I guess we can't expect miracles."

Honking horns and a few shouts from frustrated drivers forced Robertson's attention back to the traffic, which had quickly become a muddle. As he did his best to unsnarl the congestion, he said: "You and your little family are newcomers to Bartlet. Maybe you ought to think twice about interfering in matters that don't concern you. You'll only make trouble for yourself."

"So far I've only gotten trouble from you," Angela said. "And I understand that you happen to be one of the people who's not so sorry about Hodges' death. I understand you mistakenly blame him for your wife's death."

Robertson stopped directing traffic and turned to Angela. His chubby cheeks had become beet red. "What did you say?" he demanded.

Just then David slipped in between Angela and Robertson, forcing Angela away. He'd been eavesdropping on the conversation from a few feet away and he didn't like the direction it was taking.

Angela tried to repeat her statement, but David gave her arm a sharp tug. Through clenched teeth he whispered to her to shut up. When he got her far enough away he grabbed her shoulders. "What the hell has gotten into you?" he demanded. "You're taunting a man who's obviously got some kind of personality problem. I know you have a penchant for the dramatic, but this is pushing it."

"He was ridiculing me," Angela complained.

"Stop it," David commanded. "You're sounding like a child."

"He's supposed to be protecting us," Angela snapped. "He's supposed to uphold the law. But he isn't any more interested in this threatening note than he is in finding out who murdered Hodges."

"Calm down!" David said. "You're making a scene."

Angela's eyes left David's and swept around the immediate area. A number of people had paused on their way into the church. They were all staring.

Self-consciously, Angela put the note away in her purse, smoothed her dress, and reached for Nikki's hand.

"Come on," she said. "Let's not be late for the service."

With Alice Doherty recruited to watch over Nikki and Caroline, David and Angela drove to the hospital. Nikki had met Caroline after the church service, and Caroline had accompanied them to the Iron Horse Inn for brunch.

At the hospital, David and Angela met Donald Schiller and his in-laws, the Josephsons, in the lobby. They sat on the benches to the right of the entrance to discuss the proposed autopsy.

"My husband has asked you for permission to do an autopsy," Angela said. "I'm here to tell you that I will be the one to do it if you agree. Since neither the hospital nor CMV will pay for this service, I'm offering to do it on my own time. It will be free. It also might provide some important information."

"That's very generous of you," Donald said. "We still weren't sure what to do this morning, but after talking to you, I think I feel okay about it." Donald looked at the Josephsons. They nodded. "I think Mary Ann would have wanted it too, if it could help other people."

"I think it might," Angela said.

David and Angela went down into the basement to retrieve Mary Ann's body from the morgue. They took it up to the lab and rolled it into the autopsy

room. The room had not been used for autopsies for several years and had become a storeroom. They had to move boxes from the old stainless-steel autopsy
table.

David had planned to assist, but it quickly became apparent to Angela that
he was having a hard time dealing with the situation. He was not accustomed to
autopsies, and this was the body of a patient he had been treating only the day
before.

"Why don't you go see your patients?" Angela suggested when she was ready
to begin.

"You sure you can manage?" David asked.

Angela nodded. "I'll page you when I'm done, and you can help me get her
back downstairs."

"Thank you," David said. At the door he turned. "Remember, consider the
possibility of an unknown viral disease. So be careful. And also, I want a full toxicological workup."

"Why the toxicology?" Angela asked.

"I want to cover all the bases," David said. "Humor me, okay?"

"You've got it," Angela said agreeably. "Now get out of here!" She picked up
a scalpel and waved for David to leave.

David let the autopsy room doors close behind him before he took off the
hood, gown, and mask he'd donned for the postmortem. He was relieved to
have been excused. David left the lab and climbed up to the patient floor.

He fully intended to discharge Jonathan Eakins, especially after he he'd been
told by the nursing staff that there'd been no abnormal heartbeats. But that was
before he went into Jonathan's room to say hello. Instead of experiencing
Jonathan's usual cheerfulness, David found the man depressed. Jonathan said he
felt terrible.

Sensitized by recent events, David's mouth became instantly dry. He felt a
rush of adrenaline shoot through his body. Afraid to hear the answer, he asked
Jonathan what was wrong.

"Everything," Jonathan said. His face was slack and his eyes lusterless. A
string of drool hung down from the corner of his mouth. "I started having
cramps, then nausea and diarrhea. I've no appetite and I have to keep swallowing."

"What do you mean you have to keep swallowing?" David asked fearfully.

"My mouth keeps filling up with saliva," Jonathan said. "I have to swallow
or spit it out."

David desperately tried to put these symptoms into some recognizable category. Salivation keyed off a memory from medical school. He remembered it
was one of the symptoms of mercury poisoning.

"Did you eat anything strange last night?" David asked.

"No," Jonathan said.

"What about your IV?" David asked.

"That was removed yesterday on your orders," Jonathan said.

David was panicky. Except for the salivation, Jonathan's symptoms reminded him of the symptoms Marjorie, John, and Mary Ann had experienced prior to their rapid deterioration and deaths.

"What's wrong with me?" Jonathan asked, sensing David's anxiety. "This isn't something serious, is it?"

"I was hoping to send you home," David said, avoiding a direct answer. "But if you are feeling this bad, maybe we'd better keep you for a day or so."

"Whatever you say," Jonathan said. "But let's nip this in the bud; I've got a wedding anniversary coming up this weekend."

David hurried back to the nurses' station with his mind in an uproar. He kept telling himself that it couldn't happen again. It was impossible. The odds were too small.

David threw himself into a chair and took Jonathan's chart from the rack. He went over it carefully, re-reading everything, including all the nurses' notes. He noticed that Jonathan's temperature that morning had been one hundred degrees. Did that represent a fever? David didn't know; it was borderline.

Rushing back into Jonathan's room, David had him sit on the side of his bed so that he could listen to his chest. His lungs were perfectly clear.

Returning to the nurses' station David leaned his elbows on the counter and covered his face with his hands. He had to think. He didn't know what to do, yet he felt he had to do something.

Impulsively David reached for the phone. He already knew the response he could expect from Kelley and CMV, but he didn't care. He called Dr. Mieslich, the oncologist, and Dr. Hasselbaum, the infectious disease specialist, and asked them both to come in immediately. David told them he believed he had a patient who was in the very early stages of the same condition that had proved mortal three times in as many days.

While David was waiting for the consults to arrive, he ordered a barrage of tests. There was always the chance that Jonathan would wake up the next day feeling fine, but David didn't think he could risk his patient's going the route of Marjorie, John, and Mary Ann. His sixth sense was telling him that Jonathan was already locked in a mortal struggle, and lately David's intuition had not been wrong.

The infectious disease specialist was first to arrive. After a quick chat with David, he went in to see the patient. Dr. Mieslich came in next. He brought with him his records of Jonathan's treatment when he had been his patient. Dr. Mieslich and David went over the record page by page. By then Dr. Hasselbaum was finished examining Jonathan. He joined David and Dr. Mieslich at the nurses' station.

The three men had just begun to discuss the case when David became aware that the two doctors were looking over his shoulder. David turned to see Kelley looming above him.

"Dr. Wilson," Kelley said, "may I have a word with you in the patients' lounge?"

"I'm too busy right now," David said. He turned back to his consults.

"I'm afraid I must insist," Kelley said. He tapped David on the shoulder. David brushed his hand off. He did not like Kelley touching him.

"This will give me a chance to examine the patient," Dr. Mieslich said. He stood up and left the nurses' station.

"I'll use the time to write up my consult," Dr. Hasselbaum said. He took his pen from his jacket pocket and reached for Jonathan's chart.

"All right," David said, standing up. "Lead on, Mr. Kelley."

Kelley walked across the corridor and stepped into the patient lounge. After David entered the room Kelley closed the door.

"I presume you know Ms. Helen Beaton, the hospital president," Kelley said, "and Mr. Michael Caldwell, the medical director." He gestured toward both people, who were sitting on the couch.

"Yes, of course," David said. He remembered Caldwell from Angela's interviews, and he'd met Beaton at several hospital functions. David reached out and shook hands with each. Neither bothered to stand up.

Kelley sat down. David did likewise.

David anxiously glanced around at the faces arrayed around him. He expected trouble from Kelley, thinking this meeting had to do with the autopsy on Mary Ann Schiller. He guessed that was why the hospital people were there. He hoped this didn't spell trouble for Angela.

"I suppose I should be forthright," Kelley said. "You probably wonder how we've responded so quickly to your handling of Jonathan Eakins."

David was flabbergasted: how could these three be here to talk to him about Jonathan when he'd only just started investigating the man's symptoms?

"We were called by the nursing utilization coordinator," Kelley explained. "She had been alerted by the floor nurses according to previous instructions. Utilization control is vital. We feel the need to intervene. As I've told you before, you are using far too many consults, especially outside the CMV family."

"And far too many laboratory tests," Beaton said.

"Too many diagnostic tests as well," Caldwell said.

David stared at the three administrators in disbelief. Each returned his stare with impunity. They were a tribunal sitting in judgment. It was like the Inquisition. He was being tried for economic medical heresy, and not one of his inquisitors was a physician.

"We want to remind you that you are dealing with a patient who has been treated for metastatic prostate cancer," Kelley said.

"We're afraid you've already been too lavish and wasteful with your orders," Beaton said.

"You have a history of excessive use of resources on three previous patients who were clearly terminal," Caldwell said.

David struggled with his emotions. Since he'd already been questioning his competence as a result of the three successive deaths, he was vulnerable to the administrators' criticism. "My allegiance is to the patient," David said meekly. "Not to an organization or an institution."

"We can appreciate your philosophy," Beaton said. "But such a philosophy has led to the economic crisis in medical care. You must expand your horizons. We have an allegiance to the entire community of patients. Everything cannot be done to everybody. Judgment is needed in the rational use of limited resources."

"David, the fact of the matter is that your use of ancillary services far exceeds norms developed by your fellow physicians," Kelley told him.

There was a pause. David wasn't sure what to say. "My worry in these particular cases is that I'm seeing an unknown infectious disease. If that is the case, it would be disastrous not to diagnose it."

The three medical administrators looked at each other to see who would speak. Beaton shrugged and said: "That's out of my expertise; I'm the first to admit it."

"Mine too," Caldwell said.

"But we happen to have an independent infectious disease consult here at the moment," Kelley said. "Since CMV is already paying him, let's ask him his opinion."

Kelley went out and returned with both Dr. Martin Hasselbaum and Dr. Clark Mieslich. Introductions were made. Dr. Hasselbaum was asked if he thought that David's three deceased patients and Mr. Eakins might have been afflicted by an unknown infectious disease.

"I sincerely doubt it," Dr. Hasselbaum said. "There's no evidence whatsoever that they had an infectious disease. All three had pneumonia, but I feel the pneumonia was caused by generalized debility. In all three cases the agent was a recognized pathogen."

Kelley then asked both consults what form of treatment they thought should be given to Jonathan Eakins.

"Purely symptomatic," Dr. Mieslich said. He looked at Dr. Hasselbaum.

"That would be my recommendation as well," Dr. Hasselbaum said.

"You both have also seen the long list of diagnostic tests that have been ordered by Dr. Wilson," Kelley said. "Do you think any of these tests are crucial at this time?"

Dr. Mieslich and Dr. Hasselbaum exchanged glances. Dr. Hasselbaum was first to speak: "If it were my case I'd hold off and see what happened. The patient could be normal by morning."

"I agree," Dr. Mieslich said.

"Well then," Kelley said, "I think we all agree. What do you say, Dr. Wilson?"

The meeting broke up amid smiles, handshakes, and apparent amity. But David felt confused and humiliated, even depressed. He walked back to the nurses' station and canceled most of the orders he had written for Jonathan. Then he went in to see Jonathan himself.

"Thanks for having so many people come and examine me," Jonathan said.

"How do you feel?" David asked.

"I don't know," Jonathan said. "Maybe a little better."

When David got back to the autopsy room, Angela was just cleaning up. David's timing had been good. He helped return Mary Ann's body to the morgue. David noticed that Angela wasn't eager to talk about her findings. He practically had to grill her for answers.

"I didn't find much," Angela admitted.

"Nothing in the brain?" David asked.

"It was clean grossly," Angela said. "But we'll have to see what the microscopic shows."

"Any tumor?" David asked.

"I think there was a tiny bit in the abdomen," Angela said. "Again, I'll have to wait for the microscopic to be sure."

"So nothing jumped out at you as a cause of death?" David asked.

"She did have pneumonia," Angela said.

David nodded. He already knew that.

"I'm sorry I didn't find more," Angela said.

"I appreciate that you tried," David said.

As they drove home, Angela could tell that David was depressed. He'd only been answering questions in monosyllables.

"I suppose you're upset because I didn't find much on the autopsy," Angela said, pausing before she got out of the car.

David sighed. "That's just part of it," he said.

"David, you are a wonderful, talented doctor," Angela said. "Please stop being so hard on yourself."

David then told her about being hauled before the tribunal by Kelley. Angela was livid. "The nerve," she said. "Hospital administrators should not become involved in treatment."

"I don't know," David said with a sigh. "In some ways they're right. The cost of medical care is a problem. But it's so confusing when you get down to specifics with an individual patient. But the consults did side with the administrators."

At dinner, David discovered he wasn't hungry; he merely pushed his food around the plate. To make matters worse, Nikki complained that she didn't feel well.

By eight o'clock, Nikki started to sound congested and Angela took her upstairs for her respiratory therapy. When it was over, Angela found David sitting in the family room. The television was on but David wasn't watching; he was staring into the fire.

"It might be best to keep Nikki home from school tomorrow," Angela said. David didn't answer. Angela studied his face. For the moment she didn't know who she was more concerned about: Nikki or David.

When Angela first opened her eyes at the sound of the alarm, she was disappointed not to find David next to her. Getting up she pulled the drapes. The overcast skies held the promise of showers.

Angela went down to look for David. She found him sitting in the family room.

"Have you been up for long?" Angela asked, trying to sound cheerful.

"Since four," David said. "But don't be alarmed. I think I feel a bit better today." He gave Angela a half smile.

Although Angela was still concerned about David, she was pleased with Nikki's respiratory status. Nikki woke with no congestion. And she'd again made it through the night with no nightmares. Even Angela had to admit that David might have been right about the benefits of his silly prank with the Halloween masks.

Unfortunately, Angela herself had had a nightmare. It was a dream in which she came home from shopping, carrying bags of groceries, only to find the kitchen drenched in blood. But it wasn't dried blood. It was fresh blood that was running down the walls and pooling on the floor.

After Nikki's respiratory treatment, Angela listened carefully to her chest. It was definitely clear. To Nikki's delight, Angela told her she could go to school.

Despite the possibility of rain, David insisted on riding his bike to work. Angela didn't try to talk him out of it. She felt it was encouraging that he was able to muster the enthusiasm for it.

After dropping Nikki off, Angela drove on to the lab, eager to get to work. Mondays were usually busy since there was a pile-up of laboratory work from the weekend. Breezing into her office, Angela had her coat on its hanger before she noticed Wadley. He'd been standing motionless near the connecting door.

"Good morning," Angela said, again trying to sound cheerful. She hung her coat up and turned to face her chief. It was immediately apparent he wasn't happy.

"It has been brought to my attention that you did an autopsy here in the lab," Wadley said angrily.

"It's true," Angela admitted. "But I did it on my own time."

"You might have done it on your own time, but it was done in my lab," Wadley said.

"It's true I used hospital facilities," Angela said. She didn't agree that it was Wadley's lab. It was a hospital facility. He was an employee just as she was.

"You were specifically told no autopsies," Wadley said.

"I was specifically told they were not paid for by CMV," Angela said.

Wadley's cold eyes bore into Angela. "Then allow me to clear up a misunderstanding," he said. "No autopsies are to be done in this department unless I approve them. I run the department, not you. Furthermore, I've ordered the techs not to process the slides, the cultures, or the toxicological samples."

With that, Wadley returned to his office and closed the connecting door with a slam.

As usual, after one of their increasingly frequent confrontations, Angela was upset. As soon as she had composed herself, she retrieved the tissue specimens, the cultures, and the toxicological samples she had taken from Mary Ann. She then carefully packed the cultures and the toxicological material and sent them to the department where she'd trained in Boston. She had enough friends there to get them processed. The tissue samples she kept, planning on doing the slides herself.

David made the rounds of his patients, purposefully leaving Jonathan for last. When he walked into his room he was shocked. The bed was empty.

Assuming he'd been transferred to another room for some ridiculous reason as John Tarlow had been, David went to the nurses' station to ask where he could find Jonathan. Janet Colburn told him that Mr. Eakins had been transferred to the ICU by the ER physician during the night.

David was dumbfounded.

"Mr. Eakins developed difficulty breathing and lapsed into a coma," Janet added.

"Why wasn't I called?" David demanded.

"We had a specific order not to call you," Janet said.

"Issued by whom?" David asked.

"By Michael Caldwell," Janet said. "The medical director of the hospital."

"That's absurd . . ." David shouted. "Why . . ."

"We were told that if you had any questions you should call Ms. Beaton," Janet said. "Don't blame us."

David was beside himself with fury. The medical director did not have the right to leave such an order. David had never heard of anything more absurd. It was bad enough that these administrators were second-guessing him. But to intercede in patient care so directly seemed a total violation.

But David understood his argument wasn't with the nurse. He left immediately to find his patient. He arrived to discover that Jonathan's condition was indeed critical. He was in a coma and on a respirator just as Mary Ann had so recently been. David listened to his chest. Jonathan was also developing pneumonia. Twisting the IV bottle around, David saw that he was getting continuous intravenous antibiotics.

David went to the central desk to study Jonathan's chart. He quickly realized that Jonathan's course had begun to mirror David's three deceased patients. Jonathan had developed problems of the GI system, the central nervous system, and the blood system.

David picked up the phone to call Helen Beaton when the ICU unit coordinator tapped him on the shoulder and handed him another phone. It was Charles Kelley.

"The nurses told me you'd come into the ICU," Kelley said. "I'd asked them to call me the moment you appeared. I wanted to inform you that the Eakins case has been transferred to another CMV physician."

"You can't do that," David said angrily.

"Hold on, Dr. Wilson," Kelley said. "CMV certainly can transfer a patient, and I have done so. I've also notified the family, and they are in full agreement."

"Why?" David demanded. Hearing that the family was also behind the change, his voice lost most of its sting.

"We feel that you are too emotionally involved," Kelley said. "We decided it was better for everyone if you were taken off. It will give you a chance to calm down. I know you've been under a lot of strain."

David didn't know what to think, much less say. He thought about pointing out that Jonathan's condition had gone downhill just as he'd feared, but he decided against it. Kelley wasn't likely to consider anything he had to say.

"Don't forget what we said yesterday," Kelley continued. "I know you'll understand our point of view if you give it some thought."

David was of two minds when he hung up. On the one hand he was still furious to have been unilaterally removed from the case. On the other, there was an element of truth in what Kelley had said. David had only to look at his trembling hands to recognize he was overly emotionally involved.

David stumbled out of the ICU. He didn't even look at Jonathan as he passed by. Out in the hall he checked his watch. It was still too early to go to his office. Instead, he went to medical records.

David pulled the charts on Marjorie, John, and Mary Ann. Sitting in the isolation of a dictation booth, he reviewed each chart, going over the respective hospital courses. He read all his entries, all the nurses' notes, and looked at all the laboratory values and the results of diagnostic tests.

David was still toying with the idea that an unknown infection was responsible, something that his patients may have contracted while in the hospital. Such an infection was called a nosocomial infection. David had read about such incidents at other hospitals. All his patients had had pneumonia but each case had been caused by a different strain of bacteria. The pneumonia had to have been the result of some underlying infection.

The only common element in all three cases was the history. Each patient had been treated for cancer with varying mixtures of surgery, chemotherapy, and radiotherapy. Of the three treatment modalities, only chemotherapy was common to all three patients.

David was well aware that one of the side effects of chemotherapy was a general lowering of a patient's resistance because of a depressed immune system. He wondered if that fact could have had something to do with the rapid down-hill courses these patients experienced. Yet the oncologist, the expert in such matters, had given this common factor little import since in all three cases the chemotherapy had been completed long before the hospitalization. The immune systems of all three patients had long since returned to normal.

The pager on David's belt interrupted his thoughts. Looking at the LCD screen he recognized the number: it was the emergency room. Replacing the charts, David hurried downstairs.

The patient was Donald Anderson, another one of David's frequent visitors. Donald's diabetes was particularly hard to regulate. It was the main source of his frequent medical complaints. This visit was no exception. When David entered the examining stall he could immediately tell that Donald's blood sugar was out of control. Donald was semi-comatose.

David ordered a stat blood sugar and started an IV. While he was waiting for the lab result, he spoke with Shirley Anderson, Donald's wife.

"He's been having trouble for a week," Shirley complained. "But you know how stubborn he is. He refused to come to see you."

"I think we'll have to admit him," David said. "It will take a few days to get him on a new regimen."

"I was hoping you would," Shirley said. "It's difficult when he gets like this with the kids and all."

When David got the results of the blood sugar he was surprised that Donald hadn't been even more obtunded than he was. As David walked back to talk with Donald, who was now lucid thanks to the IV, David did a double take. Looking into one of the other examining stalls he saw a familiar face: it was Caroline Helmsford, Nikki's friend. Dr. Pilsner was at her side.

David slipped in alongside Caroline, opposite Dr. Pilsner. She looked up at David with pleading eyes. Covering the lower part of her face was a clear plastic mask providing oxygen. Her complexion was ashen with a slightly bluish cast. Her breathing was labored.

Dr. Pilsner was listening to her chest. He smiled at David when he saw him. When he finished auscultating, he took David aside.

"Poor thing is having a hard time," Dr. Pilsner said.

"What's wrong?" David asked.

"The usual," Dr. Pilsner replied. "She's congested and she's running a high fever."

"Will you admit her?" David asked.

"Absolutely," Dr. Pilsner said. "You know better than most that we can't take any chances with this kind of problem."

David nodded. He did know. He looked back at Caroline struggling to breathe. She looked so tiny on the big gurney and so vulnerable. The sight made him worry about Nikki. Given her cystic fibrosis, it could have been Nikki on the gurney, not Caroline.

"You've got a call from the chief medical examiner," one of the secretaries told Angela. Angela picked up the phone.

"Hope I'm not disturbing you," Walt said.

"Not at all," Angela answered.

"Got a couple of updates on the Hodges autopsy," Walt said. "Are you still interested?"

"Absolutely," Angela said.

"First of all, the man had significant alcohol in his ocular fluid," Walt said.

"I didn't know you could tell after so long," Angela said.

"If we can get ocular fluid it's easy," Walt said. "Alcohol is reasonably stable. We also got confirmation that the DNA of the skin under his nails was different from his. So it's undoubtedly the DNA of his killer."

"What about those carbon particles in the skin?" Angela asked. "Did you have any more thoughts about them?"

"To be honest, I haven't given it a lot of thought," Walt said. "But I did change my mind about it being contemporary with the struggle. I realized the particles were in the dermis, not the epidermis. It must have been some old injury, like having been stabbed with a pencil when he was in grammar school. I have such a deposit on my arm."

"I've got one in the palm of my right hand," Angela said.

"The reason I haven't done much on the case is because there's been no pressure from either the state's attorney or the state police. Unfortunately, I've been swamped with other cases where there's considerable pressure."

"I understand," Angela said. "But I'm still interested. So if there are any more developments, please let me know."

After hanging up Angela's thoughts remained on the Hodges affair, wondering what Phil Calhoun was doing. She'd heard nothing from him since she'd visited the man and had given him his retainer. And thinking about Hodges and Calhoun made her remember how vulnerable she'd felt when David had left in the night to go to the hospital.

Checking her watch, Angela realized it was time for her lunch break. She turned off her microscope, grabbed her coat, and went out to the car. She'd told David that she wanted to get a gun, and she'd meant it.

There were no sporting goods stores in Bartlet, but Staley's Hardware Store carried a line of firearms. When she explained what she wanted, Mr. Staley was instantly helpful. He asked her what her reasons were for wanting to purchase a gun. When she told him protection of her home, he talked her into a shotgun.

It took Angela less than fifteen minutes to make her selection. She bought a pump-action twelve-gauge shotgun. Mr. Staley was more than happy to show her how to load and unload the rifle. He was particularly careful to show her the safety. The firearm also came with a brochure, and Mr. Staley encouraged her to read it.

On the walk back to the car, Angela felt self-conscious about her package even though she'd insisted that Mr. Staley wrap it in manila paper; the object within was still quite recognizable. She'd never carried a gun before. In her other hand she had a bag containing a box of shells.

With definite relief Angela put the rifle in the trunk of the car. Heading around to the driver's side door she looked across the green at the police station and hesitated. Ever since the confrontation with Robertson the previous morning she'd felt guilty. She also knew David had been right; it was foolhardy for her to make an enemy of the chief of police despite the fact that he was such a dolt.

Letting go of the car door, Angela walked across the green and into the police station. Robertson agreed to see her after a ten-minute wait.

"I hope I'm not bothering you," Angela said.

"No bother," he said as she entered his office.

Angela sat down. "I don't want to take much of your time," Angela said.

"I'm a public servant," Robertson said brazenly.

"I've come to apologize for yesterday," Angela said.

"Oh?" Robertson said, clearly taken aback.

"My behavior was inappropriate," Angela said. "And I'm sorry. It's just that I've really been overwhelmed by the discovery of that dead body in my house."

"Well, it's nice of you to come in," Robertson said, clearly flustered. He hadn't expected this. "I'm sorry about Hodges. We'll keep the case open and let you know if anything turns up."

"Something did turn up this morning," Angela said. She then told Robertson about the possibility of Hodges' killer having a deposit of carbon from a pencil on his arm.

"From a pencil?" Robertson asked.

"Yes," Angela said. She stood up and extended her right palm and pointed to a small, dark stain beneath the skin. "Something like this," she said. "I got it in the third grade."

"Oh, I see," Robertson said, nodding his head as a wry smile turned up the corners of his mouth. "Well, thank you for this tip."

"Just thought I'd pass it along," Angela said. "The medical examiner also said that the skin under Hodges' fingernails was definitely his killer's. He has a DNA fingerprint."

"Trouble is, super-sophisticated DNA malarkey is not much help without a suspect," Robertson said.

"There was a small town in England that solved a rape with a DNA fingerprint," Angela said. "All they did was do a DNA test on everybody in the town."

"Wow," Robertson said. "I can just imagine what the American Civil Liberties Union would say if I tried that here in Bartlet."

"I'm not suggesting you try," Angela said. "But I did want you to know about the DNA fingerprint."

"Thank you," Robertson said. "And thanks for coming by." He stood up when Angela got up to go.

He watched through his window as Angela got in her car.

As she drove off, Robertson picked up his phone and pressed one of the automatic dialers. "You're not going to believe this, but she's still at it. She's like a dog with a bone."

Angela felt a little better for having tried to clear things up with Robertson. At the same time she didn't delude herself into thinking that she'd changed anything. Intuitively she knew he still wasn't about to lift a finger to get Hodges' murder case solved.

At the hospital, all the parking slots reserved for the professional staff near the back entrance of the hospital were occupied. Angela had to zigzag back and forth through the lot looking for a vacant spot. Finding nothing, she drove into the upper lot. She finally located a spot way up in the far corner. It took her almost five minutes to walk back to the hospital door.

"This isn't my day," Angela said aloud as she entered the building.

"But you won't even be able to see the parking garage from the town," Traynor said into the phone. His frustration was thinly masked. He was talking to Ned Banks, who had become one of the town's Selectmen the previous year.

"No, no, no," Traynor reiterated. "It's not going to look like a World War Two bunker. Why don't you meet me sometime at the hospital and I'll show you the model. I promise you, it's rather attractive. And if Bartlet Community Hospital intends to be the referral hospital of the state, we need it."

Collette, Traynor's secretary, came into the room and placed a business card on the desk blotter in front of Traynor. At that moment Ned was carrying on about Bartlet losing its charm. Traynor picked up the card. It read: "Phil Calhoun, Private Investigation, Satisfaction Guaranteed."

Traynor covered the mouthpiece and whispered: "Who the hell is Phil Calhoun?"

Collette shrugged. "I've never seen him before, but he says he knows you. Anyway, he's waiting outside. I've got to run over to the post office."

Traynor waved goodbye to his secretary and then put down the business card. Meanwhile, Ned was still lamenting the recent changes in Bartlet, especially the condominium development near the interstate.

"Look, Ned, I've got to run," Traynor interrupted. "I really hope you give this hospital parking garage some thought. I know that Wiggins has been bad-mouthing it, but it's important for the hospital. And frankly, I need all the votes I can get."

Traynor hung up the phone with disgust. He had trouble understanding the shortsightedness of most of the Selectmen. None of them seemed to appreciate the economic significance of the hospital, and that made his job as chairman of the hospital board that much more difficult.

Traynor peered into the outer office to get a glimpse of the PI he supposedly knew. Flipping through one of the hospital quarterly reports was a big man in a black and white checkered shirt. Traynor thought he looked vaguely familiar, but he couldn't place him.

Traynor invited Calhoun inside. While they shook hands, Traynor scoured his memory, but he still drew a blank. He motioned toward a chair. The two men sat down.

It wasn't until Calhoun mentioned that he'd been a state policeman that it came to Traynor. "I remember," he said. "You used to be friends with Harley Strombell's brother."

Calhoun nodded and complimented Traynor on his memory.

"Never forget a face," Traynor boasted.

"I wanted to ask you a few questions about Dr. Hodges," Calhoun said, getting to the point.

Traynor nervously fingered the gavel he used for hospital board meetings. He didn't like answering questions about Hodges, yet he was afraid not to. He didn't want to make it an issue. He wished this whole Hodges mess would go away.

"Is your interest personal or professional?" Traynor asked.

"Combination," Calhoun said.

"Have you been retained?" Traynor asked.

"You might say so," Calhoun said.

"By whom?"

"I'm not at liberty to say," Calhoun said. "As a lawyer, I'm sure you understand."

"If you expect me to be cooperative," Traynor said, "then you'll have to be a bit more open yourself."

Calhoun took out his Antonio y Cleopatras and asked if he could smoke. Traynor nodded. Calhoun offered one to Traynor, but Traynor declined. Calhoun took his time lighting up. He blew smoke up at the ceiling, and then spoke: "The family is interested in finding out who was responsible for the doctor's brutal murder."

"That's understandable," Traynor said. "Can I have your word that whatever I say remains discreet?"

"Absolutely," Calhoun said.

"Okay, what do you want to ask me?"

"I'm making a list of people who disliked Hodges," Calhoun said. "Do you have anyone to put on my list?"

"Half the town," Traynor said with a short laugh. "But I don't feel comfortable giving names."

"I understand you saw Hodges the night of his murder," Calhoun said.

"Hodges burst in on a meeting we were having at the hospital," Traynor said. "It was an unpleasant habit of his that he indulged all too frequently."

"I understand Hodges was angry," Calhoun said.

"Where did you hear that?" Traynor asked.

"I've been speaking to a number of people in town," Calhoun said.

"Hodges was angry all the time," Traynor said. "He was chronically unhappy with the way we manage the hospital. You see, Dr. Hodges had a proprietary feeling about the institution. He was also dated in his thinking. He was an old-school 'doc' who ran the hospital when it was a cost-plus situation. He had no feeling for the new environment of managed care and managed competition. He just didn't understand."

"I don't think I know too much about that, either," Calhoun admitted.

"You'd better learn," Traynor warned. "Because it's here. What kind of health plan are you under?"

"CMV," Calhoun said.

"There you go," Traynor said. "Managed care. You're already part of it and you don't even know it."

"I understand when Dr. Hodges burst into your hospital meeting he had some hospital charts with him."

"Parts of charts," Traynor corrected. "But I didn't get a look at them. I was planning on having lunch with him the following day to discuss whatever was on his mind. It undoubtedly concerned some of his former patients. He was always complaining about his former patients not getting VIP treatment. Frankly, he was a pain in the ass."

"Did Dr. Hodges bother the new hospital administrator, Helen Beaton?" Calhoun asked.

"Oh, God, yes!" Traynor said. "Hodges would think nothing of barging into her office any time of the day. Helen Beaton was probably the person who suffered from Hodges' barrages the most. After all, she had his old position. And who knew how to do it better than himself?"

"I understand that you ran into Hodges a second time that night he burst in on your meeting," Calhoun said.

"Unfortunately," Traynor said. "At the inn. After most hospital meetings, we go to the inn. That night Hodges was there drinking as usual and as belligerent as usual."

"And he had unpleasant words with Robertson?" Calhoun asked.

"He sure did," Traynor said.

"And with Sherwood?" Calhoun said.

"Who have you been talking with?" Traynor asked.

"Just a handful of townsfolk," Calhoun said. "I understand Dr. Cantor said some unflattering things about Hodges too."

"I can't remember," Traynor said. "But Cantor hadn't liked Hodges for years."

"How come?" Calhoun asked.

"Hodges took over radiology and pathology for the hospital," Traynor said. "He wanted the hospital to accrue the windfall profits those departments generated from equipment the hospital owned."

"What about you?" Calhoun asked. "I've heard you weren't fond of Dr. Hodges either."

"I already told you," Traynor said. "He was a pain in the ass. It was hard enough trying to run the hospital without his continual interference."

"I heard it was something personal," Calhoun said. "Something about your sister."

"My, your sources are good," Traynor said.

"Just town gossip," Calhoun said.

"You're right," Traynor said. "It's no secret. My sister Sunny committed suicide after Hodges pulled her husband's hospital privileges."

"So you blamed Hodges?" Calhoun asked.

"More then than now," Traynor said. "Hell, Sunny's husband was a drunkard. Hodges should have taken away his privileges before he had a chance to cause real harm."

"One last question," Calhoun said. "Do you know who killed Dr. Hodges?"

Traynor laughed, then shook his head. "I haven't the slightest idea, and I don't care. The only thing I care about is the effect his death might have on the hospital."

Calhoun stood up and stubbed out his cigar in an ashtray on the corner of Traynor's desk.

"Do me a favor," Traynor said. "I've made it easy for you. I didn't have to tell you anything. All I ask is that you not make a big deal about this Hodges affair. If you find out who did it and plan to expose the individual, let me know so the hospital can make some plans with respect to publicity, especially if the killer has anything to do with the hospital. We're already dealing with a public relations problem on another matter. We don't need to be blindsided by something else."

"Sounds reasonable," Calhoun said.

After Traynor showed Calhoun out, he returned to his desk, looked up Clara Hodges' Boston number, and dialed.

"I wanted to ask you a question," he said after the usual pleasantries. "Are you familiar with a gentleman by the name of Phil Calhoun?"

"Not that I recall," Clara said. "Why do you ask?"

"He was just in my office," Traynor explained. "He's a private investigator. He was here to ask questions about Dennis. He implied that he'd been retained by the family."

"I certainly haven't hired any private investigator," Clara said. "And I cannot imagine anyone else in the family doing so either, especially without my knowing about it."

"I was afraid of that. If you hear anything more about this guy, please let me know."

"I certainly will," Clara said.

Traynor hung up the phone and sighed. He had the unpleasant feeling that more trouble was coming. Even beyond the grave, Hodges was a curse.

"You've got one more patient," Susan said as she handed David the chart. "I told her to come right in. She's one of the nurses from the second floor."

David took the chart and pushed into the examining room. The nurse was Beverly Hopkins. David knew her vaguely; she was on nights.

"What's the problem?" David asked with a smile.

Beverly was sitting on the examining table. She was a tall, slender woman with light brown hair. She was holding a kidney dish Susan had given her for nausea. Her face was pale.

"I'm sorry to bother you, Dr. Wilson," Beverly said. "I think it's the flu. I would have just stayed home in bed, but as you know, we're encouraged to come and see you if we're going to take time off."

"No problem," David said. "That's what I'm here for. What are your symptoms?"

The symptoms were similar to those of the other four nurses: general malaise, mild GI complaints, and low-grade fever. David agreed with Beverly's assessment. He sent her home for bed rest, telling her to drink plenty of fluids and take aspirin as needed.

After finishing up at the office, David headed over to the hospital to see his patients. As he walked, he began to mull over the fact that the only people he'd seen with the flu so far were nurses, and all five had been from the second floor.

David stopped in his tracks. He wondered if it were a coincidence that the nurses were all from the same floor, the same floor where all his mortally ill patients had been. Of course, ninety percent of the patients went to the second floor. But David thought it strange that no nurses from the OR or the emergency room were coming down with this flu.

David recommended walking, and as he did so his thoughts returned to the possibility that his patients had died from an infectious disease contracted in the hospital. The flu-like symptoms the nurses were experiencing could be related. Using a dialectic approach, David posed himself a question: what if the nurses who were generally healthy got a mild illness when exposed to the mysterious disease, but patients who'd had chemotherapy and, as a result, had mildly compromised immune systems, got a fulminating and fatal illness?

David thought his reasoning was valid, but when he tried to think of some known illness that fit this bill, he couldn't come up with any. The disease would have to affect the GI system, the central nervous system, and the blood, yet be difficult to diagnose even for an expert in the field like Dr. Martin Hasselbaum.

What about an environmental poison? David wondered. He remembered Jonathan's symptom of excessive salivation. The complaint had made David think of mercury. Even so, the idea of some poison being involved seemed far-fetched. How would it be spread? If it were airborne, then many more people would have come down with symptoms than four patients and five nurses. But still, a poison was a possibility. David decided to reserve judgment until he received the toxicology results on Mary Ann.

Quickening his pace, David climbed to the second floor. What patients he had left were doing well. Even Donald didn't require much attention, although David did adjust his insulin dosage again.

When he was finished with his rounds, David went down to the first floor to search the lab for Angela. He found her in the chemistry area trying to solve a problem with one of the multi-track analyzers.

"Are you finished already?" Angela asked, catching sight of David.

"For a change," David said.

"How's Eakins?" Angela asked.

"I'll tell you later," David said.

Angela looked at him closely. "Is everything all right?"

"Hardly," David said. "But I don't want to talk about it now."

Angela excused herself from the laboratory tech with whom she was working and took David aside.

"I had a little surprise when I got in here this morning," she said. "Wadley hit the ceiling about my doing the autopsy."

"I'm sorry," David said.

"It's not your fault," Angela said. "Wadley is just being an ass. His ego has been bruised. But the problem is, he's refused to allow any of the specimens to be processed."

"Damn," David said. "I really wanted the toxicology done."

"No need to worry," Angela said. "I sent the toxicology and cultures to Boston. I'm going to do the slides. In fact, I'll stay tonight to do them. Will you make dinner for you and Nikki?"

David told her he'd be happy to.

David was relieved to get out of the hospital. It was exhilarating to ride his bike through the crisp New England air. He felt disappointed the trip was over as he pedaled up the driveway.

After sending Alice home, David enjoyed spending time with Nikki. The two of them worked out in the yard until darkness drove them inside. While Nikki did her homework, David made a simple meal of steak and salad.

After dinner David broke the news about Caroline.

"Is she real sick?" Nikki asked.

"She looked very uncomfortable when I saw her," David said.

"I want to go visit her tomorrow," Nikki said.

"I'm sure you do," David said. "But remember, you were a little congested yourself last night. I think we better wait until we know for sure what Caroline has. Okay?"

Nikki nodded, but she wasn't happy.

To be on the safe side, David insisted Nikki do her postural drainage even though she usually only did it in the morning unless she wasn't feeling well. Nikki didn't complain.

After Nikki went to bed, David began to peruse the infectious disease section of one of his medical textbooks. He wasn't looking for anything in particular. He thought there was a chance he might discover something along the lines of the infection he'd envisioned earlier in the day, but nothing jumped out at him.

Before he knew it, David was waking up with his heavy textbook of medicine open on his lap. Shades of medical school, he thought with a chuckle. It had been a while since he'd fallen asleep over one of his books. Checking the clock over the fireplace he was surprised to see it was after eleven. Angela still wasn't home.

Feeling mildly anxious, David called the hospital. The operator put him through to the lab.

"What's going on?" he asked when he heard Angela's voice.

"It's just taking me longer than I thought," Angela said. "The staining takes time. Makes me appreciate the techs who normally do it. I should have called you, but I'm almost finished. I'll be home within the hour."

"I'll be waiting," David said.

It was more than an hour by the time Angela was completely finished. She took a selection of slides and loaded them in a metal briefcase. She thought David might want to take a peek at them. Angela's own microscope was at home, so he could easily have a look if he were interested.

She said goodnight to the night-shift techs, then headed out to the parking lot.

She didn't see her old Volvo in the reserved parking area. For a moment, she thought the car had been stolen, then she remembered she'd been forced to park in the far reaches of the upper lot.

Setting off at a brisk pace, Angela quickly slowed. Not only was she carrying a heavy briefcase, but she was exhausted. Halfway across the lot she had to transfer the briefcase to the other hand.

There were a few cars in the parking lot belonging to the night-shift personnel, but they soon fell behind as Angela trudged toward the path that led to the upper lot. Angela noticed that she was entirely alone. There were no other people; the evening shift had long since departed.

As Angela approached the path she began to feel uneasy. She was unaccustomed to being out at such an hour, and had certainly expected to see someone. Then she thought she heard something behind her. When she turned she saw nothing.

Continuing on, Angela started thinking about wild animals. She'd heard that black bears were occasionally spotted in the area. She wondered what she would do if she were suddenly confronted by a bear.

"You're being silly," she told herself. She pushed on. She had to get home; it was after midnight.

The lighting in the lower parking lot was more than adequate. But as Angela entered into the path leading up to the upper lot, she had to pause for a moment to allow her eyes to adjust to the darkness. There were no lights along the path, and dense evergreen trees on both sides formed a natural archway.

The barking of a dog in the distance made Angela jump. Nervously she moved deeper into the tunnel of trees, starting up a run of stairs constructed of railroad ties. She heard crackling noises in the forest and the rustling of the wind high in the pine trees. Feeling frightened, she recalled vividly the episode in the basement when David and Nikki had scared her, and the memory made her even more tense.

At the top of the stairs the path leveled and angled to the left. Up ahead Angela could see the light of the upper parking lot. There was only another fifty feet to go.

Angela had just about calmed herself when a man leaped out of the shadows. He came up on her so suddenly she didn't have a chance to flee. He was brandishing a club over his head; his face was covered by a dark ski mask.

Staggering back, Angela tripped on an exposed root and fell. The man flung himself at her. Angela screamed and rolled to the side. She could hear the thump of the club as it sliced into the soft ground where she had been only seconds before.

Angela scrambled to her feet. The man grabbed her with a gloved hand as he began to raise his club again. Angela swung her briefcase up into the man's crotch with all the strength she could muster. The man's grip on her arm released as he cried out in pain.

With the route back to the hospital blocked by the wheezing man, Angela ran for the upper lot. Empowered by terror Angela ran as she'd never run before, her flying feet crunching on the asphalt. She could hear the man behind her, but she didn't dare to look. She ran up to the Volvo with one thought in mind: the shotgun.

Dropping the briefcase to the pavement, Angela fumbled with her keys. Once she got the trunk open, she yanked the manila paper from the shotgun. Snatching up the bag of shells she hastily dumped them into the trunk. Picking up a single shell, she jammed it into the gun and pumped it into the firing chamber.

Angela whirled about, holding the gun at waist level, but no one was there. The lot was completely deserted. The man hadn't given chase. What she heard had been the echo of her own footfalls.

"Can't you do a little better than that?" Robertson asked. " 'Sorta tall.' Is that it? That's hardly a description. How are we supposed to find this guy if you women can't describe him better than that?"

"It was dark," Angela said. She was having a hard time keeping her emotions even. "And it happened so quickly. Besides, he was wearing a ski mask."

"What the hell were you doing out there in the trees after midnight anyway? Hell, all you nurses were warned."

"I'm not a nurse," Angela said. "I'm a doctor."

"Oh, boy!" Robertson said haughtily. "You think this rapist cared whether you were a nurse or a doctor?"

"The point I'm making is that I wasn't warned. The nurses may have been warned, but no one warned us doctors."

"Well, you should have known better," Robertson said.

"Are you trying to imply that this attack was somehow my fault?"

Robertson ignored her question. "What kind of club was he holding?" he asked.

"I have no idea," Angela said. "I told you it was dark."

Robertson shook his head and looked at his deputy. "You said Bill had just been up there in his cruiser?"

"That's right," the deputy said. "Not ten minutes before the incident he'd made a routine sweep of both parking lots."

"Christ, I don't know what to do," Robertson said. He looked down at Angela and shrugged his shoulders. "If you women would just be a little more cooperative, we wouldn't have this problem."

"May I use the phone?" Angela said.

Angela called David. When he answered she could tell he'd been asleep. She told him she'd be home in ten minutes.

"What time is it?" David asked. Then after a glance at the clock, he answered his own question. "Holy jeez, it's after one. What are you doing?"

"I'll tell you when I get home," Angela said.

After she'd hung up, Angela turned to Robertson. "May I leave now?" she asked testily.

"Of course," Robertson said. "But if you think of anything else, let us know. Would you like my deputy to drive you home?"

"I think I can manage," Angela said.

Ten minutes later, Angela was hugging David at their door. David had been alarmed not just by the late hour, but the sight of his wife coming from the car with a briefcase in one hand and a shotgun in the other. But he didn't ask about the gun. For the moment, he just hugged Angela. She was holding him tightly and wouldn't let go.

Angela finally released David, removed her soiled coat, and carried the briefcase and the shotgun into the family room. David followed, eyeing the shotgun. Angela sat on the couch, embraced her knees, and looked up at David.

"I'd like to stay calm," she said evenly. "Would you mind getting me a glass of wine?"

David complied immediately. As he handed her the glass he asked if she'd like something to eat. Angela shook her head before sipping the wine. She held the glass with both hands.

In a controlled voice Angela began to tell David about the attempted assault. But she didn't get far. Her emotions boiled over into tears. For five minutes she couldn't speak. David put his arms around her, telling her that it was his fault: he never should have let her work at the hospital so late at night.

Eventually, Angela regained her composure. She continued the story, choking back tears. When she got to the part about Robertson coming in to talk to her, her anger kicked in.

"I cannot believe that man," Angela sputtered. "He makes me so mad. He acted as if it were my fault."

"He's a jerk," David agreed.

Angela reached for the briefcase and handed it to David. She wiped the tears from her eyes. "All this effort and the slides didn't show much at all," she said. "There was no tumor in the brain. There was some perivascular inflammation, but it was nonspecific. A few neurons appeared damaged, but it could have been a postmortem change."

"No sign of a systemic infectious disease?" David asked.

Angela shook her head. "I brought the slides home in case you wanted to look at them yourself," she said.

"I see you got a shotgun," David commented.

"It's loaded, too," Angela warned, "so be careful. And don't worry. I'll go over it with Nikki tomorrow."

A crash and the sound of breaking glass made them both sit bolt upright. Rusty started barking from Nikki's room, then he came bounding down the stairs. David picked up the shotgun.

"The safety is just above the trigger," Angela said.

With David leading, they made their way through to the darkened living room. David flipped on the light. Four panes of the bay window were smashed, along with their muntins. On the floor a few feet away from where they were standing was a brick. Attached to it was a copy of the note they'd received the night before.

"I'm calling the police," Angela said. "This is too much."

While they waited for the police to arrive, David sat Angela down.

"Did you do anything today related to the Hodges affair?" David asked.

"No," Angela said defensively. "Well, I did get a call from the medical examiner."

"Did you talk about Hodges with anyone?" David asked.

"His name came up when I talked with Robertson," Angela said.

"Tonight?" David asked with surprise.

"This afternoon," Angela said. "I stopped in to the police station to talk with Robertson on my way back from buying the shotgun."

"Why?" David asked with dismay. "After what happened in front of the church yesterday, I'm surprised you had the nerve to see the man."

"I wanted to apologize," Angela said. "But it was a mistake. Robertson is not about to do anything concerning Hodges' murderer."

"Angela," David pleaded, "we have to stop messing with this Hodges stuff. It's not worth it. A note on the door is one thing; a brick through the window is something else entirely."

Headlight beams played against the wall as a police cruiser pulled up the driveway.

"At least it's not Robertson," Angela said when they could see the approaching officer.

The policeman introduced himself as Bill Morrison. From the outset, it was clear he wasn't terribly interested in investigating this latest incident at the Wilsons' home. He was only asking enough questions to fill out the requisite form.

When he was ready to leave, Angela asked him if he was planning on taking the brick.

"Hadn't planned on it," Bill said.

"What about fingerprints?" Angela asked.

Bill's eyes went from Angela to David and then back to Angela. His face registered surprise and confusion. "Fingerprints?" he asked.

"What's so surprising?" Angela asked. "It's possible at times to get fingerprints from things like stone and brick."

"Well, I don't know if we'd send something like this to the state police," he said.

"Just in case, let me get you a bag," Angela said. She disappeared into the kitchen. When she returned she had a plastic bag. Turning it inside out, she reached down and picked up the brick. She handed the bag to Bill.

"There," Angela said. "Now you people are prepared if you happen to decide you want to try to solve a crime."

Bill nodded and went out to his cruiser. Angela and David watched it disappear down the driveway.

"I'm losing confidence in the local police," David said.

"I've never had any," Angela said.

"If Robertson is the only person you spoke to about Hodges today, it makes me wonder who's responsible for this brick coming through our window."

"Do you think the police might have done it?" Angela asked.

"I don't know," David said. "I can't believe they'd go that far, but it makes me think they know more than they're willing to say. Officer Bill certainly wasn't excited about the incident."

"I'm beginning to think this town is not quite the utopia we thought it was," Angela said.

David went out to the barn and cut himself a piece of plywood to fit over the hole in the bay window. When he returned to the house, Angela was eating a bowl of cold cereal.

"Not much of a dinner," he said.

"I'm surprised I'm hungry at all," Angela said.

She accompanied him into the living room and watched him struggle to open the stepladder.

"Are you sure you should be doing this?" she asked.

He flashed her an exasperated look.

"You haven't told me about your day," Angela said as David climbed up the ladder. "What about Jonathan Eakins? How's he doing?"

"I don't know," David said. "I'm not his doctor anymore."

"Why not?" Angela asked.

"Kelley assigned another doctor."

"He can do that?"

"He did it," David said. He tried to align the piece of plywood, then get a nail out of his pocket. "I was furious at first. Now I'm resigned. The good part is that I don't have to feel responsible."

"But you will still feel responsible," Angela said. "I know you."

David had Angela hand him the hammer, and he tried nailing the plywood in place. Instead, one of the other windowpanes fell out and shattered on the floor. The noise brought Rusty out of Nikki's room to bark at the head of the stairs.

"Damn it all," David said.

"Maybe we should think about leaving Bartlet," Angela said.

"We can't just pick up and go. We've got mortgages and contracts. We aren't free like we used to be."

"But nothing is turning out the way we expected. We both have problems at work. I got assaulted. And this Hodges thing is driving me crazy."

"You have to let the Hodges affair go," David said. "Please, Angela."

"I can't," Angela said with new tears. "I'm even having nightmares now: nightmares about blood in the kitchen. Every time I go in there I think about it, and I can't get it out of my head that the person responsible is walking around and could come here anytime he chose. It's no way to live, feeling you have to have a gun in the house."

"We shouldn't have a gun," David snapped.

"I'm not staying here at night when you go off to the hospital," Angela said irritably. "Not without a gun."

"You'd better be sure Nikki understands she's not allowed to touch it," David said.

"I'll discuss the gun with her tomorrow," Angela said.

"Speaking of Nikki," David said, "I happened to see Caroline in the emergency room. She's in the hospital with a high fever and respiratory distress."

"Oh, heavens no," Angela said. "Does Nikki know?"

"I told her this evening," David said.

"Does she have something contagious?" Angela asked. "She and Nikki were together yesterday."

"I don't know yet," David said. "I told Nikki she can't visit until we know."

"Poor Caroline," Angela said. "She seemed fine yesterday. God, I hope Nikki doesn't come down with the same thing."

"So do I," David said. "Angela, we've got more important things to think about than this nonsense involving Hodges' body. Please, let's let it go, for Nikki's sake if not our own."

"All right," Angela said reluctantly. "I'll try."

"Thank goodness," David said. Then he looked up at the broken window. "Now what am I going to do with this mess?"

"How about tape and a plastic bag?" Angela suggested.

David stared at her. "Why didn't I think of that?" he questioned.

TUESDAY • OCTOBER 26

Neither David nor Angela slept well. Both were overwrought, but they responded differently. While Angela had trouble falling asleep, David woke well before dawn. He was appalled to see the time: four A.M. Sensing he would not fall back asleep, David got up and tiptoed out of the bedroom, careful not to disturb Angela.

On his way to the family room, he paused at the head of the stairs. He'd heard a noise from Nikki's room and was surprised to see his daughter appear.

"What are you doing awake?" David whispered.

"I just woke up," Nikki said. "I've been thinking about Caroline."

David went into his daughter's room to talk with her about her friend. David told her that he thought Caroline would be a lot better by now. He promised to check on her as soon as he got to the hospital. He said he'd call Nikki and let her know.

When Nikki coughed a deep, productive cough, David suggested they do her postural drainage. It took them almost half an hour. When it was over, Nikki said she felt better.

Together they went down into the kitchen and made breakfast. David cooked bacon and eggs while Nikki prepared a batch of drop biscuits. With a fire in the fireplace the meal had a festive quality that felt like a good antidote for their troubled spirits.

David was on his bike by five-thirty and at the hospital before six. En route, he made a mental note to arrange for someone to fix the bay window.

Several of David's patients were still asleep and David didn't disturb them. He went over their charts, planning to see them later. When he peeked into Donald's room he found the man was wide awake.

"I feel terrible," Donald said. "I haven't slept all night."

"What's the problem?" David asked, feeling his pulse quicken.

To David's dismay, the complaints were disturbingly familiar: crampy abdominal pain along with nausea and diarrhea. In addition, just like Jonathan, he complained of having to swallow continually.

David tried to remain calm. He spoke with Donald for almost half an hour, asking detailed questions about each complaint and ascertaining the sequence in which the complaints had appeared.

Although Donald's complaints certainly reminded him of his other deceased patients, there was an aspect of Donald's history that was different: Donald had never had chemotherapy.

Donald had been initially diagnosed as having pancreatic cancer, but surgery had proved this not to be the case. He'd undergone a massive operation called a Whipple procedure which included the removal of his pancreas, parts of his stomach and intestines, and a good deal of lymphatic tissue. When pathology examined the tumor it had been determined to be benign.

Since he had had such extensive surgery on his digestive system, but had not had chemotherapy to compromise his immune system, David was hopeful that Donald's complaints were purely functional and not harbingers of whatever afflicted David's other unlucky patients.

After finishing his rounds, David called admitting to find out Caroline's room number. On his way he had to pass the ICU. Steeling himself against what he might learn, he went in to check on Jonathan Eakins.

"Jonathan Eakins died about three this morning," the busy head nurse said. "It was a very quick downhill course. Nothing we did seemed to help. It was a shame. A young man like that. It proves you never know when you're going to have to go."

David swallowed hard. He nodded, turned, and left the unit. Even though he'd known in his heart that Jonathan would die, the reality of it was hard to take. David still had a hard time absorbing the staggering fact: he had now lost four patients in a little over a week.

On a brighter note, David discovered that Caroline had responded well to her treatment of IV antibiotics and intensive respiratory therapy. Her fever was gone, her color was pink, and her blue eyes sparkled. She smiled broadly the instant David appeared.

"Nikki wants to come to visit you," David said.

"Cool," Caroline said. "When?"

"Probably this afternoon," David said.

"Could you please ask her to bring me my reading book and my spelling book?" Caroline said.

David promised he would.

The first thing David did when he got to his office was call home. Nikki answered. David told her that Caroline was much better and that Nikki could visit her that day. He also relayed Caroline's request for her books. Then David asked Nikki to put her mother on the line.

"She's in the shower," Nikki said. "Should she call you back?"

"No, it's not necessary," David said. "But I want you to remind her of something. She brought a gun home yesterday. It's a shotgun, and it is leaning against the newel post at the bottom of the stairs. She's supposed to show it to you and warn you not to touch it. Will you remind her to do all that?"

"Yes, Dad," Nikki said.

David could picture his daughter rolling her eyes.

"I'm serious," he said. "Don't forget."

Hanging up the phone, David wondered about the gun. He didn't like it. Yet he wasn't about to force the issue at the moment. More than anything, he wanted Angela to give up her obsession with Hodges' murder. A brick through the front window was all the warning David needed.

David decided to take this early-morning opportunity to get through some of the never-ending reams of paperwork he was forced to process in connection with his practice. As he laid the first form on his desk, the phone rang. The caller was a patient named Sandra Hascher. She was a young woman with a history of melanoma that had spread to regional lymph nodes.

"I didn't expect to get you directly," Sandra said.

"I'm the only one here just now," David explained.

Sandra told him she'd been having trouble with an abscessed tooth. The tooth had been pulled, but the infection was worse. "I'm sorry to bother you with this," she continued, "but my temperature is one hundred and three. I would have gone to the emergency room, but the last time I took my son there I had to pay for it myself. CMV refused."

"I've heard the story before," David said. "Why don't you come right over. I'll see you immediately."

"Thanks, I'll be right there," Sandra said.

The abscess was impressive. The whole side of Sandra's face was distorted by the swelling. In addition, the lymph nodes beneath her jaw were almost golf-ball size. David checked her temperature. It was indeed one hundred and three.

"You've got to come into the hospital," David said.

"I can't," Sandra said. "I've got so much to do. And my ten-year-old is home with the chicken pox."

"You'll just have to make arrangements," David said. "There's no way I'm going to let you walk around with this time bomb."

David carefully explained the anatomy of the region to Sandra, emphasizing how close the infection was to her brain. "If the infection gets into your nervous system, we're in deep trouble," David said. "You need continuous antibiotics. This is no joke."

"All right," Sandra said. "You have me convinced."

David called admitting to warn them Sandra would be coming. Then he gave her a written set of orders and sent her on her way.

Angela felt terrible. She was exhausted. Several cups of coffee had not been enough to revive her. It had been almost three o'clock before she'd fallen asleep, and once she had, she'd not slept soundly. She'd had nightmares again, featuring Hodges' body, the ski-masked rapist, and the brick through the window.

When she finally did wake up she was surprised to discover that David had already left for work.

As Angela dressed, she regretted her promise to David to try to forget about Hodges. She didn't see how she could "just let Hodges go" as David suggested.

Angela wondered again about Phil Calhoun. She still had not heard a word from him. She figured that the least he could do was check in. Even if he hadn't discovered something significant, he could at least let her know what he'd accomplished to date.

Angela decided to give Phil Calhoun a call, but all she got was his answering machine. Deciding against leaving a message, she simply hung up.

Downstairs, Angela found Nikki in the family room busily reading from one of her schoolbooks.

"Okay," Angela said. "Upstairs for postural drainage."

"I already did it with Dad," Nikki said.

"Really?" Angela said. "How about breakfast?"

"We had that too," Nikki said.

"What time did you two get up?" Angela asked.

"Around four," Nikki said.

Angela wasn't happy about David's getting up so early. Having trouble sleeping was often a sign of depression. She also didn't like the idea of having Nikki up so early.

"How did Daddy seem this morning?" Angela asked as she joined Nikki in the family room.

"Fine," Nikki said. "He called while you were in the shower. He said that Caroline was okay and that I can visit her this afternoon."

"That's wonderful news," Angela said.

"He also asked me to remind you about a gun," Nikki said. "He acted weird, like I wouldn't know what a gun is."

"He's worried," Angela said. "It's no joke. Guns are bad business when it comes to kids. A lot of kids are killed each year because of family-owned guns. But more often than not those cases involve handguns."

Angela walked out into the front hall and brought the shotgun back into the family room. She took the shell out of the chamber and showed Nikki how to tell there were no more inside.

Angela spent the next half hour going over the gun with Nikki, allowing Nikki to pump it, pull the trigger, and even load and unload it. When they were finished with the instruction, they went outside behind the barn and each fired a shell. Nikki said she didn't like firing it because it hurt her shoulder.

Returning to the house, Angela told Nikki that she wasn't to touch the gun. Nikki told her not to worry, she didn't want to have anything to do with it.

Since the weather was warm and sunny, Nikki wanted to ride her bike to school. Angela watched as she started off toward town. Angela was pleased she was doing so well; at least Bartlet was good for Nikki.

Shortly after Nikki left, Angela did the same. After parking in the reserved area, Angela couldn't resist the temptation to examine the spot where she'd been attacked. She retraced her steps into the stand of trees that separated the parking lots and found her own footprints in the muddy earth. With the help of the footprints she found the spot where she'd fallen. Then she discovered the deep cut left in the earth by the man's club.

The cleft was about four inches deep. Angela put her fingers in it and shuddered. She could still vividly recall the sight and sound of that club whizzing by her ear. She even could vaguely recall the glint of a flash of metal streaking by.

Suddenly, Angela realized something she hadn't focused on before: the man had not hesitated. If she had not rolled out of the way, she would have been struck. The man hadn't been trying to rape her, he'd wanted to hurt her, maybe kill her.

Angela thought back to the injuries to Hodges' skull she'd examined during the autopsy. Hodges had been hit with a metal rod. Her head could have looked just like Hodges'!

Against her better judgment, Angela put in a call to Robertson.

"I know what you're calling about," Robertson said irritably, "and you can just forget it. I ain't sending this brick up to the state police lab for fingerprints. They'd laugh me out of the goddamn state."

"I'm not calling about the brick," Angela said. Instead, she conveyed her idea that her assault had been attempted murder, not attempted rape.

When Angela was finished, Robertson was so quiet, she was afraid that he'd hung up. "Hello?" she asked at last.

"I'm still here," Robertson said. "I'm thinking."

There was another pause.

"Nah, I don't buy it," Robertson said finally. "This guy is a rapist, not a murderer. He's had opportunity to kill in the past, but he didn't. Hell, he didn't even hurt the ones he did rape."

Angela wondered if the rape victims didn't feel hurt, but she wasn't about to argue the issue with Robertson. She merely thanked him for his time and hung up.

"What a flake!" Angela said out loud. She was a fool to have thought Robertson would give any credence to her theory. Yet the more she thought about the attack, the more sure she became that rape hadn't been the goal. And if it had been an attempted murder, then it had to be related to her interest in Hodges' murder. Maybe the man was Hodges' murderer!

Angela shivered. If she was right, then she'd been stalked. The idea terrified her. Whatever she did, she'd have to be sure to make it seem as if she were giving up on the affair.

Angela wondered if she should tell David her latest suspicions. She was indecisive. On the one hand, she never wanted there to be any secrets between them. On the other, she knew he'd only use it as more reason for her to give up her probe of Hodges' murder. For the time being, Angela decided that she'd only tell Phil Calhoun—if and when he contacted her.

"I'll have a little more coffee," Traynor said as he pointed toward his cup with the handle of his gavel for the waitress's benefit. As was their habit, Traynor, Sherwood, Beaton, and Caldwell were having a breakfast meeting in advance of the monthly hospital executive board meeting scheduled for the following Monday night. They were seated at Traynor's favorite table at the Iron Horse Inn.

"I'm encouraged," Beaton said. "The preliminary figures for the second half of October are better than those of the first half. We're not out of the woods yet, but they are significantly better than September's."

"We get one crisis under control and then have to face another," Traynor said. "It's never-ending. What's the story about a doctor being assaulted last night?"

"It was just after midnight," Caldwell said. "It was the new female pathologist, Angela Wilson. She'd been working late."

"Where in the parking lot did it take place?" Traynor asked. He began his nervous habit of hitting his palm with his gavel.

"In the pathway between the lots," Caldwell said.

"Have lights been put in there?" Traynor asked.

Caldwell looked at Beaton.

"I don't know," Beaton admitted. "But we'll check as soon as we get back. You ordered lights to be put there, but whether it got done or not I'm not sure."

"They'd better be," Traynor said. He hit his palm particularly hard and the sound carried around the room. "I've had no luck lobbying the Selectmen about the parking garage. There's no way it can even get on the ballot now until spring."

"I checked with the *Bartlet Sun*," Beaton said. "They have agreed to keep the rape attempt out of the paper."

"At least they're on our side," Traynor said.

"I think their loyalty is inspired by the ads we run," Beaton said.

"Any new business to be brought up at the board meeting?" Sherwood asked.

"There's a new battle fomenting in the clinical arena," Beaton said. "The radiologists and the neurologists are squaring off for a bloody fight over which group is officially designated to read MRIs of the skull."

"You've got to be kidding," Traynor said.

"Honest," Beaton said. "If we gave them weapons it would be a fight to the death. It involves dollars and ego, a tough combination."

"Damn doctors," Traynor said with disgust. "They can't work together on anything. They're a bunch of lone rangers, if you ask me."

"Which brings me to M.D. 91," Beaton said. "He's planning on suing the hospital over his privileges."

"Let him sue," Traynor said. "I'm even tired of the medical staff's insistence that we call these 'compromised physicians' by code numbers. Hell, 'compromised physician' is a euphemism in itself."

"That's all the new business," Beaton said.

Traynor looked around the table. "Anything else?"

"I had a curious visit yesterday afternoon," Sherwood said. "The caller was a PI by the name of Phil Calhoun."

"He came to see me too," Traynor said.

"He makes me nervous," Sherwood said. "He asked a lot of questions about Hodges."

"Likewise," Traynor said.

"The problem was that he already seemed to know a fair amount," Sherwood said. "I was reluctant to give him any information, but I didn't want to appear to be stonewalling either."

"My feelings exactly," Traynor said.

"He hasn't come to see me," Beaton said.

"Who do you think retained him?" Sherwood asked.

"I asked him," Traynor said. "He implied that the family had. I assumed he meant Clara, so I called her. She said she didn't know anything about Phil Calhoun. Next I called Wayne Robertson. Calhoun had already been to see him. Wayne thought that the most likely candidate is Angela Wilson, our new pathologist."

"That makes sense," Sherwood said. "She came to see me about Hodges. She was very upset about his body being discovered in her house."

"That's a curious coincidence," Beaton said. "She's certainly having her troubles: first finding a body in her house and then experiencing a rape attempt."

"Maybe the rape attempt will dampen her interest in Hodges," Traynor said. "It would be ironic for something positive to come out of something so potentially negative."

"What if Phil Calhoun figures out who killed Hodges?" Caldwell asked.

"That could be a problem," Traynor said. "But it's been over eight months. What are the odds? The trail must be pretty cool by now."

When the meeting broke up, Traynor walked Beaton out to her car. He asked her if she'd had a change of heart about their relationship.

"No," Beaton said. "Have you?"

"I can't divorce Jacqueline right now," Traynor said. "Not with my boy in college. But when he gets out . . ."

"Fine," Beaton said. "We'll talk about it then."

As Beaton drove up to the hospital, she shook her head in dismay. "Men!" she said irritably.

After seeing off his last patient for the day, David stepped across the hall into his private office. Nikki was sitting at his desk leafing through one of his medical

journals. David liked the fact that she was interested in medicine. He hoped that
if her interest persisted, she would have the opportunity to study medicine.

"Are you ready?" she asked.

"Let's go."

It took them only a few minutes to cover the short distance to the hospital
and up a flight of stairs. When they stepped into Caroline's room, Caroline's face
lit up with joy. She was especially pleased that Nikki had remembered to bring
the books that she'd requested. Caroline was a superb student, just like Nikki.

"Look what I can do," Caroline said. She reached up and grabbed an overhead bar and pulled herself completely off the bed, angling her feet up into the
air.

David clapped. It was a feat that took considerable strength, more than
David would have guessed her slender arms had. Caroline was in a large orthopedic bed with an overhead frame. David assumed they'd put her in it for its entertainment value since the child was obviously enjoying it.

"I'm going to check on my patients," David said. He shook a finger at Nikki.
"I won't be long, and no terrorizing the nurses, promise?"

"Promise," Nikki said, then she giggled with Caroline.

David headed straight for Donald Anderson's room. He wasn't worried
about Donald's status because he'd called to check on him throughout the day.
The reports had always been the same: the blood sugars were all normal and the
GI complaints had decreased.

"How are you, Donald?" David asked as he arrived at the bedside.

Donald was on his back. His bed was raised so that he was reclining at a
forty-five-degree angle. When David spoke he slowly rolled his head to the side,
but he didn't answer.

"How are you?" David said, raising his voice.

Donald mumbled something David couldn't understand. David tried again
to talk with him, but quickly realized that the man was disoriented.

David examined him carefully. He listened intently to his lungs, but there
were no adventitious sounds, indicating that his lungs were clear. Walking out to
the nurses' station he ordered a stat blood sugar.

While the blood sugar was being processed, David saw his other patients.
Everyone else was doing well, including Sandra. Although she'd been on antibiotics for less than twelve hours, she insisted the pain in her jaw was better. When
David examined her, his impression was that the abscess was the same size, but
the symptomatic improvement was encouraging. He did not change her treatment. Two other patients were doing so well he told them they could go home
the following day.

As he was finishing his entry in the chart of his last patient, the floor secretary slipped the result of Donald's blood sugar under David's nose. It was normal. David picked up the scrap of paper and studied it. He didn't want it to be
normal. He wanted it to explain the change in Donald's mental status.

David slowly walked back to Donald's room, puzzling over his condition.

The only explanation that David could think of was that Donald's blood sugar had had a wild swing either up or down and had then corrected itself. The problem with that line of reasoning was that the patient's sensorium usually returned to normal simultaneous with the blood sugar.

David was still mulling over the possibilities when he reentered Donald's room. When he first saw Donald, David stared in utter disbelief. Donald's face was dusky blue and his head was thrust back in hyper-extension. Dark blood oozed from a half-open mouth. His body was only partially covered; the bed-covers were in total disarray.

David's initial shock quickly turned into motion. He alerted the nurses that there had been an arrest and started cardiopulmonary resuscitation. The resuscitation team arrived and followed their familiar routine. Even Donald's surgeon, Dr. Albert Hillson, came in. He'd been making rounds when he'd heard the commotion.

The resuscitation attempt was soon called off. It was apparent that Donald had suffered a seizure and respiratory arrest somewhere between fifteen and twenty minutes prior to David finding him. With that amount of time having passed with no oxygen getting to the brain, there was no hope. David declared Donald dead at five-fifteen.

David was devastated at having lost yet another patient, but he forced himself not to show it. Dr. Hillson was saddened but expansive. He said that it had been a tribute to good medical care that Donald had lived as long as he had. When Shirley Anderson came in with her two young boys, she voiced the same sentiment.

"Thank you for being so kind to him," Shirley said to David as she blotted her eyes. "You had become his favorite doctor."

After David had done all he could, he headed toward Caroline's room to get Nikki. He felt numb. It had all happened so quickly.

"At least you know why this patient died," Angela said after David had described what had happened to Donald Anderson. They were sitting in the family room. Dinner was long since over; Nikki was up in her room doing her homework.

"But I don't," David complained. "It all happened so fast."

"Now, wait a minute," Angela said. "With the other patients I could understand your confusion. But not with this one. Donald Anderson had had most of his abdominal organs rearranged if not removed. He was in and out of your office and the hospital. You can't possibly blame yourself for his death."

"I don't know what to think anymore," David said. "It's true; he was always teetering on the edge with his frequent infections and his brittle diabetes. But why a seizure?"

"His blood sugar was wandering all over the map," Angela said. "What about a stroke? I mean the possibilities are legion."

The phone startled them both. David reached for it by reflex. He was afraid it was the hospital with more bad news. When the caller asked for Angela, he was relieved.

Angela immediately recognized the voice: it was Phil Calhoun.

"Sorry I haven't been in touch," Calhoun said. "I've been busy, but now I'd like to have a chat."

"When?" Angela asked.

"Well, I'm sitting here in the Iron Horse Inn," Calhoun said. "It's only a stone's throw away. Why don't I come over?"

Angela covered the phone with her hand. "It's the private investigator, Phil Calhoun," she said. "He wants to come over."

"I thought you were letting the Hodges affair go," David said.

"I have," Angela said. "I haven't spoken to anyone."

"Then what about Phil Calhoun?" David asked.

"I haven't spoken to him either," Angela said. "Not since Saturday. But I've already paid him. I think we should at least hear what he's learned."

David sighed with resignation. "Whatever," he said.

A quarter of an hour later when Phil Calhoun came through their door, David wondered what could have possessed Angela to describe him as professional. To David he appeared anything but professional, with a red baseball cap on backwards and a flannel shirt. The sorrels on his feet didn't even have laces.

"Pleasure," Calhoun said when he shook hands with David.

They sat in the living room on the shabby old furniture that they'd brought from Boston. The huge room had a cheap dance-hall feel with such meager, pitiful furnishing. The plastic bag taped to the window didn't help.

"Nice house," Calhoun said as he looked around.

"We're still in the process of furnishing it," Angela said. She asked if she could get Calhoun something to drink. He said he'd appreciate a beer if she didn't mind.

While Angela was off getting the beer, David continued to eye their visitor. Calhoun was older than David had expected. A shock of gray hair bristled from beneath the red cap, which Calhoun made no attempt to remove.

"Mind if I smoke?" Calhoun asked as he brandished his Antonio y Cleopatras.

"I'm sorry, but we do," Angela said, coming back into the room and handing Calhoun his beer. "Our daughter has respiratory problems."

"No problem," Calhoun said agreeably. "I wanted to give you folks an update on my investigations. It's proceeding well, although not without effort. Dr. Dennis Hodges was not the most popular man in town. In fact, half the population seems to have hated him for one reason or another."

"We're already aware of that," David said. "I hope that you have more specific details to add to justify your hourly wage."

"David, please!" Angela said. She was surprised at David's rudeness.

"It's my opinion," Calhoun continued, ignoring David's comment, "that Dr.

Hodges either didn't care what other people thought of him or he was socially handicapped. As a purebred New Englander, it was probably a combination of the two." Calhoun chuckled, then took a drink of his beer.

"I've made up a list of potential suspects," Calhoun continued, "but I haven't interviewed them all yet. But it's getting interesting. Something strange is going on here. I can feel it in my bones."

"Who have you spoken with?" David asked. There was still a rudeness to his voice that bothered Angela, but she didn't say anything.

"Just a couple so far," Calhoun said. He let out a belch. He made no attempt to excuse himself or even cover his mouth. David glanced at Angela. Angela pretended not to have noticed.

"I've talked to a few of the higher-ups with the hospital," Calhoun continued. "The chairman of the board, Traynor, and the vice chairman, Sherwood. Both had reasons to hold a grudge against Hodges."

"I hope you plan to speak with Dr. Cantor," Angela said. "I'd heard he really had it out for Hodges."

"Cantor's on the list," Calhoun assured her. "But I wanted to start at the top and work down. Sherwood's grudge involved a piece of land. Traynor's beef was far more personal."

Calhoun went on to explain the Traynor–Hodges–Van Slyke triangle, concluding with the suicide of Sunny Traynor, Traynor's sister.

"What a terrible story," Angela said.

"It's like a TV melodrama," Calhoun agreed. "But you'd think that if Traynor felt compelled to do anything about Hodges, he would have done it back then, not now. Besides, Hodges had handpicked Traynor to take over the hospital board well after the suicide. I doubt he'd have done that if he and Traynor were still at odds. And Van Slyke's child, Werner, works for the hospital today."

"Werner Van Slyke is related to Traynor?" David questioned with surprise. "Now that smacks of nepotism."

"Could be," Calhoun said. "But Werner Van Slyke, Junior, had a long-term friendly relationship with Hodges. He'd taken care of this house for Hodges for years. His position at the hospital is probably more a result of Hodges' doing than Traynor's. At any rate, I don't suspect Traynor of murder."

"How can you be sure?" Angela questioned.

"Can't be sure of anything except Hodges' murder," Calhoun said. "After that we can only deal in probabilities."

"This is all very interesting," David said, "but have you come up with a suspect or at least narrowed the list down?"

"No, not yet," Calhoun said.

"How much have we spent to get to this dubious crossroad?" David asked.

"David!" Angela snapped. "I think you're being unfair. I think Mr. Calhoun has learned a lot in a short period of time. I think the important question now is whether he believes the case is solvable."

"I'll buy that," David said. "What's your professional assessment, Mr. Calhoun?"

"I think I need a cigar," Calhoun said. "Would you folks mind if we were to sit outside?"

A few minutes later they assembled on the terrace. Calhoun was utterly content with his smoke and another beer.

"I think the case is definitely solvable," he said. His broad, doughy face intermittently lit up as he puffed on his cigar. "You have to know something about small New England towns: they are more the same than they are different. I know these people and I understand the dynamics. The characters are generally the same from town to town, only the names are different. Anybody's business is everybody else's. In other words I'm sure that some people know who the killer is. The problem is getting somebody to talk. My hunch is that the hospital is involved on some level, and no one wants it to get hurt. And there's a chance it could get hurt because Hodges made the hospital his life's work."

"How have you gotten your information so far?" Angela asked. "I thought New Englanders were closemouthed, reluctant to talk."

"Generally true," Calhoun said. "But some of the best people for town gossip happen to be friends of mine: the bookstore owner, the pharmacist, the bartender, and the librarian. They've been my sources so far. Now, I just have to start eliminating suspects. But before I begin I have to ask you a question: Do you want me to continue?"

"No," David said.

"Wait a minute," Angela said. "You've told us that the case is definitely solvable. How long do you think it will take?"

"Not too long," Calhoun said.

"That's too vague," David said.

Calhoun lifted his cap and scratched his scalp. "I'd say within a week," he said.

"That's a lot of money," David said.

"I think it's worth it," Angela said.

"Angela!" David pleaded. "You told me you were going to drop this Hodges affair."

"I will," Angela said. "I'll let Mr. Calhoun do everything. I won't talk to a soul."

"Good Lord," David said dejectedly as he rolled his eyes in exasperation.

"Come on, David," Angela said. "If you expect me to live in this house then you have to support me in this."

David hesitated, then thought of a compromise. "Okay," he said. "I'll make a deal. One week, then it's over no matter what."

"All right," Angela said. "It's a deal." Then she turned to Calhoun. "Now that we have a time constraint, what's the next move?"

"First I'll continue interviewing my list of suspects," Calhoun said. "At the same time there are two other major goals. One is to reconstruct Dr. Hodges' last day, assuming he was killed on the day he disappeared. To do this I want to interview Hodges' secretary-nurse who'd worked for him for thirty-five years. The second goal is to get copies of the medical papers that were found with Hodges."

"They're in the custody of the state police," Angela said. "Having been on the force, can't you get copies easily?"

"Unfortunately, no," Calhoun said. "The state police tend to be inordinately guarded when it comes to evidence in their custody. I know because I used to work for a while in the crime-scene division up in Burlington. It makes for a kind of 'catch-22.' The state police with the expertise and the evidence aren't motivated to expend a lot of time and effort on this kind of case because they take their cue from the local police. If the local police don't care, then the state police let it slide. One of the reasons the local police don't care is they don't have the evidence to go on."

"Another reason is that they might be somehow involved," Angela said. She then told Calhoun about the brick through the window, the threatening notes, and the police's response.

"Doesn't surprise me," Calhoun said. "Robertson's on my list. He couldn't stand Hodges."

"I knew that," Angela said. "I was told that Robertson blames his wife's death on Hodges."

"I don't give that story a lot of significance," Calhoun said. "Robertson's not that stupid. I think the sorry episode about his wife was just an excuse. I think Robertson's anger toward Hodges stemmed more from Hodges' behavior, which we know was less than diplomatic. I'd bet my last dollar that Hodges knew Robertson for the blowhard he is and never gave him any respect. I sincerely doubt that Robertson killed Hodges, but when I was talking with him, he gave me a funny feeling. He knows something he wasn't telling me."

"The way the police have been dragging their feet they have to be involved," Angela said.

"Reminds me of a case when I was a state trooper," Calhoun said after another long pull on his cigar. "It was also a homicide in a small town. We were sure the whole town, including the local police, knew who'd done it, yet no one would come forward. We ended up dropping the case. It's unsolved to this day."

"What makes you think Hodges' case is any different?" David asked. "Couldn't the same thing happen here?"

"Not a chance," Calhoun said. "In the case I just told you about the dead person was a murderer and a thief himself. Hodges is different. There are a lot of people who hated him, but there's also a bunch who think he was one of the town heroes. Hell, this is the only referral hospital in New England outside of the big cities, and Hodges was personally responsible for building it up. A lot of people's livelihood is based on what Hodges created here. Don't worry, this case will be solved. No doubt about it."

"How will you manage to get copies of Hodges' papers if you can't do it yourself?" Angela asked.

"You have to do it," Calhoun said.

"Me?" Angela asked.

"That's not part of the deal," David said. "She has to stay out of this investigation. I don't want her talking to anyone. Not with bricks coming through our window."

"There will be no danger," Calhoun insisted.

"Why me?" Angela asked.

"Because you are both a physician and an employee of the hospital," Calhoun said. "If you show up at the crime-scene division up in Burlington with the appropriate identification and say that copies of the papers are needed to take care of patients, they'll make you copies in a flash. Judges' and doctors' requests are always honored. I know. As I said, I used to work there."

"I guess visiting the state police headquarters couldn't be very dangerous," Angela said. "It's not as if I'm participating in the investigation."

"I suppose it's okay," David said. "Provided there's no chance of getting into trouble with the police."

"No chance," Calhoun said. "The worst thing that could happen is they wouldn't give her the copies."

"When?" Angela asked.

"How about tomorrow?" Calhoun suggested.

"It will have to be on my lunch hour," Angela said.

"I'll come pick you up at noon in front of the hospital," Calhoun said. He stood up, thanking them for the beers.

Angela offered to walk Calhoun to his truck while David went back in the house.

"I hope I'm not causing trouble between you and your husband," Calhoun said as they approached his vehicle. "He didn't seem at all pleased about my investigation."

"It won't be a problem," Angela said. "But we'll have to stick to the one-week agreement."

"Should be plenty of time," Calhoun said.

"There is something else I wanted to tell you," Angela said. She explained her new theory on her assault.

"Hmmm," Calhoun said. "This is getting more interesting than I thought. You'd better be doubly sure to leave the sleuthing to me."

"I intend to," Angela said.

"I've been careful about not letting it be known that you've retained me," Calhoun said.

"I appreciate the discretion."

"Maybe tomorrow I should pick you up in the parking lot behind the library instead of in front of the hospital," Calhoun said. "No sense taking chances."

20

WEDNESDAY • OCTOBER 27

To David's and Angela's dismay, Nikki awoke with congestion and a deep, productive cough. Both were fearful that she might be coming down with the same illness that had briefly afflicted Caroline. David was particularly concerned because it had been his decision to allow Nikki to visit Caroline the previous afternoon.

Despite extra attention to Nikki's morning respiratory therapy, she failed to improve. To Nikki's keen disappointment, David and Angela decided she shouldn't go to school. They called Alice, who agreed to come over for the day.

Already tense from events at home, David was edgy as he started his rounds. With so many recent deaths, he was spooked to see his patients. But his worries were groundless. Everyone was doing fine. Even Sandra was much better.

"Your swelling is down," David told her as he tenderly palpated the side of her face.

"I can tell," Sandra said.

"And your fever is below one hundred," David said.

"I'm pleased," Sandra said. "Thank you. I won't even pressure you about when I can get out of here."

"Very clever," David said with a laugh. "The indirect approach is often far more effective than the direct. But I think we have to keep you until we're one hundred percent sure this infection is under control."

"Oh, all right," Sandra said, feigning irritation. "But if I have to stay, could you do me a favor?"

"Of course," David said.

"The electric controls of my bed stopped working," Sandra said. "I told the nurses, but they said there wasn't anything they could do about it."

"I'll do something," David promised. "It's a chronic problem around here, I'm afraid. I'll go out and ask about it right away. We want you to be as comfortable as possible."

Returning to the nurses' station, David found Janet Colburn and complained about the bed situation. "There's really nothing that can be done?" David asked.

"That's what maintenance told us when we reported it," Janet said. "I wasn't about to argue with the man. It's hard enough talking with him. And frankly, we don't have another bed to spare at the moment."

David couldn't believe that he'd have to go to see Van Slyke over another maintenance detail. But it seemed his choice was either to go ask why the bed couldn't be repaired, or go to Beaton directly. It was an absurd situation.

David found Van Slyke in his windowless office.

"I have a patient upstairs who was told her bed couldn't be repaired," David said irritably after a cursory knock. "What's the story?"

"The hospital bought the wrong kind of beds," Van Slyke said. "They're a maintenance nightmare."

"It can't be fixed?" David asked.

"It can be fixed, but it will break again," Van Slyke said.

"I want it fixed," David said.

"We'll do it when we get around to it," Van Slyke said. "Don't bother me. I have more important work to do."

"Why are you so rude?" David demanded.

"Look who's talking," Van Slyke said. "You came down here yelling at me, not vice versa. If you have a problem, go tell it to administration."

"I'll do that," David said. He turned around and climbed up the stairs intending to go directly to Helen Beaton. But when he got to the lobby he saw Dr. Pilsner coming into the hospital, heading for the main stairs.

"Bert," David called. "Can I speak to you a moment?"

Dr. Pilsner paused.

David approached him, described Nikki's congestion, and started to ask whether he thought Nikki should start some oral antibiotics. But David stopped in mid-sentence. He noticed that Dr. Pilsner was agitated; he was hardly listening to what David was saying.

"Is something wrong?" David asked.

"I'm sorry," Dr. Pilsner said. "I'm distracted. Caroline Helmsford took an unexpected turn for the worse during the night. I've been here almost continuously. I just went home to shower and change."

"What happened?" David asked.

"Come and see for yourself," Dr. Pilsner said. He started up the stairs. David had to jog to stay with him.

"She's in the ICU," Dr. Pilsner explained. "It started with a seizure, of all things."

David's steps faltered. Then he had to sprint to catch back up to the quickly moving pediatrician. David didn't like the idea of Caroline having a seizure. It brought back disturbing memories of his own patients.

"Then pneumonia developed rapidly," Dr. Pilsner continued. "I've tried everything. Nothing seemed to make a difference."

They arrived at the ICU. Dr. Pilsner hesitated, leaning against the door. He sighed from exhaustion. "I'm afraid she's now in septic shock. We're having to maintain her blood pressure. It doesn't look good at all. I'm afraid I'm going to lose her."

They went into the unit. Caroline was in a coma. A tube issued from her mouth and was connected to a respirator. Her body was covered with wires and intravenous lines. Monitors recorded her pulse and blood pressure. David shuddered as he looked down at the stricken child. In his mind's eye he saw Nikki in Caroline's place, and the image terrorized him.

The ICU nurse handling Caroline gave a capsule report. Nothing had improved since Dr. Pilsner had left an hour earlier. As soon as Dr. Pilsner had been fully briefed, he and David walked over to the central desk. David used the opportunity to discuss Nikki's condition with him. Dr. Pilsner listened and then agreed that oral antibiotics were indicated. He suggested the type and dosage.

Before leaving the unit David tried to bolster Dr. Pilsner with an encouraging word. David knew all too well how the pediatrician felt.

Before seeing his office patients, David called Angela to tell her about Nikki's antibiotics. Then he told her about Caroline. Angela was dumbstruck.

"You think she's going to die?" Angela asked.

"That's Dr. Pilsner's feeling," David said.

"Nikki was with her yesterday," Angela said.

"You don't have to remind me," David said. "But Caroline was much better. She was afebrile."

"Oh, God," Angela said. "It seems to be one thing after another. Can you get the antibiotics for Nikki and take them home over your lunch hour?"

"Okay," David said agreeably.

"I'll be heading up to Burlington as planned," Angela said.

"You're still going?" David asked.

"Of course," Angela said. "Calhoun called me to confirm. Apparently he's already spoken to the officer in charge of the crime-scene division up in Burlington."

"Have a good trip," David said. He hung up before he could say something he might regret. Angela's priorities irked him. While he was worrying himself sick about Caroline and Nikki, she was still obsessed with the Hodges affair.

"I appreciate your seeing me," Calhoun said as he took a chair in front of Helen Beaton's desk. "As I told your secretary, I only have a few questions."

"And I have a question for you," Beaton said.

"Who should go first?" Calhoun asked. Then he held up his pack of cigars. "May I smoke?"

"No, you may not smoke," Beaton said. "There's no smoking in this hospital. And I think I should ask my questions first. The answer might affect the duration of this interview."

"By all means," Calhoun said. "You first."

"Who hired you?" Beaton asked.

"That's an unfair question," Calhoun said.

"And why is that?"

"Because my clients have a right to privacy," Calhoun said. "Now it's my turn. I understand that Dr. Hodges was a frequent visitor to your office."

"If I may interrupt," Beaton said. "If your clients choose to withhold their identity, then I see no reason to cooperate with you."

"That's up to you," Calhoun said. "Of course there are those who might wonder why the president of a hospital would have a problem speaking about her immediate predecessor. They might even start thinking you know who killed Hodges."

"Thank you for coming in," Beaton said. She stood up and smiled. "You won't goad me into talking, not without my knowing just who's behind your efforts. My main concern is the hospital. Good day, Mr. Calhoun."

Calhoun got to his feet. "I have a feeling I'll be seeing you again," he said.

Calhoun left administration and descended to the basement. His next interviewee was Werner Van Slyke. Calhoun found him in the hospital shop replacing electrical motors in several hospital beds.

"Werner Van Slyke?" Calhoun questioned.

"Yeah," Van Slyke said in his monotone.

"Name's Calhoun. Mind if I have a chat with you?"

"What about?"

"Dr. Dennis Hodges," Calhoun said.

"If you don't mind my working," Van Slyke said. He turned his attention back to the motors.

"Are these beds a frequent problem?" Calhoun asked.

"Unfortunately," Van Slyke said.

"Since you're head of the department, why are you doing them yourself?" Calhoun asked.

"I want to make sure it's done right," Van Slyke said.

Calhoun retired to the workbench and sat on a stool. "Mind if I smoke?" he asked.

"Whatever," Van Slyke said.

"I thought the hospital was a smoke-free environment," Calhoun said as he took out a cigar. He offered one to Van Slyke. Van Slyke paused as if he were giving it considerable thought. Then he took one. Calhoun lit Van Slyke's before his own.

"I understand you knew Hodges pretty well," Calhoun said.

"He was like a father to me," Van Slyke said. He puffed his cigar contentedly. "More than my own father."

"No kidding," Calhoun said.

"If it hadn't been for Hodges, I never would have gone to college," Van Slyke said. "He'd given me a job to work around his house. I used to sleep over a lot and we'd talk. I had a lot of trouble with my own father."

"How so?" Calhoun asked. He was eager to keep Van Slyke talking.

"My father was a mean son of a bitch," Van Slyke said. Then he coughed. "The bastard used to beat the hell out of me."

"How come?" Calhoun asked.

"He got drunk most every night," Van Slyke said. "He used to beat me and my mother couldn't do anything about it. In fact, she got beat herself."

"Did you and your mother talk?" Calhoun asked. "Kinda team up against your father?"

"Hell, no," Van Slyke said. "She always defended him, saying he didn't mean it after he'd kicked the crap out of me. Hell, she even tried to convince me that he loved me and that was why he was hitting me."

"Doesn't make sense," Calhoun said.

"Sure as hell doesn't," Van Slyke said acidly. "What the hell are you asking all these questions for, anyway?"

"I'm interested in Hodges' death," Calhoun said.

"After all this time?" Van Slyke asked.

"Why not?" Calhoun said. "Wouldn't you like to find out who killed him?"

"What would I do if I found out?" Van Slyke said. "Kill the bastard?" Van Slyke laughed until he began coughing again.

"You don't smoke much, do you?" Calhoun asked.

Van Slyke shook his head after he'd finally controlled his coughing. His face had become red. He headed over to a nearby sink to take a drink of water. When he came back, his mood had changed.

"I think I've had enough of this chat," he said with derision. "I've got a hell of a lot of work to do. I shouldn't even be monkeying around with these beds."

"I'll leave, then," Calhoun said as he slipped off the stool. "It's a rule I have: I never stay around where I'm not wanted. But would you mind if I returned some other time?"

"I'll think about it," Van Slyke said.

After leaving engineering Calhoun made his way around to the front of the hospital and walked over to the Imaging Center. He handed one of his cards to the receptionist and asked to speak with Dr. Cantor.

"Do you have an appointment?" the receptionist asked.

"No," Calhoun said. "But listen, tell him that I'm here to talk about Dr. Hodges."

"Dr. Dennis Hodges?" the receptionist asked with surprise.

"None other," Calhoun said. "And I'll just take a seat here in the waiting area."

Calhoun watched as the receptionist phoned in to the interior of the organization. Calhoun was just beginning to appreciate the architecture and lavish interior decor when a matronly woman appeared and asked him to follow her.

"What do you mean, you want to discuss Dennis Hodges?" Cantor demanded the moment Calhoun stepped through Cantor's office door.

"Exactly that," Calhoun said.

"What the hell for?" Cantor asked.

"Mind if I sit down?" Calhoun said.

Cantor motioned toward one of the chairs facing his desk. Calhoun had to move a pile of unopened medical journals to the floor. Once he was seated he went through the usual routine of asking to smoke.

"As long as you give me one," Cantor said. "I've given up smoking except for whatever I can mooch."

Once they'd both lit up, Calhoun told Cantor that he'd been retained to discover Hodges' killer.

"I don't think I want to talk about that bastard," Cantor said.

"Can I ask why?" Calhoun said.

"Why should I?" Cantor asked.

"Obviously, to bring his murderer to justice," Calhoun said.

"I think justice has already been served," Cantor said. "Whoever rid us of that pest should be given a medal."

"I've been told you had a low opinion of the man," Calhoun said.

"That's an understatement," Cantor said. "He was despicable."

"Could you elaborate?" Calhoun asked.

"He didn't care about other people," Cantor said.

"Do you mean people in general, or other doctors?" Calhoun asked.

"Mostly doctors, I guess," Cantor said. "He just didn't care. He had one priority and that was this hospital. But his concept of the institution didn't extend to the physicians who staff it. He took over radiology and pathology and put a bunch of us out to pasture. All of us wanted to throttle him."

"Could you give me names?" Calhoun asked.

"Sure, it's no secret," Cantor said. He then counted off on his fingers five doctors, including himself.

"And you are the only one of this group who's still around."

"I'm the only one still in radiology," Cantor said. "Thank God for my having the foresight to set up this imaging center. Paul Darnell's still here too. He's in pathology."

"Do you know who killed Hodges?" Calhoun said.

Cantor started to speak, but then stopped himself. "You know something," he said, "I just realized that I've been spouting off despite having prefaced this conversation by saying I didn't want to talk about Hodges."

"Same thing occurred to me," Calhoun said. "Guess you changed your mind. So how about it; do you know who killed Hodges?"

"If I knew I wouldn't tell you," Cantor said.

Calhoun suddenly drew out his pocket watch, which was attached by a short chain to one of his belt loops. "My word," he said. He stood up. "I'm sorry, but I have to break off this chat. I didn't realize the time. I'm afraid I have another appointment."

Stubbing out his cigar on an ashtray in front of the surprised Cantor, Calhoun rushed from the room. He went immediately to his truck, then drove down to the library. He caught up to Angela as she was strolling along the sidewalk leading to the entrance.

"I'm sorry to be late," Calhoun said after he reached across and opened the passenger door for her. "I was having so much fun talking with Dr. Cantor I didn't realize the time."

"I was a few minutes late myself," Angela said. She climbed into the cab. It smelled of stale cigar smoke.

"I'm curious about Dr. Cantor," she said. "Did he say anything enlightening?"

"He's not the one who killed Hodges," Calhoun said. "But he interested me. Same with Beaton. There's something going on here, I can feel it."

Calhoun cracked the driver's side window. "Mind if I smoke?"

"I assumed that was the reason we were taking your truck," Angela said.

"Just thought I'd ask," Calhoun said.

"Are you sure this visit to the state police is going to go all right?" Angela asked. "The more I've thought about it, the more nervous it makes me. After all, I'll be misrepresenting myself to a degree. I mean, I work at the hospital, but I don't really need the papers to take care of patients. I'm a pathologist."

"No need to worry," Calhoun said. "You might not even have to say anything. I already explained the whole deal to the lieutenant. He didn't have a problem."

"I'm trusting you," Angela said.

"You won't be disappointed," Calhoun said. "But I have a question for you. Your husband's reaction last night is still bothering me. I don't want to cause any trouble between you and your husband. The problem is I'm having more fun on this case than on any since leaving the force. What if I lower my hourly rate. Will that help?"

"Thank you for your concern," Angela said, "but I'm sure David will be fine provided we stick to the one-week time frame."

Despite Calhoun's reassurances, Angela still felt nervous as she climbed out of the truck at state police headquarters in Burlington, but her concern was unnecessary. Calhoun's presence made the operation go far more smoothly than Angela could have hoped. Calhoun did all the talking. The policeman in charge of the evidence could not have been nicer or more accommodating.

"While you're at it," Calhoun said to the officer, "how about making two sets of copies."

"No problem," the officer said. He handled the originals with gloved hands.

Calhoun winked at Angela and whispered: "This way we'll both have a set."

Ten minutes later, Angela and Calhoun were back in the truck.

"That was a breeze," Angela said with relief. She slid the copies out of the envelope the officer had placed them in and began looking through them.

"I never say 'I told you so,' " Calhoun said with a smile. "I'd never say that. Nope. I'm not that kind of person."

Angela laughed. She'd come to enjoy Calhoun's humor.

"What are they?" Calhoun asked, looking over Angela's shoulder.

"They're copies of the admissions sheets on eight patients," Angela said.

"Anything unique about them?" Calhoun asked.

"Not that I can tell," Angela said with some disappointment. "There doesn't seem to be any common element. Different ages, different sexes, and different diagnoses. There's a fractured hip, pneumonia, sinusitis, chest pain, right lower quadrant abdominal pain, phlebitis, stroke, and kidney stone. I don't know what I expected, but this looks pretty ordinary."

Calhoun started the truck and pulled out into the traffic. "Don't make any snap decisions," he advised.

Angela slid the papers back into their envelope and gazed out at the surroundings. Almost immediately she recognized where they were.

"Wait a second," she said. "Stop a moment."

Calhoun pulled over to the side of the road.

"We're very close to the office of the chief medical examiner," Angela said. "What do you say we stop in? He did the autopsy on Hodges and a visit might generate a bit more interest on his part."

"Fine with me," Calhoun said. "I'd like to meet the man."

They did a U-turn in the middle of a busy street. The maneuver scared Angela, and she closed her eyes to the oncoming traffic. Calhoun told her to relax. A few minutes later they were in the medical examiner's building. They met Walter Dunsmore in a lunchroom. Angela introduced Calhoun.

"How about something to eat?" Walter suggested.

Both Angela and Calhoun got sandwiches out of a vending machine and joined Walt.

"Mr. Calhoun is helping investigate the Hodges murder," Angela explained. "We came up to Burlington to get copies of some evidence. While we were here I thought I'd stop in to see if there have been any new developments."

"No, I don't think so," Walt said as he tried to think. "Toxicology came back and was negative except for the alcohol level which I told you about. That's about it. As I said, nobody's making this case much of a priority."

"I understand," Angela said. "Anything more on that carbon under the skin?"

"Haven't had a chance to even think about it again," Walt admitted.

After they wolfed down their sandwiches Angela said she had to get back to Bartlet; she told Walt she was on her lunch hour. Walt encouraged her to come back any time.

The drive back to Bartlet seemed even faster than the drive to Burlington. Calhoun dropped Angela off behind the library so she could get her own car.

"I'll be in touch," Calhoun said. "And remember, stay out of it."

"Don't worry," Angela said. She waved as she got in behind the wheel. It was almost one-thirty.

Back in her office, Angela put the copies of Hodges' papers in the top drawer of her desk. She wanted to remember to take them home that evening. While she was donning her white lab coat Wadley opened the connecting door without bothering to knock.

"I've been looking for you for almost twenty minutes," he said irritably.

"I was out of the hospital," Angela said.

"That much was obvious," Wadley said. "I had you paged several times."

"I'm sorry," Angela said. "I used my lunch hour to run an errand."

"You've been gone longer than an hour," Wadley said.

"That might be," Angela said, "but I plan to stay later than scheduled, which I normally do anyway. Plus, I spoke to Dr. Darnell to cover in case there were any emergencies."

"I don't like my pathologists disappearing in the middle of the day," Wadley said.

"I was not gone long," Angela said. "I'm fully aware of my responsibilities and carry them out to the letter. I was not responsible for surgical specimens, which would have been the only true emergency. Besides, my errand involved a visit to the chief medical examiner."

"You saw Walt Dunsmore?" Wadley asked.

"You can call him if you doubt me," Angela said. She could tell that Wadley was partially mollified. She was suddenly glad she'd made the spur-of-the-moment visit.

"I'm too busy to be checking on your whereabouts," Wadley said. "The point is that I'm concerned about your behavior of late. I should remind you that you are still on probationary status. I can assure you that you will be terminated if you prove to be unreliable."

With that, Wadley stepped back through the connecting door and slammed it shut.

For a moment Angela stared at the door. She detested this open hostility with Wadley. Still, she preferred it to the previous sexual harassment. She wondered if they would ever be able to develop a normal professional relationship.

After the last office patient had been seen, David reluctantly headed over to the hospital to make his afternoon rounds. He was beginning to dread the experience for fear of what he might face.

Before seeing his own patients David went to the ICU to check on Caroline. The child was doing poorly and was clearly moribund. David found Dr. Pilsner sitting at the ICU desk in a hopeless vigil. The man was despondent. David could relate all too well.

Leaving the ICU, David started seeing his own patients. Each time he went into another room he felt anxious, only to be relieved when he discovered the patient was doing well. But when he went into Sandra's room the anxiety remained. Sandra's mental status had deteriorated.

David was appalled. The change was dramatic to him even though the nurses weren't impressed. When David had visited her early that morning she'd been bright and aware. Now she was apathetic to her surroundings and was drooling. Her eyes had lost their luster. Her temperature, which had fallen, had now crept back up over one hundred degrees.

When David tried to talk to her, she was vague. The only specific complaint he could elicit was abdominal cramps, a symptom that reminded him of other patients he'd been trying to forget. David felt his pulse quicken. He didn't think he could tolerate losing another patient.

Back at the nurses' station, David pored over Sandra's chart. The only new fact was that she'd apparently lost her appetite as evidenced by an entry in the nurses' notes that recorded she'd not eaten her lunch. David checked all the IV fluids she'd had; they were all appropriate. Then he went over all the laboratory tests; they were all normal. He was desperate for some clue to explain the change in her mental status, but there were no clues in the chart. The only idea that came to his mind was the possibility of early meningitis, or inflammation of the coverings of her brain. It was the fear of her developing meningitis that had moved him to admit her in the first place.

David re-examined her, and although he could not elicit any signs of meningitis, he went ahead with the definitive test. He did a lumbar puncture to obtain cerebrospinal fluid. He knew immediately the fluid was normal because of its clarity, but he sent it to the lab for a stat reading to be certain. The result was normal. So was a stat blood sugar.

The only thing Sandra wasn't apathetic about was pain when David palpated her abscess. Consequently, David added another antibiotic to her regimen. Beyond that he had no ideas. He felt lost. All he could do was hope.

Climbing on his bike, David cycled home. He knew he was depressed. He got no enjoyment from the ride. He felt heartsick about Caroline and concerned about Sandra. But as soon as he arrived he realized he could not wallow in self-pity. Nikki was slightly worse than she'd been at lunchtime when he'd brought home her oral antibiotic. Her congestion had increased and her temperature had reached one hundred degrees.

David phoned the ICU and got Dr. Pilsner on the line. David apologized for disturbing him but felt obliged to let him know the oral antibiotic wasn't helping.

"Let's up it," Dr. Pilsner said in a tired voice. "And I think we'd better use a mucolytic agent and a bronchodilator with her respiratory therapy."

"Any change with Caroline?" David asked.

"No change," Dr. Pilsner answered.

Angela didn't get home until almost seven o'clock. After she checked on Nikki, who was doing better after a respiratory therapy session with David, she went to take a shower. David followed her into the bathroom.

"Caroline is no better," David said as Angela stepped into the shower.

"I feel great compassion for the Helmsfords," Angela said. "They must be heartsick. I hope to heaven that Nikki doesn't come down with whatever Caroline got."

"I've got another patient—Sandra Hascher—who is scaring me the same way the others did."

Angela poked her head out of the shower. "What was her admitting diagnosis?"

"Abscessed tooth," David said. "It had responded nicely to antibiotics. Then this afternoon she suddenly had a mental status change."

"Disoriented?"

"Mostly just apathetic and vague," David said. "I know it doesn't sound like much, but to me it was dramatic."

"Meningitis?" Angela asked.

"That was the only thing I thought of," David said. "She hasn't had any headache or spiking fever. But I did a lumbar puncture just to be sure, and it was normal."

"What about a brain abscess?" Angela asked.

"Again, she's had little fever," David said. "But maybe I'll do an MRI tomorrow if she's not better. The problem is, she's reminding me of the other patients who died."

"I suppose you don't want to ask for any consults."

"Not unless I want to have her transferred to someone else," David said. "I might even get into trouble ordering the MRI."

"It's a lousy way to practice medicine," Angela said.

David didn't answer.

"The trip to Burlington went smoothly," Angela said.

"I'm glad," David replied without interest.

"The only trouble I had was when I got back. Wadley's being unreasonable. He even threatened to terminate me."

"No!" David said. He was aghast. "That would be a disaster."

"Don't worry," Angela said. "He's just blowing off steam. There's no way he could terminate me so soon after I complained about his sexual harassment. For that reason alone I'm glad I went to Cantor. The conversation officially established my complaint."

"That's not a lot of reassurance," David said. "I'd never even thought of the possibility of your being fired."

Later, when dinner was served, Nikki reported she wasn't hungry. Angela made her come to the table anyway, saying she could eat what she wanted. But during the dinner, Angela urged Nikki to eat more. David told Angela not to force her. Soon David and Angela exchanged words over the issue, causing Nikki to flee the table in tears.

David and Angela fumed, each blaming the other. For a while they didn't talk, preferring to turn on the TV and watch the news in silence. When it was time for Nikki to go to bed, Angela told David that she would see to Nikki's respiratory therapy while he cleaned up the kitchen.

David hardly had time to carry the soiled dishes into the kitchen when Angela returned.

"Nikki asked me a question I didn't know how to answer," Angela said. "She asked me if Caroline was coming home soon."

"What did you say?" David asked.

"I said I didn't know," Angela admitted. "With Nikki feeling as poorly as she is, I hate to tell her."

"Don't look at me," David said. "I don't want to tell her either. Let's wait until this bout of congestion is over."

"All right," Angela said. "I'll see what I can do." She left the kitchen and returned upstairs.

Around nine David called the hospital. He spoke at length with the head nurse, who kept insisting that Sandra's condition had not changed, at least not dramatically. She did admit, however, that she'd not eaten her dinner.

After David had hung up the phone, Angela appeared from the kitchen.

"Would you like to look at the papers we got from Burlington today?" she asked.

"I'm not interested," David said.

"Thanks," Angela said. "You know this is important to me."

"I'm too preoccupied to worry about that stuff," David said.

"I have the time and energy to listen to your problems," Angela said. "You could at least extend the same courtesy to me."

"I hardly think the two issues are comparable," David said.

"How can you say that? You know how upset I am about this whole Hodges thing."

"I don't want to encourage you," David said. "I think I've been very clear about that."

"Oh, you're clear all right. What's important to you is important; what's important to me isn't."

"With everything else that's going on, I find it amazing that you are still fixated on Hodges. I think you have your priorities mixed up. While you're chasing off to Burlington, I'm here bringing antibiotics to our daughter while her friend is dying in the hospital."

"I can't believe you're saying this," Angela sputtered.

"And on top of it, you make light of Wadley threatening to fire you," David said. "All because it was so important to go to Burlington. I can tell you this: if you get fired it will be an unmitigated economic disaster. And that doesn't even account for the jeopardy you're putting us all in by pursuing this investigation."

"You think you are so rational," Angela yelled. "Well, you're fooling yourself. You think that problems are solved by denying them. I think you have your priorities mixed up by not supporting me when I need it most. And as for Nikki, maybe she wouldn't be sick if you hadn't allowed her to visit Caroline before we knew what the poor girl had."

"That's not fair," David yelled back. Then he restrained himself. He did think of himself as rational, and he prided himself on not losing his temper.

The problem was, the more controlled David became, the more emotional Angela got, and the more emotional Angela became, the more controlled David got. By eleven o'clock they were both exhausted and overwrought. By mutual agreement David slept in the guest room.

21

Thursday • October 28

At first David had no idea where he was when he opened his eyes in the dark. Fumbling with the unfamiliar bedside lamp, he finally managed to turn it on. He looked around in a daze at the unfamiliar furniture. It took him almost a minute to realize he was in the guest room. As soon as he did, the previous night's unpleasantness came back in a flash.

David picked up his wristwatch. It was quarter to five in the morning. He lay back on the pillow and shuddered through a wave of nausea. On the heels of the nausea came cramps followed by a bout of diarrhea.

Feeling horrid, David limped from the guest bath to the master bath in search of some over-the-counter diarrhea medication. When he finally found a bottle, he took a healthy dose. Then he searched for a thermometer and stuck it in his mouth.

While waiting for an accurate reading to register, David searched for aspirin. As he was doing so, he realized that he had to keep swallowing, just as some of his now dead patients had.

David stared at his reflection in the mirror as a new fear made itself known to him. What if he had caught the mysterious illness that had been killing his patients? My God, he thought, they had the same symptoms I'm manifesting now. With trembling fingers he took out the thermometer. It read one hundred degrees. He stuck out his tongue and examined it in the mirror. It was as pale as his face.

"Calm down!" he ordered himself harshly. He took two aspirins and washed them down with a glass of water. Almost immediately he got another cramp and had to hold on to the countertop until it had passed.

In a deliberately calm manner, he considered his symptoms. They were flu-like, similar to those of the five nurses he'd seen. There was no reason to jump to hysterical conclusions.

Having taken the diarrhea medication and the aspirin, David decided to take the same advice he'd given those nurses: he went back to bed. By the time the alarm in the master bedroom sounded, he was already feeling better.

He and Angela first eyed each other warily. Then they fell into each other's arms. They hugged each other for a full minute before David spoke.

"Truce?" he asked.

Angela nodded her agreement. "We're both stressed out."

"On top of that, I think I'm coming down with something," David said. He told her about the flu symptoms which had awakened him. "The only thing that's still bothering me is excessive salivation," he added.

"What do you mean by excessive salivation?" Angela asked.

"I have to keep swallowing," David said. "It's something like the feeling you get before vomiting, but not as bad. Anyway, it's better than it was."

"Have you seen Nikki?" Angela asked.

"Not yet," David said.

After they had washed they went down to Nikki's room. Rusty greeted them eagerly. Nikki was less enthusiastic. She was a little more congested despite the oral antibiotics and the added effort at respiratory therapy.

While Angela made breakfast, David called Dr. Pilsner and told him about Nikki's status.

"I think I should see her right away," Dr. Pilsner said. "Why don't I meet you in the emergency room in half an hour?"

"We'll be there," David said. "And thank you. I appreciate your concern." He was about to hang up when he thought to inquire about Caroline.

"She died," Dr. Pilsner said. "The end came around three this morning. Her blood pressure could no longer be maintained. At least she didn't suffer, though that's not much consolation."

The news, though expected, hit David hard. With a heavy heart, he went into the kitchen and told Angela the news.

Angela looked as though she might burst into tears, but instead she lashed out. "I can't believe you let Nikki go in and visit her like you did," she said.

Stunned at the sharp rebuke, David came back. "At least I came home at lunch yesterday to be sure Nikki got her antibiotic." That said, he did feel guilty for having let Nikki spend time with Caroline.

David and Angela eyed each other, struggling with their irritation and fear.

"I'm sorry," Angela said finally. "I forgot about our truce. I'm just so worried."

"Dr. Pilsner wants to see Nikki in the ER right away," David said. "I think we better go."

They bundled Nikki up and went out to the car. David and Angela meticulously refrained from saying anything to provoke the other. They knew the other's weaknesses and vulnerabilities too well. Nikki didn't say anything either; she coughed most of the way.

Dr. Pilsner was waiting for them and immediately took Nikki into one of the examining stalls. David and Angela stood to the side while Dr. Pilsner examined Nikki. When he was finished he drew them aside.

"I want her in the hospital immediately," he said.

"Do you think she has pneumonia?" David asked.

"I'm not sure," Dr. Pilsner said. "But it's possible. I don't want to take any chances after what happened—" He didn't finish his sentence.

"I'll stay here with Nikki," Angela said to David. "You go do your rounds."

"All right," David said. "Page me if there's any problem." David was still feeling poorly himself; this latest development with Nikki only made him feel worse.

He kissed his daughter goodbye, promising that he'd be by to see her all through the day. Nikki nodded. She'd been through this routine before.

David got several aspirins from an ER nurse, then headed upstairs.

"How is Mrs. Hascher?" David asked Janet Colburn as soon as he saw her. He sat down at the desk and pulled his patients' charts.

"Nothing much said at report," Janet said. "I don't think any of us have been in there yet this morning. We've been concentrating on getting the seven-thirty surgical cases down to the operating room."

David opened Sandra's chart hesitantly. First he looked at the temperature chart. There had been no spikes of fever. The last temperature taken was just over one hundred. Turning to the nurses' notes he read that Sandra had been sleeping each time a nurse had gone into her room.

David breathed a sigh of relief. So far so good. When he was finished with the charts he began seeing the patients. All were doing well except for Sandra.

When David entered her room he found her still asleep. Moving to the bedside, he glanced at the swelling on her jaw. It appeared unchanged. He gave her shoulder a gentle shake, calling her name softly. When she didn't respond, he shook her more vigorously and said her name more loudly.

Finally she stirred, lifting a trembling hand to her face. She could barely open her eyes. David shook her yet again. Her eyes opened a bit wider and she tried to speak, but all that came out was disconnected jabber. She was clearly disoriented.

Trying to remain calm, David drew some blood and sent it off for some stat lab work. Then he devoted himself to a careful examination, concentrating particularly on Sandra's lungs and the nervous system.

When David returned to the nurses' station a short time later he was handed Sandra's stat laboratory values. They were all normal, including the blood count. The white cells, which had been elevated from her abscessed tooth, had fallen with the antibiotics and were still low, ruling out infection as an explanation for her current clinical state. That said, the sound of her lungs suggested incipient pneumonia. David wondered again about a possible failure of her immune response.

Once again David was presented with the same trio of symptoms affecting the central nervous system, the GI system, and the blood or immune system. He was seeing a complex, but he had no idea what the underlying factor could be.

David agonized over what to do next. The life of a thirty-four-year-old woman hung in the balance. He was afraid to call any consults, partly because of Kelley and partly because the consults had not provided any help in the three similar cases. And calling in consults for Eakins had resulted in David's removal from the case. David was even reluctant to order further diagnostic or laboratory tests since nothing had proved to be of any value with the other patients. He was at a loss.

"We have a seizure in room 216," one of the nurses shouted from down the hall. David went running. Room 216 was Sandra's room.

Sandra was in the throes of a full-blown grand mal seizure. Her body was arched back as her limbs contracted rhythmically with such force that the whole bed was bouncing off the floor. David barked orders for a tranquilizer. In an instant it was slapped into his hand. He injected it into Sandra's IV. Within minutes the convulsions stopped, leaving Sandra's body spent and comatose.

David stared down at his patient's now peaceful face. He felt as if he was being mocked for his intellectual impotence. While he had been indecisively sitting at the desk puzzling over what to do, the seizure had taken over Sandra's body in a dramatic gesture.

David erupted in a whirlwind of activity. Anger replaced despair as he pulled out all the diagnostic stops. Once again he ordered everything: consults, lab tests, X rays, even an MRI of the skull. He was determined to figure out what was happening to Sandra Hascher.

Fearing a rapid downhill course, David also made immediate arrangements to transfer Sandra to the ICU. He wanted continuous monitoring of her vital signs. He did not want any more surprises.

The transfer occurred within half an hour. David helped push Sandra down the hall to the ICU. Once she was moved off the gurney, David started for the ICU desk to write new orders, but he stopped short of his goal. In a bed directly across from the central desk was Nikki.

David was stunned. He'd never expected to see Nikki in the ICU. Her presence there terrified him. What could it mean?

David felt a hand on his shoulder. He turned to see Dr. Pilsner. "I can see you're upset about your daughter being in here," he said. "Calm down. I just don't want to take any chances. There are some fabulously skilled nurses in here who are accustomed to taking care of patients with respiratory problems."

"Are you sure it's necessary?" David asked nervously. He knew how tough the ICU environment was on a patient's psyche.

"It's for her benefit," Dr. Pilsner said. "It's purely precautionary. I'll be moving her out of here just as soon as I can."

"Okay," David said. But he was still anxious about this latest turn of events.

Before writing the new orders on Sandra, David went over to talk with Nikki. She was far less concerned about the ICU than David was. David was relieved to see her taking it so well.

Returning his attention to Sandra Hascher, David sat down at the ICU desk and began writing her orders. He was nearly through when the unit clerk tapped his arm.

"There's a Mr. Kelley out in the patient lounge to see you," he said.

David felt his stomach tighten. He knew why Kelley was there, but he wasn't eager to see him and didn't go immediately. He finished writing the orders first and gave them to the head nurse. Only then did he go out to meet Kelley.

"I'm disappointed," Kelley said as David approached. "The utilization coordinator called me a few minutes ago . . ."

"Just a minute!" David snapped, cutting off Kelley. "I've got a sick patient in the ICU and I don't have time to waste with you. So for now stay out of my way. I'll talk to you later. Understand?"

For a second David glared up into Kelley's face. Then he spun around and started out of the room.

"Just a minute, Dr. Wilson," Kelley called. "Not so fast."

David whirled around and stormed back. Without warning he reached out and grabbed Kelley by the tie and the front of his shirt and roughly pushed him back. Kelley collapsed into the club chair behind him. David shook a clenched fist in Kelley's face.

"I want you to get the hell out of here," David snarled. "If you don't, I don't take responsibility for the consequences. It's as simple as that."

Kelley swallowed, but he didn't move.

David spun on his heels and marched out of the lounge. Just as he was about out the door, Kelley called out to him, "I'll be talking with my superiors."

David turned back. "You do that," he said. Then he continued into the ICU. Returning to the desk, he paused. His heart was pounding. He wondered what he really would have done if Kelley had stood up to him.

"Dr. Wilson," the unit clerk called out. "I have Dr. Mieslich on the phone. He's returning your call."

"My husband teaches at the college," Madeline Gannon explained. "He gives courses in drama and literature."

Calhoun had been eyeing the many shelves of books that lined the Gannons' library walls.

"I'd like to meet him sometime," Calhoun said. "I read a lot of plays. It's been my hobby since retiring. Especially Shakespeare."

"What is it you wanted to talk to me about?" Madeline asked, diplomatically changing the subject. From Calhoun's appearance she doubted if Bernard would be terribly interested.

"I'm investigating Dr. Dennis Hodges' murder," Calhoun said. "As you know his body was recently found."

"That was distressing," Madeline said.

"I understand you worked for him for some time," Calhoun said.

"Over thirty years," Madeline said.

"Pleasant work?" Calhoun asked.

"It had its ups and downs," Madeline admitted. "He was a headstrong man who could be stubborn and cranky one minute and understanding and generous the next. I loved him and disliked him at the same time. But I was devastated by the news when they found his body. I'd secretly hoped he'd just had enough of everybody, and had gone to Florida. He used to talk about going to Florida every winter, particularly the last few."

"Do you know who killed him?" Calhoun asked. He glanced around for an ashtray but didn't see one.

"I haven't the slightest idea," Madeline said. "But with Dr. Hodges, there sure are a lot of candidates."

"Like who?" Calhoun asked.

"Well, let me take that back," Madeline said. "To be perfectly honest, I don't think that a single one of the people Dr. Hodges regularly infuriated would have actually done the man harm. In the same way Dr. Hodges would never had carried out any of the threats he voiced so frequently."

"Who did he threaten?" Calhoun asked.

Madeline laughed. "Just about everybody associated with the new administration at the hospital," she said. "Also the police chief, the head of the local bank, the Mobil station owner. The list goes on and on."

"Why was Hodges so angry with the new administration at the hospital?" Calhoun asked.

"Mostly on behalf of his patients," Madeline said. "Rather, his former patients. Dr. Hodges' practice fell off when he took over the directorship of the hospital, and then again when CMV came into the picture. He wasn't all that upset about it because he knew the hospital needed the HMO's business and he was ready to slow down. But then his former patients started coming back to him, complaining about their health care under CMV. They wanted him to be their doctor again, but it wasn't possible because their health care had to come through CMV."

"Sounds like Hodges should have been angry at CMV," Calhoun said. Before Madeline could respond, Calhoun asked if he could smoke. Madeline said no but offered to make him coffee. Calhoun accept her offer, so they adjourned to the kitchen.

"Where was I?" Madeline asked while she put water on the stove to boil.

"I was suggesting Hodges should have been angry with CMV," Calhoun said.

"I remember," Madeline said. "He was angry with CMV, but he was also angry with the hospital because the hospital was agreeing to everything CMV proposed. And Dr. Hodges felt he carried some weight at the hospital."

"Was he angry about anything specific?" Calhoun asked.

"It was a bunch of things," Madeline said. "He was angry about the treatment, or the lack of it, in the emergency room. People couldn't go to the emergency room any more unless they paid cash up front. Other people couldn't get into the hospital when they thought they needed to. The day he disappeared he was really upset by the death of one of his former patients. In fact, several of his former patients had recently died. I remember it specifically because Dr. Hodges used to yell and scream that CMV physicians couldn't keep his patients alive. He felt they were incompetent and that the hospital was abetting their incompetence."

"Can you remember the name of the patient Hodges was upset about the day he disappeared?" Calhoun asked.

"Now you're expecting miracles," Madeline said as she poured the coffee.

She handed a cup to Calhoun, who helped himself to three heaping teaspoons of sugar and a dollop of cream.

"Wait a minute! I do remember," Madeline said suddenly. "It was Clark Davenport. No doubt in my mind."

Calhoun fished out his set of the copies he and Angela had obtained in Burlington. "Here it is," he said after leafing through. "Clark Davenport, fractured hip."

"Yup, he's the one," Madeline said. "The poor man fell off a ladder trying to get a kitten out of a tree."

"Look at these other names," Calhoun said. He handed the papers to Madeline. "Any of them mean anything to you?"

Madeline took the papers and shuffled through them. "I can remember each and every one," she said. "In fact, these are the patients I mentioned: the ones Dr. Hodges was irritated about. They had all died."

"Hmmm," Calhoun said as he took the papers back. "I knew they had to be related somehow."

"Dr. Hodges was also upset at the hospital people because of the attacks in the parking lot," Madeline added.

"Why was that?" Calhoun asked.

"He felt the hospital administration should have been doing a lot more than they were," Madeline said. "They were more concerned about keeping the incidents out of the news than they were about catching the rapist. Dr. Hodges was convinced that the rapist was part of the hospital community."

"Did he have anybody specific in mind?"

"He indicated that he did," Madeline said. "But he didn't tell me who."

"Do you think he might have told his wife?" Calhoun asked.

"It's possible," Madeline said.

"Do you think he ever said anything to the person he suspected?" Calhoun asked.

"I haven't the slightest idea," Madeline said. "But I do know that he planned to discuss the problem with Wayne Robertson even though he and Wayne did not get along. In fact, he'd planned to go see Robertson the day he disappeared."

"Did he go?" Calhoun asked.

"No," Madeline said. "That same day Dr. Hodges learned that Clark Davenport had died. Instead of seeing Robertson, Dr. Hodges had me make a lunch date for him with Dr. Barry Holster, the radiotherapist. The reason I remembered Clark Davenport's name was because I remember making the lunch arrangements."

"Why was Hodges so eager to see Dr. Holster?" Calhoun asked.

"Dr. Holster had recently finished treating Clark Davenport," Madeline said.

Calhoun put down his coffee cup and stood up. "You've been wonderfully cooperative and most gracious," he said. "I'm appreciative of both your coffee and your excellent memory."

Madeline Gannon blushed.

Angela had finished her work and was leafing through a laboratory journal just prior to her lunch break when the chief medical examiner called.

"I'm glad I caught you," Walt said.

"Why?" Angela asked.

"Something extraordinary has happened," Walt said. "And you are responsible."

"Tell me," Angela said.

"It's all because of your surprise visit yesterday," Walt said. "Would you be able to jump in your car and come up here?"

"When?"

"Right now," Walt said.

Angela was intrigued. "Can you give me an idea of what this is about?" she asked.

"I'd rather show you," he said. "It's really unique. I'll have to write this up or at least present it at the annual forensic dinner. I want you to be in on it right away. Consider it part of your education."

"I'd love to come," Angela said. "But I'm worried about Dr. Wadley. We've not been on the best of terms."

"Oh, forget Wadley," Walt said. "I'll give him a call. This is important."

"You're making it hard to refuse," Angela said.

"That's the whole idea," Walt said.

Angela grabbed her coat. On her way out she glanced into Wadley's office. He wasn't there. She asked the secretaries where he was. They told her that he'd gone to the Iron Horse Inn for lunch and wouldn't be back until two.

She asked Paul Darnell to cover for her again in case there was any type of emergency. She told him that she'd gotten a specific request from the chief medical examiner to come to see something extraordinary.

Before she left for Burlington, Angela dashed up to the ICU to check on Nikki. She was pleased to discover that her daughter was doing much better and was in fine spirits.

Angela made it to the chief medical examiner's office in record time. "Wow!" Walt said when she appeared at his office door. He glanced at his watch as he stood to greet her. "That was fast. What kind of a sports car do you drive?"

"I have to admit your call whetted my curiosity. I was eager to get here," Angela said. "And to tell you the truth, I haven't much time."

"We won't need much time," Walt said. He led her to a microscope set up on a workbench. "First, I want you to look at this," he said.

Angela adjusted the eyepieces and looked in. She saw a specimen of skin. Then she saw black dots in the dermis.

"Do you know what that is?" Walt asked.

"I think so," Angela said. "This must be the skin from under Hodges' nails."

"Precisely," Walt said. "See the carbon?"

"I do," Angela said.

"All right. Take a look at this."

Angela lifted her eyes from the microscope and accepted a photograph from Walt.

"This is a photomicrograph I obtained with a scanning electron microscope," Walt explained. "Notice that the dots don't look like carbon any longer."

Angela studied the photo. What Walt was saying was true.

"Now look at this," Walt said. He handed her a printout. "This is the output of an atomic spectrophotometer. What I did was elute the granules with an acid solvent and then analyze them. They aren't carbon."

"What are they?" Angela asked.

"They're a mixture of chromium, cobalt, cadmium, and mercury," Walt said triumphantly.

"That's wonderful, Walt," Angela said. She was completely baffled. "But what does it mean?"

"I was just as perplexed as you," Walt said. "I had no idea what it meant. I even started to think that the atomic spectrophotometer had gone on the fritz until I suddenly had an epiphany. It's part of a tattoo!"

"Are you sure?" Angela questioned.

"Absolutely," Walt said. "These pigments are used for tattooing."

Angela immediately shared Walt's excitement. With the power of forensics they'd made a discovery about the killer. He had a tattoo. She couldn't wait to tell David and Calhoun.

Returning to Bartlet, Angela ran into Paul Darnell. He'd been waiting for her.

"I got some bad news," Darnell said. "Wadley knows you left town and he's not happy about it."

"How could he know?" Angela asked. Darnell was the only person she'd told.

"I think he was spying on you," Darnell said. "That's the only explanation I can think of. He came in to see me fifteen minutes after you left."

"I thought he'd gone out for lunch," Angela said.

"That's what he told everybody," Darnell said. "Obviously he hadn't. He asked me directly if you had left Bartlet. I couldn't lie. I had to tell him."

"Did you tell him I went to see the chief medical examiner?" Angela asked.

"Yes," Darnell said.

"Then it should be fine," Angela said. "Thanks for letting me know."

"Good luck," Darnell said.

No sooner had Angela returned to her office than a secretary appeared to let her know that Dr. Wadley wanted to see her in his office. That was an ominous turn of events. Wadley had never used an intermediary before.

Angela found Wadley sitting at his desk. He stared at her with cold eyes.

"I was told you wanted to see me," she said.

"I did indeed," Wadley said. "I wanted to inform you that you are fired. I would appreciate it if you would pack up your belongings and leave. Your continued presence is bad for morale."

"I find this hard to believe," Angela said.

"Nonetheless, it is so," Wadley said coldly.

"If you're upset because I was gone at my lunch hour, you should know that I drove to Burlington to visit the chief medical examiner," Angela said. "He'd called to ask me to come as soon as I could."

"Dr. Walter Dunsmore does not run this department," Wadley said. "I do."

"Didn't he call you?" Angela asked. She felt desperate. "He told me he would call you. He was excited about something he'd discovered concerning the body found in my home." Angela quickly related the details, but Wadley was unmoved.

"I've only been gone for a little over an hour," Angela said.

"I'm not interested in excuses," Wadley said. "I warned you just yesterday about this very same thing. You chose to ignore my warnings. You've demonstrated yourself to be unreliable, disobedient, and ungrateful."

"Ungrateful!" Angela exploded. "Ungrateful for what? For your sniveling advances? For not wanting to rush off to Miami for a weekend of sun and fun with you? You can fire me, Dr. Wadley, but I'll tell you what I can do: I can sue you and the hospital for sexual harassment."

"You just try it, young lady," Wadley snapped. "You'll be laughed out of the courtroom."

Angela stormed out of Wadley's office. She was beside herself with rage. As she passed through the outer office, the secretaries quickly scattered in her wake.

Angela went to her office and gathered up her belongings. There wasn't much. All the equipment belonged to the hospital. Packing her things into a canvas tote bag, she walked out. She didn't talk to anyone for fear of losing her composure. She didn't want to give Wadley the satisfaction of making her cry.

She intended to go directly to David's office, but then she changed her mind. After her recent argument with David, she was afraid of his reaction to her losing her job. She didn't think she could handle a confrontation in the hospital. So instead she went directly to her car and drove aimlessly toward town.

Just as she was passing the library she put on the brakes and backed up. She'd spotted Calhoun's inimitable truck in the parking lot.

Angela parked her car. She wondered where Calhoun might be. She decided to check the library, recalling that Calhoun had mentioned he knew the librarian.

Angela found Calhoun reading in a quiet alcove overlooking the town green.

"Mr. Calhoun?" Angela whispered.

Calhoun looked up. "How convenient," he said with a smile. "I've got some news."

"I'm afraid I've got some news as well," Angela said. "How about meeting me up at the house."

"I'll look forward to it," Calhoun said.

As soon as Angela got home she put some water on to boil. While she was getting out cups and saucers, Calhoun's truck came up the drive. Angela called out that the door was unlocked when he knocked.

"Coffee or tea?" Angela asked when Calhoun came into the kitchen.

"Whatever you're having," Calhoun said.

Angela got out the teapot and busied herself getting the tea and the honey.

"You're off kinda early," Calhoun said.

Having reined in her emotions ever since she'd fled Wadley's office, Angela's response to Calhoun's innocent comment was overwhelming. She covered her face and sobbed. At a loss for what he had said or what to do, Calhoun stood helpless.

When Angela's tears reduced to intermittent choking sobs, Calhoun apologized. "I'm sorry," he said. "I don't know what I did, but I'm sorry."

Angela stepped over to him and put her arms around him and her head on his woolly shoulder. He hugged her back. When she'd finally stopped crying he told her that she better tell him what happened.

"I think I'll have some wine instead of tea," Angela said.

"I'll have a beer," Calhoun said.

Sitting at the kitchen table Angela told Calhoun about getting fired. She explained how dire the consequences could be for her family.

Calhoun turned out to be a good listener, and he had the intuitive sense of what to say. He made Angela feel better. They even discussed her concerns about Nikki.

When Angela had talked herself out, Calhoun told her that he'd made some progress in the investigation.

"Maybe you're not interested anymore," Calhoun said.

"I'm still interested," Angela assured him. She dried her eyes with a dish towel. "Tell me."

"First of all, I discovered how the eight patients whose admission summaries Hodges was carrying around are related," he said. "All of them were former patients of Hodges' who had been shifted to CMV and had subsequently died in the months preceding Hodges' murder. Apparently each death came as a surprise for Hodges. That's why he was so furious."

"Did he blame the hospital or CMV?" Angela asked.

"Good question," Calhoun said. "As far as I could find out from his secretary he blamed both, but his main beef was with the hospital. It makes sense: he still thought of the hospital as his baby. So he was more disappointed with its perceived faults."

"Does this help us find out who killed him?" Angela asked.

"Probably not," Calhoun admitted. "But it's another piece to the puzzle. I also discovered another one: Hodges believed he knew the identity of the parking lot rapist. What's more, he thought the perp was connected to the hospital."

"I see where you are going," Angela said. "If the rapist knew Hodges suspected him, then he might have killed Hodges. In other words, the rapist and Hodges' murderer could be the same person."

"Exactly," Calhoun said. "The same person who tried to kill you the other night."

Angela shuddered. "Don't remind me," she said. Then she added: "I learned something specific about this person today, something that could make finding him a bit easier: he has a tattoo."

"How do you know that?" Calhoun asked.

Angela explained why she had gone to Burlington. She told Calhoun that Walter Dunsmore was absolutely convinced that Hodges had scraped off part of his killer's tattoo.

"Hell's bells," Calhoun said. "I love it."

When yet another nurse from the second floor called and asked to be seen for the flu, David was eager to see her. When she arrived, she was surprised that she didn't have to describe her symptoms; David described them for her. They were the same as his, only more pronounced. Her gastrointestinal problems had not responded well to the usual medications. Her temperature was one hundred and one.

"Have you had increased salivation?" David asked.

"I have," the nurse said, "and I've never had anything like it before."

"Nor have I," David said.

Seeing how uncomfortable this nurse was, David was thankful his own symptoms had waned during the day. He sent the nurse home for bed rest and told her to drink plenty of fluids and take whatever antipyretic medication she preferred.

After the last office patient had been seen, David started off to the hospital to see his patients. He'd been back and forth all day, checking on both Nikki and Sandra, so he expected no surprises.

When he entered the ICU, Nikki saw him immediately and beamed. She was doing remarkably well. She'd responded to the IV antibiotics and ministrations of the respiratory therapist. She hadn't even minded the hustle and bustle of the ICU. Still David was happy to learn that she was scheduled to be transferred out of the unit the following morning.

Sandra's condition was just the opposite, following a relentless downhill course. She'd never awakened from her coma. The consults had been no help. Hasselbaum said she didn't have an infectious disease. The oncologist merely shrugged and said there was nothing he could do. He insisted she'd had a good result from the treatment of her melanoma. It had been six years since the primary lesion on her thigh had been diagnosed, then removed along with a few malignant lymph nodes.

David sat at the desk in the ICU and leafed through Sandra's chart. The MRI of her skull had been normal: no tumor and certainly no brain abscess. David looked at the laboratory tests he'd ordered. Some were not back yet and wouldn't be for days. He'd ordered all body fluids to be cultured despite the infectious disease consult's findings. David had also ordered sophisticated searches of these same body fluids for viral remnants using state-of-the-art biotechnological techniques.

David had no idea what to do. The only possible alternative was to try to get Sandra transferred to one of the big teaching hospitals in Boston. But he knew CMV would take a dim view of such a proposition because of the expense, and David could not do it on his own.

While David was agonizing over Sandra, Charles Kelley came into the unit and approached the desk. His visit took David by surprise; the medical bureaucrats usually stayed clear of places like the ICU where they'd be forced to confront the critically ill. They much preferred to sit in their tidy offices and think of patients as abstractions.

"I hope I'm not disturbing you," Kelley said. His slick smile had returned.

"Lately you've disturbed me every time I've seen you," David said.

"Sorry," Kelley said condescendingly. "But I have a bit of news. As of this moment, your services here are no longer needed."

"So you think you can take Sandra Hascher away from me?" he said.

"Oh, yes," Kelley said with satisfaction. His smile broadened. "And all the other patients as well. You are fired. You're no longer employed by CMV."

David's mouth fell open. He was aghast. With bewilderment he watched as Kelley gave him a wave as if he were waving to a child, then turned around and left the unit. David leaped up from his chair and stumbled after Kelley.

"What about all the patients I'm scheduled to see?" David called out.

Kelley was already on his way down the hall. "They're CMV's concern, not yours," he answered without looking back.

"Is this decision final?" David called. "Or is it temporary, pending a hearing?"

"It's final, my friend." With that, he was gone.

David was in a daze. He couldn't believe he'd been fired. He stumbled into the patient lounge and collapsed into the same chair that he'd pushed Kelley into that morning.

David shook his head in disbelief. His first real job had only lasted four months. He began to consider the awful ramifications his firing would have on his family, and he began to tremble. He wondered how he would tell Angela. It was horribly ironic that only the night before he'd warned her about putting her job in jeopardy. Now here he was the one to get fired.

From where he was sitting, David suddenly spotted Angela entering the ICU. For a moment, David didn't move. He was afraid to face her but he knew he had to. He got up from the chair and followed Angela into the unit. She was standing alongside Nikki's bed. David slipped in along the opposite side.

Angela acknowledged David's arrival with a nod but continued her conversation with Nikki. David and Angela avoided each other's eyes.

"Will I be able to see Caroline when I leave the ICU?" Nikki asked.

David and Angela looked at each other briefly. It was clear neither knew what to say.

"Is she gone?" Nikki asked.

"She's gone," Angela said.

"She's already been discharged," Nikki cried. Her eyes began to fill with tears. She'd been looking forward to seeing her as soon as she got into a regular room.

"Maybe Arni will want to come in and visit," David suggested.

Nikki's disappointment made her moody and disagreeable. David and Angela knew that the ICU was taking its toll. They were afraid to tell her the truth about Caroline.

After David and Angela did what they could for Nikki's spirits, they left the ICU. They were chary with each other as they exited the hospital. Their conversation focused on Nikki and how pleased they were her clinical course was so smooth. Both of them were certain her emotional state would improve as soon as she was transferred out of the unit.

On the route home, Angela drove slowly to keep David in sight as he pedaled his bicycle. They arrived home at the same time. It wasn't until they were seated in the family room, ostensibly to watch the evening news, that David nervously cleared his throat.

"I'm afraid I have some rather bad news," he said. "I'm embarrassed to tell you I was fired this afternoon." David saw the shock registered in Angela's face. He averted his eyes. "I'm sorry. I know it'll be difficult for us. I don't know what to say. Maybe I'm not cut out to be a doctor."

"David," Angela said, reaching out and grabbing his arm. "I was fired, too."

David looked at Angela. "You were?" he asked.

She nodded.

He reached out and pulled her close. When they leaned back to look at each other again, they didn't know whether to laugh or cry.

"What a mess," David said at last.

"What a coincidence," Angela added.

They each shared the sorry details of their last acts at Bartlet. In the process, Angela also filled David in on Walt's latest discovery and her impromptu meeting with Calhoun.

"He thinks the tattoo will help find the murderer," Angela said.

"That's nice," David said. He still didn't share Angela's enthusiasm for the case, especially with the new turmoil in their lives.

"Calhoun had some intriguing news as well," Angela said. She explained Calhoun's theory that the hospital rapist and Hodges' killer were one and the same.

"Interesting idea," David said. But his thoughts were already elsewhere. He was wondering what he and Angela would do to support themselves in the immediate future.

"And remember those admission summaries Hodges was waving around? Calhoun figured out how they're related," Angela said. "They'd all died, and apparently all the deaths came as a surprise to Hodges."

"What do you mean a surprise?" David asked, suddenly becoming interested.

"I guess he didn't expect them to die," Angela said. "He had treated them before they transferred to CMV. Calhoun was told that Hodges blamed both CMV and the hospital for their deaths."

"Do you have any of the histories on these patients?" David asked.

"Just their admission diagnoses," Angela said. "Why?"

"Having patients die unexpectedly is something I can relate to," David said.

There was a pause in the conversation while David and Angela marveled at the day's events.

"What are we going to do?" Angela asked finally.

"I don't know," David said. "I'm sure we'll have to move, but what happens to the mortgages? I wonder if we'll have to declare bankruptcy. We'll have to talk to a lawyer. There's also the question of whether we'll want to sue our respective employers."

"There's no question in my mind," Angela said. "I'll sue for sexual harassment if not wrongful dismissal. There's no way I'll let that slime Wadley get off scot free."

"I don't know if suing is our style," David said. "Maybe we should just get on with our lives. I don't want to get bogged down in a legal morass."

"Let's not decide now," Angela said.

Later they called the ICU. Nikki was continuing to do well. She was still without a fever.

"We might have lost our jobs," David said, "but as long as Nikki is okay we'll manage."

FRIDAY • OCTOBER 29

Once again neither David nor Angela slept well. As was becoming his habit, David woke well before dawn. Although he was exhausted, he didn't feel ill like he had the previous morning.

Without waking Angela he went down to the family room to ponder their financial situation. He began to make a list of things to do and people to call, ranking them according to priority. He firmly believed their current plight required calm, rational thinking.

Angela appeared at the doorway in her robe. In her hand was a tissue; she'd been crying. She asked David what he was doing. He explained but she wasn't impressed.

"What are we going to do?" she cried. New tears spilled from her eyes. "We've made such a mess of everything."

David tried to console her by showing her his lists, but she shoved them away, accusing David of being out of touch with his feelings.

"Your stupid lists aren't going to solve anything," she said.

"And I suppose your hysterical tears will," David shot back.

Fortunately, they didn't let their argument go any further. They both knew they were overwrought. They also knew they each had their own way of dealing with a crisis.

"So what are we going to do?" Angela asked again.

"First, let's go to the hospital and check on Nikki," David said.

"Fine," Angela said. "It will give me a chance to talk with Helen Beaton."

"It will be futile," David warned. "Are you sure you want to expend the emotional effort?"

"I want to be sure she's aware of my complaint about sexual harassment," Angela said.

They had a quick breakfast before starting out. It felt strange for both of them to be going to the hospital yet not to work. They parked and went directly to the ICU.

Nikki was fine and antsy to get out of the unit. Although she'd found the bustle engrossing during the day, the night shift wasn't so pleasant. She'd gotten little sleep.

When Dr. Pilsner arrived he confirmed that Nikki was going to a regular room as soon as the floor sent someone to transport her.

"When do you think she'll be coming home?" Angela asked.

"As well as she's doing, she'll be home in just a few days," Dr. Pilsner said. "I want to make certain she doesn't suffer a relapse."

While David stayed with Nikki, Angela headed for Helen Beaton's office.

"Would you call Caroline and have her get my schoolbooks?" Nikki asked David.

"I'll take care of it," David promised. He was purposefully evasive. He was still reluctant to tell his daughter about Caroline's death.

David couldn't help but notice that Sandra's bed in the ICU was now occupied by an elderly man. It was half an hour before David mustered the courage to go to the unit clerk and ask about her.

"Sandra Hascher died this morning about three," the clerk said. He spoke as if he were giving a weather report; as accustomed to death as he was, he was unmoved.

David wasn't so unmoved. He'd been fond of Sandra, and his heart went out to her family, particularly her motherless children. Now he'd lost six patients in two weeks. He wondered if that was a record at Bartlet Community Hospital. Maybe CMV had been wise to fire him.

Promising Nikki that he and her mother would be back to see her later after she'd been moved to a regular room, David walked over to administration to wait for Angela.

Hardly had David sat down when Angela came storming out of the hospital president's office. She was livid. Her dark eyes shone with intensity, and her lips were clamped shut. She walked past David without slowing. He had to run to catch up with her.

"I suppose I shouldn't ask how it went," David said as they pushed through the doors to the parking lot.

"It was terrible," Angela said. "She's upholding Wadley's decision. When I explained to her that sexual harassment was at the bottom of the whole affair, she denied that any sexual harassment had taken place."

"How could she deny it when you'd spoken with Dr. Cantor?" David asked.

"She said that she asked Dr. Wadley," Angela said. "And Dr. Wadley said there had been no sexual harassment. In fact, he claimed it had been the other way around. He told Beaton that if there had been any impropriety it was that I'd tried to seduce him!"

"A familiar ploy of the sexual harasser," David said. "Blame the victim." He shook his head. "What a sleazebag!"

"Beaton said she believed him," Angela said. "She told me he was a man of impeccable integrity. Then she accused me of having made up the story to try to get back at him for spurning my advances."

When they arrived home they collapsed into chairs in the family room. They didn't know what to do. They were too depressed and confused to do anything.

The sound of tires crunching on gravel in their driveway broke the heavy silence. It was Calhoun's truck. Calhoun pulled up to the back door. Angela let him in.

"I brought you some fresh doughnuts to celebrate the first day of your vacation," Calhoun said. He passed by Angela and dumped his parcel on the kitchen table. "With a little coffee we'll be in business."

David appeared at the doorway.

"Uh-oh," Calhoun said. He looked from David to Angela.

"It's okay," said David. "I'm on 'vacation' too."

"No kidding!" Calhoun said. "Lucky I brought a dozen doughnuts."

Calhoun's presence was like an elixir. The coffee helped as well. David and Angela even found themselves laughing at some of Calhoun's stories from his days as a state policeman. They were in high spirits until Calhoun suggested they get down to work.

"Now," he said, rubbing his hands with anticipation. "The problem has been reduced to finding someone with a damaged tattoo who didn't like Hodges. That shouldn't be so hard to accomplish in a small town."

"There's a catch," David said. "Since we are unemployed, I don't think we can afford to employ you."

"Don't say that," Calhoun whined. "Just when this whole thing is getting interesting."

"We're sorry," David said. "Not only will we soon be broke, but we'll obviously be leaving Bartlet. So among other things, we'll be leaving this whole Hodges mess behind."

"Hold on a second," Calhoun said. "Let's not be too rash here. I've got an idea. I'll work for nothing. How's that? It's a matter of honor and reputation. Besides, we might be catching ourselves a rapist in the process."

"That's very generous of you . . ." David said. He started to say more but Calhoun interrupted him.

"I've already begun the next phase of inquiry," he said. "I found out from Carleton, the bartender, that several of the town's policemen, including Robertson, have tattoos. So I went over and had a casual chat with Robertson. He was more than happy to show me his. He's rather proud of it. It's on his chest: a bald eagle holding a banner that reads 'In God We Trust.' Unfortunately—or fortunately, depending on your perspective—the tattoo was in fine shape. But I used the opportunity to ask Robertson about Hodges' last day. Robertson confirmed what Madeline Gannon had said about Hodges' planning on seeing him, then canceling. So I think we're onto something. Clara Hodges may be the key. They were estranged at the time of the doc's death, but they still spoke frequently. I get the feeling living apart greatly improved their relationship. Anyway, I called Clara this morning. She's expecting us." He looked at Angela.

"I thought she'd moved to Boston," David said.

"She did," Calhoun said. "I thought Angela and I, er, now all three of us, could drive down."

"I still think Angela and I should drop this whole business, considering what's happened. If you want to continue, that's your business."

"Maybe we shouldn't be too rash," Angela said. "What if Clara Hodges can shed some light on the history of those patients who died? You were interested in that aspect of the case last night."

"Well, that's true," David admitted. He was curious to know how many similarities there were between Hodges' patients and his own. But he wasn't curious enough to visit Clara Hodges. Not after being fired.

"Let's do it, David," Angela said. "Let's go. I feel as if this town has conspired against us, and it bothers me. Let's fight back."

"Angela, you're beginning to sound a little out of control," David said.

Angela put her coffee cup down and grabbed David by the arm. "Excuse us," she said to Calhoun. Angela pulled David into the family room.

"I'm not out of control," she began once they were beyond Calhoun's earshot. "I just like the idea of doing something positive, of having a cause. This town has pushed us around the same way it's pushed Hodges' death under the carpet. I want to know what's behind it all. Then we can leave here with our heads held high."

"This is your hysterical side talking," David said.

"Whatever you want to call it is okay with me," Angela said. "Let's give it one more final go. Calhoun thinks this visit to Clara Hodges might do the trick. Let's try it."

David hesitated. His rational side argued against it, but Angela's pleas were hard to resist. Underneath his veneer of calm and reason, David was just as angry as Angela.

"All right," he said. "Let's go. But we'll stop and see Nikki first."

"Gladly," Angela said. She put out her hand. David halfheartedly slapped it. Then, when he put out his own, Angela hit it with surprising force.

David's next surprise was that they had to take Calhoun's truck so Calhoun could smoke. But with Calhoun driving, they were able to pull right up to the front door of the hospital. Calhoun waited while David and Angela ran inside.

Nikki was much happier now that she was out of the ICU. Her only complaint was that she'd been transferred to one of the old hospital beds and, as usual, the controls didn't work. The foot would rise but not the head.

"Did you tell the nurses?" David asked.

"Yeah," Nikki said. "But they haven't told me when it will be fixed. I can't watch the TV with my head flat."

"Is this a frequent problem?" Angela asked.

"Unfortunately," David said. He told her what Van Slyke had said about the hospital purchasing the wrong kind of beds. "They probably saved a few dollars buying the cheap ones. But any money saved has been lost in maintenance costs. It's that old expression: penny-wise and pound-foolish."

David left Angela with Nikki while he sought out Janet Colburn. When he found her he asked if Van Slyke had been alerted about Nikki's bed.

"He has, but you know Van Slyke," Janet said.

Back in Nikki's room, David assured her that if her bed wasn't fixed by that evening, he'd do it himself. Angela had already informed her that she and David were on their way to Boston but would be back that afternoon. They'd come see her as soon as they were back.

Returning to the front of the hospital, Angela and David piled into Calhoun's truck. Soon they were on their way south on the interstate. David found the trip uncomfortable for more reasons than the truck's poor suspension. Even though Calhoun cracked his window, cigar smoke swirled around inside the cab. By the time they got to Clara Hodges' Back Bay address in Boston, David's eyes were watering.

Clara Hodges struck David as having been a good match for Dennis Hodges. She was a big-boned, solid woman with piercing, deep-set eyes and an intimidating scowl.

She invited them into her parlor decorated with heavy Victorian furnishings. Only a meager amount of daylight penetrated the thick velvet drapes. Despite being midday the chandelier and all the table lamps were turned on.

Angela introduced herself and David as the purchasers of Clara's home in Bartlet.

"Hope you like it better than I did," Clara said. "It was too big and drafty, especially for only two people."

She offered tea, which David took with relish. Not only were his eyes burning from the secondhand smoke in the truck, but his throat was parched.

"I can't say I'm pleased about this visit," Clara said once her tea was poured. "I'm upset this ugly business has surfaced. I'd just about adjusted to Dennis's disappearance when I learned that he'd been murdered."

"I'm sure you share our interest in bringing his killer to justice," Calhoun said.

"It wouldn't matter much now," Clara said. "Besides, we'd all be dragged through some awful trial. I preferred it the way it was, just not knowing."

"Do you have any suspicions about who killed your husband?" Calhoun asked.

"I'm afraid there are a lot of candidates," Clara said. "You have to understand two things about Dennis. First off, he was bullheaded, which made him hard to get along with. Not that he didn't have a good side, too. The second thing about Dennis was his obsession with the hospital. He was at constant odds with the board and that woman administrator they recruited from Boston.

"I suppose any one of a dozen people could have gotten angry enough to do him in. Yet I just can't imagine any one of them actually beating him. Too messy for all those doctors and bureaucrats, don't you think?"

"I understand that Dr. Hodges thought he knew the identity of the ski-masked rapist," Calhoun said. "Is that a fair statement?"

"That's certainly what he implied," Clara said.

"Did he ever mention any names?" Calhoun asked.

"The only thing he said was that the rapist was someone connected to the hospital," Clara said.

"An employee of the hospital?" Calhoun asked.

"He didn't elaborate," Clara said. "He was purposefully vague. That man lived to lord things over you. But he did say he wanted to speak to the person himself, thinking he could get him to stop."

"Lordy," Calhoun said. "That sounds like a dangerous thing to do. Do you think he did?"

"I don't know," Clara said. "He might have. But then he decided to go to that abominable Wayne Robertson with his suspicions. We got into a fearful quarrel over the issue. I didn't want him to go since I was sure he and Robertson would only squabble. Robertson always did have it in for him. I told him to tell Robertson his suspicions by phone or write him a letter, but Dennis wouldn't hear of it. He was so stubborn."

"Was that the day he disappeared?" Calhoun asked.

"That's right," Clara said. "But in the end Dennis didn't see Robertson—not because of my advice, mind you. He got all upset over one of his former patients dying. He said he was going to have lunch with Dr. Holster instead of seeing Robertson."

"Was this patient Clark Davenport?" Calhoun asked.

"Why yes," Clara said with surprise. "How did you know?"

"Why was Dr. Hodges so upset about Clark Davenport?" Calhoun asked, ignoring Clara's question. "Were they good friends?"

"They were acquaintances," Clara said. "Clark was more a patient, and Dennis had diagnosed Clark's cancer, which Dr. Holster had successfully treated. After the treatment Dennis had felt confident that they'd caught the cancer early enough. But then Clark's employer switched to CMV and the next thing Dennis knew, Clark was dead."

"What did Clark die of?" David asked suddenly, speaking up for the first time. His voice had an urgent quality that Angela noticed immediately.

"You've got me there," Clara said. "I don't recall. I'm not sure I ever knew. But it wasn't his cancer. I remember Dennis saying that."

"Did your husband have any other medically similar patients who ended up dying unexpectedly?" David asked.

"What do you mean by medically similar?" Clara asked.

"People with cancer or other serious diseases," David said.

"Oh, yes," Clara said. "He had a number. And it was their deaths that upset him so. He became convinced that some of the CMV doctors were incompetent."

David asked Angela for copies of the admission sheets she and Calhoun had gotten from Burlington. As Angela was searching for them, Calhoun pulled out his set from one of his voluminous pockets.

David fumbled with the papers as he unfolded them. He handed them to Clara. "Look at these names," he said. "Do you recognize any?"

"I'll have to get my reading glasses," Clara said. She stood up and left the room.

"What are you so agitated about?" Angela whispered to David.

"Yeah, calm down, boy," Calhoun said. "You'll get our witness all upset and she'll start forgetting things."

"Something is beginning to dawn on me," David said. "And I don't like it one bit."

Before Angela could ask David to explain, Clara returned with her reading glasses. She picked up the papers and quickly glanced through them.

"I recognize all these people," Clara said. "I'd heard their names a hundred times, and I'd met most of them."

"I was told all of them died," Calhoun said. "Is that true?"

"That's right," Clara said. "Just like Clark Davenport. These are the people whose deaths had particularly upset Dennis. For a while I heard about them every day."

"Were their deaths all unexpected?" Calhoun asked.

"Yes and no," Clara said. "I mean it was unexpected for these people to die at the particular time they did. As you can see from these papers, most of the people were hospitalized for problems that usually aren't fatal. But they all had battled terminal illnesses like cancer, so in that sense their deaths weren't totally unexpected."

David reached out and took the papers back. He glanced through them quickly, then looked up at Clara. "Let me be sure I understand," he said. "These admission summary sheets are the admissions during which these people died."

"I believe so," Clara said. "It's been a while, but Dennis carried on so. It's hard to forget."

"And each of these patients had a serious underlying illness," David said. "Like this one admitted for sinusitis."

Clara took the sheet and looked at the name. "She had breast cancer," Clara said. "She was in my church group."

David took the sheet of paper back from Clara and rolled it up with the others. Then he stood up and walked over to the window. Pulling back the drapes, he stared out over the Charles River, ignoring the others. He seemed quite distracted.

Angela was mildly embarrassed at David's poor manners, but it was apparent that Clara didn't mind. She simply poured them all more tea.

"I want to ask a few more questions about the rapist," Calhoun said. "Did Dr. Hodges ever allude to his age or height or details such as whether or not he had a tattoo?"

"A tattoo?" Clara questioned. A fleeting smile flashed across her face before her frown returned. "No, he never mentioned a tattoo."

With a swiftness that took everyone by surprise, David returned from the window. "We have to leave," he said. "We have to go immediately."

He rushed for the door and pulled it open.

"David?" Angela called, astonished at his behavior. "What's the matter?"

"We've got to get back to Bartlet immediately," he said. His urgency had grown to near panic. "Come on!" he yelled.

Angela and Calhoun gave a hurried goodbye to Clara Hodges before running after David. By the time Angela and Calhoun got out to the truck, David was already behind the wheel.

"Give me the keys," he ordered.

Calhoun shrugged and handed them to David. David started the truck and gunned the engine. "Get in," he shouted.

Angela got in first, followed by Calhoun. Before the door was closed behind them, David hit the gas.

For the first portion of the trip no one spoke. David concentrated on driving. Angela and Calhoun were still shocked by the sudden, awkward departure. They were also intimidated by the rapidity with which they were overtaking other motorists.

"I think we'd better slow down," Angela said as David passed a long row of cars.

"This truck has never gone this fast," Calhoun said.

"David, what has come over you?" Angela asked. "You're acting bizarre."

"I had a flash of insight while we were talking to Clara Hodges," he said. "It concerns Hodges' patients with potentially terminal illnesses dying unexpectedly."

"Well?" Angela asked. "What about them?"

"I think some disturbed individual at Bartlet Community Hospital has taken it upon himself to deliver some sort of misguided euthanasia."

"What's euthanasia?" Calhoun asked.

"It translates to 'good death,' " Angela said. "It means to help someone who has a terminal illness to die. The idea is to save them from suffering."

"Hearing about Hodges' patients made me realize that all six of my recent deaths had battled terminal illnesses," David said. "The same as his. I don't know why I didn't think about it before. How could I have been so dense? And the same is true with Caroline."

"Who's Caroline?" Calhoun asked.

"She was a friend of our daughter," Angela explained. "She had cystic fibrosis, which is a potentially terminal illness. She died yesterday." Angela's eyes went wide. "Oh, no! Nikki!" she cried.

"Now you know why I panicked," David said. "We have to get back there as soon as we can."

"What's going on?" Calhoun said. "I'm missing something here. Why are you two so agitated?"

"Nikki is in the hospital," Angela said anxiously.

"I know," Calhoun said. "Before we went to Boston I took you there so you could visit her."

"She has cystic fibrosis just like Caroline had," Angela said.

"Uh-oh," Calhoun said. "I'm getting the picture. You're worried about your daughter being targeted by this euthanasia fiend."

"You got it," David said.

"Would this be something like that 'Angel of Mercy' case on Long Island I read about?" Calhoun asked. "It was a number of years ago. It involved a nurse who was knocking people off with some sort of drug."

"Something like that," David said. "But that case involved a muscle relaxant. The people stopped breathing. It was pretty straightforward. With my patients I have no idea how they're being killed. I can't think of any drug or poison or infectious agent that would cause the symptoms these patients had."

"I can understand why you'd be worried about your daughter," Calhoun said. "But don't you think you're being a bit hasty with this theory?"

"It answers a lot of questions," David said. "It even makes me think of Dr. Portland."

"Why?" Angela asked. She was still uncomfortable anytime his name came up.

"Didn't Kevin tell us that Dr. Portland said he wasn't going to take all the blame for his patient deaths and that there was something wrong with the hospital?"

Angela nodded.

"He must have had his suspicions," David said. "Too bad he succumbed to his depression."

"He committed suicide," Angela explained to Calhoun.

"Terrible waste," Calhoun said. "All that training."

"The question is," David said, "if someone is performing euthanasia in the hospital, who could it be? It would have to be someone with access to the patients and someone with a sophisticated knowledge of medicine."

"That would limit it to a doctor or a nurse," Angela said.

"Or a lab tech," David suggested.

"I think you people are jumping the gun," Calhoun said. "This isn't the way investigations are done. You don't come up with a theory and then go barreling off at ninety miles an hour like we're doing. Most theories fall apart when more facts are in. I think we should slow down."

"Not while my daughter is at risk," David said. He pushed the old truck harder.

"Do you think Hodges came to the same conclusion?" Angela asked.

"I think so," David said. "And if he did, maybe that's why he was killed."

"I still think it was the rapist," Calhoun said. "But whoever it turns out to be, this investigation is fascinating. Providing your daughter's okay, I haven't enjoyed myself this much in years."

When they finally reached the hospital, David pulled right up to the front door. He jumped out with Angela close at his heels. Together they charged up the main stairs and ran down the hall.

To their supreme relief, they discovered Nikki perfectly happy watching TV. David snatched her up in his arms and hugged her so tightly that she began to complain.

"You're coming home," David said. He held her away so he could examine her face, especially her eyes.

"When?" Nikki asked.

"Right now," Angela said. She started disconnecting the IV.

At that moment a nurse was passing in the hall. The commotion drew her attention. When she saw Angela detaching the IV, she protested.

"What's going on here?" she asked.

"My daughter is going home," David said.

"There are no orders for that," the nurse said.

"I'm giving the order right this minute," David said.

The nurse quickly ran out of the room. Angela started to gather Nikki's clothes. David helped.

Soon Janet Colburn came back with several nurses in tow. "Dr. Wilson," Janet said, "what on earth are you doing?"

"I think it's rather apparent," David said as he packed Nikki's toys and books in a bag.

David and Angela had Nikki half dressed when Dr. Pilsner arrived. Janet had paged him. He urged them not to remove Nikki from the IV antibiotic or the hospital's talented respiratory therapist prematurely.

"I'm sorry, Dr. Pilsner," David said. "I'll have to explain later. It would take too long right now."

At that moment Helen Beaton arrived. She, too, had been called by the nurses. She was incensed. "If you take that child out of here against medical advice I'll get a court order," she sputtered.

"Just try," Angela said.

When they had Nikki fully dressed, they led her down the hall. The commotion had drawn a flock of gawking patients and staff.

Once outside they all climbed into the truck. Calhoun drove with Nikki and Angela in the cab. David had to sit in the truck bed.

The whole way home Nikki questioned her sudden discharge. She was happy to be out, but puzzled by her parents' odd behavior. But by the time she got in the house she was too excited to see Rusty to persist in her questioning. After she played with Rusty for a bit, David and Angela set her up in the family room and restarted her IV. They wanted to continue her antibiotics.

Calhoun stayed and participated as best he could. Following Nikki's request he brought wood upstairs from the basement and made a fire. But it wasn't his nature to stay silent. Before long he got into an argument with David over the motive for Hodges' murder. Calhoun strongly favored the rapist, whereas David favored the deranged "Angel of Mercy."

"Hell!" Calhoun exclaimed. "Your whole theory is based on pure supposition. Your daughter is fine, thank the Lord, so there's no proof there. At least with my theory there's Hodges' ranting about knowing who the rapist was before a roomful of people the very day he got knocked off. How's that for cause and effect? And Clara thinks Hodges might have had the nerve to speak to the man. I'm so sure the rapist and the murderer are one and the same, I'll wager on it. What kind of odds will you give me?"

"I'm not a betting man," David said. "But I think I'm right. Hodges was beaten to death holding the names of his patients. That couldn't have been a coincidence."

"What if it is the same person?" Angela suggested. "What if the rapist is the same person behind the patient deaths and Hodges' murder?"

The idea shocked David and Calhoun into silence.

"It's possible," David said at last. "It sounds sort of crazy, but at this point I'm prepared to believe almost anything."

"I suppose," Calhoun added. "Anyway, I'm going after the tattoo clue. That's the key."

"I'm going to medical records," David said. "And maybe I'll visit Dr. Holster. Hodges might have said something to him about his suspicions regarding his patients."

"Okay," Calhoun said agreeably. "I'll go do my thing, you go ahead and do yours. How's about if I come back later so we can compare notes?"

"Sounds good," David said. He looked over at Angela.

"It's fine by me," she said. "What about having dinner together?"

"I never turn down dinner invitations," Calhoun said.

"Then be here by seven," Angela said.

After Calhoun left, David got the shotgun and proceeded to load it with as many shells as it would hold. He leaned it against the newel post in the front hall.

"Have you changed your mind about the gun?" Angela asked.

"Let's just say I'm glad it's here," David said. "Have you talked to Nikki about it?"

"Absolutely," Angela said. "She even shot it. She said it hurt her shoulder."

"Don't let anyone in the house while I'm gone," David said. "And keep all the doors locked."

"Hey, I'm the one who wanted the doors locked," Angela said. "Remember?"

David took his bike. He didn't want to leave Angela without a car. He rode quickly, oblivious to the sights. His mind kept going over the idea of someone having killed his patients. It horrified and infuriated him. But as Calhoun said, he didn't have any proof.

When David arrived at the hospital, the day shift was being replaced by the evening shift. There was a lot of commotion and traffic. No one paid the slightest attention to David as he made his way to medical records.

Sitting down at a terminal, David set out Calhoun's copies of the pages that had been interred with Hodges. He'd held on to them since their visit to Clara Hodges. He called up each patient's name and read the history. All eight had had serious terminal illnesses as Clara Hodges had said.

Then David read through the notes written during each patient's hospital stay when they died. In all cases, the symptoms were similar to those experienced by David's patients: neurological symptoms, gastrointestinal symptoms, and symptoms dealing with the blood or immune system.

Next, David looked up the final causes of death. In each case except for one, death resulted from a combination of overwhelming pneumonia, sepsis, and shock. The exception was a death subsequent to a series of sustained seizures.

Putting Hodges' papers away, David began using the hospital computer to calculate yearly death rates as a percentage of admissions. The results flashed on the screen instantly. He quickly discovered that the death rate had changed two years before when it had gone from an average of 2.8% up to 6.7%. The last year the figures were available, the death rate was up to 8.1%.

David then narrowed the death rate to those patients who had a diagnosis of cancer, whether the cancer was attributed as the cause of death or not. Although these percentages were understandably higher than the overall death rate, they showed the same sudden increase.

David next used the computer to calculate the yearly diagnosis of cancer as a percentage of admissions. With these statistics he saw no sudden change. On average, they were nearly identical going back ten years.

The increased percentage of deaths seemed to back up David's theory of an angel of mercy at work. Euthanasia would explain the fact that the relative incidence of all cancers was remaining stable while the death rate for people with cancer was going up. The evidence was indirect, but it couldn't be ignored.

David was about to leave when he thought of using the computer to elicit additional information. He asked the computer to search through all the medical histories on all the admissions for the words "tattoo" or "dyschromia," the medical word for aberrant pigmentation.

He waited while the computer searched. David sat back and watched the screen. It took almost a minute, but finally a list blazed on the screen. David quickly deleted the cases with medical or metabolic causes of pigmentary change. In the end, he came up with a list of twenty people who had been treated at the hospital with a mention of a tattoo in their records.

Using the computer yet again to match name and employment, David discovered that five of the people listed worked in the hospital. They were, in alphabetical order, Clyde Devonshire, an RN who worked in the emergency room; Joe Forbs from security; Claudette Maurice from dietary; Werner Van Slyke from engineering/maintenance; and Peter Ullhof, a lab technician.

David was intrigued to see a couple of the other names and occupations listed: Carl Hobson, deputy policeman, and Steve Shegwick, a member of the security force at Bartlet College. The rest of the people worked in various stores or in construction.

David printed out a copy of this information. Then he went on his way.

David had assumed his visit to medical records had gone unnoticed, but he was wrong. Hortense Marshall, one of the health information professionals, had been alerted to some of David's activities by a security program she'd placed in the hospital computer.

From the moment she'd been alerted, she'd kept an eye on David. As soon as he'd departed from records, she placed a call to Helen Beaton.

"Dr. David Wilson was in medical records," Hortense said. "He's just left. But while he was here he called up information concerning hospital death rates."

"Did he talk with you?" Beaton asked.

"No," Hortense said. "He used one of our terminals. He didn't speak with anyone."

"How did you know he was accessing data on death rates?" Beaton asked.

"The computer alerted me," Hortense said. "After you advised me to report anyone requesting that kind of data, I had the computer programmed to signal me if someone tried to access the information on their own."

"Excellent work," Beaton said. "I like your initiative. You're to be commended. That kind of data is not for public consumption. We know our rates have gone up since we've become a tertiary care facility for CMV. They're sending us a high proportion of critically ill patients."

"I'm sure statistics of that ilk would not help our public relations," Hortense said.

"That's the concern," Beaton said.

"Should I have said anything to Dr. Wilson?" Hortense asked.

"No, you did fine," Beaton said. "Did he research anything else?"

"He was here for quite a while," Hortense said. "But I have no idea what else he was looking up."

"The reason I ask," Beaton said, "is because Dr. Wilson has been suspended from CMV."

"That I wasn't aware of," Hortense said.

"It just happened yesterday," Beaton said. "Would you let me know if he comes back?"

"Most certainly," Hortense said.

"Excuse me," Calhoun said. "Is your name Carl Hobson?" He'd approached one of Bartlet's uniformed patrolmen as he came out of the diner on Main Street.

"Sure is," the policeman answered.

"Mine's Phil Calhoun," Calhoun said.

"I've seen you around the station," Carl said. "You're friends with the chief."

"Yup," Calhoun said. "Wayne and I go back a ways. I used to be a state policeman, but I got retired."

"Good for you," Carl said. "Now it's nothing but fishing and hunting."

"I suppose," Calhoun said. "Mind if I ask you a personal question?"

"Hell, no," Carl said with curiosity.

"Carleton over at the Iron Horse told me you had a tattoo," Calhoun said. "I've been thinking about getting one myself, so I've been looking around and asking questions. Many people in town have 'em?"

"There's a few," Carl said.

"When did you get yours?" Calhoun asked.

"Way the hell back in high school," Carl said with an embarrassed laugh. "Five of us drove over to Portsmouth, New Hampshire, one Friday night when we were seniors. There's a bunch of tattoo parlors over there. We were all blitzed."

"Did it hurt?" Calhoun asked.

"Hell, I don't remember," Carl said. "Like I said, we were all drunk."

"All five of you guys still in town?" Calhoun asked.

"Just four of us," Carl said. "There's me, Steve Shegwick, Clyde Devonshire, and Mort Abrams."

"Did everybody get tattooed in the same spot?" Calhoun asked.

"Nope," Carl said. "Most of us got 'em on our biceps, but some chose their forearms. Clyde Devonshire was the exception. He got tattooed on his chest above each nipple."

"Who got tattooed on his forearm?" Calhoun asked.

"I'm not sure," Carl admitted. "It's been a while. Maybe Shegwick and Jay Kaufman. Kaufman's the guy who moved away. He went to college someplace in New Jersey."

"Where's yours?" Calhoun asked.

"I'll show you," Carl said. He unbuttoned his shirt and pulled up the sleeve. On the outer aspect of his upper arm was a howling wolf with the word "lobo" below it.

By the time David returned home from his visit to medical records, Nikki had begun to feel worse. At first she only complained of stomach cramps, but by early evening she was suffering from nausea and increased salivation—the same symptoms David had experienced during the night. They were also the symptoms reported by the six night-shift nurses and, even scarier, by his six patients who had died.

By six-thirty Nikki was lethargic after several bouts of diarrhea, and David was sick with worry. He was terrified that they'd not gotten her out of the hospital quickly enough: whatever had killed his patients had already been given to her.

David did not share his fears with Angela. It was bad enough that she was concerned about Nikki's ostensible symptoms without adding the burden of a potential link to all those patients who died. So David kept his worries to himself, but he agonized over the possibility of an infectious disease of some kind. He comforted himself with the thought that his illness and the nurses' had been self-limiting, suggesting a low exposure to an airborne agent. David's great hope was that if such an agent was to blame, Nikki had only gotten a low dose as well.

Calhoun arrived at exactly seven. He was clutching a sheet of paper and carrying a paper bag.

"I got nine more people with tattoos," he said.

"I got twenty," David said. He tried to sound upbeat, but he couldn't get Nikki out of his mind.

"Let's combine them," Calhoun said.

When they combined the lists and threw out the duplicates, they had a final list of twenty-five people.

"Dinner's ready," Angela said. Angela had cooked a feast to buoy their spirits and to keep herself busy. She'd had David set the table in the dining room.

"I've brought wine," Calhoun said. He opened his parcel and pulled out two bottles of Chianti.

Five minutes later they were sitting down to a fine meal of chicken with chèvre, one of Angela's favorite dishes.

"Where's Nikki?" Calhoun asked.

"She's not hungry," Angela said.

"She doing okay?" Calhoun asked.

"Her stomach's a bit upset," Angela said. "But considering what we put her through, it's to be expected. The main thing is that she has no fever and her lungs are perfectly clear."

David winced but didn't say anything.

"What do we do now that we have the list of people with tattoos?" she asked.

"We proceed in two ways," Calhoun said. "First we run a background computer check on each person. That's the easy part. Second, I start interviewing them. There are certain things we need to find out, like where each person's tattoo is located and whether they mind showing it off. The tattoo that got scratched by Hodges must be the worse for wear and tear, and it has to be located someplace where it could have been scratched in a struggle. If someone has a little heart on their butt, we're not going to be too interested."

"What do you think is the most promising location?" Angela asked. "On the forearm?"

"I'd say so," Calhoun said. "The forearm, and maybe the wrist. I suppose we shouldn't rule out the back of the hand although that's not a common place for professional tattoos. The tattoo we're dealing with has to have been done by a professional. Professionals are the only ones who use the heavy metal pigments."

"How do we run a background computer check?" Angela asked.

"All we need is the social security number and the birth date," Calhoun said. "We should be able to get those through the hospital." Calhoun looked at David. David nodded. "Once we have that information the rest is easy. It's staggering what information can be obtained from the hundreds of data banks that exist. Whole companies are set up in the information business. For a nominal fee you'd be surprised what you can find out."

"You mean these companies can tap into private data banks?" Angela asked.

"Absolutely," Calhoun said. "Most people don't realize it, but anybody with a computer and a modem can get an amazing amount of information on anybody."

"What kind of information would people be looking for?" Angela asked.

"Anything and everything," Calhoun said. "Financial history, criminal records, job history, consumer purchasing history, phone use, mail-order stuff, personal ads. It's like a fishing trip. But interesting stuff turns up. It always does, even if you have a group of twenty-five people who are ostensibly the most normal people in a community. You'd be shocked. And with a group of twenty-five people with tattoos, it will be very interesting. They will not be, quote, 'normal,' believe me."

"Did you do this when you were a state policeman?" Angela asked.

"All the time," Calhoun said. "Whenever we had a bunch of suspects we'd run a background computer check, and we always got some dirt. And in this case if David is right and the killer is committing euthanasia, I can't imagine what we'd run across. He or she would have to be screwed up. We'd find other crusades, like saving animals from shelters and being arrested for having nine hundred dogs in their house. I guarantee we'll come across lots of screwy, weird stuff.

We'll need to get hold of some computer jock to help us tap into the data banks."

"I have an old boyfriend at MIT," Angela said. "He's been in graduate school forever, but I know he's a computer genius."

"Who's that?" David asked. He hadn't heard about this old boyfriend before.

"His name is Robert Scali," Angela said. Of Calhoun she asked: "Do you think he would be able to help us?"

"So why have I never heard of this guy?" David asked.

"I haven't told you every little detail of my life," Angela said. "I dated him for a short time freshman year at Brown."

"But you've been in touch since then?"

"We've gotten together a couple of times over the last few years," Angela said.

"I can't believe I'm hearing this," David said.

"Oh, please, David," Angela said with exasperation. "You're being ridiculous."

"I think Mr. Scali would probably do fine," Calhoun said. "If not, as I said, I know some companies who will gladly help for a modest fee."

"At this point, we'd do well to avoid any fees," Angela said. With that, she started to clear the table.

"Any chance of getting a description of the tattoos from medical records?" Calhoun asked.

"I think so," David said. "Most physicians would probably note them in a physical examination. I certainly would describe them in any physical I'd do."

"It sure would help prioritize our list," Calhoun said. "I'd like to interview those with tattoos on their forearms and wrists first."

"What about the people who work for the hospital?" David asked.

"We'll start with those," Calhoun said. "Absolutely. Also I've been told Steve Shegwick has a tattoo on his forearm. I'd like to talk with him."

Angela came back and asked who wanted ice cream and coffee. David said he'd pass, but Calhoun was eager for both. David got up and went to check on Nikki.

Later, when they were sitting around the table after the meal was complete, Angela expressed an interest in organizing the efforts for the following day.

"I'll start interviewing the tattooed hospital workers," Calhoun said. "I still think it's best for me to be the front man. We don't want any more bricks through your windows."

"I'll go back to medical records," David said. "I'll get the social security numbers and birth dates and see about getting descriptions of the tattoos."

"I'll stay with Nikki," Angela said. "Then when David's gotten the social security numbers and birth dates I'll take a run into Cambridge."

"What's the matter with sending them by fax?" David asked.

"We'll be asking for a favor," Angela said. "I can't just fire off a fax."

David shrugged.

"What about that Dr. Holster, the radiotherapist," Calhoun said. "Someone has to talk with him. I'd do it but I think one of you medical people would do a better job."

"Oh yeah," David said. "I forgot about him. I can see him tomorrow when I finish at medical records."

Calhoun scraped back his chair and stood up. He patted his broad, mildly protuberant abdomen. "Thank you for one of the best dinners I've had in a long, long time," he said. "I think it's time for me to drive me and my stomach home."

"When should we talk again?" Angela asked.

"As soon as we have something to talk about," Calhoun said. "And both of you should get some sleep. I can tell you need it."

SATURDAY • OCTOBER 30

Although Nikki suffered from abdominal cramps and diarrhea throughout the night, by morning she was better. She still wasn't back to one hundred percent, but she was clearly on the mend and had remained afebrile. David was vastly relieved. None of his hospital patients had shown this kind of improvement once their symptoms had started. He was confident that from here on Nikki's course would mirror his own and that of the nurses.

Angela woke up depressed about her job situation. She was surprised that David's spirits were so high. Now that Nikki was so much better, he confessed his darker fears to Angela.

"You should have told me," she said.

"It wouldn't have helped," David said.

"Sometimes you make me so angry," Angela said. But instead of pouting, she rushed to David and hugged him, telling him how much she loved him.

The phone interrupted their embrace. It was Dr. Pilsner. He wanted to find out how Nikki was doing. He also wanted to put in another plug for continuing her antibiotics and respiratory therapy.

"We'll do it as often as you tell us," Angela said. She was on the phone in the bedroom while David listened on the extension in the bathroom.

"Sometime soon we'll explain why we spirited her away," David said. "But for now, please accept our apology. Taking Nikki out of the hospital had nothing to do with the care you were providing."

"My only concern is Nikki," Dr. Pilsner said.

"You're welcome to stop by," Angela said. "And if you think that continued hospitalization is needed, we'll take her into Boston."

"For now, just keep me informed," Dr. Pilsner said curtly.

"He's irritated," David said after they'd hung up.

"I can't blame him," Angela said. "People must think we're nuts."

Both David and Angela aided Nikki in her respiratory therapy, taking turns thumping her back as she lay in the required positions. "Can I go to school on Monday?" she asked once they were done.

"It's possible," Angela said. "But I don't want you to get your hopes up."

"I don't want to get too far behind," Nikki said. "Can Caroline come over and bring my schoolbooks?"

Angela glanced at David, who was petting Rusty on Nikki's bed. He returned Angela's gaze, and a wordless communication flashed between them. Both understood that they could no longer mislead Nikki no matter how much they hated to tell her the sad truth.

"There's something we have to tell you about Caroline," Angela said gently. "We're all terribly sorry, but Caroline passed away."

"You mean she died?" Nikki asked.

"I'm afraid so," Angela said.

"Oh," Nikki said simply.

Angela looked back at David. David shrugged. He couldn't think of what else to add. He knew that Nikki's nonchalance was a defense, similar to her response to Marjorie's death. David felt anger tighten in his throat as he recognized that both deaths could have been the work of the same misguided individual.

It took even less time than it had with Marjorie for Nikki's facade to crumble. Angela and David did what they could to console her, and her anguish tormented them. Both of them knew it was a devastating blow for her; not only had Caroline been her friend, but throughout her short life Nikki had been fighting the same disease from which Caroline had suffered.

"Am I going to die too?" Nikki sobbed.

"No," Angela said. "You're doing wonderfully. Caroline had a high fever. You have no fever at all."

Once they had calmed Nikki's fears, David set out for the hospital on his bike. Once he arrived, he went to medical records and immediately set about matching social security numbers and birth dates to the list of names he and Calhoun had compiled.

With that out of the way, David began to call up each medical record to sift through for descriptions of the tattoos. He hadn't gotten far when someone tapped him on the shoulder. He turned around to face Helen Beaton. Behind her was Joe Forbs from security.

"Would you mind telling me what you are doing?" Beaton asked.

"I'm just using the computer," David stammered. He hadn't expected to run into anyone from administration, particularly not on a Saturday morning.

"It's my understanding that you are no longer employed by CMV," Beaton said.

"That's true," David said. "But . . ."

"Your hospital privileges are awarded in conjunction with your employment by CMV," Beaton said. "Since that's no longer the case, your privileges must be reviewed by the credentials committee. Until that time you have no right to computer access.

"Would you please escort Dr. Wilson out of the hospital?" Beaton said to Joe.

Joe Forbs stepped forward and motioned for David to get up.

David knew it was pointless to protest. He calmly gathered up his papers, hoping Beaton wouldn't strip him of these documents. Luckily, Forbs simply escorted him to the door.

Now David could add "bodily thrown out of a hospital" to his brief and ignominious career record. Undaunted, he proceeded to the radiotherapy unit, which was housed in its own ultra-modern building which had been designed by the same architect who had designed the Imaging Center.

The radiotherapy unit used Saturday mornings to see long-term follow-up patients. David had to wait half an hour before Dr. Holster could squeeze him in.

Dr. Holster was about ten years older than David, but he appeared even older than that. His hair was totally gray, almost white. Although he was busy that morning, he was hospitable and offered David a cup of coffee.

"So, what can I do for you, Dr. Wilson?" Dr. Holster said.

"You can call me David, for starters," David said. "Beyond that I was hoping to ask you some questions about Dr. Hodges."

"That's a rather strange request," Dr. Holster said. He shrugged. "But I guess I don't mind. Why are you interested?"

"It's a long story," David admitted. "But to make it short, I've had some patients whose hospital courses resembled some of Dr. Hodges' patients'. A few of these patients were ones you treated."

"Ask away," Dr. Holster said.

"Before I do," David said, "I'd also like to request this conversation be confidential."

"Now you're really piquing my curiosity," Dr. Holster said. He nodded. "Confidential it will be."

"I understand that Dr. Hodges visited you the day he disappeared," David said.

"We had lunch, to be precise," Dr. Holster said.

"I know that Dr. Hodges wanted to see you concerning a patient by the name of Clark Davenport."

"That's correct," Dr. Holster said. "We had a long discussion about the case. Unfortunately, Mr. Davenport had just died. I'd treated him for prostate cancer with what we thought was great success only four or five months prior to his demise. Both Dr. Hodges and myself were surprised and saddened by his passing."

"Did Dr. Hodges ever mention exactly what Mr. Davenport died of?" David asked.

"Not that I recall," Dr. Holster said. "I just assumed it was a recurrence of his prostate cancer. Why do you ask?"

"Mr. Davenport died in septic shock after a series of grand mal seizures," David said. "I don't think it was related to his cancer."

"I don't know if you can say that," Dr. Holster said. "It sounds like he developed brain metastases."

"His MRI was normal," David said. "Of course, there was no autopsy so we don't know for sure."

"There could have been multiple tumors too small for the MRI to pick up," Dr. Holster said.

"Did Dr. Hodges mention that there was anything about Mr. Davenport's hospital course that he thought was out of the ordinary or unexpected?" David asked.

"Only his death," Dr. Holster said.

"Did anything else come up during your lunch?"

"Not really. Not that I can recall," Dr. Holster said. "When we were done eating I asked Dennis if he'd like to come back to the radiotherapy center and see the new machine he'd been responsible for us having received."

"What machine is that?" David asked.

"Our linear accelerator," Dr. Holster said. He beamed like a proud parent. "We have one of the best machines made. Dennis had never seen it although he'd intended to come by on numerous occasions. So we stopped in and I showed it to him. He was truly impressed. Come on, I'll show you."

Dr. Holster was out the door before David could respond one way or the other. He caught up with Dr. Holster halfway down a windowless hallway. David wasn't much in the mood to see a radiotherapy machine, but to be polite he felt he had little choice. They reached the treatment room and approached a piece of high-tech equipment.

"Here she is," Dr. Holster said proudly as he gave the stainless-steel machine an affectionate pat. The accelerator looked like an X-ray machine with an attached table. "If it hadn't been for Dr. Hodges' commitment to the hospital we never would have gotten this beauty. We'd be still using the old one."

David gazed at the impressive apparatus. "What was wrong with the old one?" he asked.

"Nothing was wrong with it," Dr. Holster said. "It was just yesterday's technology: a cobalt-60 unit. A cobalt machine cannot be aimed as accurately as the linear accelerator. It's a physics problem having to do with the size of the cobalt source, which is about four inches in length. As a result, the gamma rays come out in every direction and are difficult to collimate."

"I see," David said, although he wasn't quite sure he did. Physics had never been his forte.

"This linear accelerator is far superior," Dr. Holster said. "It has a very small aperture from which the rays originate. And it can be programmed to have higher energy. Also, the cobalt machine requires the source to be changed every five years or so since the half-life of cobalt-60 is about six years."

David struggled to suppress a yawn. This encounter with Dr. Holster was beginning to remind him of medical school.

"We still have the cobalt machine," Dr. Holster said. "It's in the hospital basement. The hospital has been in the process of selling it to either Paraguay or Uruguay, I can't remember which. That's what most hospitals do when they upgrade to a linear accelerator like this one: sell the old machine to a developing country. The machines are still good. In fact, the old machines have the benefit of rarely breaking down since the source is always putting out gamma rays, twenty-four hours a day, rain or shine."

"I think I've already taken too much of your time," David said. He hoped to extricate himself from this meeting before Holster went on for another half hour.

"Dr. Hodges was quite interested when I gave him the tour," Dr. Holster said. "When I mentioned the fact that the old machines have this one benefit over the new ones, his face lit up. He even wanted to see the old machine. How about you? Want to run over there?"

"I think I'll pass," David said. He wondered how Helen Beaton and Joe Forbs would react if he returned to the hospital so soon after being shown the door.

A few minutes later David was on his bike crossing over the Roaring River on his way home. His morning had not been as productive as he would have liked, but at least he'd gotten the social security numbers and birth dates.

As he pedaled, his thoughts returned to what he had learned about Hodges' lunch with Dr. Holster. He wished that Hodges had shared whatever suspicions he'd been harboring with the radiotherapist. Then David recalled Dr. Holster's description of Hodges' face lighting up when he learned of the old cobalt machine's virtue of rarely breaking down. David wondered if Hodges had really been interested or if it was a case of Holster projecting his own enthusiasm on his captive audience. David figured it was probably the latter. Holster had probably come away with the impression that even David had been utterly riveted as far as the tour of the linear accelerator was concerned.

After sleeping late Calhoun didn't get back to Bartlet until midmorning. As he drove into town he decided to attack the list of hospital workers with tattoos alphabetically. That put Clyde Devonshire first.

Calhoun stopped off at the diner on Main Street for a large coffee to go, plus a look at the phone book. Armed with the five addresses, he set off for Clyde's.

Devonshire lived above a convenience store. Calhoun made his way up the stairs to the man's door and rang the bell. When there was no answer, he rang again.

Giving up after a third try, Calhoun went downstairs and wandered into the convenience store, where he bought himself a fresh pack of Antonio y Cleopatra cigars.

"I'm looking for Clyde Devonshire," he told the clerk.

"He went out early," the clerk said. "He probably went to work; he works lots of weekends. He's a nurse at the hospital."

"What time does he usually return?" Calhoun asked.

"He gets back about three-thirty or four unless he does an evening shift."

On his way out, Calhoun slipped back up the stairs and rang Devonshire's bell yet again. When there was still no response, he tried the door. It opened in.

"Hello!" Calhoun called out.

One of the benefits of not being on the police force any longer was that he didn't have to concern himself with the niceties of legal searches and probable cause. With no compunction whatsoever, he stepped over the threshold and closed the door behind him.

The apartment was cheaply furnished but neat. Calhoun found himself in the living room. On the coffee table he discovered a stack of newspaper clippings on Jack Kevorkian, the notorious "suicide" doctor in Michigan. There were other editorials and articles about assisted suicide.

Calhoun smiled as he remembered telling David and Angela that some strange things would pop up about their tattooed group. Calhoun thought that assisted suicide and euthanasia shared some areas of commonality and that David might like to have a chat with Clyde Devonshire.

Calhoun pushed open the bedroom door. This room, too, was neat. Going over to the bureau he scanned the articles on top, looking for photographs. There were none. Opening the closet Calhoun found himself staring at a collection of bondage paraphernalia, mostly items in black leather with stainless steel rivets and chains. On a shelf were stacks of accompanying magazines and videotapes.

As Calhoun closed the door, he wondered what the background computer search would uncover on this weirdo.

Moving through the rest of the apartment, Calhoun continued to search for photos. He was hoping to find one with Clyde displaying his tattoos. There were a number of photos attached to the refrigerator door with tiny magnets, but nobody in the pictures had any visible tattoos. Calhoun didn't even know which of the people photographed was Clyde.

Calhoun was about to return to the living room and go through the desk that he'd seen when he heard a door slam below, followed by footfalls on the stairs.

For an instant, Calhoun was afraid of being caught trespassing. He considered making a run for it, but then, instead of trying to flee, he went to the front door and pulled it open, startling the person who was about to open it from the other side.

"Clyde Devonshire?" Calhoun asked sharply.

"Yeah," Clyde said. "What the hell is going on?"

"My name is Phil Calhoun," Calhoun said. He extended a business card toward Clyde. "I've been waiting for you. Come on in."

Clyde shifted the parcel he was carrying to take the card.

"You're an investigator?" Clyde asked.

"That's right," Calhoun said. "I was a state policeman until the governor decided I was too old. So I've taken up investigating. I've been sitting here waiting for you to get home so I could ask you some questions."

"Well, you scared the crap out of me," Clyde admitted. He put a hand to his chest and sighed with relief. "I'm not used to coming home and finding people in my apartment."

"Sorry," Calhoun said. "I suppose I should have waited on the stairs."

"That wouldn't have been comfortable," Clyde said. "Sit down. Can I offer you anything?"

Clyde dumped his parcel on the couch, then headed into the kitchen. "I've got coffee, pop, or . . ."

"Have any beer?" Calhoun asked.

"Sure," Clyde called.

While Clyde got beer from the refrigerator, Calhoun took a peek inside the brown bag Clyde had come in with. Inside were videos similar in theme to those Calhoun had discovered in the closet.

Clyde came back into the living room carrying two beers. He could tell Calhoun had looked into his parcel. Putting the beers onto the coffee table, Clyde picked up the bag and carefully closed the top.

"Entertainment," Clyde explained.

"I noticed," Calhoun said.

"Are you straight?" Clyde asked.

"I'm not much of anything anymore," Calhoun said. He eyed his host. Clyde was around thirty. He was of medium height and had brown hair. He looked like he would have made a good offensive end in high-school football.

"What kind of questions did you want to ask me?" Clyde said. He handed a beer to Calhoun.

"Did you know Dr. Hodges?" Calhoun asked.

Clyde gave a short, scornful laugh. "Why on earth would you be investigating that detestable figure out of ancient history?"

"Sounds like you didn't think much of him."

"He was a tight-assed bastard," Clyde said. "He had an old-fashioned concept of the role of the nurse. He thought we were lowly life-forms who were supposed to do all the dirty work and not question doctors' orders. You know, be seen but not heard. Hodges would have seemed outdated to Clara Barton."

"Who was Clara Barton?" Calhoun asked.

"She was a battlefield nurse in the Civil War," Clyde said. "She also organized the Red Cross."

"Do you know who killed Dr. Hodges?" Calhoun asked.

"It wasn't me, if that's what you're thinking," Clyde said. "But if you find out, let me know. I'd love to buy the man a beer."

"Do you have a tattoo?" Calhoun asked.

"I sure do," Clyde said. "I have a number of them."

"Where?" Calhoun asked.

"You want to see them?" Clyde asked.

"Yes," Calhoun said.

Grinning from ear to ear, Clyde undid his cuffs and took off his shirt. He stood up and assumed several poses as if he were a bodybuilder. Then he laughed. He had a chain tattooed around each wrist, a dragon on his right upper arm, and a pair of crossed swords on his pectorals above each nipple.

"I got these swords in New Hampshire while I was in high school," he said. "The rest I got in San Diego."

"Let me see the tattoos on your wrists," Calhoun said.

"Oh, no," Clyde said as he slipped his shirt back on. "I don't want to show you everything the first time. You won't come back."

"Do you ski?" Calhoun asked.

"Occasionally," Clyde said. Then he added, "You sure do jump all over the map with your questions."

"Do you own a ski mask?" Calhoun asked.

"Everybody who skis in New England has a ski mask," Clyde said. "Unless they're masochists."

Calhoun stood up. "Thanks for the beer," he said. "I've got to be on my way."

"Too bad," Clyde said. "I was just starting to enjoy myself."

Calhoun descended the stairs, went outside, and climbed into his truck. He was glad to get out of Clyde Devonshire's apartment. The man was definitely unusual, maybe even bizarre. The question was, could he have killed Hodges? Somehow, Calhoun didn't think so. Clyde might be weird, but he seemed forthright. Yet the chains tattooed on each wrist bothered Calhoun, especially since he'd not had a chance to examine them closely. And he wondered about the man's interest in Kevorkian. Was it idle curiosity or the interest of a sort of kindred spirit? For now, Clyde would remain a suspect. Calhoun was eager to see what the background computer check would bring up on him.

Calhoun checked his list. The next name was Joe Forbs. The address was near the college, not too far from the Gannons'.

At Forbs' house, a thin, nervous woman with gray-streaked hair opened the door a crack when Calhoun knocked. Calhoun introduced himself and produced his card. The woman wasn't impressed. She was more New England–like than Clyde Devonshire: tight-lipped and not too friendly.

"Mrs. Forbs?" Calhoun asked.

The woman nodded.

"Is Joe at home?"

"No," Mrs. Forbs said. "You'll have to come back later."

"What time?"

"I don't know. It's a different time each day."

"Did you know Dr. Dennis Hodges?" Calhoun asked.

"No," Mrs. Forbs said.

"Can you tell me where Mr. Forbs is tattooed?"

"You'll have to come back," Mrs. Forbs said.

"Does he ski?" Calhoun persisted.

"I'm sorry," Mrs. Forbs said. She shut the door. Calhoun heard a series of locks secured. He had the distinct impression Mrs. Forbs thought he was a bill collector.

Climbing back into the truck, Calhoun sighed. He was now only one for two. But he wasn't discouraged. It was time to move on to the next name on the list: Claudette Maurice.

"Uh-oh," Calhoun said as he pulled up across the street from Claudette Maurice's house. It was a tiny home that looked like a dollhouse. What bothered Calhoun was that the shutters on the windows in the front were closed.

Calhoun went up to the front door and knocked several times since there was no bell. There was no response. Lifting the door to the mailbox, he saw it was almost full.

Stepping away from the house, Calhoun went to the nearest neighbor. He got his answer quickly. Claudette Maurice was on vacation. She'd gone to Hawaii.

Calhoun returned to the truck. Now he was only one for three. He looked at the next name: Werner Van Slyke.

Calhoun debated skipping Van Slyke since he'd talked to him already, but he decided to see the man anyway. On the first visit he'd not known about Van Slyke's tattoo.

Van Slyke resided in the southeastern part of the town. He lived on a quiet lane where the buildings were set far back from the street. Calhoun pulled to a stop behind a row of cars parked across the street from Van Slyke's home.

Surprisingly, Van Slyke's house was run-down and badly in need of paint. It didn't look like a house occupied by the head of a maintenance department. Dilapidated shutters hung at odd angles from their windows. The place gave Calhoun the creeps.

Calhoun lit himself an Antonio y Cleopatra and eyed the house. He took a few sips from his coffee, which was now cold. There were no signs of life in and around the building and no vehicle in the driveway. Calhoun doubted anyone was home.

Figuring he'd take a look around the way he had at Clyde Devonshire's, Calhoun climbed out of the truck and walked across the street. The closer he got to the building, the worse its condition appeared. There was even some dry rot under the eaves.

The doorbell did not function. Calhoun pressed it several times but heard nothing. He knocked twice, but there was no response. Leaving the front stoop, Calhoun circled the house.

Set way back from the house was a barn that had been converted into a garage. Calhoun ignored the barn and continued around the house, trying to see into the windows. It wasn't easy since the windows were filthy. In the back of the house there were a pair of hatch doors secured with an old, rusted padlock. Calhoun guessed they covered stairs to the basement.

Returning to the front of the house, Calhoun went back up the stoop. Pausing at the door he looked around to make sure no one was watching. He then tried the door. It was unlocked.

To be absolutely certain no one was home, Calhoun knocked again as loudly as his knuckles would bear. Satisfied, he reached again for the doorknob. To his shock, the door opened on its own. Calhoun looked up. Van Slyke was eyeing him suspiciously.

"What on earth do you want?" Van Slyke asked.

Calhoun had to remove the cigar that he'd tucked between his teeth. "Sorry to bother you," he said. "I just happened to be in the area, and I thought I'd stop by. Remember, I said I'd come back. I have a few more questions. What do you say? Is it an inconvenient time?"

"I suppose now's all right," Van Slyke said after a pause. "But I don't have too much time."

"I never overstay my welcome," Calhoun said.

Beaton had to knock several times on Traynor's outer office door before she heard his footsteps coming to unlock it.

"I'm surprised you're here," Beaton said.

Traynor locked the door after letting her in. "I've been spending so much time on hospital business, I have to come in here nights and weekends to do my own," he said.

"It was difficult to find you," Beaton said as she followed him into his private office.

"How'd you do it?" Traynor asked.

"I called your home," Beaton said. "I asked your wife, Jacqueline."

"Was she civil?" Traynor asked. He eased himself into his office chair. Piled on his desk were various deeds and contracts.

"Not particularly," Beaton admitted.

"I'm not surprised," Traynor said.

"I have to talk to you about that young couple we recruited last spring," Beaton said. "They've been a disaster. Both were fired from their positions yesterday. The husband was with CMV and she was in our pathology department."

"I remember her," Traynor said. "Wadley acted like a dog in heat around her at the Labor Day picnic."

"That's part of the problem," Beaton said. "Wadley fired her, but she came in yesterday and complained about sexual harassment, threatening to sue the hospital. She said she'd gone to Cantor well before being fired to register a complaint, a fact Cantor has confirmed."

"Did Wadley have cause to fire her?" Traynor asked.

"According to him, yes," Beaton said. "He'd documented that she'd repeatedly left town while on duty, even after he specifically warned her not to do so."

"Then there's nothing to worry about," Traynor said. "As long as he had reason to fire her, we'll be fine. I know the old judges that would hear the case. They'll end up giving her a lecture."

"It makes me nervous," Beaton said. "And the husband, Dr. David Wilson, is up to something. Just this morning I had him escorted out of medical records. Yesterday afternoon he'd been in there accessing the hospital's computer for death rates."

"What on earth for?" Traynor asked.

"I have no idea," Beaton said.

"But you told me our death rates are okay," Traynor said. "So what difference does it make?"

"All hospitals feel that their death rates are confidential information," Beaton said. "The general public doesn't understand how they're figured. Death rates can be a public relations disaster, something that Bartlet Hospital certainly doesn't need."

"I'll agree with you there," Traynor said. "So we keep him out of medical records. It shouldn't be hard if CMV fired him. Why was he fired?"

"He was continually at the lower end of productivity," Beaton said, "and at the upper end of utilization, particularly hospitalization."

"We certainly won't miss him," Traynor said. "Sounds like I should send Kelley a bottle of scotch for doing us a favor."

"This family is worrying me," Beaton said. "Yesterday they came flying into the hospital to yank out their daughter, the one with cystic fibrosis. They took her out of the hospital against medical advice from their pediatrician."

"That does sound bizarre," Traynor said. "How's the child? I guess that's the important issue."

"She's fine," Beaton said. "I spoke to the pediatrician. She's doing perfectly well."

"Then what's the worry?" Traynor said.

Armed with the social security numbers and birth dates, Angela headed into Boston. She'd called Robert Scali that morning so he'd expect her. She didn't explain why she was coming. The reason would take too long to explain and besides, it would sound too bizarre.

She met Robert at one of the numerous small Indian restaurants in Central Square in Cambridge. As Angela entered, Robert got up from one of the tables.

Angela kissed him on the cheek, then got down to business. She told him what she wanted and handed Robert her list. He eyed the sheet.

"So you want background checks on these people?" he said. He leaned across the table. "I was hoping that you had more personal reasons for calling so suddenly. I thought you wanted to see me."

Angela immediately felt uncomfortable. When they'd gotten together before, Robert had never intimated anything about rekindling their old flame.

Angela decided it was best to be direct. She assured Robert that she was happily married. She told him that she'd come purely because she needed his help.

If Robert was disheartened, it didn't show. He reached across the table and squeezed her hand. "I'm glad to see you no matter what the reason," he said. "I'll be happy to help. What is it you specifically want?"

Angela explained to Robert that she'd been told that a good deal of information could be obtained about a person through computer searches using just the social security number and the birth date.

Robert laughed in the deep, husky manner that Angela remembered so vividly. "You have no idea how much is available," he said. "I could get Bill Clinton's Visa card transactions for the last month if I were truly motivated."

"I want to find out everything I can about these people," Angela said, tapping the list.

"Can you be more specific?" Robert said.

"Not really," Angela said. "I want everything you can get. A friend of mine has described this process as a fishing trip."

"Who's this friend?" Robert asked.

"Well, he's not exactly a friend," Angela said. "But I've come to think of him that way. His name is Phil Calhoun. He's a retired policeman who's become a private investigator. David and I hired him."

Angela went on to give Robert a thumbnail sketch of the events in Bartlet. She started with Hodges' body being discovered in their basement, then went on to describe the fascinating clue of the tattoo, and finished up with the theory that someone was killing patients in a form of misguided euthanasia.

"My God!" Robert said when Angela ended her tale. "You're shooting holes in my romantic image of the peaceful country life."

"It's been a nightmare," Angela admitted.

Robert picked up the list. "Twenty-five names will yield a lot of data," he said. "I hope you're prepared. Did you come in a U-Haul?"

"We're particularly interested in these five," Angela said. She pointed to the people who worked in the hospital and explained why.

"This sounds like fun," Robert said. "The quickest information to get will be financial since there are quite a few databases we can tap with ease. So we'll soon have information on credit cards, bank accounts, money transfers, and debt. From then on it gets more difficult."

"What would the next step be?" Angela asked.

"I suppose the easiest would be social security," Robert said. "But hacking into their data banks is a bit trickier. But it's not impossible, especially since I have a friend here at MIT who is conveniently working on database security for various government agencies."

"Do you think he'd help?" Angela asked.

"Peter Fong? Of course he'll help if I ask him. When do you want this stuff?"

"Yesterday," Angela said with a smile.

"That's one of the things I always liked about you," Robert said. "Always so eager. Come on, let's go see Peter Fong."

Peter's office was hidden away at the rear of the fourth floor of a cream-colored stuccoed building in the middle of the MIT campus.

It looked less like an office than an electronics laboratory. It was filled with computers, cathode ray tubes, liquid crystal displays, wires, tape machines, and other electronic paraphernalia Angela couldn't identify.

Peter Fong was an energetic Asian-American with eyes even darker than Robert's. It was immediately obvious to Angela that he and Robert were the best of friends.

Robert handed Peter the list and told him what they wanted. Peter scratched his head and pondered the request.

"I agree social security would be the best place to start," Peter said. "But an FBI database search would also be a good idea."

"Is that possible?" Angela asked. The world of computer information was new to her.

"No problem," Peter said. "I've got a colleague in Washington. Her name is Gloria Ramirez. I've been working with her on this database security project. She's on line with both organizations."

Peter used a word processor to type out what he wanted. Then he slipped it into his fax. "We usually communicate by fax, but for this she'll respond by computer. With that amount of data it will be faster."

Within minutes, data was pouring directly into his hard disk drive. Peter pulled some of the material up onto his screen.

Angela looked over Peter's shoulder and scanned the screen. It was a portion of the social security record on Joe Forbs, indicating the recent jobs he'd held along with his payments into the social security pool. Angela was impressed. She was also dismayed at how easy it was to get such information.

Peter activated his laser printer. It began spewing forth page after page of data. Robert walked over and picked up a sheet. Angela joined him. It was the social security file on Werner Van Slyke.

"Interesting," Angela said. "He was in the navy. That's probably where he got his tattoo."

"A lot of the enlisted men think of a tattoo as a rite of passage," Robert said.

Angela was even more surprised later when the criminal records began coming in on another printer. Peter had to activate a second machine since the first was still busy with the social security material.

Angela hadn't expected much criminal information since Bartlet was such a small, quiet town. But like so much else about Bartlet, her assumption was wrong. The most significant item, as far as she was concerned, was the discovery that Clyde Devonshire had been arrested and convicted of rape six years earlier. The incident had taken place in Norfolk, Virginia, and he had served two years in the state penitentiary.

"Sounds like a charming fellow to have in a small town," Robert said sarcastically.

"He works in the ER at the hospital," Angela said. "I wonder if anyone knew of his record."

Robert went back to the other printer and rummaged through the data until he found Clyde Devonshire's information.

"He was in the navy too," Robert called over to Angela, who was transfixed by the criminal material still coming out. "In fact, the dates seem to indicate that he was in the navy when he was arrested for rape."

Angela stepped over to Robert to look over his shoulder.

"Look at this," Robert said as he pointed to the sequence of dates. "There are a number of gaps in the social security history after Mr. Devonshire got out of prison. I've seen records like this before. Such gaps suggest that he either did more time or was using aliases."

"Good Lord!" Angela said. "Phil Calhoun said we'd be surprised by what turned up. He certainly was right."

Half an hour later, Angela and Robert walked out of Peter's office with several boxes full of computer paper. They headed for Robert's office.

Robert's work space looked much the same as Peter's as far as equipment was concerned. The one significant difference was that Robert had a window overlooking the Charles River.

"Let's get you some financial information," Robert said as he sat down at one of his terminals. Before long, material started coming back across his screen as if a hole had been poked in a dam.

As Robert's printers snapped into operation, pages flew into the collection trays with surprising rapidity.

"I'm overwhelmed," Angela admitted. "I've never thought such reams of personal information could be obtained with such ease."

"For fun, let's see what we can get on you," Robert said. "What's your social security number?"

"No, thank you," Angela said. "Knowing the amount of debt I have, it would be too depressing."

"I'll try to get more material on your suspects tonight," Robert said. "Sometimes it's easier at night when there's less electronic traffic."

"Thank you so much," Angela said as she tried to pick up the two boxes of material.

"I think I'd better give you a hand with all that," Robert said.

Once the material was stored in the trunk, Angela gave Robert a long hug.

"Thanks again," she said. She gave him an extra squeeze. "It's been good to see you."

Robert waved as Angela drove away. She watched his figure recede in her rearview mirror. It had been nice to see him, except for the brief moment of discomfort when she'd first arrived. Now she was looking forward to showing David and Calhoun all this material.

"I'm home!" Angela shouted as she entered through the back door. Hearing no response, she went back for the second box of information herself. When she returned, the house was still silent. With a growing sense of unease, Angela passed through the kitchen and dining room on her way to the stairs. She was startled to find David reading in the family room.

"Why didn't you answer me?" Angela asked.

"You said you were home," David said. "I didn't feel that required a response."

"What's the matter?" Angela asked.

"Nothing at all," David said. "How was your day with your old boyfriend?"

"Oh, is that what this is about?" Angela said.

David shrugged. "It seems strange to me that you've kept quiet about this man from your past for the four years we lived in Boston."

"David!" Angela said with a touch of exasperation. She walked over and threw herself into David's lap, wrapping her arms around his neck. "I didn't mean to keep Robert secret. If I'd meant to keep him a secret, do you think I would have named him now? Don't you know I love you and no one else." She kissed him on the nose.

"Promise?" David asked.

"Promise," Angela said. "How's Nikki?"

"She's fine," David said. "She's napping. She's still terribly upset about Caroline. But physically she's doing great. How did you do?"

"You won't believe it," Angela said. "Come on!"

Angela dragged David into the kitchen and showed him the boxes. He took out a few pages to look at them. "You're right," he said. "I don't believe it. This will take us hours to go through."

"It's a good thing we're unemployed," Angela said. "At least we have plenty of time."

"I'm glad to hear your humor's back," David said.

They made dinner together. When Nikki woke up she joined in, though it was difficult for her to move around since she still had an IV running. Before they sat down to eat, David called Dr. Pilsner. Together they decided that Nikki's IV could be pulled and the antibiotics continued orally.

During dinner David and Angela talked about having to break the news about their employment status in Bartlet to their parents. Both were reluctant.

"I don't know what you're worried about," David questioned. "Your mother and father will probably cheer. They never wanted us to come up here anyway."

"That's the problem," Angela said. "It will drive me bananas when they start in with the 'I told you so' routine."

After dinner while Nikki watched television, David and Angela began the chore of going through the computer data. David was progressively amazed and appalled at the wealth of the material accessible to hackers.

"This will take us days," David complained.

"Maybe we should concentrate on those with connections to the hospital," Angela said. "There are only five."

"Good idea," David said.

Like Angela, David found the criminal information the most provocative. He was particularly taken by the news that Clyde Devonshire had not only served time for rape but had also been arrested in Michigan for loitering outside Jack Kevorkian's house. Assisted suicide and euthanasia shared some philosophical justifications. David wondered if Devonshire could be their "angel of mercy."

David was also amazed to learn that Peter Ullhof had been arrested six times outside Planned Parenthood centers and three times outside of abortion clinics, once for assault and battery of a doctor.

"This is interesting," Angela said. She was looking through the social security material. "All five of these people served in the military, including Claudette Maurice. That's a coincidence."

"Maybe that's why they all have tattoos," David said.

Angela nodded. She remembered Robert's comment about tattoos being a rite of passage.

After helping Nikki do her respiratory therapy, they put her to bed. Then they returned downstairs and brought the computer printouts into the family room. They began to sift through again, creating a separate pile for each of the five hospital workers.

"I expected Calhoun to have called by now," Angela said. "I was looking forward to getting his opinion on some of this information, particularly regarding Clyde Devonshire."

"Calhoun's an independent sort," David said. "He said he'd call when he had something to tell us."

"Well, I'm going to give him a call," Angela said. "We have something to tell him."

Angela only got Calhoun's answering machine. She didn't leave a message.

"One of the things that surprises me," David said when Angela was off the phone, "is how often these people have changed jobs." David was going over the social security data.

Angela moved next to him and looked over his shoulder. All at once she reached over and took a paper that David was about to put on Van Slyke's pile.

"Look at this," she said, pointing to an entry. "Van Slyke was in the navy for twenty-one months."

"So?" David questioned.

"Isn't that unusual?" Angela asked. "I thought the shortest stint in the navy was three years."

"I don't know," David said.

"Let's look at Devonshire's service record," Angela said. She leafed through Devonshire's pile until she found the appropriate page.

"He was in for four and a half years."

"My God!" David exclaimed. "Will you listen to this? Joe Forbs has declared personal bankruptcy three times. With that kind of history, how can he get a credit card? But he has. Each time he's gotten all new cards at another institution. Amazing."

By eleven o'clock, David was struggling to keep his eyes open. "I'm afraid I have to go to bed," he said. He tossed the papers he had in his hand onto the table.

"I was hoping you'd say that," Angela said. "I'm bushed too."

They went upstairs arm in arm, feeling satisfied they'd accomplished so much in one day. But they might not have slept so soundly had they any inkling of the firestorm their handiwork had ignited.

SUNDAY • OCTOBER 31

Halloween dawned clear and crisp with frost on the grimacing pumpkins perched on porches and windowsills. Nikki awoke feeling entirely normal physically, and with the festive atmosphere of the holiday, even her spirits were much improved. Angela had made it a point earlier in the week to stock candies and fruits for possible trick-or-treaters.

Angela had no interest in going to church. The idea of trying to fit into the Bartlet community had lost its appeal. David offered to take them to the Iron Horse Inn for breakfast even if they didn't go to church, but Angela preferred to stay at home.

After breakfast Nikki began to agitate to be allowed to go trick-or-treating herself. But Angela was not enthusiastic. She was concerned about letting Nikki out into the cold so soon after she'd gotten over her latest bout of congestion. As a compromise, she sent David into town to try to buy a pumpkin while she got Nikki to help her prepare the house for the children coming to their door.

Angela had Nikki fill a large glass salad bowl to the brim with miniature chocolate bars. Nikki carried it to the front hall and placed it on the table by the door.

Next, Angela had Nikki start making Halloween decorations out of colored construction paper. With Nikki happily occupied, Angela called Robert Scali in Cambridge.

"I'm glad you called," Robert said as soon as he heard Angela's voice. "I've gotten some more financial data like I promised."

"I appreciate your efforts," Angela said. "But I've another request. Can you get me military service records?"

"Now you're pushing it," Robert said. "It's much more difficult to hack into military data banks, as you might imagine. I suppose I could get some general information, but I doubt I could get anything classified unless Peter's colleague is on line with the Pentagon. But I doubt that very much."

"I understand," Angela said. "You've said exactly what I thought you'd say."

"Let's not give up immediately," Robert said. "Let me call Peter and ask. I'll call you back in a few minutes."

Angela hung up and went over to see how Nikki was doing. She'd cut out a big orange moon and now was in the process of cutting out a silhouetted witch on a broomstick. Angela was impressed: neither she nor David had any artistic talent.

David returned with an enormous pumpkin. Nikki was thrilled. Angela helped spread newspaper on the kitchen table. David and Nikki were soon absorbed in carving the pumpkin into a jack-o'-lantern. Angela helped until the phone rang. It was Robert calling back.

"Bad news," he said. "Gloria can't help with Pentagon stuff. But I was able to get some basic info. I'll send it up with this additional financial material. What's your fax number?"

"We don't have a fax," Angela said. She felt guilty, as if she and David had not joined the nineties.

"But you do have a modem with your computer?" Robert said.

"We don't even have a computer, except one for Nikki's video games," Angela admitted. "But I'll figure out a way to get the material. In the meantime, can you tell me why Van Slyke was in the navy for only twenty-one months?"

There was a pause. Angela could hear Robert shuffling through papers.

"Here it is," he said finally. "Van Slyke got a medical discharge."

"Does it say for what?" Angela asked.

"I'm afraid not," Robert said. "But there is some interesting stuff here. It says that Van Slyke went to submarine school in New London, Connecticut, then on to nuclear power school. He was a submariner."

"Why is that interesting?" Angela asked.

"Not everybody goes out on submarines," Robert said. "It says he was assigned to the U.S.S. *Kamehameha* out of Guam."

"What kind of job did Clyde Devonshire have in the navy?" Angela asked.

There was more shuffling of paper. "He was a navy corpsman," Robert said. Then he added: "My gosh, isn't this a coincidence."

"What?" Angela asked. It was frustrating not to have the papers herself.

"Devonshire got a medical discharge, too," Robert said. "Having done hard time for rape, I would have guessed it would have been something else."

"That sounds even more interesting to me than Van Slyke's going to submarine school," Angela said.

After thanking Robert again for all his efforts, Angela hung up. Returning to the kitchen where David and Nikki were putting the finishing touches on the jack-o'-lantern's grotesque face, Angela told David that Robert had more material for them that she wanted to get. She also told him what she'd just learned about Devonshire and Van Slyke.

"So they both had medical discharges," David said. It was obvious he was preoccupied.

"What do you think?" David asked Nikki as they both stepped back to admire their work.

"I think it's great," Nikki said. "Can we put a candle in it?"

"Absolutely," David said.

"David, did you hear me?" Angela asked.

"Of course I did," David said. He handed a candle to Nikki.

"I wish we could find the reasons for these medical discharges," Angela said.

"I bet I know how we could," David said. "Get someone in the VA system to pull it out of their data banks. They'd have to have it recorded."

"Good idea," Angela said. "Do you have any suggestions who we could ask?"

"I have a doctor friend at the VA in Boston," David said.

"Do you think he would mind doing us a favor?" Angela asked.

"It's a she," David said. David told Nikki that she should cut out a little depression inside the pumpkin to hold the candle. She hadn't been able to get the candle to stay upright.

"So who's your doctor friend?" Angela asked.

"She's an ophthalmologist," David said, still overseeing Nikki's efforts to stabilize the candle inside the pumpkin.

"I wasn't referring to her specialty," Angela said. "How do you know her?"

"We went to high school together," David said. "We dated senior year."

"And how long has she been in the Boston area?" Angela asked. "And what's her name?" Two could play at this jealousy game.

"Her name is Nicole Lungstrom," David said. "She came to Boston at the end of last year."

"I've never heard you mention her before," Angela said. "How did you know she came to town?"

"She called me at the hospital," David said. He gave Nikki a congratulatory pat when the candle was finally stabilized. Nikki ran to get matches. David turned his attention to Angela.

"So have you seen her since she's come to Boston?" Angela asked.

"We had lunch once," David said, "and that was it. I told her it was better that we not see each other because she had romantic hopes. We parted friends."

"Honest?" Angela asked.

"Honest," David said.

"You think that if you call out of the blue she'll help us?" Angela asked.

"To tell you the truth, I doubt it," David said. "If we want to take advantage of her employment status with the VA, then I think I should go down there. There's no way I can ask her to violate confidentiality rules over the telephone. Besides, I'd do better to explain the whole sordid story in person."

"When would you go?" Angela asked.

"Today," David said. "I'll call her first to make sure she's available. Then I'll go. I'll even stop at MIT and pick up that material you want from Robert. What do you say?"

Angela bit the inside of her lip as she pondered. She was surprised to feel such a pang of jealousy. Now she knew how David felt. She shook her head and sighed. "Call her," she said.

While Angela cleaned up the mess from the gutting of the pumpkin, David went into the family room and called Nicole Lungstrom. Angela could hear bits and pieces of the conversation even though she tried not to. It bothered her that David sounded so cheerful. A few minutes later he came back into the kitchen.

"It's all arranged," David said. "She's expecting me in a couple of hours. Conveniently, she's on call at the hospital."

"Is she blond?" Angela asked.

"Yeah, she is," David said.

"I was afraid of that," Angela said.

Nikki had the candle lit in the pumpkin, and David carried the jack-o'-lantern out onto the front porch. He let Nikki decide where she wanted it.

"It looks cool," Nikki said, once it was in place.

Returning inside the house, David asked Angela to call Robert Scali and tell him he would be stopping by. While David went upstairs to get ready to drive to Boston, Angela gave Robert a call.

"That will be interesting," Robert said once Angela explained the reason for her call.

Angela didn't know how to respond. She simply thanked him again for his help and hung up. Then she tried to call Calhoun. Once more she got his answering machine.

David came down wearing his blue blazer and gray slacks. He looked quite handsome.

"Do you have to get so dressed up?" Angela asked.

"I'm going to the VA hospital," David said. "I'm not going in jeans and a sweatshirt."

"I tried to call Calhoun again," Angela said. "Still no answer. That man must have come in late and gone out early. He's really involved in this investigation."

"Did you leave a message?" David asked.

"No," Angela said.

"Why not?"

"I hate answering machines," Angela said. "Besides, he must know we want to hear from him."

"I think you should leave a message," David said.

"What should we do if we don't hear from him by tonight?" Angela asked. "Go to the police?"

"I don't know," David admitted. "The idea of going to Robertson for anything doesn't thrill me."

After Angela watched David pull down their drive, she put her full attention on Nikki. More than anything she wanted her daughter to enjoy the day.

Motivated more by curiosity than anything else, David went to meet Robert Scali first. Hoping the man would look like a nerdy academic, David was crestfallen to discover that Robert was a handsome man with a tanned face and an athletic bearing. To make matters worse, he seemed like a genuinely nice guy.

They shook hands. David could tell Robert was also sizing him up.

"I want to thank you for your help," David said.

"That's what friends are for," Robert said. He handed over another box full of information.

"There's something new on the financial side that I should mention," Robert said. "I discovered that Werner Van Slyke has opened several new bank accounts in the last year, apparently traveling to both Albany and here to Boston to do so. I hadn't gotten that information yesterday because I'd been more interested in credit card history and debt."

"That's strange," David said. "Is it a lot of money?"

"There's less than ten thousand in each account, probably to avoid the rule that banks have to report movements of more than ten thousand."

"That's still a lot of money for a man running a maintenance department at a community hospital," David said.

"This day and age, it probably means the fellow is running a little drug ring," Robert said. "But if he is, he shouldn't be banking the money. He's supposed to bury it in PVC pipe. That's the norm."

"I'd heard from a couple of my teenage patients that marijuana was easily available in the local high school," David said.

"There you go," Robert said. "Maybe on top of whatever else you and Angela solve, you can do your part to help make America drug-free."

David laughed and thanked Robert again for all his help.

"Let me know when you guys next come to town," Robert said. "There's a great restaurant here in Cambridge called Anago Bistro. It will be my treat."

"Will do," David said as he waved goodbye. On his way out to the car, David doubted he'd feel comfortable getting together.

After stowing the computer data in the trunk, David drove across the

Charles River and out the Fenway. It took only twenty minutes to get to the VA hospital; Sunday midafternoon was a traffic low.

Walking into the hospital, David thought it was ironic how lives could intersect after years of separation. He'd dated Nicole Lungstrom for almost a year, starting in the last part of junior year of high school. But after graduation she'd gone off to the West Coast for college, medical school, and residency. At one point David had heard through friends that she'd married. When she'd called the previous year, David had learned she'd been divorced.

David had Nicole paged and waited for her in the lobby. When she first appeared and they greeted each other, they were both uneasy. David quickly learned that there was a new man in Nicole's life. David was pleased, and he began to relax.

For privacy, Nicole took David into the doctors' lounge. Once they were seated he told her the whole story of his and Angela's disastrous sojourn in Bartlet. He then told her what he wanted.

"What do you think?" David asked. "Would you mind seeing what information is available?"

"Will this be just between us?" Nicole asked.

"My word of honor," David said. "Except for Angela, of course."

"I assumed that," Nicole said. She pondered the situation for a few minutes, then nodded. "Okay," she said. "If someone is killing patients then I think the ends justify the means, at least in this instance."

David handed Nicole the shortlist of people: Devonshire, Van Slyke, Forbs, Ullhof, and Maurice.

"I thought you were only interested in two," Nicole said.

"We know all five of these people were in the military," David said. "And all five have tattoos. We might as well be thorough."

Using the social security numbers and birth dates Nicole obtained the military ID numbers on each person. She then began calling up the records. There was an immediate surprise. Both Forbs and Ullhof had also been given medical discharges. Only Maurice had mustered out normally.

Both Forbs' and Ullhof's discharge diagnoses were pedestrian: Forbs was released because of chronic back problems while Ullhof had been discharged because of nonspecific, chronic prostatitis.

Van Slyke's and Devonshire's were not so innocuous. Van Slyke's was the most complicated. Nicole had to scroll through page after page of material. Van Slyke had been discharged with a psychiatric diagnosis of "schizo-affective disorder with mania and strong paranoid ideation under stress."

"Good Lord," David said. "I'm not sure I understand all that. Do you?"

"I'm an ophthalmologist," Nicole said. "But I gather the translation is that the guy is schizophrenic with a large component of mania."

David looked at Nicole and raised his eyebrows. "Sounds like you know more about this stuff than I do," he said. "I'm impressed."

"I was interested in psychiatry at one point," Nicole said. "This Van Slyke fellow sounds like the kind of person I'd stay away from. But for all his mental trouble, look at all the schooling he went through, even nuclear power school. I hear that's quite rigorous."

Nicole continued to scroll through the material.

"Wait," David said, leaning on her shoulder. He pointed to a passage that described an incident where Van Slyke had had a psychiatric break while on patrol on a nuclear submarine. At the time, he'd been working as a nuclear-trained machinist's mate for the engineering department.

David read aloud: " 'During the first half of the patrol the patient's mania was apparent and progressive. He exhibited elevated mood which led to poor judgment and feelings of hostility, belligerence, and ultimately to persistent paranoid thoughts of being ridiculed by the rest of the crew and being affected by computers and radiation. His paranoia reached a climax when he attacked the captain and had to be restrained.' "

"Good grief," Nicole said. "I hope I don't see him in the clinic."

"He's not quite as wacko as this makes him sound," David said. "I've even spoken to him on several occasions. He's not sociable or even friendly, but he does his job."

"I'd say he was a time bomb," Nicole said.

"Being paranoid about radiation while on a nuclear submarine isn't so crazy," David said. "If I ever had to be on a nuclear submarine, it would drive me up the wall knowing I was so close to a nuclear reactor."

"There's more history here," Nicole said. She read aloud: " 'Van Slyke has a history of being a loner type. He was raised by an aggressive, alcoholic father and a fearful and compliant mother. The mother's maiden name was Traynor.' "

"I'd heard that part of the story," David said. "Harold Traynor, the fellow's uncle, is the chairman of the board of trustees."

"Here's something else interesting," Nicole said. She again read aloud: " 'The patient has demonstrated the tendency to idealize certain authority figures but then turn against them with minor provocation, whether real or fancied. This behavior pattern has occurred prior to entering the service and while in the navy.' " Nicole looked up at David. "I certainly wouldn't want to be his boss."

Moving on to Devonshire, they found less material, but it was just as interesting and even more significant as far as David was concerned. Clyde Devonshire had been treated for sexually transmitted diseases on several occasions in San Diego. He'd also had a bout of hepatitis B. Finally he'd tested positive for HIV.

"This might be really important," David said, tapping the computer screen and making reference to the AIDS virus. "The fact that Clyde Devonshire has a potentially terminal illness himself could be the key."

"I hope I've helped," Nicole said.

"Could I get copies of these records?" David asked.

"That might take some time," Nicole said. "Medical records is closed on Sundays. I'll have to get a key to get access to a printer."

"I'll wait," David said. "But I'd like to use the phone first."

After much grumbling and a few tears, Nikki finally accepted the fact that it was not in her best interest to traipse around the neighborhood trick-or-treating. The day that had started out so clear had turned gray. A distinct threat of rain was in the offing. But Nikki still dressed up in her fearful costume and derived enormous fun from going to the door and scaring the handful of children who showed up.

Angela still hated Nikki's costume, but she held her tongue. She was not about to detract from Nikki's enjoyment.

While Nikki hovered by the door waiting for more trick-or-treaters, Angela tried Calhoun one more time. Again, she got his answering machine. When she called earlier that afternoon, she'd left a message as David suggested, but Calhoun had never called back. Angela began to worry. Looking out the window at the gathering gloom, she also began to worry about David. Although he'd called many hours ago to say he'd be a bit later than expected, she thought he should have been home by now.

Half an hour later, Nikki was willing to call it quits. It was growing dark and getting late for trick-or-treaters. No one had been by for some time.

Angela was thinking about starting dinner when the doorbell chimed. Nikki had already gone upstairs to take a bath, so Angela headed for the front door. As she passed the table in the front hall, she picked up the glass bowl with the chocolates. Through the sidelight window she caught a glimpse of a reptile-headed man.

Angela unlocked the door, opened it, and began to say something about how great a costume it was when she noticed that the man was not accompanied by a child.

Before Angela could react, the man lunged inside, grabbed Angela around the neck with his left arm, and enveloped her in a headlock. His gloved right hand slapped over her mouth, suppressing a scream. Angela dropped the bowl of chocolates to the marble foyer floor where it shattered into hundreds of pieces.

Angela vainly struggled with the man, desperately trying to pull free. But he was strong and held her tightly in a vise-like grip. The only noises she could make were muffled grunts.

"Shut up or I'll kill you," the man said in a raspy half whisper. He gave Angela's head a fearful shake; a sudden stab of pain shot down Angela's back. She stopped struggling.

The man glanced around the room. He strained to see down the hallway toward the kitchen.

"Where's your husband?" he demanded.

Angela couldn't respond. She was beginning to feel dizzy, as if she might black out.

"I'm going to let you go," the man snarled. "If you scream I'll shoot you. Understand?" He gave Angela's head another shake, bringing tears of pain.

As promised, the man let Angela go. She staggered back a step but caught herself. Her heart was racing. She knew that Nikki was upstairs in the bathtub. Rusty, unfortunately, was out in the barn. He'd been a nuisance with the trick-or-treaters.

Angela looked at her attacker. His reptile mask was grotesque. The scales appeared almost real. A red forked tongue hung limply from a mouth lined with jagged teeth. Angela tried to think. What should she do? What could she do? She noticed the man had a pistol in his hand.

"My husband is not at home," Angela managed to say at last. Her voice was hoarse. The headlock had compressed her throat.

"What about your sick kid?" the man demanded.

"She's out trick-or-treating with friends," Angela said.

"When will your husband be back?" the man asked.

Angela hesitated, not knowing what was best to say. The man grabbed her arm and gave it a tug. His thumbnail bit into her flesh. "I asked you a question," he snarled.

"Soon," Angela managed.

"Good," the man said. "We'll wait. Meanwhile, let's take a look around the house and make sure you're not lying to me."

"I wouldn't lie," Angela said as she felt herself propelled into the family room.

Nikki was not in the bathtub. She'd been out for some time. When the door chimes sounded, she'd rushed to finish dressing and put on her mask. She'd hoped to get downstairs before the kids had left. She wanted to see their costumes and surprise them with her own. She'd just gotten to the head of the stairs when the glass bowl shattered, stopping her in her tracks. Helplessly she'd watched from upstairs as her mother began to struggle with a man wearing a serpent mask.

After the initial shock, Nikki ran down the hall to the master bedroom and picked up the telephone. But there was no dial tone. The line was dead. Rushing back down the hall, she'd peeked over the edge of the stairs just in time to see her mother and the man disappear into the family room.

Advancing to the head of the stairs, Nikki looked down. The shotgun was leaning against the back of the newel post.

Nikki had to jump back out of sight when her mother and the reptile man reappeared from the family room. Nikki could hear their footsteps crunching the broken glass of the candy bowl. Then the footsteps stopped. Nikki could only hear muffled voices.

Nikki forced herself to peek over the edge of the stairs again. She saw her mother and the man reappear briefly from the living room before they vanished down the central corridor toward the kitchen.

Nikki inched forward and again peered down at the shotgun. It was still there. She started down the steps, but no matter how slowly she moved, each step creaked under the weight of her light, seventy-pound frame.

Nikki only got halfway down the stairs before she heard Angela and the man coming back along the corridor. Panicked, Nikki raced back up the stairs and partway down the upstairs corridor. She stopped, intending to return to the top of the stairs and then to descend to the foyer when it was safe. But to her horror her mother and the man started up the stairs.

Nikki ran the rest of the way down the corridor and dashed into the master bedroom. She ducked into one of the walk-in closets. In the back of the closet was a second door leading to a short hall connecting with the barn. Several store rooms ran off it. At the end of the hall was a narrow, spiral staircase that led down to the mudroom.

Nikki raced down these stairs, then through the kitchen and along the first-floor corridor, finally reaching the foyer. She snatched up the shotgun. She checked to see if there was a shell in the magazine just as her mother had taught her. There was. She released the safety.

Nikki's elation quickly changed to confusion. Now that she had the shotgun in her hands, she didn't know what to do next. Her mother had explained that the gun sprayed pellets in a wide arc. It didn't have to be aimed too carefully; it would hit just about everything it was pointed at. The problem was her mom. Nikki didn't want to hit her.

Nikki had little time to ponder her dilemma. Almost immediately she heard the intruder marching her mother back along the upstairs corridor and down the main stairs. Nikki backed up toward the kitchen. She didn't know whether to hide or run outside to the neighbors'.

Before Nikki could decide, her mother appeared in the foyer, stumbling down the last few stairs. Apparently she'd been pushed. Right behind her was the reptile man. In full view of Nikki the man gave Angela another cruel shove that sent her flying through the archway into the living room. In his right hand was a pistol.

The man started after her mother. He was about twenty feet away from Nikki, who was holding the shotgun at her waist. She had her left hand around the barrel and her right hand around the stock. Her finger was on the trigger.

The intruder turned briefly to face Nikki as he walked, then did a double take. He started to raise his gun in her direction. Nikki closed her eyes and pulled the trigger.

The sound of the blast from the shotgun was horrendous in the narrow hallway. The recoil knocked Nikki over backward, yet she stubbornly held on to the shotgun. Regaining her balance enough to sit up, she used all her strength to cock the gun. Her ears were ringing so much, she couldn't hear the mechanical click the shotgun made as a fresh shell was rammed into position and the spent cartridge ejected.

Angela suddenly appeared out of the smoky haze, coming from the direction of the kitchen. Immediately following the blast she'd run from the living room into the kitchen, doubling around and back up the main corridor. She took the shotgun from Nikki, who was only too glad to give it up.

From the family room they heard the sound of a door banging open, then stillness.

"Are you all right?" Angela whispered to Nikki.

"I think so," Nikki said.

Angela helped Nikki to her feet, then motioned for her to follow her. Slowly they advanced toward the foyer. They inched past the archway leading into the living room, catching sight of the damage caused by Nikki's shotgun blast. A portion of the pellets were embedded in the side of the arch. The rest of the charge had carried away another four panes of glass from the living room's bay window, the same window damaged by the brick.

Next they rounded the base of the stairs, trying to avoid the shards of broken glass. As they approached the archway leading into the family room, they felt a draft of cold air. Angela kept the shotgun trained ahead. Edging along together, Angela and Nikki spotted the source of the draft: one of the French doors leading to the terrace hung open and was gently swinging back and forth with the evening breeze.

With Nikki clutching one of Angela's belt loops, they advanced toward the open door. They gazed out at the dark line of trees bordering their property. For a few moments they stood absolutely still, listening for any sounds. All they heard was the distant bark of a dog, followed by Rusty's rebuttal from out in the barn. No one was in sight.

Angela closed the door and locked it. Still gripping the gun in one hand, she bent down and hugged Nikki with all her might.

"You're a hero," she said. "Wait until I tell your father."

"I didn't know what to do," Nikki said. "I didn't mean to hit the window."

"The window doesn't matter," Angela said. "You did splendidly." Angela went over to the phone. She was surprised to find it was dead.

"The one in your bedroom's not working either," Nikki said.

Angela shuddered. The intruder had gone to the trouble of cutting their lines first. Had it not been for Nikki, Angela hated to think what might have happened.

"We have to make sure the man is not still here," Angela said. "Come on, let's search the house."

Together they went through the dining room into the kitchen. They checked the mudroom and the two small storage rooms. Returning to the kitchen they walked down the central corridor back to the foyer.

While Angela was debating whether to check upstairs, the door chimes rang. Both she and Nikki jumped.

Looking out the sidelights on either side of the door, Angela and Nikki saw a group of children dressed as witches and ghosts standing on their stoop.

David pulled into the driveway. He was surprised to see that every light in the house was on. Then he saw a group of teenagers leap from the porch, dash across the lawn, and disappear into the trees lining the property.

David stopped the car. He could see that his front door was plastered with raw eggs. The windows had been soaped, and the jack-o'-lantern smashed. He had half a mind to give chase to the kids but decided that the chances of finding them in the dark were pretty slim. "Damn kids," he said aloud. Then he noticed that more of the living-room bay window had been broken.

"Good gravy!" David exclaimed. "That's going way too far." He got out of the car and went up to his front door. The place was a mess. Tomatoes as well as eggs had been thrown against the front of the house.

Not until he discovered the broken glass and candy scattered across the floor of the foyer did David become truly worried. Struck by a sudden stab of fear for his family, David cried out for Angela and Nikki.

Almost immediately Angela and Nikki appeared at the top of the stairs. Angela was holding the shotgun. Nikki started to cry and ran down the stairs into David's arms.

"He had a gun," Nikki managed to tell David through choking sobs.

"Who had a gun?" David asked with growing alarm. "What's happened?"

Angela came part of the way down the stairs and sat down.

"We had a visitor," Angela said.

"Who?" David demanded.

"I don't know," Angela said. "He was wearing a Halloween mask. He had a handgun."

"My God!" David said. "I never should have left you alone here. I'm sorry."

"It's not your fault," Angela said. "But you are later than you said you'd be when you called."

"It took longer than expected to get copies of the medical records," David explained. "I did try to call on my way up, but the phone was constantly busy. When I checked with the operator, I was told it was out of order."

"I think it was deliberately cut," Angela said. "Probably by the intruder."

"Did you call the police?" David asked.

"How were we to call the police when we had no phone?" Angela snapped.

"I'm sorry," David said. "I'm not thinking."

"All we've done since the man bolted is huddle upstairs," Angela said. "We've been terrified he'd come back."

"Where's Rusty?" David asked.

"I put him in the barn earlier in the day because he got so hyper with all the trick-or-treaters coming to the door."

"I'll get my portable phone from the car and I'll get Rusty while I'm at it," David said. He gave Nikki's shoulder a final squeeze.

Outside, he saw the same group of teenagers scatter.

"You'd better stay the hell away from here," David yelled into the night.

Angela and Nikki were waiting for him in the kitchen when he returned with the phone and Rusty.

"There's a wolf pack of teenagers out there," David said. "They've made a mess of the front porch."

"I think it's because we haven't been answering the door," Angela said. "All the trick-or-treaters have been turned away empty-handed. I'm afraid with no treats we've gotten our share of tricks. Believe me, compared to what we were facing, they're nothing."

"Not quite nothing: they've broken a few more windowpanes in the bay window," David said.

"Nikki broke the window," Angela said. She reached out and hugged her daughter. "She's our hero." Then Angela told him exactly what had happened.

David could hardly believe the peril his family had been in. When he thought of what might have happened . . . He couldn't bear to entertain the awful possibilities. When another barrage of raw eggs splattered against the front door, David's anger welled. Running to the foyer, he threw open the door fully intending to catch a couple of kids. Angela restrained him. Nikki held on to Rusty.

"They're not important," Angela said. Tears welled in her eyes.

Seeing his wife start to break down, David closed the door. He had no confusion in regard to his priorities. He consoled Angela as best he could. He knew that running after the kids would accomplish nothing; he'd just be blowing off steam in an attempt to assuage his guilt.

He drew Nikki to him as well and sat them both down on the family room couch. As soon as Angela had calmed down, David used his portable phone to call the police. While they waited for them to arrive, David cursed himself for having left Angela and Nikki.

"It's just as much my fault," Angela said. "I should have anticipated we'd be in danger." Angela then conceded that the rape attempt had possibly been an attempt on her life. She said that she'd told Calhoun about it, and he tended to agree with her.

"Why didn't you tell me this?" David demanded.

"I should have," Angela admitted. "I'm sorry."

"If nothing else, we're learning that we shouldn't hold secrets from each other," David said. "What about Calhoun? Have you heard from him yet?"

"No," Angela said. "I even left a message as you suggested. What are we going to do?"

"I don't know," David said. He stood up. "In the meantime let's take a look at that bay window."

The police were in no hurry. It took them almost three-quarters of an hour to arrive. To David's and Angela's chagrin, Robertson himself came in full uniform. Angela was tempted to ask if it was his Halloween costume. He was accompanied by a deputy, Carl Hobson.

As Robertson came through the front door he glanced at the refuse on the porch and noticed the broken window. He was carrying a clipboard.

"You people having a minor problem?" he asked.

"Not minor," Angela said. "Major." She then described what had happened from the moment the man appeared to David's arrival.

Robertson obviously had little patience for Angela's story. He fidgeted impatiently as she explained all that had happened, rolling his eyes for his deputy's benefit.

"Now, you sure this was a real gun?" Robertson asked.

"Of course it was a real gun," Angela said with exasperation.

"Maybe it was just a toy gun, part of a costume. You sure this guy wasn't just trick-or-treating?" He winked at Hobson.

"Just one goddamn minute," David said, breaking into the conversation. "I don't like what I'm hearing here. I'm getting the distinct impression that you're not taking this seriously. This man had a gun. There was violence here. Hell, even part of the bay window has been blown out."

"Don't you yell at me," Robertson said. "Your good wife has already admitted that your darling daughter blew out the window, not the purported intruder. And let me tell you something else: there's an ordinance against discharging a shotgun within the town limits unless it's done at the range by the dump."

"Get the hell out of my house," David raged.

"I'll be happy to," Robertson said. He motioned for Hobson to precede him. At the door, Robertson paused. "Let me offer you people some advice. You're not a popular family in this town, and it could get a whole lot worse if you shoot at some innocent child coming by for candy. God help you if you actually hit some kid."

David rushed to the door and slammed it behind Robertson as soon as the oaf was out the door.

"Bastard!" David fumed. "Well, we no longer have any illusions about the local police. We can't expect any help from them."

Angela hugged herself and fought off a new batch of tears. "What a mess," she said, shaking her head. David stepped over and comforted her. He also had to calm Nikki, who was shocked by the sharp exchange between her father and the chief of police.

"Do you think we should stay here tonight?"

"Where can we go at this hour?" David said. "I think we should stay. We can make sure we have no more visitors."

"I suppose you're right," Angela said with a sigh. "I know I'm not thinking straight. I've never been this upset."

"Are you hungry?" David asked.

Angela shrugged. "Not really," she said. "But I'd started getting dinner ready before all this happened."

"Well, I'm starved," David said. "I didn't eat lunch."

"Okay," Angela said. "Nikki and I will put something together."

David called the phone company and reported that their phone was out of order. When he mentioned he was a doctor they agreed to send a repairman as soon as possible. Next, David went out to the barn and found some additional outdoor lighting. When he was finished, the entire outside of the house was brilliantly illuminated.

The phone repairman arrived while they were eating. He quickly determined the problem was outside; the phone line had been cut where it entered the house. While the repairman worked, the Wilsons continued their dinner.

"I hate Halloween," the repairman said when he came to the door to announce that the phone was fixed. David thanked him for coming out on a Sunday night.

After dinner David tended to additional security measures. First he boarded up a portion of the bay window in the living room. Then he went around and made sure all the doors and windows were locked.

Although the visit by the police had been exasperating, it did have one beneficial effect. After the police had been there the pesky teenagers gave up their harassment campaign. Apparently seeing the cruiser had been enough to scare them off. By nine o'clock the Wilsons had gathered in Nikki's room for her respiratory therapy.

After Nikki went to sleep, David and Angela retired to the family room to go over the material David had brought back from Boston. As an additional security aid David encouraged Rusty to leave Nikki's room where he customarily slept and stay with them in the family room. David wanted to take advantage of the dog's sensitive hearing. David also kept the shotgun close at hand.

"You know what I think," Angela said as David opened the envelope that contained the medical records. "I think the man who came in here tonight is the same person who's behind the euthanasia and Hodges' murder. I'm convinced of it. It's the only thing that makes sense."

"I agree with you," David said. "And I think our best candidate is Clyde Devonshire. Read this."

David handed Devonshire's medical record to Angela. She quickly scanned it. "Oh my," she said as she came near to the end. "He's HIV positive."

David nodded. "It means he's got a potentially terminal illness himself. I think we have a serious suspect here, especially when you combine his HIV status with the other facts like his having been arrested outside of Jack Kevorkian's house. He obviously has a strong interest in assisted suicides. Who knows? That interest could extend to euthanasia. He's a trained nurse so he has the medical expertise and he worked in the hospital so he has access, and if that isn't enough, he has a history of rape. He might be the ski-masked rapist."

Angela nodded, but she was troubled. "The only problem with all this is that it's completely circumstantial," she said. Then she asked: "Would you know Clyde Devonshire by sight?"

"No," David admitted.

"I wonder if I'd be able to identify him by his height or the sound of his voice," Angela said. "I kind of doubt it. I'd never be absolutely sure."

"Well, let's move on," David said. "The next best candidate is Werner Van Slyke. Take a look at his history." David handed Van Slyke's record to Angela. It was considerably thicker than Devonshire's.

"Good grief," Angela said as she came to the end. "What you don't know about people."

"What do you think of him as a suspect?" David asked.

"It's an interesting psychiatric history," Angela agreed. "But I don't think he's the one. Schizo-affective disorder with mania and paranoia is not the same thing as an antisocial psychotic."

"But you don't have to be antisocial to have misguided ideas about euthanasia," David said.

"That's true," Angela said. "But just because someone is mentally ill doesn't mean they're criminal. If Van Slyke had an extensive criminal history or a history of violent behavior, that would be different. But since he doesn't, I don't think he rates too high as a suspect. Besides, he may know about nuclear submarines, but he doesn't have a sophisticated knowledge of medicine. How could he be killing a bunch of patients employing a method even you can't detect if he didn't have specialized health-related training?"

"I agree," David said. "But look at this material I got from Robert today."

David handed Angela the sheet of paper listing Van Slyke's various bank accounts in Albany and Boston.

"Where on earth is he getting this money?" Angela asked. "Do you think it has anything to do with our concerns?"

David shrugged. "That's a good question," he said. "Robert didn't think so. He suggested that Van Slyke was dealing drugs. We do know there's marijuana in town, so it's possible."

Angela nodded.

"If it's not drugs it would be ominous," David said.

"Why?" Angela asked.

"Let's suppose Van Slyke is the one killing these people," David said. "If he's not selling drugs, he could be getting paid for each death."

"What an awful idea," Angela said. "But if that were the case we'd be back to square one. We still wouldn't know who was behind it. Who would be paying him and why?"

"I'd still guess it's some misguided mercy killer," David said. "All the victims had potentially fatal illnesses."

"I think we're getting too speculative," Angela said. "We've got too much information and we're straining to put it all into the same theory. Most of this information probably isn't related."

"You're probably right," David said. "But I just had an idea. If we were to determine Van Slyke was the culprit, then his psychiatric problems could work in our favor."

"What do you mean?" Angela asked.

"Van Slyke had a psychotic break under the stress of a submarine patrol. I don't find that all that surprising. I might have had one, too. Anyway, when he had his psychotic break, he had paranoid symptoms and turned against his authority figures. His history indicates he'd done that before. If we confronted him I'm sure he'd get stressed out. Then we could evoke his paranoia toward whoever is paying him. All we'd have to say is that this, quote, 'authority figure' is planning on letting Van Slyke take the blame if anything goes wrong. And since we're talking with him, obviously things are going wrong."

Angela flashed David an expression of disbelief. "You amaze me sometimes," she said. "Especially since you think you are so rational. That's the most convoluted and ridiculous idea I've ever heard. Van Slyke's history documented mania with belligerence. And you're suggesting that you could safely evoke this individual's schizophrenic paranoia? That's absurd. He'd explode in violence, and it would be directed at everyone, particularly you."

"It was just an idea," David said defensively.

"Well, I'm not going to get myself worked up," Angela said. "This is all too speculative and theoretical."

"Okay," David said soothingly. "The next candidate is Peter Ullhof. Obviously he has medical training. The fact that he's been arrested in connection with the abortion issue suggests that he has some strong feelings about moral issues in medicine. But after that, there's not much."

"What about Joe Forbs?" Angela asked.

"The only thing that makes him suspicious is his inability to handle his personal finances," David said.

"And what about the last person? Claudette Maurice."

"She's clean," David said. "The only thing I'm curious about is where she has the tattoo."

"I'm exhausted," Angela said. She tossed the papers she had in her hands onto the coffee table. "Maybe after a good night's sleep, something will come to us."

Nikki awoke in the middle of the night with another nightmare and ended up sleeping in the master bedroom. David and Angela both slept restlessly. Even Rusty seemed unable to sleep soundly, growling and barking on several occasions during the night. Each time David leaped out of bed and grabbed the shotgun. But each time it proved to be a false alarm.

The only bright spot the next morning was Nikki's health. Her lungs were completely clear. Nevertheless, the Wilsons didn't even consider sending her to school.

They tried phoning Calhoun again but got the answering machine with the same message. They discussed calling the police about the investigator but couldn't make up their minds. They admitted they didn't know Calhoun that well, that his behavior was eccentric, and that they were probably jumping to conclusions. They were also reluctant to call the local police considering the experiences they'd had with them, particularly the previous night.

"The one thing I do know," Angela said, "I don't want to spend another night in this house. Maybe we should pack everything up and leave this town to its own devices and secrets."

"If we're thinking of doing that, then I'd better call Sherwood," David said.

"Do it," Angela said. "I'm serious about not wanting to spend another night here."

David phoned the bank to make an appointment to see the president. The first opening available was that afternoon at three o'clock. Although David would have preferred an earlier time, he took what he could get.

"We really should speak to a lawyer," Angela said.

"You're right," David said. "Let's call Joe Cox."

Joe was a good friend of theirs. He was also one of the shrewdest lawyers in Boston. When Angela called his office, she was told that Joe was unavailable; he was in court and would be all day. Angela left a message that she'd call back.

"Where should we spend the night?" Angela asked, hanging up the phone.

"Our closest friends in town are the Yansens," David said. "And that's not saying much. I haven't socialized with Kevin since that ridiculous tennis game, and I don't want to call him now." David sighed. "I suppose I could call my parents."

"I was afraid to suggest it," Angela said.

David made the call to Amherst, New Hampshire, and asked his mother if they could come for a few days. He explained that they were having some difficulties with the house. David's mother was delighted. There'd be no problem at all. She said she was looking forward to their arrival.

Angela tried to call Calhoun again, with no luck. She then suggested they drive to his place in Rutland; it wasn't that far away. David agreed, so all three Wilsons climbed into the Volvo and made the trip.

"There it is," Angela said as they approached Calhoun's home.

David pulled into the parking area in front of the carport. They were immediately disappointed. They'd hoped to be reassured, but they weren't. It was obvious no one was home. There was two days' worth of newspapers piled on the front stoop.

On their way back to Bartlet they discussed the investigator and found themselves even more indecisive. Angela mentioned that after she'd hired him he'd not contacted her for days. Finally they decided they'd wait one more day. If they couldn't reach him in twenty-four hours they would go to the police.

When they got home, Angela began packing for a stay at David's parents'. Nikki helped. While they were busy with that, David got out the telephone book and looked up the addresses of the five tattooed hospital workers. Once he had them written down, he went upstairs and told Angela that he wanted to cruise by their homes just to check out their living situations.

"I don't want you going anywhere," Angela said sternly.

"Why not?" David asked. He was surprised at her response.

"For one thing, I don't want to be here by myself," she said. "Second, we now understand that this affair is dangerous. I don't want you snooping around the house of a potential killer."

"Okay," David said soothingly. "Your first reason is quite sufficient. You didn't have to give me two. I didn't think you'd be nervous to be left alone during this time of the morning. And as far as it being dangerous, these people would probably be at work now."

"Probably isn't good enough," Angela said. "Why don't you give us a hand packing the car?"

It was almost noon before they were ready. After they made sure all the doors to the house were locked, they climbed into the Volvo. Rusty hopped in beside Nikki.

David's mother, Jeannie Wilson, welcomed them warmly and made them feel instantly at home. David's father, Albert, was off for a day's fishing trip and wouldn't be back until that evening.

After carrying everything into the house, Angela collapsed on the quilted bed in the guest room. "I'm exhausted," she said. "I could fall asleep this second."

"Why don't you?" David said. "There's no need for both of us to go back to talk with Sherwood."

"You wouldn't mind?" Angela asked.

"Not in the least," David said. He pulled the edge of the quilt down and encouraged Angela to slide under it. As he closed the door he heard her advise him to drive carefully, but her voice was already thick with sleep.

David told his mother and Nikki that Angela was napping. He suggested that Nikki do the same, but she was already involved in making cookies with her grandmother. Explaining that he had an appointment in Bartlet, David went out to the car.

David arrived back in town with three-quarters of an hour to spare. He stopped alongside the road to pull out the list of tattooed hospital employees and their addresses. The closest one was Clyde Devonshire's. Feeling a bit guilty, David put the car in gear and headed for Clyde's. He rationalized his decision by telling himself that Angela's fears were unwarranted. Besides, he wasn't going to do anything; he just wanted to take a look.

David was surprised to find a convenience store at the address listed for Devonshire. He parked in front of the building, got out, and went into the store. While paying for a carton of orange juice he asked one of the two clerks if he knew Clyde Devonshire.

"Sure do," the man said. "He lives upstairs."

"Do you know him well?" David asked.

"So-so," the man said. "He comes in here a lot."

"I was told he had a tattoo," David said.

The man laughed. "Clyde's got a bunch of tattoos," he said.

"Where are they?" David asked, feeling slightly embarrassed.

"He has tattooed ropes around both wrists," the second clerk said. "It's like he was all tied up."

The first clerk laughed again, only harder.

David smiled. He didn't get the humor, but he wanted to be polite. At least he'd found out Clyde had tattoos where they could be damaged in a struggle.

"He's also got a tattoo on his upper arm," the first clerk said. "And more on his chest."

David thanked the clerks and left the store. He walked around the side of the building and spotted the door to the stairs. For a brief instant he thought about trying the door, but then he decided against it. He owed Angela that much.

Returning to his car, David climbed in behind the wheel and checked the time. He still had twenty minutes before his meeting with Sherwood: time for one more address. The next closest was Van Slyke's.

In just a few minutes David turned onto Van Slyke's lane. He slowed down to check the numbers on the mailboxes, looking for Van Slyke's. Suddenly, David jammed on the brakes. He'd come abreast of a green truck that looked a lot like Calhoun's.

Backing up, David parked the Volvo directly behind the truck. It had a sticker on the back bumper that read: "This Vehicle Climbed Mount Washington." It had to be Calhoun's.

David got out of his car and peered into the truck's cab. A moldy cup of coffee was sitting on the open glove compartment door. The ashtray was overflowing with cigar butts. David recognized the upholstery and the air freshener hanging from the rearview mirror. The truck was definitely Calhoun's.

David straightened up and looked across the street. There was no mailbox in front of the house, but from where he was standing, he could see the address painted on the riser of the porch stairs. It was 66 Apple Tree Lane, Van Slyke's address.

David crossed the street for a closer look. The house was badly in need of paint and repair. It was even hard to be sure what color it had originally been. It looked gray but there was a greenish cast to it suggesting it had once been pale olive.

There were no signs of life. It hardly looked like the house was lived in except for the indentation of tire tracks in the gravel of the driveway.

David hiked back to the garage and peered inside. It was empty.

David then returned to the front of the house. After checking to see that no one was observing him from the street, he tried the door. It was unlocked and it opened with a simple turn of the knob. He pushed it open slowly; the rusty hinges groaned.

Ready to flee at the slightest provocation, David peered inside. What furniture he could see was covered with dust and cobwebs. Taking a deep breath, David called out to determine if anybody was home.

If there was, no one answered. He strained to hear, but the house was silent.

Fighting an urge to flee, David forced himself to step over the threshold. The silence of the house enveloped him like a cloak. His heart was racing. He didn't want to be there, but he had to find out about Calhoun.

David called out again, but again no one answered. He was about to call out a third time when the door behind him slammed shut. David nearly passed out from fright. Experiencing an irrational fear that the door had somehow locked, he frantically reopened it. He propped it open with a dusty umbrella stand. He did not want to feel enclosed in the building.

After composing himself as best he could, David made a tour of the first floor. He moved quickly from one dirty room to the next until he got to the kitchen. There he stopped. On the table was an ashtray. In it was the butt of an Antonio y Cleopatra cigar. Just beyond the table was an open door leading down to the cellar.

David approached the doorway and looked down into utter darkness. Beside the doorway was a light switch. David tried it. An anemic glow filtered up the stairs.

Taking a deep breath, David started down. He stopped midway and let his eyes sweep around the cluttered basement. It was filled with old furniture, boxes, a steamer trunk, and a hodgepodge of tools and junk. David noticed that the floor was dirt just as it was in his house, although near the furnace there was a slab of concrete.

David continued down the stairs, then went over to the concrete. Bending down, he examined it closely. The slab was still dark with dampness. He put his hand on it to be sure. David shuddered. He straightened up and ran for the stairs. As far as he was concerned, he'd seen enough to go to the police. Only he wasn't going to bother with the local police. He planned to call the state police directly. Reaching the top of the stairs, David stopped in his tracks. He heard the sound of car tires in the gravel of the driveway. A car had pulled in beside the house.

For a second David froze, not knowing what to do. He had little time to decide; the next thing he knew, he heard the car door open, then slam shut, then footsteps in the gravel.

David panicked. He pulled the door to the cellar shut and quickly descended the stairs. He was confident there'd be another way out of the basement, some sort of back stairs leading directly out.

At the rear of the basement were several doors. David lost no time weaving his way to them. The first one had an open hasp. As quietly as possible, he pulled it open. Beyond was a root cellar illuminated by a single low-watt bulb.

Hearing footsteps above, David quickly went to the second door. He gave the knob a tug, but the door wouldn't budge. He exerted more strength. At last, it creaked open. It moved stiffly, as if it hadn't been opened for years.

Beyond the door was what David had been looking for: a flight of concrete steps leading up to angled hatch-like doors. David closed the door to the basement behind him. He was now in darkness save for a sliver of light coming from between the two nearly horizontal doors above him.

David scrambled up the stairs and crouched just beneath the doors. He stopped to listen. He heard nothing. He put his hands on the doors and pushed. He was able to raise the doors half an inch, but no more; they were padlocked from outside.

Letting the doors down quietly, David tried to keep himself calm. His pulse was hammering in his temples. He knew he was trapped. His only hope was that he'd go undiscovered. But the next thing he heard was the door to the cellar crashing open followed by heavy footfalls on the cellar steps.

David squatted in the darkness and held his breath.

The footfalls drew nearer, then the door to his hideaway was yanked open. David found himself staring into the frenzied face of Werner Van Slyke.

Van Slyke appeared to be in a worse panic than David. He looked and acted as if he'd just taken an overwhelming dose of speed. His eyelids were drawn back, causing his unblinking eyes to bulge from their sockets. His pupils were so dilated he seemed to have no irises. Drops of perspiration were beaded on his forehead. His whole body was trembling, particularly his arms. In his right hand he clutched a pistol which he pointed at David's face.

For a few moments neither of them moved. David frantically tried to think of a plausible reason for his presence, but he couldn't think of a thing. All he could think about was the dancing barrel of the gun pointed at him. With Van

Slyke's trembling growing worse by the minute, David was afraid the gun might go off accidentally.

David realized that Van Slyke was in the grip of an acute anxiety attack, probably triggered by his discovery of David hiding in his home. Remembering the man's psychiatric history, David thought there was a good chance Van Slyke was psychotic that very moment.

David thought about mentioning Calhoun's truck as a way of explaining his presence, but he quickly decided against it. Who knew what had transpired between Van Slyke and the private investigator? Mention of Calhoun might only exacerbate Van Slyke's psychotic state.

David decided that the best thing for him to do was to try to befriend the man, to acknowledge that he had problems, to admit that he was under stress, to tell him that David understood that he was suffering, and to tell him that David was a doctor and wanted to help him.

Unfortunately, Van Slyke gave David little chance to act on his plan. Without a word, Van Slyke reached out, grabbed David by his jacket, and rudely yanked him from the stairwell into the cellar itself.

Overwhelmed by Van Slyke's strength, David sprawled headfirst onto the dirt floor, crashing into a stack of cardboard boxes.

"Get up!" Van Slyke screamed. His voice echoed in the cellar.

David warily got to his feet.

Van Slyke was shaking so hard he was practically convulsing.

"Get into the root cellar," he yelled.

"Calm down," David said, speaking for the first time. Trying to sound like a therapist, he told Van Slyke that he understood he was upset.

Van Slyke responded by indiscriminately firing the gun. Bullets whizzed by David's head and ricocheted around the basement until they embedded themselves in an overhead floor joist, the stairs, or one of the wooden doors.

David leaped into the root cellar and cowered against the far wall, terrified of what Van Slyke might do next. Now he was convinced that Van Slyke was acutely psychotic.

Van Slyke shut the heavy wooden door with such force, plaster rained down on top of David's head. David didn't move. He could hear Van Slyke moving around in the cellar. Then he heard the sound of the hasp of the root cellar door being closed over its staple and a padlock being applied. David heard the click as the lock was closed.

After a few minutes of silence, David stood up. He looked around his cell. The only light source was a single bare bulb hanging by a cord from the ceiling. The room was bounded by large granite foundation blocks. On one wall were bins filled with fruit that appeared mummified. On the other wall shelves lined with jars of preserves reached to the ceiling.

David moved to the door and put his ear to it. He heard nothing. Looking more closely at the door he saw fresh scratch marks across it. It was as if someone had been trying desperately to claw his way out.

David knew it was futile but he had to try: he leaned his shoulder against the door and pushed it. It didn't budge. Failing in that, David started to make a complete tour of the cell when the light went out, plunging him into absolute darkness.

Sherwood buzzed his secretary and asked what time the appointment was scheduled with David Wilson.

"Three o'clock," Sharon said.

"What time is it now?" he asked. He was looking at the pocket watch he'd fished out of his vest.

"It's three-fifteen," she said.

"That's what I thought. No sign of him?"

"No, sir."

"If he shows up, tell him he'll have to reschedule," Sherwood said. "And bring in the agenda for tonight's hospital executive board meeting."

Sherwood took his finger off the intercom button. It irritated him that David Wilson would be late for a meeting that he had called to request. To Sherwood it was a deliberate snub, since punctuality was a cardinal virtue in his value system.

Sherwood lifted his phone and dialed Harold Traynor. Before he put in time on the executive meeting material, Sherwood wanted to be sure that the meeting hadn't been canceled. One had been back in 1981 and Sherwood still hadn't gotten over it.

"Six P.M.," Traynor said. "On schedule. Want to walk up together? It's a nice evening, and we won't be having too many more of these until next summer."

"I'll meet you right outside the bank," Sherwood said. "Sounds like you're in a good mood."

"It's been a good day," Traynor said. "I've just heard this afternoon from my nemesis, Jeb Wiggins. He's caved in. He'll back the parking garage after all. We should have the approval of the Selectmen by the end of the month."

Sherwood smiled. This was good news indeed. "Should I put together the bond issue?" he asked.

"Absolutely," Traynor said. "We've got to move on this thing. I have a call in to the contractor right now to see if there's any chance of pouring concrete before winter sets in."

Sharon came into Sherwood's office and handed him the agenda for the meeting.

"There's more good news," Traynor said. "Beaton called me this morning to tell me the hospital balance sheet looks a lot better than we thought it would. October wasn't nearly as bad as predicted."

"Nothing but good news this month," Sherwood said.

"Well, I wouldn't go that far," Traynor said. "Beaton also called me a little while ago to tell me that Van Slyke never showed up."

"He didn't phone?" Sherwood questioned.

"No," Traynor said. "Of course, he doesn't have a phone so that's not too surprising. I suppose I'll have to ride over there after the executive meeting. Trouble is, I hate to go in that house. It depresses me."

Just as unexpectedly as the overhead light had gone out, it went on again. In the distance David could hear Van Slyke's footfalls coming back down the cellar stairs accompanied by the intermittent clank of metal hitting metal. After that, David heard the clatter of things being dropped onto the dirt floor.

After another trip up and down David heard Van Slyke drop something particularly heavy. After a third trip there was the same dull thud that David could feel as much as hear. It sounded almost like a body hitting the hard-packed dirt, and David felt himself shudder.

Taking advantage of the light, David explored the root cellar for another way out, but as he suspected, there was none.

Suddenly David heard the lock on the root cellar door open and the hasp pull away from the staple. He braced himself as the door was yanked open.

David sucked in a breath of air at the sight of Van Slyke. He appeared even more agitated than he had earlier. His dark, unruly hair was no longer lying flat against his skull; it now stood straight out from his head as if he'd been jolted with a bolt of electricity. His pupils were still maximally dilated, and his face was now covered with perspiration. He'd removed his green work shirt and was now clad in a dirty T-shirt which he hadn't tucked into his trousers.

David immediately noticed how powerfully built Van Slyke was, and he quickly ruled out the possibility of trying to overpower the man. David also noticed that Van Slyke had a tattoo of an American flag held by a bald eagle on his right forearm. A thin scar about five inches long marred the design. David realized then that Van Slyke was probably Hodges' murderer.

"Out!" Van Slyke yelled along with a string of expletives. He waved his gun recklessly, sending a chill down David's spine. David was terrified Van Slyke would again start randomly firing.

David complied with Van Slyke's command and quickly stepped out of the root cellar. He edged sideways, keeping Van Slyke in his line of vision at all times. Van Slyke angrily motioned for him to continue on toward the furnace.

"Stop," Van Slyke commanded after David had moved some twenty feet. He pointed down toward the ground.

David looked down. Next to his feet were a pick and shovel. Nearby was the new slab of concrete.

"I want you to dig," Van Slyke yelled. "Right where you are standing."

Afraid of hesitating for a second, David bent down and lifted the pick. David considered using it as a weapon, but as if reading his mind, Van Slyke stepped back out of reach. He kept the gun raised, and although it was shaking, it was still pointing in David's direction. David didn't dare risk charging toward him.

David noticed bags of cement and sand on the floor and guessed it had been the noise of those bags hitting the floor that he had heard from the root cellar.

David swung the pick. To his surprise it dug a mere two inches into the densely packed earthen floor. David swung the pick several more times but only succeeded in loosening a small amount of dirt. He dropped the pick and picked up the shovel to move the dirt aside. There was no doubt in his mind what Van Slyke had in mind for him. He was having him dig his own grave. He wondered if Calhoun had been put through the same ordeal.

David knew his only hope was to get Van Slyke talking. "How much should I dig?" he asked as he traded the shovel for the pick.

"I want a big hole," Van Slyke said. "Like the hole of a doughnut. I want the whole thing. I want my mother to give me the whole doughnut."

David swallowed. Psychiatry hadn't been his forte in medical school, yet even he recognized that what he was hearing was called clanging or "loosening of associations," a symptom of acute schizophrenia.

"Did your mother give you a lot of doughnuts?" David asked. He was at a loss for words, but he desperately wanted to keep Van Slyke talking.

Van Slyke looked at David as if he were surprised he was there. "My mother committed suicide," he said. "She killed herself." Van Slyke then shocked David by laughing wildly.

David mentally ticked off another schizophrenic symptom. He could remember that this symptom was euphemistically called "inappropriate affect." David recalled another major component of Van Slyke's illness: paranoia.

"Dig faster!" Van Slyke suddenly yelled as if he'd awakened from a mini-trance.

David dug more quickly, but he did not give up on his attempt to get Van Slyke talking. He asked Van Slyke how he was feeling. He asked what was on his mind. But he got no response to either question. It was as if Van Slyke had become totally preoccupied. Even his face had gone blank.

"Are you hearing voices?" David asked, trying another approach. He swung the pick several more times. When Van Slyke still didn't answer, David looked over at him. His expression had changed from a blank look to one of surprise. His eyes narrowed, then his trembling became more apparent.

David stopped digging and studied Van Slyke. The change in his expression was striking. "What are the voices saying?" David asked.

"Nothing!" Van Slyke shouted.

"Are these voices like the ones you heard in the navy?" David asked.

Van Slyke's shoulders sagged. He looked at David with more than surprise. He was shocked.

"How did you know about the navy?" he asked. "And how did you know about the voices?"

David could detect paranoia in Van Slyke's voice and was encouraged. He was cracking the man's shell.

"I know a lot about you," David said. "I know what you have been doing. But I want to help you. I'm not like the others. That's why I'm here. I'm a doctor. I'm concerned about you."

Van Slyke didn't speak. He simply glared at David, and David continued.

"You look very upset," David said. "Are you upset about the patients?"

Van Slyke's breath went out of him as if he'd been punched. "What patients?" he demanded.

David swallowed again. His mouth was dry. He knew he was taking risks. He could hear Angela's warnings in the back of his mind. But he had no choice. He had to gamble.

"I'm talking about the patients that you've been helping to die," David said.

"They were going to die anyway," Van Slyke shouted.

David felt a shiver rush down his spine. So it had been Van Slyke.

"I didn't kill them," Van Slyke blurted out. "They killed them. They pushed ·the button, not me."

"What do you mean?" David asked.

"It was the radio waves," Van Slyke said.

David nodded and tried to smile compassionately despite his anxiety. It was clear to him he was now dealing with the hallucinations of a paranoid schizophrenic. "Are the radio waves telling you what to do?" David asked.

Van Slyke's expression changed again. Now he looked at David as if David were deranged. "Of course not," he said with scorn. But then the anger came back: "How did you know about the navy?"

"I told you, I know a lot about you," David said. "And I want to help you. That's why I'm here. But I can't help you until I know everything. I want to know who 'they' are. Do you mean the voices that you hear?"

"I thought you said you knew a lot about me," Van Slyke said.

"I do," David said. "But I don't know who is telling you to kill people or even how you are doing it. I think it's the voices that are telling you. Is that true?"

"Shut up and dig," Van Slyke said. With that, he aimed the gun just to David's left and pulled the trigger. The slug thumped into the root cellar door, which then creaked on its hinges.

David quickly resumed his digging. Van Slyke's mania terrified him. But after a few more shovelfuls, David took the risk of resuming talking. He wanted to regain his credibility by impressing Van Slyke with the amount of information he had.

"I know you are being paid for what you've been doing," David said. "I even know you've been putting money in banks in Albany and Boston. I just don't know who's been paying you. Who is it, Werner?"

Van Slyke responded by moaning. David looked up from his digging in time to see Van Slyke grimacing and holding his head with both hands. He was covering his ears as if shielding them from painful sounds.

"Are the voices getting louder?" David asked. Fearing that Van Slyke wouldn't hear him with his hands over his ears, David practically shouted his question.

Van Slyke nodded. His eyes began to dart wildly around the room as if he were looking for a way to escape. While Van Slyke was distracted David gripped the shovel, gauging the distance between himself and Van Slyke, wondering if he could hit him, and if he could, whether he could hit him hard enough to eliminate the threat of the gun.

But whatever chance there had been while Van Slyke had been momentarily preoccupied was soon gone. Van Slyke's panic lessened and his wandering eyes refocused on David.

"Who is it, who is speaking to you?" David asked, trying to keep up the pressure.

"It's the computers and the radiation, just like in the navy," Van Slyke yelled.

"But you're not in the navy," David said. "You are not on a submarine in the Pacific. You are in Bartlet, Vermont, in your own basement. There are no computers or radiation."

"How do you know so much?" Van Slyke demanded again. His fear was again changing to anger.

"I want to help you," David said. "I can tell you're upset and that you're suffering. You must feel guilt. I know you killed Dr. Hodges."

Van Slyke's mouth dropped open. David wondered if he had gone too far. He sensed that he had evoked a strong paranoia in Van Slyke. He only hoped Van Slyke's rage wouldn't be directed toward him as Angela feared. David knew he had to get the conversation back to whoever was paying Van Slyke. The question was how.

"Did they pay you to kill Dr. Hodges?" David asked.

Van Slyke laughed scornfully. "That shows how much you know," he said. "They didn't have anything to do with Hodges. I did it because Hodges had turned against me, saying I was attacking women in the hospital parking lot. But I wasn't. He said he would tell everybody I was doing it unless I left the hospital. But I showed him."

Van Slyke's face went blank again. Before David could ask him if he were hearing voices, Van Slyke shook his head. Then he behaved as if he were waking from a deep sleep. He rubbed his eyes, then stared at David as if surprised to find him standing before him with a shovel. But his confusion quickly changed to anger. Van Slyke raised his gun, aiming it directly at David's eyes.

"I told you to dig," he snarled.

David rushed to comply. Even then, he fully expected to be shot. When no shots followed, David agonized over what to do next. His current approach was not working. He was stressing Van Slyke, but not enough or perhaps not in the right ways.

"I've already talked to the person who is paying you," David said after a few minutes of frantic digging. "That's one of the reasons I know so much. He's told me everything, so it doesn't matter if you tell me anything or not."

"No!" Van Slyke shouted.

"Oh, yes," David said. "He also told me something you should know. He told me that if Phil Calhoun got suspicious, you'd have to take the blame for everything."

"How did you know about Phil Calhoun?" Van Slyke demanded. He began to shake again.

"I told you I know what's happening," David said. "The whole affair is about to destruct. As soon as your sponsor finds out about Phil Calhoun, it will be over. And he doesn't care about you, Van Slyke. He thinks you are nothing. But I care. I know how you are suffering. Let me help you. Don't let this person use you as a dupe. You are nothing to him. He wants you to be hurt. They want you to suffer."

"Shut up!" Van Slyke screamed.

"The person who is using you has told lots of people about you, Van Slyke. Not just me. And they have all had a good laugh over the fact that Van Slyke will be blamed for everything."

"Shut up!" Van Slyke screamed a second time. He lunged at David and rammed the barrel of the gun against David's forehead.

David froze as he peered at the gun cross-eyed. He let go of the shovel and it fell to the floor.

"Get back in the root cellar," Van Slyke screamed. He kept the tip of the gun pressed against David's skin.

David was terrified the gun would go off at any second. Van Slyke was in a state of frenzied agitation that bordered on absolute panic.

Van Slyke backed David into the root cellar. Only then did he withdraw the gun. Before David could reiterate his desire to help Van Slyke, the heavy wood door was slammed in his face and relocked.

David could hear Van Slyke running through the basement, crashing into objects. He heard his heavy footfalls on the cellar steps. He heard the cellar door slam shut. Then the lights went out.

David stayed perfectly still, straining to hear. Very faintly he heard a distant car engine start, then quickly fade. Then there was only silence and the pounding of his own heart.

David stood motionless in the total darkness thinking about what he'd unleashed. Van Slyke had dashed out of the house in a state of acute manic psychosis. David had no idea where Van Slyke was headed or what he had in mind, but whatever it was it couldn't be good.

David felt tears well up in his eyes. He'd certainly managed to evoke the man's psychotic paranoia, but the result was not what he'd hoped. He'd wanted to befriend Van Slyke and get him to talk about his problems. David also wanted to free himself in the process. Instead David was still imprisoned and he'd released a madman into the town. David's only source of solace was that Angela and Nikki were safely in Amherst.

Struggling to control his emotions, David tried to think rationally about his predicament, wondering if there were any chance of escape. But as he thought of the solid stone walls encircling him he had an acute rush of claustrophobia.

Losing control, David began to sob as he vainly attacked the stout wooden door to the cellar. He hurtled his shoulder against it multiple times, crying for someone to let him out.

At length David managed to regain a modicum of self-control. He stopped his self-destructive batterings against the unyielding door. Then he stopped crying. He thought about the blue Volvo and Calhoun's truck. They were his only hope.

With fear and resignation, David sank to a sitting position on the dirt floor to wait for Van Slyke's return.

MONDAY • NOVEMBER 1, LATER THAT DAY

Angela slept much longer than she'd planned. When she awoke around four-thirty, she was surprised to hear that David had neither returned nor called. She felt a pang of concern, but dismissed it. But as the time crept toward five, her concern grew with each passing minute.

Angela finally picked up the phone and called Green Mountain National Bank. But she only got a recording that told her the bank's hours were nine to four-thirty. Frustrated, Angela hung up. She wondered why David hadn't called on his portable phone. It wasn't like him. He'd surely know she'd start worrying if he were late.

Next Angela called Bartlet Community Hospital. She asked to be connected to the front information desk, then inquired there about David. She was told that Dr. Wilson had not been seen all day.

Finally Angela tried their home in Bartlet. There wasn't any other place she could think to try. But after letting the phone ring ten times, she gave up.

Replacing the receiver for the third time, Angela wondered if David had decided to play sleuth after all. The possibility only made her more concerned.

Angela went to the kitchen and asked her mother-in-law if she would mind if she borrowed the car.

"Of course not," Jeannie answered. "Where are you going?"

"Back to Bartlet," Angela said. "I left some things in the house."

"I want to go too," Nikki said.

"I think you'd better stay here," Angela said.

"No," Nikki said. "I'm coming."

Angela forced herself to smile at Jeannie before going over to Nikki. She took her daughter by the arm and walked her into the next room.

"Nikki, I want you to stay here," Angela said.

"I'm scared to stay here by myself," Nikki said. She broke into tears.

Angela was stymied. She much preferred that Nikki stay with her grandmother, yet she didn't have time to argue with the child. Nor did she want to explain to her mother-in-law why Nikki would be better off staying. In the end, Angela gave in.

It was close to six by the time Angela and Nikki entered Bartlet. It was still light out, but night would follow soon. Some of the cars already had their headlights on.

Angela only had a sketchy plan of what to do, and it mostly involved hunting for the Volvo. The first location she wanted to search was the bank, and as she neared the institution she saw Barton Sherwood and Harold Traynor walking toward the town green. Angela pulled over to the curb and jumped out. She told Nikki to wait in the car.

"Excuse me," Angela said as she caught up with the two men.

Sherwood and Traynor turned.

"I'm sorry to bother you," Angela said. "I'm looking for my husband."

"I have no idea where your husband is," Sherwood said irritably. "He missed our appointment this afternoon. He didn't even phone."

"I'm sorry," Angela said.

Sherwood touched the brim of his cap, and he and Traynor moved off.

Angela dashed back to the car. Now she was convinced that something bad had happened.

"Where's Daddy?" Nikki questioned.

"I wish I knew," Angela said. She made a rapid U-turn in the middle of Main Street that sent the car's wheels screeching.

Nikki reached out and steadied herself against the dash. She'd sensed that her mother was upset, and now she was certain.

"Everything will be all right," Angela told Nikki.

Angela sped to their house, hoping to see the Volvo parked near the back door. Maybe David had gone there by now. But as she pulled into the driveway, she was immediately disappointed. There was no Volvo.

Angela jerked to a stop next to the house. A quick glance told her it was just as they had left it, but she wanted to be sure.

"Stay in the car," she told Nikki. "I'll just be a second."

Angela went inside and called for David, but there was no answer. Taking a quick run through the house, she checked to see if the master bed had been disturbed. It hadn't. On her way back down the stairs Angela spotted the shotgun. She snatched it up and checked the magazine. There were four shells in it.

With shotgun in hand, Angela went into the family room and took out the phone directory. She looked up the addresses of Devonshire, Forbs, Maurice, Van Slyke, and Ullhof and wrote them down. Carrying both the list and the shotgun, she returned to the car.

"Mom, you're driving crazy," Nikki said as Angela left a patch of rubber on the road.

Angela slowed a little. She told Nikki to relax. The problem was, Angela was more anxious than ever and Nikki could sense it.

The first address turned out to be a convenience store. Angela angled in to its parking area and pulled to a stop.

Nikki looked at the store and then back at her mother. "What are we doing here?" she asked.

"I'm not sure," Angela said. "Keep an eye out for the Volvo."

"It's not here," Nikki said.

"I realize that, dear." She put the car in gear and headed for the next address. It was Forbs' residence. Angela slowed as they came to the house. The lights inside were on, but there was no Volvo.

Disappointed, Angela again gunned the engine and they sped away.

"You're still driving weird, Mom," Nikki said.

"I'm sorry," Angela said. She slowed down. As she did, she realized she was gripping the steering wheel so hard, her fingers had gone numb.

The next house was Maurice's. Angela slowed but immediately saw that it was closed up tight with no sign of life. Angela sped on.

A few minutes later, when she turned onto Van Slyke's street, Angela spotted the Volvo instantly. So did Nikki. It was a ray of hope. Angela pulled directly behind the car, turned off the ignition, and jumped out.

As she approached the car she saw Calhoun's truck in front of it. She looked in both vehicles. In Calhoun's truck she noticed a moldy cup of coffee. It appeared as if it had been there for several days.

Angela looked across the street at Van Slyke's house. There were no lights whatsoever, fanning Angela's growing alarm.

Running back to the car, Angela got the shotgun. Nikki started to get out, but Angela yelled at her to stay where she was. Angela's tone let Nikki know there was to be no arguing.

Carrying the shotgun, Angela ran across the street. As she climbed the porch steps, she wondered if she should go directly to the police. Something was seriously wrong, there was no doubt about it. But what help could she expect from the police? Besides, she worried that time might be a factor.

She tried ringing the doorbell, but it clearly didn't work. Failing that, she banged on the door. When there was no response, she tried the door. It was unlocked. She pushed it open and cautiously stepped inside.

Then, as loudly as she could, she yelled David's name.

David heard Angela's yell. He straightened up. He'd been slouched against a bin filled with desiccated apples. The sound had come from such a distance and had been so faint that at first he questioned if it had been real. He thought he might have been hallucinating. But then he heard it again.

This time David knew it was real, and he knew it was Angela. He leaped to his feet in the utter darkness and screamed Angela's name. But the sound died in the confined, insulated space with its dirt floor. David moved blindly ahead until he hit against the door. Then he tried yelling again, but he could tell it would be in vain unless Angela were in the basement.

Groping along the shelves, David seized a jar of preserves. He carried it over to the door and pounded the wood with it. But the sound was hardly as loud as he'd hoped.

Then David heard what he thought were Angela's footsteps somewhere above. Changing tactics, he hurled the jar of preserves against the ceiling. He covered his head with his hands and closed his eyes as the glass smashed against the floorboards.

Groping back to the shelving, David tried to climb up on it so he could pound directly on the ceiling with his fists. But he'd only pounded once when the shelf he was standing on gave way. The shelf and all its jars collapsed to the floor, David along with it.

Angela felt frantic and discouraged. She'd rapidly toured the first floor of the filthy house, turning on what lights she could. Unfortunately she found no evidence of either David or Calhoun, save for a cigar butt in the kitchen that possibly could have been Calhoun's.

Angela was ready to start on the second floor when she thought about Nikki. Concerned, Angela dashed out to the car. Nikki was anxious, but she was okay. Angela said she'd be just a bit longer. Nikki told her to hurry because she was scared sitting by herself.

Angela ran back into the house and started up the stairs. She carried the shotgun with both hands. When she reached the second floor, she stopped and listened. She thought she'd heard something, but if she had, she didn't hear it again. She continued on.

The upstairs of the house was even dirtier than the main floor. It had a peculiar musty smell, as if no one had been up there for years. Giant cobwebs hung from the ceiling. In the upstairs hall Angela yelled David's name several more times, but after each shout there was nothing but silence.

Angela was about to head back downstairs when she noticed something on a small console table at the head of the stairs. It was a rubber Halloween mask fashioned to look like a reptile. It was the mask the intruder had worn the previous evening!

Trembling, Angela started down the stairs. Halfway down she paused to listen. Once again she thought she'd heard something. It sounded like distant thumping.

Angela was determined to find the source of the sound. At the base of the stairs she paused again. She thought she heard pounding from the direction of the kitchen. She hurried into the room. The noise was definitely louder. Bending down she put her ear to the floor. Then she heard the knocking distinctly.

She yelled David's name. With her ear still pressed to the floor she could just barely hear David answer, calling her by name. Angela scrambled to the cellar stairs.

She found the light and headed down, still clutching the shotgun. She began to hear David's voice more clearly, but it was still muffled.

Once she was down in the basement, she yelled his name again. Tears sprang to her eyes when she heard his reply. Weaving her way through the clutter, Angela followed the sound of his voice. There were two doors. By this time David was pounding so hard Angela knew immediately which one he was behind. But there was a problem: the door was padlocked.

Angela shouted to David that she'd get him out. Leaning the shotgun against the wall, she scanned the basement for an appropriate tool. Her eyes soon came to rest on the pick.

Swinging the tool in a short arc, she hit the lock several times but with no result. Trying a different approach, she inserted the end of the pick beneath the hasp and used it as a pry bar.

Pushing with all her might, Angela was able to snap the hasp and its mounting screws out of the door. She then pulled the door open.

David rushed out and embraced her.

"Thank God you came!" he said. "Van Slyke is the one behind all this. He's killed the patients and he killed Hodges. Right this minute he's in a psychotic panic and he's armed. We've got to get out of here."

"Let's go," Angela said. She snatched up the shotgun. Together they hurried to the stairs.

Before they started up, David put a hand on Angela's arm. He pointed toward the cement slab next to the hole he'd been digging. "I'm afraid Calhoun is under there," he said.

Angela gasped.

"Come on!" David said, giving her a nudge.

They started up the stairs.

"I haven't learned who is paying Van Slyke," David said as they climbed. "But it's clear that's what's been happening. I also haven't learned how Van Slyke has been able to kill the patients."

"Van Slyke is also the one who was at the house last night," Angela said. "I found the reptile mask upstairs."

As David and Angela reached the kitchen, headlight beams suddenly filled the room, playing across their horrified faces. Van Slyke had come back.

"Oh, God, no!" David whispered. "He's back."

"I've turned on a lot of lights," Angela said. "He'll know something's wrong."

Angela thrust the shotgun into David's hands. He gripped it with sweaty palms. They heard the car door close, then heavy footsteps in the gravel of the driveway.

David motioned for Angela to step back through the cellar door. David followed and pulled the door partially closed behind him. He left it open a crack so he could see into the kitchen.

The footsteps came to the back door, then abruptly stopped.

For a few terrorizing minutes there was no sound whatsoever. David and Angela held their breath. They guessed Van Slyke was wondering about the lights.

Then, to their surprise, they heard the footsteps recede. They listened until they couldn't hear them anymore.

"Where did he go?" Angela whispered.

"I wish I knew," David said. "I don't like not knowing where he is. He knows this place too well. He could get at us from behind."

Angela turned and looked down the cellar steps. The idea that Van Slyke could suddenly jump out at them made her skin crawl.

For a few minutes they stayed put, straining to hear any noises. The house was eerily silent. Finally David pushed the door open. Stepping back into the kitchen warily, he motioned for Angela to follow.

"Maybe it wasn't Van Slyke," Angela whispered.

"It had to have been him," David whispered back.

"Let's get the hell out of here. I'm afraid if I'm in here too long Nikki will get out of the car."

"What!" David whispered. "Nikki's here?"

"I couldn't leave her at your mother's," Angela whispered. "She insisted on coming with me. I couldn't fight with her. And there was no time to explain the situation to your mother."

"Oh my God!" David whispered. "What if Van Slyke has seen her?"

"Do you think he might have?"

David motioned for Angela to follow him. They went to the door to the yard, opening it as quietly as they could. It was completely dark outside. Van Slyke's car was twenty feet away but the man was nowhere to be seen.

Now David motioned for Angela to stay where she was. He sprinted to Van Slyke's car, keeping the shotgun ready. He looked in the passenger-side window, just in case Van Slyke was hiding, but he wasn't there. David waved for Angela to join him.

"Let's skirt the gravel of the driveway," David said. "It's too noisy. We'll stick to the grass. Where did you park?"

"Right in back of you," Angela said.

David led with Angela right behind him. As they reached the street their worst fears were realized. In the light of a streetlamp next to Calhoun's truck, they could see Van Slyke's silhouette in the driver's seat of David's mother's Cherokee. Nikki was next to him.

"Oh, no!" Angela said as she impulsively started forward.

David restrained her. They looked at each other in horror. "We have to do something," Angela said.

"We have to think," David said. He looked back at the Cherokee. He was so tense, he thought he might pass out.

"Do you think he has a gun?" Angela asked.

"I know he has a gun," David snapped.

"Maybe we should get help," Angela suggested.

"It would take too long," David said. "Besides, Robertson and his crew wouldn't have any idea how to handle a situation like this—if they even took us seriously. We'll have to handle this ourselves. We've got to get Nikki far enough away so that we can use the shotgun if we have to."

For a few harrowing moments they simply stared at the car.

"Let me have the keys," David said. "I'm worried he might have locked the doors."

"They're in the car," Angela said.

"Oh, no!" David exclaimed. "He could just drive off with Nikki."

"Oh, God," Angela whispered.

"This is getting worse and worse," David said. "But have you noticed: the whole time we've been standing here looking at the car, Van Slyke hasn't moved. Last time I saw him he was in constant manic motion, unable to hold still for a moment."

"I see what you mean," Angela said. "It looks almost as if they're having a conversation."

"If Van Slyke isn't watching, we could slip behind the car," David said. "Then you could go to one side and I to the other. We'll open the front doors simultaneously. You pull Nikki free and I'll aim the shotgun at Van Slyke."

"Good Lord!" Angela groaned. "Don't you think that's taking a lot of chances?"

"Tell me a better idea," David said. "We have to get her out of there before he drives off with her."

"Okay," Angela said reluctantly.

After crossing the street a good distance back from the Cherokee, David and Angela approached the car from behind. They remained crouched down as they moved in hopes of remaining undetected. Eventually they arrived at the very rear of the vehicle and squatted in its shadow.

"I'll first slip alongside to see if the doors are locked," David whispered.

Angela nodded and took the shotgun.

David crawled along the driver's side of the car until he was even with the rear door. Rising slowly, he saw that none of the doors were locked.

"At least something is going our way," Angela whispered once he came back and told her the good news.

"Okay," David whispered. "Are you ready?"

Angela gripped David's arm. "Wait," she said. "The more I think about your plan, the less I like it. I don't think we should go up on separate sides. I think we should both go to her door. You open the door, I'll pull her out."

David thought for a moment, then agreed. The main idea was to get Nikki away from Van Slyke. With Angela's plan there was more chance they'd succeed. The problem then would be how to handle Van Slyke once Nikki was safe.

"Okay," David whispered. "When I give the signal we do it."

Angela nodded.

David took the shotgun from Angela and held it in his left hand. He moved around Angela so that he was at the right side of the car. Slowly he rounded the car and started crawling along its side, holding the gun up against his chest. When he came abreast of the rear door, he turned around to make sure Angela was right behind him. She was.

David prepared to spring forward by positioning his feet directly under his torso. But before he could give the signal to Angela, Nikki's door opened and Nikki leaned out and looked back. She was startled to see David's face so close to her own.

"What are you guys doing?" Nikki asked.

David leaped forward and pulled the door completely open. Nikki lost her balance and tumbled from the car. Angela sprang forward and grabbed her, dragging her onto the grass. Nikki cried out in shock and pain.

David trained the gun on Van Slyke. He was fully prepared to pull the trigger if need be. But Van Slyke didn't have a gun. He didn't try to flee. He didn't so much as move. He merely looked at David; his expression was completely blank.

David warily moved a little closer. Van Slyke remained seated calmly, his hands in his lap. He did not seem to be the agitated psychotic that he'd been less than an hour earlier.

"What's happening?" Nikki cried. "Why did you pull me so hard? You hurt my leg."

"I'm sorry," Angela said. "I was worried about you. The man you've been sitting with is the same man who was in our house last night wearing the reptile mask."

"He couldn't be," Nikki said, wiping her tears away. "Mr. Van Slyke told me he was supposed to talk with me until you came back."

"What has he been talking about?" Angela asked.

"He was telling me about when he was my age," Nikki said. "How wonderful it had been."

"Mr. Van Slyke's childhood wasn't wonderful at all," David said. David was still intently watching Van Slyke, who still hadn't moved. Keeping the shotgun aimed directly at Van Slyke's chest, David leaned into the car for a closer look. Van Slyke continued to stare back at him blankly.

"Are you okay?" David asked. He was at a loss for what to do.

"I'm all right," Van Slyke said in a calm monotone. "My father took me to the movies all the time. Whenever I wanted."

"Don't move," David commanded. Keeping the shotgun aimed at him, David stepped around the front of the car and opened the driver's side door. Van Slyke didn't budge, but he kept his eyes on David.

"Where's the gun?" David demanded.

"Gun run done fun," Van Slyke said.

David grabbed Van Slyke by the arm and pulled him out of the car. Angela yelled at David to be careful. She'd heard what Van Slyke had said. She told David that he was clanging; he was obviously still acutely psychotic.

David pushed Van Slyke around so that he was facing the car. Then he frisked him for any weapons. He didn't find the pistol.

"What did you do with the gun?" David demanded.

"I don't need it anymore," Van Slyke said.

David peered into Van Slyke's calm face. His pupils were no longer dilated. The transformation was remarkable.

"What's going on, Van Slyke?" David asked.

"On?" Van Slyke said. "On top. Put it on top."

"Van Slyke!" David shouted. "What's happened to you? Where have you been? What about the voices you hear? Are you still hearing voices?"

"You're wasting your time," Angela said. She and Nikki had come around the front of the car. "I'm telling you, he's acutely psychotic."

"No more voices," Van Slyke said. "I made them stop."

"I think we should call the police," Angela said. "And I don't mean the local bozos. I mean the state police. Is your cellular phone in the car?"

"How did you quiet the voices?" David asked Van Slyke.

"I took care of them," Van Slyke answered.

"What do you mean you took care of them?" David was afraid to learn what Van Slyke meant.

"They won't be able to use me as a dupe," Van Slyke said.

"Who do you mean by they?" David asked.

"The board," Van Slyke said. "The whole board."

"David!" Angela said impatiently. "What about the police. I want to get Nikki away from here. He's talking nonsense."

"I'm not so sure," David said.

"Well, then, what does he mean by the board?" Angela asked.

"I'm afraid he means the hospital board," David said.

"Board sword ford cord," Van Slyke said. He smiled. It was the first time his expression had changed since they'd confronted him in the car.

"David, the man is not connected to reality," Angela said. "Why are you insisting on having a conversation with him?"

"Do you mean the hospital board?" David asked.

"Yes," Van Slyke said.

"Okay, everything is going to be all right," David said. But he was trying to calm himself more than anyone else.

"Did you shoot someone?" David asked.

Van Slyke laughed. "No, I didn't shoot anyone. All I did was put the source on the conference room table."

"What does he mean by 'source'?" Angela asked.

"I have no idea," David said.

"Source force course horse," Van Slyke said, still chuckling.

Feeling frustrated, David grabbed Van Slyke by the front of his shirt and shook him, asking him again what he'd done.

"I put the source and the force on the table right next to the model of the parking garage," Van Slyke said. "And I'm glad I did it. I'm not a dupe for anybody. The only problem is, I'm sure I burned myself."

"Where?" David asked.

"My hands," Van Slyke said. He held them up so David could look at them.

"Are they burned?" Angela asked.

"I don't think so," David said. "They're slightly red, but otherwise they look normal to me."

"He's not making any sense," Angela said. "Maybe he's hallucinating."

David nodded absently. His thoughts were suddenly somewhere else.

"I'm tired," Van Slyke said. "I want to go home and see my parents."

David waved him off. Van Slyke walked across the street and into his yard. Angela stared at David. She'd not expected him to let Van Slyke go. "What are you doing?" she asked. "Shouldn't we call the police?"

David nodded again. He stared after Van Slyke while his mind began pulling everything together: his patients, the symptoms, and the deaths.

"Van Slyke is a basket case," Angela said. "He's acting like he just had electroshock therapy."

"Get in the car," David said.

"What is it?" Angela asked. She didn't like the tone of David's voice.

"Just get in the car!" David shouted. "Hurry!" He climbed into the driver's seat of the Cherokee.

"What about Van Slyke?" Angela questioned.

"There's no time for Van Slyke," David said. "Besides, he isn't going anywhere. Come on, hurry!"

Angela put Nikki into the back seat and climbed in next to David. David already had the car started. Before Angela could close her door, David was backing up. Then he made a quick U-turn and accelerated up the street.

"What's happening now?" Nikki asked.

"Where are we going?" Angela asked.

"To the hospital," David said.

"You're driving as bad as Mom," Nikki told her father.

"Why the hospital?" Angela asked. She reached back and patted Nikki's knee to reassure her.

"It's suddenly beginning to make sense to me," David said. "And now I have this terrible premonition."

"What are you talking about?" Angela asked.

"I think I might know what Van Slyke was talking about when he referred to 'the source.' "

"I thought that was just schizophrenic babble," Angela said. "He was clanging. He said source, force, course, and horse. It was just gibberish."

"He may have been clanging," David said, "but I don't think he was talking nonsense when he said source. Not when he was talking about putting it on a conference table that had a model of a parking garage on it. That's too specific."

"Well, what do you think he was referring to?" Angela asked.

"I think it has to do with radiation," David said. "I think that's what Van Slyke was talking about when he said he'd burned his hands."

"Oh, come on. You're sounding as crazy as him," Angela said. "You have to remember Van Slyke's paranoia on the nuclear submarine had to do with radiation, so any similar talk probably has more to do with the return of his schizophrenia than anything else."

"I hope you're right," David said. "But it has me worried. Van Slyke's training in the navy involved nuclear propulsion. That's driving a ship with a nuclear reactor. And nuclear reactors mean radiation. He was trained as a nuclear technician, so he knows something about nuclear materials and what they're capable of doing."

"Well, what you are saying makes sense," Angela said. "But talking about a source and having one are two vastly different things. People can't just go out and get radioactive material. It's tightly controlled by the government. That's why there is a Nuclear Regulatory Commission."

"There's an old radiotherapy unit in the basement of the hospital," David said. "It's a cobalt-60 machine Traynor's hoping to sell to some South American country. It has a source."

"I don't like the sound of this," Angela admitted.

"I don't like it either," David said. "And think about the symptoms my patients had. Those symptoms could have been from radiation, especially if the patients had been subjected to overwhelming doses. It's a horrendous possibility, but it fits the facts. At the time radiation had never entered my mind."

"I never thought about radiation when I did Mary Ann Schiller's autopsy," Angela admitted. "But now that I think of it, that could have been it. Radiation isn't something you consider unless there is a history of exposure. The pathological changes you see are nonspecific."

"That's my point exactly," David said. "Even the nurses with flu-like symptoms could have been suffering from a low level of radiation. And even . . ."

"Oh, no!" Angela exclaimed, immediately catching David's line of thought.

David nodded. "That's right," he said. "Even Nikki."

"Even Nikki what?" Nikki asked from the back seat. She'd not been paying attention to the conversation until she'd heard her name.

Angela turned around. "We were just saying that you had flu-like symptoms just like the nurses," she said.

"And Daddy too," Nikki said.

"Me too," David agreed.

They pulled into the hospital parking lot and parked.

"What's the plan?" Angela asked.

"We need a Geiger counter," David said. "There has to be one in the Radio-therapy Center for their certification. I'll find a janitor to let us in. Why don't you and Nikki go to the lobby?"

David found Ronnie, one of the janitors he vaguely knew. Ronnie was only too happy to help one of the doctors, especially since it took him away from the job of mopping the basement's corridor. David neglected to mention that he'd been fired from CMV and his hospital privileges had been suspended.

With Ronnie in tow, David went up to the lobby and found Angela. Nikki had discovered a TV and was content for the moment. David told Nikki not to leave the lobby; she promised she wouldn't.

Angela and David went to the Radiotherapy Center. It only took them about fifteen minutes to find a Geiger counter.

Back in the main hospital building, they met up with Ronnie in the base-ment. It had taken him a few minutes to find the key to the old radiotherapy unit.

"No one goes in here very often," he explained as he let the Wilsons in.

The unit consisted of three rooms: an outer room that had served as a re-ception area, an inner office, and a treatment room.

David walked straight back to the treatment room. The room was empty save for the old radiotherapy unit. The machine looked like an X-ray unit with a table attached for the patient to lie on.

David put the Geiger counter on the table and turned it on. The needle barely moved on the gauge. There was no reading above background even on its most sensitive scale.

"Where's the source lodged in this thing?" Angela asked.

"I'd guess it's where the treatment arm and this supporting column here meet," he said.

David lifted the Geiger counter and positioned it where he thought the source should reside. There was still no reading.

"The fact that there's no reading doesn't necessarily mean anything," Angela said. "I'm sure this thing is well shielded."

David nodded. He walked around to the back of the machine and tried the Geiger counter there. There was still no reading.

"Uh-oh," Angela said. "David, come here and look at this."

David joined Angela by the treatment arm. She pointed to an access panel that was attached by four nob screws. Several of the screws had been loosened.

David grabbed a chair from the reception room. He put it just under the arm. Standing on the seat of the chair, David was able to reach the panel. He un-screwed all four nob screws, removed the panel, and handed it all to Ronnie.

Behind the panel he discovered a circular metal plate secured with eight lug bolts. David had Angela hand him the Geiger counter. He pushed it inside the housing and tried again for radiation. There was none.

David moved the Geiger counter aside and reached in and grasped one of the lug bolts. To his dismay, it was loose. He checked all eight. All eight were loose. He began removing them, handing them down to Angela one by one.

"Are you sure you should be doing this?" Angela asked. She was still concerned about radiation, despite the readings, as well as David's questionable handyman skills.

"We have to know for sure," David said as he removed the last bolt. He then lifted the heavy metal covering and handed it to Ronnie. David peered down a long cylindrical cavity that was about four and a half inches in diameter. It looked like the barrel of a huge gun. Without a flashlight, he could only see a short distance in.

"I'm sure I'm not supposed to be able to look into the treatment arm like this," David said. "There would have to be a plug to act as a brake to stop the source when it was being moved out to the treatment position."

Just to be one hundred percent certain, David stuck the Geiger counter into the muzzle of the treatment arm. There was no reading above background.

David stepped down from the chair. "The source is not in there," he said. "It's gone."

"What are we going to do?" Angela asked.

"What time is it?" David asked.

"Seven-fifteen," Ronnie said.

"Let's get lead aprons from radiology," David said. "Then we'll do what we can."

They left the old radiotherapy unit and headed straight for the Imaging Center. They didn't need Ronnie to open the Imaging Center since it was open for emergency X rays, but David asked him to come to help carry the lead aprons. Ronnie didn't know what was going on, but whatever it was he could tell something serious was involved. He was eager to be as helpful as possible.

The X-ray technician was suspicious of David's request for lead aprons, but he decided that since David wouldn't be taking them any farther than the hospital next door, it would be okay. Besides, he wasn't used to contradicting doctors. He gave David, Angela, and Ronnie nine lead aprons as well as one pair of lead gloves used for fluoroscopy. David still had the Geiger counter, as well.

Weighed down with their burden, the three made their way back to the hospital. They got strange looks from the staff and visitors they passed on their way to the second floor, but no one tried to stop them.

"All right," David said once they reached the door of the conference room. He was practically out of breath. "Put everything right here." He dropped the aprons he was carrying to the floor next to the closed conference room door. Angela and Ronnie did likewise.

David tried the Geiger counter again. Immediately the needle pegged to the right. "Jesus Christ!" David said. "We couldn't get any better evidence than that." David thanked Ronnie and sent him on his way. He then explained to Angela what he thought they should do. David pulled on the lead gloves and picked up three aprons. He carried one in his hands while he tossed the other two over his shoulder. Angela picked up four in her arms.

David opened the door and went into the conference room, with Angela close behind. Traynor, who'd been interrupted in mid-sentence, glared at David. Those in attendance—Sherwood, Beaton, Cantor, Caldwell, Arnsworth, and Robeson—all turned to stare at the source of this rude interruption. As the assembled members of the board began to murmur, Traynor banged his gavel, crying for order.

Scanning the cluttered conference table, David spotted the source instantly. It was a cylinder about a foot long whose diameter matched the size of the bore in the treatment arm he'd examined only minutes ago. Several Teflon rings were embedded in its circumference. On its top was a locking pin. The cylinder was standing upright next to a model of a parking garage just as Van Slyke had indicated.

David started for the cylinder, clutching a lead apron in both hands.

"Stop!" Traynor yelled.

Before David could get to the cylinder, Caldwell leapt to his feet and grabbed David around his chest.

"What the hell do you think you are doing?" Caldwell demanded.

"I'm trying to save all of you if it isn't too late," David said.

"Let him go," Angela cried.

"What are you talking about?" Traynor demanded.

David nodded toward the cylinder. "I'm afraid you have been having your meeting around a cobalt-60 source."

Cantor leaped to his feet; his chair tipped over backward. "I saw that thing," he cried. "I wondered what it was." Saying no more, he turned and fled from the room.

A stunned Caldwell relaxed his grip. David immediately lunged across the table and snatched up the brass cylinder in his lead gloves. Then he rolled the cylinder in one of his lead aprons. Next he wrapped that apron in another and that one in another still. He proceeded to do the same with the aprons Angela was carrying while she stepped out of the conference room to get the others. David was anxious to cover the cylinder with as many layers of lead as possible.

As David was wrapping the last load of the aprons around the bulky parcel, Angela got the Geiger counter.

"I don't believe you," Traynor said, breaking a shocked silence. But his voice lacked conviction. Cantor's sudden departure had unnerved him.

"This is not the time for debate," David said. "Everyone better get out of here," he added. "You've all been exposed to a serious amount of radiation. I advise you to call your doctors."

Traynor and the others exchanged nervous glances. Panic soon broke out as first a few and then the remaining board members, including Traynor, ran from the room.

David finished with the last apron and took the Geiger counter. Turning it on, he was dismayed to see that it still registered a significant amount of radiation.

"Let's get out of here," David said. "That's about all we can do."

Leaving the cylinder wrapped in aprons on the table, they went out of the conference room, closing the doors behind them. David tried the Geiger counter again. As he expected, the radiation had fallen off dramatically. "As long as no one goes in the conference room, no one else will get hurt tonight," he said.

He and Angela headed toward the lobby to collect Nikki. Just before they arrived David stopped.

"Do you think Nikki will be okay for a few more minutes?" he asked.

"In front of a TV she'll be fine for a week," Angela said. "Why?"

"I think I know how the patients were irradiated," David said. He led Angela back toward the patients' rooms.

Half an hour later they collected Nikki and went out into the hospital parking lot. They took the Cherokee back to Van Slyke's so that David could get the Volvo.

"Do you think there's any chance he could hurt anybody tonight?" David asked. He motioned toward Van Slyke's house.

"No," Angela said.

"I don't think so either," David said. "And the last thing I want to do is go back in there. Let's go to my parents'. I'm exhausted."

David got out.

"I'll follow you," he said.

"Call your mother," Angela said. "I'm sure she's beside herself with worry."

David got in the Volvo and started it up. He looked at Calhoun's truck in front of him and sadly shook his head.

As soon as they got on the main road, David picked up his cellular phone. Before he called his mother he called the state police. When he got an emergency officer on the line he explained that he wanted to report a very serious problem that included murder and deadly radiation at the Bartlet Community Hospital . . .

EPILOGUE

FOUR MONTHS LATER

David knew he was late as he pulled up to a modest house on Glenwood Avenue in Leonia, New Jersey. He jumped out of the car and ran up the front steps.

"Do you know what time it is?" Angela asked. She followed David into their bedroom. "You were supposed to be home at one and here it is two. If I could get here on time I think you could have too."

"I'm sorry," David said as he quickly changed his clothes. "I had a patient who needed extra time." He sighed. "At least now I have the freedom to spend more time with a patient when I think it's called for."

"That's all well and good," Angela said. "But we have an appointment. You even picked the time."

"Where's Nikki?" David asked.

"She's out on the sun porch," Angela said. "She went out there over an hour ago to watch the '60 Minutes' crew set up."

David slipped on a freshly laundered dress shirt and did up the buttons.

"I'm sorry," Angela said. "I suppose I'm anxious about this TV thing. Do you think we should go through with it?"

"I'm nervous, too," David said as he selected a tie. "So if you want to cancel, it's fine with me."

"Well, we've cleared it with our respective bosses," Angela said.

"And everyone has assured us that it won't hurt us," David said. "And we both feel the public ought to know."

Angela paused to think about it. "Okay," she said at last. "Let's do it."

David tied his tie, brushed his hair, and put on a jacket. Angela checked herself in the mirror. When they both felt they were ready, they descended the stairs and walked out onto the sun porch, blinking under the bright lights.

Although David and Angela were nervous, Ed Bradley quickly put them at ease. He began the interview casually, getting them to relax, knowing he would be editing heavily as usual. He began by asking them what they were currently doing.

"I'm taking a fellowship in forensic pathology," Angela said.

"I'm working with a large medical group at Columbia Presbyterian Medical Center," David said. "We're contracted out with several HMO organizations."

"Are you both enjoying your work?" Bradley asked.

"We are," David said.

"We're thankful we've been able to put our lives back in some sort of order," Angela said. "For a while it was touch and go."

"I understand you had a difficult experience in Bartlet, Vermont," Bradley said.

Both David and Angela chuckled nervously.

"It was a nightmare," Angela said.

"How did it start?" Bradley asked.

David and Angela looked at each other, unsure of who should begin.

"Why don't you start, David?" Bradley said.

"My part of it started when a number of my patients began to die unexpectedly," David said. "They were patients with histories of serious illnesses like cancer."

David looked at Angela.

"It started for me when I began to be sexually harassed by my immediate superior," Angela said. "Then we discovered the body of a homicide victim entombed under our cellar steps. His name was Dr. Dennis Hodges, and he'd been the administrator of the hospital for a number of years."

With his usual clever questioning, Ed Bradley pulled out the whole sordid story.

"Were these unexpected patient deaths instances of euthanasia?" he asked David.

"That's what we thought initially," David said. "But these people were actually being murdered not through some misguided gesture of mercy, but to improve the hospital's bottom line. Patients with potentially terminal illness often use hospital facilities intensively. That translates to high costs. So to eliminate those expenses, the patients themselves were eliminated."

"In other words, the motivation for the whole affair was economic," Bradley said.

"Exactly," David replied. "The hospital was losing money, and they had to do something to stem the red ink. This was their solution."

"Why was the hospital losing money?" Bradley asked.

"The hospital had been forced to capitate," David explained. "That means furnish hospitalization for the major HMO in the area for a fixed fee per subscriber per month. Unfortunately, the hospital had estimated utilization at too low a cost. The money coming in was much less than the money going out."

"Why did the hospital agree to capitate in the first place?" Bradley asked.

"As I said, it was forced," David said. "It had to do with the new competition in medicine. But it's not real competition. In this case the HMO dictated the terms. The hospital had to capitate if it wanted to compete for the HMO's business. It didn't have any choice."

Bradley nodded as he consulted his notes. Then he looked back at David and Angela. "The new and current administrator of the Bartlet Community Hospital says that the allegations you're making are, in his words, 'pure rubbish.' "

"We've heard that," David said.

"The same administrator went on to say that if any patients had been murdered, it would have been the work of a single deranged individual."

"We've heard that as well," David said.

"But you don't buy it?"

"No, we don't."

"How did the patients die?" Bradley asked.

"From full-body radiation," Angela said. "The patients received overwhelming doses of gamma rays from a cobalt-60 source."

"Is that the same material that is used so successfully for treating some tumors?" Bradley asked.

"In very carefully targeted areas with carefully controlled doses," Angela said. "David's patients were getting uncontrolled full-body exposure."

"How was this radiation administered?" Bradley asked.

"An orthopedic bed was fitted with a heavily lead-shielded box," Angela said. "It was mounted under the bed and contained the source. The box had a remotely controlled window that was operated by a garage door opener with radio waves. Whenever the port was open the patient was irradiated through the bed. So were some of the nurses tending to these patients."

"And both of you saw this bed?" Bradley asked.

David and Angela nodded.

"After we found the source and shielded it as best we could," David explained, "I tried to figure out how my patients had been irradiated. I remembered that many of my patients had been in hospital beds that malfunctioned. They'd wound up being transferred to an orthopedic bed. So after we left the conference room we went looking for a special orthopedic bed. We found it in the maintenance shop."

"And now you contend that this bed was destroyed," Bradley said.

"The bed was never seen again after that night," Angela said.

"How could that have happened?" Bradley asked.

"The people responsible for the bed's use got rid of it," David said.

"And you believe the hospital executive committee was responsible?" Bradley said.

"At least some of them," David said. "Certainly the chairman of the board, the administrator, and the chief of the medical staff. We believe the operation was the brainchild of the chief of the medical staff. He was the only person who had the background necessary to dream up such a diabolical yet effective scheme. If they hadn't used it so often, it never would have been discovered."

"Regrettably, none of these people can defend themselves," Ed Bradley said. "I understand that all of them died of severe radiation sickness despite some heroic measures to save them."

"Unfortunately," David admitted.

"If they were so sick how could they have destroyed the bed?" Bradley asked.

"Unless the dose of radiation is so great that it is immediately lethal, there is a variable latent period before the onset of symptoms. In this case, there would have been plenty of time to get rid of the bed."

"Is there any way to substantiate these allegations?" Bradley asked.

"We both saw the bed," David said.

"Anything else?" Bradley asked.

"We found the source," Angela said.

"You found the source," Bradley said. "That's true. But it was in the conference room and not near any patients."

"Werner Van Slyke essentially confessed to us both," David said.

"Werner Van Slyke is the man you believe was the worker bee behind this operation," Bradley said.

"That's correct," David said. "He'd had nuclear technician training in the navy, so he knew something about handling radioactive materials."

"This is the same Werner Van Slyke who is schizophrenic and is now hospitalized with severe radiation sickness," Bradley said. "He's also the same Werner Van Slyke who's been in a psychotic state since the night the hospital executive committee got irradiated, who refuses to talk with anyone, and who is expected to die."

"He's the one," David admitted.

"Needless to say, he's hardly the most reliable corroborating witness," Bradley said. "Do you have any other proof?"

"I treated a number of nurses with mild radiation sickness," David said. "They had all been around my patients."

"But you thought that they had the flu at the time," Bradley said. "And there is no way to prove that they didn't."

"That's true," David admitted.

Bradley turned to Angela. "I understand you autopsied one of your husband's patients?" he asked.

Angela nodded.

"Did you suspect radiation sickness after the autopsy?" Bradley asked. "And if you didn't, why not?"

"I didn't because she'd died too quickly to manifest many of the symptoms that would have suggested radiation," Angela said. "She'd received so much radiation that it affected her central nervous system on a molecular level. If she'd had less radiation she might have lived long enough to develop ulceration of her digestive tract. Then I might have added radiation to the differential diagnosis."

"What I'm hearing is that neither of you has any hard evidence," Bradley said.

"I suppose that's true," David said reluctantly.

"Why haven't either of you been called to testify?" Bradley asked.

"We know there have been some civil suits," Angela said. "But all of them were quickly settled out of court. There have been no criminal charges."

"With the kind of accusations you've made it's incredible there have been no criminal charges," Ed Bradley said. "Why do you think there haven't been any?"

Angela and David looked at each other. Finally David spoke: "Basically we think there are two reasons. First, we think that everybody is afraid of this affair. If it all came out, it would probably shut the hospital, and that would be disastrous for the community. The hospital pumps a lot of money into the town, it employs a lot of people, and it serves the people medically. Secondly, there's the fact that in this case, the guilty, in a sense, have been punished. Van Slyke took care of that when he put the cobalt-60 cylinder on the conference table."

"That might explain why there hasn't been any local response," Bradley said. "But what about at the state level? What about the state's attorney?"

"Nationally, this episode cuts to the quick of the direction of health-care reform," Angela said. "If this story were to get out, people might begin to reevaluate their thinking on the route we seem to be taking. Good business decisions don't always equate with good medical decisions. Patient care is bound to suffer when the powers that be are too focused on the bottom line. Our experience at Bartlet Community Hospital may be an extreme example of medical bureaucrats run amok. Yet it happened. It could happen again."

"Rumor has it that you could profit from this matter," Bradley said.

David and Angela again exchanged nervous glances.

"We have been offered a large amount of money for a made-for-TV movie," David admitted.

"Are you going to take it?" Bradley asked.

"We haven't decided," David said.

"Are you tempted?"

"Of course we're tempted," Angela said. "We are buried under a mountain of debt from our medical training, and we own a house that we have not been able to sell in Bartlet, Vermont. In addition to that, our daughter has a medical condition and might develop special needs."

Ed Bradley smiled at Nikki, who immediately smiled back. "I hear you were a hero in this affair," he said.

"I shot the shotgun at a man who was fighting with my mom," Nikki said. "But I hit the window instead."

Bradley chuckled. "I will certainly keep my distance from your mother," he said.

Everyone laughed.

"I'm sure you two are aware," Bradley said, resuming a more serious tone, "that there are people who contend that you have dreamed up this whole story to make the TV money and to get back at the hospital and HMO for firing you."

"I'm sure that those who don't want the true story out will do what they can to discredit us. But they really shouldn't blame the messenger for the bad news," Angela said.

"What about the series of rapes in the hospital parking lot?" Bradley asked. "Was that part of this plot?"

"No, they weren't," Angela said. "At one point we thought they were. So did the private investigator who lost his life investigating this episode with us. But we were wrong. The one indictment that has come out of this unfortunate episode is for Clyde Devonshire, an emergency-room nurse. DNA testing has proved he was responsible for at least two of the rapes."

"Have you learned anything from this experience?" Bradley asked.

David and Angela said yes simultaneously. Angela spoke first: "I've learned that as health care is changed, doctors and patients better know all the rules of any supposed cost-cutting plan so they can make appropriate decisions. Patients are too vulnerable."

"I've learned," David said, "that it is dangerous to allow financial and business people and their bureaucrats to interfere in the doctor-patient relationship."

"Sounds to me as if you two doctors are against health-care reform," Bradley said.

"Quite the contrary," Angela said. "We think health-care reform is desperately needed."

"We think it's needed," David said. "But we're worried. We just don't want it to be a fatal cure like that old joke about the operation being a success but the patient dying. The old system favored over-utilization through economic incentives. For example, rewarding a surgeon according to how frequently he operated. The more appendixes or tonsils he removed, the more money he made. We don't want to see the pendulum swing in the opposite direction by using economic incentives to under-utilize. In many health plans, doctors are being rewarded with bonuses not to hospitalize or not to treat in some specific way."

"It should be the patient's needs that determine the level and type of treatment," Angela said.

"Exactly," David said.

"Cut," Bradley said.

The cameramen straightened up from their equipment and stretched.

"That was terrific," Bradley said. "That's plenty of material and the perfect place to stop. It was a great wrap. My job would be a lot easier if everyone I interviewed were as articulate as you folks."

"That's sweet of you to say," Angela said.

"Let me ask you guys if you think the entire executive committee was involved," Bradley said.

"Probably most of them," David said. "All had something to gain from the hospital if it thrived and a lot to lose if it shut down. The board members' involvement wasn't as altruistic as most people would like to think, particularly Dr.

Cantor, the chief of staff. His Imaging Center would have folded if the hospital went under."

"Damn!" Bradley said after he'd skimmed his notes. "I forgot to ask about Sam Flemming and Tom Baringer." He called out to the cameramen he wanted to do a little more.

David and Angela were puzzled. These names were not familiar to them.

As soon as the cameramen gave him the cue that the tape was rolling, Ed Bradley turned to David and Angela and asked them about the two men. Both said they could not place the names.

"These were two people who died in Bartlet Community Hospital with the exact same symptom complex as David's patients," Bradley said. "They were patients of Dr. Portland."

"Then we wouldn't know anything about them," David said. "They would have expired before we started working at the hospital; Dr. Portland killed himself shortly before we moved to town."

"What I wanted to ask," Bradley said, "is whether you believe that these two people could have died from radiation sickness as you allege your patients did."

"I suppose if the symptoms were the same in type, degree, and time frame, then I would say yes," David said.

"That's interesting," Bradley said. "Neither one of these two people had terminal illnesses or any medical problem other than the acute problem they'd been admitted with. But both had taken out multimillion-dollar insurance policies with the hospital as the sole beneficiary."

"No wonder Dr. Portland was depressed," Angela said.

"Would either of you care to comment?" Ed Bradley asked.

"If they had been irradiated, then the motive was even more directly economic than it was in the other cases," David said. "And it would certainly make our case that much more convincing."

"If the bodies were exhumed," Bradley asked, "could it be determined unequivocally whether or not they had died of radiation?"

"I don't believe so," Angela said. "The best anyone could say would be that the remains were consistent with radiation exposure."

"One last question," Bradley said. "Are you happy now?"

"I don't think we've dared ask ourselves that question yet," David said. "We're certainly happier than we were several months ago, and we're glad we're working. We're also thankful that Nikki has been doing so well."

"After what we've been through it will take some time to put it all behind us," Angela said.

"I think we're happy," Nikki said, speaking up. "I'm going to have a brother. We're going to have a baby."

Bradley raised his eyebrows. "Is that true?" he asked.

"God willing," David said.

Angela just smiled.

ACCEPTABLE RISK

For Jean
"the guiding light"

the Devil hath power
to assume a pleasing shape.

—*Hamlet*
William Shakespeare

PROLOGUE

SATURDAY • FEBRUARY 6, 1692

Spurred on by the penetrating cold, Mercy Griggs snapped her riding crop above the back of her mare. The horse picked up the pace, drawing the sleigh effortlessly over the hard-packed snow. Mercy snuggled deeper into the high collar of her sealskin coat and clasped her hands together within her muff in a vain attempt to shield herself from the arctic air.

It was a windless, clear day of pallid sunshine. Seasonally banished to its southern trajectory, the sun had to struggle to illuminate the snowy landscape locked in the grip of a cruel New England winter. Even at midday long violet shadows extended northward from the trunks of the leafless trees. Congealed masses of smoke hung motionlessly above the chimneys of the widely dispersed farmhouses as if frozen against the ice blue polar sky.

Mercy had been traveling for almost a half hour. She'd come southwest along the Ipswich Road from her home at the base of Leach's Hill on the Royal Side. She'd crossed bridges spanning the Frost Fish River, the Crane River, and the Cow House River and now entered into the Northfields section of Salem Town. From that point it was only a mile and a half to the town center.

But Mercy wasn't going to town. As she passed the Jacobs' farmhouse, she could see her destination. It was the home of Ronald Stewart, a successful merchant and shipowner. What had drawn Mercy away from her own warm hearth on such a frigid day was neighborly concern mixed with a dose of curiosity. At the moment the Stewart household was the source of the most interesting gossip.

Pulling her mare to a stop in front of the house, Mercy eyed the structure. It certainly bespoke of Mr. Stewart's acumen as a merchant. It was an imposing, multi-gabled building, sheathed in brown clapboard and roofed with the highest-grade slate. Its many windows were glazed with imported, diamond-shaped panes of glass. Most impressive of all were the elaborately turned pendants suspended from the corners of the second-floor overhang. All in all the house appeared more suited to the center of town than to the countryside.

Confident that the sound of the sleigh bells on her horse's harness had announced her arrival, Mercy waited. To the right of the front door was another horse and sleigh, suggesting that company had already arrived. The horse was under a blanket. From its nostrils issued intermittent billows of vapor that vanished instantly into the bone-dry air.

Mercy didn't have long to wait. Almost immediately the door opened and within the doorframe stood a twenty-seven-year-old, raven-haired, green-eyed woman whom Mercy knew to be Elizabeth Stewart. In her arms she comfortably cradled a musket. From around her sides issued a multitude of children's curious faces; unexpected social visits in isolated homes were not common in such weather.

"Mercy Griggs," called the visitor. "Wife of Dr. William Griggs. I've come to bid you good day."

" 'Tis a pleasure, indeed," called Elizabeth in return. "Come in for some hot cider to chase the chill from your bones." Elizabeth leaned the musket against the inside doorframe and directed her oldest boy, Jonathan, age nine, to go out to cover and tether Mrs. Griggs' horse.

With great pleasure Mercy entered the house, and, following Elizabeth's direction, turned right into the common room. As she passed the musket, she eyed it. Elizabeth, catching her line of sight, explained: " 'Tis from having grown up in the wilderness of Andover. We had to be on the lookout for Indians all hours of the day."

"I see," Mercy said, although a woman wielding a musket was apart from her normal experience. Mercy hesitated for a moment on the threshold of the kitchen and surveyed the domestic scene, which appeared more like a schoolhouse than a home. There were more than a half dozen children.

On the hearth was a large, crackling fire that radiated a welcome warmth. Enveloping the room was a mixture of savory aromas: some of them were coming from a kettle of pork stew simmering on its lug pole over the fire; others were rising from a large bowl of cooling corn pudding; but most were coming from the beehive oven built into the back of the fireplace. Inside, multiple loaves of bread were turning a dark, golden brown.

"I hope in God's name I am not a bother," Mercy said.

"Heavens, no," Elizabeth replied as she took Mercy's coat and directed her to a ladderback chair near to the fire. "You're a welcome reprieve from the likes of these unruly children. But you have caught me baking, and I must remove my bread." Quickly she hefted a long-handled peel, and with short, deft thrusts picked up the eight loaves one by one and deposited them to cool on the long trestle table that dominated the center of the room.

Mercy watched Elizabeth as she worked, remarking to herself that she was a fine-looking woman with her high cheekbones, porcelain complexion, and lithesome figure. It was also apparent she was accomplished in the kitchen by the way she handled the bread-making and with the skill she evinced stoking the fire and adjusting the trammel holding the kettle. At the same time Mercy sensed there was something disturbing about Elizabeth's persona. There wasn't the requisite Christian meekness and humbleness. In fact Elizabeth seemed to project an alacrity and boldness that was unbecoming of a Puritan woman whose husband was away in Europe. Mercy began to sense that there was more to the gossip that she'd heard than idle hearsay.

"The aroma of your bread has an unfamiliar piquancy," Mercy said as she leaned over the cooling loaves.

" 'Tis rye bread," Elizabeth explained as she began to slip eight more loaves into the oven.

"Rye bread?" Mercy questioned. Only the poorest farmers with marshy land ate rye bread.

"I grew up on rye bread," Elizabeth explained. "I do indeed like its spicy taste. But you may wonder why I am baking so many loaves. The reason is I have in mind to encourage the whole village to utilize rye to conserve the wheat supplies. As you know, the cool wet weather through spring and summer and now this terrible winter has hurt the crop."

"It is a noble thought," Mercy said. "But perhaps it is an issue for the men to discuss at the town meeting."

Elizabeth then shocked Mercy with a hearty laugh. When Elizabeth noticed Mercy's expression, she explained herself: "The men don't think in such practical terms. They are more concerned with the polemic between the village and the town. Besides, there is more than a poor harvest. We women must think of the refugees from the Indian raids since it is already the fourth year of King William's War and there's no end in sight."

"A woman's role is in the home . . ." Mercy began, but she trailed off, taken aback by Elizabeth's pertness.

"I've also been encouraging people to take the refugees into their homes," Elizabeth said as she dusted the flour from her hands on her smocked apron. "We've taken in two children after the raid on Casco, Maine, a year ago last May." Elizabeth called out sharply to the children and interrupted their play by insisting they come to meet the doctor's wife.

Elizabeth first introduced Mercy to Rebecca Sheaff, age twelve, and Mary Roots, age nine. Both had been cruelly orphaned during the Casco raid, but now both appeared hale and happy. Next Elizabeth introduced Joanna, age thirteen, Ronald's daughter from a previous marriage. Then came her own children: Sarah, age ten; Jonathan, age nine; and Daniel, age three. Finally Elizabeth introduced Ann Putnam, age twelve; Abigail Williams, age eleven; and Betty Parris, age nine, who were visiting from Salem Village.

After the children dutifully acknowledged Mercy, they were allowed to return to their play, which Mercy noticed involved several glasses of water and fresh eggs.

"I'm surprised to see the village children here," Mercy said.

"I asked my children to invite them," Elizabeth said. "They are friends from attending the Royal Side School. I felt it best that my children not school in Salem Town with all the riffraff and ruffians."

"I understand," Mercy said.

"I will be sending the children home with loaves of rye bread," Elizabeth said. She smiled friskily. "It will be more effective than giving their families a mere suggestion."

Mercy nodded but didn't comment. Elizabeth was mildly overwhelming.

"Would you care for a loaf?" Elizabeth asked.

"Oh, no, thank you," Mercy said. "My husband, the doctor, would never eat rye bread. It's much too coarse."

As Elizabeth turned her attention back to her second batch of bread, Mercy's eyes roamed the kitchen. She noticed a fresh wheel of cheese having come directly from the cheese press. She saw a pitcher of cider on the corner of the hearth. Then she noticed something more striking. Arrayed along the windowsill was a row of dolls made from painted wood and carefully sewn fabric. Each was dressed in the costume of a particular livelihood. There was a merchant, a blacksmith, a goodwife, a cartwright, and even a doctor. The doctor was dressed in black with a starched lace collar.

Mercy stood up and walked to the window. She picked up the doll dressed as a doctor. A large needle was thrust into its chest.

"What are these figures?" Mercy asked with barely concealed concern.

"Dolls that I make for the orphan children," Elizabeth said without looking up from her labor with her bread. She was removing each loaf, buttering its top, and then replacing it in the oven. "My deceased mother, God rest her soul, taught me how to make them."

"Why does this poor creature have a needle rending its heart?" Mercy asked.

"The costume is unfinished," Elizabeth said. "I am forever misplacing the needle and they are so dear."

Mercy replaced the doll and unconsciously wiped her hands. Anything that suggested magic and the occult made her uncomfortable. Leaving the dolls, she turned to the children, and after watching them for a moment asked Elizabeth what they were doing.

"It's a trick my mother taught me," Elizabeth said. She slipped the last loaf of bread back into the oven. "It's a way of divining the future by interpreting the shapes of egg white dropped into water."

"Bid them to stop immediately," Mercy said with alarm.

Elizabeth looked up from her work and eyed her visitor. "But why?" she asked.

"It is white magic," Mercy admonished.

"It is harmless fun," Elizabeth said. "It is merely something for the children to do while they are confined by such a winter. My sister and I did it many times to try to learn the trade of our future husbands." Elizabeth laughed. "Of course it never told me I'd marry a shipowner and move to Salem. I thought I was to be a poor farmer's wife."

"White magic breeds black magic," Mercy said. "And black magic is abhorrent to God. It is the devil's work."

"It never hurt my sister or myself," Elizabeth said. "Nor my mother, for that matter."

"Your mother's dead," Mercy said sternly.

"Yes, but—"

"It is sorcery," Mercy continued. Blood rose to her cheeks. "No sorcery is harmless. And remember the bad times we are experiencing with the war and with the pox in Boston only last year. Just last sabbath Reverend Parris' sermon told us that these horrid problems are occurring because people have not been keeping the covenant with God by allowing laxity in religious observance."

"I hardly think this childish game disturbs the covenant," Elizabeth said. "And we have not been lax in our religious obligations."

"But indulging in magic most certainly is," Mercy said. "Just like tolerance of the Quakers."

Elizabeth waved her hand in dismissal. "Such problems are beyond my purview. I surely don't see anything wrong with the Quakers since they are such a peaceful, hardworking people."

"You must not voice such opinions," Mercy chided. "Reverend Increase Mather has said that the Quakers are under a strong delusion of the devil. Perhaps you should read Reverend Cotton Mather's book *Memorable Providences: Relating to Witchcraft and Possessions*. I can loan it to you since my husband purchased it in Boston. Reverend Mather says the bad times we are experiencing stem from the devil's wish to return our New England Israel to his children, the red men."

Directing her attention to the children, Elizabeth called out to them to quiet down. Their shrieking had reached a crescendo. Still, she quieted them more to interrupt Mercy's sermonizing than to subdue their excited talk. Looking back at Mercy, Elizabeth said she'd be most thankful for the opportunity to read the book.

"Speaking of church matters," Mercy said. "Has your husband considered joining the village church? Since he's a landowner in the village he'd be welcome."

"I don't know," Elizabeth said. "We've never spoken of it."

"We need support," Mercy said. "The Porter family and their friends are refusing to pay their share of the Reverend Parris' expenses. When will your husband return?"

"In the spring," Elizabeth said.

"Why did he go to Europe?" Mercy asked.

"He's having a new class of ship built," Elizabeth said. "It is called a frigate. He says it will be fast and able to defend itself against French privateers and Caribbean pirates."

After touching the tops of the cooling loaves with the palms of her hands, Elizabeth called out to the children to tell them it was time to eat. As they drifted over to the table, she asked them if they wanted some of the fresh, warm bread. Although her own children turned up their noses at the offer, Ann Putnam, Abigail Williams, and Betty Parris were eager. Elizabeth opened a trapdoor in the corner of the kitchen and sent Sarah down to fetch some butter from the dairy storage.

Mercy was intrigued by the trapdoor.

"It was Ronald's idea," Elizabeth explained. "It functions like a ship's hatch and affords access to the cellar without having to go outside."

Once the children were set with plates of pork stew and thick slices of bread if they wanted it, Elizabeth poured herself and Mercy mugs of hot cider. To escape the children's chatter, they carried the cider into the parlor.

"My word!" Mercy exclaimed. Her eyes had immediately gone to a sizable portrait of Elizabeth hanging over the mantel. Its shocking realism awed her, especially the radiant green eyes. For a moment she stood rooted in the center of the room while Elizabeth deftly kindled the fire that had reduced itself to glowing coals.

"Your dress is so revealing," Mercy said. "And your head is unadorned."

"The painting disturbed me at first," Elizabeth admitted. She stood up from the hearth and positioned two chairs in front of the now blazing fire. "It was Ronald's idea. It pleases him. Now I hardly notice it."

"It's so popish," Mercy said with a sneer. She angled her chair to exclude the painting from her line of sight. She took a sip from the warm cider and tried to organize her thoughts. The visit had not gone as she'd imagined. Elizabeth's character was disconcerting. Mercy had yet to even broach the subject of why she'd come. She cleared her throat.

"I'd heard a rumor," Mercy began. "I'm certain there can be no verity to it. I'd heard that you had the fancy to buy the Northfields property."

" 'Tis no rumor," Elizabeth said brightly. "It will be done. We shall own land on both sides of the Wooleston River. The tract even extends into Salem Village where it abuts Ronald's village lots."

"But the Putnams had the intention to buy the land," Mercy said indignantly. "It is important for them. They need access to the water for their endeavors, particularly their iron works. Their only problem is the proper funds, for which they must wait for the next harvest. They shall be very angry if you persevere, and they will try to stop the sale."

Elizabeth shrugged. "I have the money now," she said. "I want the land because we intend to build a new house to enable us to take in more orphans." Elizabeth's face brightened with excitement and her eyes sparkled. "Daniel Andrew has agreed to design and build the house. It's to be a grand house of brick like those of London town."

Mercy could not believe what she was hearing. Elizabeth's pride and covetousness knew no bounds. Mercy swallowed another mouthful of cider with difficulty. "Do you know that Daniel Andrew is married to Sarah Porter?" she asked.

"Indeed," Elizabeth said. "Before Ronald left we entertained them both."

"How, may I ask, do you have access to such vast sums of money?"

"With the demands of the war, Ronald's firm has been doing exceptionally well."

"Profiteering from the misfortune of others," Mercy stated sententiously.

"Ronald prefers to say that he is providing sorely needed matériel."

Mercy stared for a moment into Elizabeth's bright green eyes. She was doubly appalled that Elizabeth seemed to have no conception of her transgression. In fact, Elizabeth brazenly smiled and returned Mercy's gaze, sipping her cider contentedly.

"I'd heard the rumor," Mercy said finally. "I couldn't believe it. Such business is so unnatural with your husband away. It is not in God's plan, and I must warn you: people in the village are talking. They are saying that you are overstepping your station as a farmer's daughter."

"I shall always be my father's daughter," Elizabeth said. "But now I am also a merchant's wife."

Before Mercy could respond, a tremendous crash and a multitude of screams burst forth from the kitchen. The sudden noise brought both Mercy and Elizabeth to their feet in terror. With Mercy directly behind her, Elizabeth rushed from the parlor into the kitchen, snapping up the musket en route.

The trestle table had been tipped on its side. Wooden bowls empty of their stew were strewn across the floor. Ann Putnam was lurching fitfully about the room as she tore at her clothes and collided with furniture while screaming she was being bitten. The other children had shrunk back against the wall in shocked horror.

Dispensing with the musket, Elizabeth rushed to Ann and grasped her shoulders. "What is it, girl?" Elizabeth demanded. "What is biting you?"

For a moment Ann remained still. Her eyes had assumed a glazed, faraway appearance.

"Ann!" Elizabeth called. "What is wrong with you?"

Ann's mouth opened and her tongue slowly protruded to its very limit while her body began chorea-like movements. Elizabeth tried to restrain her, but Ann fought with surprising strength. Then Ann clutched at her throat.

"I can't breathe," Ann rasped. "Help me! I'm being choked."

"Let us get her upstairs," Elizabeth shouted at Mercy. Together they half-carried and half-dragged the writhing girl up to the second floor. No sooner had they got her onto the bed than she began to convulse.

"She's having a horrid fit," Mercy said. "I think it best I fetch my husband, the doctor."

"Please!" Elizabeth said. "Hurry!"

Mercy shook her head in dismay as she descended the stairs. Having recovered from her initial shock, the calamity didn't surprise her, and she knew its cause. It was the sorcery. Elizabeth had invited the devil into her house.

TUESDAY • JULY 12, 1692

Ronald Stewart opened the cabin door and stepped out onto the deck and into the cool morning air, dressed in his best knee breeches, his scarlet waistcoat with starched ruffles, and even his powdered peruke. He was beside himself with excitement. They had just rounded Naugus Point, off Marblehead, and had set a course directly for Salem Town. Already over the bow he could see Turner's Wharf.

"Let us not furl the sails until the last moment," Ronald called to Captain Allen standing behind the helm. "I want the town folk to see the speed of this vessel."

"Aye, aye, sir," Captain Allen shouted back.

Ronald leaned his sizable and muscled frame on the gunwale as the sea breeze caressed his tanned broad face and tousled his sandy blond hair peeking from beneath his wig. Happily he gazed at the familiar landmarks. It was good to be coming home, although it was not without a degree of anxiety. He'd been gone for almost six months, two months longer than anticipated, and he'd not received a single letter. Sweden had seemed to be the end of the earth. He wondered if Elizabeth had received any of the letters he'd sent. There'd been no guarantee of their delivery since he'd not found any vessel going directly to the Colony, or even to London for that matter.

" 'Tis time," Captain Allen shouted as they approached land. "Otherwise this craft will mount the pier and not stop till Essex Street."

"Give the orders," Ronald shouted.

The men surged aloft at the captain's command and within minutes the vast stretches of canvas were pulled in and lashed to the spars. The ship slowed. At a point a hundred yards from the wharf, Ronald noticed a small boat being launched and quickly oared in their direction. As it approached Ronald recognized his clerk, Chester Procter, standing in the bow. Ronald waved merrily, but Chester did not return the gesture.

"Greetings," Ronald shouted when the boat was within earshot. Chester remained silent. As the small boat drew alongside, Ronald could see his clerk's thin face was drawn and his mouth set. Ronald's excitement was tempered by concern. Something was wrong.

"I think it best you come ashore immediately," Chester called up to Ronald once the skiff was made secure against the larger craft.

A ladder was extended into the small boat, and after a quick consultation with the captain, Ronald climbed down. Once he was sitting in the stern, they shoved off. Chester sat next to him. The two seamen amidships lent their backs to their oars.

"What is wrong?" Ronald asked, afraid to hear the answer. His worst fear was an Indian raid on his home. When he'd left he knew they'd been as close as Andover.

"There have been terrible happenings in Salem," Chester said. He was overwrought and plainly nervous. "Providence has brought you home barely in time. We have been much disquieted and distressed that you would arrive too late."

"It is my children?" Ronald asked with alarm.

"Nay, it is not your children," Chester said. "They are safe and hale. It is your goodwife, Elizabeth. She has been in prison for many months."

"On what charge?" Ronald demanded.

"Witchcraft," Chester said. "I beg your pardon for being the bearer of such ill tidings. She has been convicted by a special court and there is a warrant for her execution the Tuesday next."

"This is absurd," Ronald growled. "My wife is no witch!"

"That I know," Chester said. "But there has been a witchcraft frenzy in the town since February, with almost one hundred people accused. There has already been one execution. Bridget Bishop on June tenth."

"I knew her," Ronald admitted. "She was a woman of a fiery temperament. She ran the unlicensed tavern out on Ipswich Road. But a witch? It seems most improbable. What has happened to cause such fear of malefic will?"

"It is because of 'fits,' " Chester said. "Certain women, mostly young women, have been afflicted in a most pitiful way."

"Have you witnessed these fits?" Ronald asked.

"Oh, yes," Chester said. "The whole town has seen them at the hearings in front of the magistrates. They are terrible to behold. The afflicted scream of torment and are not in their right minds. They go alternately blind, deaf, and dumb, and sometimes all at once. They shake worse than the Quakers and shriek they are being bitten by invisible beings. Their tongues come out and then are as if swallowed. But the worst is that their joints do bend as if to break."

Ronald's mind was a whirlwind of thought. This was a most unexpected turn of events. Sweat broke forth on his forehead as the morning sun beat down upon him. Angrily he tore his wig from his head and threw it to the floor of the boat. He tried to think what he should do.

"I have a carriage waiting," Chester said, breaking the heavy silence as they neared the pier. "I thought you'd care to go directly to the prison."

"Aye," Ronald said tersely. They disembarked and walked quickly to the street. They climbed aboard the vehicle, and Chester picked up the reins. With a snap the horse started. The wagon bumped along the cobblestone quay. Neither man spoke.

"How was it decided these fits were caused by witchcraft?" Ronald asked when they reached Essex Street.

"It was Dr. Griggs who said so," Chester said. "Then Reverend Parris from the village, then everyone, even the magistrates."

"What made them so confident?" Ronald asked.

"It was apparent at the hearings," Chester said. "All the people could see how the accused tormented the afflicted, and how the afflicted were instantly relieved from their suffering when touched by the accused."

"Yet they didn't touch them to torment them?"

"It was the specters of the accused who did the mischief," Chester explained. "And the specters could only be seen by the afflicted. It was thus that the accused were called out upon by the afflicted."

"And my wife was called out upon in this fashion?" Ronald asked.

" 'Tis so," Chester said. "By Ann Putnam, daughter of Thomas Putnam of Salem Village."

"I know Thomas Putnam," Ronald said. "A small, angry man."

"Ann Putnam was the first to be afflicted," Chester said hesitantly. "In your house. Her first fit was in your common room in the beginning of February. And to this day she is still afflicted, as is her mother, Ann senior."

"What about my children?" Ronald asked. "Are they afflicted as well?"

"Your children have been spared," Chester said.

"Thank the Lord," Ronald said.

They turned onto Prison Lane. Neither man spoke. Chester pulled to a stop in front of the jail. Ronald told him to wait and alighted from the carriage.

With brittle emotions Ronald sought out the jailer, William Dounton. Ronald found him in his untidy office eating fresh corn bread from the bakery. He was an obese man with a shock of unwashed hair and a red, nodular nose. Ronald despised him, a known sadist who delighted in tormenting his charges.

William was obviously not pleased to see Ronald. Leaping to his feet, he cowered behind his chair.

"No visitors to see the condemned," he croaked through a mouthful of bread. "By order of Magistrate Hathorne."

Barely in control of himself, Ronald reached out and grasped a fistful of William's woolen shirt and drew his face within an inch of his own. "If you have mistreated my wife you'll answer to me," Ronald snarled.

"It's not my fault," William said. "It is the authorities. I must respect their orders."

"Take me to her," Ronald snapped.

"But . . ." William managed before Ronald tightened his grip and constricted his throat. William gurgled. Ronald relaxed his fist. William coughed but produced his keys. Ronald let go of him and followed him. As he unlocked a stout oak door he said, "I will report this."

"There is no need," Ronald said. "As soon as I leave here I will go directly to the magistrate and tell him myself."

Beyond the oak door they passed several cells. All were full. The inmates stared back at Ronald with glazed eyes. Some he recognized, but he didn't address them. The prison was enveloped with a heavy silence. Ronald had to pull out a handkerchief to cover his nose from the smell.

At the top of a stone staircase, William stopped to light a shielded candle.

After opening another stout oak door, they descended into the worst area of the prison. The stench was overwhelming. The basement consisted of two large rooms. The walls were damp granite. The many prisoners were all manacled to the walls or the floor with either wrist or leg irons or both. Ronald had to step over people to follow William. There was hardly room for another person.

"Just a moment," Ronald said.

William stopped and turned around.

Ronald squatted down. He'd recognized someone he knew to be a pious woman. "Rebecca Nurse?" Ronald questioned. "What in God's name are you doing here?"

Rebecca shook her head slowly. "Only God knows," she managed to say.

Ronald stood up feeling weak. It was as if the town had gone crazy.

"Over here," William said, pointing toward the far corner of the basement. "Let us finish this."

Ronald followed. His anger had been overwhelmed by pity. William stopped and Ronald looked down. In the candlelight he could barely recognize his wife. Elizabeth was covered with filth. She was manacled in oversized chains and barely had the energy to scatter the vermin which freely roamed the semidarkness.

Ronald took the candle from William and bent down next to his wife. Despite her condition she smiled at him.

"I'm glad you are back," she said weakly. "Now I don't have to worry about the children. Are they all right?"

Ronald swallowed with difficulty. His mouth had gone dry. "I have come directly from the ship to the prison," he said. "I have yet to see the children."

"Please do. They will be happy to see you. I fear they are disquieted."

"I shall attend to them," Ronald promised. "But first I must see to getting you free."

"Perhaps," Elizabeth said. "Why are you so late in returning?"

"The outfitting of the ship took longer than planned," Ronald said. "The newness of the design caused us much difficulty."

"I sent letters," Elizabeth said.

"I never got any," Ronald replied.

"Well, at least you are home now," Elizabeth said.

"I shall be back," Ronald said as he stood up. He was shaking with panic and beside himself with concern. He motioned to William for them to leave and followed him back to the office.

"I'm just doing my duty," William said meekly. He was unsure of Ronald's state of mind.

"Show me the papers," Ronald demanded.

William shrugged, and after searching through the debris on the top of his desk, handed Ronald Elizabeth's mittimus and her execution warrant. Ronald read them and handed them back. Reaching into his purse, he pulled out a few coins. "I want Elizabeth moved and her situation improved."

William happily took the money. "I thank you, kind sir," he said. The coins disappeared into the pocket of his breeches. "But I cannot move her. Capital cases are always housed on the lower level. I also cannot remove the irons since they are specified in the mittimus to keep her specter from leaving her body. But I can improve her condition in response to your kind consideration."

"Do what you can," Ronald said.

Outside, it took Ronald a moment to climb into the carriage. His legs felt unsteady and weak. "To Magistrate Corwin's house," he said.

Chester urged the horse forward. He wanted to ask about Elizabeth but he dared not. Ronald's distress was much too apparent.

They rode in silence. When they reached the corner of Essex and Washington streets, Ronald climbed down from the carriage. "Wait," he said laconically.

Ronald rapped on the front door, and when it was opened he was relieved to see the tall, gaunt frame of his old friend Jonathan Corwin standing in the doorway. As soon as Jonathan recognized Ronald, his petulant expression changed to one of sympathetic concern. Immediately he ushered Ronald into his parlor, where he requested his wife give them leave to have a private conversation. His wife had been working at her flax wheel in the corner.

"I am sorry," Jonathan said once they were alone. " 'Tis a sorry welcome for a weary traveler."

"Pray tell me what to do," Ronald said weakly.

"I am afraid I know not what to say," Jonathan began. "It is an unruly time. There is a spirit in the town full of contention and animosities and perhaps a strong and general delusion. I am no longer certain of my thoughts, for recently my own mother-in-law, Margaret Thatcher, has been cried out against. She is no witch, which makes me question the veracity of the afflicted girls' allegations and their motivations."

"At the moment the motives of the girls are not my concern," Ronald said. "What I need to know is what can I do for my beloved wife, who is being treated with the utmost brutality."

Jonathan sighed deeply. "I am afraid there is little to be done. Your wife has already been convicted by a jury serving the special court of Oyer and Terminer hearing the backlog of witchcraft cases."

"But you have just said you question the accusers' veracity," Ronald said.

"Yes," Jonathan agreed. "But your wife's conviction did not depend on the girls' testimony nor spectral demonstration in court. Your wife's trial was shorter than the others, even shorter than Bridget Bishop's. Your wife's guilt was apparent to all because the evidence against her was real and conclusive. There was no doubt."

"You believe my wife to be a witch?" Ronald asked with disbelief.

"I do indeed," Jonathan said. "I am sorry. 'Tis a harsh truth for a man to bear."

For a moment Ronald stared into the face of his friend while his mind tried to deal with this new and disturbing information. Ronald had always valued and respected Jonathan's opinion.

"But there must be something that can be done," Ronald said finally. "Even if only to delay the execution so I have time to learn the facts."

Jonathan reached out and placed a hand on his friend's shoulder. "As a local magistrate there is nothing I can do. Perhaps you should go home and attend to your children."

"I shan't give up so easily," Ronald said.

"Then all I can suggest is you go to Boston and discourse with Samuel Sewall," Jonathan said. "I know you are friends and classmates from Harvard College. Perhaps he may make a suggestion with his connections with the Colonial Government. He will not be disinterested; he is one of the justices of the Court of Oyer and Terminer, and he has voiced to me some misgivings about the whole affair, as did Nathaniel Saltonstall, who even resigned his appointment to the bench."

Ronald thanked Jonathan and hurried outside. He told Chester his intentions and was soon outfitted with a saddled horse. Within an hour he set out on the seventeen-mile journey. He traveled via Cambridge, crossing the Charles River at the Great Bridge, and approached Boston from the southwest on the highway to Roxberre.

As Ronald rode the length of the Shawmut peninsula's narrow neck, he became progressively anxious. His mind tortured him with the question of what he'd do if Samuel was either unwilling or unable to help. Ronald had no other ideas. Samuel was to be his last chance.

Passing through the town gate with its brick fortifications, Ronald's eyes involuntarily wandered to the gallows from which a fresh corpse dangled. The sight was a rude reminder, and a shiver of fear passed down his spine. In response he urged his horse to quicken its pace.

The midday bustle of Boston with its more than six thousand inhabitants and more than eight hundred dwellings slowed Ronald's progress. It was almost one by the time Ronald arrived at Samuel's south end house. Ronald dismounted and tethered his horse to the picket fence.

He found Samuel smoking tobacco from a long-stemmed pipe in his parlor following his noonday meal. Ronald noted that he'd become significantly portly over the last few years and was certainly a far cry from the rakish fellow who used to skate with Ronald on the Charles River during their college years.

Samuel was happy to see Ronald, but his greeting was restrained. He anticipated the nature of Ronald's visit before Ronald even broached the subject of Elizabeth's ordeal. In response to Ronald's questions, he confirmed Jonathan Corwin's story. He said that Elizabeth's guilt was unquestioned due to the real evidence that Sheriff Corwin had seized from Ronald's house.

Ronald's shoulders slumped. He sighed and fought off tears. He was at a loss. He asked his host for a mug of beer. When Samuel returned with the brew, Ronald had recovered his composure. After a long draft he asked Samuel the nature of the evidence used against his wife.

"I am loath to say," Samuel said.

"But why?" Ronald asked. He studied his friend and could see his discomfiture. Ronald's curiosity mounted. He hadn't thought to ask Jonathan about the evidence. "Surely I have a right to know."

"Indeed," Samuel said, but still he hesitated.

"Please," Ronald said. "I trust it will help me understand this wretched affair."

"Perhaps it is best if we visit my good friend Reverend Cotton Mather," Samuel said. He stood up. "He has more experience in the affairs of the invisible world. He will know how to advise you."

"I bow to your discretion," Ronald said as he got to his feet.

They took Samuel's carriage and went directly to the Old North Church. An inquiry with a charwoman told them that Reverend Mather was at his home on the corner of Middle Street and Prince Street. Since the destination was close, they walked. It was also convenient to leave the horse and carriage in Charles Square in front of the church.

Samuel's knock was answered by a youthful maidservant who showed them into the parlor. Reverend Mather appeared posthaste and greeted them effusively. Samuel explained the nature of their visit.

"I see," Reverend Mather said. He motioned to chairs and they all sat down.

Ronald eyed the cleric. He'd met him before. He was younger than Ronald and Samuel, having graduated from Harvard in 1678, seven years after they had. Age notwithstanding, he was already evidencing some of the physical changes Ronald saw in Samuel and for the same reasons. He'd put on weight. His nose was red and slightly enlarged, and his face had a doughy consistency. Yet his eyes sparkled with intelligence and fiery resolve.

"You have my loving solicitude for your tribulations," Reverend Mather said to Ronald. "God's ways are often inscrutable for us mortals. Beyond your personal torment I am deeply troubled about the events in Salem Town and Salem Village. The populace has been overcome by an unruly and turbulent spirit, and I fear that events are spinning out of control."

"At the moment my concern is for my wife," Ronald said. He'd not come for a sermon.

"As it should be," Reverend Mather said. "But I think it is important for you to understand that we—the clergy and the civil authorities—must think of the congregation as a whole. I have expected the devil to appear in our midst, and the only consolation about this demonic affair is now, thanks to your wife, we know where."

"I want to know the evidence used against my wife," Ronald said.

"And I shall show it to you," Reverend Mather said. "Provided that you will keep its nature a secret, since we fear its general revelation would surely inflame the distress and disquietude in Salem even more than it currently is."

"But what if I choose to appeal the conviction?" Ronald demanded.

"Once you see the evidence you will not choose to do so," Reverend Mather said. "Trust me in this. Do I have your word?"

"You have my word," Ronald said. "Provided my right to appeal is not forsaken."

They stood up in unison. Reverend Mather led the way to a flight of stone steps. After he lit a taper, they began the descent into the cellar.

"I have discussed this evidence at length with my father, Increase Mather," Reverend Mather said over his shoulder. "We concur that it has inordinate importance for future generations as material proof of the existence of the invisible world. Accordingly, we believe its rightful place should be Harvard College. As you know he is currently the acting president of the institution."

Ronald didn't respond. At the moment his mind was incapable of dealing with such academic issues.

"Both myself and my father also agree that there has been too much reliance in the Salem witch trials on spectral evidence alone," Reverend Mather continued. They reached the bottom of the stairs, and while Samuel and Ronald waited, he proceeded to light wall sconces. He spoke as he moved about the cellar: "We are much concerned that this reliance could very well draw innocent people into the maelstrom."

Ronald started to protest. For the moment he didn't have the patience to listen to these larger concerns, but Samuel restrained him by laying a hand on his shoulder.

"Elizabeth's evidence is the kind of real evidence we'd like to see in every case," Reverend Mather said as he waved Ronald and Samuel to follow him to a large, locked cupboard. "But it is also terribly inflammatory. It was at my discretion that it was removed from Salem and brought here after her trial. I have never witnessed a stronger evidence of the devil's power and ability to do mischief."

"Please, Reverend," Ronald said at last. "I should like to return to Salem forthwith. If you will just show me what it is, I can be on my way."

"Patience, my good man," Reverend Mather said as he drew a key from his waistcoat. "The nature of this evidence is such that you must be prepared. It is shocking indeed. For that reason it had been my suggestion that your wife's trial be held behind closed doors and the jury be sworn to secrecy on their honor. It was a precaution not to deny her due process but to prevent public hysteria which would only have played into the devil's hand."

"I am prepared," Ronald said with a touch of exasperation.

"Christ the Redeemer be with you," Reverend Mather said as he slipped the key into the lock. "Brace yourself."

Reverend Mather unlocked the cabinet. Then, with both hands he swung open the doors and stepped back for Ronald to see.

Ronald's breath escaped in a gasp and his eyes momentarily bulged. His hand involuntarily covered his mouth in horror and dismay. He swallowed hard. He tried to speak, but his voice momentarily failed him. He cleared his throat.

"Enough!" he managed and averted his eyes.

Reverend Mather closed the cabinet doors and locked them.

"Is it certain that this is Elizabeth's handiwork?" Ronald asked weakly.

"Beyond any doubt," Samuel said. "Not only was it seized by Sheriff George Corwin from your property, but Elizabeth freely admitted responsibility."

"Good Lord," Ronald said. "Surely this is the work of the devil. Yet I knoweth in my heart that Elizabeth is no witch."

"It is hard for a man to believe his wife to be in covenant with the devil," Samuel said. "But this evidence, combined with the testimony of several of the afflicted girls who stated that Elizabeth's specter tormented them, is compelling proof. I am sorry, dear friend, but Elizabeth is a witch."

"I am sorely distressed," Ronald said.

Samuel and Cotton Mather exchanged knowing, sympathetic glances. Samuel motioned toward the stairs.

"Perhaps we should repair to the parlor," Reverend Mather said. "I believe we all could use a mug of ale."

After they were seated and had a chance to take some refreshment, Reverend Mather spoke: "It is trying times for us all. But we must all participate. Now that we knoweth the devil has chosen Salem, we must with God's help seek and banish the devil's servants and their familiars from our midst, yet in like purpose protect the innocent and pious, whom surely the devil doth despise."

"I am sorry," Ronald said. "I can be of no help. I am distracted and weary. I still cannot believe Elizabeth to be a witch. I need time. Surely there is some way to secure a reprieve for her even if it lasts but a month."

"Only Governor Phips can grant a reprieve," Samuel said. "But a petition would be in vain. He would only grant a reprieve if there were a compelling reason."

A silence descended over the three men. Sounds of the city drifted in through the open window.

"Perhaps I could make a case for a reprieve," Reverend Mather said suddenly.

Ronald's face brightened with a ray of hope. Samuel appeared confused.

"I believe I could justify a reprieve to the Governor," Reverend Mather said. "But it would rest on one condition: Elizabeth's full cooperation. She'd have to agree to turn her back on her Prince of Darkness."

"I can assure her cooperation," Ronald said. "What would you have her do?"

"First she must confess in front of the congregation in the Salem meeting-house," Reverend Mather said. "In her confession she must forswear her relations with the devil. Secondly she must reveal the identities of those persons in the community who have signed similar diabolic covenants. This would be a great service. The fact that the torment of the afflicted women continues unabated is proof that the devil's servants are still at large in Salem."

Ronald leaped to his feet. "I will get her to agree this very afternoon," he said excitedly. "I beg you to see Governor Phips immediately."

"I will wait on word from Elizabeth," Reverend Mather said. "I should not like to trouble his excellency without confirmation of the conditions."

"And you shall have her word," Ronald said. "By the morn at the very latest."

"Godspeed," Reverend Mather said.

Samuel had difficulty keeping pace with Ronald as they hurried back to Samuel's carriage in front of the Old North Church.

"You can save nearly an hour on your journey by taking the ferry to Noddle Island," Samuel said as they drove across town to fetch Ronald's horse.

"Then I shall go by ferry," Ronald said.

True to Samuel's word Ronald's trip back to Salem was far quicker than the trip to Boston. It was just after midafternoon when he turned onto Prison Lane and reined in his horse in front of the Salem jail. He'd pushed the animal mercilessly. Foam bubbled from the exhausted animal's nostrils.

Ronald was equally wearied and caked with dust. Vertical lines from rivulets of perspiration crossed his brow. He was also emotionally drained, famished, and thirsty. But he was oblivious to his own needs. The ray of hope Cotton Mather had provided for Elizabeth drove him on.

Dashing into the jailer's office, he was frustrated to find it empty. He pounded on the oak door leading to the cells. Presently the door was opened a crack, and William Dounton's puffy face peered out at him.

"I'm to see my wife," Ronald said breathlessly.

" 'Tis feeding time," William said. "Come back in an hour."

Using his foot, Ronald crashed the door open against its hinges, sending William staggering back. Some of the thin gruel he was carrying sloshed out of its bucket.

"I'm to see her now!" Ronald growled.

"The magistrates will hear of this," William complained. But he put down his bucket and led Ronald back to the door to the cellar.

A few minutes later Ronald sat down next to Elizabeth. Gently he shook her shoulder. Her eyes blinked open, and she immediately asked after the children.

"I have yet to see them," Ronald said. "But I have good news. I've been to see Samuel Sewall and Reverend Cotton Mather. They think we can get a reprieve."

"God be thanked," Elizabeth said. Her eyes sparkled in the candlelight.

"But you must confess," Ronald said. "And you must name others you know to be in covenant with the devil."

"Confess to what?" Elizabeth asked.

"To witchcraft," Ronald said with exasperation. Exhaustion and stress challenged the veneer of control he had over his emotions.

"I cannot confess," Elizabeth said.

"And why not?" Ronald demanded shrilly.

"Because I am no witch," Elizabeth said.

For a moment Ronald merely stared at his wife while he clenched his fists in frustration.

"I cannot belie myself," Elizabeth said, breaking the strained silence. "I will not confess to witchcraft."

In his overwrought, exhausted state, Ronald's anger flared. He slammed his fist into the palm of his hand. He shoved his face within inches of hers. "You will confess," he snarled. "I order you to confess."

"Dear husband," Elizabeth said, unintimidated by Ronald's antics. "Have you been told of the evidence used against me?"

Ronald straightened up and gave a rapid, embarrassed glance at William, who was listening to this exchange. Ronald ordered William to back off. William left to fetch his bucket and make his rounds in the basement.

"I saw the evidence," Ronald said once William was out of earshot. "Reverend Mather has it in his home."

"I must be guilty of some transgression of God's will," Elizabeth said. "To that I could confess if I knew its nature. But I am no witch and surely I have not tormented any of the young women who have testified against me."

"Confess for now just for the reprieve," Ronald pleaded. "I want to save your life."

"I cannot save my life to lose my soul," Elizabeth said. "If I belie myself I will play into the hands of the devil. And surely I know no other witches, and I shan't call out against an innocent person to save myself."

"You must confess," Ronald shouted. "If you don't confess then I shall forsake thee."

"You will do as your conscience dictates," Elizabeth said. "I shan't confess to witchcraft."

"Please," Ronald pleaded, changing tactics. "For the children."

"We must trust in the Lord," Elizabeth said.

"He hath abandoned us," Ronald moaned as tears washed from his eyes and streaked down his dust-encrusted face.

With difficulty Elizabeth raised her manacled hand and laid it on his shoulder. "Have courage, my dear husband. The Lord functions in inscrutable ways."

Losing all semblance of control, Ronald leaped to his feet and rushed from the prison.

TUESDAY • JULY 19, 1692

Ronald shifted his weight nervously from one foot to the other. He was standing at the side of Prison Lane a short distance away from the jail. Sweat stood out on his forehead beneath the wide brim of his hat. It was a hot, hazy, muggy day whose oppressiveness was augmented by a preternatural stillness that hovered over the town despite the crowds of expectant people. Even the seagulls were silent. Everyone waited for the wagon to appear.

An emotional brittleness shrouded Ronald's thoughts, which were paralyzed by equal amounts of fear, sorrow, and panic. He could not fathom what he or Elizabeth had done to warrant this catastrophe. By order of the magistrates he'd been refused entry into the prison since the previous day when he'd tried for the last time to convince Elizabeth to cooperate. But no amount of pleading, cajoling, or threatening could break her resolve. She would not confess.

From within the shielded courtyard Ronald heard the metallic clatter of iron-rimmed wheels against the granite cobblestones. Almost immediately a wagon appeared. Standing in the back of the wagon were five women, tightly pressed together. They were all still in chains. Behind the wagon walked William Dounton, sporting a wide smile in anticipation of turning his charges over to the hangman.

A sudden whoop and cheer rose from the spectators, inaugurating a carnival-like atmosphere. In a burst of energy children began their usual games while the adults laughed and thumped each other on the back. It was to be a holiday and a day of revelry like most days with a hanging. For Ronald as well as for the families and friends of the other victims it was the opposite.

Warned by Reverend Mather, Ronald was neither surprised nor hopeful when he did not see Elizabeth among the first group. The minister had advised him that Elizabeth would be executed last, after the crowd had been satiated on the blood of the first five prisoners. The idea was to lessen the potential impact on the populace, especially those who had either seen or heard of the evidence used against her.

As the wagon drew abreast of Ronald and passed, he gazed up at the faces of the condemned. They all appeared broken and despondent from their brutal treatment and the reality of their imminent fates. He recognized only two people: Rebecca Nurse and Sarah Good. Both were from Salem Village. The others were from neighboring towns. Seeing Rebecca Nurse on the way to her execution and knowing her pious character, Ronald was reminded of Reverend Mather's grim warning that the Salem witchcraft affair could spiral out of control.

When the wagon reached Essex Street and turned to the west, the crowd surged after it. Standing out in the throng was Reverend Cotton Mather as the only person on horseback.

Almost a half hour later Ronald again heard the telltale sound of metal clanking against the cobblestones of the prison courtyard. Presently a second wagon appeared. In the back sat Elizabeth with her head bowed. Due to the weight of her iron manacles she'd not been able to stand. As the wagon lumbered past Ronald, Elizabeth did not raise her eyes nor did Ronald call out to her. Neither knew what to say.

Ronald followed at a distance, thinking it was like living in a nightmare. He felt great ambivalence about his presence. He wanted to flee and hide from the world, but at the same time he wanted to be with Elizabeth until the end.

Just west of Salem Town, after crossing the Town Bridge, the wagon turned off the main road and began to climb Gallows Hill. The road ascended through a scrub of thornbushes until it opened out onto an inhospitable rocky ridge dotted with a few oaks and locust trees. Elizabeth's wagon pulled next to the empty first wagon and stopped.

Wiping the sweat from his brow, Ronald stepped from behind the wagons.

Ahead he could see the noisy throng of townspeople gathered around one of the larger oak trees. Cotton Mather was behind the crowd and still mounted. At the base of the tree stood the condemned. A black-hooded hangman who'd been brought from Boston had looped a rope over a stout branch. One end he'd tied to the base of the tree while the other he'd fashioned into a noose and fitted over the head of Sarah Good. Sarah Good at that moment was precariously poised on a rung of a ladder leaning against the tree.

Ronald could see Reverend Noyes of the Salem Town Church approach the prisoner. In his hand he clutched a Bible. "Confess, witch!" Reverend Noyes yelled.

"I am no more a witch than you are a wizard," Sarah yelled back at him. She then cursed the minister, but Ronald could not hear her words, for a jeer rose up from the crowd followed by someone yelling for the hangman to get on with it. Obligingly the hangman gave Sarah Good a push, and she swung clear of the ladder.

The crowd cheered and chanted "die witch," as Sarah Good struggled against the strangulating rope. Her face empurpled then blackened. As soon as Sarah's writhing ended, the hangman proceeded with the others, each in her turn.

With each successive victim, the crowd's cheering mellowed. By the time the last woman had been pushed from the ladder and the first victims were being cut down, the crowd had lost interest. Although some people had drifted over to see the bodies tossed into a shallow, rocky, common grave, most had already started back toward town, where the revelry would continue.

It was then that Elizabeth was commended to the hangman. He had to help her walk to the ladder due to the excessive weight of her chains.

Ronald swallowed. His legs felt weak. He wanted to cry out in anger. He wanted to beg for mercy. But he did nothing. He could not move.

Reverend Mather, who caught sight of him, rode over. "It is God's will," he said. He struggled with his horse, which sensed Ronald's torment.

Ronald did not take his eyes off Elizabeth. He wanted to rush forward and kill the hangman.

"You must remember what Elizabeth did and what she made," Reverend Mather said. "You should thank the Lord that death hath intervened to save our Zion. Remember you have seen the evidence with your own eyes."

Ronald managed to nod as he vainly fought to hold back his tears. He'd seen the evidence. Clearly it was the devil's work. "But why?" Ronald shouted suddenly. "Why Elizabeth?"

For a brief second Ronald saw Elizabeth's eyes rise to meet his. Her mouth began to move as if she was about to speak, but before she could, the hangman gave her a decisive shove. In contrast to his technique with the others, the hangman had left slack in the rope around Elizabeth's neck. As she left the ladder, her body fell for several feet before being jerked to a sudden, deathly stop. Unlike the others she did not struggle nor did her face turn black.

Ronald's head sank into his hands and he wept.

Tuesday • July 12, 1994

Kimberly Stewart glanced at her watch as she went through the turnstile and exited the MBTA subway at Harvard Square in Cambridge, Massachusetts. It was a few minutes before seven P.M. She knew she would be on time or only minutes late, but still she hurried. Pushing through the crowd milling about the news kiosk in the middle of the square, she half ran and half walked the short distance on Massachusetts Avenue before turning right on Holyoke Street.

Pausing to catch her breath in front of the Hasty Pudding Club building, Kimberly glanced up at the structure. She knew about the Harvard social club only in reference to the annual award it gave to an actor and an actress. The building was brick with white trim like most buildings at Harvard. She'd never been inside although it housed a public restaurant called Upstairs at the Pudding. This was to be her first visit.

With her breathing restored to near normal, Kim opened the door and entered only to be confronted by several sizable flights of stairs. By the time she got to the maître d's podium she was again mildly winded. She asked for the ladies' room.

While Kim wrestled with her thick, raven hair which refused to do what she wanted it to do, she told herself there was no need to be nervous. After all, Stanton Lewis was family. The problem was that he had never called at the last minute to say that he "needed" her to come to dinner and that it was an "emergency."

Giving up on her hair and feeling totally thrown together, Kim again presented herself at the maître d's podium. This time she announced she was to meet Mr. and Mrs. Stanton Lewis.

"Most of your party is here," the hostess said.

As Kim followed the hostess through the main part of the restaurant, her anxiety went up a notch. She didn't like the sound of "party." She wondered who else would be at the dinner.

The hostess led Kim out onto a trellised terrace that was crowded with diners. Stanton and his wife, Candice, were sitting at a four-top in the corner.

"I'm sorry I'm late," Kim said as she arrived at the table.

"You're not late in the slightest," Stanton said.

He leaped to his feet and enveloped Kim in an extended and demonstrative hug that bent her backwards. It also turned her face a bright red. She had the uncomfortable feeling that everyone on the crowded terrace was watching. Once she was able to break free from Stanton's bear hug she retreated to the chair held out by the hostess and tried to melt into her seat.

Kim always felt uncomfortably obvious around Stanton. Although they were cousins, Kim thought they were the social antithesis of each other. While she considered herself moderately shy, occasionally even awkward, he was a paragon of confidence: an urbane and aggressively assertive sophisticate. He was built like a ski racer and stood straight and tall, overpowering people as the consummate entrepreneur. Even his wife, Candice, despite her demure smile, made Kim feel socially inept.

Kim hazarded a quick glance around her, and as she did so she inadvertently bumped the hostess, who was attempting to lay Kim's napkin across her lap. Both apologized simultaneously.

"Relax, cousin," Stanton said after the hostess had departed. He reached across the table and poured Kim a glass of white wine. "As usual you're wound up like a banjo wire."

"Telling me to relax only makes me more nervous," Kim said. She took a drink of the wine.

"You are a strange one," Stanton said playfully. "I can never understand why you're so damn self-conscious, especially sitting here with family in a room full of people you'll never see again. Let your hair down."

"I have no control over what my hair chooses to do," Kim joked. In spite of herself she was beginning to calm down. "As for your inability to understand my unease, it's entirely understandable. You're so totally self-assured that it's impossible for you to imagine what it's like not to be so."

"Why not give me a chance to understand?" Stanton said. "I challenge you to explain to me why you are feeling uncomfortable right at this moment. My God, woman, your hand is shaking."

Kim put down her glass and put her hands in her lap. "I'm nervous mainly because I feel thrown together," she said. "After your call this evening, I barely had time to take a shower, much less find something to wear. And, if you must know, my bangs are driving me crazy." Kim blindly tried to adjust the hair over her forehead.

"I think your dress is smashing," Candice said.

"No doubt about it," Stanton said. "Kimberly, you look gorgeous."

Kim laughed. "I'm smart enough to know that provoked compliments are invariably false."

"Balderdash," Stanton said. "The irony of this discussion is that you are a sexy, beautiful woman even though you always act as if you haven't a clue, which, I suppose, is somewhat endearing. How old are you now, twenty-five?"

"Twenty-seven," Kim said. She tried more of her wine.

"Twenty-seven and improving with each year," Stanton said. He smiled impishly. "You've got cheekbones other women would die for, skin like a baby's bottom, and a ballerina's figure, not to mention those emerald eyes that could mesmerize a Greek statue."

"The truth of the matter is somewhat different," Kim said. "My facial-bone structure is certainly not exceptional although okay. My skin barely tans if at all, and 'ballerina's figure' sounds like a nice way of saying I'm not stacked."

"You're being unfair to yourself," Candice said.

"I think we should change the subject," Kim said. "This conversation is not going to get me to relax. In fact it just makes me more uncomfortable."

"My apologies for being so truthfully complimentary," Stanton said, his impish smile returning. "What would you prefer we discuss?"

"How about explaining why my presence here at dinner was such an emergency," Kim said.

"I need your help." Stanton leaned toward her.

"Me?" Kim questioned. She had to laugh. "The great financier needs my help? Is this a joke?"

"Quite the contrary," Stanton said. "In a few months I'll be launching an initial public offering for one of my biotech companies called Genetrix."

"I'm not investing," Kim said. "You've got the wrong relative."

It was Stanton's turn to laugh. "I'm not looking for money," he said. "No, it's something quite different. I happened to be talking with Aunt Joyce today and—"

"Oh, no!" Kim interrupted nervously. "What did my mother say now?"

"She just happened to mention that you'd recently broken up with your boyfriend," Stanton said.

Kim blanched. The unease she'd felt when she'd arrived at the restaurant returned in a rush. "I wish my mother wouldn't open her big mouth," she said irritably.

"Joyce didn't give any gory details," Stanton said.

"That doesn't matter," Kim said. "She's been giving out personal information about Brian and me since we were teenagers."

"All she said was that Kinnard wasn't right for you," Stanton said. "Which I happen to agree with if he's forever traipsing off with his friends for ski trips and fishing forays."

"That sounds like details to me," Kim moaned. "It's also an exaggeration. The fishing is something new. The skiing is once a year."

"To tell you the truth I was hardly listening," Stanton said. "At least until she asked me if I could find someone more appropriate for you."

"Good Lord!" Kim said with mounting irritation. "I can't believe this. She actually asked you to fix me up with someone?"

"It's not my usual forte," Stanton said. A self-satisfied smile spread across his face. "But I had a brainstorm. Right after I hung up with Joyce I knew to whom I'd introduce you."

"Don't tell me that's why you got me here tonight," Kim said with alarm. She felt her pulse quicken. "I never would have come if I'd had any idea—"

"Calm down," Stanton said. "Don't get yourself in a dither. It's going to work out just fine. Trust me."

"It's too soon," Kim said.

"It's never too soon," Stanton said. "My motto is, Today is yesterday's tomorrow."

"Stanton, you are impossible," Kim said. "I'm not ready to meet someone. Besides, I'm a mess."

"I already told you that you look terrific," Stanton said. "Trust me, Edward Armstrong is going to fall for you like a ton of bricks. One look into those emerald eyes and his legs will turn to rubber."

"This is ridiculous," Kim complained.

"One thing I should admit right up front is that I have an ulterior motive," Stanton said. "I've been trying to get Edward involved in one of my biotech companies ever since I became a venture capitalist. With Genetrix about to go public, there's no time like the present. The idea is to get him beholden by introducing him to you, Kim. Then maybe I'll be able to twist his arm to get him on the Genetrix scientific advisory board. If I get his name on the prospectus it will be worth a good four or five mil on the initial offering. In the process I can make him a millionaire."

For a moment Kim didn't say anything as she concentrated on her wine. On top of her anxiety, she was feeling used as well as embarrassed, but she didn't voice her irritation. She'd always had trouble expressing herself in confrontational situations. Stanton had amazed her as he always had, being so manipulative and self-serving yet so open about it.

"Maybe Edward Armstrong doesn't want to be a millionaire," Kim said at length.

"Nonsense," Stanton said. "Everyone wants to be a millionaire."

"I know it's difficult for you to understand," Kim said. "But not everyone thinks the same way you do."

"Edward is a nice gentleman," Candice said.

"That sounds suspiciously like the equivalent of a female blind date being described as having a nice personality."

Stanton chuckled. "You know, cousin, you might be a mental case but you do have a sense of humor."

"What I meant to say," Candice said. "Edward is a considerate person. And I think that's important. I was initially against the idea of Stanton fixing you up, but then I thought how nice it would be for you to have a relationship with someone civil. After all, the relationship you've had with Kinnard has been pretty stormy. I think you deserve better."

Kim could not believe Candice. She obviously knew nothing about Kinnard, but Kim did not contradict her. Instead Kim said, "The problems between me and Kinnard are as much my fault as his."

Kim eyed the door. Her pulse was racing. She wished she could just stand up and leave. But she couldn't. It wasn't her nature, although at the moment she sincerely wished it were.

"Edward is a lot more than considerate," Stanton said. "He's a genius."

"Oh that's just great!" Kim said sarcastically. "Not only will Mr. Armstrong find me unattractive, but he'll also find me boring. I'm not at my scintillating best when it comes to making conversation with geniuses."

"Trust me," Stanton said. "You guys will hit it off. You have common backgrounds. Edward's an M.D. He was a classmate of mine at Harvard Med. As students we teamed up for a lot of experiments and lab stuff until he took his third year off and got a Ph.D. in biochemistry."

"Is he a practicing doctor?" Kim asked.

"Nope, research," Stanton said. "His expertise is the chemistry of the brain, which is a particularly fertile area at present. Right now Edward's the rising star of the field: a scientific celebrity whom Harvard was able to steal back from Stanford. And speaking of the devil, here he comes now."

Kim swung around in her seat to see a tall and squarely built yet boyish-appearing man heading for their table. Hearing that he'd been Stanton's classmate, Kim knew he'd have to be about forty, yet he appeared considerably younger, with straight, sandy blond hair and a broad, unlined, tanned face. There was none of the pallor Kim associated with academics. He was slightly stooped, as if he were afraid he was about to bump his head on an overhead beam.

Stanton was instantly on his feet, clasping Edward in a bear hug with as much enthusiasm as he'd shown Kim. He even pounded Edward's shoulder several times as some men seem impelled to do.

For a fleeting moment Kim felt sympathy for Edward. She could tell that he was as uncomfortable as she had been with Stanton's overly demonstrative greeting.

Stanton made brief introductions, and Edward shook hands with Candice and Kim before sitting down. Kim noticed his skin was moist and his grip tentative, just like her own. She also noticed he had a slight stutter as well as a nervous habit of pushing his hair from his forehead.

"I'm terribly sorry for being late," Edward said. He had a little trouble vocalizing his *t*'s.

"Two birds of a feather," Stanton said. "My gorgeous, talented, sexy cousin here said the same thing when she arrived five seconds ago."

Kim felt her face suffuse with color. It was going to be a long evening. Stanton could not help being himself.

"Relax, Ed," Stanton continued as he poured him some wine. "You're not late. I said around seven. You're perfect."

"I just meant that you were all here waiting," Edward said. He smiled self-consciously and lifted his glass as if in toast.

"Good idea," Stanton said, taking the hint and snatching up his glass. "Let me propose a toast. First I'd like to toast my darling cousin, Kimberly Stewart. She's the best surgical intensive-care nurse at the MGH bar none." Stanton then looked directly at Edward while everyone held their glasses in abeyance. "If you have to have your prostate plumbing patched up, just pray that Kimberly is available. She's legendary with a catheter!"

"Stanton, please!" Kim protested.

"OK, OK," Stanton said, extending his left hand as if to quiet an audience. "Let me get back to my toast of Kimberly Stewart. I would be derelict in my duty if I didn't bring it to the group's attention that her sterling genealogy extends back just shy of the *Mayflower.* That's paternally, of course. Maternally she only goes back to the Revolutionary War, which, I might add, is my, inferior, side of the family."

"Stanton, this is hardly necessary," Kim said. She was already mortified.

"But there's more," Stanton said with the relish of a practiced after-dinner speaker. "Kimberly's first relative to graduate from dear old Harvard did so in 1671. That was Sir Ronald Stewart, founder of Maritime, Ltd., as well as the current Stewart dynasty. And perhaps most interesting of all, Kimberly's great-grandmother times eight was hanged for witchcraft in Salem. Now if that is not Americana I don't know what is."

"Stanton, you can be such a pain," Kim said, her anger overcoming her embarrassment for the moment. "That's not information meant for public disclosure."

"And why the hell not?" Stanton questioned with a laugh. Looking back at Edward he said, "The Stewarts have this ridiculous hang-up that such ancient history is a blight on the family name."

"Whether you think it is ridiculous or not, people have a right to their feelings," Kim said hotly. "Besides, my mother is the one who is most concerned about the issue, and she's your aunt and a former Lewis. My father has never said one thing about it to me."

"Whatever," Stanton said with a wave. "Personally I find the story fascinating. I should be so lucky; it's like having had a relative on the *Mayflower* or in the boat when Washington crossed the Delaware."

"I think we should change the subject," Kim said.

"Agreed," Stanton said equably. He was the only one still holding up his glass of wine. It was a long toast. "That brings me to Edward Armstrong. Here's to the most exciting, productive, creative, and intelligent neurochemist in the world, no, in the universe! Here's to a man who has come from the streets of

Brooklyn, put himself through school, and is now at the pinnacle of his chosen career. Here's to a man who should be already booking a flight to Stockholm for his Nobel Prize, which he is a shoo-in to win for his work with neurotransmitters, memory, and quantum mechanics."

Stanton extended his wineglass and everybody followed suit. They clinked glasses and drank. As Kim set her glass back on the table she glanced furtively at Edward. It was apparent to her that he was equally abashed and self-conscious as she.

Stanton thumped his now empty glass on the table and proceeded to refill it. He glanced around at the other glasses, then jammed the wine bottle into its ice bucket. "Now that you two have met," he said, "I expect you to fall in love, get married, and have plenty of darling kids. All I ask from my part in bringing you together in this fruitful union is that Edward agrees to serve on the scientific advisory board of Genetrix."

Stanton laughed heartily even though he was the only one to do so. When he recovered he said, "OK, where the hell is the waiter? Let's eat!"

Outside the restaurant the group paused.

"We could walk around the corner and get ice cream at Herrell's," Stanton suggested.

"I couldn't eat another thing," Kim said.

"Me neither," Edward said.

"I never eat dessert," Candice said.

"Then who wants a lift home?" Stanton asked. "I've got my car right here in the Holyoke Center garage."

"I'm happy with MTA," Kim said.

"My apartment is just a short walk," Edward said.

"Then you two are on your own," Stanton said. After promising Edward he'd be in touch, Stanton took Candice's arm and headed for the garage.

"Can I walk you to the subway?" Edward asked.

"I'd appreciate that," Kim said.

They headed off together. As they walked, Kim could sense that Edward wanted to say something. Just before they got to the corner he spoke. "It's such a pleasant evening," he said, struggling a bit with the *p*. His mild stutter had returned. "How about a little walk in Harvard Square before you head home?"

"That would be great," Kim said. "I'd enjoy it."

Arm in arm they walked to that complicated collision of Massachusetts Avenue, the JFK Drive portion of Harvard Street, Mt. Auburn Street, and Brattle Street. Despite its name it was hardly a square but rather a series of curved façades and curiously shaped open areas. On summer nights the area metamorphoses into a spontaneous, medieval-like sidewalk circus of jugglers, musicians, poetry readers, magicians, and acrobats.

It was a warm, silky, summer night with a few nighthawks chirping high in the dark sky. There were even a few stars despite the glow from the city lights. Kim and Edward strolled around the entire square, pausing briefly at the periphery of each performer's audience. Despite their mutual misgivings about the evening, ultimately they were enjoying themselves.

"I'm glad I came out tonight," Kim said.

"So am I," Edward said.

Finally they sat down on a low concrete wall. To their left was a woman singing a plaintive ballad. To their right was a group of energetic Peruvian Indians playing indigenous panpipes.

"Stanton is truly a character," Kim said.

"I didn't know who to be more embarrassed for," Edward said. "Me or you with the way he was carrying on."

Kim laughed in agreement. She'd felt just as uncomfortable when Stanton was toasting Edward as when he'd toasted her.

"What I find amazing about Stanton is that he can be so manipulative and charming at the same time," Kim said.

"It is curious what he can get away with," Edward agreed. "I could never do it in a million years. In fact I've always felt I've been a foil for Stanton. I've envied him, wishing I could be half as assertive. I've always been socially self-conscious, even a little nerdy."

"My feelings exactly," Kim admitted. "I've always wanted to be more confident socially. But it just has never worked. I've been timid since I've been a little girl. When I'm in social situations, I never can think of the appropriate thing to say on the spur of the moment. Five minutes later I can, but then it's always too late."

"Two birds of a feather, just as Stanton described us," Edward said. "The trouble is Stanton is aware of our weaknesses, and he sure knows how to make us squirm. I die a slow death every time he brings up that nonsense about my being a shoo-in for the Nobel Prize."

"I apologize on behalf of my family," Kim said. "At least he isn't mean-spirited."

"How are you related?" Edward asked.

"We're true cousins," Kim said. "My mother is Stanton's father's sister."

"I should apologize as well," Edward said. "I shouldn't speak ill of Stanton. He and I were classmates in medical school. I helped him in the lab, and he helped me at parties. We made a pretty good team. We've been friends ever since."

"How come you haven't teamed up with him in one of his entrepreneurial ventures?" Kim asked.

"I've just never been interested," Edward said. "I like academia, where the quest is for knowledge for knowledge's sake. Not that I'm against applied science. It's just not as engaging. In some respects academia and industry are at odds with each other, especially in regard to industry's imperative of secrecy. Free communication is the lifeblood of science; secrecy is its bane."

"Stanton says he could make you a millionaire," Kim said.

Edward laughed. "And how would that change my life? I'm already doing what I want to do: a combination of research and teaching. Injecting a million dollars into my life would just complicate things and create bias. I'm happy the way I am."

"I tried to suggest as much to Stanton," Kim said. "But he wouldn't listen. He's so headstrong."

"But still charming and entertaining," Edward said. "He was certainly exaggerating about me when he was giving that interminable toast. But how about you? Can your family truly be traced back to seventeenth-century America?"

"That much was true," Kim said.

"That's fascinating," Edward said. "It's also impressive. I'd be lucky to trace my family back two generations, and then it would probably be embarrassing."

"It's even more impressive to put oneself through school and become eminently successful in a challenging career," Kim said. "That's on your own initiative. I was merely born a Stewart. It took no effort on my behalf."

"What about the Salem witchcraft story?" Edward asked. "Is that true as well?"

"It is," Kim admitted. "But it's not something I'm comfortable talking about."

"I'm terribly sorry," Edward said. His stutter reappeared. "Please forgive me. I don't understand why it would make any difference, but I shouldn't have brought it up."

Kim shook her head. "Now I'm sorry for making you feel uncomfortable," she said. "I suppose my response to the Salem witchcraft episode is silly, and to tell you the truth, I don't even know why I feel uncomfortable about it. It's probably because of my mother. She drummed it into me that it was something I wasn't supposed to talk about. I know she thinks of it as a family disgrace."

"But it was more than three hundred years ago," Edward said.

"You're right," Kim said with a shrug. "It doesn't make much sense."

"Are you familiar with the episode?" Edward asked.

"I know the basics, I suppose," Kim said. "Like everyone else in America."

"Curiously enough, I know a little more than most people," Edward said. "Harvard University Press published a book on the subject which was written by two gifted historians. It's called *Salem Possessed*. One of my graduate students insisted I read it since it won some kind of history award. So I read it, and I was intrigued. Why don't I loan it to you?"

"That would be nice," Kim said just to be polite.

"I'm serious," Edward said. "You'll like it, and maybe it will change the way you think about the affair. The social/political/religious aspects are truly fascinating. I learned a lot more than I expected. For instance, did you know that within a few years of the trials some of the jurors and even some of the judges publicly recanted and asked for pardon because they realized innocent people had been executed?"

"Really," Kim said, still trying to be polite.

"But the fact that innocent people got hanged wasn't what really grabbed me," Edward said. "You know how one book leads to another. Well, I read another book called *Poisons of the Past* that had the most interesting theory, especially for a neuroscientist like myself. It suggested that at least some of the young women of Salem who were suffering strange 'fits' and who were responsible for accusing people of witchcraft were actually poisoned. The suggested culprit was ergot, which comes from a mold called *Claviceps purpurea*. *Claviceps* is a fungus that tends to grow on grain, particularly rye."

Despite Kim's conditioned disinterest in the subject, Edward had caught her attention. "Poisoned by ergot?" she questioned. "What would that do?"

"Ooo-wee!" Edward rolled his eyes. "Remember that Beatles song, 'Lucy in the Sky with Diamonds'? Well, it would have been something like that because ergot contains lysergic acid amide, which is the prime ingredient of LSD."

"You mean they would have experienced hallucinations and delusions?" Kim asked.

"That's the idea," Edward said. "Ergotism either causes a gangrenous reaction, which can be rapidly fatal, or a convulsive, hallucinogenic reaction. In Salem it would have been the convulsive, hallucinogenic one, tending more on the hallucinogenic side."

"What an interesting theory," Kim said. "It might even interest my mother. Maybe she'd feel differently about our ancestor if she knew of such an explanation. It would be hard to blame the individual under those circumstances."

"That was my thought," Edward said. "But at the same time it can't be the whole story. Ergot might have been the tinder that ignited the fire, but once it started it turned into a firestorm on its own accord. From the reading I've done I think people exploited the situation for economic and social reasons, although not necessarily on a conscious level."

"You've certainly piqued my curiosity," Kim said. "Now I feel embarrassed I've never been curious enough to read anything about the Salem witch trials other than the little I did in high school. I should be particularly ashamed since my executed ancestor's property is still in the family's possession. In fact, due to a minor feud between my father and my late grandfather, my brother and I inherited it just this year."

"Good grief!" Edward said. "You mean to tell me your family has kept that land for three hundred years?"

"Well, not the entire tract," Kim said. "The original tract included land in what is now Beverly, Danvers, and Peabody, as well as Salem. Even the Salem part of the property is only a portion of what it had been. Yet it is still a sizable tract. I'm not sure how many acres, but quite a few."

"That's still extraordinary," Edward said. "The only thing I inherited was my father's dentures and a few of his masonry tools. To think that you can walk on land where your seventeenth-century relatives trod blows my mind. I thought that kind of experience was reserved for European royalty."

"I can even do better than just walking on the land," Kim said. "I can even go into the house. The old house still stands."

"Now you're pulling my leg," Edward said. "I'm not *that* gullible."

"I'm not fooling," Kim said. "It's not that unusual. There are a lot of seventeenth-century houses in the Salem area, including ones that belonged to other executed witches like Rebecca Nurse."

"I had no idea," Edward said.

"You ought to visit the Salem area sometime," Kim said.

"What shape is the house in?" Edward asked.

"Pretty good, I guess," Kim said. "I haven't been in it for ages, not since I was a child. But it looks OK for a house built in 1670. It was bought by Ronald Stewart. It was his wife, Elizabeth, who was executed."

"I remember Ronald's name from Stanton's toast," Edward said. "He was the first Harvard man in the Stewart clan."

"I wasn't aware of that," Kim said.

"What are you and your brother going to do with the property?"

"Nothing for the time being," Kim said. "At least not until Brian gets back from England where he's currently running the family shipping business. He's supposed to be home in a year or so, and we'll decide then. Unfortunately the property is a white elephant considering the taxes and upkeep."

"Did your grandfather live in the old house?" Edward asked.

"Oh, goodness no," Kim said. "The old house hasn't been lived in for years. Ronald Stewart bought a huge tract of land that abutted the original property and built a larger house, keeping the original house for tenants or servants. Over the years the larger house has been torn down and rebuilt many times. The last time was around the turn of the century. That was the house my grandfather lived in. Well, rattled around in would be a better term. It's a huge, drafty old place."

"I bet that old house has historical value," Edward said.

"The Peabody-Essex Institute in Salem as well as the Society for the Preservation of New England Antiquities in Boston have both expressed interest in purchasing it," Kim said. "But my mother is against the idea. I think she's afraid of dredging up the witchcraft issue."

"That's too bad," Edward said. Once again his slight stutter returned.

Kim looked at him. He seemed to be fidgeting while pretending to watch the Peruvians.

"Is something wrong?" Kim asked. She could sense his unease.

"No," Edward said a little too forcefully. He pondered for a minute and then said, "I'm sorry, and I know I shouldn't ask this, and you should just say no if it's not convenient. I mean, I'd understand."

"What is it?" Kim asked. She was mildly apprehensive.

"It's just that I read those books I told you about," Edward said. "What I mean to say is that I'd really like to see that old house. I know it is presumptuous of me to ask."

"I'd be happy to show it to you," Kim said with relief. "I have Saturday off this week. We could drive up there then if it's convenient for you. I can get the keys from the lawyers."

"It wouldn't be too much of a bother?" Edward asked.

"Not at all," Kim said.

"Saturday would be perfect," Edward said. "In exchange perhaps you'd like to go to dinner Friday night?"

Kim smiled. "I accept. But now I think I'd better be getting home. The seven-thirty shift at the hospital starts awfully early."

They slid off the concrete wall and strolled toward the subway entrance.

"Where do you live?" Edward asked.

"Beacon Hill," Kim said.

"I hear that's a great neighborhood," Edward said.

"It's convenient to the hospital," Kim said. "And I have a great apartment. Unfortunately I have to move come September because my roommate is getting married and she has the lease."

"I've got a similar problem," Edward said. "I live in a charming apartment on the third floor of a private house, but the owners have a baby coming and need the space. So I have to be out September first as well."

"I'm sorry to hear that," Kim said.

"It's not so bad," Edward said. "I've been meaning to move for years, but I've just been putting it off."

"Where's the apartment?" Kim asked.

"Close by," Edward said. "Within walking distance." Then he added hesitantly: "Would you care to come over for a visit?"

"Maybe another night," Kim said. "Like I said, morning comes early for me."

They reached the entrance to the subway. Kim turned and looked up into Edward's pale blue eyes. She liked what she saw; there was sensitivity.

"I want to congratulate you on asking to see the old house," Kim said. "I know it wasn't easy for you, and the reason I know is because it would have been equally difficult for me. In fact I probably couldn't have done it at all."

Edward blushed. Then he chuckled. "I'm certainly no Stanton Lewis," he said. "The truth of the matter is that I can be kind of a klutz."

"I think we have some similarities in that area," Kim said. "I also think you are a lot more socially adept than you give yourself credit for."

"You get the credit," Edward said. "You make me feel relaxed, and since we've only just met, that's saying something."

"The feeling is mutual," Kim said.

They gripped hands for a moment. Then Kim turned and hurried down into the subway.

Edward double-parked on Beacon Street across from the Boston Common and ran into the foyer of Kim's building. After ringing her bell, he kept his eye out for a Boston meter maid. He knew of their reputation from sore experience.

"Sorry to have kept you waiting," Kim said when she appeared. She was dressed in khaki shorts and a simple white T-shirt. Her dark, voluminous hair was pulled back in a ponytail.

"I'm sorry for being late," Edward said. By mutual consent Edward was dressed in a similar, casual fashion. "I had to run by the lab."

They both stared at each other for a beat, then burst out laughing.

"We're too much," Kim admitted.

"I can't help it." Edward chuckled. "I'm always apologizing. Even when it isn't warranted. It's ridiculous, but you know something? I wasn't even aware of it until you pointed it out at dinner last night."

"I only noticed it because I do it too," Kim said. "After you dropped me off last night, I thought about it. I think it comes from feeling overly responsible."

"You're probably right," Edward said. "When I was growing up I always thought it was my fault when something went wrong or someone was upset."

"The similarities are frightening," Kim mused with a smile.

They climbed into Edward's Saab and headed north out of town. It was a bright, clear day, and even though it was early morning, the sun already gave adequate hint of its summer strength.

Kim lowered the passenger-side window and jauntily stuck her arm out. "This feels like a mini-vacation," she said.

"Particularly for me," Edward said. "I'm ashamed to admit it, but I usually spend just about every day in the lab."

"Weekends too?" Kim questioned.

"Seven days a week," Edward admitted. "The usual way I can tell it is a Sunday is when there are fewer people around. I guess I'm just a boring guy!"

"I'd say dedicated," Kim said. "I'd also say you're very considerate. The flowers you've been sending me daily are glorious, but I'm hardly accustomed to such gallantry. I certainly don't deserve it."

"Oh, it's nothing," Edward said.

Kim could sense his unease. He pushed his hair off his forehead several times in a row.

"It's certainly not 'nothing' to me," Kim said. "I want to thank you again."

"Did you have any trouble getting the keys to the old house?" Edward asked, changing the subject.

Kim shook her head. "Not in the slightest. I went over to the lawyers right after work yesterday."

They drove north on route 93, then turned east on 128. The traffic was light.

"I certainly enjoyed our dinner last night," Edward said.

"Me too," Kim said. "Thank you. But when I thought about it this morning I wanted to apologize for dominating the conversation. I think I talked too much about myself and my family."

"There you go apologizing again," Edward said.

Kim struck her thigh in mock punishment. "I'm afraid I'm a hopeless case." She laughed.

"Besides"—Edward chuckled—"I should be the one apologizing. It was my fault because I bombarded you mercilessly with questions that I'm afraid might have been borderline too personal."

"I wasn't offended in the slightest," Kim said. "I just hope I didn't scare you when I mentioned those anxiety attacks I used to get when I first went to college."

"Oh, please!" Edward laughed. "I think we all get them, especially those of us who tend to be compulsive, like doctors. I used to get anxiety attacks in college before every test even though I never had any problems with grades."

"I think mine were a little worse than run-of-the-mill," Kim said. "For a short time I even had trouble riding in the car, thinking I might get one while I was cooped up."

"Did you ever take anything for them?" Edward asked.

"Xanax for a short time," Kim said.

"Did you ever try Prozac?" Edward asked.

Kim turned to look at Edward. "Never!" she said. "Why would I take Prozac?"

"Just that you mentioned you had both anxiety and shyness," Edward said. "Prozac could have helped both."

"Prozac has never been suggested," Kim said. "Plus even if it had been I wouldn't have taken it. I'm not in favor of using drugs for minor personality flaws like shyness. I think drugs should be reserved for serious problems, not mere everyday difficulties."

"Sorry," Edward said. "I didn't mean to offend you."

"I'm not offended," Kim said. "But I do feel strongly about it. As a nurse I see too many people taking too many drugs. Drug companies have got us to think there is a pill for every problem."

"I basically agree with you," Edward said. "But as a neuroscientist I now see behavior and mood as biochemical, and I've reevaluated my attitude toward clean psychotropic drugs."

"What do you mean, 'clean' drugs?" Kim asked.

"Drugs that have little or no side effects."

"All drugs have side effects," Kim said.

"I suppose that's true," Edward said. "But some side effects are quite minor and certainly an acceptable risk in relation to the potential benefits."

"I guess that's the crux of the philosophical argument," Kim said.

"Oh, that reminds me," Edward said. "I remembered those two books I'd promised to loan you." He reached in the backseat, grabbed the books, and slipped them into Kim's lap. Kim leafed through them, jokingly complaining that there weren't any pictures. Edward laughed.

"I tried to look up your ancestor in the one on the Salem witch trials," Edward said. "But there is no Elizabeth Stewart in the index. Are you sure she was executed? Those authors did extensive research."

"As far as I know," Kim said. She glanced in the index of *Salem Possessed*. It went from "spectral testimony" to "Stoughton, William." There was no Stewart at all.

After a half-hour drive they entered Salem. Their route took them past the Witch House. Edward's interest was immediately aroused, and he pulled to the side of the road.

"What's that place?" he asked.

"It's called the Witch House," Kim said. "It's one of the prime tourist attractions in the area."

"Is it truly seventeenth century," Edward asked as he stared at the old building. "Or is it Disneyland-like re-creation?"

"It's authentic," Kim said. "It's also on its original site. There is another seventeenth-century house nearby at the Peabody-Essex Institute, but it had been moved from another location."

"Cool," Edward said. The building had a storybook appeal. He was enthralled by the way the second story protruded from the first, and by the diamond-shaped panes of glass.

"Calling it cool dates you." Kim laughed. "Call it 'awesome.' "

"OK," Edward said agreeably. "It's awesome."

"It's also surprisingly similar to the old house I'm going to show you on the Stewart family compound," Kim said. "But it's technically not a witch house since no witch lived in it. It was the home of Jonathan Corwin. He was one of the magistrates who conducted some of the preliminary hearings."

"I remember the name from *Salem Possessed*," Edward said. "It certainly brings history to life when you see an actual site." Then he turned to Kim. "How far is the Stewart compound from here?"

"Not far," Kim said. "Maybe ten minutes tops."

"Did you have breakfast this morning?"

"Just some juice and fruit," Kim said.

"How about stopping for coffee and a donut?" Edward asked.

"Sounds good," Kim said.

Since it was still early and the bulk of the tourists had yet to arrive, they had no trouble finding parking near the Salem Commons. Just across the street was a coffee shop. They got coffee-to-go and strolled around the center of town, peeking into the Witch Museum and a few of the other tourist attractions. As they walked down the pedestrian mall on Essex Street, they noticed how many shops and pushcarts were selling witch-related souvenirs.

"The witch trials spawned an entire cottage industry," Edward commented. "I'm afraid it's a little tacky."

"It does trivialize the ordeal," Kim said. "But it also stands as testament to the affair's appeal. Everybody finds it so fascinating."

Wandering into the National Park Service Visitor Center, Kim found herself confronted by a virtual library of books and pamphlets on the trials. "I had no idea there was so much literature available," she said. After a few moments of browsing, she purchased several books. She explained to Edward that once she got interested in something she usually went overboard.

Returning to the car, they drove out North Street, passing the Witch House again, and turned right on Orne Road. As they passed the Greenlawn Cemetery Kim mentioned that it had once been part of the Stewarts' land.

Kim directed Edward to turn right onto a dirt road. As they bumped along, Edward had to fight with the steering wheel. It was impossible to miss all the potholes.

"Are you sure we're on the right road?" Edward asked.

"Absolutely," Kim assured him.

After a few twists and turns they approached an impressive wrought-iron gate. The gate was suspended from massive stanchions constructed of rough-hewn granite blocks. A high iron fence topped with sharpened spikes disappeared into the dense forest on either side of the road.

"Is this it?" Edward questioned.

"This is it," Kim answered as she alighted from the car.

"Rather imposing," Edward called as Kim struggled to open the heavy padlock securing the gate. "And not that inviting."

"It was an affectation of the age," Kim yelled back. "People with means wanted to project a baronial image." After removing the padlock, she pushed the gate open. Its hinges creaked loudly.

Kim returned to the car and they drove through the gate. After a few more twists and turns the road opened up to a large grassy field. Edward stopped again.

"Good Lord," Edward said. "Now I understand why you said baronial."

Dominating the enormous field was a huge, multistoried stone house complete with turrets, crenellations, and machicolations. The roof was slate and pockmarked with fanciful decorations and finial-topped dormers. Chimneys sprouted like weeds from all parts of the structure.

"An interesting mélange of styles," Edward said. "It's part medieval castle, part Tudor manor, part French château. It's amazing."

"The family has always called it the castle," Kim explained.

"I can see why," Edward said. "When you described it as a huge, drafty old place, I had no idea it was going to look like this. This belongs down in Newport with the Breakers."

"The North Shore of Boston still has quite a few of these huge old houses," Kim said. "Of course some of them have been torn down. Others have been recycled into condos, but that market is flat at the moment. You can understand why it's a white elephant for me and my brother."

"Where's the old house?" Edward asked.

Kim pointed to the right. In the distance Edward could just make out a dark-brown building nestled in a stand of birch trees.

"What's that stone building to the left?" Edward asked.

"That was once a mill," Kim said. "But it was turned into stables a couple of hundred years ago."

Edward laughed. "It's amazing you can take all this in stride," he said. "In my mind anything over fifty years old is a relic."

Edward started driving again but quickly stopped. He'd come abreast of a fieldstone wall that was mostly overgrown with weeds.

"What's this?" he asked, pointing at the wall.

"That's the old family burial ground," Kim said.

"No fooling," Edward said. "Can we look?"

"Of course," Kim said.

They got out of the car and climbed over the wall. They couldn't use the entrance since it was blocked by a dense thicket of blackberry bushes.

"Looks like a lot of the headstones are broken," Edward said. "And fairly recently." He picked up a broken piece of marble.

"Vandalism," Kim said. "There's not much we can do about it since the place is vacant."

"It's a shame," Edward said. He looked at the date. It was 1843. The name was Nathaniel Stewart.

"The family used this plot until the middle of the last century," Kim explained.

Slowly they walked back through the overgrown graveyard. The farther they went the more simple the headstones became and the older they got.

"Is Ronald Stewart in here?" Edward asked.

"He is," Kim said. She led him over to a simple round headstone with a skull and crossed bones done in low relief. On it was written: *Here lyes buried y body of Ronald Stewart y son of John and Lydia Stewart, aged 81 years Dec'd. oct. y 1. 1734.*

"Eighty-one," Edward remarked. "Healthy guy. To reach such a ripe old age he must have been smart enough to stay away from doctors. In those days with all the reliance on bloodletting and a primitive pharmacopoeia, doctors were as lethal as most of the illnesses."

Next to Ronald's grave was Rebecca Stewart's. Her stone described her as Ronald's wife.

"I guess he got remarried," Kim said.

"Is Elizabeth buried in here?" Edward asked.

"I don't know," Kim said. "No one ever pointed out her grave to me."

"Are you sure this Elizabeth even existed?" Edward asked.

"I think so," Kim said. "But I can't swear to it."

"Let's see if we can find her," Edward suggested. "She'd have to be in this general area."

For a few minutes they searched in silence, Kim going one way, Edward another.

"Edward!" Kim called.

"Did you find her?" Edward asked.

"Well, sort of," Kim said.

Edward joined her. She was looking at a headstone similar in design to Ronald's. It belonged to Jonathan Stewart, who was described as the son of Ronald and Elizabeth Stewart.

"At least we know she existed," Kim said.

They searched for another half hour but didn't find Elizabeth's grave. Finally they gave up and went back to the car. A few minutes later they pulled up in front of the old house. They both got out.

"You weren't kidding when you said it looked like the Witch House," Edward said. "It's got the same massive central chimney, the same steeply pitched gable roof, the same clapboard siding, and the same diamond-shaped panes of glass. And most curious, there is the same protrusion of the second story over the first. I wonder why they did that."

"I don't think anyone knows for certain," Kim said. "The Ward House at the Peabody-Essex Institute has the same feature."

"The pendants under the overhang are much more decorative than those at the Witch House," Edward said.

"Whoever turned those had quite a flair," Kim agreed.

"It's a charming house," Edward said. "It has so much more class than the castle."

Slowly they strolled around the aged building, pointing out its details. In the back Edward noticed a freestanding, smaller structure. He asked if it were equally old.

"I believe so," Kim said. "I was told it was for the animals."

"A mini-barn," Edward said.

Returning to the front door, Kim had to try multiple keys before she found one that unlocked the door. As she pushed it open it creaked just like the outer gate to the compound.

"Sounds like a haunted house," Edward said.

"Don't say that," Kim protested.

"Don't tell me you believe in ghosts?" Edward said.

"Let's just say I respect them," Kim said with a laugh. "So you go first."

Edward stepped through the door into a small front hall. Directly ahead was a flight of stairs that twisted up out of sight. On either side were doors. The door on the right led into the kitchen, the one on the left the parlor.

"Where to first?" Edward asked.

"You're the guest," Kim said.

"Let's check out the parlor," Edward said.

The room was dominated by a huge fireplace six feet wide. Sprinkled about the room was some colonial furniture as well as lawn tools and other paraphernalia. The most interesting piece of furniture was a canopied bed. It still had some of its original crewelwork bed hangings.

Edward walked over to the fireplace and glanced up the flue. "Still in working order," he said. Then he looked at the wall above the mantel. Stepping back, he looked at it again.

"Can you see that faint rectangle?" he said.

Kim joined him in the middle of the room and peered at the wall. "I see it," she said. "Looks like a painting used to hang there."

"My thought exactly," Edward said. Wetting the tip of his finger, he tried to smudge the outline. He couldn't. "It must have hung there a good many years for the smoke to outline it like that."

Leaving the parlor, they mounted the stairs. At the head of the stairs was a small study built over the front hall. Above the parlor and the kitchen were bedrooms, each with its own fireplace. The only furniture was a few more beds and a spinning wheel.

Returning to the kitchen on the first floor, Kim and Edward were both struck with the size of the fireplace. Edward guessed it was almost ten feet across. To the left was a lug pole, to the right a beehive oven. There were even some old pots, fry pans, and kettles.

"Can you imagine cooking here?" Edward asked.

"Not in a million years," Kim said. "I have enough trouble in a modern kitchen."

"The colonial women must have been experts at tending a fire," Edward said. He peered into the oven. "I wonder how they estimated the temperature. It's fairly critical in bread making."

They passed through a door into the lean-to part of the house. Edward was surprised to find a second kitchen.

"I think they used this during the summer," Kim said. "It would have been too hot to fire up that massive fireplace for cooking during warm weather."

"Good point," Edward said.

Returning to the main part of the house, Edward stood in the center of the kitchen, chewing on his lower lip. Kim eyed him. She could tell he was thinking about something.

"What's going through your mind?" she asked.

"Have you ever thought about living here?" he questioned.

"No, I can't say I have," Kim said. "It would be like camping out."

"I don't mean to live here the way it is," Edward said. "But it wouldn't take much to change it."

"You mean renovate it?" Kim questioned. "It would be a shame to destroy its historical value."

"I couldn't agree more," Edward said. "But you wouldn't have to. You could make a modern kitchen and bath in the lean-to portion of the house, which was an add-on anyway. You wouldn't have to disturb the integrity of the main part."

"You really think so?" Kim said. She looked around. There was no doubt it was a charming building, and it would be a fun challenge to decorate it.

"Besides," Edward said, "you've got to move out of your present apartment. It's a shame to leave this whole place vacant. Sooner or later the vandals will get in here and possibly do some real damage."

Kim and Edward made another walk through the building with the idea in mind of making it habitable. Edward was progressively enthusiastic, and Kim found herself warming to the idea.

"What an opportunity to connect with your heritage," Edward said. "I'd do it in a flash."

"I'll sleep on it," Kim said finally. "It is an intriguing idea, but I'd have to run it by my brother. After all, we are co-owners."

"There's one thing about this place that confuses me," Edward said as he glanced around the kitchen for the third time. "I wonder where they stored their food."

"I imagine in the cellar," Kim said.

"I didn't think there was one," Edward said. "I specifically looked for an entrance when we walked around the house when we first arrived, but there wasn't any. Nor are there any stairs leading down."

Kim stepped around the long trestle table and pulled aside a heavily worn sisal mat. "There's access through this trapdoor," she said. She bent down and put her finger through a hole in the floor and pulled the trapdoor open. She laid it back on the floor. A ladder led down into the darkness.

"I remember this all too well," Kim said. "Once, when we were kids, my brother threatened to close me in the cellar. He'd been enchanted with the trapdoor."

"Nice brother," Edward said. "No wonder you had a fear of being cooped up. That would have terrified anyone."

Edward bent down and tried to look around the cellar, but he could only see a small area.

"He had no intention of actually doing it," Kim said. "He was just teasing. We weren't supposed to be in here at the time, and he knew I was already scared. You know how kids like to scare each other."

"I've got a flashlight in the car," Edward said. "I'll run out and get it."

Returning with the light, Edward descended the ladder. Gaining the floor, he looked up at Kim and asked her if she was coming down.

"Do I have to?" she questioned half in jest. She came down the ladder and stood next to him.

"Cold, damp, and musty," Edward said.

"Well said," Kim remarked. "So what are we doing here?"

The cellar was small. It only comprised the area beneath the kitchen. The walls were flat fieldstone with little mortar. The floor was dirt. Against the back wall was a series of bins made with stone or wood sides. Edward walked over and shined the light in several of them. Kim stayed close at his side.

"You were right," Edward said. "Here's where the food was kept."

"What kind of food, do you suppose?" Kim asked.

"Stuff like apples, corn, wheat, and rye," Edward said. "Maybe dairy products as well. The flitches of bacon were hung up, most likely in the lean-to."

"Interesting," Kim said without enthusiasm. "Have you seen enough?"

Edward leaned into one of the bins and scratched up some of the hard-packed dirt. He felt it between his fingers. "The dirt is damp," he said. "I'm certainly no botanist, but I'd wager it would be great for growing *Claviceps purpurea*."

Intrigued, Kim asked if it could be proven.

Edward shrugged. "Possibly," he said. "I suppose it would depend on whether *Claviceps* spores could be found. If we could take some samples I could have a botanist friend take a look at it."

"I imagine we could find some containers in the castle," Kim suggested.

"Let's do it," Edward said.

Leaving the old house, they headed for the castle. Since it was such a beautiful day they walked. The grass was knee-high. Grasshoppers and other harmless insects flitted about them.

"Every so often I can see water through the trees," Edward commented.

"That's the Danvers River," Kim said. "There was a time when the field went all the way to the water's edge."

The closer they got to the castle the more awed Edward became with the building. "This place is even bigger than I had originally thought," he said. "My word, it even has a fake moat."

"I was told it was inspired by Chambord in France," Kim said. "It's shaped like the letter *U*, with guest quarters in one wing and servants' in the other."

They crossed a bridge over the dry moat. While Edward admired the gothic details of the doorway, Kim struggled with the keys just as she'd done at the old house. There were a dozen keys on the ring. Finally one opened the door.

They passed through an oak-paneled entry hall and then through an arch leading into the great room. It was a room of monumental size with a two-story ceiling and gothic fireplaces at either end. Between cathedral-sized windows on the far wall rose a grand staircase. A stained-glass rose window at the head of the stairs filled the room with a peculiar pale yellow light.

Edward let out a half-groan half-laugh. "This is incredible," he said in awe. "I had no idea it was still furnished."

"Nothing has been touched," Kim said.

"When did your grandfather die?" Edward asked. "This decor looks as if someone left on extended vacation in the nineteen twenties."

"He died just this past spring," Kim said. "But he was an eccentric man, especially after his wife died almost forty years ago. I doubt if he changed anything in the house from when his parents occupied it. It was his father who built it."

Edward wandered into the room while his eyes played over the profusion of furniture, gilt-framed paintings, and decorative objects. There was even a suit of medieval armor. Pointing to it, he asked if it were a real antique.

Kim shrugged. "I haven't the slightest idea," she said.

Edward walked to a window and fingered the curtain fabric. "I've never seen so much drapery in all my life," he said. "There must be a mile of this stuff."

"It's very old," Kim said. "It's silk damask."

"Can I see more of the house?" Edward asked.

"Be my guest," Kim said with a wave.

From the great room, Edward wandered into the darkly paneled library. It had a mezzanine accessed by a wrought-iron circular stair. The high shelves were served by a ladder that moved on a track. The books were all leather bound. "This is my idea of a library," Edward said. "I could do some serious reading here."

From the library Edward walked into the formal dining room. Like the great room, it had a two-story ceiling with matching fireplaces at either end. But unlike the great room, it had a profusion of heraldic flags on flagpoles jutting out from the walls.

"This place could have almost as much historical interest as the old house," Edward said. "It's like a museum."

"The historical interest is in the wine cellar and the attic," Kim said. "Both are completely full of papers."

"Newspapers?" Edward asked.

"Some newspapers," Kim said. "But mostly correspondence and documents."

"Let's take a look," Edward said.

They mounted the main stairs to the equivalent of the third floor since most of the first-floor rooms had two-story ceilings. From there they climbed another staircase two additional floors before reaching the attic. Kim had to struggle to get the door open. It hadn't been pried in years.

The attic space was enormous since it occupied all of the U-shaped floor plan of the house except for the area of the turrets. Each turret was a story taller than the rest of the building and had its own conical-shaped attic. The main attic had a cathedral ceiling in accordance with the roofline. It was reasonably well lighted from its many dormers.

Kim and Edward strolled down a central aisle. On both sides were innumerable file cabinets, bureaus, trunks, and boxes. Kim stopped randomly and showed Edward that all of them were filled with ledgers, scrapbooks, folders, documents, correspondence, photos, books, newspapers, and old magazines. It was a virtual treasure trove of documentary memorabilia.

"There must be enough stuff in here to fill several railroad cars," Edward said. "How far back in time does it all go?"

"Right back to Ronald Stewart's time," Kim said. "He's the one who started the company. Most of it is business-related material, but not all of it. There's some personal correspondence as well. My brother and I used to sneak up here a few times when we were kids to see who could find the oldest dates. The problem was that we weren't really allowed, and when my grandfather caught us he was furious."

"Is there as much down in the wine cellar?" Edward asked.

"As much or more," Kim said. "Come, I'll show you. The wine cellar is worth seeing anyway. Its decor is consistent with the house."

They retraced their steps down the main stairways and returned to the formal dining room. Opening a heavy oak door with huge wrought-iron hinges, they descended a granite stairway into the wine cellar. Edward understood immediately what Kim meant about its decor being consistent with the house. It was designed as if it were a medieval dungeon. The walls were all stone, the sconce lighting resembled torches, and the wine racks were built around the walls of individual rooms that could have functioned as cells. They had iron doors and bars over the openings into the hall.

"Somebody had a sense of humor," Edward said as they walked down the long central hall. "The only thing this place lacks is torture devices."

"My brother and I didn't see it as funny in the slightest," Kim said. "My grandfather didn't have to tell us to stay out of here. We didn't want any part of it. It terrified us."

"And all these trunks and things are filled with papers?" Edward asked. "Just like the attic?"

"Every last one of them," Kim said.

Edward stopped and pushed open the door to one of the cell-like rooms. He stepped inside. The wine racks were mostly empty. The bureaus, file cabinets, and trunks were pushed against them. He picked up one of the few bottles.

"Good Lord," he said. "This is an 1896 vintage! It could be valuable."

Kim blew derisively through pursed lips. "I sincerely doubt it," she said. "The cork is probably disintegrated. No one has been taking care of them for half a century."

Edward replaced the dusty bottle and opened a bureau drawer. Randomly he picked up a sheet of paper. It was a customs document from the nineteenth century. He tried another. It was a bill of lading from the eighteenth century.

"I get the impression there isn't much order here," he said.

"Unfortunately that's the case," Kim said. "In fact there is no order whatsoever to any of it. Every time a new house was built, which had been fairly frequent up until this monstrosity, all this paperwork was relocated and then returned. Over the centuries it got completely mixed up."

In order to make her point, Kim opened a file cabinet and pulled out a document. It was another bill of lading. She handed it over to Edward and told him to look at the date.

"Well, I'll be damned," he said. "Sixteen hundred and eighty-nine. That was just three years before all the witchcraft nonsense."

"It proves my point," Kim said. "We just looked at three documents and covered several centuries."

"I think this signature is Ronald's," Edward said. He showed it to Kim and she agreed.

"I just got an idea," Kim said. "You've got me interested in this witchcraft phenomenon and particularly in my ancestor Elizabeth. Maybe I could learn something about her with the help of all these papers."

"You mean like why she's not buried in the family burial plot?" Edward asked.

"That and more," Kim said. "I'm getting more and more curious about all the secrecy about her over the years. And even whether she truly was executed. As you pointed out, she's not mentioned in the book you gave me. It's pretty mysterious."

Edward gazed around the cell they were in. "It wouldn't be an easy task considering the amount of material," he said. "And ultimately it might be a waste of time since most of this is business related."

"It will be a challenge," Kim said as she warmed to the idea. She looked back in the file drawer where she'd found the seventeenth-century bill of lading to see if there were any more contemporary material. "I think I might even enjoy it. It will be an exercise in self-discovery, or, as you said in relation to the old house, an opportunity to connect with my heritage."

While Kim was rummaging in the file cabinet, Edward wandered out of the cell and deeper into the extensive wine cellar. He was still carrying the flashlight, and as he neared the back of the wine cellar he switched it on. Some of the bulbs in the sconces had blown out. Poking his head into the last cell, Edward shined the flashlight around. Its beam played across the usual complement of bureaus, trunks, and boxes until it stopped on an oil painting leaning backwards against the wall.

Remembering all the paintings he'd seen upstairs, Edward was curious as to why this one deserved such ill treatment. With some difficulty he managed to work his way over to the painting. He leaned it away from the wall and shined the light on its dusty surface. It appeared to be a painting of a young woman.

Lifting the painting from its ignominious location, Edward held it over his head and carried it out of the cell. Once in the hallway, he leaned it against the wall. It was indeed a young woman. The décolletage it displayed belied its age. It was done in a stiff, primitive style.

With the tip of his finger he wiped the dust from a small pewter plaque at the base of the painting and shined the light on it. Then he grabbed the painting and brought it to the cell where Kim was still occupied.

"Take a look at this," Edward said. He propped it against a bureau and illuminated the plaque with the flashlight.

Kim turned and looked at the painting. Sensing Edward's excitement, she followed the beam of the flashlight and read the name.

"Good heavens!" she exclaimed. "It's Elizabeth!"

Enjoying the thrill of discovery, Kim and Edward carried the painting up the stairs and into the great room, where there was adequate light. They leaned it up against the wall and stepped away to look at it.

"What's so damn striking about it," Edward said, "is that it looks a lot like you, especially with those green eyes."

"Maybe eye color is the same," Kim said, "but Elizabeth was far more beautiful, and certainly more endowed than I."

"Beauty is in the eye of the beholder," Edward said. "Personally I think it is the other way around."

Kim was transfixed by the visage of her infamous ancestor. "There are some similarities," she said. "Our hair looks similar and even the shape of our faces."

"You could be sisters," Edward agreed. "It certainly is an attractive painting. Why the devil was it hidden away in the very back of the wine cellar? It's far more pleasing than most of the paintings hanging in this house."

"It's weird," Kim said. "My grandfather must have known about it, so it's not as if it were an oversight. As eccentric as he was, it couldn't have been that he was concerned with other people's feelings, especially not my mother's. He and my mother never got along."

"The size looks pretty close to that shadow we noticed above the mantel in the old house," Edward said. "Just for fun, why don't we carry it down there and see."

Edward lifted the painting, but before he could take a step, Kim reminded him about the the containers they'd come to the castle to find. Edward thanked her and put the painting back down. Together they went into the kitchen. Kim found three plastic containers with lids in the butler's pantry.

Retrieving the painting from the great room, they started for the old house. Kim insisted on carrying the art work. With its narrow black frame, it wasn't heavy.

"I have a strange but good feeling about finding this painting," Kim said as they walked. "It's like finding a long-lost relative."

"I have to admit it is quite a coincidence," Edward said. "Especially since she's the reason why we happen to be here."

Suddenly Kim stopped. She was holding the painting in front of her, staring at Elizabeth's face.

"What's the matter?" Edward asked.

"While I've been thinking she and I look alike, I just remembered what supposedly happened to her," Kim said. "Today it's inconceivable to imagine someone being accused of witchcraft, tried, and then executed."

In her mind's eye Kim could see herself facing a noose hanging from a tree. She was about to die. She shuddered. Then she jumped when she felt the rope touch her.

"Are you all right?" Edward asked. He'd put his hand on her shoulder.

Kim shook her head and took a deep breath. "I just had an awful thought," she admitted. "I just imagined what it would be like if I were sentenced to be hanged."

"You carry the containers," Edward said. "Let me carry the painting."

They exchanged their loads and started walking again.

"It must be the heat," Edward said to lighten the atmosphere. "Or maybe you're getting hungry. Your imagination is working overtime."

"Finding this painting has really affected me," Kim admitted. "It's as if Elizabeth were trying to speak to me over the centuries, perhaps to restore her reputation."

Edward eyed Kim as they trudged through the tall grass. "Are you joking?" he asked.

"No," Kim said. "You said it was quite a coincidence we found this painting. I think it was more than a coincidence. I mean, when you think about it, it is astonishing. It can't be purely by chance. It has to mean something."

"Is this a sudden rush of superstition or are you always like this?" Edward asked.

"I don't know," Kim said. "I'm just trying to understand."

"Do you believe in ESP or channeling?" Edward asked.

"I've never thought much about it," Kim admitted. "Do you?"

Edward laughed. "You sound like a psychiatrist, turning the question back to me. Well, I don't believe in the supernatural. I'm a scientist. I believe in what can be rationally proved and reproduced experimentally. I'm not a religious person. Nor am I superstitious, and you'll probably think I'm being cynical if I say the two are related."

"I'm not terribly religious either," Kim said. "But I do have some vague beliefs regarding supernatural forces."

They reached the old house. Kim held the door open for Edward. He carried the painting into the parlor. When he held it up to the shadow over the mantel, it fit perfectly.

"At least we were right about where this painting used to hang," Edward said. He left the painting on the mantel.

"And I'll see to it that it hangs there again," Kim said. "Elizabeth deserves to be returned to her house."

"Does that mean you've decided to fix this place up?"

"Maybe so," Kim said. "But first I'll have to talk with my family, particularly my brother."

"Personally, I think it's a great idea," Edward said. He took the plastic containers from Kim and told her he was going to the cellar to get some dirt samples. At the parlor door he stopped.

"If I find *Claviceps purpurea* down there," he said with a wry smile, "I know one thing that information will do: it will rob a bit of the supernatural out of the story of the Salem witchcraft trials."

Kim didn't respond. She was mesmerized by Elizabeth's portrait and lost in thought. Edward shrugged. Then he went into the kitchen and climbed down into the cool, damp darkness of the cellar.

MONDAY • JULY 18, 1994

As usual Edward Armstrong's lab at the Harvard Medical Complex on Longfellow Avenue was the scene of frenzied activity. There was the appearance of bedlam with white-coated people scurrying every which way among a futuristic array of high-technology equipment. But the sense of disorder was only for the uninitiated. For the informed it was a known fact that high science was in continual progress.

Ultimately it all depended on Edward, although he was not the only scientist who was working in the string of rooms affectionately referred to as Armstrong's Fiefdom. Because of his notoriety as a genius, his celebrity as a synthetic chemist, and his prominence as a neuroscientist, applications for staff, doctorate, and postdoctorate positions greatly outnumbered the positions that Edward had been able to carve out of his chronically limited space, budget, and schedule. Consequently, Edward got the best and the brightest staff and students.

Other professors called Edward a glutton for punishment. Not only did he have the largest cadre of graduate students: he insisted on teaching an undergraduate basic chemistry course, even during the summer. He was the only full professor who did so. As he explained it, he felt an obligation to stimulate the young minds of the day at the earliest time possible.

Striding back from having delivered one of his famous undergraduate lectures, Edward entered his domain through one of the lab's side doors. Like an animal feeder at a zoo he was immediately mobbed by his graduate students. They were all working on separate aspects of Edward's overall goal of elucidating the mechanisms of short- and long-term memory. Each had a problem or a question that Edward answered in staccato fashion, sending them back to their benches to continue their research efforts.

With the last question answered, Edward strode over to his desk. He didn't have a private office, a concept he disdained as a frivolous waste of needed space. He was content with a corner containing a work surface, a few chairs, a computer terminal, and a file cabinet. He was accompanied by his closest assistant, Eleanor Youngman, a postdoc who'd been with him for four years.

"You have a visitor," Eleanor said as they arrived at Edward's desk. "He's waiting at the departmental secretary's desk."

Edward dumped his class materials and exchanged his tweed jacket for a white lab coat. "I don't have time for visitors," he said.

"I'm afraid this one you have to see," Eleanor said.

Edward glanced at his assistant. She was sporting one of those smiles that suggested she was about to burst out laughing. Eleanor was a spirited, bright blonde from Oxnard, California, who looked like she belonged with the surfing set. Instead she had earned her Ph.D. in biochemistry from Berkeley by the tender age of twenty-three. Edward found her invaluable, not only because of her intelligence, but also because of her commitment. She worshiped Edward, convinced he would make the next quantum leap in understanding neurotransmitters and their role in emotion and memory.

"Who in heaven's name is it?" Edward asked.

"It's Stanton Lewis," Eleanor said. "He cracks me up every time he comes in here. This time he told me he wants me to invest in a new chemistry magazine to be called *Bonding* with a foldout Molecule of the Month. I never know when he's serious."

"He's not serious," Edward said. "He's flirting with you."

Edward quickly glanced through his mail. There was nothing earth-shattering. "Any problems in the lab?" he asked Eleanor.

"I'm afraid so," she said. "The new capillary electrophoresis system which we've been using for micellar electrokinetic capillary chromatography is being temperamental again. Should I call the rep from Bio-rad?"

"I'll take a look at it," he said. "Send Stanton over. I'll take care of both problems at the same time."

Edward attached his radiation dosimeter to the lapel of his coat and wound his way over to the chromatography unit. He began fiddling with the computer that ran the machine. Something definitely wasn't right. The machine kept defaulting to its original setup menu.

Absorbed in what he was doing, Edward didn't hear Stanton approach. He was unaware of his presence until Stanton slapped him on the back.

"Hey, sport!" Stanton said, "I've got a surprise for you that's going to make your day." He handed Edward a slick, plastic-covered brochure.

"What's this?" Edward asked as he took the booklet.

"It's what you've been waiting for: the Genetrix prospectus," Stanton said.

Edward let out a chuckle and shook his head. "You're too much," he said. He put the prospectus aside and redirected his attention to the chromatography unit computer.

"How'd your date with nurse Kim go?" Stanton asked.

"I enjoyed meeting your cousin," Edward said. "She's a terrific woman."

"Did you guys sleep together?" Stanton asked.

Edward spun around. "That's hardly an appropriate question."

"My goodness," Stanton said with a big smile. "Rather touchy, I'd say. Translated that means you guys hit it off, otherwise you wouldn't be so sensitive."

"I think you are jumping to conclusions," Edward said with a stutter.

"Oh, come off it," Stanton said. "I know you too well. It's the same way you were in medical school. Anything to do with the lab or science, you're like Napoleon. When it comes to women you're like wet spaghetti. I don't understand it. But anyway, come clean. You guys hit it off, didn't you?"

"We enjoyed each other's company," Edward admitted. "In fact, we had dinner Friday night."

"Perfect," Stanton said. "As far as I'm concerned that's as good as sleeping together."

"Don't be so crass."

"Truly," Stanton said cheerfully. "The idea was to get you beholden to me and now you are. The price, my dear friend, is that you have to read this prospectus." Stanton lifted the brochure from where Edward had irreverently tossed it. He handed it back to Edward.

Edward groaned. He realized he'd given himself away. "All right," he said. "I'll read the blasted thing."

"Good," Stanton said. "You should know something about the company because I'm also in a position to offer you seventy-five thousand dollars a year plus stock options to be on the scientific advisory board."

"I don't have time to go to any damn meetings," Edward said.

"Who's asking you to come to any meetings?" Stanton said. "I just want your name on the IPO offering."

"But why?" Edward asked. "Molecular biology and biotech are not my bailiwick."

"Chrissake!" Stanton said. "How can you be so innocent? You're a scientific celebrity. It doesn't matter you know dit about molecular biology. It's your name that counts."

"I wouldn't say I know dit about molecular biology," Edward said irritably.

"Now don't get touchy with me," Stanton said. Then he pointed to the machine Edward was working on. "What the hell is that?"

"It's a capillary electrophoresis unit," Edward said.

"What the hell does it do?"

"It's a relatively new separation technology," Edward said. "It's used to separate and identify compounds."

Stanton fingered the molded plastic of the central unit. "What makes it new?"

"It's not entirely new," Edward said. "The principles are basically the same as conventional electrophoresis, but the narrow diameter of the capillaries precludes the necessity of an anticonvection agent because heat dissipation is so efficient."

Stanton raised his hand in mock self-defense. "Enough," he said. "I give up. You've overwhelmed me. Just tell me if it works."

"It works great," Edward said. He looked back at the machine. "At least it usually works great. At the moment something is wrong."

"Is it plugged in?" Stanton asked.

Edward shot him an exasperated look.

"Just trying to be helpful," Stanton joked.

Edward raised the top of the machine and peered in at the carousels. Immediately he saw that one of the capped sample vials was blocking the carousel's movement. "Well, isn't this pleasant," he said. "The thrill of the positive diagnosis of a remedial problem." He adjusted the vial. The carousel immediately advanced. Edward closed the lid.

"So I can count on you to read the prospectus," Stanton said. "And think about the offer."

"The idea of getting money for nothing bothers me," Edward said.

"But why?" Stanton said. "If star athletes can sign on with sneaker companies, why can't scientists do the equivalent?"

"I'll think about it," Edward said.

"That's all I can ask," Stanton said. "Give me a call after you read the prospectus. I'm telling you, I can make you some money."

"Did you drive over here?" Edward asked.

"No, I walked from Concord," Stanton said. "Of course I drove. What a feeble attempt at changing the subject."

"How about giving me a lift over to the main Harvard campus," Edward said.

Five minutes later Edward slid into the passenger seat of Stanton's 500 SEL Mercedes. Stanton started the engine and made a quick U-turn. He'd parked on Huntington Avenue near the Countway Medical Library. They traveled around the Fenway and then along Storrow Drive.

"Let me ask you something," Edward said after a period of silence. "The other night at dinner you made reference to Kim's ancestor, Elizabeth Stewart. Do you know for a fact that she'd been hanged as a witch, or is the story a family rumor that has been around so long that people have come to believe it?"

"I can't swear to it," Stanton said. "I've just accepted what I'd heard."

"I can't find her name in any of the standard treatises on the subject," Edward said. "And there is no dearth of them."

"I heard the story from my aunt," Stanton said. "According to her the Stewarts have been keeping it a secret since time immemorial. So it's not as if it's something they've dreamed up to enhance their reputation."

"All right, let's assume it happened," Edward said. "Why the devil would it matter now? It's so long ago. I mean I could understand for a generation or so, but not three hundred years."

Stanton shrugged. "Beats me," he said. "But I probably shouldn't have mentioned it. My aunt will have my head if she hears I've been bantering it about."

"Even Kim was reluctant to talk about it at first," Edward said.

"That's probably because of her mother, my aunt," Stanton said. "She's always been a stickler for reputation and all that social garbage. She's a very proper lady."

"Kim took me out and showed me the family compound," Edward said. "We even went inside the house where Elizabeth was supposed to have lived."

Stanton glanced at Edward. He shook his head in admiration. "Wow!" he said. "You work fast, you tiger."

"It was all very innocent," Edward said. "Don't let your gutter imagination carry you away. I found it fascinating, and it has awakened Kim's interest in Elizabeth."

"I'm not sure her mother is going to like that," Stanton said.

"I might be able to help the family's response to the affair," Edward said. He opened a bag he had on his lap and lifted out one of the plastic containers he and Kim had brought back from Salem. He explained to Stanton what it contained.

"You must really be in love," Stanton said. "Otherwise you wouldn't be taking all this time and trouble."

"My idea is that if I can prove that ergotism was at the heart of the Salem witch craze," Edward said, "it would remove any possible remaining stigma people felt who were associated with the ordeal, particularly the Stewarts."

"I still contend you must be in love," Stanton said. "That's too theoretical a justification for all this effort. I can't get you to do squat for me even with the promise of lucre."

Edward sighed. "All right," he said. "I suppose I have to admit that as a neuroscientist I'm intrigued by the possibility of a hallucinogen causing the Salem affair."

"Now I can understand," Stanton said. "The Salem witchcraft story has a universal appeal. You don't have to be a neuroscientist."

"The entrepreneur as a philosopher," Edward remarked with a laugh. "Five minutes ago I would have considered that an oxymoron. Explain to me the universal appeal."

"The affair is ghoulishly seductive," Stanton said. "People like that sort of stuff. It's like the pyramids of Egypt. There has to be more to them than mere piles of stone. They are a window on the supernatural."

"I'm not sure I agree," Edward said as he put away his dirt sample. "As a scientist I'm merely searching for a scientific explanation."

"Oh, bull," Stanton said.

Stanton dropped Edward off on Divinity Avenue in Cambridge. Just before Edward closed the door he reminded him once more about the Genetrix prospectus.

Edward skirted Divinity Hall and entered the Harvard biological labs. From a departmental secretary he got directions to Kevin Scranton's lab. He found his thin, bearded friend busy in his office. Kevin and Edward had gone to Wesleyan together but hadn't seen each other since Edward had returned to Harvard to teach.

They spent the first ten minutes rehashing old times before Edward got down to the reason for his visit. He put the three containers on the corner of Kevin's desk.

"I want you to see if you can find *Claviceps purpurea*," Edward said.

Kevin picked up one of the containers and opened the lid. "Can you tell me why?" he asked. He fingered a small amount of the dirt.

"You'd never guess," Edward said. He then told Kevin how he'd obtained the samples and the background concerning the Salem witch trials. He didn't mention the Stewart family name, thinking he owed as much to Kim.

"Sounds intriguing," Kevin said when Edward finished his story. Kevin stood up and proceeded to make a wet mount of a small sample of the dirt.

"I thought it could make a cute little paper for *Science* or *Nature*," Edward said. "Provided we find spores from *Claviceps*."

Kevin slipped the wet mount under his office microscope and began scanning the sample. "Well, there are plenty of spores in here, but of course that's not unusual."

"How's the best way to see if they're *Claviceps* or not?" Edward asked.

"There are several ways," Kevin said. "How soon do you want an answer?"

"As soon as possible," Edward said.

"DNA would take some time," Kevin said. "There are probably three to five thousand different fungal species in each sample. Besides, the most definitive method would be if we can grow some *Claviceps*. The problem is, it's not that easy. But I'll give it a shot."

Edward stood up. "I'd appreciate whatever you can do."

Taking a minute to collect herself, Kim raised her gloved hand so that her bare forearm could push her hair off her forehead. It had been a typically busy day in the surgical intensive-care unit, rewarding yet intense. She was exhausted and looking forward to getting off in another twenty minutes. Unfortunately her moment of relaxation was interrupted. Kinnard Monihan came into the unit with a sick patient.

Kim as well as the other nurses who were momentarily free lent a hand getting the new admission settled. Kinnard helped as did an anesthesiologist who'd come in with him.

While they worked, Kim and Kinnard avoided eye contact. But Kim was acutely aware of his presence, especially when their efforts on the patient's behalf brought them side by side. Kinnard was a tall, wiry man of twenty-eight with sharply angular features. He was light on his feet and agile, more like a boxer in training than a doctor in the middle of a surgical residency.

With the patient settled, Kim headed for the central desk. She felt a hand on her arm, and she turned to look up into Kinnard's dark, intense eyes.

"You're not still angry?" Kinnard asked. He had no trouble bringing up sensitive issues right in the middle of the intensive-care unit.

Feeling a wave of anxiety, Kim looked away. Her mind was a muddle of conflicted emotion.

"Don't tell me you're not even going to talk to me," Kinnard said. "Aren't you carrying your hurt feelings a bit too far?"

"I warned you," Kim began when she found her voice. "I told you that things would be different if you insisted on going on your fly-fishing trip when we'd planned to go to Martha's Vineyard."

"We never made definite plans for the Vineyard," Kinnard said. "And I hadn't anticipated Dr. Markey offering to include me on the camping trip."

"If we hadn't made plans," Kim said, "how come I had arranged to have the time off? And how come I'd called my family's friends and arranged to stay in their bungalow?"

"We'd only mentioned it once," Kinnard said.

"Twice," Kim said. "And the second time I told you about the bungalow."

"Listen," Kinnard said. "It was important for me to go on the camping trip. Dr. Markey is the number-two man in the department. Maybe you and I had a little miscommunication, but it shouldn't cause all this angst."

"What makes it even worse is that you don't feel contrite in the slightest," Kim said. Her face reddened.

"I'm not going to apologize when I don't think I did anything wrong," Kinnard said.

"Fine," Kim said. She started for the central desk again. Kinnard again restrained her.

"I'm sorry you are upset," Kinnard said. "I really thought you'd have calmed down by now. Let's talk about it more on Saturday night. I'm not on call. Maybe we could have dinner and see a show."

"I'm sorry, but I already have plans," Kim said. It was untrue, and she felt her stomach tighten. She hated confrontations and knew she wasn't good at them. Any type of discord affected her viscerally.

Kinnard's mouth dropped open. "Oh, I see," he said. His eyes narrowed.

Kim swallowed. She could tell he was angry.

"This is a game that two can play," he said. "There's someone I've been thinking about dating. This is my opportunity."

"Who?" Kim asked. The second the question came out of her mouth she regretted it.

Kinnard gave her a malicious smile and walked off.

Concerned about losing her composure, Kim retreated to the privacy of the storeroom. She was shaking. After a few deep breaths she felt more in control and ready to get back to work. She was about to return to the unit when the door opened and Marsha Kingsley, her roommate, walked in.

"I happened to overhear that encounter," Marsha said. She was a petite, spirited woman with a mane of auburn hair which she wore in a bun while working in the surgical intensive-care unit. Not only were Kim and Marsha room-mates, they were also SICU colleagues.

"He's an ass," Marsha said. She knew the history of Kim's relationship with Kinnard better than anyone. "Don't let that egotist get your goat."

Marsha's sudden appearance disarmed Kim's control over her tears. "I hate confrontations," Kim said.

"I think you handled yourself exemplarily," Marsha said. She handed Kim a tissue.

"He wouldn't even apologize," Kim said. She wiped her eyes.

"He's an insensitive bum," Marsha said supportively.

"I don't know what I did wrong," Kim said. "Up until recently I thought we'd had a good relationship."

"You didn't do anything wrong," Marsha said. "It's his problem. He's too self-ish. Look at the comparison between his behavior and Edward's. Edward's been sending you flowers every day."

"I don't need flowers every day," Kim said.

"Of course not," Marsha said. "It's the thought that counts. Kinnard doesn't think of your feelings. You deserve better."

"Well, I don't know about that," Kim said. She blew her nose. "Yet one thing is for sure. I have to make some changes in my life. What I'm thinking of doing is to move up to Salem. I've got the idea to fix up an old house on the family compound I inherited with my brother."

"That's a great idea," Marsha said. "It will be good for you to have a change of scene, especially with Kinnard living on Beacon Hill."

"That was my thought," Kim said. "I'm heading up there right after work. How about coming along? I'd love the company, and maybe you'd have some good ideas about what to do with the place."

"Give me a rain check," Marsha said. "I've got to meet some people at the apartment."

After finishing work and giving a report, Kim left the hospital. She climbed into her car and drove out of town. There was a little traffic, but it moved quickly, particularly after she passed over the Tobin Bridge. Her first stop was her childhood home on Marblehead Neck.

"Anybody here?" Kim called out as she entered the foyer of the French château–style home. It was beautifully sited directly on the ocean. There were some superficial similarities between it and the castle, although it was far smaller and more tasteful.

"I'm in the sunroom, dear," Joyce answered from afar.

Skirting the main stairs, Kim walked down the long central corridor and out into the room in which her mother spent most of her time. It was indeed a sun-room with glass on three sides. It faced south overlooking the terraced lawn, but to the east it had a breathtaking vista over the ocean.

"You're still in your uniform," Joyce said. Her tone was deprecatory, as only a daughter could sense.

"I came directly from work," Kim said. "I wanted to avoid the traffic."

"Well, I hope you haven't brought any hospital germs with you," Joyce said. "That's all I need right now is to get sick again."

"I don't work in infectious disease," Kim said. "Where I work in the unit there's probably less bacteria than here."

"Don't say that," Joyce snapped.

The two women didn't look anything alike. Kim favored her father in terms of facial structure and hair. Joyce's face was narrow, her eyes deeply set, and her nose slightly aquiline. Her hair had once been brunette but was now mostly gray. She'd never colored it. Her skin was as pale as white marble despite the fact that it was almost midsummer.

"I notice you are still in your dressing gown," Kim said. She sat on a couch across from her mother's chaise.

"There was no reason for me to dress," Joyce said. "Besides, I haven't been feeling well."

"I suppose that means that Dad is not here," Kim said. Over the years she'd learned the pattern.

"Your father left last evening on a short business trip to London," Joyce said.

"I'm sorry," Kim said.

"It doesn't matter," Joyce said. "When he's here, he ignores me anyway. Did you want to see him?"

"I'd hoped to," Kim said.

"He'll be back Thursday," Joyce said. "If it suits him."

Kim recognized her mother's martyred tone of voice. "Did Grace Traters go along with him?" Kim asked. Grace Traters was Kim's father's personal assistant in a long line of personal assistants.

"Of course Grace went along," Joyce said angrily. "John can't tie his shoes without Grace."

"If it bothers you, why do you put up with it, Mother?" Kim asked.

"I have no choice in the matter," Joyce said.

Kim bit her tongue. She could feel herself getting upset. She felt sorry for her mother on the one hand for what she had to deal with and angry with her on the other for her playing the victim. Her father had always had affairs, some more open than others. It had been going on for as long as Kim could remember.

Changing the subject, Kim asked about Elizabeth Stewart.

Joyce's reading glasses dropped off the end of her nose where they had been precariously perched. They dangled against her bosom from a chain around her neck.

"What a strange question," Joyce said. "Why on earth are you inquiring about her?"

"I happened to stumble across her portrait in Granddad's wine cellar," Kim said. "It rather startled me, especially since I seem to have the same color eyes.

Then I realized I knew very little about her. Was she really hanged for witch-craft?"

"I'd rather not talk about it," Joyce said.

"Oh, Mother, why on earth not?" Kim asked.

"It's simply a taboo subject," Joyce said.

"You should remind your nephew Stanton," Kim said. "He brought it up at a recent dinner party."

"I will indeed remind him," Joyce said. "That's inexcusable. He knows bet-ter."

"How can it be a taboo subject after so many years?" Kim asked.

"It's not something to be proud of," Joyce said. "It was a sordid affair."

"I did some reading about the Salem witch trials yesterday," Kim said. "There's a lot of material available. But Elizabeth Stewart is never mentioned. I'm beginning to wonder if she was involved."

"It's my understanding she was involved," Joyce said. "But let's leave it at that. How did you happen to come across her portrait?"

"I was in the castle," Kim said. "I went to the compound on Saturday. I have it in mind to fix up the old house and live in it."

"Why in heaven's name would you want to do that?" Joyce asked. "It's so small."

"It could be charming," Kim said. "And it's larger than my current apartment. Besides, I want to get out of Boston."

"I'd think it would be an enormous job to make it habitable," Joyce said.

"That's part of the reason I wanted to talk to Father," Kim said. "Of course, he's not around. I have to say, he has never been around when I needed him."

"He wouldn't have any idea about such a project," Joyce said. "You should talk to George Harris and Mark Stevens. They are the contractor and the archi-tect who just finished the renovation in this house, and the project couldn't have gone any better. They work as a team, and their office is conveniently lo-cated in Salem.

"The other person you should talk to is your brother, Brian."

"That goes without saying," Kim said.

"You call your brother from here," Joyce said. "While you're doing that, I'll get the phone number of the contractor and the architect."

Joyce climbed out of her chaise and disappeared. Kim smiled as she lifted the phone onto her lap. Her mother never ceased to amaze her. One minute she could be the epitome of self-absorbed immobility, the next a whirlwind of ac-tivity, totally involved in someone else's project. Intuitively Kim knew what the problem was: her mother didn't have enough to do. Unlike her friends she'd never gotten involved in volunteer activities.

Kim glanced at her watch as the call went through and tried to guess the time in London. Not that it mattered. Her brother was an insomniac who worked at night and slept in snatches during the day like a nocturnal creature.

Brian answered on the first ring. After they had exchanged hellos, Kim described her idea. Brian's response was overwhelmingly positive, and he encouraged her to go ahead with the plan. He thought it would be much better to have someone on the property. Brian's only question was about the castle and all its furnishings.

"I'm not going to touch that place," Kim said. "We'll attack that when you come back."

"Fair enough," Brian said.

"Where's Father?" Kim asked.

"John's at the Ritz," Brian said.

"And Grace?"

"Don't ask," Brian said. "They'll be back Thursday."

While Kim was saying goodbye to Brian, Joyce reappeared and wordlessly handed her a scrap of paper with a local phone number. As soon as Kim hung up from Brian, Joyce told her to dial the number.

Kim dialed. "Who should I ask for?" she said.

"Mark Stevens," Joyce said. "He's expecting your call. I phoned him on the other line while you were speaking with Brian."

Kim felt a mild resentment toward her mother's interference, but she didn't say anything. She knew Joyce was only trying to be helpful. Yet Kim could remember times when she was in middle school and had to fight to keep her mother from writing her school papers.

The conversation with Mark Stevens was short. Having learned from Joyce that Kim was in the area, he suggested they meet at the compound in half an hour. He said he'd have to see the property in order to advise her intelligently. Kim agreed to meet with him.

"If you decide to renovate that old house, at least you'll be in good hands," Joyce said after Kim had hung up.

Kim got to her feet. "I'd better be going," she said. Despite a conscious attempt to suppress it, Kim felt irritation returning toward her mother. It was the interference and lack of privacy that bothered her. She recalled her mother asking Stanton to fix her up after telling him Kim had broken off her relationship with Kinnard.

"I'll walk you out," Joyce said.

"There's no need, Mother," Kim said.

"I want to," Joyce said.

They started down the long hall.

"When you speak with your father about the old house," Joyce said, "I advise you not to bring up the issue about Elizabeth Stewart. It will only irritate him."

"Why would it irritate him?" Kim demanded.

"Don't get upset," Joyce said. "I'm just trying to keep peace in the family."

"But it is ridiculous," Kim snapped. "I don't understand."

"I only know that Elizabeth came from a poor farming family from Andover," Joyce said. "She wasn't even an official member of the church."

"As if that matters today," Kim said. "The irony is that within months of the affair there were public apologies from some of the jury members and justices because they realized innocent people had been executed. And here we are three hundred years later refusing to even talk about our ancestor. It doesn't make any sense. And why isn't her name in any of the books?"

"Obviously it's because the family didn't want it to be," Joyce said. "I don't think the family thought she was innocent. That's why it's an affair that should be left in the closet."

"I think it's a bunch of rubbish," Kim said.

Kim got into her car and drove off Marblehead Neck. When she got into Marblehead proper she had to force herself to slow down. Thanks to a vague sense of unease and vexation, she'd been driving much too fast. As she passed the Witch House in Salem, she put words to her thoughts, and admitted to herself that her curiosity about Elizabeth and the witch trials had gone up a notch despite her mother's warnings, or perhaps because of them.

When Kim pulled up to the family compound gate, a Ford Bronco was parked at the side of the road. As she got out of her car with the keys to the gate's padlock, two men climbed from the Bronco. One was stocky and muscular as if he worked out with weights on a daily basis. The other was borderline obese and seemed to be out of breath merely from the effort of getting out of the car.

The heavyset man introduced himself as Mark Stevens and the muscular man as George Harris. Kim shook hands with both of them.

Kim unlocked the gate and got back into her car. With her in the lead, they drove to the old house. They all climbed out of their vehicles in unison.

"This is fabulous," Mark said. He was mesmerized by the building.

"Do you like it?" Kim asked. She was pleased by his response.

"I love it," Mark said.

The first thing they did was walk around the house to examine the exterior. Kim explained the idea of putting a new kitchen and bathroom in the lean-to portion and leaving the main part of the building essentially unchanged.

"You'll need heat and air-conditioning," Mark said. "But that should be no problem."

After touring the exterior they all went inside. Kim showed them the whole house, even the cellar. The men were particularly impressed with the way the main beams and joists were joined.

"It's a solid, well-built structure," Mark said.

"What kind of job would it be renovating it?" Kim asked.

"There wouldn't be any problem," Mark said. He looked at George, who nodded in agreement.

"I think it will be a fantastic little house," George said. "I'm psyched."

"Can it be done without damaging the historical aspect of the building?" Kim asked.

"Absolutely," Mark said. "We can hide all the ductwork, piping, and electric in the lean-to and in the cellar. You won't see it."

"We'll dig a deep trench to bring in utilities," George said. "They'll come in beneath the existing foundation so we will not have to disturb it. The only thing I'd recommend is pouring a concrete basement floor."

"Can the job be done by September first?" Kim asked.

Mark looked at George. George nodded and said it wouldn't be a problem as long as they used custom cabinetry.

"I have one suggestion," Mark said. "The main bathroom is best situated in the lean-to as you have suggested. But we could also put a small half-bath on the second floor between the two bedrooms without causing any damage. I think it would be convenient."

"Sounds good," Kim said. "When could you start?"

"Immediately," George said. "In fact, to get it done by the first of September we'll have to start tomorrow."

"We've done a lot of work for your father," Mark said. "We could run this job just like we've done the others. We'll bill you for time and materials plus profit."

"I want to do it," Kim said with newfound resolve. "Your enthusiasm has overcome any of my reservations. What do we have to do to get started?"

"We'll start right away on a verbal agreement," Mark said. "We'll draw up contracts that can be signed later."

"Fine," Kim said. She stuck out her hand and shook hands with both men.

"We'll have to stay for a while to get measurements," Mark said.

"Be my guest," Kim said. "As for the contents of the house, they can be stored up at the garage of the main house. The garage is open."

"What about the gate?" George asked.

"If you are starting right away, let's leave it unlocked," Kim said.

While the men were busy with their tape measures, Kim wandered outside. From fifty feet away she looked at the house and acknowledged that it was indeed darling. Immediately she began to think about the fun of decorating it and debated with herself what colors to paint the bedrooms. Such details excited her about the project, but the excitement immediately conjured up Elizabeth's name. All at once Kim found herself wondering how Elizabeth had felt when she first saw the house and when she first moved into it. She wondered if Elizabeth had been equally excited.

Returning back inside, Kim told Mark and George that she would be up in the main house if they needed her.

"We have plenty to keep us busy for the moment," Mark said. "But I'll have to talk with you tomorrow. Could you give me your phone number?"

Kim gave both her apartment and work numbers. Then she left the old house, climbed in her car, and drove up to the castle. Thinking about Elizabeth had stimulated her to spend a little time looking through the old papers.

Kim opened the front door and left it slightly ajar in case Mark or George came looking for her. Inside she debated between the attic and the wine cellar. Remembering the seventeenth-century bill of lading she'd found on Saturday in the wine cellar, she decided to return there.

Striding through the great room and traversing the dining room, Kim pulled open the heavy oak door. As she started down the granite steps she became aware that the door had closed with a dull thud behind her.

Kim stopped. She had the sudden realization that it was far different being alone in the huge old house than it had been with Edward. She heard distant creaks and groans as the house adjusted to the heat of the day. Turning around, Kim looked up at the door with the irrational fear that it had somehow locked, trapping her in the basement.

"You're being ridiculous," Kim said out loud. Yet she couldn't shake the concern about the door. Finally she mounted the stairs. She leaned against the door, and as she expected, it opened. She let it close again.

Chiding herself for her overly active imagination, Kim descended and strode into the depths of the wine cellar. She hummed a favorite tune, but her equanimity was a façade. Despite efforts to the contrary, she was still spooked by the surroundings. The massive house seemed to make the air heavy and breathing difficult. And as she'd already noticed, it was far from silent.

Kim forced herself to ignore her discomfiture. Still humming the same song, she entered the cell where she'd found the seventeenth-century bill of lading. On Saturday she'd searched through the drawer where she'd found the document, but now she began to search through the rest of the file cabinet.

It didn't take her long to grasp how difficult searching through the Stewart papers was to be. She was dealing with one file cabinet out of literally scores. Each drawer was completely full, and she painstakingly had to go through document by document. Many of the papers were entirely written by hand and some were difficult to decipher. On others it was impossible to find a date. To make things worse, the light from the torchlike sconces was far from adequate. Kim resolved that on future forays to the wine cellar she'd bring additional lighting.

After only going through a single drawer, Kim gave up. Most of the documents where she could find a date were from the late eighteenth century. Hoping there might be some order to the mess, she began randomly opening drawers and sampling, looking for something significantly older. It was in the top drawer of a bureau near the door to the hall that she made her first find.

What got her attention initially were scattered bills of lading from the seventeenth century: each a little older than the one she'd shown to Edward on Saturday. Then she found a whole packet of them tied with a string. Although they were handwritten, the script was graceful and clear, and all of them had dates. They dealt mostly with furs, timber, fish, rum, sugar, and grain. In the middle of the packet was an envelope. It was addressed to Ronald Stewart. The handwriting was different; it was stiff and erratic.

Kim carried the envelope out into the hall where the light was better. She slid the letter out and unfolded it. It was dated *y 21st June 1679*. It was difficult to read.

Sir:

There hath been several days synce your letter hath arrived. I hath had much discourse with y family over your fancy for our beloved daughter Elizabeth who is a high spirited gyrl. If it be God's will ye shall have her hand in marriage provided ye shall give me work and move y family to Salem Town. Y threat of Indian raids hath made it a hazard to our lyves here in Andover and caused us much Disquietude. Ye humble servant,

James Flanagan.

Kim slowly slipped the letter back into the envelope. She was dismayed, even shocked. She didn't think of herself as a feminist, yet this letter offended her and made her feel like one. Elizabeth had been chattel to be bargained away. Kim's sympathy for her forebear, which had been on the rise, now soared.

Returning to the cell, Kim put the letter on top of the bureau where she'd found it and began looking more carefully through the drawer. Oblivious to the time and her surroundings, she went through every slip of paper. Although she found a few more contemporary bills of lading, she found no more letters. Undaunted, she started on the second drawer. It was then that she heard the unmistakable sound of footsteps above her.

Kim froze. The vague fear she'd experienced when she'd first descended into the wine cellar came back with a vengeance. Only now it was fueled by more than just the spookiness of the huge, empty house. Now it was compounded by the guilt of trespassing into a forbidden and troubled past.

Consequently, her imagination ran wild, and as the footsteps passed directly overhead, her mental image was of some fearful ghost. She thought it might even be her dead grandfather, coming to exact revenge for her insolent and presumptuous attempt to uncover guarded secrets.

The sound of the footsteps receded then merged with the house's creaks and groans. Kim was beset by two conflicting impulses: one was to flee blindly from the wine cellar; the other was to hide among the file cabinets and bureaus. Unable to decide, she did neither. Instead she stepped silently to the door of the cell and peeked around the jamb, looking down the long corridor toward the granite steps. At that moment she heard the door to the wine cellar creak open. She couldn't see the door, but she was sure it was what she'd heard.

Paralyzed with fear, Kim helplessly watched as black shoes and trousers appeared and came relentlessly down the steps. Halfway they stopped. Then a figure bent down and a backlit, featureless face appeared.

"Kim?" Edward called. "Are you down here?"

Kim's first response was to let out a sigh. Until then, she hadn't been aware she'd been holding her breath. Leaning against the wall of the cell for support, since her legs felt tremulous, she called out to Edward to let him know where she was. In a few moments his large frame filled the doorway.

"You scared me," Kim said as calmly as she could manage. Now that she knew it was Edward, she was acutely embarrassed by the extent of her terror.

"I'm sorry," Edward said falteringly. "I didn't mean to frighten you."

"Why didn't you call out sooner?" Kim asked.

"I did," Edward said. "Several times. First when I came through the front door and again in the great room. I think the wine cellar must be insulated."

"I suppose it is," Kim said. "What are you doing here, anyway? I certainly didn't expect you."

"I tried to call you at your apartment," Edward said. "Marsha told me you drove out here with the idea of fixing up the old house. On the spur of the moment I decided to come. I feel responsible since I was the one who suggested it."

"That was considerate," Kim said. Her pulse was still racing.

"I'm really sorry for having scared you," Edward said.

"Never mind," Kim said. "It's my fault for letting my stupid imagination take over. I heard your footsteps and thought you were a ghost."

Edward made an evil face and turned his hands into claws. Kim playfully socked him in the shoulder and told him he wasn't funny.

They both felt relieved. The tension that existed evaporated.

"So you've started on the Elizabeth Stewart search," Edward said. He eyed the open drawer of the bureau. "Did you find anything?"

"As a matter of fact I have," Kim said. She stepped over to the bureau and handed Edward James Flanagan's letter to Ronald Stewart.

Edward carefully slipped the note from the envelope. He held it close to the light. It took him as much time to read it as it had taken Kim.

"Indian raids in Andover!" Edward commented. "Can you imagine? Life certainly was different back then."

Edward finished the letter and handed it back to Kim. "Fascinating," he said.

"Doesn't it upset you at all?" Kim asked.

"Not particularly," Edward said. "Should it?"

"It upset me," Kim said. "Poor Elizabeth had even less say about her tragic fate than I'd imagined. Her father was using her as a bargaining chip in a business deal. It's deplorable."

"I think you might be jumping to conclusions," Edward said. "Opportunity as we know it didn't exist in the seventeenth century. Life was harsher and more tenuous. People had to team up just to survive. Individual interests weren't a high priority."

"That doesn't warrant making a deal with your daughter's life," Kim said. "It sounds as if her father were treating her like a cow or some other piece of property."

"I still think you could be reading too much into it," Edward said. "Just because there was a deal between James and Ronald doesn't necessarily mean that Elizabeth didn't have any say whether she wanted to marry Ronald or not. Also, you have to consider that it might have been a great source of comfort and satisfaction for her to know that she was providing for the rest of her family."

"Well, maybe so," Kim said. "Trouble is, I know what ultimately happened to her."

"You still don't know for sure if she was hanged or not," Edward reminded her.

"That's true," Kim said. "But this letter at least suggests one reason she might have been vulnerable to being accused as a witch. From the reading I've done, people in Puritan times were not supposed to change their station in life, and if they did, they were automatically suspected of not following God's will. Elizabeth's sudden rise from a poor farmer's daughter to a comparatively wealthy merchant's wife certainly fits that category."

"Vulnerability and actually being accused are two different things," Edward said. "Since I haven't seen her name in any of the books, I'm dubious."

"My mother suggested that the reason she's not mentioned is because the family went to great lengths to keep her name out of it. She even implied the reason was because the family considered Elizabeth guilty."

"That's a new twist," Edward said. "But it makes sense in one regard. People in the seventeenth century believed in witchcraft. Maybe Elizabeth practiced it."

"Wait a second," Kim said. "Are you suggesting Elizabeth was a witch? My idea was that she was guilty of something, like changing her status, but certainly not that she considered herself a sorceress."

"I mean maybe she practiced magic," Edward said. "Back then there was white magic and black magic. The difference was that white magic was for good things, like curing a person or an animal. Black magic, on the other hand, had a malicious intent and was called witchcraft. Obviously there could have been times when it was a matter of opinion if some potion or charm represented white magic or black magic."

"Well, maybe you have a point," Kim said. She thought for a moment, then shook her head. "I don't buy it. My intuition tells me otherwise. I have a feeling Elizabeth was an entirely innocent person caught in a terrible tragedy by some insidious trick of fate. Whatever the trick was, it must have been awful, and the fact that her memory has been treated so dreadfully just compounds the injustice." Kim glanced around at the file cabinets, bureaus, and boxes. "The question is: could the explanation of whatever it was lie in this sea of documents?"

"I'd say that finding this personal letter is auspicious," Edward said. "If there's one, there's got to be more. If you're going to find the answer it will most likely be in personal correspondence."

"I just wish there were some chronological order to these papers," Kim said.

"What about the old house?" Edward asked. "Did you make any decisions about fixing it up?"

"I did," Kim said. "Come on, I'll explain it to you."

Leaving Edward's car parked at the castle, they drove over to the old house in Kim's. With great enthusiasm Kim took Edward on a tour and explained that she was going to follow his original suggestion of putting the modern conveniences in the lean-to portion. The most important bit of new information was the placement of a half-bath between the bedrooms.

"I think it will be a marvelous house," Edward said as they exited the building. "I'm jealous."

"I'm excited about it," Kim said. "What I'm really looking forward to is the decorating. I think I'll arrange to take some vacation time and even personal time off in September to devote full time to it."

"You'll do it all by yourself?" Edward asked.

"Absolutely," Kim said.

"Admirable," Edward said. "I know I couldn't do it."

They climbed into Kim's car. Kim hesitated starting the engine. They could see the house through the front windshield.

"Actually I've always wanted to be an interior decorator," Kim said wistfully.

"No kidding?" Edward said.

"It was a missed opportunity," Kim said. "My main interest when I was growing up was always art in some form or fashion, especially in high school. Back then, I'd have to say, I was a whimsical artist type and hardly a member of the in-group."

"I certainly wasn't part of the in-group either," Edward said.

Kim started the car and turned it around. They headed for the castle.

"Why didn't you become an interior decorator?" Edward asked.

"My parents talked me out of it," Kim said. "Particularly my father."

"I'm confused," Edward said. "Friday at dinner you said you and your father were never close."

"We weren't close, but he still had a big effect on me," Kim said. "I thought it was my fault we weren't close. So I spent a lot of effort trying to please him, even to the point of going into nursing. He wanted me to go into nursing or teaching because he felt they were 'appropriate.' He certainly didn't think interior design was appropriate."

"Fathers can have a big effect on kids," Edward said. "I had a similar compulsion to please my father. When I think about it, it was kind of crazy. I should have just ignored him. The problem was that he made fun of me because of my stutter and lack of ability in competitive sports. I suppose I was a disappointment to him."

They arrived at the castle, and Kim pulled up next to Edward's car. Edward started to get out, but then he sat back in the seat.

"Have you eaten?" he asked.

Kim shook her head.

"Me neither," he said. "Why don't we drive into Salem and see if we can find a decent restaurant?"

"You're on," Kim said.

They drove out of the compound and headed toward town. Kim was the first to speak. "I attribute my lack of social confidence in college directly to my relationship with my parents," she said. "Could it have been the same for you?"

"I wouldn't doubt it," Edward said.

"It's amazing how important self-esteem is," Kim said, "and it's a little scary how easily it can be undermined with children."

"Even with adults," Edward said. "And once it is undermined it affects behavior, which in turn affects self-esteem. The problem is that it can become functionally autonomous and biochemically determined. That's the argument for drugs: to break the vicious cycle."

"Are we talking about Prozac again?" Kim asked.

"Indirectly," Edward said. "Prozac can positively affect self-esteem in some patients."

"Would you have taken Prozac in college if it had been available?" Kim asked.

"I might have," Edward admitted. "It would have made a difference in my experience."

Kim glanced briefly across at Edward. She had the feeling he'd just told her something personal. "You don't have to answer this," she said, "and maybe I shouldn't ask, but have you ever tried Prozac yourself?"

"I don't mind answering," Edward said. "I did use it for a time a couple of years ago. My father died, and I became moderately depressed. It was a reaction I didn't expect, considering our history. A colleague suggested I try Prozac, and I did."

"Did it help the depression?" Kim asked.

"Most definitely," Edward said. "Not immediately but eventually. But most interestingly it also gave me an unexpected dose of assertiveness. I'd not anticipated it, so it couldn't have been a placebo effect. I also liked it."

"Any side effects?" Kim asked.

"A few," Edward said. "But nothing terrible, and certainly acceptable in relation to the depression."

"Interesting," Kim said sincerely.

"I hope my admission of psychotropic drug use in the face of your pharmacological Puritanism doesn't alarm you."

"Don't be silly," Kim said. "Quite the contrary. I respect your forthrightness. Besides, who would I be to judge? I've never taken Prozac, but I did have some psychotherapy during college. I'd say that makes us even."

Edward laughed. "Right!" he said. "We're both crazy!"

They found a small, popular local restaurant that served fresh fish. It was crowded, and they were forced to sit on stools at the bar. They each had baked scrod and iced mugs of draft beer. For dessert there was old-fashioned Indian pudding with ice cream.

After the boisterous publike atmosphere they both enjoyed the silence of the car as they drove back to the compound. However, as they passed through the gate, Kim sensed that Edward had become demonstrably nervous. He fidgeted, brushing his hair off his forehead.

"Is something wrong?" Kim asked.

"No," Edward said, but his stutter had returned.

Kim pulled up next to his car. She put on the emergency brake but left the engine running. She waited, knowing there was something on Edward's mind.

Edward finally blurted out: "Would you like to come over to my apartment when we get back to the city?"

The invitation threw Kim into a quandary. She sensed the courage it took for Edward to invite her, and she didn't want him to feel rejected. At the same time she thought of the needs of the patients she'd be facing in the morning. Ultimately her professionalism won out. "I'm sorry," she said. "It's a bit too late tonight. I'm exhausted; I've been up since six." In an attempt to make light of the situation she added: "Besides, it's a school night and I haven't finished my homework."

"We could turn in early," Edward said. "It is just a little after nine."

Kim was both surprised and uneasy. "I think maybe things are moving a little too swiftly for me," she said. "I've felt very comfortable with you, but I don't want to rush things."

"Of course," Edward said. "Obviously I've also felt comfortable with you."

"I do enjoy your company," Kim said. "And I'm off Friday and Saturday this week if that works with your schedule."

"How about dinner on Thursday night?" Edward said. "It won't be a school night."

Kim laughed. "It'll be a pleasure," she said. "And I'll make it a point to have all my homework done."

Friday • July 22, 1994

Kim's eyes blinked open. At first she was disoriented. She didn't know where she was. There were unfamiliar shutters over the windows dispersing the early morning light. Turning her head to the side, she saw Edward's sleeping form, and it all came back to her in a flash.

Kim drew the sheet up around her neck. She felt distinctly uneasy and out of place. "You hypocrite," she silently voiced to herself. She could remember just a few days previously telling Edward she didn't want to rush things, and here she was waking up in his bed. Kim had never been in a relationship which had proceeded to such intimacy so quickly.

As quietly as possible, Kim tried to slip out of the bed with the intention of dressing before Edward woke up. But it was not to be. Edward's small, white, and rather nasty Jack Russell terrier growled and bared his teeth. His name was Buffer. He was at the foot of the bed.

Edward sat up and shooed the dog away. With a groan he fell back against the pillow.

"What time is it?" he asked. He'd closed his eyes.

"It's a little after six," Kim said.

"Why are you awake so early?" Edward asked.

"I'm used to it," Kim said. "This is my normal wakeup time."

"But it was almost one when we came to bed."

"It doesn't matter," Kim said. "I'm sorry. I shouldn't have stayed."

Edward opened his eyes and looked at Kim. "Do you feel uncomfortable?" he asked.

Kim nodded.

"I'm sorry," Edward said. "I shouldn't have talked you into it."

"It's not your fault," Kim said.

"But it was your inclination to go," Edward said. "It was my fault."

They looked at each other for a beat, then both smiled.

"This is sounding a bit repetitious," Kim said with a chuckle. "We're back to competing with each other with apologies."

"It would be funny if it weren't so pitiful," Edward said. "You'd think we would have made some progress by now."

Kim moved over and they put their arms around each other. They didn't talk for a moment as they enjoyed the embrace. It was Edward who broke the silence. "Do you still feel uncomfortable?"

"No," Kim said. "Sometimes merely talking about something really helps."

Later while Edward was in the shower, Kim called her roommate, Marsha, who she knew would be about to leave for work. Marsha was glad to hear from her and voiced a modicum of concern that Kim had failed to come home or call the previous evening.

"I should have called," Kim admitted.

"I take it the evening was a success," Marsha said coyly.

"It was fine," Kim said. "It just got so late, and I didn't want to take the risk of waking you up."

"Oh, sure!" Marsha said with exaggerated sarcasm.

"Would you give Sheba some food?" Kim added, changing the subject. Marsha knew her too well.

"Your cat has already dined," Marsha said. "The only other news is that you got a call last night from your father. He wants you to call him when you have a chance."

"My father?" Kim questioned. "He never calls."

"You don't have to tell me," Marsha said. "I've been your roommate for years, and it was the first time I spoke with him on the phone."

After Edward got out of the shower and dressed, he surprised Kim by suggesting they go to Harvard Square for breakfast. Kim had imagined he'd want to go directly to his lab.

"I'm up two hours before I expected to be," Edward said. "The lab can wait. Also, it's been the most pleasant evening of the year and I don't want it to be over."

With a smile on her face, Kim put her arms around Edward's neck and gave him a forceful hug. She had to stand on her tiptoes in the process. He returned the affection with equal exuberance.

They used Kim's car since it had to be moved; it was illegally parked outside Edward's apartment. In the square Edward took her to a student greasy spoon where they indulged themselves with scrambled eggs, bacon, and coffee.

"What are your plans today?" Edward asked. He had to speak loudly over the general din. Summer session at the university was in full swing.

"I'm heading up to Salem," Kim said. "They've started the construction on the cottage. I want to check on the progress." Kim had decided to call the old house "the cottage" in contrast to the castle.

"When do you plan to get back?"

"Early evening," Kim said.

"How about meeting at the Harvest Bar around eight?" Edward said.

"It's a date," Kim said.

After breakfast Edward asked Kim to drop him off at the Harvard biological labs.

"You don't want me to take you home to get your car?" she asked.

"No, thanks," Edward said. "There'd be no place to park it here on the main campus. To get to work I'll take the shuttle over to the medical area. I do it frequently. It's part of the benefit of living within walking distance of the square."

Edward had Kim drop him off at the corner of Kirkland Street and Divinity Avenue. He stood on the sidewalk and waved until she was out of sight. He knew he was in love, and he loved the feeling. Turning around, he started up Divinity Avenue. He felt like singing. What made him feel so good was that he was beginning to think that Kim felt affection for him. All he could do was hope that it would last. He thought about the flowers he was having sent every day and wondered if he were overdoing it. The problem was, he didn't have a lot of experience with such things.

Arriving at the biological labs, Edward checked the time; it was before eight. As he climbed the stairs he worried he'd have to wait for Kevin Scranton. But his concerns were unfounded. Kevin was there.

"I'm glad you stopped in," Kevin said. "I was going to call you today."

"Did you find *Claviceps purpurea?*" Edward asked hopefully.

"Nope," Kevin said. "No *Claviceps.*"

"Damn!" Edward said. He slumped into a chair. There was a disappointed, sinking sensation in his stomach. He'd been banking on a positive result and was counting on it mainly for Kim's sake. He'd wanted to present it to her as a gift of science to help alleviate Elizabeth's disgrace.

"Don't look so glum," Kevin said. "There wasn't any *Claviceps*, but there was plenty of other mold. One of them that grew out morphologically resembles *Claviceps purpurea*, but it is a heretofore unknown species."

"No kidding," Edward commented. He brightened at the thought that at least they'd made a discovery.

"Of course, that's not terribly surprising," Kevin said, causing Edward's face to fall again. "Currently there are approximately fifty thousand known species of fungi. At the same time some people believe that one hundred thousand to a quarter of a million species actually exist."

"So you're trying to tell me that this isn't a monumental discovery," Edward commented wryly.

"I'm not making any value judgment," Kevin said. "But it's a mold that you might find interesting. It's an ascomycete, like *Claviceps*, and it happens to form sclerotia just like *Claviceps.*"

Kevin reached across his desk and dropped several small dark objects into Edward's palm. Edward nudged them with his index finger. They appeared like dark grains of rice.

"I think you better tell me what these sclerotia are," Edward said.

"They're a type of vegetative, resting spore of certain fungi," Kevin said. "They're different than a simple, unicellular spore because sclerotia are multicellular and contain fungal filaments or hyphae as well as stored food."

"What makes you think I'd be interested in these things?" Edward asked. He thought they also looked like the seeds in rye bread. He brought one to his nose; it was odorless.

"Because it's the *Claviceps'* sclerotia that contain the bioactive alkaloids that cause ergotism," Kevin said.

"Wow!" Edward said. He sat up straight and studied the sclerotium between his fingers with additional interest. "What are the chances that this little bugger contains the same alkaloids as *Claviceps?*"

"That, I believe, is the question of the day," Kevin said. "Personally, I think the chances are reasonably good. There aren't many fungi that produce sclerotia. Obviously this new species is related to *Claviceps purpurea* on some level."

"Why don't we try it?" Edward said.

"What on earth do you mean?" Kevin asked. He eyed Edward with suspicion.

"Why don't we make a little brew with these guys and taste it?" Edward said.

"You're joking, I hope," Kevin said.

"Actually I'm not," Edward said. "I'm interested in whether this new mold makes an alkaloid that has a hallucinogenic effect. The best way to figure that out is to try it."

"You're out of your mind," Kevin said. "Mycotoxins can be quite potent, as those countless people who've suffered ergotism can testify. Science is finding new ones all the time. You'd be taking an awful risk."

"Where's your adventuresome spirit?" Edward asked teasingly. He stood up. "Can I use your lab for this little experiment?"

"I'm not sure I should be party to this," Kevin said. "But you're serious, aren't you?"

"Very much so," Edward said.

Kevin led Edward into his lab and asked him what he needed. Edward said he needed a mortar and pestle or the equivalent, distilled water, a weak acid to precipitate the alkaloid, some filter paper, a liter flask, and a milliliter pipette.

"This is insane," Kevin said as he rounded up the materials.

Edward set to work by grinding up the few sclerotia, extracting the pulp with distilled water, and precipitating a tiny amount of white material with the weak acid. With the help of the filter paper, he isolated a few grains of the white precipitate. Kevin watched the procedure with a mixture of disbelief and wonder.

"Don't tell me you are just going to eat that?" Kevin said with growing alarm.

"Oh, come on," Edward said. "I'm not stupid."

"You could have fooled me," Kevin said.

"Listen," Edward said. "I'm interested in a hallucinogenic effect. If this stuff is going to have such an effect, it will have it at a minuscule dose. I'm talking about less than a microgram."

Edward took a speck of the precipitate on the end of a spatula and introduced it into a liter of distilled water in a volumetric flask. He shook it vigorously.

"We could screw around with this stuff for six months and still not know if it can cause hallucinations," Edward said. "Ultimately we'd need a human cerebrum. Mine is available right at the moment. When it comes to science, I'm a man of action."

"What about possible kidney toxicity?" Kevin asked.

Edward made an expression of exasperated disbelief. "At this dosage? Hell, no! We're well below by a factor of ten the toxicity range of botulinum toxin, the most toxic substance known to man. Besides, not only are we in the microgram range with this unknown, but it's got to be a soup of substances, so the concentration of any one of them is that much lower."

Edward asked Kevin to hand him the milliliter pipette. Kevin did so reluctantly.

"Are you sure you don't want to join?" Edward asked. "You could be missing out on making an interesting scientific discovery." He laughed as he filled the slender pipette.

"Thanks, but no thanks," Kevin said. "I have a comfortable understanding with my renal tubular cells that we won't abuse each other."

"To your health," Edward said as he held aloft the pipette for a moment before depositing a single milliliter on the curl of his tongue. He took a mouthful of water, swished it around, and swallowed.

"Well?" Kevin questioned nervously after a moment of silence.

"A tiny, tiny bit bitter," Edward said. He opened and closed his mouth a few times to enhance the taste.

"Anything else?" Kevin asked.

"I'm just beginning to feel mildly dizzy," Edward said.

"Hell, you were dizzy before you started," Kevin said.

"I admit this little experiment lacks scientific controls," Edward said with a chuckle. "Anything I feel could be a placebo effect."

"I really shouldn't be a part of this," Kevin said. "I'm going to have to insist that you get a urinalysis and a BUN this afternoon."

"Ohooo weee," Edward said. "Something is happening!"

"Oh, God!" Kevin said. "What?"

"I'm seeing a flood of colors that are moving around in amoeboid shapes like some kind of kaleidoscope."

"Oh, great!" Kevin said. He stared into Edward's face, which had assumed a trancelike appearance.

"Now I'm hearing some sounds like a synthesizer. Also my mouth is a bit dry. And now something else: I feel paresthesias on my arms, as if I'm being bitten or lightly pinched. It's weird."

"Should I call somebody?" Kevin demanded.

To Kevin's surprise, Edward reached out and grabbed him around the upper arms. Edward held him with unexpected strength.

"It feels like the room is moving," Edward said. "And there's a mild choking sensation."

"I'd better call for help," Kevin said. His own pulse was racing. He eyed the phone, but Edward strengthened his grip.

"It's OK," Edward said. "The colors are receding. It's passing." Edward closed his eyes, but otherwise he didn't move. He still had hold of Kevin.

Eventually Edward opened his eyes and sighed. "Wow!" he said. Only then did he become aware he was gripping Kevin's arms. He let go, took a breath, and smoothed his jacket. "I think we got our answer," he said.

"This was idiotic!" Kevin snapped. "Your little antic terrified me. I was just about to call emergency."

"Calm down," Edward said. "It wasn't that bad. Don't get all bent out of shape over a sixty-second psychedelic reaction."

Kevin pointed up at the clock. "It wasn't sixty seconds," he said. "It was more like twenty minutes."

Edward glanced up at the clock's face. "Isn't that curious," he said. "Even my sense of time was distorted."

"Do you generally feel OK?" Kevin asked.

"Fine!" Edward insisted. "In fact I feel better than fine. I feel . . ." He hesitated while he tried to put into words his inner sensations. "I feel energized, like I'd just had a rest. And also clairvoyant, like my mind is particularly sharp. I might even feel a touch euphoric, but that could be because of this positive result: we've just ascertained that this new fungus produces a hallucinogenic substance."

"Let's not be so lax with the term 'we,' " Kevin said. "You ascertained it, not me. I refuse to take any credit for this craziness."

"I wonder if the alkaloids are the same as *Claviceps?*" Edward asked. "I don't seem to have even the slightest signs of reduced peripheral vascular circulation, a frequent sign of ergotism."

"At least promise me you'll get a urinalysis and a BUN or creatinine this afternoon," Kevin said. "Even if you're not worried, I still am."

"If it will make you sleep tonight I'll do it," Edward said. "Meanwhile I want some more of these sclerotia. Is that possible?"

"It's possible now that I have figured out the medium this fungus needs to grow, but I can't promise you a lot of sclerotia. It's not always easy to get the fungus to produce them."

"Well, do your best," Edward said. "Remember, we'll probably get a nice little paper out of this."

As Edward hurried across campus to catch the shuttle bus to the medical area, he was thrilled with the results. He couldn't wait to tell Kim that the poison theory involving the Salem witchcraft episode was alive and well.

As excited as Kim was about seeing the progress at the compound, she was even more curious as to why her father had called her. Confident she was early enough to catch him before he left for his Boston office, Kim detoured to Marblehead.

Entering the house, she went directly to the kitchen. As she expected, she found John lingering over his coffee and his clutch of morning papers. He was a big man who'd reportedly been quite an athlete during his days at Harvard. His broad face was crowned with a full head of hair that had once been as dark and lustrous as Kim's. Over the years it had grayed in a comely fashion, giving him a stereotypically paternal appearance.

"Good morning Kimmy," John said without taking his attention away from his paper.

Kim helped herself to the espresso machine and foamed some milk for a cappuccino.

"How's that car of yours running?" John asked. The paper crinkled loudly as he turned the page. "I hope you are having it regularly serviced like I advised."

Kim didn't answer. She was accustomed to her father treating her as if she were still a little girl, and she mildly resented it. He was forever giving her instructions on how to order her life. The older she got the more she thought he shouldn't be giving anyone advice, especially considering what he'd done to his own life and marriage.

"I heard you called my apartment last night," Kim said. She sat on a window seat beneath a bay window overlooking the ocean.

John lowered his paper.

"I did indeed," he said. "Joyce mentioned that you'd become interested in Elizabeth Stewart and had been asking questions about her. It surprised me. I called you to ask why you wanted to upset your mother like that."

"I wasn't trying to upset her," Kim said. "I've become interested in Elizabeth and I just wanted to know some basic facts. Like whether or not Elizabeth truly had been hanged for witchcraft or whether it was just a rumor."

"She was indeed hanged," John said. "I can assure you of that. I can also assure you that the family made a good deal of effort to suppress it. Under the circumstances I think it is best for you to leave it alone."

"But why does it warrant such secrecy after three hundred years?" Kim asked. "It doesn't make sense."

"It doesn't matter if it makes sense to you or not," John said. "It was a humiliation then and it is today."

"Do you mean to tell me that it bothers you, Father?" Kim asked. "Does it humiliate you?"

"Well, no, not particularly," John admitted. "It's your mother. It bothers her, so it should not be a subject for your amusement. We shouldn't add to her burdens."

Kim bit her tongue. It was hard not to say something disparaging to her father under the circumstances. Instead she admitted that not only had she become interested in Elizabeth but that she'd developed a sympathy for her.

"What on earth for?" John questioned irritably.

"For one thing I found her portrait stuck away in the back of Grandfather's wine cellar," Kim said. "Looking at it emphasized that she'd been a real person. She even had the same eye color as I do. Then I remembered what had happened to her. She certainly didn't deserve to be hanged. It's hard not to be sympathetic."

"I was aware of the painting," John said. "What were you doing in the wine cellar?"

"Nothing in particular," Kim said. "Just taking a look around. It seemed like such a coincidence to come across Elizabeth's portrait, because I'd recently been doing some reading about the Salem witch trials. And what I'd learned just added to my feelings of sympathy. Within a short time of the tragedy there was an outpouring of regret and repentance. Even back then it had become evident innocent people had been killed."

"Not everyone was innocent," John said.

"Mother intimated the same thing," Kim said. "What could Elizabeth have done for you to suggest she wasn't innocent?"

"Now you are pushing me," John said. "I don't know specifics, but I'd been told by my father it had something to do with the occult."

"Like what?" Kim persisted.

"I just told you I don't know, young lady," John snapped angrily. "You've asked enough questions."

Now go to your room, Kim added silently to herself. She wondered if her father would ever recognize that she'd become an adult and treat her like one.

"Kimmy, listen to me," John said in a more conciliatory and paternalistic tone. "For your own good don't dig up the past in this instance. It's only going to cause trouble."

"With all due respect, Father," Kim said, "could you explain to me how it could possibly affect my welfare?"

John stammered.

"Let me tell you what I think," Kim said with uncharacteristic assertiveness. "I believe that Elizabeth's involvement could have been a humiliation back at the time the event occurred. I also can believe it might have been considered bad for business since her husband, Ronald, started Maritime Limited, which has supported generation after generation of Stewarts, ourselves included. But the fact that the concern over Elizabeth's involvement has persisted is absurd and a disgrace to her memory. After all, she is our ancestor; if it hadn't been for her, none of us would even be here. That fact alone makes me surprised that no one has questioned over the years this ridiculous knee-jerk reaction."

"If you can't understand it from your own selfish perspective," John said irritably, "then at least think of your mother. The affair humiliates Joyce, and it doesn't matter why. It just does. So if you need some motivation to leave Elizabeth's legacy be, then there it is. Don't rub your mother's nose in it."

Kim lifted her now cool cappuccino to her lips and took a drink. She gave up with her father. Trying to have a conversation with him had never been fruitful. It only worked when the conversation was one-sided: when he told her what to do and how to do it. It was as if he mistook the role of a father to be an instructor.

"Mother also tells me you have embarked on a project at the compound," John said, assuming that Kim's silence meant she'd become reasonable about the Elizabeth issue and accepted his advice. "What exactly are you doing?"

Kim told him about her decision to renovate the old house and live in it. While she talked, John went back to glancing at his papers. When she'd finished his only question concerned the castle and his father's belongings.

"We're not going to do anything to the castle," Kim said. "Not until Brian comes home."

"Good," John said as he advanced the page of his *Wall Street Journal*.

"Speaking of Mother, where is she?" Kim asked.

"Upstairs," John said. "She's not feeling well and is not seeing anyone."

A few minutes later Kim left the house with a sad, anxious feeling that was a complicated mixture of pity, anger, and revulsion. As she climbed into her car she told herself that she hated her parents' marriage. As she started the engine she pledged to herself that she would never allow herself to be ensnared in such a situation.

Kim backed out of the driveway and headed toward Salem. As she drove she reminded herself that despite her revulsion toward her parents' relationship, she was at some risk to re-create a similar situation. That was part of the reason why she'd reacted so strongly to Kinnard's sporting trips when he'd had plans to be with her.

Kim suddenly smiled. Her gloomy thoughts were immediately overpowered by the memory of the flowers that had been arriving from Edward on a daily basis. In one way they embarrassed her; in another they were a testament to Edward's attentiveness and caring. One thing she felt quite confident about: Edward would not be a womanizer. In her mind a womanizer had to be more assertive and more competitive, like her father, or, for that matter, like Kinnard.

As frustrating as her conversation with her father had been, it had the opposite effect of what he'd intended: it only encouraged her interest in Elizabeth Stewart. Consequently, as Kim was driving through downtown Salem, she detoured to the Museum Place Mall.

Leaving her vehicle in the car park, Kim walked to the Peabody-Essex Institute, a cultural and historical association housed in a group of old refurbished buildings in the center of town. Among other functions it served as a repository for documents about Salem and the environs, including the witchcraft trials.

A receptionist in the foyer collected a fee from Kim and directed her to the library, which was reached by a few stairs directly across from the reception desk. Kim mounted the steps and passed through a heavy, windowed door. The library was housed in an early nineteenth-century building with high ceilings, decorative cornices, and dark wood molding. The main room had marble fireplaces and chandeliers in addition to darkly stained oak tables and captain's chairs. A typical library hush and a smell of old books prevailed.

A friendly and helpful librarian by the name of Grace Meehan immediately came to Kim's aid. She was an elderly woman with gray hair and a kind face. In response to a general question from Kim, she showed her how to find all sorts of papers and documents associated with the Salem witch trials including accusations, complaints, arrest warrants, depositions, hearing testimony, court records of the preliminary hearings, mittimi, and execution warrants. They were all carefully catalogued in one of the library's old-fashioned card catalogues.

Kim was surprised and encouraged by the amount of material that was so easily available. It was no wonder there were so many books on the Salem witch trials. The institute was a researcher's paradise.

As soon as the librarian left Kim on her own, Kim attacked the card catalogue. With a good deal of excitement she looked up Elizabeth Stewart. She was confident she'd be mentioned in some form or fashion. But Kim was soon disappointed. There was no Elizabeth Stewart. There were no Stewarts at all.

Returning to the librarian's desk, Kim asked the woman directly about Elizabeth Stewart.

"The name's not familiar," Grace said. "Do you know how she was connected to the trials?"

"I was told she was one of the accused," Kim said. "I believe she was hanged."

"She couldn't have been," Grace said without hesitation. "I consider myself an expert on the extant documents concerning the trials. I've never come across the name Elizabeth Stewart even as a witness, much less one of the twenty victims. Who told you she was accused?"

"It's a rather long story," Kim said evasively.

"Well, it certainly wasn't true," Grace said. "There's been too much research by too many people for one of the victims to have been missed."

"I see," Kim said. She didn't argue. Instead she thanked the woman and returned to the card-catalogue area.

Giving up on the documents associated with the trials, Kim turned her attention to another important resource of the institute: genealogical information on families from Essex County.

This time Kim found a wealth of information on the Stewarts. In fact they took up most of an entire drawer of the genealogical card catalogue. As Kim went through the material it became obvious that there were two main Stewart clans, hers and another whose history wasn't quite so old.

After a half hour Kim found a brief reference to Elizabeth Stewart. She was born on May 4, 1665, the daughter of James and Elisha Flanagan, and died on July 19, 1692, the wife of Ronald Stewart. No cause of death was given. A quick subtraction told Kim that Elizabeth died at age twenty-seven!

Kim raised her head and stared with unseeing eyes out the window. She could feel tiny gooseflesh rise up on the nape of her neck. Kim was twenty-seven, and her birthday was in May. It wasn't the fourth but rather the sixth, so it was close to Elizabeth's. Remembering their physical similarities from the portrait and considering the fact that she was planning on moving into the same house Elizabeth occupied, Kim began to wonder if there were just too many coincidences. Was this all trying to tell her something?

"Excuse me," Grace Meehan said, interrupting Kim's reverie. "Here's a list I copied for you of the people who were hanged for witchcraft. There's also the date of their execution, including the day of the week, their town of residence, their church affiliation if there was one, and their age. As you can see, it is very complete—and there is no Elizabeth Stewart."

Kim thanked the woman again and took the paper. After the woman left, Elizabeth dutifully glanced at it and was about to put it aside when she noted the date of Tuesday, July 19, 1692. Five people had been hanged that day. Looking back at Elizabeth's day of death, she noticed it was the same. Kim understood that just because the dates were the same, it didn't prove Elizabeth was hanged. But even if it were only circumstantial, it was at least suggestive.

Then Kim realized something else. Thinking back to the previous Tuesday, she remembered it had been July 19. Looking again at the paper Grace Meehan had given her, she discovered that the daily calendar was the same in 1692 as it was in 1994. Was this yet another coincidence whose meaning Kim had to ponder?

Going back to the genealogical information, Kim got a book that summarized the early history of her family. In it she looked up Ronald Stewart and quickly learned that Elizabeth had not been Ronald's first wife. Ronald had married Hannah Hutchinson in 1677, with whom he'd had a daughter, Joanna, born 1678. But then Hannah died in January 1679, with no cause of death listed. Ronald at age thirty-nine then married Elizabeth Flanagan in 1682 with whom he had a daughter Sarah, born 1682, and sons, Jonathan, born 1683, and Daniel, born 1689. Finally Ronald married Elizabeth's younger sister, Rebecca Flanagan, in 1692, with whom he had a daughter named Rachel, born in 1693.

Kim lowered the book and again stared off into space while she tried to sort out her thoughts. Mild alarm bells were going off in her head in relation to Ronald's character. Looking back at the genealogy book, she reviewed the fact that three years after Hannah died, Ronald married Elizabeth. Then after Elizabeth died, he married her sister the same year!

Kim felt uneasy. Knowing her own father's amorous proclivities, she thought it possible that Ronald could have suffered a similar flaw and indulged it with far more disastrous consequences. It occurred to her that Ronald could have been having an affair with Elizabeth while married to Hannah, and an affair with Rebecca while married to Elizabeth. After all, Elizabeth certainly died under unusual circumstances. Kim wondered if Hannah did as well.

Kim shook her head and silently laughed at herself. She told herself that she must have watched too many soap operas, since her imagination was taking unwarranted, melodramatic leaps.

After spending a few more minutes going over the Stewart family tree, Kim learned two more facts. First she confirmed she was related to Ronald and Elizabeth through their son Jonathan. Second she learned that the name "Elizabeth" never reappeared in the family's three-hundred-year history. With so many generations, such a situation couldn't have happened by chance. Kim marveled at the opprobrium Elizabeth had brought on herself, and Kim's curiosity waxed concerning what Elizabeth could possibly have done to warrant it.

Finally, with her superficial genealogical inquiry, Kim descended the steps of the Peabody-Essex Institute with the idea of retrieving her car and heading out to the compound. But at the foot of the steps she hesitated. The passing question that she'd entertained about Ronald's character and the possibility of foul play on his part gave her another idea. Returning inside the institute, she asked directions for the Essex County Courthouse.

The building was on Federal Street, not far from the Witch House. It was a severe Greek Revival structure with a stark pediment and massive Doric columns. Kim entered and asked to be directed to court records.

Kim had no idea whether she would find anything at all. She didn't even know if court records were saved from so long ago, nor did she know if they did exist whether they were available to the public. Nonetheless she presented herself at the appropriate counter and asked to look at any court records of Ronald

Stewart. She added that she was interested in the Ronald Stewart who'd been born in 1653.

The clerk was a sleepy-looking woman of indeterminate age. If she was surprised by Kim's request she didn't show it. Her response was to punch it up on a computer terminal. After glancing at the screen for a moment, she left the room. She'd not said a word. Kim guessed that there had been so many people researching the Salem witch trials that the town's civil servants were jaded about inquiries from that era.

Kim shifted her weight and checked her watch. It was already ten-thirty, and she'd not even been to the compound yet.

The woman reappeared with a manila pocket folder. She handed it to Kim. "You can't take this out of the room," she said. She pointed to some Formica tables and molded plastic chairs along the back wall. "You can sit over there if you like."

Kim took the folder over to an empty chair. She sat down and slipped out the contents. There was a lot of material. All of it was written in reasonably legible longhand.

At first Kim thought that the file contained only documents associated with civil suits Ronald had filed with the court for debts owed to him. But then she began to find more interesting things, like reference to a contested will involving Ronald.

Kim carefully read the document. It was a ruling in Ronald's favor involving a will contested by a Jacob Cheever. Reading on, Kim discovered that Jacob had been a child of Hannah's from a previous marriage and that Hannah had been significantly older than Ronald. Jacob had testified that Ronald had duped his mother into changing her will, thereby depriving him of his rightful inheritance. Apparently the justices disagreed. The result had been that Ronald inherited several thousand pounds, a sizable fortune in those days.

Kim marveled that life in the late seventeenth century hadn't been as different as she'd imagined. She'd been under the delusion that at least legally it had been simpler. Reading about the contested will suggested she was wrong. It also made her think again about Ronald's character.

The next document was even more curious. It was a contract dated February 11, 1681, between Ronald Stewart and Elizabeth Flanagan. It had been drawn up and signed prior to their marriage, like a contemporary premarital agreement. But it wasn't about money or property per se. The contract merely gave Elizabeth the right to own property and enter into contracts in her own name after the marriage.

Kim read the whole document. Toward the end Ronald himself had written an explanation. Kim recognized the handwriting as the particularly graceful script she'd seen on many of the bills of lading in the castle. Ronald wrote: "It is my intention that if actions pursuant to my mercantile endeavor require my prolonged absence from Salem Town and Maritime, Ltd, that my betrothed, Elizabeth Flanagan, may justly and legally administer our joint affairs."

After finishing the document, Kim went back to the beginning and reread it to make sure she understood it. It amazed her. The fact that such a document was necessary in order for Elizabeth to sign contracts reminded her that the role of women had been quite different in Puritan times. Their legal rights were limited. It was the same message Kim had gotten from the letter Elizabeth's father had written to Ronald concerning Elizabeth's hand in marriage.

Laying the premarital agreement aside, Kim went back to the remaining papers in Ronald Stewart's folder. After a handful of additional debtor suits, Kim came across a truly interesting document. It was a petition by Ronald Stewart requesting a Writ of Replevin. It was dated Tuesday, July 26, 1692, a week after Elizabeth's death.

Kim had no idea what Replevin meant, but she quickly got an idea. Ronald wrote: "I humbly beg the court in God's name to return to my possession forthwith the conclusive evidence seized from my property by Sheriff George Corwin and used against my beloved wife, Elizabeth, during her trial for witchcraft by the Court of Oyer and Terminer on 20 June 1692."

Attached to the back of the petition was an August 3, 1692, ruling by Magistrate John Hathorne denying the petition. In his denial the magistrate said: "The Court advises said petitioner, Ronald Stewart, likewise to petition his excellency the Governor of the Commonwealth for the aforementioned evidence since, by executive order, custody of said evidence has been transferred from Essex to Suffolk County."

In one sense Kim was pleased. She'd found indirect documentary evidence of Elizabeth's ordeal: she'd been tried and evidently convicted. At the same time Kim felt frustrated that the nature of the "conclusive evidence" was never mentioned. She reread both the petition and the ruling in hopes she'd missed it. But she hadn't. The evidence was not described.

For a few minutes Kim sat at the table and tried to imagine what the evidence could have been. The only thing she could think of was something to do with the occult, and that was because of her father's vague statement. Then she got an idea. Glancing back at the petition, she wrote down the date of the trial. With the date in hand she returned to the counter and got the clerk's attention.

"I'd like to see the records of the Court of Oyer and Terminer for June 20, 1692."

The clerk literally laughed in Kim's face. Then she repeated the request and laughed again. Confused, Kim asked what was so funny.

"You're asking for something just about every Tom, Dick, and Harry would want," the clerk said. She sounded as if she'd just come from the backcountry of Maine. "Trouble is, no such records exist. Wish they did, but they don't. There's no record of that Court of Oyer and Terminer for all the witch trials. All there is is some scattered testimony and depositions, but the court records themselves plumb disappeared."

"How unfortunate," Kim said. "Maybe you could tell me something else. Do you happen to know what 'conclusive evidence' means?"

"I ain't no lawyer," the clerk said. "But hold your horses. Let me ask."

The clerk disappeared into an office. Seconds later she reemerged with a heavyset woman in tow. The second woman had oversized glasses balanced on a short, wide nose.

"You're interested in a definition of 'conclusive evidence,' " the woman said. Kim nodded.

"It's pretty much self-explanatory," the woman said. "It means evidence that is incontrovertible. In other words it can't be questioned, or there is only one possible interpretation that can be drawn from it."

"That's what I thought," Kim said. She thanked the two women and went back to her material. Using a copy machine in the corner, she made a copy of the petition for a Writ of Replevin and the ruling. Then she returned the documents to their envelope and handed the envelope back to the clerk.

Finally Kim drove out to the compound. She felt a little guilty, since she'd told Mark Stevens she'd be there in the morning and already it was approaching noon. As she rounded the last bend in the road leading from the gate and broke free from the trees, she could see a handful of trucks and vans parked near the cottage. There was also a large backhoe and mounds of fresh earth. But Kim didn't see any people, not even on the backhoe.

Kim parked and got out of her car. The noontime heat and dust were oppressive, and the smell of the freshly turned earth was pungent. Kim closed the car door, and, shielding her face from the sun, she followed with her eyes the line of the trench that ran across the field toward the castle. At that moment the door to the house opened and George Harris stepped out. Sweat lined his forehead.

"Glad you could make it," George said. "I've been trying to call you."

"Is something wrong?" Kim asked.

"Sorta," George said evasively. "Maybe I'd better show you."

George motioned for Kim to follow him toward where the backhoe was parked.

"We had to stop work," George said.

"Why?" Kim asked.

George didn't answer. Instead he encouraged Kim to come over to the trench.

Hesitant to step too close to the edge for fear of its giving way, Kim stretched forward and looked in. She was impressed by the depth, which she estimated to be more than eight feet. Roots hung out of the sheer walls like miniature brooms. George directed her attention to the end, where the trench stopped abruptly fifty feet short of the cottage. Near the bottom Kim could see the damaged end of a wooden box protruding from the wall.

"That's why we had to stop," George said.

"What is it?" Kim asked.

"I'm afraid it's a coffin," George said.

"Good grief," Kim said.

"We found a headstone as well," George said. "It's an oldie." He motioned for

Kim to come around the end of the trench. On the opposite side of the mound of excavated earth was a dirty white marble slab lying flat in the grass.

"It hadn't been set upright," George said. "It had been laid flat and eventually covered with earth." George bent down and wiped away the dried dirt on its face.

Kim took an involuntary gasp of air. "My God, it's Elizabeth!" she managed. She shook her head. There were too many coincidences.

"She a relative?" George asked.

"She is," Kim said. She examined the headstone. It was similar in design to Ronald's, and gave only the specifics, namely Elizabeth's birthdate and date of her death.

"Did you have any idea her grave would be here?" George asked. His tone wasn't accusatory, just curious.

"Not in the slightest," Kim said. "I only found out recently that she'd not been buried in the family plot."

"What do you want us to do?" George said. "You're supposed to have a permit to disturb a grave."

"Can't you just go around it and leave it be?" Kim asked.

"I suppose," George said. "We could just widen the trench along here. Should we be on the lookout for any others?"

"I don't think so," Kim said. "Elizabeth was a special case."

"I hope you don't mind me saying this," George said. "But you look kinda pale. Are you okay?"

"Thank you," Kim said. "I'm fine. Just a bit shocked. I guess I'm feeling a little superstitious about finding this woman's grave."

"So are we," George said. "Especially my backhoe operator. Let me go get him out here. We got to get these utilities in before we pour the basement."

George disappeared inside the house. Kim ventured back to the edge of the trench and peered down at the exposed corner of Elizabeth's coffin. The wood was in surprisingly good shape for being buried for over three hundred years. It didn't even appear rotten where the backhoe had damaged it.

Kim had no idea what to make of this unexpected discovery. First the portrait, now the grave. It was getting harder to dismiss these as fortuitous findings.

The sound of an approaching auto caught Kim's attention. Shielding her eyes once again from the noonday sun, she watched a familiar-looking car kicking up a plume of dust as it followed the dirt road across the field. She couldn't mentally place the vehicle until it pulled up next to her. Then she realized why it had been familiar. It was Kinnard's.

With some anxiety Kim walked over to the vehicle and leaned in through the passenger-side window.

"This is a surprise," Kim said. "What on earth are you doing out of the hospital?"

Kinnard laughed. "They let me out of my cage once in a while."

"What are you doing in Salem?" Kim asked. "How did you know I was here?"

"Marsha told me," Kinnard said. "I ran into her in the SICU this morning. I told her I was coming to Salem to look for an apartment since I'm rotating through Salem Hospital for August and September. There's no way I'm going to live in the hospital for two months. You do remember me telling you about my Salem Hospital rotation."

"I guess I forgot," Kim said.

"I told you several months ago," Kinnard said.

"If you say so," Kim said. She had no intention of getting into an argument. She already felt uncomfortable enough.

"You're looking good," Kinnard said. "I suppose dating Dr. Edward Armstrong agrees with you."

"How do you know whom I'm dating?" Kim asked.

"Hospital gossip," Kinnard said. "Since you've chosen a scientific celebrity, it gets around. The irony is that I know the man. I worked in his lab the year I took off to do research after my second year of medical school."

Kim could feel herself blush. She would have preferred not to show any reaction, but she couldn't help it. Kinnard was obviously trying to upset her, and as usual he was doing a good job.

"Edward is a smart man scientifically," Kinnard said, "but I'm afraid he's a little nerdy, even weird. Well . . . maybe that's unfair. Maybe I should just say eccentric."

"I find him attentive and considerate," Kim said.

"I can imagine," Kinnard said, rolling his eyes. "I heard about the daily flowers. Personally I think that's absurd. A guy has to be totally unsure of himself to go to that kind of extreme."

Kim turned a bright red. Marsha had to have told Kinnard about the flowers. Between her mother and her roommate she wondered if she had any secrets.

"At least Edward Armstrong won't irritate you by going skiing," Kinnard said. "His coordination is such that a flight of stairs can be a challenge."

"I think you are being juvenile," Kim said frostily when she found her voice. "Frankly, it doesn't suit you. I'd thought you were more mature."

"It doesn't matter." Kinnard laughed cynically. "I've gone on, as they say, to greener pastures. I'm enjoying a new burgeoning relationship myself."

"I'm happy for you," Kim said sarcastically.

Kinnard bent down so he could see out through the windshield as the backhoe started up. "Marsha told me you were fixing this place up," he said. "Is old Doc Armstrong going to move in with you?"

Kim started to deny the possibility, but caught herself. Instead she said, "We're thinking about it. We haven't decided yet."

"Enjoy yourself one way or the other," Kinnard said with equal sarcasm. "Have a nice life."

Kinnard threw his car into reverse, shot backwards, and skidded to a stop.

Then he put the engine in drive and tromped on the accelerator. With a shower of dirt, small pebbles, and dust he shot across the field and disappeared through the trees.

At first Kim concentrated on shielding herself from flying stones. Once the danger was past, she watched Kinnard's car until she could no longer see it. Even though she'd known almost from the moment he'd arrived that his goal had been to provoke her, she'd not been able to prevent it. For a moment she felt emotionally frazzled. It wasn't until she walked back over to the trench that was now being widened and saw Elizabeth's coffin that she began to calm down. Comparing her troubles with Elizabeth's at the same age made hers seem trivial.

After pulling herself together emotionally, Kim set to work. The afternoon passed quickly. Most of her time was spent in Mark Stevens' office going over details of the kitchen and bathroom design. For Kim it was a supreme pleasure. It was the first time in her life that she was creating a living environment for herself. It made her wonder how she had allowed her career goals to be so easily circumvented.

By seven-thirty Mark Stevens and George Harris were both exhausted, but Kim had gotten a second wind. The men had to tell Kim their eyes were blurry before Kim admitted she had to get back to the city. As they walked her out to her car, they thanked her for coming and promised her things would move quickly.

Driving into Cambridge, Kim didn't even attempt to look for a parking place on the street. Instead she drove directly into the Charles' parking garage and walked over to the Harvest Bar. It was filled to overflowing with a Friday-night crowd, most of whom had been there through happy hour.

Kim looked for Edward but didn't immediately see him. She had to worm her way through the crowd standing five deep around the bar. Finally she found him nursing a glass of chardonnay at a table behind the bar. As soon as he saw her, his face lit up and he leaped to his feet to pull out her chair.

As Edward pushed the chair in under her, Kim remarked to herself that Kinnard would not have made the effort.

"You look like you could use a glass of white wine," Edward said.

Kim nodded. She could tell instantly that Edward was either excited or self-conscious. His stutter was more apparent than usual. She watched while he caught the waitress's attention and gave the order for two glasses of wine. Then he looked at her.

"Did you have a good day?" he asked.

"It was busy," Kim said. "What about yours?"

"It was a great day!" Edward said excitedly. "I've got some good news. The dirt samples from Elizabeth's food bins grew out a mold with hallucinogenic effects. I think we have solved the question of what at least kicked off the Salem witch trials. The only thing we don't know is whether it was ergotism or something entirely new."

Edward went on to tell Kim everything that had happened at Kevin Scranton's office.

Kim's response was concerned disbelief. "You took a drug without knowing what it was?" she asked. "Wasn't that dangerous?"

"You sound like Kevin." Edward laughed. "I'm surrounded by ersatz parents. No, it wasn't dangerous. It was too small a dose to be dangerous. But, being small, it certainly indicated the hallucinogenic power of this new fungus."

"It sounds foolhardy to me," Kim persisted.

"It wasn't," Edward said. "I even had a urinalysis and a creatinine blood test this afternoon for Kevin's sake. They were both normal. I'm fine. Believe me. In fact, I'm better than fine. I'm ecstatic. At first I was hoping this new fungus would make the same mix of alkaloids as *Claviceps* so it would prove ergotism was the culprit. Now I'm hoping it makes its own alkaloids."

"What are alkaloids?" Kim asked. "It's a familiar term but I couldn't define it to save my life."

"Alkaloids are a large group of nitrogen-containing compounds found in plants," Edward said. "They're familiar to you because many of them are common, like caffeine, morphine, and nicotine. As you can guess, most are pharmacologically active."

"Why are you getting so excited about finding some new ones if they are so common?" Kim asked.

"Because I've already proven whatever alkaloid is in this new fungus, it's psychotropically active," Edward said. "Finding a new hallucinogenic drug can open up all sorts of doors to the understanding of brain function. Invariably they resemble and mimic the brain's own neurotransmitters."

"When will you know if you've found new alkaloids?" Kim asked.

"Soon," Edward said. "Now tell me about your day."

Kim took a breath. Then she related to Edward everything that had happened to her, in chronological order, starting with her talk with her father and ending with the completion of the design for the new kitchen and baths for the cottage.

"Wow!" Edward said. "You did have a busy day. I'm astounded by the discovery of Elizabeth's grave. And you said the coffin was in good shape?"

"What I could see of it," Kim said. "It was buried very deep, probably around eight feet down. Its end was sticking into the trench. It had been damaged by the backhoe."

"Did finding the grave upset you?" Edward asked.

"In a way," Kim said with a short mirthless laugh. "Thinking about finding it so soon after finding the portrait makes me feel weird. It gave me that feeling again that Elizabeth is trying to communicate with me."

"Uh-oh," Edward said. "Sounds like you are having another attack of superstition."

Kim laughed despite her seriousness.

"Tell me something," Edward said teasingly. "Are you afraid of black cats crossing your path, or walking under ladders, or using the number thirteen?"

Kim hesitated. She was mildly superstitious, but she'd never given it much thought.

"So you *are* superstitious!" Edward said. "Now think about this! Back in the seventeenth century you could have been considered a witch since such beliefs involve the occult."

"All right, smarty pants," Kim said. "So maybe I'm a little superstitious. But there seem to be too many coincidences involving Elizabeth. I also found out today that the calendar in 1692 is the same as this year's, 1994. I also found out Elizabeth died at my age. And as if that's not enough, our birthdays are only two days apart, so we have the same astrological sign."

"What do you want me to say?" Edward asked.

"Can you explain all these coincidences?" Kim asked.

"Of course," Edward said. "It's pure chance. It's like the old cliché that if you have enough monkeys and enough typewriters, you can produce *Hamlet*."

"Oh, I give up," Kim said with a chuckle. She took a sip of her wine.

"I'm sorry," Edward said with a shrug. "I'm a scientist."

"Let me tell you something else I learned today," Kim said. "Things were not so simple back then. Ronald was married three times. His first wife died, willing him a sizable fortune which was contested unsuccessfully by his wife's child by a previous marriage. He then married Elizabeth within a couple of years. After Elizabeth died he married her sister in the same year."

"So?" Edward said.

"Doesn't that sound a little fishy to you?" Kim asked.

"No," Edward said. "Remember life was harsh back in those days. Ronald had children to raise. Also, marrying within in-laws was not unusual."

"Well, I'm not so sure," Kim said. "It leaves a lot of questions in my mind."

The waitress appeared and interrupted their conversation to tell them their table was ready. Kim was pleasantly surprised. She didn't know they were planning to eat at the Harvest. She was famished.

They followed the waitress out onto the terrace and were seated beneath trees filled with tiny white lights. It was a perfect temperature after having cooled down considerably from the day. There was no wind, so the candle on the table burned languidly.

While they were waiting for their food, Kim showed Edward the copy she'd made of Ronald's petition. Edward read it with great interest. When he was finished he congratulated Kim on her detective work, saying that she'd succeeded in proving Elizabeth had indeed been caught up in the witchcraft affair. Kim told him about her father's comment concerning Elizabeth's possible association with the occult.

"Which is what I suggested," Edward reminded her.

"So would you guess that the conclusive evidence had something to do with the occult?"

"I don't think there is any question," Edward said.

"That's what I thought," Kim said. "But do you have any specific ideas?"

"I don't know enough about witchcraft to be creative," Edward said.

"What about a book?" Kim questioned. "Or something she wrote?"

"Sounds good," Edward said. "I suppose it could have been something she drew as well. Or at least some kind of image."

"What about a doll?" Kim suggested.

"Good idea," Edward said. Then he paused. "I know what it must have been!"

"What?" Kim asked eagerly.

"Her broom!" Edward said. Then he laughed.

"Come on," Kim said, but she was smiling herself. "I'm being serious."

Edward apologized. He then went on to explain the background of the witch's broom, and how it had originated in medieval times with a stick that had been coated with an ointment concocted with hallucinogenic drugs. He told her that in satanic rituals it had been used to cause psychedelic experiences when placed against intimate mucous membranes.

"I've heard enough," Kim said. "I get the idea."

Their food arrived. They didn't talk until the waiter had left. Edward was the first to speak. "The problem is that the evidence could have been any one of a number of things, and there's no way of knowing specifically unless you found a description. What about looking in the court records themselves?"

"I thought of that," Kim said. "But I was told that none of the records of the special Court of Oyer and Terminer remain."

"Too bad," Edward said. "I guess that throws you back into that hopeless pile of papers in the castle."

"Yeah," Kim said without enthusiasm. "Plus there's no guarantee it would be there."

While they ate their meal the conversation shifted to more mundane issues. It wasn't until they were finishing their dessert that Edward returned to the issue of Elizabeth's grave.

"What was the state of preservation of Elizabeth's body?" he asked.

"I never saw the body," Kim said. She was shocked at such a question. "The coffin wasn't opened. The backhoe just hit the end and jarred it a little."

"Maybe we should open it," Edward said. "I'd love to get a sample—if there is anything recognizable to sample. If we could find some residue of whatever alkaloid this new fungus produces, we'd have definitive proof that the devil in Salem was a fungus."

"I can't believe you'd even suggest such a thing," Kim said. "The last thing I want to do is disturb Elizabeth's body."

"Here we go being superstitious again," Edward said. "You understand that such a position is akin to being against autopsies."

"This is different," Kim said. "She's already been buried."

"People are exhumed all the time," Edward said.

"I suppose you are right," Kim said reluctantly.

"Maybe I should take a ride up there with you tomorrow," Edward said. "We could both take a look."

"You have to have a permit to exhume a body," Kim said.

"The backhoe already did most of the job," Edward said. "Let's take a look and decide tomorrow."

The bill came and Edward paid it. Kim thanked him and told him that the next dinner was on her. Edward said they could argue about it.

Outside the restaurant there was an awkward moment. Edward asked her over to his apartment, but Kim demurred. She reminded him that she'd felt uncomfortable that morning. Ultimately they resolved the issue, at least temporarily, by agreeing to go to Edward's to discuss it.

Later, while sitting on Edward's couch, Kim asked him if he remembered a student named Kinnard Monihan, who'd done research in his lab four or five years previously.

"Kinnard Monihan," Edward said. He closed his eyes in concentration. "I have a lot of students passing through. But, yes, I remember him. As I recall he went on to the General for a surgical residency."

"That's the one," Kim said. "Do you remember much about him?"

"I remember I was disappointed when I'd heard he was taking a residency," Edward said. "He was a smart kid. I'd expected him to stay in academic research. Why do you ask?"

"We dated for a number of years," Kim said. She was about to tell Edward about the confrontation at the compound when Edward interrupted her.

"Were you and Kinnard lovers?" Edward asked.

"I suppose you can say that," Kim said hesitantly. She could tell instantly that Edward was upset. Both his behavior and speech changed dramatically. It took Kim a half hour of coaxing and convincing to get him to calm down and to understand that her relationship with Kinnard was over. Kim even apologized for bringing up his name.

In a deliberate attempt to change the subject, she asked Edward if he'd done anything about finding a new apartment. Edward admitted that he'd not had a chance. Kim warned him that September would be arriving quickly.

As the evening progressed, neither Kim nor Edward brought up the issue of whether Kim should spend the night. By not making a decision, they made a decision. She stayed. Later, as they were lying side by side in bed, Kim began to think about what she'd said to Kinnard about Edward moving in with her. It had been meant merely to provoke Kinnard, but now Kim began seriously to consider the idea. It had a definite appeal. The relationship with Edward was continuing to blossom. Besides, the cottage was more than ample, and it was isolated. It might even be lonely.

SATURDAY • JULY 23, 1994

Kim awakened in stages. Even before she had opened her eyes she heard Edward's voice. At first she'd incorporated it into her dream, but then, as she'd become more conscious, she realized it was coming from the other room.

With some difficulty Kim opened her eyes. First she made sure that Edward was not in bed, then she glanced at the clock. It was 5:45 A.M.

Settling back into the pillow and feeling concerned that something was wrong, Kim tried to hear what was being said, but she couldn't. Edward's voice was unintelligible, yet from its timbre Kim could tell that he was excited.

Within a few minutes Edward returned. He was dressed in a bathrobe. As he tiptoed across the room en route to the bathroom, Kim told him she was awake. Changing directions, he came over and sat on the edge of the bed.

"I've got great news," Edward whispered.

"I'm awake," Kim repeated. "You can speak normally."

"I was just talking to Eleanor," Edward said.

"At five forty-five in the morning?" Kim questioned. "Who on earth is Eleanor?"

"She's one of my postdocs," Edward said. "She's my right-hand person in the lab."

"This seems awfully early for shop talk," Kim said. Involuntarily she thought of Grace Traters, her father's supposed assistant.

"She pulled an all-nighter," Edward said. "Kevin sent over several more sclerotia from the new fungus last night. Eleanor stayed to prepare and run a crude sample through the mass spectrometer. The alkaloids don't seem to be the same as those in *Claviceps purpurea*. In fact they appear to be three totally new alkaloids."

"I'm happy for you," Kim said. It was far too early for her to say much else.

"The most exciting thing is that I know at least one of them is psychoactive," Edward said. "Hell, all *three* might be." He rubbed his hands excitedly as if he were about to get to work that instant.

"I can't tell you how important this could be," Edward continued. "We could have a new drug here, or even a whole family of new drugs. Even if they prove not to be clinically useful, they'll undoubtedly be valuable as research tools."

"I'm glad," Kim said. She rubbed her eyes; she wanted to get into the bathroom to brush her teeth.

"It's amazing how often serendipity plays a role in drug discovery," Edward said. "Imagine finding a drug because of the Salem witch trials. That's even better than the way Prozac was discovered."

"That was by accident?" Kim asked.

"I should say." Edward laughed. "The main researcher responsible was playing around with antihistamines and testing them in an experimental protocol that measured the effect on the neurotransmitter, norepinephrine. By serendipity he ended up with Prozac, which is not an antihistamine, and affects serotonin, another neurotransmitter, two hundred times more than it affects norepinephrine."

"That's amazing," Kim said, but she'd not been listening. Without having had her morning coffee, her mind wasn't prepared for such intricacies.

"I can't wait to get working on these new alkaloids," Edward said.

"Do you want to change your mind about going up to Salem?" Kim asked.

"No!" Edward said without hesitation. "I want to see that grave. Come on! As long as you're awake, let's go!" He gave Kim a playful shake of her leg through the covers.

After showering, blow-drying her hair, and applying makeup, Kim left Edward's apartment with him for another greasy but tasty breakfast in Harvard Square. Following their meal, they stopped into one of the many bookstores in the square. Their breakfast conversation had included a discussion of Puritanism. They both realized how little they knew about it, so they bought a few appropriate books. It was well after nine by the time they were on their way to the North Shore.

Kim drove, since they were again reluctant to leave her car in the residents-only parking area in front of Edward's apartment. With no traffic they made good time and were in Salem just before ten. Following the same route they had the previous Saturday, they again passed the Witch House.

Edward reached out and grabbed Kim's arm. "Have you ever visited the Witch House?" he asked her.

"A long time ago," Kim said. "Why? Are you interested?"

"Don't laugh, but I am," Edward said. "Would you mind taking a few minutes?"

"Not at all," Kim said. She turned on Federal Street and parked near the courthouse. When they walked back they found they had to wait. The Witch House opened at ten. They also weren't the only prospective visitors. There were a number of families and several couples already standing outside the old building.

"It is amazing the appeal the Salem witch trials have," Kim commented. "I wonder if people stop to think why it interests them so much."

"Your cousin Stanton described the episode as ghoulishly seductive," Edward said.

"That sounds like Stanton," Kim said.

"He said the attraction is that it's a window on the supernatural," Edward added. "I happen to agree. Most people are a bit superstitious, and the witchcraft story titillates their imaginations."

"I agree," Kim said. "But I'm afraid there's also something perverse about the appeal. The fact that people were executed is key. Also, I don't think it was an accident that there were many more witches than wizards. There's a gender bias as well."

"Now don't get too far out on any feminist plank," Edward said. "I think there were more females involved because of the role of women in colonial culture. Obviously they were associated with birth and death, and health and disease, a lot more than men, and those aspects of life were shrouded with superstition and the occult. They simply didn't have any other explanation for them."

"I think we're both right," Kim said. "I agree with you, but I've also been impressed with the little research I've done about the lack of legal status of women in Elizabeth's time. The men were scared, and they took it out on the women. Misogyny was involved."

At that moment the door to the Witch House opened. Greeting them was a young woman in period costume. It was then that Kim and Edward learned that the visit to the house was a guided tour. Everyone trooped into the parlor and waited for the talk to begin.

"I thought we would be allowed to wander around by ourselves," Edward whispered.

"I did too," Kim replied.

They listened while the young woman described the many furnishings in the room, including a Bible box which was said to be an invariable part of a Puritan household.

"I'm losing interest," Edward whispered. "Maybe we should go."

"Fine with me," Kim said agreeably.

They exited the building. When they reached the street, Edward turned around and faced the house.

"The reason I wanted to go in was to see how much the interior resembled the cottage," Edward said. "It's amazing. It is as if they were built from the same plans."

"Well, as you said, individuality wasn't encouraged back then," Kim remarked.

They climbed back into the car and drove the rest of the way to the compound. The first thing Edward saw was the utility trench. He was amazed at its length. It now stretched from near the castle all the way to the cottage. When they stood at the edge, they could see that it had already been tunneled under the cottage's foundation.

"There's the coffin," Kim said as she pointed to the place where it protruded. At that point the trench had been significantly widened.

"What a stroke of luck," Edward said. "It looks to me like the head of the coffin. And you were right about the depth. It's at least eight feet down, maybe more."

"The trench is only deep here by the cottage," Kim pointed out. "Where it crosses the field it's much shallower."

"You're right," Edward said. He started walking away from the house.

"Where are you going?" Kim asked. "Don't you want to take a look at the headstone?"

"I'm going to take a closer look at the coffin," Edward said. As soon as he could manage it, Edward jumped into the trench, then came walking back, descending deeper with each step.

Kim watched him with growing concern. She was beginning to worry about what he had in mind.

"Are you sure this thing won't cave in?" Kim asked nervously. She could hear bits of dirt and stones fall into the crevice when she got too close to the edge.

Edward didn't answer. He was already bending down and examining the damaged end of the coffin. Scraping some of the immediately adjacent dirt into his hand, he felt it.

"This is encouraging," he said. "It's bone-dry down here and amazingly cool." He then insinuated his fingers into the partially opened joint between the head of the coffin and its side. With a sharp yank the headpiece bent to the side.

"Good God!" Kim murmured to herself.

"Would you get the flashlight from the car?" Edward said. He was looking into the open end of the coffin.

Kim did as she was told, but she wasn't happy about what was happening. She didn't like the idea of disturbing Elizabeth's grave any more than it already had been. After venturing as close to the edge of the trench as she dared, she tossed the flashlight down to Edward.

Edward shined the light into the open end of the coffin. "We're in luck," he said. "The corpse has been mummified by the cold and the dryness. Even the winding sheet is intact."

"I think we've done enough," Kim said. But she might as well have been talking to the trees. Edward wasn't listening. To her horror she watched while he put the light down and reached into the coffin. "Edward! What are you doing?"

"I'm just going to slide the body out a little way," he explained. He got hold of the head and began to pull. Nothing happened, so he put one foot against the wall of the trench and pulled harder. To his surprise the head detached suddenly, causing Edward to fall against the opposite wall of the trench. He ended up in a sitting position with Elizabeth's mummified head in his lap. A small shower of dirt dusted down onto his own head.

Kim felt weak. She had to look away.

"My gosh," Edward said as he got to his feet. He glanced at the base of Elizabeth's head. "I guess her neck must have been broken when she was hanged.

That's kinda surprising since the method of death in those days was not to cause the neck to break but rather let the person dangle and die of strangulation."

Edward put the head down and bent the end of the coffin back to its original position. Using a rock, he hammered it into place. When he was convinced he'd returned it to its original appearance, he carried the head back down the trench to where he could climb out.

"I hope you don't think this is funny," Kim said when he'd joined her. She refused to look at the object. "I want that put back!"

"I will," Edward promised. "I just want to take a little sample. Let's go inside and see if we can find a box."

Exasperated, Kim led the way. She marveled how she allowed herself to get involved in such situations. Edward sensed her attitude and quickly found an appropriately sized plumbing supply box. He put the head into it and put it in the car. Coming back into the house, he said eagerly, "Okay, let's have a tour."

"I want that head put back as soon as possible," Kim said.

"I will," Edward said again. To change the subject he walked into the lean-to portion of the house and pretended to admire the studding. Kim followed him. Soon her attention was diverted. There had been significant progress in the renovation. They even discovered the cellar floor had already been poured.

"I'm glad I got my dirt samples when I did," Edward said.

When they were on the second floor inspecting the work being done to install the half-bath, Kim heard a car pull up. Looking out one of the casement windows, her heart skipped a beat. It was her father.

"Oh, no!" Kim said. An uncomfortable anxiety spread through her that brought instant moisture to her palms.

Edward sensed her discomfiture immediately. "Are you embarrassed because I'm here?" he asked.

"Heavens, no!" Kim said. "It's because of Elizabeth's grave. Please don't let on about the head. The last thing I want is to give him an excuse to interfere with this renovation project."

They descended the stairs and stepped outside. John was standing at the edge of the trench, looking down at Elizabeth's coffin. Kim made the introductions. John was polite but curt. He took Kim aside.

"It's a bloody unfortunate coincidence for George Harris to blunder onto this grave," he said. "I told him to keep it quiet, and I trust you will do the same. I don't want your mother to find out about this. It'll put her in a tailspin. She'll be sick for a month."

"There's no reason for me to tell anyone," Kim said.

"Frankly I'm surprised that it is here," John said. "I'd been told that Elizabeth had been buried in a common grave someplace west of Salem center. What about this stranger you have here? Does he know about the grave?"

"Edward is not a stranger," Kim said. "And yes, he knows about the grave. He even knows about Elizabeth."

"I thought we had an understanding that you wouldn't be telling people about Elizabeth," John said.

"I didn't tell him," Kim said. "Stanton Lewis did."

"God damn your mother's side of the family," John mumbled as he turned around and walked back to where Edward was patiently waiting.

"The story of Elizabeth Stewart is privileged information," John said to Edward. "I hope you will respect that."

"I understand," Edward said evasively. He wondered what John would say if he knew about the head in the car.

Seemingly satisfied, John diverted his attention to the cottage. At Kim's suggestion he deigned to look briefly at the construction. It was a quick tour. Back outside he hesitated as he was about to leave. Looking at Edward he said, "Kim's a fine, sensible girl. She's very warm and loving."

"I think so too," Edward said.

John got into his car and drove off. Kim watched him until the car disappeared in the trees. "He has such an uncanny ability to irritate me," Kim fumed. "The problem is he doesn't even realize how belittling it is to be treated like a teenager and called a girl."

"At least he was being complimentary," Edward said.

"Complimentary my foot!" Kim said. "That was a self-serving comment. It was his way of trying to take credit for the way I've turned out. But he had nothing to do with it. He was never there for me. He has no clue that being a real father or husband is a lot more than providing food and shelter."

Edward put his arm around Kim's shoulder. "It's not going to accomplish anything to get yourself all worked up about it now," he said.

Kim abruptly turned to Edward. "I had an idea last night," she said. "What about you moving into the cottage with me come September first?"

Edward stumbled over his words. His stutter reappeared. "That's very generous," he managed to say.

"I think it is a wonderful idea," Kim said. "This place has more than enough space, and you have to find a new apartment anyway. What do you say?"

"Thank you," Edward stammered. "I don't know quite what to say. Maybe we should talk about it."

"Talk about it?" Kim questioned. She'd not expected to be rejected. Flowers from Edward were still arriving at her apartment on a daily basis.

"I'm just afraid you are inviting me impulsively," Edward explained. "I guess I'm afraid you'll change your mind and then not know how to disinvite me."

"Is that really your reason for feeling reluctant?" Kim asked. She stood on her tiptoes and gave him a hug. "Okay," she added. "We can talk about it. But I'm not going to change my mind."

Later, when they had exhausted discussing the renovation, Kim asked Edward if he'd be willing to spend a little time up at the castle going through the old papers. She explained that his comment the previous evening about discovering the nature of the evidence used against Elizabeth had given her a renewed impetus. Edward said he didn't mind in the slightest and that he was happy to accompany her.

Arriving at the castle, Kim suggested they try the attic instead of the wine cellar. Edward was initially agreeable, but when they got up there, they discovered it was extremely hot. Even after opening the dormer windows, it was still uncomfortable. Edward quickly lost interest.

"Why do I have the feeling you're not enjoying this?" Kim said. Edward had taken a drawer over to the window, but instead of searching through it, he was staring outside.

"I guess I'm preoccupied about the new alkaloids," Edward said. "I'm eager to get to the lab to work on them."

"Why don't you drive back to town and go do your thing?" Kim said. "I'll take the train back later."

"Good idea," Edward said. "But I'll take the train."

After a mini-argument which Edward won because there was no way for Kim to get to the train station later that afternoon, they walked back to the cottage and climbed into the car. Halfway to their destination, Kim suddenly remembered Elizabeth's head in the backseat.

"No problem," Edward said. "I'm taking it with me."

"On the train?" Kim asked.

"Why not," Edward said. "It's in a box."

"I want that back up here ASAP," Kim said. "They'll be filling in that trench as soon as the utilities are in."

"I'll be finished with it in no time," Edward assured her. "I'm just hoping there's something in it to sample. If there isn't maybe I could try for the liver."

"We're not going back into that coffin for anything but to put this head back," Kim said. "Not with my father hovering around. To make matters worse, he is apparently in contact with the contractor."

Kim dropped Edward off at the top of the stairs that led down to the train station. Edward lifted the plumbing supply box off the backseat.

"Want to meet for dinner?" Edward asked.

"I think not," Kim said. "I've got to get back to my apartment. I've got laundry to do, and I've got to get up early for work."

"Let's at least talk on the phone," Edward said.

"It's a deal," Kim said.

As much as Edward relished spending time with Kim, he was glad to get back to his lab. He was especially happy to see Eleanor, whom he did not expect to be there. She'd gone home, showered, and slept, but only for four or five hours. She said she was too excited to stay away.

The first thing she did was show him the mass spectrometry results. She was now certain that they were dealing with three new alkaloids. After talking with him that morning she'd spent time researching the results; there was no way they could have been made by any known compounds.

"Are there any more sclerotia?" Edward asked.

"A few," Eleanor said. "Kevin Scranton said more will be on their way, but he didn't know when. I didn't want to sacrifice the ones we have until I'd spoken with you. How do you want to separate the alkaloids? With organic solvents?"

"Let's use capillary electrophoresis," Edward said. "If necessary we can go to micellular electrokinetic capillary chromatography."

"Should I run a crude sample like I did with the mass spec?" Eleanor asked.

"No," Edward said. "Let's extract the alkaloids with distilled water and precipitate them with a weak acid. That's what I did over at the biological labs and it worked fine. We'll get purer samples, which will make structural work easier."

Eleanor started toward her bench space, but Edward grabbed her arm. "Before you start on the extraction I want you to do something else," he said. With no preamble he opened the plumbing supply box and lifted out the mummified head. Eleanor recoiled at the ghoulish sight.

"You could have warned me," she said.

"I suppose I could have," Edward said with a laugh. For the first time he looked at the head with a critical eye. It was rather lurid. The skin was dark brown, almost mahogany in color. It had dried to a leathery texture and retracted over the bony prominences, exposing the teeth in a gruesome smile. The hair was dried and matted like steel wool.

"What is it?" Eleanor asked. "An Egyptian mummy?"

Edward told Eleanor the story. He also explained that the reason he'd brought the head to the lab was to see if there was anything in the cranial vault to sample.

"Let me guess," Eleanor said. "You want to run it through the mass spec."

"Exactly," Edward said. "It would be scientifically elegant if we could show peaks corresponding to the new alkaloids. It would be definitive proof that this woman ingested the new mold."

While Eleanor ran over to the Department of Cell Biology to borrow anatomical dissection instruments, Edward faced the graduate students and assistants who had come in for the day and were nervously biding their time waiting for his attention. He answered all their questions in turn and sent them back to their experiments. By the time he was through, Eleanor was back.

"An anatomy instructor told me we should take the whole calvarium off," Eleanor said. She held up an electric vibratory saw.

Edward set to work. He reflected the scalp and exposed the skull. Then he took the saw and cut off a skullcap. He and Eleanor looked inside. There wasn't much. The brain had contracted to a congealed mass in the back of the skull.

"What do you think?" Edward asked. He poked the mass with the tip of a scalpel. It was hard.

"Cut out a piece and I'll get it to dissolve in something," Eleanor said.

Edward did as she suggested.

Once they had the sample, they began to try various solvents. Unsure of what they had, they began to introduce them into the mass spectrometer. By the second sample they had a match. Several of the peaks corresponded exactly with those of the new alkaloids in the crude extract that Eleanor had run the night before.

"Isn't science great?" Edward commented gleefully.

"It's a turn-on," Eleanor agreed.

Edward went over to his desk and called Kim's apartment. As he anticipated, he got the answer machine. After the beep sounded he left a message that for Elizabeth Stewart the devil in Salem had been explained scientifically.

Hanging up the phone, Edward glided back to Eleanor. He was in a rare mood.

"All right, enough of this fooling around," he said. "Let's get down to some real science. Let's see if we can separate these new alkaloids so we can figure out what we have."

"This is impossible," Kim said. She pushed the drawer of a file cabinet closed with her hip. She was hot, dusty, and frustrated. After taking Edward to the train station, she'd returned to the attic in the castle and had made a four-hour general inspection from the servants' wing all the way around to the guest wing. Not only hadn't she found anything significant, she hadn't even found any seventeenth-century material at all.

"This is not going to be an easy task," Kim said. Her eyes scanned the profusion of file cabinets, trunks, boxes, and bureaus that stretched as far as she could see until the attic made a right-hand turn. She was daunted by the sheer volume of material. There was even more in the attic than there was in the wine cellar. And like the wine cellar there was no order in terms of subject matter or chronology. Sequential pages varied as much as a century, and the subject matter bounced back and forth among mercantile data, business records, domestic receipts, official governmental documents, and personal correspondence. The only way to go through it all was page by page.

Confronted by such reality, Kim began to appreciate the good luck she'd had in finding James Flanagan's 1679 letter to Ronald Stewart that Monday. It had given her the false impression that researching Elizabeth in the castle would be an enjoyable if not easy undertaking.

Finally hunger, exhaustion, and discouragement temporarily overwhelmed Kim's commitment to discover the nature of the conclusive evidence used against Elizabeth. Badly in need of a shower, Kim descended from the attic and emerged into the late afternoon summer heat. Climbing into the car, she began the trek back to Boston.

Edward's eyes blinked open after only four hours' sleep. It was just five A.M. Whenever he got excited about a project, his need for sleep diminished. Just now, he was more excited than he could ever remember being. His scientific intuition was telling him that he'd stumbled onto something really big, and his scientific intuition had never failed him.

Leaping out of bed, Edward set Buffer into a paroxysm of barking. The poor dog thought there was a life-threatening emergency. Edward had to give him a light swat to bring him to his senses.

After speeding through his morning ritual, which included taking Buffer for a short walk, Edward drove to his lab. It was before seven when he entered, and Eleanor was already there.

"I'm having trouble sleeping," she admitted. Her usually carefully combed long blond hair was in mild disarray.

"Me too," Edward said.

They had worked Saturday night until one A.M. and all day Sunday. With success in sight, Edward had even begged off plans to see Kim Sunday evening. When he'd explained to her how close he and Eleanor were to their goal, Kim had been understanding.

Finally, just after midnight Sunday, Edward and Eleanor had perfected a separation technique. The difficulties had been mostly due to the fact that two of the alkaloids shared many physical properties. Now all they needed was more material, and as if an answer to a prayer, Kevin Scranton had called saying that he'd be sending over another batch of sclerotia that morning.

"I want everything to be ready when the material arrives," Edward said.

"Aye, aye," Eleanor said as she clicked her heels and made a playful salute. Edward tried to swat her on the top of her head but she was much more agile than he.

After they had been feverishly working for more than an hour, Eleanor tapped Edward on the arm.

"Are you intentionally ignoring your flock?" she asked quietly while motioning over her shoulder.

Edward straightened up and glanced around at the students who were milling aimlessly about, waiting for him to acknowledge them. He hadn't been aware of their presence. The group had been gradually enlarging as more and more people arrived at the lab. They all had their usual questions and were in need of his advice.

"Listen!" Edward called out. "You're on your own today. I'm tied up. I'm busy with a project that can't wait."

With some grumblings the crowd reluctantly dispersed. Edward did not notice their reaction. He went right back to work, and when he worked, his powers of concentration were legendary.

A few minutes later Eleanor again tapped his arm. "I hate to be a bother," she said, "but what about your nine o'clock lecture?"

"Damn!" Edward said. "I'd conveniently forgotten that. Find Ralph Carter and send him over." Ralph Carter was one of the senior assistants.

Within a short time Ralph appeared. He was a thin, bearded fellow with a surprisingly broad red-cheeked face.

"I want you to take over teaching the basic biochem summer course," Edward said.

"For how long?" Ralph asked. He was obviously not enthused.

"I'll let you know," Edward said.

After Ralph had left, Edward turned to Eleanor. "I hate that kind of passive-aggressive nonsense. It's the first time I've ever asked anyone to stand in for me for basic chemistry."

"That's because no one else has your commitment to teaching undergraduates," Eleanor explained.

As promised, the sclerotia arrived just after nine. They came in a small glass jar. Edward unscrewed the lid and carefully spread the dark, ricelike grains onto a piece of filter paper as if they were gold nuggets.

"Kinda ugly little things," Eleanor said. "They could almost be mouse droppings."

"I like to think they look more like seeds in rye bread," Edward said. "It's a more historically significant metaphor."

"Are you ready to get to work?" Eleanor asked.

"Let's do it," Edward said.

Before noon Edward and Eleanor had succeeded in producing a tiny amount of each alkaloid. The samples were in the bases of small, conical-shaped test tubes labeled A, B, and C. Outwardly the alkaloids appeared identical. They were all a white powder.

"What's the next step?" Eleanor asked as she held up one of the test tubes to the light.

"We have to find out which are psychoactive," Edward said. "Once we find out which ones are, we'll concentrate on them."

"What should we use for a test?" Eleanor asked. "I suppose we could use *Aplasia fasciata* ganglia preparations. They would certainly tell us which ones are neuroactive."

Edward shook his head. "It's not good enough," he said. "I want to know which ones cause hallucinogenic reactions, and I want quick answers. For that we need a human cerebrum."

"We can't use paid volunteers!" Eleanor said with consternation. "That would be flagrantly unethical."

"You are right," Edward said. "But I have no intention of using paid volunteers. I think you and I will do fine."

"I'm not sure I want to be involved in this," Eleanor said dubiously. She was beginning to get the drift of Edward's intentions.

"Excuse me!" called another voice. Edward and Eleanor turned to see Cindy, one of the departmental secretaries. "I hate to interrupt, Dr. Armstrong, but a Dr. Stanton Lewis is in the office, and he'd like a word with you."

"Tell him I'm busy," Edward said. But as soon as Cindy started back toward the office, Edward called her back. "On second thought," he said, "send him in."

"I don't like that twinkle in your eye," Eleanor said as they waited for Stanton to appear.

"It's perfectly innocent," Edward said with a smile. "Of course if Mr. Lewis would like to become a principal investigator in this study I won't stand in his way. Seriously, though, I do want to talk to him about what we are doing here."

Stanton breezed into the lab with his usual glib hellos. He was particularly pleased to get Edward and Eleanor together.

"My two favorite people," he said, "but for different parts of my brain." He laughed at what he thought was an off-color joke. Eleanor proved to be faster than he when she said she'd not known he'd changed his sexual orientation.

"What are you talking about?" Stanton asked. He was genuinely perplexed.

"Simply that I'm confident you are attracted to me because of my intellect," Eleanor said. "That leaves your instinctual brain for Edward."

Edward chortled. Repartee was Stanton's forte, and Edward had never seen him bested. Stanton laughed as well and assured Eleanor that her wit had always blinded him to any of her other charms.

Stanton then turned to Edward. "All right," he said. "Fun and games are over. What's the story on the Genetrix prospectus?"

"I haven't had a chance to look at it," Edward admitted.

"You promised," Stanton warned. "Am I going to have to tell my cousin she's not to see you anymore because you're not to be trusted?"

"Who's this cousin?" Eleanor asked, giving Edward a gentle poke in the ribs.

Edward's face blushed with color. Rarely did his mild stutter affect his speech in the lab, but it did at that moment. He did not want to discuss Kim. "I haven't had time for any reading," he told Stanton with some difficulty. "Something has come up that might particularly interest you."

"This better be good," Stanton teased. He slapped Edward on the back and told him he was only kidding about Kim. "I would never interfere with you two love doves. I heard from my aunt that old man Stewart surprised you two up in Salem. I hope it wasn't flagrante delicto, you old rogue."

Edward coughed nervously while he motioned for Stanton to pull up a chair. He then quickly changed the subject by launching into the story about the new fungus and the new alkaloids. He told Stanton that at least one of them was psychotropic, and he told him exactly how he knew. He even handed Stanton the three test tubes, saying they'd just finished isolating the new compounds.

"Quite a story," Stanton said. He put the test tubes down on the counter. "But why did you think it might interest me in particular? I'm a practical guy. I'm not titillated by esoteric exotica, which you academics thrive on."

"I think these alkaloids could have a practical payoff," Edward said. "We could be on the brink of finding a whole new group of psychotropic drugs which at the very least will have research applications."

Stanton visibly straightened up in his seat. The casual air that he affected vanished. "New drugs?" he questioned. "This does sound interesting. What do you think the possibilities are they might be clinically useful?"

"I think the chances are excellent," Edward said. "Especially considering the molecular modification techniques which are now available in modern synthetic chemistry. Also, after the psychedelic episode with the crude extract, I felt strangely energized and my mind seemed especially clear. I believe these drugs might be more than merely hallucinogenic."

"Oh, my goodness!" Stanton exclaimed. His entrepreneurial proclivity had quickened his pulse. "This could be something huge."

"That's what we have been thinking," Edward said.

"I'm talking about you seeing a major league economic reward," Stanton said.

"Our interest is primarily what a new group of psychoactive drugs can do for science," Edward said. "Everyone is anticipating some new breakthrough in the understanding of brain function. Who knows? This could be it. If it were to be so, we'd have to figure out a way to finance its production on a large scale. Researchers around the world would be clamoring for it."

"That's fine and dandy," Stanton said. "I'm happy you have such lofty goals. But why not have both? I'm talking about you making some serious money."

"I'm not concerned about becoming a millionaire," Edward said. "You should know that by now."

"Millionaire?" Stanton questioned with a derisive chortle. "If this new line of drugs is efficacious for depression or anxiety or some combination, you could be looking at a billion-dollar molecule."

Edward started to remind Stanton that they had different value systems, but he stopped in midsentence. His face went slack. He asked Stanton if he'd said billion.

"I said billion-dollar molecule!" Stanton repeated. "I'm not exaggerating. Experience with Librium, then Valium, and now with Prozac has proved society's insatiable appetite for clinically effective psychotropic drugs."

Edward assumed a thousand-yard stare out across the Harvard Medical School quad. When he spoke his voice had a flat, trancelike quality. "From your point of view and experience, what would have to be done to take advantage of such a discovery?"

"Not much," Stanton said. "All you'd have to do is form a company and patent the drug. It's that simple. But until you do that, secrecy is paramount."

"There's been secrecy," Edward said. He was still acting distracted. "It's only been a few days that we've known we were dealing with something new. Eleanor and I are the only ones involved." He didn't mention Kim's name for fear of the conversation reverting to her.

"I'd say the fewer people you tell the better," Stanton said. "Also, I could just go ahead and form a company just in case things begin to look promising."

Edward massaged his eye sockets and then his face. He took a deep breath and appeared to awaken from a trance. "I think we are jumping the gun," he said. "Eleanor and I have a lot of work to do before we have any idea of what we might have stumbled on."

"What's the next step?" Stanton asked.

"I'm glad you asked," Edward said. He pushed away from the counter and walked over to a glassware cabinet. "Eleanor and I were just talking about that. The first thing we have to do is determine which of these compounds is psychotropic." Edward brought three flasks back to where they were sitting. He then placed a minuscule amount of each new alkaloid in each flask and filled them all with a liter of distilled water. He shook each briskly.

"How will you do that?" Stanton asked even though from Edward's story he had an idea.

Edward took three one-milliliter pipettes out of a drawer. "Anybody care to join me?" he asked. Neither Eleanor nor Stanton said a word.

"Such chickens," Edward said with a laugh. Then he added: "I'm only kidding. Actually I just want you around just in case. This is my party."

Stanton looked at Eleanor. "Is this guy nuts or what?"

Eleanor eyed Edward. She knew he was not foolhardy, and she'd never met anyone as smart as he was, especially when it came to biochemistry. "You're convinced this is safe, aren't you?" she said.

"No worse than taking a few tokes on a joint," he said. "At best a milliliter will contain a few millionths of a gram. Besides, I took a comparatively crude extract with no ill effect whatsoever. In fact it was mildly enjoyable. These are relatively pure samples."

"All right!" Eleanor said. "Give me one of those pipettes."

"Are you sure?" Edward questioned. "There's no coercion here. I don't mind taking all three."

"I'm sure," Eleanor said. She took a pipette.

"What about you, Stanton?" Edward asked. "Here's your chance to participate in some real science. Plus if you really want me to read that damn prospectus, you can do me a favor as well."

"I suppose if you two screwballs think it is safe enough, I can do it," Stanton said reluctantly. "But you'd better read that prospectus or you'll be hearing from some of my North End mafia friends." Stanton took a pipette.

"Each can choose his own poison," Edward said, motioning toward the flasks.

"Reword that or I'm backing out," Stanton said.

Edward laughed. He was enjoying Stanton's discomfiture. Too often it had been the other way around.

Stanton let Eleanor choose first, then he took one of the two remaining flasks. "This strikes me as a kind of pharmacological Russian roulette," he said.

Eleanor laughed. She told Stanton he was too clever for his own good.

"Not clever enough to keep myself from getting involved with you two oddballs," he said.

"Ladies first," Edward said.

Eleanor filled the pipette and placed a milliliter on her tongue. Edward encouraged her to follow it with a glass of water.

The two men watched her. No one spoke. Several minutes went by. Finally Eleanor shrugged. "Nothing," she said. "Except my pulse rate went up slightly."

"That's from pure terror," Stanton said.

"You're next," Edward said, motioning to Stanton.

Stanton filled his pipette. "It's a crime what I have to go through to get you on a scientific advisory board," he complained to Edward. He deposited the tiny amount of liquid on his tongue, then chased it with a glass of water.

"It's bitter," he said. "But I don't feel anything."

"Wait another few seconds for circulation time," Edward said. Edward filled his own pipette. He began to have doubts, wondering if there could have been some other water-soluble compound in the crude extract that had caused his psychedelic reaction.

"I think I'm feeling slightly dizzy," Stanton said.

"Good," Edward said. His doubts faded. He remembered dizziness had been his first symptom with the crude extract. "Anything else?"

Stanton suddenly tensed and then made a grimace as his eyes darted around the room.

"What are you seeing?" Edward asked.

"Colors!" Stanton said. "I'm seeing moving colors." He started to describe the colors in more detail, but then he interrupted himself with a cry of fear. Leaping to his feet, he began to frantically wipe off his arms.

"What's the matter?" Edward asked.

"I'm being bitten by insects," Stanton said. He continued to try to brush away imaginary pests until he began to choke.

"What's happening now?" Edward asked.

"My chest is tight!" Stanton croaked. "I can't swallow."

Edward reached out and gripped Stanton's arm. Eleanor picked up the phone and started dialing, but Edward told her it was okay. Stanton had instantly calmed down. His eyes closed and a smile spread across his face. Edward backed him up a step and sat him back down in his chair.

Stanton responded to questions slowly and reluctantly. He said he was busy and didn't want to be bothered. When asked what he was busy doing, he merely said: "Things."

After twenty minutes Stanton's smile waned. For a few minutes it appeared as if he were asleep, then his eyes slowly opened.

The first thing he did was swallow. "My mouth feels like the Gobi Desert," he said. "I need a drink."

Edward poured a glass of water and gave it to him. He drank it with gusto and had a second.

"I'd say that was a busy couple of minutes," Stanton said. "It was also kind of fun."

"It was more like twenty minutes," Edward said.

"Are you serious?" Stanton questioned.

"How do you feel generally?" Edward asked.

"Wonderfully calm," Stanton said.

"How about clairvoyant?" Edward asked.

"That's a good way to describe it," Stanton said. "I feel as if I can remember all sorts of things with startling clarity."

"That's exactly how I felt," Edward said. "What about the choking sensation?"

"What choking sensation?" Stanton asked.

"You were complaining about a choking sensation," Edward said. "You were also complaining about being bitten by insects."

"I don't remember that at all," Stanton said.

"Well, no matter," Edward said. "The point is we know that compound B is definitely hallucinogenic. Let's see about the last one."

Edward took his dose. As they did with Eleanor, they waited for several minutes. Nothing happened.

"One for three is fine with me," Edward said. "Now we know which of the alkaloids we will concentrate our efforts on."

"Maybe we should just bottle this stuff and sell it the way it is," Stanton joked. "The sixties generation would have loved it. I mean I feel great, almost euphoric. Of course, maybe I'm just reacting to the relief of the ordeal being over. I have to admit I was scared."

"I thought I experienced some euphoria as well," Edward said. "Since we both felt it, maybe it's a result of the alkaloid. One way or the other, I'm encouraged. I think we've got a psychedelic drug with some calming properties as well as some amnestic properties."

"What about this clairvoyant feeling?" Stanton asked.

"I'd like to think that is a reflection of an increase in overall brain function," Edward said. "In that sense perhaps it could have some antidepressant effect."

"Music to my ears," Stanton said. "Tell me, what's the next step with this compound?"

"First we'll concentrate on its chemistry," Edward said. "That means structure and its physical properties. Once we have the structure we will work out the drug's synthesis to obviate our reliance on extracting it from the mold. Then we'll move on to physiological function as well as toxicity studies."

"Toxicity?" Stanton questioned. He blanched.

"You had a minuscule dose," Edward reminded him. "Not to worry. You'll have no problems."

"How will you analyze the drug's physiological effects?" Stanton asked.

"It will be a multilevel approach," Edward said. "Remember, most compounds with a psychedelic effect function by imitating one of the brain's neurotransmitters. LSD, for example, is related to serotonin. Our studies will start with single-cell neurons, then move on to synaptosomes, which are ground-up, centrifuged live brain preparations, and finally involve intact neural cell systems like the ganglions of lower animals."

"No live animals?" Stanton asked.

"Eventually," Edward said. "Mice and rats most likely. Also perhaps some monkeys. But that's down the line. We've got to look at the molecular level as well. We'll have to characterize binding sites and message transduction into the cell."

"This sounds like a multiyear project," Stanton said.

"We've got a lot of work to do," Edward said. He smiled at Eleanor. Eleanor nodded in agreement. "It's damn exciting, though. It could be a chance of a lifetime."

"Well, keep me informed," Stanton said. He got to his feet. He took a few tentative steps to test his balance. "I have to say, I do feel great."

Stanton got as far as the door to the lab when he turned around and returned. Edward and Eleanor had already begun work. "Remember," he said. "You promised to read that damn prospectus, and I'm going to hold you to it no matter how busy you are."

"I'll read it," Edward said. "I just didn't say when."

Stanton made his hand into a pistol and put it to his head and pretended to shoot.

"Kim, you have a call on line one," the ward clerk called out.

"Take a message," Kim shouted back. She was at the bedside of a particularly sick patient, helping the nurse assigned to the case.

"Go take your call," the nurse said. "Thanks to you, things are under control here."

"Are you sure?" Kim asked.

The nurse nodded.

Kim scooted across the center of the surgical intensive-care unit, dodging a traffic jam of beds. Patients had been coming and going all day. She picked up the phone, expecting either the chemistry lab or the blood bank. She had calls in to both places.

"I hope I'm not catching you at a bad time?" a voice asked.

"Who is this?" Kim demanded.

"George Harris, your Salem contractor. I'm returning your call."

"I'm sorry," Kim said. She'd forgotten she'd placed the call several hours earlier. "I didn't recognize your voice."

"I apologize for taking so long to get back," George said. "I've been out at the site. What can I do for you?"

"I wanted to know when the trench will be filled in," Kim said. The question had occurred to her the day before and had produced some anxiety. Her concern was what she'd do if the trench was filled in prior to Elizabeth's head being returned to her coffin.

"Probably tomorrow morning," George said.

"So soon?" Kim exclaimed.

"They're laying the utilities as we speak," George said. "Is there a problem?"

"No," Kim said quickly. "I just wanted to know. How's the work going?"

"No problems," George said.

After cutting the conversation short and hanging up, Kim called Edward immediately. Her anxiety mounted as the connection went through.

Getting Edward on the phone was no easy task. At first the secretary refused even to try to locate him, saying she'd take a message and Edward would call back. Kim insisted and finally prevailed.

"I'm glad you called," Edward said the moment he came on the line. "I've got more good news. We've not only separated the alkaloids, but we've already determined which one is psychoactive."

"I'm happy for you," Kim said. "But there is a problem. We have to get Elizabeth's head back to Salem."

"We can take it up on the weekend," Edward said.

"That will be too late," Kim said. "I just spoke with the contractor. He told me the trench is to be filled in the morning."

"Oh, jeez," Edward exclaimed. "Things are moving here at breakneck speed. I hate to take the time off. Can't they wait and fill the trench after the weekend?"

"I didn't ask," Kim said. "And I don't want to. I'd have to have a reason, and the only reason would involve the coffin. The contractor is in touch with my father, and I don't want him to have any notion that the grave has been violated."

"Damn it all," Edward said.

There was an uncomfortable pause.

"You promised you'd have that thing back ASAP," Kim said finally.

"It's just the timing," Edward said. Then, after a slight pause, he added: "Why don't you take it up yourself?"

"I don't know if I could," Kim said. "I didn't even want to look at it, much less handle it."

"You don't have to handle it," Edward said. "All you have to do is take the end of the coffin off and stick the box inside. You don't even have to open the box."

"Edward, you promised," Kim said.

"Please!" Edward said. "I'll make it up to you somehow. It's just that I am so busy at the moment. We've started to analyze the structure."

"All right," Kim said. When someone close to her asked her to do something, it was hard for her to say no. It wasn't that she minded the drive to Salem. She knew she should check the progress at the construction site as often as possible. Maybe slipping the box into the coffin wouldn't be that bad.

"How am I going to get the box?" she asked.

"I'll make it easy for you," Edward said. "I'll send it over to you by messenger so you'll have it before you finish work. How's that?"

"I'd appreciate it," Kim said.

"Call me here at the lab when you get back," Edward said. "I'll be here at least until midnight, probably longer."

Kim went back to work, but she was preoccupied. The anxiety she'd felt when she'd heard that the trench was to be filled in so soon had not abated. Knowing herself, she guessed it would remain until she'd returned the head to the coffin.

As Kim scurried back and forth between the beds caring for her patients, she felt irritated that she'd allowed Edward to take the head in the first place. The more she thought about her putting it back, the less she liked it. Although the idea of leaving it in the cardboard box had seemed reasonable when she'd been on the phone, she'd come to realize her sense of propriety wouldn't allow it. She felt obligated to return the grave to a semblance of what it had been before it had been disturbed. That meant dispensing with the box and handling the head, and she was not looking forward to that in the slightest.

The demands of Kim's job eventually pushed her concerns about Elizabeth into the back of her mind. There were patients to be taken care of, and the hours flew by. Later, as she was concentrating on a reluctant intravenous line, the ward clerk tapped her on the shoulder.

"You've got a package," he said. He pointed toward a sheepish messenger standing next to the central desk. "You've got to sign for it."

Kim looked over at the messenger. He was intimidated by the SICU's environment. A clipboard was clasped to his chest. At his elbow stood a computer paper box tied with a string. In an instant, Kim comprehended what was in the box and her heart fluttered.

"The front desk tried to get him to take it to the mail room," the clerk said. "But the messenger insisted his instructions were to deliver it to you in person."

"I'll take care of it," Kim said nervously. She started toward the desk with the clerk following at her heels. To her horror a bad situation suddenly got worse. Kinnard stood up from behind the desk where he had been writing in a chart and was looking at the receipt. She'd not seen him since their confrontation at the compound.

"What do we have here?" Kinnard said.

Kim took the clipboard from the messenger and hastily signed.

"It's a special delivery," the clerk explained.

"I can see that," Kinnard said. "I also see that it is from Dr. Edward Armstrong's lab. The question is, what can be inside?"

"It didn't say on the receipt," the clerk said.

"Give me the box," Kim said sternly. She reached over the counter to take it from Kinnard, but Kinnard stepped back.

He smiled superciliously. "It's from one of Ms. Stewart's many admirers," he told the clerk. "It's probably candy. Pretty clever putting it in a computer paper box."

"It's the first time anyone on the staff ever got a special delivery package in the SICU," the clerk said.

"Give me the box," Kim demanded again. Her face flushed bright red as her mind's eye saw the box falling to the floor and Elizabeth's head rolling out.

Kinnard shook the box and intently listened. From across the desk Kim could hear the head distinctly thumping against the sides.

"Can't be candy unless it's a chocolate soccer ball," Kinnard said, assuming a comically confused expression. "What do you think?" He shook the package close to the clerk.

Mortified, Kim came behind the desk and tried to get hold of the package. Kinnard held it above his head, out of her reach.

Marsha Kingsley rounded the desk from the opposite end. Like most of the rest of the staff in the unit she'd seen what was happening, but unlike the others she came to her roommate's rescue. Stepping behind Kinnard, she reached up and pulled his arm down. He didn't resist. Marsha took the box and handed it to Kim.

Sensing that Kim was upset, Marsha led her into the back room. Behind them they could hear Kinnard laughing with the clerk.

"Some people's sense of humor is sick," Marsha said. "Someone should kick his Irish ass."

"Thank you for helping," Kim said. Now that she had the box in her hands she felt much better. Yet she was visibly trembling.

"I don't know what's wrong with that man," Marsha continued. "What a bully. You don't deserve that kind of abuse."

"His feelings are hurt because I'm dating Edward," Kim said.

"So now you're defending him?" Marsha questioned. "Hell, I'm not buying the spurned lover role for Kinnard. Not in the slightest. Not that Lothario."

"Who's he dating?" Kim asked.

"The new blonde in the ER," Marsha said.

"Oh, great!" Kim said sarcastically.

"It's his loss," Marsha said. "Word has it she was the role model for those dumb-blonde jokes."

"She's also the one with the body that doesn't quit," Kim said forlornly.

"What do you care?" Marsha said.

Kim sighed. "You're right," she said. "I guess I just hate bad feelings and discord."

"Well, you sure had your share with Kinnard," Marsha said. "Look at the difference with the way Edward treats you. He doesn't take you for granted."

"You're right," Kim repeated.

After work Kim carried the computer paper box out to her car and put it in the trunk. Then she vacillated what to do. She'd had plans to visit the statehouse before the issue with Elizabeth's head came up. She considered postponing the visit until another afternoon. Then she decided there was no reason she couldn't do both, especially considering that her job at the cottage had to be done after all the workers left.

Leaving her car in the hospital garage, Kim walked up Beacon Hill and headed for the gold-domed Massachusetts Statehouse. After being cooped up all day, Kim enjoyed the outdoors. It was a warm but pleasant summer day. There was a slight sea breeze and the smell of salt in the air. Walking by the Common, she heard the complaint of seagulls.

An inquiry at the statehouse information service directed Kim to the Massachusetts State Archives. Waiting her turn, Kim faced a heavyset male clerk. His name was William MacDonald. Kim showed him the copies she'd made of Ronald's petition and Magistrate Hathorne's negative ruling.

"Very interesting," William said. "I love this old stuff. Where'd you find this?"

"The Essex County Courthouse," Kim said.

"What can I do for you?" William asked.

"Magistrate Hathorne suggested that Mr. Stewart should petition the Governor since the evidence he sought had been transferred to Suffolk County. I'd like to find out about the Governor's response. What I'm really interested in finding out is what the evidence was. For some reason it's not described in either the petition or the ruling."

"It would have been Governor Phips," William said. He smiled. "I'm a bit of a history buff. Let's see if we can find Ronald Stewart in the computer."

William used his terminal. Kim watched his face since she couldn't see the screen. To her chagrin he kept shaking his head after each entry.

"No Ronald Stewart," he said finally. He looked again at the ruling and scratched his head. "I don't know what else to do. I've tried to cross-reference Ronald Stewart with Governor Phips, but I get nothing. The trouble is, not all the seventeenth-century petitions survived, and those that did are not all properly indexed or catalogued. There's a wealth of such personal petitions. Back then there was a hell of a lot of disagreement and discord, and people were suing each other just as much as they are today."

"What about the date?" Kim asked. "August 3, 1692. Is there some way you can use that?"

"I'm afraid not," William said. "Sorry."

Kim thanked the clerk and left the statehouse. She was mildly discouraged.

With the ease she'd found the petition in Salem, she'd had high hopes of finding a follow-up ruling in Boston that would have revealed the nature of the evidence against Elizabeth.

"Why couldn't Ronald Stewart have described that damn evidence?" Kim wondered as she stalked down Beacon Hill. But then the idea occurred to her that maybe it was significant that he didn't. Maybe that was some sort of clue or message in and of itself.

Kim sighed. The more she thought about the mysterious evidence, the more curious she became. In fact at that moment she began to imagine it might be associated with the intuitive feeling she had that Elizabeth was trying to communicate with her.

Kim reached Cambridge Street and turned toward the Mass General garage. The other problem that her failure at the statehouse presented was that she was being thrown back to the impossibly large collection of papers in the castle, a daunting task at best. Yet it was apparent that if she were to learn anything more about Elizabeth, it would have to be there.

Climbing into her car, Kim headed north for Salem. But it was not an easy nor quick trip. The visit to the statehouse had put her in the height of rush-hour traffic.

As she sat in the bumper-to-bumper traffic on Storrow Drive, trying to get through Leverett Circle, she thought about the blond woman Kinnard was dating. She knew it shouldn't bother her, but it did. Yet such thoughts made her especially glad that she'd invited Edward to share the cottage with her. Not only did she truly care for Edward. She liked the message that her living with Edward would send to both Kinnard and her father.

Then Kim remembered Elizabeth's head in her trunk. The more she thought about Edward's failure to come along to Salem that evening, the more surprised she was, especially since he'd promised to take responsibility for the head and was fully aware of her distaste for handling it. It was behavior at odds with his attentiveness and, along with everything else, it disturbed her.

"What is this?" Edward asked angrily. "Do I have to hold your hand continually?" He was talking to Jaya Dawar, a brilliant new doctoral student from Bangalore, India. Jaya had been at Harvard only since the first of July, and he was struggling to find an appropriate direction for his doctorate thesis.

"I thought you could recommend to me more reading material," Jaya said.

"I can recommend an entire library," Edward said. "It's only a hundred yards away." He pointed in the general direction of the Countway Medical Library. "There comes a time in everybody's life when they have to cut the umbilical cord. Do a little work on your own!"

Jaya bowed his head and silently exited.

Edward redirected his attention to the tiny crystals he was growing.

"Maybe I should carry the burden with the new alkaloid," Eleanor suggested hesitantly. "You can look over my shoulder and be the guiding light."

"And miss all this fun?" Edward said. He was using a binocular microscope to observe crystals forming on the surface of a supersaturated solution in the well of a microscope slide.

"I'm just concerned about your normal responsibilities," Eleanor said. "A lot of people around here depend on your supervision. I also heard the undergraduate summer students complained about your absence this morning."

"Ralph knows his material," Edward said. "His teaching will improve."

"Ralph doesn't like to teach," Eleanor said.

"I appreciate what you are saying," Edward said, "but I'm not going to let this opportunity slip away. We've got something here with this alkaloid. I can feel it in my bones. I mean, how often does a billion-dollar molecule fall into your lap?"

"We have no idea whether this compound is going to be worth anything," Eleanor said. "At this point it is purely hypothetical."

"The harder we work, the quicker we'll know," Edward said. "The students can do without my hand-holding for the time being. Who knows? Maybe it will do them some good."

As Kim approached the compound her anxieties increased. She couldn't forget that she had Elizabeth's head in her trunk, and the longer she spent in direct proximity to it, the more she experienced a vague, uncomfortable foreboding about the course of recent events. Having stumbled onto Elizabeth's grave so quickly in the renovation process made it seem as if the witchcraft frenzy of 1692 was casting an ominous shadow over the present.

Passing through the gate, which was ajar, Kim feared that the construction people were still there. As she emerged from the trees her suspicions were confirmed. There were two vehicles parked in front of the cottage. Kim was not happy. By that time she'd expected all of the workmen to have departed.

She parked next to the vehicles and slid out from behind the wheel. Almost simultaneously George Harris and Mark Stevens appeared at the front door. In contrast to her response, they were demonstrably pleased to see her.

"This is a pleasant surprise," Mark said. "We were hoping to get you on the phone later, but your being here is far better. We have a lot of questions."

For the next half hour Mark and George took Kim on a working tour of the renovation. The amazing progress that had been made improved her mood dramatically. To her delight Mark had brought granite samples to the site for the kitchen and the baths. With Kim's interest in interior design and her sense of color, she had no trouble making decisions. Mark and George were impressed. Kim was even impressed with herself. She knew that the ability to make such decisions was a tribute to the progress she'd made over the years with her self-confidence. When she'd first gone to college, she'd not even been able to decide on the color of her bedspread.

When they had finished with the interior, they stepped outside and began a walk around the building. Viewing the structure from the exterior, Kim told them that she wanted the new windows in the lean-to to match the small, diamond-paned windows of the main part of the house.

"They'll have to be custom," George said. "They'll be considerably more expensive."

"I want them," Kim said without hesitation.

She also told them she wanted the roof slate repaired, not replaced with a modern material, as the contractor had suggested. Mark agreed it would look far better. Kim even wanted the asphalt shingles removed from the shed and replaced with slate.

Rounding the building, they came to the utility trench. Kim glanced into its depths, where now ran a waste pipe, a water pipe, an electrical service, a phone line, and a TV cable. She was relieved to see the corner of the coffin still protruding from the wall.

"What about this ditch?" she asked.

"It'll be filled tomorrow," George said.

Kim felt an unwelcome chill descend her spine as she reluctantly imagined the terrible dilemma she would have faced had she not made the call to George that morning.

"Will all this be done by September first?" Kim asked, forcing her mind away from such disturbing thoughts.

Mark deferred to George.

"Barring any unforeseen problems we should be fine," George said. "I'll order the new casement windows tomorrow. If they're not here in time we can always hang a temporary window."

After the contractor and the architect had climbed into their respective vehicles and driven out of sight, Kim went back into the house to find a hammer. With it in hand, she opened the trunk of her car and lifted out the cardboard box.

As she followed the trench to where she could climb into it, Kim was quite astonished with her degree of nervousness. She felt like a thief in the night, and she kept stopping to listen for any approaching cars.

Once she was in the trench and had walked back to where the coffin was, a sense of claustophobia made the ordeal even worse. The walls seemed to tower above her and from her vantage point seemed to curve out over her head, adding to her fear they might cave in at any moment.

With a tremulous hand, Kim set to work on the end of the coffin. Inserting the hammer's claws, she pried it back. Then she turned to face the box.

Now that the unpleasant task was at hand, Kim revived the debate as to what she should do in relation to the box. But she didn't debate long: hastily she untied the string. As much as she hated the idea of touching the head, she had to make an effort to restore the grave to a semblance of its original state.

Lifting the cardboard flaps, Kim reluctantly looked inside. The head was facing up, balanced on a mat of dried hair. Elizabeth was staring back at Kim with her dried, sunken eyeballs partially exposed. For an uncomfortable moment, Kim tried vainly to reconcile the gruesome face with the pleasing portrait that she was having restored, relined, and reframed. The images were such stark opposites that it seemed inconceivable they were the same person.

Holding her breath, Kim reached in and lifted the head. Touching it gave her renewed shivers, as if she were touching death itself. Kim also found herself wondering anew about what had really happened three hundred years previously. What could Elizabeth have done to bring on such a cruel fate?

Turning around carefully to avoid tripping over any of the pipes and cables, Kim extended the head into the coffin. Gingerly she set it down. She could feel her hands touch fabric and other firmer objects, but she didn't try to look in to see what they were. Hastily she bent the end of the coffin back to its original position and hammered it home.

Picking up the empty box and string, Kim hurried back up the trench. She didn't begin to relax until she'd put the trash back in her trunk. Finally she took a deep breath. At least it was over.

Walking back to the trench, she looked down at the end of the coffin just to make sure she'd not left some telltale evidence behind. She could see her footprints, but she didn't think that was a problem.

With her hands on her hips, Kim's eyes left the coffin and looked up at the quiet, cozy cottage. She tried to imagine what life had been like back in those dark days of the witchcraft scare, when poor Elizabeth was unknowingly ingesting the poisonous, mind-altering grain. With all the books Kim had been reading on the witchcraft ordeal, she'd learned quite a lot. For the most part the young women who presumably had been poisoned with the same contaminant as Elizabeth were the "afflicted," and they were the ones who "called out against" the witches.

Kim looked back at the coffin. She was confused. The young afflicted women had not been thought of as witches themselves, as Elizabeth had been. The exception had been Mary Warren, who had been both one of the afflicted and one of the accused, yet she'd been released and not executed. What made Elizabeth different? Why wasn't she just one of the afflicted? Could it have been that she was afflicted but refused to accuse anyone of afflicting her? Or could she have been practicing the occult, as her father had intimated?

Kim sighed and shook her head. She didn't have any answers. It all seemed to come back to the mysterious conclusive evidence and what it could have been. Kim's gaze wandered to the lonely castle, and in her mind's eye she saw the innumerable file cabinets, trunks, and boxes.

She glanced down at her watch. There were still several hours of daylight.

Impulsively, she walked over to her car, climbed in, and drove up to the castle. With the mystery of Elizabeth so prominent in her mind, she thought she'd spend a little more time on the daunting task of looking through the papers.

Kim pushed through the front door of the castle and whistled to keep herself company. At the base of the grand staircase she hesitated. The attic was certainly more agreeable than the wine cellar, but her last visit to the attic had been singularly unsuccessful. She'd found nothing from the seventeenth century despite almost five hours of effort.

Reversing her direction, Kim walked into the dining room and opened the heavy oak door of the wine cellar. She flipped on the sconces and descended the granite steps. Walking along the central corridor, she peered into successive individual cells. Recognizing that there was no order to the material, she thought it important that she develop some rational plan. Vaguely she thought that she would start in the very farthest cell and begin to organize the papers according to subject matter and age.

Passing one particular cell, Kim did a double take. Returning to it, she gazed in at the furniture. There was the usual complement of file cabinets, bureaus, trunks, and boxes. But there was also something different. On top of one of the bureaus was a wooden box that looked familiar to Kim. It closely resembled the Bible box which the Witch House tour guide had described as an invariable part of a Puritan home.

Stepping over to the bureau, Kim ran her fingers along the top of the box, leaving parallel trails in the dust. The wood was unfinished yet perfectly smooth. There was no doubt the box was old. Placing her hands at either end, Kim opened the hinged lid.

Inside, appropriately enough, was a worn Bible bound in thick leather. Lifting the Bible out, Kim noticed that beneath it were some envelopes and papers. She carried the Bible out to the hall where the light was better. Folding back the cover and flyleaf, she looked at the date. It was printed in London in 1635. She thumbed through the text in hopes that some sheets of paper might have been stuck in the pages, but there was nothing.

Kim was about to return to the Bible box when the back cover of the Bible fell open in her hands. Written on the endpaper was: *Ronald Stewart his book 1663.* The handwriting resembled the graceful cursive script Kim recognized to be Ronald's. She guessed he'd written in the Bible as a boy.

Turning the back flyleaf, Kim found a series of blank pages with the word *Memorandum* printed at the top. On the first memorandum page following the Bible text she found more of Ronald's handwriting. Here he had recorded each of the marriages, births, and deaths of his family. With her index finger keeping her oriented on the page, Kim read off each of the dates until she came to the date of Ronald's marriage to Rebecca. It had been Saturday, October 1, 1692.

Kim was appalled. That meant that Ronald had married Elizabeth's sister just ten weeks after Elizabeth's death! That seemed much too quick to Kim, and once again she found herself questioning Ronald's behavior. She couldn't help but wonder if he'd had something to do with Elizabeth's execution. With such haste to remarry it was difficult for Kim to imagine that Ronald and Rebecca hadn't been having an affair.

Encouraged by her discovery, Kim returned to the Bible box and lifted out the envelopes and papers. Eagerly she opened the envelopes, hoping for personal correspondence, but each was a disappointment. All the enclosed material was business-related and from a period from 1810 to 1837.

Kim turned to the papers. She went through them sheet by sheet, and although they were older, they were not any more interesting until she came to one that was folded in thirds. Unfolding the multipage document, which had traces of a wax seal, Kim found a deed to a huge tract of land called Northfields Property.

Turning to the second page of the deed, Kim found a map. It was not difficult for her to recognize the area. The tract included the current Stewart compound as well as the land presently occupied by the Kernwood Country Club and the Greenlawn Cemetery. It also crossed the Danvers River, which was labeled the Wooleston River, to include property in Beverly. To the northwest it ran into present-day Peabody and Danvers, which in the deed was called Salem Village.

Turning the page, Kim found the most interesting part of the deed. The buyer's signature was Elizabeth Flanagan Stewart. The date was February 3, 1692.

Kim pondered the fact that Elizabeth was the buyer and not Ronald. It seemed strange although she did recall the premarital document she'd seen in the Essex County Courthouse giving Elizabeth the right to enter into contracts in her own name. But why was Elizabeth the buyer, especially since it was such a huge tract and must have cost a fortune?

Attached to the back of the deed was a final sheet of paper which was smaller in size and written by a different hand. Kim recognized the signature. It was Magistrate Jonathan Corwin, the original occupant of the Witch House.

Holding the document up to the light since it was difficult to read, Kim learned that it was a ruling by Magistrate Corwin denying a petition by Thomas Putnam, who wanted the Northfields purchase contract declared null and void because of the illegality of Elizabeth's signature.

To conclude the ruling, Magistrate Corwin wrote: "The legality of the signature of the aforesaid contract stands on the contract bound by Ronald Stewart and Elizabeth Flanagan dated 11th February 1681."

"My goodness," Kim murmured. It was as if she were peeking through a window on the late seventeenth century. From her general reading she knew that name Thomas Putnam. He was one of the principal characters in the factional strife that had engulfed Salem Village prior to the witchcraft frenzy and that many historians felt had been the hidden social cause of the affair. It had been

Thomas Putnam's afflicted wife and daughter who'd made many of the witch-craft accusations. Obviously Thomas Putnam had not been aware of the pre-marital contract between Ronald and Elizabeth when he filed his petition.

Kim slowly folded the deed and the ruling. She had learned something that might be important for her understanding of what happened to Elizabeth. Obviously Thomas Putnam had been upset about Elizabeth's purchase of the land, and considering his role in the witchcraft saga, his enmity had to have been significant. It could very well have catapulted Elizabeth into the middle of the tragedy.

For a few moments Kim pondered the possibility that the evidence used against Elizabeth in her trial had something to do with Thomas Putnam and the purchase of the Northfields tract. After all, such a purchase by a woman would have been a disturbing act in Puritan times considering the accepted role of women. Perhaps the evidence had been something that was considered compelling proof Elizabeth was a virago and therefore unnatural. But try as she might, Kim couldn't think of anything.

Kim placed the deed and the attached ruling on top of the Bible, and examined the rest of the papers from the Bible box. To her delight she found one more seventeenth-century document, but when she read it she was less excited. It was a contract between Ronald Stewart and Olaf Sagerholm of Göteborg, Sweden. The contract directed Olaf to build a ship of a new and swift frigate design. The ship was specified to be 128 feet in length, 34 feet 6 inches in beam, and 19 feet 3 inches in draft when fully loaded with 276 last. The date was 12 December 1691.

Kim put the Bible and the two seventeenth-century documents back in the Bible box and carried the box to a console table at the base of the steps leading up to the dining room. She planned to use the box as a repository for any papers she found that related to Elizabeth or Ronald. To that end she went into the cell where she'd found the letter from James Flanagan and brought the letter back to put it with the other materials.

With that accomplished, Kim returned to the room where she'd found the Bible box and began a search through the bureau on which the Bible box sat. After several hours of diligent work, she straightened up and stretched. She'd found nothing interesting. A quick glance at her watch told her it was nearing eight and time for her to head back to Boston.

Slowly climbing the stairs, she realized how exhausted she was. It had been a busy day at work, and she found searching through the papers tiring even if it wasn't physically demanding.

The drive back to Boston was far easier than the drive out to Salem. There was little traffic until she entered Boston proper. Getting on Storrow Drive for what normally was only a short stretch, Kim changed her mind and drove on to the Fenway exit. She had the sudden idea to pay a visit to Edward in his lab rather than phone him. Since the task of replacing Elizabeth's head had been so complication-free, she felt guilty she'd been so upset anticipating it.

Passing through the Medical School security with the help of her MGH identity card, Kim mounted the stairs. She'd briefly visited the lab with Edward after one of their dinners, so she knew the way. The departmental office was dark, so Kim knocked on a frosted-glass door that she knew led directly into the lab.

When no one responded, Kim knocked again a bit louder. She also tried the door, but it was locked. After a third knock, Kim could see someone approaching through the glass.

The door opened, and Kim confronted an attractive, slim, blond woman whose curvaceous figure was apparent despite an oversized white lab coat.

"Yes?" Eleanor questioned perfunctorily. She looked Kim up and down.

"I'm looking for Dr. Edward Armstrong," Kim said.

"He's not seeing visitors," Eleanor said. "The department office will be open tomorrow morning." She started to close the door.

"I think he might be willing to see me," Elizabeth said hesitantly. In truth she wasn't entirely sure and for a moment wondered if she should have called.

"Really, now?" Eleanor questioned haughtily. "What's your name? Are you a student?"

"No, I'm not a student," Kim said. The question seemed absurd since she was still in her nurse's uniform. "My name is Kimberly Stewart."

Eleanor didn't say anything before closing the door in Kim's face. Kim waited. She shifted her weight and wished she hadn't come. Then the door re-opened.

"Kim!" Edward exclaimed. "What on earth are you doing here?"

Kim explained that she thought it better to visit than to merely call. She apologized if she'd caught him at a bad time.

"Not at all," Edward said. "I'm busy, but that doesn't matter. In fact I'm more than busy. But come in." He stepped back out of the doorway.

Kim entered, then followed Edward as he headed toward his desk area.

"Who was it who opened the door?" Kim asked.

"Eleanor," Edward said over his shoulder.

"She wasn't terribly friendly," Kim said, unsure if she should mention it.

"Eleanor?" Edward questioned. "You must be mistaken. She gets along with everyone. Around here I'm the only bear. But both of us are worn a little thin. We're on a roll. We've been working nonstop since late Saturday morning. In fact Eleanor has been working that way since Friday night. Both of us have hardly slept."

They arrived at Edward's desk. He lifted a stack of periodicals off a straight-backed chair, tossed them in the corner, and motioned for Kim to sit. Edward sat in his desk chair.

Kim studied Edward's face. He seemed to be in overdrive, as if he'd drunk a dozen cups of coffee. His lower jaw was dancing nervously up and down while he chewed gum. There were circles under his cool blue eyes. A two-day stubble dotted his cheeks and chin.

"Why all this frantic activity?" Kim asked.

"It's the new alkaloid," Edward said. "We're already beginning to learn something about it and it looks awfully good."

"I'm pleased for you," Kim said. "But why all the rush? Are you under some sort of deadline?"

"It's purely an anticipatory excitement," Edward said. "The alkaloid could prove to be a great drug. If you've never done research it's hard to comprehend the thrill you get when you discover something like this. It's a real high, and we've been reexperiencing that high on an hourly basis. Everything we learn seems positive. It's incredible."

"Can you say what you've been learning?" Kim asked. "Or is it some kind of secret?"

Edward moved forward in his chair and lowered his voice. Kim glanced around the lab but saw no one. She wasn't even sure where Eleanor was.

"We've stumbled onto an orally effective, psychoactive compound that penetrates the blood-brain barrier like the proverbial knife through butter. It's so potent it is effective in the microgram range."

"Do you think this is the compound that affected the people in the Salem witchcraft affair?" Kim asked. Elizabeth was still in the forefront of her mind.

"Without doubt," Edward said. "It's the Salem devil incarnate."

"But the people who ate the infected grain were poisoned," Kim said. "They became the 'afflicted' with horrid fits. How can you be so excited about that kind of drug?"

"It is hallucinogenic," Edward said. "There's no doubt about that. But we think it's a lot more. We have reason to believe it calms, invigorates, and may even enhance memory."

"How have you learned so much so quickly?" Kim asked.

Edward laughed self-consciously. "We don't know anything for certain yet," he admitted. "A lot of researchers would find our work so far less than scientific. What we've been doing is attempting to get a general idea of what the alkaloid can do. Mind you, these are not controlled experiments by any stretch of the imagination. Nevertheless, the results are terribly exciting, even mind-boggling. For instance we found that the drug seems to calm stressed rats better than imipramine, which is the benchmark for antidepressant efficacy."

"So you think it might be an hallucinogenic antidepressant?" Kim said.

"Among other things," Edward said.

"Any side effects?" Kim asked. She still didn't understand why Edward was as excited as he was.

Edward laughed again. "We haven't been worrying about hallucinations with the rats," he said. "But seriously, apart from the hallucinations we've not seen any problems. We've loaded several mice with comparatively huge doses and they're as happy as pigs in the poke. We've plopped even larger doses into neuronal cell cultures with no effect on the cells. There doesn't seem to be any toxicity whatsoever. It's unbelievable."

As Kim continued to listen to Edward, she became progressively disappointed that he did not ask her about her visit to Salem and about what happened to Elizabeth's head. Finally Kim had to bring it up herself when there was a pause in Edward's exuberant narrative.

"Good," Edward said simply when she told him the head had been replaced. "I'm glad that's over."

Kim was about to describe how the episode had made her feel when Eleanor breezed into view and immediately monopolized Edward's attention with a computer printout. Eleanor did not even acknowledge Kim's presence nor did Edward introduce them. Kim watched as they had an animated discussion over the information. It was obvious Edward was pleased with the results. Finally Edward gave Eleanor some suggestions along with a pat on the back, and Eleanor vanished as quickly as she'd appeared.

"Now where were we?" Edward said, turning to Kim.

"More good news?" Kim asked referring to Eleanor's printout.

"Most definitely," Edward said. "We've started on determining the compound's structure, and Eleanor has just confirmed our preliminary impression that it is a tetracyclic molecule with multiple side chains."

"How on earth can you figure that out?" Kim asked. In spite of herself she was impressed.

"You really want to know?" Edward asked.

"Provided you don't go too far over my head," Kim said.

"The first step was to get an idea of molecular weight with standard chromatography," Edward said. "That was easy. Then we broke the molecule apart with reagents that rupture specific types of bonds. Following that we try to identify at least some of the fragments with chromatography, electrophoresis, and mass spectrometry."

"You're already beyond me," Kim admitted. "I've heard those terms, but I don't really know what the processes are."

"They're not that complicated," Edward said. He stood up. "The basic concepts are not difficult to comprehend. It's the results that can be difficult to analyze. Come on, I'll show you the machines." He took Kim's hand and pulled her to her feet.

Edward enthusiastically dragged a reluctant Kim around his lab, showing her the mass spectrometer, the high-performance liquid chromatography unit, and the capillary electrophoresis equipment. The whole time he lectured about how they were used for fragment separation and identification. The only thing Kim understood completely was Edward's obvious bent for teaching.

Opening up a side door, Edward gestured inside. Kim glanced within. In the center of the room was a large cylinder about four feet high and two feet wide. Cables and wires emerged from it like snakes from Medusa's head.

"That's our nuclear magnetic resonance machine," Edward said proudly. "It's a crucial tool with a project like this. It's not enough to know how many carbon atoms, hydrogen atoms, oxygen atoms, and nitrogen atoms there are in a compound. We have to know the three-dimensional orientation. That's what this machine can do."

"I'm impressed," Kim said, not knowing what else to say.

"Let me show you one other machine," Edward said, oblivious to Kim's state of mind. He led her to yet another door. Opening it, he again gestured inside.

Kim looked in. It was a hopeless tangle of electronic equipment, wires, and cathode ray tubes. "Interesting," she said.

"You know what it is?" Edward asked.

"I don't think so," Kim said. She was reluctant to let Edward know how little she knew about what he did.

"It's an X-ray defraction unit," Edward said with the same degree of pride he'd evinced with the NMR unit. "It complements what we do with the NMR. We'll be using it with the new alkaloid because the alkaloid readily crystallizes as a salt."

"Well, you do have your work cut out for you," Kim said.

"It's work but it's also extraordinarily stimulating," Edward said. "Right now we're using everything in our investigative arsenal, and the data is pouring in. We'll have the structure in record time, especially with the new software that is available with all these instruments."

"Good luck," Kim said. She'd derived only a sketchy idea of what Edward had explained, but she had certainly gotten a taste of his enthusiasm.

"So what else happened up in Salem?" Edward asked suddenly. "How's the renovation going?"

Kim was momentarily nonplussed by Edward's question. With his preoccupation involving his own work, she didn't think he was currently interested in her puny project. She'd been just about to excuse herself.

"The renovation is going well," she said. "The house is going to be darling."

"You were gone quite a while," Edward said. "Did you delve back into the Stewart family papers?"

"I spent a couple of hours," Kim admitted.

"Find anything more about Elizabeth?" he asked. "I'm getting more and more interested in her myself. I feel as if I owe her an enormous debt. If it hadn't been for her, I never would have come across this alkaloid."

"I did learn some things," Kim said. She told Edward about going to the statehouse prior to driving to Salem and that there was no follow-up petition concerning the mysterious evidence. She then told him about the Northfields deed with Elizabeth's signature, and how it had angered Thomas Putnam.

"That might be the most significant piece of information you've learned so far," Edward said. "From the little reading I've done, I don't think Thomas Putnam was the right person to irritate."

"I had the same thought," Kim said. "His daughter, Ann, was one of the first of the girls to be afflicted, and she accused many people of witchcraft. The problem is, I can't relate a feud with Thomas Putnam with the conclusive evidence."

"Maybe these Putnam people were malicious enough to plant something," Edward suggested.

"That's a thought," Kim said. "But it doesn't answer what it could have been. Also, if something were planted, does it make sense that it was conclusive? I still think it had to be something Elizabeth made herself."

"Maybe so," Edward said. "But the only hint you have is Ronald's petition stating it was seized from his property. I think it could have been anything indubitably associated with witchcraft."

"Speaking of Ronald," Kim said. "I learned something about him that's reawakened my suspicions. He remarried only ten weeks after Elizabeth's death. That's an awfully short grieving period, to say the least. It makes me think he and Rebecca might have been having an affair."

"Perhaps," Edward said without enthusiasm. "I still think that we have no idea how difficult life was back then. Ronald had four children to raise and a burgeoning business to run. He probably didn't have a lot of choice. I'd bet a long grieving period was a luxury he could not afford."

Kim nodded, but she wasn't sure she agreed. At the same time she wondered how much her suspicious attitude toward Ronald was influenced by her father's behavior.

Eleanor appeared just as abruptly as she had earlier and again enlisted Edward in a private yet animated discussion. When she left, Kim excused herself.

"I'd better be on my way," she said.

"I'll walk you out to your car," Edward offered.

While descending the stairs and walking across the quadrangle, Kim detected a gradual change in Edward's demeanor. As he'd done in the past, he became noticeably more nervous. From previous experience Kim guessed he was about to say something. She didn't try to encourage him. She'd learned it didn't help.

Finally when they reached her car he spoke: "I've been thinking a lot about your offer to come to live with you in the cottage," he said while toying with a pebble with his toe. He paused. Kim waited impatiently, unsure what he would say. Then he blurted: "If you're still thinking positively about it, I'd like to come."

"Of course I'm thinking positively," Kim said with relief. She reached up and gave him a hug. He returned the gesture.

"We can go up on the weekend and talk about furniture," Edward said. "I don't know if there is anything from my apartment you'd want to use."

"It'll be fun," Kim said.

With some awkwardness they separated, and Kim climbed into her car. She opened the passenger-side window and Edward leaned in.

"I'm sorry I'm so preoccupied about this alkaloid," he said.

"I understand," Kim said. "I can see how excited you are. I'm impressed with your dedication."

After they said their goodbyes, Kim drove toward Beacon Hill feeling a lot happier than she had just a half hour earlier.

Edward's excitement escalated as the week progressed. The database on the new alkaloid grew at an exponential rate. Neither he nor Eleanor slept more than four or five hours each night. Both were living in the lab for all practical purposes and working harder than they had in their lives.

Edward insisted on doing everything himself, which meant he even reproduced Eleanor's work in order to be one hundred percent certain of no mistakes. In like manner he had Eleanor check his results.

As busy as Edward was with the alkaloid, he had no time for anything else. Despite Eleanor's advice to the contrary and despite mounting rumblings from the undergraduate students, he'd given no lectures. Nor had he devoted any time to his bevy of graduate students, many of whose research projects were now stalled without his continual leadership and advice.

Edward was unconcerned. Like an artist in a fit of creation, he was mesmerized by the new drug and oblivious to his surroundings. To his continued delight the structure of the drug was emerging atom by atom from the mists of time in which it had been secreted.

By early Wednesday morning, in a superb feat of qualitative organic chemistry, Edward completely characterized the four-ringed structural core of the compound. By Wednesday afternoon all of the side chains were defined both in terms of their makeup and point of attachment to the core. Edward jokingly described the molecule as an apple with protruding worms.

It was the side chains that particularly fascinated Edward. There were five of them. One was tetracyclic like the core and resembled LSD. Another had two rings and resembled a drug called scopolamine. The last three resembled the brain's major neurotransmitters: norepinephrine, dopamine, and serotonin.

By the wee hours of Thursday morning, Edward and Eleanor were rewarded by the image of the entire molecular structure appearing on a computer screen in virtual three-dimensional space. The achievement had been the product of new structural software, supercomputer capability, and hours of heated argument between Edward and Eleanor as each played devil's advocate with the other.

Hypnotized by the image, Edward and Eleanor silently watched as the supercomputer slowly rotated the molecule. It was in dazzling color, with the electron clouds represented by varying shades of cobalt blue. The carbon atoms were red, the oxygen green, and the nitrogen yellow.

After flexing his fingers as if he were a virtuoso about to play a Beethoven sonata on a Steinway grand piano, Edward sat down at his terminal, which was on-line with the supercomputer. Calling upon all his knowledge, experience, and intuitive chemical sense, he began to work the keyboard. On the screen the image trembled and jerked while maintaining its slow rotation. Edward was operating on the molecule, chipping away at the two side chains he instinctively knew were responsible for the hallucinogenic effect: the LSD side chain and the scopolamine side chain.

To his delight, he was able to remove all but a tiny two-carbon stump of the LSD side chain without significantly affecting either the three-dimensional structure of the compound or its distribution of electrical charges. He knew altering either of these properties would dramatically affect the drug's bioactivity.

With the scopolamine side chain it was a different story. Edward was able to amputate the side chain partially, leaving a sizable portion intact. When he tried to remove more, the molecule folded on itself and drastically changed its three-dimensional shape.

After Edward had removed as much of the scopolamine side chain as he dared, he downloaded the molecular data to his own lab computer. The image now wasn't as spectacular, but was in some respects more interesting. What Edward and Eleanor were looking at now was a hypothetical new designer drug that had been formed by computer manipulation of a natural compound.

Edward's goal with the computer manipulations was to eliminate the drug's hallucinogenic and antiparasympathetic side effects. The latter referred to the dry mouth, the pupillary dilation, and partial amnesia both he and Stanton had experienced.

At that point Edward's true forte, synthetic organic chemistry, came to bear. In a marathon effort from early Thursday to late Thursday night, Edward ingeniously figured out a process to formulate the hypothetical drug from standard, available reagents. By early Friday morning he produced a vialful of the new drug.

"What do you think?" Edward asked Eleanor as the two of them gazed at the vial. They were both exhausted, but neither had any intention of sleeping.

"I think you've accomplished an amazing feat of chemical virtuosity," Eleanor said sincerely.

"I wasn't looking for a compliment," Edward said. He yawned. "I'm interested to know what you think we should do first."

"I'm the conservative member of this team," Eleanor said. "I'd say let's get an idea of toxicity."

"Let's do it," Edward said. He heaved himself to his feet and lent Eleanor a hand. Together they went back to work.

Empowered by their accomplishments and impatient for immediate results, they forgot scientific protocol. As they had done with the natural alkaloid, they dispensed with controlled, careful studies to get a rapid, general data to give them an idea of the drug's potential.

The first thing they did was add varying concentrations of the drug to various types of tissue cultures, including kidney and nerve cells. With even relatively large doses they were happy to see no effect. They put the cultures in an incubator so that they could periodically access them.

Next they prepared a ganglion preparation from *Aplasia fasciata* by inserting tiny electrodes into spontaneously firing nerve cells. Connecting the electrodes to an amplifier, they created an image of the cells' activity on a cathode ray tube. Slowly they added their drug to the perfusing fluid. By watching the neuronal responses, they determined that the drug was indeed bioactive although it didn't depress or increase the spontaneous activity. Instead the drug appeared to stabilize the rhythm.

With mounting excitement, since everything they did yielded positive results, Eleanor began feeding the new drug to a new batch of stressed rats while Edward added the new drug to a fresh synaptosome preparation. Eleanor was the first to get results. She was quickly convinced the modified drug had even more calming effect on the rats than the unaltered alkaloid.

It took Edward a little longer to get his results. He found that the new drug affected the levels of all three neurotransmitters, but not equally. Serotonin was affected more than norepinephrine, which was affected more than dopamine. What he didn't expect was that the drug seemed to form a loose covalent bond with both glutamate and gamma-aminobutyric acid, two of the major inhibitory agents in the brain.

"This is all fantastic!" Edward exclaimed. He picked up the papers from his desk that recorded all their findings and allowed them to rain down like massive sheets of confetti. "This data suggests that the potential of the drug is monumental. I'm willing to bet it's both an antidepressant and an anxiolytic, and as such it could revolutionize the field of psychopharmacology. It might even eventually be compared with the discovery of penicillin."

"We still have the worry about it being hallucinogenic," Eleanor said.

"I sincerely doubt it," Edward said. "Not after removing that LSD-like side chain. But I agree we have to be sure."

"Let's check the tissue cultures," Eleanor said. She knew Edward would want to take the drug. It was the only way to determine if it was hallucinogenic.

They retrieved their tissue cultures from the incubator and examined them under a low-power microscope. One after another they appeared healthy. There was no sign of cellular damage from the new drug, even those subjected to high doses.

"There doesn't seem to be any toxicity at all," Edward said with glee.

"I wouldn't have believed it if I hadn't seen it," Eleanor said.

They went back to Edward's bench area and made up several solutions of increasing strength. The starting point was a concentration that yielded a dose approximating the dosage of the unmodified alkaloid that Stanton had received. Edward was the first to try it, and when nothing happened, Eleanor took it. Again nothing happened.

Encouraged by these negative results, Edward and Eleanor gradually increased their dosages up to a full milligram, knowing that LSD was psychedelic at 0.05 milligrams.

"Well?" Edward questioned a half hour later.

"No hallucinogenic effect as far as I can tell," Eleanor said.

"But there is an effect," Edward said.

"Most definitely," Eleanor said. "I'd have to describe it as calm contentment. Whatever it is, I like it."

"I also feel as if my mind is particularly sharp," Edward said. "It has to be drug-related because twenty minutes ago I was a basket case, thinking my ability to concentrate was nil. Now I'm energized as if I'd had a night's rest."

"I have a sense my long-term memory has been awakened from a slumber," Eleanor said. "Suddenly I remember my home phone number when I was a child of six. It was the year my family moved to the West Coast."

"What about your senses?" Edward asked. "Mine seem particularly acute, especially my sense of smell."

"I wouldn't have thought of it until you mentioned it," Eleanor said. She put her head back and sniffed the air. "I never realized the lab was such a cacophony of odors."

"There's something else I'm feeling that I wouldn't have even been sensitive to if I hadn't taken a course of Prozac," Edward said. "I feel socially assertive, like I could walk into a group of people and do whatever I wanted. The difference is that it took three months of Prozac before I felt that way."

"I can't say I feel anything like that," Eleanor said. "But I can say my mouth is a little dry. Is yours?"

"Perhaps," Edward admitted. Then he looked directly into Eleanor's deep blue eyes. "Your pupils also might be a bit dilated. If they are, it must be the scopolamine side chain we couldn't totally eliminate. Check your near vision."

Eleanor picked up a reagent bottle and read the tiny print on the label. "No problem," she said.

"Anything else?" Edward said. "Any trouble with your circulation or breathing?"

"Everything is fine," Eleanor said.

"Excuse me," a voice called.

Eleanor and Edward turned to see one of the second-year doctorate students had approached them. "I need some help," she said. Her name was Nadine Foch. She was from Paris. "The NMR is not functioning."

"Perhaps it would be best to talk to Ralph," Edward said. He smiled warmly. "I'd like to help, but I'm rather involved at the moment. Besides, Ralph knows the machine better than I, particularly from a technical point of view."

Nadine thanked them and went to find Ralph.

"That was rather civil of you," Eleanor said.

"I feel rather civil," Edward said. "Besides, she's a nice person."

"Perhaps this is a good time for you to resume your normal activities," Eleanor said. "We've made fantastic progress."

"It's only a harbinger of what's to come," Edward said. "It's good of you to worry about my teaching and supervisory responsibilities, but I assure you that they can slide for several weeks without causing anybody irreparable damage. I'm not about to forfeit any of this excitement with this new drug. Meanwhile I want you to start computerized molecular modeling to create a family of compounds from our new drug by substituting side chains."

While Eleanor went off to work at her computer terminal, Edward walked back to his desk and picked up the phone. He called Stanton Lewis.

"Are you busy tonight?" Edward asked his old friend.

"I'm busy every night," Stanton said. "What's on your mind? Did you read that prospectus?"

"How about having dinner with me and Kim?" Edward said. "There's something you should know."

"Ah ha, you old rogue," Stanton said. "Is this going to be some sort of a major social announcement?"

"I believe I'd rather discuss it in person," Edward said smoothly. "What about dinner? It will be my treat!"

"This is sounding serious," Stanton said. "I have a dinner reservation at Anago Bistro on Main Street in Cambridge. The reservation is for two, but I'll see that it gets changed to four. It's for eight P.M. I'll call back if there is a problem."

"That's perfect," Edward said. Then he hung up before Stanton could ask any more questions. Edward dialed Kim at work in the SICU.

"Busy?" he asked when Kim came on the line.

"Don't ask," Kim said.

"I made dinner plans with Stanton and his wife," Edward said excitedly. "It will be at eight unless I hear back from Stanton. I'm sorry it's such short notice. I hope it's OK for you."

"You're not working tonight?" Kim asked with surprise.

"I'm taking the evening off," Edward said.

"What about tomorrow?" Kim asked. "Are we still going up to Salem?"

"We'll talk about it," Edward said noncommittally. "What about dinner?"

"I'd rather eat just with you," Kim said.

"You're sweet to say that," Edward said. "And I'd rather eat just with you. But I have to talk with Stanton, and I thought we could make a little party out of it. I know I haven't been so much fun this week."

"You sound buoyant," Kim said. "Did something good happen today?"

"It's all been good," Edward said. "And that's why this meeting is important. After the dinner just you and I can spend some time together. We'll take a walk in the square like we did the evening we first met. How about it?"

"You've got a date," Kim said.

Kim and Edward arrived at the restaurant first, and the hostess, who was also one of the owners, sat them at a cozy table wedged into a nook next to the window. The view was out over a portion of Main Street with its collection of pizza joints and Indian restaurants. A fire truck sped by with all its bells and sirens screaming.

"I'd swear the Cambridge fire company uses their equipment to go for coffee," Edward said. He laughed as he watched the truck recede. "They're always out riding around. There can't be that many fires."

Kim eyed Edward. He was in a rare mood. Kim had never seen him so talkative and jovial, and although he looked tired, he was acting as if he'd just had several espressos. He even ordered a bottle of wine.

"I thought you told me you always let Stanton order the wine," Kim said.

Before Edward could answer, Stanton arrived, and true to character breezed into the restaurant as if he were an owner. He kissed the hostess's hand, which the hostess endured with thinly disguised impatience.

"OK, you guys," Stanton said to Edward and Kim as he tried to help Candice into her chair. The table was narrow, and each couple had to sit side-by-side. "What's the big news between you two? Do I have to pop for a bottle of Dom Pérignon?"

Kim looked at Edward for some explanation.

"I've already ordered some wine," Edward said. "It will do nicely."

"You ordered wine?" Stanton questioned. "But they don't serve Ripple here." Stanton laughed heartily as he sat down.

"I ordered an Italian white," Edward said. "A cool dry wine goes nicely with hot summer weather."

Kim lifted her eyebrows. This was a side of Edward she'd not seen.

"So what is it?" Stanton said. He eagerly leaned forward with his elbows on the table. "Are you two getting married?"

Kim blushed. With some embarrassment she wondered if Edward had told Stanton about their plans to share the cottage. It wasn't a secret as far as she was concerned, but she would have liked to tell her family herself.

"I should be so lucky," Edward said with a laugh of his own. "I've got some news—but it's not that good."

Kim blinked and looked at Edward. She was impressed he dealt so adroitly with Stanton's inappropriate comment.

The waitress arrived with the wine. Stanton made a production of examining the label before allowing it to be opened. "I'm surprised, old boy," he said to Edward. "Not a bad choice."

Once the wine was poured, Stanton started to make a toast, but Edward quieted him.

"It's my turn," Edward said. He held out his glass toward Stanton. "To the world's cleverest medical venture capitalist," he said.

"And I thought you never noticed," Stanton said with a laugh. Then they all took a drink.

"I have a question for you," Edward said to Stanton. "Were you serious when you said recently that a new, effective psychotropic drug could potentially be a billion-dollar molecule?"

"Absolutely," Stanton said. His demeanor instantly became more serious. "Is this why we're here? Do you have some new information about the drug that sent me on my psychedelic trip?"

Both Candice and Kim questioned what psychedelic trip Stanton was referring to. When they heard what had happened they were appalled.

"It wasn't half bad," Stanton said. "I rather enjoyed it."

"I've got a lot of information," Edward said. "All of it is superlative. We eliminated the hallucinogenic effect by altering the molecule. Now I think we have created the next-generation drug to the likes of Prozac and Xanax. It seems to be perfect. It's nontoxic, effective orally, has fewer side effects and probably a broader therapeutic capability. In fact, because of its unique side chain structure capable of alteration and substitution, it might have unlimited therapeutic capability in the psychotropic arena."

"Be more specific," Stanton said. "What do you think this drug can do?"

"We believe it will have a general, positive impact on mood," Edward said. "It seems to be antidepressant and anxiolytic, meaning it lowers anxiety. It also seems to function as a general tonic to combat fatigue, increase contentment, sharpen the senses, and encourage clear thinking by enhancing long-term memory."

"My God!" Stanton exclaimed. "What *doesn't* it do? It sounds like Soma from *Brave New World*."

"That analogy might have merit," Edward said.

"One question," Stanton said. He lowered his voice and leaned forward. "Will it make sex better?"

Edward shrugged. "It might," he said. "Since it enhances the senses, sex could be more intense."

Stanton threw up his hands. "Hell," he said. "We're not talking about a billion-dollar molecule; we're talking about a five-billion-dollar molecule."

"Are you serious?" Edward asked.

"Let's say a billion plus," Stanton said.

The waitress interrupted their conversation. They ordered their dinners. After she'd left, Edward was the first to speak. "We haven't proven any of this," he said. "There's been no controlled experiments."

"But you're pretty confident," Stanton said.

"Very confident," Edward said.

"Who knows about this?" Stanton asked.

"Only me, my closest assistant, and the people at this table," Edward said.

"Do you have any idea how the drug works?" Stanton asked.

"Only a vague hypothesis," Edward said. "The drug seems to stabilize the concentrations of the brain's major neurotransmitters and in that way works on a multilevel basis. It affects individual neurons but also whole networks of cells as if it were an autocoid or brain hormone."

"Where did it come from?" Candice asked.

Edward summarized the story by explaining the association between Kim's forebear, the Salem witch trials, and the theory the accusers in Salem had been poisoned by a mold.

"It was Kim's question whether the poison theory could be proved which got me to take some samples of dirt," Edward said.

"I don't deserve any credit," Kim said.

"But you do," Edward said. "You and Elizabeth."

"Such irony," Candice said. "Finding a useful drug in a dirt sample."

"Not really," Edward said. "Many important drugs have been found in dirt like cephalosporins or cyclosporine. In this case the irony is the drug is coming from the devil."

"Don't say that," Kim said. "It gives me the creeps."

Edward laughed teasingly. He hooked his thumb at Kim and told the others that she was wont to have occasional attacks of superstition.

"I don't think I like the association either," Stanton said. "I'd rather consider it a drug from heaven."

"The association with the witch frenzy doesn't bother me at all," Edward said. "In fact I like it. Although finding this drug can't justify the death of twenty people, at least it might give their sacrifice some meaning."

"Twenty-one deaths," Kim corrected. She explained to the others that Elizabeth's execution had been overlooked by the historians.

"I wouldn't care if the drug were related to the biblical flood," Stanton said. "It sounds like an extraordinary discovery." Then, looking at Edward, he asked, "What are you going to do?"

"That's why I wanted to see you," Edward said. "What do you think I should do?"

"Exactly what I already told you," Stanton said. "We should form a company and patent the drug and as many clones as possible."

"You really think this could be a billion-dollar situation?" Edward asked.

"I know what I'm talking about," Stanton said. "This is my area of expertise."

"Then let's do it," Edward said. "Let's form a company and go for it."

Stanton stared into Edward's face for a beat. "I think you are serious," he said.

"You bet I'm serious," Edward said.

"All right, first we need some names," Stanton said. He took out a small notebook and pen from his jacket pocket. "We need a name for the drug and a name for the company itself. Maybe we should call the drug Soma for the literary set."

"There's already a drug called Soma," Edward said. "How about Omni, in keeping with its potentially wide range of clinical applications?"

"Omni just doesn't sound like a drug," Stanton said. "In fact it sounds more like a company. We could call it Omni Pharmaceuticals."

"I like it," Edward said.

"How about 'Ultra' for the drug," Stanton said. "I can see that working well for advertising."

"Sounds good," Edward said.

The men looked at the women for their reaction. Candice hadn't been listening, so Stanton had to repeat the names. After he did she said they were fine. Kim had been listening, but she didn't have an opinion; she was a bit taken aback by the discussion. Edward had shown no awkwardness in this sudden and unexpected interest in business.

"How much money can you raise?" Edward asked.

"How long would you estimate it would take before you were ready to market this new drug?" Stanton asked.

"I don't think I can answer that question," Edward said. "Obviously I can't even be one hundred percent sure it will ever be marketable."

"I know that," Stanton said. "I'm just looking for a best-guess estimate. I know that the average duration from discovery of a potential drug to its FDA approval and marketing is about twelve years, and the average cost is somewhere around two hundred million dollars."

"I wouldn't need twelve years," Edward said. "And I wouldn't need anywhere near two hundred million dollars to do it."

"Obviously the shorter the development time and the less money needed means more equity we can keep for ourselves."

"I understand," Edward said. "Frankly I'm not interested in giving away much equity at all."

"How much money do you think you would need?" Stanton asked.

"I'd have to set up a state-of-the-art lab," Edward said, beginning to think out loud.

"What's the matter with the lab you already have?" Stanton asked.

"The lab belongs to Harvard," Edward said. "I have to get the Ultra project away from Harvard because of a participation agreement I signed when I accepted my position."

"Is this going to cause us some problems?" Stanton asked.

"No, I don't think so," Edward said. "The agreement concerns discoveries made on company time using company equipment. I'll argue that I discovered Ultra on my own time, which is technically correct although I've done the preliminary separation and synthesis on company time. Anyway, the bottom line is that I'm not afraid of some legal harassment. After all, Harvard doesn't own me."

"How about the development period?" Stanton asked. "How much shorter do you think you could make that?"

"A lot," Edward said. "One of the things about Ultra that has impressed me is how unbelievably nontoxic it appears to be. I believe this fact alone will make FDA approval a breeze since characterizing specific toxicities is what takes so damn much time."

"So you're talking about getting FDA approval years sooner than the average," Stanton said.

"Without doubt," Edward said. "Animal studies will be accelerated if there's no toxicity to worry about, and the clinical portion can be collapsed by combining phase II and phase III with the FDA's expedited schedule."

"The expedited plan is for drugs targeted for life-threatening diseases," Kim said. From her experience in the SICU she knew something about experimental drug testing.

"If Ultra is as efficacious for depression as I think it will prove to be," Edward said, "I'm confident we can make a case for it in relation to some serious illness."

"What about western Europe and Asia?" Stanton asked. "FDA approval is not needed to market a drug in those areas."

"Very true," Edward said. "The USA is not the only pharmaceutical market."

"I'll tell you what," Stanton said. "I can easily raise four to five million without having to give up more than a token amount of equity since most of it would come from my own resources. How does that sound?"

"It sounds fantastic," Edward said. "When can you start?"

"Tomorrow," Stanton said. "I'll start raising the money and organizing the legal work to set up the corporation as well as to start the patent applications."

"Do you know if we can patent the core of the molecule?" Edward asked. "I'd love the patent to cover any drug formulated with the core."

"I don't know, but I can find out," Stanton said.

"While you're seeing to the financial and legal aspects," Edward said, "I'll start the process of setting up the lab. The first question will be where to site it. I'd like to have it someplace handy because I'll be spending a lot of time there."

"Cambridge is a good location," Stanton said.

"I want it away from Harvard," Edward said.

"How about the Kendall Square area?" Stanton suggested. "It's far enough away from Harvard and yet close enough to your apartment."

Edward turned to Kim and their eyes met. Kim guessed what he was thinking, so she nodded. It was a gesture imperceptible to the Lewises.

"Actually I'm moving out of Cambridge at the end of August," Edward said. "I'm moving to Salem."

"Edward is coming to live with me," Kim said, knowing it would quickly get back to her mother. "I'm renovating the old house on the family compound."

"That's wonderful," Candice said.

"You old rogue," Stanton said as he reached across the table and gave Edward a light punch in the shoulder.

"For once in my life my personal life is going as well as my professional life," Edward said.

"Why don't we site the company somewhere on the North Shore?" Stanton suggested. "Hell, commercial rents up there must be a fraction of what they are in the city."

"Stanton, you've just given me a great idea," Edward said. He turned sideways to look at Kim. "What about that mill-turned-stables on the compound? It would make a perfect lab for this kind of project because of its isolation."

"I don't know," Kim stammered. She'd been caught totally unawares by the suggestion.

"I'm talking about Omni renting the space from you and your brother," Edward said, warming to the idea. "As you've mentioned, the compound is a burden. I'm sure some legitimate rent could be a real help."

"It's not a bad idea," Stanton said. "The rent could be totally written off, so it would be tax free. Good suggestion, old sport."

"What do you say?" Edward asked.

"I'd have to ask my brother," Kim said.

"Of course," Edward said. "When? I mean the sooner the better."

Kim looked at her watch and calculated that it was about two-thirty in the morning in London, just about the time Brian would be getting down to work. "I could call him any evening," Kim said. "I suppose I could even call him now."

"That's what I like to hear," Stanton said. "Decisiveness." He pulled his cellular phone from his pocket and pushed it across to Kim. "Omni will even pay for the call."

Kim stood up.

"Where are you going?" Edward asked.

"I feel self-conscious calling my brother in front of everyone," Kim said.

"Perfectly understandable," Stanton said. "You go on into the ladies' room."

"I think I prefer to step outside," Kim said.

After Kim had left the table Candice congratulated Edward on the progress of his relationship with Kim.

"We've been enjoying each other's company," Edward said.

"How much personnel would you need at the lab?" Stanton asked. "Hefty salaries can eat up capital like nothing else."

"I'd keep the number to a minimum," Edward said. "I'd need a biologist to handle the animal studies, an immunologist for the cellular studies, a crystallographer, a molecular modeler, a biophysicist for nuclear magnetic resonance, a pharmacologist, plus myself and Eleanor."

"Jesus Christ!" Stanton exclaimed. "What the hell do you think you are creating, a university?"

"I assure you this is a minimum for the kind of work we'll be doing," Edward said calmly.

"Why Eleanor?"

"She's my assistant," Edward said. "She's the person I work with the closest, and she's crucial to the project."

"When can you start to assemble this team?" Stanton asked.

"As soon as you have the money," Edward said. "We'll have to have first-class people, so they won't come cheap. I'll be enticing them away from coveted academic appointments and lucrative positions in private industry."

"That's exactly what I'm afraid of," Stanton said. "Many new biomedical companies go belly-up from a hemorrhage of capital from overly generous salaries."

"I'll keep that in mind," Edward said. "When can you have money available for me to draw on?"

"I can have a million available by the beginning of the week," Stanton said.

The first courses of their dinner arrived. Since Candice and Stanton were having hot appetizers, Edward insisted they start. But no sooner had they picked up their forks than Kim returned. She sat down and handed Stanton his phone.

"I've good news," she said. "My brother is delighted with the idea of paying tenants in the old mill building, but he insisted that we will not pay for any improvements. That will have to be up to Omni."

"Fair enough," Edward said. He picked up his glass in preparation for another toast. He had to nudge Stanton, who was momentarily lost in thought. "To Omni and to Ultra," Edward said. They all drank.

"This is how I think we should set the company up," Stanton said as soon as he put his glass down. "We'll capitalize with four and a half million and value the stock at ten dollars a share. Out of the four hundred and fifty thousand shares we'll each hold one hundred and fifty thousand, leaving one hundred and fifty thousand for future financing and for attracting the best people by offering some equity. If Ultra turns out to be anything like it's been described tonight, each share of the stock will end up being ungodly valuable."

"I'll drink to that," Edward said, raising his wineglass yet again. They all clinked their glasses and drank, particularly Edward, who found himself enjoying the wine selection he'd made. He'd never had better white wine, and he took a moment to savor its vanilla bouquet and slightly apricot finish.

After the dinner was over and goodbyes had been said, Kim and Edward climbed into Edward's car in the restaurant's parking lot.

"If you wouldn't mind, I'd like to skip the walk in the square," Edward said.

"Oh?" Kim questioned. She was mildly disappointed. She was also surprised, but then the whole evening had been a surprise. She'd not expected Edward to have been willing to take an evening off, and on top of that, his behavior had been exceptional from the moment he'd picked her up.

"There's some phone calls I'd like to make," Edward said.

"It's after ten," Kim reminded him. "Isn't it a little late to be calling people?"

"Not on the West Coast," Edward said. "There's a couple of people at UCLA and Stanford who I'd like to see on the Omni staff."

"I gather you are excited about this business venture," Kim commented.

"I'm ecstatic," Edward said. "My intuition told me I was onto something im-

portant the moment I learned we'd stumbled onto three previously unknown alkaloids. I just didn't know it was going to be this big."

"Aren't you a little worried about the participation agreement you signed
with Harvard?" Kim asked. "I've heard about similar situations leading to serious
trouble in this town, like during the 1980s, when academia and industry became
much too cozy."

"It's a problem I will leave to the lawyers," Edward said.

"I don't know," Kim said, unconvinced. "Whether lawyers are involved or
not, it could affect your academic career." Knowing how much Edward valued
teaching, Kim was worried that his sudden entrepreneurial enthusiasm was
clouding his better judgment.

"It's a risk," Edward admitted. "But I'm more than willing to take it. The opportunity Ultra offers is a once-in-a-lifetime proposition. It's a chance to make
a mark in this world and to earn some real money while doing it."

"I thought you said you weren't interested in becoming a millionaire," Kim
said.

"I wasn't," Edward said. "But I hadn't thought about becoming a billionaire.
I didn't realize the stakes were that high."

Kim wasn't sure there was that much difference, but she didn't say anything.
It was an ethical question that she didn't feel like debating at the moment.

"I'm sorry about making the suggestion of converting the Stewart stables to
a lab without discussing it with you beforehand," Edward said. "It's not like me
to blurt something like that out on the spur of the moment. I guess the excitement of talking with Stanton got the best of me."

"Your apology is accepted," Kim said. "Besides, my brother was intrigued
with the idea. I suppose the rent will be helpful in paying the taxes on the property. They're astronomical."

"One nice thing is that the stables are far enough away from the cottage so
the lab's presence won't bother us," Edward said.

They turned off Memorial Drive and headed into the quiet, residential back
streets of Cambridge. Edward pulled into his parking spot and turned off the engine. Then he hit his forehead with the palm of his hand.

"Stupid me," he said. "We should have driven back to your place to get your
things."

"You want me to stay tonight?"

"Of course," Edward said. "Don't you want to?"

"You've been so busy lately," Kim said. "I didn't know what to expect."

"If you stay it will make heading up to Salem in the morning that much easier," Edward said. "We can get an early start."

"You definitely want to go?" Kim asked. "I had the sense you won't want to
take the time."

"I do now that we are siting Omni there," Edward said. He restarted the car
and backed out. "Let's go back and get you a change of clothes. Of course that's

assuming you want to stay—which I hope you do." He smiled broadly in the half-light.

"I suppose," Kim said. She was feeling indecisive and anxious without knowing exactly why.

Kim and Edward did not get an early start as Edward had suggested the night before. Instead Edward had spent half the morning on the phone. First he'd called Kim's contractor and architect about expanding the work at the compound to include the new lab. They'd agreed with alacrity and offered to meet at the compound at eleven. Next Edward had called a series of representatives of laboratory equipment manufacturers and scheduled them to show up at the same time as the contractor and architect.

After a quick call to Stanton to be sure the money he'd promised would be immediately forthcoming, Edward phoned a series of people whom he wanted to consider recruiting for Omni's professional staff. Edward and Kim did not get into the car for the drive north until well after ten.

By the time Edward parked in front of the stables in the Stewart compound there was a small crowd of people waiting. They had all introduced themselves, so Edward was spared the task. Instead he waved for them to gather by the padlocked sliding door.

The building was a long, single-story stone structure with infrequent windows set high under the eaves. Since the terrain fell off sharply toward the river, the back was two stories, with separate entrances to each stall on the lower level.

Kim tried multiple keys before finding the correct one to open the heavy padlock. After sliding it open, everyone entered what was the ground floor from the front and the second story from the rear.

The interior was a huge, undivided long room with a cathedral ceiling. On the rear side of the building there were multiple shuttered openings. One end of the room was filled with bales of hay.

"At least the demolition will be easy," George said.

"This is perfect," Edward said. "My idea of a lab is one big space so that everyone interfaces with everyone else."

The stairway leading down to the lower level was constructed of rough-hewn oak and pegged together with dowels an inch in diameter. Downstairs they found a long hall with stalls to the right and tack rooms to the left.

Kim tagged along and listened to the plans to convert the barn rapidly into a state-of-the-art biological and pharmacological laboratory. Downstairs there were to be quarters for a menagerie of experimental animals including rhesus monkeys, mice, rats, and rabbits. There was also to be space for tissue- and bacterial-culture incubators along with containment facilities. And finally there were to be specially shielded rooms for the NMR and X-ray crystallography.

The upstairs would house the main laboratory space as well as a shielded, air-conditioned room for a large mainframe computer. Every laboratory bench would have its own terminal. To power all the electronic equipment a huge electrical service would be brought in.

"Well, there you have it," Edward said when they had finished the tour. He turned to the contractor and architect. "Can you see any problems with all this?"

"I don't think so," Mark said. "The building is sound. But I would suggest we design an entrance with a reception area."

"We won't be having many visitors," Edward said. "But I see your point. Go ahead and design it. What else?"

"I can't see that we'll have any trouble with permits," George said.

"Provided we don't say anything about the animal aspect," Mark said. "My advice is just not to mention it. It could create problems that would take a long time to resolve."

"I'm more than happy to leave the civic relations to you experienced men," Edward said. "The fact is, I'm interested in expediting this project, so I'd like to take full advantage of your expertise. And to speed completion I'm willing to give a ten percent bonus above time, materials, and fees."

Enthusiastic and eager smiles appeared on Mark's and George's faces.

"When can you start?" Edward asked.

"We can start immediately," Mark and George said in unison.

"I hope my little job isn't going to suffer with this newer and bigger project," Kim said, speaking up for the first time.

"No need to worry," George said. "If anything it will speed work up at the cottage. We'll be bringing a big crew in here with all the trades represented. If we need a plumber or an electrician for some small task on your job, they'll already be on site."

While Edward, the contractor, the architect, and the various medical-equipment reps settled down to work out the details for the new lab, Kim wandered outside the stables. She squinted her eyes against the hazy but intense noontime sun. She knew she wasn't contributing to the planning of the lab, so she hiked across the field toward the cottage to check on the renovation.

As she neared the building she noticed the trench had been filled in. She also noticed that the workmen had reset Elizabeth's headstone into the ground above the grave. They'd laid it flat just as they'd found it.

Kim entered the cottage. It seemed tiny after being in the stables. But the work was progressing well, especially in the kitchen and the bathrooms. For the first time she could imagine what they would be like when they were finished.

After touring the cottage, Kim wandered back to the stables, but there was no suggestion that Edward and the others were anywhere near finishing their impromptu conference. Kim interrupted long enough to let Edward know she'd be up in the castle. Edward told her to enjoy herself and immediately went back to some problem involving the NMR machine.

Stepping from the bright sunshine into the somber, heavily draped interior of the castle was like stepping into another world. Kim stopped and listened to the creaks and groans of the house as it adjusted to the heat. For the first time she realized she couldn't hear the sound of the birds, which outside was loud, particularly the cry of seagulls.

After a short debate she mounted the grand staircase. Despite her recent success finding seventeenth-century material in the wine cellar, she thought she'd give the attic another chance, especially since it was so much more pleasant.

The first thing she did was open many of the dormer windows to let in the breeze from the river. Stepping away from the last window she opened, she noticed stacks upon stacks of clothbound ledgers. They were arranged along one side of the dormer.

Taking one of the books in her hand, Kim looked at the spine. Handprinted in white ink on a black background were the words *Sea Witch*. Curious about what the book was, Kim cracked it open. At first she thought it was someone's diary because all the handwritten entries began with the day of the month followed by a narrative involving detailed descriptions of the weather. She soon realized that it wasn't a personal diary but rather a ship's log.

Turning to the front of the book, Kim learned that it covered the years 1791 through 1802. Kim put the log back and glanced at the spines of the other books in the stack, reading the names. There were seven books with the name *Sea Witch*. Checking them all, she learned the oldest went from 1737 to 1749.

Wondering if there could be any from the seventeenth century, Kim looked at the books in other stacks. In a small pile near the window she noticed that there was one with a worn leather spine and no name. She got it out.

The book had an old feel much like the Bible Kim had found in the wine cellar. She opened to the title page. It was the ship's log for a brig called the *Endeavor*, and it covered the years from 1679 to 1703. Delicately turning the aged pages, Kim advanced through the book year by year until she got to 1692.

The first entry for the year was on the 24th of January. It described the weather as cold and clear with a good westerly wind. It went on to say that the ship had embarked with the tide and was bound for Liverpool with a load of whale oil, timber, ship's stores, fur, potash, and dried cod and mackerel.

Kim sucked in a mouthful of air as her eyes stumbled onto a familiar name. The next sentence in the entry stated that the ship was carrying a distinguished passenger, Ronald Stewart, Esquire, the ship's owner. Hastily Kim read on. The log explained that Ronald was en route to Sweden to supervise the outfitting and take possession of a new ship to be called the *Sea Spirit*.

Quickly Kim scanned the subsequent entries for the voyage. Ronald's name was not mentioned again until he disembarked in Liverpool after an uneventful crossing.

With some excitement, Kim closed the book and descended from the attic to the wine cellar. Opening the Bible box, she took out the deed she'd found on her last visit and checked the date. She'd been correct! The reason Elizabeth's signature was on the deed was that Ronald had been at sea when the deed was signed.

Solving even a small mystery involving Elizabeth gave Kim a sense of satisfaction. She put the deed back in the Bible box and was in the process of adding the ship's log to her small collection when three envelopes tied with a thin ribbon slipped out from beneath the back cover.

Kim picked up the slim packet with trembling fingers. She could see that the top one was addressed to Ronald Stewart. After untying the ribbon she discovered they were all addressed to Ronald. With great excitement she opened the envelopes and removed the contents. There were three letters, dated October 23rd, October 29th, and November 11th, 1692.

The first was from Samuel Sewall:

Boston

My Dear Friend,

I understand that you are troubled in spirit although I hope in God's name that your recent marriage may ease your disquietude. I also understand your wish to contain the knowledge of your late wife's unfortunate association with the Prince of Darkness, but I must in good faith advise you to forebear petitioning the Governor for a Writ of Replevin in regards to the conclusive evidence used to convict your aforesaid wife of abominable witchcraft. To the like purpose I would have you apply to and beseech Reverend Cotton Mather in whose cellar you espied your wife's infernal doings. It has come into my knowledge that official custody of the evidence has been granted in perpetuity to Reverend Mather according to his request.

I remain your Friend,
Samuel Sewall.

Frustrated that she'd found another reference to the mysterious evidence without its being described, Kim turned to the second letter. It was written by Cotton Mather.

Saturday 29th October
Boston

Sir:

I am in receipt of your recent letter and your reference to our being fellow graduates of Harvard Colledge which gives me the hope that your disposition to the venerable institution is one of loving solicitude so that you will be amenable of mind and spirit to what I and my esteemed father hath decided is the proper place for Elizabeth's handiwork. You recall when we met at my home in July I had worried concern that the good people of Salem could very well be excited to a state of unruly and turbulent spirit in regards to the Devil's presence so clearly defined by Elizabeth's actions and infernal works. It is most unfortunate that my fervent concerns have come to pass and despite my urging of a very critical and exquisite caution in the use of spectral evidence since the Father of Lies could conceivably assume the outward shape of an innocent person, innocent people's good reputation can be sullied despite the sedulous endeavors of our honorable judges who are so eminent for their justice, wisdom, and goodness. I fully comprehend your honorable wish to shield your family from further humiliation but it is my belief that Elizabeth's evidence should be preserved for the benefit of future generations in their eternal combat with the forces of evil as a prime example of the type of evidence needed to objectively determine a true covenant with the Devil and not mere maleficium. In this regard I have had much discours with my father, the Good Reverend Increase Mather who is currently justly serving as the President of Harvard Colledge. We together in like mind have decided that the evidence should be preserved at the Colledge for the edification and instruction of future generations whereof vigilance is important to thwart the work of the Devil in God's New Land.

Your servant in God's name,
Cotton Mather.

Kim wasn't certain she understood the entire letter, but the gist was easy enough to comprehend. Feeling even more frustrated about the mysterious evidence, she turned to the final letter. Glancing at the signature, she saw it was from Increase Mather.

11th November 1692
Cambridge

Sir:

I am in complete empathy for your wish for the aforesaid evidence to be returned for your private disposition, but I have been informed by the tutors William Brattle and John Leverett that the evidence has been received by the students with diligent interest and has stimulated impassioned and enlightening debate with the effect of convincing us it is God's will that Elizabeth's legacy be left at Harvard to stand as an important contribution to establishment of objective criteria for Ecclesiastic Law in association with witchcraft and the damnable work of the Devil. I beg of you to understand the importance of this evidence and agree that it indeed should remain with our collections. If and when the esteemed Fellows of

the Corporation of Harvard deem to found a school of law it will at that
time be sent to that institution.

I remain your servant,
Increase Mather.

"Damn it!" Kim said after reading the third letter. She could not believe that
she'd been lucky enough to find so many references to Elizabeth's evidence yet
still not know what it was. Thinking she might possibly have missed something,
she read the letters again. The strange syntax and orthography made reading
them somewhat difficult, but when she got to the end of the second reading she
was sure she'd not missed anything.

Stimulated by the letters, Kim again tried to imagine the nature of the incontrovertible evidence used against Elizabeth. From Kim's continued general
reading that week on the Salem witch trials, she'd become more convinced that
it had to have been some kind of book. Back in the days of the trials the issue of
the Devil's Book had come up frequently. The method that a supposed witch established a covenant with the devil was by writing in the Devil's Book.

Kim looked back at the letters. She noticed the evidence was described as
"Elizabeth's handiwork." Perhaps Elizabeth had made a book with an elaborately tooled leather cover? Kim laughed at herself. She knew she was taxing her
imagination, but nothing else came to mind.

In Increase Mather's letter, Kim noted that the evidence had elicited "impassioned and enlightening" debate among the students. She thought that description not only gave weight to the idea of the evidence being a book, but
tended to suggest it was the contents that were important, not its appearance.

But then Kim thought again about the evidence being some kind of doll. Just
that week she'd read that a doll with pins in it had been used in the trial of Bridget Bishop, the first person to be executed in the Salem ordeal.

Kim sighed. She knew that her wild speculations as to the nature of the evidence was not accomplishing anything. After all, the evidence could have been
anything to do with the occult. Instead of wild speculation she had to stick to
the facts that she had, and the three letters she'd just found gave her a very significant fact, namely that the evidence, whatever it was, had been given to Harvard University in 1692. Kim wondered what the chances were that she could
find reference to it at the institution today, and if she were to try, whether they
would laugh at her.

"Ah, there you are," Edward called down from the top of the wine cellar stair.
"Having any luck?"

"Strangely enough I have," Kim yelled back. "Come down and take a look at
these."

Edward climbed down the stairs and took the letters. "My goodness," he exclaimed when he saw the signatures. "These are three of the most famous Puritans. What a find!"

"Read them," Kim said. "They're interesting but frustrating for my purposes."

Edward leaned against a bureau to take advantage of the light from one of the wall sconces. He read the letters in the same order that Kim had.

"They're marvelous," he said when he was finished. "I love the wording and the grammar. It lets you know that rhetoric was a major course of study in those days. Some of it's above my head: I don't even know what the word 'sedulous' means."

"I think it means diligent," Kim said. "I didn't have any difficulty with definitions. What gave me trouble was how the sentences ran on and on."

"You're lucky these letters weren't written in Latin," Edward said. "Back in those days you had to read and write Latin fluently to get into Harvard. And speaking of Harvard, I'd bet Harvard would be interested in these, especially the one from Increase Mather."

"That's a good point," Kim said. "I was thinking about going to Harvard and asking about Elizabeth's evidence. I was afraid they might laugh at me. Maybe I could make a trade."

"They wouldn't laugh at you," Edward said. "I'm sure someone in the Widener Library would find the story intriguing. Of course, they wouldn't turn down a gift of the letter. They might even offer to buy it."

"Does reading these letters give you any better idea what the evidence could have been?" Kim asked.

"Not really," Edward said. "But I can understand what you mean by their being frustrating. It's almost funny how many times they mention the evidence without describing it."

"I thought Increase Mather's letter gave more weight to the idea it was some kind of book," Kim said. "Especially the part where he mentioned it stimulated debate among the students."

"Perhaps," Edward said.

"Wait a second," Kim said suddenly. "I just had another idea. Something I hadn't thought about. Why was Ronald so keen to get it back? Doesn't that tell us something?"

Edward shrugged. "I think he was interested in sparing his family further humiliation," he said. "Often entire families suffered when one member was convicted of witchcraft."

"What about the possibility it could have been self-implicating?" Kim said. "What if Ronald had something to do with Elizabeth's being accused and convicted of witchcraft? If he did, then maybe he wanted to get the evidence back so he could destroy it."

"Whooo, hold on!" Edward said. He backed away a step as if Kim were a threat. "You're too conspiratorially inclined; your imagination is working overtime."

"Ronald married Elizabeth's sister ten weeks after Elizabeth's death," Kim said heatedly.

"I think you are forgetting something," Edward said. "The test I ran on Elizabeth's remains suggests that she'd been chronically poisoned by the new fungus. She'd probably been having psychedelic trips on a regular basis, which had nothing to do with Ronald. In fact he might have been having his own if he were ingesting the same grain. I still think the evidence had to do with something Elizabeth made while under the hallucinogenic effect of the mold. Like we said, it could have been a book, or a picture, or a doll, or anything they thought related to the occult."

"You have a point," Kim conceded. She took the letters from Edward and put them in the Bible box. She glanced down the wine cellar's long hall with its complement of furniture filled with paperwork. "Well, back to the drawing board. I'll just have to keep looking in hopes of finding the evidence described."

"I finished my meetings," Edward said. "Everything is going smoothly regarding the new lab. I have to compliment you on your contractor. He's going to start today by digging the utility trench. He said his only concern was finding more graves! I think finding Elizabeth's spooked him. What a character."

"Do you want to go back to Boston?" Kim asked.

"I do," Edward admitted. "There are a lot of people I want to talk to now that Omni is soon to be a reality. But I don't mind taking the train like I did the last time. If you want to stay working here on your project, I think you should."

"Well, if you wouldn't mind," Kim said. Finding the letters had at least encouraged her.

FRIDAY • AUGUST 12, 1994

August began hot, hazy, and humid. There had been little rain all through July, and the drought continued into the following month without remittance until the grass on the Boston Common in front of Kim's apartment changed from green to brown.

At work, August brought some relief for Kim. Kinnard had started his two-month rotation at Salem Hospital, so she didn't have the anxiety of facing him daily in the SICU. Kim had also concluded negotiations with the department of nursing to give her the entire month of September free. It was put together with a combination of accumulated vacation time plus personal time off without pay. The nursing office hadn't been happy with the request, but they had compromised in order not to lose Kim altogether.

The beginning of the month also provided Kim with some time on her hands because Edward was away constantly. He was busy flying around the country on secret recruitment missions for Omni Pharmaceuticals. But he did not forget her. Despite his pressing schedule, he phoned every night around ten, just before Kim went to sleep. He also kept up the daily flowers although on a more modest scale. Now the deliveries were a single rose a day, which Kim felt was much more appropriate.

Kim had no trouble filling her time. In the evenings she continued her background reading on the Salem witch trials and Puritan culture. She also made it a point to visit the compound every day. Construction was proceeding at an extremely rapid rate. The crew at the lab was more numerous than the one working on the cottage. Nonetheless, progress at the cottage did not slow, and finish painting was begun even before all the cabinetwork had been completed.

To Kim, the biggest irony of the construction project was that her father was thoroughly impressed with her because of the work on the lab. Kim did not let on that she was not involved in that part of the renovation, and that it had not been her idea.

On every visit to the compound Kim spent at least some time in the castle, painstakingly sifting through the hoard of dusty documents and books. The results were disappointing. Although she'd been encouraged by the discovery of the three letters, twenty-six hours of subsequent search had yielded nothing of comparable value. Consequently, on Thursday the 11th she decided to follow the lead she had, and she brought the letter from Increase Mather to Boston, having built up the courage to approach Harvard.

After leaving work on August 12, Kim walked to the corner of Charles and Cambridge streets and climbed the stairs to the MTA station. After the experience at the statehouse, which she now knew was a totally hopeless venture since Ronald had never petitioned the Governor, Kim was not optimistic about finding the evidence against Elizabeth at Harvard. Not only did she think the chances of the university still having such material in its possession slim, she fully expected people at the university to think of her as some kook. Who else would come on a quest for a three-hundred-year-old object, the nature of which was never specified in what few tangible references to it she had?

While waiting for the train, Kim almost turned back several times, but each time she reminded herself that this was her only lead. Consequently she felt impelled to follow up on it, no matter what response it might elicit.

Exiting the underground station, Kim found herself in the usual bustle of Harvard Square. But once she'd crossed Massachusetts Avenue and entered the campus, the noise of the traffic and crowds was muffled with startling rapidity. As she walked along the tranquil, tree-shaded walkways and ivy-covered red brick walls, she wondered what the campus had looked like in the seventeenth century, when Ronald Stewart had attended. None of the buildings she was passing looked quite that old.

Recalling Edward's comment about the Widener Library, Kim had decided to try there first. She mounted the broad steps and passed between its impressive columns. She was feeling nervous and had to encourage herself to continue. At the information desk she made a vague request about speaking with someone concerning very old objects. She was sent to Mary Custland's office.

Mary Custland was a dynamic woman in her late thirties, stylishly dressed in a dark blue suit, white blouse, and colorful scarf. She hardly fit Kim's stereotypical image of a librarian. Her title was Curator of Rare Books and Manuscripts. To Kim's relief she was gracious and warm, immediately asking how she could be of help.

Kim produced the letter, handed it to Mary, and mentioned that she was a descendant of the addressee. She started to explain what she wanted, but Mary interrupted her.

"Excuse me," she said. She was startled. "This letter is from Increase Mather!" As she spoke, she reverentially moved her fingers to the very periphery of the page.

"That's what I was explaining," Kim said.

"Let me get Katherine Sturburg in here," Mary said. She carefully laid the letter on her blotter and picked up the phone. While she was waiting for the connection to go through, she told Kim that Katherine specialized in seventeenth-century material and was particularly interested in Increase Mather.

After making her call, Mary asked Kim where she'd gotten the letter. Kim again started to explain, but then Katherine arrived. She was an older woman with gray hair; a pair of reading glasses resided permanently on the end of her nose. Mary introduced them and then showed the letter to Katherine.

Katherine used just the tip of her finger to move the letter around so she could read it. Kim was immediately embarrassed by her own cavalier handling of it.

"What do you think?" Mary asked when Katherine was finished reading.

"It's definitely authentic," Katherine said. "I can tell by both the handwriting and the syntax. It's fascinating. It references both William Brattle and John Leverett. But what is this evidence he's discussing?"

"That's the question," Kim said. "That's why I'm here. I'd started out trying to learn something about my ancestor Elizabeth Stewart, and that goal has evolved to solving this puzzle. I was hoping Harvard could help, since the evidence, whatever it was, was left here."

"What is the association with witchcraft?" Mary asked.

Kim explained that Elizabeth had been caught up in the witchcraft trials in Salem and that the evidence—whatever it was—had been used to convict her.

"I should have guessed about the Salem connection when I saw the date," Katherine said.

"The second time Mather refers to it, he describes it as 'Elizabeth's legacy,' " Mary pointed out. "That's a curious phrase. It suggests to me something Elizabeth either made herself or acquired with some degree of effort or wealth."

Kim nodded. She then explained her idea about its being a book or writings although she admitted it could have been anything associated in those days with sorcery or the occult.

"I suppose it could have been a doll," Mary said.

"I'd thought of that," Kim said.

The two librarians conferred as how best to access the enormous resources of the library. After a short discussion, Mary sat down at her terminal and entered the name ELIZABETH STEWART.

For a minute no one spoke. The only movement in the room was the blinking of the cursor in the blank screen as the computer searched the extensive data banks. When the monitor flashed alive with multiple listings, Kim's hopes rose. But they were short-lived. All the Elizabeth Stewarts listed were in the nineteenth and twentieth centuries and bore no relation to Kim.

Mary then tried RONALD STEWART, but got similar results. There were no seventeenth-century references. Next Mary tried to cross-reference with INCREASE MATHER. There was a wealth of material, but no intersections with the Stewart family listed.

"I'm not surprised," Kim said. "I wasn't optimistic coming here. I hope you didn't find this a bother."

"Quite the contrary," Katherine said. "I'm pleased you showed us this letter. We'd certainly like to make a copy of it for our files, if you wouldn't mind."

"Of course not," Kim said. "In fact, when I'm finished with my mini-crusade I'll be happy to donate the letter to the library."

"That would be very generous," Mary said.

"As the archivist most interested in Increase Mather I'll be happy to go over my extensive files for the name of Elizabeth Stewart," Katherine promised. "Whatever the object was, there should be some reference to it, since Mather's letter confirms it was given to Harvard. The debate about spectral evidence in the Salem witchcraft trials had been ferocious, and we have extensive material on it. I have a feeling that's what Mather is indirectly referring to in your letter. So there is still a chance I could find something."

"I'd appreciate any effort you made," Kim said. She gave her phone number both at work and at home.

The librarians exchanged knowing glances. Mary then spoke up. "I don't want to be a pessimist," she said, "but we should warn you that the chances of finding the evidence itself are minuscule, no matter what it was. There was a great tragedy here at Harvard on January 24, 1764. At that time Old Harvard Hall was being used by the General Court because of a smallpox epidemic in Boston. Unfortunately a fire left in the library on that cold, snowy night sparked a conflagration that destroyed the building and all its priceless contents. That included all the portraits of the college's presidents and benefactors as well as most of its five-thousand-volume library. I know a lot about the episode because it was the worst disaster in the library's history. And not only did the library lose books: there was also a collection of stuffed animals and birds and, most curious of all, a collection that was referred to as 'a repository of curiosities.' "

"That sounds like it could have included objects associated with the occult," Kim said.

"Most definitely," Mary said. "There's a very good chance what you are seeking was part of that mysterious collection. But we might never know. The catalogue of the collection was lost as well."

"But that still doesn't mean I can't find some reference to it," Katherine said. "I'll give it my best shot."

As Kim descended the library's front steps, she reminded herself that she'd not expected to be successful so that she shouldn't be discouraged. At least no one had laughed at her, and the librarians had been genuinely interested in the letter. Kim was confident they would continue looking for references to her forebear.

Kim took the subway back to Charles Street and got her car from the hospital garage. She'd intended to go to her apartment to change clothes, but the trip to Harvard had taken more time than she expected. Instead she headed to the airport to pick up Edward, who was due back from the West Coast.

Edward arrived on schedule, and since he had not checked a bag, they bypassed the baggage area and headed directly to the parking lot.

"Things couldn't be going any better," Edward said. He was in a buoyant mood. "There's only been one person who I wanted for Omni who declined to come on board. Otherwise everybody I talk to is wildly enthusiastic. They all think Ultra is going to break the bank."

"How much do you tell them?" Kim asked.

"Almost nothing until they commit," Edward said. "I'm not taking any chances. But even with generalities they're all so eager that I haven't had to give up much equity. So far I've committed only forty thousand unvested shares."

Kim didn't know what that meant, and she didn't ask. They got to the car. Edward put his carry-on bags in the trunk. They climbed in and drove out of the garage.

"How are things going up at the compound?" Edward asked.

"Well," Kim said without inflection.

"Do I detect that you are a little down?" Edward asked.

"I suppose," Kim said. "I got up the courage to go to Harvard this afternoon about Elizabeth's evidence."

"Don't tell me they gave you a hard time," Edward said.

"No, they were very helpful," Kim said. "The problem was they didn't have good news. There was a big fire at Harvard in 1764 that destroyed the library and consumed a collection they called 'the repository of curiosities.' To make matters worse, they lost the index as well, so at this point no one knows what the collection contained. I'm afraid that Elizabeth's evidence literally went up in smoke."

"I guess that throws you back to the repository at the castle," Edward said.

"I suppose," Kim said. "The trouble is I've lost some of my enthusiasm."

"How come?" Edward asked. "Finding those letters from the Mathers and Sewall should have been a great incentive."

"They were," Kim said. "But the effect has started to wear off. I've spent almost thirty hours since then and haven't even found one paper from the sixteen hundreds."

"I told you it wasn't going to be easy," Edward reminded her.

Kim didn't say anything. The last thing she needed at that point was Edward saying "I told you so."

When they arrived at Edward's apartment, he was on the phone with Stanton before he'd taken his suit jacket off. Kim listened vaguely to Edward's end of the conversation as he related his successful efforts at recruitment.

"Good news on both ends," Edward said after hanging up. "Stanton already has most of the four and a half million in the Omni coffers and has started the patent proceedings. We're cooking with gas."

"I'm happy for you," Kim said. She smiled and sighed at the same time.

Friday • August 26, 1994

The latter days of August flew by. Work continued at the compound at a furious rate, particularly at the lab, where Edward already spent most of his time. Pieces of scientific equipment were arriving on a daily basis, causing a flurry of effort to get them properly housed, installed, and shielded, if necessary.

Edward was a whirlwind of activity, wearing many hats. One minute he was an architect, the next an electronics engineer, and finally a general contractor as he single-handedly directed the emergence of the lab. The drain on his time was enormous, and as a consequence he devoted even less time to his duties at Harvard.

The conflicting demands as a researcher and a teacher came to a head due to actions of one of Edward's postdocs. He'd had the temerity to complain to the Harvard administration about Edward's lack of availability. When Edward heard, he'd become furious and dismissed the student summarily.

The problem did not end there. The student was equally incensed and again sought redress from the administration. The administration contacted Edward, but he refused to apologize or accept the student back into his lab. As a result, relations between Edward and the administration became increasingly acrimonious.

To add to Edward's headaches, the Harvard Licensing Office got wind of his involvement in Omni. It also had heard a disturbing rumor of a patent application on a new class of molecules. In response, the licensing office had sent a slew of inquiry letters, which Edward chose to ignore.

Harvard found itself in a difficult situation. The university did not want to lose Edward, one of the brightest rising stars of postmodern biochemistry. At the same time, the university could not let a bad situation get worse since principles as well as precedents were involved.

The tension was taking its toll on Edward, especially when combined with the stresses of the excitement of Omni, the promise of Ultra, and the daily problems at the construction site.

Kim was aware of the escalating pressures and attempted to compensate by trying to make Edward's life a little bit easier. She'd begun staying at his apartment most evenings, where she'd assumed more domestic responsibility without being asked: fixing dinner, feeding Edward's dog, and even doing some cleaning and laundry.

Unfortunately, Edward was slow to recognize Kim's efforts. The flowers had stopped as soon as she began staying at Edward's on a regular basis, a cessation she thought was reasonable. But she missed the attentiveness they represented.

As Kim left work on Friday, August 26, she pondered the situation. Adding to the stress was the fact that she and Edward had not yet made moving plans even though both of them had to be out of their respective apartments in five days. Kim had been afraid to raise the issue with Edward until he'd had a less-stressful day. The problem was, he didn't have any.

Kim stopped at the Bread and Circus grocery store and bought food for dinner. She picked something she was confident Edward would particularly like. She even got a bottle of wine as a treat.

When Kim got to Edward's apartment she picked up magazines and newspapers and generally straightened up. She fed the dog. Then she made the dinner and had it ready for seven, which was when Edward had told her he'd be home.

Seven came and went. Kim turned off the heat from the rice. At seven-thirty she covered the salad with plastic wrap and put it into the refrigerator. Finally at eight Edward walked in.

"Damn it all to hell!" he said as he kicked the door closed. "I take back all the nice things I've ever said about your contractor. The guy is an ass. I could have hit him this afternoon. He promised me there'd be electricians there today and there weren't."

Kim told him what they were having for dinner. He grunted and went into the bathroom to wash his hands. Kim heated up the rice in the microwave.

"The goddamn lab could be functional in no time if these lunkheads would get their act together," Edward yelled from inside the bathroom.

Kim poured two glasses of wine. She carried them into the bedroom and handed one to Edward as he emerged from the bathroom. He took it and sipped it.

"All I want to do is to get started on a controlled investigation of Ultra," he said. "It seems that everybody wants to thwart me by putting obstacles in my way."

"This might not be the best time to bring this up," Kim said hesitantly, "but there's never a good time. We still don't have any formal moving plans, and the first of the month is almost here. I've been meaning to talk to you for a couple of weeks."

Edward exploded. In a moment of uncontrolled fury he hurled his full wine-glass into the fireplace, where it shattered, and yelled: "The last thing I need is pressure from you!"

Edward hovered over Kim. His eyes had dilated and his veins stood out on his temples. His jaw muscles were quivering and he was clasping and unclasping his hands.

"I'm sorry," Kim blurted. For a moment she didn't move. She was terrified. She'd not seen this side of Edward. As big as he was, she knew his strength and guessed what he could do to her if he were inclined.

As soon as she could, Kim ran from the room. She went into the kitchen and busied herself. As soon as the immediate shock lessened, she decided to leave. Turning from the stove, she started toward the living room and the front door, but she immediately stopped. Edward was in the doorway. To Kim's relief, his face was totally transformed; instead of rage it reflected confusion, even sadness.

"I'm sorry," he said. His stutter made getting the words out an ordeal. "I don't know what came over me. I guess it's been the pressure, although that's not an adequate excuse. I'm embarrassed. Forgive me."

Kim was immediately taken by his sincerity. She stepped over to him and they hugged. Then they went into the living room and sat on the couch.

"I'm finding this period terribly frustrating," he said. "Harvard is driving me crazy, and I desperately want to get back to work on Ultra. Eleanor has been continuing work on the drug as best she can and is getting continually good results. It's aggravating not to be able to help her, but the last thing I want to do is take my frustrations out on you."

"I've been on edge as well," Kim admitted. "Moving has always made me nervous. On top of that I'm afraid this Elizabeth thing has become something of an obsession."

"I certainly haven't been giving you any support," Edward said. "I'm sorry about that too. Let's make a pact to be more sensitive to each other."

"That's a wonderful idea," Kim said.

"I should have said something about moving myself," Edward said. "It's not solely your responsibility. When do you want to move?"

"We have to be out of our apartments by the first of September," Kim said.

"So how about the thirty-first?" Edward said.

WEDNESDAY • AUGUST 31, 1994

Moving day was hectic from the first hours of daylight when Kim got up. The van arrived at Kim's apartment at seven-thirty and loaded her things first. Then it went to Cambridge to get Edward's belongings. By the time the last chair was put in, the truck was full.

Kim and Edward drove to the compound in their own cars, with their own pets. When they arrived, Sheba and Buffer met for the first time. Since they were approximately the same size, the confrontation ended in a standoff. From then on they ignored each other.

As the movers began bringing things into the cottage, Edward surprised Kim by suggesting they take separate bedrooms.

"Why?" Kim questioned.

"Because I'm not acting like myself," Edward explained. "I haven't been sleeping well with everything that has been going on. If we have separate bedrooms I can turn on the light and read if I need to calm myself down."

"That wouldn't bother me," Kim insisted.

"You've been sleeping at your apartment the last few nights," Edward said. "Haven't you been sleeping better?"

"No," Kim said.

"Well, then, we're just a little different," Edward said. "I've been sleeping better. Knowing I'm not bothering you makes me more relaxed. Anyway, it will be a temporary arrangement. As soon as the lab opens and things settle down, the pressure will be off. Then we'll move in together. You can understand, can't you?"

"I suppose," Kim said, trying to hide her disappointment.

The unloading of the moving van went considerably faster than its loading, and soon the cottage was filled to overflowing with boxes and haphazardly placed furniture. When the truck was empty, the movers picked up their gear and the boxes that had been unpacked and stowed them in the truck. Kim then signed the moving documents and watched the movers drive away.

No sooner had the truck disappeared from view than Kim saw a Mercedes emerge from the trees and speed toward her. She recognized the car. It was Stanton's. She called up to Edward to tell him that he had company before going to the door and opening it.

"Where's Edward?" Stanton demanded without so much as a greeting.

"He's upstairs," Kim said, pointing over her shoulder.

Stanton pushed past her and yelled for Edward to come down. He stood in the foyer with his hands on his hips, tapping his right foot. He was clearly agitated.

Kim's pulse quickened. Knowing Edward's fragile mental state, she was worried that Stanton would set him off. Stanton always operated as if he had no regard for other people's feelings.

"Come down here, Edward," Stanton yelled again. "We've got to talk."

Edward appeared at the turn of the stairs. He was descending slowly. "What's the problem?" he asked.

"Oh, nothing much," Stanton said sarcastically. "It's just that your burn-rate on our capital is out of control. This lab of yours is costing an ungodly amount of money. What are you doing, paving the johns with diamonds?"

"What exactly are you referring to?" Edward asked warily.

"The whole thing," Stanton said. "I'm beginning to think you used to work for the Pentagon, since everything you order is the most expensive available."

"To do first-class experiments you need a first-class facility," Edward said. "I made that clear when we talked about forming Omni. I hope you don't think you can buy such labs at garage sales."

Kim watched the two men bicker. The longer they argued the less concern she had. Edward was angry but not out of control.

"All right," Stanton said. "Let's leave the cost of the lab alone for a moment. Instead I want you to give me a timetable for FDA approval of Ultra. I must know so I can estimate when we might see money coming in instead of going out."

Edward threw up his hands in exasperation. "We haven't even opened the doors to the lab and you're talking about a deadline. We discussed the FDA issue at the restaurant before we agreed to form the company. Have you forgotten?"

"Listen, smart-ass," Stanton shot back. "The burden to keep this operation afloat falls on my shoulders. Unfortunately it ain't going to be an easy task with the rate you are going through our capital."

Stanton turned to Kim, who was standing against the parlor wall. "Kim," he said, "tell this thickheaded dork that fiscal responsibility is a prime requirement of start-up companies."

"Leave her out of it!" Edward snarled.

Stanton apparently sensed that he'd pushed Edward too far, because he quickly assumed a more conciliatory tone.

"Let's all be calm," Stanton said, lifting his hands in supplication. "You have to recognize the reasonableness of my request. I have to have some vague outline of what you are going to do in this gold-plated lab so that I can try to anticipate and provide for our financial needs."

Edward exhaled noisily and visibly relaxed a degree. "Asking about what we will be doing in the lab is a far different question than bursting in here and demanding a date for FDA approval," he said.

"I'm sorry I'm not more diplomatic," Stanton said. "Give me an idea of your plan of attack."

"As soon as possible we'll be launching a crash course to learn everything there is to know about Ultra," Edward said. "First we must complete our knowledge of its basic chemistry, such as its solubility in various solvents, and its reactivity with other compounds. Then we have to commence controlled biological studies to understand metabolism, excretion, and toxicity. The toxicological studies will have to be done in vitro as well as in vivo on individual cells, groups of cells, and intact organisms. We'll have to start with viruses, then bacteria, and finally higher animals. We'll have to formulate assays. On a molecular level we'll have to determine binding sites and methods of action. We'll have to test under all sorts of conditions of temperature and pH. We'll have to do all this before we file an investigational new drug application with the FDA, which is what you have to do before you can even start the clinical phase."

"Good Lord." Stanton moaned. "You're making me dizzy. This sounds like decades of work."

"It's not decades," Edward said. "But it *is* years. I told you that already. At the same time I told you that it would be significantly shorter than the twelve-year average development time for a drug."

"How about six years?" Stanton questioned.

"I can't say until we begin work and start getting some data," Edward said. "All I can say is that it will be more than three years and less than twelve."

"There's a chance it could be three years?" Stanton asked hopefully.

"It would be a miracle," Edward admitted. "But it is possible. But there is another factor you have to consider. The rapid spending of capital has been for the lab, and now that the lab is almost done, spending will drop considerably."

"I wish I could count on that," Stanton said. "But I can't. Soon we will be paying the enormous salaries you promised your Ultra team."

"Hey, I had to give big salaries to get the best people," Edward said. "Also, I preferred giving higher salaries rather than more stock. I didn't want to give away too much equity."

"The equity isn't going to be worth anything if we go bankrupt."

"But we're ahead of the game," Edward said. "Most biotech and pharmaceutical companies are formed with no drug on the horizon. We've already got the drug."

"I'm aware of that," Stanton said. "But I have the jitters. I've never invested all my money in one company and then watched it being spent so quickly."

"You've invested it wisely," Edward said. "We're both going to be billionaires. Ultra is that good, I'm sure of it. Come on. Let me show you the lab. It will reassure you."

Kim breathed a sigh of relief as she watched the two men walk toward the lab. Stanton even had his hand draped on Edward's shoulder.

Once they were gone, Kim surveyed the room. To her surprise her thoughts were not on the ungodly mess the moving had created. Instead the sudden silence brought an intense sense of Elizabeth's presence and a strong recurrence of her feeling that Elizabeth was trying to communicate with her. But try as she might, Kim could hear no words. Nevertheless, at that moment, Kim was acutely aware that some of Elizabeth existed in the core of her being. And what was now Kim's home was still in some way Elizabeth's.

Kim was not entirely comfortable with these thoughts. Somehow she detected an element of distress and urgency in Elizabeth's message.

Turning her back on what should have been more pressing tasks, Kim hastily unwrapped the newly restored portrait of Elizabeth and hung it over the fireplace. With the repainting of the walls, the portrait's silhouette had vanished. Kim had to guess how high it had hung. She was following an urge to replace the painting in the exact position it had occupied three hundred years previously.

Kim stepped away and turned to face the mantel. When she did, she was shocked by how lifelike the painting appeared. In better light Kim had thought it was rather primitive. Hanging in the afternoon twilight of the cottage gave a completely different effect. Elizabeth's green eyes were hauntingly penetrating as they shone through the shadows.

For a few mesmerizing minutes Kim stood rooted in the center of the room, staring at a picture that in some respects was like looking into a mirror. Gazing into Elizabeth's eyes, Kim felt even stronger the sense that her ancestor was trying to communicate with her across the centuries. Kim again strained to hear the words, but there was only silence.

The mystical feeling radiating from the painting sent Kim back to the castle. Despite the many boxes to unpack, and despite having spent so many frustratingly fruitless hours searching through the castle's papers, Kim had a sudden irresistible urge to return. Elizabeth's portrait had renewed her motivation to learn what she could about her mysterious ancestor.

As if driven by a preternatural force, Kim mounted the stairs and headed for the attic. Once inside, she didn't hesitate nor did she take the time to open the windows. Instead she marched directly to what looked like an old sea trunk. Opening the lid, she found the usual mix of papers, envelopes, and a few ledgers.

The first book was an inventory of ships' stores. The date was 1862. Directly beneath it was a larger, primitively bound notebook with a letter tied to it. Kim gulped. She could see that the letter was addressed to Ronald Stewart.

Kim reached into the trunk and lifted out the notebook. After untying the string, she opened the envelope and slid out the letter. Recalling how carefully the Harvard archivists handled the Mather letter, Kim tried to do the same. The aged paper resisted being unfolded. It was a short note. Kim looked at the date and her anticipation lessened. It was from the eighteenth century.

16th April 1726
Boston

Dearest father,
In response to your query I esteem it to be in the meete interests of the family and the business to forebear transposing mother's grave to the family plot since the required permit would cause much disquietude in Salem town and awaken the whole affair which you suppressed with great diligence and effort.

Your loving son,
Jonathan.

Kim carefully folded the note and replaced it in its envelope. Thirty-four years after the witchcraft affair Ronald and his son were still concerned about its effect on the family despite a public apology and a day of mourning ordered by the colonial government.

Turning her attention to the notebook, whose binding was crumbling, Kim folded back the cloth cover only to have it detach in her hand. Then her heart skipped a beat. On the flyleaf was written: *Elizabeth Flanagan, her book, December 1678.*

Kim carefully leafed through the book and realized to her utter joy that it was Elizabeth's diary! The fact that the entries she saw were short and not consecutive didn't lessen her excitement.

Clasping the book with both hands for fear of its coming apart, Kim hurried over to a dormered window for better light. Starting from the back, she noticed that there were a number of blank pages. Coming to the last entry, Kim noticed that the diary stopped prior to what she would have preferred. The date was Friday 26th February 1692.

There is no end to this cold. More snow on this day. The Wooleston River is now thick with ice to support a person to the Royal Side. I am much distracted. A sickness has weakened my spirit with cruel fits and convulsions as described by Sarah and Jonathan in like manner as those I have observed with poor Rebecca, Mary, and Joanna and the same that Ann Putnam suffered on her visit.

How have I offended almighty God that he would visit such torments on his dutiful servant? I hath no memory of the fits yet before I see colors that now affright me and hear strange sounds not of this world as I feel as if to faint. On the sudden I am restored to my senses to discover I am on the floor and have thrashed about and said unintelligible mutterings or so have said my children Sarah and Jonathan who, praise the Lord, are still unafflicted. How I wish Ronald be here and not on the high seas. These molestations commenced with the purchase of the Northfields tract and the spiteful quarrel with the Thomas Putnam family. Doctor Griggs is mystified for all and hath purged me to no avail. Such a cruel winter and travail for all. I fear for Job who is so innocent as I fear the Lord seeth to take away my life and my work is not done. I have endeavored to do God's work in his land to aid the congregation by baking the rye grain to extend our stores taxed by cruel weather and poor harvest, and refugees from Indian raids in the north whom I have encouraged the brethren accept into their hearth as family as I have done with Rebecca Sheafe and Mary Roots. I have taught the older children in the manner of constructing dolls for the surcease of the torment of the orphaned infants whose trust the Lord hath given us. I pray for Ronald's speedy return to help us with these terrible molestations before the sap runs.

Kim closed her eyes and took a deep breath. She was overwhelmed. Now it was truly as if Elizabeth were speaking to her. Kim could feel the force and character of Elizabeth's personality through her anguish: caring, empathetic, generous, assertive, and courageous; all the traits Kim wished she had herself.

Kim opened her eyes and reread sections of the entry. She wondered who Job was, or if Job were a biblical reference and not a person. She reread the part about doll-making and wondered again if the evidence that convicted Elizabeth had been a doll rather than a book.

Fearing she might have missed something, Kim reread the entire entry and became impressed with the tragic irony that Elizabeth's generosity might have caused her to spread the poisonous mold. Perhaps the unspecified evidence somehow proved Elizabeth's responsibility.

For several minutes Kim stared out the window, pondering this new line of thinking. But try as she might, she couldn't think of any way Elizabeth could have been implicated. At the time, no way existed to connect the mold with the fits.

Kim looked back at the diary. Carefully, she turned individual pages and glanced at other entries. Most were short: only a few sentences for each day, which included a terse description of the weather.

Kim closed the book and then reopened it from the front. The first entry was 5th December 1678, and was written in a larger, more hesitant script than the last entry fourteen years later. It merely described the day as cold and snowy and gave Elizabeth's age: thirteen.

Kim closed the book. She wanted to savor the experience. Clutching it to her chest as if it were a treasure, Kim returned to the cottage. Moving a table and a chair to the middle of the room, she sat down. In full view of the portrait she randomly leafed through the pages. On 7 January 1682 Kim found a longer entry.

Elizabeth described the weather as being warm for the season of the year and cloudy. She then matter-of-factly mentioned that she'd been married that day to Ronald Stewart. That short sentence was followed by a long description of the fine carriage she rode from Salem Town. Elizabeth then related her joy and amazement at moving into such a fine house.

Kim smiled. As she read relatively lengthy descriptions of the rooms and their contents she understood that Elizabeth was relating her reactions to moving into the same house Kim was currently moving into. It was a charming co-incidence to have found the book on such a day, and it made the three-hundred-year interval that separated Elizabeth and Kim seem suddenly short.

Kim made a quick subtraction and realized that Elizabeth had been only seventeen when she married. Kim could not imagine herself getting married at such an age, especially considering the emotional problems she had during the first few years of college.

Looking ahead in the diary, Kim learned that Elizabeth became pregnant only a few months later. Kim sighed. What would she have done with a child at that age? It was a frightening concept yet obviously Elizabeth had dealt with it admirably. It was also a stark reminder to Kim that birth control had not been available to Elizabeth, and how little control Elizabeth had over her destiny.

Reversing her direction in the notebook, Kim glanced at entries prior to Elizabeth's marriage to Ronald. She stopped at another relatively long entry for 10 October 1681. Elizabeth recorded that on that hot, sunny day her father returned from Salem Town with an offer of marriage. Elizabeth went on to write:

I was at first troubled in spirit at such a strange affair since I know nothing of this gentleman yet father speaks well of him. Father says the gentleman espied me in September when he visited our land for purposes of timber for masts and spars for his ships. My father says it is for me to decide but that I should know the gentleman has offered most graciously to move us one and all to Salem Town where my father shall work in his company and my dear sister Rebecca should go to school.

A few pages on Elizabeth wrote:

I have told my father I shall accept the proposal of marriage. How can I not? Providence beckons as we have been living these years on poor land in Andover at constant threat of attack by red savages. Our neighbors on both sides have suffered such grave misfortune and many have been killed or taken captive in a most cruel way. I have tried to explain to William Paterson but he does not understand and I fear that he is now ill disposed toward me.

Kim paused and raised her eyes to Elizabeth's portrait. She was moved by the realization she was reading the thoughts of a seventeen-year-old selfless girl willing to give up a teenage love and to take a chance with fate for the benefit of her family. Kim sighed and wondered when the last time was she had done something completely unselfish.

Looking back at the diary, Kim searched for a record of Elizabeth's first meeting with Ronald. She found it on 22 October 1681, a day of sunshine and falling leaves.

I met today in our common room Mr. Ronald Stewart who proposes to be my husband. He is older than I supposed and has already a young daughter from a wife who died with the pox. He appears to be a good man, strong of mind and body albeit a hint of a choleric disposition when he heard that the Polks, our neighbors to the north had been attacked two nights before. He insists we move forthwith in our sundry plans.

Kim felt a twinge of guilt concerning some of her earlier suspicions of Ronald with this revelation of the cause of Ronald's first wife's death. Flipping ahead in the diary to 1690, Kim read more about fears of smallpox and Indian raids.

Elizabeth wrote that the pox was rampant in Boston and that devastating raids from the red savages were occurring a mere fifty miles north of Salem.

Kim shook her head in awe. Reading about such tribulations brought to mind Edward's remarks about how tenuous life's threads were back in the seventeenth century. It had to have been a difficult and stressful life.

The sound of the door banging open startled Kim. She looked up to see Edward and Stanton returning from their visit to the nearly complete lab. Edward was carrying blueprints.

"This place looks as bad as when I left," Edward said in a disgruntled tone of voice. He was looking for a spot to put down his plans. "What have you been doing, Kim?"

"I've had a wonderful bit of luck," Kim said excitedly. She scraped back her chair and brought the notebook over to Edward. "I found Elizabeth's diary!"

"Here in the cottage?" Edward asked with surprise.

"No, in the castle," Kim said.

"I think we should be making more progress getting the house in order before you go back to your paper chase," Edward said. "You'll have the whole month to indulge yourself up there."

"This is something even you will find fascinating," Kim said, ignoring Edward's remarks. She carefully opened the notebook to the last entry. Handing it to Edward and indicating the passage, she told him to read.

Edward put his blueprints on the game table Kim had been using. As he read the entry his face gradually changed from vexation to surprised interest.

"You're right," he said eagerly. He gave the book to Stanton.

Kim told them both to be more careful with it.

"That will make a great introduction to the article I plan to write for *Science* or *Nature* about the scientific causes of the afflictions in the Salem witch trials," Edward said. "It's perfect. She even talks specifically about using the rye. And the description of the hallucinations is right on target. Putting that diary entry together with the results of the mass spec on her brain sample closes the case. It's elegant."

"You're not writing an article about the new mold until the patent situation is more secure," Stanton said. "We're not about to take any chances so you can amuse yourself with your research colleagues."

"Of course I won't," Edward said. "What do you think I am? An economic two-year-old?"

"You said it, I didn't," Stanton said.

Kim took the diary from Stanton and pointed out to Edward the part about Elizabeth teaching others to make dolls. She asked him if he thought that was significant.

"You mean in relation to the missing evidence?" he asked.

She nodded.

"Hard to say," Edward said. "I suppose it is a little suspicious. . . . You know, I'm famished. What about you, Stanton? Could you eat something?"

"I can always eat," Stanton said.

"How about it, Kim?" Edward said. "How about throwing something to-gether. Stanton and I still have a lot to go over."

"I'm hardly set up for entertaining," Kim said. She'd not even ventured to glance into the kitchen.

"Then order in," Edward said. He began unrolling his blueprints. "We're not picky."

"Speak for yourself," Stanton said.

"I suppose I could make some spaghetti," Kim said as she mentally reviewed what she'd need. The one room that was reasonably organized was the dining room; before the renovation it had been the old kitchen. The dining table and chairs and breakfront were all in place.

"Spaghetti would be perfect," Edward said. He had Stanton hold the blue-prints while he weighted the corners with books.

With a sigh of relief, Kim slipped between her crisp, clean sheets for her first night's rest in the cottage. From the moment she'd started making the spaghetti to a half hour previously when she'd stepped into the shower, she'd not stopped working. There was still a lot to do, but the house was in reasonable order. Ed-ward had worked equally hard once Stanton finally left.

Kim lifted Elizabeth's diary off her night table. She fully intended to read more of it, but as she lay back into her bed, she became aware of the sounds of the night. The most notable was the remarkably loud symphony of nocturnal in-sects and frogs that inhabited the surrounding forest, marshes, and fields. There were also the gentle creaks from the aged house as it radiated off the heat ab-sorbed during the day. Finally there was the subtle moan of the breeze from the Danvers River wafting through the casement windows.

As her mind calmed, Kim realized that the mild anxiety she'd felt when she'd first arrived at the house that afternoon still lingered. It had merely been overwhelmed by her subsequent intense activity. Although Kim guessed there were several sources of her unease, one was obvious: Edward's unexpected re-quest to sleep apart. Although she understood his point of view better now than when the subject had first come up, Kim was still disturbed and disappointed.

Putting Elizabeth's diary aside, Kim climbed back out of bed. Sheba flashed her an exasperated look, since she'd been fast asleep. Kim slipped her feet into her mules and crossed to Edward's bedroom. His door was slightly ajar and his light was still on. Kim pushed the door open only to be confronted by a deep growl from Buffer. Kim gritted her teeth; she was learning to dislike the un-grateful mutt.

"Is there a problem?" Edward asked. He was propped up in bed with the lab blueprints spread around him.

"Only that I miss you," Kim said. "Are you sure about this idea of sleeping apart? I'm feeling lonely, and it's not very romantic to say the least."

Edward beckoned her over. He cleared the bed of the plans and patted the edge for her to sit down.

"I'm sorry," he said. "It is all my fault. I take full responsibility. But I still think it is best for now. I'm like a piano wire about to break. I even lost my cool with Stanton, as you saw."

Kim nodded while examining her hands tucked into her lap. Edward reached out and raised her chin.

"Are you OK?" he asked.

Kim nodded again, yet she was struggling with her emotions. She guessed she was overtired.

"It's been a long day," Edward said.

"I guess I also feel a little uneasy," Kim said.

"What about?"

"I'm not entirely sure," Kim admitted. "I suppose it has something to do with what happened to Elizabeth and with this being Elizabeth's house. I can't forget the fact that some of my genes are also Elizabeth's genes. Anyway, I sense her presence."

"You're exhausted," Edward reminded her. "When you're tired your imagination can do crazy things. Besides, this is a new place and that's bound to upset you to a degree. After all, we're all creatures of habit."

"I'm sure that's part of it," Kim said, "but it's not all."

"Now don't start getting weird on me," Edward said with a chuckle. "I mean, you don't believe in ghosts, do you?"

"I never have in the past, but now I'm not so sure."

"You're kidding?"

Kim laughed at his seriousness. "Of course I'm kidding," she said. "I don't believe in ghosts, but I am changing my opinion about the supernatural. The way I found Elizabeth's diary gives me chills when I think about it. I'd just hung up Elizabeth's portrait when I felt compelled to go back to the castle. And once I got there I didn't have to look very hard. It was in the first trunk I opened."

"People get a sense of the supernatural just being here in Salem," Edward said with a laugh of his own. "It has to do with that old witchcraft nonsense. But if you want to believe some mystical force guided you up to the castle, that's fine. Just don't ask me to subscribe to it."

"How else can you explain what happened?" Kim said fervently. "Prior to today I'd spent thirty-plus hours without so much as finding something from the sixteen hundreds, much less Elizabeth's diary. What made me look in that specific trunk?"

"OK!" Edward said soothingly. "I'm not going to try to talk you out of it. Calm down. I'm on your side."

"I'm sorry," Kim said. "I didn't mean to get all worked up. I just came in here to tell you that I missed you."

After a lingering goodnight kiss, Kim left Edward to his blueprints and stepped from the room. After closing Edward's door she was bathed in moonlight coming through the half-bath window. From where she was standing she could see the black brooding mass of the castle silhouetted against the night sky. She shuddered; the scene reminded her of the backdrop of classic Dracula movies which used to terrify her as a teenager.

After descending the dark, enclosed staircase that took a full one-hundred-and-eighty-degree turn, Kim navigated through a sea of empty boxes that filled the foyer. Stepping into the parlor, she looked up at Elizabeth's portrait. Even in the dark Kim could see Elizabeth's green eyes glowing as if they had an inner light.

"What are you trying to tell me?" Kim whispered to the painting. The instant she'd looked at it the feeling that Elizabeth was trying to give her a message came back in a rush along with a clear understanding that whatever the message was, it wasn't in the diary. The diary was only a tease to goad Kim to further effort.

A sudden movement out of the corner of Kim's eye brought a stifled scream to her lips, and her heart leaped in her chest. She raised her arms by reflex to protect herself, but then quickly lowered them. It was only Sheba leaping onto the game table.

Kim supported herself for a moment against the table. Her other hand was over her chest. She was embarrassed about the degree of her terror. It also indicated to her how tense she really was.

EARLY SEPTEMBER 1994

The lab was finished, stocked with reagents, and opened during the first full week in September. Kim was glad. Although she had the month off and was available to sign receipts for the hundreds of daily deliveries, she was glad to be relieved of the duty. The person who relieved her was Eleanor Youngman.

Eleanor was the first person to start work officially in the lab. Several weeks previously she'd given her notice to Harvard that she was relinquishing her post-doctorate position, but it had taken her almost two weeks to wrap up all her projects and move to Salem.

Kim's relationship with Eleanor improved, but not drastically. It was cordial but stiff. Kim recognized that there was animosity on Eleanor's part born of jealousy. At their first meeting Kim had intuitively sensed that Eleanor's reverence for Edward included an unexpressed longing for a more personal relationship. Kim was amazed that Edward was blind to it. It was also a point of minor concern for her given her father's history of licentious relationships with his so-called assistants.

The next occupants to arrive at the lab were the animals. They came midweek in the dead of the night. Edward and Eleanor supervised the unloading of the unmarked trucks and getting the menagerie of animals into the appropriate cages; Kim preferred to watch from the window of the cottage. She couldn't see much of what was going on, but that was fine with her. Animal studies bothered her even though she understood their necessity.

Heeding the advice of the contractor and architect, Edward had established a policy that the less the community knew about what went on at the lab the better. He did not want any trouble with zoning laws or animal rights groups. This policy was aided by the natural insulation the compound enjoyed: a dense forest ringed with a high fence separated it from the surrounding community.

Toward the end of the first full week in September the other researchers began to arrive. With Edward and Eleanor's assistance they secured rooms at the various bed and breakfast establishments sprinkled in and around Salem. Part of the contractual agreement with the researchers was that they come alone; they left their families temporarily behind to ease the stress of working around the clock for several months. The incentive was that everyone would become a millionaire once their stock was vested.

The first out-of-town member of the team to arrive was Curt Neuman. It was midmorning and Kim was in the cottage, preparing to leave for the castle, when she heard the muffled roar of a motorcycle. Going to the window, she saw a cycle glide to a stop in front of the house. A man of approximately her age dismounted and lifted the visor of his helmet. A suitcase was strapped to the back of the bike.

"Can I help you?" Kim called out through the window. She assumed it was a delivery person who'd missed the turnoff to the lab.

"Excuse me," he said in an apologetic voice that had a mild Germanic timbre. "Perhaps you can help me locate the Omni lab."

"You must be Dr. Neuman," Kim said. "Just a minute. I'll be right out." Edward had mentioned an accent when he'd told Kim he was expecting Curt that day. She hadn't expected the renowned researcher to arrive by motorcycle.

Kim quickly closed some fabric sample books left open on the game table and picked up several days' worth of newspapers strewn over the couch in anticipation of inviting Curt Neuman in. Checking herself briefly in the foyer mirror, she opened the door.

Curt had removed his helmet and was cradling it in his arm like a medieval knight. But he wasn't looking in Kim's direction. He was looking toward the lab. Edward had apparently heard the motorcycle and was barreling along the dirt road in his car on his way to the cottage. He pulled up, jumped out, and embraced Curt as if they were long-lost brothers.

The two men talked briefly about Curt's metallic-red BMW motorcycle until Edward realized Kim was standing in the doorway. He then introduced Kim to Curt.

Kim shook hands with the researcher. He was a large man, two inches taller than Edward, with blond hair and cerulean blue eyes.

"Curt's originally from Munich," Edward said. "He trained at Stanford and UCLA. Many people, including myself, think he's the most talented biologist specializing in drug reactions in the country."

"That's enough, Edward," Curt managed to say as his face blushed red.

"I was lucky to steal him away from Merck," Edward continued. "They wanted him to stay so badly that they offered to build him his own lab."

Kim watched in sympathy as poor Curt squirmed in the face of Edward's encomium, reminding her of their own reactions to Stanton's praise during the dinner when they'd first met. Curt seemed surprisingly bashful for his commanding size, model-like good looks, and reputed intelligence. He avoided eye contact with Kim.

"Enough of this blabber," Edward said. "Come on, Curt! Follow me with that death-wish machine of yours. I want you to see the lab."

Kim watched them caravan across the field toward the lab before she went back inside the house to finish what she had to do before heading up to the castle.

Later that day, just as Kim and Edward were finishing a light lunch, the second out-of-town researcher arrived. Edward heard the car drive up. Pushing back from the table, he went outside. Shortly afterward he returned with a tall, thin, but muscular man in tow. He was swarthy and handsome and appeared to Kim more like a professional tennis player than a researcher.

Edward introduced them. His name was François Leroux. To Kim's surprise he made a motion to kiss the back of her hand, but he didn't actually do it. All she felt was the light caress of his breath on her skin.

As he'd done with Curt, Edward gave Kim a brief but highly complimentary summary of François's credentials. But unlike Curt, François had no trouble hearing Edward's praise. While Edward went on and on, he'd locked his dark, piercing eyes on Kim in a manner that made her squirm.

"The fact of the matter is that François is a genius," Edward was saying. "He's a biophysicist originally from Lyons, France, who trained at the University of Chicago. What sets him off from his colleagues is that he has managed to specialize in both NMR and X-ray crystallography. He's managed to combine two technologies which are usually competitive."

Kim noticed a slight smile had appeared on François's face at this point in Edward's accolade. He also bowed his head in Kim's direction as if to emphasize that he was everything Edward was saying and more. Kim looked away. She had the feeling that François was a bit too sophisticated and forward for her taste.

"François will be responsible for our saving a lot of time with the Ultra research," Edward continued. "We're truly lucky to have him. It's France's loss and our gain."

A few minutes later Edward led François from the house to take him to the lab. He was eager for François to see the facility and meet Curt. Kim watched them climb into Edward's car from the window. She couldn't help marvel how such widely disparate personalities could end up doing such similar work.

The last two of the core researchers arrived Saturday, September 10. They arrived by train from Boston. Edward and Kim went together as a welcoming committee and were standing on the platform as the train pulled into the station.

Edward saw them first and waved to get their attention. As they walked toward Edward and Kim, Kim jokingly asked Edward if physical attractiveness had been one of the requirements for employment at Omni.

"What in the devil are you talking about?" Edward asked.

"All your people are so good-looking," Kim said.

"That's something I hadn't noticed," Edward said.

When the two groups came together Edward did the introductions. Kim met Gloria Hererra and David Hirsh, and she shook hands with each.

Gloria, like Eleanor, did not fit Kim's stereotypical image of a female academic researcher. But that was their only similarity. They were complete opposites in coloring and manner. In contrast to Eleanor's fairness, Gloria was olive complected with hair as dark as Kim's and dark eyes almost as penetrating as François's. In contrast to Eleanor's cool reserve, Gloria was warm and forthright.

David Hirsh reminded Kim of François. He too was tall and slender, with a panache like an athlete. He was dark but not quite as swarthy as François. His demeanor was equally urbane but more pleasant since he wasn't as bold and had a demonstrable sense of humor along with a pleasing smile.

On the drive to the station Edward described Gloria and David's accomplishments with similar detail and accolades as he'd done with Curt and François. Both Gloria and David assured Kim that Edward was exaggerating. They then turned the conversation around to talk about Edward. In the end all Kim was certain of was that Gloria was a pharmacologist and David was an immunologist.

At the compound Kim was dropped off at the cottage. As the car pulled away en route to the lab, Kim could hear more laughter. Kim was happy for Edward. She was confident that Gloria and David would be good additions to the atmosphere of the lab.

The following day, September 11, Edward and the other five researchers had a brief celebration to which Kim was invited. They uncorked a bottle of champagne, clinked glasses, and toasted Ultra. A few minutes later they fell to work at a furious pace.

Over the next few days, Kim visited the lab often to lend moral support as well as to make sure there were no problems she could help solve. She thought of her position as somewhere between hostess and landlord. By midweek she slowed the frequency of her visits considerably. By the end of the week she rarely went since every time she did, she'd been made to feel as if she were intruding.

Edward did not help. On the previous Friday he told her outright that he'd prefer her not to come too often since her visits interrupted their collective concentration. Kim didn't take the rebuff personally because she was well aware of the pressure they were under to produce results as quickly as possible.

Besides, Kim was content with her own activities. She'd adjusted nicely to living in the house and found it pleasant. She still felt twinges of Elizabeth's presence but not nearly so disturbingly intense as that first night. Indulging her interest in interior design, Kim had obtained dozens of books on wall and floor covering, drapery design, and colonial furniture. She'd brought in scores of samples which she had littered about the house in the areas she considered using the materials. As an added treat she'd spent many an hour rummaging through the area's many antique shops hunting for period colonial furniture.

Kim also invested significant time back in the castle, either in the attic or the wine cellar. The discovery of Elizabeth's diary had been a great incentive to her. It had also wiped away the discouragement built up by so many previously fruitless hours.

In the very beginning of September during Kim's first trip back to the castle after finding Elizabeth's diary, she'd found another significant letter. It had been in the same sea trunk as the diary. It was addressed to Ronald and was from Jonathan Corwin, the magistrate who originally occupied the Witch House.

20th July 1692
Salem Town

Dear Ronald:
I esteemed it prudent to draw your attention that your removal of Elizabeth's body from its interment on Gallows Hill hath been espied by Roger Simmons who in like manner did see the son of Goodwife Nurse remove his mother's body to the same end as yourself. I beg of you my friend not to flaunt this act in these unruly turbulent times lest you bring more molestation to yourself and your family for raising the departed is seen by many as witch's work. Nor would I in the mood of the public call attention to a grave for the likewise reason that it result in you being wrongfully accused. I hath spoke with said Roger Simmons and he hath sworn to me that he will speak of your deed to no man except a magistrate if he be deposed. God be with you.

Your servant and friend,
Jonathan Corwin.

After finding the Corwin letter Kim entered a two-week period of finding nothing related to Ronald or Elizabeth. But it did not dampen her enthusiasm for spending time in the castle. Belatedly recognizing that almost all of the documents in the attic and the wine cellar had historical significance, Kim decided to organize the papers rather than merely look through them for seventeenth-century material.

In both the attic and the wine cellar she designated areas for storing papers according to half-century periods. In each area she separated the material into business, government, and personal categories. It was a monumental task but it gave her a sense of accomplishment even if she wasn't adding to her collection of documents relating to her seventeenth-century ancestors.

Thus the first half of September passed comfortably, with Kim dividing her time between decorating the cottage and searching and organizing the castle's disordered archives. By midmonth she avoided the lab altogether and rarely saw any of the researchers. She even began to see less of Edward as he came home progressively later each evening and left earlier in the morning.

MONDAY • SEPTEMBER 19, 1994

It was a gorgeous fall day with bright warm sunshine that quickly brought the temperature to nearly eighty. To Kim's delight some of the trees in the low-lying marshy areas of the forest already had a hint of their fall splendor, and the fields surrounding the castle were a rich blanket of goldenrod.

Kim had not seen Edward at all. He'd gotten up before she did at seven and had left for the lab without breakfasting. She could tell because there were no soiled dishes in the sink. Kim wasn't surprised since Edward had told her several days previously that the group had begun taking their meals together in the lab to save time. He'd said they were making amazing progress.

Kim spent the morning in the cottage with her decorating project. After a week's indecision she was able to decide on the fabric for the bedspreads, the bed hangings, and the curtains for both upstairs bedrooms. It had been a difficult choice, but having finally made it, Kim felt relieved. With the fabric number in hand she called a friend at the design center in Boston and had her place the order.

After a pleasant lunch of salad and iced tea, Kim walked up to the castle for her afternoon of searching and organizing. Once inside the mansion she had her usual debate between spending the afternoon in the wine cellar or the attic. The attic won out because of the sunshine. She reasoned there would be plenty of gloomy, rainy days when the wine cellar would be a relief.

Moving all the way around to the distant point of the attic over the servants' wing, Kim set to work on a series of black file cabinets. Using empty cardboard moving boxes that had brought Edward's books to the cottage, Kim separated the documents as she'd been doing the previous weeks. The papers were mostly business-related from the early nineteenth century.

Kim had become adept at reading the handwritten pages and could file them in the proper box after a mere glance at the title page, if there was one, or at the first paragraph if there wasn't. By late afternoon she'd come to the last file cabinet. She was in the next-to-last drawer, going through a collection of ship-ping contracts, when she found a letter addressed to Ronald Stewart.

After having gone so long without finding such a document, Kim was mo-mentarily stunned. She looked at the letter as if her eyes were deceiving her. Fi-nally, she reached into the drawer and lifted it out. She held it with just the tips of her fingers the way Mary Custland had handled the Mather letter. Looking at the signature, her hopes rose. It was another letter from Samuel Sewall.

8th January 1697
Boston

My Dear Friend,
As you are undoubtedly aware the Honorable the Lieutenant-Governor, Council, and Assembly of his Majesty's Province of the Massa-chusetts Bay, in General Court did command and appoint Thursday the fourteenth of January next be observed as a day of fasting in repentance for any and all sins done against innocent people as perpetrated by Satan and his Familiars in Salem. In like manner I being sensible of my complicity serving with the late Commission of Oyer and Terminer wish to make public my blame and shame of it and shall do so in The Old South Church. But to you my friend I know not what to say to surcease your burden. That Elizabeth was involved with the Forces of Evil I have no doubt but be she possessed or in covenant I know not nor do I wish to conjecture in view of my past errors of judgement. As to your inquiry in regards to the records of the Court of Oyer and Terminer in general and to Elizabeth's trial in par-ticular, I can attest that they are in the possession of Reverend Cotton Mather who has sworn to me that they will never fall into the wrong hands to impugn the character of the justices and magistrates who served to the best of their ability albeit in error in many cases. I believe although I dared not ask nor do I wish to know that Reverend Mather intends to burn the aforesaid records. As for my opinion in regards to the offer Magistrate Jonathan Corwin made to give you all records of Elizabeth's case includ-ing initial complaint, arrest warrant, mittimus, and preliminary hearing testimony, I think you should take them and dispose of them in like man-ner for then future generations of your family will not suffer public expo-sure of this tragedy in Salem brought on or abetted by Elizabeth's actions.
Your Friend in Christ's name,
Samuel Sewall.

"For Godsake!" Edward snapped. "Sometimes you can be so blasted hard to find."

Kim looked up from the Sewall letter to see Edward standing over her. She was partially hidden behind one of the black filing cabinets.

"Is something wrong?" Kim asked nervously.

"Yes, there is," Edward said. "I've been looking for you for a half hour. I'd guessed you were up here in the castle, and I'd even come all the way up here to the attic and yelled. When you didn't answer I went down and searched the wine cellar. When you weren't there, I came back here. This is ridiculous. If you're going to spend this much time up here at least put in a phone."

Kim scrambled to her feet. "I'm sorry," she said. "I never heard you."

"That's obvious," Edward said. "Listen, there's a problem. Stanton is up in arms again about money, and he's on his way driving out here to Salem. We all hate to take the time out to meet with him, especially in the lab, where he'll want explanations about what everybody is doing. And to make matters worse everyone is on edge from overwork. There's a lot of bickering for stupid reasons like who has the most space and who's closer to the goddamn water cooler. It's gotten to the point I feel like a den mother for a bunch of bratty Cub Scouts and Brownies. Anyway, to make a long story short, I want to have the meeting in the cottage; it'll be good to get everybody out of the hostile environment. To save time I thought we could eat as well. So could you throw something together for dinner?"

At first Kim thought Edward was joking, but when she realized he wasn't, she glanced at her watch. "It's after five," she reminded him.

"It would have been four-thirty if you hadn't effectively hidden yourself away," Edward said.

"I can't make dinner for eight people at this time in the afternoon," Kim said.

"Why not?" Edward questioned. "It doesn't have to be a feast, for chrissake. It can be take-out pizza for all I care. That's what we've been living on anyway. Just something to fill their bellies. Please, Kim. I need your help. I'm going nuts."

"All right," Kim said against her better judgment. She could tell Edward was stressed. "I can do better than take-out pizza but it surely won't be gourmet." Kim gathered her things including the Sewall letter and followed Edward out of the attic.

As they were descending the stairs she handed the letter to him, explaining what it was. He handed it back.

"I don't have time for Samuel Sewall at the moment."

"It's important," Kim said. "It explains how Ronald was able to eliminate Elizabeth's name from the historical record. He didn't do it alone. He had help from Jonathan Corwin and Cotton Mather."

"I'll read the letter later," Edward said.

"There's a part that you might find interesting," Kim said. They had reached the landing of the grand staircase. Edward paused beneath the stained glass rose window. The yellow light made him appear particularly pale. Kim thought he looked almost ill.

"All right," Edward said impatiently. "Show me what you think I might find interesting."

Kim gave him the letter and pointed to the very last sentence, where Sewall mentioned that the Salem tragedy was either brought on or abetted by Elizabeth's actions.

Edward looked up at Kim after reading it. "So?" he questioned. "We already know that."

"We do," Kim agreed, "but did they? I mean, did they know about the mold?"

Edward looked back at the letter and read the sentence a second time. "They couldn't have," he said when he'd finished. "Scientifically it was impossible. They didn't have the tools or the understanding."

"Then how do you explain the sentence?" Kim said. "In the earlier part of the letter Sewall was admitting he made mistakes with the other convicted witches, but not with Elizabeth. They all knew something we don't."

"Then it comes back to the mysterious evidence," Edward said. He handed her back the letter. "It's interesting but not for my purposes, and truly I don't have time for this stuff now."

They continued down the stairs.

"I'm sorry I'm so preoccupied," Edward said. "On top of all the other pressures I'm under, Stanton is turning out to be a royal pain in the ass, almost as bad as Harvard. Between the two of them I'm ready to be committed."

"Is all this effort worth it?" Kim questioned.

Edward eyed Kim with disbelief. "Of course it is," he said irritably. "Science requires sacrifice. We all know that."

"This is sounding less like science than economics," Kim said. Edward didn't respond.

Outside, Edward went directly to his car. "We'll be at the house at seven-thirty sharp," he called over his shoulder just before climbing in behind the wheel. He started the engine and sprayed sand and dirt from beneath the wheels as he sped off toward the lab.

Kim got into her own car and drummed her fingers on the steering wheel while she mulled the problem of what to do for dinner. Now that Edward had left and she had a moment to think, she was irritated and disappointed in herself for having accepted this unexpected and unreasonable burden.

Kim recognized her behavior, and she didn't like it. By being so compliant she was reverting to more childlike conduct of appeasement, just as she had years before, whenever her father was concerned. But recognizing what she was doing and doing something about it were two very different things. As with her father, she wanted to please Edward since she desired and needed his esteem. Besides, Kim reasoned, Edward was under a lot of pressure and needed her.

Kim started the car and headed toward town for food shopping. As she drove she thought more about her situation. She certainly didn't want to lose Edward, yet over the last several weeks it had seemed as if the harder she tried to please him and the more understanding she tried to be, the more demanding he'd become.

With such short notice Kim decided on a simple dinner of barbecue-grilled steaks accompanied by salad and hot rolls. The beverage was to be either jug wine or beer. For dessert she got fresh fruit and ice cream. By six forty-five she had the steaks trimmed, the salad prepared, and the rolls ready for the oven. She even had the fire going in the outside grill.

Dashing into the bathroom, Kim took a quick shower. Then she went upstairs to put on fresh casual clothes before returning back to the kitchen to get out napkins and flatware. She was setting the table in the dining room when Stanton's Mercedes pulled up to the front of the house.

"Greetings, cousin," Stanton said as he came through the door. He gave Kim a peck on her cheek.

Kim welcomed him and asked if he'd like a glass of wine. Stanton accepted and followed her into the kitchen.

"Is that the only wine you have?" Stanton questioned with disdain as Kim unscrewed the cap.

"I'm afraid so," Kim said.

"I think I'll have beer."

While Kim continued with the dinner preparations Stanton perched himself on a stool and watched her work. He didn't offer to help, but Kim didn't mind. She had everything under control.

"I see you and Buffer get along okay," Stanton commented. Edward's dog was under Kim's feet as she moved about the kitchen. "I'm impressed. He's a nasty son-of-a-bitch."

"Me get along with Buffer?" Kim questioned cynically. "That's a joke. He's certainly not here because of me; it's because of all this steak. He's usually with Edward at the lab."

Kim checked the warming temperature on the oven and slipped in the rolls.

"How are you enjoying living in this cottage?" Stanton asked.

"I like it," Kim said. Then she sighed. "Well, mostly. The lab situation is unfortunately dominating things. With all the pressure, Edward has been on edge."

"Don't I know," Stanton commented.

"Harvard is giving him a hard time," Kim said. She purposely didn't add that so was Stanton.

"I warned him about Harvard from the beginning of this venture," Stanton said. "I knew from past experience that Harvard wouldn't be apt to roll over and play dead, not when they got wind of the potential earnings involved. Universities have become very sensitive to this kind of situation, especially Harvard."

"I'd hate to see him jeopardize his academic career," Kim said. "Before Ultra, teaching was his first love."

Kim began to dress the salad.

Stanton watched her work and didn't say anything until he'd caught her eye. "Have you guys been getting along okay?" he asked. "I don't mean to be nosy, but since I've been working with him on this project, I've found that Edward is not the easiest person to deal with."

"It's been a bit stressful of late," Kim admitted. "Moving up here hasn't been as smooth as I'd anticipated, but of course I hadn't taken into account Ultra and Omni. As I said, Edward's been under a lot of pressure."

"He's not the only one," Stanton said.

The front door opened and Edward and the researchers trooped in. Kim went out to greet them to make the best of the situation, but it wasn't easy. They were all in an irritable mood, even Gloria and David. It seemed that no one had wanted to come to the cottage for dinner. Edward had to order them to attend.

The worst response was from Eleanor. As soon as she got wind of the menu she announced petulantly that she did not eat red meat.

"What do you normally eat?" Edward asked her.

"Fish or chicken," she said.

Edward looked at Kim and raised his eyebrows as if to say: "What are we going to do?"

"I can get some fish," Kim said. She got her car keys and went out and got in the car. It was certainly a rude response on Eleanor's part, but in actuality Kim liked getting out of the house for a few minutes. The mood in there was depressing.

There was a market which sold fresh fish within a short drive, and Kim bought several salmon filets in case someone besides Eleanor preferred fish. On the drive back, Kim wondered with some trepidation what she would be encountering on her return.

Entering the cottage, she was pleasantly surprised. The atmosphere had improved. It still wasn't a joyous gathering by any stretch of the imagination, but it was less strained. In her absence the wine and beer had been opened and drunk with more gusto than she'd expected. She was glad she'd bought as much as she had.

Everyone was sitting in the parlor, grouped around the trestle table, with the portrait of Elizabeth staring down at them. Kim nodded to those who looked in her direction and proceeded directly into the kitchen. She washed the fish and put it on a platter next to the meat.

With her own glass of wine in her hand, Kim walked back to the parlor. Stanton had stood up while she'd been in the kitchen and given everyone a handout. He was now standing in front of the fireplace, directly below the portrait.

"What you are looking at is a forecast of how quickly we will run out of money at the present burn-rate," he said. "Obviously that's not a good situation. Thus I need some idea when each of you will get to various milestones in order to best advise how to raise more capital. There are three choices: go public, which I doubt would work, at least not to our advantage until we have something to sell—"

"But we *do* have something to sell!" Edward interrupted. "We've got the most promising drug since the advent of antibiotics, thanks to the Missus." Edward raised his beer bottle to Elizabeth's portrait. "I'd like to make a toast to the woman who may yet become Salem's most famous witch."

Everyone except Kim raised their drinks. Even Stanton joined after getting his beer from where he'd placed it on the end of the mantel. After a moment of silence they all drank eagerly.

Kim squirmed uncomfortably, half expecting Elizabeth's expression in the portrait to change. She felt Edward's comments were disrespectful and in bad taste. Kim wondered how Elizabeth would feel if she were there to see these talented people maneuvering for personal gain in her house from a discovery related to her misfortune and untimely death.

"I'm not denying we have a potential product," Stanton said after putting his beer back down. "We all know that. But we don't have a currently marketable product. So trust me, in the current economic climate, it is not the time for a public offering. What we could do is a private offering, which has the benefit of less loss of control. The last alternative is to approach additional venture capitalists. Of course this approach would require the most sacrifice of stock and hence equity. In fact we'd have to dilute what we already hold."

A murmur of dissatisfaction arose from the researchers.

"I don't want to give away any more stock," Edward said. "It's going to be too valuable when Ultra hits the market. Why can't we just borrow the money?"

"We don't have any collateral to secure such a loan," Stanton said. "Borrowing the kind of money we'll need without collateral means paying exorbitant interest since it will not come from the usual sources. And since it's not from the usual sources, the people you have to deal with don't allow any hiding behind a corporate shield should things go sour. Do you understand what I'm saying, Edward?"

"I get the drift," Edward said. "But investigate the possibility anyway. Let's not leave any stone unturned that would avoid giving up any more equity. It would be a shame, because Ultra is such a sure thing."

"Are you as confident of that as you were when we formed the company?" Stanton asked.

"More so," Edward said. "Every day I'm more convinced. Things are going very well, and if they continue as they are we might be in a position to file an IND—an Investigative New Drug application—within six to eight months, which is far different than the usual three and a half years."

"The faster you move, the better the financial situation becomes," Stanton said. "It would be even better if you could pick up the pace."

Eleanor let out a short, derisive laugh.

"We are all working at maximum velocity," François said.

"It's true," Curt said. "Most of us are sleeping less than six hours a night."

"There's one thing that I haven't started doing," Edward said. "I've not yet contacted the people I know at the FDA. I want to start laying the groundwork to get Ultra at least considered for the expedited track. What we'll do eventually is try the drug on severe depression as well as AIDS and maybe even terminal cancer patients."

"Anything that saves time helps," Stanton said. "I can't stress that fact enough."

"I think we get the message," Edward said.

"Any better idea of Ultra's mode of action?" Stanton asked.

Edward asked Gloria to tell Stanton what they'd just discovered.

"Just this morning we found low levels of a natural enzyme in the brains of rats that metabolize Ultra," Gloria said.

"Is that supposed to excite me?" Stanton asked sarcastically.

"It should," Edward said, "provided you remember anything from the four years you wasted at medical school."

"It strongly suggests that Ultra could be a natural brain molecule, or at least structurally very close to a natural molecule," Gloria said. "Additional support for this theory is the stability of the binding of Ultra to neuronal membranes. We're beginning to think the situation could be somewhat akin to the relationship between morphine-like narcotics and the brain's own endorphins."

"In other words," Edward said, "Ultra is a natural brain autocoid, or internal hormone."

"But the levels are not the same throughout the brain," Gloria said. "Our initial PET scans suggest Ultra concentrates in the brain stem, the midbrain, and the limbic system."

"Ah, the limbic system," Stanton said. His eyes lit up. "That I remember. That's the part of the brain associated with the animal inside us and his basic drives: like rage, hunger, and sex. See, Edward, my medical education wasn't a complete waste."

"Gloria, tell him how we think it works," Edward said, ignoring Stanton's comment.

"We think it buffers the levels of the brain's neurotransmitters," Gloria said. "Something similar to the way a buffer maintains the pH of an acid-base system."

"In other words," Edward said, "Ultra, or the natural molecule if it is different than Ultra, functions to stabilize emotion. At least that was its initial function. It was to bring emotion back from extremes created by a disturbing event like seeing a saber-tooth tiger in your cave. Whether the extreme emotion is fear or anger or whatever, the Ultra buffers the neurotransmitters, allowing the animal or primitive human being to quickly return to normal to face the next challenge."

"What do you mean by 'initial function'?" Stanton asked.

"With our latest work we believe the function has evolved as the human brain has evolved," Edward said. "Now we believe the function has gone from merely stabilizing emotion to bringing it more into the realm of voluntary control."

Stanton's eyes lit up again. "Wait a second," he said as he struggled to understand. "Are you saying that if a depressed patient were to be given Ultra, all he'd have to do is desire not to be depressed?"

"That's our current hypothesis," Edward said. "The natural molecule exists in the brain in minute amounts but plays a major role in modulating emotion and mood."

"My God!" Stanton said. "Ultra could be the drug of the century!"

"That's why we're working nonstop," Edward said.

"What are you doing now?" Stanton asked.

"We're doing everything," Edward said. "We're studying the molecule from every vantage point possible. Now that we know it binds to a receptor, we want to know the binding protein. We want to know the binding protein's structure or structures since we suspect Ultra binds with different side chains in different circumstances."

"When do you think we can start marketing in Europe and Japan?" Stanton asked.

"We'll have some idea once we start clinical trials," Edward said. "But that won't happen until we get the IND from the FDA."

"We've got to speed the process up somehow," Stanton said. "This is crazy! We've got a billion-plus drug and we could go bankrupt."

"Wait a second," Edward said suddenly, drawing everyone's attention. "I just got an idea. I just thought of a way to save some time. I'll start taking the drug myself."

For a few minutes there was absolute silence in the room save for the ticking of a clock on the mantel and the raucous cry of seagulls down by the river.

"Is that a wise move?" Stanton asked.

"Damn right it is," Edward said, warming to the idea. "Hell, I don't know why I didn't think of it before. With the results of the toxicity studies we've already done, I'm confident to take Ultra without the slightest qualm."

"It's true we've seen no toxicity whatsoever," Gloria said.

"Tissue cultures seem to thrive on the stuff," David said. "Particularly neural cell cultures."

"I don't think taking an experimental drug is a good idea," Kim said, speaking up for the first time. She was standing in the doorway to the foyer.

Edward flashed her a scowl for interrupting. "I think it is a masterful idea," he said.

"How will it save time?" Stanton asked.

"Hell, we'll have all the answers before we even begin clinical trials," Edward said. "Think how easy it will make designing the clinical protocols."

"I'll take it as well," Gloria said.

"Me too," Eleanor said.

One by one the other researchers agreed that it was a fabulous idea and offered to participate.

"We can all take different dosages," Gloria said. "And six people will even give us a modicum of statistical significance when trying to evaluate the results."

"We can do the dosage levels blindly," François suggested. "That way we won't know who's on the highest dose and who's on the lowest."

"Isn't taking an unapproved investigational drug against the law?" Kim asked.

"What kind of law?" Edward asked with a laugh. "An institutional review board law? Well, as far as Omni goes, *we* are the institutional review board as well as every other committee, and we haven't passed any laws at all."

All the researchers laughed along with Edward.

"I thought the government had guidelines or laws about such things," Kim persisted.

"The NIH has guidelines," Stanton explained. "But they are for institutions receiving NIH grants. We're certainly not getting any government money."

"There must be some applicable rule against human use of a drug before the animal trials are completed," Kim said. "Just plain intuition tells you that it is foolhardy and dangerous. What about the thalidomide disaster? Doesn't that worry you people?"

"There is no comparison with that unfortunate situation," Edward said. "There wasn't any question of thalidomide being a natural compound, and it was generally far more toxic. But, Kim, we're not asking you to take Ultra. In fact you can be the control."

Everyone laughed anew. Kim blushed self-consciously and left the parlor for the kitchen. She was amazed how the atmosphere of the meeting had changed. From its strained beginning it had become buoyant. It gave Kim the uncomfortable feeling that some degree of group hysteria was occurring due to a combination of overwork and heightened expectations.

In the kitchen Kim busied herself with getting the rolls from the oven. From the parlor she heard continued laughter and loud, excited talk about building a science center with some of the billions they foresaw in their futures.

While she was transferring the rolls to a breadbasket, Kim sensed that someone had come into the kitchen behind her.

"I thought I'd offer to help," François said.

Kim turned and glanced at the man, but then looked quickly away, surveying the kitchen. She made it seem as if she were thinking about what he could do. In reality the man disturbed her with his forwardness, and she was still uncomfortable from the episode in the parlor.

"I think everything is under control," she said. "But thank you for asking."

"May I fill my wineglass?" he asked. He already had his hand wrapped around the neck of the wine jug.

"Of course," Kim said.

"I'd love to see some of the environs when the work calms down," François said as he poured the wine. "Perhaps you could show me some of the sights. I hear Marblehead is charming."

Kim hazarded another quick glance at François. As she expected, he was regarding her with his intense stare. When he caught her eye he smiled wryly, giving Kim the uncomfortable feeling that he was flirting with her. It also made her question what Edward had said to him about their relationship.

"Perhaps your family will be here by then," Kim said.

"Perhaps," François answered.

———

After Kim finished her usual bedtime routine, she purposefully left her door completely ajar so that she could see into the half-bath the two bedrooms shared. Her intention was to stay awake to talk with Edward when he came back from the lab to sleep. Unfortunately she didn't know what time that might be.

Sitting up comfortably against her pillows, Kim took Elizabeth's diary off her night table and opened it to where she was currently reading. The diary hadn't proven to be what she'd originally expected: except for the last entry it had been a disappointment. For the most part Elizabeth merely recorded the weather and what happened each day instead of expressing her thoughts, which Kim would have found much more interesting.

Despite her attempt to stay awake, Kim fell fast asleep around midnight with her bedside light still on. The next thing she was aware of was the sound of the toilet flushing. Opening her eyes, she could see Edward in the half-bath.

Kim rubbed her sleep-filled eyes and tried to concentrate on the clock. It was after one in the morning. With some effort she got herself out of bed and into her robe and slippers. Feeling a bit more awake, she padded into the half-bath. Edward was busy brushing his teeth.

Kim sat on the closed toilet seat and hugged her knees to her chest. Edward gave her a questioning look but didn't say anything until he'd finished with his teeth.

"What on earth are you doing up at this hour?" Edward asked. He sounded concerned, not irritated.

"I wanted to talk to you," Kim said. "I wanted to ask you if you really intend to take Ultra."

"Sure do," he said. "We're all going to start in the morning. We set up a blind system so no one will know how much they are taking compared to the others. It was François's idea."

"Do you really think this is a wise move?"

"It's probably the best idea I've had in ages," Edward said. "It will undoubtedly speed up the whole drug-evaluation process and Stanton will be off my back."

"But there must be a risk," she said.

"Of course there is a risk," Edward said. "There is always a risk, but I'm confident it is an acceptable risk. Ultra is not toxic, that we know for sure."

"It makes me feel very nervous," Kim said.

"Well, let me reassure you of one significant point," Edward said. "I'm no martyr! In fact I'm basically a chicken. I wouldn't be doing this if I didn't feel it was perfectly safe, nor would I allow the others. Besides, historically we'll be in good company. Many of the greats in the history of medical research used themselves as the first experimental subjects."

Kim raised her eyebrows questioningly. She wasn't convinced.

"You're just going to have to trust me," Edward said. He vigorously washed his face, then began to towel it dry.

"I have another question," Kim said. "What have you told people at the lab about me?"

Edward lowered the towel from his face and looked at Kim. "What are you talking about? Why would I be telling the people at the lab anything about you?"

"I mean about our relationship," Kim said.

"I don't recall specifically," Edward said with a shrug. "I suppose I might have said you were my girlfriend."

"Does that mean lover or does that mean friend?" Kim asked.

"What's going on here?" Edward questioned with annoyance. "I haven't divulged any personal secrets, if that's what you are implying. I've never gone into intimate details with anyone about us. And why am I getting the third degree at one o'clock in the morning?"

"I'm sorry if you feel I'm interrogating you," Kim said. "That wasn't my intention. I was just curious what you've said, since we're not married and I assume they've talked with you about their families."

Kim had started to explain about François, but she'd thought better of it. At the moment Edward was too temperamental for such a conversation, with his fatigue and anxious preoccupation with Ultra. Besides, Kim was reluctant to cause any potential rift between him and François because she couldn't be a hundred percent sure of what François's intentions had been.

Kim stood up. "I hope I haven't upset you," she said. "I know how tired you must be. Good night." She stepped from the bathroom and started toward her bed.

"Wait," Edward called out. He emerged from the bathroom. "I'm overreacting again," he said. "I'm sorry. Instead of making you feel badly I should be thanking you. I really appreciated your putting the dinner together. It was perfect and turned out to be a big hit with everyone. It was the kind of break we all needed."

"I appreciate your saying something," Kim said. "I have been trying to help. I think I know the pressure you're under."

"Well, it should get better with Stanton temporarily mollified," Edward said. "Now I can concentrate on Ultra and Harvard."

LATE SEPTEMBER 1994

Edward's recognition of Kim's efforts at putting together the dinner on such short notice encouraged Kim to think that things would improve between herself and Edward. But it was not to be. During the week immediately after the Monday-night dinner, things seemed to get worse. In fact Kim did not see Edward at all. He'd come in late at night long after she'd gone to bed and would be up and out before she awoke. He made no effort to communicate with her at all even though she left numerous Post-it messages for him.

Even Buffer seemed to be nastier than usual. He appeared unexpectedly around dinnertime Wednesday night while Kim was preparing her food. He acted hungry, so Kim filled a dish with his food and extended it toward him, intending to put it on the floor. Buffer reacted by baring his teeth and snapping at her viciously. Kim put the food down the disposal.

With no contact whatsoever with anyone in the lab, Kim began to feel more estranged from what was happening in the compound than she had earlier in the month. She even began to feel lonely. To her surprise she started to look forward to returning to work the following week, a feeling she never expected to have. In fact, when she'd left work at the end of August, she'd thought returning to work would be difficult.

By Thursday, September 22, Kim was aware that she was feeling mildly depressed and the resulting anxiety scared her. She'd had a brush with depression in her sophomore year of college and the experience had left an enduring scar. Fearing that her symptoms might get worse, Kim called Alice McMurray, a therapist at MGH whom she'd seen a number of years previously. Alice graciously agreed to give up half her lunch hour the following day.

Friday morning Kim got up feeling a little better than she had on previous mornings. She guessed it was the excitement of having made plans to go into the city. Without her parking privileges at the MGH, she decided to take the train.

Kim arrived in Boston a little after eleven. With plenty of time to spare, she walked from North Station to the hospital. It was a pleasant fall day of intermittent clouds and sunshine. In contrast to Salem, the leaves on the city trees had yet to begin changing.

It felt good for Kim to be in the familiar hospital environment, especially when she ran into several colleagues who teased her about her tan. Alice's office was in a professional building owned by the hospital corporation. Kim entered from the hall and found the reception desk deserted.

Almost immediately the inner door opened, and Alice appeared.

"Hi," she said. "Come on in." She motioned with her head toward the secretary's desk. "Everyone is at lunch, in case you were wondering."

Alice's office was simple but comfortable. There were four chairs and a coffee table grouped in the center of the room on an oriental rug. A small desk was against the wall. By the window stood a potted palm. On the walls were Impressionist prints and a few framed diplomas and licenses.

Alice was an ample-bodied woman whose compassionate manner radiated from her like a magnetic field. As Kim knew from Alice's own admission, she had been fighting a weight problem all her life. Yet the struggle had added to Alice's effectiveness by giving her extra sensitivity to other people's problems.

"Well, what can I do for you?" Alice asked once they were seated.

Kim launched into an explanation of her current living situation. She tried to be honest and fully admitted her disappointment that things had not gone as she'd anticipated. As she spoke she began to hear herself assuming most of the blame. Alice heard it too.

"This is sounding like an old story," Alice said in a nonjudgmental way. Alice then inquired about Edward's personality and social skills.

Kim described Edward, and with the help of Alice's presence, she immediately heard herself defending him.

"Do you think there is any resemblance between the relationship you had with your father and the relationship you have with Edward?" Alice asked.

Kim thought for a moment and then admitted her behavior in regard to the recent dinner party had suggested some analogy.

"It sounds to me that they are superficially quite similar," Alice said. "I can remember your describing similar frustration about trying to please your father. Both of these men appear to have an overriding interest in their business agendas that supersedes their personal lives."

"It's temporary with Edward," Kim said.

"Are you sure about that?" Alice questioned.

Kim thought for a moment before answering: "I guess you can never be sure about what another person is thinking."

"Precisely," Alice said. "Who knows, Edward could be changing. Nevertheless, it sounds like Edward needs your social support and you are giving it. There's nothing wrong with that except I sense that your needs aren't currently being met."

"That's an understatement," Kim admitted.

"You should be thinking about what is good for you and act accordingly," Alice said. "I know that is easy to say and difficult to do. Your self-esteem is terrified to lose his love. At any rate at least give it serious thought."

"Are you saying I shouldn't be living with Edward?" Kim asked.

"Absolutely not," Alice said. "That's not for me to say. Only you can say that. But as we discussed in the past, I think you should give thought to issues of codependency."

"Do think there are codependent issues here?" Kim asked.

"I just would like it to enter into your thinking," Alice said. "You know there is a tendency for people who were abused as children to re-create the circumstances of the abuse in their own domestic situations."

"But you know I wasn't abused," Kim said.

"I know you weren't abused in the general sense of the term," Alice said. "But you didn't have a good relation with your father. Abuse can come in many different forms because of the vast difference in power between the parent and the child."

"I see what you mean," Kim said.

Alice leaned forward and put her hands on her knees. She smiled warmly.

"It sounds to me like we have some things that we should talk about. Unfortunately our half hour is up. I wish I could give you more time, but on such short notice this is the best I can do. I hope I've at least got you thinking about your own needs."

Kim got to her feet. Glancing at her watch, she was amazed at how quickly the time had gone. She thanked Alice profusely.

"How is your anxiety?" Alice asked. "I could give you a few Xanax if you think you might need it."

Kim shook her head. "Thanks, but I'm okay," she said. "Besides, I still have a couple of those you gave me years ago."

"Call if you'd like to make a real appointment," Alice said.

Kim assured her that she'd give her more notice in the future and then left. As she walked back to the train station, Kim thought about the short session she'd had. It had seemed she was just getting started when it was over. Yet Alice had given her a lot to think about, and that was precisely why Kim had wanted to see her.

As she rode back to Salem, Kim stared out the window and decided that she had to talk to Edward. She knew it would not be an easy task because such confrontations were extremely difficult for her. Besides, with the pressure Edward was under he was hardly in the mood for such emotionally laden issues like whether they should currently be living together. Yet she knew she had to have a conversation with him before things got worse.

Driving onto the compound, Kim glanced at the lab building and wished she had the assertiveness to go over there directly and demand to talk to Edward immediately. But she knew she couldn't. In fact, she knew she couldn't even talk to him even if he showed up at the cottage that afternoon unless he also did something to make her feel he was ready to talk. With a degree of resignation, Kim knew she'd have to wait for Edward.

But Kim did not see Edward Friday evening, nor all day Saturday. All she'd find was scant evidence that he came in sometime after midnight and left prior to sunrise. With the knowledge she had to talk to him hanging over her like a dark cloud, Kim's anxiety gradually increased.

Kim spent Sunday morning keeping herself busy in the castle's attic, sorting documents. The mindless task provided a bit of solace and for a few hours took her mind away from her unfulfilling living situation. At quarter to one her stomach told her it had been a long time since her morning coffee and bowl of cold cereal.

Emerging from the musty interior of the castle, Kim paused on the faux drawbridge and let her eyes feast on the fall scene spread out around her. Some of the tree colors were beautiful, but they were hardly of the intensity they would assume in several more weeks. High above in the sky several seagulls lazily rode the air currents.

Kim's eyes roamed the periphery of the property and stopped at the point of entry of the road. Just within the shadow of the trees she could see the front of an automobile.

Curious as to why the car was parked there, Kim struck out across the field. As she neared, she approached the car warily from the side, trying to get a glimpse of the driver. She was surprised to see it was Kinnard Monihan.

When Kinnard caught sight of Kim, he leaped from the car and did something Kim could not remember his ever having done. He blushed.

"Sorry," he said self-consciously. "I don't want you to think I'm just lurking here like some Peeping Tom. The fact is I was trying to build up my courage to drive all the way in."

"Why didn't you?" Kim asked.

"I suppose because I was such an ass the last couple of times we saw each other," Kinnard said.

"That seems a long time ago," Kim said.

"I suppose in some ways," Kinnard said. "Anyway I hope I'm not disturbing you."

"You're not disturbing me in the slightest."

"My rotation here at Salem Hospital is over this coming week," Kinnard said. "These two months have flown by. I'll be back working at MGH a week from tomorrow."

"I'll be doing the same," Kim said. She explained that she'd taken the month of September off from work.

"I've driven out here to the compound on a few occasions," Kinnard admitted. "I just never thought it appropriate to stop by and your phone's unlisted."

"I'd wondered how your rotation was going every time I drove near the hospital," Kim said.

"How did the renovations turn out?" Kinnard asked.

"You can decide for yourself," Kim said. "Provided you'd like to see."

"I'd like to see very much," Kinnard said. "Come on, get in. I'll give you a lift."

They drove to the cottage and parked. Kim gave Kinnard a tour. He was interested and complimentary.

"What I like is the way you've been able to make the house comfortable yet maintain its colonial character," Kinnard said.

They were upstairs, where Kim was showing Kinnard how they had managed to put in a half-bath without disturbing the historical aspect of the house. Glancing out the window, Kim did a double take. Looking again, she was shocked to see Edward and Buffer walking across the field on their way to the cottage.

Kim was immediately gripped with a sense of panic. She had no idea what Edward's reaction to Kinnard's presence would be, especially with Edward's cantankerous mood of late and especially since she'd not seen him since Monday night.

"I think we'd better go downstairs," Kim said nervously.

"Is something wrong?" Kinnard asked.

Kim didn't answer. She was too busy castigating herself for not considering the possibility of Edward's appearing. She marveled how she managed to get herself into such situations.

"Edward is coming," Kim finally said to Kinnard as she motioned for him to step into the parlor.

"Is that a problem?" Kinnard asked. He was confused.

Kim tried to smile. "Of course not," she said. But her voice was not convincing and her stomach was in a knot.

The front door opened and Edward entered. Buffer headed for the kitchen to check for food that might have inadvertently been dropped on the floor.

"Ah, there you are," Edward said to Kim when he caught sight of her.

"We have company," Kim said. She had her hands clasped in front of her.

"Oh?" Edward questioned. He stepped into the parlor.

Kim introduced them. Kinnard moved forward and extended his hand, but Edward didn't move. He was thinking.

"Of course," Edward said while clicking his fingers. He then reached out and pumped Kinnard's hand with great enthusiasm. "I remember you. You worked in my lab. You're the fellow who went on to the MGH for a surgical residency."

"Good memory," Kinnard said.

"Hell, I even remember your research topic," Edward said. He then tersely summarized Kinnard's year-long project.

"It's humbling to hear you remember it better than I do," Kinnard said.

"How about a beer?" Edward asked. "We've got Sam Adams on ice."

Kinnard nervously glanced between Kim and Edward. "Maybe I'd better leave," he said.

"Nonsense," Edward said. "Stay if you can. I'm sure Kim could use some company. I have to get back to work. I've only come over here to ask her a question."

Kim was as bewildered as Kinnard. Edward was not behaving as she'd feared. Instead of being irritable and possibly throwing a temper tantrum, he was in a delightful mood.

"I don't know how best to word this," Edward said to Kim, "but I want the researchers to bunk in the castle. It will be infinitely more convenient for them to sleep on the property since many of their experiments require round-the-clock data collection. Besides, the castle is empty and has so many furnished rooms that it's ridiculous for them to stay in their respective bed-and-breakfasts. And Omni will pay."

"Well, I don't know . . ." Kim stammered.

"Come on, Kim," Edward said. "It will only be temporary. In no time their families will be coming and they'll be buying homes."

"But there are so many family heirlooms in the building," Kim said.

"That's not a problem," Edward said. "You've met these people. They are not going to touch anything. Listen, I'll personally guarantee that there won't be any difficulties whatsoever. If there are, out they go."

"Let me think about it," Kim said.

"What is there to think about?" Edward persisted. "These people are like family to me. Besides, they only sleep from about one to five, just like me. You won't even know they are there. You won't hear them and you won't see them. They can stay in the guest wing and the servants' wing."

Edward winked at Kinnard and added: "It's best to keep the women and the men apart because I don't want to be responsible for any domestic strife."

"Would they be content to use the servants' and the guest wing?" Kim asked. She was finding it hard to resist Edward's outgoing, friendly assertiveness.

"They will be thrilled," Edward said. "I can't tell you how much they will appreciate this. Thank you, my sweet! You are an angel." Edward gave Kim a kiss on the middle of her forehead and a hug.

"Kinnard!" Edward said, breaking away from Kim. "Don't be a stranger now that you know where we are. Kim needs some company. Unfortunately I'm a bit preoccupied for the immediate future."

Edward gave a high-pitched whistle which made Kim cringe. Buffer trotted out from the kitchen.

"See you guys later," Edward said with a wave. A second later the front door banged shut.

For a moment Kim and Kinnard merely looked at each other.

"Did I agree or what?" Kim questioned.

"It happened kind of fast," Kinnard admitted.

Kim stepped to the window and watched Edward and Buffer crossing the field. Edward threw a stick for the dog.

"He's a lot more friendly than when I worked in his lab," Kinnard said. "You've had a big effect on him. He was always so stiff and serious. In fact he was downright nerdy."

"He's been under a lot of pressure," Kim said. She was still watching from the window. Edward and Buffer seemed to be having a marvelous time with the fetching game.

"You'd never guess, the way he's acting," Kinnard said.

Kim turned to Kinnard. She shook her head and rubbed her forehead nervously. "Now what have I gotten myself into?" she asked. "I'm not completely comfortable with Edward's people staying in the castle."

"How many are there?" Kinnard questioned.

"Five," Kim said.

"Is the castle empty?" Kinnard asked.

"No one is living there if that's what you mean," Kim said. "But it surely isn't empty. You want to see?"

"Sure," Kinnard said.

Five minutes later Kinnard was standing in the center of the two-storied great room. A look of disbelief dominated his face.

"I understand your concern," he said. "This place is like a museum. The furniture is incredible, and I've never seen so much fabric for drapes."

"They were made in the twenties," Kim said. "I was told it took a thousand yards."

"Jeez, that's over a half mile," Kinnard said with awe.

"My brother and I inherited this from our grandfather," Kim explained. "We haven't the slightest idea what to do with it all. Still, I don't know what my father or brother will say about five strangers living in here."

"Let's look at where they would stay," Kinnard said.

They inspected the wings. There were four bedrooms in each, and each had its own stairway and door to the exterior.

"With separate entrances and stairs they won't have to traverse the main part of the house," Kinnard pointed out.

"Good point," Kim said. They were standing in one of the servants' bedrooms. "Maybe it won't be so bad. The three men can stay in this wing and the two women over in the guest wing."

Kinnard poked his head into the connecting bath. "Uh-oh," he said. "Kim, come in here!"

Kim joined him. "What's the problem?"

Kinnard pointed to the toilet. "No water in the bowl," he said. He leaned over the sink and turned on the faucet. Nothing came out. "Some kind of plumbing problem."

They checked the other bathrooms in the servants' wing. None of them had water. Crossing to the guest wing, they found that the problem, whatever it was, was confined to the servants' wing.

"I'll have to call the plumber," Kim said.

"It could be something simple like the water has just been turned off," Kinnard said.

Leaving the guest wing, they walked through the main part of the house again.

"The Peabody-Essex Institute would love this place," Kinnard said.

"They'd love to get their hands on the contents of the attic and the wine cellar," Kim said. "Both are filled with old papers, letters, and documents that go back three hundred years."

"This I gotta see," Kinnard said. "Do you mind?"

"Not at all," Kim said. They reversed directions and climbed the stairs to the attic.

Kim opened the door and gestured for Kinnard to enter. "Welcome to the Stewart archives," she said.

Kinnard walked down the central aisle looking at all the files. He shook his head. He was floored. "I used to collect stamps when I was a boy," he said.

"Many a day I dreamed of finding a place like this. Who knows what you could find?"

"There's an equal amount in the basement," Kim said. Kinnard's delight gave her pleasure.

"I could spend a month in here," Kinnard said.

"I practically have," Kim said. "I've been searching for references to one of my ancestors named Elizabeth Stewart, who'd been caught up in the witchcraft frenzy in 1692."

"No kidding," Kinnard said. "I find all that stuff fascinating. Remember, my undergraduate major was American History."

"I'd forgotten," Kim said.

"I visited most of the Salem witchcraft sites while I've been out here on rotation," Kinnard said. "My mom came for a visit and we went together."

"Why didn't you take the blonde from the ER?" Kim asked before she had a chance to think about what she was saying.

"I couldn't," Kinnard said. "She got homesick and went back to Columbus, Ohio. How are things going for you? It looks like your relationship with Dr. Armstrong is alive and well."

"It's had its ups and downs," Kim said vaguely.

"How was your ancestor involved in the witchcraft episode?" Kinnard asked.

"She was accused as a witch," Kim said. "And she was executed."

"How come you never told me that before?" Kinnard said.

"I was involved in a cover-up," Kim said with a laugh. "Seriously, I had been conditioned by my mother not to talk about it. But that's changed. Now getting to the bottom of her case has become a mini-crusade with me."

"Have you had any luck?" Kinnard said.

"Some," Kim said. "But there is a lot of material here and it has been taking me longer than I'd anticipated."

Kinnard put his hand on the handle of a file drawer and glanced at Kim. "May I?" he asked.

"Be my guest," Kim said.

Like most of the drawers in the attic it was filled with an assortment of papers, envelopes, and notebooks. Kinnard rummaged through but didn't find any stamps. Finally he picked up one of the envelopes and slipped out the letter. "No wonder there's no stamps in here," he said. "Stamps weren't invented until the end of the nineteenth century. This letter is from 1698!"

Kim took the envelope. It was addressed to Ronald.

"You lucky son of a gun," Kim said. "This is the kind of letter I've been breaking my back to find, and you just walk in here and pluck it out like there was nothing to it."

"Glad to be of assistance," Kinnard said. He handed the letter to Kim.

Kim read the letter aloud:

12th October 1698
Cambridge

Dearest Father,

I am deeply grateful for the ten shillings as I have been in dire need during these troublesome days of acclimation to colledge life. Ever so humbly I should like to relate that I have had complete success in the endeavor about which we had much discours prior to my matriculation. After lengthy and arduous inquiry I located the evidence used against my Dearly Departed Mother in the chambers of one of our esteemed tutors who had taken a fancy to its gruesome nature. Its prominent display caused me some disquietude but Tuesday last during the afternoon bever when all were retired to the buttery I chanced a visit to the aforesaid chambers and changed the name as you instructed to the fictitious Rachel Bingham. To a like purpose I entered the same in the catalogue in the library of Harvard Hall. I hope Dear Father that now you find solace that the surname Stewart has been freed from its most grievous molestation. In consideration of my studies I can with some felicity relate that my recitations have been well received. My chamber-mates are hale and of a most agreeable nature. Apart from the fagging about which you aptly forewarned me, I am well and content and

I remain your loving Son,
Jonathan.

"Damn it all," Kim said when she'd finished the letter.

"What's the matter?" Kinnard asked.

"It's this evidence," Kim said, pointing it out in the letter. "It refers to the evidence used to convict Elizabeth. In a document I found at the Essex County Courthouse it was described as conclusive evidence, meaning it incontrovertibly convicted her. I've found several other references to it but it is never described. Figuring out what it was has become the chief object of my crusade."

"Do you have any idea what it could be?" Kinnard asked.

"I believe it has something to do with the occult," Kim said. "Probably it was a book or a doll."

"I'd say this letter favors its being a doll," Kinnard said. "I don't know what kind of book would have been considered 'gruesome.' The gothic novel wasn't invented until the nineteenth century."

"Maybe it was a book describing some witch's potion that used body parts as ingredients," Kim suggested.

"I hadn't thought of that," Kinnard said.

"Doll-making was mentioned in Elizabeth's diary," Kim said. "And dolls helped convict Bridget Bishop. I suppose a doll could be 'gruesome' either by being mutilated or perhaps sexually explicit. I imagine with the Puritan morality many things associated with sex would have been considered gruesome."

"It's a misconception of sorts that the Puritans were all hung up on sex," Kinnard said. "I remember from my history courses that they generally considered sins associated with premarital sex and lust as lesser sins than lying or the promotion of self-interest, since the latter had to do with breaking the sacred covenant."

"That means things have certainly turned around since Elizabeth's day," Kim said with a cynical chuckle. "What the Puritans thought were terrible sins are accepted and often lauded activities in present-day society. All you have to do is watch a government hearing."

"So you hope to solve the mystery of the evidence by going through all these papers?" Kinnard said, making a sweeping motion with his hand around the attic.

"Here and in the wine cellar," Kim said. "I did take a letter from Increase Mather to Harvard since in the letter he said that the evidence had become part of the Harvard collections. But I didn't have any luck. The librarians couldn't find any reference to Elizabeth Stewart in the seventeenth century."

"According to Jonathan's letter you should have been looking for 'Rachel Bingham,'" Kinnard said.

"I realize that now," Kim said. "But it wouldn't have made any difference. There was a fire in the winter of 1764 that consumed Harvard Hall and its library. Not only did all the books burn, but also what was called a 'repository of curiosities,' plus all the catalogues and indexes. Unfortunately no one even knows what was lost. I'm afraid Harvard can't be any help to me."

"I'm sorry," Kinnard said.

"Thanks," Kim said.

"At least you still have a chance with all these papers," Kinnard said.

"It's my only hope," Kim said. She showed him how she was organizing all the material in terms of chronology and subject matter. She even took him to the area where she'd been working that morning.

"Quite a task," Kinnard said. Then he looked at his watch. "I'm afraid I have to go. I've got to round on my patients this afternoon."

Kim accompanied him down to his car. He offered to give her a ride back to the cottage, but she declined. She said she intended to put in a few more hours in the attic. She said she particularly wanted to search the drawer where he'd so easily found Jonathan's letter.

"Maybe I shouldn't ask this," Kinnard said. He had the door to his car open. "But what is Edward and his team of researchers doing up here?"

"You're right," Kim said. "You shouldn't ask. I can't tell you the details because I've been sworn to secrecy. But what is common knowledge is that they are doing drug development. Edward built a lab in the old stables."

"He's no fool," Kinnard said. "What a fabulous place for a research lab."

Kinnard started to climb into his car when Kim stopped him. "I have a question for you," she said. "Is it against the law for researchers to take an experimental drug that has yet to reach clinical testing?"

"It's against FDA rules for volunteers to be given the drug," Kinnard said. "But if the researchers take it, I don't think the FDA has any jurisdiction. I can't imagine that they would sanction it, and it might cause trouble when they attempt to get an Investigational New Drug application."

"Too bad," Kim said. "I was hoping it might be against the law."

"I suppose I don't have to be a rocket scientist to guess why you are asking," Kinnard said.

"I'm not saying anything," Kim said. "And I'd appreciate it if you didn't either."

"Who am I going to tell?" Kinnard questioned rhetorically. He hesitated a moment and then asked: "Are they all taking the drug?"

"I really don't want to say," Kim said.

"If they are, it would raise a significant ethical issue," Kinnard said. "There would be the question of coercion with the more junior members."

"I don't think there is any coercion involved," Kim said. "Maybe some group hysteria, but no one is forcing anyone to do anything."

"Well, regardless, taking an uninvestigated drug is not a smart idea," Kinnard said. "There is too much risk of unexpected side effects. That's the reason the rules were promulgated in the first place."

"It was nice seeing you again," Kim said, changing the subject. "I'm glad to feel that we are still friends."

Kinnard smiled. "I couldn't have said it better myself."

Kim waved as he drove away. She waved again just before his car disappeared in the trees. She was sorry to see him go. His unexpected visit had been a welcome relief.

Returning inside the castle, Kim climbed the stairs on her way to the attic. She was still enjoying the warmth generated by Kinnard's visit when she found herself marveling over the episode with Edward. She could distinctly remember back to when she had first started dating Edward that he had reacted jealously to the mere mention of Kinnard's name. That made his response that afternoon even more surprising. It also made Kim wonder if the next time she saw Edward alone he would react with a belated temper tantrum.

By late in the day Kim was ready to give up the search. She stood up and stretched her achy muscles. To her chagrin she'd not found any other related material in the drawer, file cabinet, or even in the immediate vicinity where Kinnard had found Jonathan's letter. It made Kinnard's feat that much more impressive.

Leaving the castle behind, she started out across the field toward the cottage. The sun was low in the western sky. It was already fall and winter wouldn't be far behind. As she walked she vaguely thought about what to make for dinner.

Kim was almost to the cottage when she heard the distant sound of excited voices. Turning around, she saw that Edward and his research team had emerged from their isolation in the lab.

Kim was immediately intrigued: she stood and watched the group approach. Even from a distance she could tell that they were acting frolicsome and exuberant like a group of schoolchildren let out for recess. She could hear laughter and yelling. The men, except for Edward, were throwing a football back and forth.

The first thought that went through Kim's mind was that they had made some monumental discovery. The closer they got the more sure she became. She'd never seen them in such good spirits. But when they were within shouting distance, Edward proved her wrong.

"Look what you've done to my team!" he called out to Kim. "I just told them about your offer to let them stay in the castle and they've gone berserk."

When the group got near to Kim they let out a cheer: "Hip hip, hurray!" they repeated three times and then collapsed in laughter.

Kim found herself smiling in return. Their exuberance was contagious. They were like collegians at a pep rally.

"They really are touched by your hospitality," Edward explained. "They recognize that it is a real favor you are doing for them. Curt had even been sleeping on the floor of the lab a few nights."

"I like your outfit," Curt said to Kim.

Kim looked down at her leather vest and jeans. It certainly wasn't special. "Thank you," she said.

"We'd like to reassure you about the furnishings in the castle," François said. "We understand that they are family heirlooms, and we will treat them with the utmost respect."

Eleanor stepped forward and gave Kim an unexpected hug. "I'm touched by your selfless contribution to the cause," she said. She squeezed Kim's hand and looked her in the eye. "Thank you so much."

Kim nodded. She didn't know what to say. She was embarrassed she'd been against the idea.

"By the way," Curt said, angling himself in front of Eleanor. "I've been meaning to ask you if the noise from my motorcycle ever bothers you. If it does, I'll be happy to park it outside the compound."

"I've not been aware of any noise," Kim said.

"Kim!" Edward called out as he came around to her other side. "If it's convenient the group would like you to take them to the castle so that you can show them which rooms you want them to sleep in."

"I guess it's as good a time as any," Kim said.

"Perfect," Edward said.

Retracing her steps, Kim led the animated group in the direction of the castle. David and Gloria made it a point to catch up with her and walk alongside. They were full of questions about the castle, such as when it had been built and whether Kim had ever lived in it.

When they entered the mansion there were a lot of oh's and ah's, especially in the massive great room and the formal dining room, with its heraldic flags.

Kim showed them the guest wing first, suggesting the women stay there. Eleanor and Gloria were pleased and chose connecting bedrooms on the second floor.

"We can wake each other up if we oversleep," Eleanor said.

Kim showed everyone how each wing had a separate entrance and stair.

"This is perfect," François said. "We won't have to go into the main part of the house at all."

Moving across to the servants' wing, Kim explained about the plumbing problem but assured them that she would call a plumber in the morning. She then showed them a bathroom in the main part of the house they could use in the interim.

The men chose rooms without any disagreement although some of the rooms were obviously more desirable than others. Kim was impressed with their amicability.

"I can have the phone turned on as well," Kim said.

"Don't bother," David said. "We appreciate you offering, but it's not necessary. We'll only be here to sleep, and we're not sleeping that much. We can use the phone in the lab."

After the tour was over they all left the castle by the exit in the servants' wing and then walked around to the front. They discussed the issue of keys, and it was decided to leave the doors to the wings unlocked for the time being. Kim would have keys made as soon as she had an opportunity.

After a round of fervent handshakes and hugs and thank-you's, the researchers headed off to their respective bed-and-breakfasts to gather their belongings. Kim and Edward walked to the cottage.

Edward was in a great mood and thanked Kim over and over for her generosity.

"You've really contributed to changing the whole atmosphere of the lab," Edward said. "As you could see for yourself, they are ecstatic. And, as important as mental state is, I'm certain their work will reflect their mood. So you've positively impacted the whole project."

"I'm glad I could contribute," Kim said, making her feel even more guilty that she'd been against the idea from the start.

They arrived at the cottage. Kim was surprised when Edward accompanied her inside. She'd thought he'd head directly back to the lab.

"It was nice of that Monihan fellow to drop by," Edward said.

Kim's mouth dropped open. She had to make a conscious effort to close it.

"You know, I could use a beer," Edward said. "How about you?"

Kim shook her head. For the moment she'd lost her voice. As she followed Edward into the kitchen, she struggled to summon the courage to talk to him about their relationship. He was in a better mood than he'd been in for ages.

Edward went to the refrigerator. Kim sat on a stool. Just when she was about to broach the subject, Edward popped the top from the beer and shocked her again.

"I want to apologize to you for having been such a bear for the last month or so," he said. He took a drink from his beer, burped, and excused himself. "I've been giving it some thought over the last couple of days, and I know I've been difficult, inconsiderate, and unappreciative. I don't mean this as an excuse or to absolve myself of responsibility, but I have been under enormous pressure from Stanton, Harvard, the researchers, and even myself. Yet I never should have let such issues come between us. Once again, I want to ask you to forgive me."

Kim was taken aback by Edward's admission. It was a totally unexpected development.

"I can tell you are upset," Edward said. "And you don't have to say anything immediately if you don't want to. I can well imagine you could be harboring some ill will toward me."

"But I do want to talk," Kim said. "I've been wanting to talk, particularly since Friday when I went into Boston to see a therapist I'd seen years ago."

"I applaud your initiative," Edward said.

"It made me think a lot about how we've been relating to one another," Kim said. She looked down at her hands. "It made me wonder if perhaps living together right at the moment is not the best thing for either of us."

Edward put down his beer and took her hands. "I understand how you must feel," he said. "And your feelings are appropriate in light of my most recent behavior. But I can see my mistakes, and I think I can make it up to you."

Kim started to say something, but Edward interrupted her.

"All I ask is to allow the status quo to remain for a few weeks with me staying here in my room and you in yours," he said. "If you feel we shouldn't be staying together at the end of this trial period, I'll move up to the castle with the others."

Kim contemplated what Edward had said. He had impressed her with his remorse and his insight. His offer seemed reasonable.

"All right," she said finally.

"Wonderful!" Edward said. He reached out and gave her a long hug.

Kim held herself back a little. It was hard for her to change emotional directions so quickly.

"Let's celebrate," Edward said. "Let's go out to dinner—just you and me."

"I know you can't take the time," Kim said. "But I appreciate the offer."

"Nonsense!" Edward said. "I'm taking the time! Let's go back to that dive we went to on one of our first trips up here. Remember the scrod?"

Kim nodded. Edward drained his beer.

As they drove from the compound and Kim glanced at the castle, she thought about the researchers and commented about how exuberant they had seemed.

"They couldn't be any happier," Edward said. "Things are going well at the lab, and now they won't have to commute."

"Did you start taking Ultra?" Kim asked.

"We sure did," Edward said. "We all started Tuesday."

Kim contemplated telling Edward about Kinnard's thoughts on the subject but hesitated because she knew that Edward would be upset that she'd spoken to anybody about their project.

"We've already learned something interesting," Edward said. "The tissue level of Ultra can't be critical because all of us are experiencing equally positive results even though we're on widely different dosages."

"Could the euphoria you and the others are enjoying have anything to do with the drug?" Kim asked.

"I'm sure it does," Edward said. "Indirectly if not directly. Within twenty-four hours of our first dose all of us felt relaxed, focused, confident, and even—" Edward struggled for a word. Finally he said: "Content. All of which is a far cry from the anxiety, fatigue, and contentiousness we'd been experiencing before Ultra."

"What about side effects?"

"The only side effect that we've all had was some initial dryness of the mouth," Edward said. "Two of the others reported some mild constipation. I was the only one who had some difficulty with near vision, but it only lasted for twenty-four hours and I'd been experiencing the problem prior to taking Ultra, particularly when I got tired."

"Maybe you should stop taking the drug now that you've learned as much as you have," Kim suggested.

"I don't think so," Edward said. "Not when we are getting such positive results. In fact, I brought some for you in case you want to try it."

Edward reached into his jacket pocket and pulled out a vial of capsules. He extended it toward Kim. She shrank back.

"No, thank you," she said.

"For God's sake, at least take the container."

Reluctantly Kim allowed Edward to drop the vial into her hands.

"Just think about it," Edward said. "Remember that discussion we had a long time ago about not feeling socially connected? Well, you won't feel that way with Ultra. I've been on it less than a week, and it's allowed the real me to emerge; the person that I've wanted to be. I think you should try it. What do you have to lose?"

"The idea of taking a drug for a personality trait bothers me," Kim said. "Personality is supposed to come from experience, not chemistry."

"This is sounding like a conversation we've already had," Edward said with a laugh. "I guess as a chemist I'm bound to feel differently. Suit yourself, but I guarantee you'd feel more assertive if you try it. And that's not all. We also think it enhances long-term memory and alleviates fatigue and anxiety. I had a good demonstration of this latter effect just this morning. I got a call from Harvard announcing they've instituted suit against me. It infuriated me, but the outrage only lasted a few minutes. Ultra smoothed my anger out, so instead of pounding the walls I was able to think about the situation rationally and make appropriate decisions."

"I'm glad you are finding it so helpful," Kim said. "But I still don't want to take it." She tried to give the container back to Edward. He pushed her hand away.

"Keep it," he said. "All I ask is that you give it some serious thought. Just take one capsule a day and you'll be amazed at who you are."

Understanding that Edward was adamant, Kim dropped the vial into her bag.

Later at the restaurant, while Kim was in the ladies' room standing in front of the mirror, she caught sight of the vial in her bag. Removing it, she undid the cap. With her thumb and index finger she lifted out one of the blue capsules and examined it. It seemed incredible it could do all the things Edward claimed.

Glancing in the mirror, she admitted to herself how much she'd like to be more assertive and less fearful. She also admitted how tempting it would be to deal so easily with her low-level but nagging anxiety. She looked back down at the capsule. Then she shook her head. For a moment she'd wavered, but as she put the capsule back into the container, she reaffirmed that drugs were not her answer.

As Kim returned to the restaurant proper she reminded herself that she'd always been suspicious of quick and easy solutions. Over the years she'd developed the opinion that the best way to deal with her problems was the old-fashioned way with introspection, a little pain, and effort.

Later that night, while Kim was comfortably reading in bed, she heard the front door slam shut. It made her jump. Glancing at the clock, she saw it was before eleven.

"Edward?" she called out nervously.

"It's just me," Edward called back as he came up the stairs two at a time. He poked his head into Kim's bedroom. "I hope I didn't scare you," he said.

"It's so early," Kim said. "Are you okay?"

"Couldn't be better," Edward said. "I even feel energetic, which is amazing since I've been up since five this morning."

He went into the half-bath and began brushing his teeth. While he did so he managed to maintain a lively chatter about humorous incidents that occurred in the lab that evening. It seemed that the researchers were playing harmless practical jokes on each other.

As Edward spoke, Kim reflected on how different her own mood was from everyone else's at the compound. Despite Edward's apparent turnaround, she still was uptight, vaguely anxious, and even still a bit depressed.

After Edward was finished in the bathroom he returned to Kim's room and sat on the edge of her bed. Buffer followed him in and, to Sheba's chagrin, tried to jump up as well.

"No, you don't, you rascal," Edward said as he scooped the dog up and held him in his lap.

"Are you going to bed already?" Kim asked.

"I am indeed," Edward said. "I've got to be up at three-thirty instead of the usual five to deal with an experiment I'm running. Out here in Salem I don't have any postdocs to do my dirty work."

"That's not much sleep," Kim said.

"It's been adequate," Edward said. Then he changed the subject abruptly. "How much money did you inherit along with the compound?"

Kim blinked. Edward seemed to be surprising her every time he opened his mouth. The inappropriateness of this new question was completely out of character for him.

"You don't have to tell me if you feel uncomfortable," Edward said when he saw Kim's hesitancy. "The reason I'm asking is because I'd be willing to let you have some equity in Omni. I haven't wanted to sell any more of the stock, but you're different. You'll get a monumental return on your investment if you are interested."

"My portfolio is fully invested," Kim managed to say.

Edward put Buffer down and held up his hands. "Don't misinterpret me," he said. "I'm not playing salesman. I'm just trying to do you a favor for what you've done for Omni by allowing the lab to be built here."

"I appreciate the offer," Kim said.

"Even if you choose not to invest I'm still going to give you some stock as a gift," Edward said. He gave her leg a pat through the covers and stood up. "Now I've got to get to bed. I'm looking forward to four solid hours of sleep. I tell you, ever since I started taking Ultra I've been sleeping so soundly that four hours is plenty. I never knew sleep could be so enjoyable."

With a spring in his step, Edward went back into the bathroom and began brushing his teeth again.

"Aren't you overdoing that?" Kim called out.

Edward stuck his head back into Kim's bedroom. "What are you talking about?" he said while keeping his lower lip over his lower teeth.

"You already brushed your teeth," Kim said.

Edward looked at his toothbrush as if it were to blame. Then he shook his head and laughed. "I'm becoming the absentminded professor," he said. He went back into the bathroom to rinse his mouth.

Kim looked down at Buffer, who'd stayed behind, positioning himself in front of her night table. He was vigorously begging for some biscotti she'd brought up earlier from the kitchen.

"This dog of yours is acting awfully hungry," Kim yelled to Edward, who was now in his bedroom. "Did he get fed tonight?"

Edward appeared at the door. "I honestly can't remember," he said. Then he disappeared again.

With resignation Kim got up, slipped on her robe, and descended to the kitchen. Buffer followed close at her heels as if he understood what had been said. Kim got out the dog food and scooped a portion onto a plate. Buffer was beside himself with excitement and was both growling and barking. It was obvious that he'd not been fed, maybe even for more than one day.

To avoid being bitten, Kim closed the dog in the bathroom while she put his food on the floor. When she reopened the door, Buffer went past her like a white blur and began wolfing the food down so quickly he sounded as if he were gagging.

When Kim climbed back up the stairs, she saw that Edward's light was still on. Wanting to tell him about Buffer, she stuck her head into his room only to find he was already fast asleep. He'd seemingly lain down and fallen asleep before he'd even had a chance to turn out the light.

Kim walked over to his bedside and marveled at his stertorous breathing. Knowing the schedule he'd been keeping, she wasn't surprised at the depth of his sleep. He had to be exhausted. Kim turned out his light then went back to her own room.

MONDAY • SEPTEMBER 26, 1994

When Kim finally opened her eyes she was surprised to see it was nearly nine o'clock. That was later than she'd been getting up during the last month. Climbing out of bed, she glanced into Edward's room, but he had been long gone. His empty room appeared neat and orderly. Edward had the commendable habit of making his bed in the morning.

On her way to the bathroom to shower, Kim placed a call to the plumber, Albert Bruer, who'd worked on both the cottage and the lab. She left her number on his answering machine.

Albert called back within a half hour, and by the time Kim had finished breakfast he was at her door. Together they drove up to the castle in his truck.

"I think I already know the problem," Albert said. "In fact I knew about it when your grandfather was alive. It's the soil pipes. They're cast-iron and some of them have rusted."

Albert took Kim into each of the bathrooms in the servants' wing and took off the fronts of the access panels. In each he pointed out the rusted pipes.

"Can it be fixed?" Kim asked.

"Of course it can," Albert said. "But it will take some doing. It might take me and my boy a week."

"Do it," Kim said. "I've got some people staying in here."

"If that's the case I can get water to the bathroom on the third floor. Those pipes look pretty good. Maybe no one lived up there."

After the plumber left, Kim walked over to the lab to let the men know about the third-floor bathroom. She'd not been to the lab for some time and was not looking forward to the visit. They'd never made her feel welcome.

"Kim!" David called out excitedly. He was the first to see her come through the door that led from the vacant reception area into the lab proper. "What a nice surprise." David yelled out to the others that she was there. Everyone, including Edward, dropped what they were doing and came over to greet her.

Kim felt herself blush. She did not relish being the center of attention.

"We have fresh coffee and donuts," Eleanor said. "Can I get you some?"

Kim declined but thanked her, explaining she'd just had breakfast. She apologized to the group for bothering them and quickly told the men about the resolution of the plumbing problem.

The men were pleased and assured her that using the bathroom on the third floor was not an imposition. They even tried to talk her out of bothering to make any repairs.

"I don't think it should be left the way it is," Kim said. "I'd prefer it be fixed."

Kim then started to leave, but they wouldn't allow it. They insisted on showing her what each one of them was doing.

David was first. He took Kim to his lab bench and had her peer through a dissecting microscope while he explained that she was looking at an abdominal ganglion preparation that he'd taken from a mollusk called *Aplasia fasciata*. Then he showed her printouts of how Ultra modulated the spontaneous firing of certain neurons of the ganglion. Before Kim could even figure out what she was looking at, David took the printouts from her hands and led her into the tissue-culture incubator. There he explained how he evaluated the tissue cultures for signs of toxicity.

Then it was Gloria's and Curt's turn. They took Kim downstairs to the animal area. They showed her some pitiful creatures: stressed rats and stressed monkeys that had been raised to have severe anxiety. Then they showed her similar animals that had been treated with Ultra and imipramine.

Kim tried to appear interested, but animal experiments disturbed her.

François took over from Gloria and Curt and led Kim into the shielded room where the NMR machine was isolated. He tried to explain exactly how he was attempting to determine the structure of the binding protein for Ultra. Unfortunately, Kim understood little of his explanation. She merely nodded her head and smiled whenever he paused.

Eleanor then took over and led Kim back upstairs to her computer terminal. She gave Kim a lengthy explanation of molecular modeling and how she was attempting to create drugs that were permutations of Ultra's basic structure and that would potentially share some of Ultra's bioactivity.

As Kim was whisked around the lab, she began to notice that not only were the researchers friendly, they were also patient and respectful of each other. Although they were assertively eager to please her, they were content to wait their turn.

"This has been most interesting," Kim said when Eleanor finally finished her lecture. Kim started to back toward the door. "Thank you all for taking so much of your valuable time to show me around."

"Wait!" François said. He dashed to his desk, picked up a sheaf of photographs, and ran back. Breathlessly he showed them to Kim and asked her what she thought of them. They were brightly colored PET scans.

"I think they are—" Kim searched for a word that wouldn't make her sound foolish. She finally said: "Dramatic."

"They are, aren't they?" François said, cocking his head to the side to regard them from a slightly different angle. "They're like modern art."

"What exactly do they tell you?" Kim asked. She would have preferred to leave, but with everyone watching, she felt obligated to ask a question.

"The colors refer to concentrations of radioactive Ultra," François said. "The red is the highest concentration. These scans show quite clearly that the drug localizes maximally to the upper brain stem, the midbrain, and the limbic system."

"I remember Stanton's referring to the limbic system at the dinner party," Kim said.

"He did indeed," François said. "As he suggested, it's part of the more primitive, or reptilian, parts of the brain and is involved with autonomic function, including mood, emotion, and even smell."

"And sex," David said.

"What do you mean, 'reptilian'?" Kim asked. The word had an ugly connotation to her. She'd never liked snakes.

"It's used to refer to the parts of the brain that are similar to the brains of reptiles," François said. "Of course it is an oversimplification, but it does have some merit. Although the human brain evolved from some common distant ancestor with current-day reptiles, it's not like taking a reptile brain and sticking a couple of cerebral hemispheres on top."

Everybody laughed. Kim found herself laughing as well. The general mood was hard to resist.

"As far as basic instincts are concerned," Edward said, "we humans have them just like reptiles. The difference is ours are covered by varying degrees of socialization and civilization. Translated, that means that the cerebral hemispheres have hard-wired connections that control reptilian behavior."

Kim looked at her watch. "I really have to be going," she said. "I've got a train to catch into Boston."

With such an excuse Kim was finally able to break free from the obliging clutches of the researchers, although they all encouraged her to come back. Edward walked her outside.

"Are you really on your way to Boston?" Edward asked.

"I am," Kim said. "Last night I decided to go back to Harvard for one more try. I'd found another letter that included a reference to Elizabeth's evidence. It gave me another lead."

"Good luck," Edward said. "Enjoy yourself." He gave her a kiss and then went back into the lab. He didn't ask about Kim's latest letter.

Kim walked back to the cottage, feeling strangely numb from the researchers' intense congeniality. Maybe something was wrong with her. She hadn't liked how aloof they'd been, but now she found she didn't like them sociable either. Was she impossible to please?

The more Kim thought about her response, the more she realized that it had a lot to do with their sudden uniformity. When she'd first met them she'd been struck by their eccentricities and quirks. Now their personalities had become blended into an amiable but bland whole that shrouded their individuality.

As Kim changed clothes for her trip into Boston, she couldn't stop mulling over what was happening at the compound. She felt her misgiving—the very anxiety that had driven her to see Alice—on the increase again.

Ducking into the parlor to retrieve a sweater, Kim paused beneath Elizabeth's portrait and looked up into her ancestor's feminine yet forceful face. There was not a hint of anxiety in Elizabeth's visage. Kim wondered if Elizabeth had ever felt as out of control as she did.

Kim got into her car and headed for the train station, unable to get Elizabeth out of her mind. It suddenly occurred to her that there were striking similarities between her world and Elizabeth's despite the enormous gap in time. Elizabeth had to live with the continual threat of Indian attack, while Kim was conscious of the ever-present peril of crime. Back then there had been the mysterious and frightful menace of smallpox while today it was AIDS. In Elizabeth's time there was a breakdown of the Puritan hold on society, with the emergence of unbridled materialism; today it was the passing of the stability of the Cold War with the emergence of fractious nationalism and religious fundamentalism. Back then there was a confusing and changing role for women; today it was the same.

"The more things change, the more they stay the same," Kim said, voicing the old adage.

Kim wondered if all these similarities could have anything to do with the message she'd come to believe Elizabeth was trying to send her over the centuries. With a shudder, Kim wondered if a fate similar to Elizabeth's was in store for her. Could that be what Elizabeth was trying to tell her? Could it be a warning?

Increasingly upset, Kim made a conscious effort to stop ruminating obsessively. She was successful until she got on the train. Then the thoughts came tumbling back.

"For goodness sake!" Kim said aloud, causing the woman sitting next to her to eye her with suspicion.

Kim turned to face out the window. She chided herself for allowing her active imagination too much free rein. After all, the differences between her life and Elizabeth's were far greater than any similarities, particularly in the area of control. Elizabeth had had very little control over her destiny. She had been essentially coerced at a young age into what was actually an arranged marriage, and she did not have access to birth control. In contrast, Kim was free to choose whom she would marry, and was free to control her body insofar as reproduction was concerned.

This line of thinking kept Kim comfortable until the train neared North Station in Boston. Then she began to wonder if she was as free as she'd like to believe. She reviewed some of the major decisions in her life, such as becoming a nurse instead of pursuing a career in art or design. Then she reminded herself that she was living with a man in a relationship that was becoming disturbingly similar to the one she'd had with her father. On top of that, she reminded herself that she was saddled with a research lab on her property and five researchers living in the family house—none of which had been her idea.

The train lurched to a stop. Mindless of her immediate environment, Kim walked to the subway. She knew what the problem was. She could almost hear Alice's voice in the background, telling her it was her personality. She didn't have appropriate self-esteem; she was too pliant; she thought of other people's needs and ignored her own. And all these conspired to constrain her freedom.

Such an irony, Kim thought. Elizabeth's personality, with her assertiveness and decisiveness, would have been perfect for today's world, whereas in her own time it undoubtedly contributed to her untimely death. Kim's personality, on the other hand, which was more dutiful and submissive rather than assertive and decisive, would have been fine in the seventeenth century but was not working out so well today.

With renewed resolve to unravel Elizabeth's story, Kim boarded the subway and traveled to Harvard Square. Within fifteen minutes of her arrival she was back in Mary Custland's office in the Widener Library, waiting for Mary to finish reading Jonathan's letter.

"This house of yours must be a treasure of memorabilia," Mary said, looking up from the page. "This letter is priceless." She immediately called Katherine Sturburg to her office and had her read it.

"What a delight," Katherine said when she was finished.

Both women told Kim that the letter was from a period of Harvard history of which there was scant material. They asked if they could copy it, and Kim gave them permission.

"So we have to find a reference to 'Rachel Bingham,' " Mary said, sitting down at her terminal.

"That's what I'm hoping," Kim said.

Mary entered the name while Kim and Katherine looked over her shoulder. Kim found herself with crossed fingers without having been conscious of doing it.

Two Rachel Binghams flashed onto the screen, but both were from the nineteenth century and could have had no association with Elizabeth. Mary tried a few other tricks, but there was nothing.

"I'm awfully sorry," Mary said. "Of course you realize that even if we did find a reference, the problem of the 1764 fire would still be a rather insurmountable difficulty."

"I understand," Kim said. "I really didn't expect to find anything, but, as I said on my first visit, I feel obligated to follow up on any new leads."

"I'll be sure to go through my sources with the new name," Katherine said.

Kim thanked both women and left. She took the subway back to North Station and had to wait for a train to Salem. As she stood on the platform she vowed to redouble her efforts at sorting the impossible jumble of papers in the castle over the next couple of days. Once she started back to work she'd have little opportunity to work on it except on her days off.

Arriving back at the compound, Kim intended to drive directly to the castle, but as she cleared the trees, she saw a Salem police car parked in front of the cottage. Curious as to what that could mean, she headed in its direction.

As she approached, Kim spotted Edward and Eleanor standing and conversing with two policemen in the middle of the grassy field about fifty yards from the house. Eleanor had her arm around Edward's shoulder.

Kim parked next to the patrol car and got out. The group in the field either hadn't heard her arrive or were too preoccupied to notice her.

Curious, Kim started walking toward them. As she approached she could see that there was something in the grass that had their collective attention.

Kim gasped when she saw what had their attention. It was Buffer. The poor dog was dead. What made the scene particularly gruesome was that some of the dog's flesh from its hindquarters was gone, exposing bloodied bones.

Kim cast a sorrowful look at Edward, who greeted her with composure, suggesting to her that he'd recovered from the initial shock. She could see dried tears on his cheeks. As nasty as the dog was, she knew he cared for him.

"It might be worth it to have the bones looked at by a medical examiner," Edward was saying. "There's a chance someone could recognize the teeth marks and tell us what species of animal could have done this."

"I don't know how the medical examiner's office would respond to a call about a dead dog," one of the officers said. His name was Billy Selvey.

"But you said you've had a couple of similar episodes during the last few nights," Edward said. "I think it behooves you to find out what kind of animal is involved. Personally, I think it was either another dog or a raccoon."

Kim was impressed with Edward's rationality in the face of his loss. He'd recovered enough to have a technical discussion about potential teeth marks on the exposed bone.

"When was the last time you saw the dog?" Billy asked.

"Last night," Edward said. "He usually slept with me, but maybe I let him out. I can't remember. Occasionally the dog stayed out all night. I'd never thought it was a problem since the compound is so big, and the dog wouldn't bother anyone anyway."

"I fed the dog around eleven-thirty last night," Kim said. "I left him in the kitchen eating."

"Did you let him out?" Edward asked.

"No, as I said, I left him in the kitchen," Kim said.

"Well, I didn't see him when I got up this morning," Edward said. "I didn't think anything about it. I just assumed he'd show up at the lab."

"Do you people have one of those pet doors?" Billy asked.

Both Kim and Edward said no at the same time.

"Anybody hear anything unusual last night?" Billy asked.

"I was dead to the world," Edward said. "I sleep very soundly, especially lately."

"I didn't hear anything either," Kim said.

"There's been some talk down at the station about these incidents being due to a rabid animal," the other officer said. His name was Harry Conners. "Do you people have any other pets?"

"I have a cat," Kim said.

"We advise you to keep it on a short leash for the next few days," Billy said.

The police put away their notepads and pens, said goodbye, and started toward their cruiser.

"What about the carcass?" Edward called out. "Don't you want to take it to the medical examiner?"

The two officers looked at each other, hoping the other one would respond. Finally Billy yelled back that they thought it best not to take it.

Edward waved them away good-naturedly. "I gave them a great tip and what do they do?" he said. "They walk away."

"Well, I've got to get back to work," Eleanor said, speaking up for the first time. She looked at Kim. "Don't forget, you promised to come back to the lab real soon."

"I'll be there," Kim promised. She was amazed Eleanor cared, yet she seemed sincere.

Eleanor started off toward the lab.

Edward stood looking down at Buffer. Kim averted her eyes. The sight was grisly and made her stomach turn.

"I'm very sorry about Buffer," Kim said, putting her hand on Edward's shoulder.

"He had a good life," Edward said cheerfully. "I think I'll disarticulate the back legs and send them to one of the pathologists I know at the medical school. Maybe he could tell us what kind of animal we should be looking for."

Kim swallowed hard hearing Edward's suggestion. Further mutilating the poor dog was hardly what she'd expected from him.

"I've got an old rag in the back of my car," Edward said. "I'll get it to wrap the carcass in."

Not sure what she should do, Kim stayed by Buffer's remains while Edward went for the old towel. She was rattled by Buffer's cruel fate even if Edward seemingly wasn't. Once Buffer was wrapped in the towel, she accompanied Edward back to the lab.

As they neared the lab a disturbing possibility occurred to Kim. She stopped Edward. "I just thought of something," she said. "What if Buffer's death and mutilation had something to do with sorcery?"

Edward looked at her for a beat, then threw his head back with howls of laughter. It took him several minutes to get himself under control. Meanwhile Kim found herself laughing with him as well, embarrassed at having suggested such a thing. "Wait just one minute," Kim protested. "I can remember reading someplace about black magic and animal sacrifice going hand in hand."

"I find your melodramatic imagination wonderfully entertaining," Edward managed amid renewed laughter. When he finally got himself under control, he apologized for laughing at her. At the same time he thanked her for a moment of comic relief.

"Tell me," he said, "do you really think that after three hundred years the devil has decided to return to Salem and that witchcraft is being directed at me and Omni?"

"I just made the association between animal sacrifice and sorcery," Kim said. "I really didn't think too much about it. Nor did I mean to imply that I believed in it, just that somebody did."

Edward put Buffer down and gave Kim a hug. "I think maybe you've been spending too much time hidden in the castle going through the old papers. Once things are really under control with Omni, we should go on a vacation. Someplace hot where we can lie in the sun. What do you say?"

"It sounds fun," Kim said although she wondered what kind of time frame was in Edward's mind.

Kim did not care to watch Edward dissect Buffer, so she stayed outside the lab when he went in to do it. He came back out in a few minutes, carrying a shovel, with the carcass still wrapped in the towel. He dug a shallow grave near the entrance of the lab. When he was finished burying Buffer, he told Kim to wait a moment since he had forgotten something. He disappeared back inside the lab.

Reemerging, Edward showed Kim a chemical reagent bottle he had retrieved. With a flamboyant gesture he placed the bottle at the head of Buffer's grave.

"What's that?" Kim asked.

"It's a chemical buffer called TRIS," Edward said. "A buffer for Buffer." Then he laughed almost as heartily as he had with Kim's suggestion of sorcery.

"I'm impressed how you are handling this unfortunate incident," Kim told him.

"I'm certain it has something to do with Ultra," Edward said, still chuckling over the pun. "When I first heard what had happened I was crushed. Buffer was like family to me. But the awful sorrow I felt passed quickly. I mean, I'm still sorry he's gone, but I don't feel that awful emptiness that accompanies grief. I can rationally recognize that death is a natural complement of living. After all, Buffer did have a good life for a dog, and he didn't have the world's best disposition."

"He was a loyal pet," Kim said. She wasn't about to tell him her true feelings about the dog.

"This is another example of why you should give Ultra a chance," Edward said. "I guarantee it will calm you down. Who knows, maybe it would clear your mind enough to help you with your quest to learn the truth about Elizabeth."

"I think only hard work can possibly do that," Kim said.

Edward gave her a quick kiss, thanked her effusively for her moral support, and disappeared back into the lab. Kim turned around and started for the castle. She'd only gone a short distance when she started to worry about Sheba. Suddenly she remembered letting the cat out the night before, after she'd fed Buffer, and she hadn't see her that morning.

Reversing her direction, Kim headed for the cottage. As she walked she gradually increased her pace. Buffer's death had added to her general anxiety. She couldn't imagine how devastated she'd be if Sheba had succumbed to a similar fate as Buffer.

Entering the house, Kim called for Sheba. She quickly climbed the stairs and went into her bedroom. To her relief she saw the cat curled up in a ball of fur in the middle of the bed. Kim rushed over and snuggled with the animal. Sheba gave her one of her disdainful looks for being disturbed.

After petting the cat for several minutes, Kim went to her bureau. With tremulous fingers she picked up the container of Ultra she'd put there the night before. Once again she removed one of the blue capsules and examined it. She yearned for relief. She debated with herself the idea of trying the drug for twenty-four hours, just to see what it could do for her. Edward's ability to deal so well with Buffer's death was an impressive testimonial. Kim went so far as to get a glass of water.

But she did not take the capsule. Instead she began to wonder if Edward's response was too modulated. From her reading as well as her intuition Kim knew that a certain amount of grieving was a necessary human emotion. That made her consider whether blocking the normal process of grieving might exact a price in the future.

With that thought in mind, Kim replaced the capsule in the vial and hazarded another visit to the lab. Fearing being entrapped by more interminable demonstrations by Edward's team, Kim literally sneaked into the building.

Luckily, only Edward and David were on the upper floor and they were at opposite ends of the huge room. Kim was able to surprise Edward without the others knowing she was there. When Edward saw her and started to respond, Kim shushed him with her finger to her lips. Taking his hand, she led him from the building.

Once the door to the lab had closed behind them, Edward grinned and asked, "What on earth has gotten into you?"

"I just want to talk to you," Kim explained. "I had a thought that maybe you could include in the clinical protocol of Ultra."

Kim explained to Edward what she'd thought about grief and expanded the notion to include anxiety and melancholy, saying that moderate amounts of these emotionally painful feelings play a positive role as motivators of human growth, change, and creativity. She concluded by saying, "What I'm worried about is that taking a drug like Ultra that modulates these mental states may have a hidden cost and could cause a serious negative side effect that would not be anticipated."

Edward smiled and slowly nodded his head. He was impressed. "I appreciate your concern," he said. "It's an interesting thought you have, but I don't share it. You see, it's based on a false premise, namely that the mind is somehow mystically apart from the material body. That old hypothesis has been debunked by recent experience that shows that the mind and the body are one even in regards to mood and emotion. Emotion has been proved to be biologically determined by the fact that it is affected by drugs like Prozac, which alter levels of neurotransmitters. It has revolutionized ideas about brain function."

"That kind of thinking is dehumanizing," Kim complained.

"Let me put it another way," Edward said. "What about pain? Do you think drugs should be taken for pain?"

"Pain is different," Kim said, but she could see the philosophical trap Edward was laying for her.

"I don't think so," Edward said. "Pain, too, is biological. Since physical pain and psychic pain are both biological, they should both be treated the same, namely with well-designed drugs that target only those parts of the brain responsible."

Kim felt frustrated. She wanted to ask Edward where the world would be if Mozart and Beethoven had been on drugs for anxiety or depression. But she did not say anything. She knew it was no use. The scientist in Edward blinded him.

Edward gave Kim an exuberant hug and reiterated how much he appreciated her interest in his work. He then patted the top of her head.

"We'll talk more about this issue if you'd like," he said. "But now I better get back to work."

Kim apologized for bothering him and started back for the cottage.

Over the next several days Kim was again tempted on several occasions to give Ultra a try. Her gradually mounting anxiety had begun to affect her sleep. But each time she was on the brink of taking the drug, she pulled back.

Instead Kim tried to use her anxiety as a motivator. Each day she spent more than ten hours working in the castle and quit only when it became difficult for her to see well enough to read the handwritten pages. Unfortunately, her increased efforts were to no avail. She began to wish that she would find some seventeenth-century material, even if it had no association with Elizabeth, just to encourage her.

The presence of the plumbers turned out to be a pleasant diversion rather than an imposition. Whenever Kim took a break she at least had someone to talk with. She even watched them work for a time, intrigued with the use of the blowtorch for soldering copper tubing.

The only indication that Kim noticed that the researchers were sleeping in the castle was dirt tracked in from both entrances to the wings. Although some soiling was to be expected, she thought the amount involved suggested surprising inconsiderateness.

Edward's assertive, happy, and caring mood continued. With a gesture reminiscent of their initial dating days, Edward even had a large bouquet sent to the house on Tuesday with a note that said, *In Loving Gratitude.*

The only alteration in his behavior occurred on Thursday morning when Kim was just about to leave the cottage for the castle. Edward came through the front door in a huff. Obviously irritated, he slammed his address book down on the table next to the telephone, putting Kim immediately on edge. "Is something wrong?" she asked.

"Damn right something is wrong," he said. "I have to come all the way up here to use the phone. When I use one at the lab every one of those twits listens to my conversation. It drives me nuts."

"Why didn't you use the phone in the empty reception area?" Kim asked.

"They listen when I go there too," he said.

"Through the walls?" she questioned.

"I've got to call the goddamn head of the Harvard Licensing Office," Edward complained, ignoring Kim's comment. "That jerk has launched a personal vendetta against me." Edward opened his address book to find the number.

"Could it be that he's just doing his job?" Kim asked, knowing this was an ongoing controversy.

"You think he's doing his job by getting me suspended?" Edward yelled. "It's incredible! I never would have guessed the little dick-headed bureaucrat had the nerve to pull off such a stunt."

Kim felt her heart pounding. Edward's tone reminded her of the glass-throwing episode in his apartment. She was afraid to say anything else.

"Ah, well," Edward said in a completely calm tone of voice. He smiled. "Such is life. There's always these little ups and downs." He sat down and dialed his number.

Kim allowed herself to relax a degree, but she didn't take her eyes off Edward. She listened while he had a civilized conversation with the man he'd just railed against. When he got off the phone he said that the man was quite reasonable after all.

"As long as I'm here," Edward said, "I'll dash upstairs and get the dry cleaning together that you asked me to take care of yesterday."

Edward started for the stairs.

"But you already got the dry cleaning together," Kim said. "You must have done it this morning, because I found it when I got up."

Edward stopped and blinked as if he were confused. "I did?" he asked. Then he added: "Well, good for me! I should be getting right back to the lab anyway."

"Edward?" Kim called to him before he went out the front door. "Are you all right? You've been forgetting little things lately."

Edward laughed. "It's true," he said. "I've been a bit forgetful. But I've never felt better. I'm just preoccupied. But there's light at the end of the tunnel, and we're all about to be extremely rich. And that includes you. I spoke to Stanton about giving you some stock, and he agreed. So you'll be part of the big payoff."

"I'm flattered," Kim said.

Kim went to the window and watched Edward walk back to the lab. She watched him the whole way, pondering his behavior. He was now more congenial toward her on the whole, but he was also unpredictable.

Impulsively Kim got her car keys and headed into town. She needed to talk to someone professional whose opinion she valued. Conveniently, Kinnard was still in the area. Using the phone at the information desk in the Salem Hospital, she had him paged.

A half hour later he met her in the coffee shop. He was dressed in surgical scrub clothes, having come directly from surgery. She had been nursing a cup of tea.

"I hope I'm not bothering you terribly," Kim said the moment he sat down across from her.

"It's good to see you," Kinnard said.

"I needed to ask a question," she said. "Could forgetfulness be a side effect of a psychotropic drug?"

"Absolutely," he said. "But I have to qualify that by saying that a lot of things can affect short-term memory. It's a very nonspecific symptom. Should I assume that Edward is having such a problem?"

"Can I count on your discretion?" she asked.

"I've already told you as much," Kinnard said. "Are Edward and his team still taking the drug?"

Kim nodded.

"They're crazy," Kinnard said. "They're just asking for trouble. Have you noticed any other effects?"

Kim gave a short laugh. "You wouldn't believe it," she said. "They're all having a dramatic response. Before they started the drug they were bickering with each other and sullen. Now they are all in great moods. They couldn't be any happier or more content. They act as if they're having a ball even though they continue to work at the same feverish pace."

"That sounds like a good effect," Kinnard said.

"In some respects," Kim admitted. "But after you've been with them for a while you sense something weird, like they are all too similar and tedious despite their hilarity and their industriousness."

"Now it sounds a little like *Brave New World*," Kinnard said with a chuckle.

"Don't laugh," Kim said. "I thought of the same thing. But that's more of a philosophical issue, and it's not my immediate concern. What has me worried is the forgetfulness Edward has been exhibiting with silly everyday things. And it seems to be getting worse. I don't know if the other people are experiencing it or not."

"What are you going to do?" Kinnard asked.

"I don't know," Kim said. "I was hoping you could either definitively confirm my fears or dispel them. I guess you can't do either."

"Not with any degree of certainty," Kinnard admitted. "But I can say something you can think about. Perceptions are extraordinarily influenced by expectations. That's why double-blind studies have been instituted in medical research. There is a possibility that your expectation to see negative effects from Edward's drug is affecting what you see. I know Edward is extraordinarily smart, and it doesn't make much sense to me that he would take any unreasonable risk."

"You have a point," Kim said. "It's true that at the moment I don't know what I'm seeing. It could all be in my head, but I don't think so."

Kinnard glanced at the wall clock and had to excuse himself to do a case. "I'm sorry to cut this short," he said, "but I'm here for the next few days if you want to talk more. Otherwise I'll see you in the SICU in Boston."

The moment they parted, Kinnard gave her hand a squeeze. She squeezed back and thanked him for listening to her.

Arriving back at the compound, Kim went directly to the castle. She had a few words with the plumbers, who insisted they were making good progress but that they'd need another three days or so to finish. They also suggested they should check the guest wing for the same problem. Kim told them to do whatever was needed.

Before going down to the wine cellar, Kim inspected the two entrances to the wings. She was appalled when she saw the one to the servants' quarters. Not only was there dirt on the stairs, but there were also some sticks and leaves. Even an empty container for Chinese take-out food was in the corner near the door.

Swearing under her breath, Kim went to the cleaning closet, got out a mop and a bucket, and cleaned the stairway. The dirt had been tracked up to the first landing.

After she'd cleaned everything up, Kim walked to the front door, picked up the outdoor mat, and carried it around to the entrance to the servants' wing. She thought about putting up a note, but then thought the mat should be message enough.

Finally Kim descended into the depths of the wine cellar and got to work. Although she did not find any documents even close to the seventeenth century, her concentration served to free her mind from her concerns, and she slowly began to relax.

At one o'clock Kim took a break. She went back to the cottage and let Sheba out while she had some lunch. Before she returned to the castle she made sure the cat was back in the house. At the castle she chatted with the plumbers for a few minutes and watched Albert deftly make some seals on water-supply pipes with his blowtorch. Finally she got back to work, this time in the attic.

Kim was again becoming discouraged when she found a whole folder of material from the era she was interested in. With excitement she carried it over to one of the dormered windows.

She was not surprised when the papers turned out to be business-related. A few of them were in Ronald's easily recognizable script. Then Kim caught her breath. Out of the customs documents and bills of lading she pulled a piece of personal correspondence. It was a letter to Ronald from Thomas Goodman.

17th August 1692
Salem Town

Sir:
Many are the villainies that have plagued our God fearing town. It has been a matter of great affliction for me whereby I have been unwillingly involved. I am sore of heart that you have thought ill of me and my duty as a convenanted member of our congregation and hath refused to converse with me in matters of joint interest. It is true that I in good faith and in God's name did testify against your departed wife at her hearing and at her trial. At your request I did visit your home on occasion to offer aid if it be needed. On that fateful day I found your door ajar yet a frigid chill be on the land and the table laden with food and sustenance as if a meal interrupted yet other objects upside down or sharply broken with blood droplets on the floor. I did fear for an Indian raid and the safety of your kin. But the children both natural and the refugee girls I espied cowering in fear upstairs with word that your Goodwife fell into a fit while eating and not be of her normal self and having run to the shelter of your livestock. With

trepidation I took myself there and called her name in the darkness. She came at me like a wild woman and affrighted me greatly. Blood was on her hands and her frock and I saw her handiwork. With troubled spirit I did quiet her at risk to my own well being. To a like purpose I did likewise with your livestock which were all affrighted yet all were safe. To these things I spoke the truth in God's name.

I remain your friend and neighbor,
Thomas Goodman.

"These poor people," Kim murmured. This letter came the closest to anything she'd read so far in communicating to her the personal horror of the Salem witch ordeal, and Kim felt empathy for all involved. She could tell that Thomas was confused and dismayed at being caught between friendship and what he thought was the truth. And Kim's heart went out to poor Elizabeth, who'd been rendered out of her mind with the mold to the point of terrorizing her own children. It was easy for Kim to understand how the seventeenth-century mind would have ascribed such horrifying and inexplicable behavior to witchcraft.

In the middle of Kim's empathy she realized that the letter presented something new and disturbing. It was the mention of blood with its implication of violence. Kim didn't even want to imagine what Elizabeth could have been doing in the shed with the livestock, yet she had to admit it might be significant.

Kim looked back at the letter. She reread the sentence where Thomas described that all the livestock was safe despite the presence of blood. That seemed confusing unless Elizabeth had done something to herself. The thought of self-mutilation made Kim shudder. Its possibility was enhanced by Thomas's mention of droplets of blood on the floor in the house. But the blood in the house was mentioned in the same sentence with broken objects, suggesting the blood could have come from an inadvertent wound.

Kim sighed. Her mind was a jumble, but one thing was clear. The effect of the fungus was now associated with violence, and Kim thought that was something Edward and the others should know immediately.

Clutching the letter, Kim hastened from the castle and half-ran to the lab. She was out of breath when she entered. She was also immediately surprised: she'd walked into the middle of a celebration.

Everyone greeted Kim with great merriment, pulling her over to one of the lab benches where they had uncorked a bottle of champagne. Kim tried to refuse a beakerful but they wouldn't hear of it. Once again she felt as if she were with a bunch of frolicsome collegians.

As soon as Kim was able, she worked her way over to Edward's side to ask him what was going on.

"Eleanor, Gloria, and François have just pulled off an amazing feat of analytic chemistry," Edward explained. "They've already determined the structure of one of Ultra's binding proteins. It's a huge leap forward. It will allow us to modify Ultra if need be or to design other possible drugs that will bind at the same site."

"I'm happy for you," Kim said. "But I want to show you something that I think you ought to see." She handed him the letter.

Edward quickly scanned the letter. When he looked up at Kim he winked at her. "Congratulations," he said. "This is the best one yet." Then, turning to the group, he called out: "Listen up, you guys. Kim has found the greatest bit of proof that Elizabeth had been poisoned with the fungus. It will be even better than the diary entry for the article for *Science.*"

The researchers eagerly gathered around. Edward gave them the letter and encouraged them all to read it.

"It's perfect," Eleanor said, passing it on to David. "It even mentions she'd been eating. It's certainly a graphic description of how fast the alkaloid works. She'd probably just taken a bite of bread."

"It's a good thing you eliminated that hallucinogenic side-chain," David said. "I wouldn't want to wake up and find myself out with the cows."

Everyone laughed except Kim. She looked at Edward and, after waiting for him to stop laughing, asked him if the suggestion of violence in the letter bothered him.

Edward took the letter back and read it more carefully. "You know, you have a good point," he told Kim when he was finished the second time. "I don't think I should use this letter for the article after all. It might cause some trouble we don't need. A few years ago there was an unfortunate rumor fanned by TV talk shows that associated Prozac with violence. It was a problem until it was debunked statistically. I don't want anything like that to happen to Ultra."

"If the unaltered alkaloid caused violence, it had to have been the same side chain that caused the hallucinations," Gloria said. "You could mention that in the article."

"Why take the chance?" Edward said. "I don't want to give some rabid journalist even a tidbit that might raise the specter of violence."

"Perhaps the concern for violence should be included in the clinical protocols," Kim suggested. "Then if the question ever were to arise, you'd already have data."

"You know, that's a damn good idea," Gloria said.

For several minutes the group favorably discussed Kim's suggestion. Encouraged that people were listening to her, she suggested they should include short-term-memory lapses as well. To make her case she cited Edward's recent episodes.

Edward laughed good-naturedly along with everyone else. "So what if I brush my teeth twice?" he said, bringing on more laughter.

"I think including short-term-memory loss in the clinical protocols is an equally good idea as including violence," Curt said. "David's been similarly forgetful. I've noticed, since we're immediate neighbors in the castle."

"You should talk," David said with a chuckle. He then told the group that just the night before, Curt had called his girlfriend twice because he'd forgotten he'd called her the first time.

"I bet that went over well with her," Gloria said.

Curt gave David a playful punch in the shoulder. "The only reason you noticed was because you'd done the exact same thing the night before with your wife."

As Kim watched Curt and David playfully spar, she noticed Curt's hands and fingers were marred by cuts and scratches. Her reflex response as a nurse was one of concern. She offered to look at them.

"Thank you, but they aren't as bad as they look," Curt said. "They don't bother me in the slightest."

"Did you fall off your motorcycle?"

Curt laughed. "I hope not," he said. "I don't remember how I did it."

"It's an occupational hazard," David said, showing his hands, which appeared similar although not as bad. "It just proves we're all working our fingers to the bone."

"It's the pressure of working nineteen hours a day," François said. "It's amazing we have been functioning as well as we have."

"It seems to me that short-term-memory loss must be a side effect of Ultra," Kim said. "It sounds like you all are experiencing it."

"I haven't," Gloria said.

"Neither have I," Eleanor said. "My mind and memory are demonstrably better since I've been on Ultra."

"Same with me," Gloria said. "I think François is right. We're just working too hard."

"Wait a second, Gloria," Eleanor said. "You *have* been forgetful. What about the morning before last when you left your bathrobe in the bathroom and then two minutes later had a fit when it wasn't hanging behind your door in the bedroom?"

"I didn't throw a fit," Gloria contradicted good-naturedly. "Besides, that's different. I've been misplacing my robe way before I've been on Ultra."

"Regardless," Edward said. "Kim is right. Short-term-memory lapse could be related to Ultra, and as such it should be included in the clinical protocols. But it's not something we need to lose any sleep over. Even if it proves to occur on occasion, it will surely be an acceptable risk in light of the drug's enhancement of mental function in general."

"I agree," Gloria said. "It's the equivalent of Einstein forgetting little everyday matters while he was formulating the Theory of Relativity. The mind makes value judgments of what to keep in the processor, and how many times you brush your teeth isn't that important."

The sound of the outer door closing got everyone's attention since the lab got few visitors. All eyes turned to the door to the reception area. It opened and in walked Stanton.

A spontaneous triple cheer arose from the researchers. A confused Stanton stopped in his tracks. "What on earth is going on here?" he questioned. "Nobody working today?"

Eleanor rushed him a beaker of champagne.

"A little toast," Edward said, lifting his drink. "We'd like to drink to your heckling nature that motivated us to start taking Ultra. We're reaping the benefits on a daily basis."

Amid giggles everyone took a drink, including Stanton.

"It really has been a boon," Edward said. "We've been drawing blood on each other and saving urine to test."

"All of us except François," Gloria said, teasing the Frenchman. "He forgets more than half the time."

"We did have a slight problem with compliance in that regard," Edward admitted. "But we solved it by taping the toilet seats down and putting up a sign saying HOLD IT."

They all laughed again. Gloria and David had to put their drinks down for fear of spilling them.

"You certainly are a happy group," Stanton commented.

"We have reason to be," Edward said. He then told Stanton the good news about discovering the structure of the binding protein. He gave partial credit to Ultra for sharpening everyone's mental acuity.

"This is marvelous news indeed!" Stanton exclaimed. He made it a point to walk around and shake Gloria's, Eleanor's, and François's hands individually. Then he told Edward he wanted to talk with him.

Using Stanton's arrival as an opportunity to excuse herself, Kim left. She felt good about her visit to the lab; she had the feeling she'd accomplished something by suggesting violence and short-term-memory loss should be included in the clinical evaluation of Ultra.

Kim headed back toward the castle. The first thing she wanted to do was put Thomas Goodman's letter into the Bible box with the other memorabilia pertaining to Elizabeth. As she neared the mansion she saw a Salem police car emerge from the trees. Evidently the driver saw her, because the cruiser immediately turned onto the road to the castle, heading in her direction.

Kim stopped and waited. The car pulled to a stop, and the same two officers who'd responded to the call about Buffer got out.

Billy touched the rim of his visored hat in a kind of salute while he and Kim exchanged greetings.

"I hope we're not bothering you," Billy said.

"Is something wrong?" Kim questioned.

"We wanted to ask if you'd had any more trouble since the death of the dog," Billy said. "There's been a rash of vandalism in the immediate area, as if Halloween had come a month early."

"Halloween's big here in Salem," Harry said. "It's the time of year we law-enforcement officers have learned to hate."

"What kind of vandalism?" Kim questioned.

"The usual nonsense," Billy said. "Trash cans turned over, garbage spread around. Also more pets have disappeared and some of the carcasses have turned up across the road in the Greenlawn Cemetery."

"We're still concerned about the possibility of a rabid animal in the neighborhood," Harry said. "You'd better keep that cat of yours indoors, especially considering the size of your property and all its wooded areas."

"We think some local kids have joined the fray, so to speak," Billy said. "They're imitating what the animal has been doing. There's been too much for one animal. I mean, how many trash cans can a raccoon do in a night?" He snickered.

"I appreciate your coming by to warn me," Kim said. "We haven't had any trouble since the dog's death, but I'll be sure to continue to keep my cat close to home."

"If you have any problems please give us a call," Harry said. "We'd like to get to the bottom of this before it gets out of hand."

Kim watched while the police car made a U-turn and headed out of the compound. She was about to enter the castle when she heard Stanton call. Turning, she saw him coming from the lab.

"What the devil were the police doing here?" he asked as soon as he was within talking distance.

Kim told him about the concern of there being a rabid animal in the area.

"It's always something," Stanton said. "Listen, I want to talk to you about Edward. Do you have a minute?"

"Of course," Kim said, wondering what this could be about. "Where would you like to talk?"

"Here's fine," Stanton said. "Where to start?" He stared off for a minute then looked Kim in the eye. "I'm a bit bewildered by Edward lately and the others as well. Every time I pop into the lab I feel like the odd man out. A couple of weeks ago it was like a morgue in there. Now it's eerie the way they are enjoying themselves. It's become like a vacation retreat, only they're working as hard or harder than they did before. Their repartee is difficult to follow since they are all so damn smart and witty. In fact, it makes me feel dumb to hang around." Stanton laughed wryly before continuing. "Edward has become so outgoing and pushy that he reminds me of me!"

Kim put her hand to her mouth but laughed through her fingers at Stanton's self-deprecating insightfulness.

"It's not funny," Stanton complained, but he was laughing himself. "The next thing that Edward will want to be is a venture capitalist. He's gotten carried away with the business stuff, and unfortunately we don't see eye to eye. Now we're at loggerheads over how to raise more capital. The good doctor has become so greedy he will not sacrifice any equity. He's metamorphosed overnight from an avowed ascetic academician to an insatiable capitalist."

"Why are you telling me this?" Kim questioned. "I have nothing to do with Omni nor do I want to have."

"I was just hoping that you could talk to Edward," Stanton said. "I cannot in good conscience condone borrowing money from dirty sources through foreign banks, and I'm even sorry that I mentioned the possibility. There's just too much risk, and I'm not talking about financial risk. I'm talking about risk to life and limb. It just ain't worth it. I mean, the financial aspect of this venture should be left up to me, just like the scientific stuff should be left up to Edward."

"Does Edward seem forgetful to you?" Kim asked.

"Hell, no!" Stanton said. "He's as sharp as a tack. He's just innocent when it comes to the ways of the financial world."

"He's been forgetful around me," Kim said. "Just little everyday things. And most of the other researchers have admitted to being just as absentminded."

"I haven't noticed any absentmindedness with Edward," Stanton said. "But he did seem a little paranoid. Just a few minutes ago we had to go outside to talk so we wouldn't be overheard."

"Overheard by whom?" Kim asked.

Stanton shrugged. "The other researchers, I assume. He didn't say and I didn't ask."

"This morning he came all the way to the house to make a call so that he wouldn't be overheard," Kim said. "He was afraid to use the phone in the reception area because he thought someone would listen through the walls."

"Now that sounds even more paranoid," Stanton said. "But in his defense I've drilled it into him that secrecy is important at this stage."

"Stanton, I'm getting worried," Kim said.

"Don't say that," Stanton complained. "I came to you to relieve my anxieties, not increase them."

"I'm concerned that the forgetfulness and paranoia are side effects from the Ultra," Kim said.

"I don't want to hear this," Stanton said as he cupped his hands over his ears.

"They shouldn't be taking the drug at this stage," Kim said. "And you know it. I think you should stop them."

"Me?" Stanton said. "I just told you a minute ago I'm in finances. I don't meddle with the science side, especially when they have told me that taking the drug will speed up its evaluation process. Besides, this mild paranoia and forgetfulness are probably due to how hard they are working. Edward knows what he is doing. My God, he's tops in his field."

"I'll make you a deal," Kim said. "If you try to convince Edward to stop taking the drug, I'll try to convince him that the finances should be left to you."

Stanton made a face as if he had been stabbed in the back. "This is ridiculous," he said. "I've got to negotiate with my own cousin."

"It sounds reasonable to me," Kim said. "We'll be helping each other."

"I can't promise anything," Stanton said.

"Nor can I," Kim said.

"When will you talk with him?" Stanton asked.

"Tonight," Kim said. "What about you?"

"I suppose I could just go back and talk with him now," Stanton said.

"Do we have a deal?" Kim asked.

"I suppose so," Stanton said reluctantly. He stuck out his hand and Kim shook it.

Kim watched as Stanton started back toward the lab. In contrast to his usual sprightly step his gait was plodding, with his arms hanging straight down like he was lugging heavy weights in both hands. Kim couldn't help but feel sorry for him since she knew that he was distressed. The problem was he'd put all his money into Omni, violating one of his own cardinal rules of investing.

After climbing up to the attic, Kim walked over to one of the dormer windows that faced in the direction of the lab. She was just in time to see Stanton disappear into the building. Kim didn't have high hopes that Stanton would be successful getting Edward to stop taking Ultra, but at least she could feel that she'd tried.

That night Kim made it a point to stay awake until Edward came in just after one in the morning. She was reading when she heard the front door close, followed by Edward's footfalls on the old stairs.

"My goodness," he said, sticking his head into her bedroom. "That must be one hell of a book to keep you awake until this hour."

"I'm not tired," Kim said. "Come in."

"I'm exhausted," Edward said. He stepped into the room and absently petted Sheba while he yawned. "I can't wait to get into bed. It hits me just after midnight like clockwork. The amazing thing is how quickly I fall asleep once the tiredness comes. I have to be careful if I sit down. If I lie down, forget it."

"I noticed that," Kim said. "Sunday night you didn't even turn out your light."

"I suppose I should be aggravated with you," Edward said. He was smiling. "But I'm not. I know you only have my best interests at heart."

"Are you going to tell me what you are talking about?" Kim asked.

"As if you didn't know," Edward said teasingly. "I'm talking about Stanton's sudden concern for my well-being. I knew you were behind it the moment he opened his mouth. It's not like him to be so sympathetic."

"Did he tell you about our deal?" Kim said.

"What kind of deal?" Edward asked.

"He agreed to try to get you to stop taking Ultra if I would convince you that Omni's finances should be left up to him."

"Et tu, Brute," Edward said jokingly. "This is a fine state of affairs. The two people I think I'm closest to are scheming behind my back."

"As you said, we've only your best interests at heart," Kim said.

"I think I'm capable of deciding what's best for me," Edward said amiably.

"But you've changed," Kim said. "Stanton said you've changed so much that you're becoming like him."

Edward laughed heartily. "That's great!" he said. "I've always wanted to be as outgoing as Stanton. Too bad my father passed away. Maybe he'd finally be pleased with me."

"This isn't a joking matter," Kim said.

"I'm not joking," Edward said. "I enjoy being socially assertive instead of shy and bashful."

"But it's dangerous taking an untested drug," Kim said. "Besides, don't you question the ethics of acquiring character traits from a drug rather than from experience? I think it's fake and like cheating."

Edward sat on the edge of Kim's bed. "If I fall asleep call a tow truck to get me into my bed," he said with a chuckle. He then had another extended yawn that he tried to cover with his fist. "Listen, my dearest," he said. "Ultra is not untested; it's just not fully tested. But it's nontoxic, and that's the important thing. I'm going to continue taking it unless a serious side effect occurs, which I sincerely doubt. As to your second point, it's clear to me that undesirable character traits, like in my case my shyness, can become entrenched by experience. Prozac, to an extent, and now Ultra, to a greater extent, have unlocked the real me, the person whose personality had been submerged by an unfortunate series of life experiences that made me the socially awkward person I'd become. My personality right now hasn't been invented by Ultra and isn't fake. My current personality has been allowed to emerge despite a haze of facilitated neural responses that I'd call a 'bum network.' "

Edward chuckled as he gave Kim's leg a reassuring pat through her covers. "I assure you, I've never felt better in my life. Trust me. My only concern now is how long I have to take Ultra before this current 'me' has been facilitated so that when I stop taking Ultra I won't relapse into my shy, socially awkward old self."

"You make it sound so reasonable," Kim complained.

"But it is," Edward said. "This is the way I want to be. Hell, this is the way I probably would have been if my father hadn't been such a bore."

"But what about the forgetfulness and the paranoia?" Kim said.

"What paranoia?" Edward asked.

Kim reminded him of his coming to the house that morning to use the phone and having to go out of the lab to talk with Stanton.

"That wasn't paranoid," Edward said indignantly. "Those characters down in the lab have become the worst gossip hounds I've ever been around. I'm just trying to protect my privacy."

"Both Stanton and I thought it seemed paranoid," Kim said.

"Well, I can assure you it wasn't," Edward said. He smiled. The twinge of irritation he'd felt at being accused of paranoia had already passed. "The forgetfulness I'll admit to but not the other."

"Why not stop the drug and start it again during the clinical phase?"

"You are a hard person to convince," Edward said. "And unfortunately I'm out of energy. I can't keep my eyes open. I'm sorry. We'll continue this tomorrow if you'd like since it is an extension of a previous discussion. Right now I have to go to bed."

Edward bent over, gave Kim a kiss on her cheek, and then walked unsteadily out of her room. She heard him moving about his bedroom for only a few minutes. Then she heard the deep heavy respiration of someone already fast asleep.

Amazed at the rapidity of the transformation, Kim got out of bed. After slipping on her robe, she walked through the connecting hall to Edward's bedroom. A trail of discarded clothes led across the room, and Edward was spread-eagled on top of his bed, clothed only in his underwear. Just as what happened Sunday night, his bedside lamp was still on.

Kim walked to the light and switched it off. Standing next to him, she was amazed at how loud his snoring was. She wondered why it had never awakened her when they slept together.

Kim retreated to her own bed. She turned out the light and tried to go to sleep. But it was impossible. Her mind would not turn off, and she could hear Edward as if he were in her room.

After a half hour, Kim got back out of bed and went into the bathroom. She found the old vial of Xanax she'd been saving for years and took one of the pink, boat-shaped pills. She didn't like the idea of taking the drug, but she thought she needed it; there would be no sleep if she didn't.

Coming out of the bathroom, she closed both Edward's door and her own. Getting back into bed, she could still hear Edward but at least it was muffled. Within fifteen minutes she felt a welcome serenity drift over her. A little while later she fell into her own deep sleep.

FRIDAY • SEPTEMBER 30, 1994

At nearly three A.M. there was little traffic on the darkened streets of Salem, and Dave Halpern felt as if he owned the world. Since midnight he'd been aimlessly cruising in his '89 red Chevy Camaro. He'd been to Marblehead twice and even up to Danvers and around through Beverly.

Dave was seventeen and a junior at Salem High. He'd gotten the car thanks to an after-school job at a local McDonald's and a sizable loan from his parents, and it was the current love of his life. He reveled in the sense of freedom and unadulterated power the car gave him. He also liked the attention it evoked from his friends, particularly Christina McElroy. Christina was a sophomore and had a great body.

Dave checked the dimly illuminated clock set into the center console on the dash. It was just about time for the rendezvous. Turning onto Dearborn Street, where Christina lived, Dave hit the lights and turned off the engine. He slowed and glided to a silent stop beneath the canopy of a large maple.

He didn't have to wait long. Christina appeared out of the hedges that ran alongside her clapboard house, rushed to the car, and jumped in. The whites of her eyes and teeth glistened in the half-light. She was tremulous with excitement.

She slid across the vinyl seat so that her tightly denimed thigh pressed against Dave's.

Trying to project an air of insouciance, as if this middle-of-the-night rendezvous were an everyday occurrence, Dave didn't speak. He merely reached forward and started his machine. But his hand shook and rattled the keys. Fearing he'd given himself away, he cast a furtive look in Christina's direction. He caught a smile and worried that she thought he wasn't cool.

When Dave reached the corner he switched on his headlights. Instantly the nightscape lit up, revealing blowing leaves and deep shadows.

"Have any problems?" Dave asked, keeping his mind on the road.

"It was a breeze," Christina said. "I can't understand why I was so scared to sneak out of the house. My parents are unconscious. I mean I could have just walked out the front door instead of climbing out the window."

They drove down a street lined with dark houses.

"Where are we going?" Christina asked nonchalantly.

"You'll see," Dave said. "We'll be there in a sec."

They were now cruising past the dark, expansive Greenlawn Cemetery. Christina pressed up against Dave and looked over his shoulder into the graveyard with its stubble of headstones.

Dave slowed the car, and Christina sat bolt upright. "We're not going in there," she said defiantly.

Dave smiled in the darkness, exposing his own white teeth. "Why not?" he said. Almost as soon as the words left his mouth he pulled the wheel to the left, and the car bumped over the threshold into the cemetery. Dave quickly doused the headlights and slowed to a speed approximating a slow jog. It was hard to see the road beneath the foliage.

"Oh, my God!" Christina said as her head pivoted and her wide eyes scanned the immediate area on both sides of the car. The headstones loomed eerily in the night. Some of them gave off sudden splinters of ambient light from their highly polished surfaces.

Instinctively Christina moved even closer to Dave's side, with one hand gripping the inside of his thigh. Dave grinned with satisfied contentment.

They rolled to a stop beside a silent, still pond bordered by droopy willows. Dave turned off the engine and locked the doors. "Can't be too careful," he said.

"Maybe we should crack the windows," Christina suggested. "Otherwise it will be an oven in here."

Dave took the suggestion but voiced the hope that there wouldn't be any mosquitoes.

The two teenagers eyed each other for a moment of awkward hesitation. Then Dave tentatively leaned toward Christina, and they gently kissed. The contact instantly fueled the fires of their passion, and they fell into a wild, libidinous embrace. Clumsily they groped for each other's physical secrets as the windows steamed up.

Despite the power of their youthful, teenage hormones, both Dave and Christina sensed a movement of the car that was not of their making. Simultaneously they glanced up from their endeavors and looked out through the misty windshield. What they saw instantly terrified them. Hurling at them through the night air was a pale white specter. Whatever the preternatural creature was, it collided with a jarring impact against the windshield and then rolled off the passenger side of the car.

"What the hell?" Dave yelled as he frantically struggled with his pants, which had worked their way halfway down his thighs.

Christina then shrieked as she battled to fend off a filthy hand that thrust itself through her cracked window and tore away a handful of her hair.

"Holy crap!" Dave yelled as he gave up on his pants to fight a hand that came in through his side. Fingernails sank into the skin of his neck and ripped off a piece of his T-shirt, leaving rivulets of blood to run down his back.

In a panic Dave started the Camaro. Jamming the car in reverse, he shot backward, bouncing over the rocky terrain. Christina screamed again as her head hit the roof of the car. The car slammed into a headstone that snapped off at its base and thudded to the ground.

Dave threw the car into drive and gunned the engine. He wrestled with the wheel as the powerful engine hurled the car forward. Christina ricocheted off the door and was thrown into Dave's lap. He pushed her away just in time to miss another marble monument.

Dave snapped on the headlights as they careened around a sharp turn in the road that meandered through the cemetery. Christina recovered enough to start crying.

"Who the hell were they?" Dave shouted.

"There were two of them," Christina managed through her tears.

They reached the street and Dave turned toward town, laying a patch of rubber on the street. Christina's crying lessened to whimpering with an occasional sob. Turning the rearview mirror in her direction, she inspected the damage to her hair. "My cut's been ruined," she cried.

Dave readjusted the mirror and glanced behind them to be certain no one was following. He wiped his neck with his hand and looked at the blood with disbelief.

"What the devil were they wearing?" Dave asked angrily.

"What difference does it make?" Christina cried.

"They were wearing white clothes or something," Dave said. "Like a couple of ghosts."

"We never should have gone there," Christina bawled. "I knew it from the start."

"Give me a break," Dave said. "You didn't know anything."

"I did," she said. "You just didn't ask me."

"Bull," Dave said.

"Whoever they were, they must be sick," Christina said.

"You're probably right," Dave said. "Maybe they're from Danvers State Hospital. But if they are, how do they get all the way down here to Greenlawn Cemetery?"

Christina put her hand to her mouth and mumbled, "I'm going to be sick."

Dave jammed on his brakes and pulled over to the side of the road. Christina cracked her door and vomited in the street. Dave said a silent prayer that it all went out of the car.

Christina pushed herself back to a sitting position. She laid her head against the headrest and closed her eyes.

"I want to go home," she said miserably.

"We'll be there in a sec," Dave said. He drove away from the curb. He could smell the sour aroma of vomit, and he worried that his lovely car had been ruined.

"We can't tell anybody about this," Christina said. "If my parents find out I'll be grounded for six months."

"All right," Dave said.

"You promise?"

"Sure, no problem."

Dave hit the lights when he turned onto Christina's street. He stopped several doors down from her house. He hoped she didn't expect him to kiss her and was glad when she got right out.

"You promised," she said.

"Don't worry," Dave said.

He watched her run across the lawns and disappear into the same hedge from which she'd emerged.

Under a nearby streetlight, Dave got out and inspected his car. In the back there was a dent on the bumper where he'd knocked over the headstone, but it wasn't bad. Going around to the passenger side, he opened the door and cautiously sniffed. He was relieved when he didn't smell any vomit. Closing the door, he walked around the front of the car. That was when he noticed the windshield wiper on the passenger side was gone.

Dave gritted his teeth and swore under his breath. What a night, and he didn't even get anything. Climbing back into his car, he wondered if he'd be able to rouse George, his best friend, from sleep. Dave couldn't wait to tell him about what had happened. It was so weird it was like some old horror movie. In a way,

Dave was thankful about the broken wiper. If it hadn't happened George prob-ably wouldn't believe the story.

Having taken the Xanax around one-thirty that morning, Kim slept much later than usual, and when she got up she felt mildly drugged. She didn't like the feel-ing, but she was convinced it was a small price to pay for getting some sleep.

Kim spent the first part of the day getting her uniform ready for Monday, when she was scheduled to start back to work. It amazed her how much she was looking forward to it. And it wasn't just because of the mounting anxieties about the lab and what was happening in it. During the last two weeks she'd become progressively weary of the isolated and lonely life she'd been leading in Salem, especially once she'd finished decorating the cottage.

The main problem on both counts was Edward, despite the better mood he was in while taking Ultra. Living with him had hardly been what she'd expected, although when she thought about it, she wasn't sure what she did expect since she'd invited him to come and live with her on impulse. But she certainly had expected to see more of him and share more with him than she had. And she certainly hadn't expected to be worrying about him taking an experimental drug. All in all, it was a ridiculous situation.

Once Kim had her uniform in order, she hiked over to the castle. The first thing she did was see Albert. She'd hoped the plumbing work would be finish-ing that day, but Albert said it was impossible with the additional work in the guest wing. He told her they'd need another two days tops. He asked her if they could leave their tools in the castle over the weekend. Kim told him he could leave whatever he wanted.

Kim went down the stairs in the servants' wing and checked the entrance. To her great disappointment it was again filthy. Glancing outside, she noticed the mat was in pristine shape, almost as if they purposefully ignored it.

Getting the mop once again, Kim scolded herself for not mentioning the problem to the researchers the day before, when she'd been at the lab.

Crossing the courtyard, Kim checked the entrance to the guest wing. There was less dirt than in the servants' wing, but there was some, and in some respects it was worse. The stairs in the guest wing were carpeted. To clean them Kim had to cart over an old vacuum cleaner from the servants' wing. When she was fin-ished she vowed to herself that she would talk to the researchers about it this time.

After putting away the cleaning paraphernalia, Kim contemplated walking over to the lab. But she decided against it. The irony was that in the beginning of the month she'd not wanted to visit the lab because they'd made her feel un-welcome. Now she was reluctant to go because they were too friendly.

Finally Kim climbed the stairs and fell to work in the attic. Finding the Thomas Goodman letter the day before had kindled her enthusiasm. The hours passed quickly, and before she knew it, it was time for lunch.

Walking back to the cottage, Kim eyed the lab and again debated stopping by and again decided against it. She thought she'd wait rather than make a special trip. She knew she was procrastinating, but she couldn't help it. She even considered telling Edward about the dirt problem and having him talk to the researchers.

After lunch Kim returned to the attic, where she worked all afternoon. The only thing she came across from the time period she was interested in was Jonathan Stewart's college evaluation. Reading it, Kim learned that Jonathan was only an average student. According to one of the more verbally colorful evaluating tutors, Jonathan was "more apt at swimming in Fresh Pond or skating on the Charles River according to season than in logic, rhetoric, or ethics."

That evening while Kim was enjoying fresh fish grilled outdoors accompanied by a mixed green salad, she saw a pizza delivery service drive onto the compound and head to the lab. She marveled that Edward and his team existed on junk food. Twice a day there was a delivery of fast food such as pizza, fried chicken, or Chinese take-out. Back in the beginning of the month Kim had offered to make dinner for Edward each evening, but he had declined, saying he thought he should eat with the others.

In one sense Kim was impressed with their dedication, while in another sense she thought they were zealots and a little crazy.

Around eleven Kim took Sheba outside. She stood on the porch while her pet wandered around in the grass. Keeping one eye on the cat, Kim looked over at the lab and saw the light spilling from the windows. She wondered how long they would keep up their insane schedule.

When she felt Sheba had had adequate outdoor time, Kim carried her back inside. The cat wasn't happy, but with what the police had told her, she surely wasn't about to let the animal roam freely.

Upstairs Kim prepared for bed. She read for an hour, but like the evening before, her mind would not turn off. In fact, lying in bed seemed to augment her anxiety. Getting out of bed, Kim went into the bathroom and took another Xanax tablet. She didn't like taking it, but she reasoned that until she started back to work, she needed the respite it provided.

SATURDAY • OCTOBER 1, 1994

Kim pulled herself from the depths of a minor stupor caused by the Xanax. Once again she was surprised she'd slept as long as she had. It was almost nine.

After showering and dressing, Kim took Sheba outside. Feeling guilty that she'd been denying the animal her normal wandering, Kim was patient with the cat and allowed her to go wherever she wanted. Sheba chose to go around the house. Kim followed.

As Kim rounded the back of the house she suddenly stopped, angrily put her hands on her hips, and let out an expletive. She had discovered she'd been targeted by the vandals or the animal which the police had warned her about. Both her trash containers had been tipped over and emptied. The trash had been strewn around the yard.

Ignoring Sheba for the moment, Kim righted the two plastic garbage cans. As she did so she discovered that both had been torn at their top edges, presumably when their covers had been forcibly removed.

"What a pain!" Kim exclaimed as she carried the two containers back to where they normally stood next to the house. Looking at them more closely, she realized that she'd have to replace them since their covers would no longer be secure.

Kim rescued Sheba just before she was about to take off into the woods, and carried her back into the house. Remembering that the police had asked to be called if she had any trouble, Kim called the station. To her surprise they insisted on sending someone out.

Using a pair of gardening gloves, Kim went back outside and spent a half hour picking up all the trash. Temporarily she put it back into the two broken containers. She was just finishing when the Salem police car arrived.

It was a single officer this time who Kim thought looked about her age. His name was Tom Malick. He was a serious fellow and asked to see the crime scene. Kim thought he was making more of the incident than it deserved, but took him around behind the house and showed him the containers. She had to explain that she'd just finished picking everything up.

"It would have been better if you left everything the way you found it until we'd seen it," Tom said.

"I'm sorry," Kim said. She couldn't imagine what difference it would have made.

"Your situation here fits the same scenario that we've been seeing in the general area," Tom said. He squatted down next to the containers and examined them carefully. Then he looked at the lids.

Kim watched him with mild impatience.

He stood up. "This was done by the animal or animals," he said. "It wasn't the kids. I believe there are teeth marks along the lips of the covers. Do you want to see?"

"I suppose," Kim said.

Tom lifted up one of the covers and pointed to a series of parallel grooves.

"I think you should get more secure containers," Tom said.

"I was planning on replacing them," Kim said. "I'll see what's available."

"You might have to go out to Burlington to find them," Tom said. "There's been a run on them in town."

"It sounds like this is developing into a real problem," Kim said.

"You'd better believe it," Tom said. "The town is in an uproar. Didn't you watch the local news this morning?"

"No, I didn't," Kim said.

"Up until last night the only deaths we've had with this affair have been dogs and cats," Tom said. "This morning we found our first human victim."

"That's awful," Kim said, catching her breath. "Who was it?"

"He was a vagrant who was fairly well known in town," Tom said. "His name was John Mullins. He was found not far from here, near the Kernwood Bridge. The gruesome thing was that he'd been partially eaten."

Kim's mouth went dry as her mind unwillingly called up the horrid image of Buffer lying in the grass.

"John did have an ungodly blood alcohol level," Tom said, "so he might have been dead before the animal got to him, but we'll know more after a report from the medical examiner. The body went to Boston in hopes that we can get a lead on what kind of animal we're dealing with from tooth marks on bones."

"It sounds horrible," Kim said with a shudder. "I didn't realize how serious this was."

"Initially we were thinking about a raccoon," Tom said. "But with this human victim, and the amount of vandalism going on, we're thinking of a bigger animal, like a bear. There's been a marked increase in the bear population of New Hampshire, so it's not out of the question. But whatever it is, it's got our Salem witch industry loving it. Of course they're saying it's the devil and all that kind of nonsense, trying to get people to think it's 1692 all over again. Trouble is, they're doing a pretty good job, and their business is brisk. So is ours."

After a strong warning for Kim to be careful because of all the forestland on her property which could certainly conceal a bear, Tom left.

Before going all the way to Burlington, Kim went into the house and called the hardware store in Salem where she did most of her business. Contrary to what Tom had said, they assured her they had a full selection of trash containers available since they'd just gotten a shipment the day before.

Happy to have an errand that took her to town, Kim left as soon as she'd had something to eat. She drove straight to the hardware store. The clerk told her she was wise to have come directly. Since he'd spoken with her an hour previously, they'd sold a good portion of the trash container shipment.

"This animal really gets around," Kim said.

"You'd better believe it," the clerk said. "They're starting to have the same problems over in Beverly. Everybody's talking about what kind of animal it is. There's even odds in case you want to bet some money. But it's been great for us. Not only have we been selling a ton of garbage cans; there's been a fire sale on ammo and rifles in our sporting goods section."

While Kim was waiting by the register to pay for her purchases, she could hear other customers talking about the same subject. There was excitement in the air that was almost palpable.

Leaving the store, Kim had an uncomfortable feeling. She was worried that if hysteria broke out about this creature now that a human death was involved, innocent people could get hurt. She shuddered to think of trigger-happy people hiding behind their curtains just waiting to hear something or somebody toying with their trash. Since kids were apparently getting involved, it could easily turn into a tragedy.

Back at the house, Kim transferred the trash from the damaged containers to the new ones with their lids secured by an ingenious compression mechanism. She put the old ones in the back of the shed to use for collecting leaves. As she worked, she longed for the city, nostalgically remembering life there as being simple in comparison. She'd had to worry about muggers but not bears.

With the garbage problem taken care of, Kim walked across the field to the lab. She wasn't excited about going, but with this new development of her garbage being ransacked and a body being found nearby she felt she had no choice.

Before she went inside she checked the bins where the lab's garbage was stored. They were two heavy industrial-sized steel boxes that were lifted by the garbage truck. The lids were heavy. Kim could barely push them up. Looking inside, she could see that the lab's trash had been undisturbed.

At the front door Kim hesitated, trying to think up an excuse to use in case she was waylaid by the congenial researchers. Lunch was the only thing she could think of. She also girded herself to bring up the subject of the dirt being tracked into the castle.

Kim passed through the reception area and entered the lab proper. Once again she was surprised. On her last visit it had been a celebration; this time it was an impromptu meeting that had to be about something important. The gay, festive atmosphere that she was learning to expect at the lab was gone. In its place was a solemnity that was almost funereal.

"I'm terribly sorry if I'm interrupting," Kim said.

"It's quite all right," Edward said. "Did you want something in particular?"

Kim told them about the problem with her garbage and the visit by the police. She then asked if anybody heard or saw anything out of the ordinary during the night.

Everyone looked at each other expectantly. No one responded at first, then they all shook their heads.

"I sleep so soundly I doubt I'd hear an earthquake," Curt said.

"You sound like an earthquake," David joked. "But you're right, I sleep equally soundly."

Kim glanced around at the faces of the researchers. The somber mood she'd detected when she'd first entered already seemed to be improving. She then told them that the police thought the culprit might be a rabid bear, but that kids had been taking advantage of the situation in the name of fun. She also described the excitement that bordered on hysteria that gripped the town.

"Only in Salem could something like this get so blown out of proportion," Edward said with a chuckle. "This town is never going to recover completely from 1692."

"Some of their concern is justified," Kim said. "The problem has recently taken on a new dimension. A dead man was found this morning not too far away from here, and his body had been gnawed."

Gloria blanched. "How grotesque!" she exclaimed.

"Have they determined how the man died?" Edward asked.

"Not exactly," Kim said. "They've sent the body to Boston to be examined. There's a question about whether or not the man had been dead prior to being attacked by the animal."

"Then the animal would have been only acting as a scavenger," Edward said.

"That's true," Kim said. "But I still thought it was important to warn you all. I know that you walk late at night. Maybe you should drive the short distance to the castle until this problem has been taken care of. Meanwhile, keep your eye out for either a rabid animal or teenagers."

"Thanks for warning us," Edward said.

"One other thing," Kim said, forcing herself to switch subjects. "There's been a minor problem at the castle. There's been some dirt tracked in through the entrances to the wings. I wanted to ask that you all wipe your feet."

"We're terribly sorry," François said. "It's dark when we get there and dark when we leave. We'll have to be more careful."

"I'm sure you will," Kim said. "Well, that's all I had. Sorry to bother you."

"No problem at all," Edward said. He accompanied her to the door. "You be careful too," he told her. "And watch out for Sheba."

Edward walked back to the group after seeing Kim off. He looked at each face in turn. They were all concerned.

"A human body puts this all in a different perspective," Gloria said.

"I agree," Eleanor said.

There was silence for a few minutes while everyone thought about the situation. David finally spoke: "I guess we have to face the fact that we could be responsible for some of the problems in the area."

"I still think the idea is absurd," Edward said. "It flies in the face of reason."

"How do you explain my T-shirt?" Curt said. He pulled it from a drawer where he'd stuffed it when Kim had suddenly arrived. It was torn and stained. "I ran a test spot of one of these stains. It's blood."

"But it was your blood," Edward said.

"True. But still," Curt said, "how did it happen? I mean, I don't remember."

"It's also hard to explain the cuts and bruises we have on our bodies when we wake up in the morning," François said. "There were even sticks and dead leaves strewn about my floor."

"We must be sleepwalking or the equivalent," David said. "I know we don't want to admit it."

"Well, *I* haven't been sleepwalking," Edward said. He glared at the others. "I'm not entirely sure this isn't some elaborate practical joke after all the playing around you guys have been doing."

"This is no joke," Curt said as he folded up his damaged shirt.

"We've seen nothing with any of the experimental animals that would even suggest a reaction like you're suggesting," Edward said belligerently. "It doesn't make scientific sense. There'd be some corollary. That's why we do animal studies."

"I agree," Eleanor said. "I've not found anything in my room, nor do I have any cuts or bruises."

"Well, I'm not hallucinating," David said. "I've got real cuts here." He stuck out his hands so everybody could see them all. "As Curt says, this is no joke."

"I haven't had any cuts, but I've awakened with my hands all dirty," Gloria said. "And I don't have a nail worth mentioning left. They've all broken off."

"There's something wrong despite the fact it hasn't shown up with the animals," David insisted. "I know that no one wants to suggest the obvious, but I will! It must be the Ultra."

Edward's jaws visibly tightened and his hands closed into fists.

"It's taken me a couple of days to admit it even to myself," David continued. "But it's pretty clear I've been out at night without any recollection of going. Nor do I know what I've been up to, except that I'm filthy in the morning when I wake up. And I assure you, I've never done anything like this in my life."

"Are you suggesting that it's not an animal that has been causing problems around the neighborhood?" Gloria asked timidly.

"Oh, be serious," Edward complained. "Let's not let our imaginations go haywire."

"I'm not suggesting anything other than I've been out and I don't know what I've been doing," David said.

A ripple of fear spread through the group as they began to face the reality of the situation. But it became immediately apparent there were two groups. Edward and Eleanor feared for the future of the project while the others feared for their well-being.

"We have to think about this rationally," Edward said.

"Without doubt," David agreed.

"The drug has been so perfect," Edward said. "We've had nothing but good responses. We've reason to believe it's a natural substance, or close to a natural substance, that already exists in our brains. The monkeys have shown no tendency toward somnambulism. And I personally like the way I feel on Ultra."

Everyone immediately agreed.

"In fact, I think it is a tribute to what Ultra can do that allows us to even think rationally under these circumstances," Edward said.

"You're probably right," Gloria said. "A minute ago I was beside myself with worry and disgust. I already feel more composed."

"That's exactly my point," Edward said. "This is a fantastic drug."

"But we still have a problem," David said. "If the sleepwalking we've suggested is occurring, and if it is caused by the drug, which I think is the only explanation, it has to be a side effect that we couldn't possibly have anticipated. It has to be doing something in our brains that is unique."

"Let me get my PET scans," François said suddenly. He went down to his cluttered work space but quickly returned. He began laying out a series of brain scans of a monkey that had been given radioactively tagged Ultra.

"I wanted to show everybody something that I just noted this morning," he said. "I really haven't had time to think too much about it, and I wouldn't have noticed it except the computer picked it up when these images were in digital form. If you look carefully, the concentration of the Ultra in the hindbrain, midbrain, and limbic system slowly builds from the first dose, then, when it gets to a certain level, the concentration goes up markedly, meaning there's no steady state reached."

Everyone bent over the photographs.

"Maybe the point where the concentration increases markedly is at the point that the enzymatic system that metabolizes it is overwhelmed," Gloria suggested.

"I think you are right," François said.

"That means we should look at the key that tells us how much Ultra each of us has been taking," Gloria said.

They all looked at Edward.

"Seems reasonable," Edward said. He walked over to his desk and removed a small locked box. Inside was a three-by-five card with the code that matched dosages.

The group quickly learned that Curt was on the highest dose followed by David on the next highest. On the other end of the scale, Eleanor had the lowest with Edward just behind her.

After a lengthy, rational discussion, they came up with a theory of what was happening. They reasoned that when the concentration of Ultra got to a certain point, it progressively blocked the normal variation of serotonin levels that occurred during sleep, ironing them out and altering sleep patterns.

It was Gloria who suggested that when the concentration got even higher, perhaps to the point where the sharp upward swing of the curve occurred, then the Ultra blocked the radiations from the lower, or reptilian, brain to the higher centers in the cerebral hemispheres. Sleep, like other autonomous functions, was regulated by the lower brain areas where the Ultra was massing.

The group was quiet for a time while everyone pondered this hypothesis. Despite their emotional recovery, they all found this idea disturbing.

"If this were the case," David said, "what would happen if we were to wake up while this blockage was in place?"

"It would be as if we'd experienced retroevolution," Curt said. "We'd be functioning on our lower-brain centers alone. We'd be like carnivorous reptiles!"

The shock of this statement quieted everyone with its horrid connotations.

"Wait a minute, everybody," Edward said, trying to cheer himself as well as the others. "We're jumping to conclusions that are not based on fact. This is all complete supposition. We have to remember that we've seen no problems with the monkeys, who we all agree have cerebral hemispheres, although smaller than humans', at least most humans."

Everyone except Gloria smiled at Edward's humor.

"Even if there is a problem with Ultra," Edward reminded them, "we have to take into consideration the good side of the drug, and how it has positively affected our emotions, mental abilities, acuity of our senses, and even long-term memory. Perhaps we have been taking too much of the drug and we should cut down. Maybe we should cut down to Eleanor's level since all she's experienced are the positive psychological effects."

"I'm not cutting back," Gloria said defiantly. "I'm stopping as of this minute. It horrifies me to think of the possibility of some primitive creature lurking inside my body without my even being aware and sneaking out to forage in the night."

"Very colorfully said," Edward remarked. "You are welcome to stop the drug. That goes without saying. No one is going to force anyone to do anything they don't want to do. You all know that. Each person can decide whether to continue taking the drug or not, and here's what I suggest: for an added cushion of safety I think we should halve Eleanor's dose and use that as an upper limit, dropping subsequent doses in one-hundred-milligram steps."

"That sounds reasonable and safe to me," David said.

"To me as well," Curt said.

"And me," François said.

"Good," Edward said. "I'm absolutely confident that if the problem is as we've theorized, it has to be dose related, and there has to be a point where the chances of causing the problem is an acceptable risk."

"I'm not taking it," Gloria restated.

"No problem," Edward said.

"You won't be irritated with me?" Gloria asked.

"Not in the slightest," Edward said.

"I'll be able to be a control," Gloria said. "Plus I'll be able to watch over the others at night."

"Excellent idea," Edward said.

"I have a suggestion," François said. "Perhaps we should all take radioactively tagged Ultra so I can follow the buildup and chart concentrations in our brains. The ultimate dose of Ultra might be that dose which merely maintains a specific level of Ultra without continually increasing it."

"I'd agree to that idea," Curt said.

"One other thing," Edward said. "I'm sure I don't have to remind all you professionals, but this meeting must be kept secret from everyone, including your families."

"That goes without saying," David said. "The last thing any of us wants to do is compromise Ultra's future. We might have a little growing pains here and there, but it's still going to be the drug of the century."

Kim had intended to spend some time in the castle during the morning, but when she got back to the cottage she realized it was already lunchtime. While she was eating, the phone rang. To her surprise it was Katherine Sturburg, the archivist at Harvard who had a particular interest in Increase Mather.

"I might have some potentially good news for you," Katherine said. "I've just found a reference to a work by Rachel Bingham!"

"That's marvelous," Kim said. "I'd given up hope of help from Harvard."

"We do the best we can," Katherine said.

"How did you happen to find it?" Kim asked.

"That's the best part," Katherine said. "What I did was go back and reread the letter you let us copy from Increase Mather. Because of his reference to a law school, I accessed the Law School library data bank, and the name popped up. Why it's not cross-referenced in our main data bank I have yet to figure out. But the good news is the work seemed to have survived the 1764 fire."

"I thought everything was burned," Kim said.

"Just about everything," Katherine said. "Fortunately for us, about two hundred books out of the five-thousand-volume library survived because they were out on loan. So someone must have been reading the book you are looking for. At any rate, the reference I found indicated that it was transferred to the Law School from the main library in Harvard Hall in 1818, a year after the Law School was founded."

"Did you find the book itself?" Kim asked excitedly.

"No, I haven't had time," Katherine said. "Besides, I think it would be better if you took it from here. What I recommend is that you give Helen Arnold a call. She's an archivist at the Law School. I'll call her first thing Monday morning so that she'll expect a call or a visit."

"I'll go right after work on Monday," Kim said eagerly. "I get off at three."

"I'm sure that will be fine," Katherine said. "I'll let Helen know."

Kim thanked Katherine before they disconnected.

Kim felt ecstatic. She'd totally given up hope that Elizabeth's book had survived the Harvard fire. Then Kim questioned why Katherine had been so sure it was a book. Had it said as much on the reference?

Kim went back to the phone and tried to call Katherine right back. Unfortunately she wasn't able to reach her. A secretary said that Katherine had rushed out to a luncheon meeting and wouldn't be back to the office until Monday.

Kim hung up the phone. She was disappointed but didn't remain so for long. The idea that on Monday afternoon she would finally learn the nature of the evidence used against Elizabeth was a source of great satisfaction. Whether it was a book or not did not matter.

Despite this good news, Kim still went to the castle to work. In fact, she attacked the jumble of papers with new enthusiasm.

Halfway through the afternoon she paused long enough to try to estimate how much longer she thought it would take for her to finish sorting the material. After counting all the remaining trunks and boxes and assuming about the same number existed in the wine cellar, she figured out it would take another week if she were to work for eight hours a day.

The reality of that fact robbed Kim of some of her enthusiasm. Now that she was about to start back to work at the hospital, it wasn't going to be so easy to find the time. She was about to give up for the afternoon when she surprised herself by pulling off a stunt reminiscent of Kinnard's. She opened a drawer at random and pulled out a letter addressed to Ronald!

Sitting on a trunk by a window, Kim took the letter from its envelope. It was another letter from Samuel Sewall. Looking at the date, Kim could tell that it had been sent just days before Elizabeth's execution.

15th July 1692
Boston

Sir,
I have come from a comfortable supper with the most Reverend Cotton Mather and we did indeed discours upon the sorry plight of your wife and we are much in troubled spirit for you and your children. In a most gracious way Reverend Mather agreed to accept your distracted wife into his household to cure her as he most successfully did with the much afflicted Goodwin girl if only Elizabeth will confess and repent in publique the covenant she'd entered with the Prince of Lies. Reverend Mather is strongly convinced that Elizabeth can furnish with evidence and argument as a critical eye witness to confute the sadducism of this troubled age. Failing that Reverend Mather cannot and will not intervene in carrying out of the sentence of the court. Be advised that there is no time to waste. Reverend Mather is eager and believes that your wife can teach us all about matters of the invisible world that doth threaten our country. God bless your endeavors and I remain

your Friend,
Samuel Sewall.

For a few minutes Kim stared out the window. The day had started cloudless and blue, but now dark clouds were blowing in from the west. From where she was sitting she could see the cottage sitting among its birch trees whose leaves had become bright yellow. The combination of the old house and the letter transported Kim back three hundred years, and she could feel the utter panic brought on by the impending reality of Elizabeth's execution. Although the letter she'd just read had been to Ronald rather than from him, she got the impression it was a response from a letter Ronald had written in desperation to save his wife's life.

Kim's eyes filled up with tears. It was hard for her to imagine the agony Ronald must have experienced. It made Kim feel guilty that she'd had suspicions of Ronald back when she'd first started to learn the truth about Elizabeth.

Kim finally got up. Replacing the letter in its envelope, she carried it downstairs to the wine cellar and deposited it with the other material in the Bible box. Then she left the castle and started back toward the cottage.

Kim got halfway and slowed her pace. Glancing toward the lab, she stopped walking. She looked at her watch. It was not quite four. All at once the idea occurred to her that it would be a nice gesture to make an attempt at improving the researchers' diet. They'd seemed depressed when she'd stopped in that morning, and she imagined they must be sick of pizza. Kim reasoned she could easily repeat the steak-and-fish dinner she'd made somewhat less than a fortnight previously.

With this thought in mind, Kim changed her direction and headed for the lab. As she passed through the reception area she felt mild apprehension since she never quite knew what to expect. Entering the lab proper, Kim let the door close behind her. No one came running over to greet her.

Kim set off toward Edward's area. She passed David, who greeted her pleasantly but with hardly the buoyancy he had a few days previously. Kim said hello to Gloria, who, like David, immediately turned her attention back to her work.

Kim continued on her way, but she felt progressively wary. Although David's and Gloria's behavior was probably the most normal Kim had experienced since they had arrived, it represented another change.

Edward was so engrossed in his work that Kim had to tap his shoulder twice to get his attention. She noticed that he was making new Ultra capsules.

"Is there a problem?" he asked. He smiled and acted reasonably happy to see her.

"I wanted to make you and the others an offer," Kim said. "How about a repeat of the dinner that we had a few weeks ago. I'd be happy to run into town and get the food."

"That's very sweet of you," Edward said. "But not tonight. We can't take the time. We'll just order in some pizza."

"I promise you wouldn't have to take much time," Kim said.

"I said no!" Edward hissed between clenched teeth, causing Kim to take a step back. But Edward immediately regained his composure and smiled again. "Pizza will do just fine."

"If that's how you feel," Kim said with a mixture of confusion and apprehension. It had been as if Edward had momentarily teetered on the edge of control for a few seconds. "Are you all right?" she asked hesitantly.

"Yes!" he snapped, but then quickly smiled again. "We're all a little preoccupied. We had a minor setback but it's under control."

Kim took several more steps backward. "Well, if you change your mind in the next hour or so I can still go into town," she said. "I'll be at the cottage. Just call."

"We're really much too busy," Edward said. "You go ahead and eat, but thanks for offering. I'll let everyone know you were thinking of them."

As Kim departed, none of the researchers acknowledged her or even looked up from their work. When she got outside she sighed and shook her head. She was amazed at how changeable the atmosphere in the lab was and wondered how the people could live with themselves. Kim was coming to the conclusion that she had little in common with the scientific personality.

After dinner there was still plenty of light to go back to the castle, but Kim couldn't get herself to return. Instead she vegetated in front of the TV. She'd hoped that watching several mindless sitcoms would get the experience in the lab out of her mind, but the more she thought about her interaction with Edward and the others, the more disturbed she became.

Kim tried to read, but she couldn't concentrate. Instead she found herself wishing she'd been able to follow up that afternoon on the lead involving the Law School. Feeling progressively more nervous as the evening dragged on, Kim began to think about Kinnard. She wondered who he was with and what he was doing. She also wondered if he ever thought about her.

Kim awakened with a start despite having again taken a Xanax to slow her churning mind. It was pitch black in her bedroom, and a glance at her clock told her she'd been asleep only for a short time. Settling back into her pillow, she listened to the night sounds of the house, trying to decide what could have awakened her so abruptly.

Then she heard several dull thumps coming from the back of the house that sounded like her new rubberized trash cans hitting up against the clapboard. Kim stiffened as she thought of a black bear or a rabid raccoon trying to get at her garbage, which she knew contained chicken skin and bones.

After switching on her bedside light, Kim got out of bed. She put on her robe and slipped her feet into her slippers. She gave Sheba a reassuring pat. Kim was thankful she'd been keeping the animal inside.

Hearing the thumping yet again, Kim hurried through the short hall into Edward's room. Switching on the light, she discovered that Edward's bed was empty. Thinking he must still be in the lab, and concerned about his walking back in the dark, Kim went back into her bedroom and dialed the lab number. After ten rings she gave up.

Kim took out the flashlight she kept in her bedside table and started down the stairs. Her intention was to shine the light out the kitchen window where the trash cans were stored, hoping to scare away whatever animal was out there.

As Kim rounded the turn in the stairs, giving her a view of the foyer, she froze. She saw something that made her blood run cold. The front door was wide open.

At first Kim could not move. She was paralyzed with the terrorizing thought that the creature, whatever it was, had come into her house and was that moment stalking her through the darkness.

Kim listened intently, but all she could hear was the chorus of the last tree frogs of the season. A cool wet breeze wafted in through the open doorway and swirled around Kim's bare legs. Outside, a light rain was falling.

The house was deathly silent, giving her the hope that the animal had not come in. Kim descended the steps one at a time. After each step she hesitated and strained to hear some telltale sound of an animal intruder. But the house remained quiet.

Kim reached the open door and grasped the knob. Looking back and forth from the darkened dining room to the parlor, she began to close the door. She was fearful of moving too quickly lest she provoke an attack. She had the door almost closed when she glanced outside. She gasped.

Sheba was sitting about twenty feet away from the front of the house in the middle of the flagstone walkway. She was blissfully ignoring the drizzle while calmly licking her paw and rubbing it over the top of her head.

At first Kim could not believe her eyes since she thought she'd just seen the cat on her bed. Obviously Sheba had sensed the front door was open while Kim was checking on Edward, and had come down to take advantage of the opportunity to get outside.

Kim took several deep breaths to try to rid herself of the heavy, drugged feeling that clouded her brain. Terrified about what was possibly lurking in the nearby shadows, she was reluctant to call out to the animal, who probably would have ignored her anyway.

Sensing she had little choice, Kim slipped through the door. After a quick scan of the immediate area, she dashed to the cat, snatched it from the ground, and turned, only to see the front door closing.

Screaming a silent "no," Kim lunged for the door, but she was too late. It shut with a heavy thud followed by a sharp metallic click of the bolt engaging the striker plate.

Kim vainly tried the handle. It was locked as she'd expected. She pushed the door ineffectually with her shoulder, but it was of no use.

Hunching her shoulders against the cold rain, Kim slowly turned to face the blackness of the night. She shivered with fear and cold, marveling at her desperate circumstance. She was in her robe and pajamas, locked out of her house on a rainy night with a disgruntled cat in one hand and an ineffectual flashlight in the other, facing an unknown nocturnal creature lurking somewhere in the shrubbery.

Sheba struggled to be put down and audibly complained. Kim shushed her. Stepping away from the house, Kim scanned the front casement windows, but all were shut. She knew they were locked. Turning around, she gauged the distance to the lab, whose lights were finally off. Then she looked at the castle. The castle was farther away, but she knew the doors to the wings were unlocked. She didn't know about the door to the lab.

Suddenly Kim heard the sound of a large creature moving in the gravel along the right side of the house. Knowing she could not stay where she was, she ran in the opposite direction, going around the left side of the house, away from the approaching bear or whatever animal had been at her new trash containers.

Desperately Kim tried the kitchen door. But it was locked, as she was sure it would be. Using her shoulder, she hit it several times, but it was no use. All she managed to do was make the cat howl.

Turning from the house, she spied the shed. Clutching the cat closer to her chest and holding the flashlight like a club, Kim ran as quickly as her backless mules would allow. When she got to the shed, she undid the hook that held the door closed, opened it, and squeezed into the shed's inner blackness.

Kim pulled the door shut behind her. Just to the right of the door was a tiny, dirty window that afforded a meager view of the yard behind the cottage. The only illumination came from a pool of light spilling from her bedroom window and the luminous glow of the low swirling cloud cover.

As she watched, a hulking figure rounded the house from the same direction she had come. It was a person, not an animal, but he was acting in a most peculiar fashion. Kim watched him pause to smell the wind just as an animal might do. To her dismay he turned in her direction and appeared to be staring at the shed. In the darkness she could see no features, just his dark silhouette.

Dismay turned to horror as Kim watched the figure lurch toward her with a slow, dragging gait, still sniffing the air as if following a scent. Kim held her breath and prayed the cat would be still. When the figure was a mere ten feet away, Kim shrank back into the dark recess of the shed, pushing against tools and bicycles.

She could now hear his footfalls in the gravel. They came closer, then stopped. There was an agonizing pause. Kim held her breath.

Suddenly the door was rudely yanked open. Losing control, Kim screamed. Sheba answered with her own scream and leaped from Kim's arms. The man screamed as well.

Kim grasped the flashlight in both hands and turned it on, flashing the beam directly into the man's face. He shielded himself from the unexpected blast of light with his hands and forearms.

Kim's mouth clamped shut in surprised relief. She recognized it was Edward!

"Thank God," she said, lowering the flashlight.

Scrambling from her position wedged among bikes, lawn mower, and old trash containers, Kim burst from the shed and threw her arms around Edward. The beam of her flashlight played hapazardly in the trees.

For a moment Edward did not move. He looked down on her with a blank expression.

"I can't tell you how glad I am to see your face," Kim said, leaning back so she could look into his dark eye sockets. "I've never been so scared in my life."

Edward did not respond.

"Edward?" Kim asked, moving her head to try to see him better. "Are you all right?"

Edward exhaled noisily. "I'm fine," he said at last. He was angry. "No thanks to you. What in the hell are you doing out here in the shed in the middle of the night, dressed in your robe, scaring me half out of my wits?"

Kim apologized effusively, stumbling over her words as she realized how much she must have frightened him. She explained what had happened. By the time she was finished, she could see that Edward was smiling.

"It's not funny," she added. But now that she was safe, she smiled too.

"I can't believe you'd risk life and limb for that lazy old cat," he said. "Come on! Let's get in out of this rain."

Kim went back into the shed and with the aid of the flashlight located Sheba. The cat was hiding in the far corner behind a row of yard tools. Kim enticed her into the open and picked her up. Then she and Edward went into the house.

"I'm freezing," she said. "I need something hot like herbal tea. Would you like some?"

"I'll sit with you for a moment," Edward said.

While Kim put the water on to boil, Edward explained his side of the story. "I had intended to work all night," he said. "But by one-thirty I had to admit it was impossible. My body is so accustomed to going to sleep around one, I couldn't keep my eyes open. It was all I could do to walk from the lab to the cottage without lying down in the grass. When I got to the house I opened the door and then remembered I was carrying a bag full of the remains of our pizza dinner which I was supposed to put in the Dumpster at the lab. So I went around back to put it into our trash. I guess I left the door open, which I shouldn't have done if only because of mosquitoes. Anyway, I couldn't get the goddamn covers off the trash containers, and the harder I tried the more frustrated I became. I even hit them a couple of times."

"They're new," Kim explained.

"Well, I hope they came with directions," Edward said.

"It's easy in the light," Kim said.

"I finally gave up," Edward said. "When I came back around the house, the door was closed. I also thought I smelled your cologne. Since I've been taking Ultra, my sense of smell has improved remarkably. I followed the scent around the house and eventually to the shed."

Kim poured herself a mug of the hot tea. "Are you sure you don't want any?" she asked.

"I couldn't," Edward said. "Just sitting here is a strain. I've got to go to sleep. It's as if my body weighs five tons, including my eyelids." Edward slipped off the stool and staggered. Kim reached out and steadied him.

"I'm okay," he said. "When I'm this tired it takes me a second to get my bearings."

Kim listened to him struggle up the stairs while she put away the tea and the honey. Picking up her mug, she followed him. At the head of the stairs she looked into his room. He was on his bed asleep with his clothes half off.

Kim went into the room, and with a great deal of difficulty got his pants and shirt all the way off and put him under the covers. She turned out his light. She felt jealous how easily he could fall asleep. It was such a contrast with herself.

SUNDAY • OCTOBER 2, 1994

In the misty predawn light Edward and the researchers met halfway between the cottage and the castle and trooped silently through the wet grass to the lab. They were all in a somber mood. Inside, they poured themselves cups of morning coffee.

Edward was considerably more dour than the others, and he had improved from a half hour earlier when he'd first awakened. As he'd gotten out of bed he'd been shocked to find a carcass of a chicken on the floor that looked as if it had come from someone's garbage. It was encrusted with coffee grounds. Then he'd noticed his fingernails were filthy, as if he'd been digging dirt. In the bathroom he'd looked in the mirror and saw that his face and undershirt were both smeared with filth.

Everyone carried their coffee to the area of the lab they used for their meetings. François was the first to speak. "Even though my dose of Ultra was more than halved, I was still out last night," he said gloomily. "When I woke up this morning I was as dirty as I'd ever been. I must have been crawling in the mud. I had to wash my sheets! And look at my hands." He extended his hands, palms up, to show a myriad of shallow cuts and scratches. "My pajamas were so dirty I had to dispose of them."

"I was out too," Curt admitted.

"I'm afraid I was as well," David said.

"What do you think the chances are we wander off the property?" François asked.

"There's no way to know," David said. "But it's one hell of a disturbing thought. What if we had something to do with that vagrant?"

"Don't even bring up the possibility," Gloria snapped. "It's beyond contemplation."

"The immediate problem could be the police or some local inhabitant," François said. "If everyone in the town is as worked up as Kim says they are, one of us might be confronted if we go beyond the fence."

"It's certainly a concern," David said. "I suppose there's no way to know how we'd react."

"If we're functioning on our reptilian brains, I think we can imagine," Curt said. "It would be a survival instinct. We'd undoubtedly fight back. I don't think we should delude ourselves. We'd be violent."

"This has got to stop," François said.

"Well, I certainly wasn't out," Eleanor said. "So it's got to be dose-related."

"I agree," Edward said. "Let's halve our doses again. That will take the maximum to one fourth of Eleanor's original dose."

"I'm afraid that might not be enough," Gloria said. Everyone swung around to look at her. "I didn't take any Ultra yesterday, and I'm afraid I still went out. I'd intended to stay awake to make sure no one else did, but I found it virtually impossible to keep from falling asleep no matter what I did."

"Falling asleep quickly is something I've been doing since I began taking Ultra," Curt said. "I thought it was due to the level of activity it caused during the day. Maybe it has something to do with the drug itself."

Everyone agreed with Curt and added that when they awoke in the morning they'd had the feeling they had had a particularly good night's sleep.

"I even feel rested this morning," François said. "I find that especially surprising with the evidence that I'd been out running around in the rain."

For a few minutes everyone was silent as they pondered the dilemma posed by Gloria's revelation that even though she'd stopped taking the drug, she'd still experienced somnambulism.

Edward finally broke the silence. "All our studies show that Ultra is metabolized at a reasonable rate, certainly a lot faster than Prozac," he said. "Gloria's experience only indicates that the concentration in her lower brain is still higher than the threshold for this unfortunate complication. Maybe we should cut our doses even more, like even a factor of a hundred."

François again held out his hands for everyone to see. "These cuts are telling me something," he said. "I don't want to take this risk anymore. Obviously I'm out wandering around with no comprehension of what I'm doing. I don't want to get shot or run over because I'm acting like an animal. I'm stopping the drug."

"I feel the same," David said.

"It's only reasonable," Curt said.

"All right," Edward said reluctantly. "You all have a point. It's unconscionable for us to take any chances with our safety or the safety of anyone else. We all liked to think of ourselves as animals while we were in college, but I guess we've outgrown the urge."

Everyone smiled at Edward's humor.

"Let's stop the drug and reevaluate in a few days," Edward said agreeably. "As soon as the drug is out of our systems, we can contemplate starting again at much lower dosages."

"I'm not going to take the drug until we find an animal system that mimics this somnambulistic effect," Gloria said. "I think it should be studied completely before any more human use is considered."

"We respect your opinion," Edward said. "As I've always indicated, self-medication is totally voluntary. I should remind you that it was my intention for me to take the drug alone in the first place."

"What are we going to do in the interim for safety?" François asked.

"Perhaps we should run EEGs while we're sleeping," Gloria suggested. "We could rig them with a computer to wake us if the normal sleep patterns change."

"Brilliant idea," Edward said. "I'll see that the equipment is ordered on Monday."

"What about tonight?" François asked.

Everyone thought for a few moments.

"Hopefully there won't be a problem," Edward said. "After all, Gloria was on the second-highest dose and probably had significantly high blood levels in relation to her body weight. I think we should all check our blood levels with hers. If they're lower, maybe we'll be okay. Probably the only person who poses a significant risk is Curt."

"Thanks a lot," he said with a laugh. "Why don't you just put me in one of the monkey cages?"

"Not a bad idea," David said.

Curt took a playful swipe at David's head.

"Perhaps we should sleep in shifts," François said. "We can watch over each other."

"Sleeping in shifts is a good idea," Edward said. "Plus, if we do blood levels today we'll be able to correlate them with any episodes of somnambulism tonight."

"You know, this might all turn out for the best," Gloria said. "By stopping Ultra we'll have a great opportunity to follow blood and urine levels and relate them to residual psychological effects. Everybody should be sensitive to any 'depressive' symptoms in case there's a rebound phenomenon. The monkey studies have suggested there are no withdrawal symptoms, but that must be confirmed."

"We might as well make the best of it," Edward agreed. "Meanwhile we've got an enormous amount of work to do. And it goes without saying that everything we've been discussing must remain a highly guarded secret until we've had a chance to isolate the problem and eliminate it."

Kim looked at the clock and blinked. She couldn't believe her eyes. It was almost
ten o'clock. She'd slept later than she had since she'd been in college.

Sitting on the edge of the bed, she suddenly recalled the scary episode in the
shed. It had truly terrified her. After the event she'd found herself so wound up
that she'd not been able to fall back asleep. She'd tried for almost two hours before she gave up and took another half Xanax. Finally she'd been able to calm
down, but when she did, she found herself thinking about Thomas Goodman's
letter that had described Elizabeth's flight to the shed, no doubt under the influence of poisonous mold. Kim felt it was another coincidence that in her panic
she'd run to the very same shed.

Kim showered, dressed, and had breakfast in hopes of reviving enough to
enjoy the day. Her attempt was only partially successful. She felt sluggish from
the double dose of medication. She also felt anxious. The sheer unpleasantness
of what had happened during the night, combined with her general agitation,
was too much for the medication. She needed something more, and sorting old
documents in the castle wasn't going to be adequate. Kim needed some human
contact, and she missed the convenience and resources of the city.

Sitting down at the phone, Kim tried a number of friends in Boston. But she
did not have much luck. All she got were answering machines. She left her number on some of them but did not expect a call back until evening. Her friends
were active people, and there was a lot to do on a fall Sunday in Boston.

Feeling a strong urge to get away from the compound, Kim called Kinnard's
number. As the call went through, she almost hoped he wouldn't answer; she
wasn't sure what she would say to him. As luck would have it, he picked up on
the second ring.

They exchanged pleasantries. Kim was nervous. She tried to hide it, but not
very successfully.

"Are you okay?" Kinnard asked after a pause. "You sound a little strange."

Kim struggled to think of something to say, but she couldn't. She felt confused, embarrassed, and suddenly emotional.

"Just not answering is telling me something," Kinnard said. "Can I help somehow? Is something wrong?"

Kim took a deep breath to get herself under control. "You can help," she said
finally. "I need to get away from Salem. I've called several girlfriends, but no one
is home. I had it in mind to come into town and spend the night since I have to
be at work in the morning."

"Why don't you stay here?" Kinnard asked. "I'll just move my exercise bike
and eighty thousand copies of the *New England Journal of Medicine* out of my
guest room, and it's all yours. Besides, I've got the day off. I'm sure we could have
some fun."

"Do you honestly think it's a good idea?"

"I'll behave myself if that's your worry," Kinnard said with a laugh.

Kim wondered if she was more worried about behaving herself.

"Come on," Kinnard encouraged. "It sounds like it will do you good to get out of suburbia for a day and an evening."

"All right," Kim said with sudden determination.

"Great!" Kinnard said. "What time will you be here?"

"What about in an hour?" Kim said.

"See you then," Kinnard said.

Kim replaced the receiver. She wasn't sure what she was doing, but it felt right. Getting up, she climbed the stairs and got her things together, remembering her uniform for work. In the kitchen she put extra food out for Sheba and changed the Kitty Litter box by the back door.

After putting her things in the car, Kim drove over to the lab. Just before she entered the building she paused to think about whether she should specifically mention that she was staying with Kinnard. She decided she wouldn't bring it up, but she'd tell Edward if he asked.

The atmosphere in the lab was even more intense than on her previous visit. Everyone was absorbed in their work, and although they acknowledged her, they did it perfunctorily.

Kim didn't mind. In fact she preferred it. The last thing she needed at the moment was a long lecture on some arcane experiment.

She found Edward at his printer. His computer was busy spilling out data. He smiled at her, but the smile was fleeting. In the next second his mind was back on what was coming out of the printer.

"I'm going into Boston for the day," Kim said brightly.

"Good," Edward said.

"I'll be spending the night," Kim said. "I could leave a number if you'd like."

"It won't be necessary," Edward said. "If there's any problem, call me. I'll be here as usual."

Kim said goodbye and started for the door. Edward called to her. She stopped.

"I'm really sorry I'm so preoccupied," Edward said. "I wish we weren't so busy. We've got an emergency of sorts."

"I understand," Kim said. She looked at Edward's face. There was a hint of awkwardness she'd not seen for some time.

Kim hurried from the lab and got in her car. She drove out of the compound with Edward's demeanor on her mind. It was as if the old persona of Edward were reemerging: the persona she'd been attracted to when they'd first met.

It didn't take long for Kim to begin to relax, and the farther south she drove, the better she felt. The weather helped. It was a hot, Indian summer day with bright sunshine and fall clarity. Here and there were trees tinted with a hint of their dazzling fall foliage. The sky was so blue, it looked like one vast celestial ocean.

Sunday was not a difficult day for parking, and Kim found a spot within easy walking distance of Kinnard's apartment on Revere Street. She was nervous when she rang his bell, but he immediately made her feel comfortable. He helped carry her things into his guest room, which he'd obviously taken the time to clean.

Kinnard took Kim on an invigorating walk around the city, and for a number of blissful hours she forgot about Omni, Ultra, and Elizabeth. They started in the North End with lunch at an Italian restaurant followed by espressos in an Italian café.

For an entertaining interlude they ducked into Filene's Basement for a quick scouting of the merchandise. Both were experienced Filene's Basement shoppers. Kim surprised herself by finding a great skirt originally from Saks Fifth Avenue.

After their shopping they strolled around the Boston Gardens and enjoyed the fall foliage and flowers. They sat for a while on one of the park benches and watched the swan boats glide around the lake.

"I probably shouldn't say this," Kinnard said, "but you do look a bit tired to me."

"I'm not surprised," Kim said. "I haven't been sleeping well. Living in Salem hasn't been particularly idyllic."

"Anything you want to talk about?" Kinnard said.

"Not at the moment," Kim said. "I suppose I'm confused about a lot of things."

"I'm glad you came for a visit," Kinnard said.

"I want to make sure you understand that I'm definitely staying in the guest room," Kim said quickly.

"Hey, relax," Kinnard said, lifting up his hands as if to defend himself. "I understand. We're friends, remember?"

"I'm sorry," Kim said. "I must seem hyper to you. The fact of the matter is that I'm the most relaxed I've been in weeks." She reached over and gave Kinnard's hand a squeeze. "Thank you for being my friend."

After leaving the park, they walked down Newbury Street and window-shopped. Then they indulged in one of Kim's favorite Boston pastimes. They went into Waterstone's Booksellers and browsed. Kim bought a paperback Dick Francis novel while Kinnard bought a travel book on Sicily. He said it was a place he always wanted to go.

Late in the afternoon they stopped into an Indian restaurant and had a delicious tandoor-style dinner. The only problem was that the restaurant lacked a liquor license. Both agreed the spicy food would have been far better with cold beer.

From the Indian restaurant they walked back to Beacon Hill. Sitting on Kinnard's couch, they each had a glass of cold white wine. Kim soon felt herself getting sleepy.

She turned in early in anticipation of having to get up at the crack of dawn for work. She did not need any Xanax when she slipped between Kinnard's freshly laundered sheets. Almost immediately she fell into a deep, restful sleep.

Kim had almost forgotten how hard a normal day was in the SICU. She was the first to acknowledge that after a month's vacation she was out of shape for both the physical and emotional stamina that was needed. But as the day drew to a close, she had to admit that she'd truly enjoyed the intensity, the challenge, and the sense of accomplishment of helping people in dire need, not to mention the comradeship of shared endeavor.

Kinnard had appeared several times during the day with patients coming from surgery. Kim made it a point to be available to help. She thanked him again for the best night's sleep she'd had in weeks. He told her that she was welcome anytime, even that night, despite the fact that he was on call and would be spending the night in the hospital.

Kim would have liked to stay. After her isolation at the compound, she'd enjoyed being in Boston, and she'd become nostalgic for the time she'd lived there. But she knew she had to get back. She wasn't under any delusion that Edward would be available, but she still felt a strong obligation to be there.

As soon as Kim's shift was over, she walked to the corner of Charles and Cambridge streets and caught the Red Line to Harvard Square. The trains were frequent at that hour, and after only twenty minutes she was walking northwest on Massachusetts Avenue on her way to the Harvard Law School.

Kim slowed her pace when she realized she was perspiring. It was another hot Indian summer day, without the previous day's crystalline clarity. There was no breeze whatsoever, and a hazy, muggy canopy was stalled over the city, making it seem more like summer than fall. The weatherman warned of possible violent thunderstorms.

Kim got directions to the Law Library from a student. She found it with no difficulty. The air-conditioned interior was a relief.

Another inquiry directed her to Helen Arnold's office. Kim gave her name to a secretary and was told she'd have to wait. No sooner had Kim sat down than a tall, slender, and strikingly attractive black woman appeared in a connecting doorway and waved her in.

"I'm Helen Arnold, and I've got some good news for you," the woman said enthusiastically. She led Kim into her office and motioned for her to sit down.

Kim was struck by the woman's appearance. It wasn't what she expected at a law school library. Her hair was done in the most exquisite cornrows Kim had ever seen, and her dress was a brilliantly colored silk chemise loosely gathered at the waist with a gold chain belt.

"I spoke this morning, quite early if you must know, with Ms. Sturburg, who is a wonderful woman by the way, and she told me all about your interest in a work by Rachel Bingham."

Kim nodded through this dialogue, which Helen delivered in rapid-fire.

"Have you found it?" Kim asked as soon as Helen paused.

"Yes and no," Helen said. She smiled warmly. "The good news is that I confirmed Katherine Sturburg's belief that the work survived the fire of 1764. I am absolutely sure of this. Mark my word. Apparently it had been rather permanently housed in the chambers of one of the tutors who'd lived outside Old Harvard Hall. Isn't that good news?"

"I'm pleased," Kim said. "In fact I'm thrilled it wasn't destroyed. But you qualified your answer to my question whether you'd found it. What did you mean by 'yes and no'?"

"I meant simply that although I hadn't found the book itself, I did find reference to the fact that the work did indeed come here to the Law School for the Law Library. I also learned there'd been some confusion and difficulty of how or where to file the work, although it had something to do with Ecclesiastic Law as your letter from Increase Mather suggested. By the way, I thought the letter was a fabulous find, and I understand you have offered to give it to Harvard. That's very generous of you."

"It's the least I could do for all this trouble I've caused," Kim said. "But what about the Rachel Bingham work? Does anybody know where it might be?"

"There is someone," Helen said. "After a bit more digging around, I discovered the work had been transferred from the Law Library to the Divinity School in 1825, right after the construction of Divinity Hall. I don't know why it was transferred; perhaps it had something to do with the filing difficulties here at the Law Library."

"My Lord!" Kim exclaimed. "What a journey this book has had."

"I took the liberty of calling my counterpart over at the Divinity School Library just before noon," Helen said. "I hope you don't mind."

"Of course I don't mind," Kim said. She was pleased Helen had taken the initiative.

"Her name is Gertrude Havermeyer," Helen said. "She's something of a battleax, but she's got a good heart. She promised she'd look right into it." Helen took a piece of note paper and wrote down Gertrude's name and phone number. She then took out a single-sheet map of the Harvard campus and circled the Divinity School.

A few minutes later Kim was on her way across the campus. She passed the Physics Lab and skirted the Museum Building to reach Divinity Avenue. From there it was just a few steps to Gertrude Havermeyer's office.

"So you're the reason my entire afternoon has been wasted," Gertrude said when Kim introduced herself. Gertrude Havermeyer was standing in front of her desk with her hands aggressively settled on her hips. As Helen Arnold had suggested, Gertrude projected a severe, uncompromising temperament. Otherwise her bravado belied her appearance. She was a petite, white-haired woman who squinted at Kim through wire-rimmed trifocals.

"I'm sorry if I've inconvenienced you," Kim said guiltily.

"Since I took the call from Helen Arnold I've not had a second to do my own work," Gertrude complained. "It's taken me literally hours."

"I hope at least your efforts weren't in vain," Kim said.

"I did find a receipt in a ledger from that period," Gertrude said. "So Helen was right. The Rachel Bingham work was sent from the Law School, and it did arrive here at the Divinity School. But as luck would have it, I could not find any reference to the book in the computer or in the old card catalogue or even in the very old catalogue which we've saved in the basement."

Kim's heart fell. "I'm so sorry to have put you through all this for nothing," she said.

"Well, I didn't give up there," Gertrude said. "Not on your life. When I get committed to something, I don't let it rest. So I went back through all the old handwritten cards from when the library was first organized. It was frustrating, but I did find another reference more by luck than anything else except perseverance. For the life of me I cannot figure out why it wasn't included in the main library index."

Kim's hopes brightened. Following the trail of Elizabeth's evidence was like riding an emotional roller coaster. "Is the work still here?" she asked.

"Heavens, no," Gertrude said indignantly. "If it were, it would have been in the computer. We run a tight ship here. No, the final reference I found indicated that it had been sent to the Medical School in 1826 after being here for less than a year. Apparently no one knew where to put the material. It's all very mysterious because there wasn't even an indication of what category it belonged to."

"Oh, for goodness' sakes," Kim said with frustration. "Searching for this book or whatever it might be is getting too much. It's becoming a bad joke."

"Buck up!" Gertrude ordered. "I went through a lot of effort on your behalf. I even called over to the Countway Medical Library and spoke to John Moldavian, who's in charge of rare books and manuscripts. I told him the story, and he assured me he'd look right into it."

After thanking Gertrude, Kim went back to Harvard Square and reboarded the Red Line for Boston.

It was now rush hour, and Kim had to squeeze onto the train. There were no seats, so she had to stand. As the train thundered over the Longfellow Bridge, Kim began to think seriously about giving up the whole Elizabeth quest. It had been like chasing a mirage. Every time she thought she was getting close, it turned out to be a false lead.

Climbing into her car in the MGH garage, Kim started the engine and then thought about the heavy traffic she'd be facing on her way out to Salem. At that hour just getting through the Leverett Circle interchange would probably take close to a half hour.

With a change of heart, Kim turned her car in the opposite direction and headed for the Countway Medical Library. She'd decided she might as well follow up on Gertrude's lead rather than sit in traffic.

John Moldavian seemed perfectly suited for work in a library. He was a soft-spoken, gentle man whose love for books was immediately apparent by the affectionate and caring manner he handled them.

Kim introduced herself and mentioned Gertrude's name. John responded immediately by searching for something among the clutter on his desk.

"I've got something here for you," he said. "Where in the devil did I put it?"

Kim watched him as he shuffled through his papers. He had a thin face dominated by heavy black-framed glasses. His thin mustache looked almost too perfect, as if it had been drawn with an eyebrow pencil.

"Is the Rachel Bingham work here at the library?" Kim hazarded to ask.

"No, it's no longer here," John said. Then his face brightened. "Ah, here's what I wanted." He lifted a single sheet of copy paper.

Kim silently sighed. So much for the Gertrude lead, she thought.

"I looked through the Medical School Library records for 1826," John said. "And I found this reference to the work you're seeking."

"Let me guess," Kim said. "It was sent somewhere else."

John regarded Kim over the top of the paper he was holding. "How did you guess?" he asked.

Kim gave a short laugh. "It's been a pattern," she said. "Where did it go from here?"

"It went to the Department of Anatomy," John said. "Of course, today it is called the Department of Cell Biology."

Kim shook her head in disbelief. "Why on earth would it have been sent there?" she asked rhetorically.

"I've no idea," John said. "The entry I found was rather strange. It was in the form of a hastily handwritten card that had apparently been attached to the book or manuscript or drawing. I made you a copy." John handed the paper to Kim.

Kim took it. It was hard to read, forcing her to turn herself in order to take advantage of the light coming through the window. It seemed to say: *Curiosity by Rachel Bingham contrived in 1691.* Looking at the word "curiosity" reminded Kim of Mary Custland telling her that a "repository of curiosities" had been lost in the 1764 fire, suggesting that the Rachel Bingham work had been a part of that collection. Thinking back to Jonathan's letter to his father, Kim surmised that the handwriting she was now looking at was Jonathan's. In her mind's eye she could see a nervous Jonathan Stewart rapidly scribbling the card in a panic to get out of the tutor's chamber where he'd surreptitiously entered to change the name to Rachel Bingham. Had he been discovered he probably would have been asked to leave the college.

"I called over to the department chairman," John said, interrupting Kim's ruminations. "He referred me to another gentleman by the name of Carl Nebolsine, who's the curator in charge of the Warren Anatomical Museum. So I called him. He told me that if I wanted to see the exhibit to come over to the administration building."

"You mean he has it?" Kim asked with disbelief.

"Apparently so," John said. "The Warren Anatomical Museum is on the fifth floor of building A, catty-cornered across from the front of the library. Are you interested in going over there?"

"By all means," Kim said. She could feel her pulse quicken at the thought that she might finally have found Elizabeth's evidence.

John reached for his phone. "Let's see if Mr. Nebolsine is still over there. He was a little while ago, but I believe he has several offices. Apparently he takes care of a number of the smaller museums and collections sprinkled around the Harvard community."

John had a quick conversation in the middle of which he gave Kim a thumbs-up sign. Hanging up, he said, "You're in luck. He's still there, and he'll meet you in the museum if you head over there immediately."

"I'm on my way," Kim said. She thanked John and quickly crossed to building A, a Greek Revival structure faced with a massive pediment supported by Doric columns. A guard stopped her just inside the door but then waved her on when he spotted her MGH identity card.

Kim got off on the fifth floor. The museum, such as it was, was tucked along the wall to the left and consisted of a series of glass-fronted display cases. They contained the usual collection of primitive surgical instruments capable of making a stoic wince, old photos, and pathological specimens. There were lots of skulls, including one with a hole through the left eye socket and the top of the forehead.

"That's quite an interesting case," a voice said. Kim looked up to see a much younger man than she'd expected for a museum curator. "You must be Kimberly Stewart. I'm Carl Nebolsine." They shook hands.

"See that rod in there?" Carl said, pointing at a five-foot-long steel rod. "That's called a tamping rod. It was used to pack powder and clay into a hole drilled for the purpose of blasting. One day a hundred or so years ago that rod went through that man's head." Carl pointed to the skull. "The amazing thing is that the man lived through it."

"Was he all right?" Kim asked.

"It says his personality wasn't as agreeable after he'd recovered from the trauma, but whose would be?" Carl said.

Kim scanned some of the other exhibits. In the far corner she spotted some books on display.

"I understand you're interested in the Rachel Bingham exhibit," Carl said.

"Is it here?" Kim asked.

"No," Carl said.

Kim looked at the man as if she hadn't heard him correctly.

"It's downstairs in the storeroom," Carl said. "We don't get a lot of requests to see it, and we don't have nearly enough space to display everything we have. Would you like to see it?"

"Very much," Kim said with relief.

They took the elevator down to the basement and followed a labyrinthine route that Kim would not have liked to retrace on her own. Carl unlocked a heavy steel door. Reaching in, he turned on the lights, such as they were: several bare lightbulbs.

The room was full of dusty old-style glass display cases.

"Sorry about the mess down here," Carl said. "It's very dirty. No one comes in here very often."

Kim followed Carl as he weaved his way among the cabinets. Passing each one, Kim spied assortments of bones, books, instruments, and jars of preserved organs. Carl stopped. Kim came up behind him. He stepped aside and gestured within the cabinet in front of him.

Kim recoiled with a mixture of horror and disgust. She was totally unprepared for what she was seeing. Crammed into a large glass jar filled with brown-stained preservative was a four-to-five-month-old fetus that looked like a monster.

Oblivious to Kim's reaction, Carl opened the cabinet. He reached in and dragged the heavy canister forward, jiggling the contents so that it danced grotesquely, causing bits of tissue to rain down like a glass bubble snow-scene paperweight.

Kim clasped a hand to her mouth as she stared at the anencephalic fetus, which had no brain and a flat cranium. It had a cleft palate that made it appear as if the mouth were drawn up into the nose. Its features were further distorted by being pressed up against the glass of the container. From just behind its relatively huge froglike eyes, the head was flat and covered with a shock of coal-black hair. The massive jaw was totally out of proportion to the face. The fetus's stubby upper limbs ended in spadelike hands with short fingers, some of which were fused together. The effect was almost like cloven hooves. From the rump extended a long fishlike tail.

"Would you like me to lift it down so we can carry it out to better light?" Carl asked.

"No!" Kim said, a little too harshly. In a calmer voice she told Carl she could see the exhibit just fine where it was.

Kim understood completely how the seventeenth-century mind would have viewed such a beastly malformation. This poor creature could easily have been taken for the devil incarnate. Indeed, copies of woodcut prints of the devil that Kim had seen from that era looked identical.

"Would you like me at least to turn it around so you can see the other side?" Carl asked.

"Thank you, no," Kim said, unconsciously stepping back from the specimen. Now she knew why the Law School and the Divinity School had not known what to do with it. She also recalled the note John Moldavian had shown her in the Medical Library. It didn't say, *Curiosity by Rachel Bingham contrived in 1691*. The word was *conceived*, not *contrived!*

And Kim remembered the entry in Elizabeth's diary where Elizabeth expressed concern over innocent Job. Job hadn't been a biblical reference. Elizabeth had known she was pregnant and had already named the baby Job. How tragically apropos, Kim thought.

Kim thanked Carl and stumbled back toward her car. As she walked she thought about the double tragedy of Elizabeth being pregnant while she was being unwittingly poisoned by a fungus growing in her store of rye. In that day, everyone would have been certain Elizabeth had had relations with the devil to produce such a monster, certainly a manifestation of a covenant, especially since the "fits" had originated in Elizabeth's house and then spread to the other houses where the children had taken Elizabeth's bread. Elizabeth's assertiveness, her ill-timed struggle with the Putnam family, and her change in social status wouldn't have helped her situation.

Arriving at her car, Kim climbed inside and started the motor. For her it was now totally clear why Elizabeth had been accused of being a witch and how she'd been convicted.

Kim drove as if she were in a trance. She began to understand why Elizabeth would not confess to save her life as Ronald had undoubtedly urged. Elizabeth knew she was no witch, but her confidence in her innocence would have been undermined, especially with everyone against her: friends, magistrates, and even the clergy. With her husband away, Elizabeth would have had no support whatsoever. Utterly alone, she would have thought she was guilty of some horrid transgression against God. How else to explain giving birth to such a demonic creature? Maybe she even thought her fate was just.

Kim got bogged down in traffic on Storrow Drive and was reduced to inching forward. The weather had not improved. In fact it had gotten hotter. Kim felt progressively anxious about being cooped up in the car.

Finally she managed to get through the bottleneck at the Leverett Circle traffic light. Bursting free from the bounds of the city, she headed north on Interstate 93. With the literal freedom came a new revelation and the suggestion of figurative freedom. Kim began to believe that the shock of her visual confrontation with Elizabeth's monster had caused her to stumble onto the message that she believed Elizabeth had been trying to communicate: namely that Kim should believe in herself. She shouldn't lose confidence because of other people's beliefs, as poor Elizabeth had. She shouldn't allow authority figures to take over her life. Elizabeth hadn't had a choice about that, but Kim did.

Kim's mind was racing. She recalled all the tedious hours she'd spent with Alice McMurray discussing her low self-esteem. She remembered the theories Alice had presented to explain its source: a combination of her father's emotional detachment, her vain attempts to please him, and her mother's passivity in the face of her father's womanizing. Suddenly all the talk seemed trivial. It was as if it involved someone else. Those discussions had never punched her in the gut as the final shock of Elizabeth's ordeal had.

Everything seemed clear to Kim now. Whether her low self-esteem came from her particular family dynamics, or from a shy temperament, or a combination of the two, it didn't matter. The reality was that Kim had not allowed her own interests and aptitudes to chart her course through life. Her career choice was a good example. So was her current living situation.

Kim had to brake suddenly. To her surprise and chagrin the traffic was bogged down on the usually freely moving interstate. Once again she was reduced to moving ahead in fits and starts, bringing the summerlike heat swirling in through the open window. To the west she could see huge thunderhead clouds massing on the horizon.

As she inched forward Kim experienced a sudden resolve. She had to change her life. First she'd allowed her father to rule her despite the fact that they had no relationship to speak of. And now she'd been allowing Edward to do the same. Edward was living with her but in name only. In actuality, he was only taking advantage of her and giving nothing in return. The Omni lab should not be on her property, and the researchers should not be living in the Stewart family house.

As the traffic began to free up again, and Kim was able to accelerate, she promised herself that she would not allow the status quo to continue. She told herself that she was going to talk with Edward the moment she got back to the compound.

Knowing her weakness regarding emotional confrontations and her inclination to procrastinate, Kim also emphasized to herself the importance of talking to Edward as soon as possible now that there was reason to believe Ultra was teratogenic, or damaging to a developing fetus. Kim knew such information was crucial for studying an experimental drug not only to protect pregnant women but because many teratogenic drugs were also capable of causing cancer.

By the time Kim drove onto the compound it was close to seven o'clock. With the thunderclouds still building to the west, it was darker than normal for that time of evening. As Kim approached the lab she saw that the lights had already been turned on.

Kim parked but didn't get out of the car immediately. Despite her resolve she found herself debating whether to go inside or not. Suddenly she could think of a lot of excuses to put off the visit. But she didn't give in. She opened the car door and got out. "You're going to do this if it kills you," she said. After smoothing out the wrinkles in her uniform and brushing back her hair, she entered the lab.

As soon as the inner door closed behind her, Kim was aware the lab had had yet another change of atmosphere. She was certain that David and Gloria and maybe even Eleanor had seen her arrive, but they didn't acknowledge her. In fact, they turned away and purposefully ignored her. There was no laughter; there wasn't even any conversation. The mood was palpably tense.

The strained ambience added to Kim's anxiety, yet she forced herself to seek out Edward. She found him in a darkened corner at his computer. The pale green fluorescence from his monitor cast an eerie light on his face.

Kim approached him and stood for a moment at his side. She was reluctant to interrupt him. As she watched his hands play across the keyboard, she detected a trembling of his fingers between individual keystrokes. She could also hear he was breathing more quickly than she.

Several minutes dragged by. Edward ignored her.

"Please, Edward," Kim said finally. Her voice wavered. "I have to talk with you."

"Later," Edward said. He still did not look at her.

"It's important that I talk to you now," Kim said hesitantly.

Edward shocked Kim by leaping to his feet. The sudden motion sent his ergonomic chair skidding across the floor on its casters until it slammed into a cabinet. He stuck his face close to Kim's so that she could see red spiderwebs on the whites of his bulging eyes.

"I said later!" he repeated through clenched teeth. He glared at Kim as if daring her to contradict him.

Kim stepped back and collided with the lab bench. Awkwardly her hand thrust out to support herself, and she knocked a beaker onto the floor. It shattered, jarring Kim's already frayed nerves.

Kim didn't move. She watched Edward apprehensively. Once again he was acting like he was on the brink of losing control, just as he'd done when he'd thrown the wineglass back in his apartment in Cambridge. It occurred to her that something momentous had happened in the lab that had sparked a major disagreement. Whatever it had been, it had everybody on edge, particularly Edward.

Kim's first reaction was empathy for Edward, knowing how hard he'd been working. But then she caught herself. With the benefit of her newly acquired self-knowledge, she understood such thoughts represented a falling back on old habits. Kim was committed to heeding Elizabeth's message. For once in her life she had to stand up for herself and think of her own needs.

At the same time Kim was capable of being realistic. She knew there would be no benefit from inappropriately provoking Edward. From his behavior at the moment it was abundantly clear he was in no mood for a discussion about their relationship.

"I'm sorry to interrupt you," Kim said when she could tell Edward had regained some semblance of control. "It's obvious this isn't a good time for you. I'll be at the cottage. I do want to talk, so you come over when you are ready."

Kim turned away from his glower and started to leave. She'd only gone a few steps when she stopped and turned back.

"I did learn something today that you should know," Kim said. "I have reason to believe Ultra might be teratogenic."

"We'll be testing the drug in pregnant mice and rats," Edward said sullenly. "But at the moment we have a more pressing problem."

Kim noticed that Edward had an abrasion on the left side of his head. Then she saw he had cuts on his hands just like those she'd seen on Curt's.

Instinctively Kim stepped back. "You've hurt yourself," she said. She reached for his head to examine the wound.

"It's nothing," Edward said, roughly parrying her hand. He turned from her, and after retrieving his chair, sat down at his computer and went back to work.

Kim left the lab, rattled from her visit; she could never predict Edward's mood or behavior. Outside she noticed it had darkened significantly. There was not a breath of air. The leaves on the trees hung limply. A few birds skittered across the threatening sky, searching for shelter.

Kim hurried to her car. Glancing up into the ominous clouds that had moved ever more close, she saw short flashes of weblike lightning that stayed aloft. She heard no thunder. On the short drive to the cottage, she used her headlights.

The first thing Kim did when she got home was head for the parlor. She looked up at Elizabeth's portrait and regarded the woman with renewed sympathy, admiration, and gratitude. After a few moments of staring at the strong, feminine face with its bright green eyes, Kim began to calm down. The image was empowering, and despite the setback at the lab, Kim knew she would not turn back. She would wait for Edward, but she would definitely talk with him.

Taking her eyes off the painting, Kim wandered around the cottage that she and Elizabeth had shared. Her recent loneliness notwithstanding, it was a cozy, romantic house, and she couldn't help but wonder how different it would have been with Kinnard around instead of Edward.

Standing in the dining room, which in Elizabeth's time had been the kitchen, Kim lamented how few times the table had even been used. There was no doubt that September had been a bust, and Kim berated herself for allowing Edward to drag her along on his drug-development crusade.

With a sudden flash of anger Kim allowed herself to go a step further, and for the first time she admitted that she was repulsed by Edward's incipient greed as well as by his new persona as defined by Ultra. In her mind there was no place for drug-induced self-understanding, or drug-induced assertiveness, or a drug-induced happy mood. It was all fake. The concept of cosmetic psychopharmacology disgusted her.

Having finally faced her true feelings about Edward, Kim turned again to thoughts of Kinnard. With her new understanding, she saw that she shared a significant portion of blame for their most recent difficulties. With equal harshness that she'd expressed toward Edward's new greed, she chided herself for allowing her fear of rejection to misinterpret Kinnard's boyish interests.

Kim sighed. She was exhausted physically and mentally. At the same time, she was inwardly calm. For the first time in months she didn't have that vague, nagging anxiety that had been plaguing her. Although she knew her life was in disarray, she was committed to change, and she felt she knew what it was she had to change.

Disappearing into the bathroom, Kim took a long, luxurious bath, something she hadn't done for as long as she could remember. After bathing, she slipped into a loose-fitting jogging suit and made herself dinner.

After dinner Kim went to the parlor window and glanced over toward the lab. She wondered what Edward was thinking and when she would see him.

Kim moved her eyes away from the lab and looked at the black silhouettes of the trees. They were totally motionless, as if embedded in glass; there still was no wind. The storm which had seemed imminent when she'd first arrived home had stalled to the west. But then Kim saw a bolt of lightning. This time it arced to the ground, followed by a distant rumble of thunder.

Turning back into the room, Kim glanced again at Elizabeth's portrait over the mantel and thought of Elizabeth's gruesome, malformed fetus swimming in its jar of preservative. Kim shuddered anew. No wonder people in Elizabeth's time believed in sorcery, magic, and witchcraft. Back then there was no other explanation for such disturbing events.

Advancing closer to the painting, Kim studied Elizabeth's features. The woman's assertiveness was apparent in the line of her jaw, the set of her lips, and the forthright stare of her eyes. Kim wondered if the trait had been temperament or character, inborn or learned, nature or nurture.

Kim pondered her own newly cultivated assertiveness for which she credited Elizabeth and wondered if she could maintain it. She felt she'd made a start by going to the lab that afternoon. She was certain she wouldn't have been able to do that in the past.

As the evening progressed, Kim began to think about the possibility of changing careers and to question whether she had the courage to take the risk. With her inheritance she knew she could not use economics as an excuse. Such a lifestyle change was a daunting possibility, especially the idea of doing something artistic. Yet it was also alluring.

One of the unexpected consequences of Kim's efforts at sorting the three hundred years of business documents in the castle was the realization of how little her family had contributed to the community. The hoard of papers and the tasteless castle housing them were the two major legacies. There'd not been one artist, musician, or author among them. For all their money, they'd developed no art collections, philharmonic endowments, or libraries. In fact, they'd made no contribution to culture unless entrepreneurialism was a culture in and of itself.

By nine P.M. Kim was beyond exhaustion. For a brief moment she entertained the notion of going back to the lab, but she quickly discarded it. If Edward had wanted to talk he would have come to the house. Instead she wrote him a note on a Post-it and stuck it on the mirror in the half-bath. It said simply: *I'll be up at five and we can talk then.*

After taking the cat out for a brief sojourn, Kim climbed into bed. She didn't even try to read nor did she even consider the need for a sleep aid. In a matter of minutes she was fast asleep.

A startlingly loud clap of thunder yanked Kim from the depths of a dream in the blink of an eye. The house was still vibrating from the horrendous noise as she realized she was sitting bolt upright. Sheba had responded to the cataclysm by leaping from the bed and diving beneath.

Within minutes of the thunder came rain and gusty wind. Having held back for so long, the storm hit with unbridled ferocity. Droplets large enough to sound like hailstones battered the slate roof above Kim's head. She also heard the rain beat against the screen of the westerly-facing open casement window.

Kim dashed from her bed to the window and began cranking it shut. She could feel the wind carry rainwater into her room. Just as she was about to lock the window in place, a flash of lightning struck the lightning rod on one of the castle's turrets and filled the entire compound with a blue light.

In the instant the field between the cottage and the castle was illuminated, Kim saw a startling image. It was a ghostlike, scantily clad figure running across the grass. Although Kim couldn't be certain, since she'd had only the briefest glimpse, she thought it might have been Eleanor.

Kim winced as another clap of thunder came close on the heels of the lightning flash. Ignoring the ringing in her ears, she strained to see out in the darkness. With the driving rain, it was impossible. She waited briefly for another flash of lightning, but none occurred.

Leaving the window, Kim ran through the connecting hall to Edward's bedroom. She was convinced she'd not been hallucinating; someone was out there. Whether it was Eleanor or not was immaterial. No one should be out in that storm, especially when there was the added danger of the wild animal that had been plaguing the neighborhood.

Edward had to be told. Kim was surprised to find his door closed. He always had it open. Kim knocked. When there was no answer, she knocked louder. When there was still no answer, she looked down at the lock on the old door. A skeleton key protruded from the keyhole, meaning the door couldn't be locked. Kim opened the door.

From where she was standing Kim could hear Edward's stertorous breathing. Kim called out to him several times in a progressively louder voice, but he didn't stir.

Another flash of lightning filled the room with light. Kim got a brief glimpse of Edward sprawled on his back with his arms and legs outstretched. He was clothed in his underwear. One pant leg had not been totally removed; his trousers were draped inside-out over the side of the bed.

Kim again winced in preparation of the thunder, and it didn't disappoint her. It was as if the storm were centered on the compound.

Turning on the hall light, which spilled into Edward's room, Kim hurried over to his bedside. She tried calling to him again. When that didn't work she shook him gently. Not only didn't he wake up, his breathing didn't even alter. Kim shook him vigorously, and when that had no effect she began to be concerned. It was as if he were in a coma.

Kim turned on the bedside light to its brightest level. Edward was the picture of tranquillity. His face had a slack appearance, with his mouth open. Kim put a hand on each shoulder and shook him insistently, loudly calling his name.

Only then did his breathing change. Then his eyes blinked open.

"Edward, are you awake?" Kim asked. She shook him again and his head flopped from side to side like a rag doll's.

Edward appeared confused and disoriented until he noticed Kim. She was still holding his shoulders.

Kim watched Edward's pupils suddenly dilate like those of a cat about to spring. Then his eyes narrowed to mere slits while his upper lip curled back like a snarling beast's. Edward's previously flaccid face contorted into an expression of sheer rage.

Shocked by this horrid, unexpected metamorphosis, Kim released his shoulders and backed up. She was stunned he could be so angry at being awakened. Edward let out a throaty sound akin to a growl and sat up. He was staring at her unblinkingly.

Kim bolted for the door, aware that Edward had sprung after her. She heard him fall to the floor, presumably tangled in his partially removed trousers. Kim slammed Edward's bedroom door behind her, and, using the skeleton key, locked it.

After dashing headlong down the stairs, Kim ran to the phone in the kitchen. She knew that something was terribly wrong with Edward. He wasn't just angry about being awakened. Something had snapped in his mind.

Kim dialed 911, but as the connection went through she heard the door to Edward's bedroom splinter and then bang open against the wall. An instant later she could hear Edward snarling at the top of the stairs, followed by the sound of his coming down.

Frightened out of her mind, Kim dropped the phone and headed for the back door. As she reached it she glanced over her shoulder. She caught a glimpse of Edward crashing into the dining room table and throwing it out of his way in his haste. He was totally berserk.

Kim yanked open the door and dashed out into the rain, which was coming down in sheets. Her only thought was to get help, and the closest source was the castle. She rounded the house and struck off across the field, running as fast as she could in the soggy darkness.

A fearful bolt of lightning crackled out of the sky and illuminated the drenched landscape, briefly silhouetting the castle. The thunder followed immediately, reverberating off its looming façade. Kim did not break stride. She was thankful to see lights in some of the windows of the servants' wing.

Reaching the graveled area in front of the castle, Kim was forced to slow down. Although her panic had shielded her from most of the discomfort of running barefoot, the stones were too painful to disregard. Moving at a pace akin to a fast walk, she headed toward the side of the building, but as she neared the faux drawbridge she noticed that the main entrance was conveniently ajar.

Breathing heavily, Kim rushed inside. She ran straight through the dark front hall into the great room, where dim illumination spilled in from the huge two-story windows facing south. It was light from the surrounding towns reflected off the low cloud cover.

Kim had planned to head through the dining room to the kitchen and the servants' quarters beyond, but she hadn't gotten far when she all but collided with Eleanor. A wet, white lace nightgown clung to the woman like a second skin.

Kim stopped short, momentarily paralyzed. She now knew she'd been correct: it had been Eleanor she'd seen running in the field. Kim started to warn her about Edward, but her words died in her throat when she saw Eleanor's face in the meager light. It had the same unspeakable feral quality that she'd seen in Edward's when he awoke. To make things worse, Eleanor's mouth was smeared with blood as if she'd been feeding on raw meat.

Running into Eleanor cost Kim her lead on Edward. Gasping for breath, he staggered into the room and hesitated, savagely eyeing Kim in the half-light. His hair was plastered against his wet head. He was dressed only in his T-shirt and boxer shorts, both of which were covered with mud.

Kim turned to face him. Once again she had to catch her breath at his changed appearance. It was not that his features had altered; it was just that his face reflected a beastly rage.

Edward started toward Kim but then stopped again when he caught sight of his research partner. Ignoring Kim temporarily, he lurched toward Eleanor. When he was within arm's length, he warily put his head back as if sniffing the air. Eleanor did the same, and they slowly circled each other.

Kim shuddered. It was as if she were caught in a nightmare, watching two wild animals meet in the jungle to check each other to be sure one wasn't a predator and the other the prey.

Kim slowly backed up while Edward and Eleanor were preoccupied. As soon as she could see a clear route into the dining room, she bolted. Her sudden movement startled the other two. As if by some primeval carnivorous reflex they gave chase.

As Kim rushed through the dining room she yanked a number of the chairs away from the table and threw them behind her in hopes of slowing her pursuers. It worked better than she imagined. As if confused by the unexpected chairs and unable to adjust, Edward and Eleanor collided with them. Amid hideous, inhuman screams they fell. But the ruse did not delay them for long. As Kim passed through the door into the kitchen and cast a fleeting glance over her shoulder, she saw that they were already on their feet, throwing the chairs from their path, mindless of their bruises.

Kim started yelling for help as soon as she entered the servants' wing, but she didn't stop running. She reached the stairs and, still screaming, rushed up to the second floor. Without hesitation she burst into the room she knew was occupied by François. He was in his bed, sleeping with the light on.

Kim rushed over to him, calling his name. She shook him frantically, but he didn't wake up. Kim screamed at him and started to shake him again, but then she froze. Even with her panic she remembered that Edward had been equally hard to arouse.

Kim took a step back. François's eyes slowly opened. Just as it had with Edward, François's face underwent a savage transformation. His eyes narrowed and his upper lip curled back from his teeth. From his mouth came an inhuman growl. In an instant he'd become a demented, raging animal.

Kim spun around to flee, but Edward and Eleanor had reached the doorway, blocking her exit. Without a second's hesitation she hurled herself through the connecting door to the suite's sitting room and then exited to the hall from there. Back in the stairwell, she rushed up to the next level and entered another room she knew was occupied.

Kim stopped at the threshold, her hand still holding the open door. Curt and David were on the floor, scantily dressed and covered with mud. Water dripped from their heads, indicating they had recently been out. In front of them was a partially dismembered cat. Like Eleanor, their faces were smeared with blood.

Kim slammed the door. She could hear the others coming up the stairs. Turning around, she opened the connecting door to the main part of the house. At least she knew her way around.

Kim sprinted the length of the master suite hall. With its southern exposure it was enveloped in similar light as the great room. Kim was able to avoid the console tables, the straight-backed chairs, and the settees. But in her headlong flight she skidded on a throw rug and practically slammed into the door leading into the guest wing. After a moment's struggle with the knob, she threw open the door. The hall beyond was dark, but knowing there was no furniture, Kim ran blindly.

The next thing she knew she had collided with an unanticipated table that dug into her stomach, knocking her off balance. She fell with a tremendous clatter. For a second she didn't move, wondering if she had badly injured herself. Her stomach throbbed and her right knee was numb. She could feel something trickle down her arm, and she guessed it was blood.

Kim felt around her in the darkness. Then she realized what she had tripped over. It was the plumbers' tools and workbench. They had moved their equipment to the guest wing to check and repair the waste pipes there.

Kim listened. She could hear the distant noise of doors opening and slamming shut in the servants' wing. The sounds suggested to her that the creatures—she was loath to call them people in their current state—were searching for her randomly. They had not followed the only route possible, suggesting that they were not acting intelligently. Kim reasoned they had only limited use of their brains and were operating mostly on instinct and reflex.

Kim stood up. The numbness of her knee was changing to sharp pain. She touched it and could feel it was already beginning to swell.

With her eyes having adjusted to the dark, Kim was able to make out the workbench and some of the other tools. She saw a length of pipe and picked it up as a weapon, but discarded it when she realized it was plastic PVC pipe. Instead she picked up a hammer. But then she discarded that for an acetylene blowtorch and friction lighter. If these creatures chasing her were acting on animal instinct, they'd be terrified of fire.

With the blowtorch in hand, Kim walked as best she could to the guest-wing stairs. She bent over the balustrade and looked down. On the floor below, the hall lights were on. Kim listened again. What noises she heard still seemed to be coming from the opposite end of the house.

Kim started down the stairs but did not get far. After only a few steps she spotted Gloria two floors down on the main level. She was pacing back and forth at the base of the stairs like a cat in front of a lair. Unfortunately Gloria saw Kim and let out a screech, then started up the stairs.

Reversing her direction, Kim fled as fast as she could back down the hall. This time she avoided the plumbers' equipment. She reentered the main house and hobbled to the top of the main stairs. Behind her she heard a crash and a howl which she presumed was Gloria running into the plumbers' tools.

Kim descended the main stair, hugging the wall to keep out of view from below. After reaching the landing, she moved slowly to bring progressively more and more of the great room into view. She was relieved when she saw no one.

Taking a deep breath, Kim descended the final flight. Reaching the bottom, she hobbled as rapidly as she could toward the front hall. About ten feet from her goal she stopped. To her utter dismay Eleanor was slinking back and forth at the end of the hall, directly in front of the main entrance. She was pacing just as Gloria had been at the base of the guest-wing stairs. Unlike Gloria, she didn't see Kim.

Kim quickly stepped to the side so she'd be out of Eleanor's line of sight. As soon as she did so she realized someone was coming down the main stairs and would soon be on the landing.

With little time to debate the merits, Kim limped frantically back across the room and slipped into the powder room tucked beneath the grand staircase. As silently as possible she closed the door behind her and locked it. Simultaneously she heard footfalls on the stairs directly above her.

Kim tried to control the sound of her labored breathing as she listened to the footsteps continue their descent and then disappear into one of the thick-pile oriental rugs on the marbled great-room floor.

Kim was frightened. In fact, now that she had a moment to grasp the gravity of her situation, she was terrified. She also worried about her knee. And to add to her misery she was wet and cold and violently shivering.

Thinking over the events of the last several days, Kim wondered if the primitive state Edward and the researchers were currently suffering had been occurring on a nightly basis. If it had, and if they had had a suspicion about it, it would explain the marked change in the atmosphere of the lab. With horror Kim realized that there was a good chance the researchers were responsible for the recent troubles in the neighborhood blamed on a rabid animal and teenage vandals.

Kim shuddered in revulsion. It was plainly obvious to her that the ultimate cause was Ultra. By taking the drug, the researchers had become "possessed" in a fashion ironically similar to some of the "afflicted" people in 1692.

These musings gave Kim some hope. If what she was thinking were true, then they must revert back to their normal selves come morning, just like in an old gothic horror movie. All Kim had to do was stay hidden until then.

Kim bent down and put the acetylene torch and lighter on the floor. Groping in the darkness, she found the towel bar and used the towel to dry as much of herself as she could. Her nightgown was soaking wet. Then she draped the towel over her shoulders for a bit of warmth and clasped her arms around herself to try to control her shivering. She sat down on the toilet seat to ease the pressure on her swollen knee.

A period of time passed. Kim had no way of judging how much. The house had become quiet. But then there was a sudden loud crash of breaking glass that made Kim jump. She'd hoped they had given up searching for her, but that apparently wasn't the case. Immediately following the loud noise, she heard the sounds of doors and cabinets being opened again.

A few minutes later Kim tensed when she again heard one of them coming down the stairs above her. Whoever it was was descending slowly and stopping frequently. Kim stood up. Occasional violent spasms of shivering had made the toilet seat clank against the porcelain reservoir, and she did not want it to happen when one of them was so near.

Kim became progressively aware of another persistent sound that she could not place immediately. Finally she did, and it made her tremble more. Someone was sniffing, much the way Edward had two nights previously by the shed. She remembered Edward telling her that one of the effects they'd noticed taking the drug was how it improved the keenness of the senses. Kim's mouth went dry. If Edward had been able to smell her lingering cologne the other night, maybe he could smell her now.

As Kim struggled to control her shivering, the person above descended the rest of the way down the stairs. At that point the individual paused again before coming around to stand outside the powder room door.

Kim heard more intense sniffing. Then the doorknob was rattled as some-one tried to open the door. Kim held her breath.

Minutes dragged by. It sounded to Kim as if the others were arriving. From their collective sounds Kim could soon tell that a group of them had assembled.

Kim winced as one of them pounded a fist on the door several times. The door held, but just barely. It was a paneled door with thin veneers in each panel. Kim knew it would not withstand a concerted assault.

With her panic returning in a rush, Kim quickly squatted down in the dark-ness and felt for the blowtorch. When her hand did not immediately hit it, her pulse soared. Frantically she felt around in a larger arc. She was relieved when her fingers touched it. Next to it was the lighter.

As Kim straightened up with the blowtorch and the lighter in her hands, the pounding on the door resumed. By the rapidity of the blows she could tell that more than one of the creatures was involved.

With trembling fingers Kim tried the lighter. When she compressed it a spark leaped off into the blackness. Changing hands to hold the torch in her right, Kim twisted the thumbscrew on its side and heard a sustained hiss. Hold-ing the torch and the lighter at arm's length as she'd seen the plumber do, she compressed the lighter. With a whooshing sound the blowtorch ignited.

No sooner had Kim succeeded in lighting the torch than the door began to crack under the repeated blows. Once it began to break, it rapidly splintered, and bloodied hands appeared through fractures in the panels. To Kim's horror, the door quickly fell to pieces as the boards were torn away.

With the door gone, the researchers were like frenzied wild animals about to be fed. They all tried to rush into the powder room at the same time. In a con-fusion of arms and legs, they succeeded only in blocking each other.

Kim pointed the blowtorch at them, holding it at arm's length. It was mak-ing a throaty hissing sound. Its light illuminated their enraged faces. Edward and Curt were closest to Kim. She aimed the torch at them and saw their ex-pressions change from rage to fear.

The researchers shrank back in terror, evincing their atavistic fear of fire. Their beady eyes never left the blue flame issuing from the tip of the blow-torch.

Encouraged by their reaction, Kim stepped from the powder room, keeping the blowtorch out in front of her. The researchers responded by backing away. Kim moved tentatively forward as they retreated. As a group they moved out into the great room, passing beneath one of the massive chandeliers.

After backing for a few more steps, the researchers began to fan out. Kim would have much preferred they stay in a compact group or flee altogether, but she had no way of making them. She could only ward them off. As she moved slowly but relentlessly toward the front hall, they enveloped her. She had to swing the blowtorch around in a circle to keep all of them at bay.

The abject fear that the creatures had initially shown to the flame began to diminish as they became accustomed to it, especially when it wasn't pointed in their direction. By the time Kim made it past the middle of the room, some of them became bolder, particularly Edward.

At a moment when Kim was pointing the torch in someone else's direction, Edward rushed forward and grabbed Kim's nightgown. Kim immediately swung the torch toward him, scorching the back of his hand. He screamed hideously and let go.

Next Curt leaped forward. Kim blistered a swath across his forehead, igniting some of his hair. He yelped in pain and clasped his hands to his head.

On one of her turns Kim saw that she only had another twenty feet to go before she'd reach the hallway, but the constant pirouetting was having an effect on her balance. She was becoming dizzy. She tried to compensate by alternating the direction she spun after each revolution, but the maneuver wasn't as effective in keeping the researchers away from her.

Gloria managed to step in as Kim was changing directions and grabbed one of Kim's arms.

Kim yanked herself free of Gloria's grip, but with her balance already compromised, the sudden motion caused her to twirl out of control, and she fell. In the process of falling, her arm holding the blowtorch hit the edge of a side table with numbing force, causing her to lose her grasp on the blowtorch. The blowtorch bounced off the top of the table and hit the marble floor at a sharp angle, sending it careening across its highly polished surface. It ended up thumping against the far wall at a point where one of the immense damask silk drapes was pooled.

Cradling her injured arm with her good hand, Kim managed to sit up. Looming around and over her were the creatures, closing in for the kill. With a collective screech they fell on her in unison like animals of prey attacking an injured, doomed deer.

Kim screamed and struggled as she was scratched and bitten. Luckily the attack lasted only a few seconds. When a loud, reverberating whooshing sound accompanied by a sudden bright, hot light interrupted the frenzy, Kim was able to scramble away. With her back against a couch, she looked up at her attackers. They were all staring dumbfounded over her shoulder with their faces reflecting a golden light.

Turning to look behind her, Kim saw a wall of flames expanding with explosive force. The blowtorch had ignited the drapes, and they were burning as if they'd been doused with gasoline.

The creatures voiced a collective wail at the developing inferno. Kim looked back at them and saw terror in their wide eyes. Edward was the first to run, followed instantly by the others. But they didn't run out the front door. Instead they ran in a panic up the main stairs.

"No, no," Kim shouted to the fleeing figures. But it was to no avail. Not only did they not understand her, they did not even hear. The roar of the wall of flames sucked sound into its fury like a black hole swallowed matter.

Kim lifted her good arm to protect herself from the searing heat. Getting to her feet she hobbled toward the front door. It was becoming difficult to breathe as the fire consumed the room's oxygen.

An explosion behind her sent Kim again sprawling onto the floor. She cried out with pain from her injured arm. She guessed the blast had been the blowtorch container detonating. With renewed urgency to get out of the building, she struggled to her feet and staggered forward.

Kim lurched through the door and hobbled out into the gusty wind and driving rain. She limped all the way to the far edge of the graveled area in front of the castle, gritting her teeth against the pain in her arm and knee with every step. Turning around and shielding her face from the heat with her good arm, she looked back at the castle. The old structure was burning like tinder. Flames were already visible in the dormered windows of the attic.

A flash of lightning briefly illuminated the area. For Kim, the scene was like an image of hell. She shook her head in disgust and dismay. Truly the devil had returned to Salem!

EPILOGUE

"Where do you want to go first?" Kinnard asked as he and Kim drove through the gate onto the Stewart compound.

"I'm not sure," Kim said. She was in the passenger seat, supporting the cast on her left arm.

"You'll have to decide pretty soon," Kinnard said. "We'll be coming to the fork as soon as we clear the trees."

Kim knew Kinnard was right. She could already see the field through the leafless trees. She turned her head and looked at Kinnard. The pale, late fall sunshine slanting through the trees was flickering on his face and lighting up his dark eyes. He'd been extraordinarily supportive, and she was thankful he'd agreed to make this drive with her. It had been a month since the fateful night, and this was Kim's first return.

"Well?" Kinnard questioned. He began to slow down.

"Let's go to the castle," Kim said. "Or at least what's left of it."

Kinnard made the appropriate turn. Ahead, the charred ruins loomed. All that was standing were the stone walls and chimneys.

Kinnard pulled up to the drawbridge that now led to a blackened, empty doorway. Kinnard turned off the ignition.

"It's worse than I expected," Kinnard said, surveying the scene through the windshield. He looked at Kim. He could sense she was nervous. "You know, you don't have to go through this visit if you don't want to."

"I want to," Kim said. "I've got to face it sometime."

She opened her door and got out. Kinnard got out his side. Together they strolled around the ruins. They did not try to go inside. Within the walls everything was ashes save for a few charred beams that had not completely burned.

"It's hard to believe anyone got out alive as fast as it all burned," Kim said.

"Two out of six is not a great record," Kinnard said. "Besides, the two who survived aren't out of the woods yet."

"It's a tragedy in a tragedy," Kim said. "Like poor Elizabeth with her malformed, miscarried fetus."

They reached a hillock where they had a view of the entire incinerated site. Kinnard shook his head in disgust. "What a fitting end to a horrid episode," he said. "The authorities had a hard time believing it until the dentition of one of the victims matched the tooth marks on the bone of the dead vagrant. At least you must feel vindicated. They didn't believe a word you said in the beginning."

"I'm not sure they really believed it until both Edward and Gloria had another transformation in the burn unit of the hospital," Kim said. "That was the clincher, not the teeth marks. The people who witnessed it attested that it had been brought on by sleep and that neither Edward nor Gloria had any recollection of it occurring. Those were the two key points that were critical for people to believe what I told them."

"I believed you right away," Kinnard said, turning to Kim.

"You did," Kim said. "I have to give you credit for that and for a lot of other things."

"Of course, I already knew that they were taking their untested drug," Kinnard said.

"I told that to the District Attorney right from the beginning," Kim said. "It didn't influence him that much."

Kinnard looked back at the impressive ruins. "This old building must have burned awfully quickly," he said.

"The fire spread so fast it was almost explosive," Kim said.

Kinnard shook his head again, this time in gratitude and awe. "It's a marvel that you got out yourself," he said. "It must have been terrifying."

"The fire was practically anticlimactic," Kim said. "It was the other stuff that was so horrifying, and it was a hundred times worse than one could ever imagine. You can't believe what it's like to see people you know in such an animal state. But the one thing it did for me was underline that all drug taking, whether steroids for athletes or psychotropic drugs for character enhancement, is a Faustian contract."

"Medicine has known that for years," Kinnard said. "There's always risk, even with antibiotics."

"I hope people will remember it when they are tempted to take drugs for what they believe are personality flaws, like shyness," Kim said. "Such drugs are coming; there's no stopping the research that's going to develop them. And if someone doubts they will be used for such purposes, all they have to do is look at the expanded use of some of the current antidepressants in such questionable ways since they've been on the market."

"The problem is we're developing a culture which thinks there is a pill for everything," Kinnard said.

"That's exactly the reason that there is bound to be another episode like the one I just lived through," Kim said. "It's inevitable with the potential demand for psychotropic drugs."

"If there is another such episode, I'm sure the witch industry in Salem hopes that it will occur here," Kinnard said with a laugh. "Your experience has been a boon for business."

Kim picked up a stick and poked into the rubble of the castle. Metal objects had been distorted out of shape because of the intense heat.

"This house contained all the material legacy of twelve generations of Stewarts," Kim said. "Everything is lost."

"I'm sorry," Kinnard said. "It must be very upsetting."

"Not really," Kim said. "Most of it was junk except for a few pieces of furniture. There wasn't even one decent painting except for the portrait of Elizabeth, which survived. The only thing that I truly regret losing are the letters and papers I'd found about her. I've lost them all and only have copies of two that were made at Harvard. Now the copies are the only corroboration that exists concerning Elizabeth's involvement in the Salem witchcraft upheaval, and that's not going to be enough to convince most historians."

They stood for a time gazing at the ashes. Finally Kinnard suggested they move on. Elizabeth nodded. They walked back to the car and drove over to the lab.

Kim unlocked the door. They passed through the reception area and Kim opened the inner door. Kinnard was amazed. It was just empty space.

"Where is everything?" he asked. "I thought this was a lab."

"It was," Kim said. "I told Stanton everything had to be out immediately. I told him if it weren't, I'd donate it all to a charity."

Kinnard made a motion of dribbling a basketball and shooting it. The sound of his heels echoed in the room. "You could always convert it to a gym," he said.

"I think I'd prefer a studio," Kim said.

"Are you serious?" Kinnard asked.

"I think I am," Kim said.

Leaving the lab, they drove on to the cottage. Kinnard was relieved to see it hadn't been stripped like the lab. "It would be a shame to destroy this," he said. "You've made it into a delightful house."

"It is cute," Kim admitted.

They walked into the parlor. Kinnard walked around the room and examined everything carefully.

"Do you think you'd ever want to live here again?" Kinnard asked.

"I think so," she said. "Someday. What about you? Do you think you could ever live in a place like this?"

"Sure," Kinnard said. "After taking the rotation out here I've been offered a position with a group at Salem Hospital that I'm seriously considering. Living here would be ideal. The only trouble is, I think it might be a bit lonely."

Kim looked up into Kinnard's face. He raised his eyebrows provocatively.

"Is that a proposition?" Kim asked.

"It could be," Kinnard said evasively.

Kim thought for a moment. "Maybe we should see how we feel about each other after a ski season."

Kinnard chuckled. "I like your new sense of humor," he said. "You can now joke about things that I know are important to you. You've really changed."

"I hope so," she said. "It was long overdue." She gestured up at Elizabeth's portrait. "I have my ancestor to thank for making me see the need and giving me the courage. It's not easy breaking old patterns. I only hope I can maintain this new me, and I hope you can live with it."

"I'm loving it so far," he said. "I feel less like I'm walking on eggshells when we're together. I mean, I don't have to guess continually how you are feeling."

"I'm amazed but thankful that something good has come out of such an awful episode," she said. "The real irony for me is that I finally had the courage to tell my father what I think of him."

"Why is that ironic?" he asked. "I'd say it's perfectly in keeping with your new ability to communicate what's on your mind."

"The irony is not that I did it," she said. "It's because of the result. A week after the conversation that turned very nasty on his part he phoned me, and now we seem to be enjoying the beginnings of a meaningful relationship."

"That's wonderful," Kinnard said. "Just like with us."

"Yup," Kim said. "Just like with us."

She reached up and put her good arm around his neck and hugged him. He reciprocated with equal ardor.

Friday • May 19, 1995

Kim paused and looked up at the façade of the newly constructed brick building she was about to enter. Above the door set into the brick was a long white marble plaque on which was carved in low relief: Omni Pharmaceuticals. She was not sure how she felt about the fact the company was still in business in light of all that had happened. Yet she understood that with all his money tied up in the venture, Stanton was not about to let it simply die.

Kim opened the door and entered. At a reception desk she left her name. After waiting for a few minutes a pleasant, conservatively dressed woman appeared, to escort her up to the door of one of the company's labs.

"When you've finished your visit do you think you will be able to find your way out without difficulty?" the woman asked.

Kim assured her she could and thanked her. After the woman left, Kim turned to the lab door and entered.

From Stanton's description, Kim knew what to expect. The door that she'd just passed through did not take her into the lab. It took her into an anteroom. The common wall with the lab itself was glass from desk height to the ceiling. In front of the glass were several chairs. On the wall below the glass were a communications unit and a brass-handled door that resembled an after-hours bank drop.

Beyond the glass was a modern, state-of-the-art biomedical laboratory that bore an uncanny resemblance to the lab in the stables building in the compound.

Following Stanton's instructions, Kim sat in the chair and pressed the red "call" button on the communications console. Inside the lab she saw two figures stand up from behind a lab bench where they had been busy working. Seeing Kim, they started over.

Kim immediately felt a wave of sympathy for the pair. She never would have recognized them. It was Edward and Gloria. Both were tremendously disfigured from their burns. They were essentially hairless. Both were also facing more cosmetic surgery. They walked stiffly and pushed "keep open" IVs in front of them with hands that had lost fingers.

When they spoke their voices were hoarse whispers. They thanked Kim for coming and expressed their disappointment that they were unable to show her around the lab that had been specifically designed with their handicaps in mind.

After a pause in the conversation, Kim asked them how they were getting along healthwise.

"Pretty good considering what we have to deal with," Edward said. "Our biggest problem is that we're still experiencing 'fits' even though the Ultra has completely been cleared from our brains."

"Are they still brought on by sleep?" Kim asked.

"Not by sleep," Edward said. "They now come on spontaneously like an epileptic seizure, without any warning. The good part is that they only last for a half hour or less, even when untreated."

"I'm so sorry," Kim said. She struggled against a sadness that threatened to well up inside of her. She was facing people whose lives had been all but destroyed.

"We're the sorry ones," Edward said.

"It's our own fault," Gloria said. "We should have known better than to start taking the drug until all the toxicity studies were completed."

"I don't see that would have made any difference," Edward said. "To this day, no animal studies have shown this human side effect. In fact, by our taking the drug when we did, we probably saved a large number of human volunteers from experiencing what we've suffered."

"But there were other side effects," Kim said.

"True," Edward admitted. "I should have picked up on the short-term-memory loss as being significant. The drug was obviously showing its capability to block network-level nerve function."

"Has your subsequent research led to any understanding of your condition?" Kim asked.

"By studying each other in the throes of an attack we've been able to document what we had originally proposed as the mechanism of action," Gloria said. "Ultra builds up to a point where it blocks cerebral control of the limbic system and lower-brain centers."

"But why are you getting attacks now that the drug is gone?" Kim asked.

"That's the question!" Edward said. "That's what we are trying to learn. We believe it is through the same mechanism as 'bad trip' flashbacks which some people suffer after hallucinogenic drug use. We're trying to investigate the problem so that we might be able to figure out a way to reverse it."

"Dilantin worked for a short time to control the fits," Gloria said. "But then we began to become tolerant, so now it no longer works. The fact that it influenced the process for a short term has us encouraged we might find another agent."

"I'm surprised Omni is still in business," Kim said to change the subject.

"We are too," Edward said. "Surprised and pleased. Otherwise we wouldn't have this lab. Stanton just has not given up, and his persistence has paid off. One of the other alkaloids from the new fungus has shown significant promise as a new antidepressant, so he's been able to raise adequate capital."

"I hope at least Omni has abandoned Ultra," Kim said.

"No, indeed!" Edward said. "That's the other major thrust of our research: trying to determine what part of the Ultra molecule is responsible for the meso-limbic-cerebral blockage that we've labeled 'the Mr. Hyde Effect.' "

"I see," Kim said. She started to wish them luck but couldn't get herself to do it. Not after all the trouble Ultra had already caused.

Kim was about to say goodbye and promise she'd be back to visit when she noticed Edward's eyes glaze over. Then his entire face was transformed just as it had been on the fateful night when she'd awakened him. In an instant he was in an uncontrollable rage.

Without any warning or provocation he launched himself at Kim and collided with a thump against the thick glass shield.

Kim leaped back in fright. Gloria responded by swiftly opening Edward's IV.

For a brief moment Edward clawed vainly at the glass. Then his face went slack and his eyes rolled up into his head. In slow motion he sagged like a balloon with its air slowly let out. Gloria skillfully guided him to the floor.

"I'm sorry about this," Gloria said as she tenderly adjusted Edward's head. "I hope Edward didn't frighten you too much."

"I'm fine," Kim managed, but her heart was pounding in her chest and she was trembling. Warily she stepped close to the window and looked down at Edward lying on the floor. "Will he be all right?"

"Don't worry," Gloria said. "We're rather used to this sort of thing. Now you can see why we have these IVs. We've been experimenting with various tranquilizers. I'm pleased with how quickly this one worked."

"What would happen if both of you had an attack simultaneously?" Kim asked to try to focus her mind.

"We've thought about that," Gloria said. "Unfortunately, we've not been able to come up with any fail-safe ideas. So far it hasn't happened. I guess all we can do is the best we can."

"I admire your fortitude," Kim said.

"I don't think we have much choice," Gloria said.

After saying goodbye, Kim left. She was unnerved. As she descended in the elevator her legs felt weak. She was afraid her little visit would bring back the recurrent nightmares she'd had immediately after the terrible night.

Emerging into the warm midspring sunshine, Kim felt better. Just being outside helped, but she could not keep from replaying the image of Edward furiously slamming into the glass of his self-imposed prison.

When Kim reached her car, she stopped and turned to face Omni. She wondered what kind of drugs the company would be loosing on the world in the future. She shuddered. The thought made her vow to be even more conservative than she'd been in the past about taking drugs, any drugs!

Kim keyed open her door and got into the car. She didn't start the engine immediately. In her mind's eye, she could still see Edward's face as it underwent its ghastly transformation. It was something she never would forget.

Starting out of the parking lot, Kim did something that surprised her. Instead of returning back to Boston as she'd planned, she impulsively headed north. After the unnerving experience at Omni she felt an irresistible urge to return to the compound, where she had not gone since the visit with Kinnard.

With little traffic the trip passed quickly, and within a half hour Kim was unlocking the padlock on the gates. She drove directly to the cottage and got out. Immediately she felt an odd sensation of relief as if she were coming home after an arduous journey.

Fumbling with the keys, Kim opened the lock and entered. Stepping into the half-light of the parlor, she looked up at Elizabeth's portrait. The intense green of the eyes and the determined line of the jaw were as Kim remembered, but there was something else, something she'd not seen. It appeared as if Elizabeth were smiling!

Kim blinked and looked again. The smile was still there. It was as if Elizabeth were reacting to the fact that after so many years some good had come from her terrible ordeal; she had been ultimately vindicated.

Amazed at this effect, Kim stepped closer to the painting only to appreciate the sfumato that the artist had used at the corners of Elizabeth's mouth. Kim smiled herself, realizing it was her own perceptions that were being reflected in Elizabeth's visage.

Turning around, Kim gazed out at the view Elizabeth saw from her position over the mantel. At that moment Kim decided to move back to the cottage. The emotional trauma engendered by that last terrible night had already significantly lessened, and Kim wanted to come home to live within the penumbra of Elizabeth's memory. Remembering she was the same age as Elizabeth had been when Elizabeth had been so unjustly killed, Kim vowed to live the rest of her life for both of them. It was the only way she could imagine to repay Elizabeth for the self-understanding she'd provided.

SELECTED BIBLIOGRAPHY

1. Boyer and Nissenbaum, *Salem Possessed*. Cambridge, MA. Harvard University Press, 1974.

     For those people who might be tempted to read more about the Salem witchcraft episode, this book is one of two I'd recommend. I'm sure Kim and Edward would heartily agree. It is fascinating reading and shows how history can come to life by using primary sources dealing with ordinary citizens. It gives an entertaining look into life in New England during the last half of the seventeenth century.

2. Hansen, Chadwick, *Witchcraft at Salem*. New York. George Braziller, 1969.

     This is the second book I'd recommend about the Salem witchcraft affair. It takes the viewpoint that not everyone involved was innocent! Such an attitude surprised me at first but then turned out to be provocative.

3. Kramer, Peter, *Listening to Prozac*. New York. Viking, 1993.

     Although this book is more positive than I am about the use of psychotropic agents for personality alteration, there is a discussion of both sides of the issue. It is enlightening, enjoyable, and provocative.

4. Matossian, Mary, *Poisons of the Past: Molds, Epidemics, and History*. New Haven, CT. Yale University Press, 1989.

     This book certainly gives one an added respect for the lowly mold. For me it was particularly stimulating in regards to the storyline of *Acceptable Risk*.

5. Morgan, Edmund, *The Puritan Family*. New York. Harper & Row, 1944.

     My high school American history course didn't provide me with adequate background in relation to Puritan culture. This book helped fill the void.

6. Restak, Richard, *Receptors.* New York. Bantam, 1994.

This book is for those readers who would like a readable, stimulating, up-to-date explanation of current knowledge of brain function and the direction of research.

7. Werth, Barry, *The Billion-Dollar Molecule.* New York. Simon & Schuster, 1994.

If anyone doubts the deleterious effect of entrepreneurialism in today's scientific world, this book is a must.